MW01116116

THE SHADOW OF DREAD

THE BLADEBORN SAGA, BOOK SIX

T. C. EDGE

COPYRIGHT

Previous book in the series:

CONTENTS

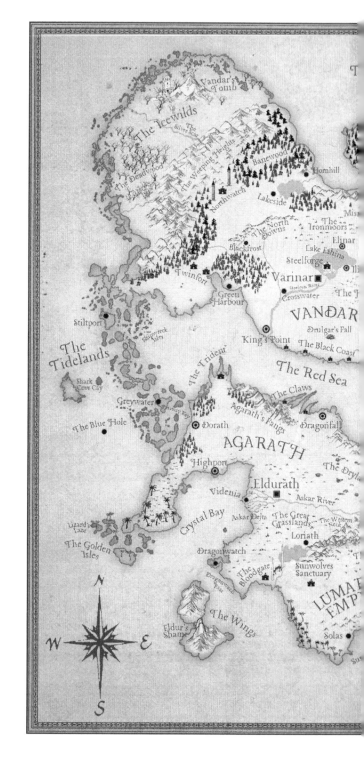

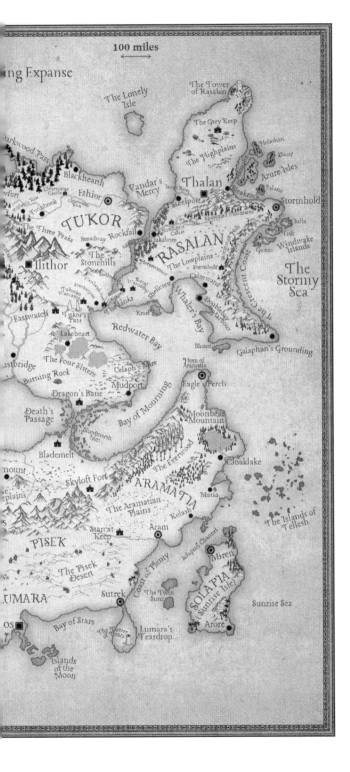

PROLOGUE

He could hear his son coming, long before he arrived. The heavy, marching step. The thunderous, bellowing voice. *He is as loud as my father was*, thought Ayrin, son of Varin. *Louder, even. That same bold blood runs thick through his veins. That same insatiable spirit.*

The king turned his eyes back down to his book, enjoying the last few moments of peace before Amron strode through the door. By the ringing of steel on stone it was obvious he was wearing his armour. *He has come from his training, no doubt. Preparing for a war that I have long denied him. His blood will be up, and his tongue will be hot.* It was the last thing he needed today.

A sigh slipped through his lips, stirring the greying bristles of his lengthening beard. Ayrin had not worn a beard as a younger man, not like his father and brother - and now his son as well - yet in his dotage the whiskers seemed to suit him. A scholar king, many called him. Ayrin the Peacemaker. Even Ayrin the Wise. True though that last might have been, he had always brushed the sobriquet aside. *My wisdom was only a gift,* he thought, *granted by one greater.*

The book before him was a gift as well, given by the same wise ruler. He had always counted it among his favourite tomes, a contemplation on the nobility of silence, and calm thought, and the great merits of taking one's time, in every endeavour they should undertake. Though the author was officially a Rasalanian philosopher called *Telys the Thinker*, Ayrin had always wondered if Thala had written it herself. His mentor's mark was all over the words; in the flow of them, in their nature, in the wisdom wrought into every page. Reading it he could almost hear her voice from beyond the grave. *This world is dimmer without her. No light has ever shone so bright.*

The footsteps were getting louder, smashing hard against the stone. When Amron of House Varin marched with such intent through the palace, the stonemasons wept, for they would have work to do. Not rarely did the man leave cracks in his wake. One of the masons had, in fact, requested that there be more rugs laid down through the halls and corridors to help soften the prince's tread. A jest, of course, or at least that's how Ayrin took it. The forced smile on the poor man's face had suggested otherwise, however.

The footfall reached its thundering apex, and the doors to his study flew open. Amron stepped inside, armour misting, skin sweating. "Father." He fell into a bow, sweat spraying off his forehead and the wet strands of hair, black as jet, flowing about his ears. In the side of his breastplate he had stuffed a cloth, which he removed to wipe himself down. "Hot out there today. The hottest of the year, I'm told."

King Ayrin had heard that as well. "You've been training daily during the heat of the day, Amron. For long hours. Do I have to ask you why?"

"I think you know why, Father." Amron headed for a side table and hooked a jug of water into his steel grasp, drinking straight from the flagon. It looked almost like a regular cup in his hand. At over seven feet in height, he made most things look small. "It'll be a great deal hotter than this in Agarath." He finished the jug, put it aside, and took up a flagon of wine instead. This one he did pour into a goblet. "Nothing to say to that, Father? You usually have a ready response."

"I have no response that I haven't given you a hundred times before. You know my thoughts on this. I have spoken to you of the risks."

"The risks of doing nothing are just as severe. I understand your position, I do, and I respect it. But this peace cannot endure forever. We're a warrior people. It's in our blood." He gulped his wine. "Are you having a cup?"

"Later. I prefer not to drink during the daytime, as you know."

Amron nodded, finished the cup, refilled it and drank again. As with his grandfather, he did everything to excess - eating, drinking, duelling - without feeling the full effects as other men did. As they became drunk, Amron remained sober. As they grew fat, he remained thick with muscle, broad at the shoulder and trim at the waist. In the duelling yard he could fight on for long hours, beating back one opponent after another without fatigue. Not since Varin had a man been so utterly born to fight. Yet so far those talents had been restricted to the sparring yard and tourney grounds, to the woods and mountains where he would hunt for prey, to the nests and dens where brigands lurked. On occasion he had encountered opponents almost worthy of his skill, but those times were few, and he had grown restless. *He wants a proper fight,* Ayrin knew. *He wants to slay dragons.*

The silence lingered for several long moments, a silence that Amron did not enjoy. It was anathema to him, this absence of noise, though to Ayrin it had always been where wonders were done. A time to think, to consider, to determine the correct course. He sat for a time, pondering. It did not take long for his son to break.

"Well? Are you going to say anything or not?"

"I *am* saying something, Amron. Silence is speech."

"Yes, so you like to say. I prefer words, however. They are rather more clear." He finished off his cup of wine and refilled it once again. "Vandar gave us his body to make weapons and armour. Tools with which to defeat our enemies. Does that not suggest to you that he wanted us to make war?"

"Weapons are used to protect what one has, as much as they are to win what one hasn't."

Amron's azure eyes descended to the desk. "Another quote from your book? Or one of your own?"

"I'm glad you think it's quote-worthy. Yes, it's one of mine."

A huffing laugh heaved from his son's chest. "A rearrangement of something Queen Thala said, no doubt. So, we protect our own. Yes, I agree with that. But what about those already fallen? What about your own father? What about vengeance?"

"Vengeance is hollow. A dark hole that can never be filled. In the end it only leads to more killing." The king felt weary already; they'd had this discussion a hundred times before. "I know you hate to hear this, Amron, but…"

"Don't say it. Do not try to convince me that the killing of Varin was necessary. He was your *father*. How can you persist in believing that?"

"It is hard to hear, I know. A terrible thing to even say. But that does not make it untrue, son. Had my father lived, he would have sought to dominate the southern kingdoms. Lori and Dor sensed this ambition. And in their fear…"

"They *murdered* him," finished Amron, looking down at his father with distaste. "They killed him during the parley, during the very signing of the peace treaty…and you tell me it was just."

"No. I did not say just."

"You might as well have." He finished his wine, smashed the goblet down, refilled it to the brim once more. All aggressive. All loud. *They cloak him like a mantle.* "Do you imagine those treacherous bastards would have killed him if Uncle Elin was still alive? No, they only did it because Elin was dead, and you were heir to the throne. They saw you as *weak*, Father. That's an opinion others share."

The king did not let the words of his son wound him. He had heard them all before, in rants and raves and muscular demands, but never did they move him. Through Thala he had learned temperance, another gift of the Far-Seeing Queen. *And not a quality my son possesses. Nor my father or brother before him.* Oh, Amron might become a great man, and a great king one day, yet if so it would not be as a wise ruler, but a warrior, and a conqueror, revered for his body and not his mind, for strength and not sagacity.

Enough time had passed. Ayrin had not moved his gaze away from his son all the while. "Men are welcome to their opinions," he said, in a calm, even voice. "They change like the wind, Amron, blowing one away and then the other. In the course of time, our legacies will solid-ify. Yes, to some I will be known as weak. A weak king who did not avenge his father. But to others, I hope, I will be seen as the king who rebuilt a kingdom, after a hundred years of war. Who strengthened and consolidated his borders and developed deeper bonds and ties with his allies. Who rejuvenated the land, re-sowed the fields and orchards, built new cities and castles, farms and market towns and monuments. How, I ask you, would more war have served us then? More men dying. More money siphoned into the forging of arms and armour. You see the world only from your own vantage, Amron. You see the great light of war, the nobility in it, the triumph. But every light that shines makes a shadow, and in that shadow, people suffer. Those are the people I looked to when this crown was placed on my head. And I hope you remember them, when it comes time for you to wear it."

Amron's jaw was tight. "I will," he said, as though his sense of civic responsibility was being called into question. "I am a man of the people as well. They cheer my name when I ride through the streets. I have Prince Amron ringing in my ears. I remind them of Varin, I'm told."

Ayrin smiled softly, proud and yet somehow sad at once. "You look like him. And you have his strength and boldness. These are qualities people love. I only wish you could show more balance, Amron. Perhaps when you are king, you will."

"When I'm king, I will do as you did. I'll build, and expand, and make this kingdom even greater. I'll raise a great new city at the mouth of the Steelrun, to watch over the Red Sea. And monuments, those too. I'll build one for you, Father. A great monument, a whole city of them, to celebrate all your *deeds*."

Ayrin studied his son; the shape of his mouth, the playful light in his eyes. "You oughtn't tease, Amron. Was I a little too boastful there, listing out my achievements as king?"

His son smiled broadly. "It was rather unlike you, I must say. But none of what you said was untrue." His voice softened. He stepped in. "And I mean it, Father. I *will* build you a city when you're gone, and I *will* have it filled with monuments to you. You *are* a great king. We might look at the world differently, but I would never diminish what you've done. You were the right king for the right time. But times… they're different now."

Different, Ayrin thought. *Worsening, and growing more bitter.* As sad as it made him to think it, he knew that war with Agarath could not be kept at bay forever, something Thala had always known. Though the Far-Seeing Queen was reluctant to speak of such things, he had learned to read her well during his years beneath her wing. Whenever the subject of war came up, he would watch her gaze, listen to the shift in her tone of voice, perceive the truth that she was unwilling to speak out loud.

He had spoken to Ilith of it too, during their private councils, when the great blacksmith king came to Varinar, or he journeyed to Ilithor to see him. Often did they speak of Thala, and the future, and the heavy burden she refused to share.

"She cannot," Ilith had told him once. "Else she break her bonds of trust with Rasalan. Should that happen he will shut his Eye, and deny her from peering through his pupil. Thala has tested those boundaries more than once before, Ayrin. She tells us only what she is able to say, and we mustn't ask for more."

Ayrin had heeded the king's advice, much as he found it difficult to do so. Now he wished Thala was still here, so he could ask her about his son. *Will he renew the war with Agarath? Will he seek vengeance for my father's fall?* She would not have answered those questions, he knew, but all the same, he'd have seen the answers in her eyes. *As I see them in the eyes of my son…*

"Is there anything I can say that would dissuade you from this course, Amron?" he asked. "This way to war. Is your heart set upon it?"

The prince's eyes were steel. "You are the king, Father. Only you can call our armies to war. As long as you live, I will obey your commands. I can wait, if I must. In respect of your achievements, I'll stir no war until I wear the crown. That I promise you. But after…"

"You will have your war." Ayrin nodded. That would be for his son to decide. "You have always been an honest man, Amron. Another might have made false promises."

"And you'd only have seen right through them. This…this is the best compromise. Only…" He let out a breath, shaking his head. "It's what I want. Battle, glory, I'll not deny it. And vengeance for Varin too. But knowing it will only come at your death, I…" He shook his head again, looking away. "It will not be the same. Every son wants to make his sire proud."

Ayrin stood from his chair. He was a tall man, as men went, even in his advancing years. Not nearly so grand in might as his son, yet strong all the same, and a brilliant swordsman once too. He stepped around his desk and put his hands on his son's broad shoulders. "I *am* proud of you, Amron. I have always been proud of you, and I *will* always be proud of you. You are my son, and I love you. And when I'm gone, you must follow your own path. If that means war, so be it. I will not be there to stop you."

Amron nodded, eyes down. "I wish it could be different," he murmured. "I wish you did not disapprove of me so."

"*Disapprove?* I do not disapprove of you, son. It is the very nature of war that has earned my disapproval. I was born during a century of it. In my youth it was all I knew. That shaped me, Amron, growing up in such a world. We have lived a different experience."

The prince gave that some thought. "Then is it any wonder how I have turned out? You were born to war and turned to a path of peace.

I was born to peace and so yearn to seek out war." He let out a sigh. "It calls to me in a way I cannot explain. I don't feel complete without it. I have never felt complete."

"You are the reflection of your grandfather. He would have said the very same thing."

There was a long pause. Amron gave a light huff to himself, then said, "That was *Ilith's* fault. If Varin wasn't complete, then the blacksmith was to blame…"

"That blacksmith built the world, Amron."

"I know. And I respect that. But he also…he also betrayed Varin. He was his friend, and he betrayed him."

This again, Ayrin thought. "He did not betray him. He protected him."

"Protected him? From who?"

"Himself. Ilith was wise enough to see that my father could not be trusted with that power."

Amron snorted. "That *power* would have saved countless lives. That power was not Ilith's to hold. You lost a brother and a sister and how many others because Ilith did not share his secret. A hundred years of war, Father. All of that could have been avoided."

It was a familiar debate, a well-worn discussion, and Ayrin was tired of it. They were never going to agree. "Come with me," he said.

Amron frowned. "Where are you…"

"Come," the king repeated. He made for the door, robes trailing in a blue billow behind him.

Amron followed, clanking heavily in his plate armour. The guards outside bowed at the king's passing, and that of the prince, then began to trail behind them at a distance as they made their way through the palace.

It was not far to the throne room. When they arrived, King Ayrin told the guards to remain outside. He stepped within with his son and asked that the heavy doors be shut. The hall was a vision of grandeur. Fluted pillars of grey-white marble rose high overhead, veined in blue. The tall frosted windows sparkled as sunlight flowed in from outside, each pane of glass a different colour. Blues were favoured, and shades of silver, the colours of the kingdom, but there were some reds and greens and golds as well, shining across the tiled stone floor. Banners hung down between them, depicting heroes of the old wars, their triumphs and victories and conquests. At the end of the hall rose the stage upon which the throne misted, forged of pure godsteel. Sitting there, a king would be enshrouded in the Soul of Vandar, given power by his presence, or so it was said. It wasn't true. Ayrin had never felt the God King's strength when sitting the throne. *Those mists just make it hard to see,* he thought, *when I look out upon my subjects.*

Amron had grown impatient. "What are we doing here, Father? If this is some kind of lesson…"

"Sit the throne, Amron."

The prince hesitated. "Father?"

"Go ahead. Seat yourself upon the chair from which your grandfather declared his wars." He waited as his son climbed the steps and took perch before him. "How does it feel?"

Amron had never liked those sorts of questions. He was a direct man, not one of deep thought. "Like I'm sitting on a throne. How should it feel?"

"Do you feel his power? Vandar's?"

Amron thought a moment. The mists poured from the arms and the back and the base, swirling and rising, only fading when they reached up to the high vaulted ceiling. Ayrin had always felt small in that throne, but Amron filled it well. *Small wonder*, the king thought. His own father had enlisted the finest of Ilith's Forgeborn to craft it, its every feature made to fit his grand, imposing proportions. Proportions Varin had shared with Elin, his eldest son, the brother who had died before Ayrin was born. *And with Amron too*, the king thought. Varin, Elin, Amron…they were all much alike.

At last his son gave answer. "Yes," he said. "I can feel it."

It felt like the answer he was expected to give. "And of Varin? What of *history*, Amron? Do you feel its weight on your shoulders?"

"I feel pauldrons on my shoulders. Just what are you trying to get at?"

Ayrin had a meandering way about him sometimes, people said. A charge he accepted. He liked to lead a man to a conclusion, rather than saying it outright, but his son was right. This was no time to be long-winded. *Time is no longer a luxury I have.*

"In that very seat, your grandfather complained of the very same thing as you do," he said. "For hours he would rage of Ilith's obstinacy, how he would not do as he demanded and reforge the Blades of Vandar. Sometimes it felt like it was the only thing in the world he wanted. It became an obsession to him, and nothing else seemed to matter, and every time Ilith came to visit, he would make his demands and requests. Sometimes directly and angrily, sometimes in a quieter, more pleading way, but always the same. And do you know what Ilith said? He said *no*, Amron. Every single time. He said no."

"Fool," Amron grunted. The mists swirled about him, obscuring his face, and in that moment Ayrin saw Varin there, not Amron, saw his father and not his son. "With such a weapon we would be unstoppable. You want peace, Father? Who would dare seek war with us when we have such power in our grasp?"

He will never see. He is so much like his grandfather. Too much, the king thought. "Absolute power is a curse. It is how tyrants are made."

The prince huffed. The sound echoed through the quiet of the chamber. "Tyrants are *weak*," he declared. "Varin would never have become one. He would have ruled with a strong fist, yes, but *fairly*. He would have let the worthy thrive."

"You speak as if you knew him. You never met your grandfather."

"You don't need to meet a man to know him." The prince slammed a fist against his breastplate, the *clang* ringing between the pillars. "I feel him in here. He speaks to me, Father, from his Table Above. *I* am his true heir, the people say."

People who never met him either, Ayrin thought. Varin had died almost two hundred years ago. There was no one left living who had known him. *Only me,* Ayrin thought.

"You don't trust me," the prince said in an indignant voice. Ayrin looked at him. Amron's eyes were hard as diamonds. The mist swirled about him, moving angrily. "Same as with your own father. You think I'll become a tyrant if I combine the blades."

I know it, a part of him thought. "I don't think that," is all he said.

"Then why? *Why* do you deny me, Father? Why?"

"I do not deny you. I do not have what you seek. Ilith took the secret to his grave, Amron. Those blades may never be reforged."

"You're lying. You've *always* lied about this. Thala told you something, didn't she? The Far-Seeing Queen, isn't that what they call her? She saw *far*. She saw the shards being hammered back together. She saw the Heart being wielded. I know she did. *Don't* lie to me, Father."

The king shook his head. "If she did, she never told me."

"You're *lying*," Amron repeated, louder. The mists billowed around him, pouring off throne and armour and blade. "Was it me? Will it be me who unites the blades? Is that what you're frightened of, Father? Is that why you hold me back?"

Ayrin felt utterly exhausted. He could not keep going around like this, repeating the same things over and over. "It will not be you," he said. "You will not combine the blades."

Amron stared at him. "So you know? You *do* know? You *have* been lying to me."

"I know you will never combine the blades. One day, perhaps another will, but not you. It will *not* be you, Amron."

The prince burst up from the throne, the mists blowing about him in a storm. "Then curse you," he shouted at him. "Curse you, Father. And Thala and Ilith too! Curse the bloody lot of you!"

Ayrin closed his eyes. He had no strength to fight him today. Not today, of all days, on the anniversary of Thala's death, long decades ago now. He had hoped only to sit and remember her, to read and write and ruminate on her wisdom. Instead he was here, with his warmonger son. A son he loved fiercely, and yet feared as well. He feared what he would become.

A conqueror, the king thought. *Ruthless and unmerciful. His armies will be enough to make him that, and his power with sword and spear.* Varin had defeated Drulgar with the Sword of Varinar alone, and so too Karagar and Eldur at the Ashmount. *He never needed the Heart Remade to win his wars and glory.*

He will not wield it, Ayrin knew, looking at his son. *He must not wield it, lest he bring the world to ruin.*

It was a sad truth, but a truth all the same. Ilith had known it of Varin, and now Ayrin knew it of his son. One day, perhaps, someone would rise up to restore the Heart. But it would not be Amron of House Varin to do it.

Another, Ayrin thought. *Another…who is more worthy.*

PROLOGUE II

3,160 Years Later…

The hall was a dead giant, a fallen god of these lands, revered. The ribs spread overhead, curving, covered in pelts and furs and skins, and from the spine, yak-hair ropes had been tied, dangling down with grinning skull-lanterns that flickered with a blood-red flame.

Tables filled the space below, long tables roughly cut of hard ironwood, coated in tar, hammered together with nails of tooth and claw. Many were packed along the benches, wise men and warrior men and warrior women too, mothers and grandmothers with children on their laps, crones and codgers, all had come. There was a murmur, like a nest of hornets, of people whispering and hissing and chattering at one another as they waited.

At the head of *Orthrand* the earth had been raised within the thick stone skull, creating a platform between the giant bear's jaws where the tribal lords would gather at times of need. They came for weddings, sometimes, and to come to terms of peace after their wars. Often those two things were linked, weddings used to end wars. Today they had come for a different reason. Today the matter was survival.

Stegra Snowfist stood upon the raised platform, garbed in his great white ice-bear cloak, broad-chested and wide-shouldered, standing at over six and a half feet tall. To his left was his teen son Svaldar, a younger version of himself, already grand and imposing. At his right stood Wagga the White, wisest of Stegra's council. The rest of his snow-brothers were arrayed below; Kusto Crowbane, Jorgen Half-Eye, Sigurt Seven-Sons, little Briggor the Big and big Arnel Hammerhand, Niklas No-Name and Verner the Herald. Verner had won his name only recently, for being the one to see the *sign*.

Others of his tribe were here too, senior men and women of the *Snowskins* clustered about one long bench beneath the platform, with their snow-white hair and milky skin and bright eyes like chips of ice. The rest of his people kept to the encampment raised outside within the frosted basin where the bear god Orthrand had died, felled by the *Red Storm* thousands of years ago. There were many out there, many thousands from all corners of the free lands and the high places of the mountains as well, the ranges the steel men called the Weeping Heights. For long days they had been gathering, arriving on their greatyaks and mammoths, their sleds and sleigh-carts, answering the Snowfist's call.

In the encampment outside they kept themselves apart, each tribe raising their tents and shelters and lean-tos away from one another, and the same was true in here. The tribes did not often mingle. Each sat along tables of their own. Next to the Snowskins sat the *Deadcloaks of the Deadwood*, heaped in their pelts and furs, brown and black and green. The *Crowmen of the Crag* wore only black, sitting shoulder to shoulder in their cloaks of raven feathers, their faces long and dour and ugly. Another table bore the strong *Stone Men* of the low ranges, who lived in their great caves…and another the *Mole Men* who dug their homes underground…and another the tribes who lived along the banks of the Silver Scar, a quiet fisherfolk who had few warriors of their own.

The people of the remote western shores were gathered in great abundance and had travelled the farthest to be here. They lived across the many small islands out there in the west of the Icewilds and wore clothes made from seal and walrus and whale, bearing weapons forged from the teeth of ice sharks and dragon seals. Their ancient leader had a necklace of massive walrus tusks around his neck which dragged him forward as he walked, and he needed to be helped along. He had brought with him his entire family, and hundreds of others besides, perhaps as many as a thousand. The family alone numbered over fifty, Stegra had heard. Everyone was enamoured with the Walrus Lord's prize, a great-granddaughter of astonishing beauty who wore a cloak of white and black made from the skin of an orca. Svaldar was in love with her, his men had said, teasing the lad last night. The way he blushed - and Svaldar never blushed - had suggested it was true.

Last were the *Wild Weepers*. They had come only this morning, a small group of them prowling down from the Weeping Heights where they made their grisly lairs. A part of Stegra had hoped they would not answer his summons. Across the free lands, the Weepers were regarded with scorn and fear. They had cuts about their eyes, and strange tattoos and markings on their skin, and wore the bones of their enemies as trophies. One had a human skull on his head, bolted atop an iron helm. Another had a man's severed arm hanging from his swordbelt, still with strips of ragged skin and wisps of cloth attached. Their leader was tall, cruel-eyed and insolent, with finger bones draped around his neck on a rope of human hair. Red scars slashed out from his eyes like a gruesome sunburst, and there were tattoos depicting scenes of torture inked into his forehead and cheeks and elsewhere no doubt too, though thankfully Stegra could not see them. The man's name was Blood-Eye. Everyone hated the Wild Weepers, who sat at the back, snickering and sneering and scheming.

Between the tables, a single long fire pit had been dug, right beneath Orthrand's spine. Flame ran along it like a long orange serpent, licking and hissing at the air with a thousand little tongues. Smoke rose in tight grey circlets, coiling to gather above them in a foggy cloud. The fire was warm, filling the hall. But even so, Stegra could feel the chill outside…that grasping, *deepening* cold. A cold that could kill them all.

He thumped the ceremonial bone-club to begin the session, smashing it hard against the huge, white-brown tooth that jutted up through the earthen platform. It rang out loudly through the smoky hall. The buzz died, and Stegra spoke.

"I am Stegra the Snowfist, Chieftain of the Snowskins," he bellowed out, through the jaws of his bear-hood cloak. "You all know me. You know I am fair, and I am fearless, but there is a fear in me now." He pointed to the rear of the *Hall of Orthrand*, where the great pelt door had been tied shut to keep away the cold. Even so, the guards there were shivering. "The white world we love is changing. The deep dark we live in is darkening. You have all felt it, you all know it, and that is why you have come."

Murmurs filled the air. Nods and grunts of agreement. No one was standing and shouting at him yet, which was good. Stegra had rarely been to one of these conclaves where arguing hadn't broken out after the first words had been said.

"It is the *End Fall*," he rumbled in his deep voice. "The last great snow that will come down upon us and bury us all beneath it…"

Now the shouting began.

At once men stood from their benches, one, two, ten of them, more, all calling over one another.

"It is just another long winter," claimed Narek of the Crowmen, son of their leader Tarek. "We have seen long winters before. And snows deeper than this."

"The Snowfist is scared of snow!" cackled one of the Weepers at the back, to jeers and laughs from his brothers. "I call you Stegra Snow*babe*, bawling in your bear cloak!"

Stegra's eyes flared. He was about to shout at the man when a great heavy voice rumbled out, "We have lived through worse. We will live through this." He was Hraka, called the Great by his people, mighty leader of the Stone Men. They wore bones and stones as armour and many were of great size, towering above even the Snowfist.

Stegra shook his head. "This is different, Hraka. It *is* the End Fall. The signs have been seen."

"What signs?" demanded the chieftain of the Deadcloaks, a

13

woman of fierce green eyes and wild jet hair called Black Merryl, who was a woods witch all knew. Her voice cut right through the din. She did not have to raise it, nor did she stand. But she was looking at him with those strange eyes that had always disquieted him. "Do you talk of your *Steel Lord*, Stegra? And your *Sea-King*? Are these the signs of which you speak?"

Laughter filled the hall. *The fools*, he thought. "These signs are true."

"True?" sniffed the witch. "But what of these lands you were granted? This blight that was cleared? Rolling hills and sweeping valleys and woodlands teeming with game. Rivers so fat with fish you need only step into the shallows and you can pluck them up with your fist. A shore, wide and open, looking out into the great beyond. You have boasted of these new lands of yours, Stegra. Now you say we should leave?"

Stegra did not like this woman. "I have not boasted," he growled, from within his hood. In it he looked like a great ice bear himself, with his huge white beard and mane of hair. "I settled there. I led my tribe to these lands. I hoped more than any man to remain, and live in peace, but I did not count on the *snow*." He looked around at the sea of faces. "You all know this is not a natural fall. It is too heavy, too constant, too *cold*. We are the Snowskins, we can fight the cold better than any of you. Yet even we fear it. Even I, the Snowfist."

"Snow*babe*," shouted that Weeper again.

Stegra thrust a finger at him. "One more word from you and I'll have your tongue."

"I'll have your *eyes*," hissed the man.

Shouts filled the air, the Snowskins and Weepers exchanging curses. Wagga the White took the bone-club from Stegra's grasp and smashed it hard against the tooth. "Quiet! Quiet! The Walrus wishes to speak!"

The voices died down. The Walrus Lord was well respected, the oldest person here by a decade. He stood with the help of two strong men wearing green-grey whale-skin cloaks. His great necklace of tusks clattered as he rose, knocking against one another. He surveyed the room through rheumy eyes, thick-bodied and stooped, with long bristles drooping down from his lips and chin. Once they were red, Stegra had been told by his father Skagar, who had been Snowfist before him, but had long since turned white and brittle.

"The snows fall thick on the western shores," the old man said, in a weak voice that one had to strain to hear. "Thicker than I have ever seen them. Many islands are lost beneath heavy drifts and the seas freeze over like never before. I am nine and ninety years old, and would live long enough to see my century on this good earth. That will not happen upon my lands, I fear. Stegra Snowfist is right. The End Fall is upon us." His men helped him sit back down to more rattling and clacking of tusks.

His words left a silence. Stegra looked across his audience, saw the nodding along the benches. The Walrus Lord was wise, all agreed. Stegra had hoped for his support and expected it as well. Why else would he have emptied out his lands? Why else would he have packed up his tribe and stacked his great sleighs and ranged all this way through the cold, dark wilds? *He has abandoned his home*, Stegra thought, *as I have. We have no choice now but to keep on going.*

Men were musing along the benches, muttering at one another. Children fidgeted in the laps of their mothers and grandmothers and sisters and aunts. Stegra looked at those he had spoken with in private conference over the last few days. Many had expressed their fears to him. Some feared to speak against their leaders, and so Stegra would not expose them now, but he knew they would break from their tribes and join him when he left. *We will become one tribe*, he thought. *As Shrikna said.*

"These blizzards will not stop," he said, ending the silence. His voice was final. He knew it was the truth. "They will fall until every tree and hill is buried beneath a hundred feet of snow. Even the Mole Men will not survive it, nor the Stone Men in their caves. There will be no food, no shelter, no relief. Every man, woman and child who remains in these lands will die."

"Says you," sneered Blood-Eye, sitting at the back. Stegra looked at him. Stegra hated him. Stegra had fought his people many times before. "You want to claim our lands in the mountains. You want to rally all these sheep and drive us out."

"If you can be driven out by sheep, you deserve it," Kusto Crow-bane shouted at him. He spat on the floor. "You shouldn't have come, Blood-Eye. No one wants you saved."

The Weepers rose as one from their table. There were only ten of them, but they were fierce warriors all, and bore cruel weapons to go with their cruel ways, each one more ugly than the last. Smoke grey steel, jagged-edged and bloodstained. Clubs with spikes and nails bearing the marks of their latest kills. Short stabbing knives that they liked to use to put out eyes. Spears with razor edges that could be swung through a man just as easily as it could skewer him. The Weepers were raiders, rapers, pillagers, who roved down through the Weeping Heights and into the Banewood, killing villagers and setting traps for passing soldiers so they could steal their weapons and make them their own. They mutilated their arms the same as they did their enemies. *And their faces*, Stegra thought, reviled.

"Put away your weapons," he said, over the noise. "Crowbane, do not inflame them."

"Why not? I'm only saying what everyone is thinking."

The Weepers stood ready for a fight. Two of them had leapt up onto the table at which they sat, brandishing bloodstained steel. *If they seek blood, all of them will die*, Stegra knew. They would kill many before then, yes, and would not care if they were women and children - nay, they would probably *target* the women and children - but none of them would make it out of the Hall of Orthrand alive, and this was sacred ground as well, where no blood should be spilt. Blood-Eye knew this. He raised a hand, and called for calm. Slowly, his men settled back down.

"We do not mean to take your lands, Blood-Eye," Stegra said. "Only to pass through them." He had spoken with some of the Crowmen already, their leader Tarek among them, who told him the passes would soon be closed and buried and there would be no way through the mountains. The Crowmen of the Crag dwelt in the lower foothills, but sometimes they ranged higher. Tarek's reports concerned him greatly. *If we do not leave soon, we will all be trapped.* "You know the high passes better than anyone, Blood-Eye. Forget Crowbane, he is an unwashed cur and has too much snow between his ears. I say it is good you have come. You are the best person to lead us out."

Blood-Eye smiled a bloody smile, his gums all red and raw. They cut those too, Stegra knew, before going into battle, to make themselves appear more fearsome. "My help," the *Wildest Weeper* said. That's what they called their leader. '*Wildest*'. "So that is why you summoned us. For our help. And I thought you cared."

"No one cares about you," thundered Arnel Hammerhand, a giant of a man. A hundred other voices echoed him, coming from the Snowskins and the Deadcloaks and the Crowmen of the Crag. Even the shy Mole Men were shaking their fists.

It was the last thing Stegra needed. "Silence!" he bellowed, trying to restore calm. "Be silent, all of you! Silence!" Wagga the White gave the tooth another clang, swinging hard with the bone club, but it did no good. The entire hall had flown into an uproar, men and women hurling insults and accusations.

"You killed my mother!" one of the young Crowmen was shrieking at Blood-Eye. His feathers fluttered, black as night, as he surged to his feet and drew out a long black dagger. "I found her with her eyes stabbed out! You killed her! I know it was you!"

"I've killed hundreds," Blood-Eye smiled.

Others were cursing them. More allegations were being hurled. One old woman said the Weepers had killed her husband and her sons. Another claimed her daughter had been raped and mutilated and left to die in the snow. One of the big Stone Men pulled a huge rock club from a strap on his back and gave a massive roar, but said no words. A few of the fisherfolk of the Silver Scar scampered away from him at that. Some were even leaving the hall, rushing for the pelt door, demanding that the guards let them through. Those men were under Stegra's charge. He waved a hand so that the people could pass if they wished, and they turned to loose the drapes. At once the winds blew in, a frosted wind sparkling with ice crystals, stirring the flames of the serpent fire, causing the tongues to lick out at strange angles, the smokes to blow in a frenzy.

Wagga was still smashing at the tooth, but the arguing did not stop. Over all that, young Svaldar was shouting of the signs. "The creatures are leaving!" the boy was saying. "Listen to my father! They are leaving these lands and going to the south! It is one of the signs! And the other…the *Ember of the Red Storm* was seen! It was seen! It is *the* sign!"

Many did not heed him, and kept on shouting. Others, those closer, heard and turned to listen. They looked at Svaldar, and then Stegra, their eyes cast into fearful frowns. A few children were crying and clutching at their mothers. All knew the story of the Red Storm, the great dragon, wreathed in red lightning, that slew the bear god Orthrand, thousands of years ago. It was an age of gods and titans, when great monsters roamed the world. The dragon came from the distant lands of the south, a spawn of the Fire God, seeking to prove its power as the titan supreme. For hours, some say days, the two giants fought, until at last the colossal bear was cast down in this valley, his armoured fur breached at the neck, his throat ripped and torn asunder. It was said the fountain of blood that rose to the sky was like a geyser a thousand feet high, red against the cold white world, that when the bear fell the ground shattered beneath him, forming the great crater in which he still lay.

A woods witch, like Black Merryl, only much older and more powerful, had stood in the distance, watching the fight. Her name was Shrikna, and it was she who spread the story, she who said that one day an ember of the Red Storm would be seen, a spark in the night sky, and that it would herald the End Fall, the great snowstorm that would engulf all the lands until the time that the world shattered and ended, or was reborn, in what the steel people called the Last Renewal.

Stegra had not believed that tale, as he had not truly believed the prophecy of the Sea-King either. But then the Steel Lord had come, and the blight had been blown away, and Amron Daecar had found his fabled snow blade to take back to his lands. When Stegra said goodbye to him he had expected to never see him again. He expected only to lead his people to their prophesied land and settle there upon the shore, hunting the woods and fishing the rivers, but then the snow had come. It started as any snowfall, a soft drift gathering on the tops of the trees and coating the ground in a pretty white blanket, but within days all the woods were armoured in ice and the rivers had begun to stop flowing. *The forests fell silent*, he recalled. *The creatures sensed it, and began to leave.* And still the snow did not stop.

It fell for a week, and then another week, and then another, and another, and not once did it stop or slow, it only grew heavier. Stegra had called a council of his own people. They discussed it at length, and he said they had a choice to make. Some of the Snowskin elders said they should go, and abandon their new lands. Others that they should stay, that they had only just arrived, and could not give up so easily. The two-hundred-year prophecy of the Sea-King had been fulfilled. This was a time to celebrate, not surrender, they said.

And so they lingered, hoping the snows would ease. They didn't. They just kept coming, and coming, and coming. Hope thinned, and more were swayed to the notion that the End Fall was upon them. Stegra and his hunters spoke of their time with the Steel Lord. They told the tribe of the scruffy little man called Walter, who was certain the Last Renewal had come, the war to end the War Eternal. It was cruel, Stegra's people lamented. So cruel that their lands should be cleared of the blight only to be taken away again. Wagga the White said that one day they could return. When the world was reborn, the snows would thaw and they could come back, but how many would be left by then? None, if they did not leave. Stegra pressed and pressed, until one day, the huntsman Verner returned from a long ranging, and what he told them sealed their course.

He had seen the Ember.

One night, he said, when camping upon a hilltop, he had seen it pass the sky, the red light moving among the clouds. It drifted slowly, gliding, he told them, before falling away beneath some hills. At once he rushed back, leaving his kill behind. When he told Stegra what he'd seen the chieftain convened his people once more. He let Verner speak, telling them of his tale, and that same night Verner was christened with his new name, Verner the Herald, the one who had seen the sign. When the huntsman was done, Stegra saw no further dissent among his people. "We leave," he had said to them. "Send out word to the other tribes. Tell them to gather at the Hall of Orthrand."

And so they had come, gathering over the last week. *And now we make our choice. Now we become one tribe.*

The noise was thick in Stegra's ears. His head was pounding, drumming with the beat of Wagga's club against Orthrand's fang. Many were staring at him, waiting for him to confirm his son's words. He pulled back the hood of his cloak, and shouted. "The Ember has been seen. As the woods witch said it would, thousands of years ago." He waved for Verner to climb the stage. The man joined him there. "Verner the Herald has seen the light spark in the sky, red as blood, spawn of the slayer of Orthrand. It cannot be denied! Tomorrow, the Snowkins will go south across the mountains. Who is with us? Who will come?"

The Walrus Lord was helped again to his feet, but many were still shouting and arguing and calling their curses and his words could not be heard. Wagga smashed harder at the tooth until he grew weary, and Svaldar took over, young and strong, pounding. Hraka the Great added his booming voice, and his Stone Men smashed clubs against the table, cracking the wood, splinters flying. "Quiet! Quiet! QUIET!" the stone lord bellowed. "I have heard enough! I will come with you, Snowfist! The Stone Men are with you!"

Stegra nodded at him. He met with the gaze of the Walrus Lord, who lowered his head, tusks clicking, and then sat back down with the help of his men. The voice of Black Merryl sliced through the tumult. Her eyes were like green moss, her hair tangled and black and wild. It was said she derived from Shrikna's line, blood of the ancient woods witch. "Is this of the Ember true?" Her eyes moved to Verner. "You saw it?"

Verner told her yes with a nod. Then another voice said, "I have seen it too."

Stegra looked around. The din was dying out now, more turning to listen. The voice was a woman's, pitched high. Stegra saw her. One of the fisherfolk of the Scar. A young woman with an ice pick at her hip and a frog spear in her grasp, wearing clothes of thick, roughspun wool and a cloak of greatyak fur.

"You've seen the Ember?" Stegra asked her. He did not know the woman's name.

She nodded. "It is why we came. We are of the high northwest, where the Scar nears the sea. I saw the light near the mountain.'

"The tomb of the steel god?" hissed Merryl. Her face twisted. "The Ember went close?"

"Only so close," the fisherwoman answered. "Then it veered away, as the mountain stirred."

"Stirred?" Stegra asked. "The mountain is dead. I saw it die." He had been there the day the caverns and chambers collapsed, the bridges and the stairs and the towers all tumbling. They only just escaped, he and the Steel Lord and Blacksteel and Walter. Before then, the mountain had been rumbling for weeks, months, even so long as a year. But that day was the worst. It felt as though the trapped spirit of the god Vandar was raging down inside the earth, giving out his final death bellow before the world came down upon him.

"It still lives," claimed the river-woman. She looked to others of her clan, in their yak-cloaks and river garb. Some of them were nodding. "It is weak, but the mountain lives."

"Not dead, but dying," rumbled Hraka the Great. "When the End Fall comes, all gods die." The huge men about him murmured in assent.

"The Ember is said to recall the Red Storm," said one of the Crowmen in a rasping voice. He was hook-nosed and big and old, ugly as sin. Stegra knew him as Drekka Darkwing, once their finest warrior, uncle to their leader Tarek. He gave his nephew wise council now, rather than the heads of his enemies. "The Ember is a spark that lights the fire, and when it burns bright the Red Storm returns."

There were shudders in the crowd, hisses as the women quietened their whimpering children. One young boy was sobbing loudly, and his mother stood and dragged him out of the hall, cursing him all the while. She had to pass the Wild Weepers to get there. All were glowering, but quiet now, still bearing their cruel blunts and blades. The accusations hurled at them had not been taken well. Blood-Eye looked like he could set fire to the hall and march out laughing, as he listened to them all die.

Stegra met his eyes. "You have heard what's been said, Blood-Eye. The signs and omens. And you have seen the snows fall thick upon your peaks. You know we have no choice. You know it. So I ask you again. Will you lead us through the mountains?"

This time no one shouted out at him, or said they were not wanted. There were no scathing words from Kusto Crowbane or Arnel Hammerhand, no insults and allegations from the others gathered in the hall. A silence fell, deep as the *Rifts of Relkor*. Blood-Eye stared out, emotionless, stretching the silence out. Then at last he grinned that bloody grin and shook his head. "No."

He turned to the pelt door, his Weepers falling in about him. Stegra's men were there, blocking the way out. They looked up at him, not sure what to do. There were only four of them, against ten. Stegra stared down the serpent fire, through the flickering flames, the rising smokes. He wanted to march down there and take Blood-Eye's head from his shoulders himself, but what could he do? The man would not be for turning, the Snowfist knew. He grunted and waved a hand. "So be it," he growled. "Let them pass."

"Craven!" someone bellowed after them.

"Betrayer!" said another.

Others shouted them off as Blood-Eye and his men slipped out into the storm, their voices full of hate. They were men of the free lands beyond the realm of the steel lords. They were kin. Dark kin, yes, but kin, and yet they were to turn their backs on their brothers and their sisters and let them die in the snow. Stegra looked down at Tarek, disgusted. "Are you with us?" he asked him.

The chief of the Crowmen nodded. "There are ways I know. Perilous ways, but if we leave soon…"

A scream ripped through the air outside.

Everyone stopped, eyes moving to the door. *Blood-Eye,* Stegra thought. They had the rage in them. The bloody gums. *They came here to kill…*

"On me, Snowkins!" The Snowfist marched down the earthen steps and through the tables, past the serpent flame. His men pressed in about him, pulling weapons from their hips and backs. There were more screams outside, ringing on the howling wind. Other warriors joined them. Hraka was calling his Stone Men to arms in their own tongue. Narek, son of Tarek, was drawing black steel from his feathered cloak and his best warriors were doing the same. Blood-Eye had brought only ten men into the hall, but outside? How many were lurking outside?

Another scream rang out, and then another, and another. Stegra was running now, his son at his hip. He reached the pelt door and swept it aside, pressing into the great white storm. The camp was spread out before him, a thousand shelters and tents raised in clusters and clumps, shadows in the mist. There was screaming out there, half heard through the storm. Shapes ghosted through squalls of snow, rushing in different directions.

"Blood-Eye!" Stegra bellowed. He set off at a hard march, boots crunching through the snow. Out of the corner of his eye he saw a group of people standing and staring out into the camp. He glanced at them as he passed and saw the Wild Weepers there, Blood-Eye with them. Some were looking up. Stegra swung about. "You! Is this you? You treacherous…"

The next scream was much closer. A woman right behind him. His eyes snapped back, his words cut off. There was a shadow above, a large shadow slicing through the sky, moving quicker than he would have believed. It went straight over them, fading into the mists with a rush of air. A stream of red light went with it, burning.

"The Ember!" someone screamed. "The Ember has come!"

Chaos erupted about him. Voices rang out across the valley. His eyes widened, bright and clear as moonstones, reflecting the sudden light of the gushing crimson flame that poured down from the skies. Tents burst afire, one and then another and then another and then another as that red river emptied upon them. Stegra watched on in horror as men scrambled out, flames pouring from their cloaks, to throw themselves down into the snow. A line of greatyaks was caught beneath the blaze, their huge fur coats combusting, the shelters on their backs throwing smoke into the sky. The animals reared, ripping at their ropes and fastenings, charging away in all directions. Two crashed into each other and fell down to die. Another went running headlong through the camp of the Stone Men, knocking giants aside as they tried to calm it, smashing into their shelters and lean-tos. Another three were lumbering away in a wild frenzy, straight through the other camps, the fires spreading.

"Bring it down!" someone bellowed. "Bring it down!"

Hraka the Great rushed passed him, with his Stone Men following in a thunder. Black Merryl was screaming out some wild incantation in words Stegra did not know, her hands raised to the skies. A sudden wind blew past him, coming from the camp, bringing with it smoke and ash that choked him. He coughed, raised a hand to his mouth. He could feel the rush of wind as the Ember flew overhead, feel the burning heat as it blew down its searing flame. "Snowskins!" he spluttered. "Snowskins, on me!" They had no weapons to kill this beast, but they had to try. He stepped forward.

There was a sound to his side, a grunt of pain. Stegra turned. Kusto Crowbane was on his knees, blood pulsing from between his fingers as he clutched at his throat. A Wild Weeper stood before him, a short savage stabbing blade in his fist. Two quick thrusts and he put out Kusto's eyes, blood gushing from the sockets. Kusto fell.

Stegra's eyes flared open in a terrible rage. He could see Blood-Eye standing there, smiling his bloody smile. "We're all going to die anyway," the Wildest Weeper said. He tore a length of serrated steel from his hip and pointed it right at the Snowfist. "Might as well kill you first."

Stegra the Snowfist, Chieftain of the Snowskins, drew an axe from the strap on his back. He looked at his friend Kusto Crowbane, blinded and dying on the floor, saw the blood spreading out across the snow, red on white, steaming. Away in the camp, the fires were spreading. A thousand voices rang out in terror on the wind. It was the end, and Stegra knew it. *So be it,* he thought.

He stepped toward his enemy, roaring.

1

Amron

He dreamt of a table, set high above the world.

Cloud cloaked it, and a vibrant golden light, raining down upon the fallen men of Varin's Order.

Cups and chalices and mugs uncountable filled the cedar wood surface, brimming with ale and mead and whiskey and wine, quaffed and refilled as the stories were sung. A hundred voices echoed out in account, some epic, some tragic, some humorous, regaling the men around them of their triumphs and toils, their victories and vices, to cheers and laughs and sombre silence as appropriate for the tale being told. The table was long, endlessly long, bleeding away to the edge of sight and sound. Into the far distance it unrolled, as straight and true as the immutable movement of time, the men sitting shoulder to shoulder to either side, drinking and feasting and singing in this, the greatest of the Eternal Halls.

The noise was cacophonous, joyful and all-consuming, a din of impenetrable merriment and mirth. Men came and went as they pleased, fading through the clouds that cloaked the hall to visit with their friends and loved ones. There were many chambers among the Eternal Halls, many rooms and gardens and terraces, some open to all, others restricted to but a few. The Knights of Varin could walk freely, the Steel Father himself had decreed. His Table was not to be a prison sentence, he had said, to shackle his knights forever to the seat they had been assigned. "Let them stand and leave and wander," he had proclaimed. "Let them visit their loved ones at their need, and return, whenever they so wish."

Yet always to the same seat, when they did. A seat determined by the sum of a man's attainments, when walking the ephemeral plane.

There were faces Amron knew. Faces of old friends, lost but never forgotten. First Blades and kings, warriors and champions, famous faces he'd seen depicted in ink and dye and wood and stone, carved and drawn and painted. At the head sat Varin himself, thunderous of voice, impossibly grand of stature, with a great blue mantle swaying at his back, silver armour of pristine brilliance shining out with a light of its own.

The very greatest of his bloodline sat about him. His eldest son Elin, powerful and proud, his youngest Ayrin, temperate and wise. Amron saw in his dream his namesake, Amron the Bold, son of Ayrin, grandson of Varin, who had renewed war after an age of peace, seeking vengeance for his grandfather's fall. He saw King Gideon the Great, who had won the War of Wrath two thousand years ago, and Balion the Brute, one of the greatest warriors the north ever known, scourge of dragons, Master of Winds and Mist. His own father had been named for Gideon, his grandfather for Balion. Both sat among the privileged few, with other great First Blades of the past; Rufus Taynar and Oswald Manfrey and more, so many more.

Amron stood aside, observing and ignored, the only man living among a great hall of the dead. *The man grows to fit the name,* he thought, recalling what his father had told him once. Now here his father was, sitting with Gideon the Great, and his grandfather too with Balion the Brute. Great names. The making of great men. He looked from one man to the next, then found that King Amron the Bold was looking right at him, and he alone among the host. "The man grows to fit the name," he said, in a thick and heavy voice. "Have you earned *mine*, Amron Daecar? You, who let my city fall."

Amron had no answer. He found his eyes moving away.

A drum-beat sounded, sudden as thunder, a single thud crashing through the hall. Amron turned his eyes back to the head to find Varin himself rising to his feet, towering above them all. He held an arm aloft, and called, "Brothers, sons, my children, my family, my friends. Another joins us. Another ascends to his seat." He gestured to the side of the hall, where the cloak of clouds began to part to make a door-way. The silhouette of a man took form, approaching. "We welcome to our family another Daecar," King Varin bellowed out. "Vesryn, son of Gideon, grandson of Balion, to take his place among us. The only other man to have fended off the Dread!"

The silence was shattered as Vesryn stepped forth to join them. A thousand voices sang out his name, and fists beat down loudly upon the table, clattering countless cups and plates and jugs.

"Vesryn Daecar!" they roared. "Daecar! Daecar! He who stood against the Dread!"

Varin was smiling and waving him over, and near the head of the table, a seat was being drawn back. Amron recognised the figure of Vesryn the Valiant, an ancient First Blade and champion for whom his brother had been named. "I give you my appellation, Vesryn Daecar," he proclaimed, to a round of raucous cheers. "Valiant is the man who stands alone against the Dread. Vesryn the Valiant is *you* now, my brother."

Vesryn shook his head humbly. "I was not alone, my lords. My brother, my nephew, we all…"

But his next words were swallowed by noise, as all the men huddled about him, demanding he tell his tale. Amron felt himself being drawn away, as though expelled by some unseen force, the clouds thickening, voices dimming. He could faintly hear Vesryn calling out for Aleron. "My seat…my seat…I will give my seat to him…" He could see Amron the Bold still staring at him, jaw fixed in disapproval. "You let my city fall. You've not yet earned my name, Amron Daecar…"

And last of all, a chant, as his body was dragged away. "Daecar, Daecar," the men of the order were crying. "Daecar, Daecar…*Daecar*…"

"…Daecar…Lord Daecar? My lord…*Amron*…"

He stirred from his sleep, eyes snapping open at once. A hand was shaking at his shoulder, black leather over dark grey steel. Before him stood a shadow in the darkness, half lit by the gentle flicker of fire from a torch.

"My lord, a messenger has come. He is waiting for you at the River Gate."

Amron cleared his throat and sat up. He'd only intended to rest his eyes a moment, but after two days without sleep… "What messenger, Rogen? From where?"

"North, my lord. From up the river."

"Crosswater?"

Whitebeard nodded. "He has a letter, he says, for your eyes only." The ranger's own eyes looked black in the dark, like a shark's, yet all the same Amron could see the worry in them. "It isn't good news I fear, my lord."

There is no good news anymore. Amron stood wearily, lumbering over to a side table to gulp down a cup of water. Pain tore through him with every step, his right thigh burning, his left shoulder jumping and cramping in spasms. He ignored it, harnessed it, as he was learning to do. *As I have to do.* At a touch the Frostblade would cast aside his ails, but he could not rely on it forever. *I will give it up,* he promised himself, as he had ten thousand times before.

He put down his cup, and met the eyes of Rogen Strand. "How long was I sleeping?" he asked.

"An hour or so, my lord."

Amron nodded. It felt shorter. A blink and no more. His head was heavy, his eyes the same, the exhaustion thick in his blood.

"You need to rest more," Rogen Whitebeard said. "If there's another attack…"

"Soon," he promised. The assault on King's Point had happened only two days ago and there had been much and more to deal with since then. In the meantime, tonics brewed by the medics would do to keep him functional. *And this*, he thought, as he hitched the Frostblade around his armoured waist. The power of Vandar himself lay within the metal. It was plenty to sustain him for now. "Lead on."

They passed through the broken doorway of the building in which Amron had taken his rest, some part of an old soldier barracks that had been only partly destroyed during the attack. Outside was a world of rubble and ash, of tumbled towers and stone-strewn squares, blackened and scorched. The survivors from the battle had taken up temporary residence in the ruin of the city, raising tents and shelters where they could, living like rats among the wreckage as they crept about, eyes skyward, ever fearing the return of the Dread. Amron Daecar shared that fear, though did not let it show. If he wilted under the weight of it all, what hope did his soldiers have? *Far too many men have deserted us already. If I crumble, the rest will follow.*

Ash coated the streets like snow, billowing and stirring with each step of his godsteel sabatons. Amron had not taken off his armour since long before the battle began, nor would he for some time to come, he knew. He felt filthy beneath it, his linens and leathers soaked and stained, his face spotted with gouts of dirt and soot, his hair an unwashed cascade of oily, greying black locks. *I feel like this city,* he reflected. *Broken and covered in grime.*

The way to the River Gate was choked with sleeping men, tucked up into whatever nook or cranny they could find; up against half-broken walls and under half-fallen roofs, in doorways and arches that once led into buildings and now led nowhere but rubble. Many huddled around fires to keep warm, muttering in muted tones, or gazing into empty space in a thousand-yard stare. Shock had gripped great swathes of them, an ailment not all would escape. Mental scars that would render them useless should they see wings in the skies again.

Others had suffered physical injury, broken limbs and savage cleaves from claw and fang and steel. Many more were burned. Great long lines of men lay down the alleys and lanes and across open stone squares with bandages wrapped about their legs and arms, torsos and necks and faces, moaning in pain as medics moved about, trying to tend to them as best they could.

Some stirred at Amron's passing, but few. Those that did tried to smile, or raise a fist in salute, or render words of courtesy for their commander and champion. Amron returned their smiles, passed on words of comfort where he could. To dying men, it was all he could give them. Solace, and a promise that their trials on this earth were done.

The great square inside the River Gate had been cleared of much of the rubble. Here the command posts were raised by whatever senior lords and captains remained, to take account of their losses and what men they had left, to list out the names of the dead and deserters, to arrange crews to search for those as yet unaccounted for, of which there were thousands lying dead beneath the rubble or trapped underground within the subterranean sanctuaries that spread beneath King's Point like a warren.

Before the fighting, Amron had ordered Lady Brockenhurst and her courtiers to take refuge in the sanctuary beneath the Spear, along with Lord Warton, her Castellan, and Walter Selleck as well. By some stroke of fortune, all of them had survived, even as the tunnels and chambers collapsed around them, the ceilings crumbling as the Spear itself came down, torn apart by the wrath of the Dread. It was Walter's doing, Amron knew. "Your luck remains, my friend," he had said to him, when greeting him after the battle. The self-styled 'luckiest man in the world' had been insistent that Vandar's *light* had deserted him. Clearly that was not so.

Others were not so fortunate. Many civilians had gone down into their refuges to take cover before the battle, and many soldiers had joined them when they saw the Dread approaching. Most still remained, dead or trapped it was hard to know for sure. Even now, the search crews could hear tapping echoing from below, hear the faint fearful sound of voices crying out for a saviour. Getting to them was another matter, however, with the city so unstable. In truth most would die down there, entombed forever in the sanctuaries that were meant to save them.

I was meant to save them, Amron Daecar thought. Dream or not, his ancient namesake had been right. *I have not yet earned the name…*

The River Gate was under the guard of Sir Adam Thorley, Commander of the Pointed Watch, the King's Point city guard. It was a charge as dead as the city itself. As dead as tens of thousands of men. "My lord," the young knight said, seeing him approach. He had with him a dozen of his men, wearing war-weary faces, all clad in doom. And the messenger, standing with his horse. By the look of that lather about the horse's mouth, he'd been riding hard for hours.

"Sir Adam. Anything new to report?"

"Yes, sire. More stragglers and deserters have returned. Mostly Vandarian. But some southerners as well. The former are being taken in by their own commanders. Captain Lythian is handling the latter."

There's no better man for it. It was not just their own men who'd deserted during the battle. Many thousands of southerners had done the same, fleeing into the woods at the sight of the Dread, and over the past two days, scores had returned, preferring to give themselves over as captives than try to make it on their own in the north, with enemies all about them. Lythian had been given the charge of handling and housing them, such as he could, though it was only a short term solution. *One problem among many,* Amron thought. *Has this messenger brought me another?*

He gave Sir Adam a nod, then turned to the man in question. "Your name," he said.

"Sir Hutchin, my lord. A knight of House Bygate, sworn to the Harrows of Crosswater." He glanced uneasily about, then withdrew a scroll from within his leather glove. "Lord Harrow had me ride here with his finest horse…with all haste, my lord. We have barely taken rest over the last two days."

"Take it now. Your duty is done." Amron turned. "Sir Adam, see that Sir Hutchin is taken somewhere quiet to sleep, and make sure his horse is fed and watered."

"Yes, sire."

Amron took the scroll, ripped the seal, and read the words. The colour drained at once from his cheeks. It was just as he had feared.

"My lord," Sir Adam prompted. "What does it say?"

Our worst nightmare. He rolled up the note, slipped it into a pocket in his cloak, and drew a breath. "Gather my council, Sir Adam. There is something they need to hear."

It did not take long for them to assemble, each man stepping through the flaps of Amron's command pavilion in quick succession as soon as they got the call. Some had been sleeping. Others were on duty elsewhere, attending to their orders. They came all the same, bleary-eyed and battle-worn, with scorch marks on their cloaks and armour and haunted looks in their eyes. Some were nursing minor injuries - Sir Quinn Sharp had a broken wrist, Sir Taegon Cargill a deep cleave across his left cheek - while others bore wounds of grief. Rodmond Taynar had lost his uncle, Lord Dalton, the First Blade dying in his arms on the battlefield from a fatal loss of blood. The Ironfoot, Lord Gavron Grave, had lost his nephew Sir Marlon. Others had seen dear friends die, those they counted as brothers. Amron had lost his brother by blood, Elyon his beloved uncle. Yet none compared to the suffering of poor Sir Torus Stoutman, whose sons Darun, Elmid, and Hoddin, had all gone to the Eternal Halls.

The pavilion was empty but for a single oakwood table and blocks of uneven stone to act as seats. There was no carpet, no furnishings, no comforts whatsoever. Two iron braziers had been brought in to provide light and warmth, yet there was a coldness here that could not be driven away by fire. Few sat. Only Lord Warton - who shuffled in, coughing - and the Ironfoot took perch; elsewise the others remained standing. Amron looked across at them all once the full complement had come, standing on the far side of the table. Some scrolls scattered it; scribbled plans, the early workings of strategy, flanked by a pair of fat tallow candles, burning low.

He decided to avoid preamble. Withdrawing the note from his pocket, he said, "Varinar came under attack two days ago, after the Dread flew north…" He looked around, saw nothing resembling shock. Desperation and despair, yes, but those were already present. In truth all had expected this. "The defences were quickly overwhelmed, Lord Harrow writes. We all saw how many dragons Drulgar had with him when he left. That many…with the Dread at the fore…"

"Is it destroyed?" Elyon asked. He stood to one side, near the canvas wall, pale-faced, still recovering from the exertions of the battle.

28

Elyon had been hit by a blast from the Bondstone, the very will of Agarath striking at his chest mid-flight and knocking him to the earth. Though his godsteel armour had protected him from the brunt of it, it had taken its toll all the same, rendering him incapable of flight ever since.

"I don't know, Elyon," Amron answered. "But after what happened here…we must assume the damage is considerable."

"How did Lord Harrow get word?" asked Sir Quinn Sharp, a Varin Knight broad-faced and homely, stout and capable. "Is he not in Crosswater?"

"A crow got out of Varinar during the attack. From your uncle, Sir Quinn. He scribbled a note, telling of the titan, towers falling, walls tumbling. Wings in the skies, blotting out the sun. The very fire of hell itself pouring from the Lowers. The note was taken to the nearest rookery and by chance the crow managed to make it to Crosswater. When Lord Harrow received it, he despatched a rider here at once."

"He's dead, then," Sir Quinn said, digesting that for a moment. "My uncle."

"We don't know that." Sir Bomfrey Sharp had been put in charge of the defence of the capital, along with Sir Hank Rothwell and Sir Winslow Bryant. All three were household knights of middling standing, the best of what was left with so many senior knights and lords away. In all likelihood, all three were dead. Along with tens of thousands of others. *Hundreds, even.* The thought was a knife in his heart. A cold knife, twisting.

Sir Taegon Cargill gave out a heavy grunt. "So your uncle's dead, what of it? We've *all* lost people, Sharp." He swung a mighty arm toward Sir Torus Stoutman, standing beside him, cloaked in sorrow. "Torus lost his *three* sons. Sons, Sharp. *Sons.* No one cares about your bloody uncle."

"This isn't a competition, Sir Taegon," Amron said. "We do not battle over grief."

"I have two sons as well," Sir Quinn retorted to the giant. "Young boys, up in the Ironmoors. They might be dead as well, so far as I know…"

"Speculation will not serve us," Lythian came in. "We deal with what we know, Sir Quinn."

"Easy for you to say. You have no children of your own."

The Knight of the Vale nodded. "A curse, it has always been said, to have no sons and heirs. Perhaps now it is more a blessing? I do not pretend to understand your fear, Sir Quinn, but…"

"My fear? My fear is enough to drive me home, sir. Return to my wife and sons and…"

"Desert?" boomed the Giant of Hammerhall. "We've got enough of those cravens already." He snorted and spat out a name. "*Stone.* If I see Sir Ramsey again, I'll pull his scrawny little head off. Don't make me do the same to you, Sharp."

Sir Quinn raised his chin. "I'm no deserter, Taegon." He looked at Amron. "I'm not, my lord. I hope you know that."

"I do." Amron had a good sense of his men. Or at least he thought he did. Once before he could sniff out a coward a mile off, but in these darkening days those margins were starting to thin. He did not begrudge a man the urge to return home to defend his family. *Yet if we all do that, what then?* Their only hope was to keep on fighting. If they splintered now, all would be lost.

Elyon took a step forward from the side, an urging look in his eye. "I have to go, Father," he said. "Varinar. I *should* have gone already."

"You've been bedridden, Elyon. This isn't your fault. There's nothing you could have done."

"I could have tracked him. Drulgar. Maybe even drawn him off." He clenched his jaw in self-rebuke, but there was only so much Elyon could do. "I'll go now. Tonight. We have to know the truth."

"We know the truth," Lord Gavron Grave rumbled. He heaved to his feet, a heavyset man of sixty-two, stamping down on his godsteel leg. "We all saw what he did to us here, and we all heard Sir Bomfrey's words. Towers falling, walls tumbling. Wings blotting out the sun. A hellish inferno. That doesn't paint a good enough picture for you, boy?"

"One man's words. One man's eyes. I can look upon Varinar from a different vantage, my lord."

Sir Storos Pentar agreed. "Varinar is ten times as large as King's Point. With ten times as many towers and ten times as many ballistas. Perhaps only a part of it was destroyed. The rest…"

"Is rubble," the Ironfoot broke in. "Same as here. Ten times the size…ten times the prize. The Dread has always wanted to see Varinar burn. There's no stopping that monster."

"I disagree." Amron would not allow this sort of thinking to infect his men. The Ironfoot was as staunch as a man could be, famous for having his own leg cut off after he broke it during a hunting accident, and replacing it with godsteel. If he could be allowed to wilt like this, then others would be sure to follow. *I'll not let this pessimism become a plague, spreading from man to man.* "The Dread *can* be defeated, Lord Grave, *never* think otherwise," he said. His tone brooked no rejection. *I must hammer this message home.* "As soon as we start thinking we are lost, then we are, and there is no coming back from it. My brother drew blood from the dragon. So did my son. And there were gashes on his face and neck when he arrived. He can be cut, wounded, weakened. Perhaps his assault on Varinar has proven his folly. A few well-placed ballista bolts would have even Drulgar reeling. It only takes one, my lord. As a man can die from an arrow to the eye, so the Dread can die from a bolt."

Lord Gavron gave a grunt, nodded, and sat again, taking the weight off his godsteel leg. "Didn't mean to sound defeatist, Amron.

30

You're right. Anything living can be killed. I'm just saying, it won't be easy."

"Killing a dragon is never easy. Less so a giant one."

Elyon gripped the Windblade, as though trying to muster his strength. "We have to know for certain. If I leave now, I can get to Varinar and back within hours."

"No, Elyon. You're not strong enough yet."

"I am. I will be." He drew the blade out a few inches, and let a gust of wind blow off it, stirring cloaks and canvas both. Some vitality returned to his cheeks. "Varinar. Elinar. *Ilivar*. If Drulgar attacked the capital, he may have flown elsewhere as well. We *need* to know." He took a step closer. "Father, *Lillia*…"

"I know." Amron couldn't let personal concerns drive his course. Lillia had been in Ilivar the last they knew, under the care of her grandfather Lord Brydon. According to Elyon, Amara had left Varinar in a bid to bring her home. It was possible she had done so, that they were back in the city when it was attacked. Or in Ilivar. Or on the road, which carried great perils of its own. In such times, he had to accept the possibility that his daughter was already dead. Accept it, and not dwell on it. Yet all the same…

He looked his son in the eye. "You know the importance of the blade you carry, Elyon. You know they may be our only chance. If you should encounter Drulgar again, or another dragon…if you should fall, and lose the blade…"

"I won't. I'm rested, Father. I'm ready."

Several other men gave assenting nods, murmuring agreement. Sir Ralf of Rotting Bridge offered counsel. "Learning the true fate of Varinar is essential. It could be as you say, my lord, and the Dread was driven away. If so there may be a chance to salvage and rebuild, regather our strength behind whatever is left of its walls."

"And abandon the coast?" asked Sir Adam, aghast. "If we leave King's Point, the Agarathi will be able to land on our shores unhindered. If they return…"

"They ran," thundered Sir Taegon Cargill. "They saw the dragon and ran. They won't be coming back."

"They expected him no more than we did," Sir Adam retorted. "They fled to their ships by instinct, in terror, but when their commanders get a grip of them, they'll be back. They will swarm us, take this city, and continue upriver to finish the job the dragons have started. The Fire Father will make sure of it. He'll destroy us all."

Chaos and calamity and the ending of the world, Amron thought.

"The Agarathi are slaves, in thrall to Eldur's rule," said Lythian. "We must work to break those chains, free them, and work with them. Our very survival depends on it."

"Work…work *with* them?" baulked Sir Gerald Strand, in a disbelieving huff. "These men came here to kill us. And now what? We're to just kiss and make up? No. I say we hang them, open their necks, throw them in the Red Sea and make it redder. Tie them to the masts of whatever ships they left behind and sink them. Send every last one of those bastards down to Daarl's Domain."

"No," Lythian said at once. "That is *not* how we treat prisoners of war here, Sir Gerald."

"Ignore him, Captain Lythian," Rodmond Taynar said darkly, staring into Sir Gerald's piggish little eyes. "We all know how Gerald treats his friends. It's no wonder he'd advocate such cruelty toward his enemies."

The doughy knight fronted up to that, swinging his soft bulk in Rodmond's direction. "And just what do you mean by that?"

"You know what I mean."

It didn't take long for Sir Gerald to puzzle it out. "King Ellis? Is that it? One little mistake, and I'm tarred forever?"

"*One* mistake? You stood by and let your own king be thrown from a balcony. If I had it my way, you'd be thrown back into your cell, Strand. How many men died here two days ago? How many thousands of good honest men. And *you* survive. At least Sir Alyn did us the courtesy of dying. But you, no. You just had to live on."

"Na..Nathaniel did too." Sir Gerald's flabby chins were wobbling. "If you're to direct your odium somewhere, Sir Rodmond, why not at…"

"Him?" Rodmond looked over to where Sir Nathaniel Oloran stood, quietly observing. "Because he knows his place. He knows not to speak unless he's got something useful to contribute. And he acquitted himself with honour during the battle. I saw. I was there. Nathaniel tried to save my uncle. But you? Where were *you*, Sir Gerald? When we all rushed out to meet the Dread, when we fought the dragons across the field, where were you?"

"I…I…"

"Nowhere. You were nowhere. Hiding, most likely. Curled up in some pit, bawling like a child and pissing yourself." He barred his teeth. Amron had never seen the young man like this before. "My uncle - your own cousin - was awoken in his sickbed, with a stab wound in his gut, and that didn't stop him donning his armour and marching out to fight at the head of his men. He fought *hard*, so hard his stitches ripped open, and the wound in his gut tore even wider. He fought on, even as he bled to death. He died a hero, Sir Gerald. And you live on, a worm…"

"Rodmond." Elyon stepped over, resting a hand on his friend's shoulder. "That'll do now. That's enough."

"Is it? You hate him as much as I do, Elyon. We *all* hate him. His very presence here insults me."

Sir Gerald's pockmarked cheeks had gone bright red. He made a harrumphing sound, as though to try to maintain some dignity. "I don't need to hear this. I'm the heir to House Strand, not some common serving man. Your great aunt Margery was my mother, Rodmond. We're family. You have no right to speak to me like this."

"I have every right. I'm your lord now."

"Lord of a dying house."

"A *dying* house?" Rodmond's fist gripped steel. "Say that again."

Sir Gerald drew back. "I only mean…how many Taynar men died here? And how many in Varinar? Your grandfather is dead, your uncle. After you…"

"Enough," Amron boomed, lest this devolve even further. "We are *all* under threat of extinction, every house in the north, great, middling and small. Every knightly house, new and renowned. Every family. Every man, woman, and child. That's the truth. When we come out on the other side of this, who knows what will be left. All we can do now is fight to retain what we have. *Together*. Enough of this bickering."

Silence followed his words, though the tension was thick enough to cut. *This isn't the time for this*, Amron realised. They needed rest, all of them. Nothing useful would be accomplished until they'd cleared their heads. "We can resume on the morrow," he decided. "Get some sleep, all of you, that's an order. Sir Adam, make sure that our borders are well watched."

"As well as they can be, my lord. I have men at every breach and broken tower, and sentries on the intact sections of wall. We'll have warning if anyone comes."

Amron nodded. *Or anything.* "Until tomorrow, then." He made to step around the table.

Elyon moved in his way. "We haven't finished, Father. I don't want to go without your permission. But I will, if I must."

Amron let out a breath. *There'll be no fighting him on this one. And he's right, we need to know.* "Fine. If you're sure you're strong enough…"

"I am."

"Then go. Rest at Crosswater if you feel you need to. See what you can learn, and return at once. I want you back here as soon as possible, Elyon."

"Yes, my lord." Elyon gave a bow, turned, took a pace, then stopped. "*King*," he said, looking at the exit flaps. He let the word hang for a moment, then turned back again to address the council. "My *king*." He met Amron's eyes. "It's time we started saying it, Father. We've never needed one more. A king, to unite us. *Inspire* us."

The men in the room shifted stance at once, sensing a moment of import, backs straightening, chins rising. Heads went up and down, nodding. Eyes steeled. Lord Gavron Grave pushed up from his stone seat; Lord Warton rose, suppressing a cough. "*King*," said Lythian, tasting the title on his tongue. "It's always suited you, Amron. About time we made it official."

Sir Taegon dropped to a knee, godsteel cracking on stone. He pulled the great warhammer of House Cargill from his back and laid it down before him. "King Daecar," he boomed. "My hammer is yours."

"And my blade," said Sir Quinn, kneeling at Cargill's side, and at once the others went to follow, Sir Nathaniel and Sir Gerald, Sir Ralf of Rotting Bridge, Sir Torus Stoutman and Sir Storos Pentar, the Iron-foot and Lord Warton, Lord Barrow, Lord Kindrick, and Lord Rodmond Taynar, Rogen Whitebeard, his faithful guard, and Walter Selleck, his faithful scribe, and Lythian, his closest friend, and Elyon, his last living son….every one of them went to one knee.

Amron watched them all go down, and accepted that it was time.

"I meant to share the rule with your uncle, Lord Taynar," he said to young Rodmond. "By rights that honour should go to you now. If you want it…"

"I never wanted it, *Your Majesty*. Not to be a lord, much less a king." Rodmond glanced across at Elyon. "Your son will tell you. I'm meant to follow, not to lead. This is your kingdom to rule."

"Yours, as it should always have been," said Lythian, looking up at him.

And from the booming lungs of Sir Taegon came the roar, "Long live the king! King Amron Daecar! Long live the king!" Without prompting, he rose to his feet, threw open the flaps, and let his bellow ring out through the ruin of the city. "Long live the king! Long live the king!" And with his great warhammer raised aloft, he marched in the smoggy night air, bellowing for all to hear.

The others took up the chant, standing and going with him, drawing their misting blades, thrusting them to the skies. Elyon and Lythian moved to Amron's sides, taking his arms, leading him forth. They marched him out into the open square, to the tents and pavilions, the captains and commanders, the banners whipping in the wind. Men emerged from inside, and appeared from broken alleys. Upon the shattered walls, the watchmen and bowmen looked down. And across the square, across the city, the chant began to echo and grow.

"Long live the king! Long live the king! *Long live the king!*"

2

Jonik

He found her standing alone, gazing up at the statue of Thala.

"Your Highness. It is time."

Amilia Lukar did not stir or turn to face him. Nor did she answer at once. A moment passed, and then another, before she cocked her head a little to one side and said, "The eyes," as she continued to stare upward, shifting her weight to the left and right. "They seem to follow you as you move. It's like she's watching us still, even after all this time."

It was where the Book of Contracts had been placed, this chamber, set upon a podium accessed up a short stone stair. The statue extended out from the wall toward it, looming over all the death and darkness that the Far-Seeing Queen had foreseen. *And written into that book,* Jonik thought. *For us mere mortals to carry out.*

"There is strange magic here, my lady," he told her. "Hamlyn carved this statue himself, some time after Thala's death. Perhaps he wrought the eyes with that particular intent, to watch those who pass below."

"Hamlyn," Amilia repeated. "Hamlyn the Humble." She took a moment to muse on the epithet. "Is that how he seemed to you, Jonik? *Humble?* This mage who presided over so much suffering?"

"He presided over fate, my lady."

"Then fate is suffering. Is that what you're trying to tell me?" She turned at last from the statue of Thala and met his steel grey eyes. Her garb was simple, warm, plain, the same colour as her long brown hair. In the contours of her face he saw shades of his mother, who was her aunt, and in the hue of her eyes as well, an arresting emerald green. *My mother, who gave her life so we could live.*

Two days. It had only been two days since then, but already the world felt different.

"I'm not trying to tell you anything, my lady. Only that we're all part of something bigger."

"As written in this famous book of yours." She turned, gesturing to the high stone plinth. "I had hoped to find it here, cousin. What do you call it? The Tome that Doomed a Thousand Souls?"

Ten thousand would be closer. "The Book of Contracts," he said.

"I wanted to see it, flip through its pages, perhaps even find my own name. I was part of the final contract, after all. My own name, my own fate, written in ink thousands of years ago." She smiled bemusedly. "Odd, isn't it? There is so much more to this world than I ever knew. So many layers beneath the surface, like an onion, waiting to be peeled."

And when you do, Jonik thought, *you cry.* He doubted his royal cousin had ever peeled an onion in her life, let alone felt the sting of cutting and preparing a hundred of them, as he once did here as a boy when he took his time in the kitchens. "There is much beyond our sight and understanding," is all he said. "As to the Book of Contracts, its use is spent. There is no sense in keeping it on display."

"I disagree. Have you visited Ilithor before, Jonik?"

The question stumped him. He frowned and shook his head. "Not yet. But when we leave…"

"There's a monument there…well, there are many, actually, but I'm thinking of one in particular. A statue, little more than a plain monolith really, that has carved into its walls the name of every Emerald Guard who has perished in his service to the crown. Brave men who died for their country, often in wars in which little was won. One might say they died for nothing, those men. Yet the monument stands and people come to honour them, every single day." She turned to the empty podium, up the short stone stair. "The book might have been something similar. A monument to those who have died for this cause. Yet instead it's been hidden away. That says a lot, don't you think?"

"It says whatever you read into it. There have been secrets here, and lies, but that time is now passed. The order has served its function."

"As has its Steward." She gave a bitter laugh. "Perhaps they have been entombed together, the mage and his favourite book."

"He never wanted this duty," he told her. "The Steward was as much a slave as any of us. And he made a sacrifice too, Amilia."

He had learned that only after. Learned that Hamlyn's life force had been spent by his final, fated toil. That in performing the *transference* he had given up his own life so that his friend and king could live. There was something tragic in that to Jonik. Ilith and Hamlyn were as brothers, once before, performing their miracles together, working wonders across the world. That Hamlyn should perish the very same day that Ilith arose had struck a chord with him. *He tended him for thou-*

sands of years. He watched over him. And he never even got to look into Ilith's eyes, as they opened. He never got to speak to him, or say goodbye…

Amilia Lukar was looking at him with eyes of green flame. "Sacrifice implies choice, Jonik. Hamlyn had the luxury of having one. *I* didn't. I was brought here against my will by that Shadowcloak in the form of Sir Munroe Moore. *Talbert*," she said, spitting the name out. "I was tricked and bewitched. And they stole a child from me." She turned her eyes away sharply, clenching her jaw.

She had suffered a great crime. Jonik understood that. "My lady…"

"No. I don't need your sympathy or your pity. I'd have aborted the child myself anyway, so what does it matter? I slew Hadrin's seed a dozen times back in Thalan. What's one more? Perhaps they did me a favour. But I never had a *choice*."

And I did, Jonik thought. He could see the accusation in her eyes, hear it sizzling on the tip of her tongue. *Aleron. I might have refused to fight him, refused to kill him. I could have done a dozen things differently back then. But no, I chose to live…* "What I did back in Varinar…"

"I don't want to talk about that," she cut in. "I've told you already. It's not the sword you blame, but the man who swings it, and you're just a sword, Jonik, a pawn in the game like me. We don't move ourselves around the board."

He nodded, eyes down. "But we can," he said quietly. "From now on…we can. The future is unseen, Amilia. From here…"

"Nothing changes. The world is still at war and I've seen what the devil looks like. I looked into his red eyes, Jonik." She looked into his. "And do you know what I saw?"

He shook his head. His voice was stiff. "No, my lady. What did you see?"

"The end. Fire and brimstone, ash and fume and death. Then darkness. A lightless void into which we'll all be swallowed up whole. So go ahead and try to help, if you want. But *don't* ask me to do the same."

She stepped away, brushing right past him, and began making for the exit. Beyond, the refuge opened out like a honeycomb, a hundred halls and chambers delved deep into the rock of the mountain.

Jonik stood his ground a moment, then followed. He had more to say, a great deal more, yet now did not seem the time. *Later*, he thought. Perhaps back in Ilithor, back in her home, she would be more amenable to listen to him, and help.

Their footsteps whispered upon the stone, scuffing softly, the only sound. High ceilings lurked in shadow above them, and statues marked the way. They looked down upon Jonik with their judging eyes; heroes of the past, kings and champions, men who had fought in wars and won them, battled through decade-long Renewals. *But not this, the Last Renewal*, Jonik thought. *None of you fought through this…*

They had not made it far before a cloaked figure emerged from a corridor, shambling along in that awkward way of his, clinging to life like a limpet. Though Hamlyn had perished of his final toil, the same could not be said of Fhanrir. As with the other three mages here - Dagnyr, Agnar, and Vottur - he remained to serve. "For as long as I still draw breath," he had said, in Ilith's presence. A part of Jonik had wanted to skewer the creature for his lies and deceptions, but now that part of him was dead.

It died the day my mother did. The day I gave up the Nightblade.

"Fhanrir," he said, as the creature appeared.

Amilia stiffened at the sight of him, shifting a little closer to her cousin. She almost grabbed his arm.

"Frighten you, do I?" Fhanrir hissed. A rotting tongue moved over rotting lips, dry as bone. Through a hole in his fleshless grey cheek the inner workings of his mouth were visible. Amilia recoiled. "Thought we were past all that, girl?"

"She's royalty," Jonik said. "You should call her…"

"I'll call her what I like. A thousand royals have come and gone in my time. Kings, queens, princes, princesses….*people*. They're just *people*, boy. None of you are special."

The mage had not softened at Ilith's rebirth. If anything he'd grown more truculent and hateful, cursing that he was still alive. Cursing that he still had to serve when Hamlyn, his trials complete, had finally earned his rest.

"What do you want, Fhanrir? Did you come to say goodbye?"

The creature made a clacking sound. "Why bother? You'll both be back." He looked at Amilia and smiled that horrid smile. "No, came to give you a message. Our master would like a word with you, before you go. You'll find him in his forge."

Something about the word rankled. *Master*. But could he deny it? *No, I have given myself up to his service, the same as these mages*. If there was a man they should all follow, a light to lead them against the spreading dark, who better than Ilith, he who built the world? *Or whatever version of him remains, in the body of his heir.*

"Fine. Thank you for telling me."

Fhanrir awarded that a snorting sound, turned, and shambled back off.

Jonik turned to Amilia. "You know the way to the portal door?"

"I think so."

"Then go. You'll find Gerrin and Harden there, with Cabel. And my mother. We plan to take her body home with us. To bury, in the palace."

She nodded. "Of course. She should come home." Her eyes swept around them, through the cavernous, soulless hall. "She doesn't belong here."

"I had hoped you would find somewhere for her, with your ancestors. I don't know Ilithor, my lady. But you…being her niece."

She touched his arm. "I'll make sure she is given a tomb to befit her. We can have a wake as well, if you like. Something small, to remember her."

I never knew her, Jonik thought. *Not really.* "Perhaps," is all he said.

She nodded at him and turned. "Then I'll see you at the door."

They parted, stepping away in opposite directions. The last time Jonik walked this route had been in very different circumstances. He and his men had been rushing along in search of his mother, intent on leaving the fort behind once and for all. Instead they had found her dead, her blood being mopped up by a half dozen Shadowknights, cloaked and armed. In the chaos and confusion of what followed, Jonik had slain several of them himself, the mage Meknyr included, before sprinting back outside into the snow with the Nightblade screaming in his head. If it hadn't been for the arrival of Ilith in his reborn form, he would have been lost.

I'd have taken it up and disappeared. The King of the Night. Lost forever.

But fate had intervened, casting aside his shackles once and for all. And from here, he would serve by choice, not coercion.

The forge was not far. From the doorway, a soft glow of orange light washed out into the corridor. Steam issued, swirling. And there too the heavy thumping of the *Hammer of Tukor.*

He reached the threshold and stepped inside, passing through steam. The air cleared before him. "My lord. You asked for me."

"I did." Ilith stood at his anvil. He wore simple raiment, the garb of a blacksmith; scuffed leather vest, stained brown breeches, sweat across his brow and glistening upon his bare, sinewy shoulders. To call him Ilith was perhaps a disservice to the body he inhabited, yet Jonik could not help it. He had never met Tyrith, had never even seen him, yet knew he shared a strong likeness to his ancient ancestor, as his mother had once told him. Ilith continued to claim that his heir remained a part of them, that they were 'both at once', 'one and the same', but if they were truly sharing the same consciousness, what did Tyrith have to contribute? He had lived for twenty five years, all of them a captive. Ilith had lived for thousands, and built the modern world. Perhaps Harden had put it best when he'd said, "If that mind they share's an ocean, the heir's contribution is no more than a pail. The demigod's all the rest." And so indeed it seemed.

"Come in, Jaycob. Did you have a nice discussion with your cousin?"

Nice would not be the word he would use. "She is still in shock," he said. "It's a lot to process…all of this."

"I quite understand. I am still processing it myself, in truth." He tapped his forehead, plastered in strands of golden, sweat-stained hair. There was a luminous quality to his skin, a radiance reserved for divinity. "Though I have Tyrith to help guide me. We are working through it all together, he and I."

There was a helm on the anvil, simple, smooth-crested, black and misting shadow. Ilith picked it up and turned, stepping over to his battered workbench. He placed the helm down, and beside it the Hammer of Tukor, resting it upon the wood with a deep, resounding *thump*. It was a simple thing, really. Not so large as depicted in statues and books, and plain of design as well, it could easily be mistaken for a regular blacksmith's hammer. *Except for those markings and glyphs*, Jonik thought. Those were etched into the head, leaking light, a sign of its godly power.

Another ancient artefact lay on the workbench as well, another gift of a fallen god. It had been removed from its scabbard, a length of steel, black as death and fuming. Jonik frowned. He hadn't expected to see it here. "I thought you were to store the Nightblade away, my lord?"

"I will. When I am done with it." Ilith took a moment to study Jonik's grey eyes. "How do you feel when near it, Jaycob? The voices are gone, I hope?"

A dip of the chin to confirm. To Jonik the Nightblade was just a sword now; wondrous, yes, powerful, there was no doubt, yet lost of its addictive appeal. In Ilith's presence, the blade's sentience was subdued. *Like a dog on his master's leash*, he thought. "What did you mean by 'done with it', my lord?"

"I have been working with it overnight," Ilith explained, gesturing to a suit of armour dressed upon a mannequin across the workshop. "Were you aware that Tyrith had been designing a suit of armour for you, Jaycob?"

His answer was no. *Though…* "I saw it," he remembered. "The black armour. Two days ago, when we came here looking for my mother. Harden suggested it would fit me well."

"It should. The suit was made to your precise proportions. Tyrith says that it was a gift for you…for the kindness your mother showed him. To help you in your onward quest. It is a fine suit, is it not? Sleek, seamless, supple."

Jonik did not disagree. "It is a work of art, truly." He paused, long enough to show his doubt. "Only…"

"Only black is no longer your colour?"

Ilith always seemed to know, as Hamlyn had before him. "It is associated with this order, with darkness," Jonik said. "If I go out there wearing black…" He was thinking of his father, his brother, all the others who might scorn him. He could imagine how Elyon would look at him and sneer, 'Once a Shadowknight, always a Shadowknight'. He sighed and shook his head. The last thing he wanted was to sound ungrateful, and yet… "If I'm to be your herald, to help them understand, then…"

"Then a brighter silver or grey would be better?" Ilith finished for him. "Yes, I quite agree. That is why I have added my own modifications, to lend light to the suit as needed." He stepped toward the mannequin, beckoning Jonik to join him. A hand waved up and down in presentation. "By day the metal will drink the light, but by night it will expel it, at your will. You are well versed in how to move unseen, I know. With this suit, you needn't abandon that instinct entirely."

"You mean…" Jonik looked over the Nightblade, resting upon the workbench. "You *used* it, to enhance the armour? You've transferred some of its power into the steel?"

Ilith smiled. "Of a sort. Though it is less a transfer of power, and more a *mimicry* of it. There are, of course, techniques in metallurgy and magic that you will not be privy to. I used one such technique, most difficult to master, to harness the unique properties of the Nightblade, reproduce them, and instil them into the armour. The magic is *lesser*, of course, an echo of what you once wielded, yet still of use when properly deployed. I thought you might appreciate it, Jaycob, as a reward for your service. Would you like to put it on?"

Jonik hesitated, even after that. Armour had never been his preference. He was bred to the shadows and the shadows didn't wear plate. Not until he journeyed to Varinar to participate in the Song of the First Blade had he garbed himself in godsteel from head to heel, and ever since then…no. *Not even when we came here*, he thought. He preferred gloves to gauntlets, and a hood to a helm, though the world was different now. A thousand perils had erupted from the earth and this suit would help protect him.

So he gave a nod, at last, and stepped toward the mannequin. "I would be honoured, my lord."

His concerns were swiftly cast aside. The suit was as supple as lambskin leather, as light as air, and the segments seemed to *fuse* together as they touched, the fit perfect. Under the Worldbuilder's watchful gaze, he wrapped the cuisses around his legs, and the greaves, slipped his feet into the sabatons. The breastplate followed, and the pauldrons for the shoulders, and the plackart and the vambraces and the gauntlets that might as well have been gloves.

When he was done, he moved about the workshop, waiting for a pinch here, or a prod there, of a design flaw that Tyrith had not considered. There were none. The armour was an extension of him, beyond anything he'd ever worn. And as he strode, and stretched, and shifted, it drank in the light of the fire, brightening to a smooth and striking silver. A gallant colour, favoured by so many great men. Yet at night he could still be at one with the darkness. *I can still embrace the man I once was…*

Ilith was observing him with that famous little grin of his. "Impressive," he said, approving. "You altered the hue of the metal without visible effort."

"My training with the Nightblade," Jonik said. Drinking and expelling light from godsteel was greatly more simple than turning invisible. It had taken Jonik years to master that art. Evidently, the skill was transferable.

Ilith returned to his workbench. The last element of armour

remained to be worn. "You will need this as well." He lifted the helm. "Much darkness and danger await you."

Darkness and danger. Those I know well. Jonik took the helm, brought it down upon his head, let it click and fuse into place upon the gorget. Then he twisted his neck to test the fit, left, right, up, down. Perfect. No hood had ever been so pliant. He took a moment to draw in light, expel it, lightening and darkening the suit at his will. Satisfied, he drew the helm up and away, shook out his long black hair, and placed it aside. Upon a work table along one wall, he saw scrolls, letters, notes. "Is there any more news from the south?" he asked.

Ilith glanced over. "Little that you do not already know."

And that was little enough. Scant scraps of news brought on the tongues of the men who had come here with Amilia. Jonik had once thought that these mages had some magical means of knowing all of what was happening beyond their borders, but that wasn't so. They gathered news like anyone else, for the most part, through rider and wing, voice and ink and scroll. There were some sorceries they could turn to, at the edge of need, to help enlighten them, but of late their focus had been the transference and the magic could not be spared.

"You will learn more when you reach Ilithor," Ilith, who had built the city, said. "From there, you must choose which way you will go. You have your instruction. Go forth from here as my herald, and my voice, and help steer the course of the other four blades to this refuge. There is no task more critical, no man better suited to it than you. I trust you to find your way."

Jonik thought for a short while, wondering on which way that might be. The blades were scattered, and in some cases their where-abouts were unknown. A part of him had hoped that Ilith would give him guidance, but it appeared that would not be so. *He wants to give me agency. To be my own man. To forge my own path.* He nodded and asked no further questions.

"Good," Ilith said. "But beware, Jaycob. What you learn one day may be different the next, and the blades may yet change hands. They will strive to remain apart, and grow increasingly corruptive. Use your words to convince, use the wisdom of your experience, but know that they may not be enough. There may come a time when trickery is needed, even force. You must be prepared to use them."

A ripple of dread moved in Jonik's heart. But he nodded. "I will do what I must."

There was nothing else to say.

Ilith stepped toward the door, where a cloak hung on a peg. He drew it over his sweaty bare shoulders, and ran a hand across his fore-head, moving aside strands of hair. Jonik donned his cloak as well, fixing it at the neck with a simple steel pin. He pulled on his leather boots, drew on his gloves, covering the armour, softening his tread.

They walked together to the portal door, moving quietly through the refuge. Ilith looked around as he went, observing the tall statues and fine carved cornices, the wide pillars and ribbed columns, the arched doorways and sculpted lintels through which they passed, chamber after chamber. Once or twice he walked to the wall and ran his hand upon the stone, feeling its age, or diverted his path so he might walk through a lance of daylight filtering down through a high window or ceiling shaft above. Motes of dust glittered, dancing, and he watched them for a moment as though seeing something Jonik did not. He seemed a man still awakening, coming out of a long undying dream. His memory of the world returning.

"Do you recall the days here, my lord? Building these halls?"

"A shadowed recollection," Ilith said, smiling, still looking around. "It is as a gloomy sky, Jaycob, though the clouds are breaking up. The sun is coming through in shafts. Every day I remember more."

But not how to reforge the Heart, Jonik knew. That secret still eluded him.

They came to the portal door a short while later, where the others were awaiting them. The chamber was plain stone, white-walled but for that door. Nothing had ever been so empty, so black, so unnerving to observe as that void.

Jonik scanned his companions, glad to see that Amilia had made it through the maze. "My lady," he said, observing courtesy with a bow. Gerrin and Harden stood to either side of her in their armour, like a pair of old grizzled knights about to step forth into battle. Cabel less so. The young sellsword wore leathers and fur, his eyes glassy and blinking, skin as pale as milk, dark hair dishevelled and wisps of beard hanging off his cheeks and chin. He still wore a bandage on his head from where Borrus Kanabar had cracked his skull, an assault that had rendered the youth abed ever since, in and out of consciousness. He would go no further than Ilithor, Jonik knew. *My company, my army… reduced to just two.* "Is everything prepared?" he asked.

Gerrin answered with a nod. "Just waiting for you, Jonik."

"Took your time." Harden peered through Jonik's woollen cloak, saw the jet black armour clinging to his skin. Recognition dawned. "That plate…"

"Later." Jonik moved his eyes to what he had been trying *not* to look at. His mother, wrapped in white linen, lying on a wooden stretcher behind them. He drew a deep breath, closing his heart, his bridge to emotion drawn up. "I'll carry her myself," he said. "Harden, take Cabel. Gerrin, accompany the princess. When you reach the other side, stay in the tunnel. Don't go wandering off."

"And if we're spat out into a wall of rock?" Harden squinted at the void like it had insulted his mother. "Lady Cecilia said the tunnels through there are unstable. Said they might have come down. The whole place might be caved in, then what?"

"Then we turn around and come back."

"And if we can't? If we get stuck?"

"We won't." Jonik didn't want to hear it. The negativity and doubt.

He had spoken to Ilith about this already, and been assured that the passage was safe. The part of him that was Tyrith had passed through the portal, after all. It had been an unpleasant experience for him. He had muttered of the things he'd seen in there, the floating shadows and glimpses of dead faces, the strange sounds that rang out through his head. But it was momentary only, a passing nightmare. *My men are stronger than that. And Amilia…her as well.*

"Enough talk," Jonik said. "Gerrin, you take Cabel through. Leave him there and come back. Harden needs to know it's safe."

Gerrin set his slab of stubbled jaw and turned, grabbing Cabel by the arm. He pulled him into motion, drawing him toward the door. "It'll be all right, boy. You'll get the help you need on the other side." The youth's eyes were big and bright with fear, where once they'd been dark and devious, the eyes of a killer. It was sad to see him fallen so low.

The pair disappeared inside.

It happened so quickly, no more than a blink; one minute they were there, then they were not, swallowed up by the lightless, soundless, void. Harden sucked a breath. "Where…they just *vanished*."

Ilith presented that smile. "The portal is no normal door, Harden. It moves matter through space almost instantaneously. It is too quick for the eyes to see."

It did not help with Harden's anxiety, try as he might to hide it. A rictus smile clung to his thin grey lips. "They'll be there, then? In Ilithor, already?"

"It will only take a few moments," Ilith confirmed. "To them it may seem slightly longer, but not to us. Sir Gerrin will return to us shortly."

He was right. Once more, it happened in a blink, Gerrin reappearing as though from thin air, *popping* into existence before them. Harden stumbled back in surprise, gasping, and almost fell. Embarrassingly, it was Amilia who had to steady him.

Gerrin went to one knee, breathing hard. He shook his head, staring down at the stone, steadying himself, then stood. Several hard blinks and he was ready to speak. "Cabel's through. Tunnel's clear. Bit of fallen debris, but…" He took a further moment to compose himself, rubbing at his eyes, grimacing. A gnarled finger stabbed into his right ear, twisting. Then he went on. "But the tunnel looks clear, from the glance I got. Won't know for sure until we start the trek, though."

Harden was staring at him. "How was it?" Jonik had never seen him so tense, this grim spare sellsword who'd travelled half the world. It was almost enough to make him laugh. Harden glanced over at him, scowling, as though knowing. Then he looked back at Gerrin. "It's not so bad, is it?"

"It's fine. *Strange*, but fine. Best just get it over with, Harden. Like jumping into a lake. Sink or swim."

"I can't swim."

Gerrin shrugged. "Just do it."

"Fine." Harden stepped forward, pausing as he stared into the shimmering nothingness, the empty space, shuddering. Jonik could almost smell the piss leaking down his leg. For a long moment he just stared, delaying. Jonik gave a silent sigh, met eyes with Gerrin, nodded, and the former Shadowmaster closed in behind Harden, quiet as a cat. One hard shove and the sellsword was tumbling forward, vanishing, his grunt of surprise abruptly cut short.

Ilith gave a chuckle. "That is one way of doing it."

"Some men need a little push, my lord." Gerrin grinned and reached out a hand, palm up. "Your Highness," he said to Amilia. "There really is nothing to fear."

The princess snorted. "Do I look frightened?" She strode forth, chin raised, her long lustrous brown hair bouncing at the small of her back. She brushed aside Gerrin's hand, said, "I'll see you in a moment," to Jonik, with a side-glance, and was gone. Not so much as a look at Ilith in parting, which Jonik understood, though didn't much like.

"Gerrin," he said, "go after her. Make sure Harden didn't land too awkwardly."

There was a twist of Gerrin's lips, and glint in his hard grey eyes, and into the void he went.

Then it was just the two of them. The demigod and his herald. "I will speak to her, my lord," Jonik said. "I know you would like her to help."

"She will. In time."

Do we have time? He decided not to ask. "I'll return as soon as I can. With another blade or bearer at my side."

Ilith nodded, staring forward. There was something sad in his eyes all of a sudden, as though a memory was resurfacing, something painful, a recollection of regret. "I was going to link all the north," he said, in a voice that was half a whisper.

Jonik barely heard him. "My lord?"

"This portal, Jaycob. It was to be the first of many, a network to connect us, bring us closer together. Can you imagine? A web of these pathways, opening to all the major cities in the north? How easy would it have been, then, to do what must be done?"

Jonik did not know what to say. He chose flattery, and truth. "You built the world, my lord. Isn't that enough? There is no one in all history so respected as you."

His smile twinkled, though a little less brightly, as a dying star in the high night sky. It seemed to Jonik that he had aged, a little. A sinking of the posture, a wrinkling about the eyes. It concerned him.

"My lord…"

"You are kind, Jaycob, to say so. Another man of great kindness said the same thing to me once. Right here, it was. Not long before I died."

Jonik waited, wondering.

"Hamlyn," Ilith whispered. A tear welled in his eye, dropping, wending down the side of his check to hold in the corner of his mouth. "Never was there anyone closer to me, Jaycob. That he died, so I could live…" He looked over. "Do you imagine a demigod's heart could be broken?"

Jonik's voice was choked. "I…suppose so, my lord."

A sad smile tugged at Ilith's lips. "Ignore me, young one. Here I am lamenting the loss of my friend and you…you stand before your dead mother. I am sorry. That was insensitive of me."

"Not at all." *I never really knew her.* He shuffled his feet, awkward. "And she is a great loss to you as well. To Tyrith, I mean…he knew her well." *Better than me.* "He was as a son to her too."

He sensed that's what it was. Demigods did not weep, as far as Jonik knew. This was Tyrith's influence, Tyrith's emotion, Tyrith's mortality and weakness.

"My lord, I should go. The others…"

"Of course. Yes, of course. They need you. The world needs you, Jaycob."

Jonik bent down to lift his mother, carefully picking her up off the floor, cradling her. He caught a whiff of putrefaction, though the worst of the decay was kept behind the layers of linen. *My own mother, rotting in my arms.* He stepped toward the door, the black void filling his vision. Behind, the light of Ilith was glowing softly, radiating from his skin, his hair. Jonik had once been told that the hottest flames burned out the fastest. He glanced back, wondering. *The spirit of a demigod, in the body of a mortal. How long can that flesh sustain him? How much time do we really have?*

In Jonik's head, a clock was ticking.

He stepped forward into the void.

3

𝕰lyon

"You're welcome to rest here as long as you like," Lord Botley Harrow said. "A minute, an hour, a day. Stay forever if you want. The gods know we could use you."

Everywhere can use me, Elyon thought. "I stopped only to speak with you, my lord. I don't mean to stay long."

"Of course. Of course." Lord Harrow lifted a hand to his mouth, suppressing an audible yawn. Such was the hour, and such the haste of Elyon's arrival, that he had not been given proper time to dress. From beneath his nightrobes, thick, tree trunk legs sprouted, muscular at the calf, with slippers on his feet. His hair was dishevelled, heavy jaw thick with two-day stubble. "You'll have to forgive the garb, Sir Elyon. If I'd known you were coming…"

"It's late, Lord Harrow. You needn't explain the nightclothes. I landed only to hear if you'd had any further word from Varinar?"

The man gave a despairing shake of the head. "None. Not since that crow came the day the city was attacked." He rubbed at his forehead. "You spoke to my man, then? Sir Hutchin. I sent him as soon as I received Sir Bomfrey's note."

"He arrived at King's Point only hours ago," Elyon confirmed. "That's why I'm here, my lord." He turned his eyes across the lord's chambers, where he'd been taken upon landing upon the high sturdy walls of Crosswater. On a table he saw a tray of sweetbreads, cheese and cured meats, with a large jug of wine on the side. He would not partake in any drinking, but the food was a welcome sight. "Do you mind if I…?"

"By all means, go ahead."

Elyon stepped over to eat. Lord Harrow went with him, poured a large cup of wine, and drank deep. "So…King's Point. How…how is it?"

Elyon took a bite of bread. "Destroyed," he said, chewing. "Almost entirely in ruin. We lost over half our men."

The stocky lord gave a sharp intake of air. "*Half?* Goodness me. And the enemy?"

"Similarly depleted. Some thousands fled into the woods across the river, when the Dread came. The rest ran for their ships and sailed south."

"They fled? Will they return, do you imagine?"

"We don't know for sure as yet." Elyon had another bite of bread, munching hungrily. "So, nothing from Varinar? What about the west? The Twinfort? Anything from there?"

"Nothing. No word, Sir Elyon."

"And the east?"

The Lord Protector of the Vanguard shook his head. "Except for that crow, everything's gone dark. No riders have come, no ships. We're living in fear that Drulgar will pass over our heads, and reduce us to ruin as well. Some of the men even reported seeing him when he flew north. From afar, yes, but even then…" He looked Elyon in the eye. "Is he as big as they say? A flying mountain…"

"More a volcano," Elyon said to that. "His blood…it's like lava. The very air around him seems to boil. It is enough to blister skin, my lord." He did not have time to discuss it in any more depth, nor did he want to think about it. He took another bite of bread, chewing quickly, to replenish his stores of energy, eating like a starved man. Of those there would be many hundreds of thousands soon. Millions, even. *These nice full plates will grow scarce*, he thought, *even for a lord like Harrow.* "Are you all on rations here?" he asked.

"We are. In preparation."

"Preparation is over. It's happening as we speak." He didn't need to define what 'it' was. "Well, I should be away then. I'd like to reach Varinar by first light if I can." *Or what's left of it.*

"As long as you're well rested, my prince? You do seem rather… shaky, shall we say?"

"I'm not quite back to full strength, but will be soon. The wind helps as I fly." Elyon finished eating, helping it down with a cup of cold water. Lord Botley Harrow followed him as he stepped out through the balcony doors and onto the terrace outside. A cold wind was blowing, whistling unnervingly through a moonless night. Elyon gripped the Windblade's haft, listened for warnings, heard nothing, and withdrew the blade. The air began to stir around him. "You called me prince just now," he said, giving Harrow a final glance. "It's official, I should tell you. Or as close as can be, before we put the crown on his head. My father…we named him king two hours ago."

A smile gripped at Lord Harrow's lips. "Well, it's about time he relented. I trust he got through the battle unscathed?"

"He is uninjured. Only tired."

"And others? You have to get going, I know, but tell me…"

48

"Vesryn's dead," Elyon said, half blurting it out. The words were a knife to his heart. He had to pray he would find Amara. Pray he found her so he could tell her that he'd released her husband, only to watch him die. *But with honour,* he told himself. *A hero. He restored his pride before he fell.* He cleared his throat, trying not to dwell on the nagging notion that it was all his fault. "And Dalton Taynar as well," he finished. "He bled out on the field, in his nephew's arms. Rodmond is now Lord of House Taynar."

"I see." Lord Harrow took a moment to digest that, performing the expected courtesies as he dulled his tone and dipped his eyes in respect of the fallen. "Their losses will both be felt keenly, I am sure. Your uncle in particular...I always liked him, despite his recent transgressions. Did he...die well?"

"As a hero," Elyon said, remembering the defiance as he stood before the Dread, remembering the crushed armour, the whispered words that had left his uncle's lips as he died. "*Aleron should have been First Blade,*" he'd croaked. "*I'll give...my seat...to him.*" His parting thoughts as he'd left this plane had been for the wrongs he'd perpetrated, for Aleron, for his part, however small it might have been, in denying his nephew the chance to forge himself into a great man, to win a famous seat of his own at Varin's Table. Elyon had passed out soon after his uncle's death, he had later learned, undone by the blast of Eldur's staff, by the godly power of the Bondstone. Yet when he awoke, alone, moved to a bed in the ruin of the city, he had wept for his uncle's loss...and those words...those words that would live with him forever.

I'll give...my seat...to him.

He drew a deep breath, steadying himself, and looked upward. "Watch the skies, my lord," he said to Harrow, without turning to face him. "I will stop again on my way back, if I can, and report on what I find." He said nothing more than that. Summoning the winds, he soared, up and away into the starless night.

The flight to Varinar was not a long one, not by the standards he set himself. Over the last months he'd flown often between Varinar, King's Point, and the cities in the east, and only days ago he'd engaged himself in his most taxing flight so far; from King's Point to Eldurath and back, with barely any rest at all. *And when I returned...*

He had anticipated the risk of finding the city under siege. He knew he might have to fly straight into battle. But Drulgar? Eldur? The Calamity and the demigod? Such world ending threats were not expected, and Elyon, exhausted, frazzled, with the Windblade in his grasp and the Eye of Rasalan on his back, had flown right down and fought them both.

Or tried to, he thought, as he glided smoothly above the dark waters of the Steelrun River, reflecting on the battle. In truth he was little more than an irritant to Drulgar, a fly to be swatted, powerless to hurt him. *No. No, that isn't true,* he tried to tell himself. *The Dread felt it when I*

drove the Windblade through his scales. He reared and roared. I made him feel pain.
It was a small thing, yes, a pinprick in his hide, but enough to give them some hope. *He is vulnerable, and he knows it. Father is right. It only takes one bolt…*

He quickened his speed a little, eager and afraid in equal parts to find out what had become of the city. The fool in him, the hopeful boy, clung to the small thin chance that he would find Drulgar dead. That he would sight that great black-red carcass lying astride one of Varinar's many hills, with a thousand ballista bolts poking from his body and one, that *crucial* one, embedded in his eye and down into his brain. He could imagine it. How the defenders of Varinar had cheered as he fell. How the man who released the mechanism that fired the bolt upon the beast would be revered as a hero for all time, honoured beside Varin himself. A common soldier. Not even a knight, less one of Varin's Order, raised above all others as the one to down the Dread.

The notion pleased him, unlikely as it might be, and he flew on, heart pounding, basking in that desperate hope. *I'll know soon*, he thought. Soon the city would unveil itself, still burning in places he did not doubt. In King's Point the fires had burned out quickly, with so many stone structures denying its spread, but Varinar was different. Though the ancient inner city had been raised in marble and fine stone, the same could not be said for the vastness of outer Varinar, where timber structures dominated sprawling sections of the Lowers. Fires were common there in summer, and had been for long centuries. Once before they had ripped through entire city regions…now there were fail-safes and procedures to contain the spread…but this was different. 'The very fires of hell itself pouring from the Lowers' Sir Bomfrey Marsh had written in his note. *There will be no stopping such a spread*, Elyon thought. *It will feast until it's had its fill, and there's nothing anyone can do to sate it.*

He clenched his jaw, the wind whipping at his hair. He had taken off his helm, attaching it to his swordbelt, to let the air rush past his cheeks, to keep him awake and alert. It knocked against his armour as he went, a wild constant rattling that seemed to announce the death of a man, woman, or child with every toll. Elyon was not certain what the population of Varinar was, though the word million had been used more than once. *And more now*, he knew. Thousands upon thousands had poured in through the gates in recent months, fleeing to the capital to escape the war. *They went there to keep their children safe. They were told the city was unbreachable…they were promised they'd have nothing to fear…*

Tap, tap, tap, went his helm.

Dead, dead, dead, he thought.

He grimaced, closing his spare hand into a fist. As he did, a faint light appeared in the skies, a soft glow on the far horizon. He narrowed his gaze, peering through the rushing air. *Fire*. It was as he'd feared. *Fire, still burning, three days on…*

The city was still long miles away, yet already he was seeing signs of destruction, a path of ruination paving the way to Varinar. Ships, blackened and burned, lay washed up against the banks of the river. Riverside inns had suffered the same fate, and hamlets built along the shore, and the jetties and little rowboats that wandered in and out of them, and the orchards and river-markets, trading posts and watch-towers that overlooked the water, all burned. The lands along the Steelrun had once been rich with life. Now they were black and dead.

On the horizon the light was growing brighter, as if the sun was rising in the north, as though all the world had been twisted and turned about, as though everything was *wrong*.

And yet there was a light now in the east as well. The rising of a true dawn. A different light, of purity and hope, climbing up to fight the fire. It spurred Elyon Daecar on, casting away the gloom in his heart. They had lost much, but not all.

There remains a lot to fight for.

The last miles passed quickly. Rising to get a better vantage, Elyon saw first the city walls, facing south. The double bulwark was thick and tall, the stone laced at intervals with godsteel supports. Built with massive bastions, the walls looked mostly undamaged. There were no major breaches. The gates and barbicans remained intact. The crenelations atop the wall walks were scarred and marked, but barely. To an invading army of men, finding a way into the city would be the first priority. Rams for the gates. Trebuchets and catapults for the walls. Ladders and siege towers to scale the battlements.

But to a thunder of dragons, none of that mattered.

They flew right over, Elyon knew. *They targeted the towers, and the turrets, and the ballistas on their turntables. They rained fire upon the battlements, inciner-ating the bowmen. The walls were of no concern to them.*

Beyond the walls, the vastness of outer Varinar spread. Elyon flew over, swerving between great black pillars of smoke, pouring from the many fires still burning in the Lowers. Far below, he could see faint signs of movement, shadows shifting through the smog. Some looked to be in groups, attempting to douse the flames. Others were sifting through the great swathes of rubble, freeing those trapped beneath, perhaps, as they were doing in the ruin of King's Point. There was some sense of order, at least. That alone gave him hope.

He scanned, as he soared, gliding slowly now to take it in. Across the breadth of outer Varinar, the destruction was severe, though far from complete. Some districts appeared to have escaped untouched, protected by one hill or another, especially in the western side of the city. The worst of the destruction was down the centre, Elyon saw, as though Drulgar the Dread had led his dragons straight for the ancient heart of Varinar, on the shores of Lake Eshina. *The city as he once knew it,* Elyon thought. *Thousands of years ago.*

His flight took him along that trail, scanning, logging the scale of the damage. Though many of the hilltop towers had been torn down, some remained standing, and he saw signs that the ballistas there were still in operation, that soldiers were still manning them, that all was not lost.

He saw dragons as well, dark carcasses in the gloom. One, and then another, and then another and another and more. They were sprawled out among the rubble, beside broken stone towers and atop still-standing buildings, hanging over the edges of the walls, filled with arrows and bolts. Some were small and thin, others big and bulky, with empty saddles on their backs or none at all, wild and riderless, minions of the Dread.

In the east, the bloom of dawn was growing brighter, casting away some of the gloom. Elyon continued north, toward the ancient inner walls, to where the Ten Hills of Varinar stood, topped with their greathouse keeps and palaces, arenas and temples. He came to a stop, hovering, and took in the scale of the devastation.

At the heart, the Royal Palace, where the Kings of Vandar sat upon the godsteel throne…where great councils had been staged… where wars had been started and ended…where history made…was no more, the great high hill on which it once stood scattered now with great blocks of rubble. There were gouge marks upon the stair leading up to it, great deep ditches torn into the stone as if Drulgar himself had ploughed straight into it, blasting the palace apart with his bulk.

Elyon looked upon the other hills, each in varying states of destruction. Keep Taynar, a spare grey castle, had been shattered down to its foundations. The same went for Keep Amadar, the greathouse of his grandfather, the once proud castle reduced to utter ruin. Through the swirling smoke and ashen air, he looked upon the keeps of Houses Oloran, Pentar, Reynar and Kanabar, all built atop their hills. All but the last were badly damaged, missing wings and towers, belfries and balconies, their yards filled with rubble, smoke rising from the wrecks.

Only Keep Kanabar looked to have been entirely untouched, away on its wide low hill in the west, lit by the light of the rising sun.

And Keep Daecar. His home. The halls and corridors where he'd played as a boy, the yard where he'd sparred with his brother. The chamber where he'd slept, the hall where they'd hosted greatlords and kings, the family feast hall where they'd dined…

Elyon looked down upon it, and breathed out. Amidst all the destruction, amidst the tumbled ruins atop the Ten Hills, Keep Daecar remained standing; burned, battered, a blackened husk, but not broken. He set his jaw, closed a fist, and spoke aloud, up there in the skies, "House Daecar still has teeth."

Across from the palace, the great amphitheatre of Varinar, where the Song of the First Blade was sung, remained standing as well, and down in the lake-side harbour some of the wharves and jetties, the strong stone docks, appeared to have escaped unscathed.

He looked north, across the dawn-lit water, to the island on which the Steelforge stood. The bridge linking it to the city appeared to have been broken in places, the stone collapsed into the lake, and the four tall towers at the corners of the Steelforge had clearly been assaulted. *But not destroyed*, he saw. Elin's Tower, and Iliva's Tower, and Ayrin's Tower were all damaged. Only Varin's Tower, facing south toward the city, had been torn down and toppled, its ruin cast into the water or left to scatter the bridge below.

He knew, Elyon thought. *Drulgar...he knew.*

The rising sun continued to cast the city in a clearer light. Elyon commanded the winds to steady him against the gusty air, and took in the entirety of Varinar once more, turning slowly in a long, solemn circle. He spent a few long moments logging what he saw, to deliver to his father on his return. Then, without further thought, he made straight for Keep Daecar.

He landed in the yard, inside the outer gate atop the hill. The stone was scorched, bits of rock and rubble strewn across the cobbles. The details had not been so clear from above, but now he saw that many balconies and terraces had been blasted apart by dragonfire, the walls torn at by their talons, the stonework and masonry pitted and scarred. Though the keep had not fallen, fire had ripped through its guts all the same. It would take years to fully restore.

He stepped forward, searching for movement, calling out as he went. "Hello? Is anyone there?" His voice echoed out across the yard, leaving behind an eerie silence. "Amara? Lil? Sir Connor? Jovyn? Anyone?"

He stepped up the stair, and into the entrance hall, passing the black and broken door. Inside was silence, soot, and smoke, the floor coated in ash. The tapestries on the walls were burned, only their iron holdings left. The wood tables were nothing but charred heaps, with bits of leg poking out here and there, as sticks in the remnants of a fire. Statues had been scorched, and sometimes misshapen. Almost everything was black.

"Amara? Lillia? Jovyn?" Elyon coughed out the names, covering his mouth as he stirred ash with his feet. His voice rang up the stairs and down them, through the corridors and halls. "Mrs Windsworth? Master Artibus? Helena? Is anyone there?"

He moved through the keep, calling out any name he remembered. The maids and cooks, the washerwomen and scullery staff, the guardsmen who manned the gate and groundsmen who tended the gardens. No replies came back. He reached his old bedchamber, found it badly damaged as well, though not like the rooms below. Old trinkets he valued were still intact; books, maps, toys he'd played with as a child, kept inside a trunk by his bed. A wooden knight that Vesryn had once carved for him. A pendant his mother had given him, only months before she died. A brooch he favoured, in the sigil of House Daecar, given by his father when he'd first won his spurs. He paused a moment to look at them, remembering simpler times, but only a moment and nothing more. It felt indulgent to lament how easy life had once been, when so many thousands, countless thousands, lay dead throughout the city.

His search continued, his voice ringing out. The upper floors were empty, hauntingly so, so he went down into the cellars and staff quarters, the storerooms built into the hill. If there were survivors, this is where they would have gone. He called out once again for the head housekeeper - "Mrs Windsworth, are you here?" - and for the head of the serving staff - "Helena, can you hear me?" - bellowing the names of a dozen others as he rushed from room to room. He saw no sign, heard no reply. In places the ceiling felt unstable, the walls groaning and threatening to fall. Thick dust filled the air, and darkness that was hard to see through.

"Amara? Lillia? Are you here? Someone answer!"

He got no answer. No one was here.

No one *alive*, at least.

He found them in one of the storerooms, in the deepest part of the castle. Over a dozen men and women, trapped when the keep was attacked. Elyon could only imagine their panic as they heard the horns ringing out from the south of the city, as they saw the shadows in the skies. *They came down here thinking they'd be safe*, he thought. *They thought the threat would pass, that the dragons would be driven away.* Instead the flames had filled the halls above and ripped through every room, cutting off their escape, drowning them all in burning smoke, suffocating them to death.

Elyon could not bear to remain there any longer. The death, the darkness, the stink, the smoke. A part of him wanted to take them away, carry them one by one up through the castle to be buried and laid to rest. But he knew he couldn't spare the time. How many thousands would suffer the same fate? Rotting where they had fallen, with no one to dig them a grave or build them a pyre, no loved ones left to speak the last rites and send them on their way with grace?

He closed a fist. Some believed that funeral rites, in whatever form they took, were the key to entry into the Eternal Halls. That those who were not officially laid to rest were doomed to wander the world as spectres, caught between the planes of the living and the dead. If so, half the city, half the kingdom, half the north would suffer the same fate. *This will become a world of ghosts*, Elyon Daecar thought. *A world haunted by a horde of lost and lonely souls.*

He returned to the main yard, shaking dust and ash off his cloak, breathing deep of the clear morning air. The sun had risen to touch the stone, bathing the carcass of the keep in a terrible new light. At the gates he found several more dead bodies, those of guardsmen, so gruesomely charred he could not tell who they once were. Their blades were scorched black, regular steel, un-misting, counting out Sir Connor and Sir Penrose and his auntie's other Bladeborn knights.

She wasn't here, he knew. *Nor Lillia.* It was small solace, faint as a candle in a storm, but something. They might have been in the palace, after all, or visiting another of the keeps, or strolling the tree-lined streets around Maple Way when the Dread and his minions descended.

Or in Ilivar, Elyon thought. His sister had been there, with their grandfather, kept in his care for the last few months. Vesryn had told him that Amara had gone to Ilivar to fetch her back, but Elyon had cause to doubt whether that had truly happened. Lord Bryon Amadar was not a man to be cowed and commanded, not in his own city, and certainly not by a woman. *He is immovable, my grandfather. Not even Father is able to bend him.*

With a stirring of the wind, Elyon rose, once more, to survey the city. In the spreading dawn light he saw pockets of people, clearing rubble or gathering provisions or tending to the many wounded. A field hospital of sorts appeared to have been established at the foot of the palace, down the southern steps, and he could see people coming and going from the harbour, wagons wending through the wreckage of the city, bringing food from the ships, perhaps, or even stocking them for the survivors to flee.

He flew right down to land where the people were thickest, drawing yelps and shrieks from several women, and causing some children to scream out in alarm. "Fear not, it's only me," he called to them. "Elyon Daecar. I'm here to help."

There were more than he'd realised. Some hundreds, soot-stained and fearful, moving up and down the nearest lanes, milling about the rubble. It was a sight he was used to from King's Point. The haunted eyes. The dirty faces. The quiet mournful shambling of the horde, as they picked through the corpse of their city. He saw a man who looked like he was in charge, and marched over to join him. It was only when he got close that he realised he was looking into the old seamed eyes of Artibus, the Daecar family physician and noted scholar. "Master Artibus…" he said, hailing him.

The old man turned, eyes widening. "Elyon? Elyon, is that you?" A smile leapt to his lips. "It's so good to see you, my boy. Come here, come here…"

He opened his arms, and Elyon stepped right into them. Artibus clung to him fiercely. He was a small man, slim and scholarly, with a bald head and long white beard, a man who had raised him, in part, helping to guide and tutor him all his life. To see him alive and well was a blessing on this bleak day.

"I feared you might have died, Artibus," Elyon said. He turned his eyes up the hill, to where the shadow of Keep Daecar loomed, wreathed in swirls of smoke. "Mrs Windsworth, Helena, all of them, they're gone."

The old man dipped his chin. There were soot stains and flakes of ash peppering his beard. "I feared as much. I had wanted to climb the hill myself, and check to be sure, but…there has been much to do here. I've barely stopped to take a breath, with all these wounded to attend."

The moaning about them was a wretched thing, men, women and children all bleating and weeping in pain and sorrow. Elyon did not doubt that such places as this will have sprung up all across the city, in whatever open squares and yards they could find unburdened by heaps of rubble. Nurses moved about, applying poultices and salves. Others were stitching wounds, or dressing them, using white cotton bandages and lengths of linen torn in strips from sheets and bedding.

Elyon looked around, wondering for a moment if his auntie or sister might be here somewhere. "Master Artibus, I didn't find Amara in the keep, or Lillia. Tell me, are they still absent from the city?"

"As far as I know," the old physician confirmed. "In Ilivar, I would hope."

And me. Elyon breathed out, a temporary relief. *Unless the Windy City is in ruin as well.* "I plan to fly there now," he said. "There are signs of destruction, east beyond the gate. Do you know if Drulgar flew that way?"

Mention of the monster made the old man flinch. A woman nearby overheard, and began babbling at once, "Dread…Dread…the Dread…the DREAD!" until a nurse came by to comfort her. Others shuddered and muttered the name. A crowd were beginning to gather around them.

Artibus shook his head. His eyes were strained, voice choked. "The people are afraid, Elyon. They fear he will return." He looked skyward, shrinking.

Elyon stepped closer. "*East*, Artibus. Did the dragon fly east?" *Show no fear. Stand tall for them.* The eyes were on him. "I need to know where he went."

The old man swallowed. "Yes…that I have heard. The soldiers at the gate there…they said…"

"He went east," a stronger voice declared. From the crowd emerged a sturdy swordsman in silver plate and blackened mail, a cloak of silver, green and blue upon his back, stitched with an elk with bladed antlers.

"You're a Kanabar man," Elyon said to him.

"Aye. Sir Miles Hewitt. Captain of the Household Guard at Keep Kanabar." He had thick brown hair, streaked in grey, a broad jaw and wide neck atop a bull's shoulders. A pair of small eyes, deep and close-set, looked west through the city smog. "Was at the keep when it happened, saw it all from there. Got lucky. Dragons didn't come out that way…not many of them, anyhow. But Drulgar? Aye? He left to the east, saw that with mine own two eyes."

Artibus nodded. "The gate guards there have reported the same. Sir Miles has been helping to restore order here, Elyon."

"Good to have you, Sir Miles."

"Many have said that the Dread was bearing wounds," Artibus went on. "I did not see myself, but there have been those who claim

56

that they saw cleaves upon his neck and face, many bolts driven into his scales…"

Elyon nodded. "I saw those cleaves to his face and neck myself. And from up close. He had them when he arrived at King's Point."

"King's Point?" repeated Sir Miles, brows knitting. "The Dread was there?"

The crowd thickened. Many were listening.

Elyon nodded. "The city is in ruin, I fear to say. But many have survived, many stout soldiers and committed commanders. My father is among them. Amron Daecar yet lives." He spoke loudly enough for the people to hear. Then he leaned in and lowered his voice. "Do you have any idea how many have died here, Artibus? Is there anyone trying to perform a count, or…" *No*, he realised. It was much too early for that, and the task here was ten times as difficult as it was at King's Point. "Who is in charge out there?" Elyon went on. "In the Lowers. Sir Bomfrey? Sir Hank? Sir Winslow? Did any of them survive?"

Sir Miles Hewitt gave answer. "Sir Hank. He is doing what he can to rally the remaining soldiers, but they're almost all Taynar men. Doesn't have the clout to command them, with Sir Bomfrey gone."

"He's dead?"

"Aye, as far as I know. Or missing. We've been doing what we can to gather information, but much of what we hear is unconfirmed and unreliable."

"There have been reports of soldiers leaving, Elyon," Artibus added, voice low. "Taynar men, returning north to the Ironmoors, rushing back to protect their families. Some are staying, but not enough to keep the peace, and in the aftermath of any battle, crime becomes rife. It has been a plague across the Lowers even since the people heard that Eldur has arisen, and now it'll grow even worse. We need soldiers. We need *leaders*, to restore order. If King's Point is truly in ruin, I would beseech your father to return."

Elyon nodded, and took a grip of the old man's arm. "I will tell him you said so, Artibus. He has always listened to your counsel."

"Listened, yes, if not always agreed. But I pray that in this case…" He cut himself off, eyes turning sharply away. A woman nearby was calling for help; a young man appeared to be convulsing, white spittle frothing from his lips. "I must go," Artibus said at once. "They need me." He was already stepping away, moving through the crowds. "I hope to see you return soon, Elyon," he called back. "Please, speak with your father. Impress upon him our need. And if you learn anything of Amara, and Lillia…"

"I'll be sure to tell you, Artibus," Elyon said, as the old man sped away to his duties. He understood that a physician's first priority was his patients. He turned to Sir Miles. "How many men do you command?"

"Score or so, from the keep. And a few knights."

"Bladeborn?"

"Aye."

"And they're here now?"

"Some. Left Sir Bismark back at the castle with a half dozen men to ward off looters. They'll be scurrying all over the city, that sort, taking advantage. Pillaging, murdering, raping, all sorts. The old man's not wrong, my lord. We need more soldiers here."

"You'll have them," Elyon said. He could not be sure if his father would leave the coast just yet, but one way or another, he would see Varinar reinforced. "In the meantime, do what you can. And send word to Sir Hank that help is coming."

"Aye. I'll do that, my lord."

Elyon nodded, turned, and began stepping away through the crowd. He needed to give himself room to take flight, and the people were pressed hard about him.

"Make way," he said. "Please, I need space."

Many eyes were on him, many lips opening and closing with questions about the dragons, and the Dread, and King's Point, and the king. Merchants and wealthy artisans, lesser lords and ladies and old rich knights who dwelled here in their fine hillside homes and grand apartments near the harbour. Elyon recognised some of them, nobles he had rubbed shoulders with at balls and banquets. He saw Lord Meleforth, a shrunken old thing, who'd once been treasurer to King Horris Reynar, decades ago. And Lord Lancelyn, a rich shipwright, who had built half the boats in the harbour. Elyon had bedded both of their granddaughters once upon a time. *Them, and more,* he thought. *A different time. A different life…*

He kept on walking, giving what answers he could to the trail of desperation pursuing him. "The king will return," he was saying. "My father…he will set things right. You don't need to worry about the dragons anymore. They have done what they came for. They won't be coming back."

A hand grabbed his arm, clinging to his steel gauntlet. "Please, don't go," a girl's voice begged. "We need you…we need you *here.*"

Others agreed, huddling about him. A hundred voices shouted for him to stay. "Sir Hank Rothwell remains in charge of the defences," Elyon called, pulling himself away. "He is working to restore order, but more soldiers will come, I promise you. Now stand back…please, stand back. I have commands to follow from the king."

He had to push at them now to make room. Gently, of course, though forcefully enough to make them see he was serious. "Stand back," he said again, more firmly. "Stand back, for your own good. Or you may get hurt. Stand back!"

He stirred the winds, causing the ash to billow, skirts and robes to rise up. Suddenly the great chorus of shouts and voices was drowned by the blowing of the breeze. It was enough to get them stepping away from him, at least, all but the same girl as before, who reached out, weeping, clinging onto his leg. "Please, please, please," she screamed.

"Stay with us! What if they return!" Some others came to prise her off him. "You said you loved me, Elyon! You said that! Don't you remember? If you love me, you'll stay!"

He frowned, looking down at her. It only hit him then that he knew her, though for the life of him he couldn't place her name. Nor what he might have said to get her into bed. *A past life*, he thought once more. *A different time, a different man.*

"Please, my lady, let go," he said, as others wrestled her free. "I will come back, I promise. But in the meantime you must do what you can to help. You're strong. I remember that. There are many here who need you. Help them. I will be back soon."

If those words gave her any solace…if she would heed them…he didn't know. As soon as she was dragged away, he thrust the Windblade skyward and took flight, leaving the grasping hands and pleading voices and desperate horde behind.

In the east, the sun was climbing, its glow dancing on the waters of the lake. The lands were scorched and blackened in patches, signalling the path of the Drulgar and his dreaded flock. *A flock greatly reduced*, Elyon thought, if the count of dead dragons had been anything to go by. Varinar might have been beaten, but it wasn't broken, and Drulgar had paid for that in blood. His vendetta against Varin and his ancient city had not come without its cost. *To his followers, and to him*, Elyon knew, as he saw the heaps and blackened lumps of dried blood across the plains. It was the molten blood of Drulgar, he knew, searing the earth where it landed. And from what he could see, there was a great deal of it.

Elyon Daecar had caught a whiff of his prey. He flew after the trail, in pursuit.

4

Saska

The report was not as she'd hoped. "Nothing," said the Butcher, shaking his large, bald, brown head, dappled with beads of sweat from the sweltering heat outside. "The snake has slithered away, I am sure of it. He escaped the city during the fighting."

"Sure?" Saska repeated. "How sure?"

"Sure enough," answered the Baker, seated behind a desk with his feet resting on the wood. The man had an apple pierced on the edge of a knife. He took a bite, chewed, and said, "There is a possibility - a small one - that the sunlord remains in the city, hidden in some den. There are hundreds of them here in Aram, these dens and little lairs, and new ones are made every day. Any house, any home, could conceivably be concealing him. Though that is looking less likely, the more we search. My brother is probably right. Most likely he is gone."

"I *am* right." The Butcher thumped his scarred chest. "My little big brother hates to admit this. But it's true. I am always right."

Little big brother. The Baker wasn't exactly little, though compared to the Butcher he wasn't large either. He was also the elder of the two, though imagining them as being born of the same mother or sired of the same father took some effort. She'd grown used to the gruesome sight of the Butcher, with the scores of scars that latticed his chest and arms and face and head, but his brother the Baker was newly introduced to her, and much different of appearance. A shorter man, he had unusually large, knuckly hands, thick forearms forested in tufts of hair, a broad, squashed nose, deeply furrowed forehead, dark, spirited eyes and missing right ear. The golden spectacles he wore rested unevenly upon those features, lending him an almost teacherly air, and he had bizarrely white teeth as well that shone unnaturally when catching the light.

They made an odd pairing, to be sure.

"How long will it take to smoke out these dens?" Sir Ralston Whaleheart asked them, in his booming voice.

The Baker gave a shrug. "How long does a man live? How long does a battle last? Questions without answers." He pushed his spectacles up his nose. They seemed to fall down regularly, owing to that missing ear. "As I say. These dens breed like the feral little creatures that live in them. One is smoked out, another is born. Lord Krator has many friends in the city."

"We killed his friends," the Wall said to that. "Antapar and Konollio and their men…"

"Were but a few. He has more. Some are known to us; we have gone to them first, and of course, most of them have gone missing as well. Others are not known. Friends of friends who can be bribed and intimidated into concealing Lord Krator from our sight. These men are without count." He took another bite of his apple, crunching. "But the foreign allies are just as numerous. If my brother is right, and the sunny snake has slithered away, then most likely he will have gone west, into Pisek. But of course, we will continue to search to make sure. I very much want to see the sunlord swing as well. Alive, he remains dangerous…and he will not forget the men who betrayed him."

The Butcher laughed and shook the scabbard of his godsteel longsword, rattling the blade within. "The snake has been defanged. I have no fear of him."

"You have no fear of anyone, brother. And a fearless man is a fool." The Baker turned his attention back upon his guests. "My brother tells me you wish to hire us, as part of your escort? You are to leave the city soon, is this so?"

The Wall nodded. "In the coming days."

The Baker manifested a coin in his hand, moving it between his knuckles, cartwheeling from one to the next. "How much are you willing to pay?"

"Whatever you want," Saska said.

"Truly? We decide our own fee?" The Baker gave a chuckle. "You may be able to outbid Denlatis after all."

Saska frowned. "What do you mean, outbid?"

"Cliffario wants us to protect him," the Butcher explained. "From the wrath of the snake. He fears that Krator will do everything in his power to kill him, if he is still alive. A fair fear, yes. He has offered much money for our swords."

A fair fear indeed. Of those who had betrayed Elio Krator, Cliffario Denlatis was king.

"We'll offer more." Saska wanted the Butcher with her, him and Merinius and the Baker as well, and whatever other Bladeborn men they had left. "My grandmother will pay."

"The fee will be high," the Baker told her. "Many of our men have died for you already. Death does not come cheap."

The Wall bristled, a snort pouring through his nose. "You are sell-swords. That's the risk you take. One we all take in war. Or would you prefer to die protecting a merchant rather than a princess?"

The Butcher smiled at that, scars drinking in the firelight. Some-times they looked like lines of flame crisscrossing his face, like he was some infernal demon risen from the depths. "I am overwhelmed to hear that you want us to come with you, Coldheart. I had feared you would wish to see the back of me and my tattered red cloak."

"Once," the giant knight admitted, in a grunt. "But you proved yourself during the battle. You and Merinius both. I would have you in the company." He looked to the Baker, less sure. Sir Ralston Whale-heart was not a man given to trusting others easily; one must work hard to enter his confidence, and even then, he kept them at a distance. "I have heard they call you the Baker for the manner in which you treat your enemies. You bake them alive."

White teeth glinted. "I do," the sellsword said, proudly. "I bake, my brother butchers. I took inspiration from the iron dragon of Eldurath, do you know of it? It is in the Golden Square, where they…"

"Roast criminals alive, I know. They are put inside the iron beast and have dragons blow their flame upon it. It is a vile torture."

"Vile to one man, victory to another. Would that not depend on the criminal, and the crime?"

The Wall did not offer an answer.

The Baker went on. "You think yourself a great knight, your honour beyond reproach. Perhaps some others do too. But not all. To many you are a monster, a brutal beast from whom men run in fear, a tale to tell children at night… 'beware the steel giant in his steel suit, if you're naughty he'll cut you in two'." He laughed. "We say this here, in Aramatia. And all across the south. The monstrous steel man who cuts children in half and drinks the blood from each end like a cup. But is this true? No, I do not think so. You do not murder children and drink their blood, Sir Ralston, and…" he leaned in, crooking a finger, reducing his voice to a whisper, "….and this is just between you and me…but I do not bake men alive either. Not often, at least, and only the very worst of them. But it is good for a sellsword captain to have a name, and so here we are, the Baker and the Butcher, names to strike fear into our enemies. But do not let that concern you, my friend. If you can trust my brother, you can trust me. And *I* fought well during the battle too."

The Wall looked at him flatly. He seemed stuck on this notion that they told tales of him killing and drinking the blood of children here. "Yes, so I've heard. I won't deny you did your part."

"Well now…" The Baker looked at his brother with brows upturned. "Praise, from the praise-less one. And so early in our acquaintance. I feel my heart may explode with pride."

"I am envious," the Butcher said, tone serious. "It took much longer for him to give me a nice remark."

62

And me, Saska thought. Praise was hard to come by from the Wall, that was true. "Don't get used to it," she warned them. "It's like trying to get blood from a stone with him."

Sir Ralston seemed to sense that it was time to leave, with all three of them ganging up on him. "When will we have your answer? We expect to depart in days."

"By which route?" the Baker asked. *And for which purpose?* his eyes inquired.

The Wall hesitated, glancing down at Saska. It remained a matter of contention, this route they would take to the north. By now they had expected to have heard back from Ranulf, but no, nothing, not a whisper, not a word. "We are still contemplating our best course. The hope was to travel north, across the Aramatian Plains and then through the Everwood, if possible."

"Yes. And then?" The Baker peered at them. "The Everwood is not where your journey is to end. My brother tells me you plan to go *much* further north than that."

"We do. Into Vandar."

"Vandar." The Baker's eyes took on a reflective look. He tapped at his chin. "Why Vandar?"

"That is not your concern."

"I beg to differ. It is of great concern to me. There is a lot of war in the north, Sir Ralston. And a lot of dragons as well."

"War is where heroes are made," was the Wall's stiff reply. "Dragonkillers live forever."

"And most who try…die. For every dragonkiller, there are a thousand dragon-diers. I have no interest in hunting dragons, if this is your quest. Marco, Garth, Stan. They already died for that."

Saska dipped her eyes at those names. *Marco of the Mistwood. Garth the Glutton. Slack Stan, with that wobbly jaw.* All had died the day they went out onto the plains so she might hone her useless dragon-killing skills. There were others too, many others who had perished for her along the way. *They all lost their lives because of me. And none of them knew why.*

She was not going to make that same mistake again. The Butcher had helped train her, and he and his brother had helped shatter Krator's coup. She owed them both for that. They deserved to know the truth.

"I'm the heir of Varin," she said.

Silence, thick as mud. It filled that dusty basement room from sandstone wall to wall.

The Wall frowned down at her. His voice was a warning. "My lady…"

"The last of his direct bloodline, granddaughter to King Lorin," she went on. "Blessed with godblood in my veins."

"*My lady,*" the giant reached out. "That's enough."

"No," she said fiercely, swerving away. "I'm fed up of hiding the

63

truth." She motioned to the sellswords. "If they're to risk their lives for me, they deserve to know why. We can trust them."

"But they haven't *agreed* yet." Sir Ralston spoke through gritted teeth. "You are too reckless. Still, *too* reckless."

Too honest more like. And too damn tired of the secrets. "I have a destiny," she said to the Bloody Trader brothers. "I'm part of some old prophecy that says I'm going to unite the Heart of Vandar, and help win the War Eternal." *Or end it.* "Only Varin's heir can wield the Heart Remade, it says...and I...I..." She looked at them, feeling foolish. Everything...all of it...it still sounded ridiculous to her. "We're going north to try to gather the Blades of Vandar, reforge them, and save the world. Now, do you want to be a part of *that*? Or would you prefer to linger here, protecting a puffed up merchant instead?" She smiled, a false fixed smile. Somehow mocking the entire thing made it easier for her still. *A child*, she thought. *I'm just a bloody child.*

Sir Ralston took her by the arm, as though to reinforce it. "We're leaving. Ignore what she said. The heat...the dust...it gets to her..." He said nothing more, as he tugged her toward the stairs. She resisted, pulling sharply away, then strode up the stone steps of her own accord. She could hear her gargantuan guardian breathing loudly behind her, each step a stamp, steel cracking against stone. When they'd gone up one level, he reached out and took her shoulder, turning her before she could go on. "What was that?" he demanded. "The Butcher I could understand, but the *other* one? This mission still depends on secrecy, Saska. By tomorrow half the city might know..."

"They won't. I trust the Butcher and I trust his brother and anyone else who we decide to bring with us...we need to trust them as well." She spun and continued on, speeding herself away from him.

The sun was at its apex when she burst out onto the baking streets of Aram. A litter awaited them, pulled along by several strong oxen; a painfully slow way of moving about the city, but with Krator and Mar Malaan and others still at large, Sir Ralston had insisted that Saska remain hidden away.

The oxen were drinking from water pails, slurping greedily. Two soldiers attended them. The rest of their Nemati escort - spearmen mostly - lingered in the shade, awaiting the return of their princess. Sir Ralston marched forward, hailing the captain, passing on orders as another soldier opened the curtain for Saska to climb in. Rolly followed her a moment later, the entire carriage groaning under his weight. A call came outside and the host moved into formation. A second later they were lurching forth, oxen trundling, mounted spearmen trotting ahead and behind, men afoot walking at their sides.

The air was still and hot behind the drapes. Saska unfurled her silver shawl and tossed it on the bench beside her. Beneath it she wore her godsteel armour, over padded garments soaked in sweat. Her plate showed many wounds, many slim scratches and cuts and scars, and beneath a few of those her flesh was stitched and bandaged. Her fight with Cedrik Kastor had not come without cost, though they were flesh wounds only, shallow and of little concern. *A few cuts to see him die*, she thought. It was a trade she would have made any time.

Sir Ralston's armour was much the same as hers, dented and rent from his brutal bout with the Emerald Guards, Sir Bernard and Sir Lothar, with minor wounds cut into the meat beneath. "We make a pair, don't we?" she said. "Maybe one day I'll have as many scars as you, Rolly."

"I hope that day never comes." Sir Ralston's body was like a tapestry of trauma, covered in burns, pits, lesions, tears, from fang and claw and fire and steel. No man living had endured what this man had. *No man living could*, Saska thought, *without succumbing to the sweet release of death.* "That was reckless," he said again, brooding, as the carriage bumped along the cobbles. "I will have to return to them later, make sure they keep it to themselves. I know why you did it, and I understand, but…"

"I'll be more judicious next time," she promised, wanting to move on. The entire topic was like a noxious fume to her; when in it she felt suffocated, unable to see through the gloom, unable to take a breath. She reached across and opened a curtain, letting a wash of hot air flow in. Dust came with it, and ash, kicked up by the hooves of the horses and the oxen and the boots of the marching men. Even here, near the docks in the south of the city, the ash had spread to coat the cobbles. She wondered, as it stirred in through the curtain, whether it had come from wood or bone. Hundreds of buildings had been burned to cinders and thousands of men had died, cremated when the wild inferno swallowed them all up whole. Now the streets and squares all the across the city were coated in the embers of the dead. *Their ashes are sprinkled everywhere,* she thought. *The city has become a cemetery, every square and street an urn.*

But none were the ashes of the man who was to blame.

None were Elio Krator.

She closed a fist. "I still don't understand how he could have escaped," she said, frustrated. "We saw the fire, Rolly. I can see how a man in godsteel plate could survive it, but…"

"The inferno was not all-consuming. There were patches where it did not catch, and Krator must have been in one of them. Take solace from the fact that Cedrik Kastor is dead. In time, Elio Krator will follow."

But not with me there to watch, she thought, as she had when Joy mauled Lord Cedrik to death, ripping at his throat and clawing at his guts, eviscerating and emasculating and tearing him apart. The scene had been so horrific that many of the men standing by had been forced to turn away, and several had even retched, heaving the contents of their stomachs into the dirt.

But not me, Saska thought. She had stood closer than anyone, and had watched with gleaming eyes. *For all the girls you abused in their cells,* she had thought. *I will watch you die, my lord.*

No sight had ever been sweeter.

She clenched her jaw. "I want him kept alive for me," she said. "If he's found, I want him chained up and locked away so I can see him die when I return. Like he did with my father. I want to watch as he's beaten to death."

The Wall's eyes were inexpressive. "You had your vengeance with Kastor. Let this one lie, my lady."

"Let it lie? He killed my father, Rolly. My grandmother is dying because of him."

"Your grandmother's illness is not the sunlord's doing. She is old. When the body grows old and frail it is more vulnerable to these maladies."

"A malady hastened by his betrayals. Don't try to tell me the stress of all this hasn't sped her decline. The doctors say she could die in weeks, even days. She might have lived on for years if it wasn't for him. And now, when I leave, I probably won't ever see her again. My own grandmother…my last living family…who I've only just met." She exhaled, loudly, shaking her head. "It makes me want to wait. To stay with her, until…"

"We cannot stay. You know that."

Of course I know it, she wanted to shout at him. She knew it. Her grandmother knew it. Everyone who knew her damnable destiny knew it. But it didn't make it any easier. She opened her lips to say a version of all that, then stopped. She'd said it all before and more than once, and if she was to say it again, the Wall was not the person to hear it. *He earns his name in these exchanges,* she thought. Her giant protector was inclined toward emotional detachment, and if she needed to vent, Leshie was the answer.

She turned her eyes back outside as they rattled along through the city, looking at the boarded doors and shuttered windows, the empty stalls and stands in the squares that only recently bustled with life. No longer. In the days before the battle, Lord Hasham had decreed a period of martial law, and for large parts of the city it was still in place as they tried to root out the malefactors and clear the rubble and dead away.

It would take weeks, months, years to make Aram what it was. And there was still the chance that further disaster would come to her. Saska could not forget her dreams, forget the spreading fires and burning forests, the mountains spouting flame. The world was firmly in the jaws of the Ever-War now, and it wasn't going to get any better.

They crossed the Amedda River, which cut down through the city to empty into the bay. Many bridges spanned its width, some simple walkways barely wide enough for two men to walk abreast, others great stone monstrosities upon which entire towns seemed to have grown, shops and taverns, winesinks and brothels, even little court-yards where tradesmen sold their wares.

Or used to. As with everywhere else, the bridges were quiet, the tradesmen gone, only soldiers walking the streets. It made for mournful viewing. Saska used to like looking down at the bridges from the top of the palace. Now, from up there, all she saw was death.

The palace itself was busier than she'd ever known it, though. In the vast entrance hall at its base, Lord Hasham had set up a bustling command centre, from where he issued his orders. There were hundreds of soldiers here, ever coming and going on patrol, sorting weapons and armour and dragging in new captives for interrogation. Those were taken to the palace's western side from the main hall, where several dark stairways led down into the dungeons. Saska had not asked what sort of methods were used to extract information from them, but she didn't imagine they would be pleasant. It was said that Iziah Hasham had several prized torturers at his disposal, and was not unwilling to use them.

The litter came to a halt at the bottom of the wide bronze steps, glimmering under the blaze of the sun. Saska did not waste a moment in escaping that suffocating wooden cell, dashing out through the curtains and scaling the steps to enter the relative cool of the atrium. Her ears were assaulted at once by the great echoing cacophony within; soldiers marching, steel ringing, voices shouting out commands. To the left of the doors, she sighted the Strong Eagle giving orders to a group of some thirty men, all wearing the scale-mail shirts and eagle half-helms of the Aram City Guard. He seemed to be issuing an instruction over a particular building that needed searching. A tip-off from a spy, perhaps, or information extracted from one of the pris-oners in the dungeons. The Wise Eagle was here as well, Saska observed, leading a prayer with a host of some fifty soldiers, all kneeling before him with their heads lowered and hands pressed together at the palm. She could guess at what was troubling them. During the battle, Aramatians had been forced to fight and kill Arama-tians and it had not sat well with many. The Wise Eagle, in his puri-fying glory, had come down to cleanse them of this sin.

Ahead, at the hall's heart, a great pavilion had been raised, its left side silver, right side white, the colours of House Hasham. Outside stood a half dozen magnificent guards in their feathered cloaks and tall white spears. Saska strode toward them, letting Sir Ralston battle the bustle of bodies behind her.

"I'm here for Lord Hasham," she said.

Saska was well known now. Where once before they might have reacted with smirks and frowns and a round of shared glances, now they only obeyed. One of the men turned and slipped inside at once. He reappeared a moment later. "You may go through, Serenity." All of them bowed as she went past.

She entered the moonlord's private sanctum, to find him alone at his desk. The desk was large, mahogany, painted as the pavilion was, silver to the left side and white on the right. Hasham himself bore the colours as well. His scale armour and feathered cloak were pristine, and the whiskers on his face and plumage of his head were similarly striking. Saska had never known anyone with such a formidable presence. It simmered off his very being like ripples of heat in the desert.

"My lord, I hope I'm not disturbing you."

He lifted his gaze. On the table were maps and diagrams detailing the destruction to the east of the city, and plans to restore it. She sighted a list - a ledger, perhaps - that appeared to instruct upon the financials of this. No doubt restoring vast swathes of an enormous city were costly. Add to that the coming famine, the ongoing war, the suspension of trade with other nations due to the perils of the seas, and the vast camp of refugees outside the walls, battling with the red flux, and Saska knew the man had much on his plate. "My lady. What can I do for you?" He set his quill pen aside in a pot.

"I don't want to take up much of your time, my lord. I only wondered if you had any news of Lord Krator? Have your torturers and interrogators learned anything new?"

"Enquiries are still being made." That was a nice way of putting it. *Enquiries*. "Did the sellswords not have anything to report? They know the underground world of this city better than I ever will."

They were sharing in that duty, this hunt for the missing sunlord. Where Hasham's men and those of the Strong Eagle went from door to door, the sellswords searched the netherworld of Aram, peeking into the grubby little places that only they knew.

Saska stepped closer to the table. A map showed the city and lands around it. She pointed vaguely to the west. "The Baker suggested he might have escaped across the border, into Pisek. So far none of their searches here have led anywhere, and it's been days, so…"

"So I think you have your answer." Hasham rested an elbow on his desk, running fingers through the thick grey bristles of his beard. He studied the same map with a pair of keen and penetrating brown eyes. "In three days Elio could have made it a hundred miles from here, perhaps double that if he keeps a strong pace. I have men watching the river to the north, and have informed Moonlord Ranaartan at Starcat Keep to maintain a constant lookout as well. I doubt he would go that way, however. East? Well, he has caused such strife in the east that he would not be welcomed there. Kolash, Matia, both sacked by his coalition. Eagle's Perch lost to Cedrik Kastor and then left abandoned. There are places in the plains he could hide, but those heights have grown treacherous now. He will know he will not last long there, not even if he has mustered a menacing host to accompany him, which I would doubt. No, more likely he and Mar Malaan and perhaps a few others tucked their tails and ran together. So west…" He nodded. "Yes, that would be my guess as well. There have been reports of men crossing the river the night of the battle, not long before sunrise. Several watchmen upon the walls corroborate this. If one of them was Elio Krator, then he is now beyond our grasp, I fear to say."

She could not hide her disappointment. "But…can't you send men to hunt him? He'll have left a trail. You have trackers…"

"I do. Fine trackers and fine hunters who I could deploy if I wished."

"But you won't? You'll just let him go free?"

The man's gaze narrowed. *Careful*, that said. "If Elio has indeed gone west, he will have ridden for an ally, and if that is the case, he will have swords about him soon. I would not expose a band of my best men to that risk, not until I have better information." He checked her eyes. "You're displeased. I understand. And so am I, do not doubt it. That man has brought this entire duchy to the brink of ruin, and as soon as I get the faintest whiff of his whereabouts, I will seek him out and destroy him, in that you have my word."

She believed him. But first he needed that whiff. And she couldn't speak for his sense of smell. "Thank you, my lord. That is all I can ask. Though…"

"Yes?"

She glanced back to the tent flaps, wondering why the Wall hadn't interrupted them yet. "Sir Ralston…he thinks I need to let my vengeance lie, but I can't, not with *him*. *If* you do find him…can you make me a promise?"

His jaw jut out. "Let me hear it first."

"Imprison him," she said. "Keep him locked away for me, so I can return to see the light leave his eyes."

The old moonlord raised a bushy grey eyebrow. He did not take long to consider it. "No," he said, firmly, and with finality. "I understand why you have made this request, but no, I cannot grant it. If Elio Krator is found and brought here during your absence, he will suffer no imprisonment or trial. Such a man is too dangerous to be left alive, and the city will demand his death. When I pit your wants against theirs, there is only one voice I will listen to. The *collective*, my lady, is always more powerful than the one. The day Krator is returned here will be the day he dies. Whether you're present for that or not is, regrettably, of no consequence."

Well, that told me. She felt the fool for even asking it. "Fine. I understand." Knowing that Krator had died to a chorus of jeers and taunts would have to be enough. *I'll have some bard sing a song about it for me*, she thought. *Maybe I'll even commission a play…a mummer's play, to mock him...*

"Is there anything else you wish to discuss?"

She shook her head. "I wouldn't want to take up any more of your time." She was halfway through turning when he stopped her.

"Oh, before you go." She turned back to see him reach into a drawer. "A letter was found this morning, in the ruin of the Tukoran encampment." He reached out. "It is addressed to you."

She frowned and stepped back over. "Does it say who from?"

"The seal is House Lukar. I suspect it is from the prince."

Robbert. She took the letter from his leathery fingers and tore the seal, withdrawing the note. She smiled as she read the words.

"What does it say?" Hasham asked.

"He apologises for the haste of his leaving, and…for everything else that happened." She looked up; Lord Iziah Hasham had taken some convincing that Prince Robbert Lukar was an ally, not an enemy, and that he and his broken army ought to be left to leave without harassment. It had not been easy, but eventually Hasham had acceded. *But still there is mistrust in him.*

"And? Anything else?"

"He says he will aim to leave these lands with all speed, and won't raise a blade against any of its inhabitants, lest they first do the same to him."

"I'm sure. And what of the bands of men who did *not* leave with him? Can he promise they will act peaceably toward our people as well?"

I would doubt it, Saska thought. As with Elio Krator's forces, the Tukorans had splintered during the battle, and many had gone racing for the hills. Now they would rove like bandits, it was feared, rogue elements stalking across their lands, plundering and pillaging as they went. She scanned the note. "He makes no mention of them. But most of his surviving men went with him. We saw that from the palace."

It had been two days ago that Robbert Lukar left, marching east toward the coast with the ragged remains of his army at his back. Saska had stood at the parapet wall of the terrace gardens, dressed in silk, her body freshly stitched and bandaged, wondering if this was the last time she would ever see the prince who had saved her life. There had never been a time in all history when the seas were so treacherous to travel. Greatsharks and greywhales in massive, wrathful pods; rare and ancient leviathans; krakens and manators and other monstrous things. If half his remaining fleet made it home to Tukor it would be a miracle. A tenth even felt unlikely. *But it only takes one ship*, she told herself. *Just the one…just his.*

Lord Hasham appeared to be thinking the same. "The seas will judge him," he intoned. "I am no godly man, as you know, but I respect the power of nature. Let the wrath of the waves decide on whether this Robbert Lukar is worthy. As to these roving bands, they will soon find that the plains of Aramatia are unfriendly to unwelcome guests. The wells and rivers are running dry and this heat is becoming unnatural. They will not survive for long." He looked at the note. "Is there more?"

She scanned it once again. After the apologies and the promises, what remained was a little more personal. Gratitude toward Del and

Leshie for saving his life. A hope that they would see one another again soon. A jape about the oddity of their meeting, there in the midst of the chaos of the fighting. And there at the end, scrawled beneath his signature, was a postscript that mentioned a gift.

"He says he left a gift for me." She looked up. "Did you find anything with the letter?"

"A chest," Hasham said. "The letter was lying atop it in the wreckage of the boy's pavilion. I had it checked, for obvious reasons. There was a concern it might contain something harmful. I had to be sure."

"And did it?"

"That would depend on your point of view. It contained godsteel, Saska. My men were unable to move it, of course, so I had the Surgeon summoned to help. He and some of his men. They hauled it up to your chambers."

Saska was already stepping back toward the flaps. "Then I'll not take up any of your time, Lord Hasham."

"Is Sir Ralston out there?" the moonlord asked.

She paused in motion. "He is."

"I'll have his report, then. Send him in, if you would."

Saska nodded, turned, and slipped out past the guards into the maelstrom of noise. It was curious how much quieter it had seemed inside that tent with only canvas walls to shield them. The Wall was taking report from the Strong Eagle, hearing of his latest operations in the city. When he saw her emerge he absented himself and stamped over, spotting the note in her grasp. "I am told there was a letter."

She waved it. "There was."

"Is it of any consequence?"

To me, yes. She folded it, stashing it in a pocket to join her other treasures; the list of jokes from Bawdry Bronn, the quill-knife Lancel had given her, the shell necklace from little Billy Bowen and the pitted piece of coral that had called to her, once, during that lazy day on the reef. All little mementoes of her time and travels, of the people who had shaped her path. "Not especially," she said. "It's from Prince Robbert. It came with a gift."

The Wall seemed to know that already. "A chest of godsteel, I'm told."

Gifts were meant to be surprises, so far as Saska knew. She gave a sigh. "Does the Strong Eagle have anything to say?"

"Nothing that will make you smile."

Little does these days, she might have said. But that was too morose. "Lord Hasham wants to see you. I'll be upstairs when you're done."

She left him, drifting through the sea of soldiers toward the grand central stair, beginning her ascent. The palace was three-tiered, towering, with many smaller levels on each, accessed by switchback stairs of stone that seemed, sometimes, to go on forever. She passed eagles along the way. Eagles in stone and eagles in iron and eagles stitched into tapestries and drapes. They perched upon the walls, clutching torches in their talons, or looming in some cold dark corner, staring out with piercing eyes. Leshie had given some of them names, though Saska never remembered which was which. They were always silly too. *Beak-Face* and *Angry-Eyes* and *Feathers*, things like that.

A third of the way up, she heard the tread of footsteps coming down. A bustle of bodies that told of a group three of four strong. She rounded a corner and saw them, moving between a patch of shadow between two torches. Then the face of the Surgeon appeared, as stony and inexpressive as the eagles on the walls.

"Serenity." He gave a bow. "We have delivered the chest to your chambers." His eyes had a soulless quality to them, those eyes that never seemed to blink. It was an affected thing, Saska suspected, a learned habit, part of his persona. The Surgeon was all about precision, and calm. Ruthless, calculating, a man of modest physical stature, but intimidating in manner and mood.

Saska could understand how this man might unnerve another, but not her. She'd seen much worse than him. "My thanks."

"There's good godsteel in there," he said. "You'll forgive me for having a look."

Stop ruining the surprise. "I would imagine a prince has access to a wealth of good godsteel, Captain."

A small smile and dip of the chin. He was clean-shaven, lightly tanned, with plain, forgettable features. "Yes. I would imagine the same."

The captain had with him three others. Two men, and a woman. The men were large, the woman larger. Saska craned her neck to look at her. "We haven't had the pleasure, as yet."

A hiss slipped through the woman's lips.

"The Tigress does not speak, Serenity," the Surgeon explained. "At least, not until she is comfortable with a person. But I know her hisses, and that one was very polite. She is not unfamiliar with courtesy."

"Courtesy I will take or leave. It's strong swords and loyalty I'm after."

"I have heard. There is a rumour that you are leaving Aram, and require an escort." He presented his men. "Let me introduce Gutter and Gore. Two of my finest implements. They look rather alike, do they not?"

"Brothers?" Saska asked.

"Cousins. But their fathers were twins to one another, and their mothers looked rather the same as well. Gutter. Gore. We bow when we meet our betters."

"Cap'n." The two men spoke in unison, dull-voiced, and bowed in time as well. They were greatly more alike than the Butcher and the Baker, that was certain, a pair of broad-shouldered men of similar stature with long, flaxen hair tumbling to their necks, one with a light wave only, the other more thickly curled. They had square chins, flat cheeks, narrow noses, piercing eyes. *Handsome*, Saska thought, taking a good long look at them. One of them had mismatched eyes, she saw. The left purple, the right clear blue. The other's were a striking hue of hazel, almost gold.

She had a question for them. "I have to ask…why Gutter and Gore?"

One pointed at the other. "He guts, I gore." He made a stabbing motion with his hand, glanced at the Surgeon as though for guidance, then bowed again. "My lady."

Fine implements, Saska thought. *But not the sharpest.* "Does every sellsword have a name?"

"Only those that earn them," said the Surgeon. "When you gut or gore a score of men, the name does tend to stick."

"And the Tigress?" Saska looked up. The woman must have been over six and a half feet tall, taller even than Lady Marian had been. And beautiful as well. Feline ochre eyes, straight black shimmering hair, skin the colour of honey. *Is that one of the Surgeon's requirements? Must all his killers be comely?* "I've heard you suffered the lash, once before," Saska said, addressing her directly. She perused her garb, a mix of godsteel chainmail and plate, with a cloak of black and orange vair flowing from her shoulders. Beneath it, her flesh was scourged, Saska had been told. The flaying had left her horribly disfigured across the breasts and back, savage stripes that won her her name, a beauty from the neck up only.

The woman hissed.

"That means 'yes'," translated the Surgeon. "One day, she may show you. Only few have ever seen them."

He was one of them, she did not doubt. *Perhaps he even stitched her up?* "You show me yours and I'll show you mine." Saska thumbed over her shoulder. "I've been whipped as well, Tigress. I'm a striped woman, same as you."

A smile, this time. And a nod.

"She likes you," the Surgeon observed, in that mechanical way of his. "I think Gutter and Gore do as well, though perhaps for a different reason. *Eyes down*," he said to them, suddenly fierce, snapping the words out. They obeyed at once, eyes to their toes. "Discipline is important in my ranks, Serenity. I am sorry if they were staring."

"It's fine. I'm used to it. Though I suggest they be careful when Sir Ralston is around. He is very protective of me."

"They mean no harm. But yes, I will make sure of that. I daresay Sir Ralston could gut and gore these two without so much as breaking a sweat." He put a hand on the Tigress's arm. Bands in black and orange were wrapped around the steel of her vambraces. "She would give him a better fight, I think. I am proud of her, perhaps you can tell. She is the greatest of all the Bloody Traders. Perhaps the most deadly sellsword in all the world."

73

"A bold claim. The Butcher might disagree with you." *Along with a hundred others.*

"Every sellsword worth his salt would disagree with me. We are a swaggering sort, a race of braggarts and boasters, with very thin skin when our competence is called into question. Now a man like Sir Ralston…he does not need to boast. He knows, in his bones, that there are few knights in this world who could conquer him, if any." That hand on the Tigress's arm again, the little proud smile to go with it. "She is the same among sellswords. A marvel of the Unseen Isles, who has slain five hundred men."

Saska had heard that one too. *That and the blood.* There were whispers going around that the Tigress liked to drink the blood of her victims, Bladeborn blood in particular, to keep herself young. That she had mage blood in her veins. Saska suspected that was just another tall tale, but if true, she cared not. *She's just the sort of woman I need. A killer, born and bred.*

"Will you come with me?" she asked.

"Yes," said the Surgeon.

She blinked. "Oh. I hadn't thought…"

"It would be so easy?"

"Well…yes. You're known as a man of careful thought. I would have imagined you'd want to consider it for a while. You don't even know where we're going."

"Vandar."

Another blink. A strong pump of the heart. "How…?"

"Ears in the walls, Serenity. Roaches in the rushes. Things are said. Things are heard. They reach my ears and I profit."

"*Profit?*" Saska felt suddenly exposed, on edge. Just one word and she was squinting at the man in doubt. "Are you trying to blackmail me, Captain?"

"No. I am trying to help you. I *have* been helping you already, in fact. Do not think me unversed in the horror that awaits us, or uncaring of the plight of this world. I know how important you are. And I am here to swear you my sword."

She looked at him, narrow-eyed. "If this is some trick…"

"No trick. Just good sense. I know who you are, who your grandfather was, and I know a little of prophecy too. Without you, all may be lost. I speak of profit, yes. There is great profit to be had in protecting you."

She still wasn't sure. Another squinting glare. Though really, that made no sense. Only moments ago she was asking him to join her, and not so long before that she was telling Rolly that anyone who joined her company deserved to know the truth. That he had somehow unearthed it first shouldn't matter. But it did, somehow. She felt less in control.

"I'll think about it," she said, after a pause. "You've just…you've taken me off-guard a bit. If the secret gets out…"

74

"Your enemies will come."

"Yes." *And one in particular.*

"It has," the Surgeon said.

Saska stiffened, peering at him. His eyes gave nothing away. "You mean…" She chose her words carefully, glancing at the Tigress, at Gutter and Gore, though their eyes were still inspecting their toes and would likely stay there until commanded otherwise. "Others who know…who I am?"

"There are. There *were*. But fear not, the Surgeon has cut these cancers free and removed the tainted flesh. They will not trouble you anymore."

She swallowed. "You've…been *killing* for me?"

He stared, cold-eyed. "I have killed, cut off tongues, fingers, hands, threatened the lives of loved ones. All for you. To shield your true identity. When a secret slips out it becomes a plague. It spreads, like the bloody flux beyond the walls. And soon everyone has it. Soon everyone knows. I have been working to contain the spread."

She knew nothing of this. "By whose authority?"

"Need," the Surgeon said. "By the authority of *necessity*." He fingered a long flaying knife at his belt, nestled beside a plain-looking broadsword and nine-inch godsteel dagger, curved and cruel. He had some smaller blades as well, surgical instruments, scalpels of various shape and size fixed to a leather belt worn diagonally across his chest. "Rest assured. Only men of ill design have been blooded over this. The flow has been staunched, for now."

Saska was beginning to understand why people feared this man. *Pete Brown*, she thought. *That's his true name.* A plain name for a plain-looking man, but behind those eyes…

She gave a firm nod, swallowing again. Once upon a time she might have condemned him for this, but not now. *The authority of necessity*, she thought. *He isn't wrong.*

"How many of your own people know?"

"Few. Only those I trust. These will be the men I bring with me, when we go."

"And all this from the kindness of your heart?" She continued to peer at him, trying to get a better read. "Or are you hoping to reap some reward, Captain, from all this fine work you've been doing?"

"My only reward will be to accompany you on your quest. And *if* it should succeed…then perhaps we can talk."

She gave a snort of laughter. *Sellswords. They're all the same.* It was all about coin after all. "That's a big risk for a risk-averse man. The Butcher told me you only ever choose the winning side."

"The winning side is invariably the one I choose."

Braggarts and boasters, she thought, pondering. Though really, what was there to ponder? She had wanted them along anyway. That they knew already of her path and purpose only made it all the easier. She reached out a hand. "I accept."

He took it in callused fingers, kissed the back of her palm to seal the contract, and released her. His lips were dry as dust, crinkly to the touch. Her hand withdrew.

"When are we to leave, Serenity?"

With this about the secret slipping out, she had no time to waste. *I cannot wait for Ranulf anymore.*

"Tomorrow," she said.

5

Lythian

"He asked for you specifically," said the burly hedge knight, breath misting in the cool of dawn. "He says he knows you, my lord. Wants to help, he claims."

"Help?" Lythian Lindar frowned. "In what regard, Sir Hadros?" The man was like a gnarled old oak, with a bulbous nose, thick with broken veins, skin like bark, and hair the colour of dirty straw. *All those days sleeping in barns*, Lythian thought. Such was the life of a homeless hedge knight, going where the winds took him, serving this lord or that master to earn a bit of coin. *Serve me well through this war, and you'll earn more than just coin*. When the dust settled on this Last Renewal, there would be a lot of empty estates and castles in need of men to restore them, the Knight of the Vale did not doubt. A man like Sir Hadros could do very well for himself…so long as he survived.

"He did not elaborate on that front, Captain Lythian," the knight told him. "Could be any manner of things, I suppose. Or some trick. Wouldn't put it past a Fireborn to try to trick us, my lord."

"A Fireborn?"

"Aye, so it would seem by his raiment. Rich scaly armour, you know the sort, and a fancy cape to match. Says he lost his dragon during the battle. Not sure if he means it was killed by one of ours or flew away. Quite a few of them abandoned their riders when the Dread showed up, that I saw. Guess that bond isn't so strong as they think."

"No," said Lythian, reflecting. He had seen with his own two eyes how easily Eldur could sever the bonds between dragon and rider, or fasten them anew. It seemed that Drulgar the Dread had the very same influence upon the dragons. *And perhaps that's something we can use*, Lythian thought. There was nothing a dragonrider feared more than the breaking of their bond. "This Fireborn. Did he give a name, at least?"

77

"He didn't. But I'm sure he'll be happy to share it with you. Older man, he is. Kinda spindly, a bit lost-looking, haunted, you know the type." Sir Hadros gave a glance around him, as men trundled here and there, collecting the dead in barrows, picking through their corpses for weapons and armour, clothes, food, whatever other provisions they could use. "Plenty of those looks about here these days, my lord. Some men just can't hack the horror of battle. Too many of them are wet behind the ears."

"This was no normal battle, Sir Hadros. I would not judge a man for withering when confronted by an ancient calamity like Drulgar."

A pair of muscular shoulders went up and down. To experienced soldiers like Sir Hadros, those who wilted in war, no matter the conditions, were considered to be lesser men. Lythian would not agree with the word 'lesser', perhaps, but they were certainly less reliable. "If you say so, my lord. Good to sort the men from the boys, though. A man shows his true face when looking death in the eye, and I'm sorry to say it, but a lot of these lads don't have it."

"And many do, Sir Hadros. Let's not deal in generalities."

"Aye, fair enough." He clapped his gloved hands together, rubbing them against the chill of dawn. "So, this Fireborn, then. You want to talk to him now, or…"

"Now," Lythian said. And the pair of them stepped away.

The captives were being kept outside the city, housed in a makeshift pen erected in the ruin of the warcamp, bordered by a ring of sharpened posts, a deep, stake-lined ditch, and watched over by a strong complement of spearmen, swordsmen, and bowmen. Before the battle that camp had been occupied by the Taynar forces; now it was a broken blackened thing, a chaos of torn tents and scorched timber, burned wagons and crippled carts. Within its rotting corpse, Lythian had ordered that accommodation be made for the southern prisoners they had taken. Many had been caught once the battle was over, throwing down their arms and surrendering. Others had run at the sight of the Dread, only to return in ones and twos and small downtrodden troops, to give themselves up and hope to be granted passage home to their own lands. Whether they would be awarded such clemency was yet to be seen. *That is a decision for our new king to make.*

"Did any others come while I was sleeping?" Lythian asked, as they walked.

"Few more trickled in, aye. Couple of Lumarans. A cat-less Starrider. Three more Agarathi, this Fireborn included. Your dragonknight's with them now." Sir Hadros squinted over toward the prisoner camp, uncertain. "You sure he's the right man for the job, my lord? This dragonknight. They're his people, after all. He might try to let them go."

"Only if I order him to, Sir Hadros. I understand your concerns, but Sir Pagaloth is sworn to me by oath, and a man of honour besides. He is aligned in our course, I assure you."

In the east the sun was climbing above the horizon, bringing light to the devastation of the coastlands, the earth churned and blackened, scarred with steaming pits. The wide handsome estuary where the Steelrun River emptied into the Red Sea was unrecognisable, choked in ash and mud and death. What thickets of trees had existed here were burned down to stumps and cinders, green turned black, life to death, all from Drulgar's passing and the destruction he wrought in his wake. From the city walls down to the shore, thousands lay dead, picked at by carrion crows and crabs, their flesh already starting to rot. Though they were doing what they could to gather their own dead for burial and cremation, the same could not be said for the enemy.

If they are truly our enemy at all, Lythian thought. *We should be fighting together in this. Drulgar…Eldur…they are a threat to us all.*

Sir Hadros wrinkled his nose. "High time we put a torch to all these corpses. This stink's only going to get worse."

"We don't have the manpower or the material," Lythian said. "We'll have to bear the smell for now."

"Sour to us, sweet to others. All that death attracts dangers, my lord." He waved a hand to the sea. "Some of the watchmen said they saw dragons during the night, swooping down to feast on the corpses down yonder near the shore. And we heard a great deal of howling too. Might just be regular wolves come from the woods, but there are sunwolves out there too now, and other older things as well. Fellwolves, grimbears, darkcats, direwolves, all sorts. I saw a stormhag myself, a few weeks ago, when crossing through the Heartlands. Tried to lure me into its lair, it did. Evil bloody witch."

"You did well to avoid a grisly fate, Sir Hadros." Lythian could not be sure if he was lying, but gave him the benefit of the doubt.

"Aye, and don't I know it. I'd sooner die in the jaws of the Dread than be boiled alive in some stormhag's pot. Not a nice way to go."

"One of the less pleasant, I agree."

They continued on past a dead dragon, its tongue lolling out of its mouth like a dog, a spear embedded in its left eye halfway up the shaft. The oaken hedge knight gestured to it with a chunky finger. "That spear's not even tipped in godsteel," he said. "There's proof if ever it's needed that any man can slay a dragon."

Lythian liked the thought. There had grown a pervading belief that only Bladeborn knights and men-at-arms could best a dragon in battle, but it wasn't so. "I should have every disbeliever brought out here to show them the evidence, Sir Hadros. It might serve to inspire them."

"We have our new king for that. If ever we needed inspiring…well, that chanting last night was enough to rouse the spirits, don't you think? Even out here we were singing out his name. *King Daecar! Amron the Great!* Taken him long enough to admit it, so the men are saying."

"And what do you say?"

"Not much. I only arrived here a few days before the battle, my lord. Not really clued in on all that's been going on. Though this about King Amron sharing the rule with Dalton Taynar…not sure who he was trying to convince with that. Even the Taynar men I've been talking to said they never saw Dull Dalton as their king."

"Less of the dull, if you would. Now is not the time to be using a man's mocking epithet. His blood has barely run cold."

"His blood ran *out*, so I hear. All of it. That's how he died."

"Yes, well…I know Dalton was not the most popular man, but he was a First Blade of Vandar, for a time, and ought to be honoured as such. We do not mock our departed, Sir Hadros. We venerate them, and praise them, and send them to the Eternal Halls with grace."

"And Varin's Table," the hedge knight put in. He slowed, then stopped, beside another fallen dragon, this one savagely butchered and beheaded with a hundred spears and arrows pricking it like a porcupine. "Captain, I wonder…"

Lythian stopped and turned to face him. "Yes?"

"Well…we've had our run-ins in the past, haven't we, you and I?"

"We have." Lythian had met the man on several occasions, and even fought with him once before when on campaign during the last war. He had not known he was here, at King's Point, let alone alive, until after the battle was over. In truth he had assumed the man to have died years ago, but apparently he was still plodding along, hoping for an opportunity to win glory and renown. *It was what brought him here*, Lythian knew. Though perhaps he didn't anticipate anything quite so cataclysmic as this. "Go on, Sir Hadros. What's the ask?"

"That." The stocky knight waved a finger at Lythian's cloak. "I want one of my own. The gods know I always have."

"Gods and men both. I remember a time many years ago when you petitioned to join the order."

"And I was close too, you might recall. Would have made a good Varin Knight if it wasn't for that trouble I got into as a boy."

Lythian thought a moment. "The desecration of the statues?"

Sir Hadron blew out through his lips. "I was young and impressionable. Just a stupid boy getting caught up with the wrong crowd, is all. We got it in our heads that King Ayrin was weak, so…well, we defaced a statue or two in the town square…"

"Ayrin's Cross, was it?"

"The worst possible place," the knight grunted. "They're all so high and mighty over there and gods do they love King Ayrin the Wise. We lads were more fond of the warrior kings, you know how boys can be. Was just a stupid thing, a bit of water and dye and now I'm branded for life. The sort of thing my father would have brushed under the rug if he was a lord, but no, I was born to a middling household knight and never had such leverage." He let out another heavy breath. "Anyhow, I suppose I was just wondering if you…"

"Might anoint you myself? Permit you into the holy sanctum of Varin's Order?"

"Aye, just that. I'd ask for a castle when all this is done, but let's be honest, I probably won't live that long. Better to plan for the afterlife, wouldn't you say? A seat at Varin's Table…now that's something to fight for."

In other circumstances, Lythian might have smiled at the man's forthrightness. It was hard to do so here, however, surrounded by such devastation and death. "That isn't my decision to make, Sir Hadros."

"Then whose is it? Dalton Taynar's dead, so is Vesryn Daecar. Leaves us First Blade-less, doesn't it? Now mayhaps Lord Amron might have retaken the mantle, but no, he's king now, so he can't be doing that. Leaves you, my lord. You're seniormost in the order…and a bloody handsome man too, I should probably add." Devastation and death or not, the man gave a winsome grin. "I'd serve you to my dying breath, believe that, Captain Lythian. And I know others would too, if given the same chance."

Lythian didn't doubt it. The lure of Varin's Table was a powerful one to be sure. But all the same, such an honour was not to be given out so freely. "Any man who joins the order must earn it, Sir Hadros."

"Or just have the right family name," the man came back, and not without a note of bitterness. "Too many Knights of Varin have bought their way into the order. You know that as well as I do, my lord."

"A fair point," Lythian admitted. Traditionally it had been much more difficult for men of lowlier birth to win their spurs. One only had to look at the likes of Gerald Strand to see that not all Knights of Varin were worth their place in the ranks. "Let me think about it, Sir Hadros, and speak with the king. I have a council meeting to attend shortly. I will try to corner him about this after, though I'm not making any promises."

The man seemed appeased by that, dipping his lumpen, bristled chin in a bow. "I'd be much obliged, my lord. Now let's go see this Fireborn, shall we? Wouldn't want to keep him waiting."

They reached the encampment a minute later, stepping through the broken barrels and shattered carts, the oddments of armour and charred corpses, the heaps of black tar that had once been mighty pavilions, reduced now to nothing but mulch. From the detritus, scraps had been gathered and made into fencing to pen the prisoners in. There was no canvas roof, no cover at all, not even for the wounded, of which there were many. Lythian took one look at the growing population. "We're going to have to expand," he said. "They'll be sleeping on top of one another soon enough."

"Won't be a problem," said Hadros the Homeless. "Not like we're lacking for space."

Lythian ran his eyes over the masses. There were several hundred of them now, born of every nation and island group south of the Red Sea, from Agarath to Aramatia, the Golden Isles to the Twin Suns. Most were common soldiers, little more than fodder for their blades, yet for every thirty of those there was a dragonknight dressed in his black scalemail armour or a paladin in magnificent robes. Fewer still were the Starriders and Sunriders, of which there were only a handful. *And now a dragonrider*, Lythian thought. *Our first.*

He spotted Sir Pagaloth across the pen, in conversation with the man in question. A quick glance was all it took. "You know him, then, as he says?" asked Sir Hadros.

"I do. I had the honour of spending time with him in Agarath."

"Aye, heard all about your travels down there."

Not all of them, Lythian thought. Regaling the hedge knight of his time in the south was not high on his list of priorities, however. "See that the pen is extended," he commanded. "Fill the ditch, pull the stakes, and remake it all some ten metres back. And perhaps you're right about the stench, Sir Hadros. It might be time to begin piling up the enemy dead for burning, if we can spare the men."

"Plenty of men sitting idle here, my lord. Might as well put the prisoners to work. They are their dead, after all."

Lythian considered it. His mind had been leaning that way as well, in truth. "Fine. But no cruelty. No lashings and beatings. I do not want to see them mistreated."

"Not in my nature, my lord. But if I might make one suggestion?"

"Go on."

He waved a hand to the east, out where the lands were burned and churned. "We pile a few choice corpses out yonder, set up a few hidden shelters in the ditches, and fill them with bowmen, spearmen, lengths of chain. Even a ballista or two if we can roll them out there."

Lythian understood. *Bait.* "You mean to catch a few more dragons, Sir Hadros?"

"Catch a few. *Kill* a few. They come sniffing around the dead again and we add them to these others." He gestured to the nearest dead dragon; there were at least a dozen of them, rotting outside the walls, and many more within, scattered about the rubble.

Lythian nodded his assent. "See it done. This works, and perhaps you'll win that cloak of yours."

"Was hoping you'd say that." The man grinned, bowed, and stamped away, the weatherworn cloak of a wandering warrior trailing proudly at his back.

Lythian's own cloak was similarly worn, though all the same, that strong Varin blue shone through all the little tears and scorch marks, the patches of soot and grime. At his neck he wore his captain's pin, fastening the cloak in place, and beneath it his armour; scratched, dented, and in need of a good polish. The last of those he could do himself, though the others…mending and tending to godsteel armour was the holy realm of the Forgeborn, blacksmiths and armourers derived from the blood of Ilith of whom scant few remained with any great skill. Several of the very best operated at the Steelforge, Forge-masters Merilore, Watling and Wainwood, and the apprentices beneath their charge. If he wanted his armour fixed and restored, they would be the men for the job.

If they're still alive, he thought. It was possible that Drulgar's assault upon the capital had extended to the Steelforge as well, striking at the very heart of Varin's Order. Amron had been hoping to send the bodies of Vesryn and Dalton there for burial, to be entombed in the crypts beside the rest of the former First Blades. Now those tombs might be under a thousand tons of rubble, the Steelforge itself reduced to rock and ruin, their reserves of swords and spears and shields, weapons and armour buried. Elyon had left only hours ago to investigate, soaring away into the skies shortly after his father was proclaimed king. By now he might have discovered the truth of Varinar's fate. His return, and his report, could not come soon enough.

But for now Lythian had to put it from his mind, to focus on matters he could control. He turned and walked along the edge of the enclosure, circling around to its eastern side where Sir Pagaloth and the Skymaster stood. He nodded to the former, and gave the latter a bow.

"Skymaster Nakaan," he said, with grace. "It is good to see you again, despite the unfortunate circumstances."

The ageing Fireborn returned the gesture, inclining his head into a courteous bow. "And you, Captain Lythian. Sir Pagaloth has just been telling me of your adventures together, since you left the Nest."

"Adventures is not a word I would use, Sa'har. Toils and trials would be rather more appropriate."

Sir Pagaloth had something of a resting frown-face, perpetually serious and sombre. "I did not use the word 'adventure'. Skymaster Nakaan is taking liberties, as he knows."

"Yes. So I am." Sa'har Nakaan showed his palms, and even raised a little smile, though one shadowed in grief and loss, the smile of a man who had lost it all. *He has haunted eyes, as Sir Hadros said, and has aged a decade since I saw him last.* The Skymaster had never been a meaty man, but now he was positively gaunt, with sunken cheeks and whitening hair and skin so parchment-thin Lythian could see the bones moving beneath his face. "I'm happy that you made it home, however," he went on. "I have worried about you…both of you…during my more…*conscious* moments. To see you both again, safe and unhurt…it is a shaft of light, on a dark and dreary day."

Lythian had always enjoyed the man's way with words. "As with you, Sa'har. But tell me, are you injured? You look…well."

"I look *old*, Lythian. And a little prematurely so. I had not realised, not until recently, just how much Ezukar's death had sapped my spirit. To be abandoned by him was hard, though ever there remained a thin hope in me that we would be reunited, one day. Once I sensed his death, however…" The pain was etched upon his face, in the lines about his eyes and mouth, the grim pallor of his skin.

"A terrible loss, Sa'har. You have my deepest condolences."

"Thank you, Lythian. It is a wound that I will always walk with, a darkening deep inside me that will never be restored to the light. The Fire Father had hoped that bonding me to another would relieve me of my troubles, but no. Bagrahar was not Ezukar, and never could be. To another I am sure he would have been a fine companion, but not me. I am better off without him. That is the honest truth."

Lythian had not heard the name Bagrahar before. "What happened, Sa'har? Was he killed, during the battle?"

"No, at least not *this* one."

"This one?" asked Sir Pagaloth. "Do you mean to say…"

"That he perished elsewhere. Yes, that is what I mean, Sir Pagaloth. Our bond may have been young and unnaturally forged, but I was still attuned enough to his spirit to know when it went dark. It was not the stark despair I felt when I knew that Ezukar was lost, not the same rending of my soul…more a cold feeling at the top of my spine, an instinct that told me he was gone. I mourn for him, as a young dragon with much to live for. He should never have left the Wings."

Like a thousand others. Unlike most of his northern brethren, Lythian had seen the beauty in the beasts, the nobility and the grace. Many of the dragons would surely have been happier remaining where they were, living out their days on those stark volcanic islands, rather than being summoned by the soul of their maker to spread his fiery will. "He followed Drulgar then? When he flew north?"

The Skymaster put his hands together and nodded. "I regret it is so. I tried to wrest control of him, and in our struggle he threw me from the saddle. As Ezukar abandoned me at Eldur's behest, so Bagrahar did for Drulgar. Now tell me, Lythian, after all of that…just where should my loyalties lie?"

"To yourself, Sa'har," Lythian said without pause. "Be loyal to who you are. A man of probity and justice. Isn't that why you're here?"

The Skymaster nodded slowly and turned his eyes to the east, to the rent and ruined lands, bathed beneath the dawn. "I landed out there, somewhere," he started, "when discarded from Bagrahar's back. I was lucky. The land was soft and churned, enough to break my fall, and we were near to the ground at the time. I escaped without injury. Many others…good Fireborn, good men and women, were not so fortunate. I suppose you saw, did you not? The riders being thrown from the backs of their dragons, to tumble into the tumult below?"

Lythian recalled it all too well. The skies had rained Fireborn and fire both. He gave a nod, and the Skymaster went on.

"I did not move for a time, after I had landed. I just lay there, hoping that some Bladeborn knight might come past and make an end of my pitiful life. What could I offer, after all? I was a dragonrider without a dragon, a man with a darkened soul, a slave in service to a lie. I deserved to die, I told myself. No one would miss an old dragon-less Skymaster like me. Yet there is a coward in all of us, Lythian, a shameful spectre who cannot always be subdued. In our weakest moments, he comes. And he came for me that day.

"So I stood, when I saw my chance…and I ran like so many others. There were many that I saw escaping into the woods. Some were alone, others in groups. They did not know where they were or where they were going. They only wanted to survive." He paused for thought. "That is a primitive instinct. An instinct that drives a man to places he never knew existed, places deep inside himself that require he do terrible things. When his survival is at stake, boundaries do not exist. And now here we are, in a world without boundaries. With northmen in the south and southmen in the north, all willing to do anything to live.

"Chaos, Lythian. A world of brutality and blood and bile. Even during my short days alone, I wondered what I would do, when my hunger grew too severe. Would I kill a man for a piece of bread? Would I steal the last rations from a child? Sooner or later, far too many of us will have to confront those sorts of questions. To steal another man's food and let him starve, or continue to starve yourself. To kill or be killed. To take one of the few spots left for the living, because believe me, they will grow scarce. For every ten men alive right now, perhaps only three or four will be alive within a year. In five years, one. In ten…" He shook his head. "Man will become a dying breed, and shrink to the edges of the world. That is what I saw in those woods, Lythian. Men running scared of monsters, with a new terror around every turn."

A battleground, Lythian thought. *A world where only the strong survive.* He took a moment to digest the man's tale, then put a hand on his shoulder and said, "Yet you returned, Sa'har. As have many others here." He looked across the pen. "They came back through fear, and in the hope of being returned home to their own lands. What of you, my friend? Is it fear that drove you here?"

"Fear? Oh, fear does not cover it, Lythian. It is something beyond fear that demanded I return. But not for myself, no. It is a deep and unsettling dread for what this world will become. What it is already becoming. Oh, as I wandered those woods I found my purpose. To help, in whatever way I can. As Sir Pagaloth has joined you, Lythian Lindar, as will I. I am yours to deploy as you see fit." Some life returned to his eyes, even as he said it, as though a weight was lifted from his shoulders. As though he was giving himself a reason to live.

Lythian's hand was still on the man's narrow shoulder. He squeezed it and withdrew. "I gladly accept, Sa'har Nakaan. What do you propose?"

The man's gaze moved eastward once more. Beyond the river lay woods of beech and birch, ash and alder, hawthorn and horse chestnut, spread over a vast land bustling with hills and valleys, rivers and lakes, flowering fields and farmlands. "There are thousands of my people scattered across these lands. Men who ran in fear of Drulgar and want no part in Eldur's war. I will help to gather them, unite them, bring us all together in common cause. If left to wander they will be reduced to their basest instincts in order to survive. They will steal, plunder, kill, and bring further chaos to these lands. That cannot be allowed."

Lythian could not agree more. "A shepherd to a scattered flock. I feel the role would suit you well. People know you, and trust you, Sa'har. Who better to be a beacon of hope for these lost men?"

Across the pen, the voice of Sir Hadros was bellowing out as he mustered the prisoners to their work. Some were being directed at wagons, to go out and collect their dead. Others were being handed spades and shovels to help with the expansion of the pen, filling the ditch and digging a new one. The hedge knight had some of the Vandarians helping as well, working alongside the southerners.

"A sign of things to come, I hope," Lythian said, observing. "All of us working together."

"We will need to," agreed Sa'har. "Though it will not be easy to convince everyone. Some animosities are delved too deep, Lythian. Look at their eyes. Even now you can see the hate."

Lythian had seen that plenty. "Hate is sometimes just a symptom of fear, Sa'har. Fear of an enemy you do not understand, whose ways are strange to you. But when these men stand shoulder to shoulder they will realise that is all they are. *Men*. Fighting for the same end."

"Then it would be wise for us to join in this endeavour, yes? To show a united front?"

"That is what I am thinking," Lythian agreed. "I will send you out with a strong cohort; some of these prisoners, and some of my own men. If there's anyone you know or trust here, by all means use them. And include some soldiers from the empire as well. We have a Lumaran Starrider here, I know, and a Piseki Sunrider. And some paladin knights from Aramatia. Gather a company to represent all nations, and I'll return later on to inspect them."

Sa'har took the order on without question. "I will see it done. But I wonder…would *you* come with us, Lythian?"

Much as he might like to, he sensed Amron would prefer he stay. "I will speak to the king, Sa'har." He checked the position of the sun. "I have a council meeting with him in a few moments."

"Then I will not keep you further. And it seems I have work to do."

Lythian nodded. "Until later, then." He gestured to Sir Pagaloth to accompany him, and the two of them stepped away. "Sir Hadros. On me," Lythian called, as they went.

The hedge knight turned, saw them coming, and bustled over to join them, breath puffing in the cold morning air. "Captain."

"I have a new duty for you."

"Oh? If it gets me closer to one of those cloaks…"

"It does. I want you to join Skymaster Nakaan in rounding up the deserters, from both sides, ours and theirs. I've asked him to assemble a suitable retinue to accompany him. You will lead the northern faction."

The man looked rather less than pleased with the task. "You want me to babysit a bunch of southerners?"

"They don't need babysitting, Sir Hadros. These will be experienced men."

"Aye, that's what concerns me. Experienced men are dangerous men."

"You're a Bladeborn knight. These are men without their mounts. A Skymaster without a dragon, Sunriders and Starriders without their wolves and cats. You'll have nothing to fear from them."

"Will they be armed?"

Lythian nodded.

"Then I'll have something to fear." Sir Hadros pointed at one of the dead dragons they'd walked past before. "Any man with a spear can kill a dragon. And any man with a length of steel can kill a Bladeborn knight. Not saying I don't trust them, my lord, but a couple of days ago we were all killing each other. Won't take much to spark violence between us."

"These are your lands, Sir Hadros. You're armoured in godsteel plate and mail, and hold a godsteel broadsword. You'll have soldiers of your own. If violence is sparked off, I should think you will come out the better. But it won't come to that. Not if we select the right men."

"And who'll be doing the choosing?"

"I will. Though if you are aware of any good honest men who hold no grudges, and are happy to assist, let me know. I will be back later. Get to it."

He turned and stepped away, Sir Pagaloth marching at his side, dressed in leathers and wool and a shirt of rusty ringmail. In such garb he looked almost northern, though the dusky skin and dark almond eyes were enough to out his heritage. "I think it's time that you were restored to your proper regalia," Lythian said to him. "Many dragonknights were slain during the battle, and we have plenty of armour to go around. And dragonsteel blades as well. I know you have missed yours, since those hunters took it from you."

"I gave the blade up willingly, Captain. For passage."

"No. They *took* it from you, Pagaloth. You must stop making excuses for all the wrongs that are done to you. You have paid your penance now." Lythian was weary of telling him that, but felt obliged to do so all the same. "Now, I want you to find armour that fits you, choose a blade to your liking, and return out here to help Sa'har in his task. When he leaves, I want you to go with him, to act as an intermediary. Is this a duty you are willing to perform for me?"

The man dipped his chin, still bearing marks and scars from when his beard had been so savagely cut at Runnyhall. "If it is your command, Captain."

"It is. And I know you have felt idle here, since we arrived. This will give you something to contribute." The dragonknight had not taken part in the battle, at his own request, preferring not to kill his own countrymen. Naturally, it poked at his pride to be standing on the sidelines, as men fought and died beyond the city walls.

They walked on for a few moments, passing the corpse of one of the dead dragons from earlier. Lythian paused to look at it, wondering about something that had long tickled at his mind. "Tell me, Pagaloth. Is it possible to bond a dragon, without the use of the Bondstone?"

The dragonknight shook his head. "Not a full soul-bonding. But there have been instances in the past of rogue dragonriders, those who did not pass the trials at the Nest, and instead journeyed to the Wings, to tame the wild dragons there. It is not the same strength of union… more similar to how a man bonds a horse. But in those terms, yes, it is possible." He looked over. "Why do you ask?"

"Just something Sir Hadros said earlier. Catch a few. Kill a few. I wonder…what if we did less of the killing, and more of the catching? If chained and caged, might that allow time for a man to tame the beast? To develop enough trust so he might ride it?"

"In theory," the dragonknight confirmed. "He would need to be Fireborn, however, and brave. Any man who tries must be willing to risk his life, Lythian."

Lythian nodded, pondering. It was a half-baked notion that would likely bear no fruit at all, but still…he was trying to think outside of the box. *If we could somehow command some dragonriders of our own…*

He continued walking, quickening his pace. The sun had risen more quickly than he'd realised and no doubt Amron was already awaiting them in his command pavilion, to resume the council meeting cut short the night before. There was much they still needed to discuss and decide. *And more now,* Lythian thought. He still needed to get Amron's official blessing for his plans.

He marched through the River Gate, to commune with his king.

6

Amilia

The cold was still in her bones, reaching in with freezing fingers to close tight about the marrow. The cold of the refuge. The cold of the mountains. The cold of the long dark journey through the tunnels.

And the cold in her heart as well.

A cloak of fine sable draped her shoulders, rich brown for Tukor, belted and tightened at the waist. Her hair was washed, skin scrubbed clean, the dirt dug out from her fingernails. She was polished, prettified, pampered, shimmering like a jewel. Amilia Lukar had hoped it might help, to restore her former beauty after long months on the road. It hadn't. Not a bit. She still felt filthy as a sty, dirty inside and out.

The wind ruffled through her long brown hair, stirring strands, as she looked out over the city. Beneath her it sprawled, tucked up in the embrace of the mountains, the White City of Ilithor in all its gleaming glory. She reached out to take up her cup of wine from the balustrade, a fine chalice of gold, inlaid with coloured gems. The wine was rich and strong and red, and she gulped it down in a single draught.

"More," she said.

Annabette scurried forward to obey.

She drank again, casting her eyes down the levels of the city. To the bridges and walkways and steep stone stairs of the Marble Steps. To the Sentinels below, bustling with barracks and training yards. To Many Markets, a further level down, where traders teemed, and peddlers hawked their wares. Last of all was White Shadow, largest of the levels, spreading and sprawling toward the boundary walls far below. From up here it was hardly more than a blur, though Amilia could see well enough the blackened square, the scorched streets, the burned-out husks of homes and hovels, taverns and pillow houses, that had been destroyed during the rioting months before.

The day my grandfather disappeared, she thought. *I hope the bastard never returns.*

A misty wind blew past her, sweeping from over the peaks of the mountains to the north, obscuring her view. She waited, sipping her wine. When the clouds had passed, she set her gaze beyond the outer walls of the city, to the great open valley beyond, with its roads and rivers and woods, opening, widening into the vastness of Southern Tukor.

My home, she thought, trying to raise a smile. For months she had longed to return, to stand on this very balcony, drink in the view and the air and the wine. But now that she was here, she felt almost nothing at all. Empty, like one of those blackened husks. *I am dead inside,* she thought. *Hadrin…my grandfather…the mages…they have killed me.*

She drank her wine down, down and down until she tasted the bitter sediment at the bottom. "More," she said, and her cup was refilled. "Just leave the jug, Annabette. And send them in. I'm ready."

The girl curtseyed, withdrew, and Amilia heard the shuffle of feet behind her. Her eyes stayed steadfast on the sweeping vista as the door to her chamber groaned open, and in walked the old men of the city, the dregs of what remained to rule. Perhaps that wasn't fair of Morwood, but Gershan, certainly, and Benton as well were a pair of old fossils who she would soon dismiss from her service.

It was Emmit Gershan, the Master of the Moorlands, who spoke first. "Your Highness," he said, in that ugly, snivelling voice of his. "So the reports are true. You're back from Rasalan. What a pleasure. A pleasure indeed."

She could almost see him rubbing his bony old hands together and licking his lips as he stared at her arse, the loathsome lecherous creature. She hated him, always had. *How my family have tolerated him for so long is baffling.* He had sat on her grandfather's council, and that of her brother too. *He won't sit on mine. I'll make sure of that.*

"We feared you were dead, Your…Your Majesty," said the old scholar and crowmaster, Archibald Benton. "Thalan. We heard of… of…of what happened. The…the dragons and…and…and…"

She closed her eyes, already irritated. That stuttering voice. The unpleasant phlegmy sound that took root at the back of his throat. *I'll dismiss him just for that. Someone save me from these fools.*

A stronger voice spoke. "My lady." It was Trillion Morwood, Lord Commander of the Watch, cutting off Archibald Benton and his dithering as a thousand others had before. "There are no reports of you arriving through the city gates. Not a single word of you passing any of the lower levels. How is it that you came to be here?"

"Magic," she said, staring out.

The man hardly heard her. "My lady?"

"Magic," she repeated, though no louder than the first time. She did not care if they heard or not, nor did she care to explain. At last she turned to face them, looking upon the three old men. Morwood, sturdy and thick-necked with a block of jaw so wide it outmatched the rest of his head. Heavy jowls drooped off his cheeks and his wispy yellow hair, with strands of grey, had gone wispier still since the last time she'd seen him. He styled it slick across a balding scalp. The man had seen about fifty winters.

The other two were much older. Rheumy-eyed, phlegmy-throated Archibald Benton, with that wine-coloured birthmark on his forehead, shaped like the foot of the crow. He had a crooked back and long white beard that had once been much more impressive. It looked rather pathetic now, as did he.

Emmit Gershan was an insult to her eyes. Part vulture, part rat, with a mean little mouth made for scowling and a nose like the prow of a longship, long and hooked. There was some spider about him too, in those juts of shoulder-bones and scrawny limbs and horrid little beady eyes. *I hate you*, she thought. Then she looked away from him and would not look back.

"I had hoped my brother would be here, Lord Morwood," she said, addressing the only one of them she had the slightest respect for. It was perhaps the last little shred of joy she had clung to, that Raynald would be here, to watch the world end with her. *But no, I don't even get that.* "Annabette told me that he's gone to war."

Morwood nodded solemnly. "Your brother is gallant, my lady. When he learned that Vandar was under threat, he mustered an army to aid them. He left several weeks ago."

"Where, exactly?"

"The Riverlands. His intention was to make for Rustbridge, to help defend the crossing. The Agarathi have been decimating the Marsh-lands and there is a fear they will not stop there. Young Raynald took it upon himself to strengthen their defence, and rush to the aid of our allies. The whole city is very proud of him."

The city is full of fools. He shouldn't have gone. No doubt he had done it because of Robbert. Amilia knew her brothers well, and with Robb at war in the south, there was no way Ray was going to sit here idle if he could march out and win his own glory.

Archibald Benton fumbled into the pockets of his oversized robes. A pair of trembling, liver-spotted hands emerged with a bundle of scrolls, tied in string. "My queen. These…these are the latest corre-spondences. A couple from your brother. Few letters come these days, but…but…"

"I'm not a queen," she cut in. She gestured for him to put the scrolls on a table. "The Rasalanians did not want me, and I did not want them. My marriage to Hadrin was a farce." *An abusive, traumatising nightmare.* She steeled her eyes, drew a breath. "What is the latest news of my grandfather? Has he been found?"

"Not officially, my lady," said Trillion Morwood, "but there are rumours. An innkeep and his wife claim that the king visited their riverside tavern some weeks ago, in the woodlands north of Tukor's Pass. They claim he has become a dragonslayer."

"He already was," Amilia said. "He killed a dragon in his youth."

"More since," rattled Gershan. "A few have been found butchered for parts. On a meadow…that was a bloody old mess, we hear. In a wood as well, near this inn. The king's been getting his hands dirty, Princess. But better the blood of dragons than children, I suppose." A smirk creased his crusty lips. She wanted to slap it off him. "You heard about that, I trust? All that slaughtering down in Galin's Post?"

"I heard."

"A dark day," Morwood intoned, jowls wobbling as he shook his heavy head. "I took a wound to the arm myself, though have healed now, thank Tukor. Many others were not so fortunate. But it's believed that your grandfather has turned to a brighter path, my lady." He smiled pleasantly. "We must hope."

She gave that a snort, turned, picked up her cup of wine, and drank. "Hope," she muttered. "I hope he's dead." She turned back to them. "Tell me true, Lord Morwood. What happened that day in the throne room? When my father died. Were you there?"

"No, my lady."

"I was told my father tried to steal the crown." Her eyes surveyed the men before her. Not for one moment had she believed that. "My grandfather is to blame, isn't he? He gave the order to have my father killed."

Lord Morwood raised a hand and coughed into his fist. Archibald Benton turned his eyes away. Gershan sneered.

"Speak," Amilia said.

The vulture did. "You want to know whose fault it was?"

She looked at him, lip pulled back.

"Your auntie's," Gershan spat. "That bastard bitch. She was always whispering away at him, pouring poison in his ear. There's plenty been said about her, my lady. Ugly stuff. None of it good. You sure you want to know?"

Her eyes were bright with disdain. "No," she said at once. *She is down in the crypts as we speak*, she thought. *Whatever she might have done in the past, she gave her life for mine. We're even. And she was just a tool, like me, and her son.*

"Oh?" Gershan chuckled. "Not even a little bit. She's dead now, so what's the bother?"

Amilia frowned. There was no way they could know that. Jonik had carried his dead mother through the tunnels and caverns himself, along that twisting, daunting route, through narrow shafts and past plunging chasms, and laid her to rest in the crypts. *Were we seen?* She couldn't think how. That side of the palace had been completely deserted when they arrived, and the rest of it was hardly much busier. *And she was wrapped up like a mummy anyway. There's no way they could have known…*

Lord Morwood gave a firm shake of the head, and directed a hard stare at Gershan. "We don't know that for certain, my lady," he said, turning to face her "Your auntie is missing, that's all. She may have returned to the Blakewood lands, or…"

"Or what?" cackled Gershan. "Gone off to fight the war? She didn't go missing, Morwood, she *vanished*." He clipped his bony fingers. "Just like that."

She went through the portal, Amilia thought, realisation dawning. *And they know nothing about it.*

Gershan put those spider-eyes on her, beady and black. "First your grandfather disappears, then your auntie, now you reappear out of thin air, all the way from Thalan." He snorted. "*Magic*, you said just now. Since when did you Lukars become mages?"

"*Mages*?" she hissed, sudden fury surging inside her. Her eyes blazed, bright and green. "You call *me* a mage?"

The old man shrugged. He looked much like a mage himself, all twisted and rotted like Fhanrir, cruel-eyed and ancient. "Well, something's not right, that's clear. You're being awful evasive, Princess."

"Get out," she said to him. "I have no need of you."

He didn't move.

"I said get out!"

He frowned at her, confused, a sneer plastered on his face. "Why? Spitting too close to the mark, am I? You got some secret to tell?"

"Just go. *Now*. Get rid of him, Lord Morwood. I cannot stand his face."

"My lady…"

"I said get rid of him!" She threw her golden chalice, hard, hitting the creature square in the jaw. There was a sickening smack as his chin split open, teeth shattering, blood bursting from the ruin of his face. The Master of the Moorlands stumbled back in shock, reeling, reaching out to steady himself, and fell heavily to the floor. Where he hit there was no rug or rushes. His head whipped back, cracking against stone. Then stillness, silence. Just the pant from Amilia's chest. "Drag him out," she commanded, breathing heavily. "Put him on a wagon and send him back to the Moorlands. I never want to see him again."

Lord Morwood stepped over, concerned, and knelt down. Blood was starting to ooze from where Gershan's head had struck the stone, horribly red on white. Morwood pressed his fingers to the vulture's neck, held them there a moment, turned his head so his ear was up against Gerhan's nose and mouth, listening.

Amilia's heart was slowly rising up her throat. "Is he breathing?"

"Faintly. He needs urgent medical attention." Morwood stood and marched to the door, pushed it open and called in the guards. They sped inside at once, armour clanking, to lift the old lord and carry him away. "Careful. Careful," Morwood told them. "Archibald. Go with them." He ushered them all out of the door, steering them away until the two of them were alone. Amilia was staring at the patch of red blood. The fragments of teeth, yellow and brown, scattered upon the stone. One of the jewels had been knocked loose of the chalice. An emerald. *Like my eyes.*

Lord Morwood went to pick the chalice up from the floor, and the emerald as well, placing them aside on a table. "He may die, my lady," he said, after a long moment. "I know you did not want to kill him, but…"

"Who says I didn't? He deserves to die."

"My lady, you don't mean that."

"He's a creature. An ugly lecherous snake, like his sigil. Everything he says is poison."

"Words, my lady. Elsewise he is harmless. If he dies…"

"I hope he does. He calls me a mage? *Me?*" The bile was creeping up her throat. She thought of the old man Talbert, who was not really a man at all, but a mage by name of Meknyr, a Shadowcloak who had taken on the guise of Sir Munroe Moore, who had tricked her and deceived her and led her into the mountains. "I *hate* mages," she raged. "I hate them. Every one!"

She turned to snatch the jug of wine from the top of the balcony. A gulp, another, and the wine was pouring down her neck, red and warm, soaking into her shirt.

Lord Morwood came up behind her. A big hand gripped her wrist. "My lady…stop…"

She struggled, half-drunk from the wine, and tore away from him. "Get your hands off me. *Don't* touch me!"

He backed away. "Princess, I'm only trying to…"

She pushed past him, away from the balcony, needing to give herself space. Echoes of memories haunted her mind. Her wrists bound to bedposts. The guards, watching on. Her husband, drunk on power, mad, crawling up between her legs… 'I want a son, Amilia, you'll give me a son…'

I killed your sons, she thought, snarling. *I slew your seed a thousand times, and I'm glad they tore your child from my womb.*

She hadn't been awake when it happened. Not since that moment at the side of the road, when Sir Munroe Moore's armour had rippled to mist and the Shadowcloak Meknyr had shown his true face. 'Beware the silver man', the dwarf Black-Eye had warned her on the boat. 'One day, he's going to change'. Those words had haunted her ever since he'd said them, yet not until that moment had she known what he meant.

After that, it was fragments only. Faint shapes and blurred recollections. Meknyr had put her into a deep sleep, though it only ever lasted so long, and when she began to come around she would blink and see snippets of the world. A cold pine forest, the trees bearded in frost. Ravens in the branches, watching. A glimpse of a high valley and mountain pass, eagles circling. Snow, falling down in sheets, heavy as godsteel plate. She had seen the black towers, high and blunt and dreaded, enshrouded in white mist. Seen the soaring peaks and prominences, their slopes draped in blankets of snow. But of her arrival at the fortress, nothing. Nor the procession into the refuge, and the cold stone slab, and the opening of her legs, the extraction…

She turned her head, unable to think about it any longer. *Tell me it was necessary all you like, Jonik, tell me it was fate…I will hate those mages forever for what they did to me.*

I never had a choice.

Lord Morwood was watching her worriedly, a deep frown etched into the flesh of his forehead. "My lady," he began once more.

She cut him off. "My auntie is dead," she said.

His frown deepened, confusion thickening.

"She is down in the crypts right now, wrapped in linen. The putrefaction has begun to set in, my lord. I suggest you summon the embalmers."

The poor man was utterly befuddled. "The crypts? How is it that she's…"

"Later. I will explain it all to you later. Where my auntie went, how I came to be here, all of it. But first, I did not come alone. I have several companions who will be returning to me soon, and they will need to be fully apprised of all of the latest tidings from beyond our borders. They have a quest of some importance to attend. Discretion is important to these men."

Lord Morwood seemed to understand, bless the man. "They intend to pass through the city unseen?"

"They do. Though in what direction, I don't yet know." Jonik's task was to gather the blades, she knew, a thankless and fruitless task that would probably just get him killed. *My grandfather attempted the same for decades*, she thought. *Look where that got him.* Whether Jonik would want to travel down through the city levels and into the south of Tukor, or through the mountain passes at the rear of the palace - a route that would take him down into Vandar via the southern reaches of the Mistwood - Amilia didn't know. That would depend upon what they learned of the locations of the remaining four blades.

Morwood rubbed at his jowls with a meaty hand. "Might I ask who these companions of yours are?"

Amilia saw no reason to deceive the man. "One you may know, from years ago. Sir Gerrin, a former Emerald Guard. He served under my grandfather."

"Gerrin." Morwood considered it, nodding. "Yes, I know of him. He was one of the king's sworn swords, for a time. And the others?"

"A sellsword named Harden," Amilia said. "He's Vandarian, from the Ironmoors." *And looks it*, she thought. The men of the Ironmoors were known to be grim and spare. "And my cousin," the princess finished.

"Your cousin?" Morwood asked. His face contorted in thought, trying to think of who that could be. Amilia didn't have many cousins. "One from your mother's side? A Kastor?"

"No, my father's," she said. "You'll know him as the Ghost of the Shadowfort, Trillion, though his real name is Jonik. He is Auntie Cecilia's son."

The man's befuddlement could not have been more acute. "Her...her *son*? I…I had no idea that she…" He wiped at his forehead, shaking his head. "Her *son*?" he said again, as though repeating it would somehow make it easier to believe. "The Shadowknight who crippled Amron Daecar? Who killed Sir Aleron in the Song of the…" He trailed off, staring at her. "Your betrothed. Your own cousin… he…*he* killed him?"

She nodded. "He did. Though under duress, my lord. I do not hold him to account for that." She paused, wondering if she should tell him, then decided there was no harm. *All the world will know soon enough.* "It was not only my betrothed Jonik killed," she said. "He also killed his own brother. Jonik is the son of Amron Daecar."

Lord Trillion Morwood, stout old Commander of the Watch, all but fell backward onto the floor. "My gods, is that…is that quite true, Amilia? You are not having a twisted jape with me?"

"No jape, my lord. It is much to get one's head around, I know. Believe me. I have only recently learned of all this as well."

"Well goodness. Goodness me." Lord Morwood staggered to the drink's table, pouring himself a cup of wine, drinking it down at once. Then he breathed out, staring down at the lacquered wood, frowning, shaking his head. Amilia gave him a moment. "And all this…" He looked over at her, horrified. "All this by the order of your grandfather?"

She nodded. "Auntie Cecilia deceived Lord Daecar into stealing his seed, back during the last war. I am told he was not aware of it. Some drug, that addled his mind into thinking it all some half-remembered dream. She acted by my grandfather's order, so she might birth a child of powerful blood, to be used as a weapon. In all this, Jonik is innocent, no more than a tool, as I have been. So you wonder why I say I hope my grandfather is dead? Well, wonder no more, Trillion. Everything he touches turns to ruin."

She filled her lungs, right up to the top, and breathed out long and slow. Somehow it felt good to get that off her chest, to share with this stout old lord the true depth of her grandfather's treachery. His devious machinations had been going on for decades. *Even King Horris Reynar's death was by his hand*, Amilia thought. The Vandarian king had died during a visit to Agarath, of heart failure the Agarathi claimed, though Janilah Lukar said otherwise. He proclaimed to all the north that King Horris had been slain by order of Tellion, the Agarathi king, just as his own brother Prince Jaylor had been murdered on Agarathi lands decades before. *He used it as a pretext to go to war*, Amilia knew. But

96

really, it was his own man, his own *tool*, who poisoned King Horris in his sleep.

It was Jonik who told her all that, having heard it first from the exiled lord, Emeric Manfrey. "He told me of his cousin," Jonik had explained to her. "A man called Sir Gerlan Stonewood. He was Vandarian, Emeric said, the son of Lord Stonewood and his own auntie, Lady Lucilla Manfrey. Sir Gerald joined the Greycloaks and was there, as part of King Horris's protective guard, when his delegation went to Eldurath. Apparently Sir Gerlan got drunk one night when he got back and confessed to Emeric that King Horris had been poisoned by his own men. He died shortly after. Hanged himself in a barn. Though not according to Emeric."

"He was murdered," Amilia said.

Jonik gave a nod. "Same as many others back then, to hide the truth. But our grandfather got what he wanted all the same. He got his war. Just the same as this one."

She turned back to Lord Morwood, putting all that from her mind. The man was still deep in thought himself, struggling to reconcile what he'd heard, but Amilia needed his attention. She had told Jonik she would help in his quest, folly that it all was, and she would. *I'll do my bit and be done with it. Then find a handsome man, to wash the taste of Hadrin away…*

"My cousin will be returning here soon," she said, drawing Morwood's kind eyes toward her. "Along with his two companions. They will have questions for you, my lord, about the state of affairs beyond our walls and borders. Are you willing to share counsel with these men?"

"If you ask it of me, it will be done, my lady."

She touched his arm. "I knew I could count on you."

That drew a smile from the jowly Watch Commander. She had known him all her life and he had a daughter of a similar age to her. In her youth they had played together. That had always made Morwood proud.

"I would like you to take them to my grandfather's council chambers when they arrive." There were maps there, she knew, and other materials that would be of use. "I will accompany you, my lord, but will not stay long. I feel I need some time alone."

His face went very serious. "I quite understand, my lady."

The wait was not so long. No more than ten minutes later, the door knocked with a forceful *tap tap tap*. Annabette, who was Amilia's most faithful handmaiden, rushed to open it, already apprised of their coming.

Lord Morwood intercepted her, however. "Let me." He ushered the girl aside, straightened out his commander's cloak, stood as tall as his height would allow, and opened out his shoulders. Then he reached out and drew open the door. "Welcome," he said, upon seeing the three men outside, in his most resounding voice. "My name is Lord

Trillion Morwood, Lord Commander of the City Watch. Please, come in."

The men filed past, Jonik in the lead, wearing that new, colour-changing armour of his under his cloak. The plate seemed to brighten a touch as he entered, though that might merely have been the firelight in the room. There was a hearth, burning bright, and several handsome sconces too with torches in their grasp. Jonik looked at Morwood, wordless, then came Harden and finally Gerrin, who stopped. "Trillion, good to see you again."

"Sir Gerrin," Morwood said.

There was a pause. "You look a tad pale," Gerrin noted. He looked over at Amilia. "I take it you've been talking about us."

"You. And a great deal more." Morwood glanced at Jonik, assessing, though the young man had already stepped out toward the balcony, to take in the ranging view.

He returned a moment later, and looked at Amilia. "He wasn't there," he said to her. "No sign of him or the blade." The disappointment was thick in his voice. "But the dragon we did find. It did not die well."

Morwood was clearly not understanding. He moved over from the door. "What dragon are you speaking of?" he demanded.

"Some purply blue beasty," said Harden, pouring himself a cup of wine. "Big one too. Found it sprawled up those steep stone stairs of yours, all cut to bits. Almost made me feel sorry for it."

"Stone stairs? What stone stairs?"

"The ones that lead up to Ilith's ancient forge," said Gerrin. "We just went up there to check if the king was dead. We are interested in retrieving the Mistblade from him, Trillion. I'm sure the princess told you?"

"No. She hasn't." Morwood looked at her.

"We didn't get that far," she said, though now that the cat was out of the bag, she might as well get into it. "They're looking for the blades, Trillion. And before you ask, no, this is not the same as my grandfather. Their cause is righteous." *Folly*, she thought, *but righteous.* "But I'll let Jonik explain the rest." She looked to the door. "And not here."

Morwood took her meaning. "The princess asked that I escort you to more appropriate chambers, for this…discussion. Please, follow me."

"What's wrong with here?" Harden asked, sipping his wine. He looked around. "Perfectly nice."

"These are the princess's private quarters," Lord Morwood told him. "A formal council chamber would be better for our needs." He marched back to the door, holding it open for them. "Please, come this way."

Harden shrugged and moved over, keeping his goblet to hand, and stepped outside with Gerrin. Jonik followed, glancing at the blood-stains on the floor, the chips of teeth. "What happened there?"

"I threw a chalice at Lord Gershan."

He raised his eyes, but said nothing. They stepped through the door, Morwood leading them on, passing through the grand palace corridors of its high, upper levels. Sir Gerrin engaged the Watch Commander in casual conversation as they went, though Amilia sensed he was trying to get a better read on him, making utterly sure he could be trusted with what they were to say.

"He's protective of you," the princess noted, walking behind with her cousin. "You're lucky to have him, Jonik. Harden too."

"I know."

They walked on a few more paces. "And your other friends? Lord Manfrey. Those sailors you travelled with? Are you to try to find them?"

"I must find the blades. I cannot give priority to personal feelings." He took another pace, another. "And nor should you."

"Meaning?"

"Meaning you can help," he said, turning his eyes forward at Morwood. "This man of yours, he seems trustworthy. Have you told him of the portal? The refuge?"

"Not yet."

"But you will?" His eyes bored into her. "He must be wondering how we all got here. You can't hide that from him forever, and Ilith does not want you to. He wants to help his people, Amilia, *all* people. You can be a part of that."

Or I can ignore it all and sit on my balcony and drink myself to oblivion, watching while the world comes crashing down around me. That had been her plan. To return here and watch the world end with her brother, but Ray was gone and Robb too, and her father was dead and mother a shrew, and what else did she have? *Nothing*, she thought. *I have nothing, and I am nothing.*

"Amilia…"

"I'll tell him," she said, sharply. "I'll tell him of this portal and refuge and Ilith and all of it. He's the Commander of the Watch and does more to run this city than anyone. He's much better placed than me to lead the people to safety."

"No. He's a lord, you're a princess. And you need to be doing more."

Need? She turned, marching away from him, unable to bear his sanctimonious preaching any longer. *Maybe I should have him hanged, after all*, she thought. *Perhaps that would shut him up.*

She turned a corner, quickening her pace, only glancing around when she'd stretched away and saw that no one was following. Jonik did not seem like a man who had the capacity for that. *That one has no idea how to handle women. A soft touch is not his strength.*

She made her way back to her chambers, walking alone and undisturbed. When she stepped inside she found Annabette on her knees, scrubbing at the blood and picking out bits of teeth from the rushes. The girl looked up, apple-faced and red from the effort, then surged to her feet. "My lady, do you need anything?"

"Wine."

Amilia found a comfortable armchair and sank into the upholstery, kicking off her slippered shoes and shaking out her hair. The hearth-fire crackled beside her, puffing up skinny little fingers of smoke. Annabette stepped over to hand her a fresh chalice, then stoked at the coals, stirring ash, and threw on another small log. She made to return to her scrubbing, but Amilia told her to sit. The girl did so, awkwardly, dropping into an armchair opposite her.

"How is your brother?" Amilia asked her.

Annabette swallowed, legs crossed demurely. "My brother, my lady?"

"Yes, your brother. The other little human that your mother pushed out from between her legs. Does he still work in the royal stables?"

She shook her head timidly. "No, my lady. He was mustered, for your brother's army. He marched with him to the south."

"A shame." Annabette was a pretty little thing, and her brother was similarly pleasing on the eye. A little feminine for her usual tastes, but perfectly comely all the same. She sat back, sipping her wine, thinking. "There's a bard," she said. "Sweetest voice I ever heard. Likes to croon for the ladies of the court. Gifford Gold-Tongue they call him. Have you heard of him, Anna?"

The girl nodded. "I remember him, my lady. He serenaded you privately, once before."

He did more than serenade me. "Does he still warble down in White Shadow?"

"I would have to ask, my lady. Most bards like to travel around."

Yes, I'm quite aware. "Do ask, then. I feel like being *serenaded* tonight."

Annabette stared at her with big round eyes. "Right…right now? Should I go myself, my lady?"

"That would be best, Anna."

The girl stood at once, moving over to the wall to slip on her hooded cloak. She was not unfamiliar with carrying out these private dispatches. "I'll be as quick as I can, my lady," she said, opening the door. "And I'll make sure that a guard is set at the door. Are you…sure you'll be OK?"

This cloying over-attention was starting to annoy her. "I'll be fine. Go."

Annabette slipped away.

Silence followed her departure, broken only by the crackle of the flame, the whispering of the winds outside. Calm though it was, tranquil even, Amilia Lukar stewed in her absence, reflecting on Jonik's words, wondering, perhaps even knowing, that he was right and hating that it was so.

You haven't seen his eyes, cousin, she thought. *Those red, pupil-less eyes. You haven't felt his power.* She had known, ever since Thalan fell, that the whole of the world would follow. So why bother hiding in that lifeless mountain refuge? *The devil will only find it eventually.*

Her wine cup was soon empty, so she stood and went to refill it, watering it down just a little so she didn't get too drunk. If the sweet-singing bard was indeed to be found, she wanted to make use of his finest asset, and sweet as his singing voice was, she had a better use for that gilded tongue of his. For that she wanted her wits about her.

So she drank with more reserve, adding ample measures of water, snacking on sweetbreads and cheese in anticipation of a night of pleasure. If Gold-Tongue was not here she would have to find someone else. A handsome soldier, perhaps, or serving man would serve. Someone beautiful, and strong. *Someone to make me scream.* She had an image of her doing so, fists squeezing the coverlets, body convulsing, just as the old snake Gershan gave out his final breath. It was a horrid thought, but she laughed out loud all the same. *That creature has had it coming for years.* It was a miracle to Amilia that someone hadn't slashed his throat open already.

She was still chuckling at that when she heard a knock at the door. Anna? Could she be back already? It seemed unlikely. *No, it'll be him, my brooding cousin. He's come to apologise, or bend my ear more like.* She was tempted to ignore it, pretend to be sleeping, but put that aside and stood.

Another knock, a little more insistent.

My killer cousin for a certainty. "Yes, yes, just a moment. Don't get your breeches in a twist."

She strode to the door, turned the handle, pulled it open and stared. It was not her cousin Jonik.

Sir Mallister Monsort smiled. "Were you expecting someone else, Your Highness?"

"I…yes, I…someone else, yes." She was momentarily lost for words, lost in those beguiling blue eyes of his, pretty as sapphires. "I thought…I thought you'd have marched to war with my brother, Mallister. He left you behind?"

"To protect your mother, yes. And now you, I suppose." His smile was the work of a master craftsman, his cheekbones high and flat. Golden hair fell in waves from his head. "How is it that you're here, my lady? When I heard…I couldn't quite believe it. I feared you had perished in Thalan."

Feared. "You feared for me, Sir Mallister?"

"Of course, yes. I think about you…all the time." A sudden blush rose up his neck and he turned his eyes away. It only made him all the more charming.

She let him linger in that state for a moment. There was hotness in her as well, spreading. *Yes,* she thought. *Yes, he will do.* She had always known Sir Mallister Monsort was an exceptionally handsome man, very much her type, and very much taken by her too. But with his sister Melany being her lady-in-waiting, she had decided it best not to muddy those waters. Mel was protective of her brother, and her brother was protective of her, but Mel was gone now, and those waters were muddy enough. *Let's swim in them together.*

"Will you come inside, Mallister?"

He swallowed. "I was told….Annabette, she caught me as she left for the city and said you were in need of protecting. I was raised to your grandfather's Six, my lady. Did you know?"

I did not know. I do not care. You can protect me from my bed. She said all of that with her eyes, as she stepped backward into her chamber, undressing him with her gaze. He followed like a moth to a flame, unable to resist her light. She looked past him, down the corridor, wondering if Anna would come back with the bard. *If she does, he can sing for us. That's all I'll need of him now.*

"Bolt the door, Mallister," she said, undressing.

7

Elyon

His grandfather stepped up onto the battlements, bedecked in pristine godsteel armour that still fit him after all this time. On his back flowed a cloak in stripes of pink and pale blue, decorated with a field of flowers in golden thread, the modest sigil of House Amadar. The soldiers deferred to their lord's coming, bowing and lowering their eyes. Elyon stood firm, awaiting him. "Grandfather," he said, inclining his head. "I'm glad to see your city is still standing."

"We have been lucky here." Lord Brydon Amadar replied. His voice was strong, detached.

He waved a hand for the nearby soldiers to give them space. At once every archer and crossbowmen withdrew at least a dozen steps, moving left and right along the battlements. They teemed in great numbers, hundreds of them lined up along the wall walks and up against the crenels, looking out over the lands below, constantly surveying the skies. Their cloaks were clean, their armour unblemished; Ilivar had not yet come under attack.

That hope had bloomed in Elyon Daecar as soon as he sighted the city from afar. There were no plumes of smoke, scratching at the sky, no tumbled towers, no blackened walls. The trail of blight he'd followed from Varinar had suggested that as well. Though it had grown harder to detect the further from the city he flew, it had become clear enough that the titan's path had taken him more south than east, and not in this direction. Elyon would return to that trail soon enough. For now, he had other matters to see to.

His grandfather was surveying his garb. "Would you like to bathe, Elyon?" he asked. "I could have your armour cleaned. And one of Rikkard's old cloaks brought out for you as well." He raised a hand to hail a man.

Elyon shook his head. "I have no time to wait for a polish. Or to wash, for that matter." He wondered if the cloak his grandfather referred to was a Varin cloak, or one of House Amadar. *Oh, how he'd love to dress me up in his own colours.* Either way, the answer was no. "I came to check on the city," he said. "And to ask of my sister and auntie." He looked into the man's hard hazel-green eyes. "Are they here?"

The Lord of Ilivar did not delay in answering. It was not the answer Elyon wanted. "No, they are not. I was hoping you might know."

Elyon frowned. "Why would *I* know? Perhaps you are not aware, my lord, but I have been rather busy of late." He'd not seen his grandfather since the day of Aleron's funeral, a lifetime ago, or so it felt. *No hug,* he thought. *Not even a 'how are you?' He says I need to bathe, and yet makes no mention of the fighting I must have seen to look this way.* Perhaps if they had met in private, the Lord of Ilivar would show more tenderness to his grandson, but not here upon the walls, before the eyes of his men.

"I have heard of your exploits, yes," Brydon Amadar said, stiffly. "This is the Windy City, founded by Iliva, who first bore the blade that now rests at your hip. We are all proud of you here."

Are you? Elyon doubted it. It would take more than killing a few dragons to make the intractable Lord of Ilivar proud. "I heard about your quarrel with Amara, Grandfather. You wanted me to give the Windblade back, I'm told. Now you say you're proud of what I've done with it. Forgive me if I don't believe you."

Lord Brydon's jaw stiffened. It was a chiselled jaw, dressed in a trim grey beard, sharply cut. His build was similarly lean, yet strong. He had the bearing of a man much younger than his sixty seven years. "You're angry with me, Elyon. That is plain."

"I'm tired. Perhaps that's plain as well. And keen to hear that my sister is safe. Now you tell me she isn't here. Where is she?"

"I don't know. Her current whereabouts are not known to me."

Elyon breathed out. "Not known to you?" he repeated, struggling to contain his frustration. "How can that be? She was in your care."

"*Was*, yes. Until she ran away, with the help of that boorish knight of hers, Sir Daryl Blunt. The gods know I attempted to find her, Elyon, but much as it pains me to say it, I failed. I had assumed she had made it back to Varinar. That is why I wondered if you might know. You came from there, I am told. Just now. You flew from the city."

"I flew from the ruin," Elyon said. "Don't tell me you don't know. You must have had word by now."

"A rider came yesterday, yes, to report the tragedy. But we knew long before that. We saw the smoke."

"The smoke? You saw it from *here*?" Elyon hadn't imagined that was possible. Ilivar was a hundred miles from Varinar. *For them to have seen the smoke from so far…*

"Yes, we saw it. I understood at once that the entire city must be burning for the plumes to be visible from here."

"Understood and did nothing," Elyon said sharply. "Why have you not sent soldiers? I saw no columns on the road, no riders in pink and blue. Varinar is in chaos. They need help. Now."

The Lord of Ilivar set his jaw. "Elyon," he said, in a hard, tense voice. "You are exhausted. No doubt you have flown a lot, and seen a lot, but…"

"I've seen more than you would believe. I've looked the Fire Father in the eye. I've ridden the back of Drulgar the Dread. Do not speak down to me. Why have you not sent soldiers to aid in the capital's relief?"

Lord Brydon's eyes were sharp enough to cut steel. He gave no reaction to what his grandson had said. Facing the Fire Father. Confronting the Dread. These were tales of a time gone by, the stuff of myth and legend, yet the old man cared more for his own authority and pride than acknowledging what his grandson had been through. "Elyon, have a care over how you speak to me. You are my grandson, yes, but my leniency has limits. Remember who you're talking to."

"The man who lost my sister," Elyon said at once. "Who plotted to have my auntie thrown into a dungeon." He had hoped to hold his tongue on all this, but no, out it came. "Have you seen Amara since then? Have you seen what they did to her?"

"She lost a finger, I'm told. Godrik Taynar lost more."

"Deservedly," Elyon seethed. "It was justice that he died."

"Justice? A finger for a life. Is that your kind of justice, boy?"

"*Prince*," Elyon said, loudly. "I am your prince, my lord."

"No, you are not," his grandfather told him. "The line of succession…"

"My father was pronounced king several hours ago," Elyon called out, turning to the men listening about the walls. "He had shared the rule with Lord Dalton Taynar, but Dalton Taynar is dead. His nephew Rodmond is now lord of his house. I watched with my own two eyes as Rodmond knelt down before my father and paid him fealty with the rest of us. He is *king*, now, without question. Amron Daecar is king. Long live the king!"

A few voices echoed him, a smattering among the throng, but they were muted and subdued, unsure of themselves at first. So Elyon bellowed it out, even louder than before - "Long live the king! King Amron Daecar! Long live the king! Long live the king!" - as more and more men took up the chant with each repetition. Before long it was spreading along the walls and into the towers, a roaring chorus, ringing out through the streets.

The look of displeasure on Lord Brydon's face was plain. Elyon stepped closer to him. "You should heed your men, Grandfather," he said. "Do not try to stand in the way of this. You'll only find yourself alone."

The lord's expression did not change. Brydon Amadar had always ruled Ilivar as if it were an island in the ocean, his authority absolute. Being isolated and alone was his preference. "Will he return to Varinar?" was all he asked, stiffly. "Nothing is official until he is crowned. There must be a coronation."

"There will be. When time allows. Right now we have other priorities." The chanting was growing yet louder. Some men were drawing blades, thrusting them to the skies. It made Elyon smile. He had not expected to spread the inferno like this, though the reaction was welcome all the same. *Let it be heard all across Vandar, and the north,* he thought. *Amron Daecar is king. Let it give us hope.*

But he could not stay much longer to listen. Already his mind was moving to more pressing concerns. "You didn't tell me whether you'd seen her," he said to his grandfather. "Amara."

"No. I did not. Though I was told she came two weeks ago."

Elyon frowned at that. "You were away?"

"Searching for your sister, yes. Amara spoke with Sir Gorton at the gate. He divulged to her that Lillia had gone missing, and your auntie left. That's all I know."

"In which direction?"

"That's all I know. You will have to speak to Sir Gorton."

"And where is he?" It was like getting blood from a stone. "Might you point me in his direction, at least?"

"He commands the Storm Gate. You will find him there." Lord Brydon looked west, pondering. "How bad is Varinar?"

"Bad. Not the western side so much, but from the South Gate to the harbour, the city is ash and rubble. The Ten Hills suffered sorely. You should know, Grandfather. Keep Amadar is a ruin."

The man showed scant reaction to that. "I never liked it," he said. "Rikkard used to say he would go and live there when he became lord. To taunt me, perhaps, or tease me. I don't know." He paused for thought. "You know my feelings about Varinar, Elyon."

Too busy. Too many noises and smells and people. Ilivar was much quieter, much cleaner, a city in the image of its lord. *And brutally defended.* One only had to glance along the walls to see that, with the bulky ballistas and chunky catapults and tall trebuchets packed behind the parapets. A part of Elyon wished Drulgar *had* flown here. It might have been enough to finish him.

"I want you to send men," Elyon said. "Not as your prince, or as my father's proxy. Not even as your grandson, or Iliva's heir as champion of her blade. No, let me appeal to your good nature, Grandfather. Your capital needs you. And you have it in your power to help. Please, send it."

The old lord considered that. "I have a duty to my people here as well. I cannot leave Ilivar undefended."

"I'm not asking you to. I'm asking you to send a portion of your strength only, those who can be spared. A thousand men will help. Five thousand would be better. Do you want me to get down on my knees and beg?"

"That would be unbecoming of a knight and greathouse heir, more so a prince and champion. Spare your knees, Elyon. I will send what men I can."

"Thank you." It was something, at least. "Today."

Lord Amadar nodded, looked to his right, and a man marched over. "Sir Geoffrey. I want you to arrange relief efforts for Varinar. Food, bandages, medicine, supplies. Load the wagons at once and have them accompanied by a strong escort. And send a mounted host ahead with all haste. Have them liaise with…" He looked at Elyon. "Who is currently in charge?"

"Sir Hank Rothwell."

"Have them liaise with Sir Hank. Help him to restore order."

Sir Geoffrey Bannard was a man of stiff posture, tight movements, and military precision. Just the sort of captain Brydon Amadar liked to keep around. He gave a sharp nod. "Yes, my lord. Who is to lead the advance host?"

"You are. Choose a suitable man to lead the baggage train. Sir Michael Tunston is reliable."

"He would be my choice as well, my lord."

"I want you ready to leave by late afternoon." He turned. "Elyon, is the road unblocked?"

"Some of the lakeside towns were burned," Elyon told him. "Those closest to Varinar. There may be some debris on the road, but elsewise the route should be passable."

Lord Amadar looked back at Sir Giffard. "Clear whatever obstacles might impede the wagons. I want at least a dozen ballista carts to go as well. If any dragon should pass, they will offer some protection."

"Very good, my lord."

"Go, Sir Giffard."

Sir Giffard gave a stiff bow to both men, and marched away. Once before, Brydon Amadar had been a fierce warrior and decisive battle commander, winning victories by the edge of his blade and the tip of his pen both, without ever having to join the fighting. Elyon had only ever seen the old greatlord hiding behind his walls, but he'd heard the stories. He was getting a glimpse of the man he used to be right now.

"Perhaps you should go as well, Grandfather," he suggested, poking at those coals. "Varinar is desperate for leadership. Your presence would be a boon."

"I am needed here. Varinar is the seat of the king."

"That seat is gone. The palace is destroyed, and the Steel Throne buried beneath it." It occurred to him that the crown would be down there somewhere too, buried beneath all that rubble, with all its little misting points. *Well, we can forge a new one.* "Father may yet remain at

King's Point. There is a fear that the Agarathi will rally and return, and he is loath to leave the coast undefended."

"A fair concern. For all the damage that dragons can do, they cannot invade or conquer. That takes men. The coast must be defended at all costs. It is our wall, Elyon. If the enemy should breach it, they will swarm." He glared south, thinking. Something seemed to be coming alive in him, the shadow of his former self, when he cared for more than his precious silver city.

"You should join us," Elyon said, once more attempting to stir him into action. "Muster your army and march south. We could use you."

Lord Amadar shook his head, but it took him a moment. It was enough to show his doubt. "My army is not what you think. I have perhaps ten thousand trained soldiers left in the city. Some will go to Varinar. Thousands of others are dispersed among the forts to the south and east of here, preparing to defend us. And there's Rikkard. I gave him five thousand of my very best when he marched to Dragon's Bane. For all I know, they might all be dead. We have had no word."

"He was well when I last saw him."

"And when was that?" His eyes were eager, though he tried to hide it.

Elyon had to think. "A week, perhaps a little more. It's hard to keep count of the days right now. We were marching the Mudway toward Rustbridge. He will be there by now, unless…"

"Unless?" his grandfather prompted.

"It's possible they came under attack, before King's Point did, and Varinar. Drulgar came from the east. Bearing wounds. I don't yet know how they were inflicted."

"And you plan to find out?"

Even the notion of it was exhausting, but what could he do but nod? "I'm going to fly there now." He might have spoken of Drulgar's blood, and the trail he'd been following, and how he had a mind to fly to the ruin of Thalan too, so he might unearth someone who might be able to peek through the pupil of the Eye of Rasalan, and give them something, anything, to work with…some glimpse of what was to come. That had been the entire reason for his heist, and yet for now the Eye was sitting idle, kept in his father's care. *Perhaps I'll fly there after I find Rikkard? Rustbridge to Thalan…how far is that. Oh, only a thousand miles…*

He grimaced at the thought. And he'd have to make it back to King's Point too. And now this with Lillia going missing, and Amara only the gods knew where. If given a choice, he would put everything else aside and spend all his efforts in finding them. *A choice every other soldier is facing*, he thought. Artibus had said as much, and it was exactly what his father feared. Every man for himself. Protect you wife, your children, your family, forget the rest. *Just as the Fire God wants. A culture-less and kingdom-less world, without nations or borders or boundaries, the strong rising, the weak falling, every one of us fighting for scraps in the mud.* Elyon could not submit to that impulse. He had to do his duty, and close his heart to his sister's fate. *As Father is.*

The chant was dying down now, leaving behind a buzzing murmur as the men discussed what they'd heard, excited by the crowning of a new king. It felt like Elyon's cue to leave, though he would check in with Sir Gorton first, down at the Storm Gate. "Is there anything you would like me to tell Rikkard, Grandfather?" he asked. "It is possible you will not see each other again."

"If that is so, then I will see him at Varin's Table." As with Rikkard, Lord Brydon had been a Knight of Varin before succeeding his father as lord of House Amadar, decades ago. "We will share words then. But I hope that isn't the case."

Elyon smiled. "I'll just tell him you miss him, how about that?" He could see that he did, even if he wouldn't say it. "Be well, Grandfather. And tell my lady grandmother I love her. I will visit her in Keep Quiet next time, I promise."

The old man shook his head. "Don't make promises you can't keep, Elyon. Lucetia is not among your list of priorities."

Cold and clear as ever. "Tell her anyway. It may give her comfort, after Lillia…"

The day was yet young, still an hour or so before noon, and where the early morning had been bright and clear, now the skies had curdled with cloud. Elyon gave his grandfather a parting nod and rose up over the battlements, soaring the short distance to the Storm Gate, facing out toward the Heartlands in a southwesterly direction. He could smell the promise of rain in the air; further south the skies looked darker. In the same direction, and wending through the open prairies from the east, thin lines of carts and wagons were making for the city, with riders among them, and men afoot, trundling along dirt roads and farm tracks, seeking sanctuary behind Ilivar's high walls.

Some had arrived already, lined up outside the gate. Some hundreds, Elyon saw; farmers, herdsmen, labourers mostly, along with their wives and children, and the occasional chicken or dog or goat, barking and bleating.

He found a soldier at the gate, inspecting the incoming carts. The smallfolk were being permitted entry, though only after careful consideration. Elyon had heard that his grandfather had kept his gates shut these last months, turning most of the smallfolk away to seek sanctuary in Varinar instead. It appeared his policy had changed. *Probably about the same time he saw all that smoke in the sky*, Elyon thought. *Brydon Amadar has a heart after all.*

The soldier stepped up to him, waving the latest cart through. The line shifted forward. "You might want to speed this along," Elyon suggested. Everything seemed very organised, very thorough, very slow. Very Brydon. *All boxes must be ticked, gods forbid.* "More are coming from the Heartlands and the prairies. It would be wise to allow them through more quickly."

"Lord Amadar wants us to check every cart carefully, for weapons and stowaways. And spies, my lord."

Spies. Gods. This wasn't a fight Elyon wanted to have. "I understand Sir Gorton commands the gate." He looked around. "I don't see him." *And Sir Gorton's is not a face one would miss.*

"Yes, my lord. He is in the gatehouse."

"Summon him, please."

"At once, my lord. Anything for the Master of Winds." The soldier sketched a graceful bow and spun away.

I am well-liked here, Elyon Daecar reflected. His status as the Lord of Ilivar's grandson might grant him that. Being the man who mastered the Windblade, so very revered in this city, was a much greater honour, however.

Sir Gorton arrived a minute or so later. His surname was Gulberry, a comical name to go with his comical appearance. Bandy-legged, wide-bellied, with close-set eyes, a piggy little nose, and unfortunately large ears, the man cut an amusing figure. Elyon recalled that his father was Sir Lorton, one of his grandfather's favoured old knights, though long since spent of his use in battle. *And never so homely as his son. I dread to think what his lady wife must have looked like…*

The knight shuffled up to him, a confused look on his face. Or perhaps that was just his face. Elyon didn't know the man well enough to say. "Sir Elyon, what a pleasure." He had been taking an early lunch, to judge by the crumbs about his lips. He brushed them away. "Have you come to see your grandparents?"

"I have just seen them. My grandfather, anyway. Did you not hear the chanting, Sir Gorton?"

"The chanting? Oh yes, yes I did." He rubbed at his chin, a non-existent thing, hardly more than a fleshy little nub poking out from his jaw. The man was beardless, and cruelly so. *His face could really use one, to give it some shape.* "Oh, of course. Your father…he has been declared king. And that makes you a prince. Apologies for the oversight, Your Highness."

"Accepted. I'm here to ask of my auntie. I'm told she came here two weeks ago."

"She did, yes. Asking of your sister."

"Which way did she go when she left, Sir Gorton?"

He strained to think, as though working out some complex mystery. "Back along the road to Varinar, my lord," he said, after a time. "She and her host took the Lakeland Pass, though…now, you'll have to forgive for me this, but…well…"

"What is it? I have no time for stammering, sir."

"I had a man follow them, just to be sure," Gorton Gulberry confessed. "He reported that they stabled their horses at one of the riverside inns a few miles from here and took a boat out onto the lake.

I took that to mean they believed your sister had done the same. From the harbour here at Ilivar, that is. The night she ran away."

Curious that my grandfather did not elucidate that detail. Elyon had half a mind to return and confront him on it, though it was possible it had slipped his mind. *Or perhaps Awkward Gorton did not tell him?* "Was Lord Amadar aware of this?" he asked, wishing to clarify. He raised an eyebrow, expectant. "He never said."

"Well, I do not think he considered it important, my lord. Unless your lady aunt possesses some staggering power of clairvoyance, she was merely guessing as to where your sister went, just the same as the rest of us. She chose to search the lake, though whether she had any success…" His sloping shoulders went up and down. "We must hope, of course. Perhaps your sister sailed for Elinar? I always thought that likely myself."

"And why is that? Did she express a particular desire to go there to you?"

"By no means. I do not recall ever speaking with your sister."

"Then why would you make that claim?" The man was starting to vex him.

"Oh, because I overheard Sir Daryl Blunt speaking of it. He was expressing his joy for a time spent in Elinar, when he was a younger man, I recall. At one of the captain's taverns here. It is a good place to meet up with others of my station, I find. I have no great fondness for drinking, you understand."

I don't care. "I am aware of Sir Daryl's liking for Elinar, Sir Gorton. He speaks of it often. There are many fine inns in the harbour and pleasant walks into the Ironmoors, and along the lake. That does not mean he would have taken my sister there. If they indeed took a boat onto the lake, they would almost certainly have made for Varinar."

And returned, if so. Two weeks was plenty enough to sail between Varinar and Ilivar a half dozen times, depending on the waves and the weather. It was a dismal thought, though far from certain. Perhaps they did make for Elinar instead, or another town along the lake. Perhaps Lillia had decided to sail straight across it and find horses on the western bank, so they could ride to Blackfrost, the old seat of House Daecar, nestled among the southern hills of the North Downs. Until Elyon knew for sure, he would hold to the hope that his sister was alive. And his auntie too, wherever she might be.

"Do you have anything else to report to me, Sir Gorton?"

The man thought for a moment, then shook his head. "That is all I know, I'm afraid. I wish I had more, but…"

You've given me more than my grandfather did, Elyon thought. "Then farewell, sir. If you hear of anything in the meantime, tell me when I return." He did not say when that might be, because he did not know himself. His next stop now would be to return to the dragon's trail, and veer east, for Redhelm and Rustbridge and Rikkard, and hope he did not find them in ruin. And after…well, he needn't think of that just yet.

For what felt like the tenth time that day, Elyon Daecar rode the winds. *A champion, a prince, a carrier crow,* he thought. *I am the eyes of the north.*

Into the darkening skies, he flew.

8

Amron

"It has caused a great deal of discord, hasn't it?" old Ralf of Rotting Bridge said, looking at the blade on the wall. "A man given to superstition might say that it is cursed, my lord. First Dalton Taynar. Then your brother, only minutes later. Are you certain this is the right course? It seems every man who takes up the sword ends up dead."

"We all end up dead eventually, Ralf."

Amron closed his steel fist around the golden hilt, lifting the blade from its fixings; a full half dozen of them, strong thick iron hooks able to bear its weight. Amron had ordered it put here after the battle, safe and secure beneath the ruin of the Spear, under guard at all times, day and night.

Not that anyone could steal it. It had taken Sir Taegon Cargill and Sir Quinn Sharp a great deal of effort to haul the sword to these vaults, so vastly heavy as it was to those unbonded to the metal. Yet to Amron Daecar it was weightless; a lethal feather in his grip. He turned it, admiring its shape, the play of golden light along its face. The Sword of Varinar had an edge that could cut anything - its central power, men said - but in reality that wasn't true. It's power was in the name, and the fame, and the men who bore it. From the moment Varin had named it for his city, and chosen to take it into battle, it had become inextricably linked with strength, fortitude, and the greatness of the Kingdom of Vandar.

And now a great man will bear it. Amron put the Sword of Varinar back onto its hooks. He turned to Whitebeard. "Let him in."

The ranger nodded, unbolting the heavy wood door. The rusted hinges screamed, and from the darkness outside, lit faintly by torches burning on the turnpike stair, Lythian Lindar stepped in.

"Amron. You called for me?"

"Come in, Lythian." Amron gestured him forward, as Rogen pushed the door shut. He turned to the blade on the wall. "I've spoken with the others. We all agree that you're best placed to succeed Dalton Taynar as First Blade. It was a short list, Lythian. Yours was the only name on it."

The Knight of the Vale wore his armour, his cloak, all sooty and stained and scorched. He went into a bow. "I'm humbled, my lord, but…"

"But nothing, Lythian. You've walked at my side all my life, and will walk at it still, as my First Blade. I've been raised to king. You deserve a promotion of your own."

"Sir Brontus might think otherwise."

"Sir Brontus might be dead, for all we know. But if not, he has no claim. When a First Blade is killed, the honour does not pass to the man he defeated in the final of the Song. The process begins again. Brontus Oloran has no more right to that blade than any other man."

"And there is the nature of Dalton Taynar's death to consider," added Sir Ralf. "We must not forget this cloaked assailant who stabbed him in his bedchamber. It was that very wound that killed him, more than any foe on the field. If this was indeed by the order of Brontus Oloran, he should be executed, not honoured."

"Well spoken, Sir Ralf," said Amron, agreeing with a hard nod. "Whether he played a part in Dalton's death or not, Brontus sullied himself with his behaviour here. You were not present, Lythian. You did not bear witness to his unseemly accusations and petty complaints. No, Sir Brontus is not a man we can rely on. But you, Lythian…there is no man more faithful, no knight more noble. So say yes, my friend. And take up the bloody blade."

But still, Lythian did not make a move. "You say you spoke with the others?" he asked.

"Every man here with a voice, yes," Amron said at once. "The response was unanimous. You're well loved, Lythian."

"That is the old me they favour. The captain and quartermaster. You know the things I've done, Amron. *They* don't."

Amron might have struck the man to try to knock some sense into him. "We've been through that. Stop wallowing, Lythian, and put it behind you. I thought you had?"

"I have. Yet it remains unknown to the men. If they find out…"

"Let them. It made no difference to me, and it'll make no difference to them. Anyone with half a brain could understand the choices you made." He wasn't going to listen to his old friend whine any longer about his part in Eldur's rise. "Just pick up the bloody blade, Lythian. By your king's command, *take it.*"

"Fine." Lythian stepped toward the wall, where the Sword of Varinar rested at chest height. He stared at it a moment, shaking his head, still tormented by doubts. A moment passed. Then another. Then he turned to Amron with a critical look in his eye. "You might have taken it down for me," he groused. "Or is this some sort of test?"

"I have faith in you. Just take it off the damn wall. I'm sure you'll be able to wrestle it to the ground."

Lythian's posture tightened. He steadied himself, studying the blade as though it was some complex mystery to be riddled out. "Is there any particular trick to it?" he asked. "Anything in particular I should know?" He looked over at Sir Ralf. "You helped Dalton, I hear, when he was struggling to master the blade. What did you tell him?"

"It doesn't matter what he told him," Amron bulled in. "You are not Dalton Taynar. Now stop delaying and pick up the blade. If you drop it, so be it. We'll go again. Pick it up."

"Damn you, then." Lythian thrust forward with his hand, gripped the handle, lifted, and pulled the Sword of Varinar from its brackets. The blade fell at once, drawn down by its enormous weight, though he managed to arrest its momentum as it swung, holding it off the ground. He turned, straining to raise it, up and up, so that the tip was pointed right at the chest of his king. There was a look of defiance painted upon the face of Lythian Lindar, the Knight of Mists. "There," he grunted. "Satisfied?"

Amron smiled. He raised a hand, sensing Lythian was about to let the blade fall back down. "No, wait. Hold on. Let me see."

The seconds passed. *One, two, three, four…*only then did the strain grow too much for the man, and he let the blade fall. Even so, he held it off the ground. Another eight or nine seconds passed in that state before he puffed out a breath, stepped to the wall, and leaned it up against the stone with a dull heavy *clunk*.

Sir Ralf was looking on in admiration. "You take to it like a duck to water, my lord. A rare thing indeed. You will take no time to master it, I feel."

"Let's hope so." Amron and the old knight of Rotting Bridge had discussed the option of Lythian being given the Sword of Varinar before the battle, as a stand-in for Dalton, though at that time Amron had been confident Dalton would carry it forth himself, no matter his physical state. In truth, he had used the man, a fact that had nibbled at his conscience ever since. At any other time Dalton Taynar should have remained abed, convalescing, but Amron had needed his First Blade to inspire the men. He had, and he had died for it. *Perhaps I never should have sent him out at all…*

It made no matter now. Whichever way he wanted to cut it, the result was the same; Dalton, dead, Vesryn, gone, the Sword of Varinar sitting vacant. While Amron would typically prefer for official procedures to be observed, there was no time for that now.

I need a man I trust to carry it, he thought. *I need someone to protect it with his life, someone who will not submit to its lure. Someone who will give it up when the time comes. I need a soldier, and I need a steward*. Lythian was one of the few who truly understood how important the Blades of Vandar were. Uniting them might be their only chance, if the prophesies were true.

He had one, his son another, Lythian would take a third. That left only Jonik and Janilah. *And the gods only know where they are…*

"I want you to make mastering it your first priority, Lythian," Amron went on. "It won't take long, if your first touch is any judge. Train with it down here for now, until you're able to carry it at your hip. Then take it everywhere. The bond will soon grow strong."

"That's what concerns me. A strong bond is hard to break." Lythian looked at the blade, grand and gold and misting, wreathed in light and history and expectation. "I did not tell you what happened with Dalton during the battle, Amron. There was a point where the blade was dislodged from his grasp, and the look in his eye…the sound of his voice as he demanded I not touch it. There was a wildness to it. A *frenzy*. That obsession…"

"Will not dominate you, as it has done others," Amron was quick to assure him. "You are *not* Dalton Taynar. You understand that your guardianship of the blade will only be temporary."

"Then why bother at all? Why not keep it here, under guard, or in Varinar should we return there?"

"Because the future is uncertain, Lythian, and our goals may yet be disrupted. In the meantime, we may well be called upon to fight, and I cannot in good conscience allow the Sword of Varinar to sit down here, idle and unused. Now, do you have any other concerns? By all means speak them, so we can move on." He waited. No further complaint was proffered. "Good. Then come. I would like to speak with Skymaster Nakaan before he leaves."

Amron made for the door, shuffling a little on his right leg as Rogen opened it back up with a scream of hinges and let him pass through. He limped his way up the stairs, heaving his weight around the spiralling stone, ignoring the jolts of pain and darting spasms in his muscles as he went. They were not so acute today; manageable, even without his tonics. Still, as soon as he stepped out into the open, he gave the pommel of the Frostblade a little touch to dismiss his ails entirely. From then on he walked upright and strong and straight-backed, through the ruin of the city and past the men. The shambling creature was a private show, only witnessed by those deep in his trust. At all other times he maintained his image - regal, powerful, dominant. *A lie.*

Sir Oswin, leal man of Sir Storos Pentar, had the charge of the River Gate today. "Has my son returned?" Amron asked him.

"No, sire, no sighting of the prince just yet."

Amron nodded, displeased.

"It's only been twelve hours," Lythian said. "Give him time, Amron."

"We don't have time." Amron had asked Elyon to assess Varinar from the skies only, to perform a fly-by, and return as soon as possible. But he knew his son. He would want to land and hear reports from on the ground. He would want to find out about Lillia and Amara and

Jovyn. He would want to know where the Dread had gone, and whether other cities had been attacked and destroyed. *He will be pulled in a hundred directions*, Amron thought. *Who knows when he'll be back.*

It was a source of great frustration to him, having to rely upon his own son to convey messages across the north. At any normal time, a thousand crows would be flying from coast to coast, city to city, kingdom to kingdom, relaying news. As a king and commander he needed to know what was happening, and yet he didn't. He was blind. And only his son had eyes.

Amron closed a fist, squeezing. His eyes moved south. Upon the broken battlements, he had positioned many watchmen, and in the southeastern corner of the city, where the massive drumtower of Bowman's Bluff had stood, a tall wooden scaffold had been erected to act as a watchtower. Their task was to look for dragons in the skies and ships on the seas, with horn-blowers ever in attendance to raise the alarm if the Agarathi armada was spotted sailing their way. Some boats had been sent out that morning as well, their purpose to watch the waters. That duty had been given to a commodore by name of Eustace Fairside, one of Lady Brockenhurst's trusted naval commanders. *The only one still alive*, Amron thought. The rest had been killed during the battle.

The king spotted the man in question upon the battlements, surveying the rough waters of the Red Sea from beside the scaffold watchtower. He strode to join him, up the broken steps and past the pitted parapets. One of the watchmen saw the king coming and hailed Commodore Fairside's attention. The man turned as Amron arrived before him, removing a monocular from his eye.

"Report, Eustace," Amron said.

The commodore was short, well upholstered, with thinning brown hair atop his head and a great, stylish moustache deeply rooted above his upper lip. It was the sort of facial hair that a man took years to cultivate to give him a particular air, and without which he would look rather plain. Three-day stubble had spouted around it, though usually the commodore was clean-shaven. He wore once-white breeches - now badly stained in soot - a dark blue frock coat with golden lapels - torn and frayed - and epaulettes to signal his rank.

"Five ships have sailed, my lord," he said, gesturing out to sea. His voice had a good strong quality to it, common among naval commanders. "Two galleys, a carrack, and two large skiffs, all swift on the water. We lost sight of them an hour ago, all except *Kite*." He presented the monocular. "If you look west, you should be able to see her. She's a few miles out from the coast."

Amron looked west, clutching at the godsteel dagger attached to his swordbelt. Faintly, he could see the shape of a vessel in the far distance, though of what type he couldn't say. "I see her, Commodore."

"Of course, yes. You have no need of my instruments to improve your sight." Eustace Fairside smiled and tucked the monocular into a pocket. "My augurs inform me that the weather is set to curdle and grow gloomy over the coming days. Propitious conditions for a hunt, my lord. It should provide ample cover."

Amron nodded. "*Kite* is making for Green Harbour, I presume?"

"Yes." Eustace Fairside nodded, his moustache waving like a fan. A stumpy finger gestured out across the Red Sea, moving from east to west. "The ships have been given orders to disperse, as you asked. *Kite* will fly west, to bring news of Green Harbour, the Twinfort, and elsewhere. *Swift* will make straight for the Trident, and get as close as she dares. The crew are brave, the captain braver. If the enemy armada has returned home to lick their wounds, there is no better boat to spot them, and get back to us in one piece. *Sparrow* will report upon the Tidelands. I would not expect her back for some time. *Tern* will sail for the Claws, and see what she sees along the way, and lastly *Thrush*… she'll sail the space in-between all that and search the Wooded Isles. It's possible some enemy ships limped there, or they may even have taken it as a short-term harbour. My birds will find out."

Birds, yes. He is fond of them, by those names. Amron had a direct question on his tongue. "Do you expect any of them to return?" He knew that Lady Brockenhurst had stopped sending out scouting ships, as they simply stopped coming back. "Answer truthfully, Commodore."

"I have hope," is all Commodore Fairside said. "But if a dragon spots them…"

He needn't say anymore. "Keep me informed."

Amron left him there, Lythian still at his side, Rogen his heel, and returned back down to the River Gate. Great stacks of arms were being gathered in the square - swords, short and long and broad, axes, spears, pikes and halberds, bows and sheafs of arrows, crossbows, shields, and armour. Most were steel and iron and wood, though there was a stack of godsteel weapons too, taken from the dead. Sir Torus Stoutman had been put in charge of taking inventory of them; a job that would keep his mind from the deaths of his sons, Amron hoped.

"We won't want for weapons," Lythian noted. They had taken many weapons from the dead southerners too; Agarathi dragonsteel swords and spears, fine curved khopesh blades and scimitars from Aramatia, brutal maces and morning stars from Pisek, Lumaran longbows and throwing knives and many more. "I wonder if some of the men might be willing to bear dragonsteel. It may not be as potent as godsteel, but its more lethal than our own castle-forged weapons. Our best non-Bladeborn swordsmen would become more deadly with dragonsteel in their grasp."

"Marginally," Amron said. "Don't oversell the properties of dragonsteel, Lythian. And I doubt too many proud Vandarians would be willing to make the switch." It was common enough for lords and wealthy merchants to hang dragonsteel weapons on their walls as trophies, but soldiers bearing them in battle…that was another matter.

"If this plan of yours works, perhaps we'll be united enough to share what we have. But that remains a big 'if' at this point. Most of our men will never stop seeing the Agarathi as their enemy. I trust you understand that?"

"I trust a man's ability to look beyond his resentments. To fight together for a common cause. We have one; our very existence. That is a reality we all must face."

Amron nodded, though gave no other reply, and passed through the gate. The man was too idealistic and it would come back to haunt him, he feared. Beneath the darkening skies, men worked tirelessly to collect the dead, pilfer them of their possessions and prizes, heap them and burn them. Many of the prisoners had now been recruited to tend to their own, mustered by the hedge knight Sir Hadros. By now a dozen great fires were pouring smoke into the air.

The host was assembled east of the prisoner camp, beside the broad stone bridge that spanned the Steelrun River a short way up the coast. Lythian had put Sir Hadros the Homeless in charge of the northern contingent, including several Bladeborn men-at-arms, a household knight or two, and a score of stout swordsmen, spearmen, and shieldmen who had plenty of experience in war. On the southern side, Sa'har Nakaan was to take charge, with some dozen of his own Agarathi, a pair of dragonknights included, and three Lightborn to represent the Empire; a Lumaran Starrider, Piseki Sunrider, and an Aramatian paladin knight. In total some fifty or so men were assembled, a strong host and one quite unlike any Amron Daecar had ever seen.

"So this is your vision of the future, is it Lythian?" he said, as he marched toward them.

The Knight of the Vale nodded. "One I hope others will come to share."

Hope will only get you so far, Amron thought. *This isn't a vision for everyone, my friend.*

That was clear by the faces of the Vandarian soldiers watching on from nearby. Many were glaring, frowning, muttering, some even making their disapproval known with shakes of the head and snorts of objection.

Walter Selleck and Sir Pagaloth Kadosk were standing together at the edge of the host. It appeared that Walter was bending the dragonknight's ear, interrogating him over the identities of the southern men of the company, digging for detail for his book. "…have only just met them, I fear to tell you," Amron heard Sir Pagaloth say, as he neared. "I know little more than you do, at this point, Master Selleck."

"Call me Walter, please."

"Call him an irritation and ask him to leave," Amron said, stepping in. He gave Walter a reprimanding look; the man was far too eager to pester and poke his nose in, and often where it wasn't wanted. "I hope he is not bothering you, Sir Pagaloth."

"No one ever accused me of being a bother, my lord," Walter said to that. Whitebeard's audible sigh said otherwise. "I'm a writer. It's my right to ask questions."

"And it's his right to ignore them. Sir Pagaloth has more important things to be doing than furnishing your tale."

Walter Selleck closed his book with a *thump*. "Then I'll be on my way."

"Don't go far. I want a word with you after."

"Regarding?"

"After." Amron turned his back on the man. There was a certain bustle of energy among the host, though the dividing lines were clear. Northmen stood with northmen; southerners with southerners, and even in those ranks, the Agarathi and men of the Empire kept themselves apart. "You have a job on your hands, Sir Pagaloth. Convincing all these men to work together."

"Skymaster Nakaan has chosen wisely. His men are all willing to cooperate."

Of course they are. They fear the axe if they don't. Amron looked at the Lightborn, the Sunrider and Starrider in particular. Both had looks of fixed grief on their faces. "What happened to their mounts? Were they killed during the battle?"

"They ran," the dragonknight said. "Sunrider Moro says his sunwolf abandoned him when the Dread came. Starrider Bellio says the same of his starcat. Both fled for the woods, they claim."

Then neither can be trusted, Amron thought. *They've only joined this mission to find them.* He did not voice the concern. He sensed a man like Sir Pagaloth would have considered that already, and if not he, Skymaster Nakaan certainly would have. The Fireborn was in discussion with the hedge knight Sir Hadros, the pair standing in the middle of the host, going over plans. "Rogen, bring them over." The ranger saw to it. A moment later, Skymaster Sa'har Nakaan and Hadros the Homeless were standing before him, the former old and wizened, the latter broad and stout.

"Your Majesty," Sir Hadros said, bowing at his thick waist. "A pleasure to see you again. We've met before, once or twice. Perhaps you don't remember?"

"I remember." Or rather, Lythian had been on hand to remind him. "You're doing this for a Varin cloak, I hear."

"Aye, won't deny it. That and unity, as Captain Lythian says." He gave a flashy grin. The man had a cocksure way about him. "Few more of us of the same mind too. Joining the order, that is. Sir Bardol, he's a knight of House Kindrick. Wants it as much as I do, that one. Then there's Ruggard Wells and Mads Miller…men-at-arms those. Know Ruggard from days gone by. Good man, better swordsman. Give him a blue cloak and he'll not let you down."

Open the order to anyone with a drop of Bladeborn blood, you mean. Amron was not about to tarnish the noble Knights of Varin by permitting that. All the same, he would not close the doors either. "Fight well, act admirably, and your cases will be considered. But I want no heroes, Sir Hadros. Do not seek out personal triumph in order to better improve your claim. You are to serve the whole. Is that understood?"

"Loud and clear."

Amron moved his eyes to Sa'har Nakaan. "Skymaster Nakaan. Well met," he said, inclining his black-bearded chin.

Nakaan returned the gesture, though his beard was thin and white and dangled from his bone of a jaw. The rest of him was a skeleton in red and brown robes, white-haired and hollow-eyed. Amron towered above him. "An honour to meet you at last, Lord Daecar. Or king, I should say. I hear you have accepted the crown."

"I serve my people. It is what they wanted."

The Skymaster smiled politely. "You have been king for twenty years. Even in Agarath we knew that you were the true power, not Ellis Reynar."

"I was steward," Amron said. "I steered the course of the kingdom, with my brother."

"My condolences for him."

"Thank you, Skymaster."

"And for your father. I am sure you know…I was wingrider to Lord Marak, once upon a time. We flew together at the Burning Rock. I was there, when your father died."

"I am aware. And I bear no grudge against you for that. My father was your enemy and he died with his blade in his grasp. It was a good death, by the natural order of things. Every warrior wishes to perish on the field of battle."

"Not all," came in Sir Hadros. "I'd sooner die in a nice warm bed with a nubile young lady nuzzling at my nethers."

Amron ignored him. "I hope you give my son the same courtesy, Skymaster Nakaan, if and when you meet. It was he who slew Ezukar."

The Skymaster nodded to show he knew. "And I have no ill will toward him for it. It is Eldur I blame for that, not your son."

"Good. Then we are of the same mind." Amron had a good long look into the Skymaster's eyes. "Lythian tells me you're free of his grip. Tell me, is the same true of Lord Marak? When I spoke to him during the battle, I could sense the conflict in him. Might he abandon the Fire Father as well?"

The man considered it, pulling at his wispy beard. "I could not say for certain," he said. "But yes, it is possible. It is a dream from which many of us are waking. But until I see him again…"

"Then you know where he is?" Amron searched his eyes once more. "I have heard differing reports, Skymaster. One man told me he saw Garlath bear Marak to the southeast. Another said they went northeast. A third claims he saw Garlath the Grand fly away weakened and bleeding from many wounds scarring his scales, barely able to stay airborne. He says he saw Lord Marak fall from the saddle, with the Fireblade in his grasp, and into the deep waters of the river. I took that claim seriously enough to have men search for him, but they found nothing. So, what do you say?"

"I say no more than what I saw."

"And what is that?"

"Little and less. The smoke, the fire, the chaos…it blinded me. I was fighting to control Bagrahar, my dragon, a fight I did not win. The Dread took him. And I was sent to the soil, humbled. That is why I am here, and free. But of Ulrik's whereabouts, I do not know."

It was not the answer Amron was hoping for. Lythian was looking at him with a frown - he had already told him all of this - but the Crippler of Kings wanted to conduct his own interrogation. Lythian was friend to Sa'har, more easily deceived if the Skymaster had a mind for it. *But no, he's telling the truth,* Amron decided. *We can trust this man.*

"And Eldur?" he went on. "Would he have returned to Eldurath?"

"Yes. That would seem likely."

"And what do you imagine his plans are now? You were with him, in the palace, and shared in his counsel. You have a knowledge of his mind that we do not. So tell me. Will he seek to assault us once again? We are concerned here of another attack."

The old Skymaster took his time, pondering. "The will of Agarath seeks chaos, calamity. It desires the end of culture, the destruction of kingdoms, the obliteration of a world that Eldur himself helped build. This is not *his* will, we must make clear. We say Eldur, but truly we are speaking of Agarath, embodied within him. I fear his power will continue to grow, as it awakens. This is just the beginning, my lord."

Amron set his jaw, steeled his eyes, and looked south across the sea. He wondered what his namesake would do if he were here now. *He would be bold*, he thought. *He would not go north, to Varinar. He would gather his forces and go south. He would find his way to Eldurath, and lay it to a terrible siege. He would take the fight to this enemy, no matter the risks and cost. He would slay the demon before he brought the world to total and unrecoverable ruin.*

History remembered Amron the Bold as the name suggested; utterly fearless and unabashedly staunch. No king had been so ruthless in his assaults upon the Agarathi - a fact that many celebrated him for, and many others condemned, for no king had been so divisive as Amron the Bold either. To many he was a hero who had finally avenged his grandfather's death. To many others, a warmonger, who had caused unutterable hurt and harm. Amron had never cared to enter that debate. *I ruled by proxy for Ellis through peacetime*, he thought. *I was more Ayrin the Wise than Amron the Bold through those years.* But now he wondered if he had grown too insular, too meek, to averse to the risks that his namesake would take. When an animal was cornered, it had no option but to attack. *And perhaps that's what we have become? A cornered animal, coiled to spring…*

The sun would soon begin to set, and already the world was

growing gloomy. Above them the skies were thickening as the augurs had promised; spring rains were on the way, and they could last for days here. "I'll not keep you any longer," Amron said. He had wanted to get a read on the Skymaster, and see Sir Hadros, and the rest of their men. What he saw was promising enough. "Prove this concept of unity for me," he said to the pair, and to Sir Pagaloth as well. "Gather as many deserters and fugitives as you can under your wing. Show them that you are one force, one fist, working toward a common goal."

"And if they don't want to join our little jig?" Sir Hadros asked. "We'll try to get everyone doing the same dance, my lord, but not everyone's going to stand in line and wiggle their legs."

It was a question with no easy answer. *The troubled cousin of unity,* Amron thought. If it was just Sir Hadros and his host hunting southerners, those who didn't submit would be slain. Add in Nakaan and his men and it wasn't so easy. *They'll want to protect their own. They might even recognise the deserters, might know them well.* Amron could see a hundred ways where this plan would turn to blood. "I will let you trust your own judgement on that," he said. "You carry my word, the word of the king. Any northern deserters who you bring back will suffer no punishment, so long as they swear to me their loyalty and service. All southern men will be given a choice; join in our cause, or be cast out to sea. We do not have the necessary food or provisions to feed thousands of prisoners, nor can we allow foreign men to wander freely across our lands."

"And those who spit on both options?" asked the hedge knight. "There might be more than a few of those."

He has me cornered. "I want blood to be avoided wherever possible. But if it must be shed, it must. Strong voices, strong wills, gentlemen. Show them the light, and they'll follow." He had nothing more to say on it. "Lythian. I will let you conclude, and see them off. I'll be in my pavilion musing on strategy." He nodded to the men, turned, and left.

Walter was waiting some ten paces behind, easily within earshot, of course. He joined Amron's side as he marched back for the gate, leaving the host behind. Rogen Whitebeard trailed them, eyes glaring left and right and above them, forever wary. Amron liked it when it was just the three of them. It reminded him of their adventures into the wilds, a simpler time. He still thought often of Stegra Snowfist and his tribe, of the beauty of the land in which they had settled. The woods, thick with game. The rivers, teeming with fish. The wide rugged coast, looking out into the endless sea. He wondered whether there were terrors rising in the Icewilds as well, as was happening across the north. Then he remembered that the terrors had always been there. *They never left,* he thought. *It was into the Icewilds that we drove them. That's the only life Stegra knows.*

"How's that fence, Amron?" Walter asked, lifting a lopsided grin. "Must be uncomfortable up there, with one leg on either side."

Amron Daecar was not amused. "You think I'm ducking my responsibility, Walter?"

"Well, you were prevaricating a bit, from what I heard."

"You shouldn't have been listening. I told you not to."

"You told me not to go far. You didn't tell me not to listen." He began opening his book. "Here, I'll show you. I drew a sketch of you all while you were talking. I sense the start of something important here."

"I know. And while you may not believe me, I see the merits in this mission as well. That is precisely why those leading it must have their own agency. I was not prevaricating. I was delegating. There is a difference."

"They seem mighty similar to me. But then, I'm just a humble scribe and carpenter. Not a great leader like you. What do I know?"

Plenty, Amron thought. Walter had always possessed a certain wisdom, he wasn't going to deny it, even if his manner of delivering it was too mocking for his tastes. He walked on for a time, silent, troubled. Through an opening in the clouds, the glow of sunlight pierced, sending a wash of light across the field. It seemed, for a moment, to illuminate the united host, bringing out the many colours of their cloaks, gleaming off their armour. It felt like an auspicious sign, that sudden light amid the gathering dark, as they mounted their horses and set out toward the bridge. *A sign from the gods, from Vandar, or just the weather of the world?* Amron Daecar couldn't decide.

The first spits of rain were coming down when they passed through the gate, across the bustling square, and stepped into Amron's tent. They pattered against the canvas, growing stronger, hitting harder. *It'll be a deluge soon.* The king removed his cloak, setting it on a peg. His armour underneath had been given a scrub that morning, the worst of the soot and stains removed. It caught the light of the brazier as good godsteel should, misting. He removed his swordbelt, setting the Frostblade aside.

"So, what did you want to speak to me about?" Walter asked.

Amron settled himself down onto a block of stone, taking the weight off his right leg. He breathed out heavily, closing his eyes against a sharp stab of pain. When it passed, he said, "The Eye of Rasalan. I want you to spend time with it."

Walter thrust his stubby fingers into his shabby beard, scratching. He looked perplexed. "I think you might be mistaking me for someone else, Amron. I'm hardly Rasal royalty. Only the line of Thala can peer into the Eye."

"I don't expect you to peer into it. I expect you to let your own light *sink* into it. Vandar is not done with you, Walter. You still have your luck. That became clear the day the Spear fell down."

"So you say, Amron. I remain unsure…"

That line was beginning to wear thin. "It is *proven*, Walter, time and again. Were it not for you, Lady Brockenhurst and Lord Florian and

Lord Warton would all be dead, and that's to say nothing of the others who were with you. Your mere presence there saved their lives. As it did Amara, years ago in Varinar. And there is Vesryn to consider as well. For months I caught you whispering in prayer every time my brother was brought up. Then the day the Dread comes, the very hour, the very minute, he appeared to take up the Sword of Varinar and face the beast as Varin Reborn. He restored his honour, and won his seat. That would not have happened were it not for you."

Rogen was at the door, standing straight as a spear. "I long suspected the same," he said. "Lady Amara…she asked you to help her husband."

"To help him go free," Walter said. "Not die. I never wanted that."

"He died well, Walter." Amron heaved to his feet, stepping to a table set up to one side. He poured the man a cup of wine and returned. "Drink. And don't doubt yourself. If Vesryn had still been in his cell beneath the palace, perhaps he'd have died anyway. We'll only know when my son returns, but until that time, let us assume the worst. What you did saved my brother from that fate. That is an extraordinary power you have, to influence events from so far away."

"I…I didn't really *do* anything. I only…" He drank his wine. "I just channelled my thoughts into his freedom, as Amara asked me. Neither of us truly believed anything would come of it. This was your son's doing, Amron. The prince released your brother, not me."

"You influenced events." Amron was convinced of that now, and hoped he could do it again. "Elyon believes that the Eye of Rasalan can be commanded by one of Hadrin's cousins. Before Thalan was destroyed, we know that they were there, some of them at least, within the walls of the city. Elyon aims to find one. And you're going to help him."

Walter visibly paled. "Go to *Thalan*? Me? But…"

Amron cut him off. "That's to be decided. It may suffice for you to spend time in the vaults, with the Eye. To channel your thoughts, as you did with Vesryn, into finding someone who can master it. The Eye of Rasalan is mysterious, Walter. Perhaps the light of Vandar that shines from you will connect to it somehow, I don't know. This is not my field. I *delegate* this duty to you."

Amron twisted his lips into a smile, and waited for the little man to chuckle. It was more of a *huff*, really, but when it came he knew he had him won over. "Fine. There's not much I could do to deny you even if I wanted to. You're the king. Your word is law. So yes, I'll do what I can, see if it makes a difference. But as I said to Amara, I'm making no promises. Most likely it'll come to nothing. When do you want me to start?"

"Right now. Rogen will take you to the vaults."

"The vaults? Beneath the Spear?"

"It's where the Eye of Rasalan is being kept. Though try not to openly declare that fact. There are few who know that it's here, and I would prefer to keep it that way." He nodded to Whitebeard, who swung a hand to open the flaps. The rain was falling harder. "Go ahead, Walter. A bit of rain won't hurt you."

"I…how long do you want me down there? In those vaults. It's hardly a pleasant place to spend time alone."

"You'll not be alone. Lythian will be with you."

"Sir Lythian?" Walter frowned. "Now surely he has better things to do…"

"He does. Training with the Sword of Varinar." Amron had it all figured out. Lythian, mastering a shard of one god's heart. Walter, himself imbued with Vandar's mysterious light, toiling with the eye of another. He had the suspicion that placing Walter at Lythian's side would help hasten his own task as well. *That luck of his…we'd be wise to use it.* "I know you two have spent scant time together, but I'm sure you'll get along. He'll be down shortly. Go ahead. Get started."

When the man had shuffled off, Amron stepped to his command table, looking over the maps and scrolls, the scribbles of strategy. Much remained uncertain. It was a puzzle without half its pieces, and until he had them, he could not confidently steer their course one way or another. It rankled him. History said that all great kings had clarity, and direction, and right now Amron Daecar had neither.

He was deep in thought, musing on much and more, when he heard a voice at the flaps. "My lord, hope I'm not disturbing you."

He raised his eyes. A spearman stood there, amour shining from the rains. His hair and beard were soaking wet. Amron could see the shadow of another man outside, all in black and heavily bearded. "Yes? What is it?"

"This man says he knows you, my lord." The spearmen moved aside, and the hunter stepped in. He looked wilder and more ragged than ever; a look that had always suited him.

"Vilmar," Amron said. "You're back."

"I am." The huntsman's voice was a growl. "And I didn't return alone."

9

Saska

Her grandmother wiped away the tear that was snaking down her cheek. "No tears, child," she whispered. "Not for me. We will see one another again. This isn't the end, I promise."

Saska nodded, sniffing, wary of the eyes around her. *Do not let them see you cry,* she thought. *Be strong. Weep alone.* She took her grandmother's old withered hand and clutched it tight in hers. "I'll come back as soon as I can. As soon as my task…as soon as it's *over*, Grandmother. I'll come back to you. I will."

A wrinkled palm cupped her cheek, cold to the touch despite the heat of the rising sun. *She'll die before I get back,* Saska knew. *Or I will.* That was just as likely. "They are waiting for you, sweetheart," the Grand Duchess croaked." She wore black, as though in mourning, black silk with a hairnet dark as jet, embracing her whitening hair. "Go. And do not look back, Saska. When you turn, *do not look back.*" She smiled and leaned in to kiss her on the forehead, pressing at her skin with lips as dry as dust. Two maids lingered behind, to steady the old woman, should she fall. Eyes down, un-listening, to be present but not seen. *Shadows,* Saska thought. *As I was, once before.*

She drew back, steeling herself. "I'll see you…soon," she said, in a voice that was threatening to break. "Whether here or…" Her eyes turned up, to the blazing blue skies. She could still see the haze of the moon up there, lingering in the firmament.

"In the stars," her grandmother finished for her, squeezing her hand. "If not on this earth, we shall see one another in the stars. And what a joy that will be…to join Lumo in her light."

Saska nodded, silent. She had often pondered which afterlife would take her…whether there was an afterlife at all. Her blood was mixed, of steel and sea and light. Would she be called to Eshina's Grove? The Great Forge? The Ocean Halls of Rasalan? Might Varin make an exception for her and summon her to his Table? If raised to the

Eternal Halls, would she be able to cross to the Stars of Fallen Souls, to wander the Blackness Above in search of her Lightborn family? To visit her grandmother and her mother and all those of the light she'd lost?

She didn't know. How could she know? *No one knows*, she thought.

But she only nodded and said, "If not here…there, Grandmother. In the stars." She looked up once again, blinking to stop the tears from welling. The others were all there, behind her, waiting. *Turn*, she told herself. *Turn, and do not look back.*

She smiled, leaned forward, kissed her grandmother on the cheek. And then she turned.

And did not look back.

Her host were assembled before her, over a hundred soldiers and sellswords strong, waiting upon the scorched cobblestones inside the Cherry Gate. She paced toward them, leaving the frail form of Safina Nemati behind, breathing deeply, heart fracturing. She wanted to turn, take one last look, call out to her grandmother that she loved her, that she was so happy she had had a chance to meet her, spend time with her, bask in the woman's fading glow. But she didn't. She couldn't. *If I turn back now, I'll never leave.*

So on she went, toward her men. Step by step, and strong.

Sir Ralston was awaiting her, with Leshie and Del. "That looked emotional," Leshie said. Her eyes were swollen with pity. "Are you…all right, Sask?"

"Fine." The word was bluntly said and that in itself said a lot. It said she didn't want to talk about it. "Is everyone ready?"

The Wall nodded. "At your command, my lady, we can go."

"Then let us go," she said.

She stepped forward, toward her horse. It was not her preference as a steed, though in her heavy plate armour, Joy was not strong enough to carry her. Thankfully, the Baker had managed to procure a number of Bladeborn-bearing horses from the ruin of the Tukoran warcamp - destriers and palfreys and a couple of swift coursers that had bolted during the fighting - that would serve to carry them. There was even one capable of bearing the Wall, a great plodding warhorse with an ill temper and penchant for biting that must have belonged to a huge Tukoran knight once before.

Sir Bernard, perhaps, Saska thought. He was not close to matching Sir Ralston's size, but was a bull of a man all the same.

Saska climbed up into the saddle of her courser, a handsome mare, chestnut brown, and all about her, others did the same. The Butcher and the Baker had with them three of their best remaining men; Merinius, Umberto, who had ridden with Saska once before, and a man they called the Gravedigger, for his cadaverous appearance. The Surgeon had brought with him the Tigress, Gutter and Gore, and two others of trusted character, he claimed. *They better be*, Saska thought. The way the Wall was eyeing them made it clear that he would have their heads off their shoulders at the first sign of disloyalty or deception.

The Butcher gave his destrier a kick and rode over, tattered cloak rippling, a broad smile on his lips. "It's finally happening, then. Exciting, no?"

It was, in part. Exciting, frightening, saddening all at once. Saska only nodded.

A bellow rang out from Sunrider Alym Tantario, the man in charge of the Aramatian escort, calling for the gates to open. Saska knew the Sunrider but barely, though Lord Hasham had assured her he was a formidable warrior, well seasoned in battle, a man of fierce loyalty and noble character who would give his life to protect her if needed. Tantario had with him almost a hundred paladin knights, mounted spearmen, mounted archers, and a small contingent of Sunriders and Starriders as well, all drawn from beneath the great wings of Houses Hasham and Nemati. Their orders were simple - get Saska to the northern coast, see her aboard a ship, and return. Only the sellswords would continue to accompany her when they made for the northern continent.

And how will we be greeted? Saska wondered, as she passed her eyes across the Bloody Traders, all in oddments of armour and mail, with multihued cloaks and strange adornments, and an assortment of savage weapons hanging at their hips and crossing their backs. They were hardly the sort of escort a princess should have, much less the heir of Varin, but what could she do? *I have Sir Ralston,* she thought. He at least was known for his commitment to duty and his honour in the northern kingdoms. *He'll be able to vouch for me, when we come across great knights and lords.*

She sighed, and not for the first time lamented that Robbert Lukar had not stayed a little longer. *I could have gone out into his encampment, spoken with him again. I could have told him who I am and what I need to do.* The foolish girl in her thought that maybe that would make a difference. That he would swear to her his loyalty and pledge that he would help. That he and Sir Lothar and Sir Bernard and Lord Gullimer and all the rest of the noble men of his army might join her too, and carry her, like a wave, toward her fated duty.

But none of that had happened. Instead she just had the sellswords.

"Form up, form up," Sunrider Tantario shouted. His men knew what to do. At once they rearranged themselves into columns, lining up to either side of Saska and her men, paladin knights and spearmen to the front and middle, bowmen to the back, with the Sunriders and Starriders prowling about the perimeter.

"Will they be like this the entire way?" Leshie asked. She didn't look pleased. "I'm not being locked in like this for a thousand miles of baking road. I want to ride and roam. *Dread* needs to stretch his legs."

Saska had to ask. "Dread?"

Leshie grinned, patting the shoulder of her little red rouncey. "That's his name. Dread. Like the dragon everyone's scared of."

"You shouldn't make jests about that name," the Wall grunted at her. "It may be that Drulgar has already attacked the north, if these rumours of his rise are to be believed."

They are, Saska thought, a shudder climbing up her spine. They had heard too many reports now, of the breaking of the Wings, of the great shadow ascending amidst the swarm, of the red lightning and black clouds, to doubt that it was true.

Leshie, as ever, wasn't taking it seriously. Her shoulders bobbed up and down in a carefree shrug, red armour clanking. "Guess we'll find out when we get there. Though that's going to take a while. Especially going *this* way."

She pointed at the Cherry Gate as it groaned open, causing ash and soot to stir. It was here that the invaders had come storming through, where the inferno had spread, where legions had died. The buildings to the sides were husks of blackened stone and charred wood, the cobbles stained with death. The stink of it was still in the air even after all these days.

"Ersella San Sabar sounds disappointed by the route," the Butcher identified. He grinned. "I understand this disappointment. The Capital Road will take much longer."

"It's the safer route," Sir Ralston Whaleheart said. "Lord Hasham insists we go this way."

"*Insists*. And where is he now? A man cannot insist if he is not coming with us. And the heir of Varin outranks him."

"Be quiet," growled the Wall, eyes moving left and right. "Lady Saska may have shared that secret with you, but otherwise it is not for spreading. Too many people know as it is."

"Strange that you care more than she does, Coldheart. It is her secret to share, not yours."

"No. It is all of ours. Because her quest affects us all. If that secret reaches the ears of the enemy, every one of us will die before we reach the north."

"Speak for yourself. The Butcher is unkillable." He thumped his chest.

"The Butcher is a fool," said his brother, the Baker. "We have established this already." He rode up to join them on a horse as stocky as he was, clopping loudly along the cobbles. "And the reason we are going along the coastal road is plain. It is safer, as the steel giant says. And no longer blocked by the coalition army. Lord Hasham is wise to advise we go this way. With fortune we will ride unimpeded all the way to Eagle's Perch. The crossing to Rasalan from there will be quick and easy. Little time for the sea monsters to seek us out for a snack."

The Capital Road, Saska thought, sighing. *Another long ride to Eagle's Perch*. She had travelled that road once before, when a captive of Elio

130

Krator, and had not expected to do it again. *We were meant to go north. To the Everwood. Ranulf was meant to return…*

"The coastal road is the sensible course," the Wall agreed. "It is paved, easy to travel…"

"Boring," said the Butcher. "The plains will be more fun."

"More *dangerous*," Sir Ralston came back. "The plains are crawling."

"There is the heat as well," added the Baker, who probably knew all about heat, with that name. He seemed much more sensible than his younger, bigger brother. "My sources tell me that the wells are drying up across the plains and the rivers are turning to dust. This heat is the sort that kills. Not to my brother, of course…no, *nothing* can kill him…but to mere mortals like us, yes. Heat is deadly, and a lack of water also. We have no choice but to travel the coast."

"And who put you in charge, Knuckles?"

"*Knuckles?*" The Baker frowned at Leshie, one corner of his mouth tugging into a grin. He wasn't familiar with her penchant for nicknames. "This is me, is it? Knuckles?"

"You have big hands," she said, pointing at them. "Too big for your little body. And oversized forearms too. They should call you the Blacksmith, not the Baker."

The Butcher chortled loudly.

The Baker smiled and said, "There is a Blacksmith already, among the Bloody Traders. A fine captain. He makes the best weapons."

Leshie groaned. "You're all just walking gimmicks."

"Says the girl who calls herself the Red Blade, for this red armour she wears." The Baker smiled, as Leshie scowled, enjoying his victory. "You are right, brother," he said to the Butcher. "She is a very funny little thing. Most entertaining. I can see why you like to keep her around."

"*Keep me*…I'm not a bloody *pet!*" She reached to the handle of her blade. That only made the Baker and the Butcher laugh all the louder. Which in turn made Leshie more angry. She drew out her blade, pointing at them, one then the other. "Call me a pet again…"

"Enough," said the Wall, in a thumping voice. "He never called you a pet, and you're far too easy to goad. Put the blade away, Leshie." He narrowed his eyes upon her until she wilted, snarling, and thrust the dagger back into its sheath. It was the one that Robbert Lukar had given her, left inside that chest of gifts. There were small rubies and garnets on the crossguard and a large red diamond glittering atop the pommel. A kingly gift, it was. A gift for helping to save his life.

The Wall turned to Saska. "My lady. Sunrider Tantario is awaiting your command."

She looked over. So he was. Tantario had his entire escort in place, perfectly spaced apart, a cage of swords and feathered cloaks, horses and camels, to shield her. The Sunrider rode down the centre of the column to join them. He wore scalemail in silver and cyan blue, his feathered cloak the same. The hues of House Tantario, she supposed. His hair was short, neat, brown, with steaks of white at the temples. He looked about forty, perhaps a little older, with skin sunbaked and heavily creased at the forehead and around the eyes. *Lots of squinting and frowning,* Saska thought. "Serenity," the Sunrider said, in a pleasant Aramatian timbre. "We are prepared to go, at your pleasure. Should I lead on?"

"Please," she said.

He bowed his head, and his sunwolf turned, claws clacking as he loped forward.

A moment later, they were moving, passing through the gate and beneath the scorched walls of Aram to exit onto the fields beyond, where many thousands had died in battle. The fires had not reached out here, though that did not mean the lands weren't stained. Of blood there was plenty, soaked into the dirt and lacquered onto the rock, mottling the lands outside the city from the walls to the ruin of the warcamp.

Del was looking at those patches, a frown of consternation on his long and horsey face. "So many," he said, quietly, over the rattling of armour, the trotting of hooves. "My friends. So many of them died here…and in the fire. I wonder…" He looked over at her. "Do you think any of them got out?"

Saska reached across to touch his arm, as they rode along side by side. "I'm sure they did, Del. Percy and Martyn weren't found among the dead. That means they left, and are probably with Robbert. They may yet get back to Tukor."

"I hope I get to see them again. And Prince Robbert, him most of all. I just…I wish he had stayed. I was his squire, Saska. I finally had something…important to do."

"You're my brother, Del. Isn't that important enough?" She grinned and jabbed at him, as she might have done once before, back on the farm at Willow's Rise. "We've come a long way, haven't we? From farmhands to freedom fighters. And look at you, in that armour. You look like a proper knight."

"*Look*, maybe. But the rest…" He moved his gaze around, eyes slightly down, peering out from beneath his tangle of wild black hair. "Everyone here's a warrior. A killer. I'm just going to get in the way."

She thought back to the steading. To the night Lord Quintan had come and mustered Del for the war with Rasalan. He had wept that night in fear, and she'd told him he'd make a good archer. Her mind had not wavered on that. So she said it again. "You have your bow, Del." It was a good bow, too, made of yew, light and strong. He wore it across his back, with a quiver of arrows for company. "If we face any fighting, you can still do your part." It went against her instincts to say that. In truth she would prefer that he find some rock to hide under, but that would hardly do much for his confidence. "You're a fine shot, Del. Always were."

132

"You were better. I just handed you the arrows and helped spot game."

She smiled to think of those days, hunting wildfowl and deer in the woods at the foot of the mountains. *Will life ever be so simple again?* Somehow she doubted it. "You've trained since then."

"Not with the bow," he told her. "I wanted to be an archer when I joined the army, but they just put me with the reserves and gave me a rusted sword. The *meat*, they called us, the senior men. *Fodder for steel.* I was lucky that I got put under Prince Robbert's charge. Sir Bernie…he took us under his wing, but even then, I barely trained with the bow."

"Then let's change that," Saska said. She twisted her neck, looking back, to where the mounted archers were trotting along at the rear of the column, a full score of them with fine white longbows captained by a veteran called Kaa Sokari. Saska had met the man only that morning, though had been reliably informed that he was a master-bowman. "See that man there," she said. "His name's Kaa, and he can shoot the wings of a fly from horseback while galloping at full speed, I'm told. If I ask him, he'll be able to train you."

The boy shook his head at once. "I don't want to be any trouble."

"It won't be trouble. When we stop to water the horses, I'll speak with him. How about that?"

He chewed on it a moment. "Only… only if you're sure." He seemed equally enthused and afeared by the thought. "Won't it be embarrassing, though? All these bowmen…they can fire from their horses, as you say. I'd struggle to hit water if I fell off a boat. They'll only laugh at me."

Saska smiled. "They won't. Every great archer has to start somewhere, and so long as you're willing to learn, that's worthy of respect. And anyway, you told me how you shot Robbert with that arrow. That's how you became his squire in the first place. And you saved his life as well. That was a good shot, wasn't it? Robbert would have died if you hadn't hit that Emerald Guard."

"I didn't hit, not really. I only grazed his armour."

"The graze was enough." She hadn't been there to witness it, but Leshie had told her what had happened. How she and Del had come rushing down the alley to find Robbert Lukar beneath a knight in an emerald cloak, driving a dagger down into his eye. Leshie had shouted out and Del had fired his bow and that had been enough to break the knight's hold. After that, Robbert had struck him in the jaw, heaved to his feet, and battered the man's head to mulch. "It was like soup," Leshie had told her later. "Red bloody soup with bits of brain and skull bobbing about in his helm. Never seen anything like it. It was *brutal*, Sask."

And well earned, Saska thought. It turned out the knight was a man called Sir Wenfry Gershan, a grandson to the Master of the Moorlands, and he'd been ordered by Cedrik Kastor to kill Robbert during the fighting, to help him steal the throne. *Well, no chance of that now.*

Saska looked down at Joy, loping gracefully along beside her horse, and imagined her muzzle all red, her eyes like silver flame, tearing and ripping at Cedrik's flesh. A smile warped her lips, as she pictured it all again. It was a memory she would treasure forever, to keep her warm when the nights grew cold.

"You saved his life," Saska said. "That's the important part. And you didn't panic either. Most boys your age would have fumbled the arrow in the string, or missed the man entirely. That you didn't speaks volumes, Del. You didn't wilt in the heat of battle."

That won her a smile of sorts, though as ever with Del it was bashful. "I guess," he said, in that mumbly voice of his. "And it was close, the arrow. To hitting Sir Wenfry. Properly, I mean."

"Do you wish it had?" Saska asked him. "Taking a life…" She paused, realising she hadn't broached this topic with him yet. "*Have* you killed anyone yet, Del? During the fighting in Kolash, or…"

"No." His eyes went down. "I wanted to, that night. I told Prince Robbert I would, but…"

"It's not a bad thing," she said. "That you haven't killed, I mean. Taking a life…that's not something everyone can do, Del. The guilt, and regret…it can become a burden."

A moment passed in silence. There was nothing but the rustle of the men around them, the clatter of hooves, the murmur of voices. Then Del asked, "How many have you killed now?" He looked over. "Have you…killed lots of people, Saska?"

She cycled through them all, one after another after another. Lords and knights and sellswords and killers, all worthy of the blade. Only Sir Jesse, perhaps, gave her cause for regret. The rest had earned their ends, and more. "I don't keep a tally, Del," she said, lying to spare him. "I don't think it does a person any good to dwell."

He nodded, thinking, then gave her a brotherly smile. "They all deserved it, I bet. Like Sir Wenfry did." His eyes darkened. "I'd have killed him, happily. He was trying to murder Prince Robbert. I'd have given my life to protect him."

"That's very brave, Del."

"I'm not lying," he said, thinking she might be humouring him. "I'm not the same boy you knew in Willow's Rise. *Man*," he corrected. "I'm a man now."

"I know, Del."

His chin lifted. "I'll protect you as well, if it comes to it. You're my sister, and…and I love you, but you're much more than that now. All of us here. It's our duty to protect you. Even me." And he nodded, firming, straightening his back. "I'll train," he said, committing. "With that archer. I don't care if it's embarrassing. I have to do my part."

I should have left him behind, a part of her thought. Rolly had suggested she do just that. That Del would only be a burden to her, causing her to worry and fret when she needed to focus on herself. He had said the same about Joy, once before, though at least Joy could defend herself. Del was not the same. *Even if he learns to master the bow, he will never be a warrior.*

But she could not say any of that to him. *He is here, now, and there's no going back.* So all she did was smile, reach across to him, and say, "I am so glad you're with me, Del."

The day was yet young. Though already it was growing hot, the horizon rippling with a blanket of burning air, bubbling and fizzing off the plains. Their course took them south, at first, along a wide paved road that led down to the coast, past the abandoned Tukoran warcamp. Much remained amid the wreckage, all left behind in their haste. She saw pavilions blowing in the hot dry wind, tents overturned, old firepits dug into the ground. Wagons sat about, empty. There was evidence of horse lines, boundary stakes and poles, the stink of latrines, and death. Some of Hasham's men and those of the Strong Eagle were still poking about, looking for anything of worth, piling whatever they found onto carts to roll back into the city. They had been joined by scavengers, jackals and vultures and big black southern crows, fighting over the last of the dead who had not yet been gathered and burned.

Saska saw an eagle too, circling above them. *Hunting mice,* she thought. No doubt there were hundreds of them here.

The trebuchets had been left behind as well. They stood forsaken, great wooden monstrosities attended by wains piled high with rocks. The bombardment had been little more than a ruse, in the end, a distraction to hide their true intent. To open the gates from within, storm inside unchallenged, and win the city. But within that plan, were plots. *Plots within plots,* Saska thought. Cedrik…he was going to betray Elio Krator, once they had won the city, take residence in the palace and wait out the war from there. They had that from one of the prisoners, a Tukoran knight in Kastor's favour. Another, an Aramatian, had said that Elio Krator was planning to do the same. A two-headed snake, devouring itself.

But neither had anticipated the deceptions of Cliffario Denlatis. Playing both sides, selecting who would win. *He was the kingmaker more than anyone,* Saska knew. *Even Vincent Rose never rose so high.*

It took some hours before they reached the sea, crossing down through a great nub of barren land that extended east from Aram. Here they met the Capital Road, a two-thousand-long coastal road that stretched all the way from Solas in the southwest of Lumara to Eagle's Perch in the northeast of Aramatia. The air was a little cooler here, owing to the breeze coming off the sea, and the road was well maintained, allowing for a swifter course. Much as Saska had wanted to go north through the plains in the hope of finding Ranulf, she knew this was the better way.

For now, anyway, she thought. *If we hear fresh tidings, we can still change our course. Ranulf may yet come back.*

The morning rolled into afternoon, the sun beating down upon them. The coast here was rocky, rugged, the waves crashing in on the surf. In places the road got so close that they could feel the spray on their faces, when the wind was right, blowing a fine briny mist across their path to give them some relief.

But mostly that wasn't the case. Though a coastal road, it often diverted inland when blocked by high stark crags and bulky headlands, wending around them, often for many long hot miles, away from the salty breeze. At these times the air grew stifling, unpleasant. Their pace began to slow, conversation halting. The energy in the company sagged.

They passed traveller inns along the way, and some small fishing villages as well. Some had been ransacked when the coalition army had passed this way. "Did you know about this, *Squire*?" Leshie asked. That was her name for Del. "You didn't take *part* in it, did you?"

She was teasing him, Saska knew at once. But he took it seriously. "*No*. Of course not. Prince Robbert would never have allowed it."

"Cedrik Kastor would," Saska said. She remembered the south of Rasalan, the Lowplains and lands around Harrowmoor. Kastor's Greenbelts had pillaged their own northern cousins, killing crofters and cobblers with impunity, stealing away their daughters. They wouldn't think twice about doing the same thing here.

"I heard that the sunlord didn't like it," Del told them. "He said that innocent Aramatians were not to be harmed."

The Butcher laughed aloud. "What the sunny snake says and what the sunny snake does are two very different things. He took Kolash, did he not? You were there. His own forces were part of the battle."

Del nodded from atop his spotted palfrey. It had a black mane, like his hair, untamed and long. "I didn't see them. I was with Prince Robbert's company. Green Company, he called us. We fought through other parts of the city…"

"But they were there, yes? In other parts of the city? Aramatian soldiers, serving Krator?"

Another nod. "I saw them, leaving their own warcamp. And returning."

"With blood on their blades. The blood of their own. This is a foul thing that Krator did. And the Port of Matia…" The Butcher's horse was much bigger than Del's, a one-eyed destrier, frothing at the mouth, a little mad like him. He loomed above the boy, looking down. "My mother was Matian, did you know that? Mine and the Baker's. She was a whore. But a nice one. That means I am half Matian. A Matian Aramatian." He smiled. One of his serious smiles. "She has been dead for many years, but I still know many people there. Some will have been murdered, because of Krator. So think again, Dellard. Do you think the sunny snake cares about harming his own people? Even innocent ones?"

Del frowned, thinking. "Well…maybe not. I did think…the inno-cents…" He looked around. "I thought he was only killing soldiers."

"Naivety, boy. Better you harden up fast, or this world will chew you up and spit you out, and tread on your mulch-corpse as it walks on by, laughing."

It was quite an image. They rode on for a while, no one saying anything. Then Del mumbled, "I'm not called Dellard, by the way. Just Del. It's not short for anything."

"I know. But I prefer Dellard, so I will call you Dellard. And in turn you may call me a name of your own choosing. Think of one, Dellard. You will have plenty of time to think."

He wasn't wrong about that. Another hour went by, and another, and another, each of them hotter than the last. The road took one of those wretched turns inland, through a series of craggy canyons where the air grew so still and close that Saska wondered if it would ever stir again. Sweat poured down her back, soaking into her linen under-clothes, the padded garments she wore beneath her armour.

That armour was polished and pristine, glittering beneath the sun in fine silver, with a soft blue undertone glimmering upon the breast-plate. The pauldrons were tessellated with squares of silver and azure, the faulds and cuisses lobstered with exquisite overlapping lengths of godsteel plate. Saska had trained for months in mismatched armour, procured by the Butcher, and shortly before the battle that armour had been upgraded. Yet nothing like this. This was a gift of Robbert Lukar, left in the chest for her to wear, thrice-beaten and more durable than anything she had worn before. She did not know who it had belonged to before - perhaps it was even his, when he was a little younger - though it fit her beautifully whoever it was.

But the blue, she thought. *The silver and blue.* Those were not Tukoran colours, but Vandarian. Robbert had seen the dagger she bore, Varin's dagger, passed down through the kings of his line. *Did he recognise it? Does he know who I am?* She could not say for sure, though that armour had certainly offered a hint. She hoped to have the chance to ask him, one day.

The maze of canyons wended a few miles inland, before opening out to a view of the plains to the northwest, barren and brown, blowing with dust, shimmering with insufferable heat. Ahead they spotted a town, windblown and dust-scarred, the buildings short and stubby and painted in a variety of colours; ochre, copper, bloody red, all peeling and stripping from the cracked, sun-baked walls.

The town seemed abandoned, not a soul stirring as they passed through and into the central square. Here they found a well, a scaffold above it, with a winch and bucket for drawing up water. "We stop here," Saska heard Sunrider Tantario call out. "Fetch water for the horses. Search the buildings."

While that was being seen to, some of the leaders gathered beside an old, dusty fountain. The Wall, Sunrider Tantario, the Baker, the Surgeon, and Kaa Sokari had assembled. Saska dismounted and strode to join them. "What are they searching for?" she asked

"Fugitives," said Tantario. "From the battle."

"And if they're found?"

The Baker made a throat-slitting gesture.

"No," Tantario said. "Any man who willingly surrenders will not be slain. He will be chained and sent to Aram to face judgement. Lord Hasham's orders, Serenity."

"Stupid orders," said the Baker, pulling off his golden spectacles. He drew out a piece of pristine cloth from a pocket and began polishing the lenses. "No captive can be trusted to return to Aram of his own accord, and thus must be escorted. The more captives, the more men to escort them. Your host will soon begin to thin, Tantario, if you follow the moonlord's command."

"I will follow them, sellsword. As I have all my life." Alym Tantario straightened out one of his ruffled feathers, raised his shaven chin, and looked at Saska. "Apologies, Serenity. I do not wish to speak so curtly in your presence, but these are my explicit commands. With luck we will not find any captives along our way, or those we do will…"

A shout sounded from inside one of the buildings.

All turned to the doorway of a single-storey house, hardly more than a block of stone, paint peeling, walls weatherworn. There were sounds of a scuffle, then a scrape of steel, and a scream. A man tumbled out backward through the door, clutching at his neck. A long dagger had been planted there. Blood ran down his craw and soaked into his feathered cloak.

Then the rest came rushing through.

One, two, ten, more of them, boiling like ants from a hill. *Tukorans*, Saska knew at once. They were pale-skinned, bearded, their foreheads and cheeks and noses red and blistered from the sun, armoured in leather and mail and bits of old plate. A few wore breastplates, gauntlets, gorgets, the essentials. She saw godsteel too, misting, saw men moving as only Bladeborn could, quicker than the rest, more deadly. Suddenly there were twenty, thirty, forty, all charging from a dozen different doors, hacking through the men who had entered to investigate.

Saska glanced aside, saw Leshie with Del, caught her eyes. *Protect him*. Leshie understood, grabbing the boy, pulling him back. *You too*, Saska thought, to Joy, and the starcat growled and pounced away. Then she tore her blade from its sheath, and launched herself into battle.

Others had already entered. The Butcher, laughing, the Tigress, hissing. The Wall was stomping forward, pulling a greatsword from its scabbard, grunting. Sunrider Tantario was calling for his men to engage, shouting, "To arms, men! For Aramatia! For Lumo!"

Arrows came spitting from the bowmen. The mounted spearmen, currently dismounted, lowered their spears and charged. Paladin knights drew great curved scimitar swords, coloured robes billowing as they entered the fray. The riders of sun and star in the company leapt in upon their wolves and cats.

Yet the Tukorans kept coming. Like lava from a fissure, they boiled up to the surface, from the vaults and baking basements in which they'd been hiding. Some took one look at the Wall, stuttered to a stop, and ran, scampering away into the hills. Most decided it was better to die here than out there, with steel in their grasp and iron in the air. Some even went right for the Wall himself as though to get it over with quickly. He obliged them, swinging through them simple as that, like a farmer scything wheat, limbs and offal flying everywhere.

Others didn't last much longer. There were some formidable fighters here, in the company, Lightborn and Bladeborn both. Saska hesitated as she set forth, realising that there was no sense in her killing Tukorans unless necessary, and with such a strong company about her, her blade wasn't needed. She stepped back instead, retreating to the rear, to watch. *The Wall will be proud of me*, she thought. *That alone was reason enough to stand down.*

She studied the men. Ahead, amid the bloodshed, the Butcher was doing what he did best, and green-eyed Merinius as well, a nimble and skilful fighter. She got her first look of the Baker in action as well; a more compact, measured combatant than his brother, though effective for all that, grinning that white smile as he cut and cleaved.

The Tigress was adding to her five hundred kills, hunting and hissing, a maelstrom of death. Saska watched her more than anyone, mesmerised by the towering woman, orange and black cloak swishing as she ducked, weaved, struck, slew, killing one man and then another with an astonishing mix of stalking grace and sudden, brutal violence.

"I said she was good, did I not?" a voice said to her. "The best sellsword in all the world."

Saska turned. The Surgeon was standing right beside her, with that proud look on his face.

She nodded at his remark. "She's…quite something. I'm glad to have her on my side."

"As I have been, through all these years. She has long been as a daughter to me, even though she is much older."

Saska took his age for about forty-five summers or so. "So these rumours…about her drinking blood, to stay young?"

"Are quite true." He raised a finger, pointing. "Look how she seeks out that Bladeborn warrior, do see you? Her eyes are set on him. She wants to be the one to slay him, my lady. Only then will she allow herself to drink the man's Varin blood."

Saska swallowed, discomfited. She could not tell if he was serious or not. "Varin's blood flows strongly in my veins," she pointed out. "More than anyone else's. She won't…"

"Seek to have a sup of yours?" He smiled one of those flat smiles of his. "No, you need not fear her, my lady. It is only the blood of the wicked she seeks."

The fighting was fierce before them, the sunbaked stone of the square quickly filling with blood and bodies. There were grunts, and death-cries, snarls and howls from the cats and wolves, horses whickering and neighing in alarm, camels honking.

"Do you not want to bloody your blade?" Saska asked the Surgeon, over all that.

"Here? No. There is no need, Serenity. Let the others have their fun." He spoke as a man used to these skirmishes, cold eyes studying the strength of friend and foe, concluding a simple victory. "Look, see Gutter and Gore?" He pointed at the pair, fighting side by side. "Now you see how they got their names."

They gut, and they gore, she thought, as the two men lived up to their tags. The other two warriors under the Surgeon's charge - a man and a woman, they were, and husband and wife if what Leshie said was to be believed - were called Scalpel and Savage. Scalpel was as advertised; precise, clean, a killer after the Surgeon's heart. Savage, too, earned the name. The woman was fury personified.

"I thought they would be the other way around," Saska said. She gestured to Savage, a diminutive, heavy tattooed woman with her hair shaven down one side of her head, braided on the other, as she screamed and ran, jumping onto the back of a big Tukoran axeman, biting at his neck with sharpened teeth, tearing.

"Ah. You thought Savage would be the man, Scalpel the woman?"

Saska nodded. "It just seemed like it would be that way."

"Indeed. But we are not always as we seem, are we?" He gave her a knowing look. "Savage is quite pleasant when the fighting is done, in truth. But when battle stirs…" The wild screaming of the axeman said it all, as she tore out a chunk of flesh from his neck, dropped off his back, drew a knife, and stabbed wildly through his armour with a godsteel blade, quick as a woodpecker. The Surgeon enjoyed that, by his smile. "But we can say the same about many other people, can we not? Look at the Butcher. All those scars, that torn and tattered cloak. He is fearsome to look upon, a pit fighter and a brute. But also a man of mirthful character when you get to know him."

A terror to his enemies, a godsend to his friends. Saska liked the Butcher tremendously.

"And you, of course."

She looked at him.

Another of his unreadable smiles. "You are more of an enigma than anyone. A slave-girl, who is a princess, who is Bladeborn and the heir of Varin. And I hear you are Seaborn too."

She nodded. "My father's mother was Princess Atia, of Rasalan. Most people believe she died of tuberculosis, but that was never true. She died birthing my father."

"As your mother died birthing you." His eyes dipped to the blade at her hip, glimmering blue and silver in its sheath. "It is said that the blood of Varin is so strong that often women perish when birthing great Bladeborn. It is an omen of greatness, some say. We must hope this is the case with you."

He sounded sincere enough, in that. "I hope the same," was all she said. Then she turned back to watch the battle.

The sun was beginning its descent into the west, turning the skies a soft shade of red, slashed through with spears of pink and vermilion, soaking the clouds in colour. The battle went from a boil to a simmer, the enemy ranks depleting. Some of them decided that they wanted to live a little longer after all, turning to run, men giving chase. Others threw down their arms where they stood, heaving and bloody, and yielded. A few fought on, the strongest of them, though soon enough those too were overwhelmed, killed or captured.

By the time it was all done, the company had lost some dozen men, each of them under the charge of Sunrider Tantario. Half of those were the men who had gone scouting into the buildings, where they were set upon without warning. The rest were made up of spearmen, swordsmen, and a paladin knight, who had been killed by the rebel leader, who had survived the battle, fighting on until the end, before being disarmed and disabled by the Wall. The giant had his great fist around the knight's neck, dragging him across the bloodied cobbles, to throw down at Saska's feet. "Their leader," Sir Ralston boomed. "His name's Sir Gavin Trent."

That name seemed familiar to her. She frowned, trying to place it.

"He was Cedrik Kastor's man," the Wall told her. "His battle commander."

Saska's lip pulled back. Sunrider Tantario was with them, and several others. The rest were gathering the dead, corralling the few other men who had given themselves up as prisoners. The red in the skies thickened and darkened to match the blood on the stone. "You were here to ambush innocent travellers," Tantario accused.

Trent gave no answer. The Wall hooked a hand under his chin, lifting him into the air. With his other hand he pulled off the man's helm, revealing a rugged face, craggy as the canyons through which they'd passed, torn with old battle-scars. "Speak," he demanded. Nothing. He squeezed, steel fingers digging into the flesh of Sir Gavin's throat. "*Speak.*"

He can't, with you holding him like that. "Put him down, Sir Ralston," Saska said. She tried not to call him Rolly during these moments.

The man was lowered, the Wall's fingers opening. Sir Gavin sucked in a sharp ragged breath, and stumbled, dropping to a knee.

"A little late to pay me fealty," Saska said to him.

He snorted, looking up at her. "I know you."

"And I you. Kastor's lapdog. He's dead, you should know."

"Figured he would be." His eyes shifted up to the Wall. "Was it you?"

"Her." Saska pointed at Joy, who had come stalking over to her side, black fur shimmering, shoulders going up and down. The silver spots on her coat were like stars, more visible when the sun was down. And those eyes, like silver flame, burning as they stared right into the man's soul. "He didn't die well, Sir Gavin. Speak, else you won't either."

The threat didn't seem to faze him. He looked at Sunrider Tantario. "We holed up here after the fighting. Seemed a good spot to catch a fish or two flapping by. Didn't expect the likes of you."

"A dozen of my men are dead."

"And five dozen of mine."

"You are enemies of this land, invaders. But my lord is merciful. You are to be taken back to Aram, to face judgement for your crimes."

Sir Gavin scoffed. "The judgement of a noose. I'd sooner die here and now." He turned to Sir Ralston Whaleheart. "You're a knight, like me. Give me the honour of…"

"Why aren't you with Prince Robbert?" Saska interrupted. She wanted to know before the man died. "He marched from Aram with what remained of your army. Why did you not go with him?"

"We did, at first…then we left him. Me and these…" He glanced over at the ruin of his little band. There must have been a good sixty of them lying scattered and dead and dying across the square. Only a handful had given themselves up. Perhaps another score had run for the hills. "The boy wanted to sail north, take us all down to Daarl's Domain. Not us. We here wanted to die with blades in our fists, not wooden decks beneath our feet. I'd die a warrior, a knight, as I have lived." He looked at Sir Ralston again. "See it done. One knight to another. See it done."

The Wall looked at Saska. She thought about it. "And your other men?"

"Them too. Line 'em up. Take their heads. You ask them if you want. See if they want to be taken back to Aram in chains. None will, I'll tell you. They'd all sooner die, here and now. By Sir Ralston's blade. That's a worthy way to go."

Saska shared a look with Sunrider Tantario. "We will have to confirm it with these men," he said. "Lord Hasham's orders are plain, Serenity. Though…"

Though you have lost a dozen men already, Saska might have said for him. They could hardly afford to be sending more back to Aram as escort for a few lowly prisoners.

Tantario clearly thought the same. "Bring them here," he called out.

There were five of them. One was a greybeard, long in the tooth, a pair of others of middle years. The youngest two were in their twenties, it looked.

"It's here, or Aram," Sir Gavin said to them. "It's the rope or the Wall. Your choice."

"What choice is that," growled the greybeard. "End it now. And be quick about it." He even lowered his head, plainly asking to be first.

The others took a moment longer to think about it, though in the end, all of them decided it was better to die a quick clean death than be marched back to Aram to die slow. Clearly, none expected mercy from the moonlord. Saska had to commend their courage, at least, to look death in the face and shrug.

"See it done, then," she said, giving out the final command once the prisoners had made their choice.

The men were positioned on their knees, lined up in single file, one behind the other, so they did not have to watch. The Wall started from the back, the greybeard first to die. "Any last words, old man?"

"Does spitting count?" The old soldier spat a gob onto Sir Ralston's greaves, the spittle sliding down an old dent in the godsteel.

The Wall gave no reaction. He merely lifted his greatsword in a heave, and swung down, cutting clean through the nape of his neck.

He stepped to the next, one of the younger men. "Any last words?"

A silent shake of the head, and another head went rolling along the cobbles.

Saska watched the executions from one side, never once turning her eyes away, unpleasant though it was. *I'm the leader,* she told herself. *I gave the final command, and should watch.* She sensed that she would earn some respect for that, from the men.

Soon enough five heads had rolled, five bodies toppling, blood flowing and pulsing to the stone. Sir Gavin Trent was the last, kneeling in front of the bodies. He turned his neck to have a look, nodding in approval. "You make a good headsman, Whaleheart. Nice and clean. You sure you didn't miss your calling?"

The Wall looked down at him flatly. "Any last words, Sir Gavin?"

The gruff battle commander gave a grunt. He looked at Saska, frowning, then at the others gathered around, the Sunriders and Starriders and paladin knights, Leshie in her red armour, Del. "Might ask what all this is about, but not sure there's much point now." He shrugged, took one last look at Saska, then lowered his head. "Ah, just get on with it, Whaleheart. Had enough of this cursed land."

Sir Ralston stepped forward, and obliged him, sending his head to join the others.

Saska looked at the corpses, the severed heads, the blood sprayed across the square. She shook her head and sighed at all the killing.

It was only day one.

10

Elyon

He woke to the sound of thunder, rumbling through distant skies.

Rain crashed hard against the ceiling of the barn, a black deluge falling, hammering at the roof. He sat up from the pile of hay he'd taken for a bed, stretching a crick in his neck. A dull throb had settled in his right arm, and his right leg had gone dead. His bladder was full to bursting. He stood, stepped unsteadily to the nearest wall, opened the small hatch in his armour that permitted a good pissing, and relieved himself, sighing deep.

Lighting flashed outside, drawing white lines between the plank walls. It lasted a split second, then darkness resumed. Thunder bellowed like a dying god.

Elyon stepped over to the wide barn door, unhooked the lock, pulled it open and looked out. A rough sea raged beyond the coastal cliffs, all white tips and waves, lashed by torrential rain. That was south. In the east, the horizon was brightening.

Another dawn, he thought. *Another day.*

He yawned, picking hay from his hair, feeling more rested than he would have supposed. Not fresh, exactly, but less heavy in the head than he had been yesterday when he'd found this little coastal farm and decided to call it a night. The farm was abandoned, its occupants most likely having fled to Redhelm to the northeast of here, the closest major city. Elyon did not yet know what had come of the Helm, or Rustbridge further east. His mission last night had been to track the trail left by Drulgar. The Pentar strongholds would have to wait.

He stepped over to his cloak, left on a rusted hook on the wall, and fixed it about his shoulders. His helm he re-attached to his belt, slipping the oiled leather strap through one of the eye slits. He had not removed any other element of his armour to sleep, hence the dead leg and throb in the arm, owing to restricted movement. Elyon did not much like sleeping in full plate, but without the luxury of company and another to keep watch, he had no choice. It was a necessity he simply put up with.

He stepped back to the door, peering out across the sea. "Where are you?" he whispered, surveying the turbulent skies. His hunt had led him here, to the southern coast of Vandar, where the trail had been lost. That meant Drulgar the Dread had most likely returned to Agarath, to rest and heal from his wounds.

Some might call that good news, but Elyon wasn't so sure. The titan's maddened quest for vengeance, against Varin and his city, had taken its toll. Dozens of his dragons had been killed and Drulgar himself was wounded, perhaps enough to make him vulnerable. Another attack on a major city might just have been enough to finish him. *It's why he did not fly to Ilivar. It's why he fled across the sea.*

Elyon closed a fist. Would the destruction of another major city or two, the deaths of tens of thousands of innocent people, and thousands of soldiers, be worth it to see the Calamity come crashing from the skies? It said a lot that Elyon could not find an answer to that. *Because if he heals, and recovers, and grows stronger. If he returns…*

He turned, stepping back from the door, brushing away the last loose strands of hay from his armour. He took a moment to nourish himself on the provisions he had brought with him - quickly dwindling - and then spent a few minutes stretching his neck, back, shoulders, legs. He had come to see that stretching was important after a long day of flying, and with many more miles to cover, he did not want to seize up in the skies and risk an unpleasant fall.

All the while the rains were weakening, the skies brightening, the stormclouds moving on to the southwest in a loud and lumbering procession. A swift sunrise rose up in the east, and it seemed that in no time at all a beautiful spring day was dawning. *Capricious gods*, Elyon thought bitterly. *They like to change everything on a whim.*

He stepped outside, the rain no more than a fine mist now, the air thick with spring scents and salt from the sea. The coastal grasses twinkled all about him, the rising sun reflecting off the plains. A few gulls were cawing overhead, complaining as they liked to do. He looked up at them. "Best move. I'll be coming your way in a moment."

He drew out the Windblade, gave it a quick wipe down with an oilcloth he kept tucked into his pocket, so that it had a nice bright shine, and summoned the winds. A vortex of air gathered and spun about its length, from tip to cross-guard, quickening, widening. Before long it was embracing him from head to heel, the rain-soaked grasses capering wildly, the door to the barn rattling on its hinges. When next he looked skyward, he saw that the gulls were flapping away.

"My thanks," Elyon said, as he thrust from the earth in flight.

The lands fell away beneath him, spreading, his view widening. The sensation was still a wonder to him, a glory that only he could know, an intoxicating thrill. He smiled. *If only others could experience it too,* a part of him lamented. But another part had no such misgivings. *Mine*, that part thought. *The skies are mine, and mine alone.*

He pushed the thought aside, a persistent nuisance in his mind, like a rat, gnawing. His father had spoken of his nightly mantra, of the pathways he was building in his head. *Pathways from temptation*, he called them. "There will come a time when we must give our blades up, son," he had said. "You may think now that it will be easy, but it will not. Speak nightly the words, 'I will give it up'. Repeat them a hundred times. Visualise handing the Wind-blade over. Visualise letting it go. Imagine a world beyond the power it bestows upon you, without flight. Do this every evening, every chance you can, and when the time comes, you will not fail."

His father had been adamant, staring at him with those steely eyes. *Does he not trust me?* Elyon wondered. *Does he see in me some weakness?*

If he did, he saw the same weakness in himself. Amron Daecar knew what it was to give up a Blade of Vandar, and in the time since then, their power was only growing stronger. *He will need to give up the power to heal*, Elyon thought. *He will accept life as a cripple, lame-legged and beset by pain.* If the king could do that, Elyon could give up flight. *I have lived my entire life without it. It is a means to an end, to help win this war, a temporary power…that is all.*

He put it from his mind, turning from it, trying not to dwell on a life earthbound…a life where travel could only be done by saddle and sole…where he would never again see the world from up here, its grand scale and scope, never feel the wind rushing through his hair, feel the power of a god, the God King Vandar, thrumming in his grasp.

I am a guardian only. A temporary champion. A servant…just a servant.

I'll give it up when I must.

He drew a deep breath, several heartbeats passing, refocussing on his task.

Drulgar, he thought. *Check the coast. Make sure he's gone.* It had taken hours for Elyon to follow the trail here, and though it appeared to end at the coast, he had to be certain of that. It was possible the dragon may have flown out to sea, and returned further along the shore. *Unlikely, but possible.* Elyon Daecar wasn't going to take any chances.

He kept to the coast, then, gliding no more than a few hundred metres from the ground. The drops of Drulgar's blood - if they could be called *drops* at all, given how large they were - were easy enough to spot. They glistened like smooth black boulders, often leaving scorched craters where they had landed, setting fire to bushes and trees as they splashed down upon the earth. *Even his blood can kill*, Elyon thought.

There were other signs of his passing too. Flattened trees, black-ened fields, buildings torn down in his wake, lakes and rivers that had boiled over as he flew by, killing all the fish. Elyon had seen them floating on the surface, the water that gave them life terraforming to some sudden simmering hell. Birds had died as well, he'd seen, their nests combusting in the trees. Others that had been flying near the dragon had perished of heat exposure and fallen to the ground, their wings and feathers singed.

It all added to the trail he had followed, making it clear where Drulgar had gone.

And it wasn't here, he thought, studying the lands along the coast. He saw no lava-blood, no dead birds and floating fish, no tracts of lands scorched by the titan's passage. He felt comfortable enough to confirm his theory that Drulgar had returned to his own lands. And given where he was, and the dragon's direction of travel, he felt he knew where. *He has returned to his Nest.*

He would need to report that to his father, as well as everything else he had seen. "See what you can learn, and return. I want you back here as soon as possible," the king had told him. No doubt he had hoped his son would return sooner, but Elyon still had much to do. East, was his next quarry.

He swung his Windblade in that direction, and made at once for Rustbridge.

It wasn't so far. No more than a hundred and twenty or thirty miles, as the crow flies. As with Ilivar the day before, he flew higher, eyes cast forward, powered by godsteel, looking for smoke plumes and signs of damage, wondering if the city was intact. Slowly, surely, it came into view. And Elyon could breathe again.

Thank Vandar, he thought.

Rustbridge still stood.

The city sat astride the Rustriver, a surging watercourse so named for the reddish tint of its water. On the river's western side the city proper stood, home to a bustling trade economy; to the east were grand fortifications, towers and battlements and siege weapons. Get through that, and an enemy army still needed to cross the river itself. No easy thing. The only bridge was narrow, fiercely defended, with drawbridges on both the eastern and western shores that could prove problematic for an enemy with designs to pass.

To the south, the Rustriver barrelled along angrily all the way to the sea, eighty miles away. There were no bridges, and only the occasional ferry crossing at places where the waters calmed. North it was little better. The river itself was served by several wide tributaries that came flowing down from the southern Hammersong Mountains. These tributaries themselves formed from branching webs of rivers and rills, hundreds of them that made up the great Riverlands of East Vandar. An enemy army could try to cross there if they wished, but that would require a long march north from the coast, with no hope of being resupplied, and worse, the attentions of the Riverlanders, who from humble fisherman to highborn lord were fiercely protective of their lands. The late Lord Wallis Kanabar had always been proud of that, Elyon remembered. "No enemy army's ever marched through the

Riverlands and lived to tell the bloody tale," he had been known to say.

That left Rustbridge. The door to the west.

And it was barred shut, Elyon Daecar saw.

The banners were in full force, fluttering and flapping in the wind. They hung off poles on the battlements, and high on the towers, and outside the many tents and pavilions mounted in the great ward within the walls. On the eastern side, the fortress side, the double walls were cast in a great half moon, curving out from the river, thick with surging, triangular bastions that made the half-moon fortress look more like a star. From the air, Elyon had a unique vantage of the fortress's unique construction. *Magnificent*, he thought.

Three double gates gave access to the fort; one at the river to the north, one to the south, and one at the centre between them, where the walls extended furthest from the waters, facing east across the plains. All the gates were portcullises, heavy with godsteel bars and chains, impossible for anyone but Bladeborn to lift. Between the two walls sunk a deep moat, spiked and flooded. Drawbridges linked the portcullises.

Inside the inner wall, the great ward was vast and open, a sprawling space designed to house armies come to defend the west. Those armies had come, Elyon saw.

He smiled, hope stirring.

He could see the banners of House Amadar at the heart of the great ward, see his uncle's pavilion in its hues of pink and pale blue, the tents of his captains and commanders ringed about it. Lord Rammas was nearby, the canvas walls of his command pavilion in a sludgy grey and brown, colours common among the Lords of the Marshes. There were others, too, tents and shelters showing greyish blue and white, Oloran colours, and those of House Kanabar; silver, green, deep river-blue, with the great blade-antlered elk of their house showing on many flags. And House Payne, of Rasalan, under the command of Lady Marian. The house of the Stormwalls, grey and black and brown. And among all that were a hundred other sigils, lord and knightly, vassals of the greathouses, spreading far and wide.

My army, Elyon Daecar thought. He had been with them at Dragon's Bane, and had fought with them when the fortress was sieged. Retreated with them to Oakpike. And found them again many days later, after he'd gone off on other errands, marching down the Mudway to defend Mudport from attack.

Folly, that had been. Mudport was already destroyed by Vargo Ven and that only left the army open to attack. Nights of raids followed, dragons swooping from the skies, and hundreds more men had been taken in the dark by the bog lizards and marsh serpents and ghoulish swamp-dwellers.

But they made it, Elyon thought. There had been thirty thousand men left after the Battle of the Bane, thirty thousand who reassembled at Oakpike, thirty thousand who marched the Mudway. Some five thousand had been lost on the road, but no more. *A strong host,* Elyon reflected.

And one of several, he saw.

The Pentar banners were here too, whipping proud in silver and red, steel and blood, tens of thousands strong. They grouped to the south of the great ward, alongside a huddle of enormous stables, and would be garrisoned at the city across the river as well. The bridge that spanned the city and the fort was busy with wagons and carts and men, supplies being brought over; food and fodder, arms and armour. *Preparing for war,* Elyon knew.

The last army was most welcome, a third force assembled in the north of the great ward, tents and shelters packed shoulder to shoulder in the shadow of the high battlements, all in tight lines and rows with many lanes and alleys between them. Those colours showed mostly brown and green. Banners fluttered with the crossed sword and hammer of Tukor. One pavilion sat in a space of its own, grander than all the rest, multi-roomed with many poles supporting its canvas walls.

Elyon smiled. It was the largest pavilion of them all, larger than those of the Vandarian greatlords and heirs. *Well, that makes sense. He is a prince, after all.*

Elyon began his descent, flying lower, looking east beyond the battlements as he went. The lands outside the fortress were open and flat for half a mile, before thickening with woodland and forested hills. The trees had once come right up to the river, but those had been cut back so that no enemy could approach unseen, concealed beneath a canopy of leaf and branch. Elyon cast his eyes that way, searching the skies, and saw wings in the distance, shadows circling. *Dragon scouts,* he thought. He did not doubt that Vargo Ven was near.

The men upon the battlements were beginning to spot him, shouting to one another, raising their fists. He flew above them, his newly oiled blade gleaming bright beneath the sun. A cheer rang out, spreading.

Men began to emerge from their tents at the sound, stopping in their duties to look up. The cheering grew louder, erupting from the lips of the soldiers he had fought with, travelled with, the men who had been there at the Battle of the Bane. He felt a rush of pride at the sound, as they welcomed back their prince, a fluttering in his heart, and for a moment it felt like victory. Despite King's Point, despite Varinar and Vesryn, hope remained.

Hope.

He saw his uncle step out of his pavilion, armoured, a cloak of Varin blue at his back. Waves of chestnut hair fell from his head, bright brown eyes peering up. A smile spread upon his lips. Elyon flew right down to greet him, landing in a swirling dismount, the canvas walls of tents and pavilions billowing, men shielding their eyes.

He stood from his knee, strode forward. "Uncle."

"Nephew."

The two men wrapped arms in a strong steel embrace, then parted.

"You got here safely," Elyon said. "Did you suffer any further attacks after I left?"

Sir Rikkard Amadar shook his head. "Ven was good to his word."

The word of a snake cannot be trusted, Elyon thought, though perhaps Vargo Ven had a few shreds of honour after all. He had met the drag-onlord at the Burning Rock, invited to join him in parley. There, Ven had said his raids upon Elyon's army would stop, that he would allow them to continue to Rustbridge unmolested under terms of a tempo-rary ceasefire. *Well, he didn't lie about that. Though he did try to kill me, as soon as the parley was done…*

Elyon looked around, saw many faces he knew among the men gathering nearby. They smiled at him, nodded. Elyon returned what gestures he could and turned to look back at his uncle. "How are the men?"

"Well enough. The Pentars have helped to resupply us, though we're on strict rationing here. It's worse for the civilians across the river. Our soldiers are being prioritised."

Elyon understood. Their strength was needed. During the march along the Mudway, Vargo Ven's dragons had made sure to target their baggage train and food stores, leaving the men to march on meagre nourishment. Most of the wagons transporting their tents and pavil-ions were left unharmed, only those containing food and fodder attacked. *The dragons could smell it,* Elyon thought. *They knew which wagons to burn.*

Rikkard put a hand on his arm. His eyes were serious. "How is it in the west?"

It was a conversation Elyon had had already. With Lord Harrow, with Artibus, with his grandfather. He turned to the tent flaps. "We should speak inside."

Rikkard nodded, waving over a spearman in Amadar pink and blue. "Send word to the others. Convene a council in my pavilion." He stepped inside with Elyon.

The interior was basic; bed, chest, command table, a few camp stools and chairs to sit on. An iron brazier sat to one side, unlit. There was a mannequin upon which Rikkard could mount his armour, a rack beside it for his weapons.

"I noticed poles outside, Uncle," Elyon said. "Something I should know about?"

He had seen them when flying over, scores of enormous great posts that rose at intervals throughout the ward, like the masts of ships, surging skyward, much higher than even the tallest pavilions. They seemed to be wrapped in lengths of tarp, so far as Elyon could tell, glistening under the rising sun.

"A new defensive system," his uncle told him. "Each post is rigged with sails of fire-proof canvas. They can be raised up to create a roof above the ward."

"The *entire* ward?" Elyon asked, surprised. It was common enough for fire-proof shelters to be raised in open squares, to defend from dragonfire, but those were typically individual structures, beneath which only a certain number of people could take shelter. This was on an altogether larger scale.

"That's the theory. I'm told they have tested the system, and when all the sails are raised, they fit together almost seamlessly. The process is very quick, apparently. The engineers here are very proud of themselves."

Elyon pursed his lips. "So if a thunder of dragons should be sighted…"

"We will not need to go running for cover beneath the battle-ments. They might try to rip at the roof with their claws, but they are very smooth, hard to grip. And to get that close would make them vulnerable to the ballistas and scorpions. It's a good system. Wine?"

Elyon frowned. "It's only morning. And wartime."

Rikkard shrugged. "Life cannot stop entirely. Perhaps you have been away too long. You know how the men of East Vandar are. Half of them fight better when they're drunk."

Elyon smiled, even let out a huff of laughter. It soured at once as he thought of what he needed to say. "Uncle…I have bad news. You remember what Ven told me. About Drulgar. How he said he had awakened." Elyon had gone straight to Rikkard and Rammas and Lady Marian after that, warning them, then flown to Varinar to warn them too. It had made no difference, in the end. Varinar had fallen all the same.

Rikkard was watching him with a knitted brow, a jug of wine in one hand, a goblet in the other. He stopped, mid-pour. "It's true," he said.

Elyon frowned. The way he said it… "You knew already?"

"There were sightings, some days ago. Most of the men here scarcely believed it at first, but more and more have come forward telling versions of the same tale. He was seen flying west, to the north of here. There was a fear he was making for Redhelm, but he flew right past the city, we've heard. We have sent out crows and riders to find out where he went, but…now that you're here." He stopped, to let Elyon speak.

"Pour your wine, Uncle," Elyon said. "I fear you're going to need it."

He told him of King's Point, of Vesryn's death, and that of Dalton Taynar. He spoke of Varinar, and the desperate state of the city. And Ilivar, blessedly untouched. "Your father is well, Rikkard. I saw some-thing in him…some fire returning to his belly. He is sending soldiers to relieve Varinar as we speak."

Rikkard nodded, digesting what he'd heard. "And the Dread has fled back across the Red Sea, you say?"

"The trail led to the coast. Most likely he has returned to the Nest."

There was a knock, a man rapping steel knuckles against a support post outside. "Come," Rikkard called out.

The same spearman stepped in. "My lord," he said. "The council members are arriving. I wanted to check with you first before I let them in."

"Good man." He clearly suspected Rikkard might want a few moments with his nephew first. Rikkard turned to Elyon. "Are you happy to share, Elyon? All of it?"

You don't know all of it yet, Uncle, Elyon thought. He had made no mention of the Eye of Rasalan, and saw no great urgency to do so. He nodded and looked at the spearman. "Send them in," he said.

Rammas was the first to enter, stamping muscularly into the pavilion, all blocky shoulders and square jaw with a tight crop of hair on his head. "Prince Elyon." He gave a curt nod. The Lord of the Marshes had always been a man of few words. He wore his dull-coloured cloak, fastened at the neck with a brooch denoting his rank of Warden of the East, a simple golden circle split by a sword with its tip pointing to his right, denoting east.

"Lord Rammas," Elyon said. "Good to see you."

Lady Marian Payne followed right after, tall and graceful in her fine, smoky-grey armour, short dark hair slicked back, intelligent blue eyes taking him in. "I smell foul news in the air."

Insightful as ever. "My lady." Elyon gave her a courteous dip of the chin. "You look well."

"I would love to say the same about you, Elyon." She stepped up to him, regarding the scorch marks on his breastplate, the godsteel distorted and melted, the deep cut that split his right eyebrow. It had been sewn up, but would leave a scar. "I hope that is the worst of your wounds?"

He nodded to confirm.

"It makes you look more like your father," Rikkard said.

"It does," Marian agreed. "No bad thing. Though his scar is bigger. How did you come by it?"

Eldur, Elyon thought. It wasn't time for that yet. "I sustained it in battle."

"And these marks on your armour? Dragonfire?"

A blast from the Bondstone. He didn't say that either. He only nodded, in a sort of diversionary way, and looked back at the flaps as another man entered. To his great surprise, it was Sir Killian Oloran.

"Kill," he said, smile quickening on his lips. "I hadn't expected to see you here."

"I arrived overnight." Sir Killian's voice was a whisper, soft as a spider's step. He looked awful. As though he had just been awoken, for this meeting, by the look of those black bags beneath his eyes. He hadn't washed in weeks, either, to judge the stink that came with him, and his once-luscious locks of long wavy hair were more brown than blond, now, owing to the mud and grime. A pair of thin lips pulled into a weary smile. "How are you, Elyon? I've heard great tales of your valour."

"And I yours," Elyon said. He gripped Killian's arm, smiling broadly. "You've been putting the fear into the enemy. Just as you said you would."

Sir Killian had gone out from Oakpike with several dozen warriors, one of three separate companies with the single directive of harrying and harassing the enemy wherever possible, killing as many as they could, as brutally as they could, to put the fear of Vandar into them. Killian had hoped it would give them time, at least, to regather their own forces after the humbling defeat at Dragon's Bane. In that he had succeeded. *But at what cost?* Elyon wondered.

"How many of your men survived, Kill?"

"Too few," said the heir of Oloran. "Though each made the enemy pay twenty times over."

Elyon nodded, not doubting it. "And the other two squads?" He glanced over at Rikkard. "Has Sir Gereon returned? Elmtree?" Sir Solomon Elmtree was Killian's man, a senior knight and commander among his Oloran forces. He had led the third squad. Barnibus had gone with him. "Have any of them returned?"

He saw shared looks, doubts. "We haven't heard of Sir Gereon's company, not for a while," Rikkard said.

"And Sir Solomon?" Elyon paused, not liking their reticence to answer him. "Barnibus? Have you heard from them?"

Rikkard seemed like he was about to speak. Then his eyes shifted to the door as another figure stepped inside, brushing past the flaps. He wore silver armour, polished and unspoiled, bordered in green around the breastplate, with darker green markings at the knuckles of his gauntlets. A fine cloak of emerald-dyed lambswool hung from his back, clasped at the neck by a golden brooch in the sigil of Tukor. Hair, a rusty brown, thick with tight waves. Green-brown eyes, the colours of his kingdom, keen and confident. Raynald Lukar looked every bit the prince he was. On his head was a small crown, modest enough, silver and set with emerald jewels.

"My lords, my lady," he said, to each in turn. Then he stepped forward and took Elyon's forearm, shaking hard. "A fellow prince, I'm told," he said, a broad smile on his lips.

Elyon smiled back. "How are you, Prince Raynald?"

"Well. Tired, but well. It was a long march from Ilithor."

"We're all happy you're here." Elyon had always liked Raynald and his brother Robbert, neither of whom seemed to have suffered from the corrupting effects of their grandfather. *No, they are their father's sons, that is certain.* "The last time I saw Rikkard, he told me there was a rumour you were marching to our aid. I was not sure if I should dare believe it. But here you are."

"Here I am." Raynald said that very proudly. "And with thirty thousand Tukoran swords and spears for company, eager for a fight."

It was a strong force, there was no doubt. Elyon looked over at Rikkard. "Are we waiting for anyone else?"

"Sir Karter is on his way," Rikkard told him. "He shouldn't be long."

It took a minute or two for the knight to arrive, Karter Pentar breathing heavily as he stepped into the pavilion. The man wore godsteel plate, mixed in with some mail, enamelled with panels of deep Pentar red. His cloak was silver, slashed with crimson cuts, clasped at the shoulders with arrow-shaped pins. He was slim of jaw, hair thinning about the crown, a smallish man of two and forty who was deceptively skilled with the blade. "Apologies if I'm late, my lords, my lady," he said." I was doing my rounds upon the walls."

"No apologies are necessary," Elyon told him. "Are your brother and father joining us?"

"No, my lord. They are both in the city." Karter's younger brother Sir Kitt had command of the city defences, Elyon recalled, while Karter commanded the fort. Both answered to their father, Lord Lester, who was the younger brother to the late Lord Porus, now succeeded by his worm of a son, Alrus. There were a lot of Pentars about these parts.

"Very well then." Elyon stepped to the command table, drawing the attention of those present. "Thank you all for coming at such short notice," he said, in official tones. "I have grim tidings from the west that I must share with you."

He looked at them in turn, took a short pause, made certain he had absolute silence, and then went straight into it. Drulgar, Eldur, King's Point, Varinar. The trail to the sea. The losses they had suffered. When he was done, a silence lingered. Rammas's expression was all anger, Killian's deep in thought, Lady Marian's face betrayed nothing at all. Raynald was staring at him with youthful wonder, even envy, or so he felt. "You…*fought* him, Elyon?" the prince said. "The titan? The…the Dread?"

"And Eldur," Elyon added. He tapped his breastplate. "The Bond-stone left this mark upon me. Lesser plate may have succumbed, but by luck I had visited the Forgemasters at the Steelforge only days before. They strengthened my armour. I advise you to do the same, if you can."

"We have a Forgeborn armourer here," Sir Karter said, swallowing. He wiped his brow of a bead of sweat. "He has a workshop over on the city side, across the river. Nothing like the Steelforge, and he has not the skill of the masters there, but at a pinch he could make improvements. I'll speak to him. See…see what he can do."

"I brought some armourers as well," Raynald added, chin rising.

"The best I could muster. All Forgeborn too, Ilith's blood. Feel free to make use of them, Sir Karter."

"My thanks," the fort commander said, smiling wanly. He looked overwhelmed by what he'd heard.

Elyon could see the council members had a hundred burning questions for him, but those would have to wait. He did not want to dwell on the dragon and the demigod right now. "You've heard my tidings," he said. "Now let me hear yours. What of Ven? Is his army near?"

Sir Karter approached the table, pulling a rolled sheepskin map from an inner cloak pocket. He laid it out. Others closed in, crowding around. "Here," Sir Karter said, pointing a finger at an open expanse a little to the southeast of Rustbridge. The map showed woods, rivers, hilly plains in that area. "It's about a one-day march from the city, my lord. The enemy army is in camp there."

Or a thirty minute flight for me, Elyon thought. "How long?" he asked.

"Two days, our scouts report. He is planning his assault, we think."

Rammas gave a snort. "Planning when to tuck his tail and run, more like. We should make sure he doesn't have a chance."

Elyon looked at the Lord of the Marshes. "You think we should attack him head-on, Lord Rammas?"

He got the expected answer. "*I* do. Amadar says otherwise, of course, but he's gone soft as sodden paper. You know my preferences, my prince."

Blood and battle. Never a backward step. "I'm familiar with them, yes."

Rikkard clearly didn't like being called soft. He gave Rammas a hard glare. "Your 'preferences' got five thousand good men killed on the Mudway. You fell for the bait and men died for it. I don't think you're in the best position to lead our course, Rammas."

"Bait?" Rammas bit back. "Mudport was burning. The greatest city in the Marshlands. *My* Marshlands. What else was I to do?"

"Think. Listen to sense. Both Lady Marian and I cautioned against exposing ourselves on the road, and so it turned out. If Elyon hadn't found us when he did, we'd have only kept on marching toward a ruin. Right into Ven's jaws. Our entire army might have been destroyed."

"Water under the bridge," Elyon said, before Rammas could respond. He didn't want this to descend into needless bickering. "Lord Rammas was only marching to defend his people. We all understand that instinct, and it was one Vargo Ven took advantage of. But we're here, now, and largely intact." He looked at Killian. "Your thoughts, Kill. Would you march out and strike?"

The heir of Oloran considered it. Calm, composed, *cold,* many called him. He was much alike to Marian in that way. *If they ever had children, she'd birth a block of ice.* "I would need to take account of our forces first. And the enemy's. I would need to study the lay of the land, consider strategy. We were soundly beaten at the Bane, we must not forget. And with the greatest fort in Vandar at our back. In the open…"

"We fought in the open at the Bane," Rammas blustered. "We met their army head-on, when we might have cowered behind our walls. That's the Marshland way. The Vandarian way. The *northern* way." He looked at Elyon, as fervent as the prince had ever seen him, eyes glittering. "We had forty thousand men then, my prince. Forty thousand, against four times that. Now we've got almost a hundred, and have taken a good chunk out of Ven's stinking horde. We'd be close to evens now, good odds for any northman. The dragon is gone, fled south, you say. Now is the time to strike. *Now*."

Rikkard was shaking his head. "We must consolidate. We march out of these walls, and we expose ourselves…"

"You're exposing yourself as a coward, Amadar. Where's your thirst for vengeance?" Before Rikkard could respond, Rammas slammed a fist down on the table, wood cracking. "We lost good men at the Bane. Ten thousand of them. Sir Rodney, Sir Grant, Sir Charles, Sir Otto and Sir Oliver, Sir Karson. All Varin Knights. *Lancel*." His eyes went to Elyon, knowing what Lancel had meant to him. "And Lord Kanabar, let's not forget *him*." Rammas squeezed a fist so tight that Elyon felt like his gauntlet might just burst asunder. "He was my lord, my commander, the Warden of the East. I'll not see him die for nothing."

"He *didn't* die for nothing," Rikkard came back, exhaling. "None of them did. We killed four men for every one we lost that night. And still lost…*because of their dragons*. We march out, and we make ourselves vulnerable. You said it yourself, Rammas. Prince Raynald's host were lucky they were not attacked on the river road. We leave these walls and thousands will die before we even get a sniff of Ven's horde."

Rammas's jaw was hard as iron. "That's a risk I'm willing to take."

"And if that's what Ven wants? If this is just another trap?"

"It isn't. It's not the same as Mudport. Ven thought the Dread would assault us here. But he didn't. And now he's stopped, unsure. *Afraid*. You mark my words, he'll go crawling back to the Bane in a day or two. Unless we get to him first."

Killian stroked his chin, pensive. Even Marian seemed half convinced, her head tilting up and down in a slow, thoughtful nod. Raynald was more open with his intentions. "Lord Rammas is right," the young prince declared. "We should march out and smash them while we can. Drive back the swarthy heathens. We win a great victory here and it'll inspire all the north." He raised a fist. "My men are with you."

Rammas nodded at that.

Elyon turned to the fort commander. "Sir Karter. Can we count on you and your men, if we decide to march?"

"I would need to consult my father, Sir Elyon. My brother and I have charge of the defence of this city, but if marching our soldiers to war, my lord father must give his consent. And for that to happen he will have to seek the permission of my cousin first. Only Lord Alrus can command a Pentar army to war. It may...take time."

"We don't have time, damn it," Rammas thundered. "Forget your crippled cousin. His courage is as lame as that leg of his. What does your father say?"

"I...I would have to speak with him, my lord. But he is a man of strict protocol, and would not want to circumvent his nephew's rule."

"Does a prince's word circumvent it?" Elyon asked.

Sir Karter looked at him, doubtful. "Sir Elyon. I know that many here in the east call you prince, but..."

"My father was declared king two days ago," Elyon cut in.

Everyone looked at him.

"My lord?" said Sir Karter.

"It is official, sir," Elyon said. "Lord Rodmond Taynar is the only man who could offer and counter-claim, and he has willingly bent the knee. From King's Point to Crosswater, Varinar to Ilivar, the news is spreading. Let it spread here too. Amron Daecar is king."

"Damn bloody right he is," grunted Lord Rammas. "Your father's always been king in the east."

Rikkard and Killian both nodded; their loyalty to Amron Daecar was without question. Taynar, Amadar, Oloran, Kanabar, all would follow him now.

And the Pentars? Elyon looked at Sir Karter. "Does that change things, sir? Would your father heed me, should I speak with him? As *prince*."

"I...well, I...I'm not sure, my lord. Even if this is true. Even if you are the Prince of Vandar, only the king can overrule a greatlord. We would need a sealed warrant from your father to circumvent my cousin's rule. It might be quicker to simply seek Lord Alrus's approval. I am sure he would be willing to consider the proposal, if you were to fly to Redhelm and speak to him yourself."

Elyon had sincere doubts about that. "You will have heard of my previous altercation with your cousin, I'm sure. If I can avoid sharing in his counsel, then I will." He would need to fly back to King's Point anyway, report to the king all he'd learned. He would get his leave, then, to march out and destroy Ven's army. "I will return to King's Point," Elyon said. "And come back with a letter of command from my father, signed and sealed." He looked at Karter Pentar. "Will that serve?"

"It...should, my lord. I cannot say for certain until I speak with my lord father."

"Then I will join you, and speak to him myself." Elyon turned to the others before Sir Karter could respond. "I want you to discuss strategy," he said to them. "Gather your best commanders and captains. Compile scout reports. Determine the truth of Vargo Ven's strength. Has he been resupplied across the Bloodmarshes? How many dragons does he have? Starriders, Sunriders. Moonbears? I want a working plan by the time I return."

The others nodded.

"How long will you be?" Rammas asked him. He opened and closed a fist. "If we wait too long…"

"I'll be as quick as I can," Elyon said. "Expect me back within a day or two." He looked at Marian Payne. "My lady, a private word, before I go?"

She dipped her chin, and stepped out through the tent flaps. Elyon went first to his uncle before following. "Barnibus," he said, as the others dispersed. "You were going to speak of him, before Raynald arrived." He checked his uncle's eyes. "Is he dead, Rikkard?"

"We don't know. Not for certain."

"But you fear he is?"

Rikkard gave a sigh. "Vargo Ven has been taunting us, Elyon. Before we arrived here from the Mudway, we were told that canvas bags of blood and gore had been dropped over the fort by dragons. Some held body parts; limbs, organs, even some heads. One of those heads belonged to one of Sir Solomon's men. And an arm, with a ring on the middle finger. Another of Solomon's company."

Elyon understood. "So you believe the entire company might be dead? Barny included?"

"It's possible. Or captured. Taken for information."

"Tortured," Elyon Daecar growled. He was starting to understand why his uncle feared a trap. "You think Ven is trying to goad us? Draw us out?"

"It's something to consider. Rammas says these are typical Agarathi terror tactics, in response to our own, but I'm not so sure. We have to consider the risk that he's trying to provoke us."

Elyon nodded. "I'll see what Father has to say of it." He clutched Rikkard's arm. "Be well, Uncle. I'll see you when I get back."

He stepped past him, out through the tent flaps, into the hectic bustle of the ward. Marian was waiting patiently outside with the few soldiers who had accompanied her to the council. Elyon recognised the man Roark among them, gruff and greying, garbed in leather and plate. *The unkillable Roark*, he thought, smiling to see him. "Still alive?" he said.

The old soldier grinned, ruts in his forehead and around his eyes deepening. "Just about. Think I'm through about eight of my nine lives by now, though."

Marian rolled her eyes. "He has taken to thinking himself a cat, Elyon."

"Or Eldur," Roark said. "He had nine lives, didn't he?"

"Eight," Elyon told him. "Or seven, actually. He never died that eighth time."

"He will," said Marian Payne.

Elyon believed it when she said it. Lady Marian just had that way about her. "How is Braddin? Is he recovered by now?"

"Getting there."

"And Lark? Is he well?" Elyon always liked to make a point of checking in with Saska's old companions whenever he got the chance. Of the four soldiers who had travelled with her and Marian, only the flat-nosed Quilter had perished, falling at the Bane.

"Keeps on warbling," Roark confirmed. "Some of his songs are getting famous too. Hear them sung about camp all the time, and not just among our own men neither. You know any of them, Sir Elyon? *King Janilah's Pride* is my favourite."

That one rang a bell. "Something about shoving forks up Janilah's arse?"

Roark barked laughter. "Just that. Shall we give out a rendition?"

"No," said Marian. She looked pointedly at Elyon. "What did you want to discuss?"

He turned his eyes through the camp. "Walk with me, my lady. Roark, free to sing that song as we go. Might give us some cover to talk."

The gruff soldier smiled, holding back with the other guards as they set off through the sprawling ward, past the sea of rippling tents. At once the strains of *King Janilah's Pride* began filling the air, starting from Lady Marian's men and quickly being taken up by other groups.

Down the North Fork we walk and ride,
We walk, we ride, for King Janilah's pride…

Elyon smiled as he heard the lyrics. "What do the Tukorans make of that, my lady? Do they not find it insulting?"

"Not that I've seen. Janilah is hardly loved, even by them." She walked on another pace. "Well? You have my attention, Elyon. Please don't keep me in suspense. What is this all about?"

"The Eye of Rasalan," he said.

She raised her eyes. "I see. Have you learned where Eldur is keeping it?"

"In Eldurath, at the summit of the palace. With King Hadrin." Elyon diverted her down a side lane between tents, looking around. It was quieter here. Roark and the others remained at the end of the alley, singing loudly, directing anyone away who attempted to take that route. Elyon looked Marian dead in the eye. "Hadrin is dead, my lady," he said. "Speared through the gut by a dragonknight. I was there. I saw. The Eye…I took it back, Marian."

She blinked at him. "You…" Her face became a frown, words momentarily escaping her. It was a rare thing indeed, to shock the spymaster Marian Payne. But shock her he had. "You *flew* there? To Eldurath? You took it from under his nose, Elyon?"

Elyon smiled, basking in her reaction. "I'm not sure I've ever seen you so taken aback, my lady."

"Do not get used to it, Elyon Daecar." Her eyes hardened on him.

"Tell me what happened."

He did as he was bidden, telling her of his heist, of Hadrin, of how the Eye had yielded to him, when he feared it would not. He spoke too of Talasha, the Agarathi princess, who had said she would follow, but hadn't. "She wanted to take Hadrin with her, but that spear in his belly put an end to that. I hoped…well I wondered if one of Hadrin's cousins might be able to use it, my lady? Their blood is almost as rich as his. Many different Bladeborn can bear a Blade of Vandar. Is the same not possible with the Eye?"

She ran a finger along the line of her sharp jaw, the set of her eyes suggesting she did not have a definitive answer. "The Blades of Vandar are one made five, Elyon. Fragments of a god's heart. The Eye is *whole*. As with the Hammer of Tukor, it may require a direct blood-link to bond it. Hadrin was Thala's heir by primogeniture, an unbroken line going back thousands of years. The cousins…" She shook her head. "I'm not sure. It may well be that one or another could peer through the pupil, but what they see beyond may be too blurred and indiscernible to be of use. And that is assuming any of the cousins are still alive. For all we know, they may all be dead."

Elyon felt a little deflated at that. He had hoped for something more. "You've had no word?"

"What few reports we've had from Thalan suggest there are survivors, that some semblance of order is being restored to the city, but that's all. Nothing about the cousins. Or Amilia Lukar. You were interested in her well-being before."

He nodded. "For my brother's sake." Amilia would have been his good-sister, had certain events not transpired. *And certain Shadowknights not appeared*. Elyon had asked that Marian check in on Amilia through a spy she had installed in the palace, though they'd heard nothing of either the spy or the princess since Thalan's fall some months ago. "I still intend to fly there, find out what has happened to her," he went on. "And learn of these cousins. But…"

"But you have more pressing matters to see to."

"Yes. My father must hear of what I've learned, my lady. If I fly to Thalan now, I won't get back to King's Point for days. I can't let him wait that long."

"I understand. Returning to him is the priority. In the meantime, I will see what else I can learn here. Of the cousins, and the Eye."

It was all he could ask of her. He turned his eyes down the lane, to where Roark and the other soldiers were standing. Sir Karter had joined them now, and was waiting patiently for Elyon to finish so he might escort him to his lord father's keep, across the bridge in the city proper. He looked less than comfortable with all the singing. "I should go, my lady. Sir Karter seems like he could do with saving."

"The world could do with saving, Elyon Daecar." She smiled at him, then turned to walk away.

He wondered if he was up to the task.

11

Amron

"How much further?" Amron Daecar asked, as they stalked through the dim and dreary woods. The trees were wet, the canopy dripping from a heavy rainfall that had racked the forest for a full two hours, before finally beginning to relent. The skies looked clearer above them now, but the rains were still dribbling through the leaves, soaking into their cloaks and hair, tapping against their armour.

"Not far," growled Vilmar the Black, brushing aside a fern.

You said that an hour ago, Amron thought. "And you're certain you're leading us the right way?"

Vilmar stopped in his tracks, looking back at him in a way few others dared, eyes narrowed to the point of slits. "You may be lord of this realm, but *I'm* the lord of these woods. Every wood, every mountain, every bog where there's a monster, *I'm* king. This is my world, not yours. Do not question my skill, Amron."

Amron sighed. The huntsman had always been ungracious, ill-mannered, churlish, but utterly without equal in his field, so he forgave him these moments of insolence. Still, Rogen Whitebeard didn't much like it. "Mind your tongue, huntsman," he rasped. "Remember who you're talking to."

Vilmar glowered back at him. "I remember, ranger. I remember a time when he was nought but a squalling babe, pink as a piglet, all wrapped up in swaddling and suckling at his mother's teat. King of Vandar now, aye. But still just a babe to me."

Whitebeard grunted an unintelligible response, and Vilmar kept on going, pushing through the ferns and the bracken and the brambles, leading them deeper into the woods. After a short time they reached a stream, shadowed by a great leaning oak with several drowsy willows standing sleepily nearby. On the northern banks was a large boulder, grey and glistening with rainwater. Amron looked at that boulder, wondering. "Is that…"

"No," Vilmar growled, turning sharply on him once more. "Not big enough. And you see the moss? The way the grass grows about its edges? Does it look like that boulder has just settled here, Amron?"

The man spoke as angrily as ever.

"No, it doesn't."

"No," Vilmar agreed. "It doesn't." He jabbed a leather-gloved finger into his rutted old forehead. "Think. Use *this* before you speak. And you, ranger," he said to Whitebeard. "Stop giving me that foul look."

"I'll give you whatever look I please, hunter. If you have a problem with that…" He drew a few inches of godsteel, steel scratching leather. "We can settle it like men."

I knew this was a bad idea, Amron reflected. Vilmar and Rogen were far too alike, and had clashed a few times during their journey from Varinar too, arguing over who was the better tracker, who had been to the more dangerous lands and slain the more dangerous beasts. It was a good contest, and one that Walter Selleck had, of course, enjoyed tremendously. But now wasn't the time for their bickering.

"Put the blade away, Rogen," Amron commanded. "And stop being so truculent, Vilmar. You snap at every question."

"Every stupid question," the huntsman growled.

"Valid questions," Amron came back, his patience thinning. "We must be seven or eight miles from the city by now. And there are Agarathi in these woods, if you haven't forgotten. How long is this going to take?"

"As long as it takes," the hunter said. He turned and kept on going.

Another ten minutes passed, the skies above darkening once more with rainclouds black as tar. Every so often, Vilmar stopped to turn his eyes about, sniffing like a bloodhound, listening. His garb was wool and fur and leather, all black, scratched and stained, his face almost entirely lost within the great forest of a beard that had grown wildly from his cheeks and chin, and the thick shock of hair that summited his dome. Two dark eyes peered out from that great thicket, resting above a nose scarred and torn by a dozen savage beasts.

"We're close," he said, in that monotone growl of his. "Keep quiet, and stay behind me. These creatures can be shy."

Another five minutes went by, then several more, and no sign of their quarry materialised. Amron was trying not to express his frustration, though it was difficult. Rogen had no such inclination to remain quiet.

"I should take the lead," he said. "Your nose is failing you, old man."

"Still young enough to put you on your backside, ranger."

Rogen Strand snorted loudly, causing a few birds to burst from an old oak tree, flapping away noisily into the skies.

Vilmar could not have looked more furious. "How did you ever survive in the Icewilds? You're loud as a broadback in must."

162

"Silent as a shadow when I need to be. A challenge. We part here, you go left, I go right. Walk a hundred paces. First to creep up on the other wins."

"Accepted," Vilmar said at once, entirely forgetting their mission.

Rogen grinned - a rare thing indeed - taking that as some sort of victory. "No man of confidence is so easily goaded. You know I'm the better tracker, Vilmar. You'd not survive in the Icewilds for more than a week or two alone."

Vilmar opened his cloak, closing fingers around a savage hunting blade, the steel black as night, misting shadow. He had a dozen other daggers and knives and little axes on his person, hanging from belts and straps that criss-crossed his chest and torso like a lattice. "I would open your neck for that, boy."

"Boy? I'm forty-one winters worn, old man."

"A boy to me. In age and skill both." A growl rumbled from Vilmar's heavy chest. "We'll settle this one day. With blood. That I promise."

"No, you will *not*," Amron said firmly. He was tiring of them, tiring of this. When Rogen and Walter entered their little verbal sparring contests, at least there was some humour to it. With the ranger and the huntsman it was just bitterness and bile, a member-measuring contest that Amron could do without. Vilmar was like a bear, Whitebeard a wolf, two bloody animals growling and snapping and circling one another. He'd had all he could take of it. "If either of you makes another challenge to the other, I'll have their tongue out. Might give me a bit of bloody peace."

"Challenge?" Vilmar repeated, with growling laughter. "This child would be no challenge to me…"

"Enough!" Amron bellowed. "Gods damn it, Vilmar, enough!" His voice stirred another flock of birds from the branches, screaming and flapping as they fled. "I'm going to give you another ten minutes. If we haven't made contact by then, then I will have no choice but to turn back. I'm starting to feel like it was a mistake coming out here."

Vilmar scowled, lips forming no reply. His black eyes met the upturned amber gaze of Rogen, seething. Then he sniffed the air, turned, and marched on, wordless.

The hunt continued, the tension between them thickening. Amron kept a few paces behind the hunter, as he had for some time now, shambling along, limping on his right leg. He had taken no tonic for the pain today, and refused to touch the Frostblade lest he must. It wasn't much helping his mood, he knew. The throbbing pain, the bickering fools, the fact that they had been going for hours, now, and were going further and further from the city of King's Point with each passing minute.

I should never have come, a large part of Amron thought. Vilmar had not said it would be so far as this, and for all he knew, King's Point might have come under attack during his absence.

"Five minutes, Vilmar," he said. "And don't bloody lie to me again."

"Lie?"

"You said they were close. A short march through the woods. That we'd be there and back within a couple of hours."

"Things change. That's the hunt. Creatures *move*, Amron. And we are on the way back to the city now. I thought your sense of direction was better."

"How can it be in these woods?" The canopy was so thick in places that they could barely see the sky, and even if they could, the sun had been blotted a long time ago by the clouds. A few hours from now dusk would be setting in. He needed to get back by then. "And what do you mean, on the way back? Are you giving up, then?"

"No. They were moving, like I told you. We have reached the last place I saw them, but they have continued on toward the coast since then. Toward *you*, Amron. They are drawn to your blade. To *him*."

For once Rogen Whitebeard did not disagree. "He is not wrong, my lord. The grulok is not like other creatures. Where a drovara or fellwolf is driven by hunger and fear and rage, by the need to survive, the grulok is designed only to serve. They are emotionless, single-minded. If they have awoken, as Vilmar claims, they will look to serve Vandar, their maker. They will find and follow his champions."

A dark smile appeared behind Vilmar's black beard. "The ranger has some wisdom, it seems. Perhaps you are not so useless, after all." His smile broadened, brown teeth in a black bush of beard. "Now come. They have passed through this way. Look here, at these trees. At this undergrowth. Does it not look trampled to you?"

Rogen nodded. Amron wasn't seeing it himself. "It looks much the same as the rest."

A disappointed sigh broke through Vilmar's lips. "Have you forgotten everything I taught you? We used to hunt often when he was a boy," he said to Whitebeard. "But since then, it has been knight this, and lord that, duels and courtly duty. You are no hunter, Amron Daecar."

Amron rolled his eyes. There were few people who could make him feel like a boy again, and the burly old huntsman was one of them. "I still hunt, Vilmar. Though…mostly by horseback." *And not for a time now*, he thought. Hunting has always been a peacetime fancy, and his days of peace were done.

"Aye. Boar hunts and bear hunts. Trifling creatures, and no threat. Leave Wolfsbane in the stables and go on foot, just you. *That* is a real hunt. Man against beast, alone in the wild." Vilmar looked him up and down, shaking his head. "And without this armour. It makes you soft."

Amron was weary of this. "I fight dragons, Vilmar. Without armour I would stand no chance. Not even Varin would have. So spare me your lectures. And find these bloody gruloks."

The rain was starting to drizzle down again, pattering upon the leaves as they passed the elms and ash, the woods thickening, opening, thickening again, sometimes blotting out the fading light, sometimes breaking into clearings where little ponds and marshy bogs had formed. Knowing now that they were at least heading in the direction of the city, Amron did not carry through on his threat to give Vilmar only ten minutes. That said, he had to trust the huntsman was telling the truth. For all he knew, they were still going directly north, right into the heart of the Wandering Wood, mile after mile from the coast.

There were more rocks and boulders here, in these parts, and some larger stone formations as well that looked, from certain angles, to have been carved by an ancient folk. Once or twice Vilmar stopped them with a raised hand, then crept closer, sniffing the air in that way of his, ears twitching like a cat, to study this boulder or that. Each time he would shake his head and return to them. "Sometimes it can be very hard to tell. And the light…it is fading."

A short while later, they came upon a thatched cabin, its roof falling through, one of its wooden walls gone to rot. With the rains falling more forcefully, they took cover for a few moments, sharing food from Whitebeard's pack, drinking from their skins. "This has been harder than I thought," Vilmar confessed to them. "These creatures are elusive, big as they are."

"How big are they?" Amron asked. Most mythical stories about the rock sentinels of Vandar claimed they could reach heights of over twenty feet. Some even said up to thirty, and he remembered a picture book he had cherished as a boy that painted a grulok as a true colossus, well over sixty feet in height, and their king as well, the book had said.

"It depends," Vilmar growled in answer. "From what I saw of them, they ranged in size. The biggest was perhaps eighteen or nineteen feet, though they often walked stooped, so it was hard to tell."

"And there were half a dozen of them, you said?"

"At the last I saw. But first, just one. Others joined later, all moving south. They must have some sense of one another. There could be many more out there, Amron. Searching for one to serve."

"They found one," the king said, taking a bite of salted pork, chewing. "Janilah Lukar."

There was a frown on Vilmar's face. "How do you know this? Why have you not spoken of it until now?"

"I have only just realised, Vilmar."

Rogen's lupine eyes showed understanding. "The wounds…to Drulgar…" he said.

Amron nodded. He had seen those slashes and cuts to the titan's neck and shoulders himself, and Elyon had described them in greater detail having walked upon the monster's back. It made a deal of sense to Amron that Janilah, in his new-found guise of dragonslayer, as the rumours said, had been joined by a few gruloks himself, and that the

Warrior King and his giant servant-soldiers had battled the Dread and Eldur already, before they flew from the east.

"It would seem likely they were made by gruloks," Amron said to the ranger.

He swallowed his mouthful of pork, washing it down with a draught from his waterskin. If he was right about all of that, he wasn't certain it was good news. That the Dread could be wounded by these creatures, yes, that was positive, and that they were indeed helping to defend Vandar's realm, that too, but more than likely Janilah Lukar had been killed in the confrontation, and if that was the case, the Mistblade may have been taken. *Without it, we can have no hope of restoring the Heart,* he thought. *We will have to win the war with its fragments instead.*

He hitched his waterskin back into place on his belt, turning his eyes out through the door of the old cabin. The rains were washing down heavily now, and did not look like they would relent any time soon. "Do we need to be here, Vilmar?" he asked.

The huntsman was still looking at him with that twisted frown on his brow. "Meaning what?"

"The gruloks. If they came to Janilah, as I think they did, then will they not come to me? You said it yourself…they were moving south, toward the city. To me. Why do I need to be here?"

"Because they slowed, Amron. I told you that. They are shy, unfamiliar with this world. The gruloks fell asleep when their master and maker died. They do not know our kind, nor half the other creatures of this world. I thought it best you come to them first. This was their world before it was ours. You must show them the proper respect."

Amron walked over to the door, hanging loose on its hinges. He looked out through the falling rain, into the trees. His eyes narrowed, peering, searching. "I understand, Vilmar. And you're right. What if I were to wait here, alone? Away from all others? Would they come to me then?"

"They may. But we're on their trail, Amron. Even the ranger knows it. We're close."

You've said that a hundred times. "And how close to the city are we?"

"A few miles, three or four. Hard to know for sure."

Whitebeard agreed. He too had a remarkable sense of place. "We can be back in an hour at a good march, my lord."

"Then I'll wait here for them. If it's as you say, and they are here to serve, then they will come to me. Both of you should go."

"Go? My lord, I do not think that wise. There are Agarathi here, as you say. And other perils. It's my duty to watch over you."

"And you will. From the trees. I do not mean for you to return to the city, Rogen. Just give me some space." He turned to look at the two men, the bear and the wolf, standing side by side in that old musky woodchopper's cabin. Vilmar, the great black shadow. Whitebeard, tall and lean, with that wolfish face and glowing eyes. "Go. Move into the trees outside and watch from there. And try not to bicker too much. You might scare them off."

There were no arguments this time, and indeed the nod that Vilmar the Black gave him suggested he thought it was a good idea. They trundled out through the door, ducking into the rains, fading quickly into the trees the way they had come. There was an old tree-stump stool at one side of the cabin, strong enough to bear Amron's weight in the plate armour he was wearing. He picked it up, moving it over to the doorway, setting it down on the threshold where the rain splashed down at his feet. Then he drew out the Frostblade, his aches and ails at once assuaged, to let its great white light spill out through the trees. Setting it across his lap, its kaleidoscopic mists rising, he sat down, and waited, listening to the calming sounds of the falling rain, to the soft and distant peals of thunder, crackling from far away.

The minutes began to tick by, the small clearing outside the cabin illuminated by the Frostblade's light. Beyond, the trees were spaced apart and shadowed, thick with brambles around their boles, thorns and bushes of holly. He closed his hand around the dagger at his hip, enhancing his senses, listening. The rains grew louder, deluging down, crashing through the leaves and the branches, splashing wildly against the forest floor.

"Did you do the same, Janilah?" Amron whispered, staring out. "Did you sit, as I am, awaiting them? Did you know that they would come?"

Despite the Warrior King's treacheries, despite ordering his son Aleron's death, he had to see Janilah as an ally in this fight. *Be well*, he thought. *Be alive. Live through this war, old king, and I shall deal with you when it's done.*

A shift of shadow in the woods caught his eye, movement behind the trunks. He searched through the sound of the rain, heard the crunch of wood, the sucking of mud, a heavy sound of grinding rock, stone rubbing against stone. He sat up at once, wondering how much time had passed. No more than five minutes or so, he guessed, maybe ten. *They were close, as Vilmar said.*

He released the dagger in his left hand, closing the fingers of his right around the Frostblade. Instinct told him to stand, to remove his cloak, to shift it from his shoulders, show himself in his armour, silver and gold and glowing. Glorious, like a great warrior of old. *Worthy of their aid.*

He removed the leather boots he had worn over his sabatons, placing them aside, and stepped out from the cabin. Rainwater washed down through his greying black hair, soaking it to the scalp, trailing through the tangles of his beard. His silver-blue eyes peered out, narrow. Through the trees he could see them more clearly now, the giant shapes, swaying, advancing.

He held the Frostblade to his side, drawing upon its power. Ice-armour formed about him, crystallising, hardening, twinkling with colour. It was not for protection that he did it, but *purpose. Show them who they want to see. Show them a man to serve.*

"My name is Amron Daecar," he said, calling over the song of the storm. "I was chosen by Vandar to bear this blade. Come forth and join me."

He raised the Frostblade higher, its light spreading forth. White shards cut through the trunks and branches, past the birch and beech and aspen, the blackthorn bushes and brambles. And there he saw them, the hulking rock giants, long-armed and wide-shouldered and stump-necked, eyes like ice staring at him through the gloom. Short, thick legs stamped forward, three-fingered hands all but trailing along the ground, granite arms swinging from side to side as they went.

Then, suddenly, one of them was stepping out, past the trees, hulking into view. Amron sucked a breath, eyes rising to its towering size. The body must have been over a half dozen feet thick, a pillar of rock, thickening at the chest. A boulder-head rested upon that short block of neck, glowing eyes staring down at him. He saw features, blunt and basic. A small mouth, vague shape of a nose, craggy jaw, chipped and pitted. The creature had holes for ears. One of its arms was shaped almost like a spear, though much thicker, a weapon for cutting and hacking and stabbing. *He could skewer right through my armour with that thing,* Amron thought, marvelling.

The king stood his ground. The blood was rushing through his veins, pulsing in his head, heart thumping at his ribs. But he stood his ground. "My name is Amron Daecar," he said, even louder than before. "Champion of Vandar, your maker, and mine. King of the realm in his name."

The grulok before him was monstrous, over three times his height, fifty times his weight. It came to a stop a mere ten feet away. Behind, others were emerging, plodding forth, arms swinging, to a rumble of grinding rock. Amron counted two, four, six of them. Vilmar had told him there were half a dozen in total but now he saw another, and another, and more, back through the trees, walking single file, hiding their numbers like any good soldier should.

He looked to their leader, with the spear for a right arm. Others had weapons of similar menace, blunts and maces, swords and spears, straight and curved, some thick, some thin, long and short, every one of them savage. Most were weapon-limbs like the leader, but a few bore them in their grasp instead, clinging on with those three-fingered hands. Amron saw one holding a tree trunk, making it a club. Another was holding a longer branch with a large shard of flint wound about its end in vines, forming a rudimentary axe.

They make their own weapons, Amron thought. He would be happy to help in that regard.

The lead grulok was staring down at him with those ice-chip eyes, lidless and unblinking, though there was a primitive intelligence in them, Amron saw. Several others were coming to a stop now, slightly to the sides and behind him, lining up, still as stone. Amron did not know what else to say or do. He twisted his neck, glancing back. "Vilmar," he hissed, through the side of his mouth. "What now?"

The huntsman either did not hear him, or chose not to appear.

"*Vilmar*," Amron repeated. "Come. Translate, or…or something."

Eventually, the huntsman came stalking out of the trees, moving slowly, tentatively, with his hands out to his sides, showing he bore no weapon. The gruloks all turned to watch him, eyes following his step, judging the threat. The leader seemed to recognise him, by the slight shift in his gaze.

"My friend," Vilmar said, in a deeper, more guttural growl than usual. "Your strength has grown since I last saw you."

The lead grulok gave a deep rumble in response.

"This is Amron Daecar, our king. He leads our people against the legions of Agarath."

More rumbles, this time, from several of the creatures. Darker, and more dangerous.

"Vandar has awoken you, to help win his war. This man…he is Vandar's chosen champion. Will you follow him? Will you serve?"

The rumbling stopped. The leader stepped forward. His primordial eyes looked at the Frostblade, and then at Amron. The giant dipped its broad rock chin at him, and from its narrow mouth, came a rumbling rockslide of a voice. Two words were all he uttered.

"We serve," the grulok said.

12

Lythian

The blade hit the ground with a resounding thump that shook dust from the ceiling of the undercroft. A heavy pant burst out of Lythian's lungs, one knee dropping to the gritty stone floor.

Sir Ralf of Rotting Bridge watched on appraisingly. "Good. Very good, my lord. You are leagues ahead of where Lord Dalton was at the same stage."

Lythian nodded, taking a moment to catch his breath, then stood. The Sword of Varinar lay before him on the floor, issuing its ethereal golden light, the ground pitted and cracked where he'd been training with it. Though, at this stage, it was hard to call it training. Bonding was more apt. Mostly, he just held onto the blade for as long as possible, letting the blood-bond build as he learned to bear its weight. On occasion, he would throw in the odd swipe or slash, even a forward thrust, to test the blade's balance. It had been one such swipe that had caused him to lose his grip, sending the sword crashing loudly to the ground.

"A break, perhaps?" Sir Ralf offered. He stood leaning against a stone pillar with legs crossed at the ankles, arms folded, dressed modestly in brown leather jerkin, godsteel mail, and an old surcoat stitched with the broken bridge of his house. "You have been going since dawn, my lord."

Lythian stared at the blade, as though it was some great riddle to be puzzled out. In truth it was merely time he needed; he had proven already that the Sword of Varinar would yield to him. How quickly, was the question. "I still have some strength to spare, Sir Ralf," he said. "I'll train until I'm spent."

He stepped forward to pick it up, heaving it from the floor and setting its point to the stone. He held it there with his sword hand as his spare hand ran across his forehead, wiping away a sheen of sweat. "The guard, Sir Ralf. I want to have a go at that mannequin."

Sir Ralf stepped to the wall, where stacks of weapons rested, swords and spears in racks, sheaves of bundled arrows. He returned with a special leather guard that could be sheathed over the Sword of Varinar, blunting its lethal edge. Elsewise it would cut through anything, if applied with proper force.

Lythian slipped the guard over the blade with his spare hand, its golden glow vanishing, then turned to face an armoured mannequin, dressed in heavy godsteel plate, dinted and old. Its mists were fading, the power in the metal close to exhaustion.

The Knight of the Vale drew in a long breath, preparing, then attacked, shifting his feet into Strikeform, lunging forward on his right leg, swinging in a side-cut. The leather guard crashed into the mannequin's midriff with a blunt thud, causing it to wobble on its heavy base. At once Lythian pulled, hauling the Sword of Varinar up with all his strength, and slashed down in a diagonal strike, left to right. Once more he struck his target, the blade crashing into the mannequin's right shoulder pauldron, its vast weight leaving a deep dent. A great shudder ran through the room from the impact, and once again Lythian lost his grip, the Sword of Varinar crashing to the floor with a shatter of stone. A web of fracture lines spread from a larger fissure, walls shaking, more dust and grit cascading from the ceiling above them.

Walter Selleck gave a cough, looking over from his wooden stool. "Careful now," he said. "Much more of that and the entire roof will collapse on top of us."

Lythian dropped his hands to his knees, panting heavily from the effort. "Isn't that…why you're here, Walter? To make sure…that doesn't happen?"

"My luck has its limits," Walter said to that. "Right now, I'm channelling it into this." He pointed at the Eye of Rasalan.

Lythian filled his lungs once again, stood, and stepped over to join him. Walter had set the Eye onto a pedestal in front of him, and had spent the entire day on his stool staring at it, murmuring to it, even stroking it, from time to time. He had also taken notes, Lythian had seen, and sketched drawings in his leather-bound book. Once or twice Lythian had caught him napping too. *Understandable.* It was hardly thrilling work.

"How are you faring, Walter?" he asked. "Do you feel any sort of…connection to it yet?"

The man's shoulders bobbed up and down. "Hard to say. I'm not expecting the pupil to open for me, Captain Lythian." He paused, checking himself. "*Lord* Lythian, I should say. The First Blade takes the title of lord, is that right?"

Lythian nodded. "Officially. Though down here, you can call me what you wish. Lythian is fine, if you prefer."

He looked at the Eye of Rasalan once more, admiring its wondrous colours, the pulsing aura that emanated from the artefact.

The orb itself was in shades of blue - sea and sky, lake and river - with a great web of golden sunlit veins branching off from a jet-black, slit-like pupil. It was said that the pupil would dilate, opening, showing visions to those who mastered it. The stronger the mastery, the clearer the vision. Even great kings and queens of Thala's line could take decades to peer clearly through the Eye.

"Have you ever been to Thalan, Walter?" Lythian asked.

"Once, yes. Many years ago."

"Did you visit the palace?"

"No, though I tried. There was some official function going on, and public visits were not being allowed."

"So you never saw the Book of Thala?"

"No, and nor did you." Walter's smile was knowing. "The one on public display there is a fake. Unless of course King Godrin permitted you to see the real thing?"

Lythian shook his head. "We were led to believe the one on display was the real one. You know the story, then?"

"Of its theft? Yes. By the order of Janilah Lukar, I heard. Though where it is now…"

"No one knows for sure," Lythian said. "But Ilithor would seem likely." He scratched his chin with a weary arm, fingers already aching from his toil, muscles burning. The strength of grip required to heft the Sword of Varinar was something he had not considered. *My hand and wrist will be a ruin come morning.* "I wonder what Janilah was searching for," he went on. "We all know he was seeking the Five Blades. Perhaps it was the location of the Frostblade that he sought?"

"The efforts of a man cannot match the power of prophecy, my lord. Amron was always going to find the Frostblade. Janilah Lukar was never one of Vandar's chosen."

Sir Ralf stepped over, his stride neat as new-barbered hair. The old man moved with a smooth grace most rare for a man of his years. "Perhaps we ought to make an effort to recover the Book of Thala?" he suggested. "Prince Elyon wishes to utilise the Eye of Rasalan, find one of King Hadrin's cousins. You are here, Walter, to lend your luck to this endeavour. But perhaps more can be done? It might be that the book contains some secret to mastering the Eye of Rasalan. Something one of the cousins could use, should they be found."

Lythian nodded. He had been wondering the same thing. It was said that the Book of Thala was passed down, from monarch to monarch, for them to add their prophecies and visions. Could it not be that certain instructions were included as well? "Elyon plans to fly to Thalan," he said. "If he does so from here, Ilithor is on the way. A short stop would not add to his workload."

There was a sharp knock at the door, a brisk *tap tap tap* on wood.

"Excuse me," Sir Ralf of Rotting Bridge said. He turned and stepped away.

The door to the undercroft and store-chamber was heavy oak,

iron-banded, with hinges that had not been oiled in decades, by the sound they made when in motion. The bolts that barred the door, too, were in need of a polish. All groaned as Sir Ralf opened the door and slipped out, returning a few moments later with a slightly amused look on his face.

"Speak of the devil, and he shall appear," he said. "I am told the prince has returned."

At last. "Where is he?"

"He landed by the River Gate, my lord, some ten minutes ago."

"Then my training for the day is done."

Lythian strode at once toward the exit, passing the Sword of Varinar that he'd left lying in its guard on the floor. He stopped, thinking that rather disrespectful, went over to it and lifted it back to its brackets on the wall, removing the guard. Golden light spilled out, the heart-light of a long-dead god. *The very core of him,* Lythian thought. *The essence of his godly strength. Now mine to protect and bear.*

Sir Ralf was watching him as he joined him at the door. "Ought you not take it with you, my lord?"

Lythian paused for thought. "No," he decided. "Amron said that I should train with it down here, at the start."

Sir Ralf corrected him. "In actual fact, I recall his exact words. He said, 'train with it down here for now, until you're able to carry it at your hip. Then take it everywhere. The bond will soon grow strong'."

Lythian gave a sigh. "Your famed powers of recall are still in good working order, I see." Sir Ralf was known to have an extraordinary memory, among his other gifts. "But all the same, what Amron said is subject to interpretation. I do not yet feel strong enough to carry it at my hip, not without causing great strain to my body. That will not serve, sir. I will leave it down here for now."

"As you wish, my lord."

Lythian turned. "Walter, are you coming?"

"Yes, just a moment." Walter was scribbling something in his book. Once done, he thrust his pencil behind his ear, slammed the book shut, stood up and picked up a dark wool blanket. He draped it over the Eye of Rasalan, concealing it, then dragged the pedestal atop which the Eye sat into a darkened corner. The undercroft beneath the ruin of the Spear was fiercely protected from above, and few even knew the Eye was here, but it paid to be careful.

Walter bustled over once that was done, book clutched at his chest, looking like a mad professor with that unwashed hoary hair and scraggly, patchy beard. "Well then, what are we waiting for?"

Lythian led the way, spiraling upward around the serpentine stair, until they reached the surface half a dozen floors up. The Spear had toppled all around them, the great tower of Amron the Bold brought down by the jaws of the Dread. Somehow this passageway leading down to the underground sanctuaries and crypts had remained intact, however, when everything else had come down around it. Amron had called that, "The Walter effect.". He had been on the third level at the time.

Sir Taegon Cargill had command of the guards today, his duty to make sure that no one went down and disturbed them. "My lord," he boomed at Lythian, bowing that enormous head. "How'd it go?"

"That would not be for me to judge, Sir Taegon."

"It went well," old Ralf said. "He will be carrying the blade at his hip in no time."

The Giant of Hammerhall squinted out into the broken city. "You be careful when you do," he rumbled. "That villain who stabbed Dalton in the guts is still out there, somewhere. Might come for you next, my lord."

It was not an unreasonable concern, though just as likely the assailant was dead, or deserted. "Others may too," Lythian said. "In these dark times, men will be drawn to the blade, Sir Taegon. I hope we can count on you to watch over us? And not submit to that lure yourself?"

The big man stood taller, squeezing past seven feet, and smashed a steel fist against his breastplate with a loud, resounding *clang*. "Never," he exclaimed. "I'm here to serve you, my lord, and the king. Be your hammer. And your shield."

Lythian smiled up at him. *There could be few better*, he thought. "We're lucky to have you, Sir Taegon," he said. "Your loyalty and strength gives us all great succour."

He dipped his chin and stepped away, moving briskly through the wreckage of the city, Sir Ralf pacing easily at his side, despite his advanced years, Walter Selleck waddling hard to keep up. It did not help that he kept that great book of his clutched to his chest everywhere he went. It was a very large tome indeed.

When they reached the River Gate they found it thrumming with its usual bustle, men coming and going, seeing to their duties. Gloomy skies glowered above them, threatening rain, though by the many puddles glistening about the cobbles a strong deluge had already fallen. Down in the undercroft, it had been impossible to tell.

Lythian looked around, searching for the prince. He saw no sign. No groups of men drawn to the prince's return, buzzing about him like flies. Elyon tended to have that effect, but so far as Lythian could see, it was business as usual here.

He marched over to the men guarding the gate. "Where is Prince Elyon?" he inquired of them. "We were told he landed here a short time ago."

"He did, my lord," the lead soldier told him. He was one of the Pointed Watch, a junior captain under the command of Sir Adam Thorley. A finger pointed out onto the open fields. "He came down just outside, and went straight out there, to talk with Sir Storos. That's him, there. In the blue cloak."

"And with the Windblade at his hip, perchance?" Walter said, with a crooked grin.

The soldier didn't catch the sarcasm. "Aye, that'd be right."

"My thanks," Lythian said. "Your name, soldier?"

"Trembly, my lord. Jett Trembly."

"Trembly," Walter repeated, smiling. "Is that your real name or did you get it the day the Dread came? Must be ten thousand Tremblys out here. Myself for one. I was quaking in my boots."

Sir Ralf gave that an amused smile. The soldier remained entirely oblivious to the man's humour, however. "No. It's my real name. Jett Trembly. I was born with it."

"So you were," said Lythian. "And a fine name too." He liked to know the names of as many men under his command as possible. With Walter's jape, he would be sure to recall this one. "You're doing a great job, Jett. Any dragon sightings today?"

"One, my lord. Far out to sea."

Lythian frowned. "Why was I not told?" A dragon at sea could augur the return of the enemy armada. "I should be kept updated on such reports at once."

"I…I'm not sure, my lord. I only heard of it while guarding the gate here. Didn't see the beast myself."

Sir Ralf of Rotting Bridge turned to look at the southern battlements, where the Bladeborn sentries were on their watch upon the broken walls. "I will look into it for you, my lord," he said.

Lythian thanked the old knight with a nod, then continued through the gate, Walter bustling along with him. The plains outside were a desolation. The blackened, scorched earth, churned and stained with blood from the battle, had now been assaulted by the spring rains, turning them into a sticky quagmire. The mud sucked at Lythian's boots as he walked, bellows of thunder in the distance growing closer with every peal.

Lythian saw Sir Storos standing with what remained of his men. That number had once been much greater, though now only Sir Oswin Cole still lived, along with a pair of non-Bladeborn men-at-arms called Tucker and Marsh, good stout soldiers both. Sir Nathaniel Oloran was there as well, to his surprise. And two others in ragged red cloaks. Agarathi, clearly. *Men taken from the prisoner camp*, Lythian thought.

He hailed them as he approached, Elyon and the others turning. A quick smile broadened on the prince's lips as he saw his old mentor appear. "I hear congratulations are in order, Lythian," he called out, stepping over. "The First Blade of Vandar. I always thought you'd make a good one."

"Congratulations for a curse," Lythian said, though with a smile. He shrugged. "You know I never wanted the honour, Elyon."

They locked forearms, shaking. "The best rarely do, *Lord Lythian*. You know, it rather suits you."

"As prince does you." Lythian looked his old squire in the eye. He needed to hear it at once. "Tell me of Varinar, Elyon. How bad is it?" He braced for the worst.

"Bad," Elyon said. "Though perhaps not as bad as we had feared. Parts of the city are salvageable, at least. But the inner city…" He shook his head. "The Ten Hills are largely in ruin. The palace, the greathouse keeps…"

"Keep Daecar?" Lythian asked.

"A husk," Elyon said. "Burned out, blackened, but standing." He turned to Sir Storos Pentar. "Keep Pentar is similar, and Keep Oloran," he said to Nathaniel. "Only Keeps Taynar and Amadar are entirely destroyed, that I saw. The rest can be restored. Keep Kanabar was untouched, that I saw."

Lythian pondered that, wondering if there was some omen in it all. Some would remark that the fate of the greathouse keeps might mimic the fate of the greathouses themselves, but Lythian preferred not to put so much stock in signs and portents. "What of the palace," he asked Elyon.

"Rubble," the prince said. "Drulgar shattered it himself with his bulk. It is chaos there, as you would expect. Fires still burning. Turmoil across the Lowers. Soldiers deserting. The cost of life…unfathomable." He breathed out, sounding exhausted, and turned to look north, into the Wandering Wood. "Sir Storos tells me my father isn't here, Lyth. That he left this morning, with Rogen Strand and an individual he described as 'more beast than man'. I take it that Vilmar the Black has returned?"

"Late last night," Lythian said. "Your father told me at dawn that Vilmar had something to show him. He took Whitebeard with him and left."

"Just the three of them? Did he say why?"

"The grulok. At least, that would be my best guess. Your father was quite tight-lipped about it. He didn't say much, in truth."

"The…grulok," Elyon repeated, flatly.

"Yes. The grulok," Lythian confirmed, nodding.

Elyon Daecar shook his head, looking bemused and weary in equal parts. "I must have missed something. I remember there was some talk of Vilmar hunting a grulok a while ago, but…why? Why would Father care to go and see it, except through some morbid fascination? Is Drulgar the Dread not enough to satisfy his need for monsters?"

Lythian had no good answer for that. "Amron assured me it was worth his time. Or, rather Vilmar did. Your father seemed rather reluctant to go when I spoke with him."

"They're soldiers," Walter Selleck put in. He had a little smile on his face, as though he was one step ahead of the rest of them. "Come on, you all know that. The grulok was one of Vandar's earliest creations in life. He made them to fight against Agarath in his wars."

"So Vilmar thinks that this grulok is going to fight *for* us?" Elyon asked.

"I would imagine so, yes. I can't think why else he would usher the king away from his army at such a time as this."

"And do we know when he'll be back?"

"Soon," said Lythian. "He left early this morning."

Elyon gave another tired shake of the head. "I'd expected a reprimand for being gone so long. Now I come back to find he's off on some misbegotten monster hunt. It beggars belief. And this…" He gestured to the traps that Sir Storos had set up, the pits and chains and shelters in which the men would hide, the rotting corpses laid out as bait. "Apparently Lythian Lindar has turned dragon-catcher. Or dragon-*tamer*, even. The world's gone bloody mad."

Walter Selleck grinned. "Something I think we can all agree on," he said.

There was muted laughter all round, except from the two Agarathi, standing aside with frowns on their faces. One wore a cloak of deep red over plain padded underclothes, the sort a dragonknight would wear under his armour, which had been stripped from him after the battle, along with his dragonsteel sword. He had stern eyes, a triangular jaw, a braided black beard on his chin. The other man was a common soldier, toad-faced and physically stout. He did not seem to have any grasp of the common tongue of the north, it seemed. The dragonknight had been whispering in translation as they spoke.

Lythian recognised the dragonknight from the prisoner camp. "Your name is Sir Hahkesh, is that right?" he said.

The man nodded. He had a bloody bandage wrapped around his head from a blow he'd taken during the battle. It had been that blow that had incapacitated him, rendering him their prisoner.

"He claims to have fire in his blood," Sir Storos Pentar said. "That one as well." He gestured to the other man, whose name Lythian did not know. "I thought it wise to bring them out here overnight, my lord, should we catch some prey."

Lythian had expected to spearhead this endeavour himself, though as soon as Amron declared him the new First Blade, he had to pass that responsibly to another. Sir Storos had already been helping him set up the traps, so seemed well-placed to take on the duty.

"Have you scoured the camp for others?" Lythian asked.

"Every Agarathi has been questioned, my lord," said Sir Nathaniel Oloran. "These were the only two willing to try."

Lythian frowned. "I did not know you were helping in this venture, Nathaniel."

"Sir Storos asked that I do so, my lord. He is short on numbers, and I have full plate armour. If we should find ourselves in a fight…" The rest needed no explanation.

"Well and good, then. So long as the king has not given you any other duty, that is? This project is somewhat…speculative, shall we say?"

Oloran smiled, his face pleasant, youthful, open. Each day it became easier to forget that he had stood by and let King Ellis be thrown from Janilah's balcony, murdered before his very eyes. *He works hard to restore his honour,* Lythian thought. He could at least commend that, treacherous as his crime had been. "I took part in the watch last night, my lord," Nathaniel said. "But this evening I find myself at a loose end, so am more than happy to help."

"He speaks a bit of Agarathi too," Sir Storos added. "That's been useful, with some of them. Not many speak the common tongue well."

Lythian pursed his lips. "You have some hidden talents, Nathaniel."

"Not so hidden, my lord," the knight smiled. "I studied the language as a younger man so I might be more useful as a Greycloak. Should the king ever have need of an interpreter, or…" He trailed off, remembering what he'd done, eyes dropping at once to the ground. As a Greycloak, the ability to speak with foreign dignitaries, and interpret for a king was no more than an auxiliary duty. The *main* duty, the one single oath they swore above all, was to protect their liege, defending them with their very lives. In that single directive, Nathaniel Oloran had failed.

"A useful skill," Lythian said, with a certain bluntness to his tone. At any other time he would have been executed for his crimes. Suffering hard manners and cold stares would be his penance for a time yet. He looked back at Sir Storos. "So these two were the only Fireborn you found?" He had expected more than that.

"The only ones with any courage," Storos said.

"They fear die," growled Sir Hahkesh. "Other men. There is fire, in blood, but not brave. But me…" He put a fist to his chest. "Me brave."

Lythian smiled at those words. "I can see that," he told him. He looked at the other man. "Your name?"

He let the dragonknight translate.

"Bah'run," the soldier said, the two syllables colliding in a thick, Agarathi grunt. "Name Bah'run."

"And you're from a Fireborn bloodline?" Lythian could believe that well enough with a dragonknight. Those were typically from noble families, rich in the blood of Eldur. But a common man?

The two Agarathi conferred, then Sir Hahkesh spoke for him. "Father was Fireborned. Mother no. She was whore. From Dorath."

The man-at-arms called Tucker gave a splutter. "A *whore*? Not many whore-sons ride dragons, that I know."

"Half of the best Bladeborn sellswords were born in brothels, Tuck," Elyon told the man. "Sired by one knight or another. They can be just as lethal as the rest of us. No reason why Bah'run can't be the same."

"I can think of a few," Tucker came back. "The fact that we don't have the Bondstone, for one."

"We've been through that," said Storos. "Lord Lythian is of the understanding that the Bondstone is not required for a man to ride a dragon. The beasts can be tamed by brave men with Fireborn blood."

"So long as they're willing to die in the attempt," Marsh put in. Both men-at-arms were burly sorts, soldiers born, survivors. They had to be, given the action they had seen. Though both wore good strong steel, it was castle-forged only, oiled against dragonflame but still vulnerable during battle in a way that godsteel was not. They had fought valiantly all the same, never shirking their duty, never showing their fear.

So when the dragonknight Hahkesh said, "We willing. Both. Both willing to die," and pointed at himself and then Bah'run, both Tucker and Marsh dipped their chins, showing them signs of respect.

"Aye, suppose you are, then," Marsh said. He had reddish hair, thinning at the crown, a fiery beard on his chin. "Not a nice way to go, though, I wouldn't think, eaten when trying to tame a dragon. But suppose there's honour in the attempt."

Lythian thought of Sir Tomos Pentar, Storos's younger brother. He remembered the deformed, pygmy drakes, crawling all over him in the Pits of Kharthar, feasting on his flesh, gnawing at his bones. It hadn't been nice at all.

Sir Hahkesh nodded firmly. "Honour in attempt," he said, agreeing. "Honour in brave. Like rider of moonbear. These bravest men. Bravest in world."

"And women," Walter added to that. "Female Moonriders are not unheard of."

"Women, yes," the dragonknight agreed. "Women Fireborned too, very brave. Misha, she our greatest."

Misha the Magnificent, Lythian thought. *The Skylady of Loriath.* She had been one of the old prophets who'd spoken of the rise of Eldur, along with Pullio the Wise and Quarl the Blind, many centuries ago. Each of them had foretold the rise of a benevolent Eldur, awakening to bring the world into balance and end the War Eternal. Somehow, all three of them had got it wildly wrong.

"How would you go about it, Sir Hahkesh?" Elyon wanted to know. "Taming a dragon? Without the Bondstone."

The dragonknight's dark eyes shrivelled to a squint, as though not fully understanding. "I use this." He put a fist to his heart again. "Fire here. It call to dragon. Some may listen, others no."

"And those that don't listen?"

"Will try to kill. Same as Lightborned, with wolf, cat, and bear. Many die this way, when try to bond animal." He waved a hand between himself and Bah'run. "No different. Without Soul of Agarath, there is more danger. But still possible to bond, when brave."

179

"And if it works? What will you do, as a dragonrider, Sir Hahkesh? Will you kill your own men? Will you turn your cloak to the north?"

"Turn…cloak?" The dragonknight did not seem to understand the phrase.

"He means to ask if you will fight on our side," Lythian said. "That can take many forms, Sir Hahkesh. We will not be expecting you to kill your own countrymen." He gave Elyon a stern look.

The prince shrugged. "I'm just wondering what the point of this is, if you're not expecting these dragonriders to actually do any fighting."

There were a few murmurs and mumbles among the others. "He's got a point, my lord," said Tucker. "I mean, Sir Pagaloth's a mean bloody swordsman, isn't he? And all he did during the battle was sit in his room twiddling his thumbs. Not much point in having Agarathi on our side if they're not going to swing a blade. Or breath fire, in this case."

More murmurs. Lythian was half tempted to just wipe his hands and be done with it, with all this naysaying. "I'm *trying* to unite us, that's all. A man can serve in other ways than by killing. For one, simply *not* killing is a form of service. If the north and south stop trying to cut chunks from one another, Eldur's armies will rapidly shrink. That alone will make him easier to vanquish. Why does no one seem to understand that?"

"Thousands of years of instinct and warrior breeding, that's why," Elyon said. "Look, I get it Lyth, I do, but I'm just saying it won't be easy. It's a good thing you're trying to do here, typically bloody right-eous and noble for the most righteous and noble man I know. And I'm right behind you, so you can count on my support. But only when it makes sense."

Lythian's brows knitted. "Makes sense? And what do you mean by that?"

"I mean that there's battle brewing in the east, and I'm not about to sheathe my sword on account of your vision of unity. Nor will I suggest it to anyone else, or try to parley with Vargo Ven. I have been there before, and it won't lead anywhere good. So battle it will be. Battle and blood. Once I get Father's approval."

His words left a short silence behind. Lythian could see the light of excitement in the eyes of Sir Storos Pentar. "You mean to say…Rust-bridge, my prince? It hasn't been attacked?"

"Nor Redhelm. You can breathe easy for now, Sir Storos. I spoke with your cousin, Sir Karter, and your uncle, Lord Lester, this morn-ing. Both are well, and willing to muster their army so long as Father signs a warrant, as king, circumventing the command of Lord Alrus." He looked around. The men were leaning in, eager to hear more. "We have the Tukorans with us too, under the command of Prince Raynald Lukar. Thirty thousand of them, eager for a fight. In sum we might have enough to destroy Vargo Ven and his horde. And free the east of the enemy's grip."

"For Vandar!" Sir Storos exclaimed, going so far as to draw out his blade, thrusting it into the drizzly skies. "Gods, how I wish I could be there too, and fight alongside my kin. Might you fly me over there with you, Prince Elyon?"

Elyon gave that a laugh, as Storos lowered his sword. "If only. At the edge of need I could probably do so, but feel I'll need my strength. And as to that, I feel the pull of my bed. And a nice large cup of wine." He smiled at them. "Good luck tonight. Lyth, are you coming?"

Lythian nodded. He gave parting words to the others before leaving. "Go well," he said to them. "If you snare a dragon, come wake me at once. And be ready to kill it, if you must. Don't throw your lives away needlessly," he added, for the sake of Sir Hahkesh and Bah'run. "If a dragon doesn't call to the fire in your blood, let it be. Do not push beyond your limits."

He left them there to climb down into their shelters, well concealed within the pits they'd dug with roofs of grass and mud. The plan was simple enough. Should a dragon swoop down to feast on a corpse, any tug or pull at the body would trigger the release of a heavy chain net, fired from a special ballista hidden in the back of a nearby wagon. Sometimes those chains would be enough to snare a smaller dragon. If a larger one descended, the men would be ready to reload and go again, as it struggled to free itself. It was a proven and effective means of trapping the beasts during battle. But in such cases, the dragons were always killed as soon as possible, slain by a storm of sword and spear. Keeping them disabled and alive was entirely new territory.

"You're a forward thinker, I'll give you that," Elyon said, as they walked back to the city. "Do you actually think that will work?"

"I would imagine the odds are low," Lythian admitted. "But it's worth a try, do you not think?"

Elyon seemed ambivalent about it. "What did Father say?"

"Much the same as you. Though he appreciates the possible benefits. If we can get a few of our own men airborne, that can only be a good thing. For scouting. Delivering messages. Transporting men and arms. Right now we're relying too much on you. I am only trying to change that."

"So you're doing this for me? To lessen the burden on my back."

"Mock me all you like, Elyon Daecar. Much of what I do, I do for you and your father."

The light was dimming quickly now, the western skies purpling in a premature dusk. Out there the clouds were not so thick, yet overhead they loomed, dark and brooding, the rains falling in a misty mizzle.

"So tell me of this battle," Lythian said. "How far is Vargo Ven's army from the city?"

"A day's march, I'm told."

"Their strength?"

"I'm not sure. I only stopped in briefly before leaving. They're compiling intelligence while I'm gone, putting together a battle plan. It should all be ready by the time I get back."

"And when will that be."

"Tomorrow."

Lythian balked. "So soon?"

"Why wait? If there's battle to be had, I need to be there."

"And you're certain this is the right course?"

"Yes," he said at once. Then, "No. I…I don't know, Lyth. You sound like Uncle Rikkard."

He took that as a compliment. "Rikkard Amadar is a sound strategic mind, a brilliant swordsman, beloved captain, and a very handsome man. I find the comparison quite acceptable."

Elyon gave a chuckle. "He would say the same about you. I long for the day that you fight alongside one another." He looked over at him. "So long as you haven't lost your taste for battle? All this talk of unity…"

"I will still do my duty, when I must, Elyon."

"But you'd prefer not to? If we could come to a ceasefire…"

"Then that would be the best thing for everyone, yes." Lythian had and always would be the servant of Amron Daecar. He would die for him, and kill for him, and do what he needed to do in order to protect his realm, his people. Yet despite all that, the thrill of battle he had felt in his youth had long since deserted him. It was a young man's game, no great joy for an ageing knight like he was, careworn and world-weary. The great glorious battles he'd fought during the War of the Continents, the Twenty-Fourth Renewal, alongside Amron and Borrus and Killian and others felt very different to those they fought now. Terrible as that war had been, it had never been like this. *We fought for land, for glory, for our families, for Vandar.* Now they were all fighting for their very survival, and the survival of the world as they knew it. It was altogether more calamitous. A world-ending war, a true apocalypse, where the very nature of existence itself was being challenged.

"There are only two entities that need to die, Elyon, for this war to come to an end," Lythian Lindar said. "All we can do is move the pieces upon the board, until we reach a point where we can make that happen. Perhaps the clash of two hundred thousand men is one such move. Or perhaps such a move can be bypassed, to seek a better end."

Elyon considered that carefully, nodding slowly as they walked. "So you think I should seek parley with Ven? Try to make him see sense again, as I did before?"

That hadn't worked out well, Lythian knew. Ven had only tried to kill Elyon as soon as the parley was done. "Do you imagine it would make a difference?"

"Honestly? No. Vargo Ven is driven by fear of Agarath and I don't think he'll want to displease him. Retreat would show weakness."

"Only the strong survive," Lythian murmured to that. They passed a great ditch, the earth torn open by the talons of Drulgar the Dread.

It brought a burning question to mind. "Do you know where Drulgar went, Elyon? After Varinar?"

He pointed. "South, across the Red Sea. I tracked his trail to the coast, east of Nightwell. I assume he has returned to the Nest. To rest and heal."

It ought to have been good news, yet somehow the idea of it made Lythian's skin crawl. That this dragon god was still out there, brooding. That he could unfurl his wings at any time and return to cast them all in his shadow.

"The optimist in me hopes he's done," Elyon was going on. "He saw Vesryn as Varin, and he took his vengeance. And then Varinar…" He had a pained look in his eye. His uncle's death had wounded him deeply, Lythian knew. "Perhaps that will be enough."

It will not be enough until all the world is burning, Lythian thought, gravely. But he said, "The Steel Father and his city were not the Dread's only rivals, Elyon. There are other challenges he may yet seek out."

Varin had always been his principal enemy, Varinar his principal target, but there were many forces of the ancient world against which Drulgar the Dread had fought. Legends of great moonbears, fighting him a dozen to one. Of the sand giants of the god Pisek, crawling across his scales. The Eagle of Aramatia driving him away with his blinding light. The old titans from an ancient time, Fronn and Galaphan and Celaph and the rest, who had all fought him in their earth-shattering battles. In these primordial wars it was not always Agarath against Vandar. The gods of north and south would clash among themselves as well, bickering, battling, forging new creatures to fight and die for them, to be raised anew if effective, and discarded if not.

Drulgar would return now to that olden world, Lythian feared. *He will seek new foes to fight. Seek opponents worthy of his wrath.*

He was musing on all of that when he heard Walter say something behind them, breaking his train of thought.

He turned, saw the little scribe pointing away to the north, to the bridge that spanned the Steelrun River a little inland. On the eastern banks, the Wandering Wood spread out, the vast forest of many smaller woods and groves into which thousands of men had fled at the coming of the Dread.

The woods that Amron had entered, early that morning. With the hunter and the ranger for company.

"They're back," Walter said. "My eyes are nothing like either of yours, but I'm sure I see three men out there."

Lythian took a grip of his godsteel dagger, enhancing his sight, the darkness receding. The Knight of Mists had excellent night vision with godsteel to grasp. He peered forward, and true enough, Amron, Whitebeard, and Vilmar the Black were returning. They made a fearsome trio, and all of them looked well and unharmed.

He breathed a sigh of relief.

Elyon did as well. "Well, his timing could not be better. Come, Lyth, let's seek his counsel. I'd be eager to hear what he…" And he stopped, voice trailing off.

Lythian did not need to ask why. He, too, was staring. And even Walter Selleck, far away as they were, could see that the king and his companions were not alone.

"Gods," the lucky little man whispered.

No, Lythian thought. *Giants.*

13

Talasha

It was a place thick with memory. A place of love and life and death. Where a demigod had lain, in stasis, unwilling to awaken despite their toils. Where a long-lost prince had spoken to his followers with passion and pride of their mission.

To find the Fire Father, and raise him from the dead. So he might bring balance to the world.

Or end it, Princess Talasha Taan thought. *Cousin Tethian was deceived by a lie.*

The air was cool here, and fresh after the recent rains, redolent of the happier times that Talasha Taan had spent in these wooded hills in the wilds of the Western Neck. It was here that she had fallen in love with Lythian, her sweet captain. She remembered fondly the days when they would hunt together for game, walking alone in the forest where their love might blossom away from the glares and mutters of the men. One day she recalled with particular fondness. A day when a fearsome storm had rolled in from the west, and they had been forced to spend the night together beneath the cover of a rocky overhang, many miles from camp.

I broke him that night, she thought, reminiscing. *I finally got him to abandon his oaths. To submit to his feelings. And to me.*

She smiled, remembering the touch of his lips, the trace of his fingers down her skin. He had been nervous, even afraid, restrained by devotion to his long-dead wife. *Yet he gave himself to me all the same. And I him.* How she missed him so.

She reached out, gripping the spit, turning it over the fire. Wild game was hard to come by here, just the same as it had been back then, but there were still some fish in the nearest river, and Talasha had managed to spear a trout; one of meagre size, yes, but it would serve for now. She reached down to grab at a handful of dried kindling, feeding the fire. The flames leapt, licking at the fish's skin, sizzling, fat popping.

Cevi licked her lips. "Is it ready yet?" she asked, breathless with anticipation.

"Soon." Talasha's stomach was rumbling as loud as her handmaiden's, but she would not yield too early to her hunger. *I have gone two days without a proper meal. Another few minutes will not hurt.*

The skies were beginning to darken, a gloomy dusk setting in. Nearby, among the old fort ruins, the shadow of Neyruu was curled up, sleeping, recovering from the wound she had taken during the flight from Eldurath over a week ago. The wound was not life-threatening, though savage enough, several deep gouges torn into her flank from another, larger dragon. Talasha had felt the pain herself, felt the bright flare of agony in her right side, as Neyruu did. She had flinched, even screamed, as she felt the claws of Paglar rake across Neyruu's scales and slice down into her flesh, tearing, felt the terrified thumping in Neyruu's heart as the bigger dragon snapped forward with his great salivating maw, trying to kill her.

He had missed. Neyruu was quicker - the swiftest in all of Agarath, Kin'rar had always claimed - and Paglar was no match for her speed. As soon as he lost the element of surprise, Neyruu tucked her wings and dove, outmanoeuvring him, then lost him in the fume of smog that hung above Eldurath's streets. The bigger dragon, a dark grey beast with touches of purple on his flanks, had continued to hunt them for a time, but soon enough his presence behind them waned and they escaped away south of the city, flying hard and swift across the Great Grasslands before veering east, into these hills.

That had not been by Talasha's command. Wounded, suffering, Neyruu had sought comfort, like an injured cat seeking a familiar place to hide and sleep and heal. So she had flown here, to the Western Neck, to the place where Kin'rar Kroll had been killed, slain by Ashun Klo in his wild state of grief on that night that Tethian had died. *The night that Eldur awoke,* Talasha thought. *The night of the parley at the Nest, when the whole world changed.*

Cevi's eyes were bulging, staring at the fish with a desperate yearning. A loud rumble filled the air, of thunder one might have thought, but no, it was only her stomach. "Surely…is it not ready yet, my lady? I don't know if I can bear this any longer."

Talasha smiled. She was glad to have her with her, more glad than she could say. "Go on then, Cevi. But be careful. The meat is very hot."

The girl grinned, took the spit from the flames, and placed it down on a rock. She blew on it fiercely, eagerly. Touched it, cringed, drew back, blew some more. Talasha's smile did not wane. "Calm, Cevi. Take your time. Give it a moment to cool."

The girl nodded, fingers fidgeting, staring at the fish all the while, willing it to cool. To Talasha, a Fireborn, the fish would be easy enough to handle. But Cevi did not have the blood of Eldur in her veins, and would only blister her fingers and mouth if she tried to eat too soon.

A few more moments passed before the fish had cooled enough for them to eat. After that they reached forward, tearing away strips of fatty meat from the bone, sucking on the skin, licking grease off their fingers after every bite. Not a bit of it went to waste, not a morsel or a scrap. Cevi even ripped off the larger bones and sucked on them, extracting every last little ounce of fat and flesh she could. It had been long days since they'd eaten properly. Nothing had ever tasted so good.

"Will you catch another tomorrow, do you think?" Cevi asked, wiping her mouth. She had a large grin on her face, a thin length of bone in her grasp. It was amazing what a good meal did for one's spirits.

"We'll see," Talasha told her. She had waited for hours to catch that one fish, exercising a patience learned during her youth hunting the delta. Talasha had always been a good huntress, though mostly with quiver and bow, not the three-pronged fishing spear she'd carved to hunt the river. Some of her fondest days in her youth had been spent around the Askar Delta, preying on duck and goose and sometimes larger birds as well. She would catch fish too, on occasion, and frogs and turtles and snakes. She even stalked and killed crocodiles, from time to time, when seeking a stiffer challenge. Though a princess by name, she'd always been a huntress in her heart. It was those skills that were keeping them alive.

The princess stood to stretch her legs, shaking out her long jet hair.

"Are you going to sit with her, my lady?" Cevi asked, looking over at Neyruu.

"Not today. She wants to be alone." Talasha could feel that well enough, and it hadn't changed for days. She understood. Neyruu and Kin'rar had been a bonded pair for long years, and their bonding had been natural. *She flew from the Wings to the Nest, and chose him, as he climbed up the Stair to the Stars, and chose her. They were bonded by tradition, by natural law. They chose one another. But us…*

It was different with them. Eldur had brought them together. The Fire Father had forged the bond. Their souls were still entwined, of a sort, but the fetters that bound them were not so strong. *I will never understand her as Kin'rar did, nor her me,* she lamented. *Our bond will never delve so deep.*

The fire was beginning to gutter out. Cevi picked up more kindling, preparing to throw it on. Talasha stopped her. "No. The fire was only for the fish. To cook. We don't need the warmth, and the light…"

Cevi's youthful face curdled. "You think we're in danger here?"

We're in danger everywhere. There is no safe place anymore. She said none of that. Cevi had been through a lot already and didn't need to hear

187

her doubts. "It's just a precaution," she told her. "The light of a fire can be visible from miles around at night. Best we put it out."

The princess stamped down on the dying flames, kicking dirt to choke the smoke. Then she picked up her waterskin, gave it a shake, felt that it was almost empty and said, "I'll go and fetch some water from the river."

The girl stood at once. "I should come with you."

"No need. The river is not far."

"But…"

"Stay, Cevi. Neyruu is near. No harm will come to either of us, I promise." She smiled, cupped the handmaid's soft tan cheek, showed strength to stymie her fear. "I'll be back soon." She picked up her fish spear, fist closing about the haft. "And who knows…maybe I'll catch another trout for breakfast?"

The girl raised half a smile at that, then sat, nervously looking around. *She doesn't like being here alone,* Talasha knew. *There are ghosts here in these woods.*

"Move closer to Neyruu, if it makes you more comfortable. She may look like she's sleeping, but she's a dragon, Cevi, and always alert. She won't let anything happen to you."

"It's…you I'm worried about, my lady. What if you get lost, in the dark. Without firelight…"

"My eyes will adjust, and I'm used to stalking in the night. I will be fine, Cevi." *And I want to be alone.*

Talasha turned and stepped away into the forest, over clumps of sedge and roots and sticks. The undergrowth here was thick and slick, damp from the rains, sprouting with bushes and thorns, and here and there were deadfalls from recent storms as well, tangled heaps of fallen trees around which she was forced to go. Talasha moved quietly, stealthily, passing beneath the branches and past the boles, letting her eyes grow accustomed to the deepening dark as the forest floor curved gently downward. Further off, she could hear the tinkling of the river, a shallow watercourse that would wend from here down through the hills toward Loriath in the west, and the great lake south of the city.

Loriath, founded by Lori, eldest son of Eldur who took the throne at his father's death. *Or disappearance,* Talasha thought. Eldur had never died, only crept away to sleep. *He feared death, as much as any man. It was his last life, without Agarath to resurrect him, and he chose to sleep instead.*

"Craven," she whispered, out loud, as she padded silently through the wood. "You were weak, Fire Father. And now look what has come of your cowardice."

She hoped, one day, to say that to his face.

A few rays of purple twilight were still piercing the high canopy, sinking down through whatever gaps and openings they could find in the trees. Talasha was no Bladeborn, bore no godsteel to heighten her senses, but knew how to move in the dark. *Night hunts on the delta,* she thought. *Creeping through the wetlands for prey, without ever making a sound or a splash.*

She clutched her spear in her grasp, prodding at the ground wherever it looked unsteady, rooting out whatever creatures might be lurking there unseen. There were snakes in these parts, she knew, and other crawly slithery things, some of which were venomous. Most likely her high hardy hunting boots and leather garb would protect her, but she could not be sure, so she took the necessary precaution, setting her feet only when she was certain it was safe.

I should be wearing my armour. Talasha owned a wondrous suit of dragonscale armour, all red riveted plates and fine links of dragonsteel mail, though it had been taken from her when she was thrown in a cell with Hadrin, the mad Rasal king. After Elyon Daecar had freed her, she had gone running to her rooms to find it, but it was nowhere to be seen. Instead she had pulled on a pair of old hunting boots, leather tunic and dark crimson overcoat, before rushing out to leap into Neyruu's saddle and fly down into the city to find Cevi. Her handmaid had, mercifully, been where she left her, in the safehouse she'd placed her in, and they had managed to escape into the skies before they were spotted.

And then Paglar came. Then the savage slash at Neyruu's flank and the desperate escape out here, into the wilds.

Talasha crept on, passing around a large deadfall. Ahead, a clearing appeared, ending in a cliff that plunged about fifteen metres to the wooded slopes below. She went to the left, where the descent was more gradual, spear in one hand, using the other to steady herself against tree trunks and stumps. When she reached the bottom of the cliff, the ground levelled out again, trees regrouping, thickening. In this part of the forest they were mostly spruce and cedar, though sometimes hulking sequoias bullied themselves into a space, dominating all the other trees and plant life around them.

The sound of the river was growing louder now, babbling down over a series of mini waterfalls and rapids to the north. She continued along her path, down another gentle decline, past one of those surging sequoias to her left, another craggy granite cliff to her right. Her eyes scanned the floor, narrow, searching, prodding with her spear all the while. Once or twice she heard a scurrying sound, and her eyes darted, but too late. Cevi might not like the idea of the princess going off after dark, but the night could be good for hunting too. *Some creatures only come out after dark*, she thought. At the river, especially, there were some nocturnal frogs and toads that would make a tasty dish.

Ahead, the trees were thinning, the movement of the river carving out a space through the woods. There were many streams and brooks here, though none were especially large or deep, not this high in the hills. Lower down they would group and merge to create fierce flowing rivers, but not here. It was one less thing to worry about. Getting swept away by a surging river, swollen by the rains, would be no way to go.

The tree line ended abruptly, giving way to a short slope that plunged down to the riverbank. Talasha used her spear to get down safely, digging the prongs into the soft muddy earth. The river was not wide - three or four metres only - and came up only as deep as her thighs. There were rocks scattered within it, around which the water rushed in frothing eddies. Talasha stepped across to one of them, moving her eyes upriver. The trout here were known to swim upstream to spawn and feed, but that season was coming to an end. *They will be further down in the valleys*, she thought. In the larger rivers, thousands of the fish were caught each year, but up here the pickings were slim.

She kept her eyes peeled all the same, her ears pricked for the croak and ribbit of toads and frogs. She had chosen the right spot, where the canopy opened above her, in line with the rising of the moon.

But these clouds…

Were it not for them, the moonlight would shine down upon the water, lighting the scales of the passing fish and shining off the wet skin of the amphibians.

Yet the skies were overcast, swamped, and dark, the moon no more than a faint glow behind them, moving up between the trees, black fingers reaching skyward. Talasha waited. The weather was prone to change quickly here, and leaden skies now did not mean leaden skies in an hour. By then they might be full of stars, the moonlight bright, her quarry exposed. *But not right now*, she thought, leaning on the butt of her spear.

That grew quickly uncomfortable, so she scanned for a wider, flatter rock, saw one further downriver, waded her way toward it, and sat, crossed-legged, at the heart of the stream. She had liked to do that as a child. Sit amid the river, with the others fishing the banks, as though claiming domain of her own private little island.

And now all this land is mine, she mused, reflecting on all those who were gone. Her uncle Dulian, slain by her brother, Tavash, who in turn had been sent to the Eternal Flame by Eldur for the crimes of avunculicide, regicide, and matricide for killing his mother. *Our mother,* Talasha thought. *Talantria, who would have been made queen at Dulian's death.* Tavash had killed her to pave his way to power, but in the end his rule had been cut short. *Not short enough. He should never have been made king in the first place. Tethian never should have left.*

But he had. The prince had gone missing many years before, drawn to the prophecies of the old wise scholars, vanishing in his quest to find Eldur's tomb and raise him from the dead. Most had thought that Tethian was dead himself, and Tavash was one of them. So he'd killed his mother, killed his uncle, and won the crown by treason.

And died for it. *Dulian, Talantria, Tethian, Tavash. My entire family, gone.*

Talasha picked up a pebble that had washed up on her rock, squeezed it, tossing it fiercely into the water. She watched the splash, spear poised. Sometimes that might be enough to attract a passing fish, but no, not this time.

Her spear settled back into her lap.

Queen of Agarath, she thought, chewing on the title. Were it not for the return of Eldur, she would be Queen of Agarath right now. She wondered on that for a while, unsure if she would even want it. *Not this Agarath, anyway.* The land she loved had been warped and twisted, and Eldurath had fallen into the grip of the zealots and fire priests. Each night, mass sacrifices were made, great fires burning bright across the city, feasting on the flesh of the non-believers.

And that was just Eldurath. Other cities had surely fallen into the same mania. And beyond them, in the lands between, the monsters ran amok, more reported every day. And there had been word of cataclysms too, great twisting storms and shuddering earthquakes and lava boiling up from the earth. Ever since Drulgar had burst out from the Wings, the world had grown increasingly unstable.

Like my dream. Talasha still remembered it clearly - the wall of fire approaching the city, the Ashmount exploding into a torrent of flame. She could only stand upon her balcony and watch as it consumed all of Eldurath, bathing one and all in Agarath's wrath and taking them to his Eternal Flame. By morning she would always tell herself it was only a dream, but how could she be sure? How could she be sure of anything anymore?

Another pebble was in her grasp. Another throw, another splash. She thrust her spear down into the river, speculative, and it came back wet, catching nothing but water. Her eyes lifted. Above, the skies were breaking up a little, thin scars appearing between the clouds. Moonlight shone down upon the woods. The river glimmered, but only for a moment, darkening once more as the scars closed up.

Her wait went on. Fingers of worry reached in, closing around her heart. She feared for what had come of the north, feared for what Eldur and Drulgar might have done. "I should have warned him," she whispered. "Elyon. I should have told him what I knew."

But there hadn't been time. Elyon Daecar had come and gone like a tornado, bringing blood and butchery in his wake. They had shared words, but few, and she had not thought to speak to him of Drulgar the Dread, of Eldur's plans, of what Hadrin had glimpsed in the Eye…

A gentle splash in the river caught her attention, a fish breaching briefly above the water before wriggling away downstream. She gripped her spear to throw, but too late. The fish was gone. She settled once more.

She saw a second ripple almost at once. A shard of moonlight shone through the clouds, and *there*, she saw the fish. She surged to a knee, steadying herself, crooking her elbow, spear clutched tight in her grasp. Aiming, her eyes moved with the fish coming her way, passing around a rock, tail thrashing as the water shallowed, then zipping away into deeper water.

She threw, unleashing the spear. A splash, a flash of movement, and the trout shot away right past her rock.

"Damn," she grunted. That one was close.

Her spear had lodged itself into the pebbly riverbed, water moving around the shaft. She went to retrieve it, wading forth into the chill water, then back to her rock, to wait.

Her thoughts continued to spiral. *King's Point*, she thought. Ulrik Marak had led the great armada there, and she knew that Amron Daecar was defending the city. Most likely Elyon would be there too, and Lythian, perhaps him as well. But there was no way of knowing for certain, and if she flew there, to that great coastal city, with its dozen thick towers and fourscore ballistas, and the thousand bowmen upon its walls…

No, too dangerous. Even if she flew with a white flag in her grasp, waving it for all to see, they would fire upon her, she did not doubt. Her only real chance had been to travel with Elyon, to have the knight as escort. But that had never been likely. Fast as Neyruu was, she had heard the Windblade could bear a man faster. *Where to go, then, when Neyruu recovers? Or do we just stay here, and hide? Or somewhere else. Somewhere far away. Do we find somewhere to wait out this war?*

But that would not be likely either. *Eventually, the fire will find us. It will spread and consume us the same as all the rest.*

Her eyes were growing heavy, thoughts circling like a bird of prey, searching for something to dive on, cling to, some morsel of hope for nourishment. Talasha Taan was a princess, even a queen. She had a duty to her people, a duty to the world, a duty to do something to help. *A good leader serves,* she told herself. *A good leader does not hide.*

She remembered, then, that she had come here for water, and had told Cevi she would not be long. The girl would be growing worried. *How long have I been out here?* By the movement of the moon, it had been over an hour. An hour of sitting, waiting, thinking. Hoping for some inspiration.

She gave it a little longer. *Another fish will come by soon, and Cevi will thank me for that.* Reaching into the cold flowing water, she filled her waterskin, took a long deep drink to refresh herself, and set it aside on the rock. She resumed her cross-legged pose, studying the water, listening for frogs and toads. She had heard the occasional croak, but could never place their position. *Somewhere in the woods,* she thought. *In some wet little bog where the rainwater has settled.*

The sound of the stream was relaxing, pleasant, a far cry from the silence of the palace. Around her the trees shook in the soft breeze, their leaves rustling, the air pristine. She filled her lungs, breathed out, filled them again, and closed her eyes. The trout was still warm in her belly, her dark leather hunting cloak enough to shield her from the chill. She could sense herself drifting, sense slumber encroaching. Feel the pull of dreams upon her…

She was back in her cell with Hadrin.

Lying on her pallet bed in the corner of the windowless chamber, high at the summit of the palace. Braziers burned softly. Shadows shifted on the walls.

The king was at his plinth, a skeleton in chains and rags, murmuring. Atop it, the Eye of Rasalan glowed.

A stronger pulse reached out from the orb, sending light to wash through the room. *Curious.* The Eye was a soft blue, veined in gold, yet that light, it was blue and *silver*. She frowned, sat up, peering through the darkness. "Hadrin. Are you all right?"

The king was on his knees, staring up at the eye with bulging eyes, shot with blood. His parched lips opened and closed, incoherent. Talasha had seen this a hundred times before. Sometimes she could divine detail from his inane ramblings, sometimes she could not, and even when she heard what he said, she didn't always understand.

"The girl…" he said. She heard that clear enough.

"Which girl?" she asked. She stood, stepping over, feet whispering on stone. "Which girl, sweet king?"

He looked up at her, seeing nothing, then back at the Eye, seeing it all. For a long moment he just stared.

"Which girl?" she asked again.

"Silver…blue…" The words were whispers, stirring the long brittle strands of hair that hung off his top lip. "A city of eagles. A…a pyramid. There is a dragon…descending…"

The princess frowned. "Who is the girl, Hadrin?"

"Silver…blue…"

She asked again, and got the same answer.

"The dragon? It is ridden?"

He stared up at the Eye, the swirling shapes and colours. The pupil, a dark slit, opening to a world of prophesy. Through it he peered, searching, searching. "A chasm…barren plains…a silver…a silver scar…" He leaned in, chest rising and falling, fingers trembling, lips murmuring. "Shadows and death. Creatures…in the night. No… no, that won't work," he said. "Steel does nothing…nothing…nothing. Fire…burn them….burn them…*burn them!*" His neck twisted, bug eyes staring up at her, wide and unblinking. Two words hissed off his lips. "*Burn them*," he said.

Talasha opened her eyes.

Her heart was thumping at her ribs, the hairs standing up on the back of her neck. A cold sweat dappled her brow. She took a deep breath, steadying, wondering why that moment had come back to her, in particular, that *memory*. Hadrin had babbled on about a hundred things, a hundred things that had not made sense to her. That had been just another of them.

Why that one? Why did I dream of that one?

193

She put it from her mind, standing, stretching. The moon had moved along its course, another hour passing by. It had felt like only moments. It was time to go, to return to Cevi. *I've been gone too long as it is.*

She turned to the riverbank and froze.

A man stood right before her, atop the muddy slope. A shadow in the dark, cloaked and cowled. The sight of him made her gasp and stumble back. "Who are you?" she blurted. "What do you want?"

There were more behind him, emerging from the woods. Two, three, four of them. One was a woman, by her size and shape, the rest men, all in ragged clothes, bits of armour and mail, tattered cloaks hanging at their backs. They looked hungry, lean, desperate. Hollow eyes caught the moonlight, gleaming.

"Who are you?" she asked again, heart thrashing. She had her spear in her grasp, though dare not raise it, lest she provoke them. "Speak."

"You know us," the lead man said. There was something in his voice she recognised. "We know you."

She peered at him as he pulled back his hood, saw beyond the fleshless cheeks and matted beard. "Tarran? Is…that you?"

A nod. "What are you doing here, Princess?"

The others stalked in behind him, glaring with hungry eyes. She recognised them as well, though had never known all their names.

"She never left," the woman said. Her voice was a rake over rock, unpleasant, a scratchy lowborn thing. She had been a washerwoman in her cousin Tethian's camp. The others were soldiers, cultists, followers. Few of Tethian's band of outlaws were half as fervent as him. They were men without a cause, suckling at the power teat. Almost no one had truly believed that Eldur would be found.

But Tarran. He had been a respected soldier, once before, Talasha remembered. *He joined Tethian for his cause. He was a man of faith.*

"Is that true, my lady?" the man in question asked her. His beard had gone to grey in patches, his hair dark as pitch, salted with strands of silver. His eyes were severe, humourless, mouth a puckered scowl. "Have you been in these wilds all along?"

"Does she look like she has," another man said, taller than the others. "Seems well fed to me."

Tarran looked her over, nodding.

"She was with that Varin Knight," said a third man, shorter, more squat, leaning on a spear at the top of the bank. "He still here with you now?" He looked around into the woods, squinting. "The Knight of Mists."

Talasha shook her head. "We left together, with…some others." She did not know what else to say. So much had happened since then. "I returned, only days ago. But I won't be staying long."

"Oh? That's a shame," cackled the washerwoman. "Be nice to have another woman around."

"Nice for us too," laughed the tall man. "You're ugly as muck, Santhra. But the princess here…"

"Quiet," Tarran said. His voice was rough, worn down by years of shouting. He let a silence settle, looking at Talasha's spear. "Did you make that yourself, my lady?"

"I did. For fishing the river."

"Have you caught anything?"

"A trout." She saw the hungry eyes and added. "We have eaten it already. I came down in the hope of catching another. And to fetch water."

Tarran's eyes ran up the slope, through the trees, behind him. "*We?* You're not alone, then?" Another silence. "We saw a finger of smoke, earlier. Is that your campsite?"

She stayed silent.

"Will you lead us there?"

No, her instincts screamed. She sensed nothing good would come of an association with this group. But for Tarran they felt rough, the worst of Tethian's followers, and few had been good to start with. Outlaws, bandits, vagrants, villains, they had joined him for food and shelter, mostly, and had never shared his vision. *Now they hope for the same from me*, she thought. *They hope I will have food to give them, valuables perhaps.* But there was something worse here too. Something she did not want to consider.

"A delay's always telling, Tarran," said a heavy-voiced man, the one who hadn't yet spoken. He was bigger than the others, broad-chested and barrel-bellied once before, though his stomach had shrunk since last Talasha had seen him. She remembered him as well. *One of Ashun Klo's brutes*. Not Grumlo or Kartheck or Rackar, no, they were all killed by Lythian and Pagaloth and Neyruu. But another of them, another crude thug. *Humghor*, the princess remembered. *That one cannot be trusted. And if one can't, none can.*

Tarran gave Talasha another moment to answer. When she said nothing, he stepped down the muddy bank and up to the water's edge. "Who are you here with, my lady? You said you returned only days ago. Do you have an honour guard with you?"

Another cackle from the washerwoman. "Course she doesn't. You think they'd let her come down here all alone, in the dark?"

Tarran considered that a moment. "Who, then? You must understand my concerns, Princess. If that Varin Knight of yours is waiting up the hill. Or the dragonknight, Sir Pagaloth…"

"Neither are with me, I assure you."

"Then who is? You said you are not alone."

"My handmaid," she decided to admit. "Cevi. You might remember her."

"I do. You had two, that I recall."

"Mirella. She…died."

The man lowered his chin. "Sad to hear, my lady. Was it…that night?"

"No, some days after. Though by an injury she sustained that night. So yes, in a fashion."

"Too many died that night," grunted the big man. "Lost my brothers. And my commander. And we all lost our prince."

"We have a princess now," Tarran said to that. The way he said it, the way he looked at her…

"What is it you want from me?" she asked him. The blood was rushing through her veins, heart pumping hard, preparing.

"Pardons," Tarran replied. "For our…associations."

Talasha frowned. The others behind Tarran nodded and murmured, understanding his intent.

"We heard that some of the old company tried to make it down to Loriath," Tarran explained to her. "They were taken as traitors and outlaws when they arrived in the city, and burned. That is why we're still lingering here, in these woods, scraping a living off the land. But with you…"

She understood. *They expect me to clear their names, award them amnesty. They have no idea what's happening out there.* She took a step away from him, right to the very edge of her rock. Only a few short metres separated them, river water rushing in between. "I will not be going to Loriath," she said, firmly. They could not know what she had done, or been through. *If they take me to Loriath, I'll be captured, returned to Eldurath.* And *him.* "I am your princess. You will obey my commands."

Laughter barked from the others. A loud snort from Humghor.

"At another time, my lady, I would agree," said Tarran. "But that time is not now." His mouth hardened. "You'll be going where I say. It's the best thing for all of us." He looked at her, something dark catching in his eyes. "Now come, or else I will ask Humghor to fetch you. I assure you, he will not be so gentle as me."

She saw the big man smile at the top of the bank, black gaps where several teeth should be, the rest of them yellow-brown and rotten. The other outlaws were there as well, up the muddy slope. Only Tarran stood at her level, slippery stones and rushing water between them.

They are hungry, tired, weak. If I run…

"Princess. You are not making this easy on yourself." Tarran paused a moment, then twisted his neck backward, growing impatient. "Humghor. Come fetch Her Highness." He looked forward again. "It is for your own good, my…"

But she was already gone, turning, driving hard with her back foot, leaping across to the other side of the river, landing with a splash where the water met the dirt. She began scrambling up the bank.

"After her!" Tarran bellowed.

She could hear grunts, curses, as the men gave chase, hear Tarran wading into the water. One of them slipped on the slope, it sounded, crashing down onto the stony shore. She glanced back, saw Humghor struggling to his feet, the taller man and squat man thrashing through the river. The washerwoman seemed disinterested in the hunt, casually following. Tarran was right behind her, closing.

The princess reached the top, raced into the trees, fish-spear in her grasp, waterskin left behind on her rock. It was a precious item, but she could not think of that now. She burst past boles of spruce and cedar, hurdling thorn bushes and spouts of sedge. Roots reached up, trying to trip her, but she hurdled those too, fleet-footed and nimble.

Darkness closed in. The river had been relatively bright, the sky open above it, but here the branches were thick as a fortress wall. All moonlight was blotted, only shadows and shapes before her. The trunks of trees she could see easily enough, and the tangles of brush on the forest floor, but smaller perils were hidden from her eyes. Her back foot caught a jut of stone, poking from the earth, and she tripped forward, arms waving, trying to restore control, and failed. The ground rushed up to greet her, the air punched from her lungs. Wheezing, she scrambled back to her feet, glanced back, saw Tarran still on her heels.

"Princess, stop! Stop, it's for your own good!"

You don't know what's good for me, she might have roared back, but there was no air in her lungs for that.

Her heart was thumping. *Neyruu,* she thought, trying to reach her. *Neyruu, hear me.* She rounded a large tree trunk, saw a clatter of boulders and rocks broken from a nearby cliff face blocking the way. She reached the rocks, saw no way through but over, and began climbing.

"Stop…you'll only hurt yourself!" Tarran was still there, the taller man fast catching. She could hear the huff and puff of Humghor crashing through the undergrowth. "Princess…stop! We're not going to hurt you!"

I can't be taken. I can't be taken. Loriath was a death sentence for her. Eldur would have sent out agents to find her, spread the word of her betrayals. *He will make an example of me. He'll put me in the belly of the iron dragon, and have Neyruu be the one to blow on it…*

She had watched men tortured inside that dragon before. Her uncle Dulian had used it for traitors and rebels, those found guilty of sedition, among others. Particular crimes were worthy of a slow death, he had proclaimed. Sometimes he would require the great and good of Eldurath to stand witness, watching as the dragons blew their flame upon their iron brother, listen to the dull hollow screams of the men and women inside, as the metal grew so hot it scorched their skin, as they were slowly roasted alive.

Talasha had always feared it. Always imagined how awful it would be. *He will know,* she thought. *He will look into my heart, and know.*

She would not let that happen. Not to her. Not to Cevi.

There was a great deal of shouting behind her now, though she wasn't listening to the words. She needed to draw them away, then she could circle back up the slope to Cevi. She continued climbing, clambering, searching for hand and footholds, pulling herself up to the top. She cut her hand on a sharp snag, felt a stab of pain, grit her teeth and kept on going, leaving blood smears on the stone. The summit was flat for a half dozen paces. She surged across to the far side, looked down, saw the rocks rolled out before her, planned a route down and began jumping from rock to rock, each lower than the last. Her ankles were strong, her legs springy, and she reached the ground without injury.

Then she kept on running.

Her breath came in pants now, in, out, in, out, lungs burning. She dared another look back and saw that Tarran and the tall man had navigated the rocks safely. Humghor was at the top, head swinging side to side, frown on his beetled brow, searching for a way down, the squat man coming up behind him. The washerwoman was nowhere to be seen.

They're tiring, Talasha thought. *They must be. They're starved.*

She kept going, thighs screaming as she reached a slope, climbing up to a higher elevation. There were a thousand small hills in these wilds, many with open clearings at the top. Legend said that those clearings were made by the dragons, in days gone by. That they would stop here on their way from the Wings to the Nest, to rest and think, deciding whether they wished to answer the call of the Bondstone, be paired with a Fireborn rider. Some would turn back, returning to the islands, others would continue going. While they waited, they would curl up on these hilltops, clearing them of trees and shrubs. Some had come to call them the *Dragonroost Hills* for that, others the *Heights of Choice*, for the final ruling the dragons came to, a choice from which they could not turn back.

There were no dragons here anymore, though, save just the one. *Neyruu,* Talasha thought again. *Neyruu, if you can hear me…*

The slope steepened. Her lungs and legs were fire, and yet she kept on going, driving hard up the hillside, kicking through snarls of bracken, thorns tearing at her hands.

She could hear Tarran and the tall man panting behind her, hear shouting further off as the others tried to find them. The dark was deep here, though further up Talasha could see the moonlight through the trees, glowing on the hilltop. She had to get there first. Get there and cross back into the woods before they saw which way she'd gone. Her legs were turning to reeds, yet she drove on all the same, harder and faster. She sensed herself stretching a lead on them, sensed their energy waning. Tarran wasn't even calling to her anymore. *He cannot spare the breath,* she knew.

The hillside shallowed again as she neared the top, the trees thinning, opening out, the high clearing coming into view. She burst into the open, looked around, saw that the plateau was wider than she'd expected. To her left it fell away sharply, a descent into a rugged mire of broken rocks that would be too slow and too dangerous to climb. To her right it looked even worse, a high cliff plummeting to darkness. Her only option was straight across.

She set into a sprint and ran.

Halfway across, she glanced back, saw her two pursuers breaching the wood and rushing onto the hilltop. They saw her at once, and gave chase, the tall man striding onward with purpose, bits of armour clanking, cloak flapping, long legs gaining ground. The woods on the other side were nearing, but she knew she wouldn't make it. He was too fast, too fast and closing.

I have to slow him.

She stopped, suddenly, and spun, hefted her spear and threw. It pierced the night air, whistling, striking the tall man in the upper thigh. Prongs bit through leather, into flesh. He stumbled to a knee, cursing. Then ripped the spear out and kept on coming.

No…

She whirled about, running for the woods, but the move had won her no time. She heard his stamp rushing up behind her, the heavy rattle of armour, felt his breath at the back of her neck. The tang of iron in the air, the stink of soiled breeches and unwashed clothes. The moon peered through the clouds, casting his shadow. He was right behind her, reaching out. Fingers snatched at her trailing leather cloak. She felt him grip, tore free, but got only a few more paces before he swung at her with her own spear, knocking her left leg into her right, tripping her.

She stumbled forward, careening into the hard rocky earth, chin smashing stone. Blood welled at once from a gash torn in her jaw. The tall man crashed down atop her, knocking the air from her a second time. She tried to struggle, to stand, but he was too heavy. "Whore for a northern knight," he spat at her. "Be a whore for me…"

She twisted, trying to scratch at him, raking fingers down one cheek. She felt his skin rip, parting. The tall man roared, eyes blazing, and swung hard, striking her in the face. A sting flashed across her cheek, eyes blurring, head fuzzing. She blinked, spots dancing in her vision, reaching feebly up, but he swatted her away.

"Whore…"

"*Enough*! Off her." She heard Tarran come running up to them. He put two hands on the tall man's shoulders, and threw him aside, releasing her of his weight. "You don't touch her, Jantor. We need her intact."

"Bitch speared me!" The tall man Jantor burst back onto his feet, wiping at his cheek, seeing the blood. "She tore my bloody face open!"

"Pin pricks. Scratches. Stop moaning and bind her hands."

"I'll have what I'm owed," Jantor growled. "Blood for blood." He turned on her and drew a dagger.

Tarran drew a sword. "I'll give you blood if you push me. She is a princess, *our* princess, and not to be touched." He stared a hard stare. "We need her. Bind her hands, I said. You've got the rope."

Jantor snorted, looked at the blade in Tarran's fist, considered, then relented. Distantly, Talasha could hear the sound of the other two men rushing across the hill, Humghor and the shorter man. They were shouting something, though she couldn't make it out. Jantor looked over, shoving his rusted dagger back into a stained leather sheath. "You hear that?"

Tarran turned to the incoming men, and then arched his neck, peering at the skies. Talasha saw him step backward, heard him draw a sharp breath, saw the shape move across the moon. There was a heavy *thwump* of wings, music in her ears. Her eyes flickered, sight fading.

Neyruu, she thought.

The rest of it was fire, and fangs, and screams.

14

Robbert

The prince's flagship was a monster, a three-decked, four-masted beast of a galleon called *Hammer*, with a bulky battering ram on the prow and an array of mounted harpoons and crossbows fixed to the thick wooden bulwarks.

Sails in brown and green fluttered proudly against the dark skies, straining against the wind, men rushing about the decks, shouting and calling. Prince Robbert Lukar stood at the quarterdeck, hair and cloak blowing, cheeks stung by salt spray, a black patch strapped across his blinded left eye. The sea about them was all white caps and rising waves, growing larger by the hour, restless, daunting.

"I don't like this," said Sir Lothar Tunney. His Emerald Guard cloak flapped wildly at his back. He reached to the port side gunwale to steady himself as *Hammer* lurched over a wave, sliding down the other side, rearing up again. Water splashed across the decks, rushing past ankles and out through the scuppers. A loud *hiss* filled the air as another wave crashed into their starboard side, sea spray spitting into their faces. Lank turned his head away, cringing. "This storm is going to sink us, Robb. And those skies…" He looked forward, wiping his eyes, peering past the tall masts and bustling seamen, the straining sails and prow. "They're only getting darker. It's a raging tempest out there."

He wasn't far wrong, Robbert Lukar would readily admit. Above them it was grey and gloomy, but in the direction they were heading, the skies were almost black. He could see thick cloudbursts out there, black bridges from sea to sky, see flashes in the dark, hear the distant growl of rolling thunder. It would be enough to set the heart of any man on edge, but Robbert Lukar would not let himself be unmanned by it. Lank had jested before that he looked like a pirate with his new eye patch. *Then this world should hold no fear for me*, the prince thought.

"We should tell the captain to turn around, Robb," Lothar was going on, as panicky as Robbert had ever seen him. "This is no place to die, on the deck of some ship. A knight should fall with steel in his fist and hard earth beneath his feet."

"Then draw your blade," Robbert told him, "if it'll make you feel any better. If we turn around we'll get broadsided. We have no choice but to continue on."

Lanky Lothar shook his head, staring out to sea. "It's not just the storm," he quivered. "There's something else out there, I can feel it. Something dark, under the waves. We should never have come this way."

There are a hundred dark terrors beneath those waves, Robb thought. "We had no choice," he said.

"We did," Lothar protested. "The plains. We could have marched across the plains, like you wanted. Crossed to Agarath from the south and gone up through the Bloodmarshes."

"Past Skyloft," Robbert said. "And Blademelt. Two of the greatest Agarathi forts and strongholds. Beset by dragons along the way. No, Lank. None of us would have made it."

"It was what you wanted."

"Once," Robbert admitted. "Before our army was decimated, and I woke up. Maybe you should do the same, Lothar. Sailing home was the sensible choice."

"Sensible? You call this sensible?" Lothar looked to the storm again, all but bawling like a babe. "We're going to die, every one of us. Every man in this fleet is doomed."

Robbert had heard enough of his bleating. "Go below decks if you're scared, Lank. Or better yet, take a dive to port, and spare me all your mewling." He threw an arm out to sea, the Aramatian coastline a faint shadow in the distance, veiled in mist. "Go ahead, swim for shore if you want. Either that, or shut up. We're here now, so deal with it."

He stepped away toward the ship captain, standing at the wheel shouting orders. His name was Ash Burton, though his men called him 'Bloodhound' for those droopy facial features and his uncanny ability to sniff out a beast at sea. "Captain Burton," the prince called to him, hailing his attention. "What does your sea nose tell you?"

The captain was a Rasal Seaborn by blood, a master of the waves who'd spent his entire lifetime at sea. He had started young, like many of his kin, becoming a midshipman when he was just a boy of eight, and had spent the next four decades using that bloodhound nose of his to hunt monsters. There were few sea-hunters so decorated as Bloodhound Burton.

"It's telling me plenty, lad," the captain said, in his barking voice. There was something of the bloodhound about that voice too, Robb thought. "Aye, the seas are teeming. Fine days for a hunter like me." A crooked smile warped his face.

Robbert Lukar was not smiling. "I asked to you be my captain to avoid these creatures, not hunt them. I asked you to get us home safe."

202

"Aye, so you did. But orders don't play well with my instincts. Hard to break the habits of a lifetime, lad."

Robbert understood that well enough. Telling Bloodhound Burton to avoid the creatures of the deep was like telling a whore to put on a chastity belt. "Try harder, then," Robbert told him. "If you lead us into trouble…"

"Lead us? Don't need to lead us. There's trouble enough out here without me having to find it."

Robbert could never tell how much he was exaggerating. Sea captains and sailors infuriated him with their tall tales and seamen stories, and these Rasals in particular. "So what are we talking? Great-whales? Krakens?"

The captain scoffed. "I eat krakens for breakfast. Killed more than one of those in my time, and big ones too." He spat to the side. "Slimy bastards are my speciality, lad. Made that oath after King Lorin died." He glanced over at him. "I sailed with him, did you know? When I was just a boy. Might have been on that ship the day he died if I hadn't come down with a fever. When the news came through that a kraken had got him I was disconsolate. Lorin had been kind to me, you see. Said I had a rare wisdom for the waves, even as a nipper, that the creatures of the deep would fear me some day." He looked out, glaring at the horizon. "Aye, and he was right in that. Been hunting monsters ever since, and krakens most of all. If I ever see *Lorin's Bane* again…"

Robbert did his best not to roll his eyes. He'd heard this story before. "You have no fear of krakens, that's clear, but I'd rather not run into one myself. Least of all the one that did for Lorin." It was a monstrous kraken, the singers liked to say, and not an acquaintance Robbert wanted to make.

"Course. You're a land-lover. Your lot always feel helpless out here."

Yes, and I don't much like it. "What of the krelia? Are we likely to meet it?"

The captain took pause, and that said it all about how feared the krelia was. "No. That one's still lurking in the Solapian Channel, so far as we know. Unless it's moved north, we should be well clear of it by now. And we'd better. I've fought most sea monsters that can be fought, but the krelia…that one's best avoided."

Robbert nodded in firm agreement. The prince was hardly an expert on sea monsters, but had heard enough to know that the krelia was a creature to steer clear of at all costs. It was the very reason why the ships had taken anchorage north of the Channel, east down the coast from Kolash, rather than sailing further south. Only a few vessels dared pass that way now, and most of them did so unaware of the threat. Some got lucky, others did not. *Bones*, Robbert thought. *Floating bones was the sign that the krelia had been feeding.*

He peered out through the mists and falling rains, looking for ships. Some were close enough to remain within sight. He could see Lord

Gullimer's fine vessel, *Orchard*, undulating along nearby, and Simon Swallow's as well, a lumbering man-of-war called *Shadow*, built from the black timber of the Darkwood north of Blackhearth, his city seat. Lord Lewyn Huffort's ship, *Landslide*, would be out there too, though right now Robbert couldn't see it. *Nor most others,* he thought.

"We've lost sight of half of the fleet," he said, turning back to the captain.

"More than half," Bloodhound returned. "And won't see most of them again until we reach our rally point at the Perch either. That's the way of the waves, lad. I'd not be surprised to find us sailing alone by the time this weather clears up. *Iulla* can be a frightful bitch."

Iulla was the goddess of storms, Robbert knew, one of many Rasalanian deities. "We're in the south, Captain. Iulla has no power here."

"All the seas are Rasalan's," Bloodhound came back. "I should know. I've battled Iulla's fury all across the world and bested her every time so far. Tonight, though…"

Ahead of them, the seas were turning wilder, and the wind blowing harder, waves rising. Robbert could see the ship's boatswain, a man called George Buckley, rushing up toward the forecastle deck, hearing reports of the state of the sails. *Hammer* was a powerful vessel, Seaborn-built and crewed, but still vulnerable in a storm like this. If a mast were to snap or a few sails tear loose, they'd be at the mercy of the winds and waves.

Captain Burton's facade had turned more serious. "You'll want to brace yourself, my prince," he said, seeing the boatswain rushing back across the decks toward him. "The next few hours aren't going to be pretty, and you'll only be getting in my way up here. Gonna need my wits about me." He looked past the prince's cloak. "Best take off that armour too."

Robbert didn't like the sound of that. It could only mean that the captain feared they would founder. "Is that necessary?"

"It's sensible. We go down, and you'll not stand a chance in godsteel. It doesn't float well, so far as I know."

If we do go down, we'll all die anyway, Robbert thought, looking to the coast once more. By now it was gone, the rains too thick to see through, at least ten miles from where they were. Perhaps a man like Bloodhound might stand a chance if the ship capsized, being Seaborn, but no normal man would survive in this. *We'll drown, sure as sunrise, or be picked off by sharks or worse.* The notion didn't hold any appeal to him. *I'd sooner just sink in my armour and be done with it.*

"As you say," Robbert said. "I trust you to see us through this storm, Captain Burton."

"I'll do my best." Bloodhound looked over to the pitiful form of Sir Lothar, clinging desperately to the port side gunwale, like a frightened girl clutching at her mother's leg. "And take your lanky friend with you. He's too tall to be out here. One bad jerk and he'll go over."

Robbert nodded to that. The man was stupidly tall. "Fine. You get us through this and there's a lordship in it for you."

"A king doesn't need a lordship," the old Seaborn captain said to him. "Every captain's the king of his ship. And I'm the king of these seas."

"Then *rule* them," Robbert said, stepping away.

He took Sir Lothar down belowdecks, as advised, the pair thrown about from side to side as they descended into the tight, claustrophobic corridors, squeezing past the sailors rushing up and down the stairs.

"The captain said to take off our armour, Lank," Robbert said, as they went. "In case the ship goes down. I suppose we ought to heed him." Whatever he'd thought about preferring to get it over quickly, that wasn't really true. More than that he wanted to live, and if that meant clinging armour-less to a bit of wreck like a limpet, floating helplessly in the raging seas, so be it. *Let the sharks come. I'll still have my sword.*

They found Sir Bernie Westermont in the prince's cabin, head in a bucket, heaving up his guts. He groaned as they entered, lifting his eyes. "I hate the sea. *Hate* it," he moaned. His skin was pale as milk, hair sweaty, body unburdened of his armour. That had not been the case when last Robbert had seen him.

"You fear we'll go down as well, Bern?" he asked, trying to stay chipper. Somehow the terrible distress of his friends made it easier. *I'm not as bad as they are, at least.*

"I've feared that from the start, Robb." Bernie tried to smile, though quickly returned his head to the pail, retching.

The others set about removing their armour, collecting the plate in chests that were strapped and bolted to the floor. The weight of it was considerable, though these ships were all adapted to carry Bladeborn men to war, and good sense dictated that only a certain number of armoured knights and soldiers be permitted on any one ship. Robbert had thus spread his forces accordingly, or what forces he had left. Many thousands had died during the fighting in Aram, and many thousands more had deserted during and after the battle, but he still had the bones of a functioning army to call upon.

And my army, he thought. *Mine, at last.* With his uncle gone, those who remained had sworn him their loyalty and agreed that returning to their ships and sailing home was the right option. *Well, all except Sir Gavin.* He'd gone off with a hundred men one night, steadfast in their loyalty to Lord Cedrik even now. *And good riddance,* Robbert thought. *Let them bake to death out there on those plains, we're better off without them.*

Robbert Lukar would not have the rest of them drown at sea on account of this cursed storm. *We've men enough here to make a difference*, he told himself. *Twelve thousand of them, all eager to get home. All eager to rejoin the fight.* They knew little of what was going on in the north, though that there was fighting to be had, Robbert had no doubt. It would give the prince a chance to restore some sense of purpose and pride, after the long disastrous campaign here under the command of his odious uncle.

Bernie continued to retch as they undressed, holding the pail between his tree-trunk legs as he sat forward on a chair, cursing his fate. He wore linens, simple garb for the heat and humidity here, soaked through and sticking to his skin. Beneath was a body thick with muscle. Bernie Westermont had the shoulders of an ox and the back of a bovidor, arms as big around as Robbert's thighs. He had some bandaging on him as well, covering the cuts he'd suffered in his duel with the Wall. They were flesh wounds only, nothing major. *His armour suffered worse,* Robbert knew. Both Bernie and Lank might have been killed a dozen times over were it not for the resilience of their plate. *Lesser godsteel would have given way. Or perhaps the Wall was holding back?*

Robbert would not say that to his companions, though. Sir Bernie was proud to have stood against Sir Ralston for so long, even cutting at the giant's armour himself once or twice to add to the Whaleheart's scars. When Lothar had joined the bout, they'd put the giant on the back foot. *But even then, I'd fancy the beast to best them,* Robb thought. Again, he kept that thought to himself.

The big man was retching again, though looked to be onto the dry heaves by now, spewing up nothing but gouts of bile and the odd bit of porridge from their morning meal. Robbert did not suffer from seasickness himself, thank the gods. Nor Lothar, and he was grateful for that. He could barely conceive of how much the tall knight would moan if he had to battle this nausea as well.

Bernie wiped his mouth with the back of his sleeve, pulled a long breath into his lungs, and breathed out. A few strands of spittle still leaked from his lips. His eyes went to the window, thick glass crossed with supporting iron bars. Little could be seen outside but mist and lashing rain. "What's it like out there?"

"Bad," muttered Sir Lothar, miserably, pulling off his padded top. He was lean to the bone beneath it, with extremely wide shoulders and tufts of tawny hair on his chest, slicked by sweat. He had a bloodied bandage around his right shoulder where Sir Ralston had cut into his pauldron, biting into the flesh beneath. He fetched a light jerkin and put it on, wincing from the pain. "And it's going to get worse."

Bernie looked at him in dull-eyed dismay. "Worse? How much worse?"

"Just that," Robbert told him. "*Much* worse. We're in for a long night, Bern."

The big man looked like he could break down and weep. "I should have just died in my duel with the Wall. At least there'd have been some honour in that."

"There wouldn't," Robbert Lukar said. "There's no honour in dying by the blade of an ally."

"Wasn't our ally then."

"He was. We just didn't know it yet."

"Still. Better way to go, falling to the blade of a knight like him." He looked to the window again, face twisting into a scowl. "Curse this storm. Meant to be calm this time of year, I thought."

"It is," Robbert said, having spoken about that to the captain already. "Bloodhound says it's unusual, this weather. Same as the heat. Much hotter than normal, he says."

"Better here, though," said Lank. "We got the wind and rain at least. That march down the coast was brutal."

And unrelenting, Robbert thought. A long hot slog down the coast under a skin-blistering sun, unbearably windless at times, parched and barren. Tukorans were not used to those sorts of conditions, and suffered worse than the Vandarians did, who basked in warm weather at certain times of year in many places across their kingdom. It wasn't the same in Tukor. Their lands were higher, colder, gloomier, more prone to turbid skies. There were some parts of Tukor where the sun never shone down, the local people liked to say. It was an exaggeration, of course, but born of truth. And it made them entirely ill-equipped to deal with the hot summer sun.

So when the rains had started the previous day, beginning as a soft, soothing sprinkle, the men of Tukor had rejoiced. It hadn't been so for the first two days of their voyage. No, the sun had been just as hot and baking as it had been during their march along the coast, but after two days at sea the clouds had come in and the rains had come down and there were cheers all about the decks. Robbert could hear them, ringing out from the other ships, which at that point were all sailing close in a grand armada of thirty vessels, all visible from *Hammer's* decks. He had seen the men come rushing out, throwing up their arms and tearing off their tops as they felt the soothing touch of the rains. Robbert had stood at the quarterdeck, smiling at their fine fortune, at the blessed relief, but Bloodhound Burton had only scoffed.

"Enjoy it while it lasts," he'd said, ominously, peering to the north with those sailor-sage eyes. "You'll all be cursing these rains soon enough, mark my words. You'll be wishing for that sun to return."

His warning had proven prophetic. Only a few hours later the seas had begun to churn, the skies darkening, and half the men were at the gunwales heaving over the sides. Then the waves grew higher and higher still, the swells surging up above the bulwarks, and the ships began to disappear, one by one. Robbert could only watch on, helpless, as his fleet was broken apart, falling behind as *Hammer* surged on. Now only a handful of them could be seen from the decks, *Shadow*, *Orchard*, a few of the others. *We're all in this alone now,* the prince thought. He just had to hope that he had a fleet left when this cursed storm finally broke.

Robbert dressed in a green linen tunic, girding his waist with a brown leather belt, slipping grippy boots over his feet. He put his swordbelt aside, right next to the cabin door, should he need to snatch it up and make a quick exit, though kept a godsteel dagger at his hip.

The ship was rocking by then, shifting violently as it bucked on the waves. The knights found good places to brace themselves against the motion, listening to the roar of wind and wave, the crash of the ocean, the storm-song of the men on deck. It was common among sailors, Rasals in particular, to embrace bad weather, and sing through the storm. *A form of prayer,* Robbert knew. *Maybe I should be praying too?*

The minutes began to tick by, turning to hours, the nerves of the knights shredded down to strips. Overhead, the prince could hear the bellowing sounds of thunder now, more fearsome than he'd ever heard before. *Tukor's dying breath,* he thought. That was what they called the sound of thunder up in the north of his kingdom. If that was so, he could not conceive of what god had perished here. It was an altogether more mighty sound, shaking him down to his bones.

A knock came at the door, and a sailor popped his head inside. He was a young midshipman, another of the many Rasals in the crew, drenched to the marrow, though smiling. *How? How can he be smiling at a time like this?*

"Captain asked that I check in on you, Prince Robbert," he chirped. He can't have been more than thirteen or fourteen winters worn, just starting out on a long career at sea. "How are you all faring?" He sounded not in the least concerned of the tempest. "I see some of the furniture has taken a tumble."

"Not just the furniture," Bernie Westermont groaned. Only a short while ago his pail of vomit had been knocked over, spilling the contents of his stomach to the floor. Some tables and chairs had also shifted position, sliding and falling with the motion of the ship, some-times flying violently across the room when assaulted by a wrathful swell. The rest of the heavy furniture - desk, bed, the chests and trunks - were all bolted down to keep them in place during heavy weather like this. Everything else had been stored before the storm hit, locked away in cupboards and cabinets built into the cabin walls.

The young midshipman looked at the vomit. "We can't be having that, not in here. I'll get it cleaned up for you, Your Highness."

Robbert shook his head. "Don't bother. I'm sure you need all hands on deck. Isn't that the phrase?"

"It is." The boy smiled at him. He was a small, stocky lad, with thick curls of russet hair on his head, darkened by the rains, and a face all full of freckles. "If you're sure, my lord."

"We can handle the sight of a spot of vomit," the prince said. "What's your name?"

The midshipman sketched a bow. "Rivers, my lord. Finn Rivers."

Rivers seemed a good name for a man of the water, Robbert supposed, though perhaps Finn Ocean would be better. "How is it out there? Are we through the worst of it yet?"

The boy almost laughed. "No, oh no, not yet. There's more to come. Never seen a storm like it, my lord."

"Seen many, have you?"

"Hundreds. Might sound silly to say, at my age, but when you've learned to walk on the decks of ships, you've already seen a lot of weather. Been at sea a decade already."

Robbert raised his eyes in appreciation of that. "You started young, same as me. My father used to put a godsteel blade in my crib when my mother wasn't looking. Sometimes he'd sneak it in there overnight, hiding it in the blankets." He smiled at that. "I've been training with the blade all of my life."

"Short life," said Lothar Tunney. "You're only eighteen, Robb."

"Whereas you're an old man, Lank?"

"Older than you."

"You're four and twenty. Stop trying to sound like a wise old head." He did moan like an old maid, though, that was true.

The midshipman Finn Rivers gave a chuckle at their bickering. "Is there anything you need, my lords? Anything else I can do for you?" He stood just inside the doorway, swaying on his sea legs as the ship lurched and rocked and groaned, moving like the ocean itself, limbs like liquid. *Seaborn, this one,* Robbert thought. There was no doubt in that.

"We're fine," he said. "Thank you, Finn."

Another smile. "Well and good, then. Let me know if you think of anything. I'll be back down in an hour or so, to check in on you again." He looked at the three of them, holding on for dear life, and seemed to find the sight most amusing, Robbert didn't fail to miss. "You keep clinging on, my lords. I'm afraid it's not going to get better for a while." He turned and slipped through the door, shutting it tight behind him.

"Damn Seaborn," Lothar grumbled after he'd left. "It's unnatural, how they can walk about in this."

Robbert looked at him. "We gain strength, speed, improved agility, and enhance our senses bearing godsteel, Lothar. I'm sure he thinks that's unnatural too." He rose from the bolted-down armchair he'd been sitting in, moving to the window, looking out. "We're lucky to have them aboard. If anyone's going to lead us through this storm, it'll be the Seaborn. This is their battleground, Lothar, same as the open field is ours."

"Not all battles are winnable, Robb. Maybe this is their Aram."

"Or maybe not." Robbert was not certain how much longer he could bear this grousing. He peered out through the window, the horizon shifting violently up and down. Sometimes he could see only the sky, then the ship would lurch suddenly the other way, and he would be looking right down into the ocean depths. For a moment he could have sworn he saw something down there, a shimmer of something - a fin or dorsal spine - breaking the surface, then moving down beneath them. He reached to grip the godsteel dagger he kept at his hip, enhancing his sight.

"What?" Lothar shifted up from the corner he was bracing in. "Did you see something?"

Robbert was still peering out, but the ship was swinging the other way now, the window showing only black sky. By the time the waters came back into view the shadow was gone. "I...I don't know," he said. "It's probably nothing."

"It's probably *something*. I heard the captain earlier. The seas are teeming, he said." Lothar stood on long, spindly legs, stepping over to join him, but the ship gave another sudden jerk and at once Sir Lothar the Looming was tumbling to the floor, keeling sideways in a tangle of limbs. There was a wet slap as he landed right where Bernie's bucket of spew had overturned.

Robbert laughed aloud. "Serves you right for all your moaning."

Sir Lothar was like a newborn deer trying to stand on ice, all arms and legs, slipping, sliding, scrambling about in the sick. Even Bernie was laughing now. "How's my breakfast taste?" he said. "Robb, look, it's got in his *mouth!*"

"Shut up Bernie! It's not funny!" Lothar spat out, trying to stand once more, but the ship moved again and he slipped, returning to the sea of vomit spread out upon the planks. "Damn it! Damn you, Bern!"

"Not my fault you're so clumsy."

"I'm not clumsy. It's the ocean, you dolt!"

"*Dolt?* Call me a dolt again, I'll press your face down into my porridge!"

Sir Lothar was on all fours. He looked over at the big man. "Dolt. You're witless as a worm, Bernie, everyone knows it."

Bernie Westermont surged to his feet. "I warned you, Lank! Don't say I didn't warn you." He took a firm pace forward, swaying with the ship. Lothar was climbing back up to stand, slick with sick, wiping his mouth and face. The two men faced off against one another across the cabin, planting their legs wide, arms out for balance. It looked like they were both waiting for the right moment, for the ship to calm for just long enough so that they could rush forward at one another. Frankly, they looked ridiculous.

And Robbert had seen enough. "Sit down," he said. "No brawling. I've had it up to here with the both of..."

A *thump* sounded beneath them, trembling up through the bottom of the ship.

Robbert looked down at the floor, frowning.

"What was that?" Lothar said.

Bernie Westermont had felt it as well. "Rocks," he offered. "Must be rocks, down there."

Lothar shook his head. "The coast's miles away. There are no rocks out here, it's too deep."

Robbert looked out of the window again, wondering. "We might be near the Telleshi Isles by now," he suggested. Running aground on some hidden shoal and gutting the hull would not serve, but if they could drop anchor near a beach or protected cove, they might be able to wait out the storm unharmed. He searched through the falling rains, hoping for some sight of land, but saw nothing but wild waves and black skies, the occasional flash of lighting.

"Do you see anything?" Bernie asked him.

Robb could only shake his head. "Nothing but sea."

"The other side, maybe?" Bern offered. Their cabin showed a view to port only. They had no sight of the ship's starboard side from here.

Lothar didn't think so. "That boy Finn Rivers would have said if we were near land. It's not land, no way, unless…"

Another *thump*, louder this time, striking hard from beneath. It was too clean to be a sandbank or rocky shoal. That would cause a grinding sound. That was more like a heavy hammer, striking at the hull.

"There's something down there," Bernie said, shuddering. "Some creature. It's right below us."

Robbert thought of the flash of movement he'd seen. The shadow, sliding beneath the ship. He had not seen it for long enough to discern its shape, though it looked big. "I'm stepping out," he said, moving from the window seat. "Stay here, both of you."

Their protests fell on deaf ears. Robbert marched straight across the cabin and moved out through the door. He could hear the commotion outside at once, the frantic shouts and calls above him. Some soldiers were stepping out of their own rooms, rushing up from belowdecks. Robbert joined them, climbing the stairs and out into the falling rains. Above him the skies were black and menacing, swollen stormclouds filling the air, lightning flashing, thunder bellowing. Faintly he could see the glow of the moon, hidden behind that great sodden swamp. *A full moon,* he thought. It wasn't always a good omen for seamen.

The captain was still at the helm, barking out his orders in a frenzy. Robbert could see men rushing to man the mounted harpoons and scorpions, fixed to the bulwarks along the main deck, and up on the forecastle too. Each had beside it a rack containing long steel bolts, to be fixed into the mechanisms and fired. Some were godsteel tipped, lifted into place by specially trained marines with Bladeborn blood. Other men snatched up hand-held pikes and harpoons, opening chests and passing them out. They lined up along the gunwales, ready, as Robbert marched up the stair to the quarterdeck, holding tight to the rail so he didn't fall. The ship was still lurching wildly, waves crashing into the walls and rushing across the decks, tripping men as they worked, who cursed and got straight back to their feet. The storm-song of the seamen had gone silent. No one was singing now.

The prince staggered to the captain, reaching to steady himself against the helm. "What's happening?" he called. "What's down there?"

"Manator," Bloodhound said. "Big one."

Manator. The creature was another of which Robbert was only vaguely familiar. "The giant eel?"

"Aye, an eel. Though a hundred feet long, all thick twisting muscle, with tusks as tall as the mizzen mast thrusting up from its lower jaws." He threw a hand back at the ship's rearmost mast, rising up from the poop deck behind them.

Robbert couldn't believe that. "That mast's got to be twenty-five feet." There was no way the manator's tusks could be that long. "How do we fight it, Burton? It's directly below us."

"We outmanoeuvre it." Bloodhound Burton filled his lungs, and at the top of his voice, bellowed, "BRACE! HARD TO PORT!" His officers echoed the call at once, spreading it down the decks, giving only a few moments' warning before he swung the wheel. The ship turned, hard, to the left, timed with the rising of the waves. Robbert held on for dear life, clutching at the rail at the fore of the quarterdeck, blinking through the lashing rain. He could hear spotters shouting from the crow's nest, saw the men on the right of the ship swing their harpoons and pikes and take aim, firing and throwing down into the sea all at once and in unison. "Miss," one shouted. "Miss," another said. Three others said the same, then a sixth called out - "Hit! Good hit in the tail, Captain!" - and other shouts came in as well. Misses mostly, a few good hits. Robbert sped to the side in a crouch, clutching his dagger to strengthen his stride, and looked over the edge. He had just enough time to see the great shape of the manator sliding away beneath them, trails of blood, black in the water, oozing in its wake.

He went back to the captain. "Is that it? Did we get it?"

Burton looked over at him. "Takes more than that to kill a manator, lad."

He spun the wheel again, righting them against the waves, before a fierce swell bore down upon them. He did so just in time; a few moments later a large wave came crashing from the prow, bursting up in a great explosion of water, showering down upon the men on the forecastle. *Close*, Robbert thought, as the ship rocked and trembled. Had that wave hit them to starboard it might have turned them over. His heart had never beat so fast, and his bowels were turning to water. *I could let them empty right here and who would know?*

The men were scrambling to reload the mounted weapons and pass out more throwing harpoons. A short silence seemed to take root, a tension thickening, the spotters in the crow's nest and up in the rigging turning their eyes out, searching. The world went queerly quiet for a moment, as though the world was taking a breath.

"A sighting!" Bloodhound Burton bellowed. "Give me a damn sighting!"

A call came from the starboard gunwale. "Nothing, Captain." And the port. "Not here either, Cap'n!" From the crow's nest the same was said.

"It's under us," Bloodhound muttered. "This one's persistent."

Even as he spoke, Robbert felt the tremor rising up through the galleon, the great crack of those enormous tusks striking at the thick wooden hull.

"Will it sink us?" the prince asked, voice a shudder. He looked about, a slow terror climbing up his spine, filling his blood. There was no land about them, no shadowed islands in the distance. Only waves, great monstrous waves dwarfing them, cast like cliffs and mountains beneath a bellowing, dreaded sky. A flash of lightning lit the world, and for a moment he saw ships, faint and fogged in the mist, battling through the storm. Then the light faded and they were gone. "Will those tusks break through the hull?"

Bloodhound Burton gave him a hard look. "Enough questions. I need to focus, Prince Robbert. Go back below where it's safe."

He turned away from him, squinting out to sea, reading the patterns of the waves. When he saw another break in the swells, he bellowed the order to brace, and then swung the wheel once more. The harpoons and mounted crossbows moved on their swivels, searching, the men standing at the gunwales, holding to the rail with one hand, pikes clasped in their other, elbows cocked and ready.

"At the forecastle!" a spotter shouted up the ship. "Shadow in the water! Twenty metres to starboard!"

The weapons aimed and fired, slicing down into the waves. Robbert heard the twangs as the mechanisms were released, heard the grunts of the men as they heaved and threw, listened to the calls of 'miss' and 'miss' and 'miss' again. Not a single man had hit their target this time.

"Damn," the captain cursed. "He went too deep."

"Moving under us again, Cap'n!"

There was another shaking tremor a moment later, and another, and another. Robbert could see the fixed tension on Burton's face, the strain in his eyes, as he tussled this ancient beast. He squinted out into the seas. Another *thump* beneath them. Another.

"We have to move, Captain!" someone shrieked. "It'll crack the hull and sink us!"

Burton gave no answer. Ahead, the waves were rolling forth in a relentless swell, big enough to capsize them should they turn. *We have no choice but to wait*, Robbert realised. Then was another blow, another.

"Brace," roared the captain's first mate, a man called Bill Humbert.

The waves crashed into them, smashing hard into the bulwarks and running across the decks, the ship tossed about like a children's toy. Men cursed as their legs were swept from under them, reaching for rigging and ropes, sliding from one side of the ship to the other. Some were swept right over, Robbert saw, disappearing into the depths.

"Men overboard," came a call.

Burton's mouth twisted, but there was nothing he could do for them. The prince could see the figures bobbing in the water, waving their arms, hear the sound of their screaming at the edge of his hearing. They looked tiny out there against the waves, specs on moving mountains, already drifting away, thirty metres, fifty, a hundred…then they were gone.

A man came rushing up from belowdecks, panting. "Captain, there's a leak," he gasped. "Water coming up into the hold."

"Seal it," Burton shouted at him. "I'm *not* losing this ship."

The man dashed away. Another shout sounded. "Sighting to starboard! Fore of the ship!"

Burton snarled like a wolf. "Ready on the port side! Ready the harpoons!" The bolts and lances were loaded, tips gleaming, misting. "Brace," Burton roared. "Hard to starboard!"

The ship swung right, wood groaning, the world a maelstrom of noise. Robbert could see the thick dark shadow coming toward them, black blood still leaking from its wounds. It was shaped almost like a tadpole, he saw, the head much larger than the body. From an extended lower mandible, the two great tusks rose up, greyish white, pitted and cracked, breaking the surface. The left tusk was chipped, he saw, a full foot shorter than the right, which was less sharp than he'd have supposed, more blunt and rounded for battering.

The weapons fired, men hurling.

"Miss," shouted a man, and, "Miss," another bellowed, but then the hits came in. "Hit to the left flank," shouted one in triumph. "Hit to the head," said another.

The creature thrashed as the spears bit down into its flesh. Robbert saw the body twist, contorting, then it thrust forward with great speed, its enormous, flattened tail propelling it into the ship's keel.

"It's going for the rudder!" Burton shouted. "Brace! Hard to port!" He swung the wheel, turning the ship, but the manator crashed into them anyway, sending the entire ship shuddering. Men were thrown from their feet, more going over and into the water. Around them the waves were growing again, the ship lost in a range of towering black peaks. Robbert could hear the sound of desperate shouting ahead. There was a horrid *ripping* sound and one of the sails tore free of the foremast, flapping wildly away into the sky. A man came rushing back. "We've lost the fore-topsail, Cap'n!"

"I know, damn it! I saw!"

"We've got to lower the others," said Bill Humbert. "There's a crack in the foremast, it won't last much longer."

"We lower the sails and we'll be at Iulla's mercy. That manator will smash us to bits." Burton looked up, saw a great wall of water rising before them, casting them all in its shadow. He had barely enough time to call for the crew to brace before the wave surged over them, cascading across the decks, sweeping more men to their doom. It reached the quarterdeck, flooding past, and for a moment Robbert thought that was it, the ship would founder, but suddenly the waters were receding, rushing away over the walls and through the scuppers, and the men were standing again, spluttering, returning to their stations.

"We can't take much more of this, Captain," called George Buckley, the ship's bosun. "We're taking on too much drink."

Bloodhound Burton scowled at him. "Are the men manning the pumps?"

"Aye, Captain."

"Then what else can we do? Unless you want to get down there with a bucket?"

"Sighting to port!" came a shout. "It's coming back!"

Burton snapped his eyes that way, scanned the seas, judging them in an instant in a way that Robbert Lukar could never hope to match. He barked his orders for the starboard weapons to be readied.

Robbert looked down, saw one harpoon unmanned. *Its operators must have gone overboard.* Without thinking, he ran for the stairs, leapt down to the main deck, speeding for the bulwark. He'd never fired one before, though they were much alike to castle crossbows, and he'd been shown how they worked during the early days of their first voyage from the north, a lifetime ago that felt, when the fleet had first sailed to siege the Perch. He went for the rack, fetched a godsteel-tipped bolt, six feet long, and fixed it into place. The captain was shouting his commands - "brace, hard to port," - as Robbert pulled back, cocking the mechanism, grabbed the handles and turned the swivel. The ship swung, as it had a hundred times, lurching wildly. Robbert saw the world turn, saw the shadow approaching beneath the waves, the tips of tusks slicing through the water. He aimed, steadying, unsure where best to fire, heard a great loud *crack* fill the air, glimpsed the foremast come crashing down, and pulled the trigger.

The godsteel-tipped harpoon went flying into the sea, taking the manator somewhere in its left flank, mid-body. The creature twisted, thrashing, and gave out some deep otherworld bellow that seemed to shake the very air. "Hit," Robbert shouted at once, breathless, and for a moment jubilant."Hit to the left flank, Captain!"

Other shouts rang out, of hit and miss, the manator diving, slithering back beneath the rough wild waters. Robbert leaned forward, seeing the shadow darken and fade away, moving beneath the ship, felt a scraping, as though the creature was brushing against the hull, moving from port to starboard. He spun, rushing across to the other side of the ship, shouting, "It's coming this way. Ready to fire!" He saw the shadow reemerge, heard the sounds of the weapons discharging, saw several savage bolts strike true. Blood burst and bubbled to the surface. Some men shouted in triumph, "Hit!"

Another man roared out, "Wave!"

Robbert turned, and saw it. The wall of water right before him, tumbling and crashing over them. He had no time to react before it smacked him hard in the chest, knocking him back and off his feet, dragging him across the ship to smash into the port side wall. For five or six heartbeats he couldn't breathe, his whole body submerged, before the water passed over. He gasped, moving up onto his knees, saw white water rushing at him again, another wave coming. He had barely enough time to snatch a breath into his lungs before it drowned him anew, tossing him into something hard. He felt a crack, a hard crack in his ribs, and coughed, losing precious air. Then he gulped a measure of seawater, scrambled back up, broke the surface, spluttering, retching.

Another wave. This one from the other side. It knocked him hard from behind, pushing him forward, bullying him across the deck. He felt himself rolling, reaching out for something to hold onto, felt the hard coarse touch of hempen rope, and clung on. The waves kept coming, rolling one after another after another, crashing in from all sides, stinging his eyes and blinding him. *We're going down*, Robbert thought. *This is it. We're going down.*

Then the ship bobbed up, bursting back above the surface, and Robbert gasped for air. The sound of the winds and waves returned, and shouting of the men, the trumpeting of the storm. Robbert was at the mainmast, he realised, clinging to a rope dangling down from the rigging. He managed to get to his feet; others did the same about him. There was a sharp pain in his side from where he'd hit the wall. He coughed, bringing up more seawater, then dared to look around.

He wished he hadn't done so.

Ahead, he saw a cliff of water, rising so high it seemed to kiss the very clouds.

Oh, Prince Robbert Lukar thought.

Then he closed his eyes and prayed.

15

Jonik

He peered into the trees, narrow-eyed, listening.

"Quiet," he said. The word was a whisper, but the men behind him heard. At once both of them stopped in their tread, freezing. No crackle of leaves and twigs underfoot. No sound of squelching mud. Even their breathing seemed to still, and grow silent. And in the silence, Jonik *heard*. The rumbling of breath, the stalking movement, the unknown creature, closing.

He turned sharply to his men, standing with their horses. The woods were thick about them, the branches deeply knotted and tangled. A hundred years of humus had formed underfoot, softening their tread, and all else too. "Something stalks us," Jonik mouthed, quiet as a crypt.

"Where?" Gerrin mouthed back.

"There." Jonik raised a finger and pointed, away to the right of the way they had come. He had sensed something lurking in this old wood, some fell creature, though had refused to go around it. That would have only added precious time, and time they did not have. *Months*, he thought. *A year at best.* That was how long the world might last before it fell to unrecoverable ruin, he deemed.

The trunks were tightly packed, the canopy dense. Roots as thick as Jonik's thigh wrestled for room beneath the earth, snarls and juts poking out from the undergrowth. This was no place to stand and fight. "We go, on my command," he whispered. He had sighted a clearing ahead, where the trees seemed to thin out a little bit, forming a glade. "Follow me. Draw swords. We leave the horses here."

Harden frowned. "We need our horses," he hissed.

"We'll draw the beast away from them," Jonik said. Thus far the horses hadn't so much as raised their eyes, or turned their heads. They were munching as the men spoke, unaware of the threat. *This creature is silent*, Jonik thought.

He pulled his bastard sword from its sheath, a weapon taken from the refuge, a pristine blade of Tyrith's forging, made with the Hammer of Tukor. Double-fullered, double-edged, with a long, two-hand grip and wide, thick cross guard, it was not the Nightblade, no Blade of Vandar, but he would deal death with it just as well. *Mother's Mercy*, he had decided to name it. He had taken it the day Cecilia died.

The others had taken blades of their own that day, both basket-hilt broadswords, honed and fierce. They scratched out into the still air, misting.

Jonik shared a look with his men, as he opened his spare hand, releasing the lead rope. The others did the same, untethering their horses.

"Ready?" Jonik asked.

Two nods.

"Go," he said.

And they ran.

They did not care to mask their tread now, did not care to creep. Jonik took the lead, the others following, dashing through the trees to where the daylight shone down. At once there was a loud, deep roaring, splitting the air, carrying far. He could hear trees crashing behind them, branches snapping, claws tearing at the ground.

"Deadfall," Jonik shouted, spying a fallen tree. He leapt right over it, a great high bound, landed and kept on going. The clearing was just ahead. He burst through into the open, the ground softening at once underfoot. Pools glistened beneath the sunlight, frogs croaking, hopping through mounds of sedge. *Damn it.* "It's a marsh!"

The others came crashing through behind him, their heavy armour sinking, boots sucking at the mud. Jonik spun. Fighting in a swamp was folly, he knew, but they had no option now. The creature was approaching, a large shadow in the gloom of the forest. He swished his cloak over his shoulder, so it wouldn't get in his way, taking a two-hand grip of his long bastard sword. Harden was struggling to pull a boot from the mud, Gerrin helping to free him. "Hurry up! It's coming!"

"What is it?" Gerrin shouted.

Jonik studied their foe, glimpsed in flashes through the trees. A powerful upper body. Long hairy arms with retractible, ten-inch claws. Shorter legs, squat and strong. Its face was bear-like, though the snout was longer and thinner, and from its rear whipped a long, hairless, rat-like tail, all muscle. Thick fur covered the rest of its body, a dense protective coat. By then, Jonik knew.

"Drovava!" he yelled.

The creature crashed into the glade, upper body slung low, ursine face swinging side to side on a thick, muscular neck. A lather foamed at its mouth and its eyes, a glowing jet black, shark-like, were glistening with the promise of meat. Jonik stood before it, ten metres away, the others behind. "Are you free of the mud yet, Harden?" he called.

218

"Was. Now my other foot's stuck. Who thought it was a good idea to fight in a bog?"

Jonik breathed out. "Gerrin, go left. Get behind it. It's weaker at the rear. I'll try to keep its attention."

The creature was watching them, studying them as they were him. It was known to be smart, cunning, and vicious. The drovara liked to eat by tearing out its prey's guts and feasting on them while the poor creature was still alive. *They are known to enjoy places like this,* Jonik knew. Dark forests, damp and dingy, where they could creep through the boles and the branches unseen. For such a big creature, it was a remarkably silent stalker.

"Watch the claws," Gerrin warned. "It's said they can slash through godsteel."

"You're kidding," Harden groaned. "And you're going to leave me here stuck in the mud?"

"Pull yourself out, then," Jonik told him. "I'll lead it away from you. That'll give you time."

He stepped to the side, crab-walking, glancing down to make sure he didn't end up like the old sellsword. Mostly the earth was just spongy, but here and there were deep muddy puddles that could trap a man if he wasn't careful. The drovara turned with him, though its tail seemed to *look* at Gerrin, as the old knight went the other way. *It's second brain,* Jonik thought. That tail was an entity in itself, some said. *Like dragons.* Their tails were known to protect their rear as well, whipping and slashing.

Jonik shared a look with his old master. He gave a nod that said 'now', and they both rushed in together.

The drovara raised a paw and slashed, five lethal daggers swiping. Jonik parried with his blade, chipping off a chunk of claw, then swung down to try to de-limb the beast. The arm drew back in time, as Gerrin leapt behind, striking down with his broadsword to try to cut the creature's spine. That tail had other ideas. With a muscular swing, it crashed into Gerrin's breastplate, sending him tumbling back down into the marsh with a splash.

"Knew it wouldn't be that easy," the old knight grunted, standing back up, swamp-water dripping from his plate. He sounded a little winded. "Gods, this thing packs a punch."

Jonik was already moving again, darting in, thrusting for the creature's broad barrel chest. It sprung back, swiping defensively, claws raking along his pauldron with a burst of sparks.

So much for that rumour, Jonik thought. Men said that the King's Wall could cut through godsteel plate in a single swing as well, though that was probably an exaggeration too. The drovara burst toward him, thrusting off powerful back legs, the mud of the marsh exploding around him, snapping with its elongated face. Jonik fended the claws again, slashed out at the neck. The creature fended with a paw, quicker than Jonik would have thought, snapping down again with his maw.

Jonik side-stepped, swung, missed, cutting air as the drovara moved away. Gerrin came in behind, duelling the tail, which coiled and lashed out like a snake, whip-quick.

Harden was still pulling at his boot. There was a great sucking sound as it began to come loose.

Lather sprayed from the monster's mouth, a stinking foam, thick and creamy. Jonik could smell the stench of death in it. He swung his blade, driving the creature back, taking another rake along his flank. More sparks. Thin scratches on the plate. The creature bellowed in rage. Jonik saw an opening, flew forward at speed, hacked down at the neck where it met the shoulder…

The edge of his longsword bit through the long fur, the flesh beneath, juddering into bone. The beast roared, rearing, thrashing away in an eruption of green-brown water. Sedge and swamp reeds flew about it as it twisted in a frenzy, blood spraying from the wound. Gerrin was coming in behind, leapfrogging the tail as it whipped at him. He hacked down through the meat, sending half the tail spinning away into the mud. Blood came gushing from the wound in a thick red spray.

Harden was free now too. He lurched forward, muddy up to the thighs on both legs, sword in his fist. They closed from three sides. The drovava's eyes flitted from one to the other, judging this triple threat of foes. It took them all in, backing away, then snarled a final time…

…and turned to bolt away into the trees, blood spraying from its severed tail as it went.

"Yeah, you better bloody well run," Harden shouted after it. "And you leave our horses alone, foul beast!"

Jonik watched it go, to be sure it would not come back. Then he wiped down Mother's Mercy and returned it to its scabbard.

"Ought we chase it down?" Gerrin asked. "Track it to its lair? That severed tail's not going to be enough to kill it, nor the cleaved shoulder. It'll still haunt these woods for whoever passes next."

Jonik gave a shake of the head. "We're not monster hunters, Gerrin. It's the *Blades* of Vandar we're after, not his beasts."

The old Emerald Guard shrugged. "As you say. We can pass on a warning at the next tavern or garrison we find. Tell them what's lurking in here. We may not be monster hunters, but there are plenty of those sorts out there who'll want a drovara's head on his wall." He wiped the blood from his blade on his cloak, then sheathed it. "Best go check on those horses. Might have bolted with all this noise."

The man's instincts turned out to be correct. They returned to where they'd left them to find all three horses gone. Jonik breathed out. It had been a poor decision to lead them through this wood, in hindsight. *I should have listened to Gerrin.* He'd warned against coming through here.

"Track them down and bring them back," Jonik commanded. "They won't have gotten far."

It took an hour. Jonik's steed, a handsome piebald palfrey that had once belonged to the royal stables, Lord Morwood had told him, was found nearby, drinking at a steam. Gerrin's, a stroppy young stallion, had gone further. He was discovered in a thick tangle of brush, staring out at the old man with terrified eyes, ensnared among a drape of twisting vines. It took Gerrin a while to cut him loose and calm him, then lead him back.

The worst was Harden's mare, though, who'd caught her leg on a hidden root and fallen. The leg was broken, and that meant one thing. "We'll have to put her down," Gerrin said. "It's the kind thing to do."

"I'll do it," Jonik told them, drawing his dagger. It was his duty, his fault. He loved horses, hated seeing them suffer, and knew Gerrin was right.

Harden had other ideas. "She was my mare, so I'll do the killing. She'd want it to be me."

Jonik could tell he wasn't going to be dissuaded on that. He gave Harden a nod, and stepped away, returning to the other horses. Harden followed a few moments later, a grim look on his face and the content of his mare's saddlebags heaped over his shoulder. "You'll have to take these, lad. Your horse is the strongest."

There was a bite to the old man's voice. He too had suggested going through the woods was the wrong idea. The other option was a circuitous route through the hills, a much longer way, though open and in places tracked with dirt paths and wagon roads. This creepy old woodland was not large, but the going would be slow, Harden had said, especially with the horses. *I should have listened*, Jonik thought again.

"I'm sorry about your mare, Harden," he said. "We'll find you another horse at the next stables we pass."

It was an empty promise. Horses capable of bearing full-armoured Bladeborn were hard to come by. Harden only nodded, choosing not to get into an argument. The gods knew they had enough of those over their long months up in the Shadowfort, bickering over the fate of the boys.

"The light is fading," Gerrin said, looking up through the twisting canopy. "Best we be gone from this wood by the time dusk falls. I'd rather not sleep here if we can avoid it."

The gloaming was upon them by the time they escaped the last of the trees, moving out onto the top of the hillside that gave views across open plains, fields and thickets that clothed this part of Southern Tukor. Jonik breathed in the clear cold air, a long deep draught to freshen his lungs. Far away to the south, the faint shadow of the twin statues of Tukor's Pass could be seen on the horizon, marking the border with Vandar, still long leagues away. Three hundred metres high those statues soared, cloaked in mist and myth. At their base, Jonik spied a soft blur of light, saw tiny little fingers of smoke swirling and twisting up from the *Valley of the Gods*.

"Do you think we'll have trouble crossing?" Jonik asked.

Gerrin didn't think so. "You have the royal seal," he said. "They won't deny us."

Jonik was not sure how much power words held in these times, nor wax seals for that matter, bearing the princess's mark or not. But he nodded, hoping Gerrin was right.

The stars were coming out, cold and distant, the moon veiled behind a silken cloud. There was a chill in the air that felt odd for this time of year. Jonik drew his cloak about himself, then climbed into the saddle of his horse. Gerrin did the same with his young stallion. Harden did not move an inch.

"I'm not riding double with you, Gerrin," the gaunt old sellsword grunted. "I'll walk till we find me a horse."

That would slow them even more, but what could Jonik say? He swung his leg over the saddle, dropping to the floor. "Take mine, Harden. I'm young enough to be your grandson. I'll walk."

"Aye." The Ironmoorer nodded his thanks and mounted up. "Don't worry, lad. We'll find you a horse at the next stables we pass." He gave Jonik a grin from up there, tapped his spurs and trotted on.

They wended a route down the hillside, the hooves of the horses silenced by the soft grasses that draped its slope. They grew up to Jonik's knees here, swaying in the breeze, crickets and critters moving and buzzing between the stalks. Tiny fireflies awoke from their slumber, dancing in their shades of green and blue. It was pretty, peaceful. Further off, a farm track cut through a copse of trees, and beyond them Jonik saw a roadside inn, with a puffing chimney, and the glow of fire behind the windows.

"We should stop there," Gerrin said. "Ask some questions." He knew the inn, it turned out. "It's called the *Crabby Onion*. Silly name, I know, but there's a story behind it." He waited for someone to ask. When no one did, he told it anyway.

Jonik was only half listening. They grew onions here, apparently, and once before there was a grouchy old onion farmer the local people called 'Crabby' for his regular foul moods. When he died - of a heart attack, it was said, brought on by one of those fearsome moods of his - his wife sold the farm and built the tavern instead, naming it in his honour.

"One of his great-grandkids still runs the place," Gerrin finished. "Guy called Burt and his wife Betty. Leastways that was the case when last I came here."

"And when was that?" Jonik asked him.

The old knight gave a shrug. "Few years, I suppose it must be. Come, let's see if they're still around."

The inn was sat alone in a field beside the road, the crops gone to rot around them. There was an unpleasant scent of decay in the air, of withered plants and death. Not far from the inn, Jonik saw the cause; a great hulking bull lay on its side, its belly opened up, innards eaten out. Crows covered the carcass like flies, screaming and flapping away as they neared, then landing as soon as they'd gone by, resuming the feast.

"The bull died recently," Gerrin said. "Looks like the work of our tail-less friend."

Jonik nodded.

The inn was two hundred metres further on. Outside, there was a stable occupied by a pair of malnourished horses. One stared at them, blind in one eye; the other was turned away, looking at the wall, scratching at the ground with a hoof and swishing its mane. There was a cat, too, which startled at seeing them and scrambled away into the shadows. A dog sat tied up outside a stinking outhouse, a large mastiff, with nary the energy to even bark. He looked thin too, beaten and bedraggled.

"Which one of those horses do you want then, lad?" Harden japed. "The mad one or the blind one?"

Jonik ignored him. Something didn't feel right. He walked up to the mastiff, scratching the big dog beneath the chin. "Not much of a guard dog are you, boy?" He looked over at the inn, frowning. He could hear voices in there, the clutter of cups, drunken chatter, laughing. The others dismounted their steeds, tying them to a post, and stepped over to join him.

"Do you know this dog, Harden?"

The old knight nodded. "I do." He reached down and stroked his head with a gloved hand. The dog cowered at his touch.

"Someone's been mistreating him," Jonik said.

"Not Burt and Betty. They love this dog."

"And those horses?"

Gerrin looked over. A few spots of rain were starting to fall, pattering gently against their cloaks. "They always kept a couple of them for getting about. Those two haven't been fed in a while, though."

Harden stepped over from the inn. He'd been peeking through the frosted window, getting a look inside. "There are eight men in there. All at one big table. Didn't see anyone else."

"No one behind the bar?"

"Not that I saw."

Jonik stepped toward the door to the inn, moving beneath the covered awning. A pair of chains rattled above him, chains that would once have borne the inn's swinging sign, which now lay aside in the mud, its painted image of a grumpy old man with an onion in his mouth cracked and broken. There were flower pots in little alcoves to either side of the door. Those too had been smashed, the flowers scattered and dead.

Jonik was sensing the worst. He raised a fist and rapped hard at the door.

The voices inside hushed. A short pause, and then he heard the sound of boots stamping over, a heavy thud of steel on wood. The door was unbolted, one and two and three of them, then opened up, a wash of firelight pouring out, the scent of smoke and spices, piss and rum and mead and roasted meat. A man in a coat of godsteel ringmail stood before him, framed by the glow, a large man with a large beard, a thick black tangle of iron wire sprouting from his cheeks and chin. He wore steel about his legs as well, and a half helm on his head in the likeness of a stag, with a pair of antlers twisting off to left and right. There was a scratch beneath his right eye, and his nose was hardly recognisable as a nose anymore, a great lumpen thing that had probably been broken a dozen times before.

He gave Jonik an appraising look, then did the same to Gerrin and Harden, standing behind in cloaks and cowls. The rain was falling harder.

"What do you want?" the big man grunted. "Got no food here for you, no beds to sleep in neither. If you're looking for ale, you can piss off. That's ours, and running low."

"We're not looking for ale," Jonik said.

"What then?"

"Information."

The man gave Jonik another long look, all the way up and down. "The inn is *full*, boy," he said. "Now off my porch if you know what's good for you." He went to slam the door.

Jonik slid his foot forward, stopping him. "This isn't your porch. Where are Burt and Betty?"

The man sneered down at Jonik's foot. "Who?"

"They're the proprietors of this inn," Gerrin said, behind. "Old friends of mine." He gripped the handle of his blade. "Where are they?"

"I'm damned if I know."

He's lying, Jonik thought. *These men are deserters, or worse.* He looked through the gap, saw another seven of them sitting about a pair of tables dragged together, all in bits of armour and mail, boiled leather and wool. There were jugs and flagons, pewter cups scattered about, some overturned, ale stains and wine stains and rum stains on the wood. He saw trenchers of carved bread, soaked in soup and stew. At the hearth fire, some meat was being roasted by another man sitting on a stool, and he saw two others appearing from a stair at the back, swelling their numbers to eleven. But no Burt, no Betty. *They're dead,* Jonik thought.

Gerrin was doubtless thinking the same. "We want no quarrel," he told the big leader. "Stand aside, let us look around, and this needn't go ill."

The man scoffed. "Ill? No, you'd best hope not, old man. Now clear off, before I lose my temper. I'm in a good mood. You don't want that to change." He kicked at Jonik's boot, thinking it nought but leather, but beneath it he wore his godsteel sabatons. His foot didn't budge. The man looked up at him and snarled. "Bladeborn, is it?" He gave them all another long look, Jonik then Gerrin then Harden. Their armour was covered in their cloaks and cowls, their blades hidden, but now he knew. "All three of you?"

"All three," Jonik said.

The man smiled, a glimpse of brown teeth behind his beard. "We got the same." He thumbed behind him. "Me, Truss, Hunter, all Varin's blood. Rest are good with the blade as well. No better knifeman than Nips, ain't that right?"

A man in the back called out approval. *Nips*, Jonik supposed he was, a cruel-faced cutthroat by the look he got of him. The rest looked unpleasant to a man, rough and unwashed, some bearded, others bearing scars and drunken scowls. It seemed as though they'd been here for a while, bedding in like rats in winter.

Jonik came out and said it. "You're deserters from Prince Raynald's army. You slipped away when he marched to the south."

That accusation caused half the men in the tavern to stand in outrage, chairs flying back, legs scraping wood. The big leader raised a hand to calm them. "Aye, so what if we are? You his little sheep dog are you, sent off to round up the herd?"

There were blades being drawn now, naked steel sliding from sheaths, daggers and swords and axes gleaming in the firelight. His boast of three Bladeborn wasn't a lie; two men behind him bore misting blades, one a short sword, the other a long one. They weren't knights, though, that was clear enough. *Freeriders and sellswords*, Jonik suspected. *Lesser sons of lowly houses at best.*

Their leader, though… The helm on his head was a fine thing, and the ringmail about him rich. Jonik sifted through the houses that had stags on their sigils. Kanabar was most famous, though that was an elk, and Vandarian too, and no good Kanabar man would ever turn deserter. He knew of House Buckland as well, who bore a stag and bear on their sigil, facing off against one another, but the Bucklands hailed from Rasalan. *Big men, though, and hairy.* He peered at the man, wondering. He'd heard that Lady Payne of Rasalan had fought with the Vandarians, so perhaps Lord Buckland had sent men to fight with Prince Raynald? Lord Morwood had not mentioned that, if so. It was a Tukoran army only, the way he told it, with banners drawn from Ilithor and the surrounding lands.

A lesser house, he thought. *Ramfort, maybe. Or Neldrey.* They had stags on their sigils, he remembered. *Or maybe that helm is stolen.* That seemed just as likely.

It made no matter either way he wanted to cut it. They were deserters, and Jonik knew what the penalty was for that.

"Tell your men to throw down their arms," he said. "We need to search this house."

The big man reached behind his back, and his hand came back

with a spiked warhammer. From each little point came a drift of mist, swirling upward. "No. Anything else?"

Jonik was not wearing his helm, nor were the others. *I have a more important duty,* he tried to tell himself. *You can't risk yourself. Just turn around and walk away.*

Instead he drew Mother's Mercy.

The big man smiled. "Fancy blade."

"You'd have liked my other one."

"I got a nice bit of steel too." He tapped the sword at his hip, which rattled in its sheath. There was something about it Jonik recognised. The cross-guard, long and twisting like the arms of a kraken; the pommel, bulbous and bumpy and a deep black-grey, like the sea-monsters's head. The likeness was good. Jonik knew that firsthand having fought a kraken once before.

He peered closer, eyes narrowing. "Where did you get that blade?"

The big man gave a chuckle. "Like it do you, boy? Aye, thought you might. Must've been some Rasal lord owned it once, what with these tentacles and whatnot. Maybe I'll kill you with it instead? How's about it? You want me to hack your head off or cave it in? Either works for me."

The rain was falling in sheets now, heavy and cold, spitting with bits of hail. Jonik reached up, unfastening his brooch, letting his sodden cloak slip to the ground. His armour had been silver, filled with light, but now it sank to darkness at his command.

The big man watched the light leech out of it, frowning. "How in the frosted hell…"

Jonik had heard enough from him. He raised a boot and kicked at the door, blasting it open, knocking the big man back, who tripped, stumbling away into the men behind him. Jonik pressed forward, thrusting for the leader, but another of the deserters got in his way and he skewered him through the chest. He pulled back, swung at another man as he roared and ran, cutting him down. There was a whistle of air and Jonik turned, jerking his neck aside as a throwing dagger came flying for his head. Nims was there, pulling another knife from his criss-cross belt. He threw again. Jonik flicked the blade away with his gauntleted hand, and the knife went plunging into the eye of another man who lurched backward, arms flailing, to crash into a table.

By then the others had followed him in, Gerrin and Harden moving left and right, cutting and engaging. The ring of battle filled the inn. The big leader roared something wordless and charged, swinging down with that godsteel warhammer, but Jonik swung hard and knocked it aside, then swung again at the flank of his ringmail shirt. Several of the little links burst asunder in a shower of silver mist. He felt the edge of Mother's Mercy cut through mail and leather and wool and flesh, then pulled back, saw the blood come sluicing from the wound. The big man roared.

The planks behind him rattled. Jonik turned. Two men were there.

One bore a battleaxe, the other a broadsword. The axe chopped down at his head, the sword lunging for his neck. Jonik whirled away, quick as lightning, hacking down through both weapons at once with his blade, shattering the steel, shards of sword and axe splintering. The axe-man went crashing to the floor at the force of Jonik's strike, chin cracking hard against the wooden deck, jaw crunching, teeth bursting from his mouth in a spray of blood and spittle. The other deserter stood there, open-mouthed, piss leaking down his leg, shivering all over. "I…I yie…"

Yield, Jonik thought, but he didn't care to hear it. He cut through his neck before the word could be uttered, carving him open to the nape. The head snapped back, almost tearing free, blood spraying up in a wild red fountain. Jonik brushed the man aside, saw the Bladeborn with the shortsword running for Harden, ghosted forward and swung right through his body, parting top from bottom. Blood and bowels, guts and gore all poured onto the floor in a great stinking splash. A man nearby let out a shuddering scream of horror and ran, and another scrambled after him, fleeing into the night.

Jonik panted like a predator and turned about, searching for his next kill. Nims was dancing about, flicking his knives, leaping from table to table as Harden chased him down. The other Bladeborn, Truss or Hunter, was duelling Gerrin, but would not last long. *You have no idea who you're fighting,* he thought. *Nor you.* He turned to the big man.

They came face to face at the heart of the room. The other men were dead or fled or dying. His foe held a hand at his side where Jonik had cut him, blood leaking out through his fingers. His other hand clung to his warhammer, a rare weapon, but Jonik didn't care for it.

"That sword," he said once more. "Where did you get it?"

The man said nothing.

"Tell me and I'll make it quick."

"Found it," he said. "On a dying man."

"Where?"

"Here."

"Here?"

"Aye. Right here in this pissing inn. There's a man upstairs, sick as a dog…didn't think he'd need it. Well, that boy who was tending him thought otherwise, but I've always hated boys. Shouted at me to leave him be, but you think I was gonna listen to that? Men were coming to take him away, he said. Bollocks, I said back. Then I cut his pretty throat."

Jonik's fist tightened about his blade. "You admit to murder?"

"Good to admit your sins before you die. Might save me."

"It won't. Where are the innkeeper and his wife?"

"Outside. We were going to bury them, but couldn't be bothered, so just threw them into the field. There's some beast out in them woods nearby, we heard. Thought we'd leave it a meal, keep it from our door."

Jonik scowled. "And this boy?"

"Him too. Annoying little runt, he was, thinking himself all high and mighty. Said he'd served with heroes. Boasted the Barrel Knight was a friend. That *ghost* as well. Lying little cretin deserved what he got."

Jonik's breath stilled in his lungs. His eyes narrowed, fist tightening about his blade. *Devin?* he thought.

He took a hard step forward.

The big man stood his ground, hefting his warhammer, pulling out that kraken-blade. Blood oozed freely from his side, trickling down through the links in his ringmail, soaking into his leathers and wools. His face twisted in pain. "Let's get this done." He thrust with the blade, bringing the warhammer down behind it.

Jonik faded left, right, swung upward. The tip of Mother's Mercy tore through the bottom of the man's bearded chin, splitting it. A gurgly grunt erupted, teeth and blood spraying. The man stumbled backward. Jonik slipped sideways, quick as a whip, slicing through his lumpen nose, then rushed forward, gripped his neck before he could fall, lifted, squeezed, saw his eyes widen, bulge, burst out from the sockets of his skull, closed his gauntlet about his throat, ripped it out as he tossed the man aside. Blood poured from his flank, and his neck, and from the hole where his nose once was. His eyes dangled out on thin tendrils of ragged sinew. Jonik spat on him, then ran for the stairs, smashing the planks beneath his weight as he rushed upward.

He reached the landing, the floor groaning as though it might collapse, saw open doors leading into the rooms where the deserters had slept. One door at the end was closed. He stamped toward it, turned the handle, pulled. The stink of piss and pestilence rolled out, thick in his nostrils. The interior was pitch dark, the drapes drawn, the patter of rain heavy on the roof. There was a groaning sound, a man in a fever lying on a bed, unwashed and uncleaned and untended and unfed.

Jonik snatched a candle from an alcove outside and stepped in, waving the light across the room. The figure in the bed had a young face, a face barely older than his, a face he knew. The kraken-blade had been his, taken from the chests that Lord Humphrey Merrymarsh had given them, an age ago when they'd landed in Calmwater after their long voyage from the south.

Jonik rushed forward, set the candle on the bedside table. He pulled off a glove and a gauntlet and put a hand to the man's fore-head. "Sir Lenard," he whispered. "Lenard, can you hear me?"

The young knight's eyes flickered, but did not open. He groaned, moving in his sleep, shifting over the soiled linens. He had not been cleaned for long days, even weeks. Jonik drew back the filthy cover, saw his skinny body beneath, the wounds that raked across his chest covered in a bloody bandage, going brown. There was a plate of food beside him, but the food was mouldy, rotten, a cup of water dry as a bone. A fury boiled in Jonik's guts. He wanted to go back down there and kill those men all over again, but that was done and they were dead.

Instead he turned and bellowed out, "Gerrin! Water! Now! Lenard Borrington is dying! Bring water! Now!"

16

Saska

The caravel was beached at the bottom of a cliff, inaccessible to them lest they risk a perilous climb down, caught on the rocks a hundred metres from the shore. The masts had all been snapped clean free, the sails shredded and torn apart, the gunwales and bulwarks battered, and the ship was listing badly. There were holes in the side of the vessel, Saska saw, and on the decks she could see what looked like bodies too, scattered here and there.

"So, what are we thinking?" asked Leshie, standing at the edge of the cliff with Saska, Del, and Rolly. The rest of the host were taking a moment to water the horses and camels, hiding from the sun in the shade of a grove of Aramatian cypress trees. There was a small roadside tavern on the other side of the Capital Road here, with a working well in the back. The innkeep and his wife and children were all hard at work bringing out trays of water for the host, and plates of fruit as well, mangos and pears, apples and dates, which the men - the sellswords in particular - were gobbling down greedily. "Do you think they foundered in that storm?" Leshie went on. "Looks like they were washed ashore."

That storm, Saska thought. They had seen it from the coast, a brutal tempest that had turned all the southern skies dark for a full two days. 'Weather of the new world', Sunrider Alym Tantario had called it. He said that this was to be expected during the Ever-War, these apocalyptic weather events. *And here was me thinking it was just gods and monsters we had to worry about.* No. Apparently, they could expect tornados and superstorms and city-swallowing earthquakes too.

"It wasn't the storm," Sir Ralston said. "That ship has been there too long."

Leshie looked up at him. "How do you know?"

"The bodies on deck. They're entering a later stage of decomposition. Those men have been dead for several weeks."

Saska took a grip of her Varin dagger, which she had come to find enhanced her sight just a little more than regular godsteel. There were several dead men on deck wearing sun-scorched cloaks and bits of rusting armour. That alone suggested they'd been lying there a while. The fact that there were crabs picking at what remained of their flesh was a better sign, however.

She nodded. "A few weeks sounds about right."

Leshie frowned at her. She wasn't able to see so far, not in such detail anyway. "I'll have to take your word for it. Or I guess we could just ask the innkeeper. He'll be able to tell us when they ran aground."

"Several weeks ago," Rolly repeated. "There's no need to trouble the man."

The Red Blade shrugged. "If you say so. So who are they, then? Tukoran?"

"It would seem likely," Sir Ralston said. "By their clothing."

"But not the ship," Saska pointed out. She knew enough about the styles of northern and southern ships to see that this caravel was of Aramatian design. The differences were subtle, if noticeable for someone looking for them, and what remained of the figurehead showed a snarling sunwolf. "It's Aramatian."

Leshie bit her lip, trying to puzzle it out. "Shall we go down and investigate?" She took a step forward, looking over the edge of the cliff. "I can get down there, no problem."

"And how would you reach the ship?" the Wall asked her. "It's a hundred metres from the beach."

"Hmmm, I wonder," the girl said, rubbing her chin. "I don't know, maybe I'd…*swim*? And *not* in my armour, before you ask. I'd take that off first, *obviously*."

The Wall shook his head. "These are shark-infested waters. You would only be risking your life and for no profit whatsoever. Most likely this ship was a part of the coalition armada that sailed south from Eagle's Perch. By the damage to the vessel it was likely attacked. Torn masts and holes in the bulwarks suggest the work of a kraken."

Leshie whistled through her lips. "That's a battle I'd have liked to see."

"Wasn't much of a battle, by the look of the ship," Saska remarked.

"I think I know who they are," said Del.

Everyone looked at him. Leshie jabbed him in the arm. "Go on then, Squire. Enlighten us."

"Sir Clive Fanning," Del said, in that way of his, as though he wasn't quite sure. Sometimes he made answers sound like questions, by the cadence of his voice, the unsure frame of his eyes. "I think, anyway."

"And who's Clive Fanning?" Saska asked him.

"He was a knight. One who spoke out against Lord Kastor, and the alliance he made with the sunlord. Sir Bernie said that he escaped, from the port at Kolash, after we'd won the city. There was a lot of trouble, after what happened with Sir Alistair. Lord Kastor killed him, for mutiny, and after that Sir Alistair's men tried to leave, but were caught and killed at the docks. But Sir Clive…he got away, I heard. Him and seventy men."

"Well…they didn't get far," Leshie said, deadpan. "We passed Kolash only days ago."

But he clearly made it through the Solapian Channel, Saska thought. That meant he must have avoided the attention of the krelia, only to then come upon a kraken instead, if what Sir Ralston said was true. That was like avoiding dying in a blazing fire, only to suffocate from ash fumes anyway. *Poor men. To get away from that bastard Kastor only to die screaming at sea…*

"Do you think anyone survived?" Del asked. "They might have swum to shore and climbed the cliff."

Sir Ralston nodded at the possibility. "I will ask the innkeeper if he has heard anything." He turned to leave the cliffside, marching away. There seemed no further reason for them to remain there, staring at the wreck, and the sun was growing fierce, so the three of them returned to the shade of the trees.

As soon as they arrived they were joined by the master archer, Kaa Sokari, who paced right up to Del with a look of hard disapproval cast onto his leathery face. "How does the spider catch the fly?" he asked. "How does the eagle snare the vole?"

Del looked stumped. "I…" He managed nothing more than a croak, then turned to look at Saska.

"No, do not look at her. You must learn to think for yourself. You must learn not to rely on others. Look at me."

Del looked back into Kaa Sokari's stern eyes.

"I ask again. How does the spider catch the fly? How does the eagle snare the vole?"

Del swallowed, trying hard not to look away from him. "They… they're born to…to…" His eyes flickered to the side, then back again.

Kaa Sokari leaned in. "Yes?"

"They're born to…to do it. To catch their prey. It's instinct."

"Yes. *Instinct.* It is something written into them, to catch these creatures on which they prey. Yet instinct is not everything. They still will fail, and try again, and fail and try and fail and try until this instinct of theirs is honed and mastered to an art. Sometimes the fly will wriggle free of the web. Sometimes the eagle will mistime its plunge and give the vole a chance to escape. But they do not stop, they do not give up. They try again, and again, and again, because they must. If they do not they will die, they will starve, and this is how *you* must think." He lifted his chin, peering down with those keen eyes of his eyes. "Where is your bow?"

"I left it…" Del pointed. "It's with my horse."

"Your horse should have a name by now," Sokari said. "You will name him by the end of this day. Yes?"

"Yes..."

"Yes, what?"

"Yes…Master.'

Kaa Sokari gave a nod. "Better. Now go, and fetch your bow. You must take these chances to train, every chance possible, to hone this instinct of yours into something worthwhile, and *not* be drawn to idle interest." He peered over to the cliffs, the seas beyond a hard flat blue,' calm after the passing of the storm. "What were you doing out there?"

"A ship…there was a shipwreck…out on the rocks…"

"A shipwreck? And this is important to you, looking at a shipwreck? More important than your training?"

The apple in Del's neck went up and down. "I don't…no, I just…I wanted to see it. That's all. I didn't think…"

"Didn't think what?"

"That we'd stop…for this long. I thought it would be quicker. I didn't think there'd be time to…to train."

"There is *always* time to train. A minute here, another minute there. They all add up." He narrowed his eyes. "Do you want to become a master archer or not?"

"I…I…"

"*I* is not an answer. The answer is *yes*, or it is *no*, in which case I will wipe my hands of you and be done. But if *yes*, you must commit. So I ask you again, do you want to become a master archer?"

Del swallowed. "Y-yes."

"Yes, what?"

"Yes, Master Sokari."

"Then what are you still doing here? Fetch your bow. There is no time to waste."

Del bowed to him in an awkward way and scampered off, bits of armour clanking.

Saska looked at Kaa Sokari. "You could go a little easier on him, Kaa."

"Easier?" The man seemed affronted by the word. "No, Sereness. You asked that I make him into a master bowman. This is a hard task that requires a hard road and a hard master. There is no other way."

I never asked that, Saska thought. She'd expected the old bowmaster to give Del a few pointers, take him aside for the occasional lesson to improve his skills. This was much more than she'd expected. *I've unleashed a monster,* she reflected. As if there weren't enough of those in this world. "Well…if you insist. Who am I to question your methods?"

"No one, my lady. Harsh as that may sound, in this particular field, you are no one to question me. Now, if you'll excuse me. We have little time before we leave, and this idle interest in shipwrecks has not helped. Your brother must become single-minded if he is to improve, Sereneness. No more coddling of him. You have a part to play in this too."

Saska took umbrage with that. "I'm not coddling him. Protecting him, maybe, but not coddling him."

"Call it what you wish. It will not serve for the boy to go crying to you when I push him too hard. For you to pat his back and say 'there, there'. This is a hard world, getting harder. There can be no space for softness." The master archer did not care to continue the debate or hear Saska's response. He sketched a bow and then turned on his heels, marching away as quickly as he'd arrived.

Leshie gave a laugh as he departed. "He's a bundle of fun, isn't he? And I thought Lady Marian was tough on us."

"Maybe it's what he needs," Saska said. She looked over. "I don't coddle him too much, do I?"

Leshie shrugged. "Not that I've seen. You're just being an older sister to him, Sask. And anyway, I don't think you're the type to coddle someone. You can be pretty hard too, you know."

I've lived a hard life, she thought. She decided not to say that, spotting Rolly as he came back over, swatting at the flies and mosquitoes as he went. They were plentiful here, and seemed to enjoy Sir Ralston's blood more than most. "Because he's so sweet," the Butcher had said. That got a good laugh from the sellswords.

"The innkeeper says he saw nothing," the giant reported. "But the cliffs are shallower further up the coast, and there is a way to climb out there. If Sir Clive or anyone survived, he says they would have gone that way."

"And what happens if we find them?" Leshie asked. "Are you to chop their heads off like you did with Sir Gavin and those others, Coldheart?"

The Wall did not enjoy the remark. "Those men asked for the blade."

"Sir Clive Fanning is not our enemy, Leshie," Saska told her. "You heard what Del said. If we were to find him or any of his men, they can join us. We'll take them home."

"Oh really? And you'd be happy to share with them who you are, will you? Soon enough everyone will know, and then what? You'll have a demon demigod breathing down your neck."

The Whaleheart nodded. There was no one more staunch in wanting Saska to keep her secret, no one more disgruntled at the fact that the sellswords all seemed to know, and no doubt half of the men under Tantario's charge as well. Trustworthy though they might be, it only took one embittered man to go blabbing the truth, or be taken and have it tortured out of them. "It would be better if we did not find anyone," the Wall said. He looked over at the Surgeon, sitting on a log sharpening one of his scalpels, the Tigress standing at his shoulder, eyes slitted, ever watchful. "There has been enough killing over your identity already."

Saska didn't disagree with a word of that. But all the same… "That was different," she felt compelled to say. "The Surgeon only killed those who would have used the secret for profit. And sometimes he didn't kill them at all. He only took out their tongues or threatened their families."

"Oh? Only that," laughed Leshie. "Isn't he just the sweetest."

"Sir Clive Fanning and his men *defied* Cedrik Kastor," Saska went on, ignoring the jest. "If any of them are alive, we will take them home. *Alive*, and with their tongues still in their mouths."

"And if the Surgeon has other ideas?" asked the Wall.

"Then you will beat them out of him, Rolly. He acted under his own authority before, but that is no longer the case. He is here under my command now, and I won't have him killing good honest men on account of who my grandfather was."

"Unless they're villains," Leshie offered, shrugging. "If they're villains, then they die. Right, Sask?"

It was murky ground, to be sure. Proving villainy and ill intent was never easy in a case such as this. Sir Ralston Whaleheart had a look on his face. "What?" Saska said.

The Wall said nothing.

"What is it?"

Still nothing.

"For Tukor's sake, Rolly, just answer me. The stone-faced treatment doesn't work with me anymore."

"It was your grandmother," the giant said, at last. "The Surgeon never acted by his own authority. He did so by that of the Grand Duchess."

Saska stared up at him, half taken aback. "Is…is that true?"

"I am not known to lie. Your grandmother did it to protect you, and spare you. You need not be troubling yourself with these petty matters. They are for us, your captains, to contend with, not you."

"I will be the judge of that. When people are dying in my name I deserve to know." Saska turned on her heels, marching through the cypress trees, stepping right up to the Surgeon. "You lied to me," she said.

The sellsword looked up from his sharpening, scalpel in one hand, whetstone in another, cloth set upon his lap with more knives and blades. He took a moment to lay down both the whetstone and the blade, then put his hands together and gave her his full attention. "How so, Serenity?"

"*The authority of necessity*, you said, about these killings. You never told me my grandmother had put you up to it."

"No. I thought that if I did, you would only have gone to her and complained. There did not seem any sense in that. With your imminent departure from the city, and your grandmother's ailing health, I sought to protect you from such bitter recriminations. You both deserved to enjoy your last moments together without this hanging over you."

Isn't he just the sweetest, Saska thought. And perhaps there was some truth in that. "I should have been told."

"You have been. Now."

"By Sir Ralston. You should have come to me with this yourself, as soon as we left the city."

"You may be right. But I saw profit in sparing you this detail. I feared it would sully your opinion of your grandmother, tar the sweet memories you made together. Why bother, when I am here to take the burden of blame? I am more than happy to carry it."

"I can tell. You're proud of what you did."

"I am proud to serve this great cause. In whatever way I can."

She met his eyes, thought about it a moment, then nodded, realising there was nothing much to this at all. She had understood when the Surgeon first told her about the killings - much as she didn't like the taste of it - and that her grandmother had played her part did not surprise her either. S*he would do anything to protect me, and shield me. Anything to win this war*. "Just tell me the truth from now on." That was, perhaps, the crux of it. "I do not like being kept in the dark."

The Surgeon gave her one of those empty smiles and bowed his head. "Yes, of course. Full candour, from now on."

She stepped away, across the sun-dappled ground, the heat already stifling. The shade could only offer so much relief when the air itself was burning. Beyond the trees, she could see Kaa Sokari leading Del out toward some rocks, using them for target practice, perhaps. There were shaded areas where they might train, but no, Sokari always sought to test Del where he could.

She spotted Sunrider Tantario stepping out of the tavern, two of his men at his sides. Saska moved back out into the blazing sun, cutting them off as they crossed to the shade. "Did you learn anything, Sunrider?"

They had gone inside to speak to the tavern guests, a protocol that they had followed for the duration of their journey. There were many such places along the Capital Road and it served to arm themselves with the latest tidings whenever they had a chance. To the same end, scouts were regularly sent ahead up the road to gather intelligence and report back. Tantario was not a man who liked surprises, Saska learned. After the skirmish with Sir Gavin Trent and his men he was not taking any chances.

"There is word of a menace on the *Matian Way*, Serenity," Tantario told her. "It may be wise for us to continue along the Capital Road, after all."

That would add long days to their journey, Saska knew. The

Matian Way was a shortcut that crossed through the hills, rather than keeping to the coastal road. It would save them having to travel around the Howling Headland, a great jut of land that extended out of the coast, south of the Port of Matia. "What sort of menace?" she asked.

"A sand drake, we believe, by the descriptions we were given. It is possible it has moved on by now, but I do not think it wise to take the risk. The heat along the Matian Way will also be quite oppressive. It will remain cooler on the coast, and more so as we move further north. By the time we get to Cloaklake the worst of it will be behind us."

Saska wasn't going to argue with the man. A sand drake she could accept. But a thickening of this stifling heat? No. "We'll stay on the coast, then. Did you learn anything else, Sunrider?"

He nodded. "One man spoke of your prince's fleet. It left its anchorage not far from here. There were some thirty of them, we are told."

"Thirty vessels?"

"Yes. They raised their sails only days ago, and took at once to deeper waters." He paused. "It is likely they were caught in the storm, my lady."

Then it's likely that Robbert is dead. She had feared that as soon as they saw the tempest, and that had been much further west. Apparently, it was even worse here. *A storm like few others, through which even Seaborn would struggle to sail.* "Prince Robbert's fate is his own, and not in our power to change," Saska said. 'The seas will judge him', Lord Hasham had told her. *Their judgements are harsh, it seems.* "Anything else?"

"Nothing to trouble you with, Serenity. Civil matters that Lord Hasham will want to hear of."

"What sort of civil matters?" Saska was heir to this duchy, technically. She ought to hear of its health.

"The sort that arise during wartime. The sort we have heard of already, in Kolash and elsewhere. Famine. Disease. Criminality on a terrible scale. Men fighting other men over stocks of food and resources. Rebellions against the local authorities in towns across the land. I am logging these events to report back to Lord Hasham upon my return." He paused. "And…"

"Go ahead," Saska said.

"There is a large town…Banassy, not far to the east of here. It is a local trading hub and port of authority, with a stronghold built into its heart containing a garrison of soldiers. Their duty is to keep order across the Howling Headland, but there are reports that the town has been taken over by a madman. One claiming he can commune with monsters."

Saska raised an eyebrow. "Monsters? To what end?"

"What end does a madman require? I would think he is driven by a dark spirit of some kind, a monster in itself. There is talk of human sacrifice, brutal executions, children being eaten by beasts in ritual sport before the very eyes of their parents. Crimes of great evil, against the natural order." He looked to the tavern, eyes creased. "There are two men in there who stood witness to this, before they managed to escape through a cistern, beneath the city walls. Their reports are… harrowing, my lady."

Saska's jaw tightened. "Are you suggesting we travel to this town, Sunrider Tantario? Liberate it from the clutches of this madman?"

"No, my lady, I would not ask that of you…"

"But you are. By telling me, you are."

He shook his head in denial. "My directive is to escort you to Eagle's Perch, and see you safely to sea. This madman will stay until I return. As with the sand drake, the risks are too great."

He was probably right about that, though by the gods she wished that was not so. *Me and my precious blood.* If it wasn't for Saska's grander mission, she would be only too happy to help. These were her people, after all. This was her duchy to protect. "I will speak with Sir Ralston and the sellswords," she said. "How far to the east is this town?"

"A three-day ride, or thereabouts."

"And it's on the Capital Road?"

He nodded. "A little inland, but yes."

"Then we will be passing by anyway. We can decide over the next few days whether we stop to help."

Saska returned to the shade of the grove, calling Sir Ralston and the sellsword captains together for a council out of earshot from the others. Leshie, of course, joined as well. "What's going on?" she asked.

Saska told them what Tantario had said.

The Wall shook his head at once. "No. If trouble comes to us, so be it. We will not go looking for it."

"You're not in charge, Coldheart," said the Butcher. "The purpose of a council is to give counsel, so the pretty princess can decide." He smiled, scars twisting, chin glistening from all the sticky fruit he'd been eating. "I say we go. We need regular battle to stay sharp and the pretty princess still needs honing. Cutting the head off a madman will serve her well."

"There is only one madman whose head she needs to cut off and it isn't this one," the Wall said. "Our mission is simple and needs no complications."

"Simple?" Leshie laughed. "You think killing a demigod is simple?"

"Killing anyone is simple. I did not say it would be easy."

Leshie clearly didn't grasp the distinction. "What's the difference?"

"A simple act is one that is easily understood," said the Surgeon, quite calmly. "That does not mean it is easy to implement. Sir Ralston is quite correct. Nothing that deviates us from our mission should be considered."

"Our mission is to win the war, isn't it?" Leshie said to that. "That means killing bad guys and slaying monsters."

"*One* bad guy. *One* monster." The Wall gave a firm shake of the

238

head. "We should take the Matian Way, as previously discussed. It will save us a lot of time. I thought that was already agreed?"

"There are rumours of a sand dragon out that way," Saska said. She hadn't told them about that yet. "Sunrider Tantario said we should stay on the Capital Road."

"Of course he did," the Baker chuckled, readjusting his golden spectacles. "This man Tantario is a proud Aramatian, and cares deeply for his people. Banassy is an important town. He will lead us to it, with this gentle coaxing, so we help to remove this madman and set the people free. We are fifteen skilled and armoured Bladeborn, who together have killed a thousand men. There could be no fiercer group in all of the south. Tantario seeks to use us."

"He is canny, this Sunrider," agreed the Surgeon. "This may be his ploy."

"A clever ploy," said the Butcher. "And a righteous one. We should go. The pretty princess needs the practice."

"She needs *protection*, not practice," the Wall said, firmly. "This town does not matter. *Nothing* matters but our mission."

The Butcher gave a laugh. "No wonder you have no wife, Cold-heart. That poor woman would always be second best."

"Enough japing," Sir Ralston thundered. "This discussion is done."

The sellsword captains all looked up at him. Then they turned to Saska. "*Is* it done?" the Baker asked her. "As fearsome as the giant is, and as passionately as he speaks, we are here to serve you, not him. We have offered honest counsel. What is your decision?"

I have no decision, she thought. "I have to think about it," she said.

The Wall did not like that answer. "We will reach the turning that takes us onto the Matian Way this afternoon," he said, staring down at her with that great bumpy boulder of a head, cut with scars and burned by the sun. His eyes were two grey pits in that thing, his brow brutish, heavy and hairless. "I hope you will have decided to take the turning by then. Any other choice would be folly." He maintained the stare for a moment longer, then turned and stamped away.

The others lingered. "You've heard my thoughts," the Butcher said. "I've got a sweet spot for Banassy, I will admit. There is a pit there, a brutal place, where I used to do some fighting when I was young. Got my first kill there, and had my first woman too, after. I was only eleven. But forget that. Whether we go there or up the Matian Way, my point stands. You need to do more fighting, pretty princess. You've not drawn your blade since Aram."

That wasn't strictly true. "I've been training every day since then." She had continued her training on the road, taking instruction not only from Rolly and the Butcher, but the Baker and the Surgeon as well. Sometimes the other sellswords joined in too to help prepare her, fighting her two-on-one, or even three-on-one, helping her understand how best to fight several foes at once. They always fought after setting camp, when the night had fallen and the air had cooled to make it more bearable. Under moonlight they'd duelled, and starlight, and beneath heavy rains as well. One night the skies had turned blood red from horizon to horizon, and Sunrider Tantario had said that there had been terrible bloodshed somewhere. *Perhaps in this town?* Saska thought. *Has he been setting me up all along?*

She didn't think so. But even if he had, she wasn't going to blame him for that. For all this talk of her destiny, there was still a good chance they were wrong. *A prophecy isn't real until it comes true,* Ranulf used to say. He had told her that prophecies and foretellings were as common as white caps on waves, and most never amounted to anything. *Maybe that'll happen with me? Maybe Tantario doesn't believe a word of it, and wants to make use of us while he can?*

And what the Butcher said…that had merit too. Training with her companions was one thing. Fighting a foe that wanted to kill her was another. She had fought a dragon and failed, fought Cedrik Kastor and failed in that as well. Both times she required saving, first by Agarosh and then by Prince Robbert and without them she'd be dead. If she was to be this saviour her grandmother said she was, she had to stop relying on others. The more she put herself in danger, *real* danger, the more she would improve. *And if I die along the way, so be it. It'll only prove the prophecy false.*

"You're right," she said, at last, looking up at the Butcher. "Next time there's battle, I'll draw my blade and join in. I won't just stand aside."

"Good." The big scarred sellsword gave her one of those good-natured grins of his. "We would not want you to rust, pretty princess."

"Nor die," said the Surgeon. "You must choose your opponents wisely, Serenity, if and when there is any fighting. Your Wall can be overbearing, but he is not wrong. Your death may doom us, and this we cannot allow." He looked over to the log he had been sitting on earlier. The Tigress still stood in the same place as before, looking over at them, staring like a cat does, still and silent, never seeming to blink. She made the men nervous, Saska had seen. Even the other sellswords looked at her with suspicion. "I will make sure the Tigress is near you," the Surgeon went on. "When we find ourselves in a fight, she will watch over you, and make sure you are safe."

The Baker gave a scoff. "It's not wise to turn your back on a tiger."

The Surgeon frowned at him. "You doubt her?"

"I've always doubted her. She is wild, *unnatural*. And those hisses…"

"Are a language," the Surgeon said. "An old language used by the people of the Unseen Isles."

The Baker snorted. "All those hisses sound the same. How can that be a language?"

The Surgeon fingered one of his many blades. "Is there no sound in the world because a deaf man cannot hear them? Nothing to see because a man is blind? That you do not have the capacity to differentiate between the hisses does not mean the differences are not there. The language is complex, and beautiful. You only need the ears to hear it."

The Baker's eyes were as flat as a tabletop. He stared at his fellow Bloody Trader captain, unimpressed, then moved his eyes to Saska. "*I* will stay near, when next we fight. Or my brother will. Forget this Tigress creature. She is crazed and wild and will pounce upon any foe she sees, leaving you vulnerable. And there is more," the Baker said, more darkly. "I have seen her *sniffing* at you, my lady. When your back is turned, and she thinks no one is watching. She sniffs at you and licks her lips. It is that powerful blood of yours. She wants herself a taste."

That made Saska shudder. She looked at the Surgeon. "You told me she could be trusted. You said it was only the blood of the wicked she sought."

"It is," the Surgeon said, body stiffening defensively. "She must enjoy the scent, that is all. It does not mean she will act upon it. The Tigress can control her impulses."

The Butcher gripped the handle of his blade. "She will, or I will kill her. I will show her how I got my name."

The Surgeon's lips twisted into a cold smile. "You would stand no chance against her."

The Butcher scowled. "Let us put it to the test, then. A duel. First blood." He drew six inches of misting steel.

"A contest?" Leshie piped in, big-eyed, enthused by the prospect. "Maybe we could all be involved? Like a tournament, to see who's the best. We could call it the Song of the Sellswords or something."

The Baker gave that a bark of laughter. "Would the Whaleheart be allowed to join in?"

"No," Leshie said, at once. "No, that would just ruin it. And he'd be all doom and gloom about it too. You know how he is. He's grumpy about everything."

"It is because his manhood is small," the Baker said, nodding as though he knew. "The giant is not in proportion. It makes him angry."

"Why?" Leshie asked. "He doesn't use it anyway."

There was more laughter at that, though Saska didn't care for it. Rolly was her protector and her guardian and she would not have him mocked like this. "No contest. No tournament. No fighting," she said. The Surgeon had spoken of the fragile ego of the sellsword, the thin skin that caused him to need to prove himself at every turn, and he'd been right, by the Butcher's reaction. Saska was not going to indulge it. "This council is adjourned."

The captains bowed and shrugged and moved off, the Butcher still grumbling complaints to his brother as they returned to Merinius and their own men. The Surgeon walked back to the Tigress, who had been watching them all along in that way men found disquieting. She might even have been listening, so far as

Saska knew. *I may have to warn the Butcher and the Baker to be careful.* It would not serve to find the Tigress supping on the brothers' blood one night.

Gutter and Gore were there as well, sitting on the same log as their captain had been on, crouching forward and looking at the ground, pointing and muttering at one another, occasionally smiling or laughing. "They're racing bugs," Leshie told her. "They're as brainless as they are beautiful, those two."

Saska looked around. "I don't see Scalpel and Savage."

"Gone off to root," Leshie said. "They're always at it."

"Go find them, bring them back. We need to get going. Kaa Sokari too."

"Why me? Kaa will only shout at me for interrupting Squire's training."

"I'm sure you can handle it."

Saska stepped away before Leshie could complain, moving back toward the edge of the grove where it met the Capital Road. The horses and camels were here, and the few sunwolves and starcats of the company too, lounging around in the shade, panting and grooming. She saw Joy among them, off to one side, and went over to scratch under her chin. *No blood*, she saw. Joy often went off hunting during these breaks, prowling away into the plains in search of food, occasionally returning with a carcass in her jaws and a muzzle all soaked in blood. Not this morning, though. She tended to have better luck at night, when her black coat made stalking easier.

"Ready to go?" she said to the starcat.

Joy's answer was to stand to her feet, reaching her fore paws forward in a great long stretch, back bending like a bow.

Saska smiled. "I'll take that as a yes."

The calls were soon ringing out for the men to muster, their waterskins filled, provisions replenished by whatever the innkeep could spare. Savage came skulking through from behind some rocks, a murderous look in her eye, her husband Scalpel fixing his swordbelt as he walked behind her, looking amused. Del and Kaa Sokari returned as well, though from another direction, Leshie shaking her head as she followed.

She walked up to Saska. "He shouted at me, like I said he would. Gave me a proper earful. And that sellsword too, that Savage bitch. She said she'd take my eyes out if she ever caught me watching her and her husband go at it again. Called me a 'red-headed pervert' and worse. Can you believe it?"

Yes, Saska thought. Leshie might look innocent as a maid, but her mind was full of filth. "You shouldn't be watching them, Leshie. I only asked you to fetch them back. Not stand and ogle. Who does that?"

"I...I didn't watch!" Leshie exclaimed. "Gods, *them*? If I was going to watch a pair do *that*, it wouldn't be *them*, Saska." She looked visibly repulsed. "You must be joking."

Saska *was* joking, of course. Though it was fun watching the girl squirm, so she decided not to say it.

The procession was soon on the road again, hooves clopping and claws scratching along the dusty cobbles beneath the blaze of the midday sun. They had ridden many miles that day already, rising as they liked to do before dawn, to steal a march on the day in the cooler conditions. Some of the men urged that they remain in the shade through the heat of the day, but that was not time Saska wanted to waste. Instead they would take it slow, taking breaks in the shade where they could, stopping at every available water source to cool their necks and faces and have a drink.

Sir Ralston came to ride beside her on his enormous warhorse, christened *Bedrock* by Leshie, for bearing the Wall atop it. One of the Red Blade's more witty nicknames. "So, what have you decided?" the giant asked her.

"I haven't. Not yet."

"Shall I make the decision for you?"

If only, Saska thought. But she had wanted to have agency, wanted to be a leader, so no, she had to make these decisions herself. "No," she said. "How long until we reach the turn-off to the Matian Way?"

"Ten miles."

"Then I have ten miles to think."

They kept an eye down the cliffs as they went, Leshie regularly riding off on her rouncey to see if there were any signs of Sir Clive Fanning and his men. Her reports were all the same. Nothing. No bodies, no torn bits of clothing or discarded armour, no steel in the sand or bloodstains on the rocks. When the cliffs shallowed, Saska even let Leshie climb down the trail the innkeep had mentioned, to have a better look. Merinius went with her, and the Butcher as well, but they only came back saying the same thing. No signs of a camp. No old fires. Nothing to suggest anyone had passed that way.

It's all for the best, Saska reflected. With all this talk about containing her secret, gathering waifs and strays along the way would be best avoided. It was one less thing to worry about.

And maybe that was the point. *I need less to think about, and worry about, not more.* The shortcut across the Matian Way would save them days, as much as a week, and perhaps the lives of some of her men as well. *I cannot save everyone,* she told herself. Every day hundreds, even thousands were dying, here in the south and across the north as well, and ridding one town of one crazed, monster-communing madman would not help her in her quest. If she did that, she'd only find herself having to stop at every beleaguered settlement, every town and village and city under siege, serving justice along the way. For every battle she embroiled herself in, she would lose another of her men, and by the time she reached the north, she might have no one left.

No, that would not serve. *I must keep my focus, keep things simple, as Rolly says.* She hated it, but it was the sensible choice. "Your brother

243

must become single-minded," Kaa Sokari had said of Del. *I would be wise to do the same,* she thought.

So when the Whaleheart next rode up to her and asked which way they would go, she gave him a definite answer, the answer the giant sought.

"We'll take the Matian Way."

17

Elyon

"Gruloks," he said.

The council members stared at him blankly.

Rammas scratched under his chin. "Rock giants?"

Elyon nodded.

"How many?" asked Rikkard Amadar.

The prince laughed and gave a shake of the head, still struggling to believe it himself. "Many," he said. "There were sixteen of them when I left. More may yet be drawn to him."

"To your father?" asked Lady Marian, standing straight-backed and stoic in her seamless smoke-grey armour.

"They're drawn to the power of Vandar," Elyon said. He drew the Windblade, causing the walls of the pavilion to billow. A few sheets of paper and scrolls went blowing from the command table. Sir Karter and Rikkard stepped forward at once to set them right. "Sorry," Elyon said. "I was trying to be dramatic."

"You mean the Blades of Vandar attract them?" Killian asked.

Elyon nodded. "Vandar made the gruloks to fight in his wars. That's why they're awakening, and being drawn to the bearers. They're being summoned to fight for Vandar."

Prince Raynald had a look of boyish wonder on his face. "Will some come *here*, then?" Once more he continued to glance at the Windblade in a manner Elyon considered covetous. *Perhaps there is more of his grandfather in him than I thought.* He had no great fear that Raynald would act upon that desire, but all the same, it stirred a reaction in him.

Eyes off. It's mine. Mine, and mine alone. The thoughts came unbidden, that rat, gnawing in his mind. He took a moment to repeat his father's mantra, briefly closing his eyes, right there before the captains and commanders of the east. *I will give it up. I will give it up. I will give it up. I will…*

245

"My lord, are you quite well? Do you need to take a short rest, perhaps, before we…"

"I'm fine, Sir Karter, just fine." Elyon opened his eyes, not caring to explain himself. He sensed the likes of Rikkard and Killian and Marian were already quite aware of his private struggles. He gave answer to Raynald's question. "I tend to move around a lot, Prince Raynald. That makes me hard to track for these creatures. And they are shy, I am told. They shun people as much as they can."

Rammas gave a snort. "Didn't imagine they could be so sensitive."

Nor did I. Though sensitive was perhaps not the right word. It seemed that the gruloks required a first meeting, somewhere private, with a bearer, before showing themselves to others. Vilmar had told him it must have been their custom, some means of testing whether the bearer was worthy of their service. It was perhaps why so many had gathered near Amron Daecar. *They gravitate toward nobility and power,* Elyon thought. *And Lythian is there also, with his bright new golden blade.*

"How does your father intend to deploy them?" Killian asked, as though they were speaking of a troop of common spearmen.

"Defence, for now. Vilmar is working with him to improve communication, so the king can more readily issue commands. A few of them are able to speak a basic form of the common tongue. A few words, here and there."

There were some murmurs at that. "Truly?" asked Rikkard. "What do their voices sound like?"

It was hard to explain. "Imagine a rockslide, and you'll be somewhere close."

Walter had suggested that they had learned to assimilate the language while they were sleeping, especially those who happened to be near people. When Vandar's power faded, long millennia ago, the gruloks had simply lain down to rest, presenting themselves as large rocks and boulders to the eyes of man. In some cases, settlements had sprung up where they were sleeping. Those were the ones who had learned to speak, according to the scribe, absorbing bits of the language during their slumber.

Elyon re-sheathed the Windblade, and walked over to the command table, putting this talk of the gruloks to one side. Sir Karter was still setting everything back in its proper place. He seemed extremely fastidious in that regard. Elyon saw the usual laid out across the large pine-wood table; maps, diagrams, battle plans, other information that would help them defeat Vargo Ven and his army.

"You've done as I asked," the prince noted.

"We've had plenty of time," Rammas returned, in his typically blunt way. "You've been gone longer than we expected. Thought you were going to come right back."

"I've been busy, my lord." Elyon pulled up a sheet detailing the enemy's strength of arms. He ran his eyes down the list of units; swordsmen, spearmen, axmen, archers, mounted units, dragonknights, paladin knights, Sunriders and Starriders, dragons. Against each unit was an estimate of numbers, given in a range. "How accurate are these numbers?" he asked.

"Hard to say," said Rikkard. "There is only so much we can do with scouting reports. But we expect the different units to be within those ranges."

The ranges were often quite broad, Elyon saw. At the bottom of the sheet, a high and low end estimate of Ven's total forces had been listed. "It says here Ven commands up to a hundred and fifty thousand men." Elyon looked up. "How can that be? He had that number at the Bane, and we've killed tens of thousands since then." *Forty thousand at the Bane,* he thought. *And how many more since?* "These numbers can't be right."

"They're not right or wrong," Rikkard said. "They're estimates. It's clear enough that Ven has been reinforced across the Bloodmarshes. That's the benefit of controlling Death's Passage…it allows him to rearm and resupply at his need."

Elyon understood all that. "Then he's left a garrison at Dragon's Bane as well? To protect the way."

"Our latest reports suggest so."

"How many?"

"Ten, fifteen thousand. Again, that is only an estimate. Some other castles are also under his control. Fort Bleakmire, Castle Crag."

Rammas's eyes darkened at the latter. It was his own seat, taken and destroyed. He had left his uncle there in command, along with others who were dear to him. *All dead now, like as not.* None of that had softened Lord Rammas's mood, which seemed as foul as Elyon had ever seen it, and that was saying something.

"So in sum Ven might have…how many? Two hundred thousand? Spread across the Marshlands?"

"It's possible, yes."

"I wasn't aware he was occupying castles." So far as Elyon knew, Vargo Ven had simply been destroying them, burning them out, and leaving them to rot.

"Some," Rikkard said. "Only those of strategic importance."

Elyon thought some more. "What about cutting off his supply lines? Starving him out. Would that be possible?"

Rikkard didn't seem to think so, nor anyone else, by those shakes of the head. "We'd have to win back the Bane to cut him off, and he's closer. If we try to march upon the fortress, he'll get there before us. Or else he'll intercept us and engage."

"*Good,*" Rammas said to that, making a fist. "We're on rations here and the food's not going to last forever. We destroy Ven's host, and his supplies will be ours. Food, fodder, all of it. We should march out and meet him while we've still got the strength to fight."

That won some murmuring from the others. The threat of famine was likely to become a major issue soon, here and elsewhere across the north, and gaining access to Ven's supplies would be a major boon. *That's if he doesn't simply burn them,* Elyon thought. He would not put it past the dragonlord to order all wagons and supply tents put to the torch should he think the battle lost.

Elyon looked back down at the battle plans laid out before him. There were several maps, each showing the position of Ven's forces and warcamp with different paths of assault. One was extremely direct, no doubt Rammas's preferred strategy. Another was more elaborate and detailed, with well-thought-out battle formations and lines of attack. That would be the combined work of Rikkard and Killian, with input from Marian no doubt. Elyon had been gone for several days - busy days, in which he had found himself drawn to other matters - but it was clear by these plans that Vargo Ven had not yet made a move to retreat back to the Bane, as Rammas had feared.

He read down the list of units once more. "It says there are two Moonriders in the host." That alone gave credence to the belief that Ven had been reinforced. There had been no Moonriders at the Battle of the Bane, after all. "Who are they? Do we know?"

"Timor Ballantris of Lumara, and Risho Ranaartan of Aramatia," said Lady Marian. "They are two of the four known remaining Moonriders in the empire. If there are more, we are not aware of them."

It sounded piteously few. "Are there more moonbears on the mountain?"

"Most likely. As with the dragons, not all wish to be bonded. But their numbers have always been fewer."

And greatly so, Elyon thought. Unless there were hundreds of moonbears stalking about the heights, the dragons had them severely unnumbered. "And who leads the empire's forces here? Is Sunlord Avam still alive?"

"We believe so," said Rikkard. "There are no reports of his death, at least, and we know he survived the Bane."

"Is there any way of getting a message to him?" Elyon asked. "Without Vargo Ven knowing."

That raised a few eyebrows. "Why would you want to do that?" Rammas asked. "You're not thinking of parleying, are you?"

That was exactly what Elyon Daecar was thinking. "The Agarathi may never agree to a ceasefire, but the men of the empire might. They are not in thrall to Eldur, as the dragonfolk are. There must be thousands of them, tens of thousands, who do not believe in this cause."

"The same could be said of any army," Rammas said to that. "Most men are mustered against their will. They want to stay and tend their farms and families, but a spear is shoved in their fist and they're pushed on down the road to war. This is no different. And you'd be barking up the wrong tree with Avam. He's a Patriot of Lumara. There'd be no getting through to him."

Elyon nodded, taking the point. He had met Avar Avam during the parley before the Battle of the Bane, and had heard the hate in his voice. *That one will never submit to a northerner.* "Another commander, then?" he offered. "Who is next in line after Avam?"

"Moonrider Ballantris, we think," said Rikkard. "Sunlord Avam is Piseki, and of a Solasi line, but Ballantris is Lumosi, born of Lumara, a moonlord in his own right, and has no affiliations with the Patriots." He looked over at Lady Marian, who seemed the authority on this subject.

"Timor Ballantris is one of Empress Valura's most loyal subjects," she informed him. "He is, moreover, the most fearsome warrior in all of the empire, and the greatest active Moonrider. It may be that when he arrived, he took command of the empire's forces, in place of Sunlord Avam. If you want to seek a conference, he would be the man to speak to."

Rammas was shaking his head, not liking where this conversation was going. "Forget all that. We have our battle plans, and Ven's out there waiting for us. What else is there to talk about? Let's just march out there and meet him."

And give Agarath the All-Father the show he craves, Elyon thought. "My father believes we should wait."

"What? Why?" blustered Rammas.

"Because rushing into action needlessly is not wise, my lord. Our urgency to act was based on the fear that Vargo Ven would leave. He hasn't, and likely won't. In time he may even grow frustrated and assault us here, which would give us the advantage. And these numbers…"

"Forget the numbers," said Rammas. "We have two men for every three or four of his. Those are good odd for us."

"And dragons?" Elyon looked down at the sheet once more. "There is no number written here."

"There can be no number with dragons," Rikkard said. "If there was a battle in King's Point, right now, would you consider yourself a part of it?"

Elyon frowned a moment, before puzzling out his meaning. "Any dragon within a hundred leagues could join the fight," he said, nodding. "I appreciate that, Uncle. But you don't even have an estimate."

"We were waiting for you for that. An aerial scout will go a long way to confirming these numbers."

That was fair. Elyon had told Lady Marian he would perform a scout of his own, and he would. "I'll see it done," he said. "Though not now. The skies are too overcast for me to get a good enough view, and it would serve to wait for clearer weather."

"That could take days," Rammas said. "What are we to do in the meantime?"

"Train, strategise, prepare."

"But not *act.*" The red was rising up Rammas's thick neck, veins pulsing. "The time is now, my prince. If we do not act, the dragon could return, and we will have lost our chance."

"That is one of my father's fears, Lord Rammas," Elyon said. "There is a concern that the Dread will bear down upon us when we expose ourselves beyond these walls. We have spoken of the risk of being attacked by dragons on the march. An acceptable risk, perhaps. But not if that dragon is the Dread. Here at least we have the protection of the towers and battlements and ballistas. But out there, no. He would obliterate the entire army."

"Or he may not. I thought you were going to fly across the sea and check."

"I did," Elyon said.

That brought silence to the room.

Elyon went on. "You wonder why I have been delayed in my return? My flight across the Red Sea is one such reason. I scouted south to check on the Dread, but the way was blocked by fume. The Ashmount *smokes*, my lords, my lady. From its summit, great plumes of black smoke fill the air, and I could not get near the Nest. Drulgar may yet be there, resting, but I cannot say for certain."

Killian was running his fingers down his sharp chin, deep in thought. "There is a relationship between the dragon and the mountain," he whispered. "Legend says that Drulgar was born from it, that Agarath forged him from its fires, building his body from the rock. These events may be linked. The smoking mountain may signal that the dragon is indeed recovering, a sign of his healing."

"Nonsense," scoffed Rammas, dismissing it with an irritated wave of the hand. "It's just a volcano, Killian. Volcanos smoke, that's what they do."

That was a possibility also, Elyon had to admit, though Killian Oloran was not a man to speak a theory unless it had been well thought out. To take it to its natural conclusion, that would mean that the volcano would stop smoking once the Dread was fully healed. Elyon put that to the group, and got a few nods of agreement, though Rammas continued to mutter that they were overthinking everything, and had gone 'myth-mad', as he called it. It was not an expression Elyon had heard before, though he got its meaning.

"Perhaps," he allowed. "But there is no harm in taking precautions. This is unprecedented ground we are treading, Lord Rammas. All eventualities must be considered."

"*All*. Yes. And that's my complaint. We spend all our time in council when we should be taking action. I lament more than ever the death of Lord Kanabar. He'd not be indulging all this prattle."

"If you are weary of listening to it, my lord, by all means go." Elyon opened an arm out to the flaps. "We will call upon you when it is time to act, if action is all you care for."

Rammas bristled at that. "You're dismissing me?"

"No. I am offering you the opportunity to leave. There is a difference." He turned back to the command table, letting Rammas do as he wished. *His warmongering is exhausting.* Elyon understood, of course. The Marshlands had been raped, pillaged, brutalised and besieged by Vargo Ven and his armies, and Rammas only wanted his chance to seek vengeance. *I want that myself, for Lancel, for Wallis, for Barnibus maybe too.* Yet that did not mean he would be drawn to rash action, spending countless lives without due thought. "I want you to try to get a message to Moonrider Ballantris," he said. "Is there a way of infiltrating Ven's army with a spy?" The question was directed at Lady Marian. "You have special ointments and potions, I know, that can be used to change a person's features, darken their skin and hair. Might you have an agent, my lady, who could pose as a Lumaran, and get close to Ballantris?"

Her face gave nothing away, as ever. "I will do what I can," she merely said.

Elyon thanked her with a nod. There was little more he wanted to say right now. "Prince Raynald, would you join me for a private word?" He looked around. "Unless there's anything else we need to discuss?"

No one came forward with anything pressing, so at that the council dispersed. Sir Karter strode quickly out, perhaps to update his lord father on proceedings, while Marian set off to her task. Rikkard and Killian remained, moving to the command table, discussing strategy. Rammas stamped out of the pavilion in a rage, seeking to purge his pent-up frustrations by engaging someone in a duel. "I need a challenger," he bellowed as he left. "Two or three good knights. And no holding back."

Raynald was smiling as Elyon joined him. That handsome smile of his father's. "Lord Rammas is a character, isn't he?" the young prince said. "I enjoy these councils for him alone. It was so dull back in Ilithor."

"It must have been frustrating, with Robb away at war?"

"More than frustrating, Elyon. What's that they say? An heir and a spare. You were the spare for Aleron, but with me it was even harder, being twins. To be left behind with the women and the old men while Robb went off to win glory?" He shook his head. "No. I wasn't going to live with that."

"So you came here," Elyon said, smiling easily. "To win glory of your own."

"I suppose that was a part of it. Personal glory. But it's about defending Tukor as well, and the north. That is my primary motivation, as I'm sure it is yours."

Elyon nodded. He'd won enough personal glory by now to fill ten lifetimes, but even so it all felt empty. If the north should perish, the world fall to ruin, what good would all that do him? "I wanted to ask you about something that may be considered sensitive, Ray. Do I have your permission to speak plainly?"

The boy looked at him curiously. "Yes. Of course. Go right ahead."

*Stop looking at the Windblade, stop staring at it with those eyes. You want it, I know you do. You want it for your own...*Elyon's mouth twisted into a rictus smile as those thoughts ran through his mind, unwelcome and uncontrolled, though they did not pass his lips. There was something about those looks Raynald gave the blade, those covetous little looks and glances, that made the whispers hiss and holler somewhere in the back of his mind. Once more he drowned them out by repeating his father's mantra. And all the while, that smile. That strange, fixed smile that made Raynald ill at ease.

"It, er...it must be something hard to express, Elyon. You look... very serious." He glanced to the side, where a table was set up with jugs of ale and wine and water. "A cup of ale, perhaps, to make it easier? Watered ale, of course. I know you're flying." He stepped away and poured, giving Elyon time to drag that smile from his lips and drown out the whispers in his head.

"My thanks, Ray," Elyon said, thick-voiced, when the prince returned. He took a sip, whispers fading, anger too, then decided it was simply best to tell the truth. "It's the Windblade," he explained. *He understands. He knows. He saw what happened to his grandfather.* "I feel it becoming more...more *protective* of me." *It wants to stay with me. With me and me alone.* "Sometimes the way you look at it..."

"You think...you think I would try to steal it from you?" Raynald looked aghast, even angered by the notion. "Gods no, Elyon. Is that why you look at me like that?"

Elyon wasn't sure what he meant. "Like what?"

"With that glare. As if you want to kill me. Perhaps you don't even know you're doing it?"

Elyon shook his head, frowning.

"Well, maybe I'm exaggerating a little. It's not so bad as all that. Just the occasional narrow-eyed glare, you know. Like I've kissed your sister or something." Raynald took a long draught of his drink. "So. This sensitive matter? Was it the Wind..." He dare not even say it. "Sorry. Your *blade* you wanted to talk about?"

Well, don't I feel the fool. "No. It's the Book of Thala. I wondered if you knew where it was?"

The young prince clearly thought that Elyon had gone mad. He gave a loud scoff. "No. Why should I know where the Book of Thala is?"

It was an honest enough answer. "No reason."

Because we're of the belief that your grandfather has it stored somewhere in his private quarters in Ilithor, he might have said instead. Lythian and Walter and Ralf had the bright idea that the Book of Thala might contain some clue they could use, about mastering the Eye of Rasalan, or combining the Blades of Vandar. Elyon had told them he would make enquiries. *Another task to add to my list.*

But clearly Raynald didn't know.

"Was that all?" the prince asked.

Elyon was inclined to say 'yes' and leave this awkwardness behind, but he had a little more to say first. "I'm planning to fly to Thalan, see what I can find out about your sister, and will stop off at Ilithor on the way. It isn't so much of a detour and I feel beholden to update them on our news. Is there anything you would like me to report, from you directly? Any word you would like me to share with your mother?"

It was the last thing in the world Elyon wanted to do, meet with that crazed old shrew who had spat in his face once before, but Raynald had earned that much.

The young prince pondered, then shook his head. "Nothing," he said. "Just make sure she knows that I'm safe. She'll like that. You don't have to visit her yourself."

"I don't mind, truly…"

"Truly?" Raynald said. "Truly I think you're a liar, Elyon. She's a bitch and we all know it. I'd not want to subject all her spiteful ramblings onto you. And I know about the spitting."

"Oh. You do?"

"An unseemly business, but sadly not unusual for her either. No, just have one of the maidservants or guardsmen bring her the news. That should serve."

"As you say."

Raynald sipped his ale. "So…Thalan. You're flying there all for the sake of my sister, are you? I didn't know you cared about her."

"She was to wed my brother."

"As my brother was to wed your sister. These things don't seem to turn out too well, do they?" His mouth hardened, as he looked at the Windblade, more pointedly this time. "That was the same night you stole it from Dalton Taynar. The night of my sister's wedding to Hadrin. That was when your auntie Amara got up and announced Robb was betrothed to Lillia."

Elyon had mixed memories of that night. The horrid spectacle of the wedding ceremony. The feast during which he pretended to get drunk. The tension of the heist, and jubilation at their triumph. The horror of what happened after, with Mel, when she confessed her part in Aleron's death and sawed open her very own throat.

"That was part of it, wasn't it?" Raynald went on. Elyon raised his eyes. "Your auntie making that great spectacle, with Wallis Kanabar? That was part of the distraction so that you could steal the blade?"

"We didn't steal it," Elyon said, defensive. He could feel his face growing hot. "We were only righting wrongs."

"Righting wrongs? What about Lady Melany? They say you killed her."

"I didn't."

"I know. I never thought you did. But others…" There was something dark happening, some anger in Raynald Lukar. "It was my father who broke you out of your cell, wasn't it? He was the one who set you free?"

Elyon's answer was silence.

"He defended you back then. I remember. When you were in your cell he would argue with my grandfather all the time, saying you had nothing to do with Melany's death, how he needed to let you go free. Well, we *all* know how that turned out. You go fleeing away into the mountains and my father goes to confess to the king. That's how it happened. He was never trying to steal the throne. He was only there for you, Elyon. *You*." He looked at the Windblade again. "If you hadn't stolen it, my father would still be alive. So maybe…" He nodded to himself, once and twice and thrice. "Maybe I'll look at it all I please, how about that? I think I've earned that much, don't you?"

Elyon did not know what to say to him. For a moment he could only stare, the words caught in his throat, memories flooding. Then he managed to mumble, "What happened with your father…"

"Save it," Raynald broke right in. "I don't want to hear your excuses."

"They're not excuses. I'm just explaining."

"Explanations, then. I don't want to hear them." He drank his ale down in one long draught. "Look. I know you cared for my father, and he you. I know you didn't want that to happen. But it did. He died and you played your part in that. Let's just leave it there." The prince turned away, setting his cup down on the table with a loud *clunk*, and strode sharply through the flaps.

Elyon could only stare after him as he went, half in shock at how quickly that had escalated. There was a sound at his side and Rikkard was there. "What was that about?"

Nothing, Elyon wanted to say. "Rylian," he told his uncle.

Rikkard understood. "He needed to let it out. He's just a boy, really, still grieving. Don't hold it against him, Elyon."

"I won't. I just…"

"It brings up memories of your own."

He nodded.

Rikkard put a hand on his shoulder. "You need to rest."

Elyon shook him free. "I need to go."

"Where?"

"Northeast. Toward the Hooded Hills first, then to Ilithor. Then Thalan."

"Then you definitely need to rest. You've only just arrived."

"I can make it to Ilithor tonight. I'll rest there."

"And the Hooded Hills? What's out there?"

"That's what I'm going to find out." Elyon finally drew his eyes from the tent flaps and turned to face his uncle. "Those wounds on Drulgar's face and neck. The ones he already bore when he arrived at King's Point. Father believes they were inflicted by gruloks. All this with them being drawn toward the Blades of Vandar…"

"Janilah," Rikkard Amadar said, seeing it at once.

Elyon nodded. "Father thinks Janilah and some gruloks fought Drulgar, somewhere to the east of here, out near those mountains. You said the Dread was spotted, flying west. Where, exactly?"

"Some fifty miles or so to the north, I think. He flew almost straight over Redhelm."

"Good," Elyon said. It would give him something to work with.

Killian stepped over, having heard them from the command table. "Amron hopes to find the Mistblade?" he asked.

Elyon turned to him. He had not spoken to Killian about all this directly, though evidently Rikkard had apprised him of everything that needed telling. "We all do, Kill. That's one of the reasons Father said to hold off on Ven for now. He's of the belief that finding the blades is a higher priority, and I'm uniquely positioned to do that." He gave the Windblade a tap, heart still racing from the confrontation with Raynald. He did not like how that had gone. *I'll smooth things over with him later.* "I can move around quickly, and know what it is to bear these blades. If I find the Mistblade I might be able to carry it."

Rikkard did not seem sure of that. "Will it not take time to bond?"

"If I want to *use* it, yes. Mastering its properties will take time. But carrying it at my hip might be possible." *The second is always easier,* he thought.

"And you don't mean to? Use it, I mean?" Rikkard bore that doubtful look in his eyes, a look he wore often these days."

"That will be for my father to decide. He will choose who the blade goes to." He had not yet spoken of Lythian, he realised. He did so now, telling them of the man's ascension to the seat of First Blade. "Father chose Lythian to *guard* the Sword of Varinar, first and foremost. He will do the same with the Mistblade, if and when it's found."

"If and when," repeated Sir Killian. "It may be that Janilah still bears it."

It may. "That is what I intend to find out. If the Dread fought a group of gruloks there are sure to be signs of destruction. I may be able to spot them from the air." He paused, then asked, "Has no one come here reporting anything like that?" He thought of the lands outside of King's Point, terraformed by the Dread's wild fury. The river, forever altered. The lands, pitted and scarred. If the same had happened to the northeast of here, someone might have seen and reported it.

But the two knights shook their heads. "Not that I'm aware," said Rikkard.

"No matter. I'll see for myself." Elyon stepped over to the table, put down his cup - he'd taken barely more than a sip of his watered ale - and turned back to the others. "I'll be back in a day or three. If I happen to spot any gruloks, I'll send them down here to help." He smiled and stepped away.

The sky was dreary outside, the winds brisk, a few spots of rain in the air. Elyon paced through the ward, taking the main thoroughfare between tents, making for Marian Payne's pavilion. Her forces numbered only two or three thousand now, the only Rasal representatives here. Roark was sitting outside on a camp stool, knocking a dint out of his breastplate with a hammer. He looked up as Elyon appeared, standing. "You again. We've got to stop meeting like this, good prince."

"Is Lady Marian inside?" Elyon asked.

"Aye. Just got back from council. I'll announce you." He moved through the flaps, stepped out again a moment, and nodded Elyon through.

He entered to find Marian crouched over a table of ointments and oils and balms. She looked over as he stepped within, straightening her back. "Elyon."

"My lady."

"You have some new task for me?"

"No task, my lady. Only a question." He took a further step inside, though this would only be a short meeting. "The cousins. Have you heard any news of them?"

"I have."

"Oh?" He hadn't expected that. "And?"

"It appears that Prince Sevrin is still alive, Elyon, or so I have been informed. He is the eldest of the cousins, and after Hadrin's death, the rightful King of Rasalan. Under his authority, the city survivors are rallying. Both Lord Buckland and the Oakenlord have sent men north to help, my sources say. It is favourable news. Sevrin is a noble man, well-liked, and there could be no one better to restore order."

"Or master the Eye," Elyon said.

"Yes. That as well. Though I still have my doubts on that account." She looked through the flaps. Beyond the great ward, with its enormous mast-like poles, the sight of the city proper could be seen across the river, faint against the bleak grey skies. "I took some time to search through the Rustbridge libraries during your absence, and Lord Lester graciously gave me access to his private shelves as well. There were some old tomes that dealt with matters mythical and arcane, though I found nothing inside any of them to help light our way. You spoke during council of unprecedented ground, and that is what we are treading here. Until such a time as Sevrin sits before the Eye of Rasalan, we cannot know for sure what will happen."

"That time is coming up shortly, my lady. I plan to fly to Thalan tomorrow."

"And the Eye? When will you deliver it back to its rightful place?"

"As soon as I can. Though all this must be done in secrecy. I have little doubt that Eldur will be hunting me, Marian. For what I did."

She nodded. "Have you felt yourself being watched? Anything out of the ordinary?"

What's ordinary these days? "Nothing," he said. "I see dragons, most

256

days, but they are fewer than they were. When I move the Eye, I'll make sure I'm not watched. Though Thalan may not be the best place to keep it. Somewhere stronger, or more secret, would be better."

She mulled on that. "Find Sevrin first," she said. "He will know best, Elyon Daecar."

"I will do that, my lady." He left her at that, giving her a bow as she returned to her task, stepping back out into the ward.

"Getting colder," Roark said outside, squinting up at the skies. "And the days are darkening too. Where you heading now, then?"

"Northeast," Elyon told him. *In search of kings and giants.*

18

Amara

"Another ship has been spotted coming from the south, Great One," said the slimy seneschal in his slimy voice, he of the lank black hair and earthy hempen garb, a skinny creep of a man, snivelling and servile. "This one is bearing soldiers, hard-eyed and lean, wearing cloaks of dull grey and blue on their backs. I fear they may seek to land here, on the island. If they do…"

The Lord of Seals raised a flipper to cut him off. He looked down the table to Amara. "Who are these hard-eyed men? These colours… they're of your kingdom, no? Vandar, was it?"

She wanted to kill him. *Soon. By the gods I promise it.* "They sound like Taynars," she said, playing nice for now. "Most likely they are fleeing north, to the Ironmoors."

"The Ironmoors?" The Great One repeated, in that horrid choked voice of his, as though his throat was constricted by the thick rolls of blubber that enwrapped his enormous neck. It seemed to amuse him tremendously to play dumb with these famous names. "Ah, yes, these hard cold lands to the north of the lake. Beyond the city of…um… what was it?"

"Elinar," the seneschal told him, always eager to please. Amara did not hate him quite so much as his lord and ruler, but that did not mean much. There were many rungs on the ladder of hate, and while the Blubber King might be at the very summit, that did not mean his thrall of a seneschal didn't warrant a place beneath him. "It is the city founded by Elin, my lord, who was the firstborn son of Varin."

"Varin…yes, Varin, I know the name." The Great One fingered his hairless chins, flesh wobbling. The rest of him was hairless too - his head, his brows, he didn't even seem to have much in the way of lashes over his eyes. "The man who built this city of yours, my lady. Is that right? This city that you say was burning."

She nodded, silent, trying not to think about it. The flames, licking at the suffocated dawn skies, the plumes of smoke, twisting up in great black columns, pouring from the burning keeps raised atop the hills. She remembered the screaming, of a hundred thousand souls, ringing out at the edge of hearing. The shapes of the dragons, moving through the mists, and that shadow, that vast winged shadow…dwarfing all others…the shadow of the Dread…

A shudder rippled through her, cold fingers climbing her spine. She reached out with a shaking hand to take up her cup of wine and drank deep. Still, even after all these days, the memories were fresh in her mind, haunting her; the shock had gone bone-deep. She gulped, feeling the warmth of the wine reach down into her chest, calming.

The Seal King was watching her through those tiny little eyes of his. "Better?" he asked her. "Wine helps. It always helps, no?"

A knife in your neck would help me more. "It does," she agreed. "The best medicine, I always say."

The whale gave a chuckle. "Others say that is laughter, but I agree with you, my lady. Wine is better, I have always thought. And food, yes. *Food.*" He licked his lips, beady eyes surveying the great feast laid out before him: plates of fish, herring and trout and salmon, pickled and salted and fried; great tubs of soup and stew and broth, made of shark and eel and seal; bowls of nuts and dried fruits; cakes, savoury and sweet, and a deal more besides. He reached out with one of his flippers and closed it around a fishcake, stuffing it into his maw. The whale was not a quiet eater. Amara stared, inwardly hateful, as he munched and chewed and slurped, crumbs tumbling to his gargantuan gut, neck bulging like a snake as he swallowed and swallowed and swallowed again.

The seneschal made a little move, just a shift of his slippered feet, to get the Great One's attention. "My lord, the boat…I fear they may attempt to make harbour here, as I say. There are several dozen armed men aboard, I am told. If they should find their way upriver…"

"Then they will steal our food and rape our women and make this little haven of ours their own," the whale said, through a mouthful of food. He chewed some more, swallowed, washing it all down with a full goblet of wine. "Oh yes, I have heard of these men of the Iron-moors. A rough folk, given to barbarism, who will take what they wish and kill to get it." The Great One took another great gulp of wine, and shook his huge round head. "No. No, no, and no again. I say *no* to that. The world may well be falling to war out there, but here, no, here we are at peace. That cannot be allowed to change."

The seneschal took his meaning, putting his hands together as he inclined his head. "I will make sure that the ship is…*diverted*, my lord. With good fortune we will be able to lure it away, beyond our shores, but I am told that it has suffered some damage. It may have no choice but to land, and…"

"And you'll deal with it, yes?"

"Yes, my lord. I…I will deal with it."

"Good. Then go, and see it done." The Great One waved those fat fingers of his, dismissing the seneschal from his hall. Thrall that he was, the slimy creature bowed that spiny back and slipped away, out through the door of hanging vines that marked the way into the pirate lord's palace, a hall woven and grown of wood and leaves over centuries. "I apologise for that unseemly interruption, my lady," the Lord of Seals said, once the man was gone. "To bring this talk to table while we're having our dinner." He shook his blubbery cheeks. "It's all such an ugly business, don't you think?"

"Very ugly," Amara agreed, glaring at him from behind the rim of her cup. She had watched him eating for days, stuffing his face on food enough to feed a hundred men. She had glimpsed his larders too, and seen the fisherfolk coming and going from the beach with nets wriggling and writhing, full to bursting. *There is food here*, she thought. *Plenty of food, but you'll not share it.*

"You think me cruel," the Lord of Lard observed, not missing that glare. "Oh, don't deny it. I can see it there in your pretty grey eyes."

"I think you're trying to protect your people," she said. *And yourself, most of all.*

"Yes, exactly. My people. There are only so many mouths I can feed, Lady Amara. I told you that, when you first came to me, do you remember? The tolls we charge, and the coin we take. It is only to feed my children."

She remembered that well enough. She'd made a jape about his own mouth costing a fortune, a jape he hadn't taken so well. She was in no mood for japing now.

The whale plucked a herring from the table and threw it down his neck like a pelican, swallowing in a single gulp. A great draught of wine followed, then more fish, a huge fistful of mixed nuts, some more herring after that as well, then another full cup of wine. All the while, the dainty little serving girl he kept at his side moved in and out, filling his bucket-sized goblet, making sure the plates were full of his favourite foods. *No wonder she is so slim, with all that rushing back and forth. And the way she ogles that food…*

"I wonder if you have given further thought to provisioning us with a boat," Amara said, to break the whale from his gluttonous feasting. "It's been long days now, and…"

"No." He shook his big bald head. "No, and no, and no again, my lady. I say *no* to that. I gave you a longship before, to take you to Varinar, and you only came right back. I cannot allow you to leave, not at this time. It is too dangerous out there. I hope you understand."

"You mean you didn't get your money," she said.

He put down his goblet and peered at her from across the table at which they sat, a huge oaken table that rested in the hall before his throne. All about them torches burned in wooden sconces on the walls and above lanterns swayed in the shadowed rafters, creaking softly. Just outside the hanging vines, a pair of burly Bladeborn guards kept watch at the door. *Could I snatch up a blade and gut the whale before they get to me?* The table was long - purposefully so, perhaps - but if she ran she might just make it.

"I promised you chests of gold and jewels to pay for passage," Amara went on. "If you give us a boat and a host of strong oarsmen, we can row to Varinar and…"

"No," he said, cutting her off. "Are you going to make me say it? No and no, and no again. I say *no* to that, my lady. You said yourself that this city of yours is in ruin, and I heard that from the captain as well. He told me about the fire, the smoke…the dragons. I will not have our boats go near that shore and risk drawing those beasts out here."

"They'll come eventually anyway. You can't hide from them forever."

"I can. And so must you. If you have an issue with that, my lady, I am perfectly willing to rid myself of a few mouths to feed and throw you and your men in the lake. If you continue to push me on this then I will have no choice but to expel you. You are grieving, I know, and I know what it is to grieve, so I will forgive you your insolences for now, but my mercy will not last. I have taken you in and given you refuge. I have fed you, clothed you, permitted you the use of my haven and my home. And for this, what do I get? Complaints and protests and these constant requests to leave." He shook his head. "Why, I ask you? If you expect to find your husband alive in that ruin, you must think again. He is dead, as is your niece, sad as it is to say. The sooner you accept that, the easier it will be for you."

Never, a part of her thought. Until she knew for sure, never…

She stood from her chair. "Do I have your leave to go?"

He frowned up at her, eyes lost in folds of flesh. "No," he said. "Sit. I am not done with you yet."

Her body was shaking with anger, but she did as she was bidden. *Wine helps*, she thought, reaching out and taking a gulp. She took another, and then another after that, struggling to compose herself. Memories haunted her. Of that first heartrending moment when she'd seen the city in flames, and broken down on the deck of the longboat, weeping for her sweet young Lillia. Sir Connor and Sir Penrose had demanded that the captain take them to shore, but he'd refused, and what could they do? The knights were too honourable to kill innocent oarsmen, and if they tried to swim in their armour every one of them would have drowned. *It might have been easier, though*, Amara thought. *I should have just thrown myself overboard, and let the lake take me.*

There were tears in her eyes, she realised, as there so often were these days. She wiped them away, turning her head to the side, but the whale had already seen. "Forgive me if I have spoken some hard truths, my lady. I did not mean to upset you."

"It's fine."

"No. When I say I know what it is to grieve, I mean it. I have lost a son before, and a daughter as well. I watched my father killed by a rival and my mother…I was forced to stand witness to her rape when I was only a boy. Oh, you think me cruel, that is clear to see, but cruelty is often complex, and comprehensible when you know its source. Mine comes from a dark place, a place I will not take you to. But this is what it has made me. I feast to drown my feelings, and I guard those under my protection at all costs. The money you promised me is not of interest anymore. Our borders are closed, to those coming in and going out, and no one, not you or anyone else, will change my mind on this." He took a pause, then said, "I will remain lenient for as long as I can. But if I get a sniff that you or one of your men are planning to kill me, or steal a boat and escape, I will have no choice but to make an example of you. A shame, what a very great shame that would be. But it *will* be done, my lady, of that you have my word." He paused once more, then looked to the vines. "Go, then, if that is what you wish. And think about what I've said. I hope, in the weeks to come, you will give up on these follies and make your home here. That would be the best thing for us all, I know. *Together*, we can be happy."

Together. The word made her want to vomit. She stood, turned, and left at once, neither bowing to him as he liked nor giving him a parting word. She marched past the guardsmen, down the long corridor of trees that led away from the palace, through the pretty grove that took root at the heart of the island. There were paths here, wood-decked and worn, the planking groaning underfoot as she marched. Little lanterns swayed in the branches and guards watched her warily as she went, hands on the hilts of their blades. They wore sealskin cloaks, scaly armour, with halfhelms wrought in the likenesses of fish and sundry sea creatures; a trout here, a leaping salmon there, a snapper and an eel, a shark and turtle, swordfish and lionfish and starfish. Amara had seen krakens too, and mermen, and other older things that lurked in the lake. Those appeared to be worn by the more experienced men, the captains who went out on their boats to ward off passing ships, or else take them in so that the duties could be paid.

Pirates, Amara Daecar thought. *This is a nest of pirates, nothing more.*

Those sailor-soldiers were not the only armed men here, though. There were Bladeborn about the island too, with godsteel mail and bits of armour, and misting blades at their hips. Some had once served in noble houses, or wandered the world as hedge knights for hire, or sought out contracts as sellswords and assassins. Amara had spoken with many of them by now, hearing their tales of how they'd come to be here, trying to detect whether any would be willing to turn their cloaks and help her. She had to be careful with that. If the Lord of Lard got wind of her sedition, he would not be best pleased, but now more than ever she knew she had no choice.

I'm not going to rot here with that whale. By now the whole of the north might be in flames, the world falling to ruin, everyone she cared for dead or dying. But as long as she stayed here, she would never know for sure. One way or another, she was getting off this rock.

The ceiling of the great cavern was twinkling with luminescent moss when she stepped out onto the beach. It was beautiful, like a starlit sky, glowing in hues of green and blue and sometimes pale shades of pink and purple as well. Beyond the shore, the waters moved serenely within the vast cave in which the island was situated, gently drifting out toward the mouth where the river wended away to the lake, miles away. While Amara had been given free rein to walk the island at her will, the same was not true of the others. They were limited in their wanderings, and watched at all times, permitted only to visit the beach on the eastern edge of the island-within-the-cave, and the little village of huts and shelters built along the shore.

At the edge of the village, a small beach hut had been provided for their use. Inside were bunks built into the walls, a trestle table between them with benches on either side. It was much alike to a ship cabin, Amara had noted when first she'd seen it. Later, the longboat captain who'd taken them to Varinar and back - and who still refused to give her his name - had told her that she was right. "We ripped it out of a galley, this one," he'd said. "Same with half the huts here. All taken from this ship or that."

Two guards were standing outside. Both were Bladeborn. One was an old knight, dressed in his former house cloak and colours of green and yellow, frayed and stained and sun-scorched. The other was a sell-sword, much younger and chirpier, garbed in a godsteel shirt of mail over boiled leathers.

"Sir Talmer," Amara said to the knight, a grim-faced man of stocky build who'd served under Lord Wallis Kanabar once, he had said. His house name was Hedgeside, a name chosen by his ancestor, who'd been a hedge knight for long years before winning acclaim during some war. For his service he was granted an estate, servants, and the accompanying lands and incomes by Lord Morris Kanabar, who was the Lord of the Riverlands at the time. He was also given the chance to choose his own name, and took on Hedgeside in honour of all his nights spent sleeping under hedges. Amara liked the tale. *That old hedge knight had a sense of humour that his descendent seems to lack.* "You're still here, I see."

The old knight nodded. "My duty isn't over yet. Will be here till dawn, my lady."

"All night? Oh, how rotten."

He shrugged. "I'm used to it by now."

Amara looked to his companion for the evening, a sellsword named Benjy Barrett. 'Brazen' Ben Barrett he liked to call himself, in that cocksure way common among his kind. He had overlarge ears, and oversized teeth, that made him look rather like a rabbit. "Brazen Ben," she said to him. "Tell me a story of sellsword adventure."

The rabbit grinned at her. "My lady, be glad to. But I reckon Sir Talmer here might object."

Amara had the same sense. Sir Talmer was a sour man, though his old acquaintance with Wallis Kanabar was something she was trying to use. "Perhaps next time, then." She leaned in. "If Sir Talmer should close his eyes for a moment, feel free to join us inside, Ben. I know Carly would appreciate it."

"Oh?" Ben's eyes showed his interest. "She mentioned me, did she?"

"Oh, Ben. She's always talking about you. A fellow sellsword and all?" A smile played about her lips as she nudged his arm. then she pulled the door and stepped inside.

The others were bathed in firelight, a torch flickering on the end wall, where a window looked out over the twinkling water. All sat at the benches, facing one another across the table, sharing a jug of mead and some plates of salted fish and bread. Sir Connor and Sir Penrose were on one side, Carly and Jovyn on the other. All had been stripped of their armour and weapons and given hempen shirts and shifts instead. Carly, of course, looked fetching anyway. *That girl would look gorgeous lathered in dung.*

"How'd it go with Lord Lard?" Sir Connor asked, shifting down the bench so Amara might sit.

She took her place next to him, as Sir Penrose poured her a cup of mead, and slid it down the table. "Thank you, Pen." She had a sip and answered Sir Connor's question. "Not well, I'm afraid. I asked if he would grant us a longship again, and he said, 'no and no and no again. I tell you no, my lady'. He says that a lot."

"He likes the word 'no'," Connor Crawfield muttered. "So, what now?"

Amara looked to the door, wondering if Brazen Ben and Sir Talmer might be listening. She could not say how good their hearing was with godsteel, though even without it, if they put their ears to the door, their voices might just carry. So she leaned in, gesturing for the others to do the same, and reduced her voice to a whisper. "He's never going to let us go," she told them, their five faces so close they almost kissed. "He made that clear tonight. He's scared, of the dragons. His borders are closed, he insists."

"They're not *his* borders," Sir Connor snorted. "These islands belong to the crown, not some fat pirate on an oaken throne."

Jovyn nodded briskly. "There are enough knights here to depose him, my lady. Men of honour. If you ask them, they'll serve you. You're the sister of the king."

"They don't care for kings out here," Carly said to that, blowing a lock of flaming red hair from her eyes. "That's why they came here in the first place. These men aren't knights anymore, Jovy. They're traitors and cravens, who have come out here to hide."

"We only need a few," Sir Connor said. "Even one might do. Someone who can get us to the armoury. After that, we'll do the rest."

Amara was torn on that. "If we take up arms against the whale, some, even all of us could die. He's got a score of Bladeborn in his ranks."

"*Weak* Bladeborn, my lady. There are two or three knights of good bloodlines here, I'll grant, but the rest...no. We'll deal with them easily enough."

"He has a hundred soldiers too," Amara said. "More, probably, out on the boats and dispersed across the islands." The Great One might have an army of thousands, for all she knew. This main island was but one of many, all with secret coves and hideouts. Some of the islands even connected to one another underground, she'd heard, with tunnels and caverns excavated beneath the bottom of the lake. She wondered if that might be their best way out of here. "I haven't yet been to the back of the Lard Lord's palace, but I'm certain there's a way down into the tunnels from there," she told the others. "We might be able to escape that way."

Sir Connor didn't think so. "We have no idea what's down there. We could run into an entire garrison, or something else we cannot anticipate. And where would we come out? My lady, I fear that option leads only to more questions. The best way off this island is by longboat."

"The oars are chained and guarded, Connor," Amara told him. "Every time a longship comes ashore, they lock those oars away. And besides, there are only five of us. We would be chased down for a certainty and recaptured. The Blubber King promises he will make an example of us if he should catch us trying to leave."

"Then we kill him," said Carly, squeezing a fist. "The walking whale needs to die, my lady. I doubt many here would miss him."

Amara didn't disagree, except for the 'walking' part. The whale had never walked, so far as she had seen. Any time she was summoned to join him, he was either seated on his huge oaken throne or stuffing his face at his table. On the odd occasion she'd seen him outside of his palace, he'd been lying on a litter, hauled about by a host of strong men. Where he went, she couldn't say. To the water, possibly. He had the look of a seal, after all. *Perhaps he swims like one too?*

The others were nodding assent. "Killing him is the only way," Sir Connor Crawfield said. "We all know the idiom about cutting the head off the snake. It applies here, my lady."

"And his men? Those loyal to him? What do you imagine they will say to that?"

"They will voice their displeasure with blades and blood, I would think. But those will be few. Carly is not wrong. I've heard the talk about the village, and from some of the soldiers as well. The whale is not well-loved."

"No," Amara said, agreeing. She remembered the look the maidservant gave the food. The Lord of Lard's 'children', as he liked to call them, did not eat half so well as their father did. *Eating those feelings of yours will not endear you to your people, my lord.* "There are other pirate lords on the other islands," she said. "Lesser lords who pay the Seal King fealty. When he dies there will be a power struggle. The people may wish to avoid that, Connor. Sometimes it is better the devil you know."

"Not a devil who feasts nightly while his people sit and starve. He is a cancer of these islands, and needs to be removed. You spoke before of the boats, passing through the lake. I have heard some of the sailors talking about them too. Most avoid the mists about these islands, but not all. These are people, good people fleeing from the war, and what is becoming of them? They are being warded off, or worse, killed. These islands could become a haven for thousands, even tens of thousands, but no, the whale refuses."

The others nodded. Carly slammed a fist on the table. Their voices were starting to rise a little, so Amara put a finger to her lips, instructing silence. Then they all looked to the door, listening, and Jovyn, who was sitting across the table in front of her, rose from the bench and put his ear to the wood. After a long moment he turned to them, and shook his head. "I don't think anyone's listening," he whispered, creeping back to retake his seat.

Amara thought it all through. The Lord of Lard needed to die, that was clear, the islands opened for others to come. Perhaps the seneschal could be entrusted with that? Slimy sycophant though he was, he had the bearing of a survivor, in the same way a cockroach does. Kill his master and threaten him with the same fate, and most likely he would yield. Amara put that to the group, and received a round of nods.

"He'll need strong swords about him," Sir Connor said. "To make sure there is no power struggle. If not some other pirate tyrant will just continue the Seal King's work."

Amara took the point, though in truth there would be nothing they could do to prevent that. She did not mean to stay or lend her aid in this endeavour. *That said...* "When we return to Varinar, we can spread the word that these islands may offer safe refuge," she proposed. "A strong cohort of trusted Vandarian soldiers ought to quell any power struggle, if that does occur."

More nods. But first they needed to overthrow the sack of suet and that required some thinking. She looked each of her faithful protectors in the eye - gloomy Connor Crawfield and spirited Penrose Brightwood, Carly Flame Mane, so fierce and feisty, Jovyn, quietly assured. "There are two Bladeborn men who guard the door to the palace. His best and bravest, I would think, utterly loyal to him and deadly with godsteel to grasp. Getting past them will not be easy."

"It will be for me," Carly said. "Get me a godsteel dagger, and I'll see this done. I'll be in and out, quick as that." She clipped her fingers. "They'll never even know I was there."

Amara had to smile at the girl's confidence. She hadn't even seen the palace, or entered the grove of trees in which it had been grown, yet she backed herself all the same. "There are other guardsmen that pepper the way. I don't see how you would be able to sneak past them all without detection, Carly." She could describe the layout, tell the girl everything she'd seen, but that would only get them so far. There were likely to be guards in places she didn't see, and if a single one of them raised the alarm, the whale would escape his well-earned fate and make an example of them, as he'd promised.

No, we have to be smarter than that.

"We need help, my lady," Sir Connor said. "Perhaps we might be able to rush the men outside right now, and take their weapons, but even if so, there would not be enough arms to go around and we would be quickly overwhelmed. We need to get access to the armoury."

The armoury was across the island, Amara knew, under guard at all times. Getting there without sufficient help would be impossible. She picked up her cup of mead and took a long drink, trying to puzzle it out. She could see no other way than waiting, right now. Much as it pained her, they needed more time to win allies, and that process was not a fast one, lest they show their hand too early.

"Sir Talmer may be willing," she said. "I have told him of Lord Kanabar's death at the Bane, and I saw the look in his eyes when I did. He fought for Wallis during the last war, and may wish to reenter this one. It may be time to ask him outright. I feel, at least, he would be a man to tender a warning, before speaking of our plans to Lord Lard."

"That would make one," Connor said. "We'll need more."

"Brazen Ben. He has a thing for Carly." Amara looked at the fiery sellsword. "Keep flirting with him, and he may bend. I do not think he would join us alone, but if we can muster a few others, I think he would help."

Jovyn was peering at the door. "They're both outside now, my lady. Brazen Ben and Sir Talmer."

"I know. I spoke to them before I entered."

"Maybe we should speak to them now," Carly said. "Invite them both in for a little chit-chat?"

Amara shook her head. That two of the men most likely to join them were stationed outside their door was no coincidence, she didn't imagine. The Lord of Seals was more wily than he looked, and might have placed them there as bait. *Or he may not*, she thought. Was she giving the oaf too much credit? She didn't know for certain, though was not quite ready to take that risk. *We must be smart*, she thought again.

"There are others," she went on, in a whisper, still leaning forward across the table conspiratorially. "Sir Hockney, Sir Mordont. I have sensed some disillusionment in both of them. Sir Ryger as well. These

267

men may have lost their way, but there is honour inside them still. We can give them a chance to regain it."

Jovyn gave that a nod. "I spoke with Sir Ryger myself, my lady. He is from Green Harbour, the same as me. He even remembers my father, Lord Colborn. He spoke well of him, and recalls him fondly. We only need to make these men remember who they once were, and what they stood for."

Amara smiled at the youth, liking that. "If we can get all five, then that should be enough. They need not bloody their blades, unless necessary…merely standing aside and not interfering may suffice, when all of you are armed. When the Blubber's King's chief protectors have been dealt with, the rest may throw down their arms."

"And if they don't?" asked Carly.

"Then we do what we must. But I hope it doesn't come to that."

Amara Daecar wrapped her fingers around her wooden cup, lifting it to the centre of the table. The others did the same until five cups were raised. There was something thrilling about all this, she had to admit, a distraction from her grief that gave her focus and drive. *Perhaps I'll thank the Lord of Lard for that when I watch the blood gush from his neck?* "We have our targets," she said. "If others present themselves, that's all the better. But be careful with who you speak to, and what you say. We're to tiptoe into this, understand? Nothing reckless, nothing overt. Not until I say so."

They nodded, all of them, and tapped their cups in a quiet toast. Then they drank to their plot, draining their mead. With that it was done. Amara stood from the bench. "Get some rest," she told them. "I will see you all in the morning."

She stepped outside, into the cool evening air, to walk the beach as she liked to do each night, pacing the shore and listening to the echoing sounds of the cavern, watching the moonlight shimmer off the water where it shone in through the mouth of the cave. The longboats would come and go at all hours too, and she liked to watch those as well. Sometimes they brought nets of fish, or the corpses of seals and sharks. At other times, they came bearing tidings, the fisherfolk whispering of the world beyond and the great darkness that was spreading. That was the sort of catch that interested Amara Daecar.

Neither Sir Talmer nor Brazen Ben Barrett eyed her with suspicion as she exited the cabin, suggesting to Amara that they hadn't been listening. "Off on your wanderings, my lady?" the sellsword asked, with his bucktoothed grin. They knew her habits well enough by now.

"I like to wear myself out before sleeping," she said. Amara did not stay with the others. Given her high station, she had been provided with a private cabin of her own - a small place, with a single bed and reading table - a little further down the beach. "Good night to you both."

"And you, my lady," said Sir Talmer, observing his courtesies with a bow.

268

Amara stepped away, sand crunching beneath her feet, a soft wind moving through her long hair. For a while she just walked, pacing slowly around the length of the island to where it merged into the rear cavern wall. The armoury was on this side, a natural cave in the rock blocked by rusted iron bars. She could see through those bars, see the chests and shelves and stacks of weapons piled and heaped inside. Two of the other Bladeborn were on guard, two she had spoken to only briefly, and didn't much trust. *Should I try?* she wondered. She decided not to bother. *We have our targets,* she told herself. *Let's stick to them for now.*

She turned the other way, moving back around the island, enjoying the soft slosh of the lapping water against the shore, the occasional splash of oars as longboats came sliding through into the cavern. She knew some of the sailors too, and their captains, though none so well as the man who had taken them to Varinar and back. *I'll get him to tell me his name one day,* she thought. For now, she simply called him 'Captain'.

After a few slow circuits, back and forth, she spotted the man in question drifting through into the cave, standing at the helm as the longship was rowed up toward the beach. She ambled over, watching as the oarsmen stepped out, taking their oars with them to be chained and stored. Some fishermen had gone with them, as was commonly the case, and had caught a large shark it looked.

The captain saw her standing nearby and stepped over. "Bull," he said, gesturing, as the fishermen hauled the heavy carcass out onto the beach, to drag it off for butchering. "Nasty beast, but a tasty one. Their fins make for a fine soup, m' lady. Have you had it before?"

"Bull shark soup? I can't say I have."

"Not even at the Great One's table?"

"Not even there. He has many soups and stews, but thus far, no bull shark, so far as I know. I did not know you got them here? The bull shark lives in saltwater, does it not?"

"Both," Captain informed her. "They can live in freshwater too, though we don't often get 'em here. Must have come in from the ocean. Through that underwater channel I told you about before."

A channel to the ocean, Amara thought. Captain had said it went all the way south to the Red Sea, and north to the Shivering Expanse as well. Apparently all sorts of sea monsters used it to reach the lake. *And those much worse than bull sharks too.* "So, Captain. How is the lake this evening?"

"Rough," the sailor told her. "The lake is often rough these days, m'lady." The man was Rasalanian, Amara had known when first hearing that voice, and Seaborn too she had surmised from the way in which he ruled the waters. Lakeborn was perhaps more suitable for him now. He was another whom Amara sought to recruit to her cause, an asset they could use to help them get safely across. It wasn't just rough waters and foul weather they might have to contend with. With all this talk of monsters beneath the waves, a man like Captain would be worth his weight in gold.

"I was told there was a ship bearing Taynar soldiers to the north," Amara said. "Did you see it out there?"

He shook his head. "Heard about it, though. They reckon it might land somewhere out on the west of the island, m'lady. Has a broken mast, I hear."

"And what will happen then?"

He pulled at his shovel-shaped beard. "Well, the Great One isn't so fond o' visitors, I'm sure you know. He'll be keeping an eye on 'em, I've got no doubt, making sure they don't get up to any mischief. Not a good place to land out there, though, on the western side. All rocks and cliffs and tangled brush. My guess is these Taynar men'll stop for the night, and set off again at dawn. Waters should be calmer then."

"And what of this broken mast? Will they be able to sail?"

"Aye, should think so. It's a galley, so they'll just get on the oars instead. Happens often enough, boats stopping off at some cove or another, then leaving a day or so later. These men'll be making for the Ironmoors, I'd think. Getting back to their families and such. None of 'em'll be wanting to stop out here long."

Amara nodded, hoping all of that was true. She had little love for the lords of House Taynar - Dalton the Dour and his father Godrik the God-awful, who had cut her finger off and locked her in a cell and died by her hand for all that - but that did not mean she wished harm upon their men. "Do you imagine lots of soldiers are fleeing the city," she asked the captain. Mostly, these ships she'd heard of had been bearing civilians. But soldiers? If Varinar was a smoking ruin, they would need such men to restore order. That they were fleeing as well did not speak well of the state of the city.

"Aye, such that I've heard. And not just by ship. There are reports of refugees fleeing by land as well. We had a scouting boat go out. Came back sayin' the Lakeland Pass was choked with wagons and wains and whatnot, all trundling north around the coast. And west as well, I heard."

West, Amara thought. Sir Connor had said that if Lillia had somehow survived the attack, Sir Daryl would have taken her west, out of the city, to the ancestral lands of House Daecar. There was a score of strongholds and castles that Lillia and Daryl might have fled to, and that at least gave her some hope. Thin hope, yes, but hope all the same. With so many survivors, who was to say Lillia wasn't among them? She looked to the mouth of the cave, more desperate than ever to leave.

Captain must have sensed it. "He still not letting you go, then?"

She shook her head, not saying anything that might implicate her or her men. "He says no boats are to come and go."

"Well that's a lie. That scout ship went all the way to the shore to gather information, after all." He gave his beard another scratch. "No, he's got another intention for you, my lady." There was some displeasure in the squat sailor's eyes. "Wants to make you his concubine or some such, I would think. Not sure I like that, I'm going to be honest."

No, nor I.

She hesitated, wondering, then seized upon her chance. "Will you help us?" she asked him. She glanced around, to make sure no one was listening, but the fishermen were busy hauling the bull shark down toward the butchering hut and the oarsmen had long since departed to stash their oars and head for the longhall, to smoke and drink and talk among themselves of tidings from far off lands. "I know you would not let us land in Varinar before, but…"

He reached out, gripping her wrist. "Careful, m'lady," he said, under his breath. "These are dangerous things you're saying."

Necessary things. "We can't stay here, Captain. You know who I am, who my brother is. He'll find out where I am eventually, and when he does…"

"Aye." He gave her a deep look, then released her wrist. His eyes moved left, right. "Fine," he said. "I'll help. But you'll need to kill him first. Else none of us will get out alive."

She looked at him. *Is this a trap? Is he trapping me?* She decided to come out and say it anyway. "We will kill him. You have my word."

"Then you have mine. A boat. Oars. Men to pull them. Once he's dead, we'll go. Let me know when you plan to do it, and I'll be ready."

She nodded, wondering if it could be as easy as all that. "Thank you," she said. "I…won't forget this, Captain."

"You thank me when we're safely gone, m'lady." He squinted across the island, in the direction of the armoury, though from here it could not be seen. "How do you plan to get your weapons back?"

"With help," she told him. "There are….a few knights we hope will join us."

"Which ones?"

She hesitated again, wondering.

The man laughed. "Don't worry, I'm not going to snitch. Been thinking of leaving this lake for a while now, in truth. Got a daughter, over in Rasalan. Estranged, but…well, with all that's happening, I mightn't get another chance to see her again. To apologise for the things I did." His eyes softened, reminiscing. There was some pain in them, like an old wound, scarred over but still troublesome, the sort that ached and itched sometimes, always there, never fully healing. "Wasn't much of a father to her, m'lady," he went on. "Always going off on some adventure or another, absent during birthdays and such, missing her grow. One day I left for so long that by the time I came back, my wife had died. Some slow sickness got into her and she suffered sorely for a full year before she passed. I wasn't there for any of it. And my daughter…she never forgave me." He looked to the mouth of the cave. "I tried for a while to make amends, but she wouldn't have it, wouldn't talk to me. So I took the craven's path and found my way out here. But now…with the world ending, and all, I wondered…I just wondered…"

Amara took his hand, squeezing tightly. "She'll forgive you, Captain. I know she will." *If she's still alive.* There was no guarantee of that, as the old sailor must have known. *He just wants a chance,* Amara thought. *A final chance to make peace before the end.*

The captain fixed her gaze again. "These knights, then," he said, clearing his throat. "You tell me who they are and mayhaps I can help you. I've been here long years, m'lady. Most o' them I know well."

She nodded, thinking, still searching the captain's eyes for any hint of deception. If this was some show then the man was a master mummer, and either way, she'd already outed her intent anyway. *But still, this isn't the place,* she thought. Someone might be watching them from afar, hidden from sight, and it would not serve to arouse their suspicions by talking like this for too long.

"Meet me later," Amara said. "We'll be able to speak then."

"Where?"

"I would hope you'd be able to tell me. Somewhere private, where we can talk freely."

He thought a moment. "You ever seen a bull shark being butchered, m'lady? Quite a sight, though not for the squeamish. You come along to the butcherin' hut in a little while, and we'll be able to talk. I'll see that we're given some space. And if anyone asks, we'll just say I was giving you a lesson on shark anatomy. You're a curious sort, that's well enough known. Might give you something to talk about with the Great One too when next you sit down for some dinner."

She nodded, thinking it through, and supposed that he was right. It would make for decent cover, she decided. "Done. I'll meet you there shortly."

"Aye, but give it an hour," he told her, looking over to the longhall at the heart of the village. It had been built from the bones of an over-turned galley. Smoke rose from the chimney and Amara could hear laughter rolling out from inside. "I'm known to like a drink or three when I come back from the lake, so best keep up appearances, don't you think?"

That made sense. "An hour, then. I'll continue my wandering until we meet. Thankfully, I'm known for that too."

"It all fits like a glove." Captain grinned, bowed, and stepped away.

Amara looked out toward the mouth of the cave, wondering what was happening in the world beyond. *Soon,* is all she thought. *I'll find out soon.*

19

Amilia

"So what happens now?" Amilia Lukar asked, looking down at the repulsive little corpse.

"Well…" Lord Morwood scratched his big nose. "Typically there would be a…a trial, I suppose. I would be called as a…as a witness and required to give my testimony, and you…well, I'm sorry to say, Amilia, but you would be found guilty. There was no premeditation, and no intent to kill, but…well, he *is* dead, my lady.."

And good riddance, she thought. Standing here before the corpse of Lord Emmit Gershan, she had wondered if she would feel anything, any guilt or remorse, anything at all, but no, there was nothing so much as a flicker of that. "Yes," she said. "I can see that plainly enough. So you're to tell me, Trillion, that I'm to be put on trial?"

"Well…in a normal case…"

She waved it away. "Let's forget all that, shall we? We'll just say he tripped and hit his head. Like my grandfather Modrik. These old men can be clumsy when they're drunk."

"Drunk? But he hadn't been drinking, Amilia."

"He didn't trip by accident either, but let's not mention that. It was only us, Archie, and Anna in the room. Let's not make this any more complicated than it needs to be."

"No, my lady. No, of course. We can just say he tripped, as you say." He had another scratch at that big bulbous nose of his. "The damage to his face, though…"

The old creature had a nasty gash on his chin, severing the flesh almost to the bone of the jaw, and a good number of his old rotted teeth had been smashed out and shattered, leaving his mouth a red ruin. That was the work of Amilia's golden chalice, hurled into his ugly smirking maw. What had killed him was the crack to the back of the skull, however. A simple fall could not possibly have done both.

But Amilia Lukar didn't care. Even if the word got out of what happened, she didn't imagine much would come of it. "I'm a princess, Trillion. Well enough liked, I'm led to believe. And this little old cretin was widely despised. Just make it all go away. I'll leave it with you." She turned to step away.

"My lady, there's another matter…"

"Yes, what now?" She turned back to face him.

"This um, *portal*, you spoke of. And the system of tunnels, through the mountain. You have not yet shown me the way, my lady. As you said you would."

"Did I? I must have been drunk."

"Well, you had been on the wine, that is true." He rubbed at his jowls, thick with stiff bristles. "You did not…make that up, did you? This of…of Ilith, and the refuge?"

I could say yes, she thought. *Pretend it was all some jest.* But no, that would be a little too petty, even for her. "I was telling the truth, Trillion." *Damn you Jonik, for making me do that.* "If you want to find this door, I advise you send men through to search for it. I wouldn't know the way back, even if I wanted to. It's a maze in there, and not a fun one, and black as pitch as well. There are chasms, ridges, tunnels so tight that anyone with a bit too much upholstery might struggle to squeeze themselves through. Now it's possible there are many different ways to reach the portal, but if there are, I don't know them. So please, leave me out of it."

"Yes, my lady. I…of course."

"Good. Then I'll leave it with you." She prepared to step away, then stopped, remembering something. "Did you send word to Lord Mortimer, as I asked you?"

Morwood gave a nod. "I had Archibald send a crow."

"Will it reach him, do you think?"

"Hard to say. There are still reports of these crow-killing dragons flying above our lands, but they're not so numerous as they once were. When Lord Mortimer writes back, we'll know that word got through, and if not, we'll write again."

It was the best Amilia could hope for, lest she send men on horseback and that would take too long. The letter had been written in her own hand, a plea to ask Lord Mortimer of Clearwater Castle to search for her dear friend Astrid, whom she hadn't seen since the loathsome mage Meknyr had lulled them all down that cold and windy road, posing as Sir Munroe Moore. Amilia had been assured during her time in the refuge that Astrid had not been harmed, that both she and Kegs the big smiling wagon-driver had been sent back the way they had come, but Amilia wanted to know for sure. *Astrid saved my life*, she thought. *And I promised her a place at my side, here in Ilithor.* If she could go looking for the girl herself, she would, but she couldn't, she was too far away. So she would have to leave it to others.

She turned and strode away, out of Lord Gershan's festering bedchamber, which had taken on the stink of a sickbay since his fall.

Now that he was officially deceased, however, he would be removed down to the crypts, and subsequently sent back up to those dreary old moorlands from whence the old lech had come. *I've done this city a favour*, she thought. *And the girls of the palace in particular.* Nary a day went by when Gershan didn't grab at some poor serving girl or chambermaid inappropriately, threatening and cajoling them into joining him in his bed. *Perhaps I'll gather them all around so they can spit upon his corpse.*

She met Sir Mallister outside the room, dressed in the triple-coloured cloak of the Six. "How is he, my lady?"

"Dead," she said.

"Oh." Mallister Monsort dipped his chin in sullen respect of the fallen. "He is in the Great Forge now, listening to Tukor in his toil. May he rest in peace."

That doesn't sound so peaceful. Amilia had never much liked the idea of the Great Forge, where the sons and daughters of Tukor all went when they died. It all seemed so terrible sweaty and noisy. The Hall of Green sounded much more pleasant, though of course that was reserved for the Emerald Guards. *Even in the afterlife, these knights get the finest treatment.* The Hall of Green. Varin's Table. Even the Suncoats of Rasalan had a great chamber to call their own, down in the sea god's halls.

They began walking down the wide carpeted corridor, the lanterns lit, dusk falling. Through the tall arched windows they saw skies soaked in sunset, great shredded banners of broken cloud rippling in russet and red. Further down, the city was starting to twinkle, ten thousand lights blinking awake.

Why would anyone want to leave? Amilia Lukar wondered. *Why exchange the wonders of Ilithor for that cold lifeless mausoleum and its population of creeping mages?* If the war was to reach them here, perhaps, but so far they had not been troubled. *And that journey to the door.* She did not imagine many would want to make it, lest Morwood and his men carve out an easier route. *What was Ilith thinking, putting his portal all the way back there?* Clearly he had intended to build a road there before he died, cutting out a great smooth corridor through the rock, bridging the chasms, for his people to move easily to the door. *Well, he's not dead anymore. Perhaps he ought to get back to work…*

Sir Mallister interrupted her thoughts. "Your mother was asking for you again, my lady," he said, as they strolled along. "She calls for you every day."

Amilia groaned internally. "I visited with her already." She'd done that a few days after her return, using that time to mentally prepare herself for the reunion she would sooner avoid. It had been a while since then, though. "Did she say why?"

"Not to me, my lady. But…she is your mother. I would not say she needs a reason to call upon her only daughter."

"No, but *I* do. And please, stop calling me 'my lady' when we're alone. I've opened my legs for you a dozen times, Mallister. I think it's about time you used my name."

The beautiful blond knight didn't seem to like that. "Well…I am still here to protect you."

She laughed aloud. "And this is where you'll refuse to cross the line? Calling me Amilia? Not staying out of my bed. That's the hill you'll die on, is it?"

He stiffened, and not in the way she liked. "There have to remain some…boundaries."

Her laughter grew only the louder at that. "Speaking of boundaries, there are some things you still haven't done to me, Mallister. Certain areas you haven't explored. I would have that rectified. *Tonight*," she said.

A shade of red was climbing his neck. *I have myself another Jeremy Gullimer,* she thought. *Only an even more beautiful, dutiful, version.*

"I was planning to…to train tonight…Amilia. I've been neglecting it, ever since you returned."

She had required a different type of training from him, that was true. Her bed-games were swordplay, of another sort. *And he's fast becoming a master, I'll grant. Not quite, but he's almost there.* She thought of the forms, Blockform and Strikeform and Rushform and the rest. She knew less than a little about all those, but of *Bedform* she considered herself an expert.

"Well, as you wish, sir. I will just get drunk and call upon someone else." She smiled playfully and skipped along, rather enjoying this newfound hedonism. There was something liberating about knowing the world would soon end. She could do as she pleased, consequences be damned, finally living without the shadow of a man - her grandfather or her husband or some ugly ancient mage - looming over her and telling her what to do.

She even whistled, as she went, smiling, laughing spontaneously. Sir Mallister followed several steps behind her, his pace steady. "I can see you glowering from here, Mally. You know, you're much more sensitive than your sister was. I don't think I ever saw her cry." She turned back, grinning, and that turned his glower into a smile. "You see, isn't that better? You don't have to take things so seriously."

She continued to skip along, skirts swishing, lips whistling, passing a few other guards along the way, who frowned at her as though she was mad. *Well, I just might be. I've seen enough to crack.* Other guards smiled, though, as a man does when they see a pretty young woman having fun, and she recognised among them one or two who she flirted with before, even pulled behind some pillar or wall to indulge in a few moments of fun. *If only the world knew.* They had always seen the Jewel of Tukor as some precious thing, so prim and proper, but the truth was far removed. *This is me, the truest me. I like to flirt and frolic and…*

"My lady, about your mother…"

Her mood took a dive. She slowed and stopped and turned. "What about her?"

"Will you visit with her, as she asks? She is alone in her apartments, isolated. Do you not feel compelled to ease her solitude?"

Oh, how beautifully he speaks. As beautifully as that face and fine courtly manner. "You visit her, then, if you're so concerned for her well-being. *You* did not have to grow up with her, Mallister. And her isolation is self-imposed."

"She suffers from agoraphobia, my lady. It is a known condition, and not her fault."

He's too sweet, she thought. *Give me a slap and I might like you better. Push me to the floor and maybe I'll love you.* She cringed at the thoughts, hating them, hating herself. She hated her mother too. "You mean she's a hermit. That's the common word for it."

"An oversimplification. She…"

Amilia cut him off. "I don't want to hear it. I'll go and see her again when I please. You're *not* going to persuade me."

"As you say." He straightened his back, and his cloak as well, putting himself in perfect order.

She had another long look at that mantle again, striped in white and green and brown. Beneath it he had on his godsteel mail hauberk, and at his hips he bore twin blades. The regalia of the Six. Another thing she hated. "I don't want to see you in that cloak again," she said, deciding that all of a sudden. "Your order is dead, Mallister. You'll wear the garb of an Emerald Guard from now on. Or your house colours should you prefer." They were pale green and gold, those colours, terribly noble and easy on the eye. His sigil was much the same, a gallant golden knight, standing heroic on a field of green. *They might have used him for the model*, she thought. "Your choice."

The muscles in his jaw were taut as a bowstring. "My lady, if I may…"

"No, you may not. Have you forgotten that it was the Six that killed my father, Mallister? They were only following orders, yes, but the very sight of that cloak insults me. The Brothers Hunt are dead, Sir Edwyn Huffort too, and I'm told the Ram of Ruxmond perished of the wounds he suffered that day. That leaves Sir Owen and Sir Kevyn, and where are they?"

"Sir Owen is missing, my lady. And Sir Kevyn…"

"Is with my brother, I know. The Bull and the Oak, the last surviving members, until you came along. Don't tar yourself with that brush, Mallister. There are things about the Six that you don't want to know, details that would make your pretty little toenails curl. You're *not* the same as the rest of them. Spare yourself, and spare me. And take off that damned cloak."

"Fine." Sir Mallister Monsort reached up to his shoulder clasps, unfixed them one by one, and let the mantle fall to the ground. "I'll be an order of *one*, then, my duty to protect you."

And love me, she thought, pathetic. *Why do I always need to be loved?*

She turned and walked on, her mood soured and spoiled. *Wine will help*, she thought. *And that bard, him too.* Annabette had managed to track down Gifford Gold-Tongue in the end, though by the time she had brought him up to the palace, Amilia was otherwise engaged. That did not mean she hadn't made use of his services since, though, bringing him to her apartments occasionally to serenade her with that tongue. Thus far, it had only been used for singing. *But tonight…*

"Are you truly going to train, Mallister? Why bother, when the world is ending?"

"That is the reason, my lady. The world is ending, and it needs my sword."

I need your sword. And not the one at your hip. "You should have marched south with my brother, then. You're wasted here with me if you want to be a hero."

"I don't want to be a hero, only to help. And your brother asked that I stay, as I told you. For…"

"Our mother, I know. A cursed duty for one so valorous and bold."

"There is honour in defending a queen."

"My mother was never queen because my father was never king…"

"I meant *you*, my lady."

Oh, was her first thought. Then she reflected on what that meant. Queen of Rasalan. Hadrin's queen. The rope around her wrists, the bedposts and the guards, her husband's haunted face. The broken body of Sir Jeremy Gullimer, hanging on the wall…

"I'm not a queen," she hissed. "Don't *ever* call me that again."

They walked along in silence, through grand golden halls with high fluted pillars and tapestries hanging on the walls, past little private alcoves in which the ladies of the court used to sit and gossip, through long white colonnades with open views through the city and valley beyond. Amilia stopped when they reached the central hall, with its great stair, curved and branched, that linked the palace's many levels. Amilia's private rooms were higher, up another two levels, among the royal quarters right at the top of the palace. But the training yards were down in the city.

"Will you make for the Sentinels, then?" she asked Sir Mallister, finally breaking the long silence between them. "How long do you intend to be?"

He seemed torn on how to answer. "I would expect to train for some hours, my lady. If you are still awake at midnight…"

"Then you can come and guard my door. From *outside*, sir. I will be fast asleep." She twisted a grin, playing her games, extracting her joys where she could. "If you should still be there in the morning, and with energy enough after your long and lonely vigil…" She turned her smile coquettish and left the rest unsaid. Below, she could hear men down in the main atrium, where the great doors to the palace opened out onto a large, walled courtyard, giving access to the city. There seemed to be some commotion, voices speaking loudly.

Sir Mallister looked that way. "It sounds like someone has entered unwelcome," he said. "I ought to find out what is happening." He turned, moving to the stairway.

And made it three paces.

A sudden uprush of air burst from beneath them, stopping Mallister Monsort in his tracks. The voices below became shouts, hollering loudly, though over that wind, Amilia could not make them out. From the main landing several levels below, a figure came rising, silver-armoured and blue-cloaked with a swirling blade in his grasp, glowing a radiant silver. Air embraced him in a spinning vortex, causing everything light and loose - skirts, cloaks, drapes and banners - to billow and stir and snap. Amilia raised her hand, shielding her eyes from that wind, hair whipping wildly. Through the gaps between her fingers she saw the figure come in to land. Then the air settled, the winds calming…

…and Elyon Daecar stepped forward.

Amilia lowered her arm, meeting his silver-blue gaze. A hush fell. His face was more bearded than the princess recalled, all windburnt cheeks and weary eyes with the weight of the world on his shoulders. Yet all the same, a tired smile tugged at his lips as he saw her, and she remembered a simpler time, in Varinar, with Elyon and Aleron and Mel and others; Lancel, Barnibus, sweet young Lillia and the squire Jovyn, cousin Amara and her husband Vesryn and Lord Amron, of course, who could ever forget him.

A better time. A happy time. "Elyon," she whispered, smiling.

"Amilia." He stepped forward. "They told me you were here. I've been wondering…we've all been wondering…with Thalan. I thought you were dead."

Only inside, she thought. "Not yet," she said. "It's good to see you again, Elyon. You look…"

"A mess," he said. "I know. I have seen much battle, my lady."

"I can tell." That was clear enough by the battle scars on his armour, the scratches and dents and marks. He had a deep gash on his right eyebrow too, sewn up and healing. On his breastplate was a large mottled burn mark that could only have been rendered by fire.

There were shouts ringing from below, the sound of guardsmen rushing up the stairs. "Some issue with the guards, Elyon?"

"Yes, they were rather reluctant to let me pass." He paused, and for the first time he seemed to notice the presence of Mallister Monsort. A tension thickened at once. "Mallister," Elyon said, awkwardly. "It's… been a while."

Sir Mallister's mouth hardened. "That's all you've got to say to me? It's been a while?" His eyes were more dark and murderous than Amilia had ever seen them. "You killed my sister, Elyon. It's been a while, yes. Been a while since you *murdered* her."

279

Elyon shook his head. "No…"

"You killed her," Mallister Monsort repeated. "You cut her throat right down to the bone."

"She cut her own throat," Elyon came back. "I loved her, Mallister. Do you think I'd have taken her life?"

"You never loved her. You just bedded her, *used* her, like you have a hundred others." Amilia could see the muscles straining in Sir Mallister's neck, limbs tensing, coiling as though ready to spring. "That girl, at the wedding. That redhead. You went off with her to have your fun, right there in front of my sister. That's love to you, is it? Taking off some random wanton while the woman you love watches on?"

"Nothing happened," Elyon said. "You don't know what you're talking about."

"I know. I know the guards burst in to find Mel's blood all over your hands. I know her screams were heard from halfway across the palace. Lady Cecilia told me that herself."

Elyon gave a scoff. "And you believed her? That scheming bitch?"

"You'll answer for what you did, Daecar," Sir Mallister growled, refusing to listen. He took a step forward, reaching to the hilt of his blade. Six inches of steel came slicing out. "My sister would never have killed herself. Never. She was strong, stronger than you. She…"

"I don't have time for this," Elyon cut in, waving him away, dismissive. "Take your grievances elsewhere, Monsort. I've things I need to discuss with the princess."

"My *grievances*? Grievances! You murdered my sister, you gods-damned bastard! I'll see you pay in blood!" The rest of his blade came ringing from its sheath, catching the light of a torch, gleaming.

"Stop," Amilia said. "Mally…just stop…"

"Mally?" Elyon looked between the two of them. "So it's Mally, is it? You two…?"

"That's none of your business," Sir Mallister snapped. He brandished the blade forward, all but ready to swing. "Come, draw your sword. Steel to steel to settle it."

Elyon looked at the blade in Sir Mallister's grasp, a flat disdainful look on his face. "I have no interest in killing you, Mallister. I have no time for you at all." He looked away, putting his eyes on the princess. "Amilia, tell your dog to stand down and return to heel before he does something he'll regret."

That didn't much help matters. "*Dog*?" bellowed the Emerald Guard. "You call me a dog for defending my sister's honour? For seeking vengeance for her death?"

"You want vengeance, find your king. Melany was working for Janilah Lukar, Monsort. For years, she told me. That's why she stole into my bed in the first place. To get close to me and my family. Close to Aleron. So she could…" He paused, breathing out.

"Could what?" Amilia asked. "What did she do?"

Elyon gave a shake of the head. "Nothing. It doesn't matter."

"It does. It does matter. What, Elyon? Tell me…"

"It was her," he blurted. "Melany. She was the one who poisoned Aleron before the final of Song of the First Blade. She confessed it to me that night. In the room. She hoped it would make me kill her, but I didn't. I *didn't*, Mallister," he repeated. "So put that bloody blade away."

Sir Mallister Monsort hesitated. A hundred things seemed to be running through his head. *He loved his sister too much*, Amilia thought. *To believe all that would be to dishonour her.* At last he shook his head. Then he reached down and ripped off a glove, throwing it to the floor. "I'll have my vengeance, Elyon Daecar," he said. "Tomorrow. Dawn. The Sentinels. Let the gods decide."

"Fine."

Sir Mallister rammed his blade back into its sheath. "Done, then. I'll see you at first light." He stormed straight past him, all but knocking into Elyon's shoulder as he marched on down the steps.

Amilia couldn't quite believe what was happening. *These men and their damnable honour.* "Elyon, you don't actually mean to…"

He kicked at the glove. "I'm honour-bound. Yes, I mean to. Maybe I'll be able to knock some sense into him."

"You'll kill him," Amilia said, gasping. "He won't stand a chance against you with that blade."

He snorted, glancing down at the Windblade. "Wouldn't stand a chance against me anyway. But don't worry, I'll fight him evenly."

There was still a great deal of noise coming up the steps, the guards puffing and panting as they finally poured out onto the landing. Amilia recognised their captain, an old palace guardsmen by name of Tollin Hodge with a sour face and milky left eye. "My lady," he said, breathless, as he saw them. "This man…there's a warrant…for his arrest. He barged straight in without my leave, and…"

"He has *my* leave now. You may go, Tollin."

The man spluttered. "But my lady…that warrant was by order… of the king." He squinted at Elyon. "He's a murderer."

"And the king? What is he?"

The old guardsman was stumped. "My lady?"

"The king, Captain. The king who issued the order. Is he not a murderer too? Do you not recall the riots in White Shadow?" She did not care to hear his answer. "Go and return to your posts. *Now*, before I issue some arrest orders of my own."

That got the men scampering back off, though old Tollin Hodge stopped to give Elyon a final distrustful squint with that good eye of his before he left. Elyon could not have looked less interested in all of that. *This is beneath him*, Amilia thought. She'd heard all about Elyon's heroics, and no doubt he'd festooned himself with a good many more triumphs since then. *I can't let them fight*, she thought. *They were friends, good friends before. No one needs to suffer for a dead girl's honour.*

"Was that true?" she asked, when the guards were gone. "What you just said. About Melany?" She could barely even say it. "She poisoned Aleron?"

"Yes." The word came out a grunt. "She told me she never expected him to die. Aleron was only meant to lose. And she had no choice, lest she incur your grandfather's wrath. The rest…"

"I know," she said.

He nodded, slowly, a hard look on his face as he reflected on those times. "I remember your scream," he said, softer. "When Aleron's throat was cut. That sound…and the crowd…and the rain…"

"I *know*," she said again, in a way that made him look at her. "About your brother," she went on. "About Jonik." She paused, watching his eyes change. "I spent time with him, Elyon. There are some things you ought to know."

He stared at her, disbelieving. "You…spent *time* with him? Where?" He looked around, eyes sharpening. "Is he here?"

"No."

"*Where is he?*" By instinct he reached to his blade, wind stirring, as though the Ghost of the Shadowfort would come creeping from the darkness, Nightblade to grasp, cackling like a demon. Amilia had thought that of her cousin too, once before. *Until I got to know him.*

"He isn't here," she said. "Though he was, briefly."

"When? When was he here? When did he leave? *When*, Amilia!"

She withdrew half a step at the force of voice. "That's a long story. I…"

"I'll hear it. *All* of it. Every word and every detail of it. Right now." His eyes blazed down upon her, those silver-blue eyes that Aleron had had. She saw in them a terrible rage, a bloodlust and something worse. Something deeper and darker. *The Windblade has a grip on him.*

"I don't want you to kill him," she said. "You need to swear me that, Elyon. By godsteel. I'll have your oath."

He laughed aloud. "*No.* That's an oath I'll never make."

"Then I'll not tell you where I met him, or when he was here, or for how long, or what he intends to do now. Your oath for information. That's the deal. Take it or leave it."

He looked at her as though she'd gone utterly mad. "He killed your betrothed, the man you loved! He killed my brother, Amilia!"

"That wasn't his choice. And you know it wasn't."

"He might have said no!"

"He's my *cousin*, Elyon."

"I know!" he shouted back at her. "I know about that. Vesryn told me. He's your cousin and he's my brother, and I don't care. I cannot make that oath, Amilia. I won't."

"Then you'll learn nothing from me." She spun on her slippers, striding away, her chest heaving up and down. *What was it with these bloody Daecars?* She'd done the same with Jonik when he was here, the night before he left. Arguing in the open corridor, turning and marching away. Jonik had not followed her then, and it seemed his half-brother was no different. Before long she found herself alone, speeding her step along a pillared colonnade, the winds blowing in through the open windows, brisk and biting, the skies dark beyond.

Much as she'd mocked Jonik's holy mission, she did not want to see them clash. *They should be helping one another, working together, not tearing at each other's throats.* It would all be for nought in the end, of course, with the world ending anyway, but why deny them the chance to try? *But if he wants to be stubborn, so be it. I'll not open my lips until he says the words.*

"Amilia." The voice was right behind her.

She spun, startled. "How in the hell did you.."

"I can move quietly when I fly."

"Well *don't* do it again." She put a hand to her chest, felt her heart smashing at her ribs. "Gods, Elyon, are you trying to kill me?"

"No, and I won't kill Jonik either." Elyon Daecar gripped the hilt of the Windblade with his right hand and reached out with his left. "My oath, by this shard of Vandar's Heart, to not kill Jonik, if and when I meet him. If that's what it'll bloody take, fine, you win. Now take my hand, and let's get this done."

She took his hand, and he spoke his oath - reluctantly, of course, but he said the words all the same. To some they were just words, wind, to be spoken and then ignored thereafter, but not Elyon Daecar. *Oh no, he's far too honourable. He makes a godsteel oath, and he keeps it. Same as all Daecars.*

She smiled once he was done, and drew her hand away. "Good. Well done. Beautifully said, Elyon."

He had a grimace on his face, almost a snarl, though Amilia only found that all the more amusing.

"You've beaten me," he said. "You have what you want - and for the life of me, I can't think why - but you have it. I'm not going to kill him. So it's your turn now. Tell me where he went. Tell me what he's doing. Tell me everything. Everything you know."

She smiled and turned to walk away from him. "Come," she said. "We'll need wine."

20

Amron

The grulok captain looked down at the weapon with his ancient ice-chip eyes, white-blue in his grey rock face. He had a ridge of mottled stone that served as a brow - it rose, suggesting an expression of interest. The sword driven into the ground was a greatsword, perhaps the largest Amron Daecar had ever seen, a full seven feet in length, the sort that only the largest Bladeborn men could bear.

A full foot longer than Vallath's Ruin, the king thought. No wonder it was down in the vaults gathering dust. *There's no one here who could wield it. No one but Sir Taegon, anyway.*

The Giant of Hammerhall had been the one to bring it out to them, the one to plant the greatsword ten inches into the earth. A giant among men though Sir Taegon was, before the grulok captain he was nought but a toddler, less than a third his height. Amron could sense the throb of anticipation among the group as they watched the grulok reach down with his long left arm and wrap his three-fingered hand about the hilt. Without any visible effort at all, he drew the greatsword from the earth, holding it up, looking at it with those small primordial eyes.

Gods, it looks no more than a shortsword in his grasp. A dagger, even.

"Astonishing," whispered Walter Selleck, shaking his head. It had been Walter who had unearthed that greatsword in the vaults, finding it during his time down there with the Eye of Rasalan. During one of his many breaks, Amron did not doubt. "That blade must weigh several tonnes."

To a normal man, yes, that would be so. To a powerful Bladeborn it would weigh almost nothing at all after bonding, and it appeared that same was true of these gruloks. Even at his monstrous size, Amron had wondered if the creature might show some toil when lifting the weight, more of a struggle when pulling it from the ground. That he did not suggested that his very nature, as Vandar's first and most fearsome creation, was partly responsible. "It is impressive, I agree," he said. "I would not expect him to gain any additional powers or physical advantages from the metal, however."

"Can you imagine?" chuckled Walter. "A Bladeborn grulok? The enemy would not stand a chance. Much less so against sixteen of them."

"Eighteen," Amron told him. "Two more appeared overnight." He gestured beyond the grulok captain, to where the rest of them rested and waited at the edge of the Wandering Wood, half in and half out of the trees. Some were standing, watching from afar, still as stone and staring. The rest were in their recuperative 'boulder-state', which they occupied most of the time unless Amron or Vilmar were attempting to communicate with them. Mostly that was done through the captain, though several others had the ability to speak a little of their language as well. It was rudimentary, but they were making progress. And Vilmar, especially, had continued to build a bond with the creatures.

"That one has blood on his spear-arm," noted Sir Taegon, peering at them through the hazy morning light. "Do they fight among themselves? Do they even bleed?"

If there had been any fighting among the creatures, Amron hadn't seen any, and nor had Vilmar - who spent almost all his time with them now - reported such. "I imagine that blood is from some other creature, Sir Taegon," Amron said. "They are very calm between themselves, and around most men as well, but are much more violent toward other beasts."

"Foreign beasts especially," Sir Ralf put in. "Perhaps a sunwolf or starcat prowled through here last night?" He rubbed his chin. "It would make me wonder how they will react to the prisoners, my lord. The Agarathi. The Lumarans. The gruloks were made to be sentinels, watchers and protectors of these lands. Should we not be concerned that one or another might walk to the camp one night, and attack them?"

It was a reasonable concern, there was no doubt, though one Amron had already thought of. "Vilmar and I have spoken with their leaders about this. They know not to attack them, and none have done so thus far. Unless provoked, I would hope they will remain placid."

They tended to shy away from large groups as well, which was partly why they were out here, away from the ruin of the city, across the river, keeping to the woods. There had been a great deal of murmuring among the men since they had arrived, though most agreed their presence was all for the best.

Ahead, the grulok captain had completed his inspection of the blade, and driven it back down into the earth. Vilmar was communicating with him, in his mix of gestures, growls, grunts, and actual words that Amron could understand. The king told the others to remain where they were, and strode forward to join them, some twenty paces away. The grulok looked down at him with those otherworldly eyes as he approached. *Assessing*, Amron thought. *Always assessing.*

"My lord," he said, observing courtesy. The gruloks seemed to like it when he was respectful to them. "The blade is yours, if you want it. And we have many more as well." He pointed to where the wagons and carts had been left nearby across the bridge, loaded with godsteel swords and axes. "You and your soldiers are welcome to use them."

He did not imagine that all of them would take up the offer. Or any, in all truth. The previous evening they had debated whether they should be giving them the godsteel at all. "It might only enrage the beasts," Lord Gavron Grave had said. "Vandar himself made these creatures with his own two hands. He is their father, as Agarath is the father of the dragons. Now imagine someone comes along and gives you a blade made from the bone of your own sire, Amron. How would you take that, I wonder?"

Not well, Amron had thought, though this was different. "They have come here to serve the bearers of the Blades of Vandar, Iron-foot," he'd said. "If the shards of the God King's shattered heart do not offend them, then why should simple godsteel?"

"It's not the same," Grave came back. "We're men. Sons of Varin. We were made to bear the metal. These monsters might turn a blind eye to that, but using it themselves?" He'd shrugged. "Well, I'm not so sure."

Nor was Amron. And still, even now, he could not say whether the grulok captain or any of his brethren would choose to make use of the blades. Many of them had weapons for arms, after all, great rock-like swords and long stabbing spears, though that was not true of all of them. Some bore primitive weapons in their grasp, and giving them godsteel blades would only make them more lethal. *And he does not seem offended,* he thought, regarding the captain. *More curious.* That was a good start, at least.

"Well, it is your choice," the king went on, when the grulok captain said nothing in reply. "The greatsword before you is the largest we have, so I thought it would suit a soldier of your station. Though you have your spear-arm, of course. So feel free to present it to another of your warriors if you prefer." He paused. The grulok still gave no response. "We have another greatsword on the wagons, though it is smaller, less than six feet in length. They are rare, greatswords. However, we have some longswords as well, and even a few bastard swords. Those will still be small to you, but…"

Vilmar the Black coughed.

Amron cut himself off.

"Too much, m'lord," the huntsman growled. "You're speaking too quickly, and he isn't understanding. Remember what we talked about? Simple words, slowly said."

Amron had not forgotten, though that did not mean he didn't struggle. He had never been particularly good at communicating with those with a poor grasp of the common tongue. "You don't have the patience," Lythian had told him once, and he wasn't far wrong. Communicating with the gruloks had been even more vexing.

But that's why I have Vilmar. And Lythian as well. The new First Blade of Vandar had visited the gruloks himself, bringing the Sword of Varinar with him one night so that the creatures could judge his character, and swear him their service, as they had Amron. It did not surprise Amron at all that the giants seemed to take a quick liking to the Knight of the Vale. Perhaps that was just Lythian's more open demeanour. Or perhaps it was the blade itself that the creatures were quickly drawn to. It was said that the Sword of Varinar carried the essence of Vandar's power more than the other four blades. It would stand to reason that the gruloks would be more compelled by it, as a result.

But it was a marginal effect, if so. *So long as they protect and serve us both, that's all for the better,* Amron thought.

"Well then," the king said. "I will leave it to you, Vilmar, to distribute the blades, as needed. Bring your report to my command pavilion later."

The huntsman nodded.

Amron looked up at the grulok captain. "My lord." He gave the rock giant a bow. "I will visit with you again soon."

The creature inclined his head in response to that, and even rumbled out a few words. "Soon," he said, in that rockslide of a voice. "We be here. Waiting." His eyes moved skyward, and out over the Red Sea. They seemed to narrow. "Protecting."

Amron returned to the ruin of the city, leaving Sir Taegon and Sir Quinn and Sir Gerald to help hand out the blades. "What if none of those…*things* want them?" asked Sir Gerald Strand, looking over at them from beside a loaded cart. It was his first time getting so close to them, an experience he did not appear to enjoy. *He fears everything, this man.* How he could be the heir of Lord Styron the Strong remained a mystery to Amron Daecar. *Sir Gerald the Jittery would suit him better.*

"Then we will return them to the city, Sir Gerald," he said. "What else would we do with them?"

Amron marched away, as the man fumbled over an answer, Sir Ralf and Walter and Rogen going with him. "You ought to send him away," Rogen growled, looking back at the doughy figure of his brother. "He is a pernicious presence here, my lord. His negativity seeps into the men."

"You exaggerate your brother's influence, Rogen. He is widely despised. No one listens to his grousing."

"That's my point. He's widely despised and no one wants him here. One day we'll find him with his neck cut open. No one's forgiven him for King Ellis."

Not like Sir Nathaniel. He at least was making a great effort to contribute, and had shown himself to be both courageous and capable during the trials they had faced. Sir Gerald was quite the opposite. "I'll think about it, Rogen. Is it his safety that concerns you?"

The ranger snorted. "No one would be happier to see that man's neck in a noose. But he is still my blood. And that counts for something."

Walter gave a chuckle. "Such a softie. I had no idea you cared."

"I don't. Perhaps I want to be the one to kill him myself, did you ever think of that?"

"If you do that, I would have to try you for murder," Amron told him. "The same goes for any man here involved in his death, should it come to that. We must maintain some semblance of law and order, even during times like this."

They made their way past the prisoner encampment, which had become a quagmire over the past week. The rains had been thick and unrelenting of late, often falling all night and showering them during the daytime as well. Rarely did they see blue skies anymore, or a rain-free day from dawn to dusk. Across the pen, huge brown puddles had formed, and elsewhere all was muck and mud. The pen had been expanded once more, though it hadn't helped, and now most of the captives spent their time huddling shoulder to shoulder beneath the shelters and awnings they had raised. It was dryer there, and less muddy, but they had little space to move. Lythian had suggested, and not for the first time, that the prisoners be brought inside the walls, if only to stave off disease, though Amron had continued to refuse him. The men would not have looked kindly on that, he knew. *They must remain my first priority. And we can ill afford revolt.*

It was not raining now, however. Overhead, the morning skies were filled with shredded grey clouds, rippling by like banners. There were banners, too, above the River Gate, and blowing from poles on the broken battlements. A few were orange and black, for House Brockenhurst. The rest were in the radiant silver and blue of Vandar, flapping in great quantity across the ruin of the city, as though in defiance of their humbling defeat.

Amron Daecar wore the same colours. His silver armour had been polished, scrubbed clean, and his cloak flowed resplendent at his back. He did not wear his Varin cloak, nor his cloak of House Daecar, but one of deep blue wool, striped silver down the centre, with the royal sigil of the kingdom stitched in fine golden thread. *The king's cloak*, Lythian had called it, when he gave it to him. It was another old relic found down in the vaults by Walter Selleck, a cloak, Lady Anne Brockenhurst had claimed, that was once worn by Amron the Bold.

Amron did not know if that was true or not - it seemed in rather too good a condition for that to be the case - though he wore it all the same. *Earn the name*, he thought, remembering his dream as he went. The judging eyes of his ancient namesake. *You let my city fall...*

Sir Adam Thorley was awaiting him at the gate. "Your Majesty. I had word that Commodore Fairside was searching for you. There is news. Another of his scouting boats has returned."

"Oh?" Only *Tern* had returned thus far, sailing back from their mission to the Claws to report that the enemy armada had not gone out that way. The other four boats - *Sparrow*, *Thrush*, *Swift* and *Kite* - had not yet been heard from, and Amron had wondered if they ever would. "Did he say which one?"

"No, my lord. I received word from a runner. He had no further information for me."

"I see. And do you know where the commodore is now?"

"He was at the harbour I believe, taking the sailors' accounts. Shall I send out word for him to join you in your pavilion?"

Amron nodded. "That would be best. And send for Lord Lythian as well. He should hear the commodore's report." He paused. "Actually, Walter, you can see to that. You've work awaiting you down in the vaults."

"Thrilling work," Walter said, sighing.

Important work, Amron thought. Or so his son believed. "Tell Lythian to come to my tent at once," he commanded. He turned away, crossing the yard to his pavilion, stepping past the guards outside and in through the flaps. Rogen remained without, Sir Ralf followed him within. The king took his position behind his desk, browsing through the letters and scrolls and rolls of parchment arrayed before him, delivered by riders from nearby forts and towns. Very occasionally, a crow would still come too, to deliver a message from further afield.

One had come from the west, bearing troubled tidings. It seemed Agarathi sails had been sighted on the water, prowling about the coast, and there had been several dragon attacks there as well. One coastal town had been burned to cinders, and another spared the same fate only by a stout defence from the local garrison, who had driven off a pair of dragons with arrow and bolt. There were fears it all augured a larger attack, and so far no word had come from Lord Randall Borrington about the current fate of the western gate.

I should have sent Elyon over there to meet him, Amron lamented. His son had been tending to other concerns, however, flying southeast across the Red Sea to report on this great ash cloud above the Ashmount - a concerning matter that they had discussed at length - and returning to Varinar as well to check on the state of the capital. In that at least the news was more promising. The fires had long since burned out in the Lowers now, Elyon had reported, and Lord Brydon Amadar's forces had arrived from Ilivar to try to restore order within the city. They had secured the gates, preventing further desertion from the fleeing Taynar soldiers, and taken control of the lakeside harbour as well so they could not flee by ship. That had not come without bloodshed, however. The captain in command of the Amadar forces, Sir Geofrey Bannard, had taken a hard line on desertion, Elyon told him.

But still nothing of Lillia, Amron thought. And Amara had not been heard from either. Try as he might to put the welfare of his daughter from his mind, he found it impossible, fretting on her fate during times of quiet, seeing her in his dreams as he tossed and turned and rolled beneath his blankets, defenceless against his fears. One dream was recurring, a nightly pain he had to suffer. In the dream he would see Lillia there, standing out on her balcony at Keep Daecar, watching as the Dread approached the city. He could see her little face, see the tears streaming from her wide-open eyes, sizzling off her skin, feel the air beginning to broil and burn as the titan and his minions approached, as the thunder clapped and skies turned to flame. He would hear the scream, ripping from her lungs, as the flames gushed down from a hundred maws, and came rolling across the city toward her, engulfing the streets and hills, the towers and walls and keeps, a great tsunami of raging red fire destroying all before it.

He could hear it, even now, the screaming of his daughter. *I wasn't even there, and perhaps she wasn't either. But still…I can hear her scream.*

His thoughts were interrupted, and blessedly so, by the arrival of the First Blade of Vandar. "You called for me," Lythian said, stepping inside.

Amron nodded, looking the man over. He sat back in his seat. "You're not wearing your blade."

"No." There were dark patches beneath his eyes, and more creases about them too, but all the same Lythian Lindar looked *strong*. There was something about becoming a bearer and a champion that gave a man an extra glow, a vitality that shone out of them even when they were physically depleted. "I needed the break from it," the First Blade went on. "I'll return to my training when we're done here." He looked at the scrolls on the table. "Anything new?"

"Not here." He and Lythian and Sir Ralf and others had already discussed the contents of these letters. "Commodore Fairside has a report, however. He should be here any moment."

Lythian nodded, stepped forward, and took a seat on a block of stone. "There's something else," he said. "Regarding the blades." He looked to the side of the table, where Amron had propped the Frost-blade up against the wood. Iridescent mist melted and rose from the scabbard. "I don't know if you feel it as well, but…"

"They don't like being close to one another," Amron said. "Yes, I've felt that too."

Lythian Lindar rubbed his chin, thick with three-day stubble. "It's concerning. I feel the spite running through the Sword of Varinar. No whispers, as yet, and no loss of control, but…there is a certain *anger* to the blade. They are like brothers, who resent one another."

Like Rogen and Gerald, Amron thought. "You'll learn to better master those feelings, in time, Lythian. Though I admit, they are becoming stronger. Perhaps it was wise of you not to bring it here."

Lythian stood and moved to a side table to pour himself a cup of water. "To think that kings and warriors of old used to bear two of them at once." He had a sip. "Balion the Brute comes to mind."

My grandfather's namesake. Lord Balion Daecar had been named for the Brute, as Amron had been named for the Bold. Balion the Brute had slain the feared dragon Larackar, bearing the Mistblade in one hand and the Windblade in the other, one of the most famous duels in Vandarian history. But that was a different time, as he told Lythian now.

"The blades were not so independent back then," Amron said. "Over time they have learned to grow apart. And Balion the Brute was well earned of his name. He was monstrously powerful, in both body and mind, and had the will to dominate both blades at once. There have been many others who have done the same, Lythian. But times are different now."

"Different, yes. Darker and more dangerous. And none of these old warriors ever had to live beneath the shadow of the Dread either." Lythian took a long drink of water, then set his cup aside. "I start to wonder how we're ever going to hammer the blades back together, Amron, if they're so adamant they remain apart."

"By strength of will, the same as the Brute," Amron told him. "That is why I made you guardian of the blade in the first place, Lythian. You have that strength, where others do not."

"So you say," Lythian muttered. "I have my doubts, as you know."

"My certainties are stronger than your doubts." *How often must I prop up his battered sense of honour?* He could hear the sound of footsteps outside, nearing, A moment later Eustace Fairside appeared, bursting along in that energetic way of his, moustache swaying with each step.

"Your Majesty." He gave Amron a bow, golden lapels catching the light of the candle on the table, then stood up straight before him. "You summoned me."

"I was told a scouting boat had returned."

"Two," said Fairside.

"Two?" Amron repeated.

"Two, yes. A mistake in communication, I think. *Kite* and *Swift* are back. And by the skin of their teeth, so they say. Both came terribly close to being attacked on several occasions."

"By dragons or ships?"

"Both. *Kite* managed to outrun an Agarathi galley not far off the coast. *Swift* was thrice spotted by dragons, who…" He cut himself off and waved a hand. "Ah. What does it matter? They're back safe now and have given me their reports." He dug into a pocket of his navy frock coat, and withdrew a scroll of scribbled notes. "Do you want to read, my lord? Or should I just tell you?"

"Speak," Amron said. Fairside's writing was very poor, he knew.

"As you wish." The commodore straightened out the scroll and cleared his throat. "Green Harbour," he then said, glancing at the letters on the table. "You had fears that it would come under assault, my lord, after these reports of dragon attacks and sails. Well, *Kite* has confirmed that fate as being imminent. If it hasn't already begun. A large fleet was seen to be amassing in the waters off the coast, preparing to lay the city to siege. But that was two days ago. By now…"

Green Harbour could be destroyed. Amron closed a fist. "How many ships?"

"Fourscore, perhaps more. Most are warships, large enough to carry several hundred men. I would estimate a force of twenty thousand at least. Agarathi and men of the empire as well. Wolves. Cats. So on."

Amron heard Lythian give a sigh. There was little likelihood that Green Harbour could repel such a force, not for long, and not if the dragons arrived in force.

"How many men do we have at Green Harbour?" Lythian asked.

Sir Ralf gave answer to that. "Our last confirmed reports from Lord Borrington suggested he was positioning most of his strength at the Twinfort. I would not imagine there are many more than seven or eight thousand men standing in the defence of Green Harbour."

"Then they will be overwhelmed."

Amron nodded agreement. He was about to speak, but stopped.

"There is more," said Eustace Fairside.

Amron looked at him. "More?"

"Yes, my lord." He sounded concerned. His eyes moved back down to his notes. "Another armada…sailing west, as reported by *Swift*. She was sent to the Trident, as you know, to see if the enemy had reassembled there. Many had, it would seem. Captain Moore told me that they sighted ships sailing in the direction of the eastern shores of the Brindle Steppe, a hundred of them at least. He could not say for sure, given the weather. There may be even more."

Amron digested that. The Brindle Steppe was a great expanse of open grassland, so named for the brownish colours of the prairie, that opened out south of the Twinfort. It was home to farmers and herders, with many small ponds and lakes and areas of swampland as well. Along the coast, small forts and watchtowers had taken root over the centuries, supplied and commanded by the Twinfort, but those were not capable of stopping such a force if they had it in mind to land there. "A hundred ships," he murmured. "We could be looking at thirty thousand men or more."

"They could be sailing to join in the attack of Green Harbour," Lythian said.

"Or the Twinfort itself," offered Sir Ralf. "This could be a two-pronged assault."

Amron had the same thought. If this second fleet landed on the eastern shores of the Brindle Steppe, they could march west and attack the Twinfort from the south. Meanwhile, the army besieging Green Harbour could pass through the Greenwood, and attack the stronghold from the rear, where it was much less stoutly defended. *And if we lose the Twinfort…if they smash through the western gate…*

Amron Daecar stood from his chair, legs scraping, and limped over toward the drinks table to pour himself a watered ale. Eustace Fairside rushed over at once. "My lord, please, let me…"

"I am quite able to pour a cup of ale, Eustace." He poured the commodore a cup as well, unwatered, and then one for Sir Ralf. He knew Lythian would not partake, with training to do, though offered all the same and got the expected response. Then he returned to his chair, sat down, and took a draught. Watered ale was about all he allowed himself these days, and only on the rare occasion too. He felt he needed one right now, as he puzzled everything out.

Eventually, he spoke. "Randall Borrington's forces number some thirty thousand, all told. They comprise his own men, Rothwell men, Crawfield men, *Daecar* men, all beneath the banners of my house." He thought some more on that. "I sent Brontus Oloran there as well, with his five thousand swords, and we've had word that Lord Strand has grown restless enough to muster his levies and march south from his castle." That was a rare piece of good news, only recently relayed to them. While so many men were deserting their posts and running off to protect their families, Lord Styron was calling his banners and marching south, to enter the fighting. So far as Amron knew, he was planning to march here, to King's Point, with a force of some fifteen thousand men. *I'll send a rider to divert him,* he decided. *It is west that his strength is needed.*

And mine, he thought.

He turned his gaze on Lythian, who was watching him like a hawk, reading him. The man knew him better than anyone else in the world. "You're going?" he asked.

Amron nodded. "It is my army, Lythian, my kingdom to defend. I cannot sit here as the enemy assaults us."

"They may not. We have not had confirmation…"

"I trust in these reports. If the Agarathi take Green Harbour, they will be able to cut through the Greenwood and come in behind Lord Randall at the Twinfort. If that happens the western gate will soon be smashed open, and they will have a free march up through our lands, massacring as they go." He paused to read Lythian's eyes. "You hate this, I know. You say the Agarathi are under Eldur's spell, that the Lumarans are being drawn along by fear. That we should be united, working together…"

"We should."

"But we aren't. And we may never do so. If an enemy is invading my kingdom, I am compelled as king to defend it. I will muster a host and march to their aid. The rest will remain here, under your command."

"No." Lythian stood from his stone chair. "I'll come with you, Amron."

The king had already decided otherwise. "You will stay here, and defend the river. I will command the gruloks to remain as well, should you come under attack. Work with Vilmar in my absence, Lythian. You have your training to do. And your other projects. There is no sense in you coming as well."

"No sense? I can see some sense in the First Blade of Vandar standing with his king in battle. There is *plenty* of sense in that."

Amron nodded, thinking of his own father, who had perished beside his king at the Burning Rock. He had been First Blade too, at the time. "One day," is all he said. "One day we will march upon Agarath, Lythian, and fight together, as we once did. And perhaps we will die together too. But not yet." He turned to Eustace Fairside, who was standing nearest to the door. "Eustace, if you'd be so good as to invite Rogen Strand inside."

The commodore did so. Whitebeard stepped in. "My lord," he growled.

"You spoke of sending your brother away, Rogen. I have a duty for him. Please fetch him from outside and bring him here."

"As you command." Rogen stepped away.

Lythian went to the drinks table, and poured himself a goblet of wine. *There goes his training for the day. Perhaps he needs an afternoon off.* "You're angry with me," Amron said to him.

"No. I understand your orders."

"But they disappoint you?"

"It is my life's honour to fight beside you."

"Even now? You speak of staying our hands and sheathing our swords, of unity and cooperation. I would think you would be happy to remain here, rather than march out and bloody your blade."

"I would always defend Vandar against an invading force. That is my first oath, and my last. Whatever my personal feelings, I will put them aside when you call upon my blade."

"And I will. But not yet."

Amron looked down at the papers and notes stacked upon the table. He had spent time strategising over the last weeks on how they might proceed, how they might claim victory over their enemy, and end the War Eternal, but his progress had been limited. *I have no control,* he thought. Elyon kept coming and going. Varinar was on its knees. There was the threat of a great clash outside Rustbridge in the east. Drulgar the Dread remained a constant menace, the shadow under which they all now lived, never knowing when he might return. *And now this.* Another invasion, in the west. Any thoughts he'd had, reckless as they might have been, of taking the fight to the enemy must now be put aside. He had wondered often what his namesake would do, whether Amron the Bold would march upon Eldurath itself, but no, that was folly and he knew it. *One day,* he thought. *One day. But not yet.*

He looked up at Sir Ralf of Rotting Bridge. "Convene my council, Sir Ralf. We must decide who will join me."

"My lord." The old knight strode away to call upon the captains and commanders.

Lythian still looked displeased, though would do his duty, Amron knew. "How many do you plan to take?" the First Blade asked.

Amron was already mulling on that. They had lost roughly half of their forces here during the assault, and thousands more had been wounded, with many deserting thereafter. Their numbers of healthy soldiers amounted to hardly more than ten thousand now, twelve or perhaps thirteen at a push. *But we have the gruloks*, he thought. They counted for an army alone, and thus far, he suspected the enemy was not aware of them. *I would keep it that way for now.*

"We will decide that in council," was Amron's answer. "Would you be willing to part with Sir Taegon?"

"That is not a question you have to ask me, Amron. He is your man, not mine."

"He is a Varin Knight, under your command. And has been helping to protect you, as you train. I would not want to deprive you of his presence unless you allow it."

"I have no authority to allow it or deny it. You are the king. Take who you will."

Amron nodded, still thinking. A man like Sir Taegon Cargill was a monstrous asset in battle, and could make a deal of difference whether fighting in the defence of a fortress or clashing in the open field. He would take Sir Torus Stoutman too, of that he was already certain. *That man needs an outlet for his grief, and I'll give it to him.* Rogen, obviously, would accompany him as well. Then there was Lord Grave, Lord Rodmond Taynar, Lord Kindrick and Lord Barrow, Sir Quinn Sharp and Sir Nathaniel Oloran and Sir Storos Pentar and many other knights and lords and captains, some of whom had command of dozens, hundreds, even thousands of men here.

He supposed that Lord Gavron Grave might be best positioned to join him, with his banners, leaving the new Lord Taynar here to support Lythian in his command. *If I leave the Ironfoot, he will only want the command for himself. But Rodmond, no, he is happy to serve.* The young man had never wanted to become the lord of his house, he had made plain, and would not cause any trouble, Amron didn't think. *And I'll leave Storos as well.* He had been with Lythian since his return to these shores, and was helping him with his traps and dragons, an endeavour that had not borne fruit thus far, but may yet. Walter would stay too, and Vilmar the Black, and Sir Adam, to remain in command of the Pointed Watch. The rest…well, he would decide on that in due course.

He pulled up a parchment and began drafting a letter, scratching with his quill. As he was doing so, Sir Gerald Strand arrived, quickly fetched by his brother. He looked worried as Rogen ushered him inside, eyes moving to Lythian and Eustace Fairside as though this was some sort of trial.

"You can relax, Sir Gerald," Amron said, waving him in. "I have a duty for you."

The doughy man moved up toward the table. "A duty, my lord?"

Amron nodded. "I need you to ride at once to Crosswater, then onwards from there until you find your father's forces. Take a few good men with you. I'll have Sir Ralf help you with that." He finished writing the letter, folded it, and stamped it with his royal seal. "Give this to Lord Styron."

Sir Gerald wobbled forward, still unsure. *He fears a trap at every turn.* "Might I ask what it says, my king?"

"In short, it is a direct command for Lord Strand to divert his army southwest. We are expecting an invasion through the western gate, Sir Gerald. Your father must help us hold it."

"I see." The man took the letter, stashing it away in his cloak. "Of course. I will set out at once."

"Good. You will find Sir Ralf outside. He will see you provisioned with swift horses and men to ride them. I want you to make all haste, Sir Gerald. Is that understood?"

The man nodded. "All haste, yes. I understand, my lord."

"Then go."

Sir Gerald Strand lumbered away, looking more springy in his step than Amron had seen for a while.

Rogen glared after him. "You may have just given him an excuse to desert."

"It was your idea, sending him away," Amron told the ranger.

"Doesn't mean I trust him."

I do, Amron thought. The last thing Sir Gerald would want would be to look like a craven in front of his lord father. And old Ralf would no doubt select some dependable men to make sure they completed their charge. "If he happens to betray my faith, Rogen, I give you leave to hunt him down and bring him to me by the collar. But I don't think it will come to that."

Amron looked through the flaps. He could see that some of the others were appearing outside, arriving from their duties, emerging from their own tents and pavilions as Sir Ralf sent word for them to gather. Some would be only too happy to march to battle, Amron knew, others less so. *But how many to take?* He was loathe to leave less than ten thousand men here to defend the coast, but would two or three thousand make a difference in the west? *If some of our best are among them, yes*, he told himself. *Every sword and spear makes a difference.*

He looked at Rogen Strand, still standing at the flaps. "Send them in," he said.

21

Elyon

"To the death," said Sir Mallister Monsort, glaring at him. "Do you agree?"

"No."

The Emerald Guard gave a snort. *He hasn't calmed since last night, then.* "I call you craven, Elyon Daecar. To the death or be called a craven."

Elyon looked around the tiered seating set about the duelling yard in the Sentinels, one commonly used by the Emerald Guards, he knew, when they competed in their intra-order tournaments. Only a few had come to watch thus far, given the early hour and impromptu nature of the duel, though more were filing in as the sun rose up in the east, touching the tops of the buildings with its warm, golden light. In the royal box, Princess Amilia was sitting comfortably on her cushioned bench, a cup of watered wine in her hand, giving Elyon a stern shake of the head. He had promised her last night that he would not kill Sir Mallister Monsort; a promise easily made. *Because I don't want to kill him,* he thought. *I just want him to see sense…*

"Call me what you wish," Elyon said, looking back into Sir Mallister's hard blue eyes. "Everywhere else they call me the Master of the Winds, the Prince of the Skies, the Lord of Storms, serial killer of Agarath's spawn. I did not get a chance to speak with you last night, Mallister, after you marched away in a huff. Had you stayed you might have learned that I am now Crown Prince of Vandar as well. And that I have ridden the back of Drulgar the Dread, where I fought Eldur the Eternal between his scales."

Mallister Monsort did not seem impressed. "Honour yourself all you like, Elyon," he said. "There are a hundred others who'd have done the same if only they'd had that blade."

That insult bristled a little. "Like you, Monsort? Do you want it for your own?"

297

"The Windblade?" The Emerald Guard looked down at it, showing scant interest. *Nothing like those covetous eyes of Prince Raynald.* "Do you take me for a Vandarian, Daecar? No, I do not want it. And I need no Blade of Vandar to best you. Simple steel will suffice." He drew his sword from right to left, cutting a line across the sand between them. "First blood, then? Does the craven agree to that?"

"That won't take long," Elyon returned. "Give me ten strikes and I'll have you cut. Don't you want to give your audience a show?"

"This show is not for them. It's for me. For *Melany*."

"I didn't kill her, Mallister."

"You did. Whether by your blade or not, she died because of you."

Elyon was much too tired to fight him with words on this. *I'll get it over quickly, cut him somewhere non-fatal.* He did not hate Mallister Monsort, far from it - the man had once been a close friend of his and he had no intention of causing him any more harm than he must. For that they would need to fight with simple steel, as he'd said.

"First blood, then," Elyon agreed. "Castle-forged steel, honed to cut and not kill. Armour for the vitals only. Limbs exposed."

Mallister Monsort nodded curtly, turned, and marched away to his corner. Elyon went to his, removing his swordbelt, placing the Windblade aside against a wall. He was still wearing the full plate armour he had flown here in last night, so took a few moments to undress, leaving himself in only breastplate, plackart, gorget, gauntlets and helm, so that any vital organs were protected, and his wrists and hands as well. His upper arms, thighs, lower legs and shoulders would be left open, though the blades used in these sorts of contests were intentionally blunted so nothing worse than flesh wounds could be rendered. It would take a man like Sir Ralston Whaleheart to hack a man's limb off with one of these blades, everyone knew.

By the time both of them were ready, the skies had brightened sufficiently for the fighting to begin. A few more spectators were trickling in, as word spread, taking seats here and there, yawning. It was not a large arena, nothing like the great amphitheatre in Varinar, though all the same Elyon could not help but think of his brother. Those days in Varinar when he had watched from the stands as Aleron destroyed all comers during the Song of the First Blade. *No one could stand against him*, Elyon thought. Even Brontus Oloran, well-fancied to prove his trickiest opponent, had been brutally swept aside by Aleron in their semi-final bout. *Jonik too. He would not have stood a chance if Mel hadn't poisoned Al's water. And now here we are, fighting for her honour. Hers. It should be me raging mad for my brother's death, not Mallister bleating about his sister's…*

Elyon marched across the sand in a hard step, to meet the man in the middle. "You need to wake up," he said sharply, as those memories rushed through his mind. "Your sister…I don't hate her for what she did. I've got every right to, but I don't. She was only a tool of the king, and given no choice, but still…you need to wake up to who she was, Mallister."

"I'll not hear of it. Never."

Fool. He's a faithful bloody fool. "Haven't you ever wondered how your father won those mining contracts? Your house was on the brink of financial ruin before then. That was Melany's doing. Janilah raised House Monsort on the back of her service."

"No." The fool shook his head, loyal like a dog. "Lies."

"For Vandar's sake, man, open your eyes."

"I'd sooner open your throat, Daecar. Let someone more worthy bear that blade of yours."

Elyon flexed his sword hand. "So be it, then. When the blood comes rushing from your flesh, perhaps you'll see the light. Let the gods decide."

Sir Mallister nodded - "the gods" - and reached up to pull down his visor. Elyon did the same, then both men took a step back, and another, until the required ten paces separated them, as per the conditions of the duel. There was no announcer, no one to call the bout to a start, no judges to award points. First blood contests were often fierce and uncomplicated and rarely lasted very long. That suited Elyon Daecar. He had much and more to do with his day, and duelling Sir Mallister Monsort over the honour of his two-faced sister was not something he wanted to waste precious time over.

"Ready, then?" he said.

"Ready." Sir Mallister put himself into Blockform, a hum buzzing through the crowds. Elyon switched his feet into his favoured Strikeform stance. His opponent inched forward, quarter pace by quarter pace, more watchful and wary than Elyon would have supposed. Anger typically made an opponent reckless, but Mallsiter was not of that sort.

He is a careful fighter, Elyon reminded himself. *And a skilled one as well.* During his days here in Ilithor before the wedding, the pair had sparred often enough, with Lancel and Barnibus and sometimes Rodmond Taynar as well, and Mallister had proven himself the equal of the others, if not quite so accomplished as Elyon. *Yet he may have improved. He is an Emerald Guard, young and strong and quick, and takes his training seriously.* Elyon's last months had been spent duelling dragons in the skies, not knights afoot. It felt strange, he had to admit, fighting without the Windblade in his grasp. *Strange…and yet strangely comforting.* There was nothing quite like engaging another knight in single, chivalric combat. *I've missed this,* he thought. It brought him back to a simpler time.

Sir Mallister was the first to break the impasse, pressing forward off his rear foot to lunge at Elyon's thigh. Elyon pulled his leg back, sidestepping in Strikeform, swinging in a sidecut. Mallister's blade met his in a *clang* of steel, and at that the fight began in earnest, the pair trading blows. Several swings and slashes connected, steel ringing out across the yard, the knights moving well on their feet to the sound of scuffing sand.

After a short, furious flurry, the pair drew apart again, circling, feeling one another out. Elyon panted a breath, smiling behind his visor. He could not tell if Mallister was doing the same, though suspected not. *I'll have him smiling by the end,* Elyon told himself. *We'll share words and wine and put all this behind us.*

He went again, moving into Glideform, assaulting the Emerald Guard with a sequence of flowing strikes. Mallister parried, fended, sidestepping away. The final strike connected with his breastplate, drawing a long thin line across the metal. An '*oooo*' went out through the swelling crowd, and a man shouted out, "For Tukor! You win this for Tukor!"

That seemed to spur Mallister on, as he spun around Elyon's back and unleashed a frenzied attack, mixing Strikeform with Rushform. *Impressive,* Elyon thought, fending furiously. When he saw a chance, he blocked with his left hand gauntlet, swiping Mallister's broadsword away, and hacked low with his own blade, trying to cut his leg. Monsort pulled back in time, Elyon's sword swiping at nothing but air, as his opponent pirouetted out of range with a charismatic flourish. There was an appreciative applause from the crowd.

"You've been training," Elyon noted, pulling a breath into his lungs.

"Not of late," Mallister returned, taking a heavy breath of his own. "My...duties have kept me busy." He glanced up into the stands, where Amilia was lounging contentedly on her bench, supping on her wine and nibbling on honeycakes, not a care in the world despite the fact that it was ending. *Or because of it,* Elyon thought. Amilia seemed resigned to the fact that they had scant time left before the whole world came crumbling down, and would enjoy that time doing as she pleased. The bard Gifford Gold-Tongue was there as well, plucking at his lute and humming a sweet melody for her, dressed in a ridiculous frilly white blouse and coloured robes that gave him the look of a preening peacock.

"I don't like that bard," Mallister growled. Elyon could see the narrow cast to his eyes through the holes in his faceplate. "He's always sniffing around."

More than sniffing. Gifford Gold-Tongue had a certain reputation, and not one limited to Ilithor either. "He used to play in Varinar," Elyon said. "I've seen him a dozen times at balls and banquets. You'll want to watch out for him, *Mally.* That tongue of his isn't just for singing."

He could all but hear the bones grinding in Sir Mallister's jaw. "I've heard...rumours, of that sort."

"They're more than rumours. Half the highborn ladies in Varinar could attest to that."

"Not Amilia. She wouldn't...not to me."

She would, Elyon might have said. There were rumours about Amilia's licentious leanings as well, and he had little doubt that Gold-

Tongue had enjoyed the pleasure of her bed in the past. He thought for a moment about using that suspicion to unhinge the man, but no, that was a little too unseemly. *I'm here to cut at his flesh, not stab at his heart. And he loves her, that's clear enough. The poor sweet fool is besotted.* So he merely nodded and said, "I'm sure you're right, Mallister. Now, are we fighting or talking? I've got other things to do."

They put themselves back into their preferred stances, feet shuffling, circling one another. The crowd stirred once more, as Elyon stepped suddenly forward in a powerful dash, feigned left and went the other way, swinging for Mallister's arm to get it done. But Monsort was good to it, parrying, twisting away as Elyon slashed again. The two men parted briefly, then drew together once more, sparks flying as steel kissed steel. Elyon could hear the murmurs in the crowd, rising and falling with each blow. Another flurry of swings, thrusts, parries and fends and the two parted, panting, for the third time. "For Tukor," came another shout from the audience. "Show that Vandarian how it's done!"

Others echoed him, and there were some jeers as well, Elyon heard, mostly from the common soldiers in the stands and the few lowborn in attendance, dressed in their roughspun wool and threadbare robes. The nobles were, naturally, much more reserved, old men and women sitting in their finery, all puckered lips and seamed, spotted skin, observing their courtly courtesies. But the soldiers were not so inclined, arriving in greater numbers now as word spread across the Sentinels, shouting out in support of Sir Mallister Monsort and hurling obscenities Elyon's way.

"I didn't know I was so misliked," Elyon said, glancing around.

"You're a murderer twice over," his opponent told him. "Sir Griffin Kastor. My sister. And some blame you for Prince Rylian too. Best take the cut and fly out of here, Elyon. Else the baying mob will set upon you."

Elyon had little fear for the mob, baying or otherwise. His reputation here didn't concern him either. *Let the commons believe what they like.* He had much more pressing concerns. "There's battle to be had at Rustbridge, you know," he said. "If you leave now and ride hard, you might just make it in time. Win some honour for yourself, Mallister. If you can wrench yourself away from Amilia's bed, that is."

The knight bristled. "I'm here by order of Prince Raynald."

"I'm sure. And you call *me* craven? Hiding here as the princess's bedwarmer when your prince, who might very well be your king, fights for his kingdom and the north."

"They were my *orders!*"

Mallister Monsort burst forward in Rushform, covering the ground at pace and swinging with powerful strikes. He was no master of the form, Elyon knew, proficient enough, but easily dealt with all the same. Elyon shifted backward, tapping Mallister's strikes away with graceful fends, wrist swishing, the crowd booing loudly. The vitriol was most unexpected, though somehow it fuelled him. *Curse you all,* he thought. *When Drulgar the Dread casts the city in his shadow, you can expect no help from me…*

"Fight back, you bastard!" Monsort bellowed at him. He rushed again, swinging, panting, Elyon dancing backward, refusing to engage. The booing grew louder. "Fight! Fight me!" Mallister was puffing now, his footing starting to falter, his early composure gone. *He wants to be doing more,* Elyon realised. *Oh, that sweetness between Amilia's legs is one thing, but glory another. And he wants it, no matter what he says.*

Elyon saw an opening and thrust forward, to prick a hole in Monsort's thigh, but his aim was off, and the blade slipped past. When he looked up he saw a glint of silver, Monsort's blade coming down to slice into his shoulder. Elyon twisted at the waist, leaning back, the edge of the steel all but grazing the tip of his nose as it cut straight past. Monsort's fist followed in behind it, gauntlet bunched, striking for Elyon's face, but he turned his head, taking the blow to the back of his helm. The impact jarred, and he staggered forward. The crowd roared, surging to their feet. Elyon regained his footing and spun back around.

"Blades only!" he yelled at him. "It's blades only, Monsort. *No* fists!"

"Who said so?"

"Those are the *rules*. First blood by the blade. They're the rules, damnit. Everyone knows."

"Vandarian rules. In Tukor it's different. Anything goes." And Monsort rushed in again.

Elyon swung in a sidecut as Mallister tried to tackle him to the ground, his blade clanging against the flank of the knight's breastplate. The crowd were in great voice now, cheering and jeering at every move. It was not what Elyon had anticipated, not the chivalric duel it had started as.

This'll become a brawl soon enough, he thought. That's how they'd first met, brawling over Melany's honour what felt like a lifetime ago. It was after the feast at the warcamp north of Tukor's Pass, when Elyon's father had come to treat with King Janilah, ask him to end hostilities with Rasalan. *The same night I found out Amilia and Aleron were to be betrothed.* Elyon had wanted to bed the princess himself before then, though ended up - drunk, of course - in the arms of Melany Monsort instead. Mallister had found them, canoodling in some corner, and knowing Elyon's reputation, had not been best pleased. *And now here we are again. Fighting for her honour. The gods sure do have a sick sense of humour…*

"I'm going to mangle that pretty face of yours, Daecar," Mallister Monsort said through ragged breaths, prowling before him.

Elyon had to laugh. "Pretty? Look in the mirror, Monsort. You're prettier than Melany was."

"Don't say her name! Never say her name!"

"I'll say it all I please. Melany. Melany. Melany. Mel…"

His fourth repeat was cut off as the dead girl's brother launched forward again, swinging wildly. Elyon was ready for it, knocking the blade aside, lowering his body to slam into Mallister Monsort's breastplate with his shoulder…

He knew at once it was a mistake.

There was a *popping* sound, a *crunch* of bone, and pain shot through his arm. Elyon gave out a roar of agony, arm falling limp, as he stumbled back.

Dislocated, he knew by instinct. He'd suffered a dislocation before and knew exactly how it felt.

It was his sword arm too.

That was not good at all.

With an agonised grimace he reached across, took the blade from his limp right arm with his left hand, raising it to fend off his opponent as Mallister came again.

I yield, he felt like calling, to protect himself from further damage, but the fury was in him now, and he would not give in so easily. Instead he thought, *I'll beat him with my left*, as he parried Mallister's sidecut, protecting his upper leg, parried again when he swung for his injured shoulder, and again when he went for his arm. Somehow he managed to defend himself, though clumsily, before backtracking and giving himself room.

Mallister stopped for a moment to observe him. "Your arm…" he said, seeing it. "Elyon, you're done. Just let me cut you and get it over with."

Elyon Daecar shook his head. He could see that Lord Morwood had arrived as well now, to sit with the princess in her royal box. *He looks like he slept even less than I did.* Morwood had been summoned by Amilia the previous evening so that Elyon might brief him on the latest tidings across Vandar - the fate of King's Point and Varinar and the news of Drulgar the Dread, foremost among them. None of that had been confirmed here before Elyon spoke of it, though of the giant dragon, rumours had begun to circulate. Morwood had gone bone pale when Elyon had told him that those rumours were true, and it appeared his skin had not returned to its usually rosy hue.

It centred Elyon's mind again on his task, his importance. His arm, his sword arm, was all but hanging out of its socket. *It took weeks to recover last time*, he remembered, in sudden alarm. *For days I could barely even raise it…*

And the things I have to do…

He thought of the list, the great long list that was growing every day. Thalan, and Prince Sevrin and the Eye of Rasalan. These new tidings he'd heard of Ilith and his refuge and his bastard brother, who was out there now, looking for the blades. Elyon wanted to find him first. *Needed* to find him first. *I have to look him in the eye and know that his heart is true.* Amilia had said they should be working together, that they were both after the same thing, driven by the same need, but Elyon wasn't sure. Over Jonik doubts would always circle like vultures over a kill. *Until I see him for myself, I'll never trust him. And even then…*

He grimaced, as another shot of pain rippled up his arm. *There's more*, he thought. *So much more*. Ven's army outside Rustbridge. The threat of invasion in the west. Lillia. Amara. Janilah Lukar, who he hadn't managed to find the previous day, the skies so swamped in thick grey cloud that a proper search had proven impossible. Jonik was looking for him too, Amilia had said. *I can't let him get to the Mistblade before I do. That's my quest, not his. Mine…mine…*

The crowd had turned ugly now, the din of their voices ringing in his ears. He looked around, shocked to see that their numbers had doubled, tripled, without him even knowing it. *Hundreds. There are hundreds*, he saw. Many of the common soldiers were on their feet, shouting abuse, and a few had even started to throw fruit, peppering the edges of the duelling grounds as they landed in a motley of colours.

"Give it up, Elyon, for Tukor's sake," Mallister called, over all of that. "I can see your shoulder's dislocated. There's no way you can fight with that arm now."

"I have another," Elyon came back, belligerent. The agony was intense. He felt like screaming, but held himself together. "And since when did you care? To the death, you said. You wanted me dead."

"I was angry. I *am* angry. When I think of my sister, and what happened that night…"

"I didn't kill her!" Elyon roared. "How many times do I have to say it! I didn't kill your damned sister!"

Mallister reached up, lifting his faceplate, jaw clenched tight. "Do you swear it by the gods? By Vandar himself? By the life of your father, your sister?"

"Yes, by them and everyone else! I swear it!"

"Then what happened? *What happened*, Elyon? I cannot believe she cut her own neck. *Suicide…*" He shook his head. "I just can't believe she would do that."

And curse herself, Elyon realised. To many, suicide was an insult to the gods that made them, a sin punishable by eternal damnation in the afterlife…an unending tumble down the Long Abyss. Mallister Monsort could not believe his sister was suffering that unspeakable fate. *He will deny it to his dying breath. How to make him see?*

"She did it for you," he said, over the shouting in the crowd, the bellowing of Lord Morwood as he tried to restore some calm. "Janilah told her he would have her whole family murdered if she didn't die by my hand that night. You. Your father. She took her own life to save yours, Mallister."

A grimace rippled across the man's face. "No…no, I can't…"

"She did it for a true cause," Elyon shouted, trying to get through to him. "It was not suicide, but *sacrifice*. There's a difference. There's some honour in that."

"Honour?" Mallister repeated. He frowned at the notion, shaking his head. "You call it honour, after what she did. What you *say* she did. To Aleron…"

Elyon had said all he was going to say. He could barely even think straight for the pain blazing in his shoulder and arm. "I've told you everything, Mallister. *Everything*. The whole truth. Do with it what you will." He raised his blade. "Now let's finish this."

The Emerald Guard shook his head, hesitating. "You can't fight on without your sword arm. You're important, Elyon. You need attention."

Elyon Daecar scoffed. "So *now* I'm important? What about the hundred others who could bear the Windblade as well as me?" He didn't care to hear what Mallister said to that, and wasn't about to let this cursed crowd get the better of him either. He bull-rushed the man, charging, swinging wildly, as Mallister Monsort reared backward, swatting Elyon's strikes aside. A hack at the lower legs missed, and a swing for his left arm as well, but all that put Mallister off balance and Elyon saw his chance, driving forward for his knees to tackle him to the floor.

The men tumbled onto the sand in a knot of limbs, plate scraping against plate, all grunts and curses. Laughter stormed through the crowd like a gale. Elyon didn't care. *If this is how they like to duel here, so be it.* The men were evenly matched in size, though Elyon had the momentum and managed to get himself on top of his opponent. *First blood*, he thought, as he threw a fist into Monsort's face, trying to split a lip or bust his nose. The Emerald Guard twisted his neck in time. Elyon's fist hit the side of his helm, glancing, punching right into the ground.

The thrust threw him off balance, and Monsort heaved at the hips, throwing him off him, then scrambled back up to his feet. Both of them had lost their blades during the tussle. Monsort saw his lying nearby, and ran for it. Elyon leapt up and gave chase, pain throbbing through his right arm. Monsort reached his blade in time, picked it up, turned and slashed at once. Elyon juddered to a halt, pulling away, the tip of the steel swishing past. He roared and rushed again, lungs burning, swinging for Monsort's face. Another glancing blow, as the man shifted sideways, and forward Elyon Daecar went, his momentum taking him to the ground.

He landed with a puff of dust and grit, the wind punched out of him. The crowd were roaring, laughing at him. *Laughing*! He gasped for air, pushing himself up to his knees, but his right arm gave way and he collapsed right back down. More laughter. Horrid, humiliating laughter. Then a huge great triumphant roar rang out, louder than everything that had come before, and the sound of men shouting out, "'Monsort! Monsort! Monsort!"

Elyon rolled over, wheezing. The skies above were a hard blue, the air chill and crisp in his lungs, the sun rising in the east. He crunched at the waist, sitting up, then laboured to stand, and saw Sir Mallister

Monsort standing before him. "It's over, Elyon," the Emerald Guard said.

Elyon plodded forward, shaking his head. "No…not yet. I'm not done with you yet, Monsort."

"It's over," the knight repeated. He gestured to Elyon's left leg. "Look for yourself."

Elyon didn't look. *I can't lose to him.* He kept on coming, step by painful step. The crowd were in uproar, rotting fruit spattering on the ground. He felt them pelting the sand behind him, and one hit him in the back, bursting.

"Look, damn you! You're cut. It's *done.*"

Elyon glanced down, saw the blood trickling down his leg from a shallow cut on his thigh. He must have inflicted it while he was down. *I never even felt it,* he thought.

"You were lying, then," Mallister said.

Elyon looked up at him, mouth twisting in disbelief. "Lying?"

"About Mel." The man pointed at the blood. "Let the gods decide, we agreed. And there it is. The red truth."

The red truth, Elyon thought. A fury was rising in him, red as well. "You're hopeless, Monsort, truly. Even now, you can't let it lie." He had held his tongue before, but no longer. "The bard has bedded Amilia, a dozen times I've heard," he spat. "He was there last night, when I left. I could hear them through the walls. Gods, you really think she could ever love you? *You?*" And he laughed. "No, it was Aleron she loved, Aleron who your sister killed. She's mocking you, you fool. She and Gold-Tongue laugh about you every night. Mallister Monsort, the pretty blond bedwarmer. The craven who shies away from battle, and bawls over his dead sister every night…"

Those were the last words that escaped the lips of Elyon Daecar. Monsort's fist came swinging, striking Elyon in the side of the helm, crashing into his jaw. The impact was powerful and sent him reeling, the sound of steel ringing out across the yard.

The last thing Elyon remembered was the mob, the roar of that loud baying mob, laughing…

…and the agony in his shoulder, throbbing.

22

Saska

The heat was unbearable.

We should have stayed on the Capital Road, she thought.

To either side, rugged rocky cliffs rose up a dozen metres high, creating a canyon through which they rode. Half of the Matian Way was like this, she had found. A hundred mile ride down a windless red ravine with nary a breath of air to cool them.

"I'm going to die," Leshie moaned. She was leaning forward in the saddle of her rouncey, head swaying from side to side as the poor horse laboured on. Their pace had reached that of a slug. They had to stop often, so the horses could rest, and they hadn't passed a stream in two days. The sunwolves and starcats were not faring any better. Even the camels were starting to struggle, and that said it all.

"You're not going to die, Leshie. We'll be out of this canyon soon."

"How soon? How do you know? It's gone on forever. It feels like it'll never end." She slumped forward, almost falling from the saddle. Saska had to reach out and pull her back up.

"Stop being so dramatic. We're all suffering the same as you are."

"No. You're half Aramatian. It's in your blood to handle heat like this, same as the others. Only Squire and Coldheart have it as bad as me, but even them…" She shook her head. "I grew up in North Tukor, Saska. *North* Tukor. The coldest, most miserable place in all the world. I'm not born for this."

"I grew up in North Tukor as well. Me and Del…"

"You grew up in Broadway, and then Ethior. They're both *south* of the Clearwater, same as Willow's Rise. Proper North Tukor is *north* of the Clearwater." She gave her a look. "Everyone knows that."

Saska sighed. She had no energy for this fight. "Fine. You win. You have it worse than anyone, Leshie. Are you satisfied?"

"I'll be satisfied when we get out of this cursed canyon. How much longer can it go on for?"

At this pace, days, Saska thought. To call it a gentle trot would be an insult to trotting, though she had been assured by Sunrider Alym Tantario that the cliffs would shallow soon enough and the plains would open out. They might get some wind, then, or at least a bit of breeze. *And water,* she thought. If we don't find a working well or water source soon…

She had barely any mental energy to take that thought to conclusion, and had reached her limits with Leshie's whining too. She gave her chestnut courser a kick, spurring the mare up the lines. The Wall was lumbering along at the front atop Bedrock, his enormous, indefatigable warhorse. Beside him, Sunrider Tantario rode his sunwolf Santarinio, a noble beast of calm disposition, gold-maned with silver streaks. Saska had half expected Bedrock to have collapsed by now beneath Sir Ralston's great weight, but the old warhorse seemed better equipped than others to handle the heat. *He just keeps on going, that one. Much like the giant on his back.*

"Leshie says she's going to die," Saska said to the two men.

Tantario raised a mild smile. "She will live, my lady. We will be free of this canyon soon, and there is a river ahead where we can bathe. When night comes, we may even feel a little cold. It is always much cooler beyond this canyon."

The Wall was watching the top of the cliffs, wary, eyes moving left and right. Given the heat, Saska and the others had seen no option but to shed their armour, stashing it in their saddle bags, if it would fit, or tying it in rope and laying it over their horse's back, to clatter and rattle as they went. They had some packhorses with them too who toiled with the rest of their gear.

Half these poor horses will die of exhaustion by the time we're done, Saska thought. Given the pace they were setting, she had chosen to walk often so as not to overburden her steed, and many of the others had done the same. The Wall had not been happy about any of that, though. Not the slow pace. Not the walking. And certainly not the fact that they had removed most of their armour. In order to keep him at least somewhat appeased, Saska still wore the fine breastplate that Prince Robbert had given her, but the rest…no. *I'd walk along naked if I could.*

"What exactly are you looking for?" she asked the giant, as he continued to watch the top of the cliffs. "Dragons? Patriots? Is there a tribe of dangerous desert people out here that I'm not aware of?"

He gave her an irritated look. "Do not play the fool, my lady. There are a thousand perils out here. We must remain vigilant at all times." He alone wore his godsteel armour, removing not a bit of it. It reminded Saska of those days on the *Steel Sister,* when Captain Rikki Bowen and his crew would go about barefoot and dressed in breezy linens, while the Wall stayed in his full plate armour, and his heavy hooded cloak, watching over her night and day. He shook his head angrily. "You should *not* have taken off your plate. A creature could come upon us at any moment, and you'd be entirely unprotected."

"I'm still wearing my breastplate," she said to that. "The rest I can put on quickly if I…"

"You will die quickly if a dragon descends upon us. Do you think you can dress in your armour more quickly than it can wreath you in flame?"

She frowned. "Is that a trick question?"

He snorted at her like a broadback. "It takes *one* moment, Saska. Just one. You should at least be wearing your helm."

"My helm?" If there was one piece of her shiny new suit of armour that she could quickly put on, it was her helm.

"Your helm, yes. To protect your head. As your breastplate does your heart."

"It's too hot. The helm is the worst. If I put it back on my head will melt. I don't think we should be doing the dragons' work for them, Rolly."

Sir Ralston gave no response to that, sensing a losing battle, and like any great warrior, he did not enjoy defeat. Saska was glad for it. The bickering she could do without. It was petty, at times even undignified, and especially so when done in front of the likes of Sunrider Alym Tantario, whom she respected greatly. That feeling had been with her ever since meeting the man, and had only grown since she had chosen to come this way.

He might have complained of my decision, she reflected, *but he didn't*. She had told him that they would remain on the Capital Road, to avoid this heat, only to change her mind later that day after taking counsel from her captains, Sir Ralston in particular. But when she had told him they would take the Matian Way, he had only nodded and said, "As you command, my lady," and had not said a word against it since.

He is a good man, and uncomplaining. The same could not be said for some of his men, though, who groused almost as much as Leshie did. Any time Tantario heard one of them moaning of the route, he would reprimand them fiercely, and remind them of their duties and their oaths. That tended to settle things down, but only for so long. *Let them complain,* Saska would think, if ever she heard a man muttering of the heat or the lack of water or the constant threat of monsters belched up by the Ever-War. *I've dragged them out here when they could be with their wives and children, back in the comfort of their homes. I've stolen from them time they will not get back, and time is short and running out. Every one of them has the right to moan.*

The sound of hooves could be heard ahead, an echoing clatter that rang out down the canyon long before the rider appeared. A returning scout, Saska knew. Tantario sent out men often to survey the way ahead, and sometimes one or two of the sellswords would go as well. On this occasion, it was a youthful spearman of House Hasham, wearing a white feathered cloak and riding a swift courser, brown with spots of grey and white.

He pulled to a stop before them.

"Your report," Tantario said.

The young man gestured down the canyon. "The road opens five miles ahead," he panted. "Just as you said, my lord."

Tantario had indeed made that claim. "And the river? Does it rush?" There were fears that it might have dried up in this fearsome, unnatural heat, but it seemed that was not so.

"It has shrunk," the scout said, "but there is enough flowing water to bathe in, and plenty to drink." He had a full waterskin at his hip, a promising sight.

"Were there any others there?" Sir Ralston asked him.

"Yes, my lord. Local goat herders and peasants from the nearby villages. Some of them were armed, to protect themselves. I saw no sign of brigands or Patriots in the area."

Alym Tantario nodded. "Well and good. We will speak to these locals when we arrive, should they still be there." He turned to Saska. "The river is a little over a mile beyond the canyon. We should be there by the turn of the hour."

The news was welcome, and spread briskly down the lines, the scout riding to the back to share it. The sense of relief was so thick Saska could almost taste it. They rode on, their pace speeding, the end of the canyon in sight. No one in the company had bathed since they had left Aram, their skin so coated in filth and grime that they all felt as though they were wearing another layer of armour. *No wonder no beasts have come sniffing after us,* Saska thought. *Even they cannot abide the smell.*

The final leg through this close, suffocating canyon passed without incident. It was decided that they would spend the night near the river, after the men had bathed, so their clothes might have a chance to dry. According to Sunrider Tantario, the lands were very open there, and it would be easy to keep watch for threats upon the plains.

There was no lie to what he said. Before long, the canyon walls began to shrink like blocks of ice beneath the summer sun, and beyond, the promised plains spread forth, sun-scorched and endless, peppered with tufts of dying grass and outcroppings of rugged rock that rose from the earth in strange twisted shapes. Saska saw one that looked like a howling wolf's head, and another reminded her of a star-cat's tail, swirling from the ground as though a giant cat had burrowed beneath the dirt, leaving only its tail above the surface. There were fingers too, all poking up in one area, like a titan's grasping hand. And grandest of all, some distance to the north, she sighted what appeared to be an enormous, colossal eagle, much bigger even than the sculpture at the Perch, rising from the ground with beak turned skyward and wings pulled back, as though yearning to soar into the skies, but forever bound to the earth.

"It looks so real," Saska said. "Like a giant, turned to stone."

"Only from this distance," Sunrider Tantario told her. "When you get closer, you see that it is only a natural feature of the world. The effect is best seen from afar, Sereneness."

"We saw it when we travelled from the Port of Matia," the Wall told her. "With the smuggler and the mute boy."

Mellio and Pig, Saska thought. Both of them had died in the Red Pits, right before Rolly was brought out to share their fate. That was the intention of Elio Krator, anyway, though the Whaleheart had had other ideas. "I never saw it."

"You were sleeping, at the time. I did not see a reason to wake you."

Tantario looked confused. "I was not aware you had passed this way before. You made it seem like you had not travelled the Matian Way."

"We didn't take the main roads," Sir Ralston told him. "We went west from Matia through the hills, taking backroads and farm tracks. When we saw the stone eagle, we looked at it from the north. It was only faint, then. It was a dusty day, I recall."

And hot, Saska thought. Those days in the back of the wagon had been sweltering, but nothing so bad as this.

The stone eagle was still within sight when they saw the river ahead, a jagged scar wending west to east through the plains, glinting silver beneath the dying sun. There were some cheers from the men at the sight of it, and raised fists too, and a few of them even gave out a shrill, eagle-like whistle that rang out across the tundra.

Eagles everywhere, Saska reflected. She had been bombarded by the sight of them in Aram - eagles made from stone and iron and silk, eagles chiselled and stitched and sewn, eagle helms and eagle cloaks and eagle masks, and a great deal more - and that had not much changed out here. *Only these ones are real,* she thought. *Alive.* She had seen them often since they'd left the city, circling high above her or perched somewhere nearby, in a desiccated tree or atop a spire of rock, and they always seemed to be watching the host as they passed.

There was an eagle at the river as well, she saw as they neared, clinging to the high branches of an old dead tree that stood alone across the far bank. The bird had a regal look to it, with that fine glossy plumage and great curved beak, the piercing gaze that always seemed to draw her eye. She went over to Kaa Sokari, as the men dismounted and hobbled their horses and camels. Sunrider Tantario was already setting a watch and rotation so that the men could bathe in peace, and had sent men out to speak with the locals too, a few of whom were still here, washing their clothes or bathing in the flowing waters a little downriver from the host.

"My lady," the master bowmen said, as she approached him. "You have a question."

"I do." She pointed. "That eagle. What sort is it?"

"What sort?"

"What species, I mean." It paid to be precise with Kaa Sokari, who was precise in all he did.

He looked up at it. "That is an Aramatian golden eagle. There are several sub-species of the golden eagle in other parts of the south, and north, but these are most common here. The colour of their plumage gives them away."

Gold, bronze, even some silver, she saw. *The colours of the duchy.* The eyes were amber, the beak sun-yellow with a black tip. "It's beautiful," Saska said.

"He is." Kaa Sokari dipped his chin in the direction of the bird. There was something of the eagle about the bowmaster as well, Saska thought. *It's those stern eyes of his, always narrowed to a glare.* He was not a large man, though wiry and strong, taut as though ready to act at all times. *Like an eagle, preparing to launch upon its prey.* "Now, where is that brother of yours? This would be a good opportunity to train, do you not agree?"

Del might say otherwise. The bowmaster had pushed him hard, a relentless shadow he could not seem to escape, though not without reward. Day by day, Del was making progress. That did not mean he much liked his master. But that was perhaps the point. *Sokari knows how to train an apprentice,* Saska thought. *And being liked has nought to do with it.* "Perhaps give him a moment to bathe first?" she offered.

The master archer looked down to the riverbank where some of the men were arrayed, disrobing. "Fine. I will give him a few minutes, but that is all. The light is fading, and the boy *must* be trained. Tell him he has five minutes only."

Saska smiled. "Are you not going to wash as well?"

"Later. I will wash when our work is done, and *not* before." The man spun and marched away.

Saska wandered down to where her brother was standing, smiling and shaking her head as she went. "Your master gives you the gift of five minutes," she told him. "So you'd better get in there, Del. Else he'll come down here and pull you out in the nude, and you'll have to train without any clothes."

Del did not look particularly enamoured by the prospect. "I don't have to wash naked, do I?"

"Yes," said Leshie. "All men have to bathe naked here. Didn't you know? It's the rule." She gestured along the banks. True enough, many of the Aramatians were unburdening themselves of all of their garments and wading into the water, entirely nude. Leshie was thoroughly enjoying the sight. "You see. Rules are rules, Del. Now show us your goods."

He took a step back from the water's edge. "Forget it, I don't need to wash. Where's Master Sokari? I'll just go and train instead."

Leshie laughed at him. "You *do* need to wash. Believe me. You stink, Squire. And more than the rest of us."

That wasn't fair. They all smelled equally awful. "You don't have to bathe naked, Del," Saska said. *And that's not something I want to see,* she omitted. "Just wash in your breeches, and they'll dry as you train." She pointed. "Not everyone's washing in the nude."

Some of the men had chosen to stay in their breeks and breech-clouts, which Leshie suggested meant they were not well endowed. "Men are very protective of their manhoods," she declared. "Thankfully, I don't have that problem." With a great deal of bravado, the Red Blade stripped off her clothes until she stood there, pale as milk and nude as a newborn, with a great big smile on her face. "You see." She even did a little twirl. "Naked and not ashamed." Then she strode into the river, washing in full view of the men.

Del was staring, wide-eyed. His mouth hung slightly open.

"OK, that'll do," Saska said, snapping him out of it. "Maybe go and wash further upriver. Or downriver. Just…not here." He didn't move. "*Go*, Del. You've only got a few minutes." She shooed him off, pushing the boy up to where the men were washing, then began removing her own clothes, until she was down to her undergarments. She had a bar of soap with her as well, wrapped in a cloth, which she fetched from her saddlebag. Then she waded into the lukewarm water, letting out a sigh of sweet relief as it trickled past her feet, her ankles, her thighs, and right on up to her hips and waist. It was wider than Saska had thought, the river, perhaps seven or eight metres across and over a metre deep. That gave enough privacy for most, who stood in the water up to their navels, scrubbing at their skin and rubbing the dirt from their clothes.

"You're not naked," Leshie observed. She sounded a little disappointed.

"No," Saska said, as she scoured herself. She looked around. "Too many men. And I'm not a showoff like you."

"You washed naked in a river before, though. You told me. That night those Patriots attacked you. And you met Joy."

Saska smiled to remember it. It probably wasn't so far from here, somewhere to the north. *Maybe even the same river,* she thought. It was not near as wide or deep, though, so probably not, unless it was just a tributary of this one. "There weren't many people about then," she said. "Only Rolly and Mellio and Pig, and a few locals at the well. And it was darker too. I don't think it would be appropriate here, Lesh."

The girl shrugged. "Guess you are a princess. Though that Savage bitch is still in her smallclothes too, I saw. And the Tigress, she's…" She looked around. "Well, I can't see her at all."

No, you wouldn't. The Tigress did not seem the sort of woman who would undress in front of these men. *If she'll wash, she'll do so in the dead of night when there's no one to see her scars.* Saska was suddenly conscious of her own, the lash marks that latticed the flesh of her back. Not many people had seen those before, or even knew of them. Rolly, yes, and Del and Leshie, who had bathed with her sometimes in the terrace pools at the top of the palace. The Butcher had glimpsed them as well, she did not doubt, but elsewise none of them knew. A part of her wanted to rush out and cover up, or else kneel down and hide in the water, but the better part of her did not care. *Let them see*, she told herself. *Let them see what the Kastors did to me. I'm not some pretty princess, as the Butcher calls me. Those scars tell a different tale.*

The sun was setting in the west, casting a golden light across the plains and gilding the surface of the river. Before long Leshie's skin was scoured raw at the chest and belly, thighs and arms. "You look redder than ever, Lesh. Or pink. Maybe we should call you the Pink Blade instead."

"Doesn't sound as good," Leshie said. She was looking upriver, eyes narrowing. "There's that bitch again," she said. "Look. Right there. Staring at me."

Saska looked, against her better judgment, and saw that Savage was indeed staring their way. Ever since the incident where Leshie caught her with her husband, the two had become bitter enemies, sharing scowls and curses whenever they got close to one another. "Ignore her, Leshie. I've told you both already, I don't want any violence."

"Yeah, and she just snorted and walked away when you did. She's going to try to get me, I know she is. When there's a battle, she'll slip a knife between my rips and claim she tripped."

"She won't. You just need to find something in common with her, and then you'll become fast friends, I know it." Leshie gave some snorting reply to that, but Saska didn't care to hear it. She looked downriver, to where Rolly and Tantario were talking with some of the villagers at the top of the banks. She was not surprised that Rolly wasn't washing. *He'll do so later, like the Tigress. He'll want the cover of night before he unveils the ruin of his body.* "I'm done, Lesh. If you want to keep on grumbling, there's a rock there that'll be only too happy to listen."

She smiled at her, then waded out, skin dripping, smallclothes soaked and cleaned. She had washed her other garments too, which she bundled on a rock as she wrapped her soap back in its cloth and set it aside. The air was cooling now, as it did at dusk, and there was even a bit of breeze, brushing through her hair and caressing her smooth olive skin. *Much colder and I may even shiver*, she thought, delirious, as she picked up her spare shift and pulled it over her shoulders.

As she was doing that one of Tantario's men came past. "Serenity. Are these your clothes?"

She looked down at the soaking bundle on the rock. "Yes, they are."

"Then I will take them for you." He reached out to pick them up.

She frowned. "What are you going to do with them?"

"Hang them to dry, my lady." Some of the men were pitching camp some thirty metres from the river, she saw, raising tents and setting lines, driving torch-poles into the ground to mark the borders and help keep watch. It had been a clear day, but the sight of the clouds suggested it might be a dark night. They were gathering, closing in. *We'll have no moon tonight*, she thought.

"Please, let me. You don't have to hang my washing for me. That isn't your duty."

"My duty is to serve." He bowed low, and smiled at her pleasantly. "It is no trouble." Then he stepped away.

It still felt strange to her, being treated like this. *Not so long ago it was me hanging clothes*, she thought. It was one of the many duties she had performed at Willow's Rise. Washing, cooking, cleaning, hunting, picking fruit and ploughing the fields and a host of others besides. She had grown used to being treated like a lady when she was Elio Krator's captive, the maids Milla and Koya and Yasha all bathing and scrubbing her nightly, dressing her up for dinner with the sunlord. And in the palace too, where her grandmother's maids and servers had attended her. But this was different. *He's Lightborn*, she thought. *Not a rider of sun or star, but a paladin knight of rich breeding. He shouldn't be hanging my clothes.*

Joy came loping up beside her as she walked down the banks to join Sir Ralston, water dripping from the bristles of her face. She smiled, scratching at the cat's head as they went. "Are you going to go hunting tonight, girl? You must be happy to be out of that canyon?"

As ever, the starcat gave no verbal response, though that didn't matter. Saska could feel what Joy was thinking. "Maybe I'll come with you? Do you think Rolly would let us?" The open plains were calling to her. She had come to like her chestnut courser, but there was nothing like riding atop Joy, bounding over boulders and scampering up rocks, feeling that power and agility beneath her as the starcat ran and sprang and leapt across the world.

A few more villagers had gathered by the time she arrived, all talking over one another in a rapid, rattle-tat tongue. Sir Ralston Whaleheart looked exasperated. "I have no idea what they're saying," he said, leaning down to Saska. "Do you understand any of this?"

Her Aramatian was pretty fluent by now, but all the same, they were talking quickly and in a local dialect that made it difficult. "I get the gist of it," she said. "They're arguing about what we should be doing to help them, I think. I'm not sure what that means, though."

The Wall grumbled and shook his head. "They were telling us just now about the troubles they have been facing," he said. "Alym was translating for my behalf until several others got involved, and all this shouting began."

"What sort of troubles?" Saska asked.

"The usual. Rioting in one town. A creature attack in another. Wells drying up. Fires ripping through local woodland."

"Ever-War stuff," Saska said.

The Wall nodded. "One of them claims that this monstrous sand drake we were told of was sighted only yesterday. He said it is burrowing underground, coming up in towns and villages and feasting on the people. It is growing bigger, he says."

That didn't make a deal of sense to her. "How can he know if it's growing bigger unless he has seen it several times?"

"That was my question as well. I sense there is much in the way of exaggeration going on here. But we must be wary of this creature, should it come. Hunting it, however, is out of the question."

"So they want us to kill it for them?"

"A request we can expect daily. Over this creature and others. But as I told you before, we must disregard these pleas. We defend ourselves if we must, but we do not seek adventure."

It was the town of Banassy all over again, and its new lord and ruler, this monster-communing madman whom Saska had elected to ignore. *I had no choice.* If they had stopped there, then how could they then deny these pleas? And the rest that would surely follow over the coming days and weeks? It was all or nothing, as the Wall had rightly pointed out. *All the people dying*, she thought, *and we'll do nothing to help.*

The villagers were still talking over one another, Alym Tantario doing his best to calm them, and hear them, as two of his men stood by, scribbling down their accounts. Saska listened in, trying to understand what was being said. She got something about a giant eagle, something about a bright light. There were bits and pieces about men going missing in the area as well, across these plains. That seemed to be the thrust of many of the villager's concerns.

Eventually, Sunrider Tantario called them to be quiet and asked for them to disperse, telling them he would do what he could to help them. Saska raised her eyes at that. Tantario did not seem the sort of man to make idle promises. "You said you'd help them," she said, when he turned to her.

"I did, Serenity. There is a garrison near here, away to the southeast, that may yet have a stock of soldiers. At your leave, I would send a man there overnight, to seek aid for these people."

"Of course," she said. "You don't need my permission for that."

He bowed. "The people will be thankful."

More thankful if we drew our own blades. It can't have been easy for him, telling all these poor beleaguered peasants that they had no means to help them. They were a powerful host, of knights and Lightborn riders, of Bladeborn armoured in godsteel plate bearing misting steel in their grasp. They would make short work of most of the troubles here. *Yet no. We must keep moving. And none of these people know why.*

"I heard something about an eagle. Was it to do with the sculpture?"

The Sunrider shook his head. "A herder made claims of a great shadow in the sky, eagle-shaped. He did not seem of sound mind, my lady. I suspect he may just have seen a dragon, or else a cloud."

Or a regular eagle, Saska thought. There were many of those here.

"There was a light also," she added. "A bright light. *Bright as the sun*, I thought he said."

"Yes, those were his words. There have been two separate reports of this, in fact. One far to the north, from several weeks ago, and one more recently, over a hundred miles to the west. Both men said the same thing. A sudden bright light, beyond the clouds, ethereal in its quality."

Saska was intrigued. "Do you know what that could be?"

He shook his head, unsure. "I could not say for certain, Serenity. There are many strange phenomena occurring, and this one is no different. It might just be another curious weather event. As with this heat, and the storm we saw over the sea."

The storm that killed Prince Robbert Lukar, Saska thought, sighing. "I heard people speaking about missing men as well?"

A dour nod from the Sunrider at that. "A troubling business. Campsites have been found abandoned in this area, we have heard. The tents and provisions all left behind, but the men and women…vanished."

"Could it be the work of the sand drake?" Saska asked.

"I would not think so. A beast like that will leave more signs of destruction. This is something different, I think. Though I am sure there is a reasonable explanation. I will continue to gather information, my lady, and see what I can find out."

To what end? she wondered. *We can't do anything to help anyway.* She only nodded and said nothing, as the sound of hammering rang out as the camp was pitched. Up the length of the river, the knights and riders, sellswords and Leshie were still bathing, the last of the daylight shining off their dampened skin. Further off, Del had already been summoned by Kaa Sokari to train before the light ran out entirely.

It was a peaceful camp, the most pleasant they'd had since leaving Aram. The trickle of the river, the laughter of the men, the line of horses and camels all drinking along the edge. *Maybe we'll stay here a day or three*, Saska thought. The air was cooler, the plains wide and open and beautiful, and that river was a great attraction too. All the same, she knew they wouldn't. Before first light they would be up and on the move once more.

Leaving the troubles of these lands behind.

23

Talasha

Be calm, she thought. *Be calm, Neyruu. They will not fire upon us.*

She could feel the dragon thrumming beneath her, sense the adrenaline coursing through her fiery veins. Beneath them, through the wisps of white cloud, the great pyramid of Aram soared high above the Amedda River, which bustled with its thick wide bridges, heaped with hovels and shops. There were men on the palace balconies, Talasha saw, and on the high city walls as well, all gesticulating and shouting to one another as they saw the dragon in the sky. On the high towers built along the battlements, great scorpions were being manned and loaded as well.

Choas, the Princess of Agarath thought. *One small dragon, and it brings chaos to the City of Eagles.*

Cevi was seated in the saddle behind her, clinging hard around Talasha's waist. "Will they attack, my lady?" the girl called out, shouting over the rush of wind. "If we try to land, are they going to fire on us?"

They may well, the princess thought. They had no white flag to raise, no way of showing themselves as friend, not foe, and would likely be peppered with bolts and arrows should they dare try to land within the walls. "We're not going to give them that chance," Talasha called back, turning her head so the girl could hear. "Don't worry, Cevi. Neyruu knows how to stay out of range. We'll land beyond the walls."

Talasha leaned low as Neyruu turned in a high wide circle, gliding above the palace. *East,* she thought, and Neyruu straightened out, passing over the wide waters of the river, over the bridges and the hills on which the noble Lightborn had their estates. To the south, the great harbour of Aram teemed with ships, moored along a hundred jetties and wharves; cogs and carracks and caravels, galleys and galleasses and galleons, massive men-of-war anchored in the bay. Of sailors there were plenty there, but below her the streets looked quiet. The market

318

squares and courtyards and broad avenues, usually bustling with life, seemed almost deserted to her eyes.

The reason became apparent a moment later, as they flew through a swirling banner of cloud, and the eastern districts of the city came into clearer view. They were scorched and blackened, the buildings burned down to rubble, the plains beyond marked and pitted. Further off she saw evidence of an abandoned warcamp - no, *two* - a pair of them separated by an open stretch of barren land with nought but a single pavilion sitting lonely between them.

There was a great battle here, Talasha realised. *No wonder the city is on edge.*

The easternmost gate was a blackened ruin, though still standing, and down there Talasha saw soldiers outside the gatehouse and watching from the wall walks. That gate was called the Cherry Gate if memory served, though if there had been cherry trees there once, that was no longer the case.

"What happened here, my lady?" Cevi called in her ear. "It's all burned. Do you think they were attacked by dragons?"

It was one possibility, though not a likely one. Aram was no northern city, not so well fortified to fend off dragons as a Varinar or an Ilithor, but all the same, it remained formidable. If dragons had done this, one or two would surely have fallen, felled by bow and bolt, but she could see no sign of dead dragons down there. *And those warcamps.* They painted a different picture.

She shook her head. "The city was sieged, Cevi," she called over the wind. She saw the damage now to the walls, the broken stone and smashed crenellations. And the trebuchets, half seen through the dusty haze outside, lined up in front of the twin camps out on the plains. "We'll land out there." She pointed beyond the walls. "The soldiers have seen us. Someone will come."

They continued beyond the gate and walls, out toward the ruin of the abandoned warcamps, far beyond the range of the city defences. As she drew closer, she saw men out there, picking through the wrecks. They looked up, hearing the thump of the wings, and took off running at once, throwing down whatever they had found, scampering away into the plains.

"Are they soldiers?" Cevi asked.

"Scavengers," Talasha said. That was obvious by their garb. "These camps were likely abandoned a while ago, Cevi. The soldiers of Aram will have taken the best of the loot."

They came in to land near a collapsed trebuchet, its great wooden scaffold shattered, huge swinging arm lying aside in a tangle of ropes and rigging. Beside it, several wagons were laden with rocks, mined from the nearby hills, she guessed. A great cloud of dust rose up as Neyruu beat her wings, landing with a heavy thump upon the barren earth.

Talasha stood from the saddle, unfastening the straps, slid down

Neyruu's wing and onto the ground, then helped Cevi dismount. Above the red and rugged plains beyond the city, a thick shimmer of heat burned atop the rocks. Cevi breathed out at once, grimacing. "It's so *hot*, my lady. There's not a breath of wind down here."

Flying was much cooler, there was no doubt. "You grew up on the Drylands, Cevi. Aren't you used to this sort of heat?"

The girl shook her head. "I've never felt heat like it, my lady." She was beginning to sweat already, a sheen glistening on her brow. She wiped her forehead with the back of her loose, linen sleeve. "Don't you feel it too?"

"Not as you do." Talasha was born of fire, able to regulate her temperature in extreme conditions, but even so, this heat was hardly pleasant. "Take shade beside Neyruu. It should be a little cooler there until we find a more permanent solution."

"It'll be cooler in the city," the handmaiden pointed out. "I saw pools on the terraces at the top of the palace. I wouldn't mind a swim, my lady. And a bath." She sniffed herself, cringing. "I smell worse than a privy."

Talasha laughed. "Don't we all."

Neyruu raised her long, serpentine neck, peering toward the city. *They're coming*, Talasha knew at once. She looked west, saw the figures riding out of the gates, a blur of motion distorted by heat and distance. "Wait here," she said to Cevi. "I will walk ahead and meet them."

"My lady? Are you certain it's safe?"

It was hard to be certain of anything anymore, though whoever was riding out to her would be wise to keep things civil. "We have Neyruu," she said. "If they want to start a fight, let them. Neyruu will finish it."

She stepped away, hardy hunting boots crunching on gravel and bits of loose stone. There were some scratches on those boots now, tears in the leather, as there were on her tunic as well. *And my chin*. She had a gash there too, and cuts to her hands, from her mad dash through the woods of the Western Neck, in flight from Tarran and his men. It would leave an unsightly scar, she did not doubt, but it could have been a whole lot worse if Neyruu hadn't come. Tarran, Jantor, Humghor and the squat man whose name she did not know had all been slaughtered. Only the washerwoman Santhra had managed to escape, but only because she had been lagging behind. *I'll bet she turned around and ran the other way when she heard the chaos atop that hill.* It might not matter either way. The wilds were no place for a woman alone, and that old crone would not last long.

The men were approaching quickly, led by a Sunrider in a white feathered cloak. Two others bounced along in the saddles of enormous camels. *Paladin knights*, she knew. They wore feathered cloaks as well, silver and black, with scalemail of the same beneath. The last of the host were Aram City Guards, riding fleet-footed horses. Upon their heads were eagle-crested halfhelms, and at their backs capes in the shape of eagle's wings billowed and whipped as they rode. Their bronze shirts of mail glittered in the waning sun, and at their hips were the scimitar swords - with eagle-wing cross-guards - that all the men of the order bore.

A cloud of red dust was kicked up at their coming, moving south to north on the faintest of breezes coming from the sea. Talasha stopped, some hundred or so metres away from Neyruu, deeming that far enough. She could feel the tension in the dragon's limbs, even from here. *Calm, Neyruu,* she thought. *They mean me no harm. Be calm.*

The procession spread as they neared her, the Sunrider taking the lead, the knights to either side, the half dozen city guards spreading to left and right. All remained in the saddle but for the Sunrider, who swung a leg over the back of his hulking wolf and dismounted, stepping forward.

"Who are you?" he demanded, speaking in his native Aramatian tongue. "Why have you come here to Aram?"

Talasha knew the language well, as she did a dozen tongues.

A dream, she might have answered. *A dream about a half-remembered memory.* Instead she said, "I wish to speak with the Grand Duchess."

"By whose authority?"

"Mine."

"And you are?"

"Princess Talasha Taan of Agarath, granddaughter to King Tellion the Proud and niece to his son King Dulian." She paused, waiting for laughter, but there was not so much as a snicker from the men.

"Princess Talasha," the Sunrider repeated. He looked at her long and hard. "Why are we to believe you? You are not known to ride a dragon."

"The dragon is newly bonded to me."

"And this garb? You look more like a huntress than a princess."

"That is a story too long for the telling right now. It is hot, and we have flown a long way to be here. We need water, food, fresh clothes if possible. And an audience with Safina Nemati."

"This I cannot grant. The Grand Duchess is sick, and not taking visitors."

"Even royalty?"

"Alleged royalty." He looked past her. "There is another with you. A girl. Who is she?"

"My handmaiden. Her name is Cevi." Talasha kept her voice perfectly even. "You have our names, Sunrider. Now I will have yours."

He lifted his chin proudly. "Samir of House Santali," he said. "Noble vassals of the Moonhouse Hasham." He peered past her once again. "Your dragon…is it named?"

She nodded. "Neyruu."

"A female?"

Another nod.

"How is it she came by that cleave on her flank?"

"By the claws of a brother," she merely said. *Let him mull on that.* There was a small part of her that wondered if Eldur's leathern reach had managed to stretch out here, that he had taken the people of Aramatia as thralls as well, but that did not seem likely. Safina Nemati was no Patriot of Lumara, no enemy of the north, and the Fire Father, in all his godly power, had no tool with which to take the Lightborn into bondage.

The Sunrider seemed to sense that she did not want to treat with him further, and nor was it his place to do so, if she was indeed who she said. *Perhaps he is starting to recognise me?* She had come to Aram several times in her life, the last occasion only a few years ago, and it was possible he saw her then. The face of a princess was not one soon forgotten, especially one so exotic and comely as hers. She was dirty, though, a little bedraggled from the flight, and that cut on her chin wasn't helping. But all the same, anyone who had laid close eyes on her before would be likely to remember. "People recall the heavenly and the hideous," her brother Tavash used to say of it. "Nothing in between." There was probably some truth in that, the princess supposed.

"I will need to return to the city, to bring word of you," Sunrider Santali said. "You may accompany us if you wish. But your dragon… she must remain out here."

Talasha would not have it. "I will stay with her," she told him. She had to consider the possibility that she would not be welcomed in the city. War did strange things to people, and she would prefer to remain beyond the walls, where she could escape at speed if needed. She pointed toward the pavilion between the two warcamps, a lonely island in a rugged red sea. "We will take cover there, while we wait."

He looked at it as though it was some foul, cursed place, lip pulling back in distaste. "That tent is tainted, my lady. It harboured men of dishonour and ignoble intent, engaging in their wicked councils. You ought not sully yourself by stepping inside."

There was clearly a story there. Two armies, separate warcamps, a tent between them for councils. *Enemies made friends,* she thought, *fighting for a common cause.* Clearly, it did not go well for them, though. "Life has sullied me enough of late, Sunrider Santali. I do not think that stepping inside a pavilion will do me any harm. We will await you there."

The tent's canvas walls were sun-scorched, discoloured here and there, brushed with dust from recent sandstorms. Piles of gritty red sand had begun to accumulate about its edges, and outside, some old posts were hammered into the ground, with hooks for holding lanterns, and holes gouged into the top into which torches could be placed. The interior was large, open, almost empty. There was only a table, and an old iron brazier that someone had tipped over, scattering ash and bits of coal into the floor. There were a few half-burned scraps of parchment there as well, though when she went to inspect them, found the writing smudged and unintelligible.

It was a little cooler inside, and as the sun continued its slow descent the insufferable heat began to wane. Cevi spent the time sitting cross-legged on the table, fanning her face with her hand, and had taken off almost all of her clothes as well. That was all well and good for now, with just the two of them. It would not serve when they had company, though.

That company took a while to arrive. Talasha waited at the flaps, staring out at the plains as they darkened beneath a purple dusk, or with Neyruu, who had curled up outside to rest, in that way of hers, with her long tail and slender neck all tucked in, one large wing draped over her body like a blanket. As soon as she heard anything - the distant cry of an eagle, the far-off howling of a sunwolf - she would raise her head at once, and peer toward the source of the sound.

She did the same when she heard the horses.

Talasha had been sitting up against Neyruu's flank, drifting in and out of dreams, when Neyruu stirred at the sound and shifted, lifting her head to look west. They were old dreams and new ones. Dreams of Eldurath, and the city aflame. Dreams of the wall of fire, approaching. The princess oft dreamed of Kin'rar too, though perhaps that wasn't a dream at all. Sometimes as she slept, she would see him, speak to him, hear his counsel and his wisdom. It was as though in her sleep she could connect more fully to the part of Kin'rar's soul that still lingered deep within Neyruu. Waking, she perceived only a half-heard voice, distant and dull, but sleeping…that was different. In their time together he would help teach her how to build the bond, to make Neyruu whole again, and Talasha as well. *He wants us both to be happy*, she thought. *Sweet Kin'rar. Even in death he cares.*

She sat up, rubbing her eyes, squinting out through the twilit lands. The sun had long since left them now and a horned moon was cruising the skies, chased down by a pack of rippling clouds, nipping at its heels like hounds. Neyruu unfurled and stood, stretching her neck to get a better view. The incoming host was larger than the one before, two dozen men approaching by horse and camel, cat and wolf.

Talasha moved at once to her feet and paced briskly back into the pavilion. Cevi had fallen asleep on the table, and in a position hardly considered ladylike. "Cevi, wake up, and put your clothes back on," she said. "They're coming. *Quickly*."

The girl sat bolt upright, and scrambled to dress, pulling on her sweat-stained, stinking linens, cringing at the stench. Outside, the riders were getting closer, hooves thundering across the plains. Talasha went back out into the moonlight. Above her the stars were waking, blinking to life. *No litter*, she thought, studying the incoming host. If the Grand Duchess were to come, she would have ridden in a royal carriage or palanquin, but there was no sign of one, and they were moving too quickly regardless.

Cevi joined her outside. "Will they have food, do you think? I'm so hungry, my lady."

They had scarcely eaten more than a few mouthfuls of berries and wild nuts and the odd boiled root since that greasy trout, and that was long days ago. If Tarran or any of the others had any food on them, the princess never had a chance to find out, not after Neyruu was done. "I would hope so, Cevi," she said.

They did not have to wait long to find out. Talasha spotted Sunrider Santali again, though he was not in the lead this time, but relegated to a subordinate position. He was one of a half dozen Sunriders, in fact, and there were several Starriders too, slinking along all black and rangy. Paladin knights completed the host, towering on their camels. This time, there were no city guards. Only Lightborn riders and noble knights, rich and powerful. *A host fit to greet a royal.*

Their leader she knew from previous visits, a man she had met on several occasions in the past, and one well-known all across the south, and perhaps the north as well. The Moonriders of the Lumaran Empire were famed warriors, after all, a rare breed, as fearless as they were formidable. This one had a distinguished face, very noble, with flowing white hair and a trim grey beard that hugged his jaw. About his shoulders fluttered feathers of pristine white and silver over a suit of glorious scalemail armour. Talasha remembered first seeing him when he came to visit her grandfather King Tellion in Eldurath, travelling in a grand delegation that included many of the noblest Lumosi and Solasi Lightborn across all the empire, from Solapia and Aramatia, Pisek and Lumara and the outlying islands as well. *He rode his moonbear then,* she recalled. It had been Talasha's first time seeing one, and as a young girl, the most awe-inspiring moment of her life. Even to this day she remembered it.

Iziah Hasham did not ride a moonbear anymore, however. Hothror had perished at the Battle of Burning Rock, and ever since then Hasham had worn only his mantle of Moonlord, not Moon*rider*. In that guise he chose to ride a glorious white warhorse, as grand in stature as he was, one of the most beautiful stallions Talasha had ever laid eyes on. She smiled to see him again. If she was not able to visit with the Grand Duchess herself, Lord Hasham was the next best thing.

He dismounted from his horse, stepping up to her, as his host came to a stop behind him. Though old now, he still seemed so grand in stature compared to most. *He reminds me of Ulrik*, she thought. Men said Ulrik Marak and Amron Daecar were much alike, two bastions of north and south, but Iziah Hasham was just as imposing, even in his senior years.

"Your Highness," he said, bowing low. His voice was strong and clear. "It is a great pleasure to see you again."

"And you, my lord. A pleasure indeed."

He smiled. "How long has it been?"

"Years. Four, by my count."

"Only four? Time passes more quickly as you grow older, Princess Talasha. You'll learn that one day, I hope."

Talasha was not yet thirty, though felt old enough. Living to be of an age with Iziah Hasham felt a long way off, in these dark times. "My lord. I was told by Sunrider Santali that Lady Safina has been taken ill. What is it that ails her?"

"A great many things," the moonlord said, sombre. "There is a cancer in her, the physicians say, that no surgery can solve. She has her good days and her bad days, my lady. Today is a bad one, I regret to say."

"That is most sad to hear." Talasha dipped her eyes. "Are there no other treatments that may help?"

"At this stage, that would seem unlikely. The Wise Eagle prays for her nightly from his roost, though, and the city gathers to join him. He claims it will help lift the sickness from her flesh, and cleanse her soul of all malady."

She detected the doubt in this voice, thick as mud. "I will pray for her as well."

"Thank you, my lady." The old moonlord glanced behind him. "Samir tells me you came to share in her counsel? Is there anything I can help you with?"

She wasn't certain, in truth, though Iziah Hasham had always been deep in Safina Nemati's counsel, her trusted friend and commander. *If Safina knows anything, it's likely Iziah does too.* "I have some questions, my lord. Perhaps you may be able to supply some answers."

"Of course. What questions, pray tell?"

Not here, she thought. There were far too many ears and eyes about, and this was a conversation to be had in private. "Will you join me in the pavilion, Iziah? I would prefer to speak alone."

He raised a grey eyebrow. "The palace would be better, my lady. I have already commanded that apartments be made ready for you and your handmaiden on the upper tier. A bath is being prepared. Food laid out. Take your time. Rest if you need to. We can talk whenever you are ready."

"I'm ready now," Talasha said. "And I don't think Cevi can wait that long to eat. Did you bring any food with you?"

"We did. But there really is no need to…"

"My lord. Please. Would you step inside the pavilion with me?" Tempting as his offer was, Talasha had not come here to stay. A soft bed, warm bath, new clothes, bellies full of food. She knew where that led. *We'll never want to leave.*

Lord Hasham looked at the pavilion in much the same manner as Sunrider Santali had. "I hope you know what transpired in there?"

She had some of it figured out by now. There had been some tattered old banners and bits of torn tent spread about in the two abandoned siege camps, and their colours gave them away. The Tuko-rans had pitched to the south, with an Aramatian host to the north. She supposed the latter must have been led by a disgruntled Patriot of Lumara, someone eager to take control of the Duchy, and that could only mean the Solasi Sunlord, Elio Krator. She had met him as well, during previous visits here, and never liked him. "I have an idea," is all she said.

The moonlord snorted. "I should have that pavilion torn down and burned," he said.

"Why haven't you?"

"Because I've had other matters to attend to. Though now that I'm seeing it…"

"Save the burning for now, Iziah. There is a table inside, and my handmaid is starved. Please, have some food laid out so we can talk."

He nodded, conceding. "As you wish." A hand was raised and a man rushed up to him. "See the food brought inside. And bring out the beef for the dragon."

Talasha raised her eyes. "You brought food for Neyruu?" She was touched by that.

"I was told by Sunrider Santali that she was injured and looked thin. As do you, my lady. Have you not been eating well?"

She smiled. "Is it that obvious?"

"Your flesh has receded since I saw you last."

"That was four years ago. I was younger then, fuller."

"And you did not have this cut on your chin either." He stepped in a little closer. "You sustained it recently," he observed. "Why has it not been stitched up?"

"I regret that I have not had access to good medical supplies of late." She smiled and took his arm, walking across the moonlit plains as the food was brought into the pavilion. Cevi was watching with eyes as big as ostrich eggs, all but salivating at the sight. The girl's youthful cheeks had been stripped of their fat, and her arms were much thinner than they once were. Talasha had barely noticed it until now. *Do I look the same?* she wondered. *Some scrawny thing, all cut up and filthy.* No wonder it had taken Sunrider Santali a moment to recognise her.

Some of the men were bringing out the beef, two great slabs of it slung over the backs of their camels. Neyruu rose up at once upon seeing it, nostrils flaring, trails of smoke rising. The knights carried it only so close, before setting it down on the ground and retreating.

"Have you had any dragon attacks here?" Talasha asked, as Neyruu's chest began to glow and brighten, a deep red-orange. A moment later she opened her maw and flame gushed out, cooking the meat to a crisp as she liked it. Then she feasted, ripping and swallow-ing. Talasha noticed how the sunwolves and starcats shrank back as they watched, hissing and growling.

"None to the city," the moonlord said. "But there is a large refugee camp to the north that has been targeted. More so since Agarosh left."

326

"The One-Eye? I thought he returned to the mountain long years ago?"

"He had, ever since Justo Nemati's death. Justo's grandniece managed to summon Agarosh to her service, however. A remarkable thing, my lady. And a remarkable girl."

She looked up at him, her interest piqued. "Walk with me," she said.

They continued to amble away across the moonlit plains, leaving Neyruu and Cevi to feast in peace. The moonlord's host remained where they were, sensing that the pair wanted to be alone. Talasha supposed a nice walk beneath the stars made for a better council chamber than that pavilion. *It stirs an anger in him just to look at it*. She would prefer his mood stay mild.

Her thoughts turned over as they went, wondering how best to approach it. She sensed she could trust Iziah Hasham, as she would have done with Lady Safina. *Speak freely*, she told herself. *This is no time to guard your tongue.*

When they were suitably far enough away from the others, she said, "I was a prisoner of the Fire Father, Iziah. That's why I look this way. Cevi, Neyruu and I have been in hiding for weeks."

He stopped at once and turned to her. There was a look of surprise on his face. "*Eldur?*"

She nodded. Then she corrected herself and shook her head. "Not truly. Eldur in form, but *Agarath* in spirit. He wields the Bondstone, Iziah, atop a black wood staff. The Soul of Agarath has corrupted the father and founder. He…he has unleashed the Dread."

The man's eyes were a fierce grey. They narrowed. "We have heard rumours," he said, in a deep, troubled voice. He looked at her again, brow descending. She saw suspicion in his eyes. "You were his prisoner, you say? Why? You are of his own bloodline, Talasha. The closest thing he has to kin."

She nodded, thinking of her brother Tavash, and her cousin Tethian. Tethian had perished the day the Fire Father awoke at the Nest, slain in his confusion as he rose from his millennia-long sleep. It was an accident, and poor reward for Tethian's work in bringing him back from the dead. Yet Tavash was different. *He sent him to the Eternal Flame. He killed him for his crimes and blasphemies. Bloodlines mean nothing to him now.*

Her answer was more simple than all that. "Because I betrayed him," she said. "Because I lost my faith in his cause, Iziah. He gave me a chance to prove myself. A task. That's why I'm here."

Doubt swirled in his eyes, sudden as a squall. That had come out all wrong, a poor choice of words on Talasha's part. "What task were you given?" the man asked her, guarded.

"He asked me to find the heir of Varin," she said.

His eyes flared, just a little, but enough. In that moment she knew for certain. *He knows. He knows of the heir.*

327

She went right on. "I was imprisoned with King Hadrin," she said quickly, to explain, lest he get the wrong idea. "He was taken captive by Eldur during the siege of Thalan and brought back to Eldurath. The Father fastened him to a plinth in chains, a plinth that bore the sea god's *Eye*. Hadrin was made to search for the heir. I was made to watch him, and report on what I learned. I *escaped* instead." She fixed him with her gaze, honest and open. "I do not serve the Fire Father, my lord. I broke from those shackles long ago."

The moonlord was silent, searching, peering into her eyes. *He fears me to be a spy*, she knew, and why wouldn't he after all that? Who better to fly down here in search of information than a princess well-liked and trusted, bearing a false tale?

She thought on her next words, choosing them more carefully. "I had a dream, Iziah," she told him. "A dream of a memory, half-forgotten. When I was locked away with Hadrin, he would ramble on about his visions, mumbling as he stared into the Eye, sometimes whispering, sometimes screaming, and rarely was he lucid. I heard him mutter a hundred prophesies, but they were all broken, fractured, a word here and a word there. Out of context, I could not piece them together, and even after he spoke them, he would soon forget…"

She thought back on those long lonely days, those nights when she would be woken by his shrieking, the rattle of chains in the dark, the shadows twisting on the walls, cast by the light of the braziers. A shudder went through her.

"One night, he spoke of a girl," she went on. "And the colours… silver and blue. At the time, I thought nothing of it. I had been sleeping when he awoke me. And when he was done…I returned to my bed. By morning it was nought but a shadow in my mind, one of many, crowding and formless. But later…only days ago, it came back to me in a dream. I could not say why, at first. Why *that* memory? Why *that* vision? But when I mulled on it, I realised it must be important. Silver. Blue. These are the colours of Varin, my lord, of Vandar. I wondered…could this girl he spoke of be the heir?"

His eyes gave nothing away. He was reading her as a scholar does a scroll, searching for any sign of deception. "Go on," he said.

"There were other words that Hadrin muttered," she said. "He mentioned a city of eagles, and a pyramid, and a dragon descending from the skies. I think that dragon was Neyruu, Iziah, bearing me. I think I am part of this vision, and that is why it came to me in the dream. It was a nudge, if you will, of fate. I was always meant to come here. I was always meant to help."

He nodded slowly. There was a change in his eyes, those dark silver eyes reflecting the light of the moon. The barren earth about them was mottled in moonlight too, clouds spotting the skies. A wind was picking up, warm from the coast, sifting through Hasham's feathered cloak and the long jet hair that hung at Talasha's back. *He believes me*, she thought.

Eventually, the moonlord spoke. "How much does the Father of Fire know, my lady? Does he set his eye upon us? Does he know…of Varin's heir?"

"He is aware of their heir's existence, from the prophecies. There was a belief that it was not literal. A spiritual heir, rather than one of true blood. I was there, in the company of his lords and captains, when it was declared that Amron Daecar was this likely man. Eldur gave Ulrik Marak an explicit command to kill him."

Hasham gave a grunt of interest. "A battle I should like to see. Was Lord Marak successful?"

She shook her head. "I could not say. I have been weeks in the wild, Iziah. Hiding. Running. What has happened in the north, I do not know. Amron Daecar may yet live. Yet with Drulgar returned…" She had no way of knowing what sort of damage the dragon had wrought. The whole of the north might be aflame by now, Amron Daecar dead and Elyon, her liberator, too…and Lythian her sweet captain as well. The thought was a cold knife in her gut. "I was freed during Eldur's absence from the city, but have little doubt he will be hunting me. This heir and I have that in common, Iziah. Whether I like it or not, I am tethered to her fate." She paused, searching his eyes. "She is this girl you spoke of, isn't she? The grandniece of Justo Nemati? Lady Safina's granddaughter?"

She saw the answer in his gaze, though he said nothing. *King Lorin's granddaughter as well*, Talasha thought. The last of the Varin kings must have had a secret son, who in turn came here and sired a child by Princess Leila. There had always been rumours about the death of Safina's daughter, and one of the whispers spoke of her death upon the birthing table. To die in childbirth was common among Blade-born, it was said. *An omen*, she thought. *The mother is a sacrifice for a great new life to come into this world.*

Her heart was beating hard in her chest. A girl. Just a girl of eighteen, nineteen, if her history was correct. Princess Leila Nemati had perished toward the end of the last war, so she could not have been any older. Had the child been kept in secret since then? Protected by her grandmother, and Lord Hasham, and others of influence and power, a secret cabal of oathkeepers? She was driven by a great curiosity now, wondering how deep this all went. There were other rumours too. Of Lady Safina's friendship with King Godrin of Rasalan. Of the King's Wall, Sir Ralston Whaleheart, fleeing south with a young companion in tow. *It's all connected*, she thought. *How long has this been in the making?*

Hasham was staring down at her with those hard, searching eyes. "It is said the thralls of the Fire Father bear a red mist in their gaze. An echo of the light that burns in his own. A light of Agarath." He stepped closer and reached out with a tough, callused hand to cup her chin. "Your eyes always had a red quality to them, my lady, but of a natural, burnished brown. I see no mist, no flicker of thralldom within them. I am going to trust you, Talasha, as I trust my instincts. Now tell me…was there anything else in this vision?"

"Yes," she whispered. *Burn them,* she thought. She told Lord Hasham the rest of it, the words that had not made sense to her. The rift. The plains. The silver scar. Shadows and death. Creatures in the night.

He listened intently, and his eyes moved east.

Then he spoke of a girl called Saska.

24

Jonik

Their party had swelled by four.

Two more horses rode along with them, one-half mad, one half-blind, with a half-starved dog and half-dead knight by name of Sir Lenard Borrington.

The young knight was slumped in the saddle of Jonik's piebald palfrey, a fresh bandage about his chest, cloak of thick wool heaped over his scrawny shoulders to shield him from this unseasonable chill. He shivered all the same, swaying, mumbling to himself as he drifted in and out of consciousness, a state he'd been in for days. Jonik walked beside him, watchful, to make sure he did not fall, leading the horse along by its rope. Gerrin went a few paces ahead, Harden behind on the spirited stallion, leading the other horses. The big mastiff plodded along at Jonik's side.

"We'll find you a new home, boy," Jonik said to him, scratching him by the ear. He had marks on his neck, the skin rubbed raw from his time tied up outside the outhouse. "When we reach the border, they'll find a place for you. No one's going to treat you badly anymore."

"You sure about that, lad?" Harden grunted from behind him. "Might be best if we just keep him ourselves. He's taken to you, don't you think?"

The dog did seem to like him, that was true, and more than he did the others. When Jonik slept at night, the dog would lay beside him. When he took his watch he would sit on watch with him. And when Jonik walked, the big mastiff rarely left his side. *He sees me as his saviour,* Jonik thought. If he was to live up to that mantle, he would have to let him go. "I like him as well, Harden," he said. "But it won't be safe for him with us. You know that."

"Aye," the man admitted. "Nice having him around, though. Had a dog like him once before. Well, was my second wife's dog, really, but he was mine for the time I was with her. Good dog, he was."

"Did he have a name?" Jonik asked. He was always learning something new about Harden. It was only recently that he found out he'd been married before, let alone to four separate women.

The sellsword scratched the tight-packed bristles of his chin, stiff and grey as he was. "You know, I forget. Something dog-like. Wolfy or Patches or Mr Barks, something like that."

"All those names are completely different," Jonik pointed out.

"Aye. Was a long time ago. Wasn't with her long, the second wife."

"I knew a dog called Toby once," Gerrin put in, slowing to join them. "Maybe we should call him that?"

Jonik shook his head. He had not named the hound because he knew they wouldn't keep him. Annoyingly, Gerrin had forgotten what Burt and Betty had called him, and the dog bowl they found inside the inn, which had once been inscribed with his name, had become so worn that the letters were unintelligible.

"Come to think of it," the old knight went on. "Maybe that was *his* name before?" He turned, looking at the dog. "Toby. *Here boy.*" When he patted his leg, the mastiff gave a growl. "Huh. Maybe not, then…"

"We're not naming him," Jonik said, with a tone of finality. "We're giving him away when we reach the border, and that's that." He looked down the track they'd been following for some hours, an old dirt road that weaved between small woods and over swollen rivers, past open fields where great puddles had formed, creating bogs and muddy marshes. The rains had fallen on and off for days, often cold, sometimes spitting with hail, and there had even been some sleet one cold misty morning as well. Gerrin knew these parts best, though Harden was a few years older. They both agreed this weather was not normal. "How far are we?"

"Close," Gerrin said. "We'll be there in an hour or so." He pointed ahead. "When we pass those trees we ought to see the statues again."

Jonik nodded. They'd seen the twin statues many times over the last few days, growing closer with each glimpse. The last had been only a few hours ago, when they'd summited a shallow rise among some grassy hills and seen them standing sentry at the border, towering a thousand feet tall, guarding the way to south and north as the sun rose in the east. Vandar faced north, glaring down at the denizens of Tukor. Tukor faced south, warily watching the men of Vandar. Both wore hard, fearsome expressions on their giant faces, as though warning any man entering their kingdom to behave, else there'd be trouble. Yet when a man returned, it was different, people said. A Vandarian who had travelled to Tukor, and was passing back south across the border, would see a different expression on the Steel God's visage. Hard, yes, but somehow more inviting. *Welcome home,* that face would say. *We have missed you. Come on through.*

And what face will I get? Jonik wondered now. He was both

Vandarian and Tukoran by blood, born of the royal houses Lukar and Daecar. *Will I be welcomed by each of the gods for that, or looked upon with suspicion?* He imagined it would be the latter. Suspicion was familiar to Jonik, a shadow that had trailed him all his life.

The dirt track led into the trees, moving through an open thicket of oak and elm. When they came out on the other side, the twin statues came into view, closer than ever, only a couple of miles away. Jonik took a grip of his godsteel dagger, enhancing his sight to get a better look. The clouds were low, the fogs thick, yet all the same he could see some damage to the twins. One of Vandar's shoulders was blackened, and it seemed to him that the fingers on Tukor's right hand - the hand that held the hammer - were chipped away, scorch marks staining the stone.

"The dragons have attacked them," Jonik observed.

"They always do," Harden said. "Every time there's war, some dragon comes and has a nibble. You'd think they'd learn by now. Those statues aren't coming down, no matter what they do. Would take a hundred of them breathing at the base to topple them, and even that would take a while. There's magic in that rock."

Ilith's magic, Jonik thought. It still felt so strange to think that he had met the demigod...stranger still that he was serving him.

They followed the road until it turned westward, leading toward the broad, stone-paved thoroughfare that passed between the statues. The twin gods were spaced two hundred metres apart, forming a valley of sorts between them in which the border town had sprung up, popularly known as the *Valley of the Gods*. Here were stables, taverns, blacksmiths, farriers, tailors, armourers and weaponsmiths, even a pillowhouse or two. Market stalls lined the route, selling foods, ales, wines and rums, clothes and jewellery, spices, medicines, ointments, shoes, weapons and armour and a whole lot more. People had always gathered here in their droves, taking advantage of the lack of duties applied to the goods they bought. Some came only to trade, others to meet friends old and new, while the rest passed south and north, moving between the kingdoms.

Today, the town was *teeming*. From the south, a great river of people, rich and poor alike, were pouring up the thoroughfare.

"Refugees," Gerrin said, as soon as they saw them. "From East Vandar, I'd guess, escaping the war. Must be thousands of them."

"Thousands of mouths to feed," grunted Harden. "That Ilith better be stocking his halls and larders. Might have a few people begging at his door soon enough."

Jonik had left that in Lord Morwood's care, seeing as his royal cousin had washed her hands of it. She would help, in time, Ilith had claimed, though that might have been more in hope than expectation. *Maybe when she sees the teeming masses gathering at the city gates, she'll decide to lift a finger to help.* He wasn't going to hold his breath.

The noise the refugees made was a doleful thing. A din of rattling wagons and weeping women, whimpering children and bawling babes. Grim-faced men tried to hold it all together, staring out with hollow eyes as they wandered up the road. Many looked starved and helpless, and the injured were in great abundance. Animals moved among them. Dogs walking forlornly, cats hissing in cages, goats bleating, chickens clucking, the occasional malnourished cow being led along on a rope.

Gerrin led them on in the opposite direction, heading south toward the border crossing. A few heads lifted and looked at them as they passed by, perhaps wondering what madness would compel them to go that way, but not many. Most were too lost in their horrors to notice.

Ahead, the great soaring statue of Tukor, the Forge God, loomed. From here Jonik could see little more than the great kite-shaped shield that he wore on his back, the hint of his right hand, bearing the hammer, a little outstretched to one side, with those tips of fingers missing. Below, great chunks of stone had fallen down onto the road, dwarfing the wagons as they wended around them, and high above birds swirled about the head and shoulders, tiny as fruit flies, giving scale to its staggering size.

Beneath the great shadow, the border guards were doing their searches, checking the carts and wagons as they passed north. There were two gates built into the walls here at the base of the statue; one for those passing into Tukor, and another for those seeking to go south, through the Valley of the Gods, and into Vandar. Despite the great flow of traffic seeking to take the former route, the guards were only using the assigned gate, rather than opening both of them to those making for Tukor. It seemed senseless to Jonik but he wasn't going to complain. The soldiers there were standing by the walls, leaning against the stone, chatting with one another, looking bored.

One moved away from the others to intercept them as they approached, dressed in a cloak of Tukoran brown and green, stitched with the royal coat of arms in fine silver thread. "Your business here?" he asked them, planting the butt of his spear on the ground.

"Passing south," said Gerrin. That was obvious, given the direction of travel they were going.

"Just you?" The guard looked them over, but this should be a formality. Typically the border soldiers were much more interested in checking those travelling *into*, rather than *out of*, the kingdom.

"Just us," Gerrin confirmed. "Though we're looking to move on these two horses." He pointed out the pair that Harden was leading on the stallion.

The guard gave them an appraising look. "That one's only got one eye."

"He still has four legs, thankfully. I would say that's more important."

"He looks starved."

"Yes. Food usually helps correct that." Gerrin smiled easily, in that way he had, an avuncular side that Jonik had not seen a great deal of during their days in the Shadowfort, as master and apprentice. Now it came out often. "Your choice. We will be happy to give them to the Vandarians instead."

The man scowled. "No. They'd only starve them some more or eat them. They eat horse over there, you know. In Vandar. *Barbarians.*" He spat to the side. There was no love lost between the border guards here at Tukor's Pass, though the rivalry was mostly in jest, Jonik knew. The chuckling of the men behind made that clear enough.

"We'll all be eating horse soon," Harden said, morosely. "That's what happens when you run out of mutton and beef." He dismounted his stallion, landing heavily in his armour, which rustled beneath his cloak. That caused the guard to raise his eyes.

"You soldiers? Sellswords?"

"The latter," Gerrin said. In a fashion it was true. They had sold their swords to Ilith now, for the price of trying to help save the world. "Looking to lend our efforts to the war."

"I see." The guard looked at the piebald palfrey, bearing the sickly form of Sir Lenard Borrington, swaddled up in that great black cloak. "And who is this? He looks in poor shape."

That was an understatement. The man had been at death's door since they'd found him, and would surely have perished already were it not for their intervention. *Those deserters…* Jonik closed a fist, trying not to dwell on their vile cruelty. Trying not to think about Devin.

"He is wounded," Gerrin said. "We will seek medical aid across the border."

"Why not here?"

"He's Vandarian."

"Ah. Well, I'll not delay you, then." He waved a hand, causing the other soldiers behind to part and let them through. As they moved past, the soldier called out, "You watch your backs in there. Those Vandarians. You cannot trust a single one of them! You hear me. Not a single one!"

That provoked more laughter from his friends. Harden, a Vandarian himself, only rolled his eyes and led the horses on.

They entered the Valley of the Gods. The border town was positively teeming. They veered at once to the side of the road, squeezing past the smallfolk making their way north, through the wagons and carts, past frightened children and noisy animals, men arguing, women shouting to be let through. Many had been here a while, Jonik sensed, all packed in tight as the soldiers made their checks. He wondered if he might take this opportunity to leap up onto some stall or shop roof and shout out to them all about the portal. *Make for Ilithor,* he might say. *There is a portal that will take you into the mountains, and the safe refuge of Ilith's sanctuary. The Worldbuilder will protect you.*

But that would sound preposterous, and they would think him only mad, so he just said nothing and kept on walking, leading his horse along.

Most of the stalls and shops were closed, Jonik saw, but as they continued south, they found that a small amount of life still lingered here. One stall was selling roasted nuts, another soup from a pot, and they saw a whore standing on the balcony of one of the brothels, scantily clad despite the chill, beckoning them to employ her services. "You three look like you need ten minutes of fun. Half an hour, I'll have you all. One after another or all together if you prefer! Give you a nice discount too."

They politely refused, Jonik hastening past her, barely even giving the woman a glance. *Jack would poke at me and tease me for that*, he thought. The big, redheaded marshlander had always made fun of him for his chastity, a matter of annoyance to Jonik, but he missed it all the same.

The statue of Vandar filled the view ahead, a work of unsurpassed magnificence. Bearded he stood, with his great blade planted into the ground at his colossal feet, a huge rippling cloak trailing heroically behind him. Jonik craned his neck up, meeting the Steel God's gaze. It was looking right down at him, in that mysterious, inscrutable way, with an expression of surpassing authority etched into his eyes. The eyes were judging him, he deemed, following him like the statue of Thala in the refuge. *Help me win my war*, they seemed to say. *Help restore my Heart.*

Jonik stopped a moment, letting the others go ahead of him. Standing there amid the bustle, he inclined his head into a bow, and said, "I will, my lord," before continuing on…and as he did so, the face seemed to change again. He saw approval in that great stone face, a look to stir the soul.

The guards at the border were judging them as well, watching as they made their approach. There were two gates here also. The layout was much the same as on the Tukoran side, with one for passing north and the other for passing south. As before, only one gate was being used for the refugees, though the wagons and carts were not being so thoroughly checked. For the most part they were being waved through without so much as a glance.

"They'll ask more questions here," Gerrin said, as they approached. "We're entering Vandar, so…"

Jonik understood. "Will Amilia's seal work?"

"Hopefully we won't need it. Sir Lenard should suffice."

A soldier stepped forward to bar their way, several others standing behind, watching. The guard wore a silver breastplate and blue cloak, stitched with the sigil of his kingdom. Banners of the same flapped against the walls. A wind was picking up and the clouds were thickening in the skies.

"Your business entering Vandar?" the man asked.

Manifold, Jonik thought. He let Gerrin do the talking.

336

"We mean to seek medical aid for our friend." He gestured to the horse. "Sir Lenard Borrington, son of Lord Randall. He is wounded and needs urgent relief."

The man looked at Sir Lenard, a single eyebrow rising. *He knows something,* Jonik sensed at once. "Sir Lenard, you say?"

Gerrin nodded.

The guard stepped forward. "Do you mind?"

"By all means."

The man drew up to the palfrey, peering closer to get a look at Sir Lenard's face. There appeared to be some recognition in the eyes of the soldier, a purse of the lips, as he nodded and stepped back. "You may pass," he said. "My men will escort you to the *Undercloak*. Lord Ghent will want to speak with you."

A pair of soldiers came forward. "This way," one of them said. He led them on, south through the gate, past the great throngs ambling north. *That went easier than I thought,* Jonik mused. A path led them over to the fortress built behind the Steel God's statue, in the shadow of his great trailing cloak. The gate here was a portcullis, and behind it they entered a courtyard of grey stone, with barracks, a stable, an armoury, storehouses, a small prayer house, and a kitchen about its border. Ahead, some steps led up to a keep of modest proportions.

"Wait here," the soldier said. He moved up the steps, as the stable-boys came over to take their horses, the other guard staying with them. A few moments later the first soldier returned. "You may enter. Follow me."

The fort commander was awaiting them in a spacious, draughty hall, standing at a table at the far end looking over some papers. He was a man of stout build, with a hard face made for frowning, fifty if he was a day. He wore a grey jerkin with a blue cloak at his back, fastened by a pin in the shape of a sword. He looked up as they entered. "I'm told you have brought Sir Lenard Borrington with you. Is that so?"

Gerrin spoke. "It is, Lord Ghent. He is badly wounded. We hoped you would be willing to…

The commander cut him off. "It's being done. I've given orders for Sir Lenard to be taken upstairs and given a room to befit his station. The doctor is being summoned as we speak. You needn't worry about him anymore. We'll see him right, you have my word." The fort commander took up a cup of wine from the table, and had a swift swallow. He swirled the wine, looking them over. "So…who are you, then? Knights? Sellswords?"

"Both," Gerrin said. "I was a knight of the Emerald Guard once before." He gestured to Harden. "He sells his sword, though is a distant kin to the Strands."

Lord Ghent smiled as though enjoying a private joke. "An Iron-moorer? Yes, you have the look, there's no doubt there." Harden was a grey man, grim and lean and hard-looking, features typical of those lands. "And how about you, young man?" Ghent said to Jonik. "Do you have a name?"

Something told Jonik he already knew. "You know my name," he said.

The commander gave a bark of laughter. It rang through the hall, up into the rafters. A nesting bird flapped away in fright. "So I do. I know all your names, in fact. He did tell me you were a perceptive young fellow. A bit of a dour lad, true, but not the monster you're made out to be. 'Greatly misunderstood' he said of you."

"Who did?" Gerrin asked.

The answer was obvious. "Borrus," Jonik said. "He passed this way not long ago."

Ghent gave another barking laugh, a short abrupt sound. "Perceptive indeed. Yes, the Barrel Knight rolled on through, and what a bloody shock it was for me to see him! Told me a funny old tale of ships and pits and long-lost knights saved from the clutches of a Piseki warlord. And much more besides. I'd heard some rumours of all that, of course, but hadn't thought much of them. Borrus Kanabar riding with the Ghost of the Shadowfort? And this Emeric Manfrey too?" He had another swallow of wine. "Nonsense, until I heard it from the horse's mouth. Before then I was one of those who wished you dead, Jonik. Now? Not so much. You sound more hero than villain to me."

Jonik could not help but smile. He even felt a bit of blush rising up his neck. "I…thank you, my lord," is all he managed to say.

"Not at all. Not at all. Now come, come. Have a cup of wine, and let's talk."

They approached the table, as Commander Ghent set about filling them each a goblet. He passed them out, looking over them as he did so. His eyes finished on Jonik again, looking at his cloak, the glimpse of armour beneath, the shape of his sword within the folds. "You don't mind if I take a look, do you? I've seen the Sword of Varinar up close a few times, when Lord Daecar has passed through, but never the Nightblade."

"You'll have to leave your post if you want to see that blade," Harden said to him.

Ghent wasn't understanding. "How's that?"

"He gave it up," Gerrin explained. "The Nightblade has been left in the Shadowfort." They had to assume that Borrus had told Ghent about all of that as well. The journey to the Shadowfort, the destruction of the order, perhaps even the Book of Contracts. *But not Ilith.* Borrus and the others had never known of him.

"Oh?" Ghent raised his eyes. "Seems odd to leave it up there. Turning over a new leaf, are you Jonik?"

"Something like that."

"Do you know which way Borrus went, Lord Ghent?" Gerrin asked.

"South, down the Rustriver. There's battle brewing that way, we've heard. Prince Raynald marched an army through here not long before Borrus appeared. Been a busy few weeks." He drank again, then refilled his cup. "But back to Sir Lenard. Was it the Crabby Onion where you found him?" He gave a sigh when they all nodded. "Then I guess my men never made it. Been expecting their return for days."

"Men?" Gerrin asked. "You sent men out to fetch him?"

"A half dozen of them," Ghent confirmed. "With a sturdy carriage so they could bring Sir Lenard back here nice and dry and out of these blasted rains. Borrus didn't want to be moving the knight in such a bad condition, so asked that I fetch him back. Him and this young lad he left to look after him." He paused, thinking. "Forget his name."

"Devin," Jonik said, feeling a hot stab of anger in his chest. "His name was Devin. And he was murdered while he waited."

Commander Ghent was not aware of that. "Oh. What happened to him?"

"A group of deserters came upon the inn," Gerrin explained. "They killed the inkeep and his wife and slew young Devin as well, leaving Sir Lenard to rot in his bed."

Ghent exhaled. "Gods. How foul. I trust you made these men suffer?"

"Not enough," Jonik growled. "They died too quickly. *Badly*, but quickly."

"Three others escaped," added Harden. "But we got the leaders."

"And you saw no sign of my men? No carriage on the road?"

They looked at each other. None of them had seen a sturdy wagon on the road, though for the most part they had kept to narrow tracks and trails down which a carriage would not be able to travel. Most likely the men had been attacked and killed by some creature before they made it to the inn. A dragon seemed the likely culprit. Gerrin put that to the fort commander, and he gave a sour nod.

"You're probably right. Those dragons swarm like flies these days, and one…" He paused, looking down over the letters and scrolls on the table. "Word's been coming in about…" He swallowed, almost unable to even say it. "The *Dread*," he managed at last. His voice was choked. "It's being claimed that Drulgar's arisen, can you believe that? They say he's as big as those twin titans out there. A thousand feet across at the wings. Picture it. Just *try* to picture it. A thing like that, haunting the skies." He gave a visible shudder. "Rumour is he's taken down Varinar. It's unthinkable."

They had heard those rumours as well, while in Ilithor. Ghent had another large gulp of his wine to steady himself. "So, you're, um…to continue south as well, I take it? The gods know we could use men like you down there."

Gerrin gave answer with a nod, choosing not to elaborate on their mission. "We are in need of a Bladeborn-bearing horse, if you have one. One of ours broke a leg, not long ago. We had to put her down."

"Ah. Terrible business, that. Always terrible to have to put down a good horse. I'll have an ask around for you. We don't have one going spare here in the fort, but perhaps they do on the Tukoran side. I'll talk with Commander Hopham, see if he can help us."

"We have a dog as well," Jonik said.

"I know. I can hear him scratching at the door." Commander Ghent smiled and called for the door to be opened. At once the big mastiff loped forward, all floppy skin and drooping chops, running up to Jonik's side. Jonik smiled, giving him another good scratch under the chin. "He was the innkeeper's dog. From the Crabby Onion. Will you find a home for him?"

"Seems *you're* his home," Ghent said. "The beast likes you."

"I know, but…"

"But you can't take him." The fort commander understood that. He stepped over, stroking at the dog's head with a stocky-fingered hand. "We'll keep him here in the fort. The men will like him."

That pleased Jonik a good deal. "Thank you, my lord."

Ghent gave the dog another scratch. "Will you be staying the night? You're welcome to sleep in here. No rooms unfortunately, but the hall will be quiet by night and we like to keep the fires going to keep it warm."

The three men convened in a silent council, meeting eyes. Then Gerrin said. "We'd be much obliged, my lord."

"Well and good, then." Ghent clapped his hands together. "Feel free to make yourselves at home. I'll go see about that horse of yours. Then we can dine and talk further. There's much and more I still want to hear." He drank down his cup, plonked it on the table, gave them a parting nod, and stamped off toward the door.

Gerrin watched him go. He had a gulp of wine and then set down his cup as well. "I'm going to go out and speak to the smallfolk," he said. "See if anyone knows anything that can help us."

Jonik nodded. Information about his grandfather's whereabouts had been in short order so far, though most of the whispers and rumours agreed that he'd turned dragonslayer, and had made for the south. There were parts of Tukor where he'd taken on some sort of mythical status. *The king who gave up his crown to walk the warrior's way.* Jonik had to hold his tongue whenever he heard men speak like that. *If only they knew the truth…*

"I'll be back later," Gerrin said. "You two just sit tight." He left the hall. Harden picked up his flagon of wine and ambled over to a seat beside the hearth. He had a happy smile on his grizzled old face. Well, *contented.* Harden never looked happy.

"You gonna join me, lad?" he called over to Jonik as he took his seat. "Come on, you deserve a break. Let's enjoy a few cups of wine."

"I'm not certain Commander Ghent will appreciate that. His stocks will be running low."

"Aye, and he's only got himself to blame, the way he drinks. You see him just now? Taking a sip between every sentence. And I'm guessing Borrus and the Blackshaws would have depleted his reserves further when they were here. Well, they don't call him the *Barrel Knight* for nothing."

Jonik smiled. He could imagine them all in here, in this very hall, feasting and drinking and arguing at one another. Borrus and Mooton and Torvyn and their men, Emeric, Jack, Turner and Brown Mouth, Soft Sid and Grim Pete, the Silent Suncoat and Sansullio and his Sunshine Swords as well. "They call him other things now, Harden. The Lord of the Riverlands and the Warden of the East."

"Aye…and the gods bloody help us." Harden gave a laugh and drank more wine. "Come lad, sit with me. No one likes to drink alone."

Jonik hesitated. He'd never been much of a drinker. "I shouldn't. Gerrin's out there, working. I ought to go and join him."

Harden didn't heed him. "You work enough. Have a cup of wine and relax."

Relax? What was that word? Jonik had never been taught how to relax. He felt restless, an urgency in him to keep on moving. *If I stop I'll never want to start again.* There remained so much to do. "I should go outside," he said again, looking at the door. "Help Gerrin…"

"Gerrin doesn't need you. He's better with the smallfolk than you are. Let him do his thing."

"I have to do *something*." Jonik started for the door.

Harden stood, stepping over to cut him off. "You've made me do this." He took him by the wrist and drew him over to the hearthside. "Now sit, damn you. And drink." He poured a cup, thrust it into Jonik's hand, glared at him with that haggard old face until he relented. "Good. Now how do you feel?"

"The same."

"Then drink more."

Jonik drank more. The wine reached down into his chest, spreading. It had a spicy bite to it, which he wasn't sure about, though after the first few gulps he started to enjoy the sensation. Wine had never been a part of Jonik's life in the way it was for other men. His tolerance was poor. *Another thing Jack used to tease me over*, he reflected.

"You're worried about them," Harden said, searching his eyes. "A part of you wants to find them."

Jonik said nothing.

"Silence is as good as words, you know. And you've got no face for lying, Jonik. Maybe that's why you were such a poor Shadowknight." He smiled. "You're too soft."

It was not an accusation he'd heard often. "They taught us not to feel. But with me…"

"You had Gerrin."

Jonik nodded. "I am how I am because of him. I had to be this way. That was fate."

"*Fate*." Harden made the word a curse. "That's all done. Aye, not

341

denying what we've seen, and been through. You had to be this way. Had to have some feeling in you. If not, you wouldn't have saved everyone from Palek's pits. You wouldn't have gathered us all to go north, and save the boys." His eyes dipped beneath a frown. "The *boys*," he repeated, and Jonik knew just who he meant. "Even that…I understand that too. The choice you made. It had to happen, for Ilith to rise, to give us a chance. I know that now. But from here…no. Bugger fate, Jonik. You make your own fate now."

Jonik mused on that. "You're saying…you think I should just abandon my oath to him? To *Ilith*. Go and find the others instead?"

"No. *You're* thinking that."

"I'm not."

"You are. A part of you."

Of course a part of me is, Jonik wanted to say. They were his friends, the only true friends he'd ever had, men he'd sailed with, fought with, men he'd saved and been saved by. If he had a choice, he would mount his steed right now and ride out to find them. He'd stand side by side with them in battle, and die with them, die *for* them if he had to. He needed to tell them what had happened to Devin, so they could sit and talk of him, drink to him, say the rites and remember him. Devin had been with Gill Turner for years, ever since he was a boy. *He was almost a son to him,* Jonik thought. *Turner was his sire and Braxton his grumpy uncle and Jack his older brother. They deserve to know, all of them. They deserve to know and they deserve to be safe.*

I don't want them to fight in any battle…

The thought terrified him. Even more so that he couldn't be there too. But there was nothing he could do about it. *Nothing. I have no choice. I've never really had a choice.*

"Ilith entrusted me to track down the blades," he said, finally. "So that's what I'm going to do."

Harden gave a deep sigh. "I know. I just want…something *more* for you. You've served all your life. And you're serving still…"

"So are you."

"I've lived. I'm an old man. I've had four wives and fathered kids. Aye, haven't told you that yet. Three of them. Two by my first, another by my third. All dead. Just don't ask me how, I don't want to go there tonight." Pain rippled across his face, the agony of memory, gone in an instant. Buried, but always there, just beneath that hard grim surface. He gulped his wine. "Point is you haven't lived. You're too young for all this. Damnit, you're too young."

"I'm old enough," Jonik said, quietly. "I'll have my time after, Harden. Once it's over. I'll live then."

"And if you don't get that chance? If you die before all this is done."

"Then I'll be dead," Jonik grunted, not liking this conversation. "And I won't much care, will I?"

He turned to look into the fire, watching the flames lick and flicker at the walls. The stone was black with soot where the smoke rose up toward the chimney shaft. Black like the fields they'd passed, and the burned farms and huts and little villages they'd seen. Black like death. Black like the Dread.

I have a chance to help, he thought. *And this old man wants me to give it all up.*

It annoyed him. He knew Harden meant well. But it annoyed him.

He stood. "I'm going outside." *And don't I feel nice and relaxed,* he thought.

Harden let him go, descending into a dark place of his own. Jonik heard him drink his cup dry, heard him refill it, and drink again, before he reached the door. The dog followed him. "No, stay here." He pulled the door open, stepped out, but the big mastiff loped past before he could pull the door back shut. He sighed. "You're staying here when we go. Lord Ghent is going to look after you."

He missed Shade, he realised all of a sudden. He missed his faithful steed, who was so much more than a horse to him. *A friend. My first friend.* Was he being taken to battle as well? Was one of the men going to armour him up in barding and ride him into the teeth of the enemy lines? It hurt him to think like that. Shade was not meant to be here. He was a horse of the Highplains, made to run free, not a warhorse. *I should have let him go when I had the chance. Now he's going to die like all the rest of them...*

He found a guard at the entrance to the keep, leaning on his spear at the top of the steps. Down in the yard, the stableboys were tending to the horses, the palfrey and the stallion and the others from the inn as well. They were being fed and watered, their coats given a brush, their hooves re-shod. Beyond, through the portcullis, the rain was coming down, but in the yard it was dry.

"Coat protects us," the guard said. He looked up. "Never rains in here."

Overhead, the enormous stone cloak of Vandar swept down from his mighty back, forming a roof high above them. Rainwater gathered and washed down its surface, cascading in waterfalls where the cloak ended. "I saw scorch marks on his shoulder," Jonik said. "And Tukor's fingers were chipped. When did that happen?"

"While back. Haven't seen many dragons here of late."

"Aren't you worried they'll come with all these people passing through?"

"It's been talked about," the guard said, shrugging. He wasn't young, nor did he seem to care. *Another old man like Harden,* Jonik thought. *A man who doesn't care if he lives or dies.* "We'll put up a fight if they do, but most dragons are frightened of the statues. They take one look at them and go flapping the other way. Only the boldest get close." He saw the dog for the first time. "I like your hound. He got a name?"

"Not yet. And he isn't mine."

343

"Oh? Seems to like you well enough."

"He's going to stay here in the fort. I'm leaving tomorrow."

"Ah. Some good news for once." The man looked at him. "That the dog's staying, that is. Not that you're leaving."

"I knew what you meant." Jonik drew a breath, pulling rain-scented air into his lungs. The rain had become a deluge. He was sick of it. *The whole kingdom will be drowned soon enough.* "Have you heard anything about Janilah Lukar?"

The question took the old soldier off-guard. He peered at him. "Why? You looking for him, are you?"

Yes, he might have said. "Just interested," he said instead.

"Well, he's an interesting man, there's no doubt. Most think he passed through here a while back. They say he used the Mistblade to go unseen. One of the scullery maids insists she saw him walk right through her kitchen. Like a blue ghost, she said."

"Is she here? I'd like to talk with her."

"I wouldn't waste your time. Woman's always been an odd one, fond of telling tall tales. There was talk of a blue ghost in Ilithor a while ago, we heard. Guessing she heard it too and just wanted some attention."

Jonik nodded. He wouldn't get much from the woman anyway, even if she was telling the truth. "We were told that Borrus Kanabar came here. Do you remember who he was with?"

"Bunch of people. Beast of Blackshaw, his cousin Sir Torvyn. Torvyn 'The Returned' they're calling him about these parts now. Was missing for two decades until recently." He frowned. "Who else? Ah, course. The exiled lord, Manfrey. Some more Blackshaw men, and a few others as well. Regular folk, they seemed, not warriors. Some sell-swords too. Their leader had skin dark as jet. Wore shiny armour under their cloaks. Caused a bit of a stir, that lot."

Same as in Blackhearth, Jonik thought. Sansullio and his Sunshine swords had not been welcomed by the soldiers there. "Was there any violence?"

"Not that I saw. They were all under the command of Lord Borrus, so who were we to argue? They didn't stay long enough either. Just went straight through and down the road while the Barrel and Sir Torvyn came to talk with Commander Ghent. All the rest just kept on going."

"They didn't stay the night?"

The soldier gave a shake of the head. "Was early when they came, lots of riding time still ahead. Continued right on toward Eastwatch. May have stayed there."

That sounded likely. Eastwatch was on the way to the Rustriver Road, and the fort was a Kanabar seat. It would make a natural stop-off if they were to continue south.

The soldier was looking out over the fortress walls. From here, the stream of refugees was visible, fighting through the winds and rains as they continued to meander up from the south. "Poor bastards. Having to travel in this weather. Never seen rains like it."

There have never been rains like it, Jonik thought. *Not here. Not this time of year.* He could see Gerrin out there, among the crowds, talking with an old couple. They looked sad and grey, their cloaks soaked through, and had a sad grey ox with them, pulling a little cart. "How many are you going to let through?"

"As many as the Tukorans will take. It's safer up there, in the north. We've been gathering supplies to send with them too, food and such. Wouldn't want it said that we're foisting all our own people onto them Tukorans without doing our part to help."

Jonik was glad to hear that. "Do you know which room Sir Lenard was taken to?"

The old soldier turned. "Take the spiral stair to the right. You'll find him on the third floor, second door along the hall, overlooking the yard. Nice room, that one. There's a small balcony too." He pointed it out, right above them.

"My thanks." Jonik dipped his head and stepped away, moving up the corkscrew stair until he reached Sir Lenard's door. He found it ajar, knocking his knuckles on the wood. The fort doctor was inside, performing his inspections, with a nurse to aid him. Jonik entered. "How is he doing?"

The doctor looked over. He was a young man, fresh-faced and clean-shaven, dressed in robes that hung loose of his slim physique. The nurse was old and frumpy. "You're the man who brought him here?"

"I am. With my companions." Jonik stepped inside and shut the door. "Will he live?"

"He should, thanks to you." The doctor gestured to the patient. "Who applied these stitches?"

Jonik moved closer. The bandaging had been removed from Sir Lenard's chest, exposing the three deep cleaves that slashed across his upper body. When they had found him in that filthy bed, they had given him water first, then made sure he was clean. The wounds had started to fester, but they'd managed to wash him, apply drakeshell powder to hasten the healing, and give him some roseweed for the pain. They'd gotten both of those from Lord Morwood. After that, there was nothing they could do but find some fresh bandages, wrap him back up, and hasten him here to the border.

As to those stitches… "We're not certain," he said. "We found him like that." His guess would be Sansullio, though. The Sunshine Sword captain was as skilled with the needle as he was with the blade, Jonik knew.

"Whoever it was did a fine job," the doctor remarked. "That said, I have had to cut away some of the flesh where it has begun to putrefy. He will scar badly, but with proper care and attention, he should survive. Do you intend on staying long?"

"We'll be leaving at dawn."

"Ah. Well, with luck he will awaken to thank you before then. I take it he hasn't been particularly conversational on the road?"

"Not especially."

"Blood fever will do that." The doctor smiled. "It was a grimbear, I'm told."

Jonik nodded. "We got that much from him." *A fearsome beast, tackled by another.* The way Sir Lenard mumbled of it, the Beast of Blackshaw had come rushing from the woods to wrestle the grimbear to the ground, killing it with his bare hands. In all truth it would not surprise Jonik if that was the case. Mooton Blackshaw was a brutally large man, and with godsteel to grasp would have the strength to match the beast.

"Then he is doubly lucky to be alive," the doctor said, with another smile. "There aren't many men who have survived a grimbear attack. After everything he's been through, he deserves a break."

"You know about the pits, then?"

"Oh yes, of course. A famous tale."

Jonik didn't want to get into it. He did not know if this doctor knew who he was, and he didn't want to know. "I'll leave you to it." He turned to step away.

"No, you needn't leave. I only need to apply these bandages, then you can sit with him. It won't take long."

Jonik thought it a better idea than returning to drink with Harden. And if Sir Lenard was to awaken, it would be nice for him to see a friendly face, he supposed. *And there's still so much I want to know,* he thought. He wanted to hear of their travels since leaving the Shadowfort. Which route they'd taken, who they'd run into, whether they'd fought dragons or other creatures along the way. He had hoped to hear all of that as soon as he set eye on Sir Lenard in the inn, but alas he'd been in no state to talk.

"I'll be on the balcony, then. Call me when you're done."

Jonik stepped outside to let the doctor do his work, the nurse bustling about with her ointments and salves. The view would usually be good from up here, Jonik imagined, a ranging view toward the south, though he could see little through the mists and squalls. Only the shadow of the people, drifting up the road in their ones and twos and little groups, pulling carts and driving wagons, sometimes sitting a horse. If Gerrin was out there still, Jonik couldn't see him. *Come back with good news,* he thought. *Come back and tell me that my grandfather has gone to battle. That he's there with all the others, and I'll not have to make that choice.*

The doctor was a quick worker. After a few short minutes Jonik heard a voice behind him. "It's done, my lord. You may sit with him now."

Jonik stepped back inside, thanking him as the doctor bowed and left, the dowdy nurse as well. When the door was closed Jonik settled onto a chair beside Lenard Borrington's bedside. The wine was moving through his blood, slowing his thoughts, making him drowsy. There was a fire here too, crackling softly, and the rain was washing down outside. It made for a peaceful setting. Before he knew it, he was closing his eyes…opening them again…closing them once more and drifting off…

Then suddenly Gerrin was there.

Jonik sat up with a start. It had darkened considerably outside, and the rain had weakened, falling in a light drizzle. The fire had burned down to its embers, a few thin tendrils of smoke coiling upward. There were some wet footprints from the open door, staining the stone, and Gerrin was standing on a rug, soaking wet and dripping.

"Sorry. Didn't mean to wake you."

Jonik blinked, clearing his throat. He felt exhausted. Sir Lenard was snoring softly. *I must have been more tired than I realised.* "So, how did it go out there?" His voice was a little heavy. "Did you…find out something about my grandfather?"

The old Emerald Guard had a grave look on his face. "I found some*one*," he said.

25

Saska

Something was pressing at her leg.

She groaned, half-asleep, and shifted in her tent. "Keep to your side, Lesh," she said in a sleepy slur. "Stop encroaching. You're *always* encroaching…"

Her eyes remained shut, and back into her dreams she slipped. This was a good one, and damn Leshie for interrupting it. She'd been with Elyon, in his pavilion at Harrowmoor, sitting together on his bed. They were talking, laughing, drinking wine and smiling at one another. He was undressed above the waist, and the sight of those muscles…

She felt that pressure at her leg again, about her calf. She pulled away. "Leshie, damn it…"

The girl was snoring soundly. She stuttered awake as Saska gave her another kick. "Wh…what are you…"

"You keep stretching your leg over to my side. I was dreaming of Elyon, and you ruined it." It was about the only escapism she had, the only time she got to indulge in her improper thoughts and memories. It happened every so often at about the same time each month. "Just keep to your side. I've asked you a hundred times."

"I didn't…I *am* on my side."

Saska rolled over to face her. She could see nought but the girl's outline in the darkness. It was a black night, dark as death. The skies above were choked in cloud, moonless, starless, lightless. Saska reached out with a hand, extending it, to touch her friend in the face.

"Hey…" Leshie swiped her away. "What are you doing?"

"Making sure you're awake. If you're going to wake me up, I'm going to do the same." *I'll never get back to sleep now*, she knew. She'd be damned if she had to lie here until dawn listening to Leshie snoring. She poked again, a finger going up Leshie's nose.

"Hey…*stop it*," the Red Blade hissed, taking her wrist, throwing her arm away. "I *didn't* kick you, all right. I was sound asleep."

"Sound asleep and *kicking*." Leshie was a sleep-kicker; Saska had worked that out a while ago.

Her eyes were adjusting, though slowly. Not often had she seen a night so black. She turned back the other way again, feeling for her Varin dagger, tucked up by her head as usual. Her armour and other weapons were stashed to one side, but her dagger she kept right there beside her. Her fingers closed about the hilt, furnishing her with its power. Gradually, her night vision improved, but only a little. *Gods. This is a dark even my blood-bond cannot penetrate.*

When she turned back around, Leshie was sitting up on her elbows, staring at the flaps. "Whose there?" the girl said. Her voice sounded curdled, frightened. But Leshie was never frightened.

Saska twisted and sat up. Her heart stilled. The light of her dagger, ethereal blue, illuminated a shape outside the tent. A shadow, large and strange. Standing still as stone.

"Whose out there?" Leshie asked again. "Coldheart, if that's you…"

The flaps shivered. Saska looked down. Through the door she saw a long, arm-like appendage reaching in through the gap, slithering toward her leg.

She sucked air, pulling her legs back. The limb was long, thin, snakelike, but ending in a hand of grasping fingers, some short, some long, two, four, six of them, more, and all of them were twisting, *changing*. More seemed to be appearing, growing from the arm, branching out like limbs from the trunk of a tree. Leshie gave out a scream, scrambling away. The arm jerked, moving at the sound, flashing out suddenly in a quick movement, like a striking snake. Ten fingers stretched and reached and wrapped, curling about her leg, pulling.

"Leshie!" Saska screamed.

She slashed out with her Varin blade, the steel slicing through the flesh of the arm and fingers. *Not flesh*, she realised. *Sand*. The severed limb collapsed to the floor in a cascade of grit and gravel, the stump writhing and pulling back, tiny bits of stone pouring out like blood. Saska breathed out in horror, drawing away to the back of the tent. Leshie's hands were groping for her blade. When she found it she ripped it from its sheath at once, pointing it at the door. Her hand was shivering.

"What…what *was* that thing?" she breathed.

Saska's voice had abandoned her. Fear filled her veins, ice cold. There were sounds of struggle outside, she heard. Muted shouts, scuffing feet, the rain of pebbles on earth. An imperilled voice shrieked, ringing across the plains.

The shadow was still at the door, blocking the way out. "Get away, you!" Leshie screamed at it. "Away! Get away!"

They could see the outline of its body. See the arm…regrowing. The sand on the floor of their tent was moving, drifting back outside.

There were more sounds out there. Panicked shouts and bellows, the roar of a sunwolf, horses whinnying in fear nearby.

The creature moved forward again, reaching in with its other arm. Leshie lurched forward. "Behind me," she said, sword brandished ahead of her. "Get behind me, Saska! Get back!"

A thunderous roar tore through the air to their right, and another shadow appeared. There was a flash, a whoosh of movement. The creature turned, as a greatsword came slicing through its body, the creature collapsing in a hail of pebbles. Saska heard the splash of ten thousand tiny stones hitting the ground, spreading out across the barren earth. An armoured arm swept the flaps aside. A round scarred head, eyes blazing, filled their view. "My lady, are you all right?"

"Fine," Saska said, breathing out. "What's…what's happening, Rolly? What was that thing?"

He had no answer. "Outside, now. *Quickly*. There are more of them. Many more."

"But our armour…"

"Leave it. It won't help. Quickly, come on."

Saska and Leshie moved out through the flaps. Her legs felt like reeds, throat clenched tight. Even with godsteel to grasp, even Varin's own dagger, her sight was blunted by this dark. Dust swirled through the spaces between the tents, mists moving. Spectres shivered through the night. "Stay close," the Wall said. "Both of you, stay with me."

The Wall led them on, through the tents. Saska saw a body outside one of them, one of Kaa Sokari's archers lying on the floor. His mouth was open, filled with sand and grit, nostrils too, eyes wide and blaring. *Suffocated*, she realised. *One of those creatures choked him dead.* Half of his body seemed to be sunk into the ground, and he was still moving, being dragged down…

"Get away from him," the Wall thundered. "Away, now!" He reached out, grabbed her by the arm, and pulled her free. Her right foot had already begun to sink.

"They're underground," Leshie shuddered. "They come from *underground*."

"Sound attracts them," Rolly said. "Quickly. We make for the river." He stepped away, all but sweeping the two girls up into his arms, but Saska pulled back.

"Del," she said. "I'm not leaving without Del."

Her brother was staying with one of the younger bowmen, in a shared tent, though she did not know where it had been pitched. Saska's was always set at the heart of the camp, though the others were more a lottery. She looked around, searching for some sight of him, but the dust and darkness disoriented her. She could not even say which direction the river was. Torches burned at the borders of the camp like distant suns, floating in a hazy night sky. But one or two only. The rest had been put out.

"I'll come back for him," the Wall said.

"It might be too late by then. No."

The Wall gave a grunt. "Fine." He seemed to know the layout of the camp better than Saska did, stamping straight past one tent and then another. On the third, a creature appeared before them, large and ghoulish, swaying side to side. It had a different shape to the other one, a fluid shape, ever-changing, but humanoid. It turned suddenly upon hearing them, rushing forward with outstretched arms to take Rolly by the neck, inhumanly quick.

The Whaleheart was quicker. He swung before they could reach him, the arms cascading in a shower of sand, then hacked its head from the top of its body. Headless, armless, it made no matter. The creature lumbered onward, the dust and stone and pebbles at its feet rolling and rising up its body, replacing what was lost.

"Die, foul creature," the Whaleheart roared, blasting it apart with the flat of his blade, sending its torso scattering away through the camp. The top half collapsed onto the bottom, then both tumbled sideward in a heap of sand and stone. He kicked through the mound with an armoured leg, scattering it further, but already Saska could see that the thing was reforming elsewhere, rising from the earth, taking shape.

Her bowels went to water. "Del" she cried out. "Del, Del!"

"He's here," the Wall said, stamping forward to a tent. He went to a knee, tore the tent flaps back. There was a *ping* as an arrow went careening off his armour, spinning out into the night. "Gods, boy, it's me, can't you see! You almost got me in the face." He stood and moved back, as Del emerged, crouching, followed by the skilled young archer he roomed with, a youth of eighteen called Jaito. Both held their bows in their fists and had quivers of arrows on their backs.

"I'm sorry, Sir…Sir Ralston, I thought…" Del saw Saska there, and Leshie, smiled briefly, then the smile was gone. His eyes were ripe with fear. There was shouting all about them now, roars and curses. More of the knights and sellswords were emerging from their tents, half-dressed, even naked but for the cold steel in their grasp. Saska could sense Joy nearby, slashing at one of the creatures with her long, razor sharp claws. *On me,* Saska thought. *Joy, on me.*

The cat came stalking out of the dark to join them, rushing up to Saska's side. She saw a swish of red following right behind, the Butcher running past in his tattered cloak and not much else. He spotted them and veered their way. "These things cannot be killed," he bellowed. "You cut them and they keep on coming…"

"The river," the Whaleheart thundered. "We make for the river. The water will hold them."

Men were still emerging from their tents. In others, the creatures crawled inside, or came up from below, dragging them down to their doom. Saska could see the shadows inside, the outlines of men struggling, choking. She looked up, hoping for a glimpse of the moon or stars, but there was nothing. *It's the dark before the dawn*, she thought. *The darkest time of day.*

"We have to help," she shouted. She pointed to one of the tents. "In there. Help him!"

No one reacted. So she did it herself, running away from the group, bursting inside the tent. There was a man inside beneath a heap of moving sand, swiping and struggling as an arm reached down his throat. She chopped at the mound with her dagger, kicked at it with her feet. It shifted, a quick movement, and a tendril came up from below to coil about her leg. It tugged, tripping her, but someone was there to catch her. Arms reached out, pulling her away.

"He's dead," the Wall was shouting. "That man is dead. There's nothing we can do for him."

They got her outside. Through the flaps she saw that Rolly was right; the man was no longer struggling. Only an arm reached up, out of the sand, as though trying to grasp for something, but soon even that was being drawn down into the earth, the world parting to swallow him up.

Horror twisted in her gut. The Butcher was shouting. "The river! The river! Run for the river!"

Saska could see some men fleeing out into the night, scattering, not knowing which way to go. All was black as tar and shrouded, a hell of shadows and death. "This way." The Wall grabbed her, pulling her onward, Leshie and Del and Jaito following, Joy prowling, the Butcher still shouting out as they went.

They passed a fire pit. The flames had been put out, covered in sand. There was a blade here, lying alone, half buried, and a wooden cup as well. "That is Tellamin's blade," Jaito said. The youth was slim as a lance, with angular features and big brown eyes. "Tellamin had the watch."

Tellamin is dead, Saska thought. He was another of the archers, though much older, a gnarled veteran of a hundred battles. *And he never even made a sound.*

The earth was rippling, moving their way like a wave. "Keep going," the Wall roared at them. "Quickly! Go!"

They rushed on, passing more tents, more shadows. Del tripped at one point, and Jaito and Leshie hauled him up, and at another Joy gave out a hiss and sprung suddenly into the air, as a cat does, as something moved below her. She landed, snarling at the ground, slashing with her forepaws.

Saska grabbed her by the scruff of the neck, pulling. "Leave it!" she shouted. Then she leapt atop the starcat, kicking with her heel, and Joy pounced away to rejoin the others.

They reached the border of the camp. The watchman had been killed here too, the earth churned and disturbed. The torch he'd been bearing lay nearby, a thin finger of smoke curling from the embers. There was nothing else. Beyond was darkness, and swirls of fog, stirred by a haunting breeze. Saska peered out, saw the faint glimmer of the river thirty metres off. She gave a shout, and they rushed across the plains.

There were men at the river already, she saw. One was bent over by the banks, vomiting. Another was fighting for breath as a friend clapped a hand against his back.

"Stay with these men," Sir Ralston commanded. "Butcher, protect them."

The sellsword nodded. Saska turned. "Where are you going?"

"Back. There are many men still in there. I have to lead them out."

She opened her mouth. Nothing came out. The Wall was already marching back toward the camp, bellowing. Another bellow came from much closer. "He's choking," shouted the man hitting his friend on the back. "Help. Nothing is working."

"Let me." The Butcher brushed the spearman aside, went behind the choking man's back, hooked his arms around his waist, and lifted, squeezing. Saska had seen the manoeuvre performed before, with several firm thrusts intended to dislodge trapped food from the throat. Several times she'd seen it, and one time it had not been successful. This was the second.

"There's too much sand, too much damn sand in him," the Butcher was grunting, as he heaved and lifted, heaved and lifted. The choking man was tearing at his throat, eyes bloodshot and blaring, sensing the terror of his own demise. "Come on, cough it up! Cough it up!"

Then suddenly the man went limp, head rolling to one side, arms falling. The Butcher shouted out a curse and laid him down on the floor, opening his mouth, blowing, hitting at his chest.

"Please, save him," the other man was saying. "Save him. He's my brother…"

The Butcher kept trying a moment longer, then stood, shaking his head. "I'm sorry. He's with the stars now."

But there were no stars. Only ink-black skies and that ghostly fog and the sound of a brother weeping.

"Someone's coming," Leshie said.

Saska turned to the plains, saw more people approaching from the camp. The Baker was among them, dressed in his underclothes, and Sunrider Tantario as well, thank the gods.

"Brother." The Butcher gripped the Baker fiercely. "The others?"

"Merinius is dead."

"*No*," Leshie shouted, at once. "He…he can't be."

"He is." The Baker turned back, snarling, searching. There was a fury in his eyes over something. Others were rushing past him, paladin knights, spearmen of Houses Hasham and Nemati, some of the other sellswords. The Surgeon was with them, and Gutter and Gore, the last of them coughing violently as he went, his doppelganger supporting him. Many had sand in their eyes, their hair. A few had clearly been dragged out from the ground before they could be sucked under, sand and grit and bits of dirt clinging to their legs and torsos and chests.

"Where is she?" the Baker demanded, striding over, eyes intense, to clutch the Surgeon by the arm. "That striped bitch, *where* is she?"

The Surgeon pulled away. "Unhand me, or you'll lose your arm."

"I saw her, over Merinius. I *saw* her," the Baker growled.

No one knew what he meant. Leshie punched the Baker in the arm. "What happened to him? Green Gaze. What happened? *Tell me!*"

The Baker pushed her away, marching back off toward the camp as his other two sellswords, Umberto and the Gravedigger, emerged. Both were sandy, stuttering, holding each other up as they came.

Leshie went to follow, but Saska held her back. "We've seen how they kill, Lesh. Merry must have been choked, or dragged under."

"But he was on guard. He had the guard tonight. He'd have been wearing his *armour…*"

"Godsteel does nothing to these devils," the Butcher growled. "The sand gets through the gaps. Down the throat. There's no blade that can stop it."

"But why?" Leshie asked, in half a whimper. She had liked the man she called Green Gaze, and had stolen into his bed once or twice as well, Saska knew. "*Why* are they killing us?"

"They are demons," one of the paladin knights said, in a ragged voice. "Sand demons of the dark deity *Hrang'kor*. He was a shadow god. The creatures are his children."

"They come at night and take your babes," another called out, panting. There was more splashing as men entered the water, wading until they were at its heart, turning their eyes about in fear. "They are shadows of death and darkness. They do not drink or feed, they only kill for the joy of it."

The disappearances, Saska thought. *I should have listened. We should never have stayed.*

Alym Tantario was shouting orders, calling for the names of the dead and the living and those who might yet be missing to be called out to him. There were dozens at the river now, more appearing from the dark of the camp every moment. The screams out there were growing quieter, the bustle of noise nearby increasing. Some men had gone to tend to the horses and camels, many of which were whinnying and honking and pulling at their lines. The sunwolves prowled about them, defending the steeds from attack, but what could any of them do? *You cut them down and they just keep on coming.*

Saska could hear the Surgeon rushing up the river, calling for the Tigress. From the darkness Scalpel came running out, stumbling as he went. He landed hard, dressed in nought but breeks, a misting blade in his grasp. He got to his knees, heaving for breath. "My wife…she is in there…help, I need help…"

"Butcher, go," Saska said at once.

The Butcher grunted, striding off. He hauled Scalpel to his feet and they rushed into the mists. A few moments later they reemerged, Savage slung over the Butcher's large, scarred shoulder, her head bouncing against his tattered cloak, one side shaved, covered in tattoos, the other flapping with long black hair which she kept braided by day. She appeared dead at first glance, but when the Butcher swung her down and lay her by the banks, Saska saw that she was breathing, though barely. There was sand about her lips and stuffed up her nose. "We need to clear that out of her airways," Saska said.

They turned her over, hitting at her back, and the sand came coughing up. The woman gasped, eyes opening, spluttering for breath.

"Take her to the water. Wash her, Scalpel." *The man looks terrified,* Saska saw. Theirs was a true love, there was no doubt. She looked out toward the camp. A worry was building in her chest. "Rolly's been gone too long. We have to go and find him."

"Let me," said the Butcher. "I do not fear these demons."

"I'm going too," said Leshie.

The next time there's battle, I'll draw my blade and join in, Saska had told the Butcher, the day they took the Matian Way. Her blade was already in her grasp, blue and silver, glowing. "And me," she said, stepping forward.

She led them on, the three of them and Joy, stalking along at her side. "Find him," Saska said to the starcat. Joy's sense of smell was astonishingly acute, her hearing and sight as well. The cat narrowed her eyes, ears opening, nostrils flaring, then ran.

"Keep up," Saska shouted, giving chase. The others raced behind. Ahead, the shadowed tents appeared, disappearing in and out of the swirling mists. Creatures moved in their ungainly gait, turning suddenly as they heard them, rushing and closing in. They ran past their outstretched arms, ducking and dashing free. Dimly, in the east, a pale light was dawning.

They reached the heart of the camp, and there he was, in battle. Sir Ralston stood surrounded, a heap of sand climbing about his right leg, another reaching for his left. He was roaring, swinging his blade, cutting the creatures down, but they kept on coming. One loomed behind him, widening like a sail, arms broadening like banners as it went to wrap him up. The Wall bellowed out into the night and gave a great, sudden twist, pulling his right leg free, turning, swinging. The sail of sand collapsed, stones scattering across the ground. They rippled, undulating, shifting, reforming…

"Rolly," Saska screamed.

He looked at her, eyes wide. "No…no, stay back! Get away!"

She ignored him, rushing in, cutting at the shapes of stone and sand. The Butcher and Leshie were there as well, and Joy, pouncing and slashing. The sand was rising about their legs, gripping, pulling. Saska felt herself drawn down as though she was standing in quicksand. She bent down, Varin dagger slicing, but it was like cutting water, and had no effect at all. Joy scrambled to her side, digging. She

355

managed to pull her leg free, stumbling back and onto solid ground. Leshie was nearby, sinking, the Butcher with her. He reached out a strong scarred arm, and she grabbed it, and he hauled her free, then staggered away.

"Stay back I said," the Wall bellowed. "Stay back!"

He was alone now. They could not get close. A dozen of the creatures shifted about him, some wrapping about his legs, others reaching out to hug his torso. The sand was climbing his chest, sluicing through the thin gaps in his plate. He swung with his blade, swung and swung again, but it made no matter. They just kept coming.

"Rolly! No!" Saska rushed again…

…the Butcher intercepted her, pulling her back. "We go in there, we all die. There's nothing we can do."

She screamed out, a wordless sound tearing from her throat. Fury boiled in her veins, and a terrible fear. "No. I won't lose him! I can't! *I can't lose him!*"

"We have to think of ourselves, Saska. Of *you*." Leshie was looking around. "There are more of them. The ground is *moving*. If we don't go now…we're all going to die…"

The sand was at Rolly's throat, passing over his gorget. She saw it filling up, rising past his granite chin, his jaw, inching above his lips, up to his nose. Soon it was only his eyes, staring at her from within that prison of sand. She couldn't move. She couldn't think.

"Saska, we *have* to go!" Leshie shouted in her ear. Her voice was strangely distant. Saska could feel the blood throbbing in her head. The Red Blade grabbed her arm, and the Butcher took the other, and together they dragged her away.

My Wall, she thought, still watching, helpless. *My guardian. My rock. My Rolly…*

Tears filled her eyes. What would she do without him?

There was a thump in the skies.

Then another.

The fogs swirled suddenly, shifting, and Saska looked straight up. *The sun is rising*, she thought, strangely. There was a glow up there, but it was too high, much too high. A deep red glow, spreading.

She blinked, saw a shape outlined above them. A slim body, long neck and tail, wings stretched wide to catch the air. Dust swam about it, obscuring its size. A shadow atop it, a figure in the saddle, and another behind. On the wind carried a voice, a woman's voice, ringing out loud and clear.

"Burn them," it called.

And from the maw, gushed the flame.

Lythian

The dragon had been torn apart, its wings snapped back and broken, the lower mandible of its jaw ripped off and cast aside. The neck was savagely crushed, spinal bones jutting out through the thick, dark grey scales. The ground was churned and ruined where it lay, and the blood was everywhere, almost black beneath the bleak grey skies. Lythian looked at the creature with a measure of pity. It had not been a pleasant end.

"He was not meant to kill it," he said to Vilmar the Black.

The huntsman snorted through the tough bristles of his huge black beard. "They were made to kill dragons. That's the whole point."

Lythian sighed. "Did you speak to him? He was supposed to *restrain* it only, Vilmar."

"I know. I made that as clear as I could, but there's no beating instinct. You can't reason with that sort of thing, can you?"

"Then why did we bother? You suggested it might work."

"It did work. The dragon is dead. That's a good thing so far as I see it."

Lythian shook his head with a measure of annoyance. The huntsman had always been of truculent disposition, and even more so as he'd grown older. "You know that wasn't my intention. I wanted it alive."

"Aye. *Hruum* wanted otherwise, though. So it's dead, and one less dragon to worry about. No sense in getting your breeks a twist over it, m'lord."

Lythian was fighting a losing battle with this dragon-catching business, that was becoming clear. "Hruum?" he asked. "That's his name?"

"Aye. At least, that's the only way I know how to pronounce it. I can't speak in that rockfall voice of theirs, but he seems to answer to Hruum, so…"

"I didn't realise they had names. You've been working with them for weeks and haven't mentioned one so far."

Vilmar shrugged. "They don't operate by the same flow of time as we do. Weeks to us is no more than an hour or so to them. The gruloks are thousands of years old." He looked at the bloody carcass again. "You want to catch a dragon alive, best revert to those other methods of yours. No grulok is going to play nice with them or go along with your fanciful schemes."

Fanciful schemes. That was a fair way of putting it. Snaring a dragon had proven more than problematic, partly owing to the fact that few ever came close to their traps. Only twice had that happened until now. On the first occasion, the chain-net fired from the ballista had malfunctioned, and the beast had startled at the noise and flapped away. On the second, the net had hit its mark, wrapping the dragon up as it feasted on the corpse left as bait. At once the beast had flown into a wild frenzy, Sir Oswin Cole later explained, blowing fire in all directions, snapping and snarling so much that the men feared to get close. "I went to reload the chain, my lord," Cole had said, "but by the time I got it all set, the dragon had untangled itself. And then, well…"

Lythian had not needed to ask what happened then. It was clear from the smashed wood and charred lengths of chain, the blackened pit and boiled mud where the ballista had been hidden in its wagon. "The dragon obliterated it, my lord," Cole had told him anyway. "I was lucky to get away. Only when Nathaniel and the others joined me did the dragon think better of the fight, and fly off. It…" He'd given an ashamed shake of the head. "It wasn't even a big one. If it was, we might all be dead."

Lythian had nodded gravely at that, pondering his folly. Losing healthy Bladeborn knights and good fighting men was not a part of his plan. He was tempted to shut down the operation there and then, but Sir Storos had come up with the bright idea of employing the use of a grulok instead. "It could hide on the ground, like a boulder," he had suggested. "We'd only need to put the bait nearby. If a dragon comes he could reach out and grab it. Do you think that might work, Lythian?"

"It might," he had said, after a short consideration. He had spoken to Vilmar about it, who had spoken to Hruum, and two days later, here they were. All staring at the butchered corpse of a young grey dragon that only made Lythian think of Neyruu, and by extension Talasha, who had become a dragonrider herself, Elyon had told him.

He shook his head and gave a sigh. "Did anyone see what happened?"

Vilmar huffed. "We know what happened."

"I want details," Lythian said. He looked to the others. "Storos?"

Storos Pentar had been in the ditch-shelter overnight, along with his men Tucker and Marsh, the Agarathi pair of Sir Hahkesh and

Bah'run, and a few other soldiers from the city. "I was sleeping," Storos said. "Denton had the watch."

Lythian looked at the man in question. He hadn't met him as yet, but that was not uncommon. Every night there were different men out here now, eager to be part of the scheme. Mostly out of morbid curiosity, Lythian knew. Few took it all seriously, and he sensed that those who raised their hands to help only wanted to have the chance of putting steel through the scales of a dragon. If one was caught in a net, after all, it was unlikely that either Hahkesh or Bah'run would realistically be able to calm it, or tame it, in which case it would need to be put down instead. *Every man worth his salt wants to call himself a dragonslayer,* Lythian knew. *They see this as an easy chance to win a bit of glory.*

"Denton, was it?" the First Blade said.

"Aye, milord." He was a common man from that voice, no older than twenty. He had a large mole where his narrow nose met the pocked flesh of his cheek, and slightly dimwitted eyes. "I'm a Brockman, King's Point born and raised." He seemed very proud of that.

Lythian could tell his loyalties from the sigil sewn onto his jerkin: a black tower against an orange sky, the arms of House Brockenhurst. That tower was meant to represent the Spear. *Perhaps put your dagger to the stitching,* he thought. *Cut that tower down.* It would make more sense like that now. "Tell me what you saw," he said.

Denton's face scrunched up. "Not much, to tell it true, milord. Was dark, real dark, you know how it gets at night."

A few other men chuckled. Clearly Denton was a bit of a dolt.

"Yes, I am aware of what happens at night, soldier. So you saw nothing?"

"Well, I saw shapes. Shadows, like. One came down from the sky. Dragon, that must have been."

"As opposed to the grulok," Tucker put in, grinning. "Would that they could fly as well."

Lythian smiled. Flying gruloks would be quite a sight, he agreed.

"Anyhow," Denton went on, oblivious to the mockery. "Dragon came down, and I heard it sniffin' about, toward the bait we set. Was thinkin' of waking Sir Storos, but thought that might frighten it off. So I stayed watchin' instead."

"And?"

"And then the giant reached out. Not the whole body. Just the hand. Grabbed the dragon by the leg, then it stood up, and tore it to pieces. I barely saw anything really. Just movement. Was dark, like I said, and I'm no Bladeborn. The noise, though…"

"We all heard the noise," said Sir Storos. "I woke as soon as the fighting began, Lythian. We all did. Never knew a dragon could scream like that."

The others nodded.

"So there was no struggle?" Lythian asked Denton. "Hruum didn't even *try* to restrain it?"

"No, milord. Not that I could see. Just went for him, all savage-like. Tore him limb from limb."

Lythian looked at the evidence of that once again. It had been a brutal killing. If Hruum, the grulok captain, and the one who conversed with them most, could not be trusted to restrain his impulses, then there would be no further sense in deploying the gruloks to this task. That was fine. It was an experiment only and Vilmar was not wrong. Another dead dragon could only be a good thing, if not the outcome he had wanted.

Storos was looking at the carcass too. "What do you want us to do with it, my lord? I don't suppose a dragon will come near if they see a dead brother down here."

"Sister," Lythian said. The dragon was female by its size and colouring, the sparkling scales of its underside. "Butcher it for parts, Storos, and store the meat in barrels, to be salted and stewed." The flesh of a dragon was tough and gamey, though nutritious. It was best boiled for hours in a pot to soften. Such a large animal was not to be wasted, times as they were. "Bury whatever's left. Deep enough so another dragon cannot smell it."

"As you say, my lord."

Sir Hahkesh did not seem pleased. "Dragon is sacred. Flesh…*no* eat." He frowned a hard frown at him.

"I'm afraid we have no choice, Sir Hahkesh. In the north we eat horse meat when times are tough. This is nothing different."

"To you." Sir Hahkesh hit his chest, then gestured to Bah'run. "We no eat dragon. No Agarathi eat dragon. Is sin. Great sin."

Lythian understood. "I will take that into account when your rations are served." Some spots of rain were falling. To the south, the seas were rough, the horizon dark. The weather was coming from there, and did not look like it was going to improve any time soon. That settled something in Lythian's mind. He had been pondering it for days, ever since Amron left, and with the rain refusing to relent, and more on the way…

It's time, he thought, nodding to himself. *The men will just have to accept it.* "Get that dragon butchered, Storos. These rains are only going to get worse."

He nodded at the knight and made to step away. A word from Storos Pentar called him back. "And after, my lord?"

Lythian turned. "After?"

"When we're done with the dragon." He left a long pause. "Shall we fetch another net-ballista out here? All this…" He gestured to the pits, the shelters, the traps. "Do you want us to continue?"

Lythian looked at each man in turn, judging their reactions. With Amron gone, he had been left in charge of the city and coastal defences and had much to occupy his time. This venture had only ever been speculative. If these men wanted to wipe their hands of it, and spend their energies on other endeavours, he wasn't going to argue.

"What do you say?" he asked. "All of you. Are you willing to keep trying?"

The men exchanged looks.

"No harm in it," said Tucker, first to speak. "Not like we're lacking for recruits, my lord. Always fresh faces out here."

The senior men came out here on rotation, Lythian knew. Sometimes Storos was in charge, sometimes Sir Oswin, and sometimes Nathaniel Oloran took command by night. Tucker and Marsh always came together, spending three out of every four nights in the shelters. The rest of the recruits came and went. Only the two Agarathi, Sir Hahkesh and Bah'run, had been here every single night, without fail. Both of them wanted their chance to try to tame a dragon, even if it meant their lives, and so far neither had been given that opportunity.

To little surprise, they both wanted to stay.

"We not stop," Sir Hahkesh said, firmly. "Me. Bah'run. We *not* stop."

Lythian smiled at the man. "I had a feeling you would say that, Sir Hahkesh."

Sir Storos Pentar pondered some more, then gave a shrug. "It's early days, my lord. And most of the men are sitting idle. Let's give it a little more time before we give up."

Lythian was happy for the show of faith, though did not let it show. "Very well, then. I'll be in the city if you need me."

He crossed the broken plains, a mile of sludge and filth and churned brown earth, walking alone beneath the drizzle. Lythian did not have his own version of a Rogen Strand to shadow him, as Amron did, though supposed he would be wise to assign someone that duty.

He pondered who that might be. Sir Taegon was gone, Sir Quinn as well, and Amron had taken Sir Torus with him too. Sir Gerald was off in search of his father - though he'd proven himself a rather poor protector in the past - and Sir Nathaniel, though still here, had the same chequered history. Lythian did not doubt that this new iteration of Nathaniel would do a fine and dutiful job, but something about it smelled off. Sir Ralf had stayed to give Lythian counsel, but the old knight was too long in the tooth to play protector now, and Sir Storos was busy with his schemes. Who did that leave? Sir Oswin, maybe? Might Sir Adam join his side, handing the keys to the Pointed Watch to another?

If Rodmond was still a Varin Knight, he would be ideal, the First Blade reflected. But the young man had become a greatlord now and the duty was far beneath him.

He put the matter aside as he veered toward the prisoner encampment, a great festering bog in the shadow of the eastern walls. Every day it grew worse, the puddles deepening, the awnings they'd set up to shelter the prisoners collapsing under the weight of the rain and torn apart by the swirling winds. Those were new, those winds. The rain had been coming down for long weeks now, unnaturally heavy and growing colder by the day, but the winds had only just started. Fierce they were, and wild, with great sudden squalls that would shred a shelter in moments if it had a mind to. That was all well and good for the men who camped in the city, protected by walls of ancient, mortared stone, but not the southerners exposed to the elements.

It's high time that was changed, Lythian thought.

He strode to the shelter erected up against the city walls, a simple but sturdy dwelling where the camp commander was based. That duty was being seen to by a knight named Sir Guy Blenhard, a biddable and affable man who no one would ever say a word against. *Sir Good Guy*, men liked to call him, or just *Good Guy* without the 'sir', which was always received with a great big smile from the man. Lythian had selected him for the duty on account of those qualities, but also his probity. If any of the prisoners were being mistreated by one of the men, he expected Sir Guy to come to him at once, and he had. Thus far his reports had included few occasions of violence, though of slurs and insults, there had been many. The offending men were usually rotated to another duty, but that was just papering over cracks, and oft as not, the new guards were just as bad.

There's too much hate here, Lythian knew. *These men are hungry, and angry, and they fear for their loved ones.* Standing out all night in the pouring rain and howling wind, their cheeks bitten at by hail, their bodies soaked to the bone, was not helping their mood.

"Sir Guy," Lythian said. The man was at his desk, heaped in a fur coat, scribbling with a quill pen, a fat tallow candle burned low beside him. There were some books on the desk as well, and a stack of papers weighed down by a stone, their edges fluttering in the breeze. The shelter had an open front, looking out over the camp, where an oil lantern swung upon the framework, creaking in the wind. Around the enclosure, the guards were standing at their posts, looking bored and miserable, glancing south at the darkening skies.

Sir Guy Blenhard looked up. "Ah. My lord. I was just compiling my latest report for you." He put his pen in a pot. "Would you like to see?"

"Tell me," Lythian said.

Good Guy read out what he'd written. His reports were always very thorough. Today, it was the usual. The typical mutters of displeasure and beginnings of dissent that were always sparking, but never quite catching alight. Mostly Lythian forgave it all. The men had the right to vent, and he would not punish the occasional grumble, but if ever something more organised arose, something approaching mutiny, he would have to act, and act quickly. Men like Good Guy were essential in that fight.

"There's been a bit more squabbling among the prisoners as well," the camp commander went on. "Tensions have been running high of late, my lord. The stronger men are all fighting to get the best spots in the shelters. The weak are being left to fend for themselves in the rain, and even their rations are being stolen."

Problems without and problems within, Lythian thought. *This is becoming more trouble than it's worth.* "Has there been any bloodshed?"

"Scant little. Mostly broken noses and split lips, nothing too bad. Without weapons they are unable to cause much harm and my men always get in there quickly enough to break them up, but stopping it entirely isn't possible. A prison camp always takes on a life of its own, my lord. There's only so much that can be done to police what goes on inside."

Lythian took the man at his word. He had some experience in this field.

"There have been a few new arrivals as well," Sir Guy finished, referring to his report. "It's all written in here, my lord. Four more men came from the woods - three Lumaran soldiers who walked together, and one Agarathi. He came alone."

"Fireborn?" Lythian asked. He was always on the lookout for more men to join with Sir Hahkesh and Bah'run.

"No, my lord. He appeared to be a normal soldier to me, by his garb and his manner. Very plain."

"Plain? What do you mean by that?"

The knight scratched his pointed chin beard. "Well, he looked rather *neater* than most others who have come from the woods. Wet and a little dirty, but not nearly so dishevelled as the rest. He did not look like he had played much of a part in the battle, my lord. No stains or rips or scuff marks, no burns or injuries. I suppose he must have run into the woods early before he could engage in any fighting, and found somewhere safe to hide."

"Suppose?" Lythian did not like the word suppose. "Have you not spoken with him yet, Sir Guy? Taken his account?"

"Not as yet, no. I'm told he does not speak the common tongue, but there are some prisoners here who have been willing to translate for me until now. I will ask one of them to help, and find out his story in due course." He looked down at his report once more, nodded, and then reached out. "For your records, my lord."

Lythian stepped in and took the parchment from him, to give to Sir Ralf later. He folded it neatly and stashed it in his pocket. Then he got to the reason he had come. "It's time to bring the prisoners inside the walls, Sir Guy. I will speak with Sir Adam to make arrangements in the city, and require that you do the same out here."

Sir Guy Blenhard gave that a thoughtful nod. Lythian did not miss the shadow of concern in his mild brown eyes. "When would you like this done, my lord?"

"At once," Lythian said. He looked away to the south. The rains were still light but would grow more fearsome in the coming hours, and perhaps last through to dawn, as they often did of late. "There's another storm approaching. I would not see these men have to suffer

363

through it, if it can be avoided. The same goes for the guards. It is a foul charge to stand on watch through this weather. They may appreciate the change in venue."

"They will, I am sure. The rest of the men, however…"

Lythian understood. This decision would not be greeted with universal approval, he knew that well enough. "They will have to accept it," he said. "Were the days bright and fine, I would not be considering this course, but they are not. The camp is a quagmire, and some of the prisoners are growing sick. If any of the men come to you with their complaints, send them straight to my door. I will deal with them."

Sir Guy Blenhard stood from his chair. "I will see to it at once. Do you know where they are to be housed?"

"Not yet. I will have to confirm that with Sir Adam."

"Very good, my lord."

Lythian left him, stepping back out into the drizzle. The rain pattered against his armour as he strode beside the wall toward the River Gate. At his hip he wore the Sword of Varinar, its soft gold mists rising from the scabbard, enrobing him in its godly light. His bond to the blade was growing, deepening, and with it came a feeling of power. *A dangerous feeling*, Lythian knew. He did not like that he liked it.

He found Sir Adam Thorley inside his modest tent in the square beyond the River Gate, where all the captains and commanders had raised their shelters. "I have need of you, Sir Adam," he said. He told him what he planned to do with the prisoners.

Sir Adam's reaction was much the same as Sir Guy's had been. Understanding and accepting, with an underlying tone of concern. "It would be wise to keep them together in one of the city squares," the young watch commander said. "They will still be exposed to the rains, but the mud will not be such an issue, and the winds are not nearly so fierce inside the city. Any shelters we build should remain standing, lest a terrible storm assaults us."

Lythian nodded. "Which one would you suggest?" King's Point, like any great city, was not without its squares and courtyards, though most of them were either heaped with rubble or too small to accommodate so many.

Sir Adam unrolled a map of the city on his table. "Here," he said, pointing at a market square near the harbour. "There's some rubble, and I know that some of the men are in camp there, but it would be the most suitable for this purpose."

Lythian wasn't certain. "Are there no unoccupied squares?" He would rather not force the men to relocate if he could avoid it.

"None that are big enough to accommodate so many." Sir Adam thought a moment, looking at the map. "There are a few halls remaining that might offer the space required, but…"

"But those are already full," Lythian finished for him. "If I force hundreds of tired and hungry soldiers out into the rains to make room for the prisoners, I will have a riot on my hands."

Sir Adam Thorley did not disagree with him. "The square near the harbour would be best, my lord. I can try to free up room somewhere for the men there to move to. Somewhere dry. That should placate them."

But for how long? It should not have been this difficult. King's Point was a large city, and until only recently several thousand more soldiers were situated here. Amron had taken Lord Gavron Grave with him when he left, along with all of the Ironfoot's men. That should have made space, but it hadn't, because the remaining soldiers had simply spread out, rushing to secure themselves a better place to rest their heads by night. There had even been reports of fighting over the choicest lodgings. Blood had been spilt, and a man had lost an eye in one such squabble, all because the soldiers were sick to the back teeth of the rain and the rationing and the discomfort of living in this cold grey broken ruin.

There had been some disgruntlement about who got to leave and who had to stay as well. Not all the men were happy to be left behind, to sit and rot and wait for the shadow of the Dread to return. *They would sooner be marching to defend the western gate. They would sooner die with swords in their hands, against a foe afoot, rather than cowering beneath the titan.* Lythian understood all that as well. He felt restless here, watching the seas and watching the skies, with his schemes all failing around him and the men beginning to darken. He would hear the whispers in the shadows, see their eyes as he passed them by. *They know*, he would think. *They know what I did. They know about Eldur, and Talasha. They are taking me for a dragonlover and a traitor, and are they wrong?*

He put those thoughts aside. They were like blunt knives in his mind, poking and prodding, and had grown worse since Amron left, since he started wearing the Sword of Varinar at his hip. Was it the men whispering, or the blade? He was so tired that sometimes he could not say whether he was awake or in some dream. *A nightmare, more like*, he thought, bitter.

Lythian looked at the map again, trying to focus on the matter at hand. "How long will it take to prepare the square, Sir Adam? I want awnings raised, covers and shelters to protect them from the rain. How quickly can you see it done?"

"How quickly do you *need* it done?" was the knight's reply.

Lythian appreciated that. Sir Adam was direct, respectful, eager to get on with the job; what every good knight and captain should be. "There is a storm approaching from the south. A bad one, by the looks of it. It may be here within the next hour or two." He left the rest unsaid.

Sir Adam Thorley was already stepping over to put on his cloak. "I'll get right to it, my lord."

Lythian nodded his thanks and left, stepping through the square to the command pavilion that Amron had vacated. The First Blade would have preferred to remain in his own, much smaller tent, but Amron had been clear that he wanted Lythian to take up here in his stead. He nodded to the guards outside, and passed within to find Sir Ralf of Rotting Bridge at his little table, set aside from the much larger oaken table from which Amron, and now Lythian, sat in command.

"Another report for your records," Lythian said, handing Sir Ralf the parchment Guy Blenhard had given him.

Sir Ralf looked it over and set it with the others. Lythian stepped over to a stone block and sat down, taking the weight of the Sword of Varinar off his worn and weary legs. A long breath escaped his lungs. Sir Ralf gave him one of those long, querying looks of his. "You look tired, my lord."

I'm more than tired, Lythian thought. He had spent the best part of the morning down in the vaults, training in the forms with the Sword of Varinar. That had taken a great deal out of him. After, he'd sat in council meetings in this very tent, dealing with mostly trivial affairs. Commodore Fairside reported that the rest of his scouting ships still hadn't returned. Lord Kindrick came demanding news about the united host. One of his favoured knights, Sir Bardol, had gone with them, along with several more of his best men, and he wanted to know when they would be back. Lythian had no answer for him. It might be days, weeks, months, before they returned. *Or never*, he had thought. That was the worst outcome.

Lord Kindrick had suggested they send out men to find them. "It's time to bring them back," the man had said. Kindrick was a typical Ironmoorer, spare and mean-looking and glum. "This whole thing. Gathering these deserters. Forget it. We send out some of our best trackers to hunt them down and tell them it's time to come back."

Lythian didn't much like Lord Kindrick, though had to admit he had a point. "I am happy to send men to find them, and report back on their progress. But if they are having some success…"

"They won't be. It'll be a failure. Was only going to be a bloody failure, we all knew that deep down."

He would never have spoken to Amron like that. Lythian knew well enough he did not command the same authority as the king here, especially with these middling Taynar underlords. "As I say. You are welcome to muster a small host to track them, and report on their progress. But I trust the leaders of that host to know when it is time to return, Lord Kindrick. If they are having no success, they will come back of their own accord."

"Or they'll have run off," Kindrick spat back. "That *Skymaster*. Was folly to put him in charge. He'll be biding his time, gathering up some of his own kin, and then he'll make his move once Sir Hadros and my men are outnumbered. He'll kill them all, I know it in my bones. We can't be trusting these Agarathi, Lindar. They're rotten to the core, all of them."

Lythian had been concerned by that. Kindrick had never been so outspoken before Amron's departure, always nodding along in agreement with any of the king's decrees. Now he had turned like spoiled milk, and that was a feeling shared among the men. Lythian gave another heavy sigh as he reflected on that. He dreaded to think what Lord Kindrick was going to say when he heard of his plans for the prisoners.

"You should rest, my lord," old Ralf said. "You have been sleeping poorly, I have noticed, since Amron left. The burden of command is a heavy weight to carry."

And my shoulders are not near so broad as his. Lythian was not made for command. He was a captain and a quartermaster, an intermediary between lords and men. Being raised so high, so fast, did not suit him. He would rest later. But for now… "There's a storm coming, Sir Ralf," he said. "I've ordered that the prisoners be brought into the city."

The old knight assimilated that stoically. "I see. And you are doubting your decision?"

"No. I stand behind it. That does not mean the men will be happy. I am not deaf to the mutterings, Ralf. Half of them want me to put the prisoners on their ships and send them away. The rest would have me drown those ships and send them to the depths of Daarl's Domain." Sir Gerald had first suggested that after the battle, and it seemed more and more of the soldiers here were beginning to agree with him.

Sir Ralf gave him what succour he could. "That is not your burden to bear, my lord. You are only following the king's orders."

"The men don't see it like that. They think I'm influencing him. They know it's me spearheading this vision of unity. Were it not for me, Amron would likely have packed the prisoners up by now and sent them on their way." He gave a weary sigh. "The men are sick of sharing their rations, Ralf. And they have every right to feel that way."

"A soldier has a right to *feel*," the old knight agreed. "But he does not have the right to act upon that feeling. These men are sworn to their captains and commanders, who are in turn sworn to you. You talk here with the king's voice. To act against you would be treason."

Act against me? Would it come to that? Lythian looked into the old man's eyes. "*Treason.* That's what they're saying about *me*, Ralf. I fear what I did…" He breathed out. His head was pounding. "There are rumours that I played a part in raising Eldur from the dead. Now with everything I'm doing. These attempts to tame dragons, to gather the deserters, my sympathy toward the prisoners…" He shook his head. "They are starting to wonder what side I am on."

"The men know which side you are on," Ralf said, firmly. "You are the Knight of the Vale, the First Blade of Vandar. *Vandar*, my lord. They *know*."

Lythian wanted to believe him. The rain was coming down a little harder outside, splashing in through the open flaps. He did not have

367

time to descend into this vortex of doubt right now. "I need to help them move the prisoners," he said, wearily. He stood, forcing himself back to his feet, and walked toward the exit. He looked out into the rain. There was a growing fear in him, a paranoia; he could hear the knives sharpening in the dark.

"I'll come with you," Ralf said, rising.

No. Stay in the tent. Stay dry, Lythian might have said. But he said nothing. He was always glad for the man's company, his counsel and calm presence. *Amron knew I'd need him. He knew I could not do this alone.*

They stepped outside together. It was growing darker, and some fires were coming alive across the square, covered in their tarps and shelters. Distantly, he could see flashes of lightning out there at sea, the far-off rumble of thunder. All agreed now that there was nothing natural about these rains, and strong though they could be during springtime here, they were never so strong and unceasing as this, never so hard and cold and black. Walter Selleck seemed to believe that such extreme weather would likely be engulfing other parts of the world as well. Heavy snows to the north, debilitating heat to the south, wild waves and tempestuous typhoons out to sea. It was part of Agarath's primordial world, the scruffy scribe had said. Nothing was mild, everything was extreme, and it was only going to get worse.

The drainage in the main square was good, though all the same, puddles had formed in places. Lythian and Sir Ralf splashed through them, marching through the River Gate and back out toward the prisoner camp. Sir Guy had already begun to get the prisoners in order, gathering them up into groups. There was plenty of shouting from the guards as they corralled them toward the plank bridge that spanned the moat they had dug around the pen.

The camp commander saw Lythian arriving and bustled over. "The men are arranged and ready to go, my lord. The women as well." He gestured. The women were few in number, less than a dozen of them from the empire, and had been kept in a shelter of their own, watched over by the commander's most trustworthy guards. There had been some concern that the other prisoners might try to assault them, but their efforts to keep them apart had ensured that had not happened.

"Very good, Sir Guy. A place is being cleared in a market square near the harbour. We'll lead them there in batches, a hundred at a time. Order your men accordingly."

Lythian returned to the city with Sir Ralf at his flank, then wended down through the alleys and roads that took them to the square in question. Here and there men had made their own nests among the tumbled stone, sleeping under archways and in whatever dry nooks and crannies they could find. Some were sleeping now, ready to take the night watch. Others sat sharpening blades or mending holes in their cloaks, trying to keep themselves busy and dry between one charge and another.

368

They're staring at me, Lythian thought. *All of them…all of them are staring.*

When they reached the square, they found Sir Adam's men hard at work raising tents and shelters. It was a large space, well littered with tumbled stone and rubble along one side, where the buildings there had collapsed. At the heart was a broken fountain, overflowing with rainwater and bits of drowned debris. It had once shown a figure of Amron the Bold, Lythian remembered. Now nothing but a lower torso and legs remained, the top half obliterated. That was not a propitious sign, with Amron Daecar marching into the jaws of battle.

Lythian did not want to think about that. No more than he did Elyon's long absence. *Too long. He's been gone for far too long…*

Some soldiers were trundling off, looking less than happy. They wore cloaks of dull grey and moody blue, Taynar colours, with pins and badges denoting their houses; Kindrick and Barrow and Rosetree. One or two glared over at him as they left. Sir Adam strode over in his long, strong step, splashing through the rains.

Lythian gestured to the departing men. "Did you not find them anywhere to stay, Sir Adam?"

"I will. For now I have told them to move elsewhere. I will see to them later, my lord." The knight pointed to a half-collapsed temple along the eastern side of the square, its domed roof caved in, walls blackened and smashed and scorched. "Some were taking cover in there. I thought it would make a good base of operations for Sir Guy and his men. It is rather draughty, shall we say, but there's enough cover inside to keep out of the rain."

Lythian recognised the temple as one raised in Varin's honour by Amron the Bold when he built the city. The particular styling gave that away. As did the broken statues he could see outside, enough of them remaining to depict Varin in his might. "Very good, Sir Adam. Is there anywhere we might keep the women?" There were some taverns and shops built along another side of the square, badly damaged. "Might one of those serve?"

"They are mostly collapsed inside, my lord. I could see about moving some rubble, however, if you would prefer to keep the women separate."

"If possible, yes." Large as the square was, it could not compete in size with the camp outside the walls, which could be expanded at their need. He had another look around as the large tarps were raised, rippling in the wind as the rain pattered down on them. "Make those as secure as possible. We don't want them tearing free when the winds pick up."

"Use the rubble," Sir Ralf advised. "If you pack heavy blocks around the beams and supports, the shelters should remain standing."

Sir Adam nodded. "I'll see it done."

The weather was worsening by the moment, sheets of black rain falling. In the west a soft blur of light remained, but elsewhere all was dark. Torches were being lit and hung about the boundary, and each of the roads and alleys leading off the square were being checked for weaknesses, where a prisoner might be able to escape. With so much tumbled stone and broken walls, every small gap and breach needed to be checked and blocked and guarded.

It took the best part of an hour to see it all done. Then the call was given, and Sir Guy Blenhard began leading the prisoners into the city. Lythian went with him, escorting each batch of a hundred, wary of the watching eyes, the muttered questions and complaints. Lord Kindrick stood beneath the porch-awning of his pavilion, staring out with dark eyes. When the third batch was escorted through, Lythian saw him shake his head and go back inside.

A city of friends, and all I see are enemies. Lythian wrapped his fingers around the Sword of Varinar, to give him strength, but somehow it just raised his doubts. He began peering back at those who peered at him. In the darkness, he could hear the whetstones scraping, and the whispers of discontent.

It took another hour to bring all the prisoners through. By then the sky was more water than air, and Lythian could not make out one man from another. The rain washed down across the cobbles, creating rivers in the alleys, a cold winter rain that made a man shudder in his furs, soaking down through wool and leather and flesh, right into a man's bones.

When the thunder began to crash around them, Lythian felt a terrible feeling of dread. He looked to the skies, wondering. But the dread was not up there, it was here.

In the shadows all around him.

27

Emeric

The smile on the face of Borrus Kanabar was as broad as any Emeric Manfrey had ever seen.

"You hear that, Manfrey," the big man said, as they trotted down the Rustriver Road. "You hear those *horns*? Now that's the sound I've longed to hear. Welcome bloody home, they say. The Warden of the East has returned!" He broke into sudden laughter, slapping Emeric hard on the back and almost knocking him off his horse. "Gods, how I've missed it! A sound to stir the heart, wouldn't you say?"

"Very stirring, yes," the exiled lord agreed.

The horns had been blaring for a full minute now, a great blasting clamour, both stirring and triumphant, ringing out from the fortress of Rustbridge. On the far banks of the rushing, red-tinged waters of the river, the city proper lay enshrouded in a cold wet fog, yet right ahead the great fort on the eastern shore loomed grand and imposing, its double walls curving in a sweeping half-moon, fortified with massive bastions that gave it the aspect of a giant star.

Men were appearing on the ramparts, rushing up at the roar of the warhorns. Fifty of them, a hundred, two hundred and three were joining the watchers and bowmen there, gathering in a great thick throng, swarming like crows on a corpse. On the fortress walls and towers, an array of banners were snapping and cracking in the wind. Red and silver for House Pentar. The green and grey and river-blue of Kanabar. The Marshland lords with their browns and greens and muddy marsh tones. The rich emerald and umber of Tukor. Between them hung smaller flags of lesser houses, lord and knightly, flapping in a hundred hues, each cast with their family sigils. Emeric saw gallant knights and posing heroes, swords and spears and bows, mountains and rocks and towering trees, bears, wolves, giants, birds, a sunburst and a strike of lightning, creatures that ran and creatures that crawled and some that slithered too.

"Strong host," remarked Sir Torvyn Blackshaw. "Lord Ghent was not lying."

"Stronger now," declared his cousin Mooton. He made a triumphant hooting sound. "Looks like we got here in time, lads. Are you ready for a war!" The Blackshaw men gave out a roar; Norwyn, Regnar, Radcliffe and Sir Bulmar. All of them were eager for blood and battle, and from what they'd heard they would have their fill.

Ahead, the twin portcullis gates were lifting, rattling and groaning as the great godsteel chains and bars rose up. Between them, the drawbridge was being lowered across the moat, and a mounted host was preparing to cross. "Seems like they got our letter, Borrus," said Sir Torvyn. "They are sending a welcoming party for you."

"For *us*, Torv," Borrus replied. He looked around at the rest of them. "For all of us," he declared. "This welcome is for all of you too."

Noble words, Emeric thought, *if inaccurate*. The host had travelled a long way together, and over that time steel-strong bonds had been built between them, but all the same there was no mistaking who this welcome host was here to honour.

The Beast of Blackshaw rode up beside him on his enormous destrier, a snorting black monstrosity as temperamental as he was. He had a knowing smile on his face. "Nervous, Manfrey?" he asked.

Emeric feigned ignorance. "And why should I be nervous, Mooton?"

The huge knight gave a grin and pointed forward. "You see those banners in green and brown. And the sigil. Now maybe it's just me, but that crossed hammer and sword seems awfully familiar, no?"

"I am aware of them," Emeric said, flatly. They had known since they crossed south at the border, and spoke with Lord Ghent of the Undercloak, that a Tukoran army had marched down here under the command of Prince Raynald Lukar. Naturally, that had led to suggestions from his companions that it might be a good opportunity for the exiled lord to have his exile ended, his castle returned to him, along with all its attendant lands and incomes, and the title of 'lord' established before his name. Borrus had joked that they had all been calling him 'lord' as a courtesy. If he should receive a pardon, however, it would become a requirement.

But Emeric was not interested in hearing it. One day, perhaps, but now? No. He had other more important concerns and was not certain a prince could enforce such a decree. "The world is teetering on the edge of doom, Mooton," he merely said. "What good will my lands and titles be then?"

"*Teetering*, yes, but it hasn't fallen yet, Manfrey. And it won't, now that *we're* back to turn the tide." Mooton smashed a fist against his chest, the uncouth battle gesture of all large, boisterous men. "Vargo Ven and his horde best beware. The Beast of Blackshaw is back, and thirsty for a taste."

Their hooves pounded hard at the packed dirty road, kicking up clods of wet earth as they went. For once it was not raining, broken clouds rippling through the skies like grey tattered banners, and through them the sun was shining, gleaming off their armour.

Borrus had come prepared. When they stopped at Eastwatch a fortnight ago, he had discarded the armour he'd taken from Lord Merrymarsh's chests and garbed himself in a fresh new suit of plate. "My spare set," he'd called it. His favourite plate had been taken to the Steelforge, he'd said, when he voyaged south with the Varin Knights Lythian Lindar and Tomos Pentar, but he had another special-made suit of armour awaiting him in the fort. It was a fine suit, Emeric had to admit, each segment fitted and smoothly linked, enamelled in shades of blue and green with the great blade-antlered elk of House Kanabar emblazoned on the breastplate in a thousand tiny godsteel studs, his helm crested with the same. His cloak was rich lambswool, trailing proudly at his back, finely chequered in the colours of his house with the elk worked in golden thread. And at his hip, Red Wrath, his ancestral blade, which had, Borrus decreed daily, a great need to sup on dragon blood. And one dragon in particular.

Emeric decided to recede a little down the column, leaving Borrus and the Blackshaws to savour this moment alone. Behind, Captain Turner was riding with his men, followed by Sansullio and his Sunshine Swords and the Silent Suncoat too in his torn yellow cloak, frayed and stained in old mud and blood. The sellswords wore cloaks to cover their glittery armour, and cowls to shield their skin. Everywhere they went, they drew looks and scowls and suspicious glances, and here it would be no different.

It will not be safe for them, no matter what Borrus says, Emeric thought. The Barrel Knight had claimed they would be safe under his protection, and true, they had been so far, but travelling the road was different to settling in a city, especially one that bristled under the imminent threat of attack and housed a hundred thousand men all armed with swords and spears. *It just takes one sword, one spear*, he knew.

There was a great deal of chattering going on among the sailors. They were pointing out this banner and that flag, marvelling at the scale of the fort, chuckling at the bridge itself, which looked terribly skinny compared to the fortress and city it linked. Mostly, though, they were interested in the approaching host, riding out with their banner-bearers and knights, a royal welcome for the Lord of Rivers.

"That's Lord Rammas there," he heard Jack say. "I saw him once, when he came to Marshbank. Sturdiest looking lord I ever laid eyes on. All muscle and grunts, that one."

Emeric knew Lord Elton Rammas, the Lord of the Marshes and acting Warden of the East, they'd heard. That would change now, of course. "I fought him in the melee at a tourney once," he told them. "Lord Rammas is about my age. Though that was over fifteen years ago, when we were barely more than boys. Still, he was thick with muscle even back then. A brutal warrior. They build them differently around here."

"Our Jack can attest to that," piped in Gill Turner, his flaxen beard blowing in the breeze, tan cloak snapping at his back. Jack was indeed a strapping man himself. "You reckon he'll remember you, lord?"

"I would doubt it. I was thin as a reed back then and did not have this beard."

Nor the cares I carry now. Emeric had been a boy lord then, still not yet free of his teens, lumbered with the rule of a famed, if fading, house after his father's death in the war. It was a life he'd lived for only a few short years, before his exile at the hands of Modrik Kastor. He clenched his jaw at the memory. It was bitter, even now. The disgrace of it, standing there before the great and good of Ilithor, hearing his 'crimes' be read out in the throne room as Janilah Lukar sat there, passing his judgements and decrees. Lord Modrik Kastor had stepped up and spoken himself of Emeric's 'unseemly behaviours', as he termed them, with his southern staff; a grating charge, sickeningly hypocritical. Few knew back then of the horrors that unfolded between the walls of Keep Kastor, but Emeric did, and no doubt that was part of the reason Modrik wanted him gone.

All I did was fall in love with a southern girl, Emeric thought. *And Modrik and Janilah conspired to see me banished for that 'sin'.* It just so happened that both of the bitter old men were grandfathers to a certain prince. *And Mooton wonders why I will not beg a pardon from him. Why should Raynald wish to overrule that charge when it was his very grandsires who sent me away?*

"Who's the one in pink and blue?" came the voice of Captain Turner, drawing Emeric from his thoughts. "Little feminine, isn't it? And that field o' flowers…"

"That's House Amadar," said Brown Mouth Braxton. "They're from the Heartlands. The flowers represent the plenty of the harvest."

"The rider's got to be Sir Rikkard," Jack said. "He's the Amadar heir, isn't that so, my lord?"

Emeric nodded, pushing those dark memories of his past aside. "Rikkard Amadar is the last living son of Lord Brydon, yes." He looked at the man riding next to him. His banner bearer held a flag of greyish blue and white. The coat of arms was a steel gauntlet, crunched into a fist. "What do you make of that one, Gill? Is it more to your liking?"

The sea captain squinted and gave a nod. "Aye, that's more like it. Simple. Powerful. Very *Vandarian.* House Oloran, no?"

"Correct. Do you know who the rider is?"

"Sir Killian," said Jack o' the Marsh, who was very well versed on banners and sigils, lords and knights and the ranks of the landed gentry. "He's heir to his father Lord Penrith's seat. They call him Gold-mane for his golden hair."

"Goldmane?" chortled Turner. "Well, might as well start calling you Redmane then, Jack. And Borrus'd be *Baldmane.*"

"Or *Nomane*," Jack put in.

That got some laughter from the men. Emeric managed a smile.

The two parties were converging quickly now. Another banner-bearer among the host bore the Pentar flag and sigil, though the knight was not one that Emeric knew. Old Lord Porus had had many sons and nephews, so he supposed it was one of them. A few others completed the ensemble, knights and retainers of princes and heirs, all men of high birth and noble standing. It was the sort of company Emeric had once *endured*, rather than *enjoyed*, company in which he had never felt particularly comfortable.

I was an outcast even before I was exiled, he reflected. He had sat with these men at balls and banquets in his youth, fought them in the joust and melee, but would any of them recall him? His *name*, yes - oh he had a famous name. But him? Well, he had cause to doubt that. *It was Sir Oswald they cared for,* he thought sourly. *I was never more than a curiosity to them. A middling lord with a famous name who never quite fit in.*

By the time the two hosts came together, Emeric had found his way right to the back, mingled in with the sailors and the sellswords, to better go unnoticed. Borrus dismounted his barded warhorse in a single leap and marched forward to embrace his friends. "Killian, you old dog!" he roared, all but pulling him down from his horse, crunching him in his embrace. "Rikkard, get that little arse of yours over here and give me a hug!" Rikkard Amadar got the same treatment, smiling all the while.

Lord Rammas did not get a hug. Instead he went to a knee. "My lord, this is yours." He reached up, presenting what looked like a brooch; Emeric was so far back it was hard to see through all the horses and heads. "Your father wore this, as Warden of the East. Now it is yours. May you wear it well."

Borrus took the brooch with great solemnity. "Thank you, Lord Rammas. You may rise, my friend." He gripped forearms with the muscled lord, shaking firmly, then turned toward the other knights and lesser lords, nodding to each, addressing them if he knew their names, before advancing toward Prince Raynald. "Your Highness, I am honoured to have you here in East Vandar. You marched with quite a host, I hear?"

Raynald was a handsome youth of eighteen who looked much alike to his father, Rylian, with warm waves of auburn hair, a strong jaw and cheekbones, and those piercing green-brown eyes that were all the rage in his family. His sense of courtesy was richly attuned, as rich as the armour and cloak he wore, glorious in green. "Thirty thousand swords, Lord Kanabar," he said, with an upward tilt of the jaw, a proud expression. "I look forward to fighting alongside you, as you once fought alongside my father."

Borrus liked that. "Well said, young prince. And days we will see restored." He paused in a weighty moment. "I was greatly saddened to hear of his death."

The boy prince dipped his eyes. "As was I, when I heard of your lord father's passing at the Bane. A great man. But I'm sure you will match him."

"Not if that beard's anything to go by," Mooton whispered, with a grin. Unfortunately, Mooton Blackshaw's whispers were like another man's roars, and everyone heard. Borrus turned to him with a glare. He had not been free of a bit of lighthearted mockery over that beard, which was not near as thick and red as his father's had been. "I'm just saying…" Mooton went on, shrugging. "All your hair's on your chest, Borrus, everyone knows that."

"Forgive my cousin, my lords," Sir Toryn interrupted, from atop his horse. He smiled to lighten the air. "He is rather clumsy with his tongue at times, though he more than makes up for it with his ferocity with axe and blade."

"*Cousin*? You are Sir Torvyn Blackshaw, then?" Raynald observed. "The knight who spent all those years in that southern pit?"

"Decades would be more accurate, Your Highness." Sir Torvyn smiled, the model of grace, though his face still twitched and jerked on occasion, a symptom of his trauma. "Without Lord Borrus I would not be here."

Emeric looked at Borrus, wondering if he would take the praise himself, but the big man knew better than to steal another's thunder. "I was present," he said, "though that honour goes to Jonik. You will know him as the Ghost of the Shadowfort, Prince Raynald."

"Yes…I did hear of that…"

"My lords." Sir Rikkard stepped forward. His armour was silver, with a shade of light blue worked into the metal of his breastplate. On his back he wore his Varin cloak. Emeric found it interesting that he chose to represent the order and not his house. He glanced around at the skies with a wary look in his eyes. "Perhaps we ought to continue this *inside* the walls. There have been some dragon attacks of late, and they may come at any time."

"Let them," Borrus said. He looked east, as though fronting up to what lay beyond. "I hear Vargo Ven is out there. I want his *head*, Rikkard. I want to carve out his brain and use it as a cup, while I toast to the memory of my father."

Emeric had a good long look at Rikkard Amadar's face. He looked weary and careworn. "We can talk about that inside, Borrus." He returned to his horse and mounted up. "Come. We have had pavilions prepared for you." He set off at that, and the rest fell in to follow, the prince and greatlord heirs and highborn knights moving to the front, Emeric lingering behind with the rest, happy to have gone unnoticed until now.

The portcullis was misting softly when they passed beneath it, curls swirling around its savage spikes. Emeric found himself riding alongside Sansullio. "This is godsteel," the Sunshine Sword remarked.

"Northern forts and cities often use godsteel in their gates and walls," Emeric said. "Though rarely so much as this. I understand only Bladeborn can raise and lower the gates here, and the same is true of the drawbridges."

"Drawbridges?" Sansullio repeated. "There is more than one?"

"Three," Emeric told him, as their horses' hooves rattled along the steel-strengthened wood of the bridge. The moat below was wide and deep, bristling with nasty spikes and stakes, half hidden in the murky water. "There is a second entrance looking east onto the plains and a third on the southern side, where the fort meets the river. Each has a double gate and drawbridge between them, same as here." They passed under the second gate, just as the first was lowered behind them, blocking off the world beyond, and entered into the great ward. At once they were assaulted by colour and noise and motion. Sansullio, who *never* lost his cool, almost lost his cool.

He gave an exhale. "There are…so many, my lord."

Yes, Emeric thought, with a twinge of concern for the sellsword. He looked across the sea of tents and pavilions, the cookfires and stables, the barrack marquees and training yards and archery ranges, the latrines and privy shelters where the nobles emptied their bowels, all contained with the vastness of the great ward of the fort at Rustbridge. The scale of it was enough to steal his breath.

"That is what a hundred thousand men in camp looks like, Sansullio." *And sounds like*, he thought, as the world erupted into shouts and barks of laughter, the ring of steel and twang of arrows, the rattling of wagons and clop of hooves and the general constant din of a thousand men in motion, bustling all about them. He gave his friend a tap on the arm as the leaders continued down a wide thoroughfare. "Come, we'd best not lose the others." He spurred his steed on, the Sunshine Swords and sailors following.

Their pavilions had been raised near the wall in the northwestern corner, close enough to the river that it could be heard rushing past outside. It was here that they stopped, handing their horses over to be taken by the grooms. "This one is not to be tied or stabled," Emeric informed them, gesturing to Shade. The beautiful black-coated Rasal thoroughbred was not like other horses, and was not to be confined. "He will go where he pleases, do you understand?"

"Aye, m'lord," one of the grooms said. "I've worked with Rasals before. I know how particular they can be."

No one had ridden Shade since they'd begun on their journey south. Once, Regnar had tried, but that hadn't gone well for him. There was only one rider Shade would permit onto his back.

Emeric found that he had been granted a private tent of his own, though it was small. Sir Rikkard Amadar showed him the way personally. "I am sorry it isn't bigger, my lord. Regretfully, space is tight, as you can tell."

Emeric had no need of further space. "I would be happy to stay with the others." The rest of the men were being barracked in communal tents; one for the Blackshaws, and one for the sailors and sellswords. "You needn't have troubled yourself on my account.."

Rikkard wouldn't hear of it. "It was no trouble, Emeric. A lord ought to have his own space."

I am no lord, Sir Rikkard, Emeric thought to tell him. But of course he knew that already. As with Borrus and the others, he was giving him the styling as a courtesy.

The heir of Amadar smiled pleasantly, then showed him a map of the encampment, which had been thoughtfully scrawled on a piece of parchment and placed upon a small table inside his tent. He pointed out where the command pavilion was, somewhere at the heart of the ward, and where Borrus's pavilion would be. He spoke too of the nearest training circle he might want to visit, and the privy outhouse that he would be permitted to use, built into the walls with a shoot that deposited a man's excretions out into the moat.

"There is a mannequin for your armour as well," the knight went on, pointing it out. "If ever you decide to remove it, that is." He said that with a knowing smile.

"Not for a while," Emeric said. "The perils of the road…"

"You will be safer here. Or will at least have more warning if there is an attack, time enough to put on your armour so you don't have to sleep in it. It's uncomfortable, I know. Do you have a squire?"

Emeric shook his head. Not once in his life had he had a squire.

"Then your armour can be removed and dressed by your own hand?" That was common enough, though most knights still preferred to keep squires to tend to their chores, and train the next generation in the chivalric arts. *A dying art,* Emeric believed. He could count on one hand the number of true knights he had known in his youth, without pride or vice, committed to the ideals.

"It's manageable, yes," he said. "Lord Merrymarsh keeps large stocks of good armour, Sir Rikkard."

"Ah yes. I did hear a rumour that you had stopped in Calmwater. You returned the long lost Lady Kathryn, did you not?"

"She was in the same pits as Sir Torvyn. Jonik was adamant that we return everyone back to their own lands."

"Jonik," repeated Sir Rikkard, mulling on the name. "The more I hear about him, the more I am convinced of his virtue. He sounds a good man."

"He is. I can attest to that personally. So will Borrus, I'm sure."

"Yet he isn't with you. When we received word from Lord Ghent that you were coming here, I had assumed Jonik would be part of your host. I wanted it to be so, in fact. I have an interest in meeting the man who killed my nephew."

Emeric detected no venom in the way he said it. "He is haunted by that, I assure you. It drives him every day to be better."

Rikkard contemplated that for a moment. "Sometimes a man has to pass through the darkness in order to walk in the light. Such it is with this war, would you not say? We are all enshrouded by it, and striving to reach the light beyond…to see the glow of that far-off dawn."

Emeric raised a brow. "You speak well, sir. Yes, this is how I feel as well."

Rikkard gave a smile, dipped his chin, and stepped over to a small possessions trunk set beside the pallet bed. He opened it and drew out three pewter cups and a stoppered clay bottle. "I took the liberty of provisioning you with a drop of wine, Emeric. I hope you don't mind if I partake?"

"By all means."

Rikkard returned to the table, placed down the cups, and poured out three portions.

"Are we expecting company?" Emeric asked.

Rikkard handed him his goblet. "She'll be along any moment."

"She?"

"Yes, the female of the species, though with Lady Marian there is perhaps some scope for debate." He smiled. "She is as fearsome as any man I have ever met. An extraordinary woman. I think you'll like her."

Emeric frowned, wondering where this was going. He had heard the name of course. Marian Payne had developed a network of spies and sneaks, always women, though it was said she was an outstanding swordswoman too, one of the finest Bladeborn in all of Rasalan, utterly redoubtable of spirit. Quite what they wanted with him, though, he could not say.

Rikkard was looking at him with a half smile on his face. "I remember getting drunk with you at a feast tourney once," he said, reminiscing. "After the war. At Eastwatch, I think it was."

Emeric recalled that as well. He recalled every tourney, every feast, every joust and melee. It was a life he'd lived for a few years only, so remembering such occasions was easy enough. "*You* were drunk, Sir Rikkard," he corrected. "I would not say the same about myself."

"Well…I was often drunk back then. The afterglow of the end of the war, and all that. Mostly I was drinking my grief, though. I lost two brothers to Vallath."

Emeric remembered that too. It was said that Rikkard Amadar would never hear a bad word said against Amron Daecar, for avenging the deaths of his older brothers when he slew Vallath at the Burning Rock.

"You know that grief, of course," Sir Rikkard went on. "You lost your father too, during the war."

"To an arrow," Emeric said. There was no great glory in that death. Just a lucky arrow that had come out of nowhere to plunge down into his eye. He had his faceplate upturned at the time, to better shout his orders to his knights. A mistake that cost him his life. Most deaths in war were luck, Emeric knew.

"And you were raised to lord thereafter," Rikkard said.

"For a time," Emeric murmured. "Before my exile. I have no lands and titles anymore, Sir Rikkard." He sipped his wine, keen to change the topic of conversation. "Ought you not be accompanying Borrus to his pavilion? He will want to convene a war council at once, I know. He has been speaking about it for days."

"I can quite imagine. Having known Borrus Kanabar for many long years, I am fully aware of his proclivities and habits. Like his father, he is bellicose, belligerent, and will no doubt be keen to march out and smash Ven's horde to pieces." He sighed, taking a sip of wine. "I tell you, Emeric, Lord Rammas was more delighted than I could say to hear that you were coming. And when I say you, I mean Borrus. Never have I seen him so restless as we awaited you, nor so courteous as when he presented Borrus with his brooch just now. Do you know what it denotes?"

"It is the brooch worn by the Warden of the East," Emeric said.

"Just that. A rank Rammas held for a short time, though only as a surrogate. He never wore that mantle comfortably, because he knows he is not worthy of it. Lord Rammas is the Lord of the Marshes, a lesser title. Borrus far outranks him, and now that he is here…"

"He will command the army to war."

"I worry so, yes. Our orders have been to stand down and wait, but those orders are growing stale. Elyon Daecar brought them, direct from the mouth of his father, but Elyon has been gone long days now and the men are growing restive. Rammas wants his vengeance for the rape and ruin of the Marshlands, and Raynald wants his glory. And what Borrus said out there, about Vargo Ven…" He paused, checking Emeric's eyes. "How did he take the death of his father?"

"Not well. He has spoken of retribution for months."

"Vengeance is never a good pretext for battle," Rikkard said, wearily. "Should tens of thousands die because of one man's fall?" He shook his head. "The king's orders are to wait, and so that is what we have been doing."

"And you fear Borrus will overrule them?" Emeric rubbed at his beard, uncertain. "I've heard Borrus talk of Amron Daecar a hundred times. There's no one he respects or admires more. If these orders truly come from the king, then…"

He did not get to finish that thought. Outside, voices rose and a moment later the door flaps swayed and the freckled face of Jack o' the Marsh peeped in. "Sorry to interrupt, my lords, but there's a lady out here who wishes to see you."

Rikkard nodded. "That will be her. You may send her in, Jack."

Jack smiled to have his name remembered. Rikkard Amadar had made a point of meeting them all when they arrived at the tents. "Yes, my lord. Of course. At once."

He disappeared, to be replaced a second later by Lady Marian Payne. She was tall, taller than Emeric was, and almost as broad at the shoulder as well. Beneath a fine silver cape she wore grey armour the colour of dark smoke, a seamless suit, sleek and slim. Her hair was dark and slicked back over her scalp, her eyes a hard icy blue. She very much met the descriptions Emeric had heard of her.

"My lady," he said, bowing his head. "A pleasure."

"The pleasure is mine."

Sir Rikkard went to hand her a cup of wine, but she shook her head.

"Thank you, but I intend to train once we are done. Save the wine, Rikkard. With the Blackshaws here, we are going to need every drop."

Emeric smiled at the remark. "You know them, my lady?"

"I was in camp at Dragon's Bane with them, before they left to join your quest. Sir Mooton would join Lord Wallis's councils, on occasion. He would drink a lot, I recall."

"A common affliction of the men of the Riverlands," said Rikkard, with a smile.

"Quite," agreed Marian. She had a long look at Emeric. "You bear a resemblance to your famed forebear. Sir Oswald was said to have a black beard and golden eyes, as you do."

"That is where the similarities end, my lady."

She cocked a brow. "A modest man. I suppose you think that is a virtue?"

"I have heard it said humility is a noble trait, yes."

"To a point. But a man can be over-humble." She continued to study him for a moment, and then said, "I am told that the Shadowknight Jonik is not with you. Pray tell, where is he?"

She had something of an interrogatory style of questioning, hardly a soft touch, but he saw no reason to lie to her. "He remained at the Shadowfort. But that was long months ago, my lady. I could not speak to his whereabouts at this time."

She nodded. "You went there to destroy the order, is that correct?"

"That was our intention, yes."

"And was it a success?"

It was not an easy question to answer. "The order was not what it seemed, Lady Payne. Jonik told us that it was founded by an ancient mage called Hamlyn, under the orders of Queen Thala. Their duty was to carry out the contracts that Thala had foreseen."

"Contracts?" asked Rikkard, frowning. "You mean assassinations?"

"Yes. There was a book, Jonik told us. It listed many hundreds of killings, going back centuries. The order's function was to prune the tree of time, so to speak, guide us to a particular destination, by the visions of the Far-Seeing Queen."

Rikkard looked half in shock. Marian less so. She had the bearing of someone who knew a great deal more than others. "Did you see this book, Emeric Manfrey?"

"Not myself. It was only Jonik who was permitted into the refuge. Sir Torvyn is of the belief that there is more that he did not tell us, secrets he was unwilling to share. That did not go down well with the men, I was told."

"*Told?* But surely you were there?"

"I left shortly after we took the fort," he explained. "We had left some of the men in camp in the foothills, and Jonik sent me to fetch them back. We were about to make our way back up the mountain when Borrus appeared, with most of the company. We joined him, and turned south."

Marian ran a finger along her sharp jaw. "I had heard you were loyal to him."

The comment rankled. "I was. I *am*. It was not my choice to leave."

"But you did."

He went silent. There was a fog in his memory around that time. Emeric had felt it, even as he descended the mountains with Sir Lenard and the Silent Suncoat. He had felt the strange pull to go south, the whispering coercions in his head. Later, when Borrus appeared, he made little complaint when the Barrel Knight swept him back into the company, and only *much* later did it occur to him that it was the work of one of the mages, some hex like the one the Steward had whispered into Borrus's ear, driving him to go south and leave Jonik behind. By the time he had realised all of that, it was too late to turn back. It had never been his intention to abandon Jonik. *Never.* He had cursed and damned himself a hundred times over for that, but there had come a time when he had to make his peace with it, and follow the whims of fate. *I will see him again,* he told himself. *I will have my chance to explain.*

He took a drink of wine and met the woman's eyes again. "Is that what you wanted to talk to me about, Lady Marian? Jonik and his mission."

"In part. I have a strong vested interest in the Blades of Vandar, Emeric. But more pressing matters have brought me here." She looked at Rikkard. There was something conspiratorial about all this. "We have been attempting to get in contact with Moonrider Ballantris," she said. "Thus far, our efforts have failed. You know of my particular talents, I trust?"

"You are a spymaster," he said. "You train young women in the arts of deception and espionage."

"I do. And that training takes *time*. Regrettably, I have no spies here at Rustbridge suited to the task I have been given. I can use balms and potions to change a person's appearance, alter their facial features and hair, the tone of their skin…but the language and the accent are much more difficult to mimic. But now you are here. And with a certain set of friends, I am told."

Emeric did not take long to understand. "You wish to use the Sunshine Swords," he said.

"Moonrider Ballantris is Lumaran," she said, in answer. "These Sunshine Swords are as well. It may be that they can reach Ballantris without stirring any suspicion. We wish to do this without the knowledge of Vargo Ven. And Sunlord Avam as well, if possible."

Timor Ballantris. Avar Avam. These were powerful figures in the south and two men Emeric had met before. The former had struck him as magnanimous, grand, a stately lord of fierce honour and a warrior of formidable prowess. The latter was a Patriot of Lumara, and that said it all. Hateful, reeking of disdain, he had looked at Emeric Manfrey like he was a stain of dirt upon his boot when they had been introduced, long years ago.

"Who is in charge of the empire's forces?" Emeric asked. It would be one of the two of them, he knew.

"Sunlord Avam," said Rikkard. "At least, that is what our latest intelligence suggests. We have no expectation that he will wish to listen to us, let alone side with us, but Moonrider Ballantris is thought to be another matter. It is our belief that many of the empire's forces are growing disillusioned and doubtful over their alliance with the Agarathi. This is not their crusade, Emeric. And it may be that they are not even aware of the rise of the Dread. Against the titan we are all natural allies."

True as that might be, it wouldn't matter, not to Avar Avam and the loathsome men beneath his charge. "Some resentments go deeper than that," Emeric said. "I lived in the south for over a decade. I saw what the hate of the Patriots can do."

He thought of *Brewilla*, the second woman he had loved, and lost. He remembered the fire that tore through his estate north of Solas, thought of the burned bodies of his staff, kind old Kestan and sweet young Puli and the rest, all eighteen of them killed by the Patriots of Lumara. He had buried Brewilla alone, out near the olive trees. He remembered the prayers he had whispered for her, and for the others, each in their own tongues. He remembered the kindness of the men as they helped gather the bodies and bury them…a grim and gory charge, but never once did they utter a word of complaint. Even now, he could see Brewilla's face, as he held her in his arms. *She looked so peaceful*, he thought. *She was always so full of starlight. And they took that light from her…*

Lady Marian Payne was watching him, reading him; every flicker of the eyes and twitch of the mouth as the memory moved through his mind. "You have suffered personally by their hand," she said. It was not a question.

"I have." His voice was blunt. In the days and weeks following the murder of Brewilla and the others, he and Jonik had sought vengeance. The perpetrators had been slain, but never he who gave the order, and still he did not know who that could be. It might have been one of a thousand men, Emeric knew, but in the end, the rot started at the top, and Avar Avam had long been one of their leaders. Avar Avam, Pal Palek, Iru Zon, Elio Krator… Even knowing that Avam was out there now, amid the enemy ranks, mere miles away…

383

A throb of vengeance beat heavy in his heart. He took a drink of wine to calm and settle his thoughts, mulling upon what they'd said. "The enemy camp," he said, after a time. "Is it well watched?"

"Their borders are secure," Marian Payne said. "The dragons keep a close watch over the host, though they prioritise the Agarathi camp, which is vast, and cannot watch every inch of ground. The camps are separated, as you would expect, between the Agarathi and the empire. So far as we have been able to discover, the empire's soldiers are evenly split between Lumarans, Piseki, and Aramatians, supplemented by men from Solapia and the smaller island nations as well. Each of them has their own camp, collected within the whole, but separate from one another. The Lumaran encampment lies along the greater warcamp's southwestern border, spread across a lightly wooded field. It is securely guarded and screened, but that does not mean an approach is impossible. The days have often been misty here, thick with fog and falling rain. Such a day would provide good cover if we decide to proceed. That is, of course, if your Sunshine Swords are willing."

"They are not mine," Emeric said. "Borrus is their patron. You would need to speak with him about severing their terms of service."

"Their terms? Do they have some formal contract with Lord Kanabar?"

"A verbal one," Emeric said. "And the Sunshine Swords are sticklers for their honour, my lady."

"So I have heard. Honourable, graceful, brave. Brave enough to act upon this task, I wonder?"

Emeric had no doubt of that, so long as Sansullio saw the merits in it. "I will speak with them," he said. "And we can make our plans."

Something about the way he said that had Rikkard Amadar raising a brow. "We? You wish to play a part in this, Emeric?"

A part, he thought. *No, a starring role.* He would not see Sansullio and his men risked without sharing in that burden. Emeric Manfrey was fluent in the Lumaran tongue and spoke it as well as any man native to those lands. If that was Marian Payne's biggest hurdle, then he would leap it himself. And what's more, he knew Timor Ballantris personally. He looked at Marian and Sir Rikkard Amadar and said, "I will see this task done myself."

28

Amara

"Is it hidden?" Amara asked.

Carly nodded. "You don't want to know where." The Flame Mane wore only a thin hempen shift and there was no place to hide a blade, lest she use her imagination. The knife was small, yes, a little stabbing dagger only, a few inches in length, and its edges were protected by a linen wrap, but still…

"I ask too much of you, Carly. There are other ways. You don't need to do this…"

"I *want* to do this, my lady. And I've had worse in there, believe me. You just make sure you get to me in time. If those two Bladeborn guards of his hear the seal whimpering, I'm not going to have much to defend myself with."

Only that little stabbing knife, Amara knew, and it wasn't even godsteel either. "We'll be there," she promised. "I won't let anything happen to you, Carly."

The once-leader of the Flame Manes had to trust her on that. She nodded, running a hand through her wild red hair, shaking it out. Her shift was tied about her waist with hempen string, illustrating the fine shape of her figure, a pair of bare legs extending from the hem, a little above the knee, and her arms were bare as well. Poor though the garb was, the girl was a vision, wild and beautiful, flame-haired and snow-skinned, almost impossible for a red-blooded male to resist. *Or a seal*, Amara thought. The Blubber King had expressed a great interest in Carly, and it was an opportunity not to be missed. "You're certain the guards will let me pass?"

"I'm certain. Just tell them you're there to speak to the Great One, and they'll escort you to him."

There was nothing else to say. With a nod from Carly to acknowledge that she was ready, the pair stepped to the door and left the cabin.

The great cavern outside was beginning to darken, dusk soon to set in, the torches being lit around the island-within-the-cave. Amara looked down the shore, and saw Captain at his longship, milling about, pretending to busy himself with this and that. A few trusted oarsmen were with him, fixing nets and stitching sails. As Amara looked his way, the Seaborn glanced over, gave her a wink, and returned to his work. *Good luck*, that wink said.

We may need it, Amara thought.

Sir Connor Crawfield was standing outside, alongside Sir Ryger Joyce, whom Jovyn had helped recruit to their cause. Sir Ryger had the guard of Amara's men today, along with the sellsword Brazen Ben, who had followed Sir Penrose and Jovyn as they took a walk along the beach, as per their plans.

"There's some suspicion from a few of the others," Sir Ryger told her, in a low growly voice. "And there's been a late change of shift too. At the armoury."

Terrific. "Who?"

"Colossus has been given the charge, in place of Wilcock, who's sick. Sir Talmer is still the other."

Wonderful. This just gets better. Wilcock was a spotty-faced sapling of a sellsword, with barely a drop of Bladeborn blood in his scrawny little veins. It was expected that he would be easy to subdue, but Colossus was another matter entirely. His name was enough to paint a picture of the man. Amara had rarely seen anyone so monstrously large. "Will Sir Talmer be able to knock him out?"

"Doubt it, at that height," growled Ryger Joyce. Sir Talmer was several inches south of six feet, Colossus several inches north of seven. "He tries, and Colossus will squash his head like a melon. Be easier just to kill him. Stick a dagger in his back when he's not looking. Pick the right spot and any man would go down, giant or not."

Amara could see a dozen ways where that could go wrong. "The plan was to sneak into the armoury unseen, Sir Ryger. That sort of bloodshed may only raise the alarm if Sir Talmer gets it wrong." She gave out a breath, doubts swirling. "Maybe we should wait. The shifts might suit us better on another day."

"Unlikely," said Sir Connor. "We were lucky to have Sir Ryger and Ben guarding us today, my lady, and even more so with Sir Talmer at the armoury. Most days we get perhaps one of our men at those stations. To have three out of four is rare. We might not have that chance again for weeks."

The man was right, she knew. Damn him. It was the slimy seneschal who set the schedule, and unless they could win him to their cause, they had no control over which guards would be at which posting at any given time. Right now those postings favoured them. The seneschal would bend the knee when it was over, Amara suspected, but until then, approaching him for help was too great a risk.

"Well?" Carly was growing impatient. "All this dithering isn't going to help us. Shall I go or not?"

"No," Sir Connor said, with a firm shake of the head. "It's a senseless risk, always was."

"It's a risk," Amara agreed, "but not a senseless one. The last thing we want is the Lord of Lard wriggling off into some secret passage we don't know about. If he escapes, we may never get away. With Carly there, we'll have someone on the inside to stop him."

Sir Connor disagreed. "We don't need that. That whale moves slower than a dying snail. If we're quick, we'll get to him first."

If. Too many ifs. They had been through all this before, arguing the merits of each option at length the previous night. In the end, it was Carly's decision. Amara looked at her, "Your choice, Carly."

"Then I'm going," the Flame Mane said, ever decisive. "That was the plan and I'm sticking to it." Before Connor Crawfield could object, she stepped away, swinging her hips and swishing her hair, making for the little wood that grew at the heart of the island.

I love that girl, Amara thought, watching her swagger off, already in character. She'd rarely met anyone so bold and wilful. "I guess it's settled, then. You two know your roles. If you hear fighting, or anything goes wrong, you get to Carly first," she said to Connor Crawfield. She looked at Sir Ryger again, saw that he bore two blades, as planned, one at each hip. *Good.* "I'm going to the others. Good luck to you both."

Sir Ryger Joyce stopped her as she stepped away. "There's going to be blood, my lady," he said, in a dark, portentous voice. "Some of the other men are growing suspicious, as I just told you. Might be a few will throw down their arms when the fighting starts, even join our side, but not all. It'll be battle at the beach tonight. I hope you're ready for that."

Amara only looked at the man. "The world is a battleground, Sir Ryger. Perhaps it's time this beach became one too?"

The others were sixty or so metres away, dawdling along the shore, Sir Penrose and Jovyn occasionally picking up a pebble to bounce along the calm crystal waters within the cave, splashes echoing. Brazen Ben Barrett walked along a half dozen paces behind them, a hand on the hilt of his godsteel sword, watchful. To anyone else, the sellsword was watching the knight and the squire, as per his duty. In truth he was glancing surreptitiously around to check the positions of the guards and sailor-soldiers, watching the waters to see which boats were coming and going, tallying up how many of the Bladeborn in the service of the Great One were on the island at any one time. *He's sharper than he looks, that one,* Amara noted. Carly had promised him a kiss on the lips when all this was done, and that seemed the only motivation the man needed to do his job, and do it well.

"It's happening," Amara whispered to him, through her smile, as she passed him by. "Be ready, Ben. We're going to divert toward the armoury."

She saw him give her a nod. "Squidge and Palmer went out that way, I saw, with a jug of ale and cups," he whispered back. "There's a willow they like to sit under, on the shore. It's in sight of the armoury cave, my lady. Be wise to wait until they're gone."

For Vandar's sake... That was another complication they could do without. Amara was half-temped to turn back, intercept Carly before she could reach the grove and tell her the plan was off...but the girl was already gone. *We're in too deep now.* "We can't delay. Carly's already left."

"Oh." Brazen Ben thought a moment. "We'll need to distract them then. I've got some dice here, my lady, always keep a couple in my pocket. Those two like a game of liars. I'll see if I can keep 'em looking away while you get into the armoury."

"And if not?"

"Then I guess I'll have to kill them. Ask them to join us first, of course, but doubt they would. Those two like it here. Won't want us causing disruption."

The same as many others, Amara knew. "And you'd do that? Kill them?" Squidge and Palmer were two fellow sellswords, both Blade-born, weak-blooded. "You've served beside them for years."

"True, but I've disliked them for years too. Got no problem with killing, my lady. Wouldn't be much of a mercenary if I did."

He's more ruthless than he looks as well, Amara noted. Brazen Ben Barrett might have the appearance of a giant grinning rabbit, but clearly there was some steel between those oversized ears of his. Amara nodded her understanding, then stepped past him and up to the others. "Did you hear all that?" she asked them.

Sir Penrose had just sent a pebble skimming along the water, leaving ripples in its wake, five, six, seven of them. "We did, my lady. Join or die."

It was a choice many would have to make. "Good. Veer toward the armoury, then. Stay relaxed. I'll see you there."

She left them to their slow circuit along the shore, moving back up the beach a little and then taking a shortcut through the trees. There were some guards posted here and there, wandering on their patrols or sitting about their little cookfires roasting fish. One young soldier was sharpening the head of a wooden fishing spear. Another was standing at a workbench beneath the creaking branches, working on a shark-head halfhelm. Most ignored her as she passed, though a few gave her courteous nods, even smiles. *Some favour me,* she thought. The same was not true of others, who only squinted at her and scowled, misliking her presence here among them. *They see a menace in me,* she thought. *Sir Ryger was not wrong about that.*

Her path took her through the grove and out onto the other side of the island. It was darker here, deeper into the cavern, and overhead the cave's rock walls rose up above her, curving into that great mossy ceiling that came alive with colour at night. Beneath the dangling leaves of an old cave willow, she saw Squidge and Palmer sitting on a pair of rocks down on the shore. They had set down their jug of ale between them and were drinking from wooden cups, sharing jokes and laughing.

Amara walked up to them. "Evening, gentlemen. Not on duty today?"

They turned, half startled to see her. "What you doing over this side?" spat Palmer, a fat-cheeked, ugly man of five and twenty. "You shouldn't be here."

"I have leave to walk the island at my will." She smiled and looked at Squidge. Despite his stupid name he was actually rather handsome. "I hear you like liar's dice, is that right?"

They both perked up. "We do. Best players on the island."

"Which island?" she asked. "This one, inside the cave, or the island proper?"

"Both," said Palmer. "And all the others too. We're the kings of liar's dice, ain't we Squidge?"

"Damn right." The man grinned and slurped his ale. "There's no one here who can beat us."

"Brazen Ben says otherwise," Amara told them. "He tells me he's much better than the both of you."

The pair of sellswords looked at one another, then laughed. "You're having us on, woman," Palmer said. "Must be. Ben's dull as dishwater. Ain't no world in which he'd beat me or Squidge at liar's. Everyone knows it."

"Not everyone," she said. "I've heard others say the same."

"Who?" demanded the ugly one, getting irate now. "What's Ben been saying?"

"That he's better than you at liar's dice," Amara said. She smiled. Her words had provoked a fierce annoyance in both of them, as she'd hoped. "I saw him a little while ago, ambling along this way. Maybe you can take it up with him personally?"

"We *will*," said Palmer, closing a meaty fist. "I'll knock that buck-toothed lackwit's front teeth down his throat. Lying bastard. He'll take it back or we'll make him."

Amara Daecar smiled. *Ah, the thin skin of sellswords.* It could always be counted on. Usually when calling into question their skill with the blade or bravery in battle, true, but clearly these two hung their hats on liar's dice instead. *To each their own.*

She continued along the shore, leaving the two men to glower and grumble, glancing into the rock pools as she went, seeing the crayfish and the crabs scuttling over the glistening stone. The armoury was near, perhaps forty metres down from the willow along the curve of the shore, built into a natural cave where the rear walls of the cavern rose up, dangling with vines and heavily clothed in lichen. The interior had been fitted with shelves and racks for weapons, and the way was blocked by thick iron bars and a gate, rusted and chained and locked.

Sir Talmer stood outside, looking a little worried. He had been expecting Wilcock too. Instead he had the gargantuan sellsword Colossus for company, garbed in a byrnie of godsteel mail with a huge greatsword slung across his back in a leather scabbard. He had long black hair that flowed all the way down to his brawny shoulders, a jaw so square and wide it looked to have been chiselled by the demigod Ilith himself. Most giant men tended to be brutish and uncomely, in Amara's experience, but this one, no. He was as dashing as he was grand.

"Oh, well hello," she said to the pair of them, feigning surprise as though she had completely lost track of her bearings. "I was in another little world there. Aren't these pools just fascinating?" She smiled and walked closer to the two men standing at the bars. "Don't you think?"

"I've no interest in those pools," Sir Talmer said to her. He gave her a hard look, as if to say, '*this isn't going to plan.*'

No, she agreed, but they had no option but to proceed.

"Well, that's sad to hear, Sir Talmer. I find the little ecosystems terribly interesting." She looked up, craning her neck to meet the eyes of the giant. They were a sky blue, very clear. *Goodness, this man is beautiful. Such a shame he has to die.* "How about you, Colossus? Do the rock pools tickle your fancy?"

"No," he thundered, in a voice that shook the air.

She leaned back. "Oh my. You need to be careful with that bass of yours, Colossus. You speak any louder and the entire cavern may collapse."

He stared, saying nothing. Not even the hint of a smile. *This man is not easily charmed.*

She smiled calmly and glanced back the way she had come. No sign of Ben just yet. "Those two are very sensitive about their skills at liar's dice," she said. "Is it played among all of the men here?"

"Most," Sir Talmer told her. "Not much else to do, half the time." It was part of the reason behind his desire to leave, she knew, the boredom of life on these isles. *And there's some honour in him as well, rusted and old, yes, and in need of a good polish, but it's there.* Sir Talmer wanted to lend his blade to the war effort, such as it was, the same as the other men they'd recruited. All were sick to the back teeth of serving the Lord of Lard.

"No battles?" Amara asked, pretending as if she didn't know. She did, of course. She had spoken to Sir Talmer and Sir Ryger and Sir Hockney and Brazen Ben and a host of others about their experiences here. Why they'd come, how long ago, what they'd been doing in the months and years and, in some cases, decades since. Though there were occasional uprisings from one local pirate lord or another, testing the Great One's rule, there had not been any significant conflict here in long years. *These men have been reduced to snaring passing ships for their tolls.* To a knight, even a disgraced one, that was an execrable existence. It was no wonder so many of them had opted to join her.

"Not for a while," Sir Talmer answered, playing along with her. He seemed to sense that she was trying to buy some time. "'Tis a rare day we draw our blades, my lady."

"It must be dull," she said, looking up. "Don't you find it dull, Colossus? Living here?" He was one of the few she hadn't spoken to much. Or at all. The man was half a mute, and rarely did he say a word. All she knew about him was that he came here with his brother, who had subsequently drowned when he fell from a longship during stormy weather. Apparently that brother had sworn the Great One his sword, and Colossus, loyal as he was, wanted to honour that. If it wasn't for that fact, she might ask that he join them right now. But alas no. *Best you join your brother instead.*

"I do not think in those terms," the giant rumbled. "I just do my duty."

Duty to a sack of suet. She glanced back again. This time she sighted the gangly figure of Brazen Ben lolloping toward the willow tree. Both Squidge and Palmer had spotted him as well. They stood up from the rocks they'd been sitting on, turning to him confrontationally, facing away from the armoury. A few shouts rang out from them, curses echoing. Both men were waving at Ben angrily.

"I wonder what that could be about?" Amara said, all innocence.

"Sellswords like to argue," growled Sir Talmer Hedgeside. "Those three especially. Been bickering for years."

Further off, Sir Penrose and Jovyn were wandering along the shore, stopping occasionally to pick up a choice pebble and skim it along the water, as they had been before.

"Those are your men," she heard Colossus say. His eyes were glaring at them. "They aren't meant to be on this side of the island."

"They're doing no harm," Amara said to that. "Goodness, all these rules."

"The Great One's rules." The giant sellsword's block-of-stone jaw clenched. *That bite could snap godsteel, I'd wager.* "You shouldn't be this close either. You are not meant to come near the armoury."

"Me?" Amara put a hand to her chest.

"Yes, you." The cliff of man looked down at her. "Why are you here?"

She glanced at Sir Talmer, saw him flexing his sword hand, moving it to the hilt of his blade.

The giant did not miss it. "What was that?" he rumbled.

Amara frowned up at him, puzzled. "What was what?"

"That look you gave him." The giant turned upon Sir Talmer, casting him in his shadow. "What did she say to you?"

"Nothing. Stand down, Colossus. You're always on edge."

The giant reached a hand behind his back, gripping the handle of his greatsword, though didn't draw it. He looked between Sir Talmer and Amara, sensing some collusion. *This isn't going well.* "What are you doing here, I asked you."

Her frown became aggrieved. "I came to look at the rock pools. What harm am I doing? You don't need to be so aggressive."

"No," Sir Talmer agreed. "Remember who you're talking to, Colossus. The lady deserves more courtesy than that. She is the good sister of a king."

The giant ignored him. "There are some rock pools up beyond the village, on the other side of the cavern. Go to them if you're interested."

"I've seen them a hundred times," Amara came back. "The ones here are better, and bigger besides. And the fauna is more interesting."

"I don't care. You can't be here."

There was more arguing up the beach. Brazen Ben stood facing the other two, who stood aggressively in front of him, gesticulating. Amara's eyes flicked across to Sir Talmer once again, hoping the giant would miss that one. She gave a nod, saw Sir Talmer grip his sword hilt, readying to draw his blade and strike.

She raised her eyes again, to the giant. He was looking down at them. *Oh,* she thought.

"I…" she started.

"Save it," he said.

Then a hundred things seemed to happen at once.

Colossus pulled his greatsword from his back, Sir Talmer ripped his broadsword from its sheath, and the latter thrust forward, driving his blade into Colossus's flank. The tip bit through the links of godsteel mail, the leathers beneath, and flesh. The giant gave out a choked howl of pain, but the sword had only made it two inches deep. Sir Talmer pulled back, swinging and slashing, hacking at the giant in a frenzy.

Amara stumbled away in alarm and turned to look up the beach. Squidge and Palmer had heard the commotion, and turned around, leaving Brazen Ben no choice but to act. Amara saw the man pull his blade, and swing, cutting through the nape of Palmer's neck, who fell forward, grasping out with his hands, blood spurting up from the back of his head. His temple smashed sickeningly against the rocks as he fell. Squidge spun at seeing, it, reaching to draw his blade, but Brazen Ben was too quick. He slashed in a sidecut, hacking off Squidge's sword arm, then followed up with a lunge through the chest and into the heart. Squidge never made a sound as he collapsed bonelessly to the ground. Then Ben was running, waving for the others to follow, and Sir Penrose and Jovyn were running too.

Amara's eyes flew back to Sir Talmer. The old knight was in Block-form, fending left and right as Colossus bore down upon him, swinging that mighty greatsword. Talmer was a skilled swordsman, though, keeping the giant off balance with his movement. Away through the trees, some shouts were ringing out. Amara looked that way and saw Sir Hockney Barrow, another of their allies, bursting out of the foliage to join them as planned, dressed in oddments of amour and bearing a longsword in his grasp. He was a large man, Hockney, and came rushing in, swinging his blade in a two-hand grip, slashing at the giant from behind. Colossus roared, his coat of mail taking the brunt of it. As soon as he turned, Sir Talmer was on him, stabbing at his back, and a moment later Brazen Ben was there as well, the three men surrounding him like wolves about a bear.

"My lady, stand back, you're too close…stand back!" That came from Sir Penrose, who came rushing up behind her, grabbed her arm and pulled her away. He had a godsteel blade in his grasp, taking it from the corpse of Squidge or Palmer, she guessed, and rushed in to use it, adding another sword to the fray. As that was happening, Jovyn was at the bars, cutting at the chains to release the door. He pulled the gate open and rushed inside, searching for their armour and weapons.

Colossus was bellowing like a broadback, turning, twisting, swinging wildly with his enormous blade. The sound of his voice echoed loudly through the cavern. *Damn it, everyone will be hearing this.* "Just finish him off," Amara shouted. "For goodness sake, it's four on one!"

Sir Penrose Brightwood obliged her. As Colossus swung at Brazen Ben, the gangly sellsword dashed back, and Brightwood came in behind. With a strong leap, he jumped up and swung down, hacking at the back of the giant's head and splitting his skull wide open, right down to the neck. Blood and bits of brain burst forth, spraying everywhere, as the giant quivered and slumped forward, landing with a heavy thump. All that was left was his last brutal roar, echoing across the cave.

Sir Talmer came up to her, panting, yet unharmed. "That wasn't meant to happen. We made far too much noise."

There was no time for regrets now. "Get the arms and armour," Amara said.

The men went to work, rushing in and out of the armoury, returning with breastplates, faulds, gorgets, gauntlets and helms, blades and sheathes and swordbelts. Amara could hear the ring of steel through the trees as they worked, feel the pumping of her heart as it hammered against her ribs.

Sir Talmer and Sir Hockney helped Penrose and Jovyn put on their armour, as Brazen Ben watched the trees. "Men coming," he warned. "We got about thirty seconds before they get here."

Amara looked over, saw the shadows approaching, lit by the lanterns in the branches. There was a lot of fighting back there, she sensed. Aside from her men here, she had a further dozen out there. Sir Ryger was one, Sir Mondant another, and Captain had recruited several others as well. One was a knight from Rasalan, Sir Montague Shaw, who'd served briefly with the Suncoats in another life, before suffering an injury. When he recovered the order had expelled him, claiming he was not up to their standards anymore. That bitterness had eventually brought him here. There were eight further sailor-soldiers with their sea-creature halfhelms and sealskin cloaks who Captain had brought on board.

And Connor, Amara thought. He would be in there too, fighting with the blade Sir Ryger Joyce would have given him. But without armour, he would be vulnerable. "Quickly!" Amara shouted. "Hurry up! We don't have all night!"

Sir Penrose had his breastplate fixed, gauntlets too, and was fastening his swordbelt as Sir Talmer clicked his gorget into place. Once that was done, he picked up a shirt of godsteel mail, as well as a swordbelt with fixed sheath and dagger, and rushed over to her. "Take these, my lady. For protection."

She didn't much like the idea of wearing a shirt of mail, but supposed it was worth the precaution. "Fine." She'd never worn such garb before. "Help me get it on, Pen."

He did so, pulling it down her head and arms and torso, the heavy links settling uncomfortably on her shoulders, then girded her waist with the belt. It pulled at one side, where the weight of the godsteel dagger was attached. Ahead, some dozen or so men were emerging from the trees, pulling blades as they rushed down to the beach. Two were Bladeborn by the mists that came with them, the rest common men. Sir Talmer stepped out, shoving Brazen Ben aside. "You needn't die," he called out to them as they ran. "None of you. Lay down your arms and you'll be spared."

The men at the front didn't heed him. The men at the back didn't hear. Sir Talmer gave a grunt, and paced forward, in the confident stride of an experienced Bladeborn knight. Brazen Ben loped out beside him.

"Pen, we need to get to Carly," Amara said. She could not remain here at the beach. She looked over. Sir Hockney was still fitting Jovyn's armour, struggling with clumsy fingers. *That'll be long years of inactivity*, she thought. *He's a blade that's turned blunt, that man.* "Jovyn, stay here," Amara called to the squire. "Hold the beach."

The youth frowned. "But..."

"No buts. Hold the beach."

She trusted the youth to do just that. He was to be a Varin Knight, a level beyond the rest of these men. Even at the tender age of fifteen she suspected he was a superior swordsman to most others on this island.

She dashed off with Sir Penrose Brightwood, rushing away as battle rang out across the strand. The godsteel mail made movement difficult for her, yet such was the strength of her Bladeborn blood that the weight would soon reduce. They passed into the woods, hurrying along a decked path, the planks rattling underfoot. Shouts rang out, and the ring of steel. The chaos was spreading like wildfire.

She guided Sir Penrose along, passing skirmishes along the way. Evidently some of the soldiers had decided to join the revolt, even using it as an excuse to settle scores with other men they did not like. Elsewhere they had already yielded, throwing down their arms, dropping to their knees. In a clearing, Amara glimpsed Sir Ryger engaged in battle with a foe, another of the Seal King's Bladeborn thralls. The fighting looked fierce, a fine knightly duel, misting steel connecting, clanging, bursting in puffs of silver smoke.

They rushed past, making hard for the corridor of trees that led to the Lard Lord's palace. Amara's thighs were aflame, her lungs burning. They turned a corner, reaching the trees, running beneath the branches. Outside the door of hanging vines, several men lay dead. One was Sir Mordant, she saw at once, his neck opened up to the bone, face twisted into an eternal rictus of pain. Another Amara recognised as one of the two burly champions who watched the Seal King's door. He was slumped forward on his knees, cradling his intestines, his belly opened up beneath his breastplate. Sir Penrose stepped forward, shoved him aside with his foot, and a nest of pink snakes slithered to the floor, steaming and stinking.

There was shouting beyond, a high-pitched screaming, the puff of men in combat, steel kissing steel. Sir Penrose swept the vines aside and rushed in. Amara followed. The earthy interior of the Seal King's palace came into view. The feasting table was overturned, plates of food and jugs of wine splashed and smashed all over the floor. About it, Sir Connor Crawfield and Carly Flame Mane were in battle with the Seal King's second guard. Connor, upright, stance wide, striking forth in clean form; Carly leaping and slashing, using her agility. There was blood all over the girl, sprayed across her face, covering her hands, further reddening her fiery hair. Sir Connor looked to have taken a wound to his left shoulder, the flesh hewn open, but it was shallow.

There was screaming in the corner of the room, a maidservant cowering away, shaking all over, urine running down the inside of her leg. Another girl was dead, lying in a pool of spreading blood, caught by an errant blade most likely. The top of her head had been sliced clean off.

Amara raised her eyes to the rear, beyond the Great One's massive oaken throne. A trail of blood led through another door of vines. There was a sound of choked whimpering back there.

"Pen, help them."

She left the knight to help finish off their foe, stepping around the overturned table, up past the stage and oaken throne, through the hanging vines. The Seal King's bedchamber was beyond, a large room, furnished with rugs, with candles burning in little alcoves along the walls and a hundred little lanterns dangling from the ceiling on vines, all at different heights, flickering in the darkness like fireflies.

The Great One lay on his enormous bed, undressed but for a sail-sized breechclout that wrapped about his immense girth. There was blood everywhere, his skin turned grey to red. A dozen stab wounds had disabled him, each shallow, cutting at his blubber. There was blood spray on the walls and the floor, gouts spattered across the room like stars in a night sky. His body was grotesque, mountainous, flesh flowing over the sides of the bed frame. A plaintive bleating sound was bubbling off his lips, eyes running with tears.

"It didn't have to be this way," Amara said, from the doorway.

He saw her, eyes widening. His cheeks and chins were quivering, blood bubbling about the corners of his blowhole of a mouth. "The girl…she…she stabbed me. She said…she said…"

"That she would lay with you if you let her leave? Yes, I know." Amara continued into the room. "Did anything happen? Did you touch her?"

"I never…we never got that far. I was only…we were only talking and then…then she reached down and…" He coughed, his entire body rippling with a great wave of bloodied blubber. Amara had seen whale hunts before, watched the great ocean beasts hauled onto shore, harpoons sticking out of their flesh, great swells of blood and oil pulsing and pouring down their hides. She was reminded of them now. "I never saw the…the knife until…" He shuddered, convulsing, and turned his head, spewing vomit across his shoulder.

Amara watched, disgusted. Yet there was a part of her that pitied him too. She had not forgotten what he'd told her of cruelty. *This man has lost a lot. A son, a daughter, he watched his mother raped and murdered, his father slain by a rival.* He had admitted his faults and follies to her, but it wasn't enough to save him. "You should have let us leave," she told him. "You would have spared yourself a deal of pain. And your men as well. Listen."

The sound of battle was still ringing out across the island, echoing between the great rock walls of the cavern. Another shudder and blubbery ripple. The Great One wretched again. "I never…I was only trying to…"

"Protect them? Or yourself?"

"Both," he admitted, coughing the word out. "Both, of course both. I am a glutton, my lady, I…admit it freely. A glutton and a pig and a cruel one too. But my children…my *children*…" His face screwed up in pain, features squashing together to hide his eyes. "I had to think of them, my lady. If I had opened these islands, we'd have been swamped and overwhelmed. When a ship goes down, most men go down with it. There are only so many…so many who can fit on a raft…"

She understood the analogy, but it wasn't going to save him. "I would consider letting you live if I trusted you," she said. "I don't. And I have made promises." She drew her knife and stepped closer.

He heaved, trying to shift his great bulk off the bed, waving a flipper for purchase. Blood bubbled up out of his wounds, scarring his belly and chest, shoulders, and arms, seeping through the slashes and cuts. He screamed out for help, tears streaming from his tiny little eyes. "Please, my lady…please, you don't need to do this. I'll serve you…I will. I'll be yours to command, your loyal servant…*please, please*…"

"It's too late for all that." She slashed at his throat, the godsteel dagger slicing through the meat and muscle. The flesh of his neck parted, opening out as the blood came gushing forth. He slapped a flipper down to stem the flow, beady eyes bulging, but it would make no difference. It was instinctive, Vesryn had once told her. Everyone did it. *Even seals, it would seem.*

She left him there to choke and die, stepping back out of the bedchamber to find that the Great One's second champion was dead. Sir Connor stood above him, valiant and victorious, pulling his blade from the man's chest. Beyond the palace, sounds of battle could still be heard, though more distantly now. "Go," Amara said at once. "I want this battle done as soon as possible."

They all made for the door, Sir Connor and Sir Penrose leading, Carly remaining at Amara's side. "You finished him off?" the girl asked, blood dripping down her face.

Amara nodded. "Cut this throat." They moved out through the hanging vines, past the bodies on the ground.

"What happened to Mondant?" Carly asked, seeing him there.

"Other Bladeborn guard got him," said Sir Connor Crawfield. "I got him back in return."

The worst of the fighting was down at the beach, as Sir Ryger Joyce had foretold, men clashing with sword and axe and spear by the light of the bioluminescent moss, glowing on the cavern ceiling. At the mouth of the cave, moonlight poured in from outside, reflecting off the water, and there Amara saw several longships and smaller fishing boats skimming out toward the river. *Fleeing*, she thought. She didn't blame them, with all this bloodshed. She left the others to add their blades to the fray - all but Sir Penrose, who remained on guard at her side - and marched straight down to where Captain stood at his boat, observing the action. His oarsmen were with him, though their numbers seemed to have swelled dramatically since last Amara saw.

"You have new friends," she said.

"I'm a popular man, always was." He grinned.

Amara recognised many of the new faces from the village. Some were men, young and old, oarsmen who she'd seen coming and going from the island. Others were fishermen, shark-killers and seal-hunters. There were some women too, sail-stitchers and net-makers, and some of them had children with them, even babes still on the breast.

"What are they all doing here?" Amara asked. "Do they want to leave?"

"After all this? Aye. Some of them are old enough to remember the old wars out here, back when the Great One won his throne. They call it the War of the Lakeland Lords. Was a bloody business, so I'm told, though before my time. They fear a repeat, now that the Great One's dead." He paused, peering at her. "He *is* dead, isn't he?"

She nodded. "He's eaten his last herring, shall we say."

Captain laughed. "The fish o' the lake will sleep easy tonight."

"So they expect the other pirate lords will make a claim for this sanctuary?"

"Aye. That's the fear, same as last time. Soon as word of all this gets out, all them bloody pirates will be at each other's throats. The Great One kept things stable, in a way. And there are some nasty men out there, m'lady. This lot here would rather take their chances somewhere else."

That was a headache Amara could do without. "There will be no civil war for control of these islands," she said. "I plan to send soldiers here to take control, but in the meantime, I hoped to put the seneschal in charge. You are quite aware of that, Captain. We have spoken of it already."

"*We* have, aye, but not these." He thumbed over his shoulder at the villagers. "They got no idea any of this would happen tonight, and are flocking to the new power, m'lady, as all serfs tend to do. That's you."

"No. I'm not staying. The new power will be the seneschal who will take temporary charge." That was assuming he hadn't already escaped. "I hope you didn't see him fleeing on some boat, Captain?"

"I saw him *try*," the Seaborn said.

"Try? What do you mean?"

"I mean he tried to scramble onto one o' those longships, but Sir Montague managed to stop him before he could. Got him penned up in the butchering hut as we speak. That seneschal's always been a little squeamish o' blood, m'lady, so Monty thought it would be a good idea to keep him there, while he awaits you."

That made Amara want to let him squirm a little longer, but she had a pressing urge to get all this business done. "I'll go and talk to him now. Make sure you impress upon these people that they will be safer staying here. Tell them help will come, and they will be protected. But if they leave, they are on their own. I cannot offer them my protection."

"Aye, m'lady, I'll tell 'em."

She walked in the direction of the butcher's hut, Sir Penrose at her side. "How's it going out there, Pen?" she asked, knowing the knight would be keeping watch.

"It's calming, my lady. I suspect it will be over soon."

"Can you see Jovyn?"

"I can. He is with Ben and Sir Talmer. There is no sign of Sir Hockney. He may have been killed at the armoury."

"Find out for me while I'm speaking with the seneschal. And lend your blade to finishing things off. Sir Montague will keep watch."

They were soon at the butchering hut, where the former Suncoat stood defending the door. "My lady. I have the seneschal."

"I heard. Thank you, Sir Montague." The man was far too well-mannered and courtly to be in a place like this, serving that disgusting whale. There were many men like that here, Amara had come to see. Disillusionment had brought them here, and shame had kept them from leaving. But Amara Daecar was giving them a way out. And for that she had their loyalty. "I take it he is unarmed?"

"Unarmed, yes. Un*harmed*, no." A smile graced the lips of Sir Montague Shaw. "He had a little dagger tucked up his right arm sleeve, and another on his leg. I took them both off him…with a little force, I confess." He paused, glancing at the door behind him. "He claims he helped in the venture tonight, my lady. That he was himself a part of the plot." A frown formed on his brow. "Is that true?"

"No. It is a bare-faced lie. I will get to the bottom of this, Sir Montague."

"I am sure you will, Lady Daecar." Sir Montague Shaw opened the door for her to pass, and she stepped inside. The door was left ajar behind her.

The interior was dim, the smell unpleasant. Dim torches burned on the plank wood walls to either side of a large, bloody table, scarred with cuts from the butcher's blade and lacquered in long years of fish guts and gore. At the far end, hooks hung down from the ceiling on lengths of chain, swaying ominously. One bore a small shark, another a large seal, which Amara supposed was fitting. There were buckets filled with entrails and old mops propped up against one wall. Pails of chum for the shark-catchers sat near the door. Amara looked at those and smiled. "You'd make good chum, don't you think, seneschal?"

The slimy little man was standing in one corner, half in shadow, a bruise already ripening on his cheek and about his left eye. There appeared to be some rips and tears on his clothing, though with that absurd, leafy garb he wore, it wasn't so easy to tell. "I would…rather not find out," he said, trying to raise that unctuous little smile of his. His eyes were hooded, shoulders tight. "You don't mean to…"

"Kill you?"

He swallowed. "I have only ever been a servant, my lady. I follow who I must, to survive."

"And you will follow me now? Is that what you're trying to say?"

He nodded nervously. "I have been doing so for some time, my lady. I…I tried to tell Sir Montague, but he wouldn't believe me. I have been helping you, whether you know it or not."

She peered at him, curious. "How have you been helping me, pray tell?"

"The…the schedule, my lady. I set it…so that you would have your own allies posted at the…"

"Don't lie to me, seneschal."

"I am *not* lying, my lady. I tell you true, I set the schedule tonight to aid you. I had heard…whisperings of your plans. For days I have come to suspect something would happen, and for days I said nothing to the

Great One. I allied myself to your cause…from the shadows, if you will. I had to protect myself as well, in case…"

"In case it all went wrong."

"Yes, my lady."

"Then how do you explain Colossus?"

He shook his head at once. "That was not my doing. Wilcock fell ill at the last moment, and Colossus took his place without my knowledge. You must see, my lady. Everything was perfectly laid out for you tonight. You cannot think that to be a coincidence, or mere chance."

"Do not tell me what I can and cannot think."

He quelled, nodding fearfully, but perhaps there was some truth to what he was saying. She puzzled on that for a moment, though in the end it did not matter. They had won the day regardless, and whether the seneschal was lying or not did not make a blind bit of difference. It was only his trust she needed now.

"The Great One is dead," she said, putting the matter aside. "His loyalists have been slain, and the rest will bend the knee. I am told that several longships managed to get away. No doubt some of the occupants of these ships will flee to other islands, and when the pirate lords discover that the Blubber King has fondled his last serving maid they will seek to take advantage. You know these men, seneschal. You know these so-called Lords of the Lake. You say you wish to serve me? Well, I will give you that chance."

He tried not to look too elated. "I…yes, of course. Whatever you need, Lady Daecar."

"My need is simple. Parley with these pirates. Tell them they will not come to harm for former crimes should they submit to the rule of the crown. Inform them that the king's soldiers will come here to take control of these islands. That they will be opened for the sanctuary of refugees. If these pirate lords welcome such terms, they will be allowed to keep their wealth, and some measure of influence here as well. If not, they will be killed." She took a pause, to make sure he understood. "What say you, seneschal?"

"I say…I say I am your humble servant, my lady. I say I am yours to command." He crept from the pool of shadow in which he'd been cowering and went down to his knees before her. She gave him the back of her hand to kiss. Then he rose, lank hair bobbing on his shoulders. "I will see it done."

"Good." She turned to leave.

He went to follow.

"No," she said, spinning back to face him. "You'll stay here for the time being, seneschal. To think things over."

"I…my lady, I don't need to think things over. I am your servant, your humble servant…"

Who deserves to squirm a little longer, she thought, stepping out through the door. "Bar it shut," she told Sir Montague. "If he makes a squeak of complaint, toss a bucket of fish guts over him. That ought to keep him quiet."

The man smiled. "Gladly, my lady."

The fighting was wilting like a weed in winter, done or thereabouts. Amara paced back along the beach until she reached the captain. "Did you tell them what I asked?"

"Aye. Will the seneschal yield?"

"Aye," she said, mimicking him.

He grinned. "Well, that's that then. Seems the lake's turning a bit rough out there, m'lady, so be best to store the oars for the night. We can leave on the morrow, when *Matmalia's* in a better mood."

Matmalia was the Rasal goddess of waves, Amara recalled. "Tomorrow is fine," she said. "Though the word 'if' is not one of my favourites, Captain. I thought you said the weather was set fair tonight?"

"Aye, I thought it would be. But the gods are capricious, aren't they? Never quite know what they're going to do."

"I suppose not. Though their cruelty is oft something one can count on." She heard a voice hailing her, and saw Sir Connor striding over. He had not yet had time to dress in his armour, though had taken no further wounds. *Thank goodness.* Her gloomy household knight had been her rock for a long time now.

He went to a knee. "My lady, the battle is done. All enemy loyalists have been defeated. The rest have thrown down their arms, and are willing to submit to your rule. Shall I gather them to swear you their oaths?"

That seemed like a pointless exercise. Most men would swear an oath one day, only to break it the next. "That won't be necessary, Sir Connor. Tell me. How fare our men? And stand, please. You're embarrassing me."

He did so. Then he said, "Sir Hockney has taken a wound to his thigh, but it does not seem serious. Sir Penrose, Carly, Jovyn are all well, as is Sir Talmer and Ben Barrett. Sir Ryger has taken command of the palace, my lady, the larders at the rear, and the way down into the underground. We should have some warning if anyone comes up from that way. And there are some others who wish to join us when we leave. They are prepared to swear you their swords."

Amara nodded. She would have time for that later. But first… "His larders, did you say?"

"Yes, my lady. They are plentiful, as you can imagine."

She did not need to imagine, having watched the Blubber King stuffing his face for weeks on end. "What happens after a battle, Sir Connor?" she asked the knight.

He cocked a brow. "Well, typically the dead are gathered and counted, funerals pyres built, graves dug, rites spoken, wounds sewn…"

That wasn't what she was getting at. "A feast, Sir Connor. After battle comes the feast." She smiled, looking at the captain, who smiled back, and the scores of men and women and children huddled about the shore. *His children,* she thought. *And the lot of them, half-starved.*

She turned back to Sir Connor Crawfield. "Tonight we feast," she said.

29

Elyon

"It will be secure here?" Elyon asked. He needed to be absolutely certain. "No one but you and I will know where it is?"

"It will remain between you and I, Prince Elyon. You have my word."

"Swear it by godsteel, my lord. I will have your oath." A part of him hated these oaths now, after that one Amilia had forced him to make, but men of honour tended to stand by them, and Lord Morwood had proven himself such a man.

"As you wish," the jowly watch commander said. He gripped the leather handle of his godsteel blade and spoke words that Elyon deemed appropriate. Then he looked at him. "Will that serve?"

"It will have to." Elyon sighed, hating this. He hated much and more these days, his damnable injury foremost among them. "Lock it up, then. But if you breathe a word of this to anyone…"

"I will curse myself to a wretched afterlife. I know the punishments for breaking a godsteel oath, good prince." He opened the chest in his chambers, an unspectacular trunk of hard ironwood, banded in lengths of old dull steel and hidden in the depths of a cupboard. "Please. Lay it here."

Elyon grimaced as he drew the Windblade from its sheath, the mists swirling and twisting uncomfortably, as though knowing it was going to be abandoned. He could hear the harsh whispers in the back of his mind, hissing their cautions and concerns. He hesitated a moment, his shoulder throbbing. After a while Morwood gave a cough.

"My lord. I think it would behove me to remind you that you did warn me you might equivocate. And that I should be firm on you when you did, and urge you to leave it here, rather than take it with you. It will be safe, you have my word. It will be waiting for you when you return."

Elyon nodded reluctantly. "Fine. I'll…I'll leave it here." He took a deep breath and placed the Windblade in the trunk before he could second-guess himself. He took a step away, wrenching against some hidden force. "Shut the chest, my lord. And do it quickly."

Morwood saw to it, shutting it, locking it. Then he stepped back and closed the cupboard door, locking that as well. Elyon was staring at the door like an addict, his obsession locked beyond two inches of solid wood. *This is good,* he tried to tell himself. *Some time away from it can only be a good thing, even if it's only hours.* He knew that was the case but it didn't make it any easier. With a great effort, he spun on his heels and marched away out of the room, Lord Morwood trailing behind him.

The corridor outside was empty. At Elyon's request, no guards had accompanied them, to better preserve his secret. He didn't trust the soldiers here. Not after all that boorish booing in the arena. He looked left and right all the same, squinting and doubtful. A hand clutched his godsteel dagger, listening for footsteps, for the sound of breathing, for spies hidden in the walls.

Morwood stepped out behind him. "Breath easy, good prince. No one knows it's here." He smiled an avuncular smile. "Now come. They'll be waiting."

It took them ten minutes to cross the palace and reach the entrance to the tunnels. The route took them along long dusty corridors and down old creaking stairs and through hidden doors in the stone walls that Elyon would never have known were there. The rest of the journey would be more taxing, he knew. A large part of him was dreading it.

The princess and her pretty blond bedwarmer were awaiting them at the gate. Elyon gave Amilia a stiff bow and Mallister Monsort a narrow glare. That only made the princess chuckle. "Oh, you two… you are funny." She gave a titter and planted a kiss on Mallister's cheek, much to Morwood's disapproval, Elyon didn't fail to note. "Now play nice, both of you. If I find that one of you has thrown the other down some chasm, I will not be best pleased, do you hear me? You're two of my favourite people and I demand you get along."

She had a chalice in her grasp, a fine golden thing with emeralds clasped in tiny brackets. "Isn't it a little early to be drinking, Amilia?" Elyon said.

"Bah." She waved a hand at him. "When the doom approaches, one must make the most of the time they have left." She had a long sip and smacked her lips, looking a little drunk already. "How do you like my chalice, Elyon? It is my favourite one. My *lucky* cup. I killed Lord Gershan with it, did you know?"

A line creased his brow. He had heard of the passing of the Master of the Moorlands, but assumed it to have been due to some other cause, old as he was. "I wasn't aware that was your doing."

She shrugged. "I threw this in his ugly old face and he fell and cracked his head on the floor. My grandfather died in a similar way, you know."

"I remember." Lord Modrik Kastor had cracked his head open on the hearth after slipping in a puddle of his own piss. "Careful you don't go the same way, Amilia. The way you're headed…"

"Guard your tongue, Elyon. You can't speak to her like that."

"I can speak to her however I damn well wish, Monsort."

"Oh boys, boys…" Amilia chuckled and moved between them. "I thought we were past all this?"

"We are," Elyon said, stiffly. They had spoken a couple of times since their bout, to try to clear the air, but ever the shadow of animosity lingered. Mallister still harboured resentment for Melany's death, and Elyon's taunting words about Gold-Tongue and Aleron and Amilia's promiscuity, just as Elyon felt a good deal of chagrin over his injured shoulder, which would never have happened if Monsort hadn't demanded a duel in the first place. Because of his injury, he hadn't been able to fly for over a week, and he had a fearsome bruise where Mallister had struck him in the jaw. By now he might have flown to Thalan, found Prince Sevrin, told him of the Eye, tracked down Jonik and Janilah Lukar, returned to King's Point to update his father and slain Vargo Ven to boot. Instead he had lurked about the palace, brooding, filling his time with drunks and old men. *And it's all his bloody fault.*

Amilia was still snickering, looking between the two men as they glared at one another. "Well, this little trip will be good for you, I think. You'll have plenty of time to talk." She smiled. "Now off you go, no time to waste. I want the both of you back home for supper."

Elyon was in no mood for her japing. "You should be coming with us. *You're* known there. We're not."

Amilia's joy curdled, just like that. "I'm not going back. Not to that place. *Never.*" She sneered at the iron gate, at the dark tunnel beyond. "I told you what they did to me, Elyon. Don't ever ask me to go back there again."

"You may say different one day, Amilia. If Drulgar comes…"

"Then I'll die on my balcony with a smile on my face. I'm not going back. You're starting to sound like your brother."

"My brother's dead," Elyon's voice was like the crack of a whip. "Jonik's no kin of mine."

She drank her wine right down to the dregs and made a bored face at him, like Lillia used to. Then she turned to Sir Mallister, smiled and squeezed his hand. "Take care of him, Mally. He thinks himself so terribly important. The *great dragonslayer*, Elyon Daecar." A titter crawled out of her throat, and with a swish of skirts, she was gone.

Elyon glowered after her. *I am important*, he thought. There was no one else who could do what he did, and her words were more than galling. "You need to rein her in, Lord Morwood. Her drinking is starting to get out of control."

The watch commander gave a dour nod of the head. "She is… incorrigible. I have spoken to her about it, but…"

"But she doesn't listen," Mallister finished, nodding to say he had challenged her with the same issue. "She's…been through a lot. Perhaps we should cut her some slack?"

"Says the man who warms her bed by night and doesn't want those slender legs to close." Elyon regretted those words as soon as he'd said them. "Sorry. I didn't mean to…"

"No. You're right." Mallister looked away, in the direction the princess had gone. Her scent was still wafting in the air, of pine and lemon, and her beauty seemed to leave behind an afterglow. He had a hopeless look on his face. "I love her. Damn it, I wish I didn't, but I do." His eyes flicked to Elyon. "And I know I'm not good enough for her, before you say anything. I know I'm not Aleron…"

"Mallister…"

"No. What you said to me that morning. You were right. About her and the rest of it. Lingering here…there's no honour in that. I should be out there with you, fighting. Not hiding here with the women and the old men…" He looked at Lord Morwood, suddenly contrite. "Meaning no offence, my lord. You hold a high office, and…"

The commander had a flat look in his eyes. "You do not need to explain, Sir Mallister." His voice was tight. He looked toward the tunnel door. "Do you remember the way?"

"I think so, my lord."

"If you get lost, use the markers. I will be sending men through later to continue building out the route, but right now it's empty. They'll be there when you come back." He looked at Elyon. "Good luck to you. I will be waiting for your return." He gave his keys a knowing rattle, and strode away the way Amilia had left.

The silence that settled was awkward. It seemed to last a lifetime. "So…you ready?" Elyon asked at last.

"No. Let me just go and pamper my cheeks and freshen my breath like a good *bedwarmer*." Sir Mallister's expression was like stone, then a small fracture appeared, and that broke into a crack, and suddenly he was laughing.

Elyon laughed along with him. "You *would* look good in make up, Mallister. It would go so well with your pretty blond hair." He laughed again and slapped him on the shoulder. "Now come on, let's go see about this demigod, shall we?"

"Oh, why not?" And together, off they went.

The route was dark, long, and at times utterly baffling, and no wonder it had taken Lord Morwood's men time to find their way. Now that they had, many sections were being stabilised and secured. The shafts were being covered over, the deep pits cordoned off, and in three separate places plank bridges had been raised over chasms to make the crossings easier. They stopped at one such place, where a bottomless rift cut clear through the heart of a great open cavern, plunging to blackness, at least seven or eight metres wide. There was a bridge there now, spanning the gap, but it had only been recently erected. Mallister pointed to the side of the cave, where a thin ridge of stone ran along the glistening wall. "We had to shimmy along that ridge to cross before," he said. "It's barely a foot wide. Not pleasant, I'll tell you."

"You came through before the bridge was built?"

He nodded. "I've been through twice now, just to learn the way. Each time I do, the men have made it safer." He looked over the edge of the precipice. "Dangerous work, though. I've heard a few have fallen. I just hope it's all worth it."

"It will be," Elyon said. "This refuge…it could house tens of thousands, hundreds even. That's worth a few men, Mallister."

The Emerald Guard nodded; they were of the same mind on this, the same as Morwood and his men, the same as any sane person would be. Through these tunnels, a portal door gave direct access to a sprawling refuge, hidden in the mountains, protected by magical seals, and watched over by a demigod resurrected in the body of his heir, some three and a half thousand years removed. That Amilia didn't want to go back was understandable, given what she'd been through, but that did not mean anyone else should share her bitterness.

They continued toward the bridge, crossing over to the other side. "I notice you're not wearing the Windblade," Mallister said.

"No." Elyon's voice tightened on instinct. "I don't need it in here."

Mallister Monsort knew him better than that. "You're worried he'll take it off you? Ilith? Don't tell me you're becoming *obsessed*, Elyon." He smirked.

"I'm not," Elyon said, too quickly, in a way that screamed the opposite. "It's just…I still need it, that's all. I've got lots of things I have to do. People are relying on me."

"Ilith would know that," Mallister told him. His face had gone more serious now. "He wouldn't take it away if he thinks you're doing some good."

Elyon shrugged. He didn't want to take that risk. "I'll give it up when I have to," he only said, eager to avoid the conversation. "But it's not time yet." He marched on, holding his torch up to light the way. Neither of them was wearing their armour, nor bearing anything more than small godsteel daggers at their hips, to make the going easier. There were some sections where it paid to dress light, he knew, requiring that you squeeze through tight gaps, though Morwood had said his workers were going to get to those sections soon, chipping away at the rock to open the passages out a bit. Elyon wondered how long that would take. *Best not dally, my lord. If you take too long, Drulgar will return, and there will be no one left to save.*

Mallister caught up with him a minute or so later, carrying a torch of his own. "I'm sorry about your arm, you know. I wasn't intending to injure you."

"No, just kill me. You wanted a death duel, Mallister."

"I was angry."

"And now?"

407

"Still angry," he said. "But…not so much at you. This whole thing with Mel…"

"We don't need to talk about it."

"I want to clear it up."

Elyon shook his head. He had said everything he could ever hope to say on the subject. "You won the duel, Mallister." Let the gods decide, they had said. "If you take that to mean I'm to blame for Mel's death, there's nothing I can do about that."

"I don't think you're to blame. I've thought about it enough now, and…" He paused. "I just want to put it behind us."

"It's behind us," Elyon said. He turned and reached out to take his forearm, and the two men engaged in a brief grip and shake. "Now let that be the end of it. My shoulder is getting stronger, and hopefully I'll be able to fly in the next few days. Properly, I mean. Without falling back to the ground."

It turned out, an injury to Elyon's sword arm was fatal to his ability to fly. He had thought - *hoped* - that he could simply use his left arm instead, but it was like starting all over again. The same as it would be if he were to try to use his left in combat. He would only make a fool of himself, and flying was the same. He needed the correct arm operational in order to soar and the dislocation to his shoulder was taking a while to heal.

They walked most of the rest of the way in silence, through tunnels and stone corridors and wide open caves, passing the occasional plunging drop, squeezing through some tight spaces. Elyon was careful to avoid aggravating his shoulder all the while, picking his way along carefully whenever the floor was uneven to make sure he did not fall. It was all easy enough in the end, though far from pleasant, and not a journey the smallfolk were likely to enjoy. The wind made strange noises here, as it came whistling eerily through the mountain, and sometimes up from the depths, growling as though some monstrous creature was trapped down there, and there was no natural light at all. All they had was their torches, which threw sinister shadows on the walls, and if they should gutter out, well…Elyon didn't want to think about that.

Eventually, they made it to a series of tunnels where in places the walls and ceilings had collapsed. Some of the tumbled stone had been shifted aside, making spaces between them, with scaffolds erected to secure the roof. There was a wooden sign here, hammered into the ground. It had an arrow scrawled onto it, and a single word: *portal*.

That made Elyon Daecar laugh. "I guess the portal's this way."

They saw it but a minute later, a shimmering black void at the end of the passage. It was quite unlike anything Elyon had ever seen. Shaped like a large door, it had no lintel, no frame, and seemed to float, undulating, between the rock to either side, opening to a lightless, soundless space that made the hair on the back of his neck and forearms stand on end. Elyon wasn't going to pretend he liked it. "I don't like it," he said.

Mallister laughed. "It's something, isn't it."

"Something I don't like." Elyon inched backward. "Supper, Amilia said." He made to turn. "We'd best be getting back."

"How about we go through first?" Mallister suggested, with an easy smile. "Who first? You or me?"

"Together?" Elyon offered.

"It's hardly wide enough. Best I go first. If you trip or fall when you're spat out the other side, I'll be there to catch you. You know, so you don't fall on your shoulder."

Elyon appreciated that. "Then I'll see you there."

Mallister took position, drew a deep breath, and stepped forward. He snapped out of existence.

Elyon blinked. "Gods," he said, out loud. The word echoed through the tunnels. It was instantaneous. He took a deep breath, wondering on the wisdom of going second. He would rather not have seen *that*, in truth. But what's done was done. He stepped to the wall, placing his torch in a sconce; Morwood's men had sensibly seen fit to hammer a couple of those onto the walls here too, one either side of the door. With luck they would still be burning by the time they got back.

He stepped to the doorway. "Well. Here goes." And without delay, he paced inside.

There was a jerk, as though some hidden force was tugging him forward, then a sense of floating. In the blackness, he perceived shapes, bodies, and those were floating too, and there was a sound of screaming, no, many different voices screaming, far away at the edge of his hearing, men and women all shrieking at once. But it was a flash, an instant, no more than a heartbeat or two, and suddenly he was stumbling forward into an echoing stone antechamber, with polished walls and high ceilings, tripping and falling to the floor.

There was a jolt through his weak right shoulder, but his left side had taken the brunt. He grunted and breathed out, pushing up with his left arm. "Damn it, Monsort! You said you would…" He looked up and cut himself off. Mallister was standing right ahead of him, in the company of a small man in old grey robes, frayed at the hems and sleeves.

"And there he is," came a nightmare of a voice, all full of mocking tones. "The Prince of Vandar, Elyon Daecar."

Elyon stood and brushed himself down. The mage was cowled, his features shadowed, though the end of his long dangly nose was visible, and he caught glimpses of the rot behind the hood, the haunting visage he'd heard tell of. "You must be Fhanrir," he said.

The creature cackled. "My reputation precedes me. Now who told you about me, I wonder? Your brother, was it? Or the betrothed of the *other* brother that he killed?"

Elyon understood at once why Amilia hated this mage. "The princess spoke of you. I have not seen Jonik since…"

"Since he killed your other brother."

"Yes." Elyon was already on edge, and Mallister seemed less than comfortable in the presence of the warlock as well. A cavernous hall opened out beyond them, and he could see many other chambers and corridors leading off it. Even from here, it was possible to get a sense of the vast scale of this place. "You were expecting us?" Elyon asked.

"No. I just like standing around here all day and night, waiting for *brilliant* men like you to grace us with their presence."

Elyon did not know how to respond.

Fhanrir snorted. "Champion of the Windblade, not *wit*. Suppose that runs in the blood. Jonik was never the sharpest either." He sneered, and Elyon caught sight of mouldy gums and brown dead teeth and purple lips cracked and split. "You *look* like him, though. Bigger, but the resemblance is clear."

Again, Elyon had no response.

"Not very talkative are you? Aye, that's like Jonik too. Dour lad, he was, hardly ever smiled." He looked suddenly up at Mallister Monsort. "How's the princess?"

The Emerald Guard stuttered to answer. "She's…well."

"Well into her latest drink, aye. You send her my regards, will you?"

"I…yes, of course."

Elyon stepped forward. "How did you know we were coming?"

"You knocked," Fhanrir said.

Elyon was stumped. "We never…"

"You *knocked*," Fhanrir repeated. "Call it a magical knocking, and not something you'd ever understand. You don't think Ilith would build a door like this without a knocker, do you? Every door needs a knocker and locks to fasten it. We got both, and I heard you coming. So here I am to greet you."

Elyon made himself bow. "And we are grateful for that, my lord."

Fhanrir only hissed and turned, bones clacking as he shambled away. Elyon and Mallister shared a look. Mallister shrugged, and then Fhanrir rasped, "*Follow*," and they did.

They were led through the refuge, and it was everything Elyon had heard: huge, cavernous, empty, cold. The statues were magnificent, and there was an unmistakable grandeur here, to be sure, but Elyon understood why Amilia misliked it. Shafts of light filtered down from high windows cut into the roof of the mountain, but there were many shadowed corners here that could do with a spot of torchlight. *This place needs a woman's touch*, Elyon thought. *And the sound of laughing children.*

"You should have brought the blade," Fhanrir said, into the silence.

Elyon let a moment pass as he puzzled out how to answer. The creature was so extraordinarily snide, that he thought he might as well fight fire with fire. "I forgot," he said.

That got a chuckle from the creature. "How's your shoulder, boy? Healing, I hope?"

"I'm on the mend," Elyon declared, unsure how he knew about his injured shoulder. Perhaps Mallister had mentioned it before he came through? *Or maybe he saw the way I was holding my arm?* They continued into another high chamber, much the same as the last, with a soaring ceiling and wide high walls and space enough to fit a thousand men, women, and children if required. "How many chambers are there here?" Elyon asked.

"Hundreds," Fhanarir said.

"Are they all as empty as this?" asked Mallister.

"Empty as your head, aye." Fhanrir shuffled on.

He took them deeper into the refuge, mocking and scorning them as they went. After a while, Elyon began to hear the ringing of a hammer, echoing out through the corridors and halls. A smile twitched on his lips, and there was a swell of nerves in his chest. He looked at Mallister and mouthed, '*the Hammer of Tukor,*' and the Emerald Guard nodded back at him, breathing excitedly.

The glow of orange light heralded their arrival at the forge. The thumping of the hammer had grown loud by then, loud enough to rattle his bones and stir dust from the ceiling of the corridor. It was a *godly* sound, like Eldur's voice had been. Fhanrir raised a hand to halt them before they entered, fleshless white fingers poking from his sleeve.

"He's been working night and day. Never stops. *Never.* I don't want you lingering here long, do you hear? In and out. And make it quick." He glared up at them through a pair of small black eyes, glowing in the shadows of his hood, then snorted and moved inside to announce them. "Found these two at the door," he said.

Ilith was at his anvil, hammering out a brand new godsteel blade, a greatsword by the size of it, much the same size as Vallath's Ruin. The demigod wore a leather vest, brown breeches tied up at the knee, the simple garb of a blacksmith. Elyon had to stop and take pause. That yellow hair, all sweat-stained and curly. The lean face and sharp green eyes. Sweat ran down his sinewy arms, glistening in the grooves of the muscles. *He looks just like the statues*, the prince thought. *And the frescoes on the walls of the Steelforge.* He had to remind himself that this was in fact Tyrith, not Ilith, at least in body, but by the gods he looked just like him. He stepped forward, opening his mouth to speak…

…but Mallister Monsort surged right past him, collapsing down to his knees. "My lord! My lord I am here to serve you!" he sang out, in a voice of sudden fervour. Elyon was taken aback. "*Anything*. I will do anything in your name, great Ilith. I will defend you, fight for you, protect you with my life. I…"

Fhanrir snorted and shuffled in to kick the Emerald Guard in the ribs. "Get up, you fool. We don't need that sort of genuflecting around here. You're embarrassing yourself."

Ilith only smiled down at the man. "You may rise, Sir Mallister. And ignore my good friend Fhanrir. He has something of a curt tongue, you may have noticed."

Mallister's blue eyes were bright with wonder. "You…you know my name, my lord?" He stayed on his knees.

"I do. Who else could you be but Mallister of House Monsort?" Ilith smiled again, and bid him rise, then looked over at the Prince of Vandar. "And you must be Elyon Daecar. A famous name of this age, I know. It is said that your family share a strong resemblance to Varin. Now that I see you, I can say that it is true."

His smile was like an old friend, familiar and comforting, and a shine of radiance seemed to fill the air around him. *And that voice…* The histories all said that Ilith had a silvery tongue, and so the case seemed to be. But then, it was *Tyrith's* voice, in truth, just as this body was Tyrith's as well. Elyon blinked, trying to puzzle that out. "Forgive me, my lord, but you…you look just like the art I have seen. The paintings and sculptures and tapestries. I wonder…"

"You wonder if the physical form of Tyrith is changing to reflect Ilith," the demigod said. "Or perhaps you wonder if this is some glamour? Some cloak of illusion I wear?"

Elyon was indeed wondering all of those things.

"Well, in actual fact neither is true. This is Tyrith's body, Tyrith's voice. The likeness is very good, that is the simple truth." He placed the Hammer of Tukor aside with a resounding *clunk*. It was smaller than Elyon would have supposed. More plain. Ilith saw him staring at it. "The painters and sculptors were more inclined to exaggerate the Hammer's size," he said. "But Tukor was never showy. He wrought his Hammer to be a simple thing, from which wonders were born. But never a wonder itself."

Fhanrir gave a snort. "Speaking of wonder, stop with your *gaping*, Monsort. You're like to make him uncomfortable, staring like that."

"No, it really is quite all right," Ilith told the mage. "Sir Mallister is just finding his bearings, isn't that so?"

"I…my bearings. Y-yes, my lord."

Ilith smiled at him. True enough, Mallister seemed rather over-whelmed by the whole experience, and more so than Elyon. Well, small wonder there. Elyon had faced Eldur atop the back of Drulgar the Dread and bore in his grasp a Blade of Vandar. He had grown quite used to these godly interactions.

"So, why is it that you're here?" Ilith asked. "Do you have some-thing particular you wish to discuss with me?"

Why are we here? *Curiosity*, Elyon thought. That was a part of it, at the least. When you hear that there's a magic portal door and a demigod beyond it, it does rather tickle your interest. "We wanted to see the refuge, my lord," he thought better to say. "There are many frightened people in your city, and your kingdom, and across the north as well. We came to check whether you're ready to receive them. And how many you might host."

"Ah, now there is the crux of it. How many? Well, as you can see we do not lack for space. Did Fhanrir give you the tour?" He laughed and waved that away. "Of course he didn't. Fhanrir brought you straight here, I know. He is something of a curmudgeon and is not one to suffer…"

"*Fools*," Fhanrir came in. "I'm not one to suffer *fools*, Ilith."

Ilith chuckled pleasantly. "Everyone is a fool to you, Fhanrir. I remember you as a boy. You were sour-tempered even then."

A boy, Elyon thought. It was hard to imagine. That would be thousands of years ago. *Gods, what must that be like, to live so long? And here?*

Ilith turned to the knights. "You ought not take offence to his discourtesy; truly, it is nothing personal. That is just his way. But the years have only made him harder, I fear, and he has seen more of those than any of us. But what was I saying? The refuge. Yes. You have not been given a tour, but even so, you have a sense of its scale. We could host half the world here if we wished, but space is not the problem. It is food. Mages though we might be, we cannot conjure beef and barley from thin air. We have been working to stockpile what resources we can, but we could use some more help on that account. We are few here, Elyon Daecar. How are the tunnels coming along? I understand they are being reinforced."

"They are passable, my lord, though the journey is not easy. Lord Morwood is securing the route, and gathering up food and supplies. He has many men working for him."

"And why has this lord not come himself?"

Fear, Elyon thought. No one had come yet since Amilia and Jonik had left. "He wanted me to have that honour first," he lied. "I will report to him on my return. He will visit you soon."

"Wonderful," muttered Fhanrir. "More of you fools to deal with."

Elyon ignored him. That seemed to be the best way with Fhanrir. "Instructions will be given to anyone coming here to bring as much food with them as they can carry," the prince said. "We have had word of travellers on the road. Refugees from the south, coming up from Vandar in great numbers. My own kinsmen are sending carts and wagons laden with onions, turnips, carrots, potatoes, sacks of wheat and barley and other grains. Casks of cured meat and pickled fish and…"

"And we don't need an inventory," Fhanrir snapped. "They're bringing food. We get it."

"Security is another issue," Elyon went right on. "You say you have men here, my lord? How many?"

"Not enough," Fhanrir answered. "Agnar, Dagnyr, Vottur. Those are mages. We have some men as well, bringing supplies up the mountain." He thought a moment. "A dozen, maybe."

413

Elyon was shocked; the mage had answered without spite for once. He knew those names as well, of the mages, having heard them from Amilia. Vottur was Fhanrir's great-grandson, if he remembered correctly. "Lord Morwood commands hundreds," he said. "He is Commander of the City Watch and there are thousands of soldiers in the city as well. I'm sure some of them can be spared."

"And what about you, Sir Mallister?" Ilith asked, looking at the young Emerald Guard. "You wish to serve, you say. Perhaps you can help us usher the people here?"

Mallister swallowed. "Um…yes, my lord. What…whatever you need of me." He bowed his head low.

Ilith saw right through him. "You would prefer to serve with the blade," he said. "Please, Mallister, do speak plainly."

The Emerald Guard looked terribly awkward. "Well I…I am no steward, my lord. I am born and bred to fight, and I would sooner…I would prefer to…"

"Serve by killing," Fhanrir came in roughly. "That's how you'd like to serve your lord and master? By taking life?"

"I…" Mallister seemed unable to respond. Everything the creature said was so hot with scorn. "What…whatever you need, Lord Ilith. If you require something else of me, then…"

"A man must serve in whatever function best suits him, Mallister Monsort. As a man born and bred to fight, then fighting it must be, but fighting takes many forms. You want to seek battle in the south, but there is a battle to be had here as well. We need more swords and shields. Security, yes, as Elyon says, to keep the peace, but it's more than that. There are dark forces in these mountains, and they are trying to find their way in."

"Then your shield I will be," Mallister said, in a stirring voice. He fell to a knee once more. In lieu of his godsteel broadsword, he withdrew his dagger, and placed it on the floor. It shone in the light of the forge, misting. "My…sword is yours, Lord Ilith," he proclaimed. "I swear to you my oath and service until my dying day."

"And I gladly accept it, Mallister Monsort. We will all feel safer here with you to help protect us."

But from what? Elyon wondered what sort of dark forces he meant. Beasts? Monsters? Something worse? The brood of *Brexatron*, perhaps? Was one of them lurking here? He was about to inquire of that when Ilith said, "It is a shame, Elyon, that you did not bring the Windblade with you. I should have liked to have seen it again, after all these years. Did you forget it, pray tell?"

Forget. That was the lie he gave to Fhanrir. Did Ilith know of that? *Can he read my thoughts?* "No, my lord," he said. Lie though he could to the mean little mage, he would not do so with the Forgeborn King. "I left it behind on purpose," he admitted.

"Oh? And why is that, Elyon? Do you believe I would have taken it from you?"

Yes, he thought. "No," he said.

"No?" Fhanrir rasped, snorting at him. "*He* made it, *boy*. Ilith, with his magic. Dark magic too, that was, like nothing you'd ever believe. How else do you shatter the heart of a god? He'll take it back if he pleases, and you'll have no say in the matter."

Elyon disagreed. "I still have things I must do with it. I am its guardian, and will bring it here when…"

"Guardian?" Fhanrir scoffed. "Thief, more like."

Elyon would not hear of it. "I never stole the blade. I took it back from one who did, and will bring it here when I must."

"*Must?* No, *boy*. You'll bring it here when you're *told*. Ilith tells you to fetch it, and you *will*."

Elyon shook his head.

"No? You're to say no? *You?*" Fhanrir's nostrils flared open. "*Entitled*," he rattled. "You stink of *entitled*, and *thief*. The same as that miserable brother of yours. He tried to steal his too. Did you know that? Was one step away…just one step…"

"I'm *not* going to steal it," Elyon said hotly. "I'm *not* my brother."

"You are. You two are just the same." Fhanrir gave out that odious laugh of his. "You see this, Ilith. The boys are as weak-willed as each other. *You*," he said, in a deeper, guttural voice, looking at Sir Mallister Monsort. The knight's eyes snapped over to him at once, as though drawn on a string. "You go back to the palace, right now, and fetch it. You bring the Windblade here."

"*NO!*" Elyon said, too loudly. The word rang out through the forge, rolling into the corridors beyond, out through the vastness of the refuge. The sound seemed to go on forever; *no…no…no…* "I…I have so much…there's a lot I still need to do." The word was still echoing; *no…no…no…* Elyon could hear it screaming inside his head as well. The others had gone deathly silent. *They know. They see. They're going to take it from me.*

Fhanrir broke the quiet. "Thief," he hissed, lifting and pointing a withered finger. "You're going to steal it. You're going to *run*."

"No, I…" Elyon shook his head in denial. He looked at Ilith. The demigod was observing him cautiously. "I won't, my lord. I am no thief, I swear it."

"I know that, Elyon Daecar," the Worldbuilder said. "But I can feel the fear in you too. You are afraid to be parted from it."

I shouldn't have come, he thought. *I should never have come here.* "At least let me explain," he blurted. "Let me tell you the things I must do. There are matters, with the Eye of Rasalan, and the cousins of the king. That is a quest I must see through, my lord."

Ilith nodded pensively. "Perhaps that is so. But you also must weigh the *risk*, Elyon. You may not be a thief, but sooner or later, you will be overwhelmed. The force you carry at your hip is pernicious, sentient, and more powerful than you can know. There is no man living who can truly dominate a Blade of Vandar. Eventually, all bearers will fall."

415

Elyon shook his head. "My father…"

"Will fall, in time. He may take longer to do so, but eventually, even he will succumb. The blades *must* be brought to me before that happens. We do not have very much time, Elyon. The shadow is stirring, and my strength…it is waning."

"It's time to let it go, boy," Fhanrir said. "You've killed a dragon or two…good for you. But nothing you're doing's making a blind bit of difference. So you bring it here."

"But…"

"But you won't. Because you're frightened. Just a frightened little boy afraid to lose his favourite toy. You like flying, don't you, *boy*? You like being up there in the skies, looking *down* on everyone else." Fhanrir sneered at him in disgust. "Monsort, go back to the refuge and get it. If he tries to stop you, run him through."

Sir Mallister balked. "My lord?"

"You deaf as well as stupid? You heard me."

"I…" Mallister looked at Elyon, alarmed, and then Ilith, desperate. "My lord…?"

"Don't look at him. You *look at me*, Monsort." And he did, unable to resist the power of the mage's voice. "Aye, you're serving *us* now. You're here to protect us from dark forces at the door, and this man…" He pointed at Elyon. "Oh, there's a darkness in him. So you know what to do, don't you? There's a monster in our midst and he needs slaying…"

"*Enough*," Ilith said. "Fhanrir, enough. You have made your point."

Fhanrir sniffed. "I've more to say."

"You've said plenty. Wait outside, both of you. I would speak with Elyon alone."

"Fine." The mage clipped his fingers at Mallister as though he was a dog. "Come, boy. Seems we're not wanted here." They left through the door, moving out into the corridor.

Silence filled the air at their parting. It lasted a while.

"Elyon," Ilith said softly. "Look at me, child."

Elyon's eyes were down, lowered in shame at Fhanrir's rebuke. He did not feel the prince anymore, nor the champion, no Master of Winds and Lord of the Skies and serial slayer of Agarath's spawn. Just a boy, as the mage kept calling him, a silly boy with a head full of dreams. Slowly, he raised his eyes.

"We all stumble occasionally, Elyon," Ilith whispered. "We may trip and even lose our footing, but that does not mean we must fall. Fhanrir prods and probes in order to unveil your weakness, but in doing so, I can see your *strength*." He stepped closer to him. Elyon could feel the warmth of his radiance, his divinity. Callused hands came up to rest on his shoulders. Ilith was not tall, not in the body of Tyrith. But he seemed a giant to Elyon all the same. "You hold no avarice in you, child. You have no great want of honours and spoils and to you the triumphs of battle have grown stale. You act selflessly, and for others. You love, and you care, and you are not given to self-conceit or pride. These qualities will stand you in good stead. They are a shield of light against the darkness…and I believe in you, Elyon Daecar."

The words were like sudden sunlight piercing the storm, bathing Elyon in their glow. "You…you believe in me, my lord?"

"I do. I believe in you, and I will trust you. But that is not enough. *You* must believe and trust in *yourself*." He paused, searching his silver-blue eyes. "Do you?"

Fhanrir had stricken him with doubt, but Ilith had blown it away like autumn leaves in a fierce gust of wind. *He believes in me. The king who built the world.* Ilith had spoken of wonders earlier. The greatest wonder in all history was him. "I…I do, my lord," Elyon croaked. Ilith's faith was like a new suit of armour, stronger than anything he wore. "Now…now I do."

Ilith gave a tender smile. "Good. That is all I wanted to hear. So you go, and do what you must. Fulfil your quest, and be a hero to those who need you. I will trust you to bring me the Windblade when the time is right."

Elyon drew a breath. "I will not let you down, Lord Ilith." He spoke with great gravity. "I promise it. I won't."

"I know, Elyon. You won't. Because you know what will happen if you do."

He did. He knew.

"You have much to do, Elyon Daecar. This I know as well; I can see it in your heart. A great list, a great burden, such a weight to carry. But…if I may…permit me to lay one last task upon your table?"

Elyon went down to a knee. "Of course, my lord. Anything."

"*Smile*," the Worldbuilder said. He reached down and put a hand to Elyon's bearded cheek. "A world without smiles is not one I care to live in, Elyon . So go from here with a smile on your lips, and remember why you're fighting. You will feel better for it, I promise."

Elyon stood, and as he did so, a true smile touched his lips.

"Well," Ilith whispered, smiling fondly as well. "Now isn't that better? Is not a smile a touch of light, ushered from the soul?"

Elyon could not agree with the demigod more. *Light from the soul,* he thought. It was one request he was happy to fulfil.

30

Amron

The air was still thick with the stink of smoke, and ash coated the cobbles like new fallen snow.

Amron Daecar sat in the saddle atop Wolfsbane, his mighty black destrier, staring out across the docks of Green Harbour. Scores of ships lay twisted and broken in the water, masts poking up from the depths in a horror of grasping, blackened fingers. Through the swirling smog, it was hard to make out their colours, though here and there a tattered length of sail flapped and fluttered, in black and red and gold.

"How many were there?" Amron asked. He was trying to get a count of the Agarathi ships, but that was proving impossible in this smog. It was more than just the fume of smoke that had risen from the burning corpse of the city, and those ships. This was a coastal mist, thick and unnatural like the rains. *And cold,* Amron thought. They were a hundred leagues northwest of King's Point here and he could feel the bitter chill in the air. "We heard an armada of eighty vessels was bearing down on you, Sir Harold. Was that number correct?"

Sir Harold Conwyn confirmed with a stiff nod. He was a short man of three and thirty with a broad nose, large red cheeks, and short, stubbly beard. One of Randall Borrington's knights, Amron knew. He had met Conwyn several times in the past and found him a genial sort. "Eighty would be about right, my lord."

"Most are burned," the Ironfoot observed, glaring out at the ships. "Was it *you* or *them* that did that?"

Sir Harold seemed confused by the question. "My lord?"

Amron explained. "What Lord Grave means to ask is…did you burn the ships with your defensive weapons, or were the dragons to blame?"

That did not much allay the knight's confusion. "The dragons? No, my lords, the dragons wouldn't burn their own ships." He seemed bemused by the suggestion.

Grave grunted, and his horse snorted, as though in agreement with his rider. That horse was called *Ironhoof* and was shod in godsteel shoes. They misted as he trotted. "You weren't there at King's Point, Harold. The dragons didn't seem to care who they slew. Rained fire down on us all, Vandarian and Agarathi alike."

"Well, um…not here, my lords, no." Sir Harold gestured with a gauntleted hand to the harbour walls and gate behind them. Atop the battlements were catapults and ballistas, twisted and shattered, though a few of them were still operational. "We threw burning barrels of pitch from the catapults and flaming bolts from the ballistas. Managed to burn ten or so ships before they came ashore. The rest rammed right into the jetties and wharves, harder and faster than you would believe. Then they came spilling out in their thousands. Like termites, they were, swarming from their nests, all black and red and angry. There was a wildness to them, Lord Daecar. The screams they gave out…the sound they made…" He shuddered. "I've never heard anything like it."

He is too young to have seen the last war, Amron knew. The king was well acquainted with the Agarathi warcry, a noise made to unman their enemies on the field. He still remembered the first time he'd heard it. A thrilling sound, he had found it to be, heralding the joys of battle. But that wasn't the case for everyone. "How did they get through the gates?" he asked.

"From the inside, my lord. They had ladders to scale the walls, dozens of them. We fought them off for a time, and went blade to blade on the battlements, but eventually they overwhelmed us and managed to get the gate open. After that they came flooding through."

Amron turned his eyes about. The docks were piled high with corpses, scattered about like burial mounds, and further back beyond the harbour gates, many fires were still smouldering, sending up plumes of thin black smoke. "How many did you kill, Sir Harold? I want numbers."

The man took a moment, then said, "Three, four thousand I would guess. We haven't had a chance as yet to perform a precise count, my lord."

"And in the waters?" asked the Ironfoot. Well, *demanded*. Lord Gavron was prone to demand, not ask. "You said you sank ten ships before they landed. How many drowned?"

Sir Harold scratched at his dimpled chin. "I would think at least two thousand drowned, Lord Grave, perhaps more. And there were some skiffs that foundered as well." He pointed out a few such wrecks, washed up among the tangled masts and hulls and sails. "They came from the bigger galleons that dropped anchor in deeper waters. The rest of them died trying to win the gate, or else when battling through the city."

419

Amron was performing the calculations. "So up to six thousand died in total? From a force of how many?"

"Some twenty thousand I would think, my lord, perhaps as many as twenty-five."

"Then up to twenty thousand may still be alive," Amron said, musing.

"Yes, my lord. Once they won the gate, we couldn't do much to stop them moving through the city and into the woods to the north. Sir Tefler tried to harry them as best he could, but their numbers were too many."

"Where is Sir Tefler now?" Amron wanted to know. He was a senior knight of high battle acclaim. Lord Borrington had mentioned in his most recent letters - though those were months old now - that he'd put Sir Tefler in charge of the forces here.

"Dead," Sir Harold Conwyn said, with a sigh. "He was at the Green Gate...tried to hold it, but with that many dragonkin coming up the Mossway." He shook his head. "Lord Westwood perished too. Dragon got him as he crossed the ward of the castle. And his son, Sir Wilas. He was grief-struck, my lords, and wanted vengeance. He gathered a host and went out through a postern door to meet the Agarathi blade to blade at the docks. I told him it was folly, but...well, he wouldn't listen. They overwhelmed him within minutes. Wasteful death, it was."

"A valiant death," the Ironfoot put in. "Same as Tefler's." He gave Sir Harold Conwyn a judging look. "And all of that left *you* in charge, did it?"

"Yes, my lord. I was Sir Tefler's second-in-command."

"Did you harry them?" Grave demanded. "When the Agarathi broke into the woods? Did you give chase?"

"I...no, my lord. I was trying to consolidate, and..." He looked at Amron. "I hope I made the right choice, Your Grace. We had lost thousands of our own, and I didn't think...sending men to give chase...well, I thought it would be too wasteful. Against so many..."

"You made the right choice," Amron told him, if only to calm his stuttering. He needed to get this done as quickly as possible. "What are your current numbers, Sir Harold?"

The knight's eyes twisted in thought. "Not sure on the exact figure, my lord, but I'd guess at some four thousand, give or take."

"And wounded?" Amron asked.

"Five hundred or so," said Conwyn. "Perhaps a quarter of those are at death's door, though we've hope for the rest. None have the strength to fight, mind. We've got others nursing minor wounds, but they'll be ready to go back into battle if they must."

"They must," Amron said at once. "I plan to march at once for the Twinfort and need every sword and spear I can muster. How long ago did the Agarathi break through?"

Sir Harold thought a moment. "Coming up on three days now."

420

"And they did not try to occupy the city?"

"No. Just rushed through like a black-red river, and straight out into the Greenwood."

As I expected, Amron thought. "Green Harbour is the back door to the Twinfort," he said. "They aim to go west through the forest and attack it from the rear. There is another army marching across the Brindle Steppe. Perhaps you've heard? They hope to take the fort from both sides." He spoke with a rush to his voice. He had only just arrived in the city, and had no intention of staying any longer than he needed. "Harold, how quickly can you muster your men?"

The knight was not used to this level of command. He fumbled for an answer for a while, then said, "How quickly do you need them?"

"As quickly as possible. I want to leave within the hour."

The man balked. "One hour, my lord? I've got men scattered all over. Half are horror-struck from the fighting, and the rest are broken from lack of sleep. Been days since most got any good rest. And the food…the men are hungry, my lord. The city storehouses were all targeted by the dragons, and…"

Amron did not need to hear of all of these ails and issues. They were the same as those occurring across half the kingdom. He raised a hand to stop him. "See it done, Harold. I will hand over some men to help you. You may leave a small garrison here to defend the city. Five hundred should serve. The rest will come with us, and must be ready to move at speed. I want them gathered beyond the western walls in an hour, ready to march."

"An…an hour. Yes, my lord. I'll…see it done."

"Good." Amron wheeled Wolfsbane around and trotted back the way they had come, with the Ironfoot at his side. He had brought with him a small guard of twenty knights and men-at-arms, though the rest of his army had been left outside the walls. Sir Quinn Sharp had command of the guard. "Sir Quinn. I want you to help Sir Harold muster his soldiers to leave. Have your men move through the city and get them armoured and on their feet. You have an hour."

The broad-faced Varin Knight gave a single affirming nod. "As you command, my king."

Amron spurred his heels and moved back through the harbour gate, Grave and Rogen Strand following. Green Harbour was not a large city, but it had once been a pretty one, full of timbered taverns and inns and shops along a waterfront bustling with trade. There was a famous fish market here, a famous summer market too, and each year the main city square played host to a festival of theatre and art. Now all of that was burned to cinders, and the foul smell of death was heavy in the air.

Ash was stirred at their passing, kicked up by the hooves of their horses. Amron coughed and covered his mouth as they rode north-ward along the Mossway - the main thoroughfare that cut up through the city from gate to gate, linking the harbour with the Green Gate that gave access to the woods. The portcullis was still raised when he arrived, and the drawbridge that spanned the short moat was down. Amron nodded to the soldiers and rode right by. Grave slowed a moment to say, "If you've got loved ones here, say your goodbyes. We're riding west in an hour," before trotting past.

The woods grew close outside the walls, and in places their branches reached up over the ramparts as though trying to clamber inside. The men were spread out among the boles, taking this rare chance to rest. Some were lying up against the trunks, sleeping; others had started little cookfires with dry kindling they kept in their packs, shielded from the rains. They had pots of broth on the boil and were handing them around to anyone who wanted some. Steam rose up through the canopy, curling into the thick green leaves. Above, the sky was more clear than it had been in long days. Most of the march had been under the rain and that had only made it all the harder, though Lord Gavron's men were a hardy sort in the image of their lord and the complaints had been kept to a minimum.

Sir Taegon Cargill was waiting for them when they returned, alongside Sir Torus Stoutman. The former overtopped the latter by over two feet. Both wore godsteel from head to heel, and Sir Taegon wore his rich Varin cloak, fastened at the neck with a brooch in the shape of a warhammer that looked just like the one he kept strapped to his back.

"Sir Taegon," Amron said. "You look thirsty for a fight."

The Giant of Hammerhall smashed his chest with a clang of steel. "Always. What're your orders, my king?"

Amron looked at Torus. "I want the both of you to ride ahead and catch a whiff of the enemy's scent. Take fifty of our best men. I want you to harry their rear and slow them down."

Sir Torus was smoking his rosewood pipe, which Amron took as a good sign. He had given up on all such joys during their weeks in King's Point, as the man mourned the death of his sons. The grief was still there, but less acute, and the long days on the road had helped him get a grip of his demons. *Battle and blood will help more*, Amron knew. "How many Agarathi are we talking?" Stoutman asked.

"Fifteen to twenty thousand."

Torus spat smoke. "Fifteen to twen…you're out of your godsdamn mind!" He grinned like he used to, big and broad, through the bushy tangles of his beard. "Fifty against fifteen thousand. Aye, I like those odds." He tapped at Sir Taegon with the back of his knuckles. "How about it, Hammer? Shall we go win this battle alone?"

"I'll do the winning. You can watch, Halfman."

"Nothing reckless," Amron was quick to say. "They have a three-day lead, though their army is afoot. Chase them down and raid their rear and flanks. Do it by night if you can. The woods can be confusing west of here, and even men who walk them their entire lives can get turned around sometimes. Focus on chaos and disruption. I'll have riders coming and going, so watch your tail as well. I want to know how you're faring."

"Aye," said Stoutman. "When should we leave?"

"You know the answer to that, Torus."

"I'll pack my bags, then." The dwarfish knight had a deep swallow of smoke, blew out and strode away. The Giant of Hammerhall bent his back in a bow, then turned, stamping after him.

Lord Gavron watched them go. "Maybe we should put all our mounted strength into this, Amron?" the gruff old lord suggested. "Conwyn will have horses. We add them to our own, and we might have a good enough host to cause the Agarathi some trouble."

Amron thought on that for a moment. Only one in five of their own men was ahorse. If Sir Harold had a similar number to hand it would prove a worthy weapon should they find the enemy unawares. A night charge by warhorses was a fearsome prospect, more so when you were already lost and tired and struggling to find your way through a fearsome wood. And the Greenwood was just that, on the western side especially. It was wilder that way, with crags and cliffs and rugged hills with hidden caves and eerie valleys between them. There was no road along the coast from here, not west, and what tracks there were could be hard to find lest a man know the way. Few enemy armies had ever managed to assault the rear of the Twinfort for this very reason - getting there was by no means easy. It would be plenty to put many an Agarathi horde on edge.

And then the thunder of hooves in the night, he thought. *The ring of steel and scream of a brother, dying right beside you. And the trailing mist of godsteel as a knight charges past.* Armies had broken and scattered under those conditions in the past. *We would do well to do the same.*

"It's a good notion," Amron said eventually. "We'll remain together for now, but if we hear that we are closing in on them, it may be worth sending a charge. The coming days will tell."

"Then we need to be in striking distance. That means setting a good pace." Grave was already looking over his men. "Mine will keep on going hard, I'll make sure of it. Not so certain of these Green Harbour men. Not after what Conwyn said."

"They're not all Green Harbour men," Amron pointed out. The west was being defended by the Borringtons and Crawfields and Rothwells and their banners, and all paid fealty to House Daecar. "These are my people, Ironfoot. Many are men of the North Downs. I'll see that they don't hold us up."

The host took two hours to assemble outside the walls. It was longer than Amron had wanted, but in all truth his hopes of getting it all done within the hour were unrealistic to the point of being unattainable. He had anticipated that, and two hours was a reasonable effort. "How many?" he asked Sir Harold Conwyn, as the men trailed out through the Green Gate in a solemn, weary stream, to join the rest of the host.

"Three thousand four hundred and twenty-six, my lord."

"Very exact. Mounted?"

"We have three hundred and eighty men ahorse. Most are light cavalry, my lord, but we have some heavy horse as well. A hundred and twenty, I believe. There are fourteen Bladeborn knights in the company, some of whom you will know, and several times that number in sellswords and freeriders with a drop or two of Varin's blood. None of the knights are fully armoured, except for Sir Trystan. The rest all have the essentials of godsteel plate, however, with good castle-forged steel to fill in the gaps."

Amron nodded. "I'd like to see them," he said. "Line them up for inspection, Sir Harold."

The Bladeborn knights were brought forward, each of them wearing their house colours and arms. Amron recognised some of them and knew a few by name. Five were Green Harbour men, household knights to Lord Westwood and the other noble houses here. Of them Amron knew only Sir Lambert Joyce, who had commanded Lord Westwood's guard. He had a brother, Amron recalled, who had gone missing a long while ago. Another claimed to know Amron by way of House Colborn. "I served Lady Colborn for a time, my lord," the tall knight said. "She told me her boy Jovyn was squire to your son Elyon."

Amron had half forgotten that Jovyn's family hailed from Green Harbour. "That is true, Sir…"

"Sir Dederick, my lord, of House Dudden. We are a small knightly house, founded by my grandfather. I serve beneath the banners of Westwood now."

Sir Lambert nodded. "And he does so well, my king. Sir Dederick has proven himself most reliable."

"I should hope so," Amron said. Reliability was the minimum standard for any good knight or serving man. "Tell me, is Lady Colborn well?" He directed the question to any of the Green Harbour men who might know, Sir Harold included.

It was Sir Lambert who gave answer. "I understand that she left, some weeks ago, my lord. To seek safer pastures."

"Most of the city evacuated before the fighting," Sir Harold Conwyn put in. "We knew we would be targeted eventually, so Lord Westwood put the call out to empty the city as best we could. Most made for Crosswater, to take ship up the river to Varinar. But now… well, I'm not sure what has become of them."

It was an all too familiar tale.

The rest of the knights performed their courtesies, as Amron spoke to them one by one. Sir Trystan was a proud, golden-haired youth of seventeen, the last living son of Lord Tymon Spencer. House Spencer had become wealthy from mining operations in the North Downs, where they had struck upon a rich vein of gold. The lord had spent a small fortune garbing his son in full plate, and a fine suit it was, gilded and gleaming, lobstered and sleek. As his last living heir, Trystan must be protected, Lord Spencer had been known to say.

The other knights were all older. There were hedge knights here, and household knights, and a former Varin Knight as well. Amron smiled at seeing that last. "Sir Bryce. I had not expected to see you here." Byrce Coddington had retired from the order a decade ago, after long years of noted service. He had settled into a stout little keep of his own, east of the Greenwood, with servants and staff to attend him. "How are you, old friend?"

"Pissed off," the old man grumbled. "Was enjoying the quiet life before all this war broke out. Got a library full of books that need reading, and a cellar full of wine that needs drinking. Well, now all of that's burned and ruined, and my staff are scattered and dead. So I'm here again, with godsteel to grasp, and my mood is red as blood."

Amron could tell. Bryce had always been intense and the years had not softened him. "Well, I'm glad to have you. Ride with me at the front, Bryce. You can catch me up on the battle."

"Oh, there was a battle here, was there?" he snorted. "More like a grown man shoving a toddler aside. Might have been different with you here, Amron, but this lot…" Clearly, he did not think much of the other knights. "They're wet, most of them. Green as summer grass and just as easily felled. Sir Tefler did what he could to lead them, but after he died…"

"We did our best," said Sir Harold, overhearing. He looked insulted. "Every man here fought as well as he could."

Bryce Coddington gave a throaty laugh. "All relative, I suppose. Can see why you never made the order, Conwyn, if *that's* your best."

Sir Harold looked at a loss for words. He turned to Amron. "My king, I assure you I am a capable fighter. You know that yourself. You have seen me in the melee and the lists, and…"

"Playfighting," broke in Sir Bryce. "That's all those tourneys really are, a bit of pretty swordplay. How did your first taste of the *real* world go down, Conwyn? Not quite the same, is it?"

The man had no response. Sir Bryce turned away from him. "So we're on a hunt are we, my lord?" he said to Amron. "Heard you've sent the Giant of Hammerhall ahead with Torus Stoutman? You don't mind if I ride to catch up, do you? One of these other lads can fill you in on the battle if you want. But as I say, not much to tell."

Amron could see that there were some fractured relationships here. And he knew Sir Bryce as a fierce combatant. That was a decade ago, but still…those were skills a man never lost. "Do you have a mount?"

"No. Was planning to run after them." He smiled gruffly. The flesh about his face was haggard and folded, heavily seamed about the eyes and forehead, with patches of stiff grey whiskers on cheeks and chin. "Course I've got a horse."

"Very well. Then go. Did you bring any men with you when you came here?"

"No. Just me. Had a squire but he died on the journey. Wasn't much use anyway, if I'm honest. Good lad, but *good* isn't enough to survive these days, is it?"

"No, I suppose not." Amron thought a moment. "If you must have your taste of blood, fine, but I would prefer you not to ride alone. Pick out a few of these knights and take them with you. Sir Harold, see him supported by some men-at-arms as well."

"Yes, my lord. How many?"

"A dozen will serve."

That was all done within a short ten minutes, and away Sir Bryce Coddington went, riding hard into the murky woods on the back of his barded horse, with young Sir Trystan Spencer, tall Sir Dederick Dudden, and an old, one-eyed hedge knight called Sir Cod Murray for company. After that Amron gave his speech, calling forth to the gathered men to inspire them and speed them on the march. He spoke of the families whom they must avenge, the living loved ones they must protect, how a man defending his own country counted for ten invaders on the field of battle. They were words he had spoken a hundred times before, dressed up in a hundred different ways, but the essence was always the same.

"Standard battle script," the Ironfoot called it after. "But it's the delivery that's important."

Amron nodded and steeled his eyes. He hoped he would continue to deliver for his people…with script and steel both.

31

Pagaloth

Sir Hadros had the map. He laid it out in the draughty wood cabin they'd taken for a council chamber, using stones to hold it down at the edges. The wind rattled through the rotting timber walls, the floorboards creaking and cracking as the men moved in to look. Outside, the weather was dreary, the skies grey and overcast yet the rains had not yet come. They would, Sir Pagaloth knew. *They come every day out here.*

"Here," the hedge knight said. He prodded at a blur of ink that marked the small wood they were in, of elm and oak and ironwood, one of a hundred that clothed this vast verdant land. "That's us right there."

"You're sure?" asked Ruggard Wells, squinting.

"Aye, sure as when I mounted your sister, Rug. But we don't want to talk about that now, do we?"

Wells glared at him. He was a grizzled old man-at-arms of fifty winters, with grey streaks in his beard, eyes hard as flint, and a dome as bald as an egg. He said nothing.

"The *Smallwood*," Skymaster Sa'har Nakaan noted, looking at the name scrawled onto the map. "That is a little…what is the expression? A little on the nose?"

Hadros gave a chuckle. "Aye, you're not wrong, Skymaster. Half the names around here are the same. The Littlewood. Light Elm Forest. Teen Oak. All things like that." He pointed them out, prodding here and there. "All part of the greater Wandering Wood. Once before these valleys were all forested, but they were cut back for roads and farms and such, making all these little pockets. It's only the local people who use these names, though."

Sir Bardol was studying the map with a dour look on his face. There was nothing new there. "We're a long way from home," the knight observed, in that toneless, perpetually unhappy voice that made

427

Pagaloth want to fall asleep or slap some life into him. "It will take us ten days to corral the deserters back to the city. *At least* ten days," he groaned.

"Especially if these damnable rains keep coming," Hadros added in, "and they don't look like they're going to relent any time soon. Before long every wood will become a bog and every valley a sea. Hell, we'll be swimming back at this rate." He made a face. "And I'm not one for swimming."

Sir Bardol shook his head. "Nor I." He was a haggard, angular man, old beyond his thirty-five years, with thin folds of dark skin beneath his eyes that made him look constantly exhausted. "I think it may be time to turn back, Hadros. Four hundred men is enough."

The hedge knight nodded thoughtfully, rubbing at his lumpen chin, stiff with short brown bristles, going grey in places. He looked to the other members of the council, a strange motley of men from north and south. "What do the rest of you say?"

"No," grunted the Piseki Sunrider Tar Moro. He wore brown and golden robes, mud-spattered and rain-soaked, over scalemail armour in links of fine bronze steel. "There are more men out there," he said. "*Many* more. We should not stop yet. There is more work to be done."

"You mean you want to keep looking for your precious wolf," scoffed Ruggard Wells. "We're *not* going on for the sake of your pet, Moro. Just admit that's all you care about. You could care less about finding more deserters. You think every one of them is a craven anyway." He snorted. "Might say the same about your wolf. It ran away as well."

Moro turned on him. "You dare…"

"Dare? What's so daring about calling it how it is? Your wolf's a frightened little pup and your cat's no better, Bellio. They're both dead. Just accept it."

Moro's dark eyes burned with rage. "*When* I find Natallios, I will demand a death duel with you, Vandarian. You will see then that he is not a coward, when he rips out your throat and opens your belly."

"All right, calm down there Moro," Hadros said, pulling the man away. "You two and your bickering…" He sighed. "Now let's get back to the matter at hand. Moro, you want to keep going. Bellio, I'm guessing you're the same?"

Starrider Anson Bellio was as pleasant as Sunrider Moro was peevish. He was slim as a dagger, youthful and handsome, with mysterious, purply-brown eyes and smooth dark ebony skin. He wore dark leather garments with a black cloak sprinkled with silver spots. "I miss Eleesia deeply," he said, in that long-suffering way of his. "I will not deny it. My heart breaks each day to think…"

"All right, no need to go reciting poetry, Anson. You miss your starcat, we know that, but it's been long weeks now and there's been no sign of either of them. Best let it lie." He looked at the Piseki Sunrider. "Both of you."

428

"Never," grunted Moro.

Bellio only lowered his eyes, his anguish marrow-deep.

Hadros looked at Sa'har. "Skymaster. Your thoughts?"

Sa'har Nakaan was stroking at the wisp of white beard on his chin as he perused the details of the map. "We are told there is a large group of deserters gathered here," he said, in his quiet croak of a voice. A thin finger reached out of his crimson robes, gesturing to a dot on the sheepskin scroll, marked with the name *Fronnfallow*. There was a skull sign next to it, the skull of a wolf it looked, which did not seem a positive omen to Sir Pagaloth Kadosk. "If we are to return to King's Point, it would be sensible to travel to Fronnfallow first. We can turn west after."

"Or we just turn west *now*," Ruggard Wells came in. He squinted down at the map as though it was some fell creature to be feared. "Fronnfallow's a dark place, and best avoided. There are ghosts there in those ruins, spirits of *Fronn* himself. I say we go back right now. No good will come of us going there."

Sir Hadros gave a bark of laughter. "Since when did the dead frighten you, Ruggard? It's the living that concern me more."

"The dead inhabit the living," the old man-at-arms warned. "You know the stories, Hadros. Those spirits get into the living wolves and make them monstrous and mean. They grow unnatural in size and strength and you can hear them howling from a hundred leagues away, like they're *Fronn* himself come back from the dead."

Hadros did not seem in the least bit fazed. "Well, we've heard no such howling and Fronnfallow's only a few hours march away. So I'm guessing we're fine. And if these wolf-spirits are infesting the local lupine population, then I doubt we'd be hearing about a group of deserters in camp there, would we? Men don't put down roots when there are monsters about." He looked at the map again, jabbing at it like he was trying to get its attention. "I say we go. If there are some deserters camping there, as that Agarathi claimed, we can assimilate them and then head home."

"You're making a mistake…" Ruggard started.

Hadros cut in. "You're as fretful as a maid on the morn of her wedding, Rug, and doing yourself no favours with all this naysaying. When we get back to the Point, and I report to Captain Lythian and the king, what do you want me to tell them? That Ruggard Wells, the battle-hardened old warrior, moaned every step of the way? That he was unmanned by children's tales of spirits and ghosts? Or that he was valiant and bold and a good fit for a Varin cloak?" He met the man's eyes. "Aye, it'll be the latter I'll wager. So stop with your bleating. We're going, and that's that."

"Fine," Wells grunted. "But if you think Daecar's going to let us all into the order for this, then you're as mad as Miller is. That's *never* going to happen."

"Not for you. You're just an angry old man who no one likes. But me? Oh, I'm getting my cloak, Rug. You just wait and see."

Seats and steeds, Sir Pagaloth thought. That's all it came down to with these men. The Bladeborn were trying to win their seats to Varin's Table. The Lightborn were here to track down their cats and wolves after they'd run from the battle. They were selfish motivations, even in part dishonourable. *Only Sa'har and I are truly driven by Lythian's ideals*, Pagaloth reflected. But it had served to keep them moving forward until now, and the peace had thus far been kept. It was a tense unity, and one built on unstable foundations, but so far they were proving that it could, theoretically, be done.

"Any more questions?" Hadros asked the group.

No one ventured anything.

"Good. Then let's get going." Sir Hadros brushed aside the stones and rolled up the map, stashing it back in his cloak. He stepped outside into the biting winds, the rest following. Mads Miller had guard of the door. He was another man-at-arms, another Bladeborn, though younger and much less grim and grumpy than Sir Bardol and Ruggard Wells. Miller was afflicted by some bizarre malady that made his features jerk and spasm at random. As a child the other boys had laughed at him and called him mad, but apparently that wasn't enough. He was 'more than mad' they said, so they decided to use the plural form of the word, and he had been 'Mads' Miller ever since.

"What's the plan, then?" Miller asked, as the leaders filed out. "Where we headed?"

"Fronnfallow," said Sir Hadros. "Then home."

"*Fronnfallow?*" Mads' left eyelid flickered. Pagaloth could not tell if that was fear or just a part of his tick.

"Aye. Fronnfallow." Hadros turned to the group. "Get the men ready to go. It's a six-mile march and best we make haste while it's still dry." He looked up through the thin canopy. The skies were light enough to suggest no rain was imminent, but that could change quickly. The weather gods here were capricious, Pagaloth had come to see. In Agarath the weather was much more predictable. "Right. Let's get to it." Hadros clapped his gloved hands together with a slap of leather, and marched off to deliver his orders.

The deserters were assembled in a clearing where the trees thinned out, all standing and sitting about beneath the bleak grey skies awaiting their next instruction. There were some four hundred in total, over two hundred of them Agarathi. The rest were a mix of men of the empire - Lumarans, Piseki, Aramatians, Solapians - with some soldiers who hailed from the Islands of the Moon and the Twin Suns and the Golden Isles as well. Some thirty northern deserters had also been found, mostly Taynar soldiers from the Ironmoors who had fallen in beneath the command of Sir Bardol, who was a knight of House Kindrick, bannermen to the Taynars. Sir Hadros had given every northman a choice when they were dragged before him; to help guard the rest of the deserters, or else stay among them, as prisoners, and be brought before the king upon their return to the Point. "You know what happens to deserters," Hadros the Homeless would always say, and that would be enough for them to swear their oaths and serve their duty.

Some of the southern deserters had been assimilated as well, taken in under the command of Sa'har or Moro or Bellio, or the paladin knight Sir Quento, who had charge of the Aramatian contingent, but they were few. The majority were watched over, day and night, and had been disarmed of their weapons to limit the threat of violence. Most of those had given themselves up willingly, though, and sought no quarrel. They had been hunted down and captured in their groups, often hiding away in old huts and barns and abandoned farmsteads, and rarely did they put up a fight when they heard the thunder of hooves arriving outside their door. As soon as they saw that it was not merely northmen on their trail, but a united host sent to bring them all together, they would see the sense in giving in. Sa'har in particular was a boon. He was a man of heroic tale to the Agarathi, widely revered, and had worked wonders in helping to usher the Agarathi deserters beneath their banners of unity.

Pagaloth walked with him now to where the two hundred Agarathi captives were waiting. The Skymaster found an old tree stump on which to stand, and climbed up, raising his hands. The men gathered around. "My friends," Sa'har called out. "We will be travelling a little to the northeast, a two-hour march, to a place called Fronnfallow. Some of our brothers are in camp there, we are told. When they see us here united, I am sure they will want to join. After, we will return to King's Point." A murmur rippled through the crowd, men turning to look at one another, worried and wary. "Do not be afraid, my friends," Sa'har said, raising his voice over the din. "The Vandarians mean you no harm. I have spoken to their king and he has assured us that all deserters and captives will be treated with honour and respect. On that you have my word."

His word was enough to settle them down, and after that, they gathered themselves up to leave. Pagaloth stood watching for a while, scanning the men before him. After a time he shook his head. "I don't see him," he said to Sa'har. "The man who told us of the deserters at Fronnfallow."

The old Skymaster had a quick look. "Ah. He is right there, Pagaloth." He pointed to a man of middle years, with long greying hair and a kind face. He was standing with some of the others, speaking to them, his hands moving in gesticulation. They seemed enthralled.

But Pagaloth only frowned, confused. "That is…no, Skymaster, you are mistaken. That is not the man who spoke of Fronnfallow. He was younger, dark-haired."

Sa'har Nakaan favoured him with a pleasant, teacherly smile. "I do not fast forget a face, Sir Pagaloth. Come, let us speak to him. He can tell us himself."

They moved through the crowd. There was a lot of shouting going on in a lot of different tongues as the men of the empire were being mustered up to leave, called to action by Moro and Bellio and Quento and their own men. Pagaloth could see Hadros's outriders trotting away into the woods on all sides, to keep watch for threats and give warning should a beast be spotted. That had happened on occasion. One rainy afternoon a fellwolf had been sighted, and Hadros and his men had gone forth to battle a grimbear once as well.

There had been some dragon sightings too, though mostly from afar. The most recent had been two days ago. Mads Miller had said the dragon had a *rider* on his back, but an hour later, when the same beast was spotted flying back south, Ruggard Wells had seen it and countered the younger man's claim. It was *riderless*, Wells said. Hadros only shrugged and said ridden or riderless, it didn't matter so long as the beast made no move to attack.

The grey-haired man was still talking to the group of Agarathi as they neared. There were some twenty of them, all staring at him, silent. Then suddenly the man broke off from his speech and turned, smiling. "Skymaster Nakaan. Sir Pagaloth." He fell into a low bow. Without a word, the twenty deserters turned and stepped away, drifting off here and there into the crowd. "Is there something I can do for you?"

Pagaloth watched the men go. There was something strange about the way they dispersed in different directions like that. He looked at the grey-haired man, studying his features. "Your name is Ten'kin, is that right?"

The grey-haired man smiled. "That is correct. Ten'kin. We have spoken before, Sir Pagaloth."

No, Pagaloth thought. *It was the other man I spoke with, the younger man with the dark hair. The other man was called Ten'kin*. Confusion blew through him like a cold wind.

"You look perplexed," Sa'har noted, with that same teacherly smile. He gave a little laugh. "I do think our noble dragonknight is overworked and under-rested, Ten'kin."

"What is the trouble?" Ten'kin asked, innocently.

"Nothing." Pagaloth shook his head. *Overworked and under-rested*. Perhaps that's all it was. "I wanted to ask of Fronnfallow. You said you came from there?"

"Yes. I did."

"And there are men in camp there, is that right?" He waited for the man to nod. "Why did you leave?"

Ten'kin frowned and looked at Sa'har Nakaan, who said, "We have been through this already, Pagaloth. Ten'kin was sent out to find others, to bring them together. That is when we found him."

"I…" Pagaloth rubbed his forehead, trying to remember. His sleep had been a paltry thing of late, there was truth in that, and maybe it had addled his sense of recall. He had another look at the man Ten'kin. He was old, into his fifties, much older than he had thought, and those eyes…*were* they kind? He thought they were kind before, but there was something strange in them as well, something empty. His lips were in a smile, but those eyes… it was like they were features of two separate faces, not in sync with one another. "My lord," he said, turning to Sa'har. "A word in private, please."

The Skymaster looked befuddled, but nodded and stepped away with him all the same. Ten'kin watched them go, smiling his empty smile. "I do not trust him," Pagaloth whispered, when they had gone beyond the reach of his hearing. "There is something off about that man. How can we be sure he is who he says he is?"

"And who do you think he is, Sir Pagaloth?"

Pagaloth frowned at the question. "A common soldier, from the battle. He was…a spearman? Or…or was he a…" He could not recall. "I do not know, Sa'har."

Sa'har smiled once again, a patient smile. "He was no soldier, Pagaloth. No man of the sword or the spear or the bow. He is Fireborn, a dragonrider, who lost his dragon as I did."

"He…" Pagaloth shook his head. That was not how he remembered it. "No, my lord. That…that isn't the case."

"Now come, Pagaloth. You are beginning to vex me in this. We have spoken of this already. Two nights ago, when Ten'kin came to us. Do you not remember? I told you he was a dragonrider."

Two nights ago… "I don't…I don't remember any of that, Sa'har." His eyes moved back into the crowd of Agarathi deserters, all in their scratched and stained leather armour and robes. A few dragonknights moved among them, and here and there a fallen Fireborn dragonrider as well, in his coloured cape and fine dragonscale armour. He could not see Ten'kin anymore, and nor was that a known name. The *true* dragonriders of Agarath were famed all across the kingdom, rejoiced in song and tale at taverns and feast halls and palaces from Skyloft to Highport, from the Trident down to the Bloodgate. Everyone knew their names. Everyone. *But not the new ones*, Pagaloth thought. Not the *unnatural* ones, bonded by Eldur. "I don't trust him, Sa'har. If he's a dragonrider, why is he wearing plain garb?"

Sa'har Nakaan chuckled in bemusement. "*Plain* garb? You consider fine scales of dragonskin plain, Pagaloth? His soft silken cape in crimson and green? My, you must have some rich tastes."

Pagaloth breathed out, astonished. "You are toying with me, my lord. You must be. He…he was wearing plain clothing, Sa'har. Leathers, linen."

Sa'har Nakaan's face went serious. "Pagaloth, my dear boy. I do not know if this is some misjudged jape on your part, but perhaps now is not the time? We have a distance to go still and I find myself in no mood for…"

433

"Listen to me, Sa'har." Pagaloth grabbed him roughly by the arm, shaking. "Something is amiss here. That man..." He looked around. "Whoever he is…he is in your head. Think, *really* think. What was he wearing?"

Sa'har tried to pull away from him, but Pagaloth held on tight. Some of the nearby Agarathi were starting to notice. "I just told you, Pagaloth. Let me go. Just let me go."

"Yes. Let him go, Sir Pagaloth." The voice belonged to Sir Hadros. "Just what's going on here? You two having a lover's tiff, are you?"

Pagaloth hastened toward the hedge knight. "Hadros, there is a man among us, pretending to be someone he is not. Ten'kin. The man who told us about Fronnfallow. I think he is harbouring some dark intent."

Sir Hadros looked over at Sa'har, then back at Pagaloth. "Are you sniffing a trap, Sir Dragonknight?"

Pagaloth wasn't sure. He was suddenly unsure of everything. The men were all looking at him, frowning; some were glaring. "I…I don't know," he said, quieter now. "I just…you need to speak to him yourself. You have to take precautions."

"I *always* take precautions," the stout old knight said. "You hear those hooves, Pagaloth? You see those horses heading out? Those'll be the outriders, my eyes and my ears and my nose as well, and better than this lumpy old thing." He prodded at his own nose to show him. "And I've sent a pair of scouts ahead as well, just to be safe, Miller and Doris. If they come back saying there's something nasty awaiting us at Fronnfallow, or anywhere close, I'll turn us right around. We won't get within a mile of the place until I know it's safe to proceed." He put a hand on his shoulder. "Yes?"

What could Pagaloth do but nod? The men were looking at him like he was a madman, and frankly, he felt like one right now. It had come on so quickly. "Yes," he said, at last. "I am…tired," he admitted. "Perhaps that's all it is."

Hadros gave him a shake. "You're a wary sort, Sir Dragonknight. No wonder you made a good sworn sword to Captain Lythian." He drew his hand from his shoulder. "Now come, ride with me at the front. We'll be the first to hear if there's trouble ahead."

Pagaloth nodded doubtfully, but did not deny him. He turned to have a final word with Sa'har but the Skymaster had already moved off, drifting away into the crowds. *Perhaps he has gone to speak with Ten'kin*, Pagaloth thought. *Later*, he told himself. *I will let things settle and speak with both of them later.*

He mounted up and rode to the front of the lines with Hadros. There were calls to get the host moving, ringing out through the woods, and the men moved into motion. Almost at once the rain began to come down, sprinkling softly through the trees, pitter-pattering on the leaves and soaking into their cloaks.

The hedge knight scowled at the skies. "Damn this weather. Was a few hours without rain too much to ask?" He snorted. "Bardol says Vandar's weeping, for all the bloodshed across his lands. What do you make of that, Sir Dragonknight? You think a dead god can cry?"

"I think men find ways to explain things they don't understand," Pagaloth said. "For that they often look to the gods."

"Aye. We're of the same mind there. So…you going to explain what that was about?" He glanced behind them. "Not like you and the Skymaster to feud."

"It was a misunderstanding," Pagaloth said.

"Aye, about this Ten'kin. Well, we'll get to the bottom of it later, Pagaloth. Just watch yourself, you hear? I didn't much like the way those men were looking at you. Like you were some foreigner to them. Never good to alienate your own."

Pagaloth wasn't certain what he meant. "Foreigner? I am a dragonknight of Agarath. I have always served my people."

"I'm not saying you haven't. Just that there were some dark looks in your direction, and those eyes…I didn't like them. Some of those men don't trust you."

Pagaloth was getting a sick feeling in the pit of his stomach. "Why should they not trust me?"

"Why do you think? You've got a northern stink about you now. Well, maybe stink's not the right word. To me it's a pleasant smell, but I'm Vandarian, so it would be. To the rest…" He shook his head. "Guessing they know all about your time with the captain, in service to some northern lord. Your hair's been shorn and your beard's been cut, and even your skin's gone a little lighter out of the sun. They don't see you as one of their own anymore."

A man of no nation, Sir Pagaloth thought. He had become a pariah the moment he swore his sword to Lythian, abandoning his oaths as a dragonknight. He was a rogue now, an exile and an outcast, but above all he remained a patriot to the true nature of the land he loved. *I will see it restored,* he told himself. *And my honour with it.*

They rode on in silence for a time. The rain made a peaceful tinkling as it fell through the trees, and the rustle of the four hundred men at their back had a calming quality to it as well.

"So, you never heard of Fronn before?" Hadros asked, after a while.

Pagaloth looked over at him.

"I saw you in the cabin. Your face. You don't know the story, do you?"

The dragonknight shook his head.

"Aye, well let me tell you then. We got some time to kill, so why not?"

The hedge knight set into his tale as they continued through the trees, telling of the giant wolf god Fronn and how he'd been slain here long millennia ago by Drulgar in his rage. "Was a time of titans," Hadros said. "That dragon wanted to prove himself the meanest, so he

435

went out on his hunts. Three times he tried to slay Fronn, and three times he failed. The first time, the wolf howled so loud the dragon tucked its leathery tail and flapped away in fright. On the second, he leapt so high he managed to get onto Drulgar's back, scratching and biting at him until the dragon gave up and flew home. The third time, Fronn outran him, dashing about across these here lands, avoiding his attacks. The dragon plunged down upon him a thousand times and a thousand times the wolf sprung away, snarling and mocking. That's how these dales were formed, during that battle, the legend goes. Eventually, the Dread got tired and flew south as he had those first two times. He was so tired, in fact, that he slept for five hundred years, brooding all the while." He shrugged. "Or so the singers like to say."

By then they had left the wood behind and were crossing one of those valleys, a misty vale peppered with stands of tall elm trees and lonely old oaks. The grasses had grown high between them, stroking at the flanks of their horses as they went, and here and there massive puddles had formed, large as lakes, pooling in the lowlands.

"This rain," Hadros grunted. "Wasn't joking about swimming home, was I?" He gave a bitter laugh that lacked his usual vigour. A shadow passed his eyes as he looked forward, across the sloping rise and beyond. "He died just over those hills," the hedge knight went on. "Down in a dale on the other side. In places you can still see his bones poking up from the dirt, though most of them are covered over by now. Massive they are. Gives you a good idea of how big Fronn was, though supposing we don't need to imagine it all anymore…not since we saw the Dread."

"What happened?" Pagaloth asked. "The fourth time Drulgar came?"

The knight gave a deep sigh. "Nothing good, Sir Dragonknight. Nothing good at all. All that mocking…the running about and leaping on his back…well, the Dread didn't much care for that. After that long sleep of his he came back bigger and meaner than ever, and well, wasn't much of a contest then. Tore Fronn up, ripped him limb from limb. The bones….they're spread over miles. Each year there are still blood blossoms around them, big red flowers that bloom where the blood soaked into the soil. And the trees weep red sap too, as though they remember what happened. Ah. Maybe they do? Some say there's memory in the soil, that their roots can see the past. Always thought there was something sad about that. All these trees crying over the memory of a god."

Pagaloth had not taken the knight for a sensitive man. "And the wolves? These spirits Ruggard spoke of?"

"Nonsense. The wolves are drawn to that vale, is all that is. Fronn was their god. They come to remember him, and not just regular wolves. Nowadays, aye, but once before there were fellwolves and direwolves and shadowwolves stalking these lands, and most of those are monstrous big. Guess that's where the rumours started."

"We saw a fellwolf only days ago," Pagaloth reminded him. "Could a pack of them have gathered there?"

The man thought about it, scratching his bulbous nose. "Aye, suppose it's possible. If so these Agarathi won't be many. Not much a dragonkin can do against a fellwolf, Pagaloth. A man like you, maybe, but there aren't so many Agarathi who can beat the Barrel Knight in single combat." He gave him a grin.

"You heard about that?"

"Sure did. Captain Lythian told me, the evening before we left. He thinks a lot of you, you know. And I can see why." He smiled a sincere smile then his eyes moved forward again. "Ah…there's Mads returning now. Come, Dragonknight, let's ride ahead." He spurred his destrier into a gallop and raced off across the valley.

Pagaloth rode hard to keep up, the wet grasses slapping at his blood bay courser as he went. The rains were still falling in an incessant drizzle, cold enough to give a man a chill, and a deep fog was settling about the lands, souping down in the valley. Pagaloth could not abide it. He craved some heat in his flesh, some sun on his skin. *No wonder they think me half northern. This rain is soaking the south out of me.*

Sir Hadros came to an abrupt stop ahead, pulling hard at the reins. His horse reared and gave a loud whinny as Mads Miller and the other scout, a young spearman called Cam Doris, came racing up to join him. Pagaloth slowed as he approached, glancing back. The mists moved heavily, a shroud that veiled the land in a wet grey cloak. He could barely see anyone back there, save a few shadows in the fog.

"What news?" the hedge night called. "Did you find the Agarathi?"

Miller was breathless. He panted hard, giving a shake of the head. "Nothing, my lord. There's…no one there."

"What do you mean, no one?"

"I mean…" Mads shared a look with Cam Doris. "There was no one, my lord."

"Then he lied, this Agarathi?" Hadros looked at Pagaloth with a frown. "Ten'kin, was it? Well we best find him as you say, Pagaloth, ask him a few questions…"

"No, my lord," Miller came back in, still fighting to catch his breath. "He didn't lie…well, not about that. They *were* there, the deserters. Just not anymore. They'd left."

"We saw firepits," added Cam Doris, taking up the tale. "Two dozen of them, maybe more. Some of the trees had been chopped up for firewood and there were signs that men had slept there on the ground. Hundreds of them, I'd say."

Mads Miller nodded. "Five hundred, Sir Hadros. Perhaps more than that."

"*Five hundred?* Gods. Where could they have gone?"

"Were there tracks?" Pagaloth asked. His eyes moved left and right and then behind him. The rest of the host were following, more shapes

437

appearing in the fog. He wasn't liking any of this. A cold tingle was climbing his spine.

"Not that we saw," Miller said. "Though we didn't stay long to look for them. Creepy place, my lord. And quiet. Quiet like I've never heard."

"Was there any blood on the ground?"

The two scouts shook their heads. "Didn't see any."

"Then they didn't leave because they were attacked," Pagaloth said. "They *chose* to leave."

A few horses were coming in behind them. Sir Bardol came cantering up with Ruggard Wells close on his heels. Their horses were snorting mist and stamping at the ground. Sir Bardol took a moment to gain control of his mount as Ruggard scowled and looked around. "Curse these mists. Can barely see beyond the tip of my damn nose." He looked at Miller. "What'd you find?"

"There was no one there," Sir Hadros answered for him. "Agarathi had already moved off, Rug. Hundreds of them by the sound of it."

Sir Bardol came wheeling around on his stallion, still struggling to get it to calm. "Hundreds? Well that's too many, Hadros. We can't take hundreds more on. We don't have the manpower to…" His horse reared suddenly, giving out a great neigh as it threw him from the saddle. The knight landed with a splash and a grunt, the air pressed out of him. He got to his knees, wheezing, rainwater running down his arms. The other horses were flicking their manes, stamping at the ground, tails whipping.

"Godsdamnit, what's got into them?" Hadros swore. "Someone help him up. Doris, get him back in the saddle."

No sooner had Cam Doris dismounted than his horse went bolting away, running hard into the fog, swallowed out of sight. Doris cursed loudly and went to chase after it, but Hadros called him back. "It's gone, damnit. Bard, stop mucking about and stand up. You're winded, not wounded. Stand up, man!"

Somewhere far off, a sharp cry rang out, echoing through the vale.

Pagaloth's eyes shot left.

The Bladeborn reached to clutch godsteel.

Only Hadros had enhanced hearing. He stared a moment, squinting. "One of the outriders," he said, in a choked voice.

The air went still, a sudden silence falling. There was only the rustling of the men coming down the slope, the tinkle of the rain, the whisper of the grasses as they swayed in the wind. Pagaloth looked out into the fogs across the valley. There were shadows there, of trees unmoving, tall and thick and ominous. But deeper, somewhere deeper, more shapes were appearing. A wall of motion, approaching.

"It's them," Hadros said. He drew his broadsword, its mists swirling and curling, adding to the fog. "Agarathi." His men drew their blades. Hadros turned to Pagaloth. "Find the Skymaster at once. *At once*, Pagaloth. We're going to need him."

Pagaloth understood. He turned his courser about and rode hard up the hill, passing some of the riders coming down as he went. Sunrider Moro was one of them. "What's happening, Pagaloth? What is going on?" the Lightborn demanded.

The dragonknight ignored him, racing toward the Agarathi host, ambling along at the back. "Skymaster Nakaan," he called out, moving into the thick of them. "Skymaster Nakaan. We have need of you!" The men kept on sliding past him like ghosts, cloaked and cowled. "Sa'har! Sa'har, you are needed at once!"

He could not make out one man from another. They all looked much the same until he got right up close to them, and saw their garb, the features of their faces beneath their hoods. Many were staring blankly. There was something strange about the way they walked. Down the hill, he could hear Sir Hadros' voice calling out to the incoming host. *"Halt there, in the name of the king! Take another step and we will be forced to engage!"* Sir Pagaloth turned a full circle, calling out Sa'har's name. The men kept sliding past, silent. *"We are here united!"* Hadros was saying. *"Put up your steel and lay down your arms! Now! Now, else you will give us no choice…"*

"Sa'har!" Paglaoth bellowed. "Sa'har, where are you?"

"Here," hissed a voice.

The dragonknight spun on his horse. The men were drifting past like a slow-moving river, but one stood still before him, a stone in the stream, the others eddying around him. He pulled back his hood and gave an empty smile.

"Ten'kin," Pagaloth growled. He reached to clutch his dragonsteel blade.

The man grinned at him. "Why draw steel? We are allies, Sir Pagaloth, *brothers*. We are all the *Children of Eldur*." His voice was warm and pleasant, a honeyed potion in his ear. Pagaloth blinked and saw him as a younger man, kind of face and dark of hair. He blinked again and he was old, grey-haired and empty-eyed and cold.

"Who…who are you?" he demanded.

"A man of *loyalty*," Ten'kin said. "A humble son to a godly father. He sent me here to correct the course of these men. To make them see the error of their ways. But *you*…" He shook his head. "You have proven troublesome, Pagaloth. You are stubborn, and wilful. But most of all, too *northern*." He hissed and spat to the side.

"*Priest*," Pagaloth rasped, drawing out his blade. "You spread the will of Eldur."

"I speak with his *voice*." The last word was like a crack of thunder, awesome and powerful. His courser startled, rearing. Pagaloth fought to stay in the saddle and failed. He flew into another man, the pair tumbling into the sodden grasses in a tangle of limbs. Pagaloth grunted, scrambling to collect his sword, rushing back to his feet. He caught a glimpse of the other man's eyes as he stood as well. They were glazed. Red. *Thrall*, Pagaloth thought. He looked around in a

439

sudden panic, the fogs swirling about him. "Sa'har!" he roared. "Sa'har!"

"You will not turn him," Ten'kin said. Pagaloth rounded on the priest. His horse had regained its feet and was charging away through the mists, knocking aside the slaves as he went. The last of them were drifting by, moving down the hill. He could hear the clash of fighting breaking out below…screams ripping through the fog…cries of pain. "The good Skymaster is back where he belongs," Ten'kin told him. "He knows where his loyalties lie. *I* have reminded him."

"*No*," Pagaloth said.

"No?" the man repeated, laughing. It filled all the air, rumbling like thunder across the vale. Pagaloth recoiled. He recalled the voice of Eldur when he had come to the Nest. That whisper that filled the world. "All of Eldur's children beckon to his voice," Ten'kin said. "Even you, *northman*. Even you will join us."

Pagaloth grit his teeth and backed away, shaking his head.

More laughter erupted from the depths of the priest, and suddenly he appeared to Pagaloth as a man in robes of red flame, with fire leaping from atop his head, an inferno burning in his eyes. The drag-onknight stepped away from him, backtracking, tripping on something underfoot, slipping into the sodden grasses. Through the fogs the priest was walking closer, whispering all the while. "Come, child, join us. It is no use to resist. If not me, *another* will ensnare you…"

Never, Sir Pagaloth thought, closing his mind to the man. He stormed to his feet and ran, charging back down the hill. The clamour of combat rang out, the peal of steel on steel. Men were roaring in a dozen tongues. He saw the Agarathi deserters leaping and lurching, reaching for the men of the empire, scratching and biting. Sunrider Bellio was on his horse, wheeling, swinging with his scimitar sword. The slaves moved in around him with their grasping fingers and pulled him down. One snatched away Bellio's dagger and began stabbing down and down and down; another disarmed him of his sword and began hacking in a wild frenzy.

Pagaloth could hear Sunrider Moro roaring somewhere in the fog. He caught a glimpse of Sir Quento stirring his own guards to the fight. The waterlogged lands at the base of the hill were growing red with blood and bodies. From the north, hundreds of Agarathi were charg-ing, screaming their warcry…

A hand came down on his shoulder. "Join us."

He spun. The face was not one he knew. A braided beard, hair in rings, almond eyes glazed red. Pagaloth knocked the man's hand away and turned.

"Join us or die," another man said, standing before him.

Pagaloth put his shoulder to the man, bursting past. Ahead he saw Sir Hadros and Ruggard Wells fighting back to back, their blades mist-ing, Agarathi after Agarathi dying on their steel. The bodies were piling high, but they would soon be overwhelmed. The shadows were closing, closing…

"Pagaloth."

The voice was weak as a whisper, but he heard it amid the din. His gaze surged toward the sound and he saw him. Sa'har Nakaan, standing with that glazed look in his eye, a shrivelled old man in his limp red robes, soaked and stained and frail.

"I'm sorry, Pagaloth." The Skymaster reached down to his side and drew his dragonsteel dagger. "I cannot go back…I…I *will* not go back…" His hand was shaking, his eyes were tortured. Slowly, forcefully, he lifted the blade to his neck.

"Sa'har! No!"

Pagaloth set off, but too late. The steel bit through skin and flesh, its red edge slicing open the meat and muscle. Pagaloth reached him, snatching out at his scrawny wrist, pulling the blade away, but the damage was done. The Skymaster collapsed into his arms, blood pulsing from his open throat. Pagaloth brought him down to a knee. He looked into the old man's eyes and saw the deep grief there, the fractured soul, saw the light fading and the red glaze clearing.

"Sa'har…*Skymaster*…" Tears welled in his eyes. "What…what am I to do?" He looked around. He did not know north from south, friend from foe, he did not know where to go. "I…I…"

A trembling finger reached to his lips, old and thin and grey. The blood was sluicing from Sa'har Nakaan's neck, weakening with each pulse, running down into his robes. He opened his mouth, tried to speak. Pagaloth could not hear. He turned his head and leaned right down and from the lips of his friend he heard the faintest whisper.

"*Run*."

32

Saska

Saska had always wondered what it would feel like to fly.

Who hasn't? she thought. *Didn't everyone have the same dream?*

She'd first imagined it in Lord Caldlow's kitchens when she was just a little girl. There was an old scullery maid there called Ada Smalls - an ironic name, Saska had always thought, because Ada was far from small - who would sit her down on her massive squashy knee sometimes, and turn through the pages of a picture book, one of heroes and villains and gods and monsters going back ten thousand years.

The illustrations had been awe-inspiring to the little outcast with the olive skin. Even now she could remember them; the huge great sprawling battles across monstrous forts and windswept plains. The legendary heroes of both north and south, with their misting blades of many colours and fearsome dragons of the same. She could still see them all so clearly. The fiery swirling form of Agarath in a death duel with Vandar, bright and silver and mighty. Tukor, forging his Hammer to help shape the world. Rasalan rising from the ocean to present his Eye to Thala. The famed fight between Varin and Drulgar, with his son Elin and daughter Iliva lying dead and defeated upon the field. The Battle of Ashmount, where Varin slew Karagar, son of the Dread, and drove Eldur away into shame.

Back then they'd all seemed like myth and legend to Saska but old Ada always assured her they were true. The sand giants of the god Pisek. The eagleriders of the Calacania. The great Rasalanian hunters who would take down giant leviathans with their ships. Saska had marvelled at them all, always tugging at the old woman's skirts to go fetch the book and sit her down so she could look at them all again. Sometimes Ada would swat her away and tell her to get back to her chopping, and Saska would have to cut another hundred onions or turnips or carrots before she might get another glimpse. At other times she'd find Ada asleep on her kitchen stool, snoring softly between meals, and would sneak into her room and take a look for herself. Once, the scullery maid had caught her, and spanked her red as the dawn, but Saska didn't care. Back then that was the only punishment she ever got. Life was easy in Lord Caldlow's keep, before he sold her to Modrik Kastor.

But of all the illustrations, perhaps her favourite ones were of the dragonriders. The ones that showed them close up, showed their faces, as they soared the skies like gods, their hair whipping behind them, colourful capes trailing like banners in the breeze. She liked to think of what it would feel like, to have the wind rushing past her cheeks and rifling through her hair, to hear the roar of air in her ears, to feel the soft wet touch of the clouds and see the world from high up there, spreading to the edge of sight.

But today, she had to imagine it no more.

Today she *knew* how it felt.

Neyruu banked left, turning with the wind, and Saska's heart gave a sudden leap.

"How was that," Talasha called to her, as they soared high above the arid plains. "Too much too soon?"

Saska's lips split into a smile. "No," she shouted into Talasha's ear. "*More*. I want more."

She grinned like a goon, looking out at the lands below, wondering if this was all some dream. She could see *so much* from up here, the whole world it felt, but the skies went so much higher still.

All the way to eternity, she thought. *To the Blackness Above and beyond.* She could see the coast to the east, see the city of Cloaklake to the north, and Eagle Lake beyond it, the biggest lake in all the empire. To the west were high rugged hills, clothed in green and brown trees, and there were some rivers there too, thin silver scars wending toward the sea. She saw settlements dotting the lands. Coastal fishing villages and goat farms across the plains and inns and taverns and little hamlets along the Capital Road. A starcat was racing across the lands below, black as a shadow, dashing into some trees. She wondered for a moment if it was Joy, out hunting, but if so she'd gone a long way from the company, who were trudging up the road in the direction of the city, where they would rest the night, Saska knew.

The Agarathi princess was looking back at her with an amused smile on her lips. "Are you *sure*, Saska? Neyruu can be *a lot* more acrobatic than this. Baby steps, remember. That's what Sir Ralston said."

"Everything is baby steps with Rolly," she called back. "I'm *sure*, Talasha. Do your worst!"

The princess gave out a laugh. "You're not ready for my worst." She hunkered down, streamlining her posture, and Saska did the same. "Hold on tight," she said.

And then the world became a blur.

By the time they came in to land, sometime later, Saska was part-elated, part-besotted, and a large part sick, her insides churning and

443

threatening to evacuate as Neyruu flapped down upon a high barren perch in the hills to the west of the city. She sucked air, one breath and then another and then another, great gulps to try to recompose herself.

Talasha was smiling all the while. "If you're going to be sick, best wait till we get to the ground. Neyruu won't appreciate you vomiting down her wing."

That only made Saska chuckle, which made her insides churn some more, but somehow she managed to hold it all together. Another few breaths and she was ready to dismount, swinging a leg over the double-saddle hitched around the dragon's shoulders and neck, then sliding down to the ground. She landed with a crunch of grit and gravel on the high rocky outcropping. Her legs were a little wobbly, her head a little dizzy, but by the gods was it all worth it.

"All good?" Talasha asked.

"Good," Saska said, grinning that dumb grin, and realising that she was part-envious too. Elated from the thrill of the flight, besotted by the dragon (and her rider too, she had to admit), sick from the swerving, twisting, plunging motion, and very much envious that Talasha Taan could bond such a magnificent beast and she could not. And that only made her feel part-guilty as well, for betraying Joy. It was a lot of parts, in all.

She staggered to a rock and sat down, wiping the sweat from her sticky brow. Talasha had brought them down to a fine spot. The view was ranging, looking out over the ocean and the city and the lake, though for all that it was no match for the endless vistas one got from the back of a dragon.

Talasha took a perch next to her. "So, how was it? Actually, you don't need to answer. Your grin rather gives it away." She laughed in that warm, sultry way of hers and handed Saska her waterskin.

Saska drank deep, wiping her mouth with the back of her loose, linen sleeve when she was done. She wore no godsteel armour - it would only weigh the dragon down - and was garbed instead in much lighter fabrics. It felt nice to feel the air on her skin. She had another drink and then handed the waterskin back.

"Thirsty work, isn't it? There's something about flying that dries out the throat." Talasha refreshed herself with a long draught, then hitched the skin back to her belt. "You handled yourself well, I thought. You followed every instruction I gave you."

Saska was good at following instructions, and they weren't exactly complicated. The meat and mead of it was simply 'do what I do'. When Talasha shifted forward in the saddle, Saska was to follow. When she leaned left, go left; right, go right. "Just don't follow me if I fall," she had quipped before they set off. "Try to hang on and Neyruu will bring you safely back."

Sir Ralston hadn't liked that joke.

"I'm used to it," Saska said. "Well, not *that*, exactly. But Joy is pretty acrobatic too when she bounds over rocks and scrambles up

444

cliffs." It wasn't the same as descending in a steep vertical plunge or performing a barrel roll - a manoeuvre that Talasha had performed on three occasions, each one quicker than the last - but there were *some* similarities at least. "When I first rode Joy I used to fall off sometimes, though. Guess the training paid off. Wouldn't be so good to fall from a dragon."

Talasha smiled and shook her head. "The word 'splat' comes to mind." Her laugh was musical. Saska found herself staring into her deep brown eyes, flecked with sparkles of red, admiring that luxuriant jet hair that tumbled in waves from her head. Even with the deep cut on her chin, Talasha Taan was about the most beautiful woman she had ever set eyes on. The fact that she had saved Rolly's life from those sand demons only made her all the more wonderful.

The day was dwindling, the sun speeding its way to the west, though still the air was hot. In the days since Talasha had joined them, there had been a minor easing of the insufferable temperatures, but not much. Certainly not as much as Sunrider Tantario had said when he'd told her the days would grow much cooler north of the Port of Matia.

They had grown cooler, though the word 'much' ought to have been omitted. She couldn't blame Tantario for that, though. From what they'd heard, there had been more sandstorms than ever before in the plains and over in Pisek, more storms at sea than would usually fit into a ten year cycle, and even reports of earth-shattering earth-quakes and sinkholes too, sucking settlements down into the voids beneath the earth.

Every day, more tidings reached them when they passed the inns and taverns and met travellers on the road. And of course, so came the requests. 'My village has been plagued by a pride of night-lions. Please kill them.' 'My farm was raided by bandits. They stole my daughters. Please save them.' 'I seek help for a band of refugees crossing the plains to the north. We are trying to get to safety, but every day is a new threat. Please protect us.'

They were relentless, a daily barrage of begging, and to each and every one of them, Saska could only say 'no'. She had to harden her heart to them, she told herself, but every rejection pained her. To see their desperate faces, the hands held together in prayer, grown men dropping to their knees as they wept for the loss of their loved ones. At first it had been Tantario who took their pleas, Tantario who gave the rejections, Tantario who they cursed, but Saska would not let that continue. She made a point now of being there too. "This is my decision, my fault," she would tell them, in her broken, not-quite-fluent Aramatian. "If you're going to blame someone, blame me." And they did.

She had been hissed at, sworn at, heckled and even spat at once too. Sunrider Tantario had barked for that man to be taken and beaten for his insolence, but Saska told him 'no'. He was venting, afraid, grieving. She could handle a bit of spit. Most just scowled at her though, muttering in their own accents and dialects as they left, never being told the true reason for their rejections. It was wretched work, and more than once Tantario had said she did not need to carry that burden. But to that she said 'no' as well. She would stand before every petitioner, every supplicant, hear every plea. Their anguish and their fury and their fear was her fuel. It reminded her of the importance of her task. *I will stop this suffering,* she would tell herself, as they hissed and swore and spat at her. *One day, they'll see it. They'll understand, in the end.*

The shadows of the hills were lengthening across the plains, stretching all the way toward the Capital Road as it ran northeast up the coast, thin as a strand of silk from here. She could see her host moving in their ragged column, a force further depleted by the terror at the river, trudging in a mournful procession.

Two dozen men, she thought, sighing. *Each of them a brother or a friend to one man or another.* They had all been affected by it, though none so much as the men under Tantario's charge. Many of them had complained of the heat during their journey. Now they complained of the dead. Their brothers-in-arms were gone, slain by sand and shadow, and how long until they followed? Tantario continued to assure her they would escort her to the Perch, but perhaps it was time she let them go. She had the sellswords, and Rolly, and Leshie and Del, and now Talasha Taan as well. *Perhaps that is enough,* she thought. *Maybe we should just take ship from here and brave the waves, as Robbert Lukar did.*

"You seem distressed, Saska. What is it you're thinking of?" Talasha smiled sympathetically. "I am sure you have much on your mind."

A million things, and a million more. "As do you," she only said. "We're both being hunted, my lady. That's a worry we share."

"A worry, yes. And I understand my presence here is not accepted by all."

"No," Saska admitted. Talasha did not ride with them, but soared the skies, circling high above, watching for trouble and often finding places like this where she would rest and let the others catch up. Even at night she would remain apart, owing to Neyruu, who the men did not want around, and the beasts feared. "They wonder….well, *some* wonder…"

"Whether I should be here at all," Talasha finished for her. "They fear I am an agent of Eldur, here to bring the doom."

It was ridiculous, but true. "A few have muttered that concern, Sunrider Tantario says. I haven't heard it myself, but he is very keen to keep me informed. Most think no such thing, though. They know you're here to help, as you did at the river, but…"

"But they are concerned my mere presence will attract danger? Yes, I suspected that would be the case. That is why I try to keep my distance, Saska. If Neyruu senses any threat, I will be able to lead it away from you. This will give you time to escape, or go unnoticed."

Saska breathed out a sigh, wishing she had a better way to thank her for her kindness. Talasha was a princess, and perhaps even a queen, and she should *not* have to spend her days circling the skies, acting protector like some common guard. That she had to deal with all this doubt and suspicion only made it worse.

"You don't have to stay, you know," she told her awkwardly. She turned her eyes to the east, out past the coast and across the darkening sea. Out there, somewhere, the Telleshi Isles sprawled, a thousand drops of land in the ocean, some stark and tall and unwelcoming, others tropical and idyllic, with sandy beaches and quiet palm-fringed coves. "You could find a place to be safe out there, my lady, on the islands. You and Cevi and Neyruu. You could wait out the war in peace. Eldur may never find you."

"And if the war doesn't end? If the world only grows worse? No, Saska. I was *meant* to come here, to help you. King Hadrin saw it in the eye, what happened at the river. My place is with you."

Saska nodded, looking at her toes, shifting her feet. Talasha was everything a princess should be, beautiful and kind and refined, a singer and a dancer and a linguist and a poet, educated to the highest standards, all that she would never be. *Yet here she is, to serve me. It should be the other way around…*

Talasha put a hand on her arm. Her touch was as warm as the summer sun. "There is a saying we have in Agarath," she said. "The translation to the common tongue is not so elegant, but in essence it means 'when the thrill dies, the path darkens'." She looked at her. "Do you understand?"

Saska thought about it a moment. She had an idea, but shook her head. She didn't want to sound foolish or get it wrong, not in front of Talasha.

The princess smiled as if she knew. "Let me explain, then. The thrill sets our hearts soaring. It sharpens the mind and tingles the limb. When in it we feel alive, but once it is done, and we stop, and it leaves us, our thoughts can turn to darker things." She brushed her cheek with a finger, right by the corner of her mouth. "You were grinning up there, exulting in the flight. But here, beyond the thrill, your mind is growing full of doubts. It is better that we walk, Saska, and keep the blood from stilling." She stood. "Come. There is a path I saw, down to the plains. You will feel better when you start moving."

Beautiful and kind and *wise*, Saska thought. She stood and made to follow as the princess led her on.

The trail was an old goat path, most likely used by the herders when they travelled to Cloaklake and back from their farms among the hills. They took the path down, a narrow winding track that ebbed back and forth along a path of loose scree. Neyruu did not follow, though she unfurled herself and moved to the edge of the ridge, watching as they descended with those keen, intelligent eyes.

Saska felt better at once, less doubtful, more hopeful. A smile moved back to her lips as she reflected on the wonders of dragonflight. "Will you take me up again?" she asked, after a while. "I'd like to get to know the sensation more. I might fly myself one day, so…"

"*Might?*" Talasha stopped and turned to her. "I didn't come here to help you for 'might', Saska Varin."

Saska cringed at the name.

"You don't like it?" Talasha asked. "You are Saska of the House of Varin, are you not?"

"So I'm told."

"So you *are*. Again, why else did I come here? Well, to help fortify your sense of worth, for a start. You have to start believing in yourself, sweet girl." She cupped her cheek and smiled. Talasha was barely more than a decade older than her, but somehow she had a motherly air. *Older sisterly, more like,* Saska reflected. *Or perhaps like a young aunt.*

"That comes and goes," Saska admitted. "Believing in myself. Half the time I feel like I'm just wandering along through a dream I can't awaken from. Day to day…everything feels real, but when I sit and think about what's to come…" She shook her head. "I don't know. It's just…a lot."

"A lot can be broken down into little bits. That is what you are doing. Each day is like another block of stone, to add to the great fortress that is Saska of House Varin." She smiled. "One day you'll be a towering structure, and all will quell to look upon you. And the Windblade will be a part of that. I saw it in use, and that shard alone astonished me. I cannot imagine what you will become when you bear all five at once."

A god, a part of her thought. It frightened her, the idea of wielding all that power, as it did what she'd be expected to do with it. "It may not come to that," she decided to say. "There might be another."

"Another heir? Did your mother have twins?"

"No, I mean…"

"I know what you mean. Lord Hasham spoke to me of your doubts, and your friend Leshie has as well." She raised a brow. "She told me something else of interest too. About Elyon Daecar. You know him well, I understand?"

Damn you, Leshie. "We have…history."

"*Good* history, I'm led to believe. She says that Elyon will be more than happy to yield the Windblade to you."

Saska sighed. "Leshie likes to talk, my lady. Elyon and I…we care about one another, I think. At least…he did, before. Now…I don't know. I'd hope that he'll remember me well, but with everything he's been doing, in the war, and…" She'd heard all about it. How Elyon had saved the princess and stolen back the Eye, how he'd slain all those dragonknights as easy as if he was carving up a cake. The gallantry of

448

that, the depth of bravery and brilliance…Leshie had said she'd never heard anything so heroic, and even the Wall had been impressed. To Saska, it only made her see how far she had to go. Elyon was performing astonishing feats, and who was she to deny him that? "I just…I fear to ask him to give it up. And the others…his *father*." She shuddered to think of it. Who was she to ask the great Amron Daecar, the Hero of the North, to lay down his blade for some slave-girl from North Tukor? And all on account of a grandsire who'd died two decades before she was even born? "When I think of all of that, I just…I struggle, Talasha. I struggle." She had no better word to express it.

"I know you do, sweetling. But that struggle is not yours alone. We are all here for you." She took her arm and gave a tug, urging Saska on.

They continued down the trail, walking through the dusk as it went from russet to red to purple. By the time they reached the foot of the hills, where they opened out into the rugged plains, the skies had fully darkened and a cloaked moon was floating in the skies. The road was long miles away from here, much too far to walk. "We'd best fly," Talasha said. "I will take you back, and fetch Cevi. Then return here for the night."

"Are you sure, my lady? Would you not like a bed to sleep in tonight? It'll be safe in Cloaklake, Alym says."

They'd heard as much from the travellers who had come from that way, at least. It seemed that civil order was being upheld in the city and there had been few riots, few occasions of looting and criminality, and no attacks from dragons or other creatures. Sunrider Tantario had said that he would see them hosted in one of the city strongholds, with fine views of the lake, and that for once they could all rest in feather-beds for the night and maybe, if they were fortunate, he would find a willing lord who would host them for a feast. That had cheered the men somewhat. How long it would last was anyone's guess. Saska's guess would be - not long.

"Thank you, Saska. But no. I would prefer to remain with Neyruu. I enjoy sleeping beneath the comfort of her wing."

Talasha smiled and summoned her dragon, and they mounted up, gliding low and swift across the plains, the wind rushing through Saska's hair. The sensation had her smiling again. After a short time, the company were sighted, gathered at a public well where a clutch of shops and inns had sprung up a half mile south of the city. Neyruu came down nearby, landing on the moonlit tundra, and they went the rest of the way on foot. When they emerged from the darkness, Sir Ralston stamped over. "You were gone longer than I expected."

"We flew a while, talked a while," Princess Talasha said. "All these men, Sir Ralston…I feel that Lady Saska is starved of female company."

"Do not let the Red Blade hear you say that," Rolly said. It was the

449

first time Saska had heard him use Leshie's self-styled nickname. "She likes to be the one to whom Saska vents."

"Who says I was venting?" Saska groused. "Maybe we were talking strategy?"

"Were you?"

"Well…of a sort." Saska looked to the others. The men were doing their usual investigations, talking with the tavern guests and inn-dwellers, hunting down travellers to gather up intelligence. She could not see Alym Tantario there, nor Leshie, nor Del.

When she asked of them, the Wall said, "Alym has gone into the city to see about those featherbeds. Leshie went with him, and some of the other sellswords. Your brother is training. Kaa Sokari took him…" He looked about. "I am not sure where. Further down toward the sea, I think."

That was on the far side of the road, where some rocks and stands of trees clothed the coastline. Beyond, the waters glimmered beneath the moonlight, calmer than they'd been in a while. Saska thought she could see some shadows out there in the dark. Of late Kaa Sokari had been setting Del the challenge of firing blind, and in darkness, to better test his senses when striking for a target. Sometimes Sokari himself *was* the target, running about with a small wooden shield, shouting for Del to hit him. It seemed a little risky to Saska, but who was she to argue? Just so long as it was Del with the bow and Sokari with the shield, she didn't have much cause for concern.

The Wall turned his eyes out to the gloomy plains. "So, how was it? Flying?"

"Good," Saska said. *Amazing, exhilarating, I wish I'd been born Agarathi*, she thought. It would not serve to express that to Rolly, though. "I think it'll stand me in good stead when I train with the Windblade." *When*, she thought adamantly. *When. Not if.*

The Wall nodded. "It will. I saw the acrobatics. How did that make you feel?"

"A little sick," Saska confessed. "But that's normal. Next time I'll know what to expect."

"Next time." The Wall looked like he wanted to pour his usual pail of cold water over that, but he knew it was for a worthy cause, not just a way for Saska to seek out some chancy thrill. "Yes. Next time. Though now that you're back down, I would ask you to put on your armour. The essentials at least. We are entering a busy city and must take the proper precautions." He looked at Talasha. "Will you be coming as well, Your Highness?"

"Into the city? No. I will be fetching Cevi and taking my leave."

The Wall did not try to persuade her otherwise. Grateful as he was to her for saving his life, he seemed to prefer to keep her at arm's length. "I will fetch her for you." He bowed and stepped away.

He returned shortly after, with Cevi in tow, having found her with the horses. The handmaid loved horses, Saska had noticed, and always smiled when she saw them. The camels not so much. They were loud, she had said, and didn't smell so nice. Saska quite agreed. With her handmaid returned, Talasha retreated back into the darkness to rejoin Neyruu, telling them she would find them come morning.

It was the same each night, and no matter how many times Talasha said it was her preference, the sight made Saska feel guilty. "The men should be more inviting to her," she grumbled, as the princess took her leave. "You as well, Rolly. You're only alive because of her."

"I give her every courtesy."

"But not every kindness. She has flown across half the world to be here. And she's a princess. She should be *leading* this host, not trailing behind it."

The giant did not like that. "She is Agarathi. Derived from the line of Lori. Eldur's blood runs thick in her veins."

"Yes. I know. That's why she's able to bond a dragon."

The Whaleheart ignored her sarcasm. "A dragon bonded to her by Eldur. *He* gave her that dragon. He can just as easily take it away."

"It? Her name is Neyruu."

"I know her name. Forgive me if I do not feel as you do, Saska. You have Lumo's Light in you, I do not. The bonding of beasts is unfamiliar to me."

This was old ground, worn and trodden and it needed no further footfall. Saska changed the subject. "I think it's time to leave them behind," she said, looking over at the men. A pair of them were pulling up a bucket from the well, a few others watering the animals, and some dozen or so would be gathering intel, but the rest were just standing around, looking worn and weary, gazing out in the direction of the city. This promise of feasts and featherbeds seemed the only thing keeping some of them going. "I don't like the tension here anymore. There's an ill feeling in the air, and we'd be best rid of it." She looked up at him. "I think we should go west. If we ride hard across the plains, we could reach the Everwood in a week."

"The Everwood?" He exhaled. "Saska, we have been through this…"

"Ranulf may still be there. He might be trying to seek the permission of the Calacania still…"

"He might. Or he might not. It is possible that Ranulf Shackton is dead. We cannot go that way. We must keep to the Capital Road."

She knew he was going to say that. *Why do I even bother?* "Then we sail from here. We're a long way out of the krelia's reach now, and if we hug the coast…"

"No. You have seen the seas. The storms come from nowhere and cannot be predicted. The waves rack the coast so fiercely it's said that great chunks of cliff are falling away. Taking ship would be folly until we must. We would only follow Robbert Lukar down to the depths."

451

"He's alive," she found herself saying, if only to argue. "Robbert's still alive, I know it."

"I hope so. The boy is brave, but courage counts for nothing at sea. Not to a Bladeborn."

"He has Seaborn with him too. Del told us. All the best ships were crewed by Rasals. If there's anyone who could get him home…"

"It is them. I know. But this weather is not usual. The heat, the storms, the sinkholes. The extremities of the world are becoming uninhabitable, and this world is surrounded by *sea*. When we reach Eagle's Perch, we *must* take ship…we will have no choice but to cross from there, but here? No. We will stay on the road."

"'That is *my* decision,' Saska snapped at him. "Not yours. Mine."

He stared at her, silent, his horribly pocked and pitted head cast in grim detail by the moonlight. It took only a few moments for her to realise she was being unreasonable, arguing for the sake of it. Not for the first time, not even for the hundredth, she realised she was not made to be a leader. But she had to keep trying. Much as she wanted to hand over the reins, she couldn't, and wouldn't, give up so easily.

"I'm sorry," she murmured. "I'm just frustrated. All the muttering from the men. The pleas of the smallfolk. And with the sellswords being at each other's throats as well…" She gave a sigh. That was another concern. The Butcher and the Baker had no love for the Tigress, and had only grown more suspicious of her since that night at the river. "There's going to be blood between them one night, I know it. This business with Merinius…"

"The Baker has no proof of that," Sir Ralston came in. His upper lip did flicker, though, showing how much he was disturbed by the Baker's accusation. "He saw a shadow, hovering over Merinius's body, no more. It may just have been one of those creatures."

"And blood on the sand," Saska said. "Where Merry died. He says there was blood."

No one else had seen it, but the Baker swore that the Tigress had cut open Merinius's neck, and drank his blood as he lay dead at the border of the camp. The sand demons of *Hrang'kor* may have killed him, like they had two dozen others, but the Baker was adamant the Tigress had supped when she might have tried to save him, before his body was dragged beneath the dirt.

It was a foul allegation to be sure, and Saska's skin had crawled when she'd heard it. The Surgeon had continually claimed that the Tigress only ever drank the blood of the Bladeborn men she slew, evil men or so he called them, men who deserved it. But Merinius was far from evil. He was a bright-eyed man, kind and faithful, and everyone had liked him. No one argued that the Tigress had killed him herself, though there was a growing sense that the Baker was not lying, and that she had seen a chance to have a taste of Bladeborn blood and taken it, thinking no one would ever know.

Now the talk had turned to casting her out. The Baker and his brother did not want to fight beside her, and yet if Saska dismissed the Tigress from her service, she would only lose the Surgeon as well, and with him Gutter and Gore and Scalpel and Savage, all of whom had proven their worth. So far Saska had prevaricated over that problem, hoping it would go away, and that tensions would settle, but they hadn't. Only two nights ago, the sellswords had come together in a fierce clash of words over it all, the Surgeon defending the Tigress's honour, calling the Baker a liar, the Baker and the Butcher angrily pointing fingers and making their gruesome claims. In the end, it was one word against another and the matter had been put to bed. *But not to sleep*, Saska knew. This grim business was like to rear its ugly head once more, and when it did, it would be more than a clash of words she'd have to worry about.

She sighed again. Of the two factions of Bloody Traders, she would sooner keep the Baker and the Butcher, and with them Umberto and the Gravedigger, their men, but she would prefer not to have to make that choice. "How are we to solve his, Rolly? The Butcher has asked that we settle it with steel. Blade against blade, to let the gods decide her guilt. Do you think I should let them?"

He pondered it. "They will not accept anything less than a fight to the death, Saska. This will be no duel to first blood. You would have to be happy accepting that the Butcher may die."

She hated the idea of losing him. And would the Baker stay in her service if his brother was slain? Would the Surgeon if he lost the Tigress? "Do you think the Butcher would lose?"

"There is every chance. I have seen the Butcher fight up close many times. He is a formidable warrior. But the Tigress is as well, from the glimpses I have seen of her. Such a fight could go either way."

She ran a hand across her forehead. It came back slick with sweat. It was still so close here, so damnably humid. It wasn't helping with anyone's mood. "We need to find a way to bring them back together. This division weakens us all."

"Battle usually does that. A common foe." He shrugged. "Saving that, time can prove a healer. My advice is to let this play out naturally. If these men are truly committed to you, they will put their personal resentments aside and work out how to get along."

Saska preferred that option. "We'll give it time, then." The men at the well were stirring, and that could only mean one thing. She peered up the road toward the glow of the city, and saw a host of riders returning. "Tantario," she said. "Let's hope he has good news."

That hope, like many others, was dashed when they went to greet him. Sunrider Tantario dismounted his sunwolf Santarinio with a grave look cast on his face. The men gathered around to listen. "There has been an earthquake," he told them. "Beyond the city. It has torn a great rift in the earth, we are told. The Capital Road is impassable that way."

There were murmurs from the men. "Then we stop here," said one. "We can go no further. We return to Aram."

Tantario glared at him. "We will continue to the Perch, as ordered by Moonlord Hasham. How often must I say it?"

Once more, Saska thought. *Always once more.*

"What of the feast?" called another of the men.

"And the featherbeds," said a third.

Tantario shook his head. "We will camp here tonight. There are fears that the earth will tremble once more, and the city is no longer safe. Many buildings have collapsed, even some of the stone towers, and sinkholes are appearing. Tomorrow, we will head for the lake and take barges across the water. This will take us back onto the road." He talked sharply, in a voice that brooked no dissent, and before any of the men might call out their complaints, he looked to Saska and said, "Serenity. Does that serve?"

Everyone looked at her. She could feel their eyes upon her. "If...if you think it's the right course, Sunrider."

"It is the only course," he said. Then he stepped closer to her. "Walk with me, my lady."

They left the others behind, grumbling and grousing, and moved out across the yard to where the animals were tied and stabled. From the coast, Saska saw the shadowed forms of Del and Kaa Sokari reappear, much to her relief, and Jaito as well, Del's tent-mate and friend who'd been helping him with his training. She was musing on how glad that made her, for Del to have his own friend here, when Alym Tantario said, "I am sorry for my men, my lady. They shame me with their behaviour, and I assure you, it is quite unlike them. They were all chosen for this charge for their sense of duty, and yet too many are now losing their faith. I can only apologise. I hope you will accept it."

She smiled at his grizzled face, deeply rutted at the eyes and forehead. It seemed to Saska that more lines had appeared during their weeks on the road, and they still had so far to go. "You don't need to apologise, Alym. They are sun-weary and grief-struck and afraid, that's all."

"They are *soldiers*. Fine spearmen and knights, even Lightborn. They should know better how to control their emotions. But there is a rot in too many of them, eating away. It is the shroud of the Ever-War, permeating all. The creatures. This weather. Even the men are being corrupted."

"Then send them home," Saska found herself saying. "Let them return to their wives and their children."

He frowned at her. "I cannot. Men of duty and oath are the last bastion against anarchy. If they should be allowed to abandon their posts, every city and town will fall to ruin." He shook his head. "We will take you to Eagle's Perch, as is our charge. The road is impassable here, as I said, and to go west around the lake would take time, and prove perilous. Crossing the lake would be quickest, though is not

454

without its dangers." He looked into the darkness. "I had hoped to speak to Princess Talasha about that. I take it she has found somewhere to rest for the night?"

"The hills," Saska said, looking to the shadows in the distance. "She'll spend the night up there."

"Then I will speak to her on the morrow." His jaw was tight, his eyes tense and weary. "It will take several days to cross the lake, my lady. And the barges are not large enough to take us all. We will have to take three, for the men and the mounts. But even then it will be tight, and these divisions…"

She understood. "We'll split them up accordingly. Make sure the sellswords are separated. And the worst of the dissenters too."

"That would be wise," he said.

The look on his face suggested this was not the option he would have preferred. But no road was safe anymore. The sea was crawling, the plains as well, and the lake seemed the lesser of those evils. All the same, Saska could not help but think of Robbert Lukar, and the words that Lord Hasham had said.

"The seas will judge him," the old moonlord had intoned.

And now the lake will stand judgement on us, she thought.

33

Jonik

They rode in the shadow of the Hooded Hills, a solemn troop of four.

There was something sinister about this place. It had crept up on them over the last hour, a brooding menace suffusing the thick, misty air. The wind moaned and whined in strange plaintive voices, as though calling out in torment, and the trees seemed to shy at their passing, creaking and cowering away.

"It's like the very land is afraid," Harden said warily, riding beside Jonik on his weary old warhorse. It was the best that Lord Ghent could procure for them at the border, a stubborn old gelding whose best days were long behind him. Much like Harden, a man might say, but he kept on going like the old sellsword too. "Can the wind be in *pain*, do you think? The sounds here…"

"It's just the lay of the land," Jonik said. "The way the wind moves through the valleys and trees."

"And this mist? It's unnatural."

A lot was unnatural these days. "It's a thick morning fog, is all. Our minds are playing tricks on us." He gave his piebald palfrey a rub on the neck. "If the horses aren't worried, there's no reason we should be."

"You sure about that, lad?" Harden murmured, looking around. "These mists…Who knows what's hiding behind the veil? Might be all sorts lurking just out of sight."

"Nothing that I can hear," Jonik said. He had his hand clutched to the grip of Mother's Mercy, and had not let go for a long while. He had heard no growling, no low deep breathing, no skittering of feet, no crunch of twigs among the trees. Just that wailing wind, and its haunting laments. He wondered what the Rasalanians would make of it. They had lots of gods for the weather of the world. *Gustas* was their god of fierce winds, he knew, and *Tish* their goddess of the breeze. Did they have a deity for all this eerie keening? Some dead god, perhaps, who had perished in some foul way? If they did, Jonik hadn't heard of it. "We're just spooked because we know what happened here," the former Shadowknight went on. "That's all it is."

The others were riding a little way up the slope, fading in and out of the fog, a dozen horse lengths away. Around them, the trees shivered in their clumps and thickets, shadows in this thick grey gloom, but every once in a while the mists cleared and the lands opened out, showing the distant shadow of the Hooded Hills to the east, the rolling grassy hills and wetlands around them, spreading far and wide.

They seemed to be thinning again now, those mists, waning as they made their way up the slope to the top of the rise. Jonik peered forward, to where Gerrin and Sir Owen were riding side by side, approaching the crest of the hill. The latter was sitting up stiff in the saddle, taut as a bowstring, staring forward. "We're close," Jonik said to Harden. "I can hear Sir Owen's heartbeat getting faster. He recognises this place."

Harden looked over at him. His haggard old face was twisted into a frown. "You can hear his heart from *here*?"

Jonik smiled. "You don't believe me?"

"When you had the Nightblade, aye, maybe, but now…"

"The Nightblade didn't enhance my hearing any more than regular godsteel. Or my sight. And if it did, it was marginal and I barely even noticed." He looked forward again. "He's anxious." He could hear it when he focussed, that *thud thud thud* in Armdall's chest, growing harder and stronger as they climbed. "This is the hill they fought on. It must be. We'll see it when we reach the top."

His own heart was starting to thump harder in anticipation, because he had heard from Sir Owen Armdall exactly what to expect. A land torn and broken, with steaming fissures and blackened trees melted down to stumps, where Drulgar the Dread, with Eldur the Eternal atop him, had fought a host of giants and a certain mad king with a Blade of Vandar in his grasp.

It had been a long week since the Oak of Armdall had told them that, since Gerrin had found him at the border. Jonik had been sleeping at the time, dozing beside Sir Lenard Borrington's bedside when Gerrin stirred him awake. "Did you find out something about my grandfather?" Jonik had asked him, rubbing his eyes and clearing his throat.

"I found some*one*," the old knight had responded. "Come, he's waiting in the yard."

He'd led Jonik down the spiral stair and through the keep, past the night guards and out into the yard of the Undercloak. There they had found him, sitting on a stump outside the stables, hunched forward in a sodden cloak, greenish grey and travel-stained. The knight had a cowl over his head, but at once Jonik saw the long tangle of beard, the matted hair, the glint of godsteel gorget about his neck. The knight looked up, hearing their approach, and then Jonik saw his eyes. They were the eyes of one haunted, eyes that had beheld things no man should ever perceive. His skin was mud-spattered, cheeks gone gaunt, and there were webs of wrinkles about his eyes. Jonik had heard it said that the Oak of Armdall was the model of chivalry, a dashing knight, beautiful and brilliant and young. What he saw was a broken thing, old before his time, a shadow of the man he was.

"Sir Owen," Gerrin said. "This is him, the one I told you about."

The sworn sword had stood and looked at Jonik for a long moment, as though searching for some resemblance. "The king's grandson," he said. "You don't look like him."

Jonik hadn't cared to respond to that. He looked into the Oak's haunted turquoise eyes. "Where is he? Is he dead?"

Sir Owen gave a forlorn nod. His voice was hollow, blunt. "He must be," he said. "No one…no one could have survived that."

"Survived what?" Jonik asked.

And that was when he told his tale.

Jonik had been speechless. He had stood for a long time in mute astonishment once Sir Owen was done. Then he had asked the only question that mattered. "Where is the Mistblade, Sir Owen?" Fear cut through him like a knife. "Did he take it? Eldur?"

"Not that I saw," the Oak answered in a shaky voice. "The demon…he never left the back of the dragon. I wanted to help, to fight with him, your grandfather, I did, but…" He turned his eyes aside. "There was nothing I could do."

"You've done enough bringing this news to us," Jonik told him. "Did you try to search for him after?"

"After," the knight nodded. "Once the dragon was gone, I…I tried. But there was no sign. He must have fallen…"

"Or left," Gerrin had put in. "Could he not have faded to mist and given chase, Sir Owen? You said he had *wanted* this fight, against Eldur…"

"Against the demon, not the Dread. He never expected *him.*"

"Even so. If he survived…"

"He *couldn't* have survived. Not that." His eyes swam with the horror of it. "And he wouldn't have left me. I was his faithful servant. His sworn sword."

"Will you be mine?" Jonik asked him. The question took Sir Owen off guard. Even Jonik had not expected to utter it. "I have to find the Mistblade, Sir Owen. That is of vital importance. Will you swear me your sword and lead us to where they fought?"

The knight stared at him. "I don't know if…I'm not sure I can go back. I tried to find him, as I said, but…"

"Four of us will have better luck," Jonik said. "You're coming with us, Sir Owen. It's what my grandfather would have wanted." He did not know why he said that or where it came from, but it seemed to work. He saw some measure of duty in the man's gaze, a need to serve and help. "Will you swear me your sword?"

"I…yes, I…I will."

"Then swear it," Jonik had said, and shakily, Sir Owen Armdall went down to one knee…and their company took on a new member.

Harden, as ever, was not so happy about it. "You think we can trust him?" he asked now, as they rode behind, some thirty paces back. "Begging your pardons, Jonik, but your grandfather was a known loon, and Sir Owen his most loyal disciple. He might have some hidden plan up his sleeve."

"Like what?"

"I don't know. Give me time to think about it."

"You've had time. He's been with us for a week."

"Maybe he's not dead," Harden said. "Janilah. Maybe he's off somewhere, hiding in the woods, and he's planning to creep out and kill us one night."

"Why?" Jonik asked, humouring the old man. "I'm his grandson. Why should he want to kill me?"

"For the Nightblade."

"I don't have the Nightblade."

"Aye, but does the Oak know that? You've not pulled out Mother's Mercy since he joined us, and…"

"He's seen the crossguard, the handle, the pommel, and the sheath," Jonik interrupted. "That should be enough for him to know it isn't the Nightblade, Harden."

"Aye. So why haven't you told him?"

Jonik was confused. "Told him what?"

"About everything. Ilith and the refuge and all that. Leaving the Nightblade behind. You haven't told him."

"He hasn't asked."

"Exactly. He hasn't asked about the Nightblade…and you haven't told him…so that means you don't trust him…and he…well, he doesn't want to get into those sorts of conversations, because he's planning to betray us anyway." He smiled craggily, as though terribly proud of himself for coming up with such utter nonsense.

Jonik was less impressed. "Are you done? Can we focus on the task at hand now?" He made sure the sellsword wasn't going to say anything more, then gestured up the slope. "The hilltop is just ahead. If you're so worried about Sir Owen Armdall's loyalties, by all means keep scowling at him, but so far as I see it, he's the best chance we have right now of tracking down the Mistblade, and that's all that matters." He gave his horse a spur and left the old man behind.

Within a quick canter he had caught up with the others. Gerrin looked back. His eyes were wary. "Sir Owen says this is the place. The old castle ruins are right ahead, where they made their camp. The battle took place beyond."

Not much of a battle, so far as Jonik had heard it. The word battle conjured a good contest and fair fight, two foes evenly matched, or at least enough to put the outcome in doubt. There had been no doubt as to who was going to emerge the victor in this fight, even with the gruloks involved. The demigod and the Dread could fell entire armies by themselves. An old man and his small cohort of giants were never going to be enough to stop them.

You were a fool, Grandfather, Jonik thought. *You were blinded by your arrogance, and you died for it, and you've only yourself to blame.*

The hilltop was wreathed in mist, like the valley they'd ridden through below. It hung heavy and still over the sodden, muddied earth, as though trying to shield the world's eyes from what had happened here. That dark, ominous feeling still lingered in the air, and the wind was still making that plaintive, wailing noise. Sir Owen's chest was going up and down. "I see the ruins," he whispered, staring forward. "Right there. Near those trees."

The castle had belonged to some river lord once upon a time, though had never been particularly grand. From the earth, the old stones poked out like grey finger bones, and in places the ground was churned and scarred. It was where the gruloks had rested, Sir Owen explained to them. "The night we arrived, the king sat out alone in the rain. He knew there was a grulok out there, and he was right. It came from the darkness, and then a bunch of others appeared. They'd been here for thousands of years, King Janilah said. Waiting for him to come. He said it was fate."

The others shared a look. None of them wanted to discuss the whims of fate anymore.

Further south, across the hilltop, the mists swirled upon a land scarred and broken. They got only glimpses of it, but it was enough. Jonik saw chasms torn open in the earth, black mud boiled by flame, trees burned down to stumps. It had been a fine open grassland before, Sir Owen had said. "But the dragon and the demon…they turned it to a hell."

Jonik was seeing that now, though only in the aftermath. Before, fires had blazed high across the hill, the fissures had gushed a black fume, and the very air had seemed to fizz and simmer, the Oak explained. He had been told to stay back by his king and had fought that command at first, but when the Dread drew closer, his own courage had fled him, he admitted. "I ran," he'd said, in shame. "Took cover further back, and if I hadn't, I'd be dead. There was nothing I could do. Even the gruloks…I saw them swatted aside like they were nothing. A few cut him, but they were just scratches. I saw one bitten into a thousand pieces, and another was knocked a hundred metres through the air." He swallowed. "But mostly it was smoke and fire I saw. And the titan's shadow. And that red light, from Eldur's staff. It made a sound, like ten thousand men screaming at once. I thought I was going to die just hearing it."

But that had been then. Now, what they saw was a land black and dead and shattered. No smoke, no flame, just a lingering shadow of dread.

"Let's leave the horses here," Gerrin said, dismounting. So far as they could see, the devastation had stopped just short of the ruins. "Is there any cover here to make a fire, Sir Owen?"

"There's part of an old roundtower still standing, further in," Armdall said. "That's where we had our camp."

"Let's see it restored. We can begin our search after. Hopefully these mists will have cleared a bit by then."

It was strange, Jonik mused, to think that a once great king had made camp here, in these mossy old ruins out in the middle of nowhere. The rotted remains of the curtain wall were barely visible among the weeds and sprouts of sedge, the gate had long since gone to rust and blown away, and the yard was full of thorn bushes and saplings. Some had been singed by the hot winds that blew from the battlefield, it looked, carrying here with its burning ashes, though the rains had served to prevent any true fires from catching. Further in, the wooden shelter Sir Owen had erected in the wreckage of the round-tower was still there. It had a roof of latticed branches and twigs, covered in grass and leaves to keep off the rain, and beneath that a small firepit had been dug, scattered with bits of charred wood. Jonik imagined his grandfather sitting here, night after night, brooding on the coming of his foe. He had turned pious, Sir Owen had told them, and called himself Vandar's herald and his will. He was doing this all selflessly, to try to defeat the enemy and end the war.

Jonik did not believe a word of it. Janilah Lukar had never done anything selflessly, not in all his life. *No, he did this for himself*, he knew. *He hoped Vandar would honour him for defeating Eldur in battle. He still wanted a Table of his own, the old fool.*

"Let's see about getting a fire started," said Gerrin. "Sir Owen. You took care of that I presume?"

"I did. I built the fires and hunted game and went off in search of tidings." He sighed, shaking his head. "I came back one day telling the king his grandson was leading a host to Rustbridge. I urged him to leave, to take command of the army. The gruloks might even have followed him, I said, but he wouldn't listen. If he had, he might still be alive."

"Then good thing he didn't," grunted Harden. "That man earned his death a hundred times over for the things he did."

Sir Owen lowered his eyes "He was trying to turn to a better path," he said, in a small voice. "Doesn't every man deserve a second chance?"

"Are you speaking for yourself, Sir Owen?" Jonik asked him. He'd heard about the death of Rylian Lukar in the throne room. He knew it was Sir Owen Armdall who was the one to deal the killing blow. "You have things to make up for as well."

"We all do," said Gerrin. "There's not a man among us without a chequered past. But honour isn't a straight path, not like some men will say. Sometimes a dark deed can lead to a bright beginning. Isn't it

461

all just about perspective, in the end?" He let them ponder that a moment, then said, "So how about that fire, Owen? Where's best to gather good wood?"

An hour later, the fire was roaring happily, they had a stack of good kindling gathered beneath the shelter, and Jonik had used Mother's Mercy to slice up some logs as well. When he was done with that, he drew out an oilcloth to wipe down its edge, sitting on a stump. Sir Owen came over. "That blade…do you mind if I ask…"

"I don't wield the Nightblade anymore, Sir Owen."

"No. I realised you didn't have it the day we met at the border. Was it…taken from you?"

"I gave it up willingly." He slid Mother's Mercy into its scabbard. "Harden thinks you're going to betray us. Is that true?"

"Betray you? No." He sounded offended. "Why would I?"

"I never said you would. But Harden's more cynical." Jonik folded his oilcloth and deposited it into the pocket of his cloak. "So everything you've told us is the truth?"

"Yes, every bit of it. I've led you here, have I not? The ruins…the lands…it's all as I've said."

"And my grandfather? You're quite certain you don't know where he is?"

"I told you. He was consumed in the fume and I didn't see what happened to him. I would guess he fell into a chasm. Though it's possible he was…well…"

"Go ahead. Say it."

"*Eaten*," Armdall finished. "Once or twice I saw the dragon's head plunge down from the skies. It's possible the king…I don't think so, but…it's possible he may have been swallowed."

With the Mistblade in his grasp, Jonik thought. That would be a calamity. When he'd told Ilith he was going to set out to fetch the Blades of Vandar for him, he had not reckoned on delving into the internals of a colossal, world-ending dragon god. He smiled at the absurdity of it. "Well, let us hope your first instinct is correct. I would sooner spelunk down into those rifts out there than down the throat of the Dread."

The Oak gave a small smile, perhaps the first Jonik had seen from him. "Yes, I'd say that would be preferable. Though may I ask…the Mistblade, you say it's of vital importance that you find it. Why is that? Do you intend to try to combine them, as your grandfather once did?"

Jonik saw no reason to lie to him. "I do. Though not for me. I serve a greater power, Sir Owen, but I'll say no more on it for now." He looked across the hilltop, at the black and broken land beyond. "The mists are a little thinner," he noted. "Come, you can show us where you last saw him."

Sir Owen led them out, leaving Harden to prepare a broth. It was well into the afternoon, and Jonik had no expectation of finding either his grandfather or the Mistblade today. He would call this a first scouting, to get a better feel for these lands. Across the hill, the waning mists unveiled the true breadth of the battlefield, the earth torn with great vents and deep pits, some so deep the bottom could not be seen. Most were thin, but here and there a wide chasm yawned open, metres wide, its walls plunging down into the earth with roots and rocks and little ledges poking from its sides. Down some, stagnant pools of rainwater had gathered. Down others, hot air rose, and with it came a haunting sound, echoing from beneath the earth. That movement of the winds, Jonik took that for. *Or some fell creature, lurking below.*

Gerrin went around with a parchment in his grasp, scribbling a map with a quill pen, guessing at the width and depth of each rift. When he could not see the bottom, he simply drew a cross. Soon there were many rifts with crosses beside them. "So where abouts was the king, then?" the old Emerald Guard asked.

Sir Owen shook his head, turning around a full circle. "Somewhere around here. I could not say with any certainty."

"So he might have fallen into any one of these cracks?"

The Oak nodded.

"Did you climb down to check any of them?" Jonik asked.

"A couple of the shallower ones. But I was afraid I wouldn't be able to get back out, without ropes or anyone to help me. So my search was limited. And the ground was unstable."

Jonik learned that to himself a short while later, when he inched too close to one of the edges and the earth gave way beneath him. His left foot went first, slipping, then his right, and he'd have gone tumbling down were it not for Sir Owen, who dashed in and grabbed his arm, hauling him back.

"Thank you," Jonik said, panting. His heart had leapt into his mouth for a moment. Most likely this armour would have protected him from the fall, but there was no guarantee of that. "I can see how my grandfather might have fallen in."

Armdall nodded solemnly. "Even if he survived the fall, he'd have starved to death by now. With all the rain, water shouldn't be a problem, but food…I doubt there would be much of that down there."

Just worms and roots, Jonik thought. There was also the chance he was crushed to death, or entombed when some chasm wall collapsed on top of him. That would be a foul fate, lying trapped under a thousand tonnes of rock, with nothing to do but mull on your mistakes and follies until your body eventually gave out. Perhaps that was what had happened. And perhaps it would be just.

Gerrin came over from a nearby fissure he'd been mapping. "Wide one, that, and deep," he said, shaking his head. "It's a lot worse than I thought, Jonik. We'd do well to consider going for help. It'll take a hundred men to search these chasms and even then it could take weeks."

"We are the help," Jonik said. "I'd rather not bring anyone else into this if I can avoid it."

"Then I guess we have to hope we get lucky." Gerrin looked at Sir Owen. "Maybe Vandar will guide us, how about that? He brought Janilah here after all. Only fair that he helps us find him." He turned his eyes across the plains as the mists continued to clear. To the south, the signs of the Dread's passing were clear. Some thickets out there were burned, and the grasses had been scorched to black. Once the dragon and the demigod had dealt with the king, the battle had evidently continued to the west. Down the slope, more pits and scars peppered the land, and here and there were boulders and rocks as well.

"Are those gruloks?" Jonik asked.

Sir Owen's answer was indefinite. "It's hard to say. Even when you get right up near them, they're impossible to distinguish from regular rocks."

"Could we try to wake them?"

"I…wouldn't," the man said. "If you still had the Nightblade, they might have come to you willingly, but you don't. They may only try to kill us."

Come to me willingly, Jonik thought. That gave him an idea. "If the Mistblade fell into one of these chasms, wouldn't the gruloks gather close to it?"

Gerrin thought the notion had merit. He had a look around, searching for a place where there were many rocks and boulders close together. There were none, however, and their hopes were quickly dashed. "Maybe all the gruloks here were killed?" he offered. "How many of them did you see die, Owen?"

"Some…from afar. That one that was bitten…" He gestured to a scattering of stones at the edge of one rift. "That's probably it, right there. And those down the hill…they might all be dead as well. There were about a dozen of them here, I remember. If any of them lived, they might have gone off looking for another to serve."

"Did you see any moving away, once the dragon had gone?" Jonik asked.

"None. Though there was a lot of smoke still. I could easily have missed them."

Jonik pondered which Blade of Vandar would be closest. The latest tidings they'd heard said the Frostblade and Sword of Varinar were still a thousand miles to the west, and Elyon was known to move about a lot with the Windblade. *We could use him here*, Jonik thought. As ever, thinking about his half-brother made him nervous, but he tried to push that aside and think of the greater good. With the Windblade, Elyon would be able to fly down these chasms one after another just like that. And if he were to find the Mistblade somewhere down there, he'd have the strength to bring it up as well.

But Elyon wasn't here, and he was, so he'd have to do this alone.

"We'll start with the smaller rifts," he decided. "That will give us a better understanding of what we're dealing with, and we can go from there. Best we go down in minimal armour. Full plate will be too heavy for the ropes."

Gerrin agreed. "Just the essentials should serve. To protect us should we fall."

Jonik looked to the skies. It was getting late and would soon be dark. "Should we start now or tomorrow, do you think?"

Gerrin thought about it. "There's still some more mapping to do. And we haven't covered the whole battleground yet. I'd say we get a good night's rest and then attack it full-on in the morning."

Jonik agreed with the plan. Tomorrow, the hunt would begin.

34

Lythian

A hand shook him awake. "My lord, there is trouble."

Lythian blinked, escaping the sweetness of his dreams. Dreams of the princess he should never have loved, of tenderness and warmth. There was no sweetness here in this ruin, no warmth to be had. Only rain and wind and darkness. "What is it, Sir Oswin?" His voice was hoarse, his head heavy. "What trouble?"

"It's the prisoners, my lord. There has been some bloodshed, I am told."

Lythian grunted as he sat up, swinging his legs off the pallet bed he slept on in his tent. He rose wearily, picking up the Sword of Varinar as he did so, which he kept on hand beside him. Sir Oswin had been assigned to watch over him as he slept. He did not know how long that had been, but it felt scant, the skies still black as pitch outside. For once it did not seem to be raining.

"What time is it?"

"Dead of night, my lord. Some two hours until dawn."

"My cloak," Lythian said. As Oswin went to fetch it from its hook, Lythian pulled on a godsteel hauberk, glittering in the torchlight. Of late he had taken off his plate armour to sleep, to help improve his rest, but there was no time to put that on now. The chainmail would serve. Atop it he garbed himself in his blue woollen cloak, fastening it quickly at the neck with his First Blade pin. Then the pair of them stepped outside.

The night was quiet, the air cold and still. A rare thing. One of Sir Guy Blenhard's men was waiting, a guard Lythian new as Marc Torrence, a good and faithful fellow and a man from Sir Guy's own lands, a little north of the city. Presumably he was the one to rush here and tell Oswin of the trouble. "What's going on, Marc?"

"Blood and butchery, m'lord, in the square." He had a flush to his cheeks and a slight pant to his voice to suggest he'd run to get here. "Good Guy told me to come fetch you at once."

Blood and butchery. That sounded worse than the squabble he was thinking of. "How bad is it?"

"Bad, m'lord, and was getting worse when I left."

Lythian frowned. "It's still going on?"

Torrence nodded. "Aye, m'lord."

The First Blade of Vandar set off at a hard march, Sir Oswin trailing behind him, Marc Torrence hurrying to keep up. Two men-at-arms were standing guard outside the silver-blue pavilion of Lord Rodmond Taynar, wearing the gloomy colours of his house. As they passed by, the young lord emerged, rubbing at his eyes, peering at them. "What's the commotion?" he asked sleepily. "Are we under attack?"

"Nothing so bad as that, Lord Taynar," Lythian said. "There is some fighting in the prisoner camp. Nothing you need to worry about."

He marched past at a speedy clip, pressing onward through the square and toward the lane that took them south through the city in the direction of the docks. The noise grew louder as they went. Loud enough to awaken others along the route, who came crawling from their shelters and tents and out of broken doorways. All peered at the skies concernedly. Some shouted out, asking if the dragons were coming. Many were already rushing for their weapons, scrambling to prepare for a fight.

Lythian put their minds to rest. "We're not under attack," he called to them. "Go back to sleep. If there are dragons you'll hear the horns."

Some heeded him, returning to their dens, but not everyone. By the time they came to the prisoner square, a trail of some dozens were following behind, eager to find out what was happening. As soon as they arrived, Lythian looked out across the cobbles and saw chaos. Scores of men had been killed or maimed. The noise was cacophonous, the fighting ongoing. Men moved through the flickering light of the torchfires, hacking and slashing and screaming.

Lythian turned to Sir Oswin and the men who'd gathered behind him. "Help break them up and stop this damned bloodshed," he commanded fiercely. He looked to the temple along the eastern side of the square. Sir Guy Blenhard was on the steps, calling orders and trying to restore calm. Lythian marched to join him. "What in the blazes is happening here, Guy? Who started this?"

Sir Guy turned to him. He looked visibly pale and was only half-dressed. "I...I don't know, my lord. I was sleeping when the fighting broke out. My men give different reports."

Lythian breathed out in anger. That wasn't good enough. "Get this place in order. Now! I want the fighting stopped and the perpetrators caught." His eyes went toward the tavern in which the women were being kept. It looked undisturbed, a pair of guards stationed there. Most of the prisoners were watching in great huddles, staying as far back from the bloodshed as they could. They were Lumaran, Piseki, Aramatian, Lythian saw, under the command of the few knights and nobles in their ranks. Few of those were engaged in the bloodshed. The vast majority of the dead were Agarathi, and those still fighting were Agarathi too, identified by the reds and crimsons of their torn and tattered cloaks, the almond eyes and dusky skin, the black hair twisted in braids.

At least fifty of them still seemed to be fighting, some with weapons, others without. Those without were screaming, leaping, clawing at the northern soldiers, trying to stab out their eyes with their thumbs. *Gods, what madness is this?* Those with blades were hacking, swinging, cutting wildly, a frenzy to their movement. Many were singing out their battlecry as they fought.

"How were those men armed?" Lythian shouted. "Where did they get those weapons?"

"I don't know, my lord," Sir Guy told him. "They must have stolen them."

"Stolen them?" He looked again. By his count at least fifteen or twenty of the prisoners bore northern steel in their grasp, swords and daggers and axes. They would have had to pilfer two dozen corpses to arm themselves like that. So far as Lythian could see not nearly that many Vandarians lay dead. *How could they possibly have stolen them?*

Lythian clung hard to the Sword of Varinar, knuckles whitening. The blade was urging to be drawn, to be swung through one man and then another, to drink in dragonkin blood, to see an end to this madness and win the men back to his side. He was tempted. Gods he was tempted to put an end to all of this folly and give up on all his failed designs. His hand twitched. An inch of golden steel glimpsed the night air, glowing, but at once he shoved it back down.

No, he thought. He need not bloody his blade, and nor did he want to. These prisoners were under his protection. They had come here willingly, in many cases. He did not believe that they had been stirred to violence without cause. *Northmen did this. My men.* He took his hand off the blade.

"Tell me what happened, Guy. Damnit, I want to know how this began."

The camp commander stuttered nervously.

"Speak, damnit!"

"It was them," said a voice. Lythian turned, saw one of the guards there, a grim look on his face. He was a Barrow man, out of the Iron-moors, with that burial mound sigil of House Barrow sewn into his jerkin. "That Agarathi lot. They just went wild and started screaming and attacked. I saw."

"From where?"

The man waved a hand. "There. Had the guard of that alley, and saw it all. You ask others, m'lord. They'll say the same thing."

Lythian did not trust this man. He turned back to Sir Guy. "You said there were differing reports."

He nodded. "Willim said he saw a few of the guards enter the pen. He heard a *clatter*," he told me. "Then sudden shouts and screams."

"A clatter?" Lythian looked around. "Where is he?" Willim Winters was another of Sir Guy's own men, a trusted man-at-arms who lived on his estate.

"In the fighting, my lord. Somewhere. I can't see through this damnable dark."

Lythian gave out a grunt. He could not stand by idle while the men were dying. Agarathi or Vandarian, it made no matter, they should not be fighting at all. He stormed off down the steps, shouting, "Make way," as he went. The guards in the cordon turned, saw him coming, and backed off so he could pass. Lythian stepped straight into the square, past the posts and fencing that had been erected around the boundary. Ahead of him, to the right of the shattered fountain of Amron the Bold, dozens of men were still doing their death dance. Lythian marched straight into the fray, grabbed the first Agarathi he saw by the shoulder, turned him, and put his fist into the man's jaw, knocking him unconscious. A second whirled, screamed, and ran at him. He too was soon on his arse. Then a third made the same mistake, leaping from the side with a dagger in his grasp. Lythian Lindar flicked a wrist, backhanding the man to the floor, and kept on going.

By then he was in the thick of it, blades flashing all around him. A dinted steel broadsword came whizzing past, cutting down upon the head of an Agarathi prisoner who was looking the other way. Lythian dashed forward, swinging upward with his arm, knocking the blade aside. It made not a mark on his chainmail. The guard stumbled back from the impact, eyes flaring in confusion as if Lythian had materialised from thin air. "Enough killing! Enough!" the First Blade bellowed at him. Others heard, saw their commander there with them, seeming unsure what to do. "ENOUGH!" Lythian roared again.

He spun about, hoping his presence would be enough to settle things. Some of the Vandarians were lowering their arms, backing down. Others had not seen or heard him and were still hacking away at limbs and torsos and necks and heads. The dead were thick on the ground, the blood wet upon the cobbles, the stink of iron hot in the air. A trio of crazed Agarathi were staring at him. All of a sudden they screamed their warcry and rushed. Lythian heard a shout of "My lord!" and saw Sir Oswin Cole hurrying forth with his misting longsword.

He raised a hand and shouted, "No! Enough killing!" and stepped forward, ducking into the first Agarathi with his shoulder. The man went flying backward as though he'd been hit by a bull in full flight,

469

tumbling insensate to the ground. A second was caught by Lythian's elbow as he ducked, which smashed against his chest, and off he went as well, barrelling into a group of other men, knocking them off their feet. The third stumbled past him, pirouetting and swinging with an axe, a wild crazed light in his eyes.

Lythian blinked. *Red*, he thought, disturbed.

He lost his focus for a moment, but regathered it in time to slide sideways, the axe rushing down past him. Instinct wanted him to rip out his godsteel dagger and cut the man through, but he kept it sheathed, needing only its power and not its edge; his fist would do. As the Agarathi heaved to hack at him once more, Lythian phased forward and struck him in the chin, using but a fraction of his strength lest he knock his head clean off. The man joined the rest on the ground.

The First Blade looked about once more. The fighting was fading, but still shadows moved about him. Sir Oswin had taken up his call - "Enough killing! Enough killing!" - and was showing the way by knocking an Agarathi out, as Lythian had, with a strong clean hook to the jaw. Lythian met eyes with him, nodded, then saw past Sir Oswin's shoulder. Through the churn of bodies, a man was grinning right at him. There was a mad triumph in his eyes, a queer mania, but Lythian saw him only in a flash. A second later a body moved past and blocked him and when next he looked, the grinner was gone.

He stood a moment, disquieted. There was something about the look on his face…

"My lord!" Sir Oswin shouted. "Look out!"

Lythian snapped out of it, saw the knight's eyes looking behind him, flared in warning, and threw himself away at once. A sword came slashing through where his head had been. Sir Oswin Cole roared a cry of "For Vandar!" and flew forward, spear-tackling the assailant to the ground. More of the men echoed him, calling for Vandar and for the king, and the violence erupted anew. Swords slashed out, axes hacked down, blood sprayed across the cobbles.

Lythian Lindar had seen enough. He pulled the Sword of Varinar from its sheath and raised it to the skies. A golden light spread forth to fill the square, and the last few Agarathi hissed and shielded their eyes, shying away. "Enough! I say enough!" His voice was a thunderclap, given power by the blade. His very eyes shone like golden flame. "Enough killing! *ENOUGH!*"

His words rang out through the square, the city, echoing off the broken towers and walls. The final few Agarathi quailed, stunned, and Marc Torrence and Willim Winters sped in to disarm them, knocking them down. Quiet settled across the square. Slowly, Lythian lowered the blade, returning it to its sheath. Darkness drank the light once more, the golden mists receding, until only the glow of torchlight remained, flickering in the gusting wind.

Lythian turned to the men. "Marc, Will. Bind the unconscious and gather the weapons. Sir Oswin, on me." He spoke calmly, marching back the way he had come to rejoin Sir Guy Blenhard on the steps. "It's done," he said. "Get this place in order. Seal the square and start asking questions. I want to know what happened. *Exactly* what happened. I will be in my command tent when you're done."

He returned to his pavilion within the main square by the River Gate. Outside, the lords and captains had already gathered, roused by Lord Rodmond Taynar. "I thought you would want to convene a council," the young greatlord said.

I want to wake up and find this is just some nightmare, Lythian thought. But he only said, "Thank you, my lord. You did the right thing."

Rodmond smiled. He had the skinny features of his uncle Dalton, the lean build of the men of his house, but had always been much more palatable of character. He'd been a Varin Knight for several years, and all of those serving under Lythian's command as captain. It made him naturally obedient to him, despite the great power he now wielded as Lord of House Taynar. *Power he never wanted, same as me.*

They gathered in the command pavilion. Sir Ralf had already lit the braziers to ward off the darkness and chill. They were approaching the midst of the Vandarian summer, where the days would typically grow hot and muggy, yet this weather was autumnal, almost wintery, and there had been news of snows further north. A part of Lythian would welcome it if it decided to come down here. The constant rain was beginning to drive them all to madness, and strange things were starting to happen.

But for now it remained dry, the skies black, cold and quiet. Lythian removed his swordbelt and set the Sword of Varinar against the wide oaken table, just where Amron would rest the Frostblade. His cloak he removed as well, though not his chainmail. He sat in Amron's seat, and would speak with Amron's voice.

"What happened?" asked Lord Barrow, once Lythian had taken his seat. He was grey like the grave, his sigil appropriate, with tufts of hoary hair to either side of a banner of baldness from forehead to crown. It made him look older than his forty-five years. *We are almost of an age*, Lythian thought. *Yet he looks like he could be my father.* "Lord Rodmond said there was trouble with the prisoners."

Lythian nodded. "The square broke out into a riot. Involving the Agarathi and the guards. Scores are dead."

Lord Kindrick gave a snort of triumph. "I warned you, Lindar, didn't I warn you? Said something like this would happen."

"He is the First Blade of Vandar," said Rodmond. "You will use the proper courtesies, Lord Kindrick."

The lesser lord bowed to his better. "Of course. You're right, Lord Taynar." He smiled as sweetly as that weaselly face would allow. "*Lord* Lindar. I did warn you that this was a mistake."

Lythian did not recall that occasion. "When, exactly? And what mistake are you referring to?"

"Bringing the Agarathi into the city. I said it would come back to haunt you."

Lythian was still struggling to recall. He frowned hard at the man. There was still an anger in him, the embers of the battle. His blood was up, his eyes intense. "I did not speak to you that night," he said bluntly. "I gave the command and moved the prisoners. You only stood by and watched."

"Yes. I watched, and I shook my head at you. I thought that made my feelings clear."

Old Lord Warton gave a cough. His voice was tremulous when he spoke. "Are you to say that...that some of the soldiers *provoked* the prisoners to...to violence, my lord?" His words were punctuated by more coughing, a malady that had afflicted the poor man for long years, and which tended to irritate those around him.

"Yes, my lord. That is certainly one possibility."

Sir Fitz Colloway gave a haughty laugh. "Now you can't be serious, my lord. Why would they do that?"

You know why. Colloway was five and twenty, a man who thought he was a great deal more handsome and important than he was. He wore a constant smirk on his lips and slicked his hair back over his scalp with oil. A nephew of Lord Rosetree, Sir Fitz had taken on command of the Rosetree men after his lord uncle perished during the battle. Some four hundred, all told. A paltry number in all honest truth, but it had been enough to earn Colloway a place at this table. *That is how few we are now,* Lythian reflected. *Nine thousand and change. And hardly the best or the bravest.*

"There have been tensions between the soldiers and the prisoners for weeks," the First Blade said. "I am told by Sir Guy that some men were seen entering the pen before the fighting began. He mentioned hearing a *clatter.* I believe some blades were thrown down, and some of the Agarathi provoked into picking them up and using them."

Lord Barrow guffawed. "My own men stand guard about that square. None of them...not a single one...would ever do anything so reckless."

Lythian looked at him flatly. "You have over two thousand men here mustered from your lands. Are you to tell me you know them all?"

The lord fronted up to that. "I know the character of my people, Lord Lythian."

Lythian considered that an empty boast, but didn't say it. "I'm not suggesting it was your men, Lord Barrow. Sir Guy is making inquiries as we speak."

"Sir *Good Guy*," smirked Colloway. "Sir *Arselicker*, more like. He'll just tell you whatever you want to hear. He's a sycophant, that man."

"Do you know him well, Sir Fitz?"

The knight shrugged. "I know a suck-up when I see one, my lord."

Lythian shook his head. "Sir Guy is known for his honesty. That is why I assigned him to watch over the prisoners in the first place."

Kindrick sniffed at that. "Exactly. *You* assigned him. He's *your* man, not ours."

Lythian's patience with this Ironmoor lord was growing desperately thin. "Since when did this become about me against you?" he demanded.

"Since you started accusing our men of killing prisoners."

"I have not accused your men. I have said the men have not yet been identified. The guards are drawn from all parts of our forces. Yours and those of Lady Brockenhurst as well…"

"So it could be Brock-men who did it?" Sir Fitz said.

"Or no one," said Lord Kindrick. "You heard a *clatter*? Is that all you're going on? A clatter?" He laughed.

Lythian's upper lip twitched. "More information will come through shortly."

Kindrick had a gulp of wine. "You *want* this to happen. You want it to be northmen to blame." He drank again. "Gods forbid your precious Agarathi might have started it."

Lord Rodmond frowned at him. "Just what are you insinuating?"

Kindrick looked over at him lazily, an ingratiating smile on his lips. "Nothing. Just words. They're just words, my lord. Nothing to worry about."

He has no respect for him, Lythian thought. *Or for me.* Tension thickened in the room, a short silence brewing before they heard the sound of footfall outside. The flaps swayed open and Sir Adam Thorley stepped in, Sir Storos Pentar right behind him. "My lord, we heard what was happening," Sir Adam said. He had been sleeping, that was evident by the puffy eyes and messy hair. Storos had been taking a watch on the walls tonight, Lythian knew, though might well have wandered out toward the traps as well to check in on his men. The muddy boots would indeed suggest he had spent time beyond the walls.

Lythian invited them both to sit, as Sir Ralf served the wine. Outside, the first faint signs of dawn were beginning to glow. It was going to be a long morning, Lythian sensed. He sensed too he was going to have to make some difficult decisions by the end of it, depending on what Sir Guy Blenhard reported. *I cannot let this stand*, he thought. *If Vandarians are to blame, I must come down on them hard.*

And then he thought of the grinning man. Had he imagined that? And the Agarathi with the red eyes? Had he imagined that too? *They were crazed,* he thought. *Wild.* Was that just driven by hunger and hate, by the slurs and the taunts and the mocking of the men who guarded them? Or was something more sinister happening here?

He mulled on that as the debate went on.

"We need to get rid of them," Lord Barrow declared of the prisoners. He waved a hand as though his word was final. "These Agarathi clearly cannot be trusted. The others from the empire…mayhaps they can be kept here for now, but the dragonkin, no. Load them up on a ship and send them away. It's time, my lords. Let them fend for themselves at sea."

"A leaky ship with torn sails and wonky masts," smirked Sir Fitz Colloway. "We let these creatures crawl off to Agarath, and they'll only be re-armed and sent right back. They're wild, every one of them."

"Would you listen to yourself, Colloway," Sir Storos scoffed at him. "Only a fool makes such broad claims."

"And only a sympathiser would deny them."

Sir Storos shook his head, exasperated. "Do we have to invite this child to these councils? Lord Taynar, it is well within your power to dismiss him. All he ever does is smirk and spit this bile."

Rodmond glanced at Lythian, then said. "He does have a point, Fitz. You say little that is constructive."

"And you say little without Lord Lythian allowing it," the haughty knight came right back. He sweetened the insult with a smile. "Apologies, my lord. That came out wrong. I only mean to say…"

"You think I have no mind of my own?" Rodmond bristled.

"No, of course you do. Only…"

"Only what?" He stared at him. "Speak."

"I only meant to say that you served under Lord Lindar for a long time, in the Varin Knights. Those habits are hard to break, and..."

"And you were never a Varin Knight at all," Rodmond dismissed. "Frankly, you are nothing. Go. Get out of my sight."

"My lord?"

"Did you not hear me? I said go."

Sir Fitz Colloway stood, sketching a stiff bow. "I serve at your pleasure, Lord Taynar." He stalked off out of the tent. Kindrick's eyes followed him darkly, the shadow of a smile on his face.

Lord Barrow was the best of the three. "I apologise for the boy, my lord," he said to Rodmond. "His uncle favoured him, but he has much to learn of command and courtesy."

"And me?" Rodmond challenged. "I am five years his junior. A boy, as you would say."

"A boy raised to rule."

"No. I never expected to rule. Nor did I want to, which I have made quite clear. But fate has handed me the reins of House Taynar and I will steer her as best I can. Perhaps I do seek guidance from Lord Lythian, as I did King Daecar before he left. A wise man knows to learn from his elders. Would that not be the case, my lord?"

Lord Barrow nodded agreement. "Well said. I quite agree."

The tension was somewhat defused by Colloway's departure, though they still had Lord Kindrick to contend with. "Fitz is a fool," he said, in his grating voice. "Young and spirited and a little bit stupid as well. But what he said is not wrong. We have heard what those Agarathi did out there tonight. Who's to say the rest won't rise up and go wild as well?" He looked around. "They have to die. All of them. This is war and they *have to die*. We can't keep sharing our rations with

474

them. While we eat the flesh of dead dragons, they eat the flesh of our livestock, pork and beef and mutton stew." He snorted at the notion, over-exaggeration though it was. "Is it any wonder the men took action?"

Lythian sat uneasily at the command table, peering across at the man. "So you're admitting the men took action?"

Lord Kindrick sniffed. "In defending themselves when these barbarians rose up in riot. Yes. They took action. And rightly."

"That is yet to be seen."

Kindrick spat a breath. "Why do you *always* defend them? You're the First Blade of Vandar. *Vandar*, not Agarath. It's your sworn duty to defend this realm from those heathens and I'm sorry to say it, *my lord*, but you're doing a piss-poor job of it." He gulped his wine, gave a snort, then stood. "I take no pleasure in saying that, but your time in the south's made you soft and every man in this city knows it. Best you have a good long think on that, my lord. It's high time you set your priorities straight." He stiffened that weasel face of his into a look of great gravity and turned to leave the tent without another word.

Lord Barrow gave out a solemn sigh at his parting. "I must apologise again, my lords. He is tired and fretful and worries sorely for his wife and children back home. It is a malady we all have to bear, I fear, though affects us all very differently. He blames the Agarathi for his toils." He stood from his stone seat. "Might I suggest we adjourn until a later time? We have all woken suddenly and it would serve to cool our tongues. We can reconvene when there is something new to report."

It was a sensible suggestion. Lythian nodded, silent, and the men rose from their perches and moved off, leaving him alone with only Sir Ralf for company. For a long moment the First Blade brooded, saying nothing. Eventually, Ralf spoke. "What do you plan to do?" the old man asked. "If Sir Guy should report that some of Barrow's men, or worse Kindrick's, were responsible for the violence…"

"Then they will be dealt with…and harshly." His voice was hard, his eyes sharp. "I have made plain the punishments, Ralf."

He closed a fist and felt a fearful rage move through him.

Life for life, he thought.

35

Amilia

The wind was fierce in her face, blowing up from Vandar's Mercy. Much as it was pleasant to see the view from here, Amilia Lukar was cursing herself for ever agreeing to this. "Are you quite ready, Elyon?" she called, over the noisy gusts. "You promised me that we would return to Ilithor by dusk, and we're barely even halfway to Thalan."

The prince was on one knee, rolling his right shoulder in its socket. He winced on occasion, and Amilia could almost hear the clicking of the joints even over the wind and the crash of waves below, smashing distantly against the Tukoran cliffs. "Just give me a minute," he said. "I need to do my stretches so I don't seize up."

It was mid-morning, and the air was bitter cold. Amilia had dressed appropriately at Elyon's advice, wrapping herself in rich furs and wools over godsteel mail and studded leathers to protect her, but the winds knifed through her all the same. Somehow it was even worse here on the hilltops by the coast than up there in the skies. Up there she had the world to look down on, at least, and there was something about the fear of flying that seemed to keep her warm. But standing on this hilltop was unbearable; it was a cold fierce enough for the deep of winter, but summer had only just begun.

"Just hurry up," she said. "I'm *freezing*, Elyon. If I stand here any longer, you're going to have to thaw me out."

"And if I don't stretch properly, we could crash, and die," he came back at her. "So just suck it up and stop complaining. I'll be done in a moment."

She made a rude gesture at him, then dug into her cloak pocket to pull out a skin of wine, taking a long drink. Elyon frowned at her. "Oh, you didn't think I'd come without refreshments, did you?" *At least if we crash, I'll be half drunk*, she thought.

"What is *wrong* with you?" he said. "We're going to meet the new King of Rasalan. You shouldn't be drinking, Amilia."

She shrugged and had another drink, then another just to ram the point home. "You should just be happy I'm here. I might have said 'no', you realise. Thalan's not somewhere I ever wanted to go back to."

"Yes, and I appreciate that. But this drinking…"

"Has got to stop," she said for him. "Save it, Elyon. I've had that from Morwood and Mallister already, and I don't need it from you as well." She had a last swig for good measure, stoppered the skin with a cork, and put it back into the large inner pocket of her cloak. Then she drew it tight about herself, fastening it with her leather belt. "Are you ready yet? Just give me a timescale, at least. If you're going to take another ten minutes, I'll take a walk to keep warm."

"No." He performed a final roll of the shoulder and stood. "I should be OK to go now. Come on. Let's get you strapped up."

The harness had been of Elyon's own design - with the help of old Archibald Benton - and allowed him to fly with another person strapped up to his chest. Amilia would prefer to straddle his back like she was sitting a horse, but was told that was not possible, and far too dangerous. She'd been drunk when she made the suggestion. She walked up to Elyon and slid her arms and legs through the leather loops, then he tightened them all up to make sure she was secure, harnessing her into place. "Good?" he asked.

"None of this is good, Elyon. But yes, I feel quite secure."

"Let me know if you feel any of the straps loosening, and I'll land. Do you want me to go at the same pace as before, or a little faster?"

She twisted her neck back to look at him. He was so close they could kiss, pressed up behind her like that. "How much faster can you go?" So far as she could tell, they'd been going rather quickly already.

"Much," he said, smiling at her. "Though with my shoulder, I'd best take it easy. Thalan is still over two hundred miles from here, so we may have to stop again, but I'll try to make it in one go if I can." He paused. "Is there anything else you want to say before we take off?" Talking when in flight could be difficult, with the rush of the wind, Amilia had found. "Do you need to make water?"

She huffed at that. "I'm not a bloody child, Elyon."

"No. You're just a drunken princess who may need to take a piss. And I'd rather you didn't do it when we're airborne."

"I'm fine. Let's just go. I can hold my bladder if I must." She did not like feeling demeaned like this, though supposed he had a point. Two hundred miles was a long way.

"Just tell me if you need to go, and I'll land. I wouldn't want you soiling yourself before we meet the king." She could almost see him smiling behind her. Before she could conjure a response, he raised the Windblade and stirred the winds, and that deafening rush filled the air.

Amilia braced as her feet left the ground; it was not a sensation she would fast get used to and her heart was pumping hard, yet there was an undeniable thrill to it as well. Much as she liked to tease Elyon Daccar, she trusted him to fly her safely, and if a dragon should happen by, well, perhaps there would be a thrill in that as well. Fighting through the skies, battling in the clouds…Amilia wondered what it would be like to have an up-close view of all that, though in truth she'd rather not find out. Her stomach was sensitive enough as it was, and no doubt Elyon would do a great deal of jerking and twisting and somersaulting to outmanoeuvre his foe, and she would prefer not to choke on her own vomit. That would not be a princessly way to go.

Elyon lifted them up slowly at first, then a little faster, and at once the world spread out beneath them. Amilia cast her eyes around. To the far south, she could see the towers of Rockfall, Lord Huffort's city seat, tiny as children's toys at the base of the mountains. Northwest, more distant, the shining waters of the Clearwater Run jagged their way through the rugged lands of North Tukor. As they flew higher she could see the city of Ethior out there, the city of her lady mother and her kin, hardly more than a black smudge at the edge of her sight, built upon the river's southern banks.

East was their direction of travel, though. Within moments they were flying directly over the choppy waters of the Sibling Strait, right where it opened out to form the great bay of Vandar's Mercy. The story was as old as time. The god Vandar had been sick of the squabbling between the brother-gods Tukor and Rasalan, so had come here and torn them apart, forming the bay and strait as he did so, ripping the lands of the gods asunder.

Amilia didn't believe that, of course, though she liked the tale. There were a hundred others like it, in which the gods had shaped the world. How Vandar had made the islands of the Bloodmarshes with his warhammer, smashing the land-bridge that linked the continents into a thousand tiny pieces. How the Hammersong Mountains had been raised from all the thudding of the forge god's hammer, and so named thereafter as Ilith took the hammer up at Tukor's death, singing his sweet melodies as he struck at his anvil, the sound of both *hammer* and *song* ringing out through the peaks. In the far south they said that Solapia had been Lumara's favourite child, and so the goddess of the sun and the moon and the stars had made Solapia an island all of her own, where she could live in peace.

There were so many stories like that. Every land and every people had been raised by the gods and their followers and moulded in their image. It had all happened over such a long time, over countless millennia, right back to the beginnings of the world, but now it all seemed to be collapsing in on itself so quickly.

And what would be left if Elyon and his ilk prevailed? Even if they won - and the princess thought that most unlikely - the cost of life would be unimaginable. Hundreds of thousands had already perished, and great forts and cities across all the north were toppling like trees beneath the woodsman's axe. Thalan was lost, and now even Varinar, the great impregnable city of the Steel Father, had been cast beneath the shadow of the Dread. *How long until the same happens to us?* the princess fretted. *How long until Ilithor falls?*

She did not like to confront all of that. She only wanted to drink, and dance, and sing, and take Mallister Monsort into her bed as often as she liked, and perhaps others as well, to indulge in the fruits and vices of the world before it all came crashing down. *And why shouldn't I?* she thought, and not without a note of bitterness. *Why should I not be able to enjoy these dying days in pleasure, and in peace?*

And yet…it was growing harder to silence the voices, to sit by idle while others worked to save the world. *As I drink and dance, the world is dying. As I sing a thousand more are slain. When I scream in the throes of pleasure in my bed, how many thousand are screaming in terror?* Those thoughts gnawed at her, and her guilt was building. Little by little, her hedonism was losing its lustre. And so came the creeping, gnawing thought - *maybe I should do something to help?*

The air was getting colder, burning at her cheeks. She blinked from her thoughts and looked forward. Ahead, beyond the eastern shores of the Sibling Strait, she saw the Oakwood fringing the coast of Rasalan. There was a glitter of white atop the trees. *Snow?* she thought. *At this time of year?* She heard Elyon calling out to her, pointing his spare hand away to the north. "The Mercy is freezing over," he shouted into the wind. "There are floes of ice out there."

She squinted through the rush of air and saw that he was right. A thick carpet of ice was forming atop the waters, with broken floes jostling and bustling in the waves. That usually happened at the height of winter, and only during the coldest.

"It's the same to the south," Elyon was going on. "It's raining almost nonstop across the southern parts of Vandar."

"And the north?" she shouted at him.

She saw him shake his head. "This is as far north as I've gone." He gestured forward. "Look. There's snow up there, in the Highplains. The Izzun River is choked with ice."

She saw that too, as they flew closer to the river's mouth where it opened into the bay. Some ships were resting along the banks, and there were others that looked to have been caught in the floes as they crashed together and merged, right in the middle of the river. There were some men down there, small as fleas, trying to break the ice and get themselves moving, but it was a losing cause, that was clear. South of the Izzun, the harbour city of Steelport was much the same, its docks frozen over, the galleons and galleys and cogs and other trading vessels all stuck in the ice.

"The clouds are thickening ahead," Elyon called. "It's snowing out there." His teeth were starting to chatter, and the wind was cutting bone deep. "I'm going to have to go faster, Amilia. Thalan isn't far now and I'd sooner not freeze to death in flight."

Amilia agreed. "I can't feel my face." Much more of this and she'd get frostbite on her nose, and her cheeks were stung red and raw by the wind and cold. "Go as fast as you need to. Just get us there *safe.*"

The extra speed only made it all the more loud and painful. The wind stabbed at her like a thousand small needles, cutting at her cheeks and eyes and lips. She squeezed her eyes shut and clamped her mouth tight, praying for it all to end. She could feel a crust of hoarfrost forming on her eyebrows, filling her nostrils, dangling off her lashes.

After a long while she heard a shout. "*There*, Amilia. We're almost there."

Thank the gods. She opened her eyes with some effort; the cold had almost glued them shut. Through the sudden white world through which they were flying she could see the city spreading out before her, ghostly in its pale misty mantle, a city of spectres and death. She had flashbacks from the night it fell. The dragons and the fire and Eldur with his red eyes, and that voice from another world, filling all the air. The rush through the palace and the secret tunnels Astrid knew, and the gasping, leg-burning escape into the Highplains to the north. The City of Thalan had become a hell that night, visited by the wrath of a god. *And now that hell has frozen over,* Amilia thought, as they flew across its stiff dead corpse.

They passed over the harbour where the city straddled the Izzun River. The boats were thick below them, clustered and frozen at their docks. The masts wore white cloaks, and from the rigging icicles hung down. Beyond, the city stepped up through its levels, its whitewashed walls and painted roofs, in ocean-blue and sun-yellow, all covered in a layer of snow. Great piles of rubble lay scattered where buildings had toppled, half hidden under their freezing blankets, and the open squares were deserted. At the rear, rising up with the Snowmelt Mountains to its back, the Palace of Thalan still stood above it all. The balconies were broken, the walls pitted and scarred, and some of its towers had fallen, but it still stood. To one side, Amilia saw the Tower of the Eye rising up near the cliffs, the rotunda at its summit torn open by the claws of Garlath the Grand.

"That's where I saw him," she said, with a shiver to her voice. "*Eldur.* That's where he took the Eye."

And Hadrin, she thought, remembering how her rat of a husband had whimpered and obeyed, taking the Eye off its tessellated stone pedestal, to fly away with the Father of Fire. That did not go well for him, Amilia had learned. Her husband had spent the following months chained to a plinth in a windowless chamber, scorned and mocked, his clothes worn down to rags, his flesh all but melted off his bones. She had the story from Elyon, who had been there to see her husband die. It gave her such joy to hear it, after all he'd inflicted upon her. "Tell me again," she would say to him, as she cuddled in her chair by the fire. "Tell me how he died, Elyon. Tell me of his fear." And she would sit there and listen, drinking down her wine, imagining the death of her rat-king husband over and over again, smiling.

She was not smiling now, though. There was nothing to smile about here.

"We'll land there," Elyon called back to her. "Just outside the palace. I see guards."

His eyesight was clearly much better than hers, because she hadn't seen a soul thus far. But as they flew lower, and came down to land, the faces started to show themselves. They poked from out of their broken hovels and peered from shattered windows. She sighted cloaked figures slipping away down alleys like mice, saw footprints in the snow. Through the palace windows, some fires were burning in its grand and stately rooms, glowing softly behind the shutters and boards, and outside on the steps were a host of guards, huddling about an open fire on stools and blocks of stone.

The soldiers saw them coming down. There were voices, shouts, and several of them stood and drew swords. The others made no effort to move. The rush of air softened as Elyon came in to land in a slow dismount, stirring loose snow from the surface of the icy cobbles and causing the flames of the fire to dance. Their feet crunched down through a film of ice, and Elyon dismissed the winds. All went calm and still.

"Are you OK, my lady?" he asked. "Not too cold, I hope?"

"I've never been colder," she replied. "Just happy to have landed." *And dreading the return journey already,* she decided not to say.

The guards were stepping over, brandishing their blades. They sheathed them at once as soon as they saw who it was. "Elyon Daecar?" one of them said, realising. He turned to the others. "It's Elyon Daecar."

The rest of the guards approached through the cold white mists, moving from the heat of the fire. There were whispers and murmurs among them as Elyon began undoing the straps, unfastening Amilia from her harness. It was only then that one of the guards recognised her, looking almost like a small bear in that enormous fur cloak of hers, and all the other layers beneath. "Your Majesty? Queen…Queen Amilia?"

She looked at the man who had uttered those words. He was one of the guards who had served here during her time, one she recognised. His name slipped her mind, though. "I am not your queen," she said. "We have come for another reason."

Another of the men moved forward, brushing past the rest. He had a black beard sprinkled white with frost, black hair, and fierce eyes of the same colour. "My lady, I am the captain here. How might I be of service to you?"

"My companion here wishes to speak with Prince Sevrin. He is still alive, we have heard. And *king*, if so."

The men exchanged looks. The captain spoke. "Prince Sevrin

481

refuses to name himself king until he has knowledge of his cousin's fate. Until Hadrin is proven as deceased, he…"

"Here is your proof," Amilia cut in. She opened her arms out to present Elyon Daecar. "He has a story to tell, but not to you. Bring word of our arrival to the king. We shall wait within the hall."

The captain commanded for the doors of the palace to be unbarred and opened. Inside it was much warmer. The main hall had a large and elegant hearth, beside which a great pile of firewood had been stacked, and the flames were crackling pleasantly. There was a stale scent of smoke in the air, from the fires that had torn through the palace long ago, and ash still sat in little heaps and drifts here and there.

"My lady, please wait here," the captain of the guard said, voice echoing softly. He called for two seats to be set by the fire. "Is there anything I can get you while you wait?"

"Nothing. Thank you.'

She lowered herself down onto the seat, enjoying the licking warmth of the flames as they thawed the cold from her bones. The chair was sturdily built, capable of bearing the weight of godsteel, so Elyon decided to sit as well, stiff and grand in his armour and over-cloak, resting the Windblade beside him, along with the pack he had brought with him, containing the book. He removed his helm to let his black hair tumble down over his forehead, and his beard was growing longer. Amilia regarded him for a long moment. With the hair and beard, and the new scar across his right eye, he was starting to look the spit of his father. *Even more than Aleron did,* she realised. *Maybe this is always how it was meant to be. Elyon was always the true heir.*

"I hope the book didn't get too wet," she said, looking at the bag beside his chair.

He checked to make sure, but did not seem too concerned. The bag had a waterproof lining, he told her, should they encounter rain. "I didn't expect snow, though," he said, with half a laugh. "It's almost like the seasons are reversing."

"Or changing forever," she said, feeling a pang of tiredness. Flying was weary business, even as a passenger. She yawned, lifting a dainty hand to cover her mouth, as her mother taught her. "This fire is far too soothing. I could sleep right here, couldn't you?"

He nodded wearily. "I wonder…would you mind if we stayed here, for the night? Pending what happens. I just…with the snow and the cold and how long it's taken to get here…"

"We're not going to make it back for dusk, are we Elyon?" She smiled at him, to show him it was fine. "I'm happy to stay if you are. These halls…" She looked around. "They don't seem so bad now that Hadrin's gone. It's like the evil has been removed, scoured away by fire. There's something peaceful about it, something almost pretty." She frowned at her own words. "Is that bad to say? To find beauty in all this death and ruin?"

482

"It's important to find light even in the dark," he told her. "That doesn't mean you don't care."

"Really?" As far as she was aware, Elyon understood her to only care about herself. "You think I care?"

He laughed softly. "You're not a monster, Amilia. So you think the world is going to end, that's your right. It doesn't mean you *want* it to. I'm sure you'd sooner live into your dotage as a crazed old drunk, still bedding handsome spearmen and stableboys."

She chuckled, removing her gloves, and reached her hands closer to the flames to warm them. "I guess that wouldn't be so bad." Little clumps of snow and frost were melting off her cloak and hair, trailing down her neck. She shivered as a drop snaked down her spine, and then reached up to touch her cheek. It felt sore, windburnt, bitten by the chill. "I need a mirror," she said. "I must look awful after that."

"You look beautiful. You don't have the capacity to look awful."

She smiled at him. "It's nicer when we're kind to one another, don't you think? In another life, it might have been me and you who were betrothed. Do you think we would have been happy?"

He met her eyes, wondering on the question for a moment. "Maybe," he said at last. "I'd have to put a curb on your drinking, but…" His lips twisted into a smile. He had done more of that of late - smiling - since his visit to the refuge, and seemed in better spirits. "We'd have had pretty children, at least."

"Not with all the drinking. That isn't good for an unborn child, I've heard." She grinned and withdrew her wineskin. "Fancy a taste?"

He seemed to have lost his strength to fight her on it. "Hand it here," he said.

They shared the wine as they waited, passing it back and forth, whispering into the quiet of the hall, laughing and smiling. After a while they heard the tread of footsteps outside. The door swung open, stirring ash from the tiled floor, and a small troop of guardsmen entered in yellow cloaks, with a young man at their head. He had a neat, confident step, a pleasant, narrow face, and keen golden eyes. He was not large, nor small, very much of average height and build, though trim, lean in a good way, and had a fine head of wavy chestnut hair that bounced winsomely as he walked toward them.

"Your Highness, Your Highness," he said to them as he approached. "What an honour to host you in our humble home." He smiled a courteous smile and performed an elegant bow, the links and scales of his whaleskin armour catching the light of the fire. It was a beautiful suit, in shades of gold and royal blue, and over it he wore a fine cloak of lambswool at his back, split blue and yellow for his kingdom. "I am so sorry to keep you waiting. I hope you will forgive me."

"You're forgiven," Amilia said, standing to face him. "I'm sorry, but I don't think we've met."

"No, we haven't, my lady. My father had planned to introduce us after the coup, though when it failed we never had that chance." He

483

smiled at her. "I am Devrin, Prince Sevrin's son and heir. It is an honour to finally meet you."

She let him kiss the back of her hand. "And you," she murmured, remembering how Sevrin had spoken of his son, that time they met down in the cellar. He had said he was not near as ugly as the rest of them - in a tone of jest, of course - and he wasn't far wrong. Despite the narrow facial features, Devrin looked almost nothing like his father or his uncle or his crazed, wiry-haired aunt. Nor Hadrin, that was for certain. The family tended to be rather weaselly of feature, but there was little of the rodent about this man. *He might even be called handsome,* she thought. Not an Aleron or an Elyon or a Mallister Monsort, no, but perfectly acceptable in his way. "I'm happy to hear you survived, Prince Devrin. Tell me. Did your uncle Garyn live through the attack? Your auntie Cristin?" She had met them both that day in the cellar as well.

The young prince dipped his eyes. He was older than her and Elyon, though not by much. Perhaps five and twenty, she thought to look at him. "I regret to say that Uncle Garyn perished in a blaze, my lady. Auntie Cristin, however, still lives, and we are all most grateful for that." His eyes lifted. "You did not meet the others, did you?"

"No. Just those three."

"Ah. Well I'll not trouble you with their fates, then." He kept his eyes on her for a long moment, smiling, then seemed to remember himself, snapping out of his trance. "Well, um, let's not keep my father waiting. Princess Amilia, Prince Elyon, this way please." He glanced at Amilia again, smiled, and set off through the palace.

She followed behind with Elyon, moving through the hall and into the adjoining chamber beyond. She knew the palace well, though mostly the apartments at the back, and the fine high terraces she liked to sit on, watching the city below. It was about the only pleasure she had here. Well, besides Sir Jeremy Gullimer.

Elyon gave her a nudge. "I think he likes you, Amilia," he whispered under his breath. He had a little smile on his face. "Devrin could hardly stop staring."

"I'm used to it," she said. That was just the plain truth; Amilia had been stared at by people all her life. "And let's not pretend you didn't stare at me when we first met as well, Elyon. I remember how you undressed me with your eyes that night at the feast."

He laughed aloud. "And since. Many times." That was in jest, she supposed. *Though…*

Their path led them through the public parts of the palace, across an inner courtyard, past the stately rooms where balls and functions were held, and finally to the king's private audience chamber, or one of them. He had several, Amilia knew, though this one had not been touched by the fires, or so it seemed as they entered.

The rugs within were warm and fresh, the walls clean and hanging with rich tapestries, the furniture unspoilt. A fire was crackling in the hearth, attended by a pair of armchairs and a table between them. Another table was busy with flagons and jugs and cups, and there were some plates of food there too. A set of doors led to a large covered balcony, with fine views of the city. The view had somewhat worsened of late, though the balcony itself remained intact. It was out there that they found King Sevrin, standing at the balustrade, looking over the ruin of Thalan. His son performed the introductions.

"Father. I have brought Princess Amilia to you, and Elyon Daecar, the Prince of Vandar, and Master of Winds."

"Thank you, Devrin." King Sevrin turned. He was cloaked in a rich mantle of dyed sable. Beneath it he wore a fitted leather doublet, embroidered at the chest with the speared leviathan and golden sunrise of his kingdom. He was a small man, weak-chinned and growing gaunt, with wispy strands of grey hair blowing from his scalp. There was perhaps a mild resemblance to his son, in the narrow shape of his face, and the keen nature of their eyes, but one had to look hard to see it. No doubt Devrin's mother had been something of a beauty to make up the difference. The king's lips swelled into a smile. "Amilia…how happy it makes me to see that you are well. We had men looking for you for weeks after the city fell. I began to fear that you were buried somewhere in the rubble, or taken off by some foul beast." He stepped forward. "To see you here before me…oh, it warms my heart, child, on this cold and drear day."

She smiled back at him and gave a bow. "As it does mine to see you in this palace, my lord. I feared that all of you would have perished. But now the city and the kingdom are *yours*, as they should have been."

"Ah, but what is left? I rule a ruin, child, and the world is only growing darker." He paused to look at Elyon. "An honour to meet you, Prince Elyon. I know your father. A great man."

"Thank you, my lord. He is."

"And so are you, I am hearing. You are performing miracles with this wondrous blade of yours." He looked at it, though there was no desire in his eyes. Amilia had seen how Bladeborn men looked upon the Windblade, with that gleam that Elyon didn't like, but Sevrin was Seaborn and had no such interest.

"I am only doing what many others would, in my position," Elyon said, humbly.

"I think that rather unlikely, Elyon," Sevrin told him, with a smile. He turned to look at his son. "Devrin, be so good as to see our royal guests refreshed. What would you like?" he asked them. "Wine? Port? Ale? You look like a man who might drink ale, Elyon."

"An ale would be nice, thank you."

"And you, Amilia? More wine?"

More, she thought. He could probably see the stains on her lips and teeth, perhaps even smell it on her breath. "Please," she said.

"And the same for me," Sevrin told his son. "Nice and warm, Devrin, as I like it."

The prince bowed and stepped away. As he did so, Elyon swung the bag from his shoulder and placed it on a fine stone table, circular in shape, with chairs set around it for lazing here during warmer days. The snow was falling prettily beyond the high awning, some flakes drifting in, capering on the breeze. There was a certain purity to snow that Amilia liked, hiding all the horror beneath. A body lying dead in an alley was grim and woeful to look upon. Cover it in snow, and it became nothing but a pretty pile, soft and white and pristine.

"How long has this snow been falling?" Amilia asked.

"A few weeks," the old king answered, tiredly. "It has come on very quickly, and unexpectedly. When we saw the first flakes falling, we were all quite bemused. When those flakes swelled and thickened and the ice started forming on the river, we began to grow worried." He sighed, looking out. "We are finding people dead in their homes. Families frozen even as they huddle together for warmth. Mothers with babes in arm. Fathers clutching at their daughters. The old, lying in their beds, locked in eternal embrace. We have been working hard to bring firewood to the people, to gather them in safe spaces and halls, but many fear the crowds. They stay in their homes and sometimes we don't know they're there until we find them frozen and dead. And all so quickly. It has happened so very quickly."

Amilia sympathised with the poor man. It was a foul inauguration of his time as king. To rule the frozen ruin, as he called it. She reached out a put a hand on his arm. "We have things we must tell you, my lord," she said. "Elyon has brought you a gift."

The king frowned, turning, as Elyon opened his bag and withdrew the Book of Thala, large and leather-bound and ancient. "It was in Ilithor," Elyon said. "Janilah Lukar was the one who stole it."

Sevrin did not show much surprise. "We suspected so." He moved forward, running a hand across the old cover of the book. "Have either of you looked inside?"

Amilia hadn't, not herself, though Elyon had spent time with Archibald Benton scouring through its pages. Her grandfather had recruited the scholar and his underlings to search for passages that might reveal the location of the Frostblade, the old man had confessed to them, though that was a long while ago now. In the end they'd found nothing, and there were many passages they did not have the skill to translate. *And the mystery of the missing page,* Amilia thought. But that was not for her to worry about.

"I have looked," Elyon said, in answer. "Though the words mean nothing to me. Others have translated certain passages, my lord. I have them all here as well." He pulled a heap of notes and scrolls from the bag, tied up in string. "I hope there is something here that will help you, King Sevrin. To master the Eye of Rasalan."

Sevrin gave a soft laugh. "The Eye is not here, young prince. It was stolen the night my cousin was taken. And I am not king, not yet. Until I have confirmation of Hadrin's death…"

"I saw him die," Elyon said. "And I took back the Eye." He looked at him intensely. "*Could* you master it, if I should bring it here?"

That was a lot for the king to take in, though Sevrin was a man of stout character, if not appearance. He took a moment to digest it. "I would try, certainly. But you must know…"

"I know," Elyon said. "I have spoken about this with Lady Marian Payne, and she has made it quite clear that your sight through the pupil may be limited. You may not be the direct blood of Queen Thala, but you are as close as can be, and it is said that you are the son Godrin should have had. Until we try, we will not know. And perhaps…" He looked at the book. "Perhaps you will find something inside that will help."

Sevrin nodded to that, pulling at a small length of beard trailing from his chin. His eyes flitted to the bag. "Unless the Eye of Rasalan is smaller than I remember, you do not have it with you. Pray tell, where is it?"

"King's Point," Elyon said. "I wanted to come and find you first before I flew it here."

"I see. Then you have a lot more flying to do, Elyon Daecar. I do hope this is worth your time."

Elyon smiled. "I hope the same."

"A hope we all share," said Prince Devrin, stepping back out onto the balcony with a tray of drinks in his grasp. He frowned at the book as he set the tray down on the table, plucking up the cups and chalices to hand them out. "A handsome tome," he noted. "It looks familiar."

"The Book of Thala," his father said.

The prince smiled. "Truly? Or is this one of your japes, Father?" He looked at the others. "He is fond of japing. Not so much these days, perhaps, but…"

"No jape, Devrin. Elyon has the Eye of Rasalan in his safekeeping. He plans to bring it here. To help to win the war, I presume?" he asked Elyon.

The Prince of Vandar nodded. "Any glimpse of the future may help us, my lord. However blurred or trivial."

Devrin had a sip of his mulled wine. "Well in that case we should go north at once, Father," he declared breezily. "Perhaps not *at once* at once, no it's getting a tad late for that. But tomorrow. We should leave tomorrow morning, so we make it in time."

Amilia didn't know what might be to the north, though Sevrin seemed to understand. "That is a long journey, son. Four hundred miles as the crow flies, and in this snow…" He shook his head. "The way would be slow and the seas are too iced over to take a ship. And besides, I cannot leave the city. I am king now, officially. I must stay to tend my flock."

Devrin disagreed. "If the Eye is to open for you, Father, it will be there. We must go to where Great Rasalan's presence is strongest. To where he first presented his Eye to Thala."

487

Something triggered in the memory of Amilia Lukar. She recalled a conversation with Sir Munroe Moore as they journeyed across the Highplains, following the siege of the city. He had spoken of the Grey Keep and the many watchtowers that stood sentry along the northern coast, high on the cliffs. They were there to keep a lookout for threats and invaders, but there was one tower that held a different history and purpose.

"The Tower of Rasalan," she murmured, remembering. Sir Munroe had said that kings and queens went there at times of need, retreating from the pressures of their rule to sit for long days, even weeks, with the Eye, to better understand and unravel its mysteries. Many of Thala's prophecies had been foreseen there, she knew.

Prince Devrin was looking at her, smiling broadly now. "Yes," he said. "Exactly so, my lady. We should go to the Tower of Rasalan, Father. It's remote. And safe. If the enemy should find out of us…"

"*Safe*," Elyon said. That was always of utmost importance to him. "How safe is this tower?"

"Very. Thala herself enshrouded it in seals and deceptions to hide it from the sight of her enemies. And yes, Father, four hundred miles is a long way, but not if we use the thoroughbreds. They can go for days without tiring and know the lay of every rock and stone, even under the snow." He paused, taking a breath. "Father, we *must* go. You have been saying we have to do more to help, for months you've been saying that. This is our chance to do something in this war. I can muster a company to leave by morning."

The old king had a smile on his face, part defeat and part pride and part doubt. But it seemed the impassioned plea of his son had won him over. He looked at Elyon, raised his cup, and Elyon did the same. "A toast to providence," he said. "We can make our plans over dinner."

36

Talasha

She could feel Cevi drifting asleep behind her in the saddle.

"Cevi. Stay alert. You still have a job to do."

The girl's voice was sleepy. "Yes, my lady." She gave out a yawn, stretching her arms, as they glided slowly above the fleet, Neyruu filling her wings with air to try to match their speed. That wasn't possible, of course - the barges were painfully slow - but she was trying her best. When she got too far ahead she would circle slowly around. *And again and again and again,* Talasha thought. *Endlessly. For days.* Cevi yawned again, trying to shake herself awake. "I'm meant to be looking left, right, my lady?"

"Right," Talasha said.

"Oh. I thought I was looking left?"

"Yes, you are, Cevi. I meant right, as in 'yes'."

"Right," Cevi said. "So I'm looking left, then?"

"Right," said Talasha, and they both began laughing.

They needed that, sometimes, because by the fires of Agarath, this was dreary work. For three days they had been circling above the barges, watching for shadows in the water, searching for creeping threats. There were a hundred predatory creatures that might be lurking in this lake, Sunrider Tantario had told them, and they had to keep watch for them all. So far they'd seen seals, the occasional lake shark or freshwater whale, something that looked ominously like a kraken, with its long tentacles and bulbous body, and about a hundred million birds, all bobbing on the water and nesting on the many little islands that peppered the lake like freckles on a gigantic face.

There were many species of bird, Talasha had seen, terns and ducks, geese and kingfishers, herons and cormorants and gulls, all screaming and squabbling for space. Talasha knew birds well, from her days hunting the Askar Delta, though many of these were different, not least the eagles. Of those there were many, perching in the tall trees that grew upon the islands, cruising on their hunts, even circling above the barges sometimes too. They seemed to have the rule of the lake, Talasha had noticed. And no wonder. It was called *Eagle Lake*, after all.

But as yet, the barges had gone undisturbed, and no creature had paid them much notice, save for a pod of porpoises that had swum alongside them for a while, leaping and jumping out of the water. A big whale had come close as well, though it seemed a passive beast, and had only been curious, before descending back into the grey-blue murk almost as quickly as it had appeared. The kraken, too, had proven no danger, because it wasn't a kraken at all. The big bulbous body had turned out to be nothing but a large knot of kelp, and the tentacles its fronds, waving in the currents. Thankfully, Talasha had realised that before raising the alarm. She was misliked enough as it was without giving half the men heart attacks.

It just takes one time, though, the princess reminded herself. At any moment some vengeful fiend could come surging up from the deep, and she needed to be on hand to spot it, call the danger, and help fight it off. She twisted her neck back. "Are you keeping watch, Cevi?" The girl's breathing had started to take on that slow heavy rhythm of a sleeper. "Next time you fall asleep, I'm going to have Neyruu do a barrel roll. We'll see if you'll still be sleeping when you're crashing into the lake."

"Sleeping?" Cevi yawned again. "I would die, my lady."

"The long sleep, then."

They were two hundred metres above the boats, so yes, Talasha supposed a fall from this height would be fatal. Occasionally they flew higher, to get a broader perspective, and sometimes they would fly lower, to share a word with Saska Varin or Sunrider Tantario or the King's Wall, Sir Ralston Whaleheart, but mostly they remained at this height where they could get a good view of the waters around the barges, and quickly swoop down if required.

Her eyes swung to the right, searching for shadows. There was an island a little way off, teeming with birds, and some seals lazing on a rock, but of perils she saw none. "Anything on that side, Cevi?"

The delay was telling. "I…no, nothing, my lady…"

"You were dozing again."

"No. I just…I didn't hear you." Her voice was thick with sleep. "There's nothing on the left. No shadows under the…the water."

Talasha looked to make sure. This whole left, right business was merely to keep Cevi engaged, and most of the time, Talasha would look in every direction possible, to north and south and east and west, straight down and straight up as well. The girl was right, though; nothing brewing on the left of the barges, which were floating along in that glacial way toward the northern shores.

"How long do you think it will take for them to land?" Cevi asked. She rubbed her eyes. "We're getting close."

"Another hour or so, I would say." The barges were the slowest vessels Talasha had ever laid her eyes on, and the currents here did not help. They seemed to be moving against them, the winds as well, and the wide, flat boats were not blessed with many sails. They had a pair each, and not the biggest, and a few holes for oars, but not enough. With the weight of the horses and camels and all those sellswords with their godsteel, it was taking an utter age to cross. *The war will be over by the time we get there,* she thought.

They had gone too far past them, so circled back around, moving with the winds this time. It was quicker like that, and Neyruu struggled to fly slowly. The poor dragon had grown desperately frustrated these last days, never able to swoop and dive and plunge as she liked to, never zipping along at speed. Only at night did Talasha let her stretch her wings, once the barges had pulled up against some island so the men could sleep. She would permit Neyruu a quick dash about the lake, though only a short one, before they found an island of their own nearby, much to the displeasure of the resident birds, who weren't much for sharing.

But sleep would not come easy. Not to Talasha, or to Cevi, or to Neyruu. The birds would often squark and complain, there would be seals barking and grunting and splashing nearby, and the winds were prone to howling. Sometimes it rained as well, a hard hot rain, as if the very clouds were boiling. It was the weather of the new world, the world since Eldur awoke, and would only grow more extreme, Sunrider Tantario had said.

They circled back around again until they were right above the fleet, looking north. There were three barges, so calling it a fleet was somewhat of a stretch, and the men had been dispersed accordingly. At the head was its flagship, such as it was, containing most of the company's leaders. Saska Varin was there, with Sir Ralston, who would never be parted from her, and Sunrider Tantario as well. The girl Leshie travelled with them, and the boy Del, and Del's bowmaster, Kaa Sokari. He was training the young Tukoran in the archery arts, even as they sailed the lake, using the birds for targets. So far as Talasha could tell, the boy was a reasonable bowman. Sokari never had him firing at the birds bobbing on the water; no, only those in flight, and she had seen him take down at least four or five of them that way.

The sellswords liked to watch, she saw, applauding the boy's successes. The scarred one called the Butcher was travelling with them, and the bespectacled one called the Baker, and the two men under their charge. The rest of the Bloody Traders sailed in another barge, under the rule of the Surgeon, a small man of plain countenance who commanded a small host of oddities, not least this tall Tigress woman

491

who had caused such discord among the men. *Well, perhaps I should make friends with her,* Talasha reflected. *Us fellow disruptors must stick together.*

The Surgeon and his band of comely killers shared their boat with a mix of spearmen, archers, paladin knights with their camels, horses and a few other Lightborn, with their sunwolves and starcats, who hated the water most of all. The rest of the men squashed into the last and largest barge, with the remainder of the animals. If one ship was to go down, Talasha supposed it would be best if it was that one. Those were the men who distrusted her the most, and frankly, they were of scant importance to her. *Good men, I'm sure, but their lives do not matter.* Only Saska mattered to Talasha, she and her captains. The rest she could do without.

The minutes dawdled sedately by, the last hour passing without incident. Talasha could see men appearing at the jetties on the northern shore, waiting to anchor the barges. A small ferry-town huddled about the banks, nestled in among the trees of the Green Cloak, the forest that bordered the lake. Just beyond that, the trees had been cut back, and the lands opened out, spreading into pastures and plains, split by a wide wagon track that would lead back toward the Capital Road that hugged the Aramatian coast.

"They made it," Cevi said, yawning. "That last hour…it went so quickly, my lady."

Because you were dozing. Talasha had decided not to keep fighting that battle and just let the girl sleep.

"Will we land to talk to them?"

"Later." The only times she joined the company was by night, once they had made camp, or if one of them hailed her. Then she would swoop down and hear what they had to say, but that happened rarely, and only when there was a problem. "We'll wait until they stop for the evening."

"Will they stop *here*?" She could hear the hope in Cevi's voice. The town was not large, but seemed cosy enough and would offer them a pleasant sanctuary through to dawn. There were some places in the world where you still wondered if there was a war going on at all. This was one of them. The town looked unmolested, and she could see villagers going about their chores. Old crones weaving baskets. Women picking along the shore, searching for crabs and clams among the rocks. There were some small fishing boats on the water, fighting off the birds as they tried to get at their catch. Three men in aprons were butchering the carcass of a large seal, she saw, and many were gathering now to help unload the barges as they came in. She caught sight of woodchoppers in the trees as well, and fruit-pickers with bags slung around their shoulders, working the orchards. It was a pretty place, the princess decided. A part of her hoped it stayed that way, though the rest of her knew it wouldn't. Eventually some creature would come prowling, or they'd be set upon by bandits. That was just the way of it these days. *Nowhere can escape that shadow,* she thought.

"They may," she merely said, in answer to Cevi's question. "But there's another three hours of daylight left, so they might choose to get back on the road. The coast is only fifteen miles from here. If they're quick, they'll make it by dusk."

That was not for her to decide, though. She was an observer and an outsider, more of a guardian than a guide, and had told herself that she would not interfere lest she must.

The barges were soon being pulled in and fastened, the men stepping eagerly onto the docks. After that, the horses and camels and other animals were unloaded. The few starcats that travelled with them did not wait their turn, scrambling at once over the sides of the boats to dash away into the trees, leaping and jumping and stretching their legs. Talasha could see Saska down there, shaking her head and laughing as Joy ran for a tall sentinel tree and climbed frantically up into the branches, as though needing to expend all the pent-up energy accumulated during the crossing.

They continued to circle all the while, taking a wide gliding arc around the company to watch as they disembarked. After another two circuits all the men and mounts were ashore and saddling up to continue up the track. Tantario and his quartermaster were standing with a few costermongers, buying food from a line of wagons, and some of the others were refilling their stocks of fodder for the animals, to be carried by a small troop of packhorses. The rest were already moving up the road through the ferry-town, as more of the villagers tried to hawk their wares; handmade jewellery and homespun clothes, local liquors and wines of questionable vintage, oils and ointments, salts and spices, hides and pelts and furs.

There were few takers, though. Most of the men simply ignored them, riding on by. One of the sellswords - the one called Scalpel, it looked - had taken his wife Savage to peruse the jewellery, and the girl Leshie appeared fascinated by a cloak of red feathers, but elsewise they rode right on. Soon Tantario and his men had completed their resupply and were mounting up to join them, and after that they formed into their columns and continued at a light canter up the road and into the plains.

Talasha made to follow, flying high over the tops of the trees. There was a hot wind on the air, and above them some ugly clouds were gathering, staring down with menacing smiles. She had not often seen clouds like them. Such twisted shapes and unruly motion. There had been thunder one night, and it had sounded like laughter to her ears, the wild cackling of some unseen god. In her mind she saw only Agarath, red and dreaded in his wrath, and it had made her shiver and curl her knees up to her chest, a terror running through her.

It was a foul thing to live in fear of your own god, she mused, as they glided above the host. Were the Vandarians ever the same? The Tukorans? Rasalanians? Did *their* gods ever give them sleepless nights as well?

493

"My lady, they are hailing us," said Cevi, interrupting her thoughts. Talasha looked down. Below, she could see arms waving for her, calling her to join them. She gave Neyruu a silent command and the dragon descended, landing up the road from the host, suitably far so as not to frighten the animals. "Stay here," she told Cevi, as she unstrapped herself and dismounted. She paced down the track toward the host.

Some of the captains rode out to meet her; Saska Varin, Tantario, the Whaleheart, a few others. She sensed concern among them. "Is there trouble?" she called out.

"Dark wings in the distance," Sunrider Tantario replied. He gestured back in the direction of the lake. "A dragon has been sighted."

"Where?"

"To the west, before the clouds came in. A dark shape, with flashes of violet."

Talasha frowned. "Violet?" She threw her eyes back at Neyruu, who was tensing now, lifting her head and looking around. Talasha felt a dull pain flare in her side. Her heart gave a thump. "How long ago was the dragon seen?"

"A few minutes. The beast was far, many miles away. But approaching, Sir Ralston says."

Sir Ralston. Of course it had been the giant who'd sighted the dragon first. That man was always on edge. "Take cover in the trees," Talasha warned them. Her voice was sharp. "Quickly. I will lead him away."

"Him?" Saska Varin looked worried. "*Who,* Talasha?"

"Paglar. He has found us." She saw the puzzled faces, though did not have time to explain. "Go. *Now.* I will lead him off and then return." She turned and ran.

Cevi was looking down from the saddle, her face cast in terrible worry. "My lady, what is happening? Neyruu is afraid."

Talasha could feel it, the thrumming in the dragon's heart. A rumble crackled through the sky, that wild laughter of Agarath the All-Father. It was coming from the west. The clouds were thick out there, black as tar and twisted. She scrambled right up Neyruu's flank, past the three deep gouges torn by Paglar's talons, and fastened herself into the saddle. *Fly,* she thought, and Neyruu took off running, flapping her wings, soaring at once into the skies, each wingbeat taking them higher. Within a few moments the company were receding below them, making for the trees. Saska was lingering behind, staring up at her in confusion. *Go,* Talasha thought to her. *Go. Hide. I will not let him find you.*

Neyruu banked and made back for the lake, and suddenly Saska Varin and the rest were gone from view, lost among the trees. The storm seemed to have come from nowhere, as though spat down from the ether by some foul sky demon, coughing out blackness and hate.

Cevi still wasn't understanding. "My lady, where are we going?" she asked, in half a panic. "I don't understand. Are we leaving them? I thought…"

"Paglar has found us, Cevi. We need to lead him away from Saska."

"*Paglar?*" she squeaked. "No. He will *kill* us, my lady. If he catches us…"

"He won't catch us." Neyruu was much the quicker dragon and would be able to outmanoeuvre him, as she had in Eldurath the day they'd escaped. "We'll fly him back west and lose him there." Standing and fighting was not an option. Neyruu was quicker, but Paglar at least three times larger, and would make short work of her if he got her in his jaws.

Talasha narrowed her eyes against the fierce wind, the air tugging at her cloak and hair. Below them, the blue-grey waters of the lake were growing restless, white caps appearing, waves sloshing against the banks. She caught a glimpse of the villagers from the ferry-town throwing tarps over their wagons and calling in the fishing boats. The world had gone suddenly gloomy, just like that, the trees swaying and bending in the wind, the birds screaming and flying away in their flocks. It was as though some fell god had come, reaching out to embrace the lake in its long dark shadow.

"I see him," Cevi whimpered.

Talasha looked and saw him too. Paglar was coming right for them, smoke-grey and purple and powerful, closing quickly.

"How did he find us, my lady?" Cevi wailed. "It's been *weeks*. How could he track us so far?"

Eldur, Talasha thought. He had set Ezukar to hunting Elyon Daecar and unleashed Zyndrar the Unnatural upon his father Amron too. She had little doubt that Paglar had been instilled with the same single focus; to track her down and kill her. *And we must hope it is just me he wants,* she thought.

"He's getting closer," Cevi said. "We should turn back, lead him to the company. The Bladeborn…they will kill him, my lady. The giant… he has killed dragons before."

One dragon, she thought. *And a small one, no bigger than Neyruu.* "We can't take that risk."

Cevi continued to wail and whimper behind her, begging and pleading, but she ignored her, focusing on her quarry. The dragon was closing on them fast, his wing-skin rippling in the wind as he flew. Twin horns curved back from the sides of his head, dark and demonic, and from his neck and shoulders jutted a hundred savage spikes. The breath stilled in Talasha's lungs. Was he bigger than before? There was something strange about him, something different, nightmarish. Even from here she could see the red light of his eyes, burning like twin suns in that smoke-grey skull.

"Hold on, Cevi," she called. "Hold on tight. We're going to fly above him."

She felt the girl hunker down, heard her rapid breathing at the nape of her neck. Almost at once Neyruu gave several quick beats of her wings, lifting them up too swiftly for Paglar to counter. The big dragon roared and rose, wings thumping, but they flew right over the top of him, beyond his snapping maw. Talasha glanced back, her heart in her mouth for a moment, fearing Paglar would keep on going for the company, for Saska, but no, he arced around and made to follow. The race was on.

She kept her distance, leading him off as she had intended, westward across the lake. When they reached the clouds, a hot rain was falling, and Neyruu ducked lower, plunging down toward the islands, swerving around them. Seals barked and slipped away into the water, disappearing. Birds thrashed and fled in their thousands. On one of the islands, a trio of fishermen stood with nets and spears, their skiff pulled up onto the rocky beach. They dashed for cover as Neyruu passed, and Talasha felt a furnace wind behind her. When she turned the island was aflame, and smoke rose joyously from Palgar's maw.

"He's gaining on us," Cevi squealed.

She was right. The big dragon was faster than before, and Neyruu was tired from her long days circling. *Up*, she thought. The western banks of the lake were nearing, and the clouds would offer them sanctuary. Neyruu did not heed the command. The storm was no friend to her, the clouds a foe, and she liked to see where she was going. "Up," Talasha said, tugging the reins for all the good it would do. "We'll lose him in the clouds. *Up*, Neyruu!"

The dragon ignored her. Talasha gave out a fitful grunt, but she had to trust that Neyruu knew what she was doing. She glanced back. No more than a hundred metres separated them. Several islands had been lit by Paglar's passing, she saw, spewing black smoke into the skies. There were cooked birds on the water and a seal was flopping on the banks of one isle, scorched and dying. Ribbons of flame spat out from between her pursuer's teeth, warped into some maddened grin.

Talasha shuddered. *Faster*, she urged. *Faster*. They reached the lakebank, where the trees rose up to clothe its fringe. The forest was a thin green mantle, stretching for a few miles inland only. Beyond it unfolded a wide and open land of grass plains and shallow rock valleys and the occasional spread of hills and highlands. Further off lay the great forest of the Everwood, full of mysteries, and to the northwest the lonely mountain where the moonbears dwelled. Talasha did not mean to go that far. *We need only outrun him*, she thought. *Once we lose him, then…*

Neyruu banked so suddenly and sharply that Talasha was thrown forward in the saddle. Her straps strained with a stretch of leather, holding her in place. She felt an impact against her back, a hard strike, as though someone had punched her. It was Cevi. The girl had been thrown forward as well, and knocked out, her head rolling limp on her shoulders, her body swaying left and right.

"Neyruu! What are you doing!"

She had scant time to worry for her handmaid. There was a bigger problem at hand. Palgar was coming right for them, maw widening, flame gushing out in a smoking red river. Talasha raised an arm on instinct to shield herself from the heat, but an instant later it was gone. Neyruu shot up, lifting on the hot air, and then down in a precipitous dive, swinging in behind the bigger dragon. All of a sudden they were giving chase, the hunter becoming the hunted, Paglar's long tail whipping and fending as Neyruu swerved and snapped down upon it.

"Neyruu! Neyruu! *What* are you doing!"

She had no control of the dragon. Helpless, she clung to the reins, firming her thighs, tensing her core to fortify her posture. Behind her, Cevi was swinging wildly from side to side in her harness. Paglar turned in sharp movements, left, right, left again, right, diving down and flapping up, trying to wriggle free of his pursuer, but Neyruu was the sleeker flyer. She kept right behind him, nipping at his tail, biting down on it once and twice and thrice as Paglar gave out a fearsome bellow, spewing flame down to the trees.

He'll burn down the whole forest, Talasha thought. Great swathes of the wood were catching, the fire spreading in a swift inferno. "Neyruu, up, up!" she shouted. The dragon ignored her. She pulled at the reins, kicking out with her heels as though urging on a horse, but that was nothing to such a large beast. She was ten times the size of a horse, with scale armour in place of skin. Her kicks and jerks were soft as kisses to the dragon. "Neyruu! Up! What are you doing! Up!"

The trees ended abruptly, and Paglar went plunging straight down to land upon the sparse sedgy grasslands beyond. His talons tore great chunks of earth from the soil as he twisted about, blood spraying from his bitten tail. The clouds overhead were still spitting their warm rain, and up there Talasha saw lightning, great nets of silvery light spreading, heralds of thunder. But west the sun was still visible, moving beneath the swamp of cloud to set above the hills, gilding their slopes in a warm golden glow.

For a moment, Talasha Taan was captivated by the wild beauty of it all. The sun and the lightning and the clouds, the colours, the two dragons doing their death duel, brother fighting sister. Through the distant clouds, shafts of light were showering down, and a great rainbow had formed, curving across the plains, magnificent in its multicoloured radiance.

The roar from Paglar's maw only added to the moment, an echoing bellow that seemed to match the thunder above him, mixing with it, overlapping. It was a challenge for her to land and face him, but Neyruu was no fool. With a hiss of her own, she shot right over him, circling as he turned and scrambled, firing lances of flame to the skies. Neyruu ducked them, jerking out of the way, turning her body to protect Talasha and Cevi on her back. Then suddenly Talasha felt the deep heat inside her, the furnace fires boiling in Neyruu's chest, and the dragon turned, flying over Paglar, dousing him in a great torrent of flame and smoke, a thick black smoke that spread and billowed, enshrouding him and blinding him.

Then she plunged, right down atop him, reaching out with her taloned feet, raking and clawing at him like a crazed crow defending her young. Talasha coughed and covered her mouth and her nose. The smoke stung her eyes. She could see nothing but black. But she could hear plenty; the ripping of scales, the rending of flesh, the roaring of Paglar as he thrashed beneath them.

Then as abruptly as Neyruu had descended she beat her wings and up she went, firing herself out of the shroud, and not a moment too soon. Paglar's mighty jaws snapped after her, reaching up on a long thick neck, crunching down on fume and air. Neyruu was gone, rising, circling. Paglar bellowed and beat his wings in a frenzy, dispersing the smoke. It spread and weakened and grew thin, turning from black to charcoal to a light flint grey. Talasha could see the cuts and gouges on the dragon's back and neck, but they were superficial, and only enraged him further.

You'll never kill him, she thought.

She sensed Neyruu knew that too. She was circling her foe, keeping a wide berth, trying to recover some strength. Was it anger that drove her? Vengeance for those three deep gouges Paglar had torn down her flank? *No, she is only trying to protect us,* Talasha was starting to realise. If they fled the dragon now, he would only find them later. *He will not stop,* she knew. *Not until one of us is dead.*

Neyruu turned, Paglar roared, and the battle resumed in earnest. Talasha was a passenger, an observer, and Cevi no more than dead weight on her back. It would be different with Kin'rar, she knew. He had been a born rider, in tune with Neyruu's every thought and feeling, their connection as strong as steel. The Fireborn dragonriders went through years of training with their steeds, learning attack patterns, forging together a style of combat that suited them. Like the Bladeborn with their fighting forms, the dragonriders too had their preferences. *But I am no dragonrider,* Talasha thought. *I am no Kin'rar Kroll.*

So she could do nothing but cling on and hope, raising her hand against the sudden burst of flame and smoke, coughing as it rushed down into her lungs, blistering and burning. Before long they were fighting upon a field of fire, pitted and scarred, and Talasha's stomach was starting to lurch. She wretched and gagged, the motion too much, too fierce and fast and frenzied, heaving up clots of bile. Breathing became difficult, the air was choked and black. She shut her eyes and tucked her chin and prayed to some formless god for it to end.

Then suddenly there was a fierce impact, shuddering hard against Neyruu's side, and the dragon tumbled across the field. She landed with a crunch of scales and horns, raking ruts in the earth as she ground to a stop. Talasha breathed hard, hanging sideward in the saddle, opening her eyes. She could see Paglar lumbering forward in a burning rage, feel the ground shaken by his tread. His tail was lashing behind him. *That tail. It must have hit her.*

"Up, Neyruu,!" Talasha screamed. "Up! Up!" The dragon staggered to stand, unsteady. A storm of flame was brewing in Paglar's maw. "Up! Up!"

The torrent of fire came gushing. Neyruu gave a weary beat of her wings, and half running, half flying, she fled. The flames receded behind them, but Paglar was setting into a charge, thumping his wings to follow. Talasha could feel Neyruu's exhaustion, her fear and her pain, but her instinct to survive was stronger. She took flight, wings working hard at the grey, smoky air, ascending, as fast as she could, up toward the clouds.

Paglar was close, matching her wing-beat for wing-beat. *He is not tiring,* Talasha thought, in fear. *This is it. He'll catch us eventually.* Cevi was still swaying in the saddle, oblivious, and perhaps that was for the best. The fear of death was always worse than the dying itself, it was said.

But Talasha was sensing her doom. They could try to get back to the company, as Cevi had pled, and let the Whaleheart and the sellswords swarm Paglar with their swords, but something told her they wouldn't make it that far. Neyruu was depleted, or near enough that made no matter, and their only hope now was the storm. And Neyruu had realised that too.

Weary, battle-beaten, she pressed skyward as steeply as she could, thumping hard through pillars of smoke rising up from the woods beneath them. A great conflagration was engulfing the Green Cloak, a ring of fire spreading to girdle the lake. *Where Agarath's minions go, fire follows,* the princess thought numbly. She could hear the Fire God laughing in the skies, and the twisted forms of tar-black clouds seemed to gather to form his face, lit from below by the flames. It was the face of doom, and into it Neyruu flew, right up through the fiery maw of the god, punching through cloud and fume and rain.

They were not alone. Paglar gave chase, the smog swirling about him, and with each flash of silver lightning, each deafening peal of thunder, he drew closer.

Talasha twisted her neck to look back. *It should not have been this way,* came a bitter, angry thought. Paglar's jaws snapped down so close they bit through the tip of Neyruu's tail. The dragon screeched, and propelled herself onward, but it won her only yards. Talasha felt her pain. The flash of it, searing, where her tail might be, a phantom blaze that rippled through her, and there were tears in her eyes, she realised, tears of horror and hate streaming down her cheeks.

It should not have been this way. He was meant to rise benevolent.

But that had never been true, Saska Varin had told her. The wise masters had all been lied to. Pullio the Wise, Quarl the Blind, the Skylady of Loriath. All had prophesied the second coming of the

Father and the Founder, rising from his tomb to bring the world to balance, but that balance did not require his strength, it only required his death. For millennia Rasal manipulators had worked toward that end, with their whispers and their spells and their potions, all guided by the foresight of Thala. It was they who seeded the prophesies into the minds of Pullio and Quarl and Misha. They who lurked in the shadows, corrupting their dreams with their magic. No good gods-fearing Agarathi would resurrect Eldur only to see him slain, so they had twisted the truth, this lie of his benevolence, and in that form, the prophecy had spread.

Talasha had been part of that prophesy, that lie. *I was the first to find him in the depths of the mountain*, she thought. *I was there the day he awoke at the Nest, my heart bursting with hope to see him open his eyes and end the war once and for all.* But no sooner had that red gaze awakened than Talasha's hope had turned to fear, as she watched her cousin die, saw Ulrik Marak swatted aside, stood in horror as Eldur summoned the dragons to his will, enslaved by the Soul of Agarath. Tethian had died that night, and Kin'rar too, and Mirella only days later, and how many others since? *And now I'm to follow, at last*, she thought. *To join my brother in his Eternal Flame.*

The tears were rolling down her cheeks. She could feel the hot breath of Paglar behind them, feel the force of his power as he thrashed through the skies. Blood sprayed out from the tip of Neyruu's tail. She was starting to slow. Paglar snapped down hard, a crashing of a thousand teeth, but Neyruu swerved to the side, and he missed. Another snap, another jerk, another savage bite and Paglar only ate air. A thrumming sound filled the air, of satisfaction, Talasha thought, as Paglar closed on his prey. She dared to look back at him, at his massive smoke-grey maw, right there, saw the burning hate in his eyes, but there was joy within them too, as he savoured the thrill of the kill.

It was then that Cevi stirred awake, into that smoking, fiery hell.

She lifted her head and opened her eyes, blinking, looking around in confusion and fear as it dawned on her what was happening. *Just don't look back*, Talasha thought. When the girl did, she screamed.

Talasha reached behind her to take her hand, twisting in the saddle. "Look at me, Cevi," she told her. "*Look at me.*" The girl looked at her, her eyes bulging in horror. Tears crawled from her eyes, drawing thin lines down her sooty cheeks. "It's OK, Cevi. Just look at me, that's it. Keep your eyes on me, my sweet."

Paglar's jaws were opening wide. Talasha saw the flame boiling within, ready to pour upon them. She squeezed Cevi's hand as tight as she could. "It's going to be all right," she called to the girl. "Just keep your eyes on me. It will be quick, I promise. There's not going to be any pain…"

A light reflected in Cevi's eyes, golden as the dawn.

It brightened, spreading through the clouds, casting away gloom and fume and smoke. There was a great flash of golden lightning, strands stretching and reaching across the world like a net, and the thunder that followed sounded strange.

Like an eagle, screeching, Talasha thought dimly…though godly, other-worldly, divine.

She turned in time to see him…

…descending from the skies.

37

Emeric

The Moonrider did not remember him, and why should he? *I am wearing a different face,* Emeric Manfrey thought, and it was not a mask that could be easily removed.

"It is me I assure you, my lord," he said, speaking in the Lumaran tongue. His long years living in the south had taught Emeric how to speak as a native, without so much as a hint of accent to betray his Tukoran roots. In the past, the pallor of his skin had done that. Not so today, with his features changed and darkened with the aid of Marian Payne. Emeric had seen himself in the mirror before leaving. It was him, but not him, a Lumaran version of Emeric Manfrey, the features delicately toned and altered by balm and potion to pass him off as one of their own.

Timor Ballantris was looking at him curiously, searching his face for the man behind the mask. The Moonrider was tall, lean, bald-headed, clean-shaven, with rich dark skin and piercing purple eyes, some fifty years in age. The few thin lines around his eyes and mouth and forehead spoke of a man of staid expression. "You look different, Emeric Manfrey," he remarked. His voice was deep, calm. "You can see why I would have trouble believing you."

"I understand, of course." Emeric thought that now might be a good time to speak in his own mother language, so switched to the common tongue of the north, with that distinctive Tukoran brogue. "Perhaps now you may be more convinced of my identity?" he said, with a smile.

The Moonrider cocked his head a little to one side, bemused. "A switch in tongues and timbres serves as a nice trick. But I will need more proof than that." He wore a magnificent cloak of black and blue lion fur, white at the collar, with a belt of silver medallions fastened about his waist. His armour was scalemail, in intricate links of black and blue and silver as well, set on a mannequin to one side, glittering in the torchlight.

Emeric felt rather naked without his own plate armour, but walking into the enemy encampment bedecked in godsteel from head to heel was not likely to go down quite so well. Instead he was armed and armoured as the others were; in the fine gold garb of the Sunshine Swords. "What proof do you require, Moonrider Ballantris?" he asked.

The man continued to study him. "How many times have we met?"

Emeric did not need to think about it long. "Four, my lord."

"Where was the first occasion? When?"

"In Lumos, eleven years ago. It was my first time to the Glass City. You had heard that Sir Oswald's descendent had come to settle in the empire and were eager to meet him." It was a tale as old as time for Emeric. Even in the south, Sir Oswald Manfrey was a famous name. "You spoke to me with grace, I recall."

"And what did we discuss?"

"My exile," Emeric said. "You had some choice words to say about it."

"What were those words?"

"Not ones I would care to utter again." Emeric smiled. He had been required to shave his beard for the disguise, and his cheeks and chin felt terribly cold without its warm black cloak. "You taught me many new expletives that day that I had not heard before."

A smile formed on the moonlord's lips. "I am always happy to expand another's vocabulary. Even then, your grasp of our tongue was quite exemplary, but your use of curses was sadly lacking." He looked behind Emeric, to where several soldiers stood with long blue spears, their handles black. "You may leave us. He is who he says he is."

The soldiers bowed and left them alone, moving through the flaps of the stately pavilion. The rest of the Sunshine Swords had been left outside to wait, save Sansullio, who stood to one side, politely observing. The morning was wet, cold, and misty, a thick fog hanging over the fields and woods. Emeric and the sellswords had used it to mask their approach, as planned. With Sansullio taking the lead, getting through the cordon of guardsmen at the camp border had been simpler than Emeric could have hoped. It seemed that they were not the only company of Sunshine Swords here; several other groups had sworn their swords to the war effort, and they were simply assumed to be one of those, passing on patrol through the camp.

Timor Ballantris began walking side to side, his cloak of dyed lion fur waving gently. He held his elbow in his palm, hand to his mouth in thought. "I have every right to kill you," he said, after a time. "We are at war, I am sure you know. Why did you not come with a banner of peace? A white flag would have protected you."

Emeric had to doubt whether that was the case. Either way, it hadn't been an option. "It is important that Dragonlord Ven is not aware of this meeting, my lord. Nor Sunlord Avam. I sought a privy conference."

That made the man frown. "Sunlord Avam is in command of our forces here. If he should discover that I entertained a spy in my tent…"

"There is no reason why he should. And I am no spy, but an emissary."

"A secret emissary. Some would call that a spy. Avar would certainly be one of them, as would Lord Vargo. You have put me in danger coming here."

That gave Emeric pause. Not often did a man like Timor Ballantris exhibit concern. "That was not my intent, my lord."

"And what is your intent?" The Moonrider's fierce eyes shifted to Sansullio, and back to Emeric again. "I hope you are not here to try to seduce me to your side, Emeric. If you are, you had best save your breath and leave the way you came."

"I know you would not join us. Not directly, in any case."

"Directly? So you expect me to join you *indirectly*, is that so?" The man's hackles were rising more than Emeric would like, and that put him on dangerous ground.

It was dangerous enough coming here, he thought.

"We have heard rumours of division among your ranks, my lord," Emeric said, choosing his words carefully. "That is only natural. I know how tense relations have been in the south, between Empress Valura and the Patriots. I know what happened at the warmoot. Valura was strong-armed into action against her will, through threat of violence and civil war. I understand. She had no choice, lest her people suffer, and she lose her rule. But that does not mean she wanted any part in this conflict."

"No," Ballantris agreed, blunt-voiced. "I stood at her side at the warmoot, Emeric. I spoke against the war, the same as Moonlord Hasham, and Grand Duchess Nemati, and several other prominent figures. But we were outvoted. The Patriots came in force and with the backing of their Agarathi allies. Empress Valura kept her own counsel; she was there to listen and to hear, not to speak, as is custom. But privately, I heard her thoughts. No. Of course she did not want this war. But that was not her choice. As sovereign, she must hear her people. The vote was cast, and here we are."

"But not you," Emeric said. "I am told you were not present at the Battle of the Bane, my lord. Nor Moonrider Ranaartan. You were sent later…by Empress Valura, is that not so? To balance the scales, and speak with her voice."

The moonlord considered that at length. "My voice is not so large or loud as you may think, and the time for speaking is done. That was what the warmoot was for. By sacred tradition, we declared ourselves allies to the Agarathi, and Empress Valura herself commanded us to muster and march here. That I came later is of no significance. Nor are my personal beliefs."

Emeric understood. "You serve," he said. "Whether you agree or not, you obey."

"I must," said Ballantris. "This is not a time for half-measures, and the empress is not as strong as her mother was. She bows to strength, and what are the Agarathi if not strong? Were it mere civil conflict against the Patriots she feared, perhaps she would have taken a harder line, but it isn't. To stand against them both would be to court her own destruction."

"And what of the *world's* destruction?" Emeric asked. He fixed the man with a steely look. "Are you aware that the Dread has risen, my lord? Have you heard of the ruin he has wrought?"

A shadow passed the eyes of Timor Ballantris. He did not speak for a moment. Then he looked at Sansullio and asked, "Is this true?"

The Captain of the Sunshine Swords gave a nod. "It is true, Moonlord."

"You've seen him? The Black Calamity? With your own two eyes?"

"No, Moonlord. Not with my own eyes."

"Then how can you be sure? Who told you of these reports?"

"Many, Moonlord. It is claimed that the dragon flew to the Vandarian city of King's Point and reduced it to rubble. Then he continued north to Varinar. This city, too, has fallen beneath his shadow."

"*Varinar?*" The man snorted and shook his head. "Varinar has never fallen. Not once since its founding."

"There's a first time for everything," Emeric Manfrey said dryly. It was as Marian and Rikkard had suspected. "We feared you did not know, Timor. That is part of the reason I have come; to expose to you the truth. Your allies have been lying to you."

Sansullio nodded. "Many of our own people have abandoned the Agarathi in the west," the sellsword said. "We have heard these tales, and I believe them. They must fear the same will happen here. So they have kept the truth from you."

Timor Ballantris walked toward the tent flaps, moving them aside, looking out. Through the bustle of Lumaran tents and pavilions, the edge of the Piseki encampment could be seen through the trees. "Avam," he grunted. "*He* will know, I am sure of it. I have seen signs of deception from him. And fear, that as well. There have been times when he has wanted to tell me something but has lost his nerve. Lord Ven must have threatened him to silence. I must speak with him at once."

"Vargo Ven?" Emeric asked. "My lord, is that wise? If you speak against him…"

"Not Ven," Ballantris interrupted impatiently. "It is Avar Avam with whom I must share words." He drew back, letting the tent flaps sway shut. The rain was coming down softly outside, the noise of camp forming a general din. Emeric could hear the screech of dragons in the distance, as they flew on their patrols, the occasional *thwump* of wings overhead. Ballantris continued his pacing. "Where is the Black Calamity now?"

"Flown south, we heard," Emeric told him. "Across the Red Sea. It's understood he returned to the Nest, to heal. There is smoke pouring from the summit of the Ashmount, my lord. Some believe this may be connected."

"Connected how?"

"It's thought the smoke signals the dragon's healing. When it ends, he is healed, and will return."

Timor Ballantris did not think much of that theory. "I have never heard of such a thing. But that mountain…it is a dreaded place, full of foulness and sorcery. The fume heralds some fell darkness, of this we can be sure." His jaw had tightened into a grimace, purple eyes gleaming with concern. "The Dread came for Varinar first, but he will not stop there. Millennia ago, the city of Lumos stood against him as well. Lumo beat him back with her light, as did Calacan further east, and the darkness was driven away. But there was always a fear it would return. And now…if what you say is true…"

The moonlord paced, shaking his head, thinking. Lumos was to a Lumaran as Varinar to a Vandarian; their capital and spiritual home, the beating heart of their holy nation. Unique in its construction it was beautiful and formidable at once. *But no Varinar,* Emeric knew, *leastways not in its impregnability.* History said that Lumos's greatest defence was her citizens, both man and beast, and above all the power of the moonbears had kept her foes from the door. In battles past they would gather in great numbers to protect her, and once before they had come together, the singers said, to fight the Dread as well in an epic contest the bards liked to call the *Battle of Crystal Wall.*

That must have been going through the mind of Timor Ballantris as he paced. He balled his hand into a fist. "I should have known," he said, eyes narrowing in self rebuke. "*Tathranor* has not been himself of late. He must have sensed the Black Calamity's return, but I was too blind to see it."

"You ought not blame yourself, my lord," Emeric said. "Many of us have been deceived."

"Deceived. Bullied. Coerced. Such as it always is with the Agarathi." A muscle in his jaw gave a ripple. "I cannot in good conscience fight with them. If this is true…I *cannot.*"

Emeric could have grinned in glee, but he held his lips in a line, and said, "What do you intend to do?"

"Confront Sunlord Avam. Learn the truth of what he knows. Put my fist through his face, perhaps? Oh, how I would like to…" He glowered a moment, then went on. "But that would not be wise. Avam commands the loyalty of many men here, and I would first need to speak with my own allies. Ranaartan. Grintillio. Tar Von Toro. We will confront Avam together."

"To what end? Sunlord Avam is a Patriot. He would sooner see all the world burn than join with the north."

"Join?" Ballantris said. "No, we will not join you, Emeric. After what you have said, I have no choice. I must muster my host and march home. The defence of Mother Lumara comes first."

Emeric furrowed his brow. "My lord, if I may...by the time you get home, there may be nothing left. You are a thousand leagues away. Your best defence is to fight. Here. Now. You are a Moonrider. Risho Ranaartan as well. Together you could make a deal of difference."

Timor Ballantris shook his head. "If we fight against the Agarathi here, the dragons will descend upon us. I have no doubt that Tathranor could fell one, perhaps two or even three of them, but when a dozen all attack us at once, we will stand no chance. You overstate what difference we will make."

"And if you break camp and march south, what do you imagine Vargo Ven will do?"

"*Ven.*" The moonlord growled the name out. "That man is too sure of himself by half. He would have plenty to say of our departure, I have no doubt. But to seek blood would weaken and deplete him, making him vulnerable to your host. He would not dare."

That was not what Lady Payne had said. "I am told he is driven mad by fear of Eldur. Would you risk it, my lord?"

"Risk? You talk to me of risk, Emeric? We are both risking much even having this conversation. Does your life mean so little to you?"

"Not as much as other men," he said.

That caused the man to smile. Then the smile withered into a hard look, and he searched Emeric's face once more, looking for the man he knew beyond the make-up. "This...*disguise*. Why bother, Emeric? Why have you come at all? Captain Sansullio might have told me this."

"I know you, Timor. I can speak for the north."

"No." Ballantris stepped closer. He loomed above Emeric, several inches taller, though slim and athletic in build, long-armed and lithe as a lance. His great cloak smelled of damp and battle. "There's more to it than that. Your honour. Your lands and titles. You are here to restore them, is that not so?"

It was a fair assumption, but wrong. Emeric shook his head. "A man takes no titles to the Eternal Halls. My lands would be useless there."

"Then what is it?" He angled his head a little to one side, peering at him, then he nodded. "Vengeance," he said. "I heard what happened to your estate. You seek vengeance for the murder of your staff. They were dear to you, I know. And one more than the rest."

Emeric did not say her name. He only thought it. *Brewilla.* "I sought vengeance...for a time," he admitted. "In Solas. We hunted the men who wronged me. But I have moved to another path now."

"Have you?" The question was thick with doubt. "Your face may look different, but I know those eyes. There is a hate there that you have not quenched." He paused and then said it. "Are you here to kill Sunlord Avam?"

"No," Emeric said at once. "I am no assassin."

"No. Just a spy." Ballantris stood close before him, reading him like an unrolled scroll. "I don't believe you. Were I to give you sanctuary here, you would stay, would you not? I could put you in a tent, near the border with the Piseki camp. I could tell you of Avam's guards and habits, his schedule. I know that is what you want."

Emeric was struggling to get a read on the man. *He is testing me,* he thought. *He is too righteous to knowingly harbour an assassin in his camp.* "That is not my wish," he said.

A huff slipped through Timor Ballantris's lips. "So you say. But let me ask again…why you? You are not even Vandarian. Not even a lord in truth. An exile, who has lived long in disgrace. You know me, yes, but that is not enough. Or were you the only one willing to shave your beard? You look younger without it, let me say. As young as when I first met you."

Emeric had to smile, remembering those times. "It was not meant to be me," he confessed. "I arrived at Rustbridge only recently. Prior to that certain parties were attempting to contact you, to arrange a parley."

"Who?"

"Prince Elyon Daecar. It was his desire to speak with you. His eyes that have seen the Dread, his blade that has cut him. He hoped to meet you in secret, and somewhere neutral."

"And yet you are here in his stead. Where is he?"

No one in Rustbridge knew the current whereabouts of Elyon Daecar. They had expected him back a long while ago, and his lack of return had given them cause to worry. "Missing," Emeric answered. "For some weeks now."

"A shame," Timor Ballantris said. "I would have liked to have spoken with him, hear all this from his own lips. Though perhaps it is for the best, Emeric. Lord Vargo is not fond of the boy. He has vowed to kill him many times in my hearing. A petulant man, is Vargo Ven. His company has grown insufferable to me. It will give me great plea-sure to rid myself of it, for good and all."

Emeric remained wary of how that might unfold. "And if he does seek blood?"

"Then he will have it. I will challenge him myself for our right to leave, and take pleasure in that as well." There was a glint in his eye, of the sort common among peerless warriors. "Tathranor will shred the scales off Malathar's back. He will flay the dragon living, Emeric, and when he's done he will feast on his flesh."

Emeric should like to see that battle. "I do not doubt it, my lord."

Ballantris snorted, as though not believing him. "So you came in the prince's stead. You came to spread this news of the Dread. But not to kill Sunlord Avam, you claim." He looked at him, judging. "Perhaps you are telling the truth in that. Without godsteel, you would stand no chance."

I have godsteel, Emeric thought. It was not a blade, no weapon at all, but a tiny disc, sewn into his armour, to grant him the power of his blood-bond should he need it. Lady Marian Payne had given it to him as a gift. Paired with the fine scimitar sword he carried at his hip, he would be lethal, godsteel sword or no.

He said none of that, however. Instead he peered at Timor Ballantris and said, "If you want Avam dead, say it plainly, my lord."

"I want him dead," the moonlord said, at once, in a voice as blunt as an un-honed blade. "Is that plain enough? I want them all dead. Zon, Palek, Avam, Krator, and all the rest. The Patriots are a blight on our empire, a plague I have long fought, but I cannot knowingly harbour an assassin in my host. My honour compels that I cast you out." He looked at him, wrestling against his own sense of morality. "I think it is time for you to go, lest I weaken. I thank you for bringing me these tidings, grim as they are. You have given me much to ponder."

Emeric gave a bow. He only hoped it would be enough. "Thank you for the audience, my lord. Will it be safe for us to depart the way we came?"

"I will see you led to the camp border. Beyond that, I cannot vouch for your safety."

It was the best he could hope for. "Thank you." He turned to Sansullio. "Let us go."

"No," said Timor Ballantris. "Only you. Sansullio and his men will remain here."

Emeric frowned. "My lord? They came here under my protection, as free and independent men."

"They are *Lumaran.* They are skilled soldiers. They will join my company, and march with me when I leave. All men of the empire must answer the call to defend her." The man looked at Sansullio. "Is that not so?"

The sellsword captain nodded. "It is, Moonlord."

"And…it's what you want, Sansullio?" Emeric asked. He would be sad to see them go, but perhaps it was for the best. He had feared for their safety in Rustbridge, after all, and the Sunshine Swords had already spoken to Borrus, telling him they would not raise their blades against their own. *They will only be sitting idle in the city*, he reflected. *Better they return to their own lands now, and help defend them if they can.*

Sansullio smiled handsomely and said, "It has been an adventure, Lord Emeric. And an honour to know and serve you, and Lord Jonik, and the others as well. But Mother Lumara calls us home. And we must answer." He gave a bow.

Gracefully spoken as always, Emeric thought. He would miss the man very much. "Then I will take my leave alone."

"No," Timor Ballantris said again. Emeric looked at him, vexed. Was he having some sudden change of heart? "It would be better for you to leave under cover of night if you are to go alone. I am denying you the guard you came with and cannot in good conscience send you into the wild in broad daylight. And the rain is waning."

It was. Emeric could hear its patter fading on the walls of the pavilion. Sunlight could be seen cutting slits through the flaps, and the walls were brightening as the light kissed the canvas. As ever, the weather had changed abruptly. "It is still morning," the exile said. "Dusk is not for long hours."

"Good. That will give me time to confer with Risho and the rest as to what you have told me. You will stay here, in the meantime. Make no attempt to leave the pavilion, or you will end up with the others."

Emeric did not know what he meant by that. "Others, my lord?"

"Yes. The captives." Ballantris frowned. "Were you not aware?"

Emeric had heard that some men of prominence were missing, principally from the squadrons that had ranged through the Marsh-lands, terrorising the Agarathi outriders and supply lines. "There are some knights," he said. "Men who have not been seen for some time." He was thinking of Sir Soloman Elmtree, an Oloran man, and Sir Barnibus Warryn, who was a close friend to Elyon Daecar, Sir Rikkard had told him. Apparently bags of blood and body parts had been dropped over the fortress by dragons, and some of the parts had been identified as belonging to men whom Elmtree and Warryn were travel-ling with. He wondered if Timor Ballantris had any knowledge of that.

"No," was the man's answer, when Emeric asked him. His face curled in disgust. "Another notion of the noble dragonlord, I would think. I would have spoken against it, Emeric."

Emeric nodded. "Are you willing to give me the captives' names, Timor? It would give the men some succour to know of their fates, good and bad."

"In the interest of sharing, yes, I will tell you." Timor Ballantris spoke the names, then, one and then another and then another. As feared, both Sir Soloman and Sir Barnibus had been taken hostage by the Agarathi host, kept in a cage, chained and beaten.

But there were others who predated them, men who had been fettered here for some time, taken during the Battle of the Bane after the northern host fled in retreat. And one name, above all, set Emeric's heart to thumping.

Lord Wallis Kanabar was still alive.

38

Amara

"It's snowing," Sir Connor Crawfield said, stepping into her room. He went to the window and threw open the curtains. A cold light spilled in, and about the edges of the panes a thin crust of frost had formed. Beyond, flakes fell serenely from a pure white sky, a soft coat settling upon the grassy fields. "It started a little before dawn, my lady. I suggest you wrap up warm today."

Amara rubbed her eyes and sat up from her bed, swaddled in her blankets. Her bones were stiff, and she felt old as sin, her rump sore from the saddle. She stared out of the window, disbelieving. "Snow? In summer? Has that ever happened before?"

"I'm not the person to ask, my lady. Will you take your breakfast in here?"

"No. I'll join the men on the benches." She sniffed the air. The scent of bacon was rising from the common room below. It made her stomach churn hungrily. "I won't be long."

Sir Connor nodded and left her to dress on her own. By rights she should be wearing some colourful summer dress, light and breezy in linen or silk. Instead she pulled on winter wear; a thick grey gown over dark woollen stockings, leather riding boots for her feet, a warm fur overcoat with a scarlet scarf tied about her neck. Her gloves were supple leather, soft as a babe's backside, lined inside with vair. Those she kept in the pockets of her cloak to wear when they set out riding.

The common room was busy with men, packed shoulder to shoulder along the benches. By now Amara had some dozens in her company, all sworn to her service, and a good many of them were Bladeborn. They were all chattering with one another as she entered, talking about the snow, the war, dragon sightings, and other such tidings; most of them grim Amara did not doubt. A fire burned warmly in the hearth, driving away the unseasonal chill, and the innkeep and his wife and three daughters were bringing out the food;

plates of crispy bacon, fresh-baked buttery bread, bowls of soup floating with chunks of onion and turnip, great pots of porridge with jars of honey on the side. It was quite the morning feast, and the men were munching eagerly. They hadn't eaten half so well since their last night on the island, when they'd plundered the Seal King's larders and set up a banquet on the beach.

The innkeep bustled right over as soon as he saw her. He was a small, unattractive man with lank greying hair and a long, misshapen nose. Old, yellowing bruises marked his eyes and upper cheeks. "M'lady. Mornin' to you. I hope the food is to your liking? And the bed. You slept well, I pray?"

"As well as can be expected at such a time."

She hadn't slept well, in truth, though that was not on account of the bed. Ever since she'd returned to Varinar…ever since she'd learned the truth of her husband's fate…her sleep had been plagued by dreams of his passing. *A heroic end,* she thought, stiffening against the grief. *He restored his honour before the end. He died on the field of battle, bearing a Blade of Vandar, fighting the Dread himself.* For long weeks she had feared him crushed beneath the palace, locked down in his cell, alone and helpless as the city fell to ruin above. That he had perished with such gallantry was a blessing, she knew. *He so feared the Long Abyss,* she thought, part proud and part sad and a whole lot heartbroken. *But he earned his absolution. My dear sweet Vesryn…he will be welcomed to Varin's Table with cheers and open arms.*

The innkeep stuttered uncomfortably. "M'lady, if I may, I'd like to ask you about…"

"Payment," Amara said, cutting him off. She drove all thoughts of her husband aside; there would be time to grieve him later. Right now it was Lillia who drove her on, Lillia whose fate remained uncertain, Lillia who had seen her and her company marching out of the western gates of Varinar no more than a day after they had arrived in the thin desperate hope of finding her. "You will be fairly reimbursed for your trouble, fear not." She gestured across the room. "Speak with my man Sir Connor. He will see you paid."

The innkeep held his hands together and bowed. "My thanks, Lady Daecar. Oh, you are kind. These are trying times and your generosity means the world, it surely does."

"It is not generous to pay fairly for board and lodging. That is your due."

"A due unpaid by others, m'lady. We've had all sorts passing us these last weeks, those escapin' the city and the war and whatnot, and not all have been so kind as you. They take what they will and leave without payment, and if ever I should try to protest, they threaten me with bare steel, even beat me. I have been struck many times, m'lady, as my face will attest. And my daughters…" He wiped at his long, runny nose, looking pained. "I will not even speak of it. I only thank the gods that they are alive, and untaken from me."

Alive but not unspoiled, Amara thought grimly, to judge the girls' red and weepy eyes, the marks on their smooth young skin that could only have been made by the rough touch of base men. At any other time such crimes would be reported to the local magistrate or lord, and the culprits hunted and hanged, but there was no recourse for that now. It irked her more than she could say.

"I am sorry for your troubles," she said, giving him what succour she could. "If you want to better protect your family, I suggest you pack a wagon and make for Varinar. You may have heard unsettling tales of its fate from passersby, but there is a measure of order being restored now that the forces of Lord Amadar have reached the city. You will be safer there."

The man's eyes showed doubt. "They say the Dread will return, m'lady. Here…well, he won't touch us here. We're too small a morsel, but Varinar…"

That was a shadow under which they all lived now. "It is your choice, of course. If you decide to leave, come to me and I will write you a letter of patronage. It will ensure that you and your family are housed and situated somewhere safe upon your arrival. But be quick about it. I expect to depart as soon as I've filled my stomach with your fine-smelling soup and bacon." She smiled. "And I will have a cup of watered wine as well."

The man's face went terribly apologetic. "Begging your pardons, m'lady, but we have no more wine. You drank the last of our reserves last night."

"Some honeyed ale, then, if you will."

She continued through the common room, smiling at the men as she passed, sharing gestures of greeting. At the far end, Master Artibus - whom she had found tending the wounded in Varinar - was sitting alone at an alcove table, quietly breaking his fast. It was Artibus who had told her of Vesryn, Artibus who had spoken of Elyon's visits, and Artibus who had asserted with confidence that Lillia and Sir Daryl had not returned to the city before she fell. Amara remained unsure of that - after all, how many thousands were still trapped under rubble, or too badly burned to be identifiable - though she had to cling to the slim possibility that he was right. The old scholar was currently hunched over a bowl of steaming soup, idly spooning measures into his mouth as he scribbled notes in an old book. Artibus was always scribbling something, his mind never at rest. He looked up as she sat down.

"How's the soup?" she asked.

"Very pleasant. If a touch too salty for my tastes." He smiled his kindly old smile and glanced to the nearest window. "Have you seen the snow?"

"From my room, yes. It's whiter than your beard, Artibus. Awfully strange, don't you think?"

"Very strange," the man agreed thoughtfully. "Though far from the only queer climatic event we have heard of. Elyon spoke of heavy rains in the south, much stronger than normal for this time of year, and there have been rumours of superstorms and earthquakes as well. One herdsman told me of a rift that had opened in the Heartlands, miles long and a hundred metres wide. He said that there was a great rumbling down there, made by a creature of immense size. And when he peered over the edge to look, he saw a great shadow, moving in the depths. He claims it to be *Brannatar*."

Amara cocked a brow. "Brannatar? The giant boar?"

"So he said. And why not, with Drulgar risen? They were all bitter enemies once, you know, these titans."

"Better than you do," she said. Amara had always been more interested in myth and mystery than Artibus and was more fully versed in it as well. The old scholar was driven by logic and learning and misliked things he couldn't understand or decipher through some theory, but that was not true of Amara Daecar. She liked the ancient and arcane. "Accounts differ as to what happened to him," she said, taking on the role of scholar in this field. "Some say the Dread slew him in a fierce battle, as he did Fronn in their fourth fight. Others that it was the wolf himself who killed the boar; they clashed often, legend says, as wolves and boar will do. Those of a sweeter sensibility prefer to think that Brannatar never died at all, and instead entered into a long hibernation, where he has rested for thousands of years." There was even a place called *Brannatar's Burrow*, some hundred miles west of Ayrin's Cross where it was said the great boar had delved his den. "Let us hope the last of those is true, and he has indeed returned. Perhaps one of those great tusks of his will do for the Dread, Artibus? They are said to be as tall as sentinel trees; plenty long enough to skewer him, don't you think?"

Artibus had a spoonful of soup. "More likely the dragon will feast on roasted boar, Amara. But I take your point."

The innkeep came bustling over with her cup of honeyed ale, smiling obsequiously as he set it down on the table before her. One of his daughters followed. The youngest, she was, a waif of a girl no older than ten - and blessedly without any bruises that Amara could see. She had a pot of soup under her arm and set about serving it with a ladle, filling Amara's bowl with the steaming broth. Last of all came the wife, a short and stumpy woman with a great sagging bosom poorly contained by her stained apron, who put a plate of crispy bacon before her.

"Hope you like it, m'lady," she said, performing a clumsy curtsey. "Saved the best rashers for you, I did."

"That was very thoughtful of you." Amara had a bite and could confirm that the bacon tasted as good as it smelled. "Delicious," she said, licking her lips. The soup, too, was thick and filling and not so salty as Artibus made out. "I hope we have not emptied out your larders with this feast?"

"No, those *monsters* did that," said the wife, with a snap to her voice.

She wrapped a protective arm around her little daughter. "They took it all, m'lady, the *bastards*, excusin' my tongue. This is from our personal stores. Got a secret pantry dug down beneath the boards here." She tapped a heavy foot on the wooden floor. "Those *whoresons* never found it, thank the gods. Excusin' my filthy tongue, m'lady."

"That is quite all right. Do you have much food left down there?" She tapped a riding boot on the floor.

"Not much, I'll confess it, not much at all." She looked at her earnestly. "So we'll be having that letter…if you're still willing? My husband just told me, m'lady. Very kind of you to help. Very kind indeed."

"It is no trouble at all." Amara had sensed that this woman was the decision-maker around here. "Artibus, a sheet of parchment, if you will. And melt some wax for my seal." She set about writing her letter, scribbling a few words to the effect of 'help this family with food and lodging', then folded the note, added a drop of sealing wax, and pressed down with her personal seal. She handed the letter to the wife who took it greedily. "See this into the hands of Sir Hank Rothwell or one of his men when you arrive at the western gate. He will see that you are provided for."

"Oh m'lady, thank you, thank you." The frumpy woman took her hand and kissed it wetly. "We'll be leavin' right away." She looked at her husband, who still seemed less sure. "*Right away*," she repeated to him. "*You* can't protect our girls, so we'd best find someone who can."

"I…what was I to do? They'd have killed me dead, woman. Dead. Is that what you want?"

"I'd sooner see you dead than my little darlings violated. Now get upstairs and start packing our things. Go on, *get*." She kicked at him. "*Get. Get…*"

The husband moved off, glowering.

"Sorry for the show," the dowdy woman finished. "Not meanin' to be unseemly in front of you, m'lady."

"It's quite all right." Amara had a sip of sweetened ale. "Would you like any help packing your wagon? I have plenty of men here who would be willing to lend a hand."

The woman was obviously going to protest to that, so Amara took matters in hand herself. She waved over Sir Penrose Brightwood. "Pen, choose three men to help this family gather their belongings and pack their wagon." To the woman she said, "I would be happier knowing you are on the road when we leave."

The innkeeper's wife seemed at a loss for words. "Your kindness, Lady Daecar. It is…it is such a rare thing these days."

"One kind act begets another," Amara responded. *And I have much to make up for,* she knew, reflecting on Rylian, and the Flame Manes, and the innocents who had perished in her island-within-an-island coup. "Pen, see to it. And tell the rest of the men to get moving. I want to be on the road as soon as possible."

515

Sir Penrose bowed and stepped away, selecting three men for the charge, calling for the rest to finish their breakfast and gather their things. In short order all of them were gobbling up whatever food remained in their bowls and plates and heading out to saddle their horses. As soon as the first man opened the door, a wintry wind came blowing in, stirring the flames of the fire. Several curses were loudly uttered as they shouldered out into the cold.

Sir Talmer Hedgeside marched over. "My lady. Sir Montague and Brazen Ben went out a little earlier, to scout the road. Thought you should know."

"Thank you, Talmer. Any disturbances overnight?"

"Nothing, my lady. I've taken report from all the men who had the watch, and they tell me nothing unusual happened. Except the snow."

"Ah, the snow. A curious business, wouldn't you say?"

"Most curious, my lady. What do you make of it, Master Artibus?"

Artibus set down his quill pen and set about clearing his throat. Amara knew what that meant. A lecture was imminent and she had no time for that right now. "You can discuss it on the road," she said. "Artibus will have plenty of time to expound upon his latest theories then, I'm sure. Just try not to fall asleep….we wouldn't want you taking a tumble from the saddle, Sir Talmer." She smiled at the old scholar and then looked at the door. "Is my horse being saddled?"

"Jovyn is seeing to it, my lady," Hedgeside told her. "That boy never stops. Seems awful eager to get moving every day, don't you find?"

There was no mystery there, not to Amara and Artibus, though Sir Talmer was not yet aware of it. "He is in love with my niece Lillia," she said. "I daresay he wants to find her as much as I do. Perhaps even more."

The stocky old knight gave a rugged smile. "Young love. Nothing sweeter. I hope we find her, truly I do. For all your sakes."

Amara Daecar hoped for nothing more. She spooned a final measure of soup into her mouth, wiped her lips with a cloth, and stood, walking briskly outside into the bitter cold air. It hit her like a brick wall. "Gods be good. It's even colder than I'd thought."

"Will be worse to the north," Sir Talmer said, following her out. He gestured northwest up the road as it wended off between the hills, dappled with their woods of spruce and pine. The elevation of the lands rose a little from here, and the snow looked thicker out there as well. "Might not be the worst thing, my lady. Dragons aren't so fond of the cold, they say. This sort of weather…might just be enough to ward them off."

"We must hope."

Amara Daecar pulled her cloak tighter, teeth chattering. Some of the men were already ahorse, waiting beside the road in their heavy cloaks over suits of armour, swords hanging at their hips, axes at their backs, shields fixed to the flanks of their mounts. The rest were still at the stables, fixing saddles and bridles and arms.

It had become a much stronger host than Amara could have hoped for. She had counted on Connor and Penrose and Jovyn and Carly for long months now, and she had her men from the coup as well; the knights Sir Talmer and Sir Ryger, Sir Montague and Sir Hockney, still nursing his injured leg, and the sellsword Brazen Ben Barrett, who Carly had come to call Rabbit for his goofy teeth and big ears. But there were more now too. Some of those had joined them either during, or after, the island coup, all swearing their oaths and fealties. One was a burly Tukoran from the verdant valleys east of Ilithor, a knight called Sir Gobert Fuller who said he had met Amara once when they were both young.

"I even danced with you at a banquet in the palace, you may recall," he'd said when he knelt before her on the beach, laying his blade before her, bloody from the battle. She didn't recall, of course; it was far too long ago, his was hardly a storied house, and she'd had a hundred suitors back then before her cousin Janilah gave her hand to Vesryn Daecar. But she only smiled and said, "Of course, Sir Gobert. I remember every dance," winning a shy smile from the big Tukoran.

There was another knight from Pentar lands, a Sir Hugo Dain who claimed to be a distant relative to the late Lord Porus, through one of his many wives. Sir Hugo was sad to hear that Lord Porus had perished. And angry when he found out that his eldest son Alrus had lived long enough to succeed him. "Never liked Alrus," he had told her, with a bite of bitter memory. "Petty man. And *weak*. I served under him once, before he dismissed me from his service, and disgraced me." That was why he ended up on the islands, he went on to explain. "All I did was talk with his lady wife, show her some kindness," he said. "That's all it was, just some talking, laughing, but spineless Alrus saw more in it than there was and sent me away. Jealous man, my lady. Gods help us if he's Warden of the South."

Three other Bladeborn had joined during the coup, a trio of mercenaries called Baxter, Ballard, and Brandon, who tended to stay together. Baxter was tall and thin, Ballard short and fat, and Brandon somewhere in between, a handsome man with flowing auburn hair and a cocksure smile. Carly called them the *Three Bees* and made a buzzing sound when they passed.

They had all joined her on the island, but the rest had been added in Varinar; common fighting men from Daecar lands under the banners of Houses Crawfield and Rothwell, Blunt and Brightwood and Gully who had asked to join her on their journey west, so they might aid in the return of the little Lady of House Daecar. Whether that was their true motivation or not Amara couldn't say. All of them hailed from the lands to which they were headed and no doubt wished to learn what had become of their kinsmen out there, but they were all good stout men, mixed in age, and loyal to the Daecars without question. So she happily invited them aboard.

But alas not everyone had joined her. Captain, regrettably, had gone east instead of west, taking off some of the other sailor-soldiers and oarsmen he had recruited from the island. Amara did not begrudge him that. She had shared in Captain's tale, after all, and knew he wanted to return to Rasalan, to his daughter, and beg forgiveness for abandoning her long years before. When they had parted in Varinar, Amara had wished him all the luck in the world and said, "Now perhaps you'll finally tell me your name, Captain?"

To which the old Searborn had said, "Next time, my lady," with a grin touched with sadness. "Let's leave something to look forward to, should we ever see each other again."

Amara had smiled and agreed and embraced him, thanking him for leading them safely across the lake. Then she wished him luck in finding his daughter. She knew she would never see him again.

But her host was a strong one, well armed and well armoured. The Great One's armoury had helped with that - the gluttonous oaf had plenty of good godsteel stashed away in there, it turned out - as had the plate they had scavenged from the ruin of Keep Daecar. They had an armoury of their own there, down in the storerooms below the keep, and Amara had permitted the men to take what they wished. She did not think Amron would mind. Most of it was not his, or Aleron's, or Elyon's, or Vesryn's - no, the Knights of Varin tended to keep their spare armour in the Steelforge - but old plate worn by the household knights that was only sitting there gathering dust.

And ash, Amara thought, with a pang of grief. Walking through the ruin of the keep had been distressing, reflecting on the many memories they had shared there as a family, seeing ghosts in every blackened, burnt-out room. She had wandered through with Artibus, and the pair had spoken softly of happier times. And she had spent an hour alone in her bedchamber as well, weeping over the loss of her husband, emptying her eyes of tears. She had laid upon the half-burned bed, curling up in the ashes, and it was as though she could hear his voice calling to her from the Eternal Halls. *Take care of her*, Vesryn's ghost had said, as he had in the dream, the one she'd had before awaking on the longboat, before she saw Varinar burn. *Promise me you will.*

"I will," she had whispered back, sniffing and wiping her eyes. It was Lillia her late husband was whispering of, she knew; it could only have been Lillia. "I'll find her, and I'll protect her. I won't stop until I do."

And that had brought them here, far now west of the city. Amara and her company of *Knights Assorted*, hailing from this land and that, all vowing to serve.

Before long the host was mounted and ready to leave, and the snow was falling a little thicker. Jovyn led Amara's mare over to her and helped her up into the saddle, where she settled uncomfortably, her thighs sore from the previous days' riding, rump all battered and bruised. They had gone hard up the High Way since leaving Varinar, staying most nights in holdfasts, eating with this lesser lord or that landed knight in his little keep or castle. Most had been generous enough to let them share their table, though oft as not the food was meagre and bland. Were these old knights and lords serving up their worst and saving their best for their own? Amara did not doubt it. Thus far, the war had not touched this part of Vandar, and the gentry were seeking to batten down the hatches if they could.

That vexed Sir Connor Crawfield, of course. "They should be joining the fight," the dour knight had complained. "I understand an old lord hiding behind his walls, but to keep men there with him, men of fighting age?" That had been the case wherever they had stopped. Each small lord had kept his retainers about him for protection, and to preserve the little food they had from roving bands of brigands.

When Amara explained that, Sir Connor only shook his head and said, "Hiding is not a strategy, my lady. An old man may care to live for another half year, but what of his sons and nephews and liegemen? They have their lives ahead of them, and he's holding them back to die slow. Every single one of them ought to be adding his blade to the war."

And of course, he had made that request each night, once the company had taken themselves off to sleep. "I would talk with your men before we go," Sir Connor would say, to whatever liver-spotted lord or knight was hosting them. "If any man should wish to join us, that is his choice. You do not have the authority to keep him against his will."

He got the usual rebuttals. Lord Mandrake, who was so ancient Amara assumed he had perished at least a decade ago, but was still clinging to life like a limpet, told the younger man that no greatlord had called the muster of these lands, and he was under no such obligation. Lord Gaston, who was much younger than Mandrake, though still at least sixty and almost as fat as the Great One had been, said much the same, and added that his sons and knights were not Blade-born, and would likely perish before they even reached any functioning army, far away as they all were. One-armed Sir Barloff Terring was more irritable and truculent still, and told them that they'd had their walls assaulted by at least three parties of Taynar men trying to win the keep, and he had no intention of giving up his men to leave him vulnerable. "Had to fight them off with bolt and arrow," the miserable old knight said. "Why should those men be free to wander, pillaging and stealing, while my own men are sent off to die?"

"Because the king demands it," Sir Connor had said, bristling.

Sir Barloff looked around his draughty old hall. "What king? I don't see him. Now he comes and stands before me, mayhaps I'll yield, but until then…" He'd shaken his small bald head and sent them on their way.

There was nothing to be done about it, Amara knew. To her mind, a few men here and there weren't going to make a blind bit of difference, but Connor Crawfield saw it differently. "Every little helps, my lady," he had said. "These old fools are only burying their heads in the sand. That sort of thinking weakens us all."

The Captain of the Guard rode up to her now, his stallion snorting mist, hooves kicking up clods of mud and snow. "My lady. The men are all prepared to leave and the innkeep has been paid," he said. "He and his family will be leaving shortly." He gestured to the wagon, packed high with possessions. A pair of dray horses had been hitched to it, but the going would be slow in this weather. So far as Amara saw it, they should be travelling lighter, but that was no longer her concern.

"Let us go," she said.

They set off north by west along the High Way, riding into the teeth of the wind that came sweeping in from the hills. Thus far the sight of keep and castle had been plentiful, and there were many settlements and towns here in the hinterlands within a week's ride of Varinar, but beyond this point the world grew wilder and less populous as they entered the great vastness of northwest Vandar. From here they could expect long rides between safe harbours, and there was no guarantee that they would be able to make it from one to another within a day.

That was clearly on the mind of Sir Ryger Joyce, as he came riding up to join her. "My lady," he said, in that low growl of a voice. "What is the destination today?"

Sir Connor answered for her. "We hope to make it to Lord Gully's keep," he told the Green Harbour knight. "It is a full day's ride from here, a half dozen miles north of the road. A stout castle on a windswept plain."

"Or *snow*-swept," Joyce said. "Will we make it in this weather?"

Sir Connor's delay was telling. "We will arrive late, if we make it at all," he admitted. "If the snow slows us too much, there is a small hilltop fort called Raymun's Watch that may be able to host us instead. But our preference would be Gully's keep."

"His son was a knight of our household," Amara added in. "Sir Gilmore. He perished when Varinar was attacked, and I would like to be the one to tell Lord Gully myself. If he is there."

There was no guarantee of that. Any keep or castle could conceivably have been attacked and burned by dragons, though that seemed less likely out here than in the south or east of the kingdom, where the fighting had been fierce.

"And your niece," Sir Ryger said. He was an attractive enough man, stern and unsmiling, and wore a green cloak over silver armour. Carly liked to call him Ryger the Tiger, or just Tiger Ryger, for his growly voice and striped hair, which was a reddish brown with streaks of grey at the temples. "You think she might have gone there?"

"It is possible, yes. Lillia was fond of Sir Gilmore, as the rest of us were. Sir Daryl may have taken her there."

"Or a dozen other places, so I've heard," said Sir Ryger. "Meaning no offence, my lady, but how long are we going to search for her? It could take months to scour every keep and castle in the northeast."

He was not wrong. And it could all come to nothing in the end. "I would hope to learn more of her whereabouts soon," she only said. She doubted that Sir Daryl would have settled permanently in Gully's keep, small and poorly provisioned as it was, but if he had passed this way with Lillia he might well have stayed the night. If so, Gully would know where they had gone. And the lands of Daryl's lord grandfather were only a half week away besides, and he surely would have stopped in there. If old Lord Blunt had not heard from his grandson, then Amara would begin to fear the worst. Until such a time as she spoke with him in his hall, she would hold to hope, however.

Eventually, she said, "I will not keep you to your oaths that long, Sir Ryger." Those oaths had been to serve her, though she knew these men wanted more. The knights she had taken from the lake in particular were all keen to restore their honour. Spending months in search of a teenage girl would not grant them that. "I know it is battle you want, and you'll have your chance to seek it, I'm sure. That is not something I would ever deny a knight."

The Green Harbour man bowed from the saddle of his horse. "My thanks, Lady Daecar. That is all I ask."

Her words were proven to be strangely prescient. Several hours later, as they stopped at an icy stream to water the horses, Sir Talmer called out that Sir Montague and Brazen Ben were returning. They were easy enough to differentiate even at a distance. Ben with those big ears, flapping in the wind like sails; handsome Sir Montague in his golden cloak, a relic of his time among the Suncoats half a lifetime ago. Their horses even matched them. Montague's was an athletic courser, racing along proudly; Ben's a rather more ungainly young stallion, with a slightly clumsy-looking stride.

But in the flush of their faces, both looked alike, and the fervent light in their eyes as they came reining up before her. It was Sir Montague Shaw of Rasalan who spoke. "Lady Amara, we sighted a great host ahead," he said, panting. "They are marching west along the High Way in great columns, bearing banners of gold and brown."

"*Strands*," added in Ben Barrett, with that bucktoothed grin. His cheeks were as red as Carly's hair…redder than they'd gone when she followed through with her promise to kiss him after the coup, in full view of all the men during their feast down on the beach. "Those banners, m'lady. They bore his standard. The bare-chested knight wrestling the giant."

There was no standard in the north quite so macho as that of House Strand. Amara had to smile. "Lord Styron," she said. "How large is his host?"

"Hard to say for sure, my lady," said Sir Montague. "The snows fall even thicker further west, and they served to obscure his numbers. Ten thousand at least. Perhaps double that."

"That would be his entire strength," said Sir Connor, thinking. He looked at Amara. "He must be marching toward the Twinfort, my lady."

They had heard rumours that Styron the Strong was coming down from the Ironmoors, where he ruled over a great tract of land beneath the banners of House Taynar. It was assumed he was heading to King's Point to help protect the coast, but if an enemy assault was expected upon the western gate then perhaps his course had been diverted.

Others had gathered around to listen. Jovyn was one of them. "That would take them past Blackfrost," the squire said. "My lady, ought we not ride to join them? We could accompany them there."

They had intended to make for Blackfrost eventually, though via a more circuitous route, pending what they heard of Lillia. Sir Connor, as always, knew what his lady was thinking. "We can send riders out," he said to her. "To Lords Gully and Blunt and others, to hear tidings of Lady Lillia. But it would be wise to join Lord Strand, my lady. A strong host we may be, but against certain perils we remain vulnerable." He let her think it over a moment, turning to the scouts. "How far away are they?"

"A good long gallop," Sir Montague said. "We only sighted them distantly, and from a rise. But they're moving more slowly than we are. At a hard push we might reach them by nightfall."

"Or tomorrow at an easier pace," Connor said. He seemed to notice that Amara did not want to subject herself to a 'good long gallop'. He addressed her once more. "My lady. I suggest we make for Raymun's Watch for the night. We should reach it shortly after dusk at this pace. I will send men to speak to Lord Gully. Tomorrow, we can ride for Lord Styron's host."

They all seemed to be of the same mind, the men nodding and murmuring, and who was she to deny them? She smiled at Sir Connor, nodding assent, and then turned to look at Sir Ryger Joyce. "Well, Sir Ryger, it looks like you may yet get your wish," she said.

39

Amron

Wolfsbane hurdled a root, his godsteel barding rattling.

The caparison he wore across his back fluttered heroically against the dim hue of dawn, trailing with small ribbons in the colours of his kingdom. Across the wooded valley, warhorns rang out, blowing loudly to mark the break of day…and battle. Amron hoped they would provide distraction.

Draw the enemy eye, he thought.

He burst out into the open where the Agarathi had stopped for the night, spread out across the vale. The trees were sparse, the canopy thin; Amron's sight pierced far and wide. He could see the tents at the heart of the night camp, see the men emerging from within, rushing to snatch up sword and spear. Hundreds were still lying here and there on the ground, waking to the sudden commotion, throwing off their blankets and scrambling to their feet. There was shouting, barks of command as the horde stirred to life, men mustering to meet the challenge of the warhorns, coming from the hill.

We caught them unawares. It was just as he'd hoped.

Right ahead, the guards at the camp border were turning to meet them, swishing about in their crimson cloaks, lowering their long black spears. Shouts of alarm spread like wildfire. Amron rushed forth. Two spearmen thrust up at Wolfsbane as he reached them, but the steel just pinged right off the barding, and the men were bashed aside. "For Vandar!" the king bellowed, barreling straight through the men beyond. "For Vandar!" echoed a hundred other riders, smashing through the lines.

Amron bore the Frostblade in his grasp, misting ice. He swung it left and right, twisting at the torso, hacking men apart as Wolfsbane galloped fiercely onwards. In the span of ten heartbeats ten men were dead, crushed and cleaved, Wolfsbane trampling grown men like they were nought but crops in a field. A trail of iridescent dust marked their passing, glittering off the edge of the blade with each swift swish and slash, ice particles sparking and melting in shades of red and blue and green and gold and a hundred other hues. "For Vandar!" Amron roared again. "For Vandar! *FOR VANDAR!*"

The horns were still blowing from the north, ringing out from the wooded slopes at the edge of the vale. Their cadence had quickened now; a series of shorter, sharper peals to call the men to charge. Sir Torus Stoutman would be blowing on one of them, Sir Bryce Coddington another, Sir Lambert Joyce a third, the three knights leading the charge of the men afoot, six thousand Vandarians with naked steel in their grasp.

For Vandar! they called as one. *For Vandar! For Vandar!*

The sound was stirring. Amron led his host onward, mowing the Agarathi down. In front came the barded beasts, many of them monstrous warhorses strong as broadbacks. Sir Taegon rode the biggest of them, *The Hammerhorse* he called him, a broad-shouldered, muscular brute who stood a full hand and a half taller than even Wolfsbane. The giant bore his greatsword in one hand, his warhammer in another, bellowing "Hammerhall!" at the top of his lungs. Others called out for their houses, their homes, their kingdom and their king. "*To the Grave!*" roared Lord Gavron and his men; the words of their house. Tall Sir Dederick Dudden shouted, "*Green Harbour!*" The boy Sir Trystan Spencer rode in the van as well, his gilded armour gleaming in the dawn, his fine slim horse barded all in gold. Further down the lines Amron sighted Sir Quinn Sharp leading fifty riders into the teeth of the camp, and behind them all came the bulk of the charge led by Sir Harold Conwyn.

The enemy broke before them.

They ran them down like weeds in winter.

Such was the power of the sudden charge. They had marched hard to catch up with their enemy, and this was their reward. This valley, sparse with trees, the earth flat and open with scant roots and rocks to trip them. The trees thickened upon the slopes to the north and they had provided ample cover for the bulk of the army to work around their flank unseen. Overnight, Rogen Strand had crept out with the best killers he could find to silence the sentries, so their advance would not be known.

And it had worked. Everything that they had hoped for, planned for, had worked.

But it felt too easy.

And Amron Daecar didn't like it when things felt too easy.

"My lord, we have them! We have them, my king!" Sir Harold came riding up from behind him, panting, his blade dripping red. His pockmarked face was split in a smile and there was an enraptured energy to his voice. It was the thrill only blood and battle could bring. "They're falling like wheat to the scythe!"

Dozens of riders were charging past. Only a few had been taken down by spear-thrusts and sword cuts to the legs. Hundreds of Agarathi lay trampled and maimed about them, moaning and dying. Men slowed on their horses, thrusting down with their lances to finish them off, or letting their horses crush them. Others dismounted to slash open throats and drive cold steel down into their hearts.

The light of dawn was spreading through the trees, dappling the forest floor, thick with bodies and blood. Amron rode onward, making for the heart of the camp. He found Sir Taegon there with the Ironfoot, riding from tent to tent, slashing them open to see if anyone was hiding inside. Horses reared and kicked out at canvas walls. Lord Gavron's men dismounted to search, their black and grey cloaks emblazoned with the godsteel scythe of House Grave. It was an apt sigil for such a day, Amron thought. He looked around. The north rang to the sound of battle. He could see his six thousand men afoot out there, swarming upon the enemy as they came boiling from the trees.

But it all looked wrong. *Felt* wrong.

He knew why. "They're not all here," he said.

Sir Harold Conwyn was still with him, and Rogen Strand as well, all in black and grey. His horse was black to match him. "My lord?" said Conwyn.

"Look around." There were pockets of fighting, but they were far too few. There was noise, but not enough. Amron had been in battles great and small and this was a small one. Hardly more than a skirmish. "We outnumber them," he said. "There can't be more than a few thousand Agarathi here." He was getting a horrible feeling in the pit of his stomach. "Did you get it wrong, Sir Harold? The numbers of Agarathi. At Green Harbour."

The stocky knight shook his head. "No, my lord. No, there were twenty thousand at least, maybe more." His eyes roamed the vale, looking concerned and confused. "Perhaps this is their rearguard camp? They may have set their main one up ahead... somewhere safer?"

It was a possibility. The cold fist in Amron's gut was suggesting something more disturbing, however. "I fear we have been tricked," he said, the truth of it dawning. His voice was thick. He looked around, jaw tightening. "This is no army, Sir Harold. It's *bait*."

Some of the others were starting to come to the same realisation. Lord Gavron rode over from the trampled tents, Ironhoof snorting fog from his nostrils. "There are no captains here," the lord growled. "No dragonknights. I know dragonsteel when I see it, Amron, and these black spears they're carrying *aren't* it."

"They're water men," thundered the voice of Sir Taegon nearby. He had dismounted The Hammerhorse to fight afoot. A half dozen bodies were decapitated and dismembered about him. He kicked a torso aside, entrails tumbling from its open gut in a gory red splash.

"Weakest men I ever fought. Not one of them can fight worth a damn. And half of them are *boys.*"

Amron had only just noticed that. Many of the dead faces looking up at him were young, green as summer grass. He felt sick all of a sudden. *They left their worst behind…their least experienced. The rest…*His eyes moved west through the open vale to where the woods thickened anew, knotted and gnarled, dense with oak and ash. "Rogen, gather up your trackers and scout west at once. I need to know how far they've gone."

"Gone?" rumbled Cargill, as Whitebeard kicked his spurs and rode away.

"To the Twinfort," Amron said. "This host was left here to slow us, delay us, confuse us." He gave a bitter shake of the head. "It's all been a ruse, Taegon."

The Giant was starting to pull it all together. He ripped off his greathelm, crested with a warhammer crushing the head of a dragon, and threw it on the ground in a rage. "Treacherous bastards! I'll kill them. Kill them all!" He kicked out at his helm with a great clang of steel, sending it flying into a tree where it got lodged in the bark with a *crack*. "*Cowards!*" he thundered. "They left these water boys behind and ran."

"Fool," the Ironfoot said to that, snorting the insult out. "They didn't *run*, Cargill, they went off *laughing*." He looked about, snarled, then spat. "The Twinfort's only a day and night's march from here, Joyce says. How long have we been chasing ghosts, Amron?"

It wasn't a question he wanted to confront. For days Taegon and his men had been raiding the enemy rear, killing dozens of men each night, but they were nothing but lambs to the slaughter. As this smaller host kept a slow pace, leading them on this merry chase, the rest might have stormed ahead at speed, making for the rear of the Twinfort. Quick as that, victory had turned to bitter defeat. It was not a taste Amron Daecar much liked.

Sir Quinn Sharp rode over to join them, puffing and panting. "This is all wrong, my lords. We outnumber them two to one. Where are the rest of their men?"

"Where do you think? We've been tricked, Sharp." Taegon Cargill marched over to collect his helm, ripping it from the tree. "The dragonfolk have gone and conned us."

"The Twinfort?" Sir Quinn said. "How far ahead are they?"

"The ranger's gone to find out," said Lord Gavron. He glowered toward the western edge of the valley. Rogen was hastily gathering up several other men and was dismounting from his black steed to slink away into the trees on foot. "It's worse in there," the Ironfoot went on. "Fifteen miles of thick forest, dark as sin. Full of monkey lizards and tree wolves and greatboars big as broadbacks. Hard to navigate, you said that yourself, Amron. How the hell did they outrun us? We've got hundreds of Green Harbour men here. These are *their* lands, and they've been outwitted."

I've been outwitted, Amron thought. This was his army, his kingdom, his *failure*. Could they be wrong? Might the enemy have been scattered by Taegon's raids? Did they splinter and get separated during the night? He doubted it, but would know for sure. "Sir Quinn. Start asking questions of our southern friends. See what you can find out."

"Let *me*," the Giant of Hammerhall said, hefting his enormous godsteel warhammer. "Sharp's soft as his mother's teats. *I'll* get them talking."

Sir Taegon strode off, hunting for a man alive among the legions lying dead. There was still noise enough across the valley to know the battle would go on for a time yet, but it was as good as won already. "We need to get this over quickly," Amron said. "Sir Quinn, get back out there and make haste. Have our injured gathered; we're not going to be able to take them with us unless they can fight. Leave what men we can spare to tend them, treat them, and try to get them safely back to Green Harbour."

Sir Quinn put his heel to his horse and rode off.

Amron closed a fist around the hilt of the Frostblade, squeezing tight. He must have lost his focus; he could feel the deep ache in his left shoulder and right thigh, even with the blade in his grasp. Was he growing immune? He couldn't think about that now. He concentrated a moment, drinking in the Frostblade's powers of healing, and his pains dissolved.

Lord Gavron gave a grunt. "It's their dragons," he said. "We didn't count on their dragons, Amron."

Amron looked at him.

"They've been leading them," the Ironfoot explained. "These woods are thick and hard to pass. We know that. Joyce and his men have all said it. But none of us have counted on their dragons showing them the way. They fly above them and find the right path. Around this hill. Through that valley. Across this gulley. And they've been warding off other beasts as well." He snorted and spat once more. "No wonder they've moved so quickly. They've had eyes in the skies unlike us."

He was right, Amron knew. They had not seen dragons during the march, not with the mists and fogs that cloaked the forest, the cold wintry skies, but no doubt they had been out there, guiding and protecting their own. He was starting to fear the worst, fear that the enemy had stretched too big a lead, and if they had…

"There's smoke in the air," said a rough voice. Amron turned. Sir Bryce Coddington had come over from the main force, sour-faced and blood-spattered, wearing his old armour and Varin cloak, a warhorn hanging at his hip. His cheeks were flush from battle.

"Where?" Amron asked.

The old knight scowled west. "That way. Far off and *unpleasant*."

Amron's nostrils flared open, drawing in the air in a long, deep breath, eyes closing to focus. Beneath the rotting smell of wet leaves, the earthy tones of mud and bark and branch, the tang of iron and putrid stink of bladders and bowels being emptied...beneath all that was an undertone of smoke, trailing in on a westerly breeze. Coddington was right. It was coming from a long way away, carrying a distinctive, unpleasant scent.

"Brimstone," the king said. "*Dragonfire*."

Sir Harold frowned warily. "Could they be burning the woods? To make it easier for their men to pass?"

Sir Bryce looked at the younger knight like he was a halfwit. "They burn the forest and it'll only alert Lord Borrington that they're coming. No, boy, they'll want to sneak out behind the Twinfort, all silent like. If there's something burning out there, it's *stone*. Towers and walls and *men*. The Twinfort's under siege."

A ripple of worry went through the men.

Amron would not have it

"We don't know that yet," he said firmly. He looked up, checking the skies. It was a clear morning, though not often did that last, and shortly after dawn the mists and fogs would descend to reduce visibility. But if they could reach some higher ground before that happened, perhaps they might be able to see across the forest to where the smoke was coming from. He turned to Sir Harold. "Take some men and scale the slopes. Climb trees if you must. Look for smoke rising from the west, Harold. Go. *Right now*."

Sir Harold swallowed and bolted off. He was replaced almost at once by Sir Taegon who came marching back over, his gauntleted hand gripping a long black braid. The head to which it was attached swayed freely...without a body. Cargill threw the head down before him. It bounced against Amron's boot and settled in the mud. "That one laughed at me," the giant rumbled angrily. "I asked him where the rest were, and I pointed west, and he just laughed. So I'm guessing they went west."

That was growing obvious now. "Find others," Amron said. "Try to get them to talk before you take their heads, Taegon."

The giant shrugged, grunting, and lumbered back off.

Sir Bryce Coddington was looking down at the decapitated head. It had landed face up. The eyes were open, staring, the mouth twisted into a grin. There was something horrifying about that. A red mist was slowly fading from the man's gaze. "There's something strange about their eyes," the old knight said. "Saw the same in Green Harbour. It's like they have no control. Wild, they are."

"They're slaves," growled Lord Gavron. "Thralls to Eldur. We saw it at the Point. Some break free, but not all." He stepped in and kicked the head away, unwilling to look at it any longer. "The men aren't going to like this, Amron," he said. "They thought this was it. Battle, victory, and then some rest. Well earned too. Now we march on without so much as a second to stop and take stock."

"There's no choice…" Amron started. He was weary too. Weary to his bones, but they had to keep going.

"I know," Grave came in impatiently. "I'm sixty-two years old, Amron. Most men my age can barely get out of bed in the morning. Hell, if there's a man here older than I am, I don't know of him."

"I'm close," said Sir Bryce. "Though I got all my limbs at least."

The Ironfoot grunted laughter. It died as soon as it lived. "Just saying it's going to be an ugly march. And horses won't be much good in there either." He looked at the tangle of dark green forest ahead. "Gonna be slow, a full day and night of marching. We'd best set a strong watch and rearguard. Half the men are going to want to slip away after this."

"I'll leave that with you." The Ironfoot had no tolerance for desertion. The king thought a long moment, wondering if he might give the men a few hours to rest at least. They had barely slept for days and most had stayed up through the bitter cold of the night, preparing to launch their attack. The fear that coursed through a man's veins on the eve of battle kept him alert, but after…after he was prone to collapse when the thrill rushed out of him…and marching for another day and night was about the last thing he wanted to do. They'd expected to have a great fight on their hands; six thousand men afoot and five hundred ahorse against an Agarathi horde some twenty thousand strong. A brutal battle. A stirring victory. The long rest for the dead and a shorter one for the survivors, but a rest all the same. Then onto the Twinfort to join their strength to Lord Borrington and beat back the Agarathi invaders.

None of that had happened. The battle had not been brutal, the victory was not stirring, and they would have no rest. *And when we reach the Twinfort…*

Amron didn't want to think about that just yet.

"Get them ready," he said. "I want us marching within the hour."

40

Robbert

The Eagle of Aramatia loomed high above them, staring out to sea with those fierce stone eyes.

"What do you imagine he's looking at?" asked Bernie Westermont, perching on the forecastle gunwale with his great wide rump. His eyes went lazily to the east, out across the open waters that spread restlessly toward the horizon. "You think there's anything out there, Robb? Other continents, like they say?"

Robbert Lukar didn't think it mattered what he thought. "Give me proof and I'll believe it. Otherwise it's just a matter of faith." It was his own lands that the prince cared about, lands he was desperate to return to. He scanned the horizon, eyes moving east to south in a slow arc, clutching hard at his blade. "Still no sails," he muttered. "No ships."

Bernie put a big hand on his shoulder. "More will come, Robb. We just have to wait."

I don't want to wait, Robbert thought. But he didn't want to leave either, and that was the problem. Only a fraction of his fleet had managed to battle through the storm and limp to their rendezvous point here at Eagle's Perch. *Six ships. Just six, out of thirty.* And most of them battered and bruised.

He supposed he should be thankful that any of them had survived, not least his own ship *Hammer.* By some miracle, they had seen off the brutal onslaught of the manator's massive tusks, and the even more brutal onslaught of the mountainous waves as well. Several times they had been enveloped by the sea, the waves rising up like great liquid cliffs around them, black and fearsome, to collapse and swallow them whole…and each time *Hammer* had bobbed its way back to the surface, belligerently refusing to founder. That another five vessels had survived as well ought to have been cause for celebration. But that meant there were two dozen that had likely gone down. *Along with most of my army*, he thought.

It had left him with less than three thousand men - three thousand down from twelve - and most of them serving under the banners of Lord Lewyn Huffort whose loyalty was questionable at best. Huffort's powerful flagship *Landslide* had escaped the worst of the storm by taking a daring line toward the coast. It was risky, the man himself had admitted, but his ship captain had said it was their best hope of survival. He was right. In the end, they'd suffered nothing worse than a shredded sail or two before they broke through the storm and sailed serenely up the coast to the Perch.

They were the first to get there, the first of the six so far. It took four days for the second ship to arrive, another of Lord Huffort's bulky galleons - *The Stone Maiden* - carrying almost five hundred men. The third was a Kastor vessel with green and black sails called *Blood Bear*, the fourth a much smaller caravel ironically named *Mountain* which had been supplied by Lord Malcolm Marsh, a Huffort bannerman. Those four had assembled over the course of ten days before *Hammer* finally limped in to join them, in need of serious repairs to the hull and mainmast, which had been torn down during the storm. Three days later, one of Simon Swallow's ships - *Blackthorn* - had found its way to the rendezvous as well.

But that was the last, a further three days ago now. *And still no sign of Lord Swallow himself*, Robbert thought. And more importantly, Lord Gullimer, who he favoured as his right-hand man. His own ship, *Orchard*, was nowhere to be seen.

Robbert sighed and wiped a length of cloth across his forehead. It was another hot, windless day in the sheltered bay where they had taken sanctuary, protected by the high cliff walls around them. There were some natural stone jetties here, carved and hacked into shape by the Aramatians, forming a small harbour of sorts at the base of the bluffs. Beyond a narrow fringe of stony beach, the cliffs rose up high and sharp, cut with a perilous switchback stair that must, Robbert Lukar assumed, have claimed the lives of more than a fair few men over the years.

Thankfully, none were *his*. Robbert had ordered that a watch be kept on the coastlands above, to look out for incoming ships and other threats, and no one had tumbled to their demise just yet. He could see Sir Lothar Tunney on the steps now, picking his way carefully down, holding onto the ropes hammered into the cliff-side for support. He had with him several others, relieved of their duties by the new company of watchmen who'd just gone up to take their shift. Lank's godsteel armour glinted brightly in the sun, which was arcing up from the east in its morning ascent. It cast the sandstone colossus of Calacan in a glowing light, clinging with its enormous talons on the cliffs, mighty wings outstretched, gazing out to sea with that eternal stone gaze.

"You ever noticed how they all look to the ocean?" chirped a voice.

Robbert turned from the forecastle of *Hammer* and saw that the young midshipman Finn Rivers was approaching. Behind the boy, soldiers and sailors alike sat and lazed about the decks in various states of undress, seeking what shade they could from the searing morning sun. As soon as it summited the cliffs and headed west, the entire bay would be plunged into shadow, but for now the decks were baking.

Robbert looked at the boy. "You mean the eagles?" he asked.

The stocky young sailor nodded happily. "Every one of them. You'll never find a stone eagle in Aramatia that's looking inland. Every statue, every fountain, every sculpture…even the iron ones that adorn braziers and the wood ones cast above inns and tavern doors…they all look out to sea."

"Why?" Bernie asked, interested. Finn Rivers was full of interesting facts.

The boy gave a grin. "Like you said earlier, my lord. About the continents. Calacan was always flying off searching for new lands, the Aramatians say, so they honour him by making sure he's looking out to sea when they build or carve his likeness. They believe there are many other lands out there, the Aramatians do. Some are battlegrounds, like this one. Others are peaceful. The gods haven't ruined those ones yet." He gave a chuckle. "I've heard it said there might be dozens of them, even as many as a hundred or more. Some are much smaller than ours, but others are much bigger, with their own versions of our gods and different ones too, and huge kingdoms and nations and sprawling empires filled with all sorts of weird and wonderful people, with powerful magic and strange sorceries we've never even heard of. I should like to travel to see them one day. When I'm older I'll build a giant ship, the biggest one ever seen, and find a crew more brave than any that came before, and we'll punch through the Stormy Sea and see what lies beyond."

"Others have tried that before," Robbert said. Finn Rivers was not the first boy to dream of exploring beyond the net of perilous seas and oceans that surrounded these two continents. "I am not aware of anyone who has made it back, though."

"That doesn't mean they didn't find anything," the lad said. "Maybe it *is* possible to break free of the seas, only when you do you can't come back. I'd make sure my crew understand this. Only those willing to never return would come with me."

Bernie Westermont pursed his large lips and turned his eyes over the gilded waters. "What sort of people are out there, then? On these other continents. Are they like us?"

"No one knows for sure," said the short, freckle-faced teen. "But there are probably all sorts, same as here. Some think the people of the Unseen Isles came from another land originally. They're very tall. Like giants. And they have a strange language too."

Bernie scrunched his eyes. "You just said no one could return here if they leave. How could these people have made it from another land?"

Sometimes, when Bernie and Finn spoke, it was the thirteen-year-old who seemed the elder of the two. Even at so unripe an age he had a mature and teacherly manner. "Well, maybe it was the same where they originally came from? They were able to leave and not return from their own lands, and that's why they settled on the Unseen Isles."

"The Tigress was from there," Robbert said. "She was a sell-sword," he explained to the boy. "And even taller than Bernie is."

Finn Rivers nodded briskly. "They're all like that, I've heard. Some of the men can be over eight feet tall. That's as tall as the Wall. And their *biggest* are even taller. Those of purer blood. When they came here, they mixed with regular people, Aramatian and Solapian merchants mostly, who went to the islands to trade, and also Lightborn and even Bladeborn too. After a while the blood thinned and they grew smaller, but still, there are some huge people out there."

"Where *are* the Unseen Isles," Bernie asked, frowning and scratching at his scabby chin. He had a nasty graze there from when he'd taken a tumble during the storm.

"South of Solapia," the prince answered. He looked at Finn Rivers for confirmation; the boy was a fount of such knowledge, they had found, always chipping in with these little details. He had proven of great entertainment and insight during the long days it took to get here after the tempest, battling through a series of smaller 'sub-storms', as Captain Burton had called them, as well as a four-day period where they had languished, becalmed, upon a strange and silent silver sea.

That was almost more frightening than the storms had been. For those four days, the waters had gone still as a millpond, the winds dying as though the world had come to a sudden, abrupt end. They could see no land, and some of the men had started to fret that the storm had driven them out beyond the known oceans and into the empty void where thousands of other vessels had been known to vanish in the past. Even Bloodhound Burton had seemed wary for a while, with their water stocks running low, and the sun beating mercilessly down upon them. Men were prone to go mad in those conditions, he'd said, though once again the gods had proven themselves generous when they stirred the winds back up into a frenzy, and they drove themselves west toward the coast.

It's all these Rasals aboard, Robbert Lukar had decided. The Seaborn were the people of the ocean god Rasalan and he was doing what he could to help them. Every day they sang their songs of prayer, remaining upbeat even in the direst of circumstances, and if it wasn't for Bloodhound, there was no way they'd have lived through that tempest. *The way he moved the ship on the waves…the way he outmanoeuvred and outwitted that manator.* Lank had said later that the captain had been sent by Rasalan to save them, and tongue in cheek though the comment was, he did not seem to be far wrong.

Finn Rivers nodded. "Hundreds of miles south of Solapia," he confirmed to the prince. "Almost directly south of the city of Azore. The Unseen Isles aren't on most maps, because they're too far away. That's why they're called 'unseen'. People say they're the farthest islands from the continents. Right at the edge of the world that we know."

Bernie peered up at the great sandstone carving of Calacan again. "What happened to him, then? Did he get lost when he flew out searching for other lands?"

Finn Rivers nodded solemnly. "So some say. The goddess Aramatia made a land of her own, the local people believe. She wanted her own island, like her sister Solapia, so she went off to try to make one, far away across the sea. Only…she never came back. And Calacan grew so worried that he would fly out searching for her. And then he went missing too."

"Maybe they both found peace," Bernie said, in a hopeful voice. He looked to the eastern horizon. "Did anyone go looking for them? Like sailors and explorers? If Aramatia made a land of her own it would be a peaceful one, wouldn't it? She wasn't so fond of war like some others, I've heard."

"She was a goddess of life and love and beauty," Finn Rivers agreed. "If there's a land of her own making out there, I'll bet it's real nice."

He gave a grin, and that made Bernie grin too, though Robbert's face was stone. Much as he liked the sentiment there, he didn't want to let his own thoughts drift in that direction. *If we wanted to find somewhere even half peaceful, we would have staggered toward the Telleshi Isles*, he thought. But it was war Robbert wanted to seek, his own lands he wanted to defend. All this airy talk of mythical lands and goddesses and giant eagle-titans wasn't going to lead anywhere.

He left them at the prow, stepping down through the men, offering what words of encouragement he could. The humidity was wretched down in their bunks and cabins, so most had come up for air, and the decks had grown crowded. Many had taken to sleeping on the little beach as well, finding little nooks among the rocks, erecting their own little shelters to stave off the sun.

Robbert joined Captain Burton on the quarterdeck. He held a monocular to his eye and was scanning the sea.

"See anything out there?" the prince inquired.

"Whales," Bloodhound said. "See them. *Smell* them." His nostrils flared. "Pod of them cruised past, few miles out."

"Going which way?"

"North. Toward Bhoun."

It was an island on the south coast of Rasalan, barely a hundred miles away, named for the god of whales. Apparently, the giant animals were drawn to the waters between the island of Bhoun, and Galaphan's Grounding, further to the east, where the whale titan

Galaphan had died and washed ashore. Some said that was due to old age. Others that Galaphan had been mortally wounded fighting Izzun, the kraken titan, in a bout that turned the sea to a great red-white froth, and created giant whirlpools that sucked a thousand ships down to Daarl's Domain. According to the tale, Izzun, too, had died from wounds taken during the battle. Like the gods, the monstrous beasts of their making were often at war with one another, back during the early days, fighting for supremacy of land and sea and sky.

"Hand that over, will you," Robbert said. He took the monocular from Burton and put it to his working right eye. The black patch he wore over his blinded left had become bleached and salt-stained now, the rest of his face kissed with a bronzing tan. He gave the sea a look, spotting no ships, no whales, nothing at all, then handed the monocular back, clutched at his godsteel dagger, and squinted out, looking again.

Burton frowned at him. "What are you doing?"

"Checking to see if my eyesight is better with godsteel or that little gadget of yours."

"And?"

He shrugged. "About the same. Hard to know with nothing to look at." He performed the same experiment, this time looking up at the stone eagle on the cliffs above them, then over at Lank as he continued down the steps. He was nearing the bottom now. With both godsteel and monocular Robbert could see the beads of sweat on the knight's forehead, the focused cast to his eyes as he took each step one at a time. Sir Lothar was not especially fond of the climb, clearly. "My sight's better with godsteel, but it's marginal." He gave the monocular back again. "I've decided to head straight for Vandar," he said. "Not Mudport, maybe, but one of the harbours further up the coast. I can't waste time marching through Rasalan. The fighting's in Vandar, Captain, and that's where I need to be."

Bloodhound scratched a grey-whiskered jowl in thought. They had heard from the occasional passing ship that the Marshlands had become a warring wasteland, overrun by the hordes of Agarath and their allies. There was even a rumour that a Tukoran army had been mustered to join the fighting, marching from Ilithor under the command of Robbert's twin brother. If that was true, he had to do whatever he could to get to them. The idea of fighting beside Ray made him smile. *For Father,* he thought. That's what they would say to one another, before they took to the field. *Even if we didn't say it with words,* he knew. *We'd say it with our eyes, and our hearts.*

That's how it had always been between them. Robbert always knew what Raynald was thinking, and vice versa. A glance here, a smile there, a little gesticulation that only they knew. In battle that made them almost one, knowing what the other would do. *And maybe that's what I need,* Robb reflected. He'd lost the use of his left eye, but Ray would more than make up the difference.

535

"The crossing will be difficult," the captain said, after a while. "We've been lucky since that manator, but that's not likely to last. The amount of greatwhales we've been seeing…and that kraken the lads spotted a few days ago. Those beasts are drawn to fight, as Izzun and Galaphan were. Might be we'll slip by unnoticed, but if not, we'll be in a spot of bother, lad, make no mistake. And we can expect to see dragons soon enough too."

"We have no choice," Robbert said. "The way from Rasalan will take weeks of hard riding, and months if we're forced to march afoot." Which they would be. Robbert had some horses in the holds, but not many, and there was no way he'd be able to find mounts for three thousand men at any Rasal port, no matter how big. "I can't wait that long, Captain. When we leave, we're sailing west. There's no other option."

"Aye, so it is then. But just remember what you told me, princeling."

Robbert remembered. "I told you to get us home safe. You've done a fine job in that so far."

"Aye. *So far.* Now I'm not one to go running scared of krakens, as you know, but if you want to avoid a tussle, you're going to have to trust me to steer our course. We'll start west once we pass the Horn, but if I get a sense that it's too dangerous, I'll have no choice but to turn us north. Just making you aware."

Robbert had to trust the captain's judgment on that. He nodded to say he understood and looked across his little fleet of six. Each of the ships was tied up against a stone jetty, fastened to iron pylons with lengths of hempen rope, moving and creaking gently on the water. *Blackthorn* was still under repairs - she had taken a savage gutting from a rocky shoal only a few miles down the coast, puncturing her hull in several places, and the Seaborn were working underwater to fix her, holding their breath for long minutes at a time. Some could do so for upwards of ten, fifteen, even twenty minutes or more, Robbert had heard. Bloodhound claimed he could hold his breath twice as long as any of them, of course, though hadn't yet risen to any requests to prove it.

Hammer was also undergoing some reinforcements from the battering the manator had given them, overseen by the boatswain George Buckley and the ship's chief carpenter, Wick Ashton, both Seaborn of middling blood. By now all the masts had been fixed, the sails stitched back together, holes and breaches covered over and filled in with thick black tar, but there were a couple of areas down at the belly of the beast that still needed a bit of attention.

"Will they be ready when I give the order to sail?" Robbert asked.

"Buckley says we'll be fixed up by tomorrow," Bloodhound confirmed. "*Blackthorn* the same. Might want to give it an extra day or two to make sure, though."

536

Two, three days, Robbert thought. If no more ships came in that time, he would call the command to leave.

A glint of sunlight on steel caught his eyes and he saw Sir Lothar long-striding down the rocky beach with that absurd gait of his, moving toward the stone pier at which *Hammer* had been moored. Lank gave an order to his men as they reached the ship, and off they went to seek their rest, staggering away to find some shade. Lank crossed the gangplank and joined Robb and the captain at the helm. He looked weary after a long night up there on the clifftops.

"Anything?" Robbert asked him.

Sir Lothar had a half smile on his lips. A tired smile. "There's a ship incoming," he told his prince. "It's still far off, and looks in poor shape, but it's one of ours."

"Gullimer?" Robbert looked at his tall friend in hope.

But Lank's head went left and right. "One of Lord Simon's. Another Swallow ship."

Robbert nodded. It was good news. Not the ship he wanted to see, but any of them was a boon to his cause. He heard a hammer of feet across the decks, and looked up to see that Lord Huffort was stamping their way, having left his cabin aboard *Landslide*, moored across the pier. Both of the ships were mighty galleons, with three great decks and four soaring masts furled with sails coloured in the hues of their houses. Huffort had been here for weeks now and had grown restive in that time.

"My prince." The large, lantern-jawed lord greeted him with a perfunctory bow. He wore a linen shirt, cotton breeches, and a cloak of soft light wool, quartered in shades of brown and grey.

"My lord," Robbert returned. "Sir Lothar was just updating us on his night on watch."

The Lord of Rockfall nodded. That was clearly the reason why he had joined them. "And what did you spy from the cliffs, sir?"

"Little and less than little," Lank replied. "And a little less than that. There's no one on the nearest road, no enemy soldiers coming up the coast, no beasts or monsters prowling the plains. We did spot an eagle or two, but when is that not the case? Oh. And a ship. As I was just telling Prince Robbert and Captain Burton. One of Lord Swallow's is heading this way."

Huffort seemed mildly disappointed to learn it wasn't another of his own. "One of Simon's. But not *Shadow?*"

"Not big enough or black enough. It is most likely to be *Greystar* or *Wild Raven,* according to Sir Gregory."

"Sir Gregory," repeated Huffort. "Why isn't he reporting this himself?"

"He is weary from the watch," Lothar said. "I am just as capable as saying the names of ships as Sir Gregory is, my lord."

Huffort made a doubtful sound. He did not much like Sir Lothar, and the feeling was most assuredly mutual. "And when this ship gets here?" Huffort looked at Robbert with a set of demanding eyes. The man was grouchy, hard-headed and craggy-faced. He had coarse prickly stubble on his head, severely balding at the crown, and coating his slab of jaw as well. "Are we to hoist anchor and sail home, Robbert?"

"In a day or three," the prince told him.

"And *where*?" The word was loaded with doubt. Lord Lewyn Huffort had made his preferences known several times already. He wanted to sail north, to Bhoun, then cruise the Rasal coastline westward through Whaler's Bay. If they came afoul of some monster or other mishap, they would be close enough to shore to reach safe harbour somewhere, he argued. If not, they could continue to sail the coast until they reached the Links, and then sail up the Sibling Strait to Rockfall, his city seat on the eastern shores of Tukor. Lord Lewyn Huffort believed that was the safest route. Once there, he would muster the remainder of his levies and march to war. Or so he claimed.

Robbert believed otherwise. Huffort might look like a warrior, and might have even fought as one once upon a time, but he'd shown himself to have a coward's heart of late. The prince knew his true intent. *He wants to hide in his city*, Robbert thought. Rockfall was built into the base of the mountains and had strong underground bunkers well stocked with food and resources. The lords of his line had always used them as a private sanctuary, concealing their wives and young children and their favoured attendants and retainers during times of war. Not the population of the city, no, it was far too small for that, and gods forbid Huffort had to share his air with them, let alone his stocks of meat and mead, but his loved ones would be safe. It seemed clear to Robbert Lukar that the man wanted to retreat there, bar the door, and pray that when he re-emerged at last, the war would be done and won.

It vexed him greatly. And he was not about to let the man abandon his oaths of duty.

"We'll be sailing west," Robbert Lukar said, to answer Huffort's question. "Across the Three Bays, directly for the Vandarian Marshlands. The north needs us, my lord. I suggest you spend time polishing your armour and honing the edge of your blade. We will be in battle soon enough."

The lord looked at him with a set of flat, impassive eyes. "You are not taking account of my counsel?"

"I have heard your counsel, and I appreciate your wisdom," Robbert told him, with grace. "However, I have decided we must act more expediently. You yourself brought us this rumour that my brother Raynald may be marching to war. If this is so, we cannot abandon him. It is our duty to make haste to his side." *And my duty*, Robbert thought, *to take command of the men of Tukor, and lead them forth into battle, as king.*

Huffort remained unmoved. "That was only a rumour. Most likely Prince Raynald is still in Ilithor. The quickest way to reach him would be by sailing up the Sibling Strait."

Robbert Lukar was not going to listen to this. "I have heard your counsel," he repeated. "But we *will* be sailing west, my lord, and to war. It is escalating too quickly for us to drag our feet. We must act. And now."

Robbert saw the man's upper lip twitch. He saw him close and open a fist. But Huffort only sketched another bow, and said, "As you say, my prince," in a voice as stiff as a corpse. "I will see to honing my blade, then." He turned abruptly and walked away.

Robbert watched him leave. "The gods cursed me when they put him in my lap," he said, once the man was out of earshot. "It would have been better if he'd died with my uncle in Aram."

"Or at sea," Sir Lothar put in.

Robbert nodded. He did not like to wish such a foul fate upon a man, but Lewyn Huffort had proven a pebble in his shoe for too long, and had been very much his uncle's creature. He turned back to the sea, putting the man from his mind. Vaguely now he could see the shape of a ship, taking a wide course around the coast, moving past the headland. Bloodhound snatched up his monocular and planted it to his eye. "*Wild Raven*," he said. "I can see her figurehead on the prow."

"How many men aboard?" Robbert asked.

"Some three hundred, when we put to sea," Lothar answered. "Though they may have lost men during the storm."

That was likely. Robbert well remembered how dozens had gone over the sides of *Hammer*, sucked off into the churning black waters. The very thought of it set his heart to racing. *If I never step foot aboard another ship after this, it'll be too bloody soon.*

It took them another hour for *Wild Raven* to reach them, Captain Burton assessing the damage as the ship approached the stone harbour. She had lost her mainmast, the same as *Hammer* had, and most of her sails had been torn loose or so badly tattered they barely caught the wind. Without oars she had clearly struggled to make good headway. "How long will she take to repair?" Robbert asked.

"Depends if they've got damage to the hull," Burton said. "Though doesn't look like it, the way they're sitting in the water. So might just be the sails that are the problem. We can sort those out quickly enough."

It was favourable news. So too the tidings that they had lost only a handful of men during the storm. Robbert had that from the Emerald Guard Sir Colyn Rowley who'd been in command of the Swallow soldiers aboard. As soon as *Wild Raven* was tied up to a free pier Robbert stepped aboard for his inspection. The men were ragged, malnourished, and badly dehydrated, but alive. Robbert ordered for water to be brought aboard at once, as Sir Colyn spoke of their journey.

"Got blown miles off course by the storm," the knight said. He had been a comely man before the voyage. Now his face was slim to the bone, his forehead and cheeks sun-scorched and blistered, and his hair had turned from brown to blond and started to thin and even fall out in places. But the relief in him was palpable. "Couldn't even say where, Prince Robbert. Threaded through the northern islands of the Telleshis, we think. Saw shapes out in the gloom, sometimes, distant islands they must have been, but we were pushed right beyond them. Out to the ends of the world, we were. Never seen anywhere so silent and still."

"We had the same experience on *Hammer*," Robbert said. "For four days we were becalmed."

"Was closer to twelve for us. A few of the men went mad and started seeing things in the water. Giant monsters, some said, circling below us. Another claimed to have seen all the way down to Daarl's Domain. He started screaming, that one, in a way I've never heard. So loud his throat was shredded and blood started to come up through his teeth. He wasn't the same after that. Even when we got him calmed, his eyes…they just stared out all day long, as he sat on the deck muttering and mumbling. Two others even jumped in and started swimming under. We managed to fish one out, but the other just kept going down and down until he drowned. We got his body when it came back up, but why he did it…" He shook his head. "Couldn't fathom it. Must have gone sun-mad or something."

Robbert shuddered to hear all that. "But you made it," he said, gripping the knight's arm. He had some two hundred and seventy men with him, he told Robbert, though some were ill from scurvy and others so badly dehydrated they had developed kidney failure and debilitating seizures. Many of the rest were in poor health, though would quickly be revived with better nourishment and hydration. "I hope to leave within two or three days, Sir Colyn. That ought to give your men some time to rest and recover. And to repair your ship."

"I could use some help in that, my prince. We have little in the way of spare sails and we lost our mainmast, as you can see."

"*Blackthorn* has a spare," Robbert said. "I will send Sir Gregory over to you. My boatswain Buckley can help with your sails."

"We would be much obliged." Sir Colyn smiled wanly. "Have you sent out foraging parties?" He squinted up the cliffs, cast high above them. Beyond, the blue skies were beginning to curdle with cloud, dark and grey. It looked like rain to Robbert Lukar.

"We have sent men to Eagle's Perch, though they found little in the way of food. Some casks of dried beef, a barrel of oats, not much to sustain us." The fortress had not been revived since they had occupied it moons ago, and sat almost entirely deserted. Robbert had made certain that Lothar or Bernie accompany the men, to make sure there was no killing of innocent civilians, though he could not say what had happened before *Hammer* arrived. Huffort had claimed to have remained down here while he waited for other ships to appear, though Robbert had a suspicion that the lord had already sent men out to scour the city in an attempt to fill his own holds.

I might have to perform an inspection, he thought. He would not put it past Lewyn Huffort to have squirrelled away stocks of food for his own men. House Huffort had never been one for sharing; a miserable and miserly series of men had ruled from Rockfall for centuries, of which Lord Lewyn was just the latest.

"We will try to forage a little further afield in the coming days," Robbert went on. "But I would not count on us finding much. Most likely we will have to make do with what we have until we reach Vandar."

"Vandar, my lord?"

Robbert nodded and told him of his plans. Sir Colyn seemed in agreement with him, unlike certain others. "We're dying a slow death, all of us," the knight said, looking over the small, broken fleet. "Might as well die doing something useful." The Emerald Guard looked south, squinting toward the headland. "We saw another pair of ships, I should say. Not three, four days ago. They were distant, and looked badly damaged, but seemed to be making their way here, if slowly. I caught some flashes of red and green, my lord. On the tattered sails."

"Red and green?" Robbert repeated. Those were the colours of House Gullimer. "Might it have been *Orchard*, Sir Colyn?"

"I believe so, my lord, yes I do. She was sailing with another of Lord Gullimer's vessels, and they looked to be tied together, that I saw. Though I could not say for certain. They were many leagues away, and we did not get a long look at them." He rubbed at a scraggly flaxen beard. "I wonder if you might consider sending someone out to search for them, Prince Robbert. They may be in dire need of water and rations, as we were. I would go myself, if I could, but with the damage we have suffered…"

"You've done quite enough, Sir Colyn, and have earned your rest." Robb looked across his little fleet. "I'll send *Landslide*," he decided. He was not going to let the apple lord die without an attempt to save him, and Lord Huffort's flagship was best placed to brave the waters again, big and bulky and undamaged as it was. It would be nice to rid himself of Huffort for a day or two as well. *The man is restless here. I'll give him something to do.*

Some rain was starting to fall, and the wind was picking up, a hot wind blowing from the ocean. Across the decks of every vessel, empty buckets and pails and barrels were brought out to catch the rainwater. The ragged men of *Wild Raven* were opening their mouths and looking skyward, sighing in sweet relief. Some were weeping, hugging one another. Sir Colyn smiled. "We haven't felt a drop of rain for long days. It has come at just the right time."

541

Not for Orchard, Robbert thought. If these winds continued to strengthen, the waves were sure to follow, and both beleaguered boats could yet be sunk. He told Sir Colyn to begin repairs right away, and that he would send both Buckley and Sir Gregory to help him, then paid a visit to Lord Huffort's large, spacious cabin aboard *Landslide*. There, he gave a direct command to the lantern-jawed lord to unmoor on the morning tide and sail south down to the coast, to find *Orchard* and her companion ship and tow them both back if required.

Naturally, Lord Lewyn did not seem pleased with the charge. "We're meant to be sailing *north*, not south," he groused. "How far do you want me to go?"

"As far as is required," Robbert said.

"And if another storm picks up? You'd risk me and my men to this folly? I have almost six hundred soldiers aboard."

"Those can stay here," Robbert told him. "Take only the captain and his crew. If *Orchard* is foundering, her men may need to come aboard. You can clear space overnight."

"In *this* weather?" The rain was falling much harder already, and a grey fog was closing in. "Be reasonable, Robbert. At least let them sleep belowdecks tonight. By morning the rain will have cleared and they can move onto the beach then."

"Fine," Robbert said. "But I want you ready to sail by dawn, Lewyn. If *Hammer* was not still undergoing repairs, I would go myself. But alas that is not the case, so it must be you. Or would you prefer to see Lord Gullimer left out there to die? Along with hundreds of men?"

Huffort grunted and shook his head. "Of course not." He thought a moment, and there was a slight shift in his eyes. "I'll see it done, if that's your command."

"It is," Robbert said, firmly.

"Then we'll be gone by morning, fear not."

Robbert left him as quickly as he'd come. Spending any length of time with the man only ever served to put him in a foul mood. He purged himself over the following hours by helping to oversee the repairs to the ships, taking reports from scouts and scavengers as they returned from the cliffs above, distributing water and rations to the starving men aboard *Wild Raven*, checking on the horses and mules and watching the seas for signs of sails. With luck Lord Gullimer would be sighted by nightfall and he could give Lord Huffort a reprieve.

He wasn't. The fog was too thick to see through, the rains too heavy, and none of the watchers came down from the cliffs telling Robbert that *Orchard* was near. All the same, the prince went to bed that night more hopeful than he'd been in a while. Another ship had come in, along with the loyal knight Sir Colyn Rowley, who had served beneath his father for many years, and with luck Lord Wilson Gullimer, and several hundred more men, would soon be joining him as well.

It would bring their total numbers up toward four thousand,

perhaps a few more. It was hardly much of an army, but enough to make some difference. He smiled to think of how his brother would react to his return, and his lords bannermen and captains and knights. And when he slept that night, he dreamt of fighting beside Ray on the battlefield, back to back, as one, slaying both man and beast, fighting for the pride of their father, the great Rylian Lukar, as he watched on from the Hall of Green.

He was awoken by a hard shake to the shoulder.

Bernie Westermont loomed above him. His face was cast in a glare of anger. "What is it, Bern?" Robbert asked, voice cracked from sleep. He blinked and sat up and glanced outside through the window by his bed. It was dark still, and foggy, and the rain had not stopped falling. A thin line of colour marked the eastern horizon.

"*Huffort,*" the big knight said, making the name a curse.

Robbert frowned. "What's he done now?"

"Come. You'd best see."

Robbert threw on a pair of breeches and stepped outside, unclothed above the waist. The rain washed down across his agile, youthful frame. The light was so poor and fog so thick that he could barely make out the rest of the fleet, moored along their stone jetties. But it was clear enough that *Landslide* was gone.

And she was not the only one.

"He took them," Bernie said. "*The Stone Maiden* and *Mountain*. Huffort took all his ships."

"To find Gullimer?" Robbert asked, his head still heavy with sleep. It was a naive question, and he realised the truth at once.

Bernie Westermont said it for him. "He sailed north, Robb. *Home*. That traitorous bastard has abandoned us."

543

41

Lythian

The doomed were led out at dawn, a line of four men accused of murder and mutiny.

Outside the broken city walls, a stage had been erected, looking east toward the sunrise. Shards of pale light shone down through the clouds, and a soft cool rain was falling, sprinkling from the skies. It was almost pretty, Lythian thought. He closed a fist, knowing what he had to do.

One of the men was weeping, the youngest of them, a youth of only seventeen. He served Lord Barrow, and had been a stableboy in his former life before the muster called him to war. The lord himself stood at Lythian's side, shaking his head. "This is foul, my lord. *Foul.* He is only a boy. He did not know what he was doing."

He knew, Lythian thought. *He was drawn along by the older men, but he knew.* "No man can escape justice, Lord Barrow," is all he said. He spoke in a strong, clear voice, standing tall and straight-backed, bedecked in his misting armour. From his shoulders trailed the cloak that marked him as the First Blade of Vandar, and from his hip glowed the great golden blade that only such a man could bear. He had decided to portray an image of total strength. *No more doubt,* he thought. *No more weakness. Play the role with pride.*

The young weeper was walking at the back. Before him went three others, two in the service of House Kindrick and one of the Rosetree men. They were part of a larger group, it had been discovered. There had been eight of them originally, though three had perished during the fighting with the prisoners, and another had died of his wounds a few days later.

Dead by their own steel, Lythian thought. As he had suspected, the men had conspired to gather weapons from the armoury, and throw them down upon a group of Agarathi men they had previously identified as violent. Men they had taunted for weeks, Lythian knew, mocking them and goading them and stirring them into a frenzy. It seemed that this was a long-term plan, involving more men than had likely been identified.

There are some out there now, the First Blade thought, looking across the crowds gathered upon the muddy plains below the stage. Hundreds had come out to watch, perhaps as many as a thousand, and many more were observing from the battlements and broken walls. Most wore hooded cloaks to shield themselves from the rains, shadowing their faces and their dark, hateful eyes. Lythian looked out at them, a fixed expression of defiance on his face. He wondered for a moment what would happen if they all attacked him at once. *How many would I kill before they overwhelmed me? Fifty? A hundred? Might I slay them all?*

The thought moved through him darkly. His jaw stiffened as he embraced it. There was a hate rising in him, approaching like a tide he could not seem to stop. It had crept upon him, day by day, fuelled by the whispers and the rumours and the dark glances of the men. *Men*, he thought bitterly. *Roaches would be a better term for them.* Too few of them were good and honourable, and some had started to leave. Amron had staunched that wound for a time, but the deserters had begun to slip away again, escaping through the breaches in the walls in ones and twos and little groups, up to a dozen disappearing each night.

He grimaced, gazing out, wondering which of the men would be gone by tomorrow. It was a leak he could not stop, a *drip drip drip* of deserting men driven to return home to their loved ones. If that was a motive he could understand, it was not one he was able to forgive. *I will leave this gallows here,* he thought. *I'll decree that any man caught trying to flee will get a length of rope as well…*

"You're going to regret this, Lindar," sneered a voice. "You hear me. You kill those men and…"

"And *what?*" Lythian turned, cloak swaying, to look Lord Kindrick in the eye. He loomed over him. Lythian was no Amron Daecar, but he was no small man either, and in his armour he was grand as a god. "If I kill these men, then what will happen to me?"

Kindrick shrunk away at the force of his voice. His eyes moved aside like the frightened weasel he was. "It'll…it'll rest on your conscience, is all. These men…they didn't do anything. They…"

"We have testimony from trusted men that says otherwise. These men plotted to cause a riot. They stole weapons from the armoury. Several of them walked into the square and armed the Agarathi prisoners. They *armed* them, my lord. That in itself is treason. And how many died as a result? How many, Kindrick? *Answer me.*"

"Six…sixteen, my lord."

"Sixteen *northmen*. Four were their allies and deserved what they got. That leaves another *twelve*. A dozen men who had no part in these plans, and yet died as a result of them. And how many Agarathi were slain?" He waited. "*How many?*"

"I…I don't know, my lord." His voice was a squeak. "Sixty, or…"

545

"*Ninety-four,*" Lythian said. "It was butchery, sparked off by the men lined up before you. And you dare tell me *I'll* regret this?" Lythian's hand was on his blade, the knuckle-plates of his gauntlets crunching and grinding together. A mist pulsed and swirled up out of the golden scabbard, moving sharply, *angrily*. Kindrick drew back from him, inching away as a man does from a predator about to pounce, eyes lowered. Some of the men in the crowd nearby had heard, and were watching, but Lythian Lindar was past caring. He bore the greatest blade in all the world, and held one of its greatest offices. It no longer mattered to him what lesser lord worms like Kindrick and his men thought.

He turned away, showing the man his back. "Sir Guy. Get them noosed."

Sir Guy Blenhard had command of the executions. The four plotters had been led beneath the gibbet, their heads covered in soaking black hoods. Before each of them a stool awaited. Good Guy gave a nod and his men began moving the prisoners forward, forcing them up, tightening nooses about their necks. The youngest one at the back was sobbing uncontrollably, piss leaking down his leg, begging for mercy. *I should have muzzled them*, Lythian thought. The other three men made not a sound.

Before long all of them were in place. It was time for the last words.

One by one, their hoods were pulled back, so they could observe the time-honoured custom. Lythian had warned them already not to make a show of it. "Die with dignity," he'd said in the dungeon where the men were being kept. "Speak a prayer or tell your mother you'll see her soon. Incite hate or anger and you'll see a slower end."

He wondered now if that threat would be heeded. The first man was the eldest, but still no older than thirty-five, a bull-shouldered blacksmith who'd hacked up half a dozen Agarathi with a massive axe he'd made. "Made it special," he'd sneered at Lythian, when he confessed his part in the crime. "Nice edge for killing scum."

I ought to have given him the same edge, Lythian thought. *I should be doing this myself.* That was the way of it among the Varin Knights. In the few occasions where treason had been committed in the ranks of the order, it was the First Blade who swung the sword. But these men weren't Varin Knights, or knights at all. They weren't men-at-arms or long-serving soldiers, but swineherds and farmhands and butchers out for blood who did not deserve to see their lives ended by the First Blade of Vandar.

So the rope it would be.

Sir Guy stood before the man. "Any last words?" he asked. "Speak them now, and go in peace."

"Peace?" the blacksmith snorted. "I've seen men hanged before, Blenhard. Ain't nothing peaceful about it. Just see it done. I'm proud of what I did and would do it again. So you kick that stool you snivel-ling runt. I've made my peace with *that*."

"As you say." Sir Guy kicked the stool. The man did not go in peace.

It took a while for him to stop wriggling, and all the while the youngest of the prisoners continued to sob and whimper, his legs so weak it looked like he might collapse. There was a certain cruelty to making him go last, but that was custom too. The four men had drawn lots and here they were. It just so happened that those lots had lined them up from oldest to youngest, but there was nothing Lythian could do about that. *The gods are cruel*, he only thought. *This is their doing, not mine.*

The second man's hood was removed. He was thin as a spear, gaunt-faced and grim, the very vision of an Ironmoorer, and one of Kindrick's men. Lythian had seen him guarding his lord by night sometimes, and walking in his retinue as he moved about the city. Sir Guy invited him to speak. "Any last words?" he asked, as he had the first. "Speak them now, and go in peace."

The gaunt man sneered, the rope tight about his throat. "Was Vandar's work we did. Work that our First Blade refuses to do himself." He managed to gather a gob of spit, to send out in Lythian's direction. "You should be ashamed of yourself, *traitor*. We all know what you did…"

Sir Guy Blenhard kicked the stool to shut him up and the man went jerking on his rope. His gaunt face reddened, eyes blaring, legs flailing. There was murmuring in the crowd.

We all know what you did.

Lythian looked over at the sea of hungry men, their eyes burning with questions and doubts. He had spoken now to his close allies of what he'd done during his time in the south, spoken of Tethian and Marak and Talasha and Eldur. Ralf already knew; now Sir Adam did as well, and Sir Guy and Sir Storos, who had felt aggrieved that Lythian had not told him the full truth already "We travelled together, Lythian," he'd said, hurt. "We have been brothers-in-arms for long months. Why didn't you tell me?"

I was afraid, Lythian had thought. "I worried you would condemn me," were the actual words he said.

Storos had thought about it long and hard, then given a shake of the head. "If the king does not condemn you, nor will I. I trust that what you did, you did for the right reasons. But I cannot say that everyone will be so understanding."

No, Lythian thought now, seeing them all there, standing in the rain. He had wondered if he should gather them all together, stand before them and tell the truth of his tale. Rumours were dangerous, wise old Ralf had said, and the men were beginning to warp events as the whispers went from ear to ear. Some said he had willingly participated in releasing Eldur from his tomb, giving his own Bladeborn blood to resurrect him. Others were certain he had done it for the love of his Agarathi 'whore', that she had put some dark spell on him and used him to unleash the devil. They even knew of Starslayer, and how he'd lost it in those depths. A sacrifice, many claimed. He presented it before the demon, his own ancestral blade. The demigod drank the mists and laughed, and was reborn in his fiery gown.

"You must tell them the truth," Ralf had urged him, but what good was the truth to them now? That they could think so little of him, believe him capable of such treachery was the only truth Lythian cared for. He looked at the eyes, shadowed in their hoods, and felt that hate clawing at his heart. *The things I have done in service of this kingdom. The sacrifices I have made to help keep them safe...* "Let them share in their lies," he had only said to the old knight. "Those who matter know the truth of who I am." *And the rest can go to hell.*

The gaunt man had gone quiet, his arms hanging limp at the sides. Lythian wanted this done. He met eyes with Sir Guy with a look, and the third plotter had his hood removed.

The man was more noble than the rest, the son of a wealthy merchant who had travelled with him to the south. He had seen first-hand how his sire was treated by the Agarathi. How uncouth they were, how barbaric, how his father had been bullied and abused by their unseemly tradesman, how the peasants had pelted them with pebbles and stones as they passed. "You suffered the same, didn't you?" the young man had said to Lythian in the dungeons. "You were a prisoner there, in Eldurath. You were mocked and scorned and debased by these people. How can you *not* hate them?"

Because I was a kingkiller to them, he thought. *They believed I murdered their beloved Dulian.* He had since seen great kindness from many other Agarathi, from Kin'rar and Marak and Pagaloth and Talasha, from Sotel Dar and Sa'har Nakaan and Prince Tethian, even him. His answer had been more simple than that. "There is light and dark in every one of us," he'd told the merchant's son. "I tend toward the light, and you've let yourself be drawn to the dark. What you did was wrong. And on the morrow, you will pay for it."

And here he was, paying.

"Any last words?" Sir Guy asked him. "Speak them now, and go in peace."

"I said what I needed to say to the First Blade last night," the merchant's son called out. "To the men here, gods-speed to you in the battles to come. And may I just say, *open your eyes.* There will be no unity between the men of the north and south. *Never.* Let it be known that these were my last words. Let my father hear them, and rejoice." He turned his eyes down at Sir Guy, and nodded.

The stool was kicked away.

The rain had started to come down harder, and more men were pulling up their hoods. The shards of light that had been cast by the dawn were gone, the clouds closing up to cover all the world in shadow. In that sudden grim darkness, the weeping boy's hood was removed, and at once he looked across at the three men to his right, dangling dead on the ends of their ropes. "No…" he said, in slow encroaching horror. "No, please…no no!"

"Spare him!" came a call from the crowd. "Spare him, my lord! Show mercy!"

The rest responded, a hundred more calling out. "Mercy!"… "Spare him!"…"He's just a boy! *A boy*!"… "Show him mercy, my lord. Mercy!"

Lythian closed his ears to them. He could not bow to the mob. "Sir Guy, ask the question."

The knight hesitated. "My lord, perhaps we should…"

"Ask the question," Lythian repeated.

Sir Guy drew a breath, turning to the weeping teen. "Any…last words?" he asked him. He had to speak up; the noise was growing louder. "Speak them now…and go in peace."

The boy did not seem to hear him. He looked at the dead men again, swinging on their ropes as a breeze picked up. Some crows had already come down to perch upon the gibbet, cawing impatiently, waiting for their feast. "Please…please…I don't want to die…" He looked at Sir Guy. "Please…please *don't*!"

The knight looked pained. He turned to Lythian. A voice spoke behind him. "My lord, perhaps on this one occasion…"

"No," Lythian said, resolute. He met the eyes of young Rodmond Taynar. "No, my lord." Loath as he was to command a greatlord, he spoke here with the king's voice, and outranked him on that basis. "We cannot make exceptions. He must die along with all the rest."

"I know, my lord, but…" Rodmond looked out into the crowd, concerned. "If we follow through, we may start a riot. The men…"

"Cannot rule us, Rodmond," Lythian cut in. "They *cannot* rule our course." He looked back at Sir Guy Blenhard and gave a stiff nod of the head. "Kick the stool," he commanded.

The knight stepped a little closer, to better hear him over the clamour. "My lord?"

"I said kick the stool. He has had his chance."

"You hear them…" raked a voice. "I said you'd regret it…wasn't I lying, was I?" Lythian spun in anger upon the weasel Lord Kindrick, but this time the man did not draw back. "You have a chance here, Lindar," he said, emboldened by the crowd. "You let that boy go free, and maybe you'll get the men back onside. Show mercy, as they say. I can help."

"Help?"

He smiled. "All this about *Eldur*. I'm sure there's a good explanation. Let me hear it. Let me speak it to the men. You let that lad go and I'll help smooth it all over."

Lythian was half tempted to accept, but for that nagging doubt that this lord was behind it all. *I will not accede to him. I will not give him that power.* "No," he said, firmly. "It cannot be one rule for him and another for everyone else. He is old enough to take a wife and sire a son, to work a farm and fight a war. Then he is old enough to answer for his crimes." He turned back to Sir Guy, who cringed at the look Lythian gave him. "See it done," he said.

The knight obeyed with great reluctance. He stepped back to the wailing boy. "I'm sorry. I…I have no choice, you understand? Your own actions got you here." There was a final pause, a last intake of breath, and then Sir Guy Blenhard kicked away the stool. At once the boy's wailing was caught in his throat, his body jerking horribly from side to side as he fought against his own bodyweight, eyes bulging from his skull, veins swelling in his neck.

The sight was as ugly as the din. Lythian watched the boy wriggle, watched him struggle, watched him die. Something inside him was dying as well. Or perhaps it was already dead?

How had it come to this? How had he become so hated? There was a time when Lythian Lindar was amongst the most beloved men in the north, unimpeachable in his honour, near-peerless with the blade. There was no man in the world more proficient in the art of Strikeform, no man so well regarded for his staunch commitment to the chivalric ideals. *I am still that man,* he told himself. *It is the world that has changed around me.*

He had been mocked and locked up in Runnyhall, put on trial when he arrived at Redhelm, questioned and queried relentlessly over what happened to him in the south. The lies and half-truths and secrets had eaten away at him. Now this. Commanding an army of the hungry and the hateful. Lingering here with all his failed schemes, his hopes of unity crushed.

He could not stand here any longer. The youth was giving his last jerks and twitches and the noise was dying with him, the crowd growing quiet. A lull lingered, for a moment, another. Then someone shouted out, "Bastard!" and that set them off again, the calls of 'mercy' and 'save him' turning to heckles and shouts of 'traitor' and 'dragonlover' and 'scum'.

Sir Adam Thorley stepped up to his side. "My lord, we'd best go. The crowd is getting ugly."

Crowd, Lythian thought. It was meant to be an army, not some baying mob. He turned on his heels, brushing straight past Lord Kindrick as he left. Sir Adam's men fell in around them, and Sir Oswin and Sir Stroros and Sir Ralf as well. *My allies,* he thought. *But for how long? How long before they turn against me as well?*

He walked in a state of funereal gloom, his face a mask of sombre dignity, his boots sucking and pulling at the mud as he went. Behind, the men were screaming their obscenities, and on the battlements above he could see them looking down at him, silent. He imagined their faces, twisted in contempt, imagined the grunts and mutters they were sharing, the curses whispered beneath their breath. Sir Ralf had told him that it wasn't so. Many of the men still admired him, the old man claimed, and respected his drive to seek unity. Not just men among the Brockenhurst banners, but hundreds of good men from the Ironmoors too, even those serving under Kindrick and Barrow. Sir Adam had said the same. The Pointed Watch were with him, he assured the First Blade. They would not waver in their allegiance and would follow him until the end.

The end, he thought. *Perhaps this day is the start of it.*

He passed through the River Gate, across the dirty cobbles of the square, and made for the sanctuary of his tent. The others did not follow him through. He could hear talking outside, hear the strains of debate, and then old Sir Ralf entered through the flaps. "I told them you would prefer to be alone, my lord. If that includes me, by all means, tell me to go."

"No. Stay." Lythian removed his cloak, unbuckled his swordbelt, and took his seat, pouring two cups of watered wine. He invited Ralf to sit, and the old man settled down, his posture upright and neat. A long moment passed as Lythian digested what had just happened. "Did I make the right choice, Ralf? Tell me true."

"You did," the knight said without hesitation. "A true lord does not bend to the bleating of the sheep. The boy…the drawn lots. I do not believe it was by chance that he was last. Nor that all of those soldiers calling for mercy were so perfectly spaced apart." He paused to check Lythian's eyes. "Perhaps you did not notice? There were calls coming from every corner of the crowd. That was *arranged*, my lord."

Lythian nodded, pondering. "Kindrick?"

"I would think so. He and Sir Fitz. Of Lord Barrow I am not so sure. He is a decent man and a calmer head. I do not doubt that some of his captains will have contributed their men, however."

This was a riddle Lythian could not puzzle out. "What am I do to, Ralf? I look into the crowd and see an enemy behind every hood. No matter who they are, or what they're truly thinking, I see hate and anger."

"It isn't so," Sir Ralf assured him. "I was watching the crowds as well, and many were there to see justice be served. They agree with what you did."

"Then I'm growing paranoid," Lythian grunted. "This hate I see, this anger…" He gave a sigh and shook his head. "I don't just see it. I *feel* it too."

The old knight crossed one leg over the other. "In yourself?"

Lythian drank his wine. Even now the anger was in him, bubbling up through his veins. "I have never been a hateful man, nor one given to rage. Only recently. Since Amron left, and…" He knew the cause, as did Sir Ralf of Rotting Bridge. "The blade," he said. "Having it at my hip all day and beside my bed at night…that constant connection, the growing bond…" He looked at it, resting by the table. "It is trying to lead me astray, Ralf. And a part of me…a part of me *wants* to be led."

"You cannot allow it…"

"I know. I know my role. I speak the words Amron taught me. I recall his lessons. But it is a double-edged sword. To guard the blade I must keep it close, and yet keeping it close…it makes me vulnerable. And now, with all this brewing dissent…" He blew out a breath once more and drank a gulp of wine. "We all know what happened to Janilah Lukar. Are they trying to make me do the same? Are they so desperate to see me fall?"

"That was different," Ralf told him. "The Warrior King was following a dark path, and it led him to that dark day." He had slaughtered dozens, it was said, when he went on a rampage through Galin's Post in Ilithor. Not only men and women, but children as well, some as young as three or four if the rumours were true, cut down in their mother's arms. It was the baying of the crowd that sparked him, they'd heard. The jeers and accusations and pelted fruit. They had scant stocks of fruit here in the ruin of King's Point, and what they did was not to be wasted. *Elsewise I'd have received my measure as well*, the First Blade thought.

"My path is righteous," Lythian said. "Is that what you're saying?"

"You know it is," Sir Ralf told him. "Perhaps the most righteous of all."

Lythian did not know how the old man had come to that. "I have the rule of a ruin, Ralf. Every scheme I try ends in failure and death. Tell me how my path is more righteous than the others."

"Because you carry the blade only to protect it, not wield it. You bear it for a single function, and outcome."

"Amron and Elyon walk toward the same outcome."

"But by a different route. A route that takes them through battle and glory. You have no such outlet." Ralf uncrossed his legs and leaned forward. "The blade must yearn for blood and battle. It cannot be easy keeping those instincts in check."

Like the gruloks, Lythian thought. Hruum had torn that dragon limb from limb even though he'd been told to restrain it. The same was true of the blade. Ralf was right, it wanted blood. And every day Lythian denied it that impulse, the blade's grasp upon him tightened, swelling his rage.

"It may be time to put it back into the vaults," he decided. "It can be protected there."

"The armoury was protected as well. Yet those men gained access anyway."

"They won a guard to their cause," Lythian came back. "It would be my men on the door. Loyal men."

But even that had its risks. A man's loyalty could be unquestioned one day, and grow fractured the next. *I wonder what it feels like*, he would think. *To touch it, just the once.* For a while he would deny the urge, but before long it would grow too strong. *Just the one time, just once,* he would tell himself, as he took the stair down and unlocked the door, as he crept forward to the blade on its brackets, as he reached out, tentative yet eager, to close his fingers about the glowing, golden hilt. A smile would breach his lips, a wanton smile, desirous, at the sensation of power. It was unlike anything he had ever felt, molten steel coursing through his veins, and for a moment he would feel invincible.

But just this once, he would repeat in his head. *I am loyal to the First Blade. Just this once,* he would say.

Yet that very same night he would dream of it. He would toss and turn and awake in a cold sweat, his mind a fog of golden mist and urging whispers, and know that he needed to feel that power again. It could *not* be just this once. *Twice,* he would say. *Just once more,* he would promise. But soon once more would become twice more, and twice more thrice more, and soon he would be building a bond of his own, creeping down in the dead of night, hopelessly and utterly lost.

And one day I will open my tent and see him standing there with it, Lythian thought. *He will curse me for a craven, for keeping it down there gathering dust, and he will cut me through with the blade I am sworn to protect. No,* he told himself. *No, it cannot be that way.*

Ralf was watching him all the while. "You bear it easily now," he observed. "Its weight is no burden to you. If battle comes here, by all means use it, but until that time, may I suggest you create some separation. When you sleep at night, leave it across the tent, not beside your bed. When you hold your councils do not rest it there, beside the table, but further away. When you walk the walls and do your rounds, you must wear it at your hip. There can be no helping that. But when in here, put it aside."

Lythian considered it. It was a good suggestion, and perhaps the best he could do, though would have a limited impact. Even now, he felt his eyes drawn to it. Like an addict, checking to make sure it was still there. "I will do as you say, Ralf," he said. "I thank the gods every day that Amron left you here with me."

The old knight bowed his head. "I am honoured to offer you whatever wisdom I can, my lord. You have many friends here, please believe it. Let that thought strengthen you, when…" He cut himself off. There was shouting outside. At once Ralf was moving to his feet. "Excuse me just a moment. I will see what the commotion is."

Lythian waited, brooding, as Ralf of Rotting Bridge slipped back outside through the door. His eyes moved to the Sword of Varinar. *If it's him…Kindrick, or any of his lickspittles…* A part of him wanted to snatch the blade up and slay the lot of them. These were lesser lords and unworthy knights, rats and roaches feasting on the crumbs from the greatlord's table. Lythian had sat at that table all his life, beside Amron. *Amron…curse you. Curse you for leaving me here…*

He was so entombed in his spiral of thoughts that he did not see the young man enter.

"Lythian, you look awful."

He looked up. "Elyon." He took in the sight of him, unsmiling. "You've been gone a long time."

"I know." Elyon moved to the table to fill a cup of wine. "Believe me, it wasn't by choice. And I'm not going to be staying long." He had a large gulp, looking beside himself with exhaustion. There was a leather bag strapped to his back, some sort of harness fixed about his chest. "Father's gone, I'm told. To defend the western gate. How long did he…"

"I thought you were dead," Lythian said, interrupting. "Where have you been all this time? It's been weeks."

"Figuring things out. Discovering the right path. Nursing an injured shoulder. Meeting a demigod." Elyon smiled wryly. "How about you? The men…" He glanced back at the tent flaps. "They look miserable out there, Lyth. I suppose those four hanged men have something to do with it?"

"They earned it," Lythian said.

"I'm sure they did," agreed Elyon Daecar. He spoke in a way that said he didn't care. Not of this little army here, and this broken ruin of a city, and the petty squabbles and disagreements of the men within it. Elyon was above all of that now. He soared higher than other men. "How is Walter Selleck? Does he still spend his time with the Eye?"

Lythian nodded sourly. "Every day. For hours. It's a dull charge, Elyon, and I'm not sure…"

"I'll give him a more exciting one." Elyon drank down his wine and refilled his cup. He gave one of the straps of his harness a flick and said, "I'm going to show him how it feels to fly."

42

Amron

It was as he'd feared. As all of them had feared.

Beyond the treeline, across the flat and open pass that formed the western gate, the two great strongholds of the Twinfort were burning.

Great roiling plumes of smoke poured up from the many high towers, billowing into the grey morning skies, black as tar and roaring. Flames in orange and red licked ravenously from a thousand windows. The *Last Bastion* - a towering wall two hundred feet tall that linked the two citadels - was pitted and battered and scarred by dragonfire. At the heart of the great bulwark stood an immense godsteel-plated gate called the *Fists*, five feet thick and impregnable. The gate comprised of two great doors, shaped like closed fists, knuckles locking tight as they punched into one another. No dragonflame could melt it. No ram could knock it through. But it stood open all the same, the fists parted, and the dead were thick about it.

"We failed them," said Sir Harold Conwyn.

No, I failed them, Amron Daecar thought. He could only stare a moment from the edge of the Greenwood. Thousands lay dead across the field. Thousand of North Vandarians. Thousands of Daecar men. The Agarathi trick had worked; they had come out here, right here at the edge of the forest, and assaulted the Twinfort from the rear. They had engaged Lord Borrington's host in battle and caught them unawares, opening the gate. And then the rest had come pouring through, from the south. An Agarathi horde that was said to be even bigger. Thirty, forty thousand strong. *I failed them,* he thought again. *As I did at King's Point. I have not yet earned the name.*

"There's still some fighting," Sir Quinn Sharp called out. He pointed to where small pockets of men fought amidst the swirling smoke. "My lord, we must ride to help."

"For Vandar!" bellowed Sir Taegon Cargill, and the Hammerhorse thundered away. Sir Quinn followed, and hundreds more, riding to the defence of their realm.

Amron did not go with them. The heat of the battle had cooled long ago and what skirmishes remained were minor. "Sir Harold, Sir Lambert, do what you can to help the injured," he commanded. "Secure the pass to the north. It is possible the enemy will return."

He wheeled Wolfsbane toward the eastern citadel and set off at a hard canter.

Lord Gavron Grave rode with him, and Sir Torus and Sir Bryce as well, Rogen Whitebeard following behind with a host of Grave men-at-arms. Amron scanned the battlefield as he went, trying to get a better read on what had happened. The dead were spread far and wide, filling the entire breadth of the pass between the forests. That pass was known as the western gate, a broad plain of gentle hills and rocky knolls littered with forts and goat farms and forester huts, some twenty miles wide at its broadest point and over a hundred miles in length. Here at its southernmost point where the Twinfort had been raised the Greenwood and South Banewood grew close enough to kiss, and between the two forts and forests the fighting had clearly been fierce. But for every dead Vandarian Amron saw two or three dead Agarathi, and there were dragon carcasses too, scattered here and there. That at least made him feel a measure of pride.

"My lords, movement on the walls," came a shout behind.

Amron looked forward, saw the shapes appearing through the smoke. Men on the ramparts, hundreds of them; bowmen, crossbow-men, pikemen, spearmen, men with swords and men with axes. They peered over the broken crenellations of the towering Last Bastion, and from the smoking battlements of the two strongholds as well. Twins they were, and so the Twinfort had been named, one identical to the other down to the very last block of stone. Both stood behind the Last Bastion to the east and west, shielded on their other three sides by dual curtain walls cut with portcullis gates facing north into Vandar. Past the gates plunged moats deep and dangerous, armed with jaws of spikes and traps.

The gates into the eastern fort were raised. The king sighted a small host of riders approaching from the yard inside. They wore cloaks of Borrington blue, with the pickaxe-and-ore sigil of their house worked in silver thread. There were others moving in and out across the bridge, carrying stretchers and pulling carts, heaped with men cut and burned and dying. They were Borrington men, Rothwell men, Crawfield men, men of houses Gully and Blunt and Spencer and Brightwood and twoscore more, all men of North Vandar, all men who served beneath the power of House Daccar. And sprinkled among them, Olorans and Mantles and Flints from Sir Brontus's five thou-sand swords.

The captain of the host reined up before him. Amron knew him as one of Lord Randall's favoured knights; youthful, strong, devoted, the eldest son of Lord Hightree of the Downs. "Sir Reginald," he called to him. "Where is Lord Borrington? I must speak with him at once."

"He is inside, Lord Daecar, in Farwatch Tower." Sir Reginald Hightree's eyes were grave. "He took a wound…to the neck. You had best come at once."

They swung about and made back for the fort, riding beneath the walls and across the bridge. Smoke eddied, black and grey, in the great yard beyond, and men moved about like spectres in the ashen mist. There were many of them; hundreds, perhaps even thousands. The yard rang to the sound of coughing, shouts and orders, the clatter of hooves, the moaning of men in pain. A field hospital had been set up to one side. The worst of the flames were being kept to the fort's southern side, Amron saw, flames raging in the guts of the towers that looked out over the Last Bastion to the south. He could feel the heat of the fires in his face, fighting against the chill. One of the towers had toppled, crashing down over the walls.

"How is the west fort?" Amron asked Sir Reginald. They dismounted to let a host of sooty-faced grooms take their horses. They were young, frightened, but awed to see the rugged face of Amron Daecar before them, to see the Frostblade glowing at his hip.

"No worse than us, my lord," said Sir Reginald. "Reports are coming across, but so far we've not had time to piece it all together. It's been hectic. The enemy came from the woods in the dead of night and took us by surprise. It had been quiet before then. *Too* quiet. We've been dealing with raids and sallies from the south, but last night those all stopped. Then suddenly there was shouting, screaming, fighting. Before we knew what was happening, the men outside had been slaughtered and the gate was being opened. We rushed out of the garrisons to try to hold them at bay, but when the Fists were opened…" He blew out a breath. "They poured through like water from a broken dam, tens of thousands of them, wild and screaming. We assaulted their flanks and drew some of them into combat, but most just kept on going, right up the pass. I fear they will try to make for Varinar, my lord."

Amron put a hand on his shoulder to calm him. "How bad are your losses, Sir Reginald?"

The man shook his head. "I could not say for certain. Thousands fell outside. Perhaps thousands more when the forts were besieged. The dragons came in force, and at once, focusing on the towers to declaw us. Most of our siege weapons were destroyed. And the last weeks, my lord…we have lost many men trying to hold the enemy back as they crossed the Brindle Steppe. But you…" he looked at the Ironfoot, and Stoutman, and Coddington, and the other men-at-arms behind with Rogen Strand. "I heard shouts from the battlements that you have brought a host, Lord Daecar? You came from the woods, as they did…"

"We chased them here," Amron said. "But too late." He was not about to explain how they were deceived, not now. "I have some six thousand swords and mounted spears with me."

"Six thousand?" The man seemed disappointed. "We may not have more than double that after the losses we have suffered. Only twenty thousand combined, perhaps. The enemy has four times that number."

"*Four?*" blared Lord Gavron. "We chased no more than twenty here. You're to say the host from the south numbered *sixty thousand* men?"

"It is a guess, my lord, but yes, roughly that. And dragons. They came from the Trident in a great armada and crossed the Brindle Steppe. We rallied to slow them but they were too strong. And as soon as they opened the Fists…" He coughed, a cloud of smoke passing from a burning tower. "It was mayhem, my lords. We were outnumbered and outmatched."

And outwitted, Amron thought bitterly. It hurt like a punch to the gut.

But he'd heard enough for now. "Farwatch," he prompted. "Take me to Lord Borrington."

The rest were left behind, save the Ironfoot, and Rogen, who walked as Amron's shadow. Farwatch Tower stood at the northeastern corner of the fort, thick and strong and tall, and a watchtower first and foremost without defensive weaponry built upon its dome. The dragons had not targeted it for that reason, Sir Reginald explained, only singeing and scorching the stone as they flew by but elsewise leaving it alone.

They found Lord Borrington in a warmly furnished bedchamber, high up in the tower with ranging views in all directions from its tall, narrow windows. There were rugs on the stone floor, tapestries depicting famous victories here at the Twinfort hanging between the slitted windows. A large bed rested against one wall; atop it lay the lord, feverish beneath sweat-soaked covers, his neck wrapped up in a bandage. It was dark with blood on one side. There was an acrid tone of pestilence in the air and a doctor stood at a side table, fiddling with his pots and potions.

"Arrow," Sir Reginald said, in a quiet voice, before they entered. "Slipped right between his gorget and helm. Unluckiest shot I ever saw."

"Will he live?" Amron asked.

"I'm not dying from *this*," rattled a voice like death. Lord Randall's eyes opened a crack. A thin smile crept onto his lips, crusted with blood. "Amron. Is that you, old friend? I thought I recognised that heavy tread."

Amron moved up to his bedside. "It's been too long, Randall."

"Blame the crows," Borrington said. He shifted to sit up against the headboard; Amron helped him, propping him against his pillows. "I've sent more than I care to count your way. Did you not…" Lord

Randall's face spasmed in pain. Clearly talking was of great discomfort to him. "Did you not receive any of them, Amron?"

"Not for long months."

"But you're here."

"We had word from Green Harbour. The city is lost, Randall."

"Ah. So that's where those Agarathi came from." His smile was wan, his skin pale; sweat dappled his brow despite the chill. "They got the gates open, I suppose you saw? Killed thousands. But my host…" He winced again, coughed. "We have strength enough still to oppose them."

Amron gripped the man's hand. Lord Randall had always been his staunchest bannerman, the Borringtons second only to the Daccars in power in the west of the realm. He was stout, severe, but a fierce and noble friend. Not a man to laugh like his younger brother Robert, who had the command of Northwatch Castle, but that was oft the curse of the elder son. *I never laughed half so hard and often as Vesryn*, Amron thought. *And Aleron and Elyon were the same*. Heirs always tended to be more grim and solemn than younger sons, though these days all men were much the same, and all laughter seemed to have left the world. There was too much hurt for that now.

"When did you take the wound, Randall?" Amron asked him. It was not fresh, that was clear.

"I led a skirmish against the Agarathi," he said in a whispered rasp. "A week or so ago. Didn't fix my helm properly to my gorget, Amron. More fool me." He smiled grimly. "Been in this bed ever since. But I'll be damned if I die in it. No. Not until I see my son again. He's back, you must have heard? Lenard. Returned after three long years, Oloran told me."

Amron had heard that from Elyon. It was his *other* son, his secret son, the son he'd never known he had, who had saved Sir Lenard Borrington and many others from those pits, Lady Kathryn Merrymarsh and old Lord Leyton Greymont among them. There was a great nobility in what Jonik had done, saving those stricken souls.

He smiled down at his friend. "I pray you get to see him again, Randall. I still remember the day he went missing."

"From a brothel," the man's father said, with a grunt. "Lenard always had a weakness for women, stupid boy. Maybe he's learned a thing or two from this experience?"

Amron couldn't think what. He had been drugged, so the story went, kidnapped and taken south on a ship from Green Harbour. He could not imagine how harrowing it must have been to fall asleep in the arms of some nubile girl, only to take in that bleak southern hell.

Where he was now, however, no one seemed to know. The latest they had heard, he was travelling with Jonik to siege the Shadowfort. Was Sir Lenard still with him? Might he not have come home only to perish in that quest? Amron didn't want to put that notion into the sick lord's mind. Hope was a good healer, he knew, and he wanted him to come back strong.

"You say Sir Brontus told you?" he asked. "Of your son's return?"

Lord Randall nodded, about to speak, then began coughing some more, and groped for a cup of water by the bedside. The doctor bustled over, but Amron waved him back. He served Lord Randall himself, holding the cup to his lips. "Brontus, yes," the lord croaked when he'd drank his fill; no more than a few sips, painfully swallowed. "Told me your Elyon had brought the news from the east. He flies everywhere, they say, though not here. I could have used him, Amron. And you." His weary eyes flitted to the Frostblade. "Ah. There it is. It's got the power to heal, they say." He pointed gingerly to his neck. "Would you mind?"

Amron gave a low chuckle. "That's not how it works, Randall. I wish I could, but…"

"I know. I know. Only the man bonded to it can heal."

Amron took his arm. "Where is Sir Brontus now? Did he live through the fighting?" Amron had endured some bitter exchanges with Brontus Oloran in King's Point and that was part of the reason he had sent him here, to bolster the western gate. That did not mean he hoped him ill. To the contrary, he prayed he was well. Brontus was a brilliant Bladeborn knight and swordsman, and the king needed every one of those he could get.

But Randall Borrington's mouth only twisted as he said, "*Gone*. Took off with some of his men one night and vanished."

Amron was taken aback. "He *deserted*? Where?"

"Deserters don't tend to tell you where they're deserting to, Amron," Borrington said in a dry rasp. "The man never wanted to be here, he made that plain. Had some choice words to say about you, though I put him down quickly enough. Bitter man. All this business with the Sword of Varinar. Threatened to take his men and march back to his lord uncle's lands to spite you, but Lord Mantle wouldn't have it. In the end Oloran just took off with Steelheart and a few others." If he'd had the energy to spit, he might have. "Cowards," he said instead. "But at least we kept his men. Lord Mantle's taken a firm charge of them. He's disgusted by what Brontus did."

Amron was glad to hear that there was a firm hand here to guide the Oloran host. "What of Sir Marcus Flint? Did he leave with Brontus too?"

"No. He stayed, like Mantle. Good men, those two. I thought Brontus was as well until he got here. Always complaining. Bleating of his injustices."

"He was the same at King's Point," the Ironfoot came in. He limped heavily over from the doorway. "Lord Borrington." He gave a courteous bow. Borrington was the greater lord, an order of magnitude more powerful in lands and incomes, and a warrior to boot, and that made him worthy of Lord Gavron's respect. There weren't many men who fit that profile. "Sorry for the neck. And for sending Oloran over to you. You ask me, you're better off rid of him."

Lord Borrington nodded from his bed. "How's the foot, Lord Grave? Not yet rusting, I hope?"

Gavron gave his best version of a smile. "No. Just the rest of me. They'll find me one day…a dusty old skeleton with a pristine godsteel leg. And sooner than I'd hope." He snorted to himself, then said, "There was an attempt on Dalton Taynar's life. While back. A man got into his bedchamber and stabbed him in the gut. That wound… weakened him enough that he bled out on the battlefield. Whoever it was murdered a greatlord. *My* greatlord." He glanced at Amron. "We think Brontus was to blame. And now you say he deserted…" Amron knew what he was getting at. "When was that craven last seen? That's what I want to know."

Lord Randall frowned, thinking. "How long was it, Reggie?"

Sir Reginald stepped over. "It must be close to three weeks now, my lord." He looked at Amron. "When was it that Dalton was attacked, Lord Daecar?"

"Long before then," Amron said, scratching at his soiled black beard. Crusts of dirt fell away. It had been a good long while since he'd washed. The timings didn't line up, though he had never thought it was Brontus himself who had committed the act. More likely a catspaw left behind to slink through the shadows, and seek revenge on his behalf.

Or was it more than vengeance? Was his coming here, and then leaving weeks later, a part of some larger scheme? A slither of concern moved up his spine. He didn't like the stink of this one.

But he had to put the matter aside. Men were deserting every day, and in their thousands, from a hundred posts across the north. Green boys fleeing to their mothers was one thing. Deserting Varin Knights was another, and Brontus Oloran, whether he'd had a part in Dalton's death or not, had now made his own life forfeit. When caught, he would be condemned to die, just the same as Sir Ramsey Stone, who had abandoned Lord Dalton during the fighting. *I need warriors, and knights, and as many as I can muster…but not cowards.* Amron would come down hard upon such men.

He drew a breath and refocused on the matter at hand. The Fists had been prised open, the enemy had breached the Last Bastion, and tens of thousands of Agarathi were now pouring up the pass, right through the western gate. He had an army a fraction of that size to call upon, and those he had led from King's Point were almost too exhausted to go on. Much as he might want to rally them and give chase right now, he knew he couldn't. The men needed to rest, to sleep, to regroup. It was no good hurrying after the enemy if they had no strength to fight when they caught them.

He went to the north-facing window and looked out. But for the smoke and morning mist, the view from here would range for long leagues. He might even be able to see the enemy marching away into the distance. But he couldn't. The skies were choked and grey. "They came in the night you said, Sir Reginald?"

The knight spoke behind him. "They did, my lord. Most of the fighting happened under cover of dark. By dawn the horde had begun moving up the pass, but for a few stragglers who stayed to hold their rear. They will be a half-day march away by now."

Amron continued to stare out, considering. When the wind came just right, pulling off the mist and fume, he caught glimpses ahead. A frown furrowed his brow. "There's snow," he said, surprised. "A few miles to the north." The air had grown colder the further north they'd gone from King's Point, the mornings dawning with a hard and bitter frost, but they had not seen snow as yet.

"It started only days ago," Sir Reginald said. "We were all shocked when we first saw it."

Amron mused in silence for a moment. Snow was no friend to the Agarathi, and if it fell thickly to the north, it would slow them, weaken them, even kill them. The dragonfolk were not conditioned to fighting in such conditions; to the men of the north, it was as common as mud in a marsh to battle beneath a blizzard, but not them. "This helps us," he said. "They will not be properly garbed for such weather. Many might freeze."

"Dragons aren't fond of snow either," said the Ironfoot. "It messes with their fires when the air's too cold, and they don't like that. Makes them scared."

"And we have you," added Lord Randall, in his choked whisper. "Now maybe I'm wrong, Amron, but I'd guess the Frostblade's not a bad weapon to wield in the snow."

Like the Windblade in the storm, Amron thought. Elyon spoke of how at home he felt in the tempest, how the thunder and lightning enlivened him, made the Windblade sing. Could it be the same for him here? He had travelled the Icewilds with the blade, true, but back then he was new to its power. *And battle brings out the best of us*, he knew. *Maybe…maybe…*

He stepped away from the window, crossing the room to look south. It was like looking upon another world. Past the burning towers and licking flames, the Brindle Steppe spread out to the edge of his sight, dull in shades of brown and green, a vast scrubland speckled with ten thousand little ponds shining silver beneath the sun. There were signs of the abandoned enemy camp out there, raised beyond the range of their trebuchets and catapults. Hundreds of small tents; dozens of larger pavilions, their canvas walls in red and black and gold, rippling in the wind. Most had slept upon the open ground, however; he saw old cookfires and pits staining the earth for miles, bare patches in the tundra when dragons had curled to rest, called *dragon circles* in the north. They ringed the border of the camp, shielding them from harm. There looked to be some dozens of them, though from here it was hard to be sure.

The size of the camp supported what Sir Reginald had said. *Sixty thousand men*, Amron thought. *And added to the rest…*

He pondered a little longer, then turned back to face the others, all hard northmen to their bones, like thousands of others below. Randall Borrington, even with an arrow-shaped hole in his neck, had the air of a defiant man. He would play no part in any battle, not for a while, but that wound would not be the death of him, Amron knew. "Rogen," he said. "Come in. I'd like you to meet Lord Robert's older brother."

The ranger appeared from the darkness beyond the chamber, clad in smoke grey godsteel, stained and scratched, with an overcloak of black wool draped heavily from his shoulders. His hair and beard were black and grey-streaked, ragged, long like his face, eyes amber and upturned, wolf and steel.

Lord Randall gave him an appraising look. "The ranger," he said. "Yes, I've heard about you. You served under Robert for long years, is that so?"

"Since I was a boy, my lord." Rogen rasped.

"And his best, I've heard it say." He continued to study him. "You accompanied Amron to the Icewilds. Led him safely there and back. And now here you stand, his shadow and protector. That's quite the story you're building, Rogen. Perhaps Amron ought to make you a knight."

"That is not what I want."

Lord Randall gave a smile. "No. I can tell. Not a man for all this courtly nonsense."

"I escaped that fate when my lord father sent me away."

"A lesser son, are you? It's often the case with the best rangers, Robert would always tell me. Good houses, lesser sons, rich Bladeborn bloodlines. I suppose you hailed from a strong house, did you?"

Amron smiled at the choice of words. "His father is Lord Styron Strand, Randall. *Strong* is in his blood." He looked at Rogen, hard and lean and lupine, and sensed something brewing in the air, some faint hope that the enemy might have made a grave mistake. "The Agarathi should have put you to the sword, Randall," he said. "They should have taken their time to kill every last one of you before moving up the pass. Now all they've done is enter the bear pit…and there are wolves about."

"Wolves?" Lord Borrington was not understanding. "We're a quarter their size, Amron. The Agarathi may be a bear, and us a wolf, but I count only the one."

"*Two*," Amron said, hoping he was right…hoping Sir Gerald had ridden hard and done as he'd asked. "And big ones, Randall, more direwolves than common wolves… more than a match for a frightened Agarathi bear, trudging through the northern snow."

563

Borrington's brow twisted into an impatient frown. "Wolves, dire-wolves, fellwolves, call us what you will. I still only count the *one*."

"Two," Amron said again. "Because if the gods are good, Lord Styron will be marching to our aid. And that bear will have nowhere to run."

43

Jonik

He climbed up over the lip of the rift, the rope straining against the weight of his godsteel.

"Anything?" Gerrin asked, as Jonik got to his feet and brushed himself down. The word was not loaded with hope.

"Nothing," Jonik said.

The old Emerald Guard gave a nod; it was hardly an unexpected result. For long days they'd been searching the chasms and rifts and thus far their search had yielded no reward. They had begun optimistically, *excitedly*, even, but by now their enthusiasm had withered away like a desiccated plant caught in the grips of an unending drought.

"Right." Gerrin pulled out the map he'd made and scribbled through the chasm from which Jonik had returned. There were a lot of scribbles on the parchment now. He looked across those that remained, and tapped the tip of the quill down at random, selecting one of those they hadn't yet searched. "This one," he said. "Who's next?"

Sir Owen stepped forward. "It is my turn, I believe."

Of course it was his turn. His turn came after Jonik's turn, and Jonik's came after Sir Owen's turn, and so on and so forth. Barring the occasional descent by Gerrin, those two had taken the lion's share of the spelunking duties, owing to their age and vigour. Harden claimed he was too old for this sort of nonsense and had only taken his turn once. Apparently that was enough. "I'll only fall and hurt myself, and you'll have to come down and fetch me back," he had said. "No sense in adding to your workload. I'll stay at the top from now on."

Jonik supposed there was some sense in that, and hadn't disagreed. From that point on, he and Owen Armdall had searched eight or nine out of every ten trenches, with Gerrin making up the difference when they had exhausted themselves from their toil.

"Right then," the former Shadowmaster said. "Let's get you roped up, Owen…"

"Wait," Jonik said. He looked at the map in his old master's grasp. The chasm he was pointing out was another of the *shallow* ones, those of which you could see the bottom when standing at the edge. There were dozens of those spread all across the hillside, all of varying depth, and they'd searched over half of them, all to no avail. Jonik shook his head. "We're never going to find anything in these baby rifts," he said. "It's time we went deeper. Adult." He jabbed out at random, prodding a finger at one of the rifts marked with a cross, signifying that they could not see the bottom. "That one. It's time, Gerrin."

The old Emerald Guard rubbed at his grey-bristled chin. "Why that one?"

"Why not? They may all link together down there anyway. Some of the shallow ones do." Sometimes, when searching the bottom of a ravine, they had gone through a tunnel or cave and ended up in another, saving them time by searching two at once, or even three on one occasion. Jonik had the sense that there was a great underground world beneath them just waiting to be explored. Great caves and echoing caverns and colossal chambers with lakes and rivers within them. It was impossible to say how deep it all went unless they went down there and had a look. Maybe he was wrong. Maybe not. But from up here they'd never know. "We have to try," he finished.

Harden's face was dour. "We don't know what's down there. But my guess is nothing good. There are too many monsters roaming the world to have come from the woods and mountains." He scowled over the edge of the nearest rift. "Half have been hiding underground, I'll wager. And many will still be there."

Gerrin agreed with the old sellsword. "We've all heard the noises…" he started.

"That's just wind," Jonik came in. He only half believed it. "It's just the sound it makes when it rises from below us."

"Sometimes. Not always. I know a growl when I hear one."

"That's just your mind playing tricks." A part of Jonik agreed that there would be creatures down there in the depths, but that didn't serve his argument, so he chose to ignore it. "If the Mistblade is down there, we have to find out."

"It could be anywhere, lad," Harden said. "Might have fallen through the world and come out the other side for all we know. Perhaps it's time to give this up."

"*Give it up?*" Jonik couldn't believe what he was hearing. "Are you ready to roll over and die so easily, Harden?"

"Been ready for that for a while, in fairness." His grey lips twisted into a smile. Then he shrugged. "I'm not saying give up completely. Just that we need help. There aren't enough of us for a project this size."

"There might be if you pulled your weight." Jonik couldn't refuse the barb. He blew out a breath, frustrated. "Do you want to go and join the others, is that it? Ride off to Rustbridge and die alongside them?"

"I'd sooner not die at all. But aye. We ride to Rustbridge and maybe we find them. We could bring them all back here to help…be one big happy family again. A dysfunctional family of sailors and sell-swords and soldiers, aye, but still…"

Jonik would not let the old man tempt him. "We don't know what's happening in the city and cannot spare the time." He poked at the map again. "*I'm* going. If anyone wants to join me, they're welcome."

"I'll go," Sir Owen said at once. He had proven most dutiful had the Oak of Armdall. "If there are creatures down there, it would be wise to go together. All of us."

"No," Gerrin said. "We'd best keep someone up here should things go wrong. We all know who that's going to be."

Everyone looked at Harden.

The old man folded his arms. "What is this, some guilt trip? Well bugger you all. I'm beyond caring. You go for all I care. I wouldn't go down there for all the godsteel in the Steelforge."

That settled it. They returned to their camp to prepare, gathering provisions, dressing in the essentials of armour, hitching their sword-belts around their waists. Sir Owen made the bright suggestion that they gather up a large stack of green maple leaves to mark a trail, should they find the depths hard to navigate. Harden stood by all the while muttering of their folly and shaking his head.

"How long do you expect me to wait if you don't come back?" he asked.

"We will come back," Jonik said.

Harden gave a sigh. "I appreciate the optimism, lad, but that's not an answer. How long?"

"You be the judge."

"Give it three days," Gerrin said. "If we're not back by then, then you might want to consider going for help."

Harden grunted. They stepped out to the edge of the chasm Jonik had chosen, picking past the many rifts and scars into which they'd already spelunked. Some were shallow, barely four or five metres in depth, savagely gouged open by the claws of the Dread. Those had not required a proper searching; even from the side, you only had to glance down into them to see that there was no dead king lying down there, no misting blue blade resting among the rocks.

Others were much deeper, opened not by the titan's claws, but his weight, the earth shattering and ripping apart as he landed and moved, fighting off the gruloks. The force of it had been beyond Sir Owen's capabilities to describe. "Like a mountain had fallen over," was his best effort, when telling them how the entire world had shuddered beneath him. It had caused the entire landscape to break apart, like a block of stone struck by a hammer, fracturing into a hundred cracks and fissures. It was a job for a much larger company of men, in that

Harden was not wrong, and Gerrin had suggested that as well the day they'd arrived…but Jonik didn't want to. This was his mission, his duty. *If I can't find that blade, no one can,* he told himself.

And something was telling him to go deeper…*much* deeper. Was it just his gut instinct? A feeling? Or something more? In the quiet of night, when all was silent and still, Jonik might have sworn he'd heard a whisper, somewhere in the back of his head…the whisper of a voice he recognised, different but somehow the same…calling out to be saved. He could not say if that was just a dream, or desire, or the echo of a memory, but it nagged at him all the same. And it frightened him a little as well, he had to admit. Ilith had drawn him back from the precipice when he was about to plunge into the abyss, but Ilith wasn't here. What if he should find the Mistblade, and be consumed by it as he was the Nightblade? What if he could not resist the lure?

He turned away from such concerns. Gerrin was at the edge of the chasm, stamping down at the earth with his feet, making sure it was steady and secure. Behind, Sir Owen waited with the stake, three or so metres back. "Is this a good spot, Sir Gerrin?" the younger knight asked him.

Gerrin nodded. "It seems secure enough to me. Go ahead, Owen."

The Oak lifted the thick wooden stake above his head and drove it hard down into the ground, its sharpened end stabbing down through a foot or so of soil. Then he drew out his godsteel dagger, spun it around in his grasp, reached up and began hammering at the stake's flattened top with the pommel. The weight of the godsteel, and the strength it gave him, made the rest of it simple enough. When the stake had been driven some five or so feet into the earth, the knight set about fastening the rope, then tested it, pulling and tugging with all his strength to make sure it would not yield. Jonik joined in for good measure; even with their combined strength, the stake did not budge.

"Should hold," Jonik said. "Though probably best we don't all go down at once." He looked at Gerrin. "How's the climb?"

"Sheer for about fifty feet. Then there's a ledge wide enough to stand on. Looks secure. Beyond that the hand and footholds are plentiful, as far as I can see. There's another platform below, but after that the dark takes over."

Such as it was with the deeper chasms; the darkness that pooled down there, and the mists and fogs that still lingered, made it impossible to know their true depths. Sometimes they had dropped stones and rocks and listened for them to hit solid earth, hearing them crash and echo up from below, but they never knew if they'd hit the bottom or just landed on some ledge instead. When they did hear any sound, they would count out the time, and that would give them an estimate of the depth, which Gerrin would scribble on his map. Some of the rifts had no such estimate. The ones where they'd dropped stones and heard nothing at all. No echo far beneath them. No distant splash of water. Nothing. And this was one of them.

"What if the rope's not long enough?" Harden asked. He peered over the edge, as the rope tumbled into the abyss.

"Then we'll figure something out," Jonik said. They had brought half a dozen long coils of rope with them from the Undercloak, and for this particular descent several of them had been lashed together, creating a rope almost two hundred metres long. If that didn't serve, they had one last coil that they could use to lengthen it. "Best bring the other roll down with us as well," Jonik said to Sir Owen. "We can tie it to the bottom if we need to."

"And if that's still not enough?"

"I don't know, Harden. We'll have to climb back up and choose another rift. Or just climb the wall without the rope if it's doable."

Harden shook his head. "Too risky. Perhaps you save yourself the trouble, and choose a shallower one? Why this one?"

"Because it's deep."

"*Too* deep. There are others that…"

Jonik was done with the man's complaints. "I'll go first. Test that ledge and what's below. When I find sure footing further down, I'll call up. You can follow me after."

"Should be me going first," Gerrin protested. "You're more important…"

"And younger, stronger, and a better climber," Jonik came in. He would hear no arguments about it. He stepped to the edge, peering to the ledge fifty feet below. Then without thinking further, he picked up the rope, closed his grip about it, and swung himself right over the side, abseiling down the wall.

The godsteel gave him strength, imbuing him with the necessary power and agility to make light work of the climb. With one hand clutched about the rope, he eased his grip just enough to slide gracefully down toward the platform. A tightening of the pressure brought him to a gentle stop, and he pushed his legs off the wall, landing on the ledge with a hollow *thud*. It was broad, narrow, but strong, and quite capable of bearing their weight.

"How is it?" he heard Gerrin call. The men above were peering over the edge, their faces framed by the wan light of the grey morning skies. A trickle of rain pattered into Joink's face as he looked up at them. "Strong enough for us to follow?"

"I'd say so," Jonik called. Further down, through wisps of fog, he could see the other landing Gerrin mentioned some hundred feet beneath him, barely visible in the darkness, half shrouded by the eddying mist. Between the two ledges, the face of the chasm was rough and craggy and uneven, with many cracks and crevices wrinkling it like the face of some ancient crone. The rope dangled down to bundle on that landing below, where it coiled about itself several times like a snake before disappearing away over the side. What lay beyond, Jonik couldn't see from here. "Just wait until I've gone a bit further down," he went on. "I'll shout up when I make the second ledge and tell you what I see."

He gave the rope a tug, just to test the strain, and then continued on his way down. By now, after long days of this, he had the tension just right. He slid down the rope, feet tapping along the wall, the hemp gliding easily against the crisp leather of his glove. Beneath gloves and cloak and boots, he wore armour; gauntlets, greaves, gorget, breastplate, sabatons, and in his pack he carried his helm. Not quite a full suit, but plenty enough to protect him should he find himself in a fight, without overly weighing him down and putting too much strain on the rope. All the same, he could feel the hemp groaning and complaining as he went. *Play nice now,* he thought. The last thing he needed was the rope snapping.

He reached the next ledge without incident. Above him now, the others were barely visible, coming and going from behind the swirls of fog. He took a moment to check the ledge, stamping a foot, feeling out its strength, before confirming that it was solid and secure. Then he called that up to the others and told them to join him. As he waited, he looked over the edge…down into the blackness of the void.

Gerrin arrived first. When he landed he called up for Sir Owen to come, then took a knee at Jonik's side. "No bottom, then?"

Jonik shook his head. They were about fifty metres down, and he could see no ledges beneath him. The light here was too thin, the fog too thick. If they continued from here, it would be a plunge to the unknown. "What do you think? Just slide down, and hope for the best?"

"Either that or go back up," Gerrin said.

"We can't do that. Harden will only gloat."

A gruff smile split Gerrin's lips. "Better to die down here than allow *that.*"

"He'd gloat about that as well," Jonik said dryly. "Might be no winning here, Gerrin."

The old knight gave a laugh, as Sir Owen came sliding smoothly down to join them, landing with a rustle of leather on the rock. He stepped over, peering into the abyss. "Anything?"

Jonik shook his head. "Just mist and darkness." He turned his eyes across the ledge; it was roughly rectangular in shape, three metres by two. He saw a suitably sized stone, picked it up, told the others to be silent, and then tossed it over the edge, between the two rock walls. It pierced the fog, swallowed from sight, and Jonik counted, *One, two, three, four, five, six, se…* He cut himself off. There was a faint clattering echo coming up from below. "Six seconds," he said.

The others nodded. "I counted the same," said Sir Owen.

Both of them looked at Gerrin, who frowned in thought, performing his calculation. He was their resident expert in the field of motion and acceleration. "Be about a hundred and seventy metres," he said, after a short moment. "Though impossible to say if it hit another ledge or the bottom of the chasm."

"We can throw more stones," Sir Owen suggested. "If they all hit at six, we'll know it's the bottom."

They all thought that a good idea, so picked up what stones they could find on the ledge, and set about tossing them away at different angles, counting them out each time. The experiment confirmed that there was solid ground less than two hundred metres below them… though whether the bottom of the rift or not, they could not say for certain. One stone, alas, made not a sound, which suggested there might be a rift within a rift down there, shafts and tunnels that plunged much further down.

"The rope won't take us to the bottom," Gerrin pointed out. "We'd best pull it up and tie on the other coil, to be safe."

It took a few minutes to drag the rope up to their ledge and lash the length that Sir Owen had brought onto the end, extending it by another forty metres. Then they threw the bundle over and let it tumble into the darkness. All that rope made for a significant weight, and when they added their own, it would put the anchor on the surface under significant strain. "Best hammer in a horseshoe," Jonik said.

Sir Owen saw to it, and indeed it had been his idea in the first place, these horseshoe anchors. From his pack he drew out a spare shoe, filed and sharpened at the points, pressed the rope up against the rock wall, and hammered the horseshoe over it using his godsteel dagger. The rift wall was solid stone here, and the anchor held fast. Sir Owen gave it a strong tug to make sure, then nodded.

"Good," Jonik said. "Gerrin, call up to Harden and tell him what's going on. I'll shout out if I find a footing further down. Listen for me." He took the rope and went to the side of the ledge, pressed his feet against the wall, and slid down into the abyss.

The smog swallowed him up almost at once. It souped heavily, wet and cold against his skin, and a shiver ran down his spine as he entered a strange and eerie place, of shifting mists and unsettling shapes, of sounds echoing oddly through the gloom. The daylight faded as he descended, the dark deepening until there was almost no light at all. Some thirty metres down from the ledge, teeth of sharp stone protruded out of the chasm walls, as though the rift was no rift at all, but the jaws of some monstrous beast, ready to snap shut and devour him. He hastened through the field of fangs, sliding deeper. Another twenty metres down, he saw a faint glow peppering the rock, of lichen and moss, radiating a soft green and white light. Here and there long vines sprouted and hung down, and he heard the faintest sound of dripping water, tapping far beneath him.

A chill wind rose from below, stirring the hem of his cloak as it whispered by. He could feel the airflow broadening beneath him, moving through a much larger space. He continued down the rock face, another five metres, eight, ten, and then all of a sudden the rift wall gave way beneath him, curving sharply inward as the rope fell away, dangling into the abyss.

He stopped above the void, peering down. *A cavern*, he realised. *A great open cavern.* The dripping water was coming from the ceiling, leaking from cracks in the stone. Across on the other side of the chasm, he could see more vines trailing from the rocky roof, drooping and swaying into the shifting fog. He found a wide crack in the wall and drove the toe of his boot forward, to take the weight off his arms. *How far have I gone?* Another seventy metres or so he would guess and that meant there was still a hundred to go. *A hundred metres…*he thought…*with nothing but the rope to hold onto.* Where the wall ended, empty space reigned. *And if the rope should snap or come loose…*

No. It was securely fastened at the surface, and Sir Owen had hammered another anchor in above them. If they could add another one or two, there would be no reason why the rope should come loose. He filled his lungs and called up. "Gerrin, Owen…can you hear me?" His voice sounded strangely muted, strangled by the fog.

He waited for their reply. It came a moment later. "We hear you, Jonik," came Gerrin's small voice. "What do you see?"

"There's a cavern," he answered. The rift wall ends about seventy metres below where you are now. Sir Owen, you'd best hammer in another horseshoe or two on the way down to secure the rope."

"I will," Sir Owen called out.

"Can you see the bottom below you?" Gerrin asked.

"It's a hundred metres, Gerrin. What do you think?" He glanced down. "I see some luminous lichen and moss, some trailing vines and growth on the ceiling and walls. But not much else. When I reach the floor, I'll call out again. Hopefully you'll be able to hear me."

There was a short pause. Then Gerrin spoke. He sounded uncertain. "A hundred metres is a long way, Jonik. Down is one thing, *up* another. That's not an easy climb without a wall to steady you."

He wasn't wrong, but Jonik was not about to turn back now. "No one ever said this was going to be easy, Gerrin. I'm going to slide down now. I'll shout when I reach the bottom." He did not want to linger here, above the abyss, thinking about it too much. Without further delay, he clutched a little more tightly at the rope, let his legs swing back off the wall, and slowly…ever so slowly…eased his grip and slid down.

The air changed almost at once as he escaped the narrow space between the chasm walls. He could feel it, the way it opened out, the way the sound spread and echoed. His leather glove ran smoothly along the hempen rope, warm from the friction, his pace steady. The mist thinned as he went, and the darkness began to recede. Less than halfway down, he could see the faint outline of the chamber beneath him, vast and open, given shape by the light of the moss. More of it grew in patches on the floor, and he saw glow worms too, and the flicker of fireflies, drifting in red and purple and blue. It was beautiful, otherworldly. Further off, he could hear the echo of rushing water, and on the floor of the cavern he saw darker scars and pits where it went deeper, down into the very bowels of the earth.

Many rocks lay scattered across the cavern floor and there were some large outcrops too, jutting up in distorted shapes, their bases and walls clothed in bioluminescent fungi. The rope trailed down onto one of them, a large, flat-topped block of rough stone, and that was where Jonik landed, on a perch some six metres above the ground.

He let out a breath as his feet reached solid earth; they felt a little shaky, tremulous from the descent. He turned a full circle, awestruck, searching for where the cavern ended, but not all of the walls were visible. On one side it bled into darkness beyond his sight, stretching away in a field of broken rock. Some formations were colossal, as big as tumbled towers. One looked like the peak of some huge mountain, poking up from somewhere lower, and he could see a thin waterfall hissing down out there, appearing from the mists above and vanishing through a pit.

How big is this place? he wondered, astonished. Through vents and shafts warmer gusts of air blew up from below, coming from places much further down. He could see almost directly down one of them from atop the rock. Down it went, down and down to darkness. *If the Mistblade fell down one of those…*

The scale of the task was dawning on him, even if it hadn't already. *One step at a time*, he told himself. *Just take it one step at a time.*

It did not take long for the others to join him. First Gerrin appeared from the gloom, sliding down to land on the upthrust of rock, then a short time later Sir Owen followed, reporting that he had hammered in two more horseshoes to better secure the rope. That was good. It was their only lifeline, their only way out of here. They were some two hundred and twenty metres beneath the surface, Jonik had to remind himself, and he could feel it too; that weight of rock above him. Through the drifting mists, he could just about see the thin line of the rift opening far above, faint as a torch flicker in a black storm. Harden would be up there now, already wary Jonik did not doubt, and not much liking being left alone. *Three days*, he thought. *We have three full days to explore.*

The others were looking out through the cavern in awe. Their expressions reflected how Jonik felt. "So…what now?" Sir Owen asked. He looked around, wide-eyed and open-mouthed, peering at the tunnels and caves and pits and shafts that led beyond the cavern. "There are two dozen ways out of here. Which route shall we take?"

Jonik only had one answer to give them, and it wasn't one they were going to like. In the back of his mind he could hear the faintest of whispers, no more than a breath across a field, dimly heard, calling out to him. Calling for help.

He looked at Sir Owen and gave answer. "Down," he only said.

44

Saska

"They stole away during the night," Sunrider Tantario informed her. "I would think they returned to the lake, Serenity, to take the barge back across the water."

Saska took the news calmly. In fact, she took it well. Far too many of Tantario's men had turned sour and bitter these last weeks, and it served her to see them gone, lest they cause her any problems. "What do you mean to do, Alym?" she asked.

The Sunrider was not one to suffer such insubordination. "I have their names," he said. "Desertion is as firmly dealt with here as it is in the north, especially so for men of high birth. These men abandoned their charges. When caught, they will suffer the penalty."

Death, she thought. In the north, desertion meant death. "They don't deserve that, Alym," she said. "Can't you show them mercy? They've helped get us this far, haven't they?"

"Would that I could, Serenity, but that is not my gift to give. When caught they will be returned to Aram, and if your grandmother or Lord Hasham should wish to grant such clemency, they may. My duty is simply to deliver them."

Then it's death. Her grandmother might grant a stay of execution, she supposed, but she might well be dead by now, and that would put Lord Hasham in charge. *He* certainly wouldn't.

The Surgeon withdrew a scalpel from his cross-belt of knives and instruments. He turned its edge against the sun, inspecting it. "When a cancer infects the body, it must be cut away," he declared. "These men need to die, Sunrider Tantario. *At once*. We cannot wait for them to be caught and returned to Aram. They carry too precious a secret to be spared."

Saska vented a sigh. The Surgeon was nothing if not dedicated to keeping her secret from spreading, for which she was grateful, even if it all made her skin crawl whenever he spoke about it. But *these* men?

Moan as they had, and mislike her as many of them had come to, she did not believe they would go that far. "They're not going to speak of who I am," she said, trying to dismiss it. "They know the price, and they swore their oaths."

"They swore oaths that they would escort you to Eagle's Perch as well," Sir Ralston reminded her. He stood above them all in his scarred and scratched armour, all in steel from head to heel but for the greathelm he held in the crook of his arm. "An oath they broke last night."

"One broken oath oft leads to another," the Surgeon added, casually spinning the scalpel between his fingers. "An oathbreaker is not a man who can be trusted. He is a weak man, a *rotten* man, who must be cut free lest he infect the healthy flesh." He stabbed the scalpel back into its sheath. "I will do this. Give me leave to chase them down, and I will bring you back their heads."

"No," Alym Tantario said. "This is not of your concern. You are not Aramatian."

"No," the Surgeon agreed. "I am a man of the world. And it is the world I seek to protect. The deserters hold knowledge that can hurt us all. They must die, and soon."

The Sunrider looked exhausted. His skin was wan, his eyes shadowed and bloodshot, and the ruts in his forehead had turned chasm-deep. Saska felt for him. These men had been honourable once, chosen for her escort for that reason, but a rot had got into their souls. He did not want to see them killed, and certainly not like that, hunted by some sellsword. That they were so close to Eagle's Perch, close to the fulfilment of their duty, only made it all the harder. "You are a cruel man, Captain," he said to the Surgeon in a small voice. "You have travelled with these men, broken bread with them, set camp with them, fought with them…and yet you would speak of taking their heads so casually." He gave a dispirited sigh, shaking his head. "If this is to be done, my own men must do it. I will speak to my captains, and…"

The Baker cut him off. "Your men cannot be trusted, I regret to say. They are friends with these deserters, and may only join them, or show them mercy. If they're to die, and I agree, they *must*, then godsteel will see it done." He looked at the Surgeon in a moment of solidarity, and perhaps in that Saska could salvage something from this misfortune. *A common foe*, Rolly had said, as a way to bring the sellswords together after all that foul business with Merinius. Perhaps these deserters were just that. "I will go as well," the Baker said. "Umberto will come with me, and the Surgeon may choose one of his own. The four of us will make quick work of these cowards."

The word *coward* only made Alym Tantario cringe. "They were not cowards, once," he murmured sadly. "They were good men, gallant and noble. The Ever-War has brought them to ruin."

The Surgeon did not think much of that excuse. "The Ever-War shows a man for what he is. It is a torch in the dark, shining the light of truth upon him. Your men have proven themselves craven, Tantario. They will be well rid of. We will see it done." He looked at the Baker with a nod, and the Baker nodded back.

Alym Tantario had no further fight in him, though the last word would have to be Saska's. Such as it was when they gathered for these councils and made these decisions. *And now the lives of over a dozen men rest with me,* she thought. Well, she had no choice. "See it done, then," she told them. She took no pleasure in giving the command, but they all knew it was the only option. "Surgeon, take the Tigress with you. I would see you mend your rift on the way."

The Baker's jaw was tight. He did not want to ride with that woman, but that was the point. Saska had some naive hope that the Tigress would save the Baker's life in battle, and that would put an end to it, but doubted the gods were so kind.

"You had best get moving," Sir Ralston boomed, before the Baker might conjure a complaint. "They have a two hour head start and will be riding hard. Ride harder until you catch them. And harder still when you're done. We're not going to wait around for you."

The Bloody Trader captains nodded, turned and left them, moving toward the small lake beside which they had camped for the night. The horses had been hobbled there, where the grasses were thick, and they could take a drink. Beside the placid waters, their small campsite was being struck beneath the glow of the rising sun, the men moving about listlessly as they took down the tents and readied to leave. The gleaming company that had left Aram had become a beaten, broken thing, dragging its bedraggled bones down the road, step after weary step. It made Saska sad to see.

She returned to her own tent to find Leshie putting on her armour. "What's happening with those deserters, then?" the Red Blade asked, as she pulled on her gauntlets. There were tiny rubies in the knuckles that twinkled as they moved. If Leshie should live through the war, that armour alone would make her a very rich woman if she ever had a mind to sell it.

"The sellswords are hunting them," Saska answered.

"Which ones?"

"The Baker, Umberto, the Surgeon and the Tigress."

Leshie made a whistling sound. "Nice team. They'll probably kill each other on the way, but nice." She clicked her gorget about her neck before fixing her crimson cape at the shoulders with clasps of plain ornamentation. Last of all came her swordbelt, oiled red leather with her dagger on one hip and shortsword on the other, sheathed in scarlet scabbards. "They're going to kill them, then? Or bring them back?"

"Kill them," Saska said.

Leshie understood. "Shame, but needs must." She stepped out into the sunlight, brushing the door flaps aside. Her eyes roved the camp, the sparse trees, the little lake and shore beyond. Saska was not certain what she was searching for until she asked, "No princess, then? She still hasn't returned?"

"No." Saska's voice was dull. Princess Talasha Taan had not been seen since she led away that dragon, the day they reached the northern shore of Eagle Lake. A part of her feared she was dead. A bigger part would not let herself believe it. "She'll come back when she's ready," she made herself say. *Fate brought her to us. Why bother if she was only going to die?* "It's only been a few days."

Leshie's eyes showed doubt, but she knew better than to express it. Instead she grinned and said, "She'd better. That woman owes me a flight, Sask. I'll be damned if she dies before I get one."

That made Saska smile. Leshie always knew how to make her smile.

The company was soon ready to leave, the tents packed and loaded on the horses. The sun rose to gild the cobbles of the Capital Road as it wended up the coast. To the east, the seas swelled treacherously upon the horizon, though closer to shore it looked calmer. It was prone to change quickly, they all knew. One only had to look away for a moment and look back, and all of a sudden the tranquil waters would have churned into a frenzy of white caps and waves, and who knew what lurked beneath.

Sometimes, when the road was right up near the shore, they would see pods of greatwhales prowling about, looking for trouble, their water spouts spurting high and angry. Who they were so angry with, or why, no one could say, but all the same the victims of their rage were in great evidence. Every day they saw ships beached in bays and coves, or snagged on shoals further out to sea, and it seemed no one was to be spared. The waves and the whales and all the other beasts beneath the water did not seem to care which ships they attacked. They had seen trading cogs washed ashore, and fishing carracks with their bellies torn open, and strong war galleys shattered and smashed, and even massive, bulky galleons, triple-decked and four-masted, lying broken in the surf.

Some beaches were so crowded with wrecks that they had become more wood than sand, and on one island out to sea, a ship had even seemed to have been thrown from the water, to lie in ruin on the side of a jagged hill. What creature had done *that* no one could say. It was not a big ship, but still. Could a leviathan throw a boat so high like that? Had the waves grown so grand as to deposit the boat up there?

The Butcher said it was Galaphan, the great titan whale, risen from the dead to claim his dominion over the waters. Leshie said that was stupid. Galaphan had died thousands of years ago and his body had washed ashore. "It's still there, dummy," she'd scoffed to the Butcher. "The whale bones. The Rasals celebrate important events there. Isn't that right, Coldheart?"

The Wall was loath to get involved in their arguments but admitted that Leshie was correct. "I have seen the bones of Galaphan many times. He is dead, Butcher. And isn't likely to rise again."

Some others said that maybe the great kraken Izzun still lived, or that there was a giant manator out there somewhere, strong enough to knock a ship right through the air with a blast of its great long tusks. Del had wondered if there were creatures down there that no one knew about, things never seen before. "Maybe the gods have created something new?" he offered.

"The gods are gone, boy," the Baker had said to that. "Their creating days are done."

In the end, it came down to Alym Tantario to tell them that in any mystery, the simplest solution was usually the most likely to be true. "It was the storm," he thus declared. "A great wave lifted that ship up there." Saska agreed he was probably right. But the guessing was fun as well.

As the morning moved languidly along, they saw several more vessels scragged on rocks and stranded at the bases of cliffs, to add to the others they'd seen. Some were so battered that they were barely recognisable as ships at all. Others were seen only distantly, snagged out in some bay or beached against a coastal island. When the sun was high in the sky, they stopped at a stream to water the animals and cool their necks. Joy loped over for a drink, lapping in that ridiculous way cats did, barely taking in a drip of water with each lick. It made Saska chuckle as she knelt beside her, cupping her hands to the run, splashing it against her face.

The Wall stepped over, casting her in the shade. "My lady. There is another ship."

She gave her face another splash. "There's always another ship." She assumed he had left off the 'wreck' for the sake of brevity. "Why is this one special?" It was not common for Rolly to announce such trivial matters to her.

"Kaa Sokari says it has sails in green and red."

She did not immediately know why that should be considered important. Then she thought about it a little more. "The apple lord?"

"It may be so. Or one of his vessels."

Saska stood, intrigued. "Where is it?"

"Another few miles up the coast. Sokari spotted men down there, on the beach. They are trying to make repairs."

Saska looked back to the road, where a short stone bridge spanned the stream. Kaa Sokari was there now, speaking with Sunrider Tantario and the Butcher. "Joy, on me." She paced over to join them, the starcat loping at her side, Rolly following. "What's this about a ship?" she asked. "It's one of Lord Gullimer's, Sir Ralston says."

The other men broke off from their discussion. "The sails would suggest so," confirmed Kaa Sokari.

"And these men? How many are there?"

"We didn't stop to take a count."

"Give me an estimate, then."

"Hundreds," the eagle-eyed bowmaster said. "They've set camp on the beach while they make repairs. They are not in good shape, it did not seem to me."

"We might want to give them a wide berth," Sunrider Tantario offered. "There is a path inland I know. It will lead us safely around them."

Saska shook her head. "These are Lord Gullimer's men. *Robbert's* men. Not his uncle's. We're not enemies with them."

"Pardons, Serenity. But we cannot be certain of this. If there are hundreds, they could overwhelm us. They will have Bladeborn with them, no doubt. And we've just sent away four of our own. That is not a risk we can take."

Saska disagreed. They were Tukoran, and only trying to get home to help fight in the war. At the least she wanted to know which ship it might be. "We need Del," she said, looking around. "Someone fetch him."

The Butcher saw to it. With a swish of his tattered red cloak he strode off, returning a short while later with the lanky youth all but grasped by the scruff of the neck. He pressed him into the centre of the circle. "Describe Lord Gullimer's flagship," Saska said to him.

Her brother frowned in thought, in that way he had, as though trying to puzzle out an impossible riddle, and never quite sure if he was getting it right or wrong. "It's a…a galleon, I think. Or…or maybe a carrack, I'm not sure. They call it *Orchard*, for his sigil, Lord Gullimer's. The sails are green and red for apples, and the figurehead is a hand, holding an apple too." His face scrunched up as he tried to recall anything else, but that would serve just fine.

"Well done, Del. That's enough." Saska always liked to praise her adopted brother, to help build his confidence. She looked at Kaa Sokari. "Is that the ship you saw?"

The archer gave a nod. "The fist figurehead. Yes. That is her."

"Then I'm going," Saska said. For once she did not equivocate. "Kaa, is the beach easy to access?" Much of the coastline here was high and rugged, though sometimes the lands sloped down toward broad stretches of beach.

"It is reachable."

Alym Tantario still seemed dubious. "Serenity, are you sure about this?"

"Certain." Lord Wilson Gullimer had gone for help when she fought with Cedrik Kastor. *And even after I stabbed him*. She might well have been slain by the odious greatlord were it not for him, and besides, he might know what had become of Prince Robbert. It was not an opportunity she could pass up. "Sir Ralston, you can accompany me. Butcher, you too." The sight of those two ought to be more than enough to deter any ill-advised heroics. A white flag would serve as well. "Sunrider Tantario, do you have a truce banner?"

The man confirmed as much.

"Good." Saska looked at her brother. "Del, you can be my banner-bearer. It'll help show good faith."

The boy swallowed nervously, and nothing more needed to be said.

Five minutes later, the company was back on the road, and an hour following that, they had reached the rocky headland at a brisk canter. Saska commanded that the rest of the company remain there while she went down to the ship, then set off with Rolly and the Butcher and Del, crossing a land of parched earth dotted with sprouts of brittle sedge. The slope was moderately steep, though manageable for their horses. Saska's mare trotted gracefully beside Bedrock, who lumbered along in that thunderous way of his, while the Butcher's red stallion and Del's spotted, black-maned palfrey followed just behind.

They made quite a quartet, Saska had to admit. *How must we look, coming down this hill.* The Butcher with his shredded red cloak and shredded grinning face; Sir Ralston Whaleheart, the biggest and most serious man in all the world. Del was rather normal by comparison, though was evidently having trouble holding up the white banner properly, as Saska could hear the Butcher laughing and japing as they went. "Not like that, Dellard. You're going to drop it. Hold it straight, boy. *Straight.* How hard is it? Your arms are too thin and weedy. You need some muscle, boy. Some meat on those skinny bones."

"Shut up," Del snapped eventually. "I'm doing the best I can, Meshface."

The Butcher's laugh was as loud as a thunderclap. "*Meshface?* This…*this* is your nickname for me? Meshface?"

"For…for the scars. They look like a mesh." Del's voice was very small and embarrassed. "I thought it was good."

"No. It is not good. You have had many weeks to think of a nickname for me, as I asked you, and this is what you come up with?" The Butcher sounded grossly disappointed. "You do not have Ersella's talents, Dellard. Perhaps you need to train with her, as you train with Kaa Sokari?"

Saska could imagine the sort of training Del might like to engage in with Leshie. Ever since she'd undressed right there before him at the river, he had looked at her differently, and Leshie had teased him relentlessly over it. "Quiet now," she told them. "They've seen us."

They were nearing the bottom of the slope now, where it flattened out into a rugged mire of pitted grey rocks bordering the edge of the beach. Beyond, the small camp was pitched on the hard-packed sand, no more than a few tents and shelters and lean-tos, and further back, the battered body of *Orchard* lay beached among the shells and pebbles and seaweed. Men were hard at work with hammers, knocking in nails and fixing what wounds they could, while others picked through the rocks in the surf and a little further to sea, searching for usable drift-wood to patch holes in the bulwarks and bow.

Ahead, a host of soldiers were approaching, armed with swords and shields, a dozen or so in number. They looked ragged and half-starved, sunburned and bearded, and their cloaks were salt-stained and discoloured. Saska made out some browns and greens and faded reds, but they were scorched by the sun, sand-scoured and torn. Beneath those cloaks they wore oddments of armour, scratched and stained, much of it leather, but here and there a bit of castle-forged plate and even some misting godsteel.

Saska could not see Lord Gullimer among them. "Del, do you recognise anyone?"

"I think…that one…" He tried to point, but realised he had to keep hold of the banner with both hands, lest he drop it. "The one with the yellow beard and dark hair. And the godsteel sword. That's Sir Kester Droyn. He's one of Lord Gullimer's knights."

"Should we stay ahorse?" Saska asked the others.

"That would be best until we know their intentions, and they ours," the Wall told her.

"Dellard must dismount, however," the Butcher put in. "He must plant the flag. This is how the parley is done."

Del looked at Saska, unsure. The Wall nodded. "Go ahead, boy. Plant the flag."

The youth dismounted with a certain lack of grace, almost dropping the banner as he did so, then hastened forward to plant it in the dirt. He did so with great toil, but eventually got the flag standing straight, or near enough, before scrambling back to his horse to mount up. He seemed vastly happy to see his duty done.

The man Del named as Sir Kester took the lead as the band approached, turning his head to shout a command as they picked through the last of the rocks. A soldier came forward, bearing a white flag of his own, though a rather more shoddy version. He planted it down in the earth five metres from their own. "We have parley," Sir Kester Droyn declared ringingly.

"We have parley," repeated the Wall.

The Gullimer knight looked at him. He knew him, obviously. Everyone knew the Wall on sight even if they'd never met him. "We had not thought to have seen you here, Sir Ralston." Sir Kester had yellow eyes to go with his yellow beard, but his hair was almost black. He looked no older than five and twenty. "Nor you, my lady," he added, smiling at her.

My lady. They know me as well, then. She should not have been too surprised by that. Doubtless her story had spread by now among the ranks of Robbert's army. Several dozen of the prince's men had watched as Joy tore Cedrik Kastor's throat out, after all, and mauled him to a bloody mess, Lord Gullimer himself among them.

"My name is Sir Kester Droyn," the knight told them, not knowing that they knew. "Of Smallweather." He inclined his head in a courteous bow. Beneath a cloak of soft grey wool, slashed with crimson stripes, he wore godsteel breastplate, gauntlets, gorget and greaves over a chainmail hauberk of regular steel. His cloak was held at the throat by a brooch in the likeness of a howling wolf with a bloody maw. If that was his sigil, it was not one Saska knew. Nor Smallweather, wherever that was. "May I ask why you have come?"

"To see Lord Gullimer," Saska said. "Is he here?"

"He is, my lady." Droyn motioned behind him. Among the shoddy tents and shelters was a larger pavilion, though not by much. "His lordship commands from there. I will bring you to him."

"We would sooner invite Lord Gullimer to join us out here," the Wall rumbled.

Saska raised a palm. "No. It's fine." She was not about to summon a lord to come out to her, a middling lord though he might be. This was his camp and she would go to him, as a courtesy if nothing else. She dismounted her mare. The other soldiers were peering at her like she was some strange creature, and truly, she was. Not often was a lady seen dressed in a suit of such exquisite godsteel plate, with a broadsword at one hip and an ancient, glowing dagger at the other. *Imagine if they knew whose dagger that once was. And who I am.* The deep olive skin tone, radiant blue eyes and youthful visage only made her all the more queer to these men. "Sir Ralston will come with me, as escort," she said.

Sir Kester nodded. "As you will, my lady." He gave the Butcher a side glance, not much liking what he saw, then noticed Del for the first time. The shadow of recognition crossed his eyes, but he said nothing. "And these others?"

"Will stay here," Saska said. "I trust that will maintain the terms of parley?"

"It will, my lady."

Sir Ralston swung a massive leg over Bedrock, landing on the ground with a thump that shook the earth. Several of the men quelled from him, but not Sir Kester Droyn. He looked up at the giant with a smile. "You are even larger in person, sir," he observed.

The Wall only grunted, as if he'd heard that a thousand times before, and plonked his greathelm down upon his head, clicking it into his gorget. "Lead on, Sir Kester," he boomed from within that bucket.

Sir Kester nodded, turned, and led them across the rocks. He had a courtly way about him, offering Saska a hand each time they reached a treacherous section. She did not need his aid, of course, but accepted anyway, to show her thanks. He seemed happy with that. "I never liked Lord Cedrik," he confided in her, as they went. "Not to say his manner of death was my preference, but perhaps there was some justice in that."

"There is justice in the Long Abyss," Saska said.

"Indeed. And his crimes will see him there, I am certain. One does not lightly break the terms of parley, my lady. That alone is enough to incur the wrath of the gods."

Harrowmoor, Saska thought. She had been a spy in the warcamp when Lord Cedrik incited blood at the parley outside the fortress walls. His crimes preceding that were of greater consequence to her, however. "Did you know him well?" she asked.

"Not well, no. More by *reputation*. There was a knight, a friend of mine…Sir Alistair Suffolk. A good and noble man. Sir Alistair the Abiding, we called him. Not a man to suffer gross injustice and villainy, my lady, such as Lord Cedrik and his Greenbelts perpetrated. Alistair saw fit to challenge him before the men and even threw down his gauntlet and demanded a duel to the death. Lord Cedrik's response? To drive a dagger into his neck when he wasn't looking." His face twisted in disgust. "He proved his ignobility *then*, if not before."

Before, Saska thought. *Long before, Sir Kester.*

Droyn glanced back behind them. "That boy with you…he was one of Prince Robbert's charges, was he not?"

"His squire, for a short time."

"Ah. The squire." He smiled. "Yes, I thought it was so. I heard he helped to save our noble prince from that snake Sir Wenfry Gershan. He is well thought of around here."

That made Saska happy to hear.

"The prince left a chest of treasures, as a reward," the knight went on. His eyes gave her a quick study. "This plate of yours…"

"Was a gift of Robbert's, yes," she confirmed. "And Del's armour as well, and his bow." She felt a pang of nerves as she prepared to ask the next question. "The prince…do you know what has become of him, Sir Kester?"

"Alas no, my lady," he said, with a deflated sigh. "Our fleet suffered sorely during the storms, and of the prince there had been no sign. We lost sight of *Hammer* long weeks ago. As we did *Landslide* and *Shadow* and most others. After a time there was only us and *Harvest*." He gestured with a hand to the waters of the bay. Some two hundred metres from the shore Saska could see masts poking out from the surf, a ship submerged beneath. "We had lashed ourselves together as we battled up the coast, but it soon became a losing struggle. Eventually, the tides and currents ran us aground, but *Harvest* didn't make it. The old girl had her belly torn upon by a shoal, and went down, but we managed to get her men ashore. Most, at least. Some were taken by sharks."

Of those men there were many, Saska saw. *Hundreds*. Kaa Sokari had not been wrong. "You were trying to get up the coast, did you say?"

"Yes, my lady. When we left our anchorage to the south it was agreed that we would regroup in the waters below Eagle's Perch, should we be scattered by storms. Whether anyone made it there, though…" He gave a shrug.

By then they had passed the last of the rocks and entered the small encampment. Men stopped in their tasks to watch her pass, eyes squinting in recognition. Their ordeal at sea had not been pleasant, that was clear. Many had crusted sores on their faces and red blisters on their hands and feet, with dry cracked lips that spoke of men in desperate want of water. Here and there a cookfire chugged smoke, with fish roasting on spits, and Saska saw a small shark as well, and a bucket of crabs all scrambling over one another as they tried to escape their tin prison. But elsewise food appeared scarce.

They found Lord Gullimer's pavilion at the heart of the makeshift camp, its walls of common canvas rippling limply in the coastal wind. A banner had been posted outside bearing the apple orchard sigil of his house, and Saska could hear the strains of raised voices coming from within.

"Wait here a moment. I will announce you." Sir Kester Droyn stepped inside. The voices died away abruptly, sinking to murmurs, and a few moments later some disgruntled men came bustling out, muttering among themselves. One was so lost to his grumblings that he almost stepped right into the Wall, and staggered away in fright when he saw him. "It is quite all right, Lord Tymson," Sir Kester chuckled. "The Whaleheart is here under terms of parley." He opened out a hand. "Please, come this way."

The pavilion interior was as simple as its exterior. On a floor of hard dark sand and chunks of stone, a small pallet bed had been unrolled and there was a table as well, no more than a ragged slab of driftwood raised on legs of the same. A few camp stools had been brought in, and from the support poles hung a pair of oil lanterns, currently unlit.

"My lady." Lord Wilson Gullimer stood beside the driftwood table, bearded, sunburned, and somewhat shabby, but still handsome for all that. When last she'd seen him, he'd been dressed in full plate armour, stained by blood and battle, with a sooty cloak at his back. Now he wore but linens and leathers of simple styling, and no cloak at all in the heat. "Pray forgive the inelegance of my dress," he said. "My finer clothes are aboard the ship and I had not expected such company." He looked at Sir Kester. "Serve the lady a cup of wine, if you would. Sir Ralston, will you partake?"

The Wall removed his greathelm, and shook his great head. "My thanks. No."

"As you wish."

Sir Kester went to the driftwood table and did the honours, pouring two cups, one for Lord Gullimer and one for Saska. She didn't really want any, but knew it was polite to at least take a sip. She did so. She was no expert in wine, but this was sour stuff, most unpleasant.

Her face must have shown that, because Lord Gullimer gave a hoarse laugh. "Poor fare, I know, but it's all we have left. Soon the rum will run dry and we'll have real problems." He had a drink of his own and set his cup aside on the table. "The men can do without water, but rum? Gods forbid they should die sober."

"You're not going to die," Saska found herself saying. She was not sure what else to say, in truth. Or even why she was here. She had wanted to find out about Prince Robbert, and she had. What else was she hoping for? *I can't help them,* she told herself. *Not after waving away a hundred other pleas.*

"I'm glad you think so, my lady. But some will, and soon. We have many sick men among us, and some wounded as well. And these waters are perilous to fish. Only this morning a man was taken by a shark, and another so badly bitten he is likely to follow come nightfall."

Saska did not imagine being killed by a shark was a pleasant way to go. "Do you have medicine with you…for the sick?"

"Scant little. *Harvest* had some decent stocks in the hold, but retrieving it isn't so easy. Not with those sharks prowling about the bay. I believe they call that a conundrum." He gave a bitter hack, picked up his cup, took a sip, and set it down again. "So how is it you've come to be here? You're a long way from Aram, Lady Saska."

"That is not your concern," the Whaleheart said.

"My concern?" Lord Gullimer repeated, studying the giant with a frown. "No, I suppose you're right. I have enough here to be concerned about, Sir Ralston, than to worry over you. But I *am* interested." He looked at Saska again. "You won a great victory in Aram, my lady. I would have thought it prudent to remain there, rather than venturing a thousand miles from home."

Aram isn't my home, she thought. Willow's Rise was the only proper home she'd ever known, and who knew what had become of it? "I came to find out about Prince Robbert," she only said. "Sir Kester says you lost him during the storms."

"Weeks ago, yes. We've had a sighting or two of some other vessels, but for the most part the fleet is scattered and likely destroyed. How we managed to limp this far, only the gods will know. But far as we've come, I fear we will go no further. Alas my *Orchard* has grown withered, and I do not believe she'll bear new fruit."

"We saw the ship," the Wall said. "You're to say she can't be repaired?"

"Well enough to be seaworthy? I would doubt it. Lest a strong mast should float ashore, and we find some bales of sailcloth among the flotsam, I fear she may be lost to us."

"This land is not empty of trees," the Wall told him. "One ought to serve for a mast."

"One problem among many," the apple lord said. "We lack for nails as well, and tar, and our defensive weapons have been ravaged. We have four hundred and fifty men among us, from *Orchard* and *Harvest*, too many to fit on a single vessel. I fear a strong wind will see us founder, much less a storm of the like we have seen. And already the men are talking of marching. Perhaps you heard the voices before you entered? Half the men want to rest here a while and hope the ship is repaired, while the rest would have us continue afoot to the northern coast. Eagle's Perch," he said. "That was our rendezvous point." He pointed to a map on the table, an old crumpled thing curling at the corners, the ink all smudged and faded. "It's not so far from here, only a hundred miles or so. Even with our wounded we might be able to make it in less than a week, and who knows, perhaps we'll find help there? Another of our ships, or…"

"My lord," came a voice.

Gullimer looked past them, to the flaps. Another of his ragged band was peering inside. "Yes? What is it, Jacob?"

"Pardons, my lord. A ship has been sighted. It is approaching from the north."

Lord Wilson Gullimer gave an abbreviated nod. "How far?"

"Long leagues still. It is faint, some way out to sea. A large galleon, we think."

"Tukoran?"

"Yes, my lord. It looks to be so."

Saska frowned. She did not know why any Tukoran vessel would be coming *south* at this time, and galleons were typically warships.

"If you'll excuse me for a moment." Lord Gullimer stepped past them, moving for the exit. "Sir Kester, entertain our guests while I'm gone. Tell them that joke you know."

Sir Ralston turned upon the young knight once the lord had left. "This joke, then. Let's hear it."

Sir Kester rather fumbled over the punchline - who wouldn't, with the Wall staring down at you like that, colossal void of humour that he was - but Saska found herself chuckling anyway. It was a ribald joke, of the sort that Bawdy Bron Bowen used to tell her when she sailed on the Steel Sister, and only reminded her of her time with the crew. She still had Bawdy Bron's parchment of jokes with her, as she did her shell necklace and quill-knife and the pitted coral that called to her, and sometimes she liked to read them through when she was feeling low. By now she knew most of them by heart. "I know some jokes too," she said. "Would you like to hear one, sir?"

The man's yellow eyes lit up like the sun. "Yes…of course, I'd love to." He poured himself a cup of wine and waited, eager to hear it.

Saska made something of a pig's ear of the ending herself, but kind as he was, Sir Kester repaid the compliment and unleashed a guffaw of laughter. "Very good, my lady, very good. I have another, in actual fact. Let me see if I can recall it…"

He did, and this time his delivery was on point. Saska laughed, long and true, and after that they went back and forth, exchanging jokes and never getting a punchline wrong. Rolly did not much enjoy it. Though once…maybe even twice…Saska was sure he cracked a smile.

By the time Lord Gullimer came back, Saska and Sir Kester were red-faced and breathless, and the entire jug of wine had been drunk down to the dregs. The lord walked in, took one look around, then smiled broadly. "Your joke went down well then, I see," he said to Kester Droyn.

"And the rest," the knight chuckled. "This young lady is full of mischief, my lord, let me tell you. The jokes she knows. Goodness."

Gullimer smiled. "I should like to hear them." He looked in fine spirits all of a sudden. "Perhaps you would care to share some with me, my lady, while we await him?"

"Him, my lord?" Saska wasn't understanding.

"We won't be waiting," the Wall came in, with his great warhorn of a voice. His mouth twitched, as though he knew something Saska didn't. Or feared something, more like. "We will be leaving at once."

Saska glared at him, taking charge. "*I'll* be the judge of that, Sir Ralston." Her eyes returned to the handsome Lord of Watervale. "Who is coming here, my lord?"

"Well…I cannot be completely certain, my lady, but the flying of the royal standard has me rather convinced."

Her lips quickened into a smile. "You mean…"

"Yes, Lady Saska," he said. "*Hammer* is fast approaching. And unless I am mistaken, the man who gave you that armour is aboard."

45

Pagaloth

He could hear their voices muttering through the branches.

They're right below me, he thought.

Sir Pagaloth Kadosk had only just awoken from a short and troubled sleep, nestled among the high branches of an old oak tree. He had lashed a rope around him so he did not fall. Quickly, quietly, he worked the knot loose and coiled the rope, sitting up tight against the trunk. The leaves were thick and green and dripping, the rain falling from a slate-grey sky, the light thin and sickly. Pagaloth peered down through a gap in the canopy and saw men moving beneath him, glimpsed red cloaks and black armour and tall dragonsteel spears.

Dragonknights, he thought. *I live in fear of my very own order.*

Sir Pagaloth did not make a sound. He pulled his legs in, so that they did not dangle or rustle through the leaves, and kept himself perfectly still. He ached all over. Sleeping tied atop a tree branch was not comfortable, he had discovered, nor restful, and he felt weary to his bones. How much sleep had he had since he'd run from the battle? An hour here, an hour there, never much more than that. He could not even say how long it had been since he'd been running, or in which direction he had gone. Every day dawned grey and wet and foggy, and rarely had he glimpsed the sun. *A week? Has it been as long as two, three?* His exhaustion and discomfort were only matched by his hunger. His stomach felt so empty he could eat an entire boar and still have plenty of room for another.

The men below were talking to one another in hushed voices as they passed, though one had stopped to kneel on the ground near the oak's broad trunk, brushing his hand through the undergrowth, searching for tracks. *Don't hear me. Don't see me. Don't look up*, Pagaloth prayed. He had been careful to cover his trail when he made camp in this tree, though a skilled tracker might still see signs.

He drew a long deep breath into his lungs, trying to energise himself should he need to run. He had a way down through the branches planned out. If he was quick, he might be able to reach the ground before they had him surrounded, and then it would be a footrace once more. He'd found himself involved in two of those already, in the days since the battle, and had managed to outrun his opponents each time.

But now? *I'm too tired, too weak, too hungry.* Desperation would only take a man so far when his vital needs were not met, and it had been too long since he'd had a proper meal.

Keep going, he thought. *Just keep on going. There's nothing here for you.* The tracker was still on his knee, searching the ground, eyes sweeping across the forest floor. Pagaloth saw another man step over to join him. He glimpsed a pin that marked his rank as captain. Words were shared, too low for him to hear, and then the captain looked up, peering through the branches.

Pagaloth froze, pressing himself against the bark. He had draped his cloak over him to better hide him among the leaves, and hoped he appeared no more than a shadow from down there. He dare not look. Hooded, he sat as still as a statue, listening for sudden shouts and commands below.

But there was nothing. Just the murmur of voices, then the rustle of armour, the tread of men continuing on through the trees. Pagaloth did not stir. He sat as he had been, cloaked and cowled and patient as a stalking cat, waiting for the sounds to recede. Then he waited some more, and some more after that. *This might be some trick. They might come back.* It was a risk he was not willing to take, so he stayed where he was for what felt like an hour, before finally climbing down.

He reached the forest floor, carefully descending through the thick, rough branches. When he landed he looked around. The tracks of the dragonknights were clear, moving away through the wooded valley and into the mists, though in what direction he couldn't say. The skies were so clogged even the glow of the sun was veiled. Pagaloth turned and went the opposite way.

The Wandering Wood was a giant maze, he had come to find. Vast, unending, a hundred separate woods that all looked much alike, clothing a thousand rolling hills and valleys that he could not tell one from another. His days here had been more frustrating than he could say. He had no map, no guide, no horse, no one here to help him. When he did see the glow of the sun, he would make for the west at once, to try to get back to King's Point, but those occasions were rare, and it was far too easy to get turned around again. For all he knew, he was further away than ever before. *Perhaps I'm wandering toward the South Downs instead? I might be hundreds of miles away by now.*

Navigating was no easier by night. If the skies had cleared to show the stars, Pagaloth had not seen them. Each night was black as the bottom of some pit, it was almost always raining, and that rain was turning *cold.* He slept where he could, but staying dry had proven impossible. One night he'd crawled into cover beneath the tangled branches of a deadfall, but had been awoken when a great river of rainwater came flooding down into his den. Another night, he had found a barn, long since abandoned and almost entirely overgrown, deep in some forgotten part of whichever smaller wood he was in. He had thought it safe enough to sleep in, so forged himself a nest of leaves, only for the roof to crumble as he drifted off to sleep, bringing rotted wood and rainwater down atop him.

Since then, he had chosen trees. The canopies were often thick enough to keep the worst of the rain off him, and if he lashed himself to a wide branch, he supposed he would not fall. That experiment had almost failed two nights ago, when the rope came loose in the night, and he woke with a start, about to roll off the edge, but he'd stopped himself just in time. Now he double and triple-checked his knots to make sure they held fast.

But sleep, when it did come, was almost impossible in anything more than fits and starts. He had to be on his guard all the time. From the fell creatures that might catch his scent and climb up to have a taste. From the Agarathi patrols, prowling about in numbers far greater than he had thought possible. Had more of them come from the south on ships? Most of the forts along the Black Coast had been destroyed now, and the Vandarian defences were shredded and dispersed. For all he knew thousands more of his kin had poured across the Red Sea, raiding and pillaging, shepherded by the fire priests who spoke with Eldur's voice.

That thought disquieted him. He needed to get back to King's Point and warn Lythian and Amron Daecar. If one of those priests should manage to infiltrate the prisoner camp, he would quickly muster all the Agarathi to his will. *Like Ten'kin*, he thought, bitterly. The man had been like a plague in their ranks, secretly taking the Agarathi deserters back into thraldom beneath the Fire Father's wing. Pagaloth remembered the look in Sa'har Nakaan's eyes as he cut at his own throat, sawing back and forth to empty his own lifeblood to the earth. The fear of being taken back into bondage had been too much for him to bear. *He had sooner died than served, but how many are so strong as that? Am I? If they find me…will I be able to resist?*

Sir Pagaloth walked on, bitter and alone, aimlessly wandering through the Wandering Wood and wondering, now, if that's why they'd been so named. *A man could wander here forever and never find his way out. Where is west? Where, damnit?* He kicked out at a stone, sending it spinning off into the fog. *Run*, Sa'har Nakann had told him, and he had…but now a part of him wished he hadn't. *I might have stayed and fought. Maybe they even won?*

He scowled at his own stupidity. It was a foolish notion and he knew it. Five hundred foes had descended upon them that day, pouring out through the mists of that valley, and the Agarathi deserters they had gathered had turned on them too. There was no winning that fight. Sir Hadros, Sir Bardol, Ruggard Wells and Mads Miller, Moro and Bellio and Sir Quento, the paladin knight. Most likely all were dead. *They were my companions, my confederates, and I left them there to die.* He had to, lest get caught himself, and turned a slave, and for some foul purpose…but all the same it shamed him.

He gripped the hilt of his dragonsteel sword, tightening his fingers around the leather grip. Around him the woods were thinning, the trees spreading. Banners of mist rippled by, drawn along on a whispering breeze. He could almost hear the voice of Ten'kin in the way it rustled and moved. *Come, child, join us. It is no use to resist. If not me, another will ensnare you…*

Another. How many of them are there? The dragons had brought some of the priests over from the south, Pagaloth had no doubt, and perhaps more of them had been sent in ships, protected by companies of spearmen and knights. For all he knew there were dozens of them spreading the will of Eldur through these lands…

The cracking of a twig caught his attention, somewhere to his left. The dragonknight froze to look around, listening for the tread of pursuers. He squinted at the drifting fogs, looking at every trunk and tree as though an enemy might come out from behind it.

He stood still for several minutes, turning slowly, listening, until he was satisfied there was no one there. The only sound was the keening wind, whispering in Ten'kin's voice, the soft distant babble of a stream somewhere away to his right…and the rumbling in his stomach, cramping from lack of food. All he had eaten in long days were berries foraged from fruiting bushes, and those were scant enough. Most he found had been picked clean, by man and beast both, and game was scarce. He had been close to catching a wild turkey once, but the bird had been spooked by the approach of a patrol and Pagaloth had been forced to abandon the hunt and flee.

On he went, knowing not where. His head felt as foggy as the woods, his legs weak as river reeds, and not for the first time he wondered if he was dead. Had he perished in the battle after all? Was this some purgatory for the things he'd done in the past? Lythian had told him a hundred times that he'd paid his debts, but Pagaloth was not so sure. *I should have trusted Kin'rar and Marak back then,* he thought. *I should never have spoken of their plot.* It was his duty, required of his honour, but who was he to talk of honour against men like Ulrik Marak and Kin'rar Kroll and Lythian Lindar, the Knight of the Vale? *I am but a spec on this earth compared to them. I should have let them kill Tavash, as they'd planned. Perhaps then none of this would have happened.*

He had thought about it so often since then…how different things might have been had he simply kept his mouth shut. Tavash would never have been king. Lythian and Borrus and Tomos would never have been imprisoned and mocked and scorned. Sir Tomos would not have died. Lord Marak and Skymaster Kin'rar Kroll would never have fled to Tethian's side. They would not have saved Lythian and Borrus from the Pits of Kharthar that day. Without Ulrik Marak, and Kin'rar, and Lythian, they never would have been able to get to the Wings. How could they have done so without Neyruu and Garlath to fly them there? How could they have made it down to the depths of Eldur's Shame without Lythian and his ancestral blade? The prophecy of the Fire Father's awakening was fated, some said, and had those events not transpired in that order, Eldur would have awoken anyway by some other means. *But maybe not,* Pagaloth thought. *If only I had stayed true to the men I admired, if only I had not betrayed them, all of this might have been avoided. It is my fault the world is falling to ruin. My fault. And this is my penance.*

The thoughts swirled darkly, but there was no point in thinking like that now. He had sworn his oath to Lythian and it was his duty to get back to him. *I must tell him what has happened. Tell him his hopes for unity have been dashed.* He ground his jaw at the thought of it, and held tight to his dragonsteel blade. *Ten'kin. If ever I see him again, I will take his head from his shoulders, and spit on the ruin of his corpse.*

He walked for long hours, trudging through the woodland and an open valley beyond, across a lofty hillside cloaked in mist, down the slope into another identical wood, always hoping for some sight of the sun. The gods did not grant him so much as a glimpse. The skies were dark grey and murky, the air bitter cold. There were sores all over his body from where his armour had chaffed him, the padded clothes he wore beneath soaked through by the rain. He felt soggy, chilled to the bone, sluggish and slow. He came to another hill, and climbed the sodden slope, stepping through the roots and rocks and soft humus on the forest floor, step by weary step. When he reached the summit, the trees thinned, and he looked around in hope, but saw nothing. Just the same grey skies, the same thick fog. *Have I been here before?* he wondered. *Have I been walking in circles all along?*

He could not say. The way down on the other side was more thickly forested, and what light there was withered and died, strangled by the branches and boles. Through a thick gloom he drifted, eyes scanning lazily for berries and edible roots. At the base of a large maple, he saw a cluster of mushrooms and knelt to pick them. His first instinct was to devour them instantly, but he inspected them first, turning them between his fingers, looking at the stalks, rings, gills and caps, and concluded that they were likely edible. Then he devoured them hungrily, chewing through the spongy flesh, eyes moving about in search of more. He found another spouting nearby, and another, and soon his belly was not so empty. It was scant nourishment, almost tasteless when uncooked, but would serve for now.

On he went. At the bottom of the forested hillside, a great muddy river was rushing stroppily through the vale, choked with sticks and branches and bits of debris. Pagaloth wondered if a river had ever rushed through here before. Most likely this one was new. Much of the land had become flooded and waterlogged, collecting in basins and valleys, but when some natural dam burst, the waters would come pouring out, always moving downhill, storming away to freedom.

They will make for the sea, Pagaloth thought. He had wondered if he should do the same - at least the rivers would lead him, if not the sun and stars - but decided against it. If he reached the coast he would know where he was, but those lands were open, offered little cover, and he would struggle to go unnoticed.

The river was too fierce and hazardous for him to cross safely here, but upstream he found a fallen tree that cut across its length, creating a place to ford. He picked carefully across, the water rushing up to his thighs, testing every step before moving forward. When he got safely across, he found another shallow hill before him, overgrown with high stiff grass and thornbushes. He continued upward, fighting through the tangles as his legs screamed out at the toil. His efforts were not in vain. At one bush, he found a great bounty of blackberries and feasted greedily, pricking his fingers a hundred times as he plucked them free and threw them into his mouth, chewing and swallowing, not caring a jot for the pain. He ate until he felt satisfied, then stashed the rest of the berries in his pack for later, not missing a single one.

By then the light was fading, and he would need to think about where to sleep for the night. At the top of the hill, the winds blew wildly, buffeting him as he struggled on, tugging insistently at his cloak. Ahead, the lands lengthened and flattened out. Through the bands of fog he glimpsed a broad plain, the shadow of another forest beyond. His heart sank. For a moment…just a brief moment…he'd wondered if the open plain augered the end of the Wandering Wood. But no. He was still in its midst, hopelessly and helplessly lost.

He sagged, though had no choice but to keep on going. The open land made him wary. His eyes flitted left and right and behind him, searching the mists, and often he stopped to stand still and listen. Distantly, he heard the howling of wolves, that long sorrowful sound that set a chill in the dragonknight's bones. Common wolves he could fight off, perhaps, but anything larger would make a meal of him. Fellwolves, direwolves, shadowwolves and worse all prowled these parts, and those were all one family. There were bears and boars, slithering serpents and savage cats of similar peril, and more ancient creatures besides lurking in the dark.

The wind blew loud in his ears as he crossed the field, the fogs thickening and weakening and thickening again. Sometimes he could barely see his hand before his eyes. Then suddenly the air would clear and he would be granted a broader view. At one such time he sighted what looked like a building away to his right. He saw it in a glimpse and stopped, waiting for the mist to clear once more. On his second sighting, he realised it must be an inn, raised here in this field between the woods. It was small, a timber structure of two storeys, with a stable annexed to its flank. There was no light glowing behind the shutters.

He saw no horses in the stalls, no movement outside, but could not be certain from this far.

He pondered what to do. It was possible the Agarathi had taken it for a base, dousing their torches and candles to lay a trap. Just as likely there was no one there, and he might be able to scavenge some food from the larder. Might there be an innkeep in hiding, with his family? *He could have a map*, Pagaloth thought. *Information. He might be able to show me where to go…tell me where I am…*

The thought of it was too tempting. He crept closer, moving through the tall tufts of swaying grass, trying to stay hidden as he approached. The wind gusted across the plain, loud and then quiet and then loud again, never resting. Pagaloth drew as near as he dared, then crouched in cover to watch. Rain pattered down upon his shoulders, but it was gentle now, and he could see the faintest colour in the sky, the blurred red hue of sunset beyond the clouds. *West*, he thought. He logged its position against the inn. At worst, he would find a tree nearby to camp in, then return here at daybreak, and go west from there.

He watched the inn for long minutes, searching for a glimmer of light, a flicker of movement behind a window. When the wind died, he closed his eyes and listened for voices or the tread of a boot on floorboards, the whicker of a horse. There was nothing. He turned his eyes behind him, and then left and right along the track. He saw no one out there. *I'm alone*, he thought.

He stood and strode forward.

First, he checked the stalls, and as expected, he saw no horses. Then he went around the back of the inn, peering through cracks in the shuttered windows, and saw no one. At the front door, he drew out his dagger, better for combat in close quarters should he need to fight. The mushrooms and berries had driven away the worst of his hunger, and there was a little more strength in his limbs. He reached for the handle. Turned it. It made a horrid whining sound as he pushed forward, and stepped in.

He moved his eyes across the darkness. The common room was silent and still, shadows of tables and chairs here and there. Dust motes flickered in the faintest of light. The inn looked long abandoned, its hearth cold, the air stolid and stale. The dragonknight moved quietly, light on his feet, but the floorboards creaked all the same. The sound seemed loud as a thunder strike in the silence, echoing eerily through the house. He reached a door that went back to the kitchens and pushed it open. The cabinet doors and drawers were all opened, their contents removed. He saw some jars and pots, but they were empty or elsewise of no use to him. If there had been food here, either the innkeep had taken it with him when he left, or someone had come by and cleaned them out.

He turned back into the common room, moving to a set of wooden stairs that led to the upper floor. The boards groaned as he

594

climbed. At the top he found a landing that gave access to several rooms. There was a ladder, too, that permitted access to a loft where smaller sleeping cells would be. Pagaloth went room by room, hoping to find a map, a letter, anything that might tell him where he was, but found nothing. He climbed the ladder to the loft, but found nothing up there either. Just a bundle of clothes, heaped to one side, old and moth-eaten, and a small leather-bound book that had been left behind, forgotten beneath a bed.

He sat a moment, flicking through the pages. The book was a compendium of flora and fauna found in the Wandering Wood. He searched for a chapter on mushrooms, found the ones he'd eaten earlier, and confirmed that they were edible. It was one less thing to worry about.

A horse whickered outside.

His heart gave a lurch and he was on his feet in an instant. There was a small window in the loft, looking over the field. He paced over, looked out. A troop of men were coming up the road from the south, a dozen of them, perhaps two. Several had already reached the stables and were dismounting their steeds, moving to the door.

Pagaloth spun at once, speeding for the ladder, tossing the book onto the bed. He could hear men stamping into the common, heavy boots rattling against the boards, talking to one another in Agarathi. He wondered if he should stay up here and hide. Draw the ladder up so they couldn't find him. Then he heard a man call out, "Search the building. Every room. If there's anyone hiding here, I'll know of it."

That sealed it. Quick and quiet as a cat, Pagaloth descended the ladder and dashed into one of the rooms with a window that gave access to the outside. He made it just in time as a pair of soldiers stamped up the stairs, crimson-cloaked and leather-armoured with tattoos around their eyes, declaring their kills. "I'll take this one," he heard one of them say. "You start there."

Pagaloth slipped behind the cover of the door, melting into shadow. He drew a breath to still his heart. He could hear the soldier walking along the landing, see the shadow passing the door. He slid his dagger from its sheath, waiting.

The man pushed the door open with a creak. He stepped in two paces and turned his eyes around. Pagaloth pounced, emerging from the shadows to slap a hand over his mouth, muffling his screams. His dagger flashed up, driving deep into the flesh of his neck. The soldier gave out a shudder of pain, jerking his legs as Pagaloth dragged him into a darkened corner. The boots thumped against the ground too loudly. Pagaloth pulled out the knife with a fine spray of blood, turned it, slammed it down into the man's chest, puncturing his heart. The jerking stopped at once as his body fell limp. As quietly as he could he laid him on the ground, cursing that it had come to this.

"Jangor, you all right in there?"

The other man had heard. He was right outside, stepping in.

"If this is some joke, I…"

Pagaloth lunged out from the darkness, slashing at the man's throat, cutting it to the bone. His head snapped back, blood gushing out in a wild red fountain, a gurgled scream spluttering from his mouth. He reached for his blade and stumbled back into a closet, crashing against the wood. The sound rang out through the inn. At once there was shouting down below, voices calling, the thunder of stamping boots slamming up the stairs.

Pagaloth spun, rushing for the window, pulling the shutters apart. There were too many for him to fight alone. The wind howled in from outside. He could hear men running up onto the landing, hollering as they came. One leg went through the window, and then the other, until he was perched on the edge. The drop was not far; down into some bushes below, growing at the side of the inn. He had time enough to glance back and see the men rush in as he threw himself out, landing in the shrubs with a crash of twigs and branches.

"After him!" a voice bellowed.

Pagaloth scrambled to his feet, pulling free a foot caught among the vines. He stumbled out onto the road. Above the skies were breaking up, and he saw his first sight of stars in long days. The rain had stopped falling, and the fog had started to clear. *Damnit. Why now?* The one time he needed those mists to conceal him and they were gone. *Curse the gods!*

He set off at a run, making for the woods. Men were crying out behind him, rushing to mount their horses and give chase. Several others had vaulted through the window in pursuit and were following him afoot. A sharp wail suggested a man had landed poorly, but Pagaloth gave him no mind, dashing through a pool of moonlight, turning off the road and away to the nearest trees.

A spear came whistling past him, so close it almost shaved the skin off his neck. It slammed into the ground ten paces ahead, quivering. "Alive!" he heard a man bellow. "We take him alive!"

He reached the trees, rushing beneath the canopy…and all hope of escape was gone.

Far as he could see they spread out evenly, widely spaced, the forest floor flat and mottled in open patches of hard-packed dirt and slanting rays of moonlight. There were no hazards to trip horses, or slow them, no rivers into which he might jump and swim and flee, no rocky cliffs he could scale to win his freedom. It was the plainest wood he had ever seen, as though some cruel god had made it just so to taunt him. *Curse the gods!* he thought again. He drew out his sword and turned.

There was a man right behind him, who had not expected him to whirl. Pagaloth took him off guard, saw the eyes widen as he swung and cut the man down. A host of others were following, though they were not all together, and coming in ones and twos. Pagaloth roared and ran at the nearest pair, hoping to thin out the herd as best he could. He was on them in a flash. His dragonsteel sword caught the moonlight, rippling red between the fullers, as he cut down at one man's hand, shearing through the fingers and slicing off half the palm as he snatched for his sword. The man stared at his mangled hand in mute shock. Then the pain came and he screamed.

The other foe was a dragonknight, the one who had thrown his spear. He had a sword as well, ripping it from its sheath. Further back a voice was still calling for them to take him alive, but the dragonknight paid it no mind. "Traitor!" he roared. Then he stormed forward with all his rage.

Pagaloth swung up to fend off his attack, and they clashed loudly, steel on steel. The impact jarred. Pagaloth moved back, letting his enemy come onto him, then turned his next cut aside, pirouetting around the knight's back, slashing off half his cloak and raking a line across his scale armour.

The man with the mangled hand was still screaming, clutching at his wrist, watching in horror as the blood burst and pulsed from his palm. Pagaloth swung about, silencing him with a flashing upcut that sliced through his low jaw, and in the same move danced back about to face his foe.

"Traitor!" roared the dragonknight again, seeing his companion crumple in a bloody heap. He came at him, blade swishing. Pagaloth's caught the attack six inches from his eyes. The blades trembled against one another, ringing. His foe scraped his blade away, edge to edge, then swung in a brutal sidecut. Pagaloth turned it, tracked backward, cutting hard at his opponent's flank. His steel bit into the thick scales of his dragonhide armour, lodging there a moment. With a heave Pagaloth ripped it free. A trickle of blood came with it, red on black. The man grunted, swinging at him again. Behind, Pagaloth could see the rest of the host coming his way. *Too close*, he thought. *Too many.* There were another five, six, seven of them afoot, racing into the trees. Behind came the mounted men, kicking their spurs, brandishing spears and swords, their tips and edges winking in the moonlight.

He would be overwhelmed in short order, he knew. *Unless…*

He whirled, suddenly, ramming his bloodied blade back into its sheath and surging away through the woods in a sprint. The move caught his foe unawares. "Coward!" he bellowed, disdainful. Then he grunted and made to follow.

Pagaloth Kadosk had always been quick. He drew upon his reserves of strength now, hurtling with all his speed. Some of the men were left behind; others raced to keep up, but none were as pacy as he was. It was the horses who would catch him. And the first one to reach him…

He glanced back. One was closing fast, galloping past the boles, kicking up clods of dirt. The forest floor shivered, leaves stirring. Shouts rang out through the trees. Pagaloth knew it was his only chance. He reached for his dagger as he ran, drawing it out. Ahead was a large oak, thick-trunked and wide. He kept up his sprint until he passed it, then abruptly changed direction, dashing to the right. The rider shouted a curse and pulled the reins, twisting to give chase, but Pagaloth had stopped and turned. He steadied his footing, drew a breath, took aim at his target and threw.

The dagger sliced the air. The rider had barely enough time to blink before it struck him in the eye, gouging a path to his brain. His head cracked back. The horse gave out a ringing neigh and reared, but Pagaloth was already there, hurrying forward to snatch the reins. With his other hand he reached up, grabbed a fistful of cloak, and tugged hard, pulling the dead rider from the saddle. Then he vaulted up, swinging his leg over, kicked his heels into the horse's flank and roared, "*Heyah!*"

The steed set off at a wild gallop. Hope soared in him. The trees were spaced out and even ahead, and suddenly that favoured him. *Ride hard!* he thought. *Ride until you can ride no more!* He would lose the men afoot like this, and if he could only outpace the other riders…

A *thump* rippled through the horse's rear. The beast screamed and buckled, its front legs collapsing beneath it. Pagaloth went flying from the saddle, gouging a muddy track in the ground where he landed. He crawled to all fours, wheezing. The horse was trying to stand, failing, screaming as it fell back down. A long black spear protruded from its rump, blood trailing down through its glossy coat. Behind, mounted dragonknights closed in, the rest hurrying to catch up, shouting as they came. Pagaloth glimpsed a man in robes back there, robes red as a bloody dawn. *No…*he thought.

"Get him up," someone said.

Men were pulling to a stop around him, dismounting. Pagaloth staggered to his feet, reaching to draw out his sword. In a blink three dragonknights had him surrounded. He panted, trying to recover his breath, then lashed out at the first he saw. The knight swiped his attack aside. The two others came in behind him. He felt hands on his wrist, shaking his blade loose, an arm around his neck, choking him. He struggled against them, but it was no use. A boot kicked at the back of his leg with a sharp stab of pain, driving him down to his knees. Two men held him there as others gathered around, panting and scowling and cursing. Their eyes showed hate and their lips were twisted. Pagaloth glimpsed red in their gaze.

Their captain stepped through, waving as he came. "Someone silence that damn horse."

"We should silence *him* too," said another man. He snatched a dagger from his belt and took a menacing pace forward. "*Northern* scum. He killed Jangor and Taglo and…"

"*No.*" The word snapped from behind them. Pagaloth cringed at the voice, saw the men part to make way, lowering their heads and falling silent. The priest fluttered forward in his fiery red robes, slashed in crimson and ruby and amber. He wore a kind smile beneath cold, empty eyes. "Do not fear, Sir Pagaloth," he said. "It is warm in the Father's embrace."

Pagaloth's lips tore open to snarl a reply, but a hand came down to silence him. He bit out at the flesh, felt his teeth sink through meat and muscle. The man yelped and yanked, but he clung on like a dog, feral and wild. Several more figures rushed in to prise him off, and a fist closed to slam into his jaw. His head snapped to one side, mouth full of flesh and blood, bared teeth glistening red. The priest smiled at him all the while. "Do not be too rough with our friend," he said to the men. "He will be one of us… soon enough."

Pagaloth spat out a glob of meat. "No…I'll never…"

"Never? Never *ever*?" The fire priest laughed and stepped in, cupping his chin firmly, lifting his head. When Pagaloth looked up he saw eyes of molten flame staring down at him, swimming with chaos. "I disagree, young one. All join the path eventually."

"Not *all*."

The voice was new. It rumbled deeply from behind the throng. Pagaloth raised his eyes to search beyond them. The dragonknights and spearmen were all turning to look. Several drew back a step at what they saw. A few more drew their blades. One even went down to a knee and bowed his head.

The fire priest swung about, hissing. "*You*," he said. "You have turned from the way?"

"I walk my own way." Lord Ulrik Marak reached to his hip and pulled the Fireblade from its sheath. Flame leapt from its edge, a glow of warm amber light spreading through the glade. "Step away from him," he said.

Pagaloth blinked in shock. More men were drawing steel. The fire priest gave a cackle. "Fool," he said, in that ringing whisper. "Even you cannot fight the will of Agarath, Marak."

Ulrik Marak's face was stone. His eyes moved across the host, one by one. Scales in red and black wreathed his hulking frame; the Body of Karagar, son of the Dread. But the dragonlord's eyes were clear. "Lay down your weapons. I will not give you another chance."

"Do no such thing!" The priest's voice snapped out, shattering through the cold night air. His face twisted in manic glee. "Take him!" he called. "The Fire Father demands it! Take him! Take him! Take him!"

The men obeyed like the slaves they were.

They died like the slaves they were.

46

Robbert

"Whales," Bloodhound Burton said.

"Where?" Robbert scanned across the rough, choppy waters, but he couldn't see them. No shadows, no fins, no spouts. Nothing.

"Yonder." The captain threw out a hand, away to the east. "They're far, but closing. Might have caught our scent. Or not. I'll keep my nostrils open for them, princeling. Be a shame to founder now, wouldn't it?"

Yes, Robbert thought. They had almost five hundred men aboard, and some special guests as well. Being sunk by a pod of grumpy great-whales was not on his agenda. "Tell me if they come too close," he said, "I ought to report to the princess."

"The princess, aye." Burton had a twinkle in his eye. "Pretty girl, isn't she?"

Beautiful, Robbert thought. Pretty didn't do her justice by half. "She is comely, yes."

"And young. Not far off your own age, lad. You'd make a fine pairing, wouldn't you say?"

Robbert did not want to engage in this discussion. He would only say something to implicate himself, and Bloodhound's nose wasn't the only good sense he had. *He knows*, he thought. *He's probably seen me looking at her.* Gazing might be a better word, though he would hope he stopped short of ogling. That would not be particularly princely of him.

"Well, just a thought," the Seaborn said. "Might be the world could do with healing when all this is done, and you being royalty…"

"Yes, Bloodhound, thank you." Robbert didn't need a lesson on marriage pacts to form alliances if that's what the old sailor was getting at. His own mother and father had been wed for that reason, and their union had always been loveless. "In any case, I'm given to understand that she is rather fond of *another* prince. Elyon Daecar,"

Robbert said, in case Burton wasn't aware. "She stayed with him in his tent during the siege of Harrowmoor. She was a spy back then."

"And a slave before it," Burton said, with a whistle. "Interesting life she's led, this girl. And that blade she has at her hip. The dagger, not the sword. Those glyphs and symbols…well, I could swear I've seen it before. Reminds me of one King Lorin used to wear, way back when I was just a tot. Not the same one, of course…couldn't be…but similar." He scratched at a stubbly jowl. "I did tell you about Lorin, didn't I? How I sailed with him? Those fine words he said to me."

The man was being facetious and rather silly, Robbert knew. There was no subject he liked to drone on about more than his days sailing with King Lorin in his youth. The day Lorin fell to that kraken, Ash Burton, nought but a boy of eight or nine back then, had come down with a fever. But for that sickness, he might have been aboard the doomed vessel, he claimed, and ever since then he'd dedicated his life to hunting the monsters of the deep…and krakens in particular. "Yes, Bloodhound," Robbert said dryly. "I am aware."

The captain grinned knowingly. "Well now…I'm sure there's an anecdote or two I haven't told you. But I'll save those for later. You'd best be off to your princess, and I'd best keep my nose open for them whales. When there are whales about, krakens aren't far behind. And if I get a whiff of one of them slimy devils…"

"You'll race away from it," Robbert said. "No heroics, Captain. We've precious cargo aboard."

The prince spun away, pacing down the stairs from the quarter-deck. The men teemed about him, working the sails and rigging, and down belowdecks they were crammed in even tighter. *They'd best get used to it*, Robbert thought. He still had some fourteen hundred men waiting for him beneath the cliffs, and his three remaining ships - *Bloodbear*, *Blackthorn*, and *Wild Raven* - were not so big as *Hammer* was. *We'll make do*, he told himself. *Huffort gave us no choice in that when he left with half my ships and men.*

Robbert had given Saska his own cabin for the voyage back to his fleet, to be shared with Leshie and Del and whomever else she cared to invite inside. Outside the door she had posted the Butcher and another of her sellswords, a furious little woman called Savage who'd been one of the Surgeon's killers. Robb remembered her from the warcamp outside Aram. Her hair was long and black and braided on one side and shaven and tattooed on the other. "Pretty prince," the Butcher said. "Here to see the pretty princess?"

It struck him as odd that he was being barred from his own cabin. *I made that bed, though*, he thought. And now Saska was the one sleeping in it. The thought made him swallow. "Yes," he only managed. "Is she decent?

When the Butcher grinned, the scars in his face deepened and glistened redly. "She is a very decent lady, yes. So I would not be getting any ideas, pretty prince…pretty as you are."

"And what ideas do you suppose those are?"

"Ideas that will not please Coldheart."

"The King's Wall?" Robbert was no stranger to nicknames, though these…he could barely keep up. Many of them had been bestowed by Leshie, he did not doubt.

"He is always watching," the Butcher said. "So be careful, pretty prince. His wrath is a fearsome thing."

I know. Bernie and Lank can attest to that. "Whatever you're implying would be none of his business. Now step aside. And less of the 'pretty' if you would. I'd prefer you call me handsome."

He smiled and brushed past them, the little woman Savage sneering at him as he went. That one seemed very odd. Through the door he found Saska, Leshie, and Del all sitting cross-legged on the floor in a wide circle playing some sort of game involving a small tin cup and piles of pebbles. He paused at the sight of them. They looked like a band of common youths, all sitting there like that without their armour, and in a fashion they were. Del was no more than a farm-hand, Leshie a serving maid, and Saska, well…she'd grown up in a dozen guises, never knowing her true identity. Joy sat with her, curled into a great black ball. It made him smile. "What are you playing?"

"Pebbles," Del said, grinning up at him. His tangled black hair fell in random strands about his forehead. Del had a rather horsey face to fit his gangly build, but his skills with the bow were improving daily, Robb had heard. "You throw pebbles in the pot. First one to get all their stones in sits out. He's the winner."

"Or she," corrected Leshie.

"Or she," agreed Del. "Then we play on until there's only one left with stones, and they have to do a forfeit for losing."

It was not a complex game, though the addition of the forfeit rather spiced it up. The prince did not miss that the slim youth Jaito was here as well, sitting aside in a chair. He stood as soon as Robbert laid eyes on him, and inclined himself in a bow. "Your Highness."

"Hello, Jaito. Were you playing the game as well?' Robbert liked the archer's good sense of courtesy.

"I was, my lord. I won. So I am sitting out."

That did not surprise him. "You ought to be good in games of accuracy," he said. "Fine archer as you are."

"I am capable, my lord," the youth said, smiling. He had angular features, large brown eyes and a strong inner confidence, Robbert decided. He and Del had shared a tent during their journey from Aram, and had become fast friends along the way. So much so that Jaito had volunteered to join them on their journey north when the rest of Saska's Aramatian escort were relieved of their duties and left behind.

Robbert ran his eyes over the remaining pebbles. "What sort of forfeits do you do?" he asked.

"Depends," Del said. "The others decide." His face went red. "I lost the last game, and they made me quack like a duck. I had to go down the corridor flapping my arms." He glared at Leshie. "Everyone laughed at me."

"Yes, because you looked stupid." Leshie was laughing now; obviously it had been her doing. "I want Savage to play with us, so she'll lose, and I can make her look stupid too. I hate that woman."

There was a story there, Robb did not doubt, though he didn't care to hear it right now. "Saska. A word, if I may."

"Of course." Saska stood, brushing down her skirts. The light and breezy linens she wore only served to give him a better look at her nubile figure, which was just as prepossessing as her face. Her hair had been cleaned and brushed and tumbled down to her shoulders in a flow of deep brown waves, lustrous and thick, and her eyes were bright and pretty as sapphires. Not for the first time, Robbert found himself staring at her a second or two longer than he should. "Shall we talk over here?" Saska offered, moving toward the window. Joy stood and stretched and went to follow, nuzzling at her side as she went.

Robbert walked behind across the spacious cabin, trying not to look any lower than Saska's hips. When they reached the window, she took a perch on the cushioned seat, Joy planting her head in her lap for a good bit of scratching. "So needy," the princess said, smiling as her fingers worked through the dense black fur. A deep purr began to rumble from the starcat's chest, and Robbert marvelled at how calm and beautiful she was, so far removed from that stalking beast that had torn his uncle apart.

The sound of a pebble rattling through tin rang across the room. "That's another one, Saska," Leshie called over. "We're going to continue whether you're here or not…so I'd be quick if I were you."

Saska sighed. "She'll think of some nasty forfeit for me, no doubt," she said. "So…what was it you wanted to talk about?"

Robb leaned forward, to get a better look through the black iron bars that crossed the window. "Captain says there are whales about," he told her. "He picked up a pod of them heading our way. I just thought you should know."

She furrowed her brow and had a closer look out over the water. It brought her very close to him. She smelled of warmth and sunshine. Robbert swallowed. "I don't see any."

"No. No…you wouldn't, not from here." He drew back from her. "They were spotted east, so…"

"Oh. I thought you were looking for them? Why did you peer through the window?"

"I was just looking." *And trying to get closer to you,* he supposed, though he hadn't thought about that consciously. "But you can see the coast now. Look. We should be there in an hour or so."

"So long as those greatwhales don't get us," Saska offered. "Or something else."

"Krakens," Robb said. "Bloodhound says krakens and whales are often seen together. They're enemies, you know. From the time of Galaphan and Izzun."

She knew about that, *obviously*. There was something about her that made Robbert feel like she knew much more than he did about a great many things. Maybe that was Marian Payne's training? He'd heard it said that the spymaster was very stoic and phlegmatic and Saska seemed somewhat similar. *She's like a riddle I can't figure out*, he thought. *A riddle within a riddle, even.* Then again, Leshie had trained under Marian as well and that one was an open book.

"My lady, I wanted to ask as well…"

…about why you're heading north, he was about to say, before the door to the cabin swung open and Sir Ralston Whaleheart ducked inside.

He had to turn sideways to fit through the entrance, massive as his shoulders were, and wore his full plate armour even at sea. There were some thin cuts in the plate where Bernie and Lank had beat his defences during their duel, and some older dints and wounds as well. It was not a polished set, far from gleaming, and in need of a good Forgeborn armourer to set it right, but that didn't matter. His father had always said it wasn't the armour, but the man inside it that counted, and so far as Robbert Lukar saw it there was no man living as formidable as this giant.

Saska looked over from the window seat. "Is something wrong, Rolly?"

The Wall bristled at the name.

"Oh…sorry." Saska made a face and whispered to Robbert, "He doesn't like it when I call him that in company. Especially not around a prince. He thinks it undermines him."

"It is unbecoming," the giant rumbled. He stamped forward, the reinforced wood groaning beneath his feet. *My poor ship. And it thought Bernie was bad.* The only piece of armour the Wall didn't wear was his greathelm, held in the crook of his arm, an ugly bucket with an eyeslit and vents. His head was as large as a boulder, grey and scarred and pitted. The Whaleheart was not a handsome man. "There are reports of a dragon, my lady. I wanted to give you fair warning, should it come close. And suggest it may be time to start putting on your armour."

"A dragon." She shifted on her seat, and Joy jerked to attention. "Where?"

"A distant sighting. Over the cliffs near Eagle's Perch."

"The Perch?" Robbert turned to look back out of the window, but could not see well enough from here. "My fleet is there."

"*Fleet?*" chuckled the Butcher. He was leaning against the door-frame, legs casually crossed at the ankles. "Does three little ships make a fleet?"

"You shouldn't be in here unless invited," Robbert scolded him. "And yes, it does. You only need three ships for a fleet, and I have four. You're standing in the fourth." He turned back to the Wall. "Where is the dragon now?"

"Sir Kester says he lost sight of it beyond the clifftops, Your Highness. It seemed to be coming down to land, though he could not be sure from so far away."

"Thank you, sir." Robbert nodded and strode to the door, passing the others at their game, and brushing right past the Butcher to make it quite clear who was in charge. He did not like the man's insolence and didn't know him well enough yet to enjoy his sense of japery. Saska swore by him, but still, he was struggling to warm to these sellswords. The woman Savage was still at her post outside.

"You," she said.

Robbert whirled on her, aghast. "*You*? I am a prince, likely a king. You do not call me 'you'."

She looked at him flatly. "I heard that little red pervert say my name. What did she say about me?"

Vandar, give me strength. Robbert had no interest in their petty squabbles. "Call me 'you' again and I'll have you thrown overboard." He spun and continued down the corridor, and almost ran right into Lank as he came loping down the stairs.

"Ah, Robb, was just coming to tell you…"

"About the dragon," Robbert said. "The Whaleheart just informed us."

"Droyn saw it from the crow's nest. He's with Bloodhound now, and Gullimer. Apparently there are…"

"Some whales out there, coming our way," Robb finished for him.

Sir Lothar Tunney gave a bemused laugh. "Well, it seems I'm not needed around here anymore. Might as well un-swear you my sword and take a ship to the Telleshis. Join a clan of outcasts…one with some pretty maids, ideally. Might get a year or two of fun before the war finds me."

"Months more like. And you'd only sink on the way. And good luck finding a girl who fancies you, Lank. Women don't tend to swoon over giraffes."

"I was good enough for your sister. She fancied me."

Robbert laughed aloud. The notion of it. "Keep dreaming, Lothar." He strode right past him and out into the daylight, and the fog of noise on deck. The tall knight followed, easily keeping up with that absurd stride of his as Robb fought his way through the sailors and soldiers, some at work, others idle, and returned to the quarterdeck where the captain stood working the wheel and barking commands. The seas were uneasy, but big as *Hammer* was, she drove across the waves smoothly enough. Lord Gullimer was there with Sir Kester Droyn, the former in his essentials of armour and green and red cloak, the latter in light leathers to better scale the rigging. Dryon was a fearless sort, and had happily scampered up to the nest to keep lookout, taking a godsteel dagger with him to improve his sight. His blood-bond granted him particularly good vision, Robb knew.

"I heard about the dragon," the prince said, arriving. "Where was it, Droyn? Point out exactly where you saw it."

The knight of Smallweather obeyed. His finger gestured to the cliffs above his fleet. "Right there, my prince. I lost sight of it when it came down to land."

"And it hasn't been seen since?"

"No, my lord."

Robbert nodded. "How about these greatwhales, Captain?"

"Cruising," Bloodhound said.

"Cruising?" Robb repeated. "Or *closing*?"

"Bit of both. I don't get the sense that they're hostile. Not against us, at least."

"Then who?" asked Lothar.

"Krakens," Robbert said. "Whales hate krakens, Lank."

"Aye," agreed Burton. "That's something old Bloodhound shares with them. Ever since I sailed with King Lorin as a boy." He smiled. "You *have* heard about that, haven't you? My days as a nipper riding the waves with the king?" He saw the look on Robbert's face. "Well, reckon I might have mentioned it once or twice in the prince's hearing, and this lanky knight here too, but not you, Lord Gullimer."

"No," Gullimer admitted. "At least not from the horse's mouth. I have heard second-hand reports, Captain Burton. Your adventures on the high seas are well known. My own captain speaks very highly of you."

"Oh? Truly? Well doesn't that make me mighty proud to hear. If you'll indulge me, I'll be happy to share a tale or ten. We got a bit of time before we reach the fleet, so…"

These were not tales that Robbert needed to hear again. "Sir Kester, keep watching the skies. Report to me if that dragon is seen again."

Robbert returned to the smaller cabin he shared with Lothar, his tall friend striding at his heel. The space was much smaller than his own royal cabin, but he didn't mind that. It was worse for Lothar; the bunk could not fit him properly and Robbert could only imagine how bad it must be for the Whaleheart squeezing himself into a bed. *Wherever he sleeps*, Robbert thought. *Or…does he sleep?* He wasn't sure on that account. Mostly the giant just prowled about the decks by day and night, never resting in his vigilance.

"A week, Robb," Lank said, as they entered the cabin. "A week or even less if we're lucky and we'll be back home. Gods, I can't wait to feel northern soil beneath my feet again."

Bloody soil, Robbert thought, *thick with the dead*. The way they'd heard it, the Marshlands had been bled dry. If they landed there, it would be a wasteland they'd enter, of burned cities and scorched forts and armies of scavenging crows. "We have to get there first, Lothar," he said. "We've hundreds of miles of open sea to cross, and there are some beasts about who might object to our passing. I'll get excited when we're a few hundred *metres* from shore, not *miles*."

"And the princess?" Lothar asked. "Has she said where she wants to go yet? Except *north*."

"No. I was about to ask just now before the King's Wall interrupted."

"Queen's Wall," Lank corrected. "Or…no, *Princess's* Wall? Doesn't sound so good, does it."

"She'll be the Grand Duchess when her grandmother dies," Robbert said. "Not sure Grand Duchess's Wall sounds any better to be honest."

"She might be Grand Duchess already." Lank went to his chest of armour; it was time to dress, now that they were nearing the coast. And especially so if there was a dragon to fight. "Odd that she's going north at all. Do you think they'll accept her as their leader, the Aramatians? I mean, she has the skin tone and the starcat, but all that godsteel and the Tukoran accent….personally I see her more as one of us than one of them, don't you?"

Robb nodded. "The eyes as well." That bright blue was much more common in the north. He crossed to his own chest and opened it up. A fog of mist poured out of it, his armour packed neatly inside. "Bloodhound said the dagger she wears reminded him of one King Lorin used to have. I thought it was familiar as well, the night we met her in Aram. I don't know, Lank…all of this. The Whaleheart being sent to protect her. All this with her grandmother and Godrin, and that rumour that she's Seaborn too. I think she's important, and not just as her grandmother's heir. I don't want to drag her into danger if that's where we're going."

Lothar gave him a long look. "Robb, you can't let her change our course, just because you're smitten."

"I'm not smitten."

"Besotted, then. Infatuated. Maybe you prefer one of those words."

"Use whatever word you like, that's not what this is about."

"Then what is it about? *She* joined *us*, remember, and heir of Aramatia or not, *you're* the Crown Prince of Tukor and maybe even our king. You have a responsibility to sail home and help defend the north. We can't change course on her account, no matter who she is." Lothar bent down to pick up a shoulder pauldron. "And all this cloak-and-dagger stuff isn't helping. You need to sit her down and get the truth from her, Robb. You're a king. Our king. You can't be letting a woman dictate to you."

She isn't dictating to me, Robbert wanted to protest, but he had no taste for that fight right now. "There's time," is all he said. "Stop rushing me, Lank. Not everyone walks as quickly as you."

Robbert finished dressing in silence, then returned to the decks to watch the cliffs grow high above him. Before long Bloodhound was barking his orders from the helm, and the crew were reefing and relaxing the sails, driving the prow of *Hammer* safely toward its stone jetty. Robbert was most relieved to see that the other three ships of his fleet were still intact and, blessedly, not burning.

He joined Lord Gullimer on the forecastle deck, the apple lord standing at the very front of the ship next to *Hammer's* powerful ram forged in the likeness of her namesake. "A sad sight," the lord intoned, looking across the paltry armada. His cloak flapped listlessly, as though to match his mood. "To think we set out from Tukor with almost twenty times the number." He sighed. "Such is war, alas. One campaign can begin with great promise, and end in sour defeat. Oft as not luck and leadership are the deciding factors, and I fear we've been miserly provisioned in both."

Robbert hoped he was referring to his uncle's leadership, and not his own. "We still have strength enough to make a difference, Wilson. It only takes one blade, my father used to say. History has taught us that."

It was said in the north that the War of the Continents ended by the edge of Amron Daecar's sword. One man. One duel. One good strike to slay the dragon Vallath and cripple the prince Dulian, and then the mercy to spare his life. It was not as simple as that, of course. There were a hundred events that needed to occur for that war to end, as with any war, but history did have the habit of distilling things down into important moments, and that one at the Burning Rock was the pivot that people pointed to when they spoke of the end of the war, for right or wrong.

And this one? Robbert wondered. *How will this one end?* Not by the edge of his own blade, he knew that much. All his life he'd fancied himself a great warrior in the making, a dragonslayer-to-be like his father and grandfather before him, but those dreams had been dashed the day Sir Wenfry Gershan stabbed out his eye. *I'll never be a great hero*, he thought, dourly. He would be capable, yes, but capable was not enough anymore. It left a bitter taste in his mouth to know he would never rise to such heights.

The ship was fast approaching the wharf, where men stood waiting to catch the ropes and tie them to the iron posts hammered into the stone. Others were preparing to slide across the gangplanks so that they could disembark from *Hammer's* decks. Beyond, the stony beach bustled with shelters and tents, and a small field hospital had been set up as well. Most of the sick had come from *Wild Raven* after their long days becalmed at sea. Lord Gullimer's host would add some more, Robbert knew, though he was not intending to wait upon their convalescence.

That appeared to be on Gullimer's mind as well. "How long do you expect to stay?"

"A day, two at most." The war was calling him, and he must join it as soon as he could. "If we can sail on the morning tide, we will."

There was a lot of shouting going on around them, as soldiers left the beach and the decks of their moored ships to gather about at the prince's return. Men were pouring up from the bowels of *Hammer* as well, more than Robbert would have let himself believe once upon a time. Before this campaign, he'd had scant experience of ships, and it was always a wonder to him how many men could fit belowdecks. Any time he went down to visit them, he would see how tightly packed they were, down in their cramped quarters with their bunks piled one atop another. And when they poured up the steps, they were like ants crawling from their hill, boiling out in a great long stream of stinking, ragged men.

My army, he thought.

The ship was bumping up against the jetty, and the gangplanks were being slid into place. Robbert remained at the forecastle deck for a moment, scanning for his captains below. He could not see Bernie down there, but he did sight Sir Colyn Rowley, who had charge of *Wild Raven*, and Sir Gregory Jarvis as well, the knight in command of *Blackthorn*. Both were pushing forward through the men on the docks, as Sir Lothar strode down to greet them. Robbert still did not move. They would come to him, he knew.

They bustled forth almost at once, Lank waving men aside to let them pass. Across the decks, Lord Gullimer's men were streaming off, eager to feel firm ground beneath their feet. The sellswords had all gathered around Saska and the Whaleheart, who was giving an address, while Captain Burton remained at the wheel, bellowing out this order and that. Through all that noise and ruckus, the three knights arrived. Sir Colyn and Sir Gregory both inclined themselves into bows. "Your Highness, we praise Tukor for your safe return," Rowley said.

"Praise Bloodhound," Robbert replied. He wasn't sure what Tukor had to do with it. "What news, Sir Colyn? Is *Wild Raven* ready to sail?"

"She will be, my prince. Give her one more night and she'll be ready to spread her wings."

Black wings, Robb thought. *Wild Raven* was made from the timber of the Darkwood like all the Swallow ships.

Sir Gregory looked over Gullimer's men. "Lots of apples, but no *Orchard*," he noted.

"We had to leave her behind." The damage had been too severe, and it would have taken long days to set her right. It had been a great sadness to Lord Gullimer to abandon his ship, but their need for haste had not given them a choice. "And *Harvest*," Robbert added. "She foundered near the shore." He had a pressing question on his lips. His eyes moved to the top of the cliffs and he asked it. "We saw a dragon. Has there been word of it?"

"Sir Bernard is up there now, with some others," Gregory said. "I came down to report to you when we saw the ship approach."

"And? Is this beast not hostile?"

"No. It is a smaller dragon, my lord. And bearing three souls. Two women and a man. They landed some distance from us, and appear to be waiting. Westermont is keeping watch."

Robbert was confused. "Waiting? For who? Me?" He looked over. Saska appeared to be learning the same news, and a smile was rising on her lips. *She knows who they are*, he realised. If that were so, she'd made no mention of having a dragonrider in her party. *Gods. This girl and all her secrets.* "Pray excuse me." He stepped across the decks to join her. "My lady, a word." He took her arm and ushered her away from the others, Lank's words ringing in his head. "Saska, no more secrets. It's time you told me the truth. The full truth, and…"

And she kissed him. The connection lasted but a short moment, but it was electric. Robbert felt a giddy wave of excitement spread through his body as his lips met hers, soft and warm. Then Saska drew back, just as quick. "Sorry," she said. "That wasn't my doing."

Robbert frowned. His mind was all ablur. "Not your doing? I don't…"

"Leshie. I lost the game, after you left. So…"

Oh. The truth came down on him like a sack of rotten spuds. "That was a…" He glimpsed Leshie watching from across the decks, a broad grin on her freckly little face. "That was your forfeit?"

"But a good one," Saska said, quickly. "Much better than quacking like a duck."

"Yes." Robbert Lukar felt like the biggest fool in the world all of a sudden. His elation had shrivelled to bitter disappointment, and a shade of red was climbing his neck. Saska saw and her eyes turned pitying and that only made it all the worse.

"Robbert, I…"

"It's fine." He raised a hand. Others were looking, he just knew it. He needed to push right past this and forget it ever happened. *I'm a king, Lank's right. A king does not blush.* "This dragon…I'm told it's bearing three passengers." He spoke in a voice as rigid as an old tree stump. "Do you know them, or…"

"It was nice, you know," Saska said.

Robbert met her eyes. He had been looking away all the while.

"It was, Robbert. "Forfeit or no, I…"

He didn't want to talk about it. "The dragon," he prompted. "Do you know the riders?"

A moment passed as she looked at him. Then she nodded and said, "The two women. The man…I'm not sure, but…" She reached out and took his hand, squeezing, brushing all that awkwardness aside. "Come, Robb. There's someone I want you to meet."

47

Elyon

In the cold grey morning light, he watched them come. Streams of people, snaking up through the snowy city, from White Shadow to Many Markets to the Sentinels and the Marble Steps, through the squares and up the stairs and past the gates and across the bridges, ushered along by an army of soldiers many hundreds strong.

It was a sight to warm Elyon Daecar's heart despite the deep chill in the air. "How many have gone through the tunnels so far?" he asked Lord Trillion Morwood, as they stood on the high palace balcony overlooking the city of Ilithor.

"Some thousands," Morwood told him. "We started only three days ago, but we have not lacked for volunteers, as you can see. We have worked hard to make the passages safe, Prince Elyon. I've had men going back and forward for a fortnight, carrying provisions. Every man, woman, and child is being told to take as much food as they can."

Elyon nodded. "Are you prioritising the Tukorans?"

"No. Tukoran and Vandarian alike are being allowed through. Princess Amilia decreed it so."

Elyon raised a brow. "She's helping?"

Morwood had a fatherly smile on his lips, a proud smile. "She is, I am glad to report. She goes among the people and helps to give them strength and succour. There is a certain power that women like Amilia possess. Their beauty and radiance can be inspiring. Many of the people have chosen to journey into the mountain on account of her word alone, and much of that has to do with you, I think."

"Me?" Elyon asked.

"I do believe so, yes. She has been drinking less and doing more ever since you flew together to Thalan. I daresay your actions have helped inspire *her*, good prince. There is no one in the realm who is doing more than you."

Elyon appreciated that. "My thanks, Trillion. That is kind of you to say."

"Not at all. I do not see truth as kindness, Prince Elyon. Only truth." He smiled. "Did you rest well?"

"Well enough," Elyon lied. He and Walter Selleck had arrived long past midnight when the city was sleeping, and had been ushered straight to private bedchambers by the palace steward and his guards. He had slept perhaps four hours before rising at dawn, stiff, tired, and dreading the day to come. Taxing as yesterday's flight had been, today would be longer, harder, and most importantly, colder. He looked out over the city again. "How long has the snow been falling, Trillion?" It was not so the last time he was here.

Morwood looked out in consternation. "Ah. The *snow*. Yes. It reached us several days ago. People are saying it heralds some great doom, this snowfall in summer. It has all the city frightened."

"Good. Use it. The more people who flee in fear to the refuge the better."

The Watch Commander nodded. "As you say. We have criers out there, calling out of the Dread's return, but too many refuse to believe it. They trust their eyes, Elyon, and their eyes see the snow. That at least we can use."

Thousands, Elyon mused. Thousands in three days was a good start, but how many were there here? How many Ilithorans and smallfolk from across Tukor? How many Vandarian refugees camped outside the city walls? He could see the vastness of their numbers grouping down there in the valley. If the Dread should come again, it would be a slaughter, and there was no knowing when that might be.

"What of Sir Mallister? How has he taken to his new role?"

"Very well, I am reliably told. He has some three dozen under his command now. They're keeping a tight watch on the peaks and passes."

It sounded much like a new order, Elyon thought. He wondered what his Shadowknight brother would make of that. "Have there been any attacks?"

"On the refuge? No. But Mallister and his men have gone out on hunts, I know. Mountain wolves, mostly, great white ones I'm told. There is a large pack of them up there that howl through the night. But there are worse things too. I understand there are fears of a greatbat lair, but as to that, ah…" Lord Morwood broke off as Walter Selleck came stepping through the hall to join them, accompanied by a pair of palace guards. "You must be Walter," Trillion Morwood said. "A pleasure to meet you."

"And you, my lord." Walter bustled forward.

"Did you sleep well?"

"Oh yes, very well thank you. The featherbed made quite the change from King's Point, I must say." He chuckled. "What do you stuff in your pillows around here? Goose down, is it?"

"The Aramatian Wanderer," Morwood said, smiling. "Finest down in all the world." He looked him up and down, most amused. "Are you sure you have enough layers on, Walter?"

The two soldiers behind were grinning, and rightly, because Walter Selleck cut a frankly ridiculous figure. He wore so many layers of wool and fur he looked positively round. "If you're offering to give me that fine cloak of yours, I'm not going to say no."

Morwood gave a laugh. "Very droll, Walter. Yes, I'd heard that about you."

"I'm glad to hear my reputation precedes me." Walter turned to Elyon. "Are you ready for round two, good prince?"

"No. But we'd best get going anyway. Come, let's get you strapped up."

The soldiers were dismissed, snickering, leaving only Morwood there to observe as Elyon fixed Walter Selleck into place. It required a slight loosening of the straps given Walter's absurd garb, but Elyon supposed the man knew what he was doing, having ventured into the Icewilds not once, but twice before.

"Oh. I should say. We had word from Rustbridge. It seems that Borrus Kanabar has returned, if you'll believe it."

Elyon stopped in his work and looked at Morwood. "*Borrus*? He's back?"

"So we hear. And Lord of the Riverlands and Warden of the East now as well."

Elyon took a moment to digest that. "How long has he been there? In Rustbridge?"

"On that I could not say. Word came from a rider sent up from the Undercloak, so I would imagine it's been a while now."

Elyon didn't like the sound of that. Borrus would have taken charge, no doubt, and he was not a man to sit idle for long. *He'll want vengeance for his father. And Ven will try to goad him out.* "But no word yet of battle?" he asked Morwood.

"Not that we've heard."

That didn't mean much. Not in this crow-less kingdom. Elyon felt a new urgency pulsing through his veins. *I've been gone too long*, he fretted. For all he knew, there was battle to both the east and west and here he was, flying about with a scruffy old scribe dealing in hope and hunches.

"We'd best go, Trillion. Express my apologies to the princess for not seeing her on this visit. I will return as soon as I can. And please, hasten as many people into the tunnels as possible. Tell them that people are freezing to death in Thalan, and it won't be long before that happens here."

"I will do as you say, Prince Elyon. Be safe up there, and Tukor be with you." He gave a bow.

Elyon nodded back, then waddled with Walter to the edge of the balcony to give themselves room to take off. On his back he bore his satchel bag, the Eye of Rasalan wrapped up safely within, alongside Walter's things. He drew the Windblade from its sheath and pointed it skyward. "Ready?" he asked, lamenting that it was Walter, and not Amilia, for the hundredth time. *Her hair smelled nice*, he thought. Walter's scraggly dome gave off a sour odour that was much less pleasant, and he did not much like the musty smell that came off his clothes either. The winds would help with that, and the cold as well. *My nostrils will be frozen shut soon enough, and I won't have to endure it.* Would that Walter's lips might freeze as well. The man did like to chat.

"I'm ready, yes. What pace will you set today?"

"A quick one. This cold could kill us, Walter. We may have to stop and find shelter if it gets too bad."

"I know what a killing cold is, my prince. I'm not wearing all this fur to be fashionable."

The notion of Walter Selleck doing anything to be fashionable was preposterous. Aside from city strays and alleyway bums, Elyon had never known anyone to dress so poorly. He smiled, letting out a bit more light from his soul, as Ilith had commanded. Walter at the least was an amusing fellow. Smiling came easily in his company.

"Hold tight," Elyon said. "I'm going to start quickly and gain some speed. And think *positive* thoughts, Walter. Channel your luck into our safe passing."

"And the finding of this tower," the man added. "I know."

Elyon nodded. The winds stirred, thickened, strengthened, and into the skies they shot, fired like a bolt from a ballista, straight and true. A hundred metres, two, three, and the city was beneath them. *The White City*, he thought, as they soared toward the mountain peaks that enclosed it, making for the northeast. It was named that for the colour of the stone. Today it might have been for the snow.

He wondered how far south they'd go. Already half the north was covered in a white shroud, and the rest of it was still battling the rains, drowning beneath the deluge that seemed never to cease. In King's Point the whole coast had turned into a soggy mire, and the broken river was fat and swollen, rushing wildly into the Red Sea. The city had become a grim place. A dark place. And more so than before. *Ever since my father left*, he thought. *Since Lythian took charge and the vultures began to circle.*

He had not stayed long in the city. But it took him only moments to see that Lythian was not himself. He had grown as grim as that ruin, and paranoid, with eyes that saw a shadow around every corner, and ears that heard the sound of knives sharpening in the dark. Lythian had not been the same since he went to Agarath, in truth, but now he'd grown truly dour. It was the blade, Elyon knew. It was the rain and the ruin and the ragged army that his father had left him, starved and bored and resentful. Lythian was a dragonlover, they said, and a traitor. Word of what he'd done in the south had spread and men were deserting by the day, abandoning his command. Sir Ralf had confided that many of the men still stood in support of the First Blade, but Lythian seemed unable to see it. Day by day, a dark shroud enveloped that ruin, as though the Dread had cursed it with his coming, and Lythian was stuck at the heart of it.

Elyon feared for his friend. He feared for what would become of him the longer he lingered there.

Below them, the lands had turned white from horizon to horizon. Only here and there were places that the snowfall had not reached. Towns rose up from the white wilderness and roads had been covered over and lost. The rivers had started to freeze, as the Izzun had further east. The cold was reaching down into Elyon's bones, but he flew on, and on, driving himself as fast as he could bear. So fast and so loud that even Walter could not speak, his words lost to the roar of the winds.

After several hours, Elyon sighted the great city of Ethior below, sitting on the southern banks of the Clearwater Run where it curved in a great snaking bend, frozen stiff as a corpse. There, upon its own hill as though mimicking the greathouse keeps in Varinar, stood Keep Kastor, soaring above the river and the city spread beneath it. Elyon had never visited. He had never seen the keep up close, or walked through the streets of the city. No doubt Ethior was beautiful; he had heard it was so. An ancient city, founded by Ilith's great-grandson Ethin, it had once been a great light in the north of Tukor. But all the same Elyon scowled to see it, thinking only of the Kastors and their perversions, thinking of Saska, who had suffered there, thinking of those lash scars on her back inflicted by Lord Modrik and his cruel son Cedrik. He had his own scars now to match her, ten deep cuts that had almost killed him. For killing Sir Griffin, but in truth that was her. *She got me these scars*, he thought. *She turned my back to a twin of her own, and I'd have done it again for her, a thousand times again…*

He wondered where she was now. He wondered what had come of her. How many times had he wondered that? How many times had he told himself he would fly south to find her? *Always once more*, he thought.

Soon Ethior was fading into the distance behind them, and so too all thoughts of Saska. Elyon set his mind forward, to his quarry. Ahead, the great open sea of Vandar's Mercy spread forth toward the Rasalanian coast. It was frozen over, Elyon saw. The last time he was here with Amilia, he had seen some floes and bergs jostling in the restless water, but now they had grouped and gathered and formed a great plain of unbroken blue ice that bridged the two northern kingdoms. *Gods*, he thought, astonished. Even in the depths of the cruelest winter the cold did not grip like this.

He slowed a little, the winds quietening, so he could speak. "How are you, Walter?" he called. "Not dead yet, I hope?" The man had been rather too quiet for his liking.

Walter twisted his neck with some effort. There was frost forming in his patchy beard, and tiny icicles dangling from his eyelashes. "I should have put on another layer," he said, with a wry smile. His lips were going blue. "Perhaps we ought to land and build a fire to warm up?"

Elyon would sooner push through if they could. At least cross the Mercy first, and find a fire already burning. Gathering firewood and trying to start one in this weather would be no easy task. "Can you hold on a little longer? If we make it to Thalan, we can stop there for a short while. It would be sensible to hear tidings before we continue north."

Walter gave no complaint to that, and seemed in no state for a lengthy discussion. That served Elyon just fine. He had left Thalan with a promise from King Sevrin that he would make haste for the Tower of Rasalan at once, but he would sooner find out for sure before braving those frozen skies. "Hold on, then. The winds are with us, Walter. They should speed us hence."

It was an hour and a half later before Thalan unveiled itself, appearing from that wintry white shroud much as it had the last time. It had that same cursed sense about it as King's Point, touched by darkness, befouled the day Eldur came. About the squares and streets the snow had continued to climb, and now much of the city was lost beneath it. Ship masts and spires and towers alike poked out from the great high drifts, and deep trenches had been cut and shovelled to permit passage down certain streets. Others were snowed under, the houses lining them too, and Elyon wondered how many dead lay within. *When first the Fire Father came thousands were lost beneath the rubble. Now it is snow that entombs them.*

He landed outside the palace, just as he had before. A half dozen men sat shivering around their fire, breath misting, rubbing their hands. "We need fire, food, and to speak with the man in charge," Elyon called, as he unstrapped Walter from his chest with stiff and clumsy fingers. "Quickly. Who commands now King Sevrin has left?"

One of the guards stood, a big bearded Buckland with the stag and bear sigil. "Princess Cristin has that honour."

"Take us to her," Elyon commanded.

The princess was to be found in her own private solar, a bush-haired old rodent of a woman knitting by the warmth of the fire. She wore heaps of robes in many colours, her spindly fingers poking from extravagantly dagged sleeves, working the needle skilfully, *click click click*.

"My lady, you have a visitor," the Buckland man said.

"Two of them, it looks like." She peered at them through small dark eyes. "Who are you?"

Elyon opened his mouth.

"No, don't tell me, I know who you are." She gave a cackle and waved them over. "Come, share my fire. You must be cold. You *look* cold. And handsome as they say, that too, oh yes. The spit of your father. Devrin must be wary of you." She laughed again.

616

Elyon stepped over to join her. "Your Highness." He bowed his head.

She bowed hers, though didn't stand. "Your Highness. There, courtesies done." Her eyes flitted to Walter. "And you must be the lucky one. Did it keep the dragons away, that luck of yours?" She waved a hand to dismiss the Buckland man and went right on. "Well you must have. You're here, aren't you? And dragons don't like the cold. Even that *big* one…he's not going to want to come up here, else his fires will go out, and when a dragon's fire goes out, it *dies*, no matter how big." She reached to a side table and took up a cup of spiced wine. "Will you have a cup? I know you're flying, but one won't hurt. Or two or three. Have you ever flown drunk, Elyon Daecar? Probably not. You're very sensible, I hear. Now, anyway. You used to be a hoot, but no longer. But times are different, isn't that so? We change to match the times, yes we do."

This woman was clearly mad. Amilia had not been lying. "I will have a cup, thank you."

She clipped a finger, and a servant appeared from nowhere. The wine was served. It was warm and nicely spiced, just what Elyon needed to thaw. The room was much the same, warm and spiced with quirky furniture from all across the world; rich rugs from Pisek, tapestries from Vandar, a large bed of Agarathi ashwood, celestial crafts from the Islands of the Moon. The shelves were cluttered with ornaments and stacks of old books, and above the fireplace was painted a great golden tree, filling all the wall, branching with hundreds, even thousands of names.

Cristin saw Elyon admiring it. "You like my tree, do you? Well, not mine really. I didn't commission it, but it's mine now that I'm living here. *Finally*. Ah, it's been a long wait, but I'm here now, aren't I? And so are *you*."

Elyon frowned at her. She was truly an oddity and this room matched her well. He turned his eyes to regard the mural. "The line of Thala," he said.

"What else? Yes, that's our house. My name is up there somewhere at the top. Right next to my brother's." She twisted in her chair and pointed. "That's him, with the golden wreath painted around his name. They came and added that only days ago; had to climb a ladder to get up there. Marks him as king, that wreath. There above him, that's Devrin and Milessa. They're first and second in line. I'm third, and how about that? Me. Third in line to the throne." She laughed manically.

"That is…quite something, my lady."

"You think so? Quite something. Something *more* would be if I *became* queen of this ruin, and who knows…maybe I will. Or already *am*."

Elyon furrowed his brow.

"You're confused. Let me explain. I'm third in line. My brother is king and he's gone off up into those frozen wastes with his son and heir, the fools. Well you've seen the city, Elyon. You've seen how bad it's become. How frightful must it be *up there*? It makes you wonder, doesn't it? I love them both, and gods forbid anything has happened, but let us not be naive. Both of them might already be dead."

"I do hope not, my lady."

"That would make Milessa queen," the woman babbled on. "She's a pretty enough girl, like her brother, but a bit of a lackwit I'm afraid. She wouldn't want it, the crown. Oh no. And no one would want to see *her* wearing it either. So it would go to me. Me. Queen." She cackled again and her eyes glittered madly. "Do you think they'd want that? Me being queen?"

No, Elyon thought. "I could not say, my lady," he said.

"Or *will* not say. You're too polite for that. Of course they wouldn't. A mad old shrew like me! Oh no. Oh no."

Elyon stared at her. He could not tell if she was being serious or not. "My lady, how long ago did the king and the prince depart? They told me they would do so the day I left."

"And they did. Right away. Devrin's a positive chap, isn't he? I'm sure you saw that. He had his old man mustered to go in a jiffy, and off they went into that frozen wasteland to die." She drank her wine. A bit dribbled down her long pointed chin, but she did not wipe it off or seem to care. "Gods forbid. No, they'll be fine, I'm sure. Sparky as Devrin is, Sevrin's much more staid. He'll have them turned back if he thinks they're in trouble. How do you expect to find them? In this weather?"

"It's the Tower of Rasalan we need to find," Elyon said.

She cawed like a crow. "You think they'll be there already? Good gods no. It's four hundred miles. Not much for you, I'm sure, but on horseback that can take a while, and in this cold…even the thorough-breds are going to struggle. They may be light and graceful beasts, but they can't walk on snow so far as I'm aware."

That was not what Elyon wanted to hear. "Prince Devrin told me a week would be enough. It's been longer, my lady. Are you certain…"

"Certain? Do I look like the sort of person who's certain about anything? Maybe they're there. Maybe not. Maybe they've turned back. Maybe they're dead." She shrugged her bony shoulders, and her bush of wild greying hair bobbed up and down. Elyon half expected some birds to come flapping out of it. "But you'll find out, won't you? That's why you're here. To fly up there and give them the Eye."

He nodded. "Yes. We've come a long way, and…"

"And far enough, maybe? I'm Sevrin's sister, and I've got the same blood as he does. Well, maybe not *all* the same. There was always a rumour that Sevrin was Godrin's son, same as Hadrin, but no one really believed it. Godrin would never have betrayed his brother Tayrin. He was our father, Sevrin and me. Well, *me*, certainly. Sevrin…" She shrugged. "Mayhaps he's my cousin and not

618

my brother, but it all comes down to the same thing in the end, doesn't it? We're all much alike as you can see. Not a comely flock, no…well, Devrin's handsome enough and that lackwit sister of his too, but only because their mother was a beauty. Not as beautiful as *your* mother, though…no, who was? Ah…the Lady Kessia," she swooned. "Was there ever a finer-looking woman? I hear your little sister's much the spit of her, as you're the spit of your father, is that right?"

"It is said."

"Amilia's a real beauty too. *The Jewel of Tukor.* Oh, she is some looker. And was to wed your brother, I know, until…well, best not get into that." She slurped more wine. "But you're still here, and quite the hero. Is she in love with you, do you think?"

The question took him quite off guard. "Amilia? No. Of course not. She sees me as a brother."

"You're certain? Quite certain?" She leaned forward, peering at him. "Hmmmm, I'm not so sure, but let's hope you're right for Devrin's sake. He is quite taken with her, you know."

Elyon had noticed that when last they were here. "Yes, I…"

"Anyway, what was I saying?" the mad woman barrelled on. "Far enough, yes…maybe you've come far enough? If you've got the Eye of Rasalan with you, maybe *I* can see through it? I've got some experience with balls and orbs, you know." She cackled again. "No, truly…I have seen it once or twice when Uncle Godrin showed me. I was just a little girl back then, but he said some curious things. 'One day you'll help shape the future, sweet Cristin,' he told me. And I *was* sweet back then. A sweet girl, always smiling. I've turned sour now, and strange, I'm told. Do you find me strange, Elyon Daecar?"

He did not know what to say to that. Sidestepping the question seemed best. "My lady. Do you know what your uncle meant, when he said that?"

"That I'd help shape the future?" She smiled at him queerly, as though she knew something he did not. "Well…my uncle was always terribly cryptic, Elyon. Perhaps he knew I would become queen. That would be enough to shape the future, would it not? Or something much more simple than that. When you give a starving child some food, and they live, and go on to do great things, you shape the future. When you stop someone before they commit great evil, you shape the future. A gift can shape the future, would you not say?"

He was not sure what she meant. "A gift, my lady?"

"A gift, yes. If I gifted you a great weapon for you to slay your enemies, that would shape the future. If I gifted you knowledge, that would too. It is power, they say, the knowing of things. *Words* are power. And goodness, my uncle liked words. Words and riddles and puzzles and mysteries. Everything he saw in the Eye." She looked at Elyon for a good long while, reflecting on something, some old memory. She seemed very sad all of a sudden. Then she broke out of it and waved a hand. "So, the Eye. Come then, let's see it." She pointed to a small table set before her. "Right there will do."

Elyon saw no reason to refuse her, and nor did he have that right. Her name was on that great golden tree, after all, and Thala's blood ran richly through her veins. He motioned to Walter to open the bag on his back, and the scruffy scribe did as bidden, drawing it from its cloth wrappings inside and placing it on the table before her. Her dark eyes reflected its gold and blue glow, swirling within the orb. Veins of golden light spread from the thin black pupil, shut tight to Elyon's eyes, and to Walter's as well, but to her?

Elyon watched, curious. He thought of those words Godrin told her. Was she lying about them? Misremembering? Was that just the sort of thing a kindly old uncle would say to a sweet young niece, to inspire and nurture her? *One day you'll help shape the future.* Maybe he was talking about the Eye. And this moment. Perhaps she would see something to show the way?

Silence enrobed the chamber. The crone princess stared long and true at the orb, smiling in that odd way of hers, stroking a hand across its surface. Her gaze moved here and there as though following the swirls of blue and golden light, admiring their languid motion. Her eyes narrowed and her weaselly face scrunched up, and it seemed to Elyon that she was holding her breath and, frankly, trying too hard.

"My lady, if I may."

"You may *not*. Be silent, Elyon Daecar. I am trying to concentrate." She glared up at him, then returned her eyes to the pupil, willing it to open. Elyon's hope faded. He had the distinct sense that he was wasting his time. At last the woman gave out a whooshing breath and leaned back, irritated. "Stupid thing. It's broken. Where have you been keeping it? Down in some dusty old vault, I'm told. Well, you've ruined it. Oh, the colours shift prettily enough, but that pupil's closed, and closed for good. Rasalan wants no further part of this. We're on our own, yes we are."

Elyon wouldn't believe it. "Your brother may have better fortune," he said. *Or cousin. That about Godrin being his sire…*

"He will try, of course. Sevrin always tries hard, not like me. That's if you find him."

"We will." Elyon gestured for Walter to take back the Eye of Rasalan. *Just the words of a kind uncle*, he decided. The woman would be no help to him. He waited for Walter to return the Eye into the bag, and then inclined himself into a bow. "We will be on our way, Your Highness. Thank you for the wine and the warmth."

"You're going already?"

"Yes. There are hours of daylight left, and I would prefer to make haste." He dipped his chin and stepped toward the door, Walter following.

"Wait," Cristin said.

Elyon stopped, sighing, and turned. "Yes, my lady?"

"I haven't yet given you your *gift*." She clipped her fingers and her servant materialised from an alcove. Cristin whispered something in the man's ear, and he slipped away once more, returning a moment later with a small wooden box in his hands. "Come," the crone said, waving Elyon over. "For you, my *handsome prince*. The gift is inside."

Elyon moved forward, intrigued. He took the box, wondering if this was just another part of her theatrics. *A gift can shape the future*, he thought. The box was plain, scratched, its hinges starting to rust. They creaked shrilly as Elyon opened the lid and looked within. *A scroll?* He reached in and took it out. It was old, sealed, dusty. The seal was the king's. "What is this?" he whispered.

"A warhammer. What do you think it is? You have eyes, don't you?"

"I meant…" He turned it over between his fingers. The seal had not been broken. There was no indication that it was addressed to him. "It's for me?"

"Yes."

"From…"

"My uncle Godrin," she said.

"Godrin? But…"

"But he's dead. I know. A while ago now. Did you ever meet him?"

Elyon shook his head. "I never had the pleasure," he murmured, looking at the scroll.

"A pleasure it would have been…or a pain. My sweet old uncle was like that. Some men could not abide his riddles." She drank her wine. "He said some curious things to me, as I told you. I'd help shape the future. That was one. Another was that one day I'd live in this very chamber, right here in the palace. I'd live here and a *handsome prince* would come, swooping from the skies. Well…you can imagine how that made a little girl feel. A handsome prince? Coming for me? Goodness, what could be more exciting? Trouble was, I didn't live in the palace back then. So I went to my father…the gods know how many times I went to him…and asked if we could come live here too, so I could be here in this bedchamber for when my handsome prince arrived, but no…he would never have it. 'My brother is the king, not me,' he would say. He was bitter about that, being the younger brother, so he'd had us moved out of the city and over to Bleakrock instead. Dismal place. Well, it's in the name, isn't it? Have you ever been? Well good, don't bother. It's drear and cold and always wet. I hated it, and for a time I hated my father for making me live there. 'There's a handsome prince coming for me,' I'd tell him. 'But only to the palace. I *have* to live in the palace'.

"Well, he didn't care for that. Nonsense, he called it. More lies from his older brother. He saw me for what I was, I suppose. Just an ugly little girl, with a weasel face and frizzy hair, and not all that important. Mayhaps he'd have made me a good pairing when I grew older, but no, I wanted this prince, this handsome prince who'd fly to my bedchamber. It was a dream for me, and became an obsession. So much so that one day I ran away. I couldn't cope anymore. Years had passed since my uncle's promise, and I fretted every night in my bed, in that horrid keep that overlooked the bleak grey sea, that this prince was coming and I wasn't there. I *had* to be there. I *had* to.

"So I ran away. It took me almost a week to get here, and when I arrived, my old uncle Godrin put his hands on my shoulders and said, 'Not yet, sweet Cristin. One day you'll live here, in this room in the palace, but not yet. Be patient. This prince will come. He will fly to the city to meet you, and when he does, you must give him this. Can you do this for me, sweet girl? Will you be patient, and wait for him? And keep our little secret?'"

Elyon looked at the poor woman, frowning sympathetically. It was not a sweet tale, the way she told it. "That was cruel of him," he said. "To give you that false hope."

"Ah. Well…some might say. And me being such an ugly little girl. He did not intend it like that, no, but…" Her smile went sad. "But you're here now. At last. Not in the way I'd hoped, but…" She nodded to the scroll. "I never looked. He told me not to, so I never did. He must have known you would come. My uncle…they say only Thala saw more clearly through the Eye than he did. So you read that note, Elyon Daecar. Read it and fulfil a dead man's riddle, and leave this sour old woman to rest."

Elyon did as she bid him. He broke the seal, unrolled the scroll, and read, running his eyes down the dead king's words.

In Godrin's graceful script was written a story. A love story, an adventure story, a story of shipwrecks and slavery and sacrifice. A story about a sister and a king, a nephew and a princess…a story about a girl in silver and blue.

48

Ranulf

"Feeling better, Ranulf?" the princess asked, as he stepped around the rock to rejoin her.

He brushed himself down and smiled wanly. "Yes, thank you, my lady. It must have been something I ate."

Talasha Taan arched a sleek, black eyebrow. "Something you ate? Yes. It had nothing to do with the *flight*, of course." She smiled at him. "I did not take you for a braggart, Ranulf Shackton. Why not admit to this failing? You do not have the stomach for dragonflight, there is no shame in it."

Ranulf wiped away a bit of spittle from his chin with the back of his dusty sleeve. "I am a good friend to failure, my lady. It is failure that makes a man. Or woman, as the case may be."

"Yet you still contend that it was something you ate that brought on this sudden sickness?"

"Of course. Something I ate, most certainly." He grinned playfully. His stomach had been doing somersaults ever since they landed and it had taken his head a good long while to stop from spinning as well. It was, of course, the flight that had done it. He knew it, she knew it, but his pride demanded he spin the lie. *I am the famed adventurer Ranulf Shackton*, he told himself. *I have scaled the highest peaks and sailed the wildest seas. I ought not be unmanned by a short hundred-mile flight.*

"Well, just make sure to watch what you eat from now on," the princess said, gamely playing along. "We have a much longer flight to make, and cannot be stopping every five minutes so you can bring up your breakfast and lunch."

And dinner. The flight would be long enough to include all three meals, he judged. It might even take days. A long flight, a dangerous one, and an increasingly *cold* one too. "I will keep to a diet of fresh fruit and nuts, my lady," he said. "They have always agreed with me." He was not certain how long he could keep up this charade before he began to annoy her, but the princess seemed a good sport when it came to his jests. He had not known her long, but in their short days together she had supplied him with an ample allowance of laughter and smiles to accompany his silly japes.

As if she needed to be any more delightful. Hers was an exquisite beauty, exotic and rich and wild, yet she more than matched it with her wit and charm. *And that laugh. Gods. Has there ever been a sweeter sound?* It was small wonder the Varin Knight Lythian Lindar had fallen in love with her. *Ah, poor Lythian. He does so struggle in that cold wet ruin of his.*

"Saska struggled with her first flight as well, you know," Talasha said. "Well, perhaps struggled is not the right word. Certainly not like *you.* She became somewhat queasy when we landed, though quickly settled after a few deep breaths. And I did subject her to rather more acrobatics. *Our* flight was terribly dull."

"Not to me, my lady. One always remembers their first."

She tipped her head back and laughed. "Too true. First flight. First fornication. I do hope your first coupling with a woman was better for you, Ranulf Shackton. Or did you throw up on her as well? Neyruu is not best pleased."

Ranulf lowered his eyes. "Why do you think I've been hiding around that rock?"

She grinned and looked out across the dusty plain that led eastward to the clifftops. The soldiers and watchmen were still watching them warily, their blades drawn and arrows nocked just in case Neyruu should stir.

"They are still terribly tense," Talasha observed.

"They are Tukoran, and there's a dragon about. Of course they're tense."

"A small dragon who clearly means no harm. If we wanted to attack them, we'd have done so already. And you claim this Bernard Westermont to be a great Bladeborn knight and Emerald Guard…the personal bodyguard of the crown prince, no less. He should have no fear of a little dragon, Ranulf. She is only a gentle soul."

A gentle soul who fought savagely against Paglar, Ranulf thought. *And not so little as you're making out.* Still, Paglar was a great deal larger, and without the intervention of mighty Calacan he would have caught his prey eventually and conducted Neyruu, Talasha, and Cevi to a most unpleasant and untimely end. Instead it was *he* who became the prey, as the Eagle of Aramatia soared down from the storm in a net of golden lightning to tear Paglar wing from limb.

A battle I should have liked to see, Ranulf thought…though he had to settle for hearing a pair of secondhand reports instead, firstly from the *Fourth Elder*, who had witnessed the fight through the eyes of one of her bonded eagles, and secondly from Talasha herself when she arrived at the Everwood the following day. That had been by invite of the *First Elder*, the oldest and wisest and most powerful of the twelve, the First Elder who was in fact the *tenth* First, as he'd told Ranulf the very first time he'd met him. *The day Calacan returned to the world*, Ranulf thought. *The day I scaled the steps to the high eyrie atop the First Tree and saw him plunge down from the skies…*

It still gave him shivers, even now. The sound the great eagle made. The width of his wings as he opened them wide and bathed all the Everwood in a wash of golden light. He had not seen him since that day, leastways in nothing more than distant glimpses as Calacan soared on his patrols, high in the skies, warding off threats and protecting his borders. Paglar had been foolish enough to enter uninvited, and thus Calacan had destroyed him. Others would not yield so easily. One in particular. *And he is stirring.*

A screech rang out through the air, the high-pitched call of an eagle. Ranulf understood. "They're nearing the top of the steps, my lady," he said to Talasha Taan. Ranulf could speak eagle now. The clicks and whistles and cries made for a fairly basic language, but during his time with the Calacania he had learned to comprehend their tongue.

"Your bird told you?" The princess peered at him.

"*Kamcho*," Ranulf said. That was the name of the eagle he had chosen. And the eagle who had chosen *him*. It had been a mutual pairing, as did happen when man and beast built their bonds. One day, shortly into his time with the Calacania, the First Elder had invited Ranulf to join him atop his eyrie. There, rather than discuss with Ranulf the fate of the world, and describe to him the events he had witnessed, he had opened out a feathery arm and presented to him a great convocation of eagles.

"Choose," the ancient had said. The command had been given to both Ranulf and the gathered birds, and so followed a period of deliberation as Ranulf walked among them, the eagles peering at him with those piercing eyes, some flapping up close to take a good long look, even nipping gently at his hand as he reached out to touch them. Eventually a strong bird with plumage in gold and blue had come forward. Ranulf knew several of their names by now and this one he knew as Kamcho; handsome, strong, quick and courageous, with eyes of burnished gold. Somehow he knew he was the one, and it seemed that Kamcho did as well. When the eagle opened his wings and gave a screech, then flapped up to land upon Ranulf's shoulder, the choice was made and the bond was sealed.

"A fine pairing." The First Elder had smiled at them both with that face three centuries old. "Kamcho's colours are the same as your homeland, Ranulf. Yes, a fine pairing indeed. You shall do well together, I think."

In the days that followed Kamcho had accompanied Ranulf everywhere. He stayed by him at night when he slept in his hammock, and soared about him by day as he strolled through the glade. When Ranulf climbed the trees and met the Elders in their eyries Kamcho would be there, circling and watching. Soon enough his clicks and whistles and cries were as familiar to Ranulf as the speech of man, but that was just the start of it. One day, soon after Ranulf and Kamcho had made their choice, they were invited to join the First Elder again.

"Sit down, Ranulf. Take a drink of water."

The water was from the Spring of Aramatia, rich in magical properties, a source of great power. Ranulf drew on its sweet taste as he perched in a seat of woven branches, looking out across the Twelve Trees and the Greater Everwood beyond.

"Tell me of your great-great-grandfather," the First Elder said. "Do you know much about him?"

"Only what I heard from my grandmother as a boy." Ranulf Shackton was not the only adventurer in his family. Though his parents had been somewhat strangled of that ambition, that was not true of those who came before. His grandmother herself had been a dedicated climber and his great-great-grandfather had travelled through much of the southern continent, visiting lands so far off as the Unseen Isles if the tales were to be believed. "His name was Edmond," Ranulf recalled. "He was said to have some southern blood in him, a touch of olive in his skin. And keen eyes."

The First Elder smiled. His robes of feathered plumage were mixed silver and bronze and gold, and a great long beard, white as snow, flew from his chin like a banner. "More than a touch, Ranulf. He was sired here in this very glade."

Ranulf frowned. He must not have heard. "Apologies, Great Elder, I…"

"His mother, your great-great-great-grandmother, visited us once before," the ancient went on. "She stayed with us for some months, oh, it must be almost two hundred years ago now. I was a young man back then, barely more than a century old. I knew her well, though not as well as the Eighth Elder of that time. They fell in love, Ranulf. The Eighth was young, headstrong, and your great-great-great-grandmother was a beautiful woman. When she left us she did so carrying his child. That Eighth Elder is long dead now, of course, and your great-great-great-grandmother as well, but the seed that was planted lies dormant in you. The power of *Light*, Ranulf. I did tell you there was light in you, did I not?"

Some of that light shines in you, Ranulf Shackton. He had said that the day they met. "I…I did not think you meant…" The truth of it was dawning. "There is *Lightborn* blood in me. Elder blood?"

"A smidge of it, yes. Diluted by time and generations of breeding, but enough for you and Kamcho to develop a more special bond. Speech is one thing, sight and senses another. The water from the Spring will hasten your learning, Ranulf. Drink freely, and drink often. You will not be with us long."

From that moment on, Ranulf's bond to Kamcho took on a different meaning. Day by day, week by week, he learned to see through his eyes.

Now, standing by that rock on those dusty plains, he closed his eyes and focused. Slowly, vaguely, the world came into view from high above him, a blur of blue, of sky and sea, and the golds and browns of the cliffs and plains. He could see the blotchy forms of the Tukoran soldiers below and himself, even *himself*, standing in the distance with the princess by the rock, with Neyruu nearby, and Cevi sitting up against her, enjoying the shade of her wing.

His sight remained blurred, indistinct, but the details were growing clearer every day. Kamcho flew over the edge of the cliff, over the fleet far below, bobbing against their piers. Thousands spread out onto the beach and there was a great rush of motion down there. He saw the great sculpture of Calacan soaring from the cliffside, a sculpture of great likeness he could now attest. As Kamcho circled back around Ranulf sighted the switchback stair, zig-zagging up the face of the rock. The company were at the top now, just about to take the last turn that would bring them up over the lip.

He smiled and withdrew, opening his eyes to return once more to himself. Talasha was looking at him strangely. "You are a curious fellow, Ranulf Shackton. You can truly see through him. This eagle of yours?"

"Vaguely, yes."

"And you never knew? Of this power hidden in your blood?"

"Never." Everything happened for a reason, Ranulf Shackton had come to find. Talasha's coming to the Everwood was one such event. They were twined, now, in their quest. A long bleak flight awaited them. *And it will be cold up there.*

The company were stepping up the last of the stairs and joining the other men on the clifftops. Ranulf felt a pang of nerves to reunite with Saska again. "How do I look, my lady? Presentable, I hope?"

"You smell of vomit, Ranulf Shackton."

He sighed. "You are cruel, Lady Talasha. How long are you going to mock me over this?"

"Oh, as long as we know one another." She spoke with a smile. "Best refresh your breath with a swig of that water of yours. And wipe your chin again. You missed a bit."

She grinned and set off across the dusty plain, commanding Cevi to remain behind and keep Neyruu company. Ranulf wiped his chin again, though there was no need. The woman was merely teasing him. By then the host at the cliffs had doubled in size, and a party of considerable power, both in land and title and sheer brute force, was approaching across the barren rock.

Saska and Leshie were leading from the front. Both of them were grinning, turning their heads to speak to one another as they came, laughing and shaking their heads. Behind came the Wall, with the Butcher and the Baker for company. Some of the other sellswords had made the climb as well, out of interest most likely; Ranulf knew them by description, if not by sight. So too Robbert Lukar, whom he'd never met, yet who was said to be much alike to his father in look, and so it did seem. He walked at the back looking somewhat perplexed. "A handsome young man," Talasha observed, upon seeing him. "Even with the eyepatch. Who is this tall one who walks beside him?"

"That would be Sir Lothar Tunney. He is the second of Prince Robbert's guards, along with Sir Bernard."

"He must be seven feet."

"I believe he is six feet and eleven inches." No doubt that was of great upset to him, to miss out on that vaunted number by so small a margin.

Leshie took it upon herself to rush ahead as they neared, lifting a finger to point right at him. "*I know you.* I'm sure of it. I know that silly old face." She hurried along in her fetching red armour, a red silken cape trailing at her back, grinning massively. "Bloody hell, Ranulf. Now don't tell me you *flew* here?"

"I had that pleasure, Leshie, it's so."

"*It's so,*" the Red Blade repeated. "Gods, I don't miss *that* stupid phrase of yours. *It's so.* What does that even mean?" She snorted, hugged him, grinning and laughing and then drew back and turned to the princess, performing a clumsy curtsy. "Your Highness. We've been worried about you. Saska especially. She…"

"Can speak for herself," Saska said, stepping in behind her. Her eyes flitted between the princess and the adventurer. A smile simmered on her lips. It felt to Ranulf as though she wanted to rush in and embrace them both, though she held her reserve, ever wary of how she appeared. "I'm sure there's quite a tale to tell here. How is it you came to be together?"

"Oh, that is a story for Ranulf to tell, I think." Talasha smiled and drifted in to take Saska's hands in her own. "I'm sorry I left for so long. We had a spot of trouble with Paglar."

"Paglar?" repeated Leshie. "That was the big dragon at the lake?"

"A fearsome beast, but ultimately overmatched. Drulgar is not the only titan to have returned."

The two girls shared a confused look, as the Butcher stamped forward, smirking from ear to ear. "Ersel!" he roared. "Ersel San Sabar!" He stepped straight in to pick Ranulf up off his feet in a chest-crunching bear hug. "What a joyous day! Ersel San Sabar has returned to us. I have missed you, Ersel!" He shook him from side to side. Ranulf's legs swung freely like a rag doll. "Where have you been? The Everwood. Yes, we know. But why is the true question? Why have you not returned? And these others who went with you? The Sunrider and his men and that funny little gardener…"

"Let him go and perhaps he'll answer." That came from the Wall, a booming thunderclap of a voice that was not easy to mistake for another. "He can barely breathe, Butcher. Put him down."

"Ah. Sorry, Ersel. I am getting overexcited to see you, I think." The Butcher lowered him to the ground, and Ranulf tried to remain dignified while refilling his lungs. A great paw shook his shoulder. "So? So? Let us hear this tale from the famous tale-teller. *Wine*. Yes, there is wine aboard the ship. We should go down and drink wine and you can speak of your adventures."

"You'll forgive my brother. He is a child in a man's body." The Baker pushed his golden spectacles up his nose. "A very ugly scarred man, and a very simple child." He smiled, showing his odd, unnaturally white set of teeth. "How are you, Ranulf Shackton? Still trying to avert your eyes from Ana, is it not so?"

"*Ana?*" The Butcher burst out laughing. "Yes, you tried so hard *not* to look, Ersel. A very pretty girl. Do you remember her?"

How could I forget? It had been Ranulf's first meeting with the Bloody Trader brothers in their pavilion outside Eagle's Perch. Never in his life had Ranulf Shackton entered a scene of such debauchery, with couples writhing in every corner and naked singers prancing about among the cats and dogs and goats that roamed freely through the scented smoke. Ana had been the nude girl who served their wine, a very nubile girl whom Ranulf had been very careful not to look at below the eyes. Of course, that had been of tremendous amusement to the sellswords. "I recall Ana, yes," he said.

"You could have recalled her better if you'd taken her to bed, Ranulf," the Baker informed him. "We did offer."

"And I politely declined. I remember."

"A gallant fool you are, Ersel San Sabar." The Butcher laughed fondly. "Not so Denlatis, oh no. He took Ana to union many times that night, kept her up through dark and dawn." He prodded Ranulf in the chest. "Do you think you could do that, Ersel? Keep a pretty girl up all night?"

Ranulf smiled politely. "A gentleman never tells."

"You are saying that Denlatis is not a gentleman? Yes, yes! You are right! All that silk and satin and he still has the stink of a dock-man's son." The Butcher laughed loudly. "Ah, but he has risen yet higher, Ersel. Denlatis pulled a great trick on the Sunny Snake, and it won him the hand of the Lady Asherah Tamaar. Can you imagine? He is one of the most powerful men in Aramatia now."

"And one of the most frightened," the Baker added. "He is terrified that Krator will seek vengeance."

"I know about Cliffario," Ranulf said.

"How?" the Butcher demanded. "Where did you hear of this?"

"The Second Elder told me. He had an eagle watching at the time." Ranulf suspected that would stump the big sellsword, and duly it did. The Butcher frowned, the scars twisting on his forehead. It gave Ranulf enough time to slip away to the others.

Prince Robbert and Princess Talasha were being introduced as he joined them. Saska did the honours. "Robbert, I'd like you to meet Talasha." The prince gave a well-rehearsed bow, the princess a smile and a playful curtsy. "I think you'll get along well."

"Oh, I am quite sure of it," Talasha said. She kept eye contact with the prince, who seemed more shy in her company. That was only natural. He was a boy of eighteen, Talasha a decade his senior and ravishingly beautiful, wielding her beauty like a well-honed weapon. "I am told you have had some struggles at sea, Prince Robbert. A manator attacked you, am I right? And you were becalmed for several days."

"Four, my lady. Another of my ships…*Wild Raven*…she was becalmed for twelve."

"Twelve? Goodness, that would drive me mad."

"It had that effect on some of the men, I am told." The prince frowned. "How did you know of this?"

Talasha gave a playful shrug. "I have my ways. Ranulf Shackton is a great fount of knowledge, it turns out, and news." She turned to introduce him. "And here he is now."

Ranulf stepped in and bowed. "Your Highness. A pleasure."

Robbert regarded him with a furrowed brow, intrigued. "You knew my grandfather. He kept you in a cell once in the palace."

"He did. A snug place. If a little cold and dark for my tastes."

The prince favoured that with a smile. "My captain says you sailed with him once. Ash Burton. You went with him on a kraken hunt."

"A failed one," Ranulf recalled. "Bloodhound was most wroth about that, of course. He has no great love for those creatures." *And a great penchant for talking often and loudly of his days sailing with King Lorin*, Ranulf thought. Now here they were, standing in the company of Lorin's granddaughter and heir. How queer the world was sometimes.

He looked at her now. Pleasant as it was to meet a prince and reunite with some of his old friends, it was Saska he wished to speak with. And alone. Talasha knew that as well. She stepped in to take Robbert's arm, smiling sultrily. "My prince, why don't you tell me more about your time at sea? I'm sure you've got many exciting stories to tell." She looked around. "The rest of you. Come along. Let's leave Saska and Ranulf to talk in peace."

Leshie gave a face. She hated being left out. But Saska nodded and off she went with the others. Sir Bernard Westermont had remained aside all the while and was looking at the Wall warily. Saska shook her head. "There's been lots of drama," she told Ranulf, when they were alone. "Bernie and Lothar fought Rolly in Aram. These last few days Lothar's had a chance to speak with Rolly on the ship and clear the air, but not Bernard." She looked at him. "Aram. Do you know about all that? I guess Talasha must have told you. Krator and Kastor and everything?"

"She didn't need to tell me, Saska. I knew already, as it happens."

The girl was baffled. "How? Did you speak to a traveller, or…"

"The Elders have a particular power," he explained. "A power to see through the eyes of their bonded eagles. Lumo gifted them her light, long ago. At Thala's request. They have been keeping watch."

Saska took that in staidly. The girl was no stranger to shocking disclosures. "They've been watching me?" she asked, quietly. "We've seen lots of eagles, since we left Aram."

"Most eagles are just eagles, Saska. But, yes, through some the Elders were watching. They have been keeping track of your progress and have kept me well-informed of your journey. And much else from across the world."

Her eyes went apprehensive at that. "The north...so you know... you know what's happening there?" She paused. "Drulgar. Is he..."

"Resting," Ranulf said. "But not for much longer."

The First Elder had glimpsed it. The broil of fume and ash rising from the Ashmount, and the dragon stirring from his Nest. One of his eagles had dared to get close, and there far below, his eyes pierced through both smoke and sky and saw the Calamity shifting on his perch as his minions screeched and flew about him, tiny against his unthinkable bulk. Soon he would return to scorch and sunder all his enemies. Cities that defied him. Titans that challenged him. And those who kept watch...all would suffer from his wrath. It would herald the beginning of the end. And time was growing short.

Ranulf said nothing of that. It would only add to her burdens, and of those she had plenty already.

"Talasha..." Saska glanced over as she strolled along with Robbert Lukar. "She said earlier that Drulgar wasn't the only titan who's returned. What did she mean by that?"

"She was referring to Calacan. It was the Eagle of Aramatia who slew Paglar."

The heir of Varin blinked. "*Calacan?* We heard...a few times we heard of a giant eagle shape in the skies. From travellers. And a light. A great gold light. But...I never thought..."

"It's true. I saw him descend from the skies myself, the day he returned. Calacan has been protecting the borders of the duchy, warding off dragons primarily, but there is only so much he can do. His power will not be sufficient to keep the Dread at bay."

She stared out, trying to imagine it. "Is he...Calacan...how *big* is he?"

"Not near Drulgar's size. But larger than other dragons. And there have been other stirrings as well. On land and at sea." He could not list them all, not now, and did not want to frighten her unduly. "Saska, you should know..."

"My grandmother," she said at once. Her eyes went flat as though she already knew. As though she'd prepared herself to hear it. "She's dead, isn't she?"

"No." It was one of the most satisfying words Ranulf Shackton had ever said. "She remains abed most days but occasionally takes to her feet. Her condition has not improved, but nor has it worsened. We can take some comfort from that."

She nodded. "It's still just a matter of time. I know I'm never going

631

to see her again." She seemed resigned to that now. Sometimes it was easier to give up on hope than let yourself be disappointed. "So, what is it? The thing I should know?"

"It's…I'm sad to say that Sunrider Tantario has perished. He and the rest of his men were caught in a sinkhole as they slept two nights ago. None survived, Saska."

Her eyes stared blankly, like she was dead inside. "He deserved more than that," she said, in a low whisper. "All of them." She dwelled on it a moment, then snorted balefully. "My secret. Must everyone die to keep it?"

"It was just a sinkhole, Saska. A natural event."

"Natural? There's nothing natural about this. I had a dozen men killed only days ago, Ranulf. To keep my secret. Now the gods have seen fit to finish the job." She scowled and shook her head.

Her soul is scarred, Ranulf thought. He wondered if she would ever recover from all the things she'd done, all the decisions she was being forced to make to forge her into the person she must become.

Ranulf knew what had happened with the deserters. He had been told how the Baker and Umberto and the Surgeon and the Tigress had caught up to them and killed them, brutally and without mercy. It had not been a fair fight, or a long one. By nightfall the four sellswords had returned to Saska to report to her their success. The following morning, Sunrider Tantario and the remainder of his men had bid Saska goodbye and left her in the protective custody of Prince Robbert, to sail on the final stretch to Eagle's Perch. *And then they died*, Ranulf thought. *After all that, the earth claimed them, to be crushed by rock and stone.*

It was a tragedy, and unfair. But that was the world. It was tragic and unfair.

"It's snowing in the north," Ranulf said. The change of topic had her frowning at him, but he needed to move things on. "Heavily, Saska. Thalan is snowed under, Ilithor is following and even Varinar too. In the south of the continent the rains are coming down so hard that great swathes of land are underwater. I know Alym Tantario spoke of this. He called it the weather of the new world, brought on by the Ever-War and he was right. The sinkhole that claimed his life was one such event. The storms that racked Prince Robbert's fleet another. The heat is becoming more severe further to the south, and the cities of Sutrek and Lumos are suffering. There have been other weather events as well. Great tornados. Violent earthquakes. In the far west a tsunami swept inland to drown the Golden Isles. Thousands were killed in an instant. And still, there is more to come."

"I know," she said. A muscle tensed in her jaw. "We've heard about the troubles in the south. And the north…we suspected as much. Every day thousands are dying, Ranulf. I know that, and not just from the weather. That's why I need to go north. That's why you went to the Everwood in the first place. To help us find a safe way to cross. Yet you never came back. Not even a word."

"I wanted to. I…"

"It wasn't your doing. I understand. And I don't blame you. All this…" She looked east, over the seas. "It's like the edges of the world are closing in. It's like…an eye dimming. You know how that happens when you faint. How your sight dims at the edges and then suddenly everything goes black. The whole world is like that, Ranulf. We have to stop it before it goes dark."

It was well put. *An eye, dimming.* "There's still time," he said. "Things are not so hopeless as they might seem."

"And when Drulgar comes again? When he comes after *me*? It won't matter where I am or who I have protecting me. He'll kill us all, Ranulf."

"Drulgar the Dread is his own master. He might not care even if he knew of you. More likely he would relish the challenge of facing the Heart Remade. Once all his enemies lie dead at his feet, what else is there? I do not think you need to worry about him. Not yet."

She gave a huffing laugh, shaking her head at how absurd it all was. "I'll take your word for that. But those blades have to be reforged first, and…"

"And that's why I have to go," Ranulf said.

She looked at him. "Go? But you've only just come back."

"I know." He took her hand. "I don't want to. I *have* to. I'll return as soon as I can."

She looked at him, and saw the truth. "The secret," she said. "From the stolen page. You know where you have to go?"

He nodded, remembering the day he'd torn that page from the Book of Thala. How he'd finally translated King Godrin's words and found a coded message sent to him through time. He'd been instructed to burn the page, and he had, memorising its contents, writing it out every night and burning it anew before he slept to make certain he recalled it. It was the lost formula to combining the blades, the key to reforging the Heart. And for a long while it existed only in the head of Ranulf Shackton. Until the day he finally came to Aram and passed that knowledge to the Grand Duchess as well.

She told me she would memorise it herself, he thought…but that could no longer be trusted. *She said she would keep the written copy safe…*but he could not rely on that either. For many moons he had wondered where the knowledge would take him, and to whom it would be delivered, but he need wonder no longer. The First Elder had seen it, the awakening in the distant north. He had told Ranulf where he must go.

And now I have a dragon to bear me there. He wished he could take Saska with him, but he couldn't. She would have to remove her armour, and that would make her vulnerable, and besides, he knew she'd never leave her friends behind. Leshie, Sir Ralston, her brother Del. Even if she could wrench herself free of them, what of her starcat Joy? No. She would have to remain with the company for now, and continue by sail and saddle and sole. *We'll find you again,* he thought in silent vow. *When we're done, we'll fly back and find you.*

Ranulf Shackton reached into his pocket and removed a piece of parchment, folded to make a neat square. "Take this," he said, handing it to her.

She took it, brow furrowing. "What is it?"

"The formula. Written out again in my own hand."

She looked up. "But why?"

"Insurance. In case I don't make it." He had no intention of dying along the way, but it always served to be careful. "Just keep that tucked away somewhere safe. When I come back, we can burn it together. How about that?" He smiled.

She didn't. "You'd better come back, Ranulf. Find me. Promise me you will?"

"I will. I promise."

"You'd better." She hugged him, hard, and then let him go. "So where? Where *are* you going?"

"North," he said. "Far to the north. Talasha has kindly volunteered to fly me there to see him."

"Him? The person who'll reforge the Heart? Who is it, Ranulf. *Who?*"

"Oh, no one special." He smiled, eyes twinkling in anticipation. "Just a demigod," he said.

49

Emeric

"Tell me again what he said," Borrus Kanabar demanded. "Again, Emeric. Tell me again."

He had told him a dozen times over almost half as many days, and it wasn't getting easier with each repetition. "Your father is being held in the heart of the Agarathi warcamp, chained at the ankles and neck to a post. An iron cage has been erected around him. He has grown thin, his beard has been shorn, and he looks old and frail. The Agarathi mock him daily. He suffers as you did, during your time in Eldurath. He…"

"*Enough.*" Borrus cringed, barely able to hear it any longer, recalling the torments he'd suffered. "Enough Emeric, *gods*. The way you speak…with such dispassion."

"That isn't fair," Sir Rikkard Amadar said. "You've asked Emeric to tell that tale a dozen times, Borrus. He does as you ask without complaint."

"Complaint? Complaint, you call it?" The Barrel Knight slammed a hand down upon the table. "*I'm* the one who has the complaint here, Rikkard! My father…the idea of him being abused and starved and debased…such a man as he? Such a great bloody man as *he!*"

"We all agree he is a great man," Rikkard said calmly. "And it pains us all to know that he has been a captive of the enemy for so long. But shouting and screaming will not help. Pull yourself together, Borrus. You are acting like a child."

The Barrel Knight could hardly have looked more furious. A shade of deep red was rising up his neck and a vein the size of a small grass snake pulsed angrily across his temple. "I should throttle you, Amadar! The gods know I should bloody well throttle you! *I'm* the Lord of the Riverlands, damnit, and Warden of the East."

"No," the heir of Amadar said, giving a neat shake of his head. "You *were* the Lord of the Riverlands and Warden of the East…until we found out your father was still alive. Now Lord Wallis still holds those titles."

"Blast you, Rikkard! You and your bloody semantics. You know what I meant. Lord or heir, it matters not. My father is incapacitated!"

"Yes. We know. And we are trying to figure out how to change that."

They had been at it for days, though were going around in circles. Any plan they had conjured to try to steal Lord Wallis and the other hostages back had run into a brick wall as thick as the Last Bastion. The Agarathi camp was vast, a day's march from here, and there was no way to get to them without stirring up the hornet's nest. *Or the dragon's lair,* Emeric thought. If they attempted to free them, the hostages would die, and so too their would-be rescuers. The only sure option was to engage in diplomacy. But so far that had failed as well.

"Send another rider," Borrus said, to anyone who would listen. He looked across the council members gathered in his pavilion. "Sir Karter. One of yours. Send an envoy with a mounted guard."

Sir Karter Pentar hesitated.

Sir Rikkard spoke for him. "They'll only send back their heads. It would be a waste of time and men." He had the right of that, Emeric knew; their previous attempts to parley with the dragonlord had all gone much the same. Horses and riders went out. Horses and *heads* came back, stuffed in their own saddlebags.

"Then what? *What* do you suggest, Rikkard?" The pain was clear on Borrus's ruddy face. "We cannot free him by force. Ven won't agree to parley. So *what*? What am I to do?"

"March on them," said Lord Rammas of the Marshes. "We have no other choice."

Borrus shook his head at once. "They'll kill him if I do." He hit the table again with his fist, but it was weaker, disconsolate. That was Borrus Kanabar. He blew hot and cold and he was cooling again, sinking into despair. "I should never have let you go, Emeric. I'd made my peace with my father's death. Now I find out he's still alive, suffering, *dehumanised*. I know how the Agarathi are. I know how they like to treat their prisoners, and my father…my father…"

"We should march," repeated Lord Rammas. Emeric wondered how many times he had said those words, or some version of them, during their long encampment here. According to Rikkard it was many times daily, and he barely said anything else. 'He's like a trained raven, that one, always quorking the same thing,' the knight had said. "We cannot let your father's suffering continue," the Lord of the Marshes went on. "Nor the others. Death would be better."

"He's right," declared Mooton Blackshaw, standing from his stool. He towered above all but Borrus in the room. "I loved your father the same as you, Borrus, but we have to accept that he's dead. The longer he suffers, the worse it will be. Lord Rammas is right. We should march."

Once more, Sir Rikkard was the voice of reason. "Amron ordered us to stand fast, I'll remind you all," he said. "He is our king. His word is absolute."

"His word is *old*," came back Mooton Blackshaw. "It might as well be sprouting mushrooms it's been rotting so long."

"King Daecar isn't here," put in Prince Raynald Lukar. He looked around the room to make sure he had been heard and had their attention. "How long do we submit to his ruling when he does not know what is happening here? And Elyon…who knows where *he's* gone. I saw his *eyes*, my lords. The Windblade may have led him astray, and there's no knowing when he'll be back. I say *we* decide upon our own fate. We cannot be led by a man a thousand leagues away."

Rammas and Mooton both nodded agreement. Others murmured their own doubts, and the debate went on. It would lead nowhere, Emeric knew. Much the same had been said the day before, and over the days before that as well, and for all Borrus's bluster, he did not want to risk the sacrifice of his father without exhausting all attempts to save him.

"I need to think," the Barrel Knight said, after they'd gone around in circles a few more times. "We'll reconvene later once something new comes to light." He waved them away, and off they went, streaming from the tent and into the rain. Rammas stepped in for a private word, but Borrus flicked a wrist and said, "Not now, Rammas. I know what you're going to say. *Not now*."

The rest filed out until only Torvyn Blackshaw and Emeric remained. Borrus sagged down into his seat, hooking a cup of wine in his grasp, drinking deep. "Go on then, Torv. You've got something to say, I can smell it."

"Nothing that hasn't already been said."

The Barrel Knight huffed. "I'm sure. And you, Manfrey?"

Emeric stepped forward. "I could try to reach out to Moonrider Ballantris again," he said. "Lady Marian has sufficient ingredients, she says, to disguise me as before."

Borrus thought little of that. "Nothing will come of it," he dismissed. "We've lost Sansullio now, and his men. You'd never make it there alone."

"I made it back alone."

"That was different. The moonlord let you go. But getting back in by yourself…no. And what would happen if you did? You think Ballantris would urge that my father be freed? You think he would care, or that Vargo Ven would listen? No, is the answer you're looking for. Ballantris told you he planned to muster his men to leave at once, is that not so? Then why hasn't he? His army is still in camp so far as we know."

"These things take time. His allies…"

"What allies? That's Avar Avam's army out there, not his. This Moonrider thinks a lot of himself, doesn't he? They're all like that, these Moonriders, pompous and superior. He thought he could snap his fingers and Avam's host would rush to heel. He thought he would tell Vargo Ven he was leaving and the dragonlord would meekly smile and let him go. Well neither of those things have happened. More likely Avam brought *him* to heel. Perhaps your precious Moonrider is dead."

Sir Torvyn gave a solemn nod, the lid of his left eye flickering. "He may be right, Emeric. Vargo Ven will not take kindly to any attempts to undermine him."

"If he has killed Moonlord Ballantris, we would know of it," Emeric claimed.

Borrus snorted. "How do you come by that? They're a day's march from here, twenty miles as the crow flies. Our scouts and outriders don't get anywhere near…"

"Near enough to hear Tathranor seek his vengeance," Emeric told him. "You have seen moonbears on the battlefield, Borrus. They are a force of total destruction, and their rage cannot be matched. Not even by a dragon. Tathranor would kill a thousand men getting to Ven. It would take half a dozen dragons to stop him."

"They *have* half a dozen dragons. They might have ten times that, for all we know. I don't doubt the moonbear would kick up a bit of a fuss, but Ven's power would quickly subdue him. He'd only need to send out Malathar for that." He drank his wine. "But I take your point. All that fighting would cause a stir, and no doubt we'd have heard it. So Ballantris lives. What of it? Maybe he's been thrown in with my father? That ought to keep the bear at bay."

It was a possibility, there was no denying it. But there was another that Emeric Manfrey preferred. "Timor may yet side with us," he said, with the thin strains of hope in his voice. "His allies might have convinced him of that wisdom, as I failed to do. It will take him months to march his army home, and anything could befall them on the way. Turning on Ven once the fighting begins would be the wiser course."

"Of course it would be," Borrus said. "The best way to defend is to attack, that's what we say around here. Talk to Rammas. He'll tell you. Well…sometimes that man takes it a little too literally, but the point still stands. I…" He cut himself off at the sound of the horns. All of them turned sharply to the flaps. The sound was low, a long deep wailing. Borrus frowned. "These Pentars…I can't figure out their calls. What does that one mean?"

Sir Torvyn answered. "Scouts returning."

He was right. Emeric walked to the flaps and stepped out. A steady, slanting rain was falling, as it did most days, and the great ward at Rustbridge had turned grey and soggy, its drainage system tested to its limits. Emeric could hear shouting from the walls as the horn-blast trailed off, echoing out over the open plains east of the city.

He walked to the crossroad a short distance away, where the main thoroughfare led to the eastern gates. The portcullises were rising, the drawbridge falling, the Pentar captain there shouting commands in his red and silver cloak. Into the city Emeric saw a small host of riders returning, dressed in grey and brown, leather and light chainmail, saddled atop swift slim coursers all frothing at the mouth. Emeric saw Sir Karter appear, hastening out to take report from the scouts. The conversation looked tense.

"What's happening?" Borrus asked. He had followed Emeric outside, Sir Torvyn as well, and all of a sudden the lords of Rustbridge were emerging from their pavilions to converge at the cobbled cross-road. A moment later Sir Karter Pentar came running.

"My lords," he said, breathless. "The enemy host…they're *moving*."

"Moving?" repeated Borrus. "Where?" He looked at Emeric, as though to wonder if they'd been wrong. Had Ballantris finally stirred his army to leave? Was Vargo Ven retreating back to the Bane, fearing he no longer had the strength to challenge them?

All such questions passed through the mind of Emeric Manfrey. Until Sir Karter shook his head and said, "*Here*, my lord. They are coming *here*. They struck their camp this morning and are marching west with all their strength. They may intend to siege the city."

"Or they're just moving camp," said Rikkard Amadar. He had stepped from his pavilion with Sir Killian in tow. "Their grounds may have become waterlogged in this rain. It is not uncommon to move camp after so long in one place."

Sir Killian looked to Emeric. The heir of House Oloran was a quiet, intense man who rarely spoke unless he had something to say. When speaking with the blade he was most garrulous, however, Emeric knew, one of the finest swordsmen in the north. "Was their camp waterlogged, that you saw?" he asked in his whispered voice.

"I did not see enough of it to judge, Sir Killian," Emeric answered. "But what I did see…no, the ground was muddied, but not overly drenched."

"They're not moving camp for the hell of it," snorted the Beast of Blackshaw. He took Borrus by the arm. "We need to beat the drums, Barrel. Get the men ready to attack."

"*Defend*, you mean," Rikkard Amadar said. "We have high walls and deep moats and battlements bristling with bowmen and ballistas, spitfires and scorpions. Leaving the fort would be folly until we are certain what they plan to do."

Borrus pulled his arm from Mooton's grip. "You talk too much, Moot. Too much and too loudly." He thought a moment, then told Sir Karter Pentar to raise the canopy roof. "If the dragons come in force, we'll need that shield. See to it, Sir Karter. And triple your guard on the walls. I want a bowmen at every crenel, and every scorpion and trebuchet loaded and manned. They will stop out of range, we can be sure, but it pays to be prepared." He looked around. "Where is Lady Payne? She was not at council earlier."

"She finds our company overbearing," said Sir Rikkard. "Rammas, mostly. And Mooton is too boisterous for her tastes."

"He's too boisterous for everyone's tastes," Borrus said to that. "Even I'm growing tired of him." He did not bother softening the insult with a smile. "Emeric, you go see her...she seems to like you. Tell her what's happening if she doesn't already know and then head back to the others. If we're to come to blows, I want the Silent Suncoat in the van. That man's mere gaze is like to freeze a dragon in its tracks. And someone go speak with the prince. Tell him..." He paused. "Actually, I'll see to it. The lad deserves me to pay him a visit over there. He's always asking." He waved a hand to dismiss them. "Go. See to it." And off he marched, Sir Torvyn at his side.

Emeric made for the small Payne encampment, an orderly place raised amidst the larger Vandarian host. The Payne forces numbered only about two and half thousand, Emeric knew, and were the sole Rasalanian representatives here. There had been some hard words said over that. But for Tandrick Payne, the Rasal greatlords had not sent aid and had chosen to defend their own lands and borders instead. Emeric would not judge them harshly for prioritising their own people, though others were not so forgiving. The word craven had been bandied about a fair bit. Perhaps that was the reason Lady Marian did not attend council so often as the others. Listening to the likes of Rammas and Mooton Blackshaw curse her countrymen did not make for pleasant hearing, and who knew the truth of what was happening over there in the east? They might have sent a great host afoot, only for it to be besieged by dragons on the road. The lords of the bays may have pulled together a grand armada, only for it to founder as it crossed the seas, assaulted by wing and fin. They did not know, that was the truth of it. And no amount of fist-shaking was going to help.

The Payne colours were grey and brown, their sigil a range of hills beneath a raging black storm. The standard flicked and flapped on banners and was stitched into every cloak. The black storm seemed apt to Emeric Manfrey. It was said to denote the Stormy Sea that raged beyond the Stormwall Hills from where Lord Tandrick ruled. But Emeric supposed that black storm could mean something else. The storm of war, black and wild, enshrouding the world in its shadow.

The gruff soldier called Roark was sitting on a stool outside Lady Payne's pavilion, sharpening his blade with a whetstone. It was common steel, castle-forged. Across the flaps sat another soldier, much younger, plucking on the strings of a lute and humming to himself happily. It was a pleasant sound, an oasis within the growing din that was spreading through the great ward as a hundred thousand men stirred to life. The man Roark lifted his eyes as Emeric approached. "Lot of noise about," he remarked.

Emeric nodded. "Is Lady Payne inside?"

"She's putting on her armour," Roark said. "In case there's trouble." He stood from his stool and looked east. "We hear the dragonfolk are flappin' our way. That so, my lord?"

Word travels fast here. "Yes, it's true. They will be here by dusk."

"Dusk. It's always dusk, isn't it?"

Emeric did not catch the man's meaning. "Would you check if the lady is decent, please."

"Decent? Well listen to him, Lark." Roark laughed. The soldier-bard called Lark plucked a string and warbled a line from a song, some ballad about decency no doubt. "Aye, I'll check." The old soldier disappeared and reappeared a moment later, quick as that. "She's *decent*," he confirmed, finding the word awfully funny for reasons Emeric couldn't fathom. "In you go, my lord."

Emeric passed inside. "My lady," he said, bowing. She was half-dressed in her armour, working from the bottom up. Her torso, chest, and arms were garbed in a padded undertunic, over which her sleek plate would nestle snugly. The usually slicked-back hair was all awry and messy, hanging over her forehead in strands. She swept a hand to put them into place.

"Emeric," she said. Marian Payne did not call him 'lord' as others did, who observed it as a courtesy. There was no malice in that, only truth. The lady was not one to be overly sentimental. "To what do I owe this pleasure?"

"I came to inform you that the enemy host is moving. But I see you already know."

"Yes. The blaring horns and shouting on the walls did rather spike my interest." She raised a brow at him. "You ought to do as I am, and armour up, Emeric. The host may still be miles away, but their dragons could come at any moment."

"I will as soon as I leave you."

She waited. "And was that it? You came to tell me something I already knew. Or was there something else you wanted?" She lifted her breastplate from its mannequin, sliding it into place with a series of satisfying clicks. "Or perhaps you just came to watch me dress."

"No, my lady. Just to update you on what was happening." He paused. "Borrus wondered why you were not at council."

"Was anything of interest said?"

"No," he admitted. "It was much the same as usual."

"Then you have your answer. I never did attend every council at Dragon's Bane, and nor have I here. Most are tedious affairs that cover the same ground. There's often a lot of shouting and drinking. I come when I have something to say or there is something interesting to hear."

She was a blunt woman, to be sure, though Emeric had found her self-possession quite impressive. There were not many women like her in the north, if any. Warrior women were much more common in the south.

She took up a shoulder pauldron. "You are lingering, Emeric Manfrey," she observed. "Lingerers always have something on their mind." She clicked the pauldron into place, fitting seamlessly with the rest of her armour, and took up its twin. "Would you like me to make you Lumaran again, is that it? The host is moving closer. Perhaps with all that commotion you might have a chance to infiltrate their ranks unnoticed, and cut the throat of Avar Avam."

He smiled at that. "Do not put such thoughts into my head, Lady Payne. If I slay Sunlord Avam it will be on the field of battle, with godsteel to grasp."

"Yes, to defeat your enemies on the battlefield is more noble, of course. That would suit you better. You do not live in a world of spies and sneaks like I do. I have always found your ideals of honour too restrictive myself."

"They are what have always guided me," he said. "Even during my exile."

"Sir Oswald would be proud."

He furrowed his brow at that. "You need not mock me, Lady Payne."

"I'm not mocking you, Emeric. I'm praising you, so take it. You've shown great strength to continue living a life of probity after what you went through." She clicked her right pauldron into place. "How have the Tukorans reacted to your return? I have not asked you yet."

"Well enough," he said, though it was much more complicated than that. Some of the older men still seemed convinced of Lord Modrik's slanderous accounts and had not taken kindly to his arrival. They looked away as he passed them, muttering unheard remarks, and once or twice he'd been spat at as he went by. But those occasions were few and far between. Most of the men were too busy with their own concerns to spare much of a thought for a lord long exiled and recently returned. "Not everyone knows who I am. Some have had kind words for me. The rest all ask of my ancestors as though I knew them personally." His smile was long-suffering. "I've had that all my life."

"People are interested in heroes," Lady Marian said. She took her left rerebrace and wrapped it about her arm. "Do they ask of Lord Bedrik as well?"

"You know your history, my lady. Yes, some have done so."

Lord Bedrik Manfrey was Sir Oswald's grandson, and a staunch ally of Galin Lukar, who was Lord of Redhelm, Warden of the South, and the First Blade of Vandar at that time. When Galin threw down the Sword of Varinar and called his banners to march upon Tukor, Lord Bedrik had gone with him to help siege Ilithor and win the kingdom. The rest was well known. Galin Lukar ousted the last of the Ilithian kings and granted his bannermen lands throughout Tukor. Lord Bedrik was given a tract in the north, and the castle he named Osworth, in honour of his famous grandfather. They flourished, for a time, but not long. Over the centuries their power began to wane, and when Emeric's father Lord Emerson perished in the war, the strength of House Manfrey had all but been forgotten. *I was the last flickering light of a once great house,* Emeric thought. *And then Lord Modrik Kastor waved a hand, and the flame went out for good.*

He gave a bitter shake of the head. "Some say my house is cursed," he said. "That Lord Bedrik damned us when he joined Galin Lukar in his invasion of Tukor. Sir Oswald was one of the greatest ever Vandarians, and his grandson abandoned the kingdom that made him. I like to think that, sometimes…that we were cursed. It helps to mask my own failures."

"What failures are you referring to?"

He looked at her. She had stopped dressing and was staring right at him. "My exile, my lady. Most would consider that a failure. No matter the circumstances and injustices. I presided over the fall of my house."

"And you will preside over its restoration," she told him.

He shook his head. "Prince Raynald doesn't have the power. Only a king can grant a pardon."

"Which he very well may be, should his brother not return. But that is not what I am talking about. Tell me, Emeric…who was Sir Oswald before his rise?"

He sensed a trap but answered anyway. "A knight. Of promise…if not renown."

"And who did he become?" She smiled and answered for him. "He became the First Blade of Vandar. A hero without equal who sits at the side of Varin for all time, his knights will have you believe. His deeds granted him a lordship, and a house of his own, that famous name you bear. But men don't care about lands and the titles, Emeric Manfrey. They care about feats. They care about his duel with Karlog and Bagazar. They care about his triumphs with the Sword of Varinar, and the many battles he won by the edge of his blade. So you go out there and wipe away your dishonour with deeds. With feats and triumphs. *That* is what men care for."

She was right, he knew, and her words had stirred him. Men did not remember lords, they remembered heroes. If he wanted to restore the name of Manfrey, he would do it by the blade Sir Oswald bore, the eagle-blade at his hip. He gave Lady Payne a low bow. "Thank you, my lady. I will leave you to finish dressing."

Roark was standing outside with a smile. "Stirring stuff," he said. "I don't often hear her talk like that. She must see something in you, my lord."

"Do you always listen in on her private audiences, Roark?"

"Not always. Sometimes it's Lark or Braddin with their ear to the flaps." He grinned at him. Coarse grey stubble covered his cheeks and chin. "Best go get armoured, though. You're not going to be killing any dragons like old Oswald wearing nought but leather and fur."

Emeric took the old soldier's advice, returning to his own small tent in the northwestern corner of the ward. The noise of the encampment was so loud that he couldn't even hear the river rushing outside. He pushed through the churn of men heading for the walls to find the sailors in conference outside their communal tent. They had a fire going, covered with a tarp to keep off the rain. Grim Pete was cooking a pot of something over the flame and Soft Sid was adding some logs when Emeric arrived. The others were talking in heady tones.

Jack spun to him at once when he saw him appear. "My lord…they say the Agarathi are coming? Is it true?"

"Yes, Jack."

"How far?" asked Braxton, standing.

"They'll be here by nightfall. We don't yet know if they will divert their course. They may be bluffing, or trying to unsettle us."

Grim Pete shuddered. "We'll be expected to fight, then? If it comes to that."

"Every man capable of bearing steel ought to take up arms," he said. "You'll be in the reserves, Pete. There's no safer place on the battlefield."

"There's no *safe* place on the battlefield," Captain Turner said to that. "Not when there're dragons about." He sat on a camp stool in his tan coat, rain dripping from his flaxen beard. "You lot go ahead and fight. I'll be taking the bridge over into the city when the fighting starts." He had a bite of bread. "Call me coward all you like. I'm an old sailor and no fighter and I'll only get in the way. Said that a thousand times."

Emeric nodded. "No one will object to you sitting this one out, Gill."

Pete's eyes widened in hope. "And me?"

"That is not for me to say. I am not your commander."

Soft Sid stood from the fire, towering above them all. He towered above everyone, even Mooton. "I'm fighting," he said, in his enormous voice. He had a childlike slowness to him. "Me too. *I* fight." He slapped his chest and frowned.

Emeric smiled at him. "You'll kill many men, Sid. Make sure you're well armoured and there will be few men who can match you."

The giant grinned.

"But I hope it will not come to that. We have high walls and a shield above our heads. If sense prevails, we'll be here a little while longer at least." Emeric sniffed the air. "What's on the pot, Pete?"

"Onion broth. Bit of turnip in there too, m'lord. Not much to it, really, but it warms the belly."

"I'll have a bowl when it's ready. Just let me dress in my armour, and I'll be back out."

By the time he'd done all of that, the Silent Suncoat had joined them, sitting by the fire with that thousand-yard stare in his eyes. He still sent a chill down the spine of most who looked upon him, but the men had grown well used to him by now. "Borrus wants you in the van," Emeric told him. "If and when the time comes."

The man nodded. He wore fine godsteel armour beneath his tattered yellow cloak, both plate and mail, polished and gleaming. From the armoury of Lord Humphrey Merrymarsh the knight had taken a helm crested with a crab, its claws outstretched and open, ready to pinch. Emeric had wondered if that was some clue to his true identity. House Swiftwater's sigil was a crab with godsteel claws, so perhaps he was a relation? Or maybe he just liked the helm? To this day, the big knight had not spoken a word about his past, or a word at all, mute as he was. *He speaks with steel, and that's all that matters.* The man was a fearsome swordsman.

"Here, m'lord, a bowl of broth as requested."

"Thank you, Pete." Emeric took the bowl and sat at the fire. The Blackshaws had joined as well, the big burly men all sitting around, eating and sharpening their blades and boasting to one another, as they liked to, occasionally breaking into laughter as one of them made a bawdy jest. Sir Bulmar had the charge of them. He was the only one without a beard and easily the most genteel. He sat with Jack, sharing what advice he could impart.

"You'll fight with us, when it all begins," Emeric heard the knight say. "All of us together…we'll be stronger like that."

"You're honorary Blackshaws now," declared Regnar.

Sir Bulmar nodded. "Any battle goes easier when you trust the men about you. Those bonds are important, Jack. You have the back of the man next to you, and he'll have yours. A fist is stronger than an open hand, remember that." He made a fist to show him.

Jack gave a nod and fixed his jaw, trying to look brave. But his eyes showed the truth. *He's nervous*, Emeric thought, *and so he should be.* He was nervous as well, in truth. Emeric Manfrey had crossed swords plenty enough over the years, but he'd never fought in a battle like this. He missed out on the last war on account of his age, and though he might have been there as a squire, his father had insisted he remain at Osworth should it go ill for him. "Our house needs an heir," Lord Emerson had said, the day he rode to war. "If I should not return, do us proud, Emeric. May you bear many sons. And bring honour to our name."

They were the last words his father had spoken to him before he smiled down from his horse and called his men to ride, and off they went in a column, cantering off to die. *Last words, and a last request, and I failed him in all of it.*

He sat alone and ate his soup, brooding on what was to come.

A quiet had fallen over the great ward following the early furore. Across the battlements, the bowmen took their places, and by now every man had put on his armour and readied his weapons to fight. In that state the hours ticked by. A sense of anticipation prevailed, until at last they heard the horns once more. Everyone stopped what they were doing and their eyes went east. A darkness was creeping out upon the world, the unseen sun moving away west beyond the hills. *It's as though it wants to hide,* Emeric thought.

"They're here," Sir Bulmar said.

Emeric rejoined the others in council, and everyone came in their best, bedecked head to heel in steel with the fine rich cloaks of their kingdoms and houses and orders falling resplendent at their backs. Even Lady Marian had come this time.

"They've stopped at the treeline," Sir Karter Pentar reported. His armour was silver and red, like his cloak, enamelled on the breastplate and pauldons. "They cannot come much closer, else we'll bloody their nose with our trebuchets. Would you like me to fire a warning shot, my lord?"

"No," Borrus said. "Save the ammunition, Sir Karter. We'll need every rock and barrel."

"Do we have a notion of their strength?" asked Prince Raynald. "Are they all here? All of them?"

"We're unable to tell from the towers," Sir Karter answered. "I have sent outriders around their flanks to try to ascertain the truth of that, young prince. If they have left anyone behind, we will know of it soon."

"Then there's not much to do but wait," said Sir Rikkard. "I want to have a look at them."

"As do I," said Borrus, and quick as that the council was done.

Emeric joined them on the ramparts, scaling the stairs behind the east gate to peer across the plains. The dying light made it difficult to see much of anything, and the misty rains did not help, but all the same he could see the distant glow of firelight out in the distance, hundreds of tiny orbs floating among the trees half a mile away. His eyes ran slowly left to right, and even as he did so, more fires were blinking to life. It looked like all of them to his eyes.

"Do you see your friend Ballantris out there, Manfrey?" Borrus asked him. "That bear of his should be easy enough to spot."

"Look to the fringes," Sir Killian whispered. "Moonbears do not like crowds."

They all looked but none could see either Tathranor or *Jahendroth*, the young bear of Risho Ranaartan. Of dragons, however, there were many sightings, rippling like ghosts through the fogs that souped above the trees. Borrus stared out with a scowl. "I want Malathar," he said, as he often did. "I cut him up two decades ago, and this time I'll finish the job."

"You're two decades older," Rikkard informed him. "Don't over-stretch yourself or try to play the hero, Borrus. Lancel did that at the Battle of the Bane, and he paid for it with his life."

"Lancel," Borrus huffed. "Good lad. Decent sword. I don't want to speak ill of the dead, but I'm ten times the swordsman he is. When I come at Ven in Rushform he won't have a clue what hit him. I've been training daily, Rikkard. For months now. I trained at sea and I trained when we rode up through the mountains and I trained when we came back down again. I'm as good as I've ever been…better, even. And Malathar's two decades older too, don't forget. He's turned fat in his dotage I've heard. Heavy and slow and I'll have him."

"I'll get him if you die, Borrus, don't you worry," put in Mooton Blackshaw.

Borrus turned to him with a look of mild contempt. "You think too highly of yourself, Moot. I love you, I do, but you've become a braggart without backing it up." He took him by both shoulders as the two massive men stood face to face. Borrus put his forehead to Mooton's, pressing. "Prove it to me. Prove you're as fearsome as you say. I want you killing dragons, Moot. The gods know you're born for it, so do it. *Do it.*"

"I will." Mooton drew back. He had a fire in his eyes. "For your father, Borrus. And for you."

"For Vandar," Killian whispered.

They all agreed with that. "For Vandar," they said together. *For Tukor,* Emeric thought.

But not yet. For an hour they stood on the battlements until the light faded to black, and the mists closed in, and even the fires were blotted out. Emeric returned to the others at the northwestern corner, updating them on what was happening. "They're setting their camp," he told them. "There's unlikely to be any fighting tonight, and if there is, it'll be dragons. We'll let the ballistas take care of them."

"And if they attack us in force?" asked Brown Mouth Braxton. "We know what happened at the Bane. They took down the fort, and that's never happened before. There's magic in that stone, and they took it down all the same. They do the same here, and all of us could burn."

"If they wanted to do that, they'd have done it already, Braxton. No, I think they wish to engage us in the field. Their dragons numbers have been depleted and are growing precious. Men are much cheaper. So sit fast for now, and try to get some rest if you can. I'll be in my tent if anyone needs me."

He retired to his private sanctuary, taking with him a cold bowl of soup. For a while he sat and ate, listening to the gentle murmuring through the camp. Here and there men were singing, their voices rising like islands of noise in a sea of silence, but mostly it was quiet out there. Eventually, the pull of sleep nagged him into his bed. He remained armoured, just in case, removing only his swordbelt and helm, easing down onto the sturdy pallet he slept on. Sleep took him gradually, and the familiar faces in his dreams. The women he had loved. The men he had hated. The swirl of a thousand formless shapes asking for him to regale them of tales of Sir Oswald.

And then Sir Oswald himself stood before him. He looked much the same as the reflection Emeric saw in the mirror, only taller, broader, harder, wiser, stronger, better in every way. Sir Oswald came to him often, but in the dream he never spoke. He just looked at him, judging, searching his soul, shaking his head, and no matter what Emeric said, no matter where he turned, the great man was there, watching, displeased.

He was awoken by the sound of the horns.

His eyes snapped open and he scrambled at once to his feet, rushing groggily out into the ward to find that dawn was breaking, a red light bloodying the eastern walls. He had slept long hours somehow, all through the night. The horns were loud and coming from all quarters, a wild urgent blaring to call the men to assemble.

Emeric blinked and rubbed his eyes, remembering that he'd left his helm and swordbelt in his tent. He rushed to fetch them and burst back out, fixing his belt as he ran to the others. Jack was already awake, Braxton emerging sleepily from the tent they all shared as Soft Sid and Grim Pete followed him out. The Blackshaws were pouring from their tent as well.

"What's going on?" Jack asked. "Are we to march out to meet them, my lord? I heard someone say we would."

"I don't know, Jack." Emeric looked around. "Stay together, all of you. Captain Turner, best make for the city. I'll find out what's happening." He spun on his heels and dashed off.

Borrus's pavilion was in an uproar when he arrived. Everyone was shouting over one another, trying to be heard. Borrus stood behind the command table, hands to the wood, face red and boiling with rage. Emeric saw a bloody bag there, on the table. Sir Karter Pentar's hands were bloody as well.

Emeric moved over to Sir Rikkard. "What's happening, Rikkard? All the men are forming up."

Rikkard hardly seemed to hear him, Mooton was shouting so loud, roaring about smashing the enemy to pieces, while Rammas was repeating, "We have to march! We have to march!" as though incapable of saying anything else. Sir Torvyn was calling for calm thought, Killian Oloran looked like he wanted to put his thumb through someone's eye, and Prince Raynald's mouth was moving, but Emeric could not hear the words through all that. Lady Marian stood silent to one side, watching everyone else.

"Rikkard," Emeric repeated, grabbing his arm. "That bag? What's…"

"Sir Soloman," Rikkard told him darkly. "And that one…" A grimace passed the knight's lips and Emeric saw another bloody bag on the table, behind the first. "It's Barnibus. Their…their heads."

Emeric felt a sickened churn in his guts. "The dragons. They dropped them, as before?"

Rikkard nodded. "A short while ago. Sir Karter brought them in. There are others. Men are fetching them now, and…"

…and Emeric knew why Borrus was staring down at the table, red-faced and raging. He knew why the horns were blazing and the men were forming up. They all knew it, and all feared what was to come next. And just as Emeric was making that realisation, the tent flaps swayed open and a man burst in with another bloody bag in his hand.

The pavilion fell to a deep and sudden hush. "Bring it here," Borrus said. His voice was choked. The man came forward and put the bag on the table with a soft *clunk*. "Open it."

"My lord, I don't…"

"Open it," Borrus repeated. "*Now*."

The man's fingers fumbled as they undid the ties and the canvas bag fell open. Emeric peered forward. He caught a glimpse of a bald head, scraps of red beard, a skull smashed and maimed. There were cuts and lesions all over the face and cheeks and around the eyes as well. One of the eyes looked like it had been put out by a hot poker. "Gods," whispered Raynald Lukar. "Is that…"

"My father," Borrus said. He stared at the decapitated head of Lord Wallis Kanabar, battered and beaten and broken. For a long moment he just stared. And then his lips skinned back, and he bared his teeth, and from his lungs bellowed an anguished roar that needed no translation.

A roar to herald battle, and blood.

50

Elyon

The Tower of Rasalan emerged from the wintry shroud, suddenly and unexpectedly and very *luckily*, Elyon thought. He allowed a laugh, a burst of mist puffing from his lips. "Well Walter, I finally believe it," he shouted over the blusterous wind. "That luck of yours is truly something."

The man gave a humble chuckle from his harness. "I *think*, and it is *so*." A blue grin twisted on his frosted lips. "If only more people knew, good prince. I'd be worshipped as a god."

The comment was in jest, but there was some truth in there, to be sure. The light of Vandar shone from him, and if *that* didn't make a man godly, Elyon didn't know what did. "We can land there. I see...I think I see figures, Walter."

At the base of the ancient coastal tower, two large fires burned from within a pair of great iron braziers, cut into shapes of waves around the rim. Between the braziers, a great double door stood open, wood studded in iron, and three cloaked figures were to be seen outside. One was pointing skyward in their direction. Waving, it seemed to Elyon. The enthusiasm of it suggested it was Devrin.

They came in to land, piercing the icy wind, both of them frozen right down to the core. The flight from Thalan had been the most unpleasant of Elyon's life, though the letter from the dead king had kept his mind warm and busy. *Saska*, he thought. *Gods, so it's you.* He was still coming to terms with that, and would for some time, he suspected. *I need to find her at once. I need to find her and bring her to the refuge. To Ilith. I need to help her.*

But he had this to do first. This quest with the cousins and the Eye that had, through the mad old princess, turned into something much more. *One great quest will fail, but one greater will light the way.* Those words had been part of his father's quest to find the Frostblade, uttered by some Sea-King hundreds of years ago, but perhaps it was apt now too.

He did not know if they would see anything in the Eye, but that didn't matter to him now. This quest might fail, but it had led him to another. One greater. It would lead him back to *her*.

He smiled as his feet touched down on the icy earth, crunching through a film of frost. The fires blew wildly within the braziers, as though mimicking the crazed spray of ocean waves in a storm, spitting smoke into the ice-white skies. The warmth was welcome, and necessary. There were times when Elyon feared his sword arm had frozen solid in flight, outstretched in the direction of travel, never to thaw again. Well, that wasn't so, he was happy to find. With a film of ice breaking from his cloak and armour and hair, he lowered the Windblade and thrust it back into its sheath. He was shivering violently, his fingers fumbling to unstrap Walter from the harness.

"Let me help." One of the three figures came forward, reaching out to work the straps free. Within the heavy hood of thick wolf fur, Elyon espied the friendly face of Prince Devrin, son of the king.

"Devrin," Elyon said. "You made it."

"As did you, Elyon. And right on time. There must be something more than coincidence in that."

Elyon frowned. "How long have you been here?"

"Oh. About fifteen minutes. We're just getting the horses unsaddled inside. I rode ahead with a half dozen others. My father is a little behind. I don't suppose you saw him on your way?"

Elyon had seen shapes beneath him, a short while ago, but had put it down to rocks or boulders of which there were tens of thousands scattered across these bleak and windswept lands. "I was flying too fast to make anyone out clearly."

"Well, no matter. They'll be along shortly. An hour, perhaps two, I would hope. If not Father may have to spend another night on the ice." He sounded unconcerned. This prince had a rare zest to him, there was no doubt. His fingers worked the last of the straps, setting Walter loose. "Come inside, my friends. I sent my man Geffray to light the fires in the small hall, and small it is. It should warm up quickly enough."

Once they'd passed through the double doors, two guards pushed them closed, shutting off the howling wind. The entrance hall was thick stone, large and open, with stalls for the horses along one wall, stacks of weapons and armour and hooks for cloaks along the other. Firewood was piled high either side of the door, and sweepings of old hay were scattered across the paved stone floor. A half dozen Rasal thoroughbreds were in their stalls, their saddles and bridles being removed, hay laid out in troughs before them. *My bastard of a bastard brother has one of those*, Elyon thought. The beasts were rarely beautiful and graceful, capable of scaling cliffs like mountain goats and highly intelligent too. Most ran free up here in these wilds, and those that were taken to bond by a master were extremely particular about that choice.

651

"I hear only a fraction of them are ever saddled," Elyon said.

"A small fraction, yes," confirmed Devrin. "They are drawn to nobility, it's said."

Elyon grimaced as he thought of his brother. "How was the journey from Thalan? Your auntie had doubts as to whether you'd have made it by now. Or at all. She feared you dead."

"My auntie? You saw her?"

"In the palace." *And that special room of hers*, he thought, reflecting on her sorry tale. "We stopped there several hours ago."

"Several hours. And now here you are. While for us it's taken over a week." He gave a laugh. "The journey was cold, Elyon. Very cold, very windy, very long. But not so bad as we'd feared once we got beyond the snow. I do not know if you noticed from the skies, but about a hundred and fifty miles north of Thalan, the entire Highplains are frozen over and hard as rock. That made the going much easier for the horses."

They passed the stalls, moving toward a stair at the back that wound upward through the tower. "The small hall is on the floor above," Prince Devrin told him. "Then above that we have two floors of bedchambers, with the royal rooms above those. Then it's a way up to the top of the tower. It's a rotunda, perhaps you saw? With an open front of thick glass that gazes northward toward the ocean, right where Rasalan rose up to present Thala with the Eye, so legend says." He spoke with his usual energy. "Speaking of. I hope I don't need to ask, but…"

"I have the Eye in my bag," Elyon confirmed. "Along with Walter's possessions."

"Walter. Of course." Devrin turned to him. "Apologies for my lack of courtesy, Walter. I'm rather excited and weary at the same time." He smiled and took the man's arm, shaking. "A pleasure to meet you."

"And you, Your Highness." Walter performed one of his functional bows. "These bedchambers you mentioned. Will I be getting one of my own?"

"Of course. You'll be our honoured guest. Most of the men will sleep in the hall. My father has another dozen still with him, guards mostly, but he brought his steward too, and his horsemaster, and a cook. The cook came ahead with me to get a start on dinner. Oh, we won't want for good food, Walter, never fear. Hemmet does wonders even with basic ingredients. The miracles he can conjure with spices… ahhh. But come, let me give you a quick tour."

The prince seemed to know the tower well. He took them first to the small hall, where the man Geffray was lighting the fires, then up to the next level to show Walter his bedchamber. It was modest, but pleasant, with a window that looked west, providing views out to sea and down the frozen coast, a double bed warmly furnished in fur blankets, a thick rug on the floor, and a writing desk. Walter seemed happy to see that. "I like to write," he declared. "Perhaps Elyon told you?"

"He did mention that, yes."

Elyon removed his bag and handed Walter his things, his great tome of sketches and scribbles included, with fresh rolls of parchment, quills, ink pots, and clothes. There were few of those, because Walter was wearing most of his wardrobe. The scribe took his book with great affection and laid it on the table, positioning it neatly. "I'd love to take your portrait, if you'll allow it, good prince," he said. "You and your father. Perhaps both of you at once might be nice?"

"I'm sure he'll be agreeable. There is a small hearth as well, as you can see. I shall have Geffray light a fire for you." Devrin turned to Elyon. "I presume you will be staying the night before you leave?"

Elyon was about to keel over. He nodded.

Devrin laughed. "A foolish question. We'll have a room prepared for you. Feel free to stay longer if you wish."

"My thanks. One night will serve."

The tour took them next to the royal chambers, which occupied the entire fourth floor, comprising bedchamber, large solar, library, audience chamber, and privy. The library was of great interest to Walter Selleck. "What a trove," he said, looking around at the shelves. "I wonder what wonders are in here?"

Prince Devrin chuckled at the use of words. "It is said my great uncle Godrin read every book in here three times over during his reign."

Elyon looked across the high shelves and stacks, the thick leather-bound books and ten-tome volumes, the scripts on philosophy and history and culture and art. There must have been several thousand books in here, and frankly, that sounded like a tall tale to Elyon Daecar. *No man reads thousands of books,* he thought, *let alone three times over.* "He must have come here often," he only said.

"Oh he did. All monarchs would retreat to his sanctuary from time to time, to better connect with Great Rasalan. I understand my great uncle did most of his best work here."

"You mean his visions?"

Devrin's eyes wrinkled with excitement. "My father and I spent the week scouring his pages of the Book of Thala, Elyon, and those translations you provided us. Each night in our tent, we sat together for hours and read them. Fascinating stuff, truly. Though there is a page missing, did you know? In the book."

Elyon knew. "A man named Ranulf Shackton stole it." That was what Archibald Benton had said, anyway. Apparently Janilah Lukar had been most wroth about that and had sent a Bloody Trader captain called the Surgeon after him. But that was all a long time ago now.

Prince Devrin was smiling. "Ranulf Shackton is a famous name," he said. "A great adventurer of our people. And a friend of my great uncle if I'm not mistaken. Why do you imagine he would steal a page?"

"I suspect because it contained an important secret that he did not want to fall into the wrong hands." Elyon had an idea what that secret was, and had a mind to try to find Shackton himself. He wondered if he might find the man with Saska. She had always spoken very highly of him, he remembered, and Ranulf had been the one to put the first piece of the puzzle of her identity into place, when he found out she was the secret child of Leila Nemati.

I wonder if he knew the rest? Or knows it now? Most likely he did. Elyon did not delude himself into thinking that he was the only one. *Just the latest*, he thought. Saska's grandmother had long been part of this scheme, Elyon knew that from the letter, so if nothing else he would fly to Aram and see if Saska was still with her.

At last, he thought ruefully. *To Aram at last.* He had told himself he'd go a hundred times, and now it had become his top priority. *Well, one of them, anyway*, he thought. One high peak among many. He still must return to his father, and his war in the west. He still yearned to find his missing sister. And Rustbridge. He had been gone from there for far too long and now Borrus was back as well. And what of the other blades? He had told Ilith he would help find them, and bring them to him, as he'd told his father the same. Jonik was out there now, working for Ilith as well, and Elyon still did not know what to make of that. A part of him did not trust the Shadowknight, as a part still didn't trust himself. *He is tainted, as I am. He knows what it is to have a god in his head.*

He put that aside. In the end it did not matter who gathered the blades, only that they *were* gathered and brought to the refuge for Ilith to hammer back together. *And soon*, Elyon knew. *Soon. Time is short.* At least now he knew who would wield the Heart Remade. *Gods, can it be true? She is so young, untrained, so new to godsteel. And a woman.* Gifted, yes, but she would need to be trained. No doubt the King's Wall had been seeing to that, and others as well, but none of them knew what it was to bear a Blade of Vandar. *I do. I know, and I must show her, teach her, help her. We cannot hammer the blades back together and expect her to wield them at once.*

His thoughts were spiralling. When he withdrew from them he found that Devrin and Walter had moved off, as the prince showed the scruffy scribe around the library, pointing out this book and that. "Ah, here's one of interest to you," Devrin was saying. He pulled out a dusty leather tome, the surface cracked and frayed, and laid it on a table with a *thud*. "*Oddities and Anomalies*," he said. "*Unique Powers from Across the World*. I daresay you would fit in here yourself, Walter, with this *luck* of yours."

Selleck gave a chuckle. "It'll make fine night-time reading, good prince. Might I pick a few books out, to take to my bedchamber?"

"By all means. There is one on Vandar's Tomb somewhere, I think, listing all the official and successful journeys there. You could be in that one too." Devrin smiled and returned to Elyon. "Well, shall I show you the rotunda? It's just up the stairs."

They left Walter to pick through the library; the man would have ample time to explore every nook and cranny of the tower in the coming days, and the rotunda in particular would become like a second home to him. For now it was only the two princes who wound about the spiral stair, moving up the worn stone steps, smoothed by time, level by level as the tower narrowed and thinned toward the top. Devrin carried a flaming torch before him to show the way, stopping to light the candles sitting in small niches along the outer wall. When they reached the top of the stair it straightened out, leading right up into the domed rotunda at the tower's summit, a large half-orb empty of all furnishings but for the plinth set at its hearth, a stone pillar tessellated in squares of gold and blue. The walls were thick stone, painted in veins of gold, windowless but for the great glass aperture that looked straight out over the endless sea. On the floor was a wondrously detailed mosaic depicting the day Rasalan rose from the frothing ocean to gift his sight to Thala. The tower did not exist then, so the demigoddess stood only on the clifftop, looking over the raging waters as the ocean god came up from his halls.

"Beautiful, isn't it," Devrin said. "I've always wanted to see it."

Elyon frowned. "You've never been here?"

"Up here? No. This is the preserve of kings and queens. I have come to the tower before, long ago, but was only permitted into the guest quarters." He looked about the walls; there were more candles in niches, and a few torches in sconces too. "Let's see how it looks when given more light." The prince moved about the circumference, firing the torches and the candles, filling the dome with warmth and radiance. "Ah…the detail. I could stand here all day admiring it."

Elyon had rarely seen such a fine work of art. It felt almost wrong to be walking on it, but he supposed so few people ever came up here that the mosaic would not be unduly damaged by their footfall. All the same, he went about more carefully than he normally would, worried the weight of his plate might crack or tarnish a tile. After a full slow circuit, he found his way to the window that gazed out over the frozen sea. It was broadly oval in shape, somewhat like a pupil. "It's like a giant eye," Elyon said.

"That was the intention," Devrin agreed. "When the Eye of Rasalan is placed on the plinth, its power is amplified, it is said. The weaker monarchs would only glimpse through the pupil here, in the tower. There is one rather similar to it, back in Thalan. The Tower of the Eye it is called."

Where Hadrin was taken, Elyon thought. Amilia had pointed it out when they first flew to Thalan.

"Typically the Eye would be kept there while a monarch was in Thalan. But here they would see more clearly." Devrin smiled and filled his lungs, terribly excited. "Well, perhaps you can place the Eye down now, Elyon? I am my father's son. Now he will curse me for a monster forevermore for this, but maybe I'll have a little gander first, see if I might glimpse something for you?"

For us, Elyon thought to correct him. This was about everyone, not just him. But he only took the orb from the bag on his back and set it on the plinth. A smile graced his bearded lips as he placed it there. It sat snugly in the depression, a perfect fit. It felt good - *right* - to bring it back to its proper place, and to finally complete his quest.

Devrin looked at the Eye like it was an old friend of his, though more likely he'd glimpsed it only a handful of times in his life, if that. He moved about it in a slow walk, admiring it from all angles, smiling and turning his head here and there. "I suppose my auntie Cristin asked to have a look as well, did she?" He glanced over, seeing the answer in Elyon's eyes. "Did she have any luck?"

"None. She said it was broken. That the pupil was shut for good."

Devrin smiled. "Perhaps she's right. I daresay we will find out in due course. Though…" He continued to circle it, like a very friendly bird of prey. "I can feel a certain *power* coming off of it. A throbbing essence, if you will, spreading from its core. Do you feel it as well?"

"Not like you do."

"No. It is steel that calls to you, not the timeless motion of the sea." He took another slow step, another.

Elyon watched him, as the prince moseyed along on a second circuit. He seemed to be biding his time, embracing the essence of the orb, letting its aura enrobe him, fill him. *Not like Cristin. She tried too hard and gave up too easily.* Devrin did not seem that sort and his father, too, would be greatly more patient. "Your auntie said something interesting about your father," Elyon said, as the prince walked.

Devrin kept his eyes on the orb. Another step. Another. "Oh? And what was that?"

"She spoke of a rumour regarding his sire."

"Ah, *that.* A well-worn thing among the members of my family. There is no proof of it either way, though some like to point at my grandfather's general sense of discourtesy toward his king brother as reason to believe it. Not many take it seriously, though. Why do you mention it?"

"Because of that." Elyon pointed at the orb. "If your father is Godrin's son, not Tayrin's, his sight will likely be stronger." He was not the eldest son, no, not the firstborn and thus not direct in the line of Thala by primogeniture, so in that sense it probably didn't matter, but all the same, Elyon had been intrigued by it. Simply being born of Godrin's loins, brilliant as he was, might have fostered Sevrin with more power, and Devrin too by extension.

Might this have even been foreseen? By Godrin or even his father King Astan before him? Elyon didn't much want to take that thought to completion, ugly as the implications were. A father, guiding his eldest son to sire a child by the wife of his brother. There was much about all this that could be perverse, even if it was necessary. *Like tricking a poor girl into thinking a handsome prince was coming for her*, he thought. *Gods, that poor woman. No wonder she's turned so crazed.*

Devrin had stopped before the Eye, his hand to his chin, rubbing. "Well…here goes, then," he said. "Let's see if Great Rasalan's got anything to show me." He stepped toward the glowing orb, put his hands to the stone plinth to either side, locked eyes with the pupil and leaned in. A second later he leaned back. "My father is here," he said.

Elyon frowned. "Great Rasalan showed you *that*? That isn't so exciting, Devrin."

"No, I mean…I heard them outside. A horse whicker. It must be them arriving."

Elyon had heard nothing. He reached to grip the handle of his dagger, enhancing his hearing, and true enough there was the sound of horses and men below, and the howling wind blowing in through the open doors. "You're right. Good ear, Devrin."

"We Seaborn have decent senses, you know. Helps us under the water." He smiled and then looked at the Eye once more and the smile slipped from his lips. "Well, my chance is gone. Knowing my father he will command me to stand down. Etiquette must be followed, Elyon. Gods forbid I might have better sight than him." There was the smallest hint of rancour in his tone, hidden amidst the jest. "Well, let's leave it here. Come, I'll announce you."

They sped together down the spiral stair. Walter was waiting where it passed the library and joined them as they descended, a stack of books clutched in arm. He took a short moment to deposit them into his room, then they continued back down into the entrance hall with the stables and the wood and the weapons. Men were dismounting and unpacking their saddle bags, bustling about, stabling the horses.

Devrin saw his father among all that and moved forward at once. "Father, you made it. I have prepared the tower for your arrival. The fires are roaring and Hemmet is preparing the food. Oh, and Elyon is here with his friend Walter Selleck."

King Sevrin's face looked like it was carved from a block of ice, white-blue and frosted over as it was. The rest of him was fur speckled in hoarfrost. "Prince Elyon. You didn't have to await my son too long, I hope?"

"No, my lord. He awaited us, in truth."

"Oh?"

"They arrived only fifteen minutes after I did, Father. No more than an hour ago."

Sevrin cocked a brow. "Intriguing. And you must be Walter Selleck."

"Last I checked." Walter gave that functional bow. "A pleasure, Your Majesty."

"Majesty. I don't feel so majestic right now. Your Frozenness would suit me better, yet I thank you for the courtesy, Walter. But that'll serve on the titles. We'll dispense with them here in the tower. My lord will do, or Sevrin when we're alone. And we'll be alone plenty enough, I would think."

657

It was hoped that Walter's luck might help Sevrin to open the Eye. It would be an extremely dull charge, Elyon knew, standing by for hours on end while the king peered endlessly into that orb. He would be tasked with writing down anything he heard as well. As Elyon understood it, Sevrin might mutter something without remembering, and someone must be on hand to record it.

"I have shown our guests around, Father," Devrin put in. "And I brought Elyon to the rotunda. We left the Eye up there."

Sevrin looked at his son. "I asked you to wait for me, Devrin. Before visiting the top of the tower."

"Yes, Father. I would have, but for Elyon. We thought it prudent to set the Eye in place as soon as possible. So it might settle."

Sevrin gave a small grumble. "I did want to share that moment with you, Devrin, but so be it. It's done now." He removed his gloves and flexed his thin, bony fingers, trying to get some life back into them. Both were white from the cold. "Is the small hall warm?"

"Pleasantly so, Father."

"Then let us retire there." He turned to the man who was likely his steward, fussing with some bags. "Bertrand, take my things to the royal apartments. And make sure a fire is lit. I want the room warm for when I take to my bed."

The steward nodded acknowledgement, and off they went up the stairs.

The small hall was aptly named, a small hall with only a few long tables and benches lined up down its length. There was no king's table, no stage at the top where a monarch might sit and cast his judgements. That was not the way of the humble Rasal people. Instead a monarch would go among his men and subjects, of which there were only ever few here, sitting with them as they ate at whatever table he so chose.

On the eastern and western walls of the hall were built great chimneyed hearths. Both were firing splendidly as they entered. Two men were going around, wiping the tables and benches of dust, setting out plates and cutlery. One stepped away as he saw them enter, and returned as they sat with a tray topped with a large jug of wine and cups. Their chosen table was near the western hearth, and Sevrin sat closest to the blaze, reaching out to warm his hands against the flames. He flexed his fingers again, feeling the blood return. "I've never felt a cold like it, truly. A beastly thing. Be thankful you flew, Elyon. How long did it take you to get here?"

"We left Ilithor not long past dawn."

"Oh. You came that far in one day?"

Elyon nodded as Devrin served the wine. Steam rose from the top of the jug. "We stopped for a short time in Thalan, to confirm you'd left. That added some length to the journey."

"And tomorrow? You're to leave come the dawn, I suppose?"

"That is the plan." Elyon did not say where, because even he did not know. He needed to sleep first, and already he could feel the pull of it in his head. He had a long drink of wine to warm his insides. The fire crackled relaxingly, and he felt a deep thick pang of weariness fill his blood.

King Sevrin smiled at him. "You look even more tired than I feel, Elyon. Can you hold on to eat? You must be hungry after your flight."

Famished, Elyon thought. He had barely enough strength to say it all of a sudden, the last of his energy leeching out of him like the final spurts of blood from a severed throat.

"Well, let's get you fed, then." Sevrin waved a man over and asked for them to bring out whatever the cook Hemmet had already prepared.

The stew was delicious, rabbit cooked slow with carrot and onion, a simple broth brought alive by the seasoning. Elyon began by eating with accustomed grace, before Sevrin disavowed him of the notion and after that he ate like a man starved, slurping, gulping, tearing at chunks of bread with his teeth, munching on thick moist cheese and cuts of beef so tender they fell apart in his mouth. By the time he was done he jested he might have to have the Forgemasters at the Steelforge let out his armour a little, when next he visited Varinar, and that led into a discussion on the state of the city and other such affairs.

Elyon found a second wind, but it lasted only so long before the warmth and the wine and the food in his belly demanded he take his leave. By then the other men were sitting about the tables as well, and there was talking, laughter, hearty voices to be heard. It reminded Elyon of a simpler time. Here in this remote old tower, four hundred miles from the nearest city and hidden away from the rest of the world, he felt safe. It was an odd feeling. Even in Ilithor, far from the fighting, he knew a thunder of dragons could come at any time. He knew the Dread might descend upon them. But here… no. It was a haven in the frozen wastes, looking out over the frozen seas, enrobed and enclosed in a thick white mist. No one would find them here.

Prince Devrin accompanied him to his room. It was grander than Walter's, with a larger bed and richer furnishings, but Elyon did not care for them. The bed was all that mattered. "Will your father spend time with the Eye tonight?" he asked, as Devrin was leaving.

The prince paused at the door. "He will pay a visit, I'm sure, before taking to his bed. Who knows, perhaps you will awaken to good news and the birth of a brand new vision?"

"Good news would depend on the vision," Elyon said to that. Just as likely a vision would spell doom.

Devrin smiled. "Quite so." He reached for the door handle. "Goodnight, then. Sleep well."

Elyon crawled into his bed a few minutes later, unarmed, unarmored, naked but for a pair of cotton breeks that had seen some better days. The fire had warmed the room nicely and beneath the furs sleep took him quickly. He entered a dreamless space, a void beyond thought and time, and woke to the pale light of an icy sunrise, slanting through the frosted window.

He sat up, rubbing his eyes, yawning like a lion. He had slept all through the night and felt all the better for it. The fire had long since burned itself out, his breath misting in the chill. He took a moment to stretch and limber up, working his shoulder around the socket, then put on his padded underclothes, armour and furs and cinched the Windblade around his waist.

If Elyon had hoped the night might have given the king a chance to glimpse something in the Eye, he was mistaken. "I had a brief look," King Sevrin informed him, when Elyon found him down in the entrance hall, brushing his fine Rasalanian thoroughbred. "But nothing, as yet. It will take time. When next you return, I will have something for you, Elyon." He put his hand on Elyon's arm and smiled. "So, where next? It is clear out there, nice and crisp…good air for flying I would think. Where will the wind take you, young prince?"

Elyon had a few options in mind, and today, shorn of Walter's not inconsiderable weight, he would be able to fly swift and true. He was about to answer when they heard a shrill cry outside, the high-pitched call of a bird of prey piercing the morning air. The horsemaster stepped interestedly to the open door and peered out. "An eagle," he said. "It's circling above us."

"So far north?" Sevrin was intrigued. "What sort of eagle is it, Rodney?"

The horsemaster held a gloved hand to his eyes and squinted. "Huh."

"*Huh*? Is that a new species of eagle I'm not aware of?"

"Sorry, m'lord. It's…well, it's not northern, is what I mean. Not by that size and colouring. Looks southern to me. Aramatian I'd guess."

"Aramatian?" Elyon repeated. A line furrowed his brow. "I didn't know eagles migrated so far."

"Well…they don't. Mayhaps a short ways to find better hunting grounds, but this sort…known to live at Eagle Lake, if memory serves. Plenty of good hunting to be had there. All them birds and fish and such."

Sevrin drifted toward the door, Elyon following. The air was still, biting cold but not blowing like it had the day before. In the skies above the tower the eagle was circling in a high wide arc, but what prey it might be hunting Elyon couldn't say. It looked majestic up there against the frozen white skies, gliding on its glorious plumage, strong wings in gold and bronze and a gilded black-tipped beak.

As the prince stepped out through the door, the bird gave another whistling cry, tail feathers fluttering as it furled itself into a sudden plunge.

"It's seen something," the horsemaster Rodney announced. "Mouse or vole, most like."

The eagle had seen no mouse or vole. Halfway through its dive it opened its wings once more, slowed abruptly, and came gliding right toward them to land on the lip of one of the great iron braziers.

"Well I never," Rodney said, nonplussed. "Friendliest eagle I ever saw." He took a step forward, smiling, reaching out a gloved arm.

"What's that in its talon?" King Sevrin asked.

"Huh," Rodney said. "Looks like a scroll, m'lord."

Elyon frowned. Since when did eagles become carrier crows?

The eagle flapped its wings, leaping from the rim onto Rodney's arm. The man gave out a huff of delight. "You're an inquisitive one, aren't you." The eagle was large, a strong bird. Rodney was a solidly built man, but the weight of it had his arm tensing to bear it, powerful talons clutching at the old leather of the horsemaster's elbow-length glove. "Now what's this about a scroll, then? Mind if we take a look?" He reached forward with his spare hand, speaking softly as he did so. The man was clearly versed in conversing with animals. Ever-so-deftly, he plucked the scroll from the eagle's ankle. No sooner had he done so than the bird beat its wings and took flight, giving out another piercing call as it rose into the frigid skies and bore itself back to the south.

All three men watched it go in amazement. Then Rodney handed the scroll to King Sevrin. "For you, m'lord. The seal is unmarked."

The small king took it, broke the plain wax seal, unrolled it and read the words. "It's not for me," he said.

He handed it to Elyon Daecar.

51

Pagaloth

The fire priest fell to the mud with a splash, his legs giving way beneath him.

"To your feet," Ulrik Marak commanded roughly. "Stand. Or you will be dragged."

The priest scrambled up clumsily, wiping the mud from his face. His wrists were bound in rope, mouth gagged with a filthy cloth, eyes staring out in boundless hate as the dragonlord stared back impassively. Mud and rainwater coated the priest's once red and orange robes, the fine thread spoiled and ruined. He had fallen many times that day, and bore the marks to show it. His hands showed cuts and bruises, he had a deep gash on his left cheek where a branch had whipped back at Marak's passing, slicing the flesh open, and he had started to walk with a limp having landed awkwardly on his hip when stumbling over a root.

The dragonlord seemed to take pleasure in the man's pain. "I don't think he likes me," he said, staring into those cloudy red eyes. "Perhaps it's the gag, Pagaloth, what do you think? Should we take it off him?"

"No," the dragonknight said at once. "My lord, if we do that…"

Marak snorted and waved it away. "Nothing will happen," he dismissed. "Not to me, anyway."

"You? My lord, I'm not sure I understand."

"You will. We'll be there soon enough, Pagaloth. And you will." He turned forward and kicked his spurs, urging his horse onward. The rope that tethered the priest to the mount grew taut, then tugged him forward at the wrists, and on they went through the wood.

The day was as grim and wet as those that had come before, but for once Pagaloth felt rested and full, his hunger satiated at last. The rabbit stew had seen to that, cooked in a pot above the hearth fire in the common room of the inn, where they had camped for the night following the slaughter. Lord Marak had taken the watch, to allow

Pagaloth to get some sleep. "Save your protests," he had said. "I've had rest enough of late, and you look about ready for the pyre. Find a bed upstairs and sleep soundly. I want you back to full strength, Pagaloth. You'll be perfectly safe with me."

Sir Pagaloth did not doubt it. He had seen what the man had done. The Fireblade was as lethal as the finest godsteel and granted Ulrik Marak the same set of powers. Whirling through the woods like a flaming cyclone, he had made short work of the fire priest's company, sparing only the man himself.

"We should kill him," Pagaloth had insisted, once the bloodshed was complete. "He is too dangerous to be left alive." He had thought of the damage Ten'kin had done. Thought of Sa'har, taken back under Eldur's spell. If the same happened to Lord Marak…

But the dragonlord shook his head. "I have another use for him. Bind him and gag him, Sir Pagaloth. We will leave at first light."

They had, though *where*, Marak still hadn't told him. The dragonlord had been miserly with his tale thus far, though had demanded Pagaloth tell his. When the dragonknight spoke of Lythian, and his plan for unity, Lord Marak only grunted and gave a sour shake of the head. When he told the dragonlord of what had happened to their party, about Ten'kin and the ambush and the self-sacrifice of Sa'har Nakaan, his eyes had darkened with grief and he had turned his head away. Sa'har had been his dearest friend, his wingrider, the closest thing he had to a brother, and for a fleeting moment Pagaloth had wondered if he might rip the Fireblade from its sheath and give the priest a grisly death in retribution. But he had only closed his eyes, as though remembering fonder times, and then ridden on in solemn silence, never speaking a word.

Later, as they forded a swollen stream, Pagaloth had mustered the courage to ask of Garlath. "No one knows what happened to you after the battle, my lord," he had said. "Some say Garlath took a wound…a wound bad enough to kill him." He had paused, checking the dragonlord's eyes. "Is he…"

"Garlath is very much alive."

"But…you did not come on him, when you found me. You rode a horse."

"A horse served my needs."

They continued on through the rustling waters, the priest splashing and slipping on the stony bed behind them. Pagaloth glanced back at him. "And…how *did* you find me, my lord? Or was it him you were hunting?"

"Him," Marak said at once. "Finding you was mere happenstance." The dragonlord looked over at him, granite-jawed and grim. "Some would call that fortune, even fate. Others a second chance." His eyes bored into him. "Do you still curse yourself for your betrayal, Sir Pagaloth?

The dragonknight lowered his eyes. "Every day, my lord."

"Good. Guilt can drive a man to make amends, whether that guilt is valid or not." He'd looked him up and down, appraising. "There's fire in your blood." It wasn't a question.

Pagaloth answered anyway. "Yes, Lord Marak. On my mother's side."

"And rich enough, so I remember." He'd given a smile, hard and knowing. "Well, we'll see about that later. Now come, we have a way to go yet. I want to get there by dusk."

They had spoken little since, leaving the dragonknight to ride in mystery, trying to puzzle out Lord Marak's meaning. The rain had waxed and waned, reliable only in its presence, coming down in black sheets sometimes, and sometimes falling gently, but never once deigning to cease. The lands, too, were much as they'd been. Eerie woods and waterlogged valleys, rushing rivers and haunting fogs. Pagaloth heard howling, as he did most days, and once the low rumbling of something much bigger as well, echoing through some dark thicket. The fire priest's eyes widened in fear at that, his bleats of alarm muffled by his gag.

"The *will of Eldur,*" Marak mocked. "Terrified of some mortal beast." He reached back, tugging on the rope, and the priest went stumbling forward. "Quiet now, priest. You wouldn't want to draw it near."

The priest had been silent since, just staring at them with those hostile eyes as they drew him along on his rope. By now the light was just starting to fade, leeching out of the overcast skies. They rode on through the woods, entering a thicker forest, the canopy dense above them. It grew dark in there, as though night had come on suddenly, and they moved slowly on their steeds, carefully picking through the roots and grasping growth of the forest floor.

Then suddenly the trees ended, abruptly and dramatically, and light filled the world once more. Right ahead of them, the earth fell away into a great abyss, as though some god had hacked down at the land with a colossal axe, splitting it asunder. The rift must have been a hundred metres across, cutting right through the heart of the forest. "Gods," Pagaloth whispered. "What happened here?"

"Earthquake," Lord Marak said. "This rift wasn't here a month ago."

Pagaloth trotted his horse as close to the edge as he dared, his eyes roaming left and right, trying to see where the rift began. Both ways it bled beyond his sight, trees cloaking its sides. From its sheer far wall, Pagaloth could see thousands of roots dangling out of the rock like strands of hair on a thinning scalp, some thin and wispy, others thick and long. He was amazed at how deep some of them went. And how many there were. It gave him a new appreciation of just how much was going on beneath his feet. "This canyon's got to be miles in length," he said.

"It is," Marak told him.

664

"How do we cross it?" Lest their horses learn to fly he couldn't think of any way but to go around. "Ought we track back through the forest, my lord?"

"No. We are here."

"Here?" He did not understand.

"We go down, Pagaloth. There is a way a little further along the edge where we can descend."

Down. Pagaloth leaned forward, looking over the lip. The plunge was almost vertical, with thick shafts of rock poking out here and there. In a net of roots and vines he saw a fallen tree, suspended above a cloud of mist, which souped between the canyon walls some thirty or so metres below them. He could not see the bottom through it. "How deep does it go?"

"We have not tested its depth. There is a plateau on which we have made our camp. But in places it goes much deeper. That is not of our concern."

We. Our. "I thought it was just you. Are you to say there are more of you?"

"Five," he said. "And one prisoner." He glared at the priest. "Now that you are here, we are six, Pagaloth. And the dragons."

"The…" He turned to look into Marak's craggy face, as bluff as the sheer rock wall across from them. "Dragon*s*, my lord? There is more than one?"

"You heard what I said, Sir Pagaloth." Marak turned his horse to the right. "This way." He tugged the rope, getting the priest moving. "We'll have to leave the horses at the top."

A little further along they came to a small glade, just a short way back from the edge of the rift. Marak dismounted his horse and instructed Pagaloth to do the same. There were two others here already, munching on the soft grasses. A fence of vines had been drawn around the trees to pen them in, though they had some space to canter about if they wished. "Where did you get them?" Pagaloth asked.

"I found them wandering in the woods, not far from here. I thought we might make use of them, and so it has turned out. Flying is not always the best way." He untied the rope that bound the fire priest to his horse, though left him fettered at the wrists. The man's eyes were red and wild and bloodshot. Marak smiled at him. "I can't have you falling on the way down, so will carry you. Try not to thrash too much." He bound his legs to hold them tight, at the ankles and knees both, then ran another length of rope around the priest's body, before lifting him onto his broad shoulders and looping the rope around his arms. He tied it all fast, securing the man, as he hissed and spat into his gag.

Below, Pagaloth heard a deep rumbling. He recognised the sound. "Garlath," he said.

Marak dipped his chin. "I would summon him to carry us, but

665

there's nowhere here for him to land. And the climb is easy enough. I hope you have no fear of heights, Pagaloth."

"None."

Marak nodded, pleased to hear it. "Come. Use the roots and rocks as handholds. Follow me and you'll be fine."

The descent began nearby. The edge here had crumbled unevenly, creating a place where great ledges and rocky steps worked down toward the roiling fog. At the very top, a tree had tumbled over the lip, its twisting network of roots clinging on stubbornly, anchoring it to the wall. The branches made for a good way down to the first shelf, some ten metres below. Marak went first, the bark grinding beneath his boots, moving more deftly than one would think for such a large man as he lowered himself from branch to branch. Pagaloth followed, marking where he put his feet and hands.

When they reached the shelf, Marak went to its left side, showed Pagaloth the way down, and set off. Here the section was more steep, and they had to climb down handholds on the rock wall itself. At the bottom, a large chunk of rock thrust out of the wall like a spearhead, pointed and triangular. It sat in line with the fog, so close he could reach out and touch it, hanging strangely and uniformly in the air. Below, Pagaloth could hear the shriek of dragons, echoing through the chasm.

"The next part is hardest," Lord Ulrik Marak said. "The mist makes it hard to see. Watch closely. Step where I step."

Pagaloth nodded. Marak had not been wrong. Muffled screams moaned through the priest's spit-soaked gag as he lay slung across Marak's shoulders, staring down into oblivion. The dragonlord flicked a hand back, striking him in the side of the head. "Be silent, priest. I must concentrate." He stopped for a moment, clinging to the wall, figuring out which of two footholds to choose. He reached out a leg to test one, but the wall gave way, stone tumbling and echoing. "It'll be the other one, then," Pagaloth heard him say. He did not seem overly concerned, and that gave the dragonknight faith.

All the same, he'd never been so frightened…not that he'd ever admit it. In these thick wet mists he could not tell whether the floor was a metre below him or ten or a hundred. It set his heart to pounding, a heavy pulse throbbing in his neck. He could feel the cold sweat on his palms, a chill running down his spine. One wrong move and he would tumble into the void, never knowing when the earth would rush up to meet him. "How far is it?" he heard himself say, trying to drive the fear from his voice.

Lord Marak did not deign to answer. And he didn't need to. No sooner had Pagaloth asked the question than the mists melted away, just like that, and they landed on a rough rock shelf beneath the cloud of fog, floating now queerly above them.

Pagaloth looked up, then down, astonished. Beneath him, the cavern spread forth, in places falling to black pits, in others cast with great rocky shelves and ledges as large as market squares. On one, no more than sixty feet down, he saw a camp laid out. A fire burned at the heart of a ring of tents. There were some crates, boxes, bags here and there. Around the fire seats of stone had been arrayed. Pagaloth spied three figures there, a woman and two men, their voices rising in echoes. The woman wore a cloak in sky blue and ochre, split unevenly, two-thirds and one. The slim man who sat near her had a chequered cape on his back, greyish white and lime green. The third figure was large, round-shouldered, and garbed more plainly in boiled leather and an overcloak of undyed wool.

Upon several other ledges, dragons lay curled and sleeping on private roosts, a half dozen of them that he could see. A pair more were circling, stretching their wings and diving into the darkness below, only to burst up from somewhere else, screeching all the while. Those screeches sounded almost gleeful, playful to Pagaloth's ears. On a great shelf overlooking all of them, Garlath the Grand had made his nest. He sat up, wings furled, eyes gleaming in the dimness, watching over it all. His scales were silver and blue.

Pagaloth was at a loss for words. "What…what is this place?" he managed to whisper.

"Home," was Ulrik Marak's reply. "For now."

The final descent was simple enough, a zigzag back and forth across the rocks where a great heap of stone had tumbled from the rift wall, giving passage down to the camp. The figures around the fire spotted them coming, calling out their greetings and standing from their stones. Once they reached the shelf, Lord Marak slipped his arms through the loops and swung the fire priest down to the floor. He landed with a thump. "Found a replacement," he said. "And another recruit." He gestured to Pagaloth.

The three strangers looked at him…though not all were strangers, he realised, as soon as he came face to face with them. One he knew, the woman in ochre and blue. "Lady Kazaan," he said, shocked to see her here. He recalled his courtesies and gave her a respectful bow. She was in her middle years, spare and lean, with black hair slashed with a strand of white on one side. Thin wrinkles spread from a set of hard lilac eyes, her mouth a puckered aperture in a thin and pointed jaw. Lady Adelle Kazaan was a known figure in Eldurath, rich and high-born, the head of her dragonhouse since the death of her husband in the war. He had been a rider of some repute, Pagaloth remembered. "We met once," he told her. "I rode escort for you when you travelled to Videnia, to celebrate the summer festival."

She peered at him. "I do not remember."

"I was young, my lady. It was many years ago."

"I see. And who are you?"

"Sir Pagaloth Kadosk," he said. "Dragonknight."

She knew the name. "Your uncle was Sir Lendroth."

"He was, my lady. I squired for him in Eldurath, for a time. He taught me much of what I know." *And then he died*, he thought. His uncle had ridden to war, along with his father and brothers and other uncles, and none of them had come home. Not long after, his mother had taken her own life, unable to bear the grief. *The war killed her too*, Pagaloth thought bitterly. He was all that remained of his family now.

It seemed to him that Lady Kazaan knew that story. It was rare, even among the tragedies of the war, for a man to lose so much. Her eyes showed a flash of sympathy, then hardened again. She looked at Marak. "Where did you find him?"

"South of here. He was being chased by a patrol." He looked down at the fire priest, squirming on the floor in his hempen bounds. A kick to the midsection stilled his wriggling. "This one was with them. We killed the rest."

The slim man in the chequered cape knelt down, taking the priest's face in his grasp, turning his head toward him. He looked long and deep into his eyes. "Plenty of hate in there," he mused. "Looks like he's been in for some rough treatment."

"He has fallen once or twice," Marak explained.

The man stood up again. He looked at Pagaloth, smiling. He was about Pagaloth's own age, perhaps a few years older, with eyes of burnished brown and thick waves of dense black hair cascading from his head. His jaw was peppered with patchy stubble. "My name is An'zon Graz. You have likely heard of my house, if not me."

All of that was correct. House Graz, like House Kazaan, was another well-known family with a storied history and rich holdings. The name An'zon was not familiar to him, however. Most likely he was of a lesser branch, and a lesser son. "I have," Pagaloth said, inclining his head.

"And this is Rhok." An'zon gestured to the other man in the boiled leather jerkin and plain frayed cloak. He cut an imposing figure, broad in the chest and well endowed about the gut, heavy and tall. A braided beard hung off his rounded chin, trailing to his belt, tucked in beneath his girth, and there were many tattoos inked about his dark, angry eyes. Pagaloth had commanded many men like him in the past. He was of humble birth, but had fought in the last war, and taken many lives. Those tattoos told that story. As did the well-worn longsword he wore on his left hip, the savage dirk on his right. "Rhok joined us only two weeks ago," An'zon Graz went on. "He was saved, same as you."

Pagaloth was still missing a few pieces to this puzzle. Though much of it he was putting together. "You're all riders," he said. He had glimpsed the colours of the dragons as he climbed down the final section. One had been mottled in shades of white and lime green; the dragon of An'zon Graz. Another, larger, long-bodied and broad-winged, was plated in light blue scales along its right side and back, with ochre armour on its right. A match for the cloak that Dragonlady Adelle Kazaan wore. Neither were known Fireborn riders, and thus both would have been bonded to their beasts only recently. *By Eldur,* Pagaloth knew. *Yet now they have turned against him…*

"Guilty as charged," An'zon Graz said, with a pleasant smile. He had a carefree way about him. "You have questions, that is clear. How much have you told him, Lord Marak?"

"Enough," Marak said. He looked pointedly down at the priest; clearly, he preferred not to talk in front of him. "Rhok. Take him away to his cell." His eyes lifted beyond the fire and ring of tents. There were some partings in the rock wall back there, openings leading to caves. A light flickered down one of them. "Is Angrar there?"

"With the other one," Rhok confirmed. His voice was heavy and blunt.

Marak flicked a hand. "Take the priest to him. Do not let him see."

Rhok understood. He reached into his cloak and withdrew a length of black cloth, kneeling down to wrap it around the fire priest's eyes, blinding him. His big hands worked roughly. When the blindfold was tightly fastened, he grabbed the priest suddenly by the neck, squeezing tight with his fingers, digging into the cords of his throat. Pagaloth frowned, perplexed, as the priest thrashed and wriggled as he was choked, his neck bulging and turning red. No one made any move to interfere. They only watched, impassive, until Rhok released his grip, and the priest lurched for breath on his gag, sucking air fiercely through his nostrils.

A nod from Marak said that was enough. Rhok stood, grabbed the priest by the scruff of his neck, and dragged him off toward the cave as though he was nothing but some beast being taken to the butcher's table.

Pagaloth felt a small measure of pity for the man. "Why did he do that?"

"It is better when they hate us. Rough treatment stokes their ire."

"And now? What are you going to do with him?"

"Leave him to stew," Marak said. "For a day or so, in silence and darkness. His hate and fear will grow."

"The voice is more powerful like that," put in An'zon Graz. "All that anger and hate…it fuels them. It's a better test."

"Test?" Pagaloth was not fully understanding. "You mean to say… you are exposing yourself *willingly* to the voice? You're…" And then it came to him. "You're building a resistance to its power. An immunity."

"Yes," said Ulrik Marak. "As a knight armours his body for battle, so we are armouring our minds. The plate we wear has grown strong, Pagaloth. This is not the first priest we have found."

Replacement, he thought. That is what Marak had called him.

"The other one died three days ago," Graz explained. "We had him here for weeks, but every barrel runs dry eventually. He stopped trying to turn us, and his voice grew thin. Then we came in one morning and he'll bitten off his tongue and choked on his own blood. The one before that managed to dash his head against the wall. Now

669

we keep them bound and watched at all times. These priests are precious commodities."

Pagaloth had so many questions. "But…if they know what you're doing…why would they…"

"They cannot help themselves," sniffed Lady Adelle Kazaan. "They are slaves. Their purpose is to spread his will. And this is what they try to do. Again and again. Until they are spent."

"And you?" Pagaloth looked at them. "How did you come here, after the battle?"

"By fortune and the good favour of the gods," An'zon said. He put a hand on Lady Kazaan's shoulder and she quickly shook it off. "The good lady and I were two of the lucky ones, Sir Pagaloth. Many riders were thrown from their dragons - perhaps you saw? - but I suppose our bonds were tighter. I saw Lord Marak fly east on Garlath and something urged me to follow. We found Lady Kazaan a day later, flying aimlessly across the woods. That was when we discovered this rift and took it for a camp. The others joined later."

"They're Fireborn?"

"Not like us. But yes, there is fire in their blood."

Marak stepped in, brushing An'zon aside. "Garlath is not a dragon to yield to anyone, Pagaloth, not even Drulgar the Dread. He is stronger than that, and has broken free, as I have. As you can see, others have been drawn to him. He is a power of his own now. And they are his flock."

As if on cue, a great rumble spread through the wide walls of the chasm. Smoking flame gushed through the teeth of Garlath's maw, curling and rising to join the roof of fog above them. Several other dragons screeched out, unfurling and flapping their wings. The air stirred and blew, the flames of the fire flickering.

Marak smiled. "Garlath is no one's slave," the dragonlord said proudly. "And nor am I. We are done serving another." He reached out with a powerful arm and took Pagaloth by his shoulder. "Your mother's side, did you say?"

The dragonknight took a moment to riddle out his meaning, then nodded. "Yes, my lord. I had faint hopes of becoming a rider myself, as a boy. I was told the fire was too weak."

"A weak fire can still grow. You only need the right fuel."

Wings thumped the air. Several of the dragons rose up on their roosts, screeching. The sound stirred his soul. There was a great beating in the chest of Pagaloth Kadosk.

"You have a noble heart," Marak said to him. "They can sense it in you."

He thought of his betrayals. He thought of the chaos he'd caused. He was about to shake his head in denial when one of the dragons took flight from his perch, beating his wings in a hard ringing thunder, crashing down to land before them.

The earth trembled at his feet, pebbles dancing on the shelf. The dragon stretched out his long slender neck, nostrils opening wide, sniffing. Pagaloth felt the hair stand up on the back of his neck as those glowing golden eyes peered down into his very soul. Scales in royal red and copper glittered on the dragon's flank. There were tears in the dragonknight's eyes. Those were the colours of his house.

"You have been chosen," Lord Ulrik Marak said, in a voice of great weight. "Step forward, Sir Pagaloth Kadosk. The first ride will seal the bond."

52

Amara

She could have throttled her dead.

"You have a lot to answer for, young lady," she said, with tears in her eyes, as she strode into the dim-lit bedchamber. "So much to answer for."

She could have throttled her dead...but instead she wrapped her into an embrace so fierce she felt she might never let go. *Let it be real*, she thought, shutting her eyes tight. *Let this not be some cruel dream.* Her fingers pressed hard into Lillia's back, as though making sure, and her lips split into such a smile that she felt the skin might tear at the corners of her mouth.

She held her there so long that eventually Lillia squirmed. "I've missed you too, Auntie, I have. But the adventure's been fun. Daryl is such a hoot."

A hoot? Fun? Adventure? Amara Daecar could have throttled her dead...but instead she only laughed out loud, a manic chortle pouring from her lips. Lillia looked at her like she was crazed, and perhaps she was. Driven mad by fear and grief and now this wild and blazing relief to have found the girl at last, safe and entirely unharmed.

"Auntie...you're...are you all right? You're scaring me a little."

Amara's crazed laughter crumbled and collapsed into tears, and they were streaming down her cheeks, hot and fierce. She snapped her arms around Lillia again, clutching for her life. "I feared you were dead. I've been searching...we've all been searching for so long..."

"Searching? Oh...because I ran from Grandfather? I had no choice, Auntie. He wasn't letting me train at all, and I missed you and Jovy too much. Is he here with you? Did you bring him too?"

"He's here," Amara wept. She drew back, clutching her cheeks, smiled as she looked into her sweet beautiful young face, hugged her again, and then moved her to the bed. She sat her down and perched right next to her. She could not be certain what she had been told, but it was important she set some things straight at once. "Lillia, you need to know…about your uncle."

"I know," the girl said. "Cousin Gereth…he told me."

"What did he say?"

"That Uncle Vesryn died a hero." Her big blue eyes dipped down. "I mourned him, but…but the *way* he died. They say…" She looked up again. "They say the Dread is back. That's how Uncle Vesryn was killed. Fighting him. And Father and Elyon were there as well, but they lived…" Her voice weakened. "I heard, anyway. Though, now…I don't know if…if they're…"

"They are alive," Amara said, though she could not know that for sure. But she believed it. She had to believe it. "Your father has been declared king. He has marched west to defend the Twinfort."

"The Twinfort? I thought he was at King's Point?"

"He was."

"What about Elyon?" Lillia's face scrunched up, demanding. "If you've been looking for me, why hasn't *he* come? He can *fly*. He'd have found me easily if he'd tried. It wasn't that hard. We were on the lake for a long time, and then on those islands, and then back on the lake again. And then we came here."

Here was Blackfrost, the city seat of House Daecar, perched in the southern foothills of the pine-forested North Downs. After all that chasing, all those weeks and months in the saddle and under sail, the girl had come back home all along. *Sir Daryl*, Amara thought. *Bless that man.* He would have a lordship for this, she would make sure of it. *Well, a better one.* Daryl was already set to become Lord Blunt at his grandfather's death, but Amara would make certain his lands at least were vastly expanded. "Elyon has been busy, Lillia," she said. "He is helping to win the war, like your father. They do not have time to worry about you. And they wouldn't have to if you had stayed where you were. You never should have left Ilivar."

"I *hate* Ilivar," the girl seethed at once. "It's too clean and boring. And Grandfather's castle. *Keep Quiet*," she hissed. "I hate it even more. Even the servants go around afraid of him. Not like ours. In Keep Daecar, and here. The servants here are happy and friendly. They smile and aren't afraid to talk to us, because we're nice to them, and treat them well. But with Grandfather they cower and move like corpses, all stiff and worried they'll do something wrong." She shook her head. "I hate Grandfather most of all."

"You don't mean that," Amara made herself say. She had no love for Brydon Amadar, but he was still Lillia's grandfather, and a great-lord, and she must respect him. "Your grandfather has his faults, I will not say he doesn't, but he loves you, Lillia. He only wants to see you safe."

"He wants to see me become my *mother*," she bit back. "He doesn't really love me. He loves her. The ghost of her. But I'm *not* her. I'm never going to be her."

Amara smiled. "You always were more wilful, child," she said, cupping her cheek. "Brydon will say that is my fault. I never did raise you right."

The girl frowned angrily. "You did so. You raised me brilliantly. I like who I am."

"So do I, child. Though your grandfather thinks you are too wild and reckless, qualities that I have imparted upon you. Your mother would have brought you up to be more demure…"

"More *dull*," Lillia said to that. "That's what Grandfather was trying to do. Make me dull and stamp the life out of me. I feel sorry for my mother growing up in that place. And I'm glad you raised me. You've been an amazing mother."

Amara could have wept all over again to hear her say those words. "Sweet child. You are kind."

"I'm just telling the truth. I don't even remember my real mother anymore. You're the only mother I've known, and…"

And the door knocked, interrupting her. Amara sniffed, wiped her eyes, and cleared her throat. "Come in."

Sir Connor Crawfield stepped inside. Lillia gave him a hard frown. "You interrupted me," she said. "I was saying something nice, and you interrupted me."

The household knight gave an apologetic bow. "My lady. I am sorry for the intrusion."

"Oh shut up and come here." Lillia skipped right over to hug him, grinning as she buried her head into his chest and wrapped her skinny arms around his back. "I'm just teasing you, Con. You were always easy to tease."

"As it please you, Lady Lillia." Sir Connor curled a single arm around her, smiling. "It is good to see you again. We have all been very worried."

"It's OK. Sir Daryl kept me safe. We came right here when we heard about Varinar." Lillia pulled back and looked up at him. "Were you with Auntie Amara as well? When she searched for me?"

"Yes, my lady. You gave us a good runaround."

Lillia grinned fiendishly, as though it was all a game. Amara could have throttled her dead. "So you went to that island as well? On the lake?" She looked over at Amara. "Did you meet that fat pirate? The Great One, they called him." She made a disgusted face. "I've never seen anyone so grotesque. He took my necklace, to pay for passage. The one Mother gave me before she died. And Daryl's sword. That slimy one took them."

The seneschal. Amara stood from the bed and opened her wolfskin cloak, reaching into her pocket to retrieve the necklace in question. She had demanded the obsequious little seneschal give it back, along with Daryl Blunt's blade, and duly he had. She stepped over and reached around Lillia's neck, setting the necklace back into its proper place. "There. Much better." It was gold, a chain of fine links, with a pendant showing the Daecar family crest; a knight on horseback, thrusting aloft his misting blade. *Small wonder Lillia grew up wanting to swing a sword*, Amara reflected. It was one of the few pieces of jewellery she liked.

Lillia held the pendant in her hand, smiling at it. "How did you get it back for me?"

"I asked nicely."

Lillia smirked. "You demanded, more like. I know you, Auntie." She clasped the pendant tight in her grasp, squeezing, then let it fall to the soft pale skin of her throat. "It means a lot. Thank you. I thought I'd never see it again." She smiled again. The reaction was pleasing to Amara, and as she'd hoped. "Did you get Daryl's sword back as well?"

Sir Connor gave answer. "I have just returned it to him now, Lady Lillia." He gave Amara an urging look. "My lady, the lords and captains are gathering downstairs in the audience chamber. There is…news."

Amara heard the tone. It was not good news, that was plain. "Thank you, Connor. I'll go and join them now."

"Who?" Lillia asked. "Who else is here with you?"

Oh, just an army twenty thousand strong, Amara might have answered. *And my own new order of Knights Assorted.* She did not have the time to explain that now. "I'll let Jovyn tell you all about it," she said. "He's right outside. Is that correct, Connor?"

The knight nodded. "That is correct, my lady. And most eager to see the little lady, I do believe."

Lillia grinned enormously. "Why didn't you say so?" She rushed straight for the door, her cotton nightgown fluttering. It was late, long past midnight, and Lillia had been sleeping when they arrived, tucked up in her bed in her private chamber in the castle. Her long brown hair bounced at the back of her neck as she ran, barefoot, across the rugs and cold bare stone. Through the door she went, and out into the hall beyond. "Jovy!" Amara heard her cry, elated. "Jovy, Jovy, Jovy!" The rest was screams and laughter.

Amara Daecar smiled. "Well. Let's leave them alone, shall we? These two young love birds can do without us watching, Connor."

The word 'watching' made the knight raise his eyes.

"No, I don't mean *that*. Goodness, Connor Crawfield, you do have an unsavoury mind." She prodded the knight in the arm. "Come, we'll take the back way out."

They left through the adjoining solar and down a long corridor until they reached the central stairway. Blackfrost Castle was not large as castles went, a stronghold moderate in its majesty, but strong all the same, rich in rugs and tapestries and decorative beams of darkened pine. It was one of the few stone structures in the city, a list that included the walls, gatehouse, defensive towers, and several other minor keeps and storehouses raised by the small lords and city elites. Elsewise Blackfrost was primarily a timber city, a city of pine and pure air and snow, pretty in its winter blanket and handsome through spring and summer. Though summer now, it wore its winter coat, and that was of constant bemusement to everyone. *A particularly thick winter coat*, Amara thought. *And growing thicker still.*

The castle was as familiar to her as an old friend, and the audience chamber made no exception. Hearths burned brightly in large alcoves to each side, and dark timber beams warmed the walls and ceilings, blessing Blackfrost Castle with a rustic feel to match the city below. At the heart of the room, a great carved pinewood table stood grandly, the chamber's fabled centrepiece. First commissioned by Lord Bayron Daecar four centuries ago, it showed a map of the world as it was known, with islands and mountains, cities and woods and landmarks all carved out in intricate, three-dimensional detail.

Vesryn had loved coming here with Amron when they were boys, Amara knew. *They used to play at war*, her husband had told her, storming castles and devising battle strategies as they acted out the next great Renewal. Their grandfather Balion had paid a wood carver to sculpt hundreds of little figures for them to use in their games. Knights with their miniature blades, warriors on barded horses, archers and spearmen, kings and commanders, dragons and dragonriders and riders of sun and star and moon, paladin knights and dragonknights and sea monsters and siege weapons. It was her husband's favourite room in the castle, Amron's as well. *And mine*, she thought. *It became mine too. We would sit in here and drink wine and talk all through the night.* Sometimes it would just be her and Vesryn. Sometimes Amron would be there too, with Kessia, and when Aleron first came along, and then Elyon, the boys would run around the table playing *catch the dragon* as the adults watched and laughed.

That was another time, though. Kessia was gone, dead long years now, and Aleron as well. Elyon was only the gods knew where, Amron away defending the borders. *And Vesryn…my sweet Vesryn…*

She put old memories aside and strode into the room. At the table at which her family once gathered were assembled men strange to this city, standing around in strained debate as servants moved among them bearing trays of spiced beer and mulled wine well earned after their long cold march through the snow.

Lord Styron Strand stood at the heart of it, his son and heir Sir Gerald at his side, pockmarked and lumpy where his father was broad and strong. Amara was impressed by how powerfully built Lord Styron remained at his age. The man was into his mid-sixties but still looked like he could rip a man's head off with one good grab and twist of those muscular hands. Gerald cut a pathetic figure beside him.

The rest of the lord's captains and commanders stood attendance about him, lesser lords and knights all. Amara knew most of them from one feast or tourney or another, and even those she had never met had been introduced to her during the preceding days, as they marched with Lord Styron's host along the High Way.

Senior among them was hook-nosed Lord Abel Darring, called Daring Darring or Darring the Daring by those who liked to overstate his courage and fearlessness. Young Lord Victor Manson had come in for the same treatment. They called him Victor the Valiant, Amara had heard, or sometimes Manly Manson. That last one was particularly eye-roll-inducing, though the man was stout and had a deep bass voice, so perhaps there was some truth to it. Sir Gervis Manson, Lord Victor's younger brother by a year, was commonly referred to as Gervis the Unshrinking, and handsome Sir Robin Fallow had been granted the name Robin the Resilient for reasons Amara could only guess at. Either the lords of Lord Styron's bleak hard lands were staunch and gallant to a man, or else they were all rather fond of over-inflating their precious egos. Amara Daecar thought a mix of the two was likely.

In Lord Styron Strand, however, the name 'Strong' was more than appropriate and had been won and proven during a lifetime of triumph and achievement. Physically imposing, with a build to match Amron, and the dominant, unyielding personality of a man like Brydon Amadar, Styron Strand was a formidable man. He wore a short, triangular beard on his wide chin, grey and peppered with the occasional coil of wiry brown, and kept his hair cut trim at the sides and back. The natural course of time had done that duty for him on the top, where he'd gone bald long ago. His eyes were deepset, greyish green in colour. From them a great web of deep wrinkles spread, cutting ruts in his leathery skin, and his forehead was a lattice of lines and old scars. His cloak had been removed and hung on a hook near the door, leaving him in his godsteel armour from head to heel. The steel showed old scars from battles gone by, enamelled at the breast-plate in umber brown with pauldrons and vambraces in a dark yellow-gold, the colours of his house. Across his breast, a bare-chested man wrestled with a giant. The Strand house crest looked good on Lord Styron the Strong. Less so on Gerald, one had to admit.

The lord looked up as he saw her coming, waving the men around him to silence. They had been talking loudly as she entered, and included some of her own knights. Sir Penrose, Sir Talmer, Sir Ryger and Sir Montague were all present, as was Sir Gereth Daecar, Amron's cousin and Warden of the North Downs. The remainder of Amara's men would be down with the rest of Styron's host, camping within the city walls.

"My lady," Lord Styron said. "Be welcome." His voice matched him, a strong clear tone.

This is my home, Amara thought. *I welcome you, not the other way around.* She only smiled as she approached.

"Get the lady a cup of wine," Strand went on, as though it was his own castle. "Quickly. And for Sir Connor as well."

The wine was warm, pleasantly spiced, just the tonic on a cold bitter night like this.

"How is your niece, my lady? Was the reunion all you'd hoped?"

Amara had another drink of wine before answering. "It was too short," she said. "But elsewise, yes, a happy moment for me."

"And her as well, I'm sure."

Amara nodded. She would have time for a proper reunion later. Right now the concerned faces and strained eyes consumed her interest. "There is news, I'm told."

"Yes." Lord Styron walked along the top end of the table and around to Vandar, his men moving aside for him. He reached and tapped a steel finger at Blackfrost. "We're here."

"Yes. I am aware."

The man smiled. Unlike Lord Bryon Amadar, Styron the Strong *did* smile occasionally. His finger slid just a little bit south, moving beyond the southern edge of the North Downs. "*They're* here."

"They?"

"The Agarathi. A great host. Some seventy, eighty thousand strong we are told. They'll be here by dawn."

Amara blinked up at the man. "Sorry...I must have misheard. I could have sworn you said there were sixty or eighty *thousand* Agarathi heading our way."

Lord Styron nodded. "And dragons. Those numbers we don't know. They have been melting the snow with their fire to speed the enemy's advance, it would seem. Smart. Though it will tire and weaken them. Dragons don't like the cold, my lady."

She stared at him. "Are they to attack?" Her heart gave a thick beat, squeezing up her throat. She had only just found Lillia again. *Now this?* "Blackfrost is not built to withstand *dragons*, Styron. Let alone such a massive horde."

"I have a strong host of my own," the lord reminded her.

"One a quarter of the size," Amara came back.

"A northman counts for five Agarathi," declared Lord Victor Manson. Amara did not know where he came up with that number. "And in this weather? Ten."

She blew out a sigh. "And a dragon counts for a thousand northmen. You see, Victor. I can spout nonsense too." Her mind was whirling, leaping from one thing to the next. If they were so close... "The Twinfort," she said, trying to swallow her heart back down. "They breached the *Twinfort?*" It was unthinkable. The Last Bastion was unbreakable, many believed. But the same fools said that about Dragon's Bane too, and Varinar, and looked how that turned out.

"We must assume so," Lord Styron said. His voice was calm.

Amara's was not. "Then the men there....Lord Borrington's host..."

"We don't know what has become of them."

"We can guess," Amara said. "Randall is hardly likely to have opened his gates to let them pass unchallenged, Styron. And what of Amron?" She looked at Sir Gerald. He had been the one to tell them of Amron's plans to march west to help defend the Twinfort, carrying with him the order for his father's host to divert there as well. "You said Green Harbour was going to come under attack?"

The doughy, pock-faced knight licked his lips. "Yes, my lady. Lord Daecar…the king, he marched there to defend it. Whether he got there in time…"

"Clearly not," Amara said. She had it figured out even if the dimwit was struggling to piece it together. "The Agarathi must have come in *behind* them," she stated to the group. Some men nodded and gave agreeing murmurs. Lord Strand smiled. "They got the Fists opened from the rear."

"You always had a piercing mind, Lady Amara," Styron observed. "Yes, I think you're right." He waved a hand over the map, gesturing to King's Point, then Green Harbour, then the Twinfort, and all the coastlands and woods in between, carved into the old pine. "Amron was always going to be in a race and it would seem he had been pipped to the post. As to his fate, and that of Lord Borrington, we can only speculate. But the signs are not good."

No, Amara thought, agreeing. For all they knew this horde might once have been twice the size, only to lose half its strength defeating both Amron and Lord Randall and battling their way up the western gate. What remained was plenty large enough to deal with Styron's twenty thousand swords, she feared. "How many men do you have, Gereth?" she asked the castellan, clutching at straws.

Gereth Daecar limped forward on his maimed men. "Scant few, my lady. Most of our strength was sent to the Twinfort. We can count on some two thousand fighting men in the city. If we send all the grey-beards and green boys to the armoury, perhaps we can double that number."

Amara had always loved how small Blackfrost felt compared to Varinar and Ilithor. Now she cursed its frail little size. "That won't be enough. Not near enough to repel them."

Lord Abel Darring gave her a curious frown. "I was not aware you were an expert in siege strategy, Lady Daecar."

"I'm an expert in common sense. Now I'll admit it's been a while since I polished my skill at sums, but it would seem we're a tad outnumbered."

Lord Darring of the questionably daring disposition smiled at her. He had a hooked beak of a nose and a thin jaw, not your typical hero. His smile was ugly as well. "Lord Manson has the right of it," he said. "Man for man, we are much the stronger. I would not pay too much attention to numbers, my lady, they can be terribly misleading. And we have these walls as well, and some stout towers to help defend us. Behind them we can outlast this horde and watch smiling as they freeze to death."

This man is a fool. "You think they will sit back and lay us to a long siege?" She laughed at him. "I have spent years in this city, my lord.

Those towers you speak of are few and the walls might as well be wet paper for all the good they will do when the dragons get a sniff of us. Have you not been paying attention? Dragon's Bane has fallen, and King's Point has fallen, and *Varinar* has fallen. Against them we are nought but a daub and wattle dwelling cowering in the shadow of a castle. It is dark, I know, so perhaps you haven't had a proper look. Come dawn you'll see how vulnerable this city is. Even calling it a city is a stretch."

Her speech did not endear her to Lord Darring the Not-So-Daring. "Are you done? Or can the men continue their discussion?"

Sir Gereth Daecar rounded on him. "You'll not speak to her like that in my halls, Lord Darring. Amara's voice has always been welcomed in council here."

"A council of cripples and harlots," Darring said, unwisely.

Several blades came ringing from sheaths and Amara's Knights Assorted leaped to defend her honour. "Guard your tongue or lose it," Sir Connor Crawfield growled.

Lord Darring thought little of the threat. He gave a sniff. "You at least have some honour about you, Sir Connor, but these…" His eyes passed over Sir Talmer, Sir Ryger, and Sir Montague. "Cravens and runaways, the lot of them. I ought not have to share my air with them."

"Then bugger off outside," spat Sir Talmer Hedgeside. "I've had enough of you and your slurs, Darring."

Lord Styron raised a hand. "As have I," he said, unexpectedly. "These men strayed from the path, but they have admitted to their follies and righted their course. You will extend them the proper courtesies, Abel."

"My lord? They're traitors and cowards, every one of them…"

"Enough. I have spoken." Lord Strand's power was absolute among his men, and Darring quickly submitted. "And if you lay such an insult upon either Lady Daecar or Sir Gereth again, I will happily let Sir Connor carry out his threat. I will even hand him my own blade for the task. Do you quite understand me, Abel?"

The foul little lord gave a bow. "I do, my lord."

Strand stared down at him. Amara had never liked the man so much. He let a long moment of silence pass and then turned to Sir Gereth Daecar. "Tell me of the mountain stronghold, Sir Gereth. How many can it hold?"

"The entire city at a push." Gereth's voice was a little stiff. Crippled though he might now be, he'd once been a great warrior, and did not much care to have his disability highlighted so crudely. *No more than I like being called a harlot*, Amara thought. She would shed no tears to hear of Darring's death during battle, to be sure.

"Then push," Lord Styron said. "Ring the city bells and get them waking. If I'm to defend this city, I would sooner do it knowing the smallfolk are withdrawn."

It was one of Blackfrost's best defences. Her provision of towers was poor as northern cities went, her walls were not laced with godsteel like others, and she hardly boasted the sort of siege weaponry to make a dragon think twice, but of a good strong sanctuary for the commons to retreat to, she was well blessed. For long centuries the North Downs had been mined of tin and iron and deposits of precious metals, and its interior was as pocked as Sir Geralds cheeks with vast open caverns and deep mining shafts. There were tunnels that led there, smoothed out and reinforced over the years, through which the smallfolk would flee at times of need. If the city should fall, there were ways out that led away to the north. Amara wondered what they would find on the other end. *Snow* was a firm bet.

Sir Gereth Daecar gave a nod. "I shall see to it at once, Lord Strand. Ought I send the old and young to the armoury as well?"

"It cannot hurt to have a few more swords."

Amara pondered the awakening that awaited these poor souls. As their mothers and wives and children were being ushered to the caves, they would be ushered to the armoury to take up sword and spear. *Boys as young as Lillia*, Amara knew. *And men as old as Artibus.* War was cruel, she'd always thought. No matter how romantic the bards tried to make it.

The command was quickly passed along to the city captains. A minute later the bells began ringing out through the snowy streets to herald the approaching doom. Amara took Lord Darring's advice and left the men to their debate, moving over to the high windows to look out as the lights winked awake through the drifting snow. She could only imagine the panic that was permeating this city she loved so much. From here she could see the vague outline of the walls below her, see the tents pitched in whatever square and quad the men could find. Elsewise the city was white, every thatched roof heaped with snow, the pretty winding streets of Blackfrost lost beneath that thickening winter coat.

It would be warmer inside the mountains, she told herself. They would get great fires going to beat off the chill, and the little children would like that better. And if they went far enough and deep enough, they wouldn't even hear the strains of battle outside, as their fathers and brothers and sons fought and died. She liked that thought as well.

Sir Connor stepped over from the table to join her. "My lady. You should think about going as well. To the caverns."

She had not even considered herself as yet.

"And Lady Lillia," the knight added.

Amara nodded. "She won't like it." The girl would probably want to put on her own armour and fight, but that would not happen. "Have a man sent to wake Artibus, Connor. He sleeps soundly and the bells may not wake him up here. Carly too." The Flame Mane had also been given her own room in the castle. Most likely she'd have gone to visit Lillia by now.

"As you say, my lady. I will leave a pair of guards to protect you. Who would be your preference?"

"You," she said. "But I know you'll want to fight."

He nodded, and she would not want to deprive the defence of the city of such a gallant knight. In Connor the descriptor was well-earned. *Sir Connor the Courageous,* she thought, smiling. "Perhaps Daryl will want to continue in the role?" she offered instead.

"Sir Daryl would be a good choice."

His laughter will boom all through the caverns. No man in the world had a laugh like Sir Daryl Blunt.

"And Carly," Connor said. "She is a gifted fighter, but too reckless for this sort of battle. I fear she would do something rash and get herself hurt or killed.

Hurt or killed. That could be said for any of them. *All* of them. Amara's face twisted in sudden grief at the thought of losing him. "Connor…"

"My lady." He put his hand on hers, squeezing. "It will be OK. I promise."

She smiled weakly, and glanced over at the others. Sir Penrose was dear to her too, another of her longtime protectors. The others she had come to like during their short time together. *And Jovyn. He will be called upon to fight as well.* A part of him would want to stay with Lillia, but his sense of duty would compel him to battle. All of them could be dead by this time tomorrow. How had it come so quickly to this? *They were meant to be marching to help defend the Twinfort, not defending Blackfrost from a monstrous horde.*

"It will be all right, my lady," Connor Crawfield repeated, to comfort her. "They may pass us by. We are not the banquet they're here for."

Varinar, she thought. No doubt they were making for Varinar, to occupy the ruin of the city. No enemy army had ever done that before. This war was a war of firsts. "You don't really believe that, Con."

"No," he admitted. "We know from the east that their intent is to slaughter our people. I fear they will do the same here." He tightened his grip on her hand. "My lady, if the battle goes ill, you must not delay. Take Lillia and head north through the mountains. Lead the people. Keep them safe."

It was so much. Too much to take on. "I will," she croaked. Though where, she could not say. She kissed him on the cheek, her sweet loyal knight. "Don't die, Connor. That is a command. Don't die." The man always followed her commands. Always.

"I will do my best, my lady."

The men at the table were devising their defence strategy. City maps had been brought out and Sir Gereth was delineating the strength of their siege weapons. Amara felt sick. She had hoped to find Lillia here, and she had, but the rest was not as she'd planned. Lord Strand was to march his host down to the Twinfort. There he would meet Amron and Lord Randall Borrington and together they would hold the western gate, repelling the Agarathi invaders while Amara and Lillia remained here, sharing stories as they sat by the fire, waiting for word of a great northern triumph. And now this. *The gods are cruel.* Her stomach churned unpleasantly.

"My lady. You have gone pale," Conner observed.

"It's the wine. Poor stuff." Her guts gave a lurch, but she managed to keep it down. "I think I'll retire to my bedchamber."

"Your…Amara, do you not think you should make for the mines?"

"Later. There is a way through the back of the castle. I'll stay until the last moment, Con." *Can the gods not at least grant me that?*

She said her brief goodbyes before leaving. She would likely not see many of these men again. Sir Ryger Joyce gave her a bow and Sir Montague knelt and kissed her hand. Sir Talmer Hedgeside smiled a grizzly old grin and told her it had been an honour to serve her. "You gave us this chance, my lady. To restore our honour. None of us will ever forget that."

"Do us proud," she only said, smiling sadly back.

Sir Gereth limped up to her. "Will you fight?" she asked him.

"I'll command," he said. "Amron tasked me with defending this city, Amara. A good captain goes down with his ship."

The way he said it…with such solemnity. She sniffed and wiped a tear from her eye. The emotion was swirling and roiling within her, and she sensed she was about to make a fool of herself. *The weakness of women,* she thought. *That's what they'll be thinking.*

She was spared that fate by a loud knock at the door. Lord Styron waved a hand and beckoned a man to open it, and into the chamber marched one of Sir Gereth's guardsmen. "My lord," he said, addressing Gereth. "Men have come. They seek urgent audience."

"Men? What men?"

"They are outside, my lord. Ought I let them in?"

"Go ahead."

Amara watched with the others as the small host moved through the door and into the warmth of the audience chamber. There were four of them, each wearing frosted black cloaks well spattered in mud, blades at their belts, wild dirty beards poking out from under their hoods. "Who are you?" Lord Styron the Strong demanded. "Show your faces. What business do you bring?"

"The word of a king." Rogen Whitebeard drew back his hood and showed his long lupine face.

Sir Gerald's eyes went wide as saucers to see his younger brother appear. He gaped for words. "Rogen? How are you…What are you…"

"He just said," dismissed their lord father. "Quiet, Gerald. Men are speaking." The big old lord stepped away from the table and toward his youngest son. The son he'd sent away as a boy to be raised a ranger at Northwatch Castle. The son he blamed for the death of his wife, or so Amara had heard. "Rogen," the lord said, looking down at him, but not by much. Rogen, too, was a tall man. "I've heard great things of the man you've become. You've made an old father proud."

The ranger's amber eyes glimmered red in the firelight. Amara saw hate in the way they shone. "My lord," he simply said, in his rasping voice, ignoring the rest. He reached into his cloak and pulled out a scroll. "From the king."

The other newcomers were peeling back their hoods. Amara did not recognise them. They were scouts, scouts and messengers from Amron's host. Her heart gave a hopeful beat, thrusting at her ribs. She met eyes with the ranger, who dipped his long chin at her, and so too Sir Gereth, whom he'd met when passing this way with Amron and Walter Selleck after their time in the Icewilds. Lord Styron had taken the scroll and was reading it with narrow eyes.

He passed it to Lord Darring, to read and hand down the line. "We're going to have to change our strategy," Styron told the men. "Rogen, son, will you stay with us?"

"I must return to the king."

"I understand. You did well to flank around the enemy. All of you." Lord Strand acknowledged the other scouts.

"We will do well to repeat the trick," one of them said in a lowborn drawl. "But best be quick about it, m'lord. That fat old horde out there isn't getting any further away."

"We need to go," Rogen said. He looked at his older, uglier, softer brother with a hard look, ignored his father, and turned away.

Lord Styron came up behind him, and put a big hand on his shoulder. "You did well, Rogen. I *am* proud of you."

The ranger shifted the man's hand off and left, taking his men with him. Amara raced after him and met him out in the corridor. "Rogen…"

He turned. "Lady Daecar."

"Amron…is he…" She looked up. At just that moment Lillia was coming down the corridor with Jovyn, Carly, and Artibus all in tow. It seemed the whole castle was gathering all of a sudden.

"Rogen Strand? Is that you?" Artibus had met the man during his time in Varinar.

Lillia came rushing right up to Amara. "They say the Agarathi are coming. That we're to go into the caves? Not me, Auntie. I can fight."

Amara was about to shake her head when Carly took the girl's arm and drew her away. "Battle's no place for us girls, Lillia."

Lillia tugged back. "You've killed fifty men, you always say. You'd belong in any battle and so would I."

"Not this one," Carly said.

"But I want to…"

"No," Amara came in. "Carly's right. You'd only get in the…" Her stomach heaved and let fly, bringing up the contents of her dinner. Mostly it was just wine. She managed to turn away so it splattered against the wall, a splash of chunky red.

"My lady…" Jovyn rushed up to her. "Are you all right?"

"Fine. I'm fine." She took a breath and rubbed the red spittle from her mouth, feeling ashamed. This was not the first time she had been sick over the last week, though the first time she'd vomited so publicly. Artibus was watching her with a strange look in his eye. She sucked more air into her lungs and stood up, battling the nausea. "I'm sorry. I don't know what has come over me." She composed herself and turned to Whitebeard. It was obvious that the ranger wanted to be away. "Amron," she managed, weakly. "Is he…"

"Father?" Lillia broke in. "What about Father?"

The ranger did not seem to know who to answer. Everyone was crowding around and Amara's stomach was still roiling horribly. "The king closes," Whitebeard said. "You must hold on until he gets here. Lord Strand has the king's command. Speak to him. He will tell you. But I must go." He bowed and turned to leave, striding down the corridor.

Lillia blinked after him. "That's the ranger? That Whitebeard guy?" The one who took Father to the Icewilds?"

"That is correct, Lillia," said Artibus. "Who could be better to reach us in this snow?"

Amara was thinking the exact same thing. *Close*, she thought. *He is close.* Her hope was rising like the coming of dawn, but her stomach was doing the same. She could feel another wave of nausea rushing through her, her guts twisting, and put a hand on the wall to steady herself. Jovyn was still there. "We need to get you to your bed, my lady. Carly, will you help me?"

Before she had gone more than a few short steps, her belly heaved again, and more wine came up. Lillia was utterly bemused. Artibus's eyes had turned knowing. It was her niece who gave a laugh and said, "You need to stop drinking so much wine, Auntie. Who knows…you might be pregnant."

I cannot get pregnant, Amara Daecar thought. Then she saw the look on Artibus's face, and Carly saw it, and Jovyn too, and Lillia, who swallowed her laughter. She stepped in. "Auntie…you're not…*are* you?"

"I don't…I can't…" She had no words. *Cursed*, she thought. Vesryn always said he had cursed them, made them barren, due to his betrayals and crimes. *But he restored his honour,* she told herself. *He fought the Dread and died a hero… and…and…*

Take care of her, Vesryn had said in the dream. *Promise me you will…*

Lillia was looking at her with amazed eyes. "Gods, Auntie. Pregnant? You're *pregnant*?" She stared at her in a state of shock, then gave a huffing laugh and said, "But you can't be pregnant. You're so…so *old!*"

Amara Daecar could have throttled her dead…

…but instead she curled an arm about her belly, thought of her sweet dead husband…and wept.

685

53

𝕰meric

He opened his eyes to darkness.

He coughed, gasping for air.

A great weight was pressing down on him. Dimly, he could hear the clash of battle, ringing all around him.

It took him a moment to remember. *The dragon,* he thought. He could smell its leathern stink, the brimstone and the blood. It had collapsed atop him when he cut it though, pinning him to the ground with its bulk. Slimy entrails squirmed in the earth where he lay, massive intestines and bowels as big as a rowboat. The stink was unbearable, suffocating. His stomach heaved and churned.

He was prone, face down. Mud and blood oozed in through the eye-holes of his visor, and he could taste it on his lips. He braced his shoulders and twisted his head to the right. He could see nothing but scale armour and thick bone horns digging down into the dirt. He grimaced, labouring to look left.

Light.

There was a narrow gap ahead, a furrow of earth beneath the beast, ploughed during their duel. Emeric heaved and pulled his right leg up and to his side, his armour scraping against scale, then pressing hard against a horn to propel himself toward freedom. He made it half a foot. His left leg followed the same motion, and he achieved another six inches. Bit by bit, he squirmed his way forward, slithering along like a snake. Blessedly, he still held his blade in his grasp. Without its strength he'd almost certainly be dead, pinned beneath the beast forever.

The battle had been short and fierce, and the dragon had come from nowhere. One moment Emeric was duelling a host of dragonknights with Sir Rikkard Amadar and the next he sensed a great presence come down behind him, and he whirled in time to face his foe. "We take him together!" Rikkard had bellowed. Emeric had nodded and the two of them rushed in.

Then the tail had lashed out, whipping through a drift of smoke, and Rikkard never saw it coming. It struck him in the chest, sending him careening away across the field and that was the last Emeric had seen of him. He'd faced the dragon alone, then, a beast with great curved black horns atop its head, eyes of wild and swirling red, a long and thin crocodilian jaw. From the lower mandible another long spike protruded, and out of its rough armoured hide were a thousand more, all fanning backward toward a long lashing tail that ended in a serrated blade.

Emeric did not recall much of the fight. It was all swirls of smoke and bellows of rage, that deadly tail sweeping from the left and right, the snapping of that long thin maw. But somehow, at some point, he'd managed to get himself close enough to slide beneath it, swinging up in a fearsome arc to open up the beast's underbelly. The entrails had splashed down, the dragon had collapsed, and that was about the last that the exiled lord remembered.

Until now, as he continued to squirm onward, past scales and horns, dragging and pushing, dragging and pushing. He did not know how much time had passed as he lay entombed, but the light had changed, he saw. *Was I under there for an hour? More?*

He wriggled his way out at last and stood on shaking legs, leaning his back against his vanquished foe, breathing deep of the open air, suffused with smoke and sulphur, the bitter taste of bloody iron and foul reek of men in death. He was lacquered in dragon blood from head to heel, his cloak sticky and sodden, and it had even sluiced through the thin gaps in his plate armour to coat his padded underclothes as well. It was on his skin, sinking down into his flesh. *No bath will ever get rid of it*, he thought. *I'll stink of dragon guts forever.*

He turned his eyes around, trying to get his bearings. He could see Rustbridge far to the west, its towers burning, great pillars of black smoke churning and chugging to the skies. Dragons wheeled about it like crows above a corpse, diving and plunging, belching their flame, as the ballista bolts flew out to meet them. East the world was aflame as well. He could see the woods in which the enemy had made their camp blazing in a great conflagration, greasy smoke swirling upward in great roiling columns to coat the sky in tar.

South and north he saw pockets of men clashing amid the flames and the smoke, which puffed up from a thousand fires spread wide across the field. The dead were innumerable. Tens of thousands. Men and horses, camels and cats, wolves and dragons. The dying were an even stronger force, and the noise they made was wretched. Everywhere grown men were crying out for their mothers, weeping as they crawled through the mud. Some were aflame, running amok in their agony, red streamers moving through the smoke before falling down dead. Others dragged themselves along, missing arms and legs. A man was knelt over in the filth, scooping up his own guts as they slipped and slithered through his bloody muddy fingers. Another was moving around in circles, armless, searching for his missing limb.

Emeric Manfrey drew a long breath. He had never seen anything like it, not by half, not by a quarter or a tenth of a hundredth. It was his first true battle. *This is hell*, he thought.

He took a step forward, looking left and right, wondering where Rikkard had gone. Could that blow have killed him? More likely he'd returned to find the dragon dead and never knew that Emeric was under it. The dead were thick here where the dragon had fallen. Emeric picked through the corpses, moving through a banner of smoke that came swirling from a nearby blaze. He turned his head, coughing. His chest felt tight, his lungs burning.

"Tukoran," said a voice.

He spun. A dragonknight was charging him with his dragonsteel spear, three others coming in behind. One was hefting his spear to throw. Emeric shifted to one side, stumbling as he did on the trailing leg of a dead horse. A spear came whistling, missing him by inches as it burst into the horse's flank with a wet *crack*. Emeric rolled and stood, setting his feet, then surged forward in Rushform.

The dragonknights were skilled and quick. The first man thrust with his spear; Emeric swung, deflecting it with a crisp *ring*. The others came in around him, spreading to make room. "He's a dragonkiller," one said, in Agarathi, but the exile understood. "The blood…"

"Kill him."

They rushed as one. Emeric squatted and leapt, vaunting over them to escape the circle. Curses barked into the air. Red cloaks whipped and snapped as they turned. The one who'd thrown his spear retrieved it, pulling it out of the horse with a burst of blood and bone. He was tall and lean, spattered in blood. All of them wore black armour of dragonscale, but this one had fine dragonclaw clasps that marked him as their captain, a dragon maw roaring from the crest of his helm. He shouted something Emeric didn't hear and suddenly there were more of them. Emeric glimpsed them arriving through the smoke. Another two, three, four. He turned a full circle, counting them out. One was limping, blood leaking from a wound to his calf. Another moved exhaustedly and would not pose much threat, and a third had a savage cut that raked across his eye, blinding him. Emeric understood how to fight when surrounded. *Target the weak. Break the circle.*

He lurched for the limper, feigning one way and then the other. The man was too weak to push off that leg and his defence was slow. Emeric hacked down through his attempt to parry, and his godsteel blade cut deep into his armour where the shoulder met the neck. He heaved back, blood swishing, flesh parting. The man gave a grunt of pain and collapsed to a knee, and quick as that, Emeric punched the tip of his blade through his eye and out the back of his head.

He whirled out of the circle once more, but the other men were already regrouping. Dragonknights were some of the best-drilled soldiers in the world, skilled and brave, their formations honed and adapted to defeat and overwhelm Bladeborn knights in combat, and their dragonsteel weapons were capable of deflecting godsteel where other common blades would shatter. The armour, too, did not yield so easily when struck by Ilithian Steel.

And Emeric was *tired*. The battle had taken it out of him, and not just the bout with the dragon. He'd been fighting long hours before then, dragged this way and that across the open field and he knew not how many he'd killed. Fifty men might have died by the edge of his steel. Or double that. Or more.

It did not serve to think about it. *Add another seven*, he told himself, as the dragonknights moved and closed in. *One and then another and then another. Pick them off. Choose the weakest.*

He went for the man with one eye. The knight was ready for him, expecting him, and backtracked at once as the rest rushed in from all sides. Emeric skidded to a stop and swung his eagle-blade in a full arc, deflecting spears and swords. One got through, a spear tip prodding hard at the flank of his breastplate, juddering to a stop. Emeric tore out his dagger and swept the spear away, launching himself at the nearest attacker. His cut was quick and savage. It hacked at the dragoknight's arm, strong enough to part armour and leather and flesh, jarring into bone. The man let out a throat-splitting cry. Emeric tore the blade away and hacked again in a blink, frighteningly quick, right at the same spot, and the man's arm went spinning into the filth.

The exile turned, just as another spear plunged hard into his gut, but his armour was more than a match for it. It would leave a dent, no more. Emeric drove his dagger into the neck of the assailant. Another two dragonknights hacked down at him with swords. He swung, deflecting, and pirouetted back out of the circle.

Five, he thought. Another was dead and the armless man was no longer a concern. He'd die of loss of blood soon enough. The rest moved back around him, more cautious now. Their captain was bellowing orders in Agarathi, a language Emeric understood well enough, but spoke poorly. It was the tongues of the empire he'd mastered, those of sand and sun and star, not the dragon-tongue. Another bark from the leader and the five closed in. Emeric kicked out at a body. The corpse went rolling over into the legs of the nearest knight and the exile followed right in. He thrust too quickly for the dragonknight to counter, taking him in the gut. A burst of blood spat from the man's mouth. The rest roared and rushed.

Then there was a great bellow behind him. "Stop toying with them, Manfrey! There's better prey to hunt than these!"

Emeric caught a glimpse of silver armour, enamelled brown and black at the shoulders and chest, a great thicket of beard atop a neck so thick the armourers had baulked when it came time to make a gorget to fit it. Mooton Blackshaw was a fearsomely large man, but that neck…there was nothing like it. He gave a laughing bellow as he entered the fray, monstrously quick for such a brute, a huge smile splitting his wild hairy face. The first swing of his greatsword took a dragonknight at the waist, cutting right through him and parting top from bottom. The second came down so hard and true it parted the captain lengthways instead, from crown to groin. Emeric watched as the body peeled apart, right side and left side falling opposite ways as gore and organs tumbled out, steaming, to splash bloodily into the mud.

"Ha! I've wanted to do that all my life. Usually they move, but that one was just right." The Beast of Blackshaw laughed thunderously at his success. "You'll remember that one, Manfrey. I want you telling everyone when the battle's done."

Emeric wasn't going to fast forget it. Nor the two remaining dragonknights who had seen a losing cause and run. Mooton snorted. "Cowards. Too many cowards out here." He took Emeric by the shoulder with an enormous paw, and shook him. "So? How many have you killed? Not more than me, I'll bet. I've probably killed a thousand men by now."

As ever, Mooton Blackshaw was given to hyperbolic exaggeration. "I'm not keeping count."

"No, you wouldn't. You're too well-behaved for that, but us Blackshaws…" He paused to give him a look up and down. "You're covered in blood, Manfrey." The big man leaned in, sniffing. He gave an ugly cringe. "Dragonblood," he spat. "It's all over you."

There was worse than blood all over him. "I killed one," Emeric told him, without pride. He motioned into the moving smokes. "Back there, somewhere."

Mooton did him the honour of believing him. "Ha! Well good for you. I hacked the head off a beast myself. Like the King's Wall did in the last war. You know that story? How big was yours?"

This was hardly the time to compare notes. "Where are the others, Mooton? I haven't seen anyone for a while."

"Damned if I know. I lost track of Torv and the Barrel a while ago. Might be a mile away. Or two. It's crazy, isn't it? This battle. Gods, I feel alive!" He laughed and thumped his chest with a great *clang* of steel. "Come, let's find them. Just listen out for a man bellowing for Vargo Ven and we'll track Borrus down soon enough."

If he's still alive, Emeric thought. There were no guarantees of that, even for the formidable Barrel Knight.

They stepped away through the battlefield. Here and there men clashed around them, but Mooton paid them no mind unless they got too close. When he saw a dragon flying overhead, he bellowed out, "Fight me, devil-spawn!" raising his blade in challenge. "Come fight the Beast of Blackshaw!" But the dragon soared right by, and just like that it was gone, swallowed up by the billowing smoke. Mooton snarled in disdain. "They're all like that. They don't engage like they should."

"They're not Fireborn," Emeric said. "They're dragons." The

distinction needed no explaining. Riderless dragons were not bound by the honour-duels of the Bladeborn-Fireborn clash.

Mooton knew that too. "They fear me," he declared anyway. "And I can't blame them. They all saw me behead their brother and now they want no part of me. Ven's the same, no doubt." He stopped to pick up a spear staked into the ground, casually hefting it at a passing rider. It was a paladin knight charging through upon a huge barded camel, his silken cloak streaming at his back in shades of white and gold. The spear took him right in the neck and the knight went flying from the saddle. Mooton grunted. "Might have just killed an ally there," he said. "Hard to know, isn't it? With these from the empire."

Emeric stopped to frown at him. "What do you mean?"

"What do I mean? What do you think I mean? Your friend Ballantris has turned his cloak against the Agarathi, *that's* what I mean. I saw him myself. Him and that great moonbear of his. He came leading a host of his own against the dragonfolk. Took them in the flank and near scattered them too." He scratched at his beard. There was blood in the twisting tangles of hair, and bits of bone. He picked out a chunk of skull, frowning bemusedly as he inspected it, then flicked it from his steel fingers with a *ping*. "Never know what you're going to find in there," he said. "That's part of the fun of having a big beard."

"The Lumarans have joined us?" Emeric pressed. He was not aware of that.

The big man shrugged. "Don't know about *joining* us. But I saw some of them attack the Agarathi, that I'll swear by. That's *your* doing, Manfrey. Whatever you said to that Moonrider must have gotten through to him. You'll have your lordship back for this, I'll bet." He smiled at him, then his eyes flitted to some nearby fighting, and he roared and charged, adding to his tally of kills.

They'd reached a small slope by then, topped with an old stone watchtower. Emeric continued up the rise, beating back any enemy who came near him. The fighting was well dispersed now. Not like the beginning, when the armies had first come together. Back then the press had been so thick it was hard to move, the noise so loud it was impossible to hear the thoughts inside your own head. It was all shouts and grunts and curses and barks of pain, the screaming of dying horses, the howls of dying men, sounds so near they seemed like they were calling right in his ear. He at least had the fortune to be armoured all in godsteel, but that was not true for almost everyone else. *How many times might I have died without it?* How many swords and spears and axes had come crashing against his armour, only to bounce away, barely leaving a mark?

He pushed aside his guilt for that and continued up the slope. There was fighting at the top, a host of Tukoran pikemen in brown and green cloaks defending the tower against a surge of Agarathi, coming up from the other side. Emeric did not know why they were protecting the tower, other than to give them somewhere to rally, a physical point that they must defend. From the windows, archers had taken their places and were firing down on the enemy host. On the steps outside the thick wood doors, the men held tight together, defending the way in with their lives, thrusting out with their pikes and spears. A man in an emerald cloak and armour was shouting commands, a big ugly bald man who Emeric knew to be Sir Kevyn Bolt, once of Janilah's Six. That gave him pause. He was one of the prince's guards now.

Sir Mooton came striding up the hill behind him, a new crop of butchered bodies sown in his wake. His beard had been splashed in a fresh coat of blood which dripped grimly through his smile.

"That'll be another ten," he said proudly. When he joined Emeric, he saw the watchtower, the archers at the windows, the violent press around the door. He did not stop long to consider what might be happening. "What are you standing here for, Manfrey? Those are your people dying out there." He raised his greatsword aloft and gave a mighty roar, shouting, "Blackshaw!" and "Elmhall! and "Vandar!" as he charged.

Emeric followed after him, thrusting and cutting his way through the throng until he reached the tower steps. He pushed his way up toward Sir Kevyn Bolt, hailing him loudly. The man turned. "Manfrey." He wore the essentials of godsteel armour, the rest castled-forged but strong, his cloak torn and singed. In his grasp he held a blade with a bull-head pommel, one of two he kept at his hip. That was custom among the Six, to have dual blades. Though no longer a sworn sword, he'd served at Prince Raynald's side, acting as part of his protective escort and had ridden at his flank when first they stormed the field.

The tower, the knight, the desperate defence. It painted a story.

"Where is the prince?" Emeric shouted. The noise was fearsome, the shouting and cursing.

Bolt thumbed at the door. "Inside. He took a wound. The bastards are trying to get at him." The bald knight looked out; more foemen were coming up the hill in a flood as though sniffing the blood of a prince in the water. Further off a dragon was wheeling around, a big dragon, umber brown with scales of mossy green coming their way with a rider on its back. "That dragon's coming back," Bolt said. "Wants to finish the job." He spat

"We have to get the prince out." Emeric spun and pushed at the door. It didn't yield.

"It's barred," Bolt shouted at him. "From the inside."

Fools. If that dragon burned the tower down they'd be trapped. Emeric kicked at the wood. "Open up. It's Emeric Manfrey. Quickly!"

He heard the bolts go, heard whatever they were using to block it moved aside. The door opened a crack and a pair of eyes peered out to confirm it was him. Then it opened wider, enough so Emeric could slip inside. The roar of battle weakened as the door was pushed shut again.

Emeric took the room in at a glance. Crates and casks sat along the curve of a wall to the right, being hastily searched by a pair of soldiers. To the left a stair crawled around the interior, leading to the upper floors, the tower-top above them. Bowmen were shouting and firing up there, their voices echoing down through the stone drum.

The prince was up against the far wall, holding a steel hand to his gut. His helm rested on the floor beside him, his skin wan, hair wet, mouth bloody. Several men-at-arms were fussing about him. One was a knight that Emeric knew; Sir Ernold Esterling, called Ernold the Shy, another Emerald Guard in the prince's service. The sobriquet 'shy' was ironic. Sir Ernold was anything but.

The man heard him enter and stood to face him. "Manfrey. Bloody good to have you. How is it out there?"

"Not good." Emeric stepped forward. "The men are overwhelmed and more enemy soldiers are coming up the hill. We have to get the prince out."

Prince Raynald Lukar groaned, propping a bloody hand to the stone floor to try to stand. He winced and flopped back down.

"Be still, my prince," said one of the armsmen at his side. He turned and barked to the men searching the crates. "Quickly. Find something, damnit."

The boy did not look in good shape. "What happened?" Emeric asked Sir Ernold.

"Dragon," the knight told him. "Tail-blade cut through his armour. Savage strike. He's got a six-inch gash across the gut. It's deep, Emeric. He takes his hand away and who knows what'll come squirming out."

"I found some," a man shouted. He stood from a crate and raised aloft a bale of clean bandages, as though he'd won a great duel. At once they surged into action, wrapping the prince up, but it would only do so much. He needed that wound sewn and seared shut, else he'd bleed out, and there was no way he'd be able to fight in his condition.

There was a roar outside, shuddering through the air. Panicked shouts rang out from the bowmen above them. Then screams as the fire took out the men on the roof, shattering the stone summit. Emeric looked up as the stone came down, a shower of debris collapsing through the hollow tower to crash down onto the floor. "Look out!" He shoved Sir Ernold aside as men threw themselves over the prince, stone blocks and shards of timber smashing against their shields.

It all happened in an instant. Above them, fire swirled where the tower ceiling had been breached, and Emeric could see clear sky above. There was a deep thwump of wings as the dragon wheeled about. "We have to get him out!" The tower would not survive for long before collapsing. Sir Ernold nodded and rushed to the door, but Emeric shouted, "No. We go out the back."

"There is no back."

"We'll make one." The exile heaved his blade and began hacking at the stone of the rear wall. Sir Ernold hurried to join him. Chips and sparks flew as they carved open a rough door, kicking with their boots to widen it, stone and mortar tumbling. "Get the prince up!" Emeric shouted, as the open field appeared through the breach. "Get him up! Carry him!"

"I can walk." Prince Raynald laboured to stand, swatting aside the men who tried to help him. They'd wrapped him around a dozen times in the bandaging, but already the blood was starting to seep through, red on pristine white. How long it would hold Emeric Manfrey could not say, not without inspecting the wound. "You're going the wrong way," the prince said. His voice was hoarse, but determined. "They're out that way." He pointed at the door and grimaced in pain. "We have to fight. I cannot abandon my men."

Sir Ernold Esterling moved over to him. "That is noble, my prince, but Emeric is right. Our first priority is to protect you." No sooner had he said the words than the dragon swept by in another assault. The tower shook as more stone came down, fire flooding through the open roof. "Now! Out now!"

They rushed for the breach, Sir Ernold bundling the prince out into the open air. The rest of the men followed, just as the flames licked down to tongue at the floor. They hissed and spat, raging for a moment and then retreating just as quickly. Emeric pressed back inside the tower, through the smoke and fume, and pulled open the door. The battle had swelled outside. Mooton was in the midst of it, swinging wildly with his greatsword in one hand and his greataxe in the other, the rest of the Tukoran soldiers trying to keep the horde at bay. More were coming up the hill, hundreds of them screaming their warcry. "Sir Kevyn!" Emeric shouted.

The Bull of Bolt turned.

"We're taking the prince through the back. Hold them. Hold them here, sir!"

The man nodded.

Emeric spun. He did not want to leave Mooton, but what could he do? I am Tukoran, no matter where my life has taken me. Raynald is my prince, no matter who his grandfathers were. Emeric had a duty to help protect him.

He rushed back through the tower and out of the breach. Sir Ernold was shouting commands as he took the lead. To either side of the prince, several other household knights and men-at-arms formed a cordon, while another helped him along. It was a force of only a dozen.

Emeric hurried to join Sir Ernold at the front. The Emerald Guard was of an age with the exile, not yet forty, with a high forehead, thinning hair at the crown, short brown beard well salted at the sides, and a misshapen nose that had never properly set after a bad break. He

694

scowled at the skies; the dragon had circled off out of sight to the south, and they had to hope it would keep nibbling at the tower or else fly off after some other prey. "The city's too far," Esterling called. "And burning besides. We'd never make it."

"We make for the woods," Emeric said. They were burning badly to the east, but further north small thickets clothed the land and among the boles they might find salvation; a place to stop and take stock and try to mend their prince.

Sir Ernold had the lead and did not see any other way. He shouted a command and set off at a run, the company pressing on through the swirling smoke, puffing and boiling from fires and pits. The earth was treacherous underfoot. Bodies lay everywhere, men of north and south scattered as far as the eye could see. *Is there no end to this battlefield?* Emeric had always heard tales of the Battle of Burning Rock, but the scale of it always sounded unimaginable. Two hundred thousand men and mounts clashing across miles of hills and plains. That might have described today. *The Battle of Burning Woods*, he thought. *The Fight of the Barrel Knight's Folly.*

Borrus had been a fool. He would not hear of Rikkard and Torvyn's calls for calm. He did not listen to sense. The moment he saw his father's head in a bag, that was it. He'd bellowed for the men to muster and charge, and out of the gates they'd stormed. Oh, it was a stirring sight, no doubt. All those banners cracking in the wind. The warhorns blasting their long rousing calls as they poured out into the dawn. But how many had died for it? How many tens of thousands of men and boys had Borrus doomed when he looked into that bag?

Emeric could not think of that now. What's done was done, and the horse had bolted, and now they must make do. Yet all the same he could not help but wonder which of his friends were dead. The men he'd travelled with since the Tidelands in particular. Jack and Braxton, Pete and Sid. Even Turner, back in the city, was not safe from harm. These men were sailors, not soldiers, and none of them should be here. *Sir Bulmar will watch over them,* he tried to tell himself. *The Blackshaws will keep them safe.* But that was the thought of a child, devoid of sense and logic. In truth the Blackshaws too could be dead. It would take one dragon, one gush of flame, one charge of dragonknights or a surging horde and that would be it, none would survive.

A shout intruded on his thoughts, and that was all for the good. It came from one of the men defending the flank. "Sunriders!" he called. "Brace!"

Emeric turned in time to see the pack charging through the smoke. It was not just Sunriders; several Starriders prowled and leapt among them, and there were paladin knights too atop their mighty camels, all loping and galloping in a fierce formation, crying out and swinging their curved blades as they went.

"Defend the prince!" bellowed Esterling.

Men jumped ahead of him, throwing up their shields, as Sir

Ernold and Emeric and a pair of other men rushed for the front, blades brandished. The riders were on them quickly, a storm of shouts and thrown spears. Emeric deflected one with his blade, pinging it away into the fog. Another took one of the men-at-arms in the chest, punching through his caste-forged breastplate as he was thrown backward off his feet. The company came charging through, knocking two more of the guardsmen aside, hacking with swords and long-axes. A scarcat leapt atop one man, slashing with its claws before pouncing away as the defenders lashed out.

And then they were past, surging beyond them. Amid the din Emeric heard their commander give a shout in Piseki; an order to circle and charge again. His hopes that they would carve their way onward through the battlefield were dashed. "They're coming back!" he roared.

They turned to meet him. Emeric got a better look at them this time. They were a gleaming force, lords and Lightborn, and the Sunrider in their middle, the leader…

The garb gave him away. The rich armour, beautifully detailed. The fine cape that waved at his back in dark gold and shimmering black. On his head was a helm with a sunwolf roaring from its crest, wolf claws holding his cape at the shoulders. Beneath the dark leather saddle on which he sat charged an enormous sunwolf, thick-shouldered and powerful in the chest, with a bright golden mane flowing out from its armour. Blood covered the beast's maw and stained the fur around its face. It was the wolf *Gragaro*, ridden by the Sunlord Avar Avam.

Emeric's eyes narrowed upon them.

"Form up! Form up!" shouted Sir Ernold. He swung his cloak over his shoulder and stepped forward, holding his longsword in two hands.

Emeric glanced at Raynald. The boy prince was held down by two men as he fought to stand and fight. *Brave boy*, Emeric thought. He turned his back and faced the enemy, eyes trained on Avam as they came again. Spears flew and blades met, steel clanging and kissing. Another two of their own were killed, and Sir Ernold cut a paladin down, but Emeric's thrust at the sunlord missed its mark and the company went charging by.

"We have to move!" someone shouted, one of the men huddled over the prince. "They're picking us off. We have to run!"

"We can't," Sir Ernold shouted back. "They'll charge us down. Our only chance is to…"

A dragon bellowed. Emeric swung about and saw the air shifting as the beast crashed down to land before them, the earth shuddering underfoot. The Fireborn in its saddle wore bright green and muddy brown, a mockery of the colours of Tukor to match his leathern steed.

"He's back," cried a voice. "He's found us again."

"He's mine." Prince Raynald battled the men away and pulled the sword from his hip. The blood had darkened and spread across his

696

bandage. "You," he tried to shout. "Fireborn. Finish the job if you dare. I challenge you to a duel, an honour-duel, just me and…and…" And he fell forward, passing out into the mud.

The dragonrider gave a cruel laugh. "Boy," he sneered in a brutal attempt at their northern tongue. "Sick boy. Dead boy." Emeric did not know him. The dragon he rode was large and fearsome, thick and muscular, a brute. There were some cuts to his shoulder and neck, leaking blood. Emeric wondered if the prince had inflicted them before the tail ripped his belly open.

The exile went out to meet him, striding forth alone. The dragonrider laughed again as he saw him stepping near. Smoke swirled and snorted from the dragon's nostrils, fire burning deep and hot in its chest. Emeric could hear the sunlord and his company racing back across the field to his right, snapping and snarling. Sir Ernold was shouting for them to brace, to protect the prince, but they were outmatched and outnumbered, and would shortly be overwhelmed.

Emeric stood to face this new foe. His feet shifted into Glideform, quickest of the stances, best to avoid attacks. The dragon reared in response; it was larger than the one he'd slain. Its rider stood in the saddle, tore his blade from its sheath and raised it. *This is it,* Emeric thought. *This is where it ends.*

A new roar filled the world.

A deep thunder thick with rage, trembling the very air.

The dragon's great head swung north toward the sound, its body tensing, lowering. It stood bulky as a warship, claws digging into the earth, a tongue hissing and quivering from its open mouth.

The smoke ahead of it moved, eddying. The ground shook, *boom doom, boom doom,* like a drumbeat. *Boom doom, boom doom,* it came, *boom doom, boom doom,* it neared, growing louder and stronger, and then suddenly *he* was there.

Tathranor, monstrous in white, his fur hardened to a thousand savage crystal spikes. Between the great moonbear's shoulders stood Timor Ballantris, armoured in glittering scalemail in silver and blue and black. Down his back draped his cloak of lion fur, striped black and blue and white at the collar. Tall he stood, and grand and peerless. He raised his own gleaming sword aloft and shouted, "*Jah Kavosh!*" at the dragonrider, as Tathranor thundered on.

The dragon coiled its bulk, tearing great ruts in the earth as he sprung forward. Tathranor met it upon an open stretch of field, lifting his enormous forepaws from the earth to grapple and tackle the dragon to the ground. Emeric watched in awe as they crashed down into the earth. The sounds they made. The way the world shook. Great clods of dirt flew and rained about them, fire gushing, smoke swirling thick and black. The moonbear roared and the dragon screeched as they wrestled amid the burning shroud.

Emeric tore his eyes away and turned. He could not watch, nor could he help. Behind him, Avam's Lightborn host was charging through Raynald's guard. Emeric saw Sir Ernold knocked aside by a massive camel, but the Emerald Guard landed in a graceful roll and sprung right back to his feet, hurling a spear he found in the mud to catch the paladin knight in the back. Two other men were engaging a Sunrider. Another knelt with the unconscious prince, trying to revive him. A starcat was racing in behind him, preparing to leap, but Emeric tore his dagger from its sheath and threw in a single motion, catching the cat in the shoulder. It stumbled and fell, gouging a rut in the earth, the Starrider caught in the stirrups as he tried to crawl free. Emeric got their first. Cat and rider both fell to the edge of his blade as he cut them down with two quick swings.

The rest of the host were coming back around. Some were dead, others fled, the animals bolting at the sight of the moonbear. But not the sunlord. He charged low in the saddle, shrieking some Piseki battlecry as he made for the dying prince, the rest fanning out to face the others. *No,* Emeric Manfrey thought. *He'll not die today.*

He stepped ahead of Raynald Lukar and put himself into Block-form, blade held vertically before him, feet set, stance wide. "Sunlord Avam," he called out. "Do you remember who I am?"

The man did not give answer.

I will remind you, Emeric thought.

He shifted stance in a blink, feet switching to Strikeform and forward he flew. His enemy did not expect it. In a blur Emeric was on him, skidding low to the ground to cut at Gragaro's legs. The wolf saw him coming, leapt up, but Emeric expected it, following up with his steel. He cut the beast's hindquarters, slicing hard through armour and fur and flesh to part the meat of his trailing leg. The sunwolf howled and tumbled. Avar Avam was thrown forward, crashing into the body of a dead camel. Dazed, he tried to climb to his feet, tripped and fell. Emeric pressed on Gragaro, the wolf rising, limping, bleeding. Savage fangs flashed against firelight, snarling, red with the blood of the dead.

He sprung forward, Emeric swished sideward, and his eagle-blade flashed down. Blood soaked out through the sunwolf's mane as he fell, whimpering, to die.

The exile strode up to the sunlord. "Do you remember who I am?"

The man was still dazed from his fall.

"I asked you a question." Emeric reached out to pick him up by the throat and tore away his helm. The face behind stirred an old recollection of the one and only time they'd met. "Do you remember me, Avar?"

The man blinked. His nose was bloody, lip split. He had the tan skin of the Piseki, the thick black hair and brows, the dark eyes. He did not look fearsome, not like this. *He is afraid,* Emeric thought.

"You…I do not know you…"

Emeric lifted his visor. "And now?"

The man's brow furrowed. "I…I don't…who…"

Emeric threw him back down to the ground. The man was nothing without his sunwolf and no threat to him anymore. He turned around to check the battlefield. The last of Avam's company were running away through fire and smoke and Emeric saw why. Ahead, not far from where the prince lay, Tathranor stood upon the field, his immense forepaws dripping blood, ragged strips of dragon flesh trailing from between his claws. The points of his spiked crystal armour gleamed red with blood and between his mighty jaws hung the head of his foe, tongue lolling, eyes rolling, faint wisps of smoke curling up from between its teeth.

Timor Ballantris stood triumphant in his saddle. He looked at Emeric, and nodded salute. Then with a thunderous roar, the moon-bear swung about and charged away, flinging the dragon's head aside as it went.

Emeric watched them fade into the shroud. But only for a moment. Much remained to be done, and there was a prince nearby who needed saving. But first…

He turned to look down upon Avar Avam, squirming at his feet. He did not need the man to acknowledge him. He only needed him to die.

His blade cut easily into the sunlord's throat.

"For Brewilla," Emeric said, as he twisted.

54

Lythian

Lythian almost felt sorry for him. *Almost*. "Rope or blade?" he asked. "I'll be kind and give you the choice."

"My lord...please...please, I'm too young to die."

Lythian disagreed. "I lost a son on the birthing table, Sir Fitz. *That* was too young to die. You're five and twenty, and a *knight*. Now grow up and die like a man." He did not care to soften his words, not with a lickspittle like this. "So let me ask you again. Rope or blade? Choose now or I'll make the choice for you."

"B-b-blade, my...my lord."

"The right answer." Lythian waved a hand. "Get him on his feet." Sir Storos and Sir Oswin did the honours, hauling Fitz Colloway up. The knight groaned in pain from the wound he'd taken to the ankle. "Take him out into the main square with the others. Have them gagged and bagged. I want to get this done quickly."

The man was dragged away, kicking and screaming and pleading for his life, but Lythian did not hear him. He had made his decree that any man caught deserting would die, and that counted double for knights.

It was raining outside the stone undercroft where Sir Fitz was being kept, a strong fall from grey skies cut with thicker bands of black. Away to the south, the Red Sea was raging wildly, and east the swollen Steelrun River ran furiously into the sea, carrying with it fallen trees and branches and broken boats, even corpses sometimes as well, all swept from the woods and the waterlogged coastlands.

Sir Ralf of Rotting Bridge was waiting outside the building, his grey hair soaked to the scalp. "Another dour day for another dour duty," he said in a solemn voice. "Is it just me, or does the rain seem to fall with more purpose on these occasions?"

"The rain is always falling," Lythian said. *And men are always deserting.* Decree death upon them as he did, that had not stopped the tide.

Every night at least thirty or forty men still crept from the city, escaping through whatever breach they could find, and only one or two in every twenty were ever caught and captured.

Sir Fitz had been one of the unlucky ones. An archer had spotted him slipping away with his men and fired, catching Colloway in the ankle, and that had set his fate. A few of his more loyal soldiers had stayed back to help carry him as the others ran off, but Sir Adam's men had caught up to them quickly and dragged them all back to the city. Well, there was some honour in what those men did, Lythian supposed, trying to save their captain, but it would not be enough to save them. They were deserters too and would pay the headsman's price.

He strode to the main yard where the men in question were waiting, his stride like his face; purposeful, hard, mirthless. It was a foul business, there was no doubt, plenty enough to scourge the soul of even the noblest man, and Lythian's had been whipped red and raw by all the lives he'd been required to take.

He hated it. He hated it as much as he hated the men who made him do it, but mostly he had come to hate himself. He remembered an executioner from his youth, a cold-eyed monster who handled the killings in the town of Mistvale where he'd grown up. *I am become that man*, he thought, as he took the blade from Sir Adam Thorley. *A cold-eyed monster, soulless and uncaring.*

The blade Sir Adam gave him was an executioner's sword, a long plain blade of common godsteel to ensure a clean true strike. Lythian would not anoint the Sword of Varinar in the blood of these deserters. Several hundred men were gathered in the square and on the ramparts around the River Gate, standing in the rain or beneath the awnings of their tents. *Shadows and scowls*, Lythian thought. In the dark of the afternoon he could not make out one man from another. They stood about, still and silent. The only sound was the lash of the rain, washing across the cobbles, and muted whimpers of the doomed men sobbing in their gags.

All six were lined up on their knees before him, soaked to the bone, their hands tied behind them. Each had a bag over his head and a gag in his mouth to prevent him from making too much noise. Lythian gestured to the first man and his bag and gag were removed. The man blinked into the sudden light, taking a deep breath. His eyes were red from tears, and he was young, no older than twenty. "Any last words?" the First Blade asked him. "Speak them now, and go in peace."

The young soldier blubbered something about not wanting to die, how he loved his mother, how he was a good man and only wanted to go home and fight for his family. There was nothing happening here, he said. They were all just waiting to die anyway, and for what? Couldn't he return to his loved ones instead? Lythian closed his heart to him as he swung the blade, detaching his head from his shoulders. It bobbled into a depression between a crossroad of cobbles. Blood drained out, spreading through the grooves.

Lythian went to the next man. "Remove the hood." He stared down, dead-eyed, as he asked him for his last words and saw the man's mouth move in reply, saw his face twist and contort in fear and desperation. But he didn't hear the words. He did not see the face. He heard only muffled noise and perceived only a blurred facade. *Close your heart,* he told himself. *You do not have a choice.* He swung the blade.

And down the line he went. One man and then another and then another had their bags and gags and heads removed, with a few unheard words spoken in between. There was a strong chance there were some decent men among them. Not every deserter was craven as not every knight was courageous, but Lythian was only a conduit for Amron's law. *His,* he thought. *Not mine. His orders, his kingdom, his rule… his blade.*

At last he came to Sir Fitz Colloway. "Remove the bag and gag." It was done. The skinny young knight let out a great breath of anguish and began pleading at once for his life.

"My lord…you mustn't! You mustn't…please…"

Lythian looked at him blankly. "Any last words? Speak them now, and go in peace."

"My lord, no! *NO!* I have command of four hundred men here… they count on me, if you do this, they'll…"

Lythian swung the blade in a swift cut and Sir Fitz Colloway went bleating into the afterlife. The First Blade turned a half circle to face Sir Adam Thorley. "Your blade." He handed it back, dripping blood to the wet grey stone. "Have them buried outside. If there are men here who knew them, permit them to go and speak the rites and remember them as they will. Tell me when it's happening. I would like to be there to pay my respects."

Sir Adam took back the blade. "As you command, my lord."

Lythian returned to his private tent, set aside from the rest toward the edge of the square, the tent Amron had given him, like the rule of this ruin and the curse of the blade. He took the Sword of Varinar off his hip at once, and stored it in a chest set as far from him as possible. Separation was important, he had learned, and yet he must always keep it in sight to guard it. Sir Ralf followed him in. "Would you like me to summon the other lords?" the old man asked.

Lythian wanted no such thing. He wanted to sit and stew in silence, but he could not. "Yes. Thank you, Ralf."

They did not take long to come. Lord Tanyar, Lord Barrow, Lord Warton, the old castellan of the Spear. Sir Storos Pentar came as well, and Sir Nathaniel Oloran. Both had worked hard on Lythian's scheme to catch and tame a dragon, but what had come of that? Nothing. Just mockery. With the rains refusing to ease, Lythian had finally brought that project to a close, admitting his folly and failure.

Lord Barrow coughed violently as he sat on a stone block. "That cough isn't getting any better," Sir Storos observed.

"Thank you...for noticing," Barrow said between hacks. The cough was almost as bad as Lord Warton's perpetual blight and had been growing worse each day. "It's these rains. And the cold. It'll improve once the weather clears."

Then it'll never improve, Lythian thought. He could not remember a time when it wasn't raining. He could not remember seeing a shred of blue in the sky, or the sound of silence. The wash of rain was constant. It splashed against the stone of the city and pattered incessantly on the roof of his tent, sometimes loud, sometimes softer, but never stopping for good. No doubt it was one reason for all these desertions, escaping these insufferable rains.

He looked over the men. "Thank you for coming," he said in an empty voice. "Drink wine if you want. And there's some ale." He waved at a sideboard. "I don't mean to keep you long." A few of them partook. Cloaks were hung on pegs and shaken free of the rain, and Sir Nathaniel went to warm his hands against a brazier. Once the men had settled, Lythian spoke. "Six more dead," he said. *Six more scars on my soul, to add to all the rest.* "And over forty deserted. How much longer must we suffer this?"

Sir Storos drank his wine. "Permission to speak frankly, my lord."

Lythian gave a lazy flick of the hand. "Go."

"I fear there's nothing more we can do that we haven't already tried. We've closed what breaches we can and have archers on the walls. Men still go. They're like rats and roaches, and they find a way. And forgive me, Lord Barrow, but your men aren't doing much to stop them."

Barrow harrumphed. It was a ridiculous sound coming from him. He wasn't big enough to carry it off, or old enough, or important enough. "I take umbrage with that, Sir Storos."

"I thought you might."

"My men are not helping these deserters." He looked over at Lythian. "My lord, I tell you they're not."

Lythian didn't care. His dull expression said as much. "You're not to blame, Lord Barrow. But if your men are caught aiding anyone leaving, they'll have to face the blade as well. Have that spread among your captains. Any guard turning a blind eye to desertion is as bad as a deserter himself."

Lord Rodmond cleared his throat. "My lord. Is that not too much? Oft as not the deserting parties outnumber the guards. If they try to stop them, it will only come to blood. And these are friends of theirs, kinsmen."

Taynars, Lythian thought. He was surrounded by them, cursed by them. They called him dragonlover and sympathiser and traitor. Once, a man had stepped right up in front of him and spat into his face. "For the hanged," he'd said. Lythian might have hanged him as well, but instead he'd only let Sir Oswin put his fist through his face, shattering his jaw. Another man had dared insult Talasha in his hearing, and he'd suffered the same fate…by Lythian's own hand. Now they only muttered behind his back, scowling as he passed.

Kindrick was to blame. The weaselly little lord had taken two hundred men and run when Lythian discovered his part in the butchery at the prisoner camp. He'd have taken ten times that if he had the time, Lythian knew, and perhaps he was even planning more than that. A coup. Mutiny. The rule of this rotting ruin. A part of Lythian would happily have let him have it, but the weasel had slipped away before he could collar him.

After that, the desertions had come thick and fast. Forty here, fifty there, never less than several dozen each night, and some were even leaving by day. By now a thousand must have abandoned him, all fleeing back home to their lands across the Ironmoors. And in a week, what then? How about a month? Would he even have an army left when Amron returned? Would it even matter if he did?

Lythian had cause to doubt it. He had perhaps eight thousand men left here, hungry, cold, wet, and weakening. And they were never the best. What good would they do in any battle? *Numbers,* he thought. *That's all they'd be. Bodies to make up the numbers.*

Rodmond Taynar spoke again. "My lord. I would ask you not to make this decree. Killing deserters is one thing, but if a man only turns a blind eye, then…"

"Fine. We'll stick to the current ruling. But I want more archers on the walls who'll be happy to fire when they see a man running. In the dark they won't know who it is, and that should make it easier." He looked over. "Nathaniel. See to it."

Nathaniel Oloran nodded. "As you command, my lord."

Not a word of complaint, as ever, Lythian noted. The tar of being a known traitor had forged the man into a very dutiful knight. It was curious how things went sometimes.

"My lord," said Lord Rodmond. He had a frown on his face, and clearly disagreed with the order. "I'm not certain that firing into the backs of fleeing men is honourable."

"Deserting is not honourable."

"No. But this is not common desertion. This war is unprecedented, and what that soldier said, the first one…about us doing nothing here…"

"We're here by the command of the king, Lord Taynar."

"Yes. And of course we should obey. But I wonder if a certain amount of desertion should be considered permissible."

"Permiss…" Lord Warton started, incredulous, before he was consumed by a bout of coughing.

"Yes, my lord," Rodmond said. "We are only cutting off our nose to spite our face. These men can still do some good to protect the people, even if it is their own. Isn't that the cause we're all fighting for, in the end? Our own survival."

Lythian sighed. It was something he might have once said himself, a well-meaning thought and yet a naive one all the same. "We cannot have one rule for one man, and a different one for another. We have set the precedent now, Rodmond. If we decide that men can freely leave, how many do you imagine will want to stay?"

The young lord frowned in troubled thought. "I would say the Brockenhurst men will stay, my lord. This is their city, their land."

"And the rest? Your own men, Rodmond? Yours, Lord Barrow? How many will choose to stay in this wet and rotting ruin if given the chance to return to their wives and children, their mothers and sisters? I tell you few. Duty and honour only go so far when you're hungry and cold and sitting idle, fearing for your loved ones."

Lord Barrow gave that a grave nod. "I fear Lord Lythian has the right of this. If we open the gates, thousands will go. That can't be done, Lord Taynar. Not here. Not anywhere. It'll lead to chaos across the north."

"No…I don't mean to open the gates. I just…firing at fleeing men. Like Sir Fitz. There is something about it that sits poorly with me, is all."

There is much about this that sits poorly with me, Lythian thought. "You're still young, Rodmond," he only said. "You'll get used to it." He didn't mean that to sound dismissive, though it probably did. He rested his forearms on the table, thinking. "I want a closer eye kept on the Rosetree men," he commanded. "Not all will have taken kindly to Sir Fitz's death."

That would be for Lords Taynar and Barrow to contend with. Barrow nodded and coughed into a dirty square of cloth. The gouts of blood did not look healthy. "As you say, my lord. I'll have my men looking for…for troublemakers…among them…"

"My thanks." Lythian had found Barrow to be more accommodating these last weeks, despite their early differences. Unlike Kindrick, he'd played no part in the slaughter of the prisoners, and had cursed his fellow lord for a traitor when he heard he had taken off. Barrow had even suggested they send out men to hunt Kindrick down, but Lythian had decided against it.

No, I'll want that pleasure myself one day, he'd thought. He'd even dreamed of it by night, and more often than he'd care to admit. Lythian Lindar, noble Knight of the Vale…turned dark harbinger of justice and vengeance. In his dreams he would stalk the north in search of deserters and act judge, jury and executioner upon them. Some he might forgive if he felt the pull of mercy, but *never* a lord in command of thousands, *never* an anointed knight. Oh, those men would suffer the full brutality of his retribution, and nothing so simple as hacked-off heads either. No, he would take his time with them, and that's just

705

what he did in the dreams. They were dark dreams, bloody dreams, dreams from which he woke feeling hateful, and angry, and dangerous. And all the while, the Sword of Varinar would be calling from its chest, whispering, hissing, fuelling his rage with its want for blood and battle.

He was looking at it now, he realised. Staring straight at the chest. He dragged his eyes away and saw that the men were averting their eyes from him, uncomfortable. "My lord," prompted Sir Ralf. "You were talking about the Rosetree men."

Lythian nodded. How long had he been staring at the chest? "I've said what I need to say. You heard what Fitz said, before he died. We can't have his four hundred men causing problems."

"Three hundred," said Sir Storos. He had a gulp of wine and went to fill his cup. *Another ally drifts*, Lythian thought. Even Storos had grown listless of late, drinking at any chance he got to wile away the long dull days here in this city of ghosts. "At least a hundred have deserted by now."

Barrow coughed into his cloth again. "I'll see to it…as I said. Some will try to run. The rest…I'll keep a watch on the rest…but Fitz…he was never much liked among them. Most saw him as…as an upjumped fool."

Lythian nodded. It was an apt description of the knight. He looked up as Sir Adam Thorley entered, ducking through the flaps. "Are they ready, Adam?"

"They are, my lord."

Lythian stood. "We'll reconvene at a later time," he said to the others. "See to your duties." He went to collect the Sword of Varinar from its chest, lifting the great golden blade from inside. When he turned he found Barrow watching him. "A problem?"

"No, I…I was not aware you kept the blade in a trunk, is all."

"Occasionally. For safekeeping." Lythian did not need to explain his mental struggles to this man. Only his close allies were privy to that, and Barrow was not a part of that circle. No doubt he had guessed, though. *All that staring*, Lythian thought. He had no idea he was even doing it, and that was a troubling thought.

He stepped out of the tent with Sir Adam Thorley, fixing his swordbelt as he went. The rain soaked through his hair at once, trickling down his spine. "Have many gathered to pay their respects?"

"A few dozen, my lord."

A few dozen, Lythian thought. It was hardly a strong show of support for Sir Fitz, and many of those would have come for the other five men. *Not much liked*, he reflected. Barrow was not wrong. Lythian wondered idly how many would gather if it was Amron, or Elyon, lying in some grave. *What if it was me?* Once before many might have come, but now…

He heard the sound of splashing footsteps behind him, and Lord Rodmond came up to join them. "I ought to be there too," the young lord said. "To pay my respects."

706

Lythian nodded. "As you say."

They walked out of the gate together, a few of Rodmond's guards trailing behind in the dull blue cloaks of his house. A little south of the gate, near the outer curtain wall, some firm ground had been found and into it six graves were dug, dirt heaped at their sides. At another time the bodies might be returned home to their loved ones, but not now. The likes of Sir Vesryn Daecar and Lord Dalton Taynar had been placed in the crypts, to be brought to the Steelforge to rest with the other First Blades at a later time, but these common men and deserters would be granted no such honour.

They should feel lucky they get their own graves, Lythian thought. Some of the men had even cut headstones to mark them, and Lythian had allowed that as well. *I permit much*, he reflected. *But why? Why do I even bother? They all just hate me anyway.*

He was not wanted here, he knew, but duty compelled him to come. Men glared at him through baleful eyes as he took his place nearby, standing a little aside so as not to interfere. Once all had gathered, men stepped forward to tell stories, speak verses, sing their sombre songs. Some trinkets were thrown into the graves of each man. A necklace of stones here. A favoured blade and scabbard there. A letter from a loved one. The toy of a favourite child. Lythian watched alone. Some might think his presence perverse, but no, it was honour that brought him here. *I still have my honour*, he told himself. *I am cursed, tainted by the touch of Eldur…but it is honour that still defines me.*

The rain was falling in a thick black deluge by the time the burials were done. Lythian took his leave before the men dispersed, returning to the River Gate where Sir Adam stood waiting. "I'm going to visit with Vilmar. Keep watch for my return; I may not return for some hours."

"Do you want an escort, my lord?"

"I want to be alone."

He stepped away across the broken coastlands, walking through the deepening puddles and bogs beneath a tar-black sky. The mud was so deep in places it went right up to his knees, and sometimes he had to veer around great tracts lest he get caught in the mire. He thought of Pagaloth as he went, and Sa'har Nakaan and Sir Hadros. They'd still had no word from them, and the men that Lord Kindrick had sent out to bring word had not come back either.

Small wonder. He could not imagine how it must be in those woods now. The rain would make navigation hard and there would be new rivers where there were none before, washing through the valleys, new lakes forming between the hills. Here at least the men had shelter, but out there? *They're not coming back*, he thought. His hopes for unity were as dead and done as his failed attempts to catch dragons. *It was always folly, all of it. Everything I touch is cursed.*

The river had become a wild thing. The drawbridge that spanned it was kept down, and the water rushed over it in places now, rising higher and higher each day. To each side debris had become caught and was starting to clog on the banks, piling high with wood and bits of broken stone, bloated corpses trapped and crushed amid the tangles, of man and horse and deer. South of the bridge, the water-course spread and opened out into a great estuary where the Dread's coming had warped its shape, breaking the banks and causing it to wash over the lands, carving new furrows of its own. Now a half dozen smaller rivers rushed into the Red Sea with islands rising up between them.

Lythian crossed the bridge, the water surging past his ankles and washing the mud from his boots. On the other side the land was a little firmer. He walked toward the edge of the woods where it gazed south toward the sea. A small fire was flickering in the trees, burning beneath a raised canvas roof tied between the branches. There was a hammock there too, swaying in the breeze. Vilmar the Black sat hunched before the flames, turning a rabbit on a spit. He wore black from heel to head, a huge bush of beard pouring out from under his hood. His dark eyes did not lift at Lythian's arrival. "Knew you were coming," he growled. "They always stir when you do."

Lythian scanned the trees, saw the shapes scattered among the trunks. Most of the gruloks were sleeping, indiscernible from boul-ders. A few had awoken at his arrival, as they were prone to do when he came with the Sword of Varinar. They stood gigantic, over twenty feet tall, staring from the dark with those ice-chip eyes. Several others were staring out to sea. "What are they looking at?" Lythian asked.

"Agarath. They're always staring out that way."

Lythian looked a little closer. By his judgement they were looking more south-east than due south. Eldurath was due south, he knew. Further east meant they were staring at the Nest, or perhaps even the Ashmount. "Do they sense something out there, do you think?"

"Dragons," Vilmar grunted. "That big one. He's waking up again, Lythian. That's what Hruum thinks."

Lythian scanned the giants, searching for their captain. "Is he awake now? I'd like to speak with him."

"Sleeping. But you'll get nothing much more than that."

Lythian stepped closer to the fire. "If he knows something…"

"Then what? There's nothing we can do about that big one anyway. He'll wake when he wakes and we'll all do what we can to outlive him. There's no preparing for that." He turned the spit. "Want some rabbit? It's almost done."

Lythian removed his cloak and threw it over a low branch. "That'd be nice." He envied the huntsman sometimes, living out here alone. He turned over a fallen tree stump and sat down, the wood crunching beneath his weight. "Any trouble of late, Vilmar?"

"Not like you've got," the man said. "A few wolves came sniffing around last night, but I scared them off easily enough. That's bread and butter for me." He prodded the fire. "How many did you kill today, then?"

"Six. Sir Fitz was one of them."

Vilmar shrugged. "You expect me to know who that is? I can't keep up with all you lordlings."

"He had command of the Rosetree men after his uncle's death in the battle."

"Battle? Wasn't much of a battle, far as I've heard." He inspected the meat, then pulled the rabbit from the flames, laying it on a cut stone. "Help yourself." He tore a length of flesh from the bones and chomped hungrily. Lythian ate with a little more dignity.

For a long time neither man spoke. Lythian was happy for it. To be away from the city and all its ghosts. He could breathe out here, and think a little more clearly. He felt less angry, more focused, and perhaps it was the presence of the gruloks that did it. He didn't know for sure. "Have any more of them come?" he asked eventually.

Vilmar crunched a bone between his jaws. "Not since the last time. Still twenty-two in total."

When Amron left there had only been sixteen. *Can I take that as a small success when he returns?* Lythian wondered. *Will that balance out my other failures?* He scoffed in self derision. "Are there any more out there?"

"What? Twenty-two not enough for you?"

"I'm only wondering."

The huntsman could turn truculent just like that. "Aye. Well don't worry about all that wondering. If more come, they come. Same as the dragon. Nothing you can do about it. Now are we talking or eating?"

"Some men can do both at once."

That only won him a scowl, and if he said anything more, he'd likely lose a share of his dinner, so he kept his mouth shut from there on out. Only once the rabbit was picked clean of its bones - the ones Vilmar didn't eat, anyway - did Lythian say, "I want you to ask them to clear the clog at the bridge. I don't know if you've noticed, but there's lots of debris there, and…"

"And the bridge might break if it keeps accumulating. Well, we can't be having that, can we? How would you come and pay us your little visits?" The huntsman picked out a splinter of bone from his teeth and tossed it into the trees. "I'll ask them when the time is right."

"And when is that?"

"When it's right. I got a sense of these things."

Lythian had a sense too. He sensed it was time to leave him. He stood from his stump. "A pleasure as always." The man only growled an unintelligible response and the First Blade started back for the city.

He felt heavier every step of the way, knowing what awaited him. By now the dark had turned so thick he could scarcely see more than a dozen paces ahead. The river ran wilder than ever when he reached it, roaring and rushing past and over the bridge. Lythian stomped across in his heavy plate armour, labouring through the mud on the other side. He wondered if what Vilmar said was true, about the Dread. Was he about to come again? Could they beat him back a second time if he did? He did not know how. *He'll destroy us all,* he thought. *We're broken and divided and weaker than we were the last time. We've had no time to prepare. He'll lay waste to every one of us.*

He plodded along, his mood sinking the same as his boots as they pressed down into the mud. Ahead, the faint light of the city could be seen, blurred by the rain and fog. He pushed on through a quagmire, the filth rising up past his knees. Gradually the walls took shape before him, smashed and broken, and the River Gate, still standing strong. He saw the shadows of men on the ramparts, walking on patrol or leaning at the crenels. The guards above the gate saw him coming and the call was raised for the doors to open. Lythian stepped through, trailing mud. Sir Adam was there to greet him. "My lord. You were gone a long time."

Lythian had no response.

"Will you retire to your tent, my lord?"

He nodded. It was late and he was bone-weary.

"I shall have two of my best sent to stand guard," Sir Adam told him. He looked around. "It's a dark night, my lord. I'm told a storm is coming."

Another storm. They came often now, booming and bellowing. Lythian had already heard the crackle of thunder approaching from the east, and it was coming nearer with each rumbling peal.

"There are concerns of a large breakout tonight, my lord," the young Watch Commander went on. "Lord Barrow came to me while you were gone. Whispers from some of the Rosetree men, I understand. He has set more bowmen in place on the northern walls to deter an escape, and Sir Storos and Sir Oswin are with him, and Oloran as well. I fear Storos is eager for a fight. He will raise his blade to any deserter. There may be blood tonight."

Lythian had no complaint with that. "These deserters know the risks. Have some more of your own men deployed to patrol the streets, Sir Adam."

"As you say, my lord. Ought I wake you if there's trouble?"

"Only if it's serious." He did not need to explain what that meant. Lythian trusted Sir Adam Thorley to come to his own judgment on that.

He continued through the yard, boots splashing in the puddles. The pavilions were scattered around him, dark and ghostly in the rain and mist, occupied by this lesser lord and that unheralded knight, their roofs and walls sagging and drooping. The tent of Lord Kindrick had collapsed from the weight of the rain with no one to tend and restore it, and Sir Fitz's abode would likely do the same now. Some others had suffered similarly; Fitz Colloway was not the first knight to have abandoned him and nor would he be the last. As he crossed the yard, a loud rumble of thunder bellowed across the skies, closer than ever. Even the lightning that preceded it struggled to pierce the gloom.

The brazier was still lit inside his tent, though the flames had burned down low. Lythian removed his sodden cloak and hung it on a hook, then unfastened his swordbelt and placed the Sword of Varinar back in its chest. He went to the brazier, picked up the iron poker and stirred the coals. Sir Ralf was the one to keep the fire lit, but the old knight would have taken to his bed by now, retiring to his own small tent a little way through the ward. *He knows I want to be alone,* Lythian thought. *And no doubt he's grown tired of my dour company.* He could hardly blame him if that were true.

He removed his armour and poured himself a cup of wine from the sideboard to help him sleep. He sat and drank it down, brooding, listening to the falling rain, the raucous thunder. Faintly, he heard voices and movement outside and knew that Sir Adam's men had taken their posts. That gave him some comfort. He finished his cup and poured another, drinking until he tasted the dregs. It was bitter stuff, the last of the wine they'd scoured from the city cellars, the sort of cheap swill that sailors and dockworkers drank down with great enthusiasm, never knowing any better.

But it helped him sleep, so he drank a third cup, and a fourth after that, sitting at his desk all the while. Idly, he fingered through some old maps and letters, but for what? He wasn't here to devise strategy. He had no battle plans to make. His task was just to sit and wait. *And rot,* he thought. He pushed the papers aside and poured himself a fifth cup.

Eventually, the pull of sleep took hold of him. He stood, heavy-headed and heavy-legged and moved wearily to his bed, easing down onto the hard mattress and pulling the covers over. The brazier was burning softly, and outside more thunder rumbled through the skies, rolling from the east. *Maybe it's not thunder,* Lythian thought drowsily. *Maybe it's the roar of the Dread, coming to finish the job.* A part of him would relish it. *Come,* he thought. *Just come and get it done.* He turned onto his side, staring at the trunk across the room, cloaked in darkness, listening to the whispers hissing from inside. *If the dragon should stir, at least I'll get to use you,* he thought. *Just the once. I deserve that, don't I? To go to battle with you just the once?*

Sleep took him slowly. He dreamed of a spectre, stalking the lands, the harbinger of justice, slaying deserters. He moved from town to town in a heavy wool cloak, unsmiling, unblinking, killing as he went. *I am death,* he thought, as he took one life and then another. *I am justice.* He bore the Sword of Varinar, blood swishing from the edge of the blade, red on gold, gouts and godly mist mingling as he swung and cut and swished and hacked.

He knew some of the faces of the men he slew. Kindrick. Colloway. Sir Ramsey Stone. The big blacksmith he'd hanged and the merchant's son too. But most others were nameless, faceless, shapes and shadows cut through by his blade and with every kill the Sword of Varinar called for more. *More!* it shouted. *More!* it screamed. *More! More! More! More! More!*

"Shhh, *quiet*," whispered a voice.

Lythian stirred from his sleep.

His eyes cracked open into darkness.

He was facing away from the chest now, facing the canvas wall of the tent; he must have rolled over in his sleep. The echo of his dreams moved lazily through his mind. The spectre of death, the harbinger of doom. The demands of the blade and the…

That voice again, behind him. "Shhh, be quiet. Lift it quietly. *Quietly*, Symon."

Lythian's pulse began to rise. There were men behind him, inside his tent. *Symon*, he thought. *Steelheart?* He could hear the low grunts of exertion, the scrape of metal on wood. "It's so heavy," a man hissed.

"We just need to get it outside," said another. "To the others."

"On me. *Heave*," commanded the first.

They're at the chest, Lythian realised. *The sword…*

He drew a deep and steady breath, trying to remain calm. He was unarmored, defenceless. How had these men gotten in? He had guards outside, two guards. Slowly, he turned over, praying no one was looking. The wood beneath him gave the lightest creak and he froze, but the intruders were busy and didn't hear. He completed his turn. The brazier was almost entirely burned out, but it emitted enough light to show shadows. There were four of them, hunched over the trunk across the room, struggling to lift the Sword of Varinar from its chest. Inside the flaps, two bodies lay inert. *The guards. They killed the guards.*

Lythian reached slowly to take the dagger from beneath his pillow. His fingers closed around godsteel and his sight improved at once. The men were all cloaked, cowled, with swords poking out from the folds. They would be in armour, he knew. Outside, the rains were still coming down thick and hard. A crash of thunder bellowed through the skies, and beneath the cover of that noise, the men heaved a little louder, pulling the blade up and out to stand it on its tip. "Take it, Brontus. You can carry it. I know you can."

Brontus Oloran took the blade's handle with both hands and heaved it from the floor. The others helped him to get it up onto his shoulder. Lythian slid his legs from the bed, and the wood beneath him gave a groan.

One of the men heard. "He's awake," he said, turning, throwing open his cloak. A broadsword scraped from its sheath. "He wasn't supposed to wake."

Lythian stood, letting the covers fall from his frame. He felt groggy from the wine. "Drop the sword, Sir Brontus," he said. "It isn't yours to take."

Brontus Oloran turned to him. His face was warped and wild,

reddening from the weight of the blade. "It should have been mine," he rasped. "It should have been! Dalton cheated. He cheated me!"

"You were beaten fair and square."

"Says who? Amron? Elyon?" Brontus panted a breath. "You weren't even there!"

"I have heard a dozen tales of your bout."

"It was the rain. The rain. It helped him. I was winning easily before…"

"Drop the blade," Lythian repeated, more firmly.

"No. It's mine. Mine, Lythian. *MINE*."

Sir Symon Steelheart stepped between them. His coiled golden hair was dark with rain and he looked nothing like the pretty man who pranced along at Oloran's side. There was a cold pallor to his face, and he'd grown out a thatch of beard. His eyes were hard and deadly. "Go, Brontus," he said. "We'll take care of him." He drew his blade and pointed it forward. "We didn't want to kill you, Lindar. That's not why we're here."

Lythian looked at the dead guards. "And them? They were good men."

"Necessary sacrifices."

"The blade should have been mine, Lythian," Brontus said again, breathing heavily now. "I should have had it before Dalton. You know it. And now he's dead. You've got no right to it."

Lythian stared at him, holding his knife to his side. He was concerned by how well the man was bearing it. "King Daecar made me its guardian," he said. "This is bigger than you know, Brontus. Now put it down, and go. This needn't come to blood."

"Your blood," sneered the man beside Steelheart.

"I don't want that," said Brontus. "I don't, Lythian. We've served together for years. Just give me what I'm owed and I'll leave."

Lythian knew that could never happen.

So did Sir Symon Steelheart. "He's not going to yield, Brontus. We have to kill him. We have no choice now."

"I told you *no*," Brontus commanded, as a blast of thunder shattered the skies. "Perner, disarm him. Do it quickly." He turned to lurch outside.

The man Perner pressed forward, but Lythian was quick as a cat. He slipped sideways and slashed out, cutting at the man's neck with his dagger. Perner reared, blood spouting from his open throat, hand snapping down on his craw. Symon Steelheart whirled forward with the fourth man, a big bearded brute, and the two of them slashed out with their blades. Lythian staggered backward, rolling over his desk, then leapt up over it and slashed down. He caught Steelheart with a glancing blow that cut open his pretty cheek to the bone. The man bit back a roar, swinging in an upcut…but Lythian vaulted away behind the table and kicked it forward, sending it crashing into the two men.

By then Brontus was staggering away with the full weight of the

Sword of Varinar on his shoulder, escaping through the flaps. Lythian went to chase, but Steelheart flew in front of him. Blood was pouring from his open cheek. "Just give it up, Lindar. That's his blade. *His*. You've got nothing to do with this."

The bearded man reached out and swiped the table aside. He stood to Lythian's right, Steelheart to his left, the exit beyond. Lythian glared at them. "You're deserters." That was the only thing that made sense. Amron had sent them all to the Twinfort, and they'd left to steal the blade. "You've abandoned Lord Borrington's command."

"We don't serve him. We serve Brontus."

There was some noise outside. Voices and movement. Brontus had more men out there. Lythian went to roar for help, but his voice was weak, his head heavy, and a bellow of thunder interrupted him.

Steelheart laughed. "Guess Vandar's deserted *you*," he mocked. "He heard about what you did, Lindar. Down in the south. Maybe this is your punishment?"

Lythian lunged at him, clumsily, slashing with his dagger, but the big man came in from the side, swinging with a mailed fist. Lythian swerved away, but never saw the second blow coming. It swung up from below, crunched hard into his gut, punching all the air from his lungs. He doubled over, gasping, staggering away. He tried to call out, tried to breathe, but he couldn't.

The big man followed after him, stamping through the tent. Lythian backtracked, felt canvas behind him, turned and slashed, cutting a strip in the wall. He stumbled out into the rain, desperately trying to call out. Distantly, he could hear the sound of fighting somewhere to the north of the city. The yard was deserted. He could not see the River Gate through the rain, nor the walls and the men atop them. He took a step, another, and finally drew breath. Ralf's tent was near. And Lord Rodmond's. He had to reach them…

He lurched out across the cobbles, but got only a few feet. A steel boot swung out and took away his legs and he went crashing down to the stone. His chin struck hard, head juddering. He felt a man coming up behind him, felt a boot pressing down on his back, hard and heavy, crunching his spine. Then Steelheart was on a knee, right there beside him. "You've had your day, Lindar. But it's over. And you're done."

The Knight of the Vale had time enough to snatch a breath, but not time enough to shout. Something hard came down at the back of his head. And that was that.

Done.

55

Amron

Lillia, Amron Daecar thought, as he charged. *For Lillia, and for Amara, and for Blackfrost and for Vandar.*

He raised the Frostblade and gave out a shuddering roar. "Blackfrost!" he bellowed, as he saw the city under siege before him. "Blackfrost! Blackfrost! For Vandar!"

A thousand voices echoed him. Ten thousand. Twenty. Borringtons and Crawfields and Rothwells and Blunts, Gullys and Spencers, Sharps and Cargills and Graves led by the Ironfoot, Mantles and Flints under the banners of House Oloran. A middling host in size. A powerful one in strength. *For Vandar!* they roared. *For Vandar! For Vandar!*

The Hammerhorse was thundering at his side, matching Wolfsbane stride for stride. Lather foamed from the horses' mouths, clods of dirty snow flying backward at their charge. Sir Taegon Cargill tore his godsteel warhammer from his back and lined up the nearest foe. Amron had his eyes trained on his own, just fifty lengths away. Ahead, the rearguard lines of the enemy army were bracing for impact, lowering their spears and pikes as they hastened into a tight formation. Thousands of them spread across the open field outside the city, all shouting out and crying commands as Amron led his host through the midmorning mists. Muddy puddles of melted snow glittered beneath the sun, and the earth was churned and scorched by the passing of the horde. For once it was not snowing. For once the skies were clear. Arcing east to west, the summer sun shone down from on high. *Vandar's Smile*, Amron Daecar thought. *He favours us this day.*

"For Vandar!" the men were chanting. "For Vandar! For Vandar! For Vandar!"

The northern warhorns sang out everywhere, a great chorus to stir the soul, and ahead the Agarathi were responding with their shrieking battlecry. The thrill was thick in Amron Daecar's veins. This was like a battle of old. A battle of the last war. Dragons in the skies and a great horde ahead. A thunderous charge of misting knights with thousands of northmen at their backs. A city under siege, a desperate defence, a heroic charge to break the lines. For a moment Amron forgot the Dread, forgot Eldur, forgot the snows in summer and the unending rains, forgot the fall of the Bane and the Point and Varinar and the ending of the world. Today it was just this city, this battle. It was Blackfrost, his home, and his family within it. Lillia, Amara, Artibus, Gereth, young Jovyn was in there too, Whitebeard had said. They were safe in the mines, but for how long? If the enemy broke through…how long?

The enemy spears glinted against the sun, their black tips winking, lowering to meet them. To left and right three hundred riders fanned out, three hundred knights and lords and men-at-arms all armoured and armed with cold bare steel. Behind followed another line, and another, a thousand heavy horse to shatter the siege, punching through the lines like a fist. Amron thrust the Frostblade aloft, and let it catch the glow of the sun. Light shone out, bright and brilliant, and colour spread like a sunburst upon the field. The enemy soldiers turned their heads from the sudden glare, shying away, and into them the cavalry stormed.

The crash and clangour of steel on steel rang out, the thunder of ten thousand hooves. Men were trampled and smashed aside. Riders swept blades left and right, hacking and hewing; others went flying from the saddle, caught by pike and spear and bolt. Behind them followed the rest of the riders, two thousand strong, and the men afoot, swordsmen and spearmen, axemen and shieldmen, men with pikes and men with maces, bowmen, archers, crossbowmen to the rear, flying their arrows and bolts.

The Agarathi spearmen were falling before them like winter wheat beneath the scythe, crushed by the fury of the charge. The lines were smashed and broken. Beyond, tens of thousands more swarmed the field, spread across an open tract that led to the city walls several hundred metres away, framed by the snow-coated downs.

The outer bulwark had been breached, Amron Daecar saw, the battlements blackened and burnt, men lying dead in their droves, ballistas broken, flaming, catapults smashed and shattered. The fighting was ferocious where the walls had come down, toppled by dragonfire, opening gaps into the city. The enemy horde crowded in their thousands, trying to fight their way in as the Strand host held them back. Dragons circled like vultures above, slithering through plumes of dense black smoke that belched up from the squat stone towers, plunging and diving, savaging men with fang and claw.

My city, Amon thought, racing harder, faster.

"Blackfrost!" he bellowed, "Blackfrost!" as he led the riders on, cutting into the meat of the enemy host, sweeping the Frostblade left and right. With one great swish he sent a thousand arrows of ice cutting into the foemen before him. With another a blanket of frost fell upon them, slowing them, freezing them, and his riders ran them down. Behind him his men cheered out his name. Ahead the enemy shrank back in fear. A great screech pierced the sunlit skies. "Dragons!" bellowed the Ironfoot. "Brace for dragons! Dragons!"

The warhorns blew their warning, three blunt blasts, short and low.

"Arrows!" called out Lord Mantle, leading the Oloran host. "Spears! Prime spears!"

Flights of reeds and quarrels stormed skyward from behind them. Spears shot upward into the cerulean blue, thrust by the arms of Bladeborn men given strength by their bond to the steel. The first dragon to near was a small one, fleet and thin. It twisted through the hail of arrows, spinning, diving, but a spear caught it in the wing. The webbing tore, fluttering, and the dragon screamed and fell. Two more spears plunged into it, at shoulder and neck as it came crashing down into the bulk of the army below who swarmed it like wolves on a kill.

A second dragon followed behind, bigger, a thick bulky brute. It snapped its jaws and tried to gush flame, but its furnace fires would not catch in the bitter cold. A roar of rage bellowed and down it came, sweeping through a clot of Rothwell men, talons grasping and tearing. More spawn of the fire god followed, divebombing like seabirds, one and then another and then another, ploughing through tracts of northmen in leather and steel. They plunged and rose, plunged and rose, pulling men to the sky to rain down upon the host in a deluge of blood and bodies.

By then it was chaos. The riders charged onward; the foot spread wide. The Agarathi horde screamed their warcry and pressed. Ten thousand puffs of breath filled the air, snorting from mouths and maws and nostrils, and steam rose from the tops of heads to mingle into a great cloud. Atop Wolfsbane, Amron rode forth into the jaws of the enemy strength, leading a charge of his bravest and best; Sir Taegon and Sir Torus and Rogen Whitebeard in his dark grey armour and black cloak, bitter Sir Bryce Coddington and biddable Sir Reginald Hightree, the Varin Knights Quinn Sharp and Marcus Flint in their rich blue Varin cloaks. The Ironfoot veered west with his Grave and Ironmoor men; Lord Mantle charged east with the Olorans, his bat-like cloak flapping in his wake. Sir Harold Conwyn and Sir Lambert Joyce were with the foot, leading the Green Harbour forces.

"For Vandar!" Amron bellowed. All around him, thousands of Agarathi swarmed. He cast the Frostblade to the air once more. Power thrummed through it, so fierce it seemed to tremble and vibrate in his grasp. The cold, the snow, the ice enlivened it. The air sparked and glittered in a hundred hues. A shroud of icy barbs and bolts gathered and coalesced, hardening, sharpening, and he swung down and forward in a mighty arc. A score of soldiers flew backward off their feet, peppered with spikes and daggers of ice. *Again*, Amron thought, as he swung. *Again, again, again.*

Men fell before him. His knights spread out. Some stayed ahorse, charging and swinging. Others leapt off the backs of their steeds to hack and cut the Agarathi down on foot. The Giant of Hammerhall bore warhammer and greatsword at once, rampaging through the host as the Hammerhorse stampeded at his side, monstrously heavy in his godsteel barding. Whitebeard too was on his feet, a whirling black menace with Sir Bryce at his side. Amron glimpsed young Tyrstan Spencer in his gilded armour, bright as a beacon, wheeling about on his horse. The boy had gotten himself separated from his men and the Agarathi were scrambling to pull him down, several dragonknights rushing toward him with their tall black spears primed to thrust and stab.

"Rogen!" Amron bellowed. "Help Sir Trystan." He flung a hand.

The ranger dashed off, and Sir Bryce rushed to follow. There was a roar behind him and Amron jerked the reigns, tugging Wolfsbane around. A dragon filled his view, jaws agape as it plunged toward him. Amron swung the Frostblade upward at once, sending a spray of icy spears into the dragon's jaws. The beast's roar cut off abruptly as they pierced the soft meat and muscle inside his mouth, cutting deep. Another swing of his blade and a thicker, longer spear shot forth to plunge into the beast's neck, sending it reeling down to crash into the battlefield, scattering men and mounts as it gouged a rut into the muddy wet earth.

Men roared out Amron's name. The air filled with the strains of, "Daecar! Daecar!" More of the leathern beasts were coming, too many to count. Amron peered across the battlefield. The enemy were still thronging at the breaches across the walls. Some looked to be battling their way in. How bad had Styron's host suffered? They were meant to come pouring from the gates when the enemy turned to meet Amron's charge. *They're weakened,* the king knew. *It's all they can do to hold the Agarathi at bay.*

A sudden fear engulfed him. *Lillia. If they break through…*

"My lord!" shouted a voice. Sir Torus Stoutman came riding up to Amron's side, knocking men out of the way on his small barded horse. The dwarfish knight was armoured head to heel in steel, his great thicket of a beard poking out from beneath his faceplate. He raised a finger and pointed. "That one's for you, Amron."

Amron looked over. A huge dragon was hurtling their way, much bigger than the one he'd just slain, the largest brute on the field. Forest green scale armour with horns in shades of red and vermilion. A barrel chest, strong wide wing arms, webbing rippling pink against the sun, veined in blackish blue. It had a classic look, a fearsome beast of strong proportion, near as large as Garlath and Malathar. Amron knew him as Angaralax, and his rider as Axallio Axar, the finest young drag-onrider to appear since the end of the last war. He had been there, at the Battle of King's Point, the day Drulgar and Eldur came. *Second in command to Ulrik Marak,* Amron knew. *Now their leader.* "AXALLIO AXAR!" he called.

Amron raised the Frostblade in challenge. Angaralax gave out a resounding roar in response. Axar ripped out his blade and lifted it against the blue skies, his green and red cape fluttering in the wind. Amron could not hear his voice from here, but those raised blades were a sign. He glanced at Sir Torus Stoutman. "Torus, fight your way to the city. Clear the breaches so Lord Styron can join us. Take Sharp and Flint and their men."

"Aye, my lord."

Stoutman rode off, hollering and calling for the two Varin Knights to go with him. At once a host of riders hundreds strong was mustering another charge, cutting their way toward the walls as hundreds more followed afoot.

Amron vaulted down from the saddle. "Do what you do best," he said to Wolfsbane, smacking him on the armoured rump with a ringing clang of steel. The beast reared up and kicked out. His neigh was loud and long, Wolfsbane's version of a roar, and off he charged, swinging his head side to side as he stampeded through the battlefield.

Amron turned. Men were starting to clear away as they saw Angaralax approach. That was like the last war too. Bladeborn and Fireborn meeting in honour-bound combat. There were too few proper Fireborn riders left for that, but Axallio Axar was one such man. Amron favoured him for that. He stepped forward, encrusting himself in a thicker layer of ice, shining like a sculpture, a glitter of iridescent dust sparkling about him. The Frosblade was thrumming in his grasp, exultant. It thirsted for dragon-death and was having its fill.

"Axar!" the king roared, raising the blade once more in salute.

Angaralax thumped down to land upon the earth before him. The world gave a shudder, puddle water rippling, a hot wind rising to stir the king's cloak. A broad space was opening around them, men racing away to battle elsewhere. Amron had flashbacks of the Battle of Burning Rock. The same had happened that day, with Vallath and Dulian, though he'd only had eyes for his foe. He would give Angaralax and Axar the same respect.

"Amron Daecar," the rider called. He was a burly man, strong like his steed, with a ledge of thick brow protruding over his eyes to leave his gaze in shadow. His dragonscale armour was a dark pine green, his hair short and beard shorter, both black as a raven's wing. His voice was thick and blunt."Marak was meant to kill you at King's Point."

"He tried."

"Did he? I saw your duel from the air. There was more talking than fighting. You have become soft men."

"And you are here to do what he could not?"

Axallio Axar gave a firm nod. "I should have been given that honour from the start. I asked the Father and the Founder, but Marak took it from me." He scowled. "Lord Eldur chose poorly that day. Now Marak has fled, and left you to me."

Fled or dead? Amron thought. He still did not know. "Are we fighting or talking?"

The comment rankled the younger man. "This is how it is done," he called out, in a bitter shout. "Is that not so, Daecar? Some talking at the start. Then the fighting. It was so with Dulian, yes. I have heard the tales of how you taunted him that day, before you crippled him and killed half his soul. They call it mercy here, but no. It was cruelty. Evil. You are a villain, Amron Daecar."

Amron did not care to listen to the man's meaningless bombast. He knew what had happened that day. He knew it was not mercy, as they said. *He threatened to kill my sons*, he thought. *Those words could not be spared.* "How old are you, Axallio?" he asked.

The man grunted and lifted his chin. "Four holy turns."

Thirty-two. The number eight was sacred to the Agarathi. Some called it a holy turn, the passing of eight years. "Just a boy, then."

"A boy who has ridden Angaralax for a dozen years," the Fireborn snarled at him. "Our bond is unbreakable, you will see." He leaned back in the saddle, as though to prove it, and Angaralax reared up high, pausing to stand tall with wings outstretched before smashing his bulk back down. The earth trembled. Smoke drifted out through the dragon's teeth. Amron did not quell. The dragon was formidable, there was no doubt, but he'd faced Drulgar now. *A child*, he thought. *That is all the rest are.* "Marak and Garlath. Ven and Malathar. Not even Dulian and Vallath can match us."

Amron doubted it. "Are you afraid, Axallio?" he asked.

"Afraid? Of you?" The man laughed aloud. "I fear no one, Daecar. Nothing. You may hold this god-shard, but that is nothing to me. Gather them all. Reforge them. I still would not quiver. Varin's heir or no, I hold no fear of you."

The man was lying. Amron had fought enough Fireborn to know that. "I will give you one chance. Fly home, leave this land, join the rebellion against your master. Do this and I will spare you. Do it not and you will die."

The man's face went red with rage, and Angaralax bellowed a fearsome roar. That was as good an answer as any.

"So be it," Amron murmured. He stepped forward to engage.

The dragon stirred at once, shifting backward and twisting its bulk to swing out a lashing tail. Amron knew he would. He'd faced enough dragons in his time to know they often led with the motion of the beast, bracing his feet. The air sparkled, frosting, as he swung his blade in a rapid horizontal arc. A spray of ice blew over his foe, spreading into a thick white cloud, slowing the tail as it whipped around. Amron shifted stance, heaving the blade high, and swung down with all his might. His timing was perfect. The steel hacked down through the scale armour, through horns and spikes, biting deep into the meat and muscle. The beast bellowed. The tail kept coming. It slammed into Amron's chest, knocking him back a pace or two as ice exploded from his breastplate, reforming almost instantaneously as he heaved the blade back out with a spray of frost and blood.

The dragon swung back around. Blood sluiced freely from the wound, but the tail was thick and it would take a lot more than that to sever it. Angaralax slammed his forefeet into the ground, ripping away chunks of mud and earth, head tipped high and roaring. Amron saw his chest beginning to glow, the fires stirring. He swished the Frostblade. A cloud of frozen air swamped the beast, steaming as it enrobed him. The king swished again, and again, and again. And then he swished some more.

The dragon's motion was slowing, each swing of the Frostblade a new frigid fetter to chain him. Amron could see Axallio Axar shouting wordlessly as the air froze and closed about him. His silken cape had turned stiff as stone, frost forming on his armour. Angaralax was widening his wings to try to thump the air and take flight, but the wings were too slow, the webbing rigid. Amron swished and swished and swished. His power was unlimited here.

I gave you a chance, he thought. The Frostblade swung back and forward in an ice-white blur. *You should have taken it, Axallio.* The air had become a pale wintry shroud, the shadow of the dragon encased within it. Its motion slowed, slowed, and eventually stopped. Amron took a pace through the mist. Dimly he could hear the crazed strains of battle around him, but here he seemed to be in another world. It had even begun to snow, he realised, a localised storm formed by his blade. *Would that every battle could be fought here*, he thought. He had never felt so invulnerable.

He reached the frozen dragon, with the frozen rider atop him, entombed in a layer of glass-like ice. Axar's face was twisted into a white rictus of pain, his eyes open, panicked, staring, but dead. The man was gone, Amron knew. The body could not sustain such a swift decline in temperature and be revived, not without fatal effects. The dragon, though...

Already he could see it warming from within, the ice cracking and breaking from the scales, the glow of its furnace flame spreading from its molten core. Amron did not know how long it would take to become fully mobile, and nor did he want to wait to find out. It felt wrong to slay a beast this way, like killing a man when he was down and defenceless, a dishonourable act, but he had no time for such misgivings.

He will kill many if I do not, he told himself, as he moved over to the beast's head, and saw the open eye staring at him, hating him, saw the fear in it and the rage. The huge head was raised too far off the ground for him to cut at it, the neck lifted high, but that was no hurdle to Amron Daecar. With a small measure of reluctance, he raised the Frostblade, pointing its tip up at the softer underside of the dragon's jaws, and summoned the power of Vandar within it. A spear of clear ice coalesced, hard as crystal and sharp as godsteel. He thrust upward. The spear launched forth to drive deep into the beast's jaws, cutting up and through the roof of his mouth. A shudder ran through the dragon's mighty body, more flakes of ice cracking and falling. He saw the pupil in that eye dilate. Blood gathered to dribble out through its teeth, hot and steaming as it fell.

But the beast was not yet dead. Another spear was fired upward, shattering into the first. Already it was melting, dripping icily down to mingle with the blood. The second spear drove through the first and both surged deeper, piercing through the bone of the beast's upper jaw. Another ripple went through it. More blood gushed, mingling with the meltwater to turn pink as it splashed onto the ground. The brain was pierced, Amron knew. He could tell from the way the eye ripened and rolled over. Still, he summoned a third spear for good measure, to be absolutely sure.

When that was done, he took a moment to look upon his fallen foe, watching as the fires dimmed within its cavernous chest, the furnace guttering out as the forge shut down. The ice thawed enough for it to slump and sag at the body, crusts of frost breaking off as it crashed suddenly down to sprawl dead upon the field, half-frozen limbs jutting out at odd angles. Axallio Axar remained fixed to his saddle, poking out unnaturally, frozen like a statue. Amron shook his head at him, disappointed. He was no Dulian, no Ven, no Ulrik Marak. *Just another gallant fool*, the king thought. *Who thought he was a hero.*

The white pall around him was weakening, lances of sunlight piercing the shroud. The din of battle returned to his ears. He turned, moving away from the fallen beast. Gradually, the battlefield opened back out before him, a chaotic swell of frenzied fighting. His host were battling in pockets, he saw, each an island in a sea of red and black. Some islands were large, others small, but in many the tides were coming in as the Agarathi numbers told. *They are overwhelming us*, the king fretted. It was not meant to go this way.

A shout hailed him. He saw the young face of Sir Reginald Hightree racing over on his armoured horse, fighting his way toward his king with a strong guard of men-at-arms in Borrington blue. "My king. Angaralax, I saw him come down to face you. Is he…"

"Dead," Amron confirmed. "And Axallio Axar." His eyes flitted to the city walls, still some distance away. He could not say for certain how well Sir Torus was faring, but it seemed to him that the knight's charge had been held. "We need to secure the city, Sir Reginald. Come with me. All of you."

He marched on foot, Hightree and his men forming a cordon to his left and right. In short order they came upon the Giant of Hammerhall, an island unto himself, grunting as he swung and chopped with greatsword and warhammer. The man looked to be tiring. Dozens of men lay butchered about him. He was bleeding from a small hole in his left leg, where the cuisses met the poleyn protecting his knee. "Damned dragonknight got me," he bellowed, in a fury. "Got him back, and the rest of them."

"We're making for the city, Sir Taegon," Amron said. "Where is the Hammerhorse?"

"With Wolfsbane," the giant knight grunted. He grimaced as he put weight on his wounded leg. If the spear had cut into his knee that could be a serious problem. "They're competing. For kills. Least it looked that way to me."

Amron might have smiled at another time. The notion of horses competing for kills in battle amused him. "We'll leave them to it. On me, Sir Taegon."

The giant joined them, half limping as he went. The air was beginning to thicken with a mix of steam and smoke, swirling from the burning city on a southerly wind, and above them the skies were curdling. When a cloud passed over the sun, Amron felt a tingle slither up his spine. *Vandar's Smile*, he thought. *Blotted. He turns from us.*

It was not true, he hoped, but the omen did not encourage him. Nor Lord Strand's lack of showing. He marched on, casting frost as he went to drive the enemy away. Sir Reginald called out what he saw, counting dragon numbers such as he could. "At least thirty," he shouted out. Most were smaller, riderless, darting down and up and down and up, picking weaker men for foes. Some circled high, waiting for their time to strike, like eagles hunting prey. At one point Amron was certain he saw a true eagle above them, by the shape of it, but it was hard to say for sure. Ahead, the city came and went between banners of smoke and fog. His glimpses were dire. Another breach had opened up in the walls, he saw, and a river of red and black was pouring inside, clambering over the broken stone.

"The city," he roared out, to the men he passed. "Make for the city! Secure the streets!"

Others echoed him. He heard a warhorn blow a loud blast nearby, others responding across the field. A man in black ghosted through the fog, blood spattered across his cloak. "Rogen," Amron called to him.

The ranger hastened to join him. "Sir Trystan is dead," he reported. "A dragonknight stabbed a dagger through his eyehole before I could get to them. I failed you."

He failed himself. The boy was reckless and paid for it dearly. "You did what you could," he told the ranger. "What of Sir Bryce?"

"Fighting with Conwyn and Joyce. They were leading a charge for the easternmost breach last I saw. The Agarathi...they were breaking through."

"My lord...to the left," warned a voice.

Amron turned that way and saw a great swell of enemy soldiers pouring toward them in a sudden charge. The Borrington men surged to defend him, clashing with sword and spear and shield. Several dragons were following them in, diving as one, two, three, four of them reached out with their great sharp talons to snatch men from the saddle and flap away. Sir Taegon roared and tried to leap, swinging his greatsword, but his leg buckled and he fell to one knee, smashing a fist into the ground in rage. The dragons wheeled around for another pass. Amron turned with them. Men were shouting around him. "Watch the right," they called. "East. They're coming from the east."

Then suddenly another man shrieked out 'west' and another said 'to the left...the *left!*' and Amron did not know where to look. All of a sudden dragons were coming down from everywhere, from left and right and east and west, from the city ahead and the torn earth behind. "Protect the king! Protect the king!" Sir Reginald was shouting, and then Whitebeard was there right with him, and Sir Taegon surged to his feet and lurched over as well. Men gathered to form a shield wall, but Amron wished they hadn't.

"Move aside!" he commanded. "Give me room. I need space!" He swung an arm, shifting men out of the way, and tried to swing the Frostblade upward as a dragon flew by, but another armsman got right in front of him. "Damn it," he cursed. He had to be careful here not to freeze his own men. "Stand aside, that is an order. All of you...step away and give me space!"

Some heard, calling for others to move back, but the Agarathi were thick about them. "Protect the king! Protect the king!" No sooner had Amron found a bit of room than others came rushing in to fill the space, their backs to him, shields held close, swords and spears and pikes facing out.

"Move aside," the king roared again. "Rogen, Taegon, help make room! Make room!"

But Taegon Cargill was no longer there. Amron glimpsed the giant knight in the throes of combat with a dragon, his warhammer cast aside as he swung with his two-handed greatsword. Men were being scattered as the beast twisted and turned, his tail whipping them aside. Shields went flying from grasps, and swords and spears. Amron saw a blade come tumbling down to drive into the neck of a young Mantle man in his black cloak and bat sigil. Another was knocked out by a heavy godsteel shield, to be trampled by a charging horse. Sir Taegon was swinging, roaring. He gave a great hack, but the dragon jerked away, spinning fiercely to trip Taegon up with its tail. Then the battle churned about them and Amron saw no more.

"Rogen!" he bellowed. "Sir Reginald! Clear a path!"

Whitebeard was there, ahead of him, rasping out the king's orders, but Sir Reginald too had been drawn into the fighting to Amron's left. The dragons were still diving, one and then another and then another, like nesting birds harrying and harassing some predator trying to steal their eggs. He swung his eyes about, calling for Wolfsbane, trying to whistle as he did when hailing him, but the horse was nowhere to be seen. The world had closed about him, thickening and tightening. The Agarathi legions were pressing from all sides.

Suddenly a bright amber light filled his sight as a dragon glided atop them. "Shields!" came a shout, and men swung their shields upward, the flames licking down through the spaces between them. Amron needed no such defence in his icy armour, yet the men flew to defend him all the same. Cloaks caught fire, and beards and hair. Burning men threw themselves into the snowy mud, rolling and screaming. Some were trampled in the chaos and never stood. Others staggered back to their feet, muddied and scorched.

"Spears!" someone was calling. "Spears!" They flew at the passing dragons, most missing or glancing harmlessly away. A few struck their targets. One dragon roared and twisted and fell, disappearing into the swarming horde. But they kept coming. Clawing and snapping and killing. Amron felt the heat of one behind him, and spun about as it reached out to grasp him. He ducked, the long talons raking at his armour, tearing off chunks of ice that quickly reformed. Another followed right behind, snatching up one of the Borrington men-at-arms to drag him into the skies. A thick curtain of smoke drifted over from the city. Mist rose from bodies and mouths, breath fogging; flakes of snow and ash were swirling. Another man was snatched away. Behind, the glow of firelight told of another spear of flame. Amron whirled, thrusting the Frostblade at the firebreathing beast, but his ice spear missed, vanishing into the shrouded air.

"Target the fire-breathers!" he roared. "Take them down! Take them down!"

The air was suffocating. Everywhere was steel and fangs and fire. Claws raked and ripped and tore at the men about him, tugging them skyward to fall bloodily back down where they landed hard on the soldiers below. He pushed, driving men aside, trying to fight his way toward the enemy ranks, but he was trapped, enclosed. "Make way! Make way!" He raised the Frostblade, sending a pulse of white light across the field. "Make way! Move aside! *Move*!"

A searing heat blew across him, and suddenly he felt talons closing about his sword arm. The dragon thumped its wing, struggling to lift him. Up he went, a metre, two. Men saw and reached out, grabbing to pull him back down, but then another dragon was there, bathing them in flame. The king was drawn upward, through ash and smoke and mist, his captor beating the air into a furious storm to lift him in his armour. His rerebrace and vambrace and gauntlet all groaned as the talons tightened.

He kicked hard with his legs, trying to dislodge himself, and snatched out his dagger with his spare hand to slash at the dragon's foot. Blood came down in black-red rain, but the dragon did not release him. A smaller beast descended, flapping, snatching at a leg, and together they drew him higher…higher…

He saw the city, no more than a hundred metres away. The fighting looked to have spread into the streets and lanes and squares. Banners flew the standards of Lord Styron Strand and his underlords. Amron saw them in flashes, the steel-horned goat of House Darring, the

725

Manson hornets with their godsteel stingers, the Fallow axeman in a field of stumps. They were fighting back. At one breach a swell of them came boiling out to join Sir Torus Stoutman and his host. Further east, Sir Lambert Joyce was battling with the Green Harbour men, their banners rippling in the cold wintry wind. He glimpsed a black tide of Mantles crashing against a wall of gold and red, saw the Ironfoot leading a charge of Graves and Taynars. And west...west...

There were shapes out there, in the snow. Shapes coming around the hills. A great blur of them, of men it looked. *But who?* he thought. *Who?*

A spear came flying from below, puncturing the smaller dragon in its flank. The beast roared and reeled away, releasing Amron's leg. The king slashed with his dagger, again and again. More spears pierced the air. "Avoid the king! Avoid the king!" One missed him by inches, driving up and past him to deflect off the dragon's thick hide. The din of thumping wings made a fearsome racket. Smoke billowed about him, seeping in through the seams of his armour, through the eyeslit and vent holes of his faceplate. The king coughed, spluttering. His eyes watered and stung. Blinking, he lashed out again as more spears pinged and bounced. The beast was tiring, his weight too much...but suddenly there was another grasping at him. He had a sensation of movement as the battlefield ghosted by below him. They were taking him, flying him away. *To Eldur*, he thought. *They're going to fly me all the way to Eldur...*

He shut his eyes and focused. His arm was locked tight in the dragon's grip, but he still clung to the hilt of the Frostblade. Its magic required movement, but not always. *Ice*, he thought, summoning its power, and from its edge came a sudden blast of frozen air. The dragon gave a hiss of alarm, grip weakening, and Amron Daecar seized his chance. He heaved, ripping his arm free, and slashed out.

And suddenly he was falling.

The mists engulfed him. He could hear the din of battle below. He fell three metres, five, eight. Then a hard juddering impact struck him in the legs, a dragon flying by, charging him. His armour clanged loudly and he went spinning into a dizzying fall.

A searing agony tore through his right thigh and left shoulder, a thousand daggers stabbing at once. He screamed. The blow had knocked the Frostblade loose. Spinning, he saw it, tumbling away into the masses below.

No...

Then it was gone, lost, as he spun away and saw only sky. By flashes he saw it, sky and earth, sky and earth, as he fell head over heel, tumbling. The ground was fast approaching. Pain ripped through his shoulder and thigh, blinding. He saw a dragon coming and braced. The collision was terrible, a hard shoulder to his chest. He flew sideward twenty, thirty feet, his head rattling in his helm, and crashed down to land amid a clot of foes.

At once the blows came, steel smashing and stabbing wildly at his armour. He could hear the rough Agarathi, the shrieking battlecries. He struggled to his feet, swinging out with his dagger to clear them away. The pain in his shoulder was unbearable. His right leg could barely bear his weight. A dragonknight pushed forward, all in black and red, and thrust hard with his spear. The tip took him in the gut. He twisted as it scraped across his armour, reached out and snatched it away, spun it around and skewered the man in a single motion. His brothers roared and piled on, trying to stab through the tight seams between his plate. He swung the spear to hold them off but there were too many.

Their weight pressed him down, overwhelming him. Dimly he could hear men coming to his aid. His crippled leg gave way. Mud splashed up as he fell. The world was all scraping and shrieking and hate, as they tried to get at the weak meat behind the steel.

You let my city fall, he heard Amron the Bold say. *You have not yet earned the name.* He thought of his dream, of Vesryn arriving at Varin's Table. He imagined the Steel Father watching him now, and his brother, and his father and his grandfather and his namesake, and all the great men who came in between. *This is how I die. A cripple in a steel suit, crushed and suffocated.*

Darkness consumed him. The mass of bodies was blotting out the light. He got his right hand beneath him and pushed up, but the enemy swarmed anew, pressing him right back down. The pain was so intense he could barely think. He heaved again, but it was no use, the agony had stolen his strength. He blinked, trying to stay conscious. The edges of his vision were closing…closing…

Sudden shouts rose all about him. Agarathi words he did not know. From his right side a roar spread, of voices united, and a chorus of battle rang out. The press weakened atop him. Light pierced the swamp of bodies. Men were shouting in a dozen different tongues. There was a great rumbling voice, deep as a mine shaft, and Amron glimpsed a giant rush into the fray swinging an enormous stone club. Others followed after him, monstrous men in furs and pelts, grey-skinned and bearded, driving the Agarathi back.

Amron got to a knee. Hundreds of new combatants were rushing by him in a flood. He blinked, lifting his faceplate to rub the mud and smoke from his eyes.

Then a voice roared behind him. "Steel Lord! No, it cannot be you? Ha! It is! What are you doing down there? Get up, get up!"

Amron remained on his knee, trying to catch his breath. His vision was blurred by pain but that voice…He peered at the big figure all in white. He could not believe what he was seeing. "Stegra? Is that…"

"Who else? Of course it is me!" The Snowfist marched toward him and pulled him up to his feet. He was dressed in his snowbear cloak, armoured beneath in layers of thick hide. His skin was milk-white, his beard a drift of new-fallen snow, his eyes an icy blue, clear as a spring.

"Where is your frosty blade, Lord of Daecar? You need it, I think, in this snow."

Amron was at a loss for words. "I…it fell…" He gestured away, but did not know where the blade could be. The city was away now to the east. To the west a great host was pouring through the low snowy hills, thousands of them, the strangest army Amron had ever seen. There were tribesmen, Snowskins and Stone Men and Deadcloaks and Crowmen of the Crag, soldiers and rangers from Northwatch, common men mustered from the distant lands of the north, from Lakeside and Hornhill and the deep places of the Banewood, fierce forest men bearing woodaxes and crofters with sharpened hoes, farmhands with pitchforks and fisherfolk with their spears and nets. They came in their thousands, *tens* of thousands, Amron saw, a great vast march of men and even women flowing down from the north. Amron gaped to see them all. "How? *How*, Stegra?" is all he managed.

"How is a big question. One word, but a big question. The asking of it should come later, my friend. Yes, later, once these fire people are gone." He hefted a long godsteel blade. Stegra had Bladeborn blood in him, Amron knew, from some ranger long ago. He turned his head. "Svaldar, Hammerhand, keep going! There are fire men to kill! Go! Put them out!"

Amron saw them, the tribesmen he'd travelled with. Svaldar son of Stegra and Arnel Hammerhand, Wagga the White and Briggor the Big and Jorgen Half-Eye and others. They rushed right past, Svaldar leading them on, and with them went Crowmen in their black feather cloaks and Deadcloaks in their pelts, the giant Stone Men, lumbering and bellowing, many a match for Sir Taegon in size and some of them even larger. Against this new force the enemy were wilting, many of them turning to flee back down the pass, and even some of the dragons were flapping away.

"Ha!" Stegra bellowed. "You see. I raise my blade and they flee before me. I knew these flame men were weak. Fire does not like snow, my friend. Now where is that blade? I want to see it again."

Amron did as well. He turned his eyes across the battlefield, searching. Then a hand came down on his shoulder and he turned to look into the face of Lord Robert Borrington, the scaly burn scars that mottled the right side of his face twisted by his grin. "Well now, there's a man I've longed to see."

"Robert."

"Amron." The Lord of Northwatch tugged him into an embrace; he'd always been greatly more garrulous and tactile than his older brother Randall. Amron grimaced in pain as he felt the jolt go through his left shoulder. "Ah. The pain is still with you, then?"

Always. And worse than ever. He only nodded. "Is this your doing? This army?"

"In part. Mostly it was down to the snow."

"The End Fall," the Snowfist put in, suddenly serious. "The free lands are buried, Lord of Daecar. Even us Snowskins had to flee. The Ember of the Red Storm was seen. It heralds the last days. The battle for the dawn, as Shrikna said."

Amron did not know what that meant. He would have time to hear of it later. He scanned the field. More foemen were fleeing. From the city he could see black and red and gold in retreat, see Lord Styron's host emerging to chase them down. Dragons were screeching and flapping away as flights of arrows and bolts filled the sky.

Amron limped back into the thick of it, a shambling wreck, his armour scratched and stained and covered in mud. *Amron the Bold*, he thought. *Amron the Broken.* Ahead, he saw a group of men crowding around something, and hastened toward them, led by the whispers. The Frostblade lay half buried in the mud, the shard of a god's heart slick with blood and filth. Amron breathed out in relief to see it. As he bent down he almost fainted from the pain, but as soon as his fingers touched the hilt…as soon as he felt the connection, the bond….all his ails were gone.

He stood, restored, tall and mighty, the fire in his veins replaced by ice, driving the pain away. The sensation was more powerful than ever, the contrast acute. He drew a long deep breath, trying not to dwell on what would come *after*, when he gave the blade up. That time was near, so very near now. Living without it had become an unbearable thought.

But he would give it up when he must. *I will*, he told himself. *I will.*

He turned to the men gathering around him, a pocket of calm in the chaos. "Clear the enemy from the city. Drive them from the field. Harry them if you can. But beware the dragons, they will seek to defend their retreat." He nodded. "Go."

Shouts rang out as his orders were passed on. The warhorns blew long and low as riders mustered to give chase. Just then, Wolfsbane came cantering through the fogs, snorting and swishing his mane. Amron smiled, wondering how many men he'd slain, and climbed up into the saddle.

Lord Robert was still afoot. "And where will you go?" he asked him.

Amron turned Wolfsbane toward the city. "To see my daughter," he said.

56

Jonik

"We need to go back," Gerrin warned, wiping his bloody blade clean on his cloak. That blood was thick, viscous, black, like no blood they had ever seen. "We're not prepared for this. And there's no way out of this cave."

The old knight's eyes strained to see through the dark of the cavern. This one had no luminous moss, no glow worms and flickering fireflies, no phosphorescent fungi, nothing. *Just those giant insects,* Jonik thought, clinging fast to Mother's Mercy. They had come upon a nest of them, some strange, overlarge species of beetle with long pincer-legs, thick-armoured shells, roving antennae and hellish faces with a thousand beady little eyes. The largest were as big as dogs; no great threat to them when they came one at a time, or even ten at a time, but should a hundred of them come scuttling out of the darkness, they might have a problem on their hands. Jonik could hear them now, squeaking and chittering in their holes and crevices. This entire cave was their home, he realised. They had slashed a score of them dead, but there were many more out there, and those noises sounded like the bugs were making a plan, communicating. At any moment they might come storming out in force and overwhelm them, and Jonik was not about to be defeated by a beetle.

"Fine. We'll track back and find another way," he said, acceding.

They moved away slowly, eyes swaying through the gloom all the while, searching for movement. The beetles seemed satisfied to let them go, quieting down as they reached the mouth of the cave and stepped back into the tunnel. Once there, Gerrin turned around to lead them hastily on, Jonik behind him, Sir Owen watching their rear should the bugs mount a sortie and seek vengeance for their fallen kin. They went like that in silence, snaking back up the passageway, ducking where the ceiling narrowed, climbing when the way grew too steep. Ten minutes later, they emerged back into the large chamber above it.

They took stock there, considering their next course. There was a little more light in this cavern. On one wall a curtain of vines draped down, peppered with growths of glowing fungus, and that gave illumination enough for them to see. "What were they?" Sir Owen asked, peering back down the tunnel. His voice was thick with disgust; Sir Owen Armdall had no great fondness for things that crept and crawled. "I never knew insects could grow that large."

"They are creatures of the old world," Gerrin told him, giving his blade another wipe on his cloak. "Everything was bigger back then. They…" He cut himself off with a curse. "Damn this sticky blood. It's ruining my cloak." He turned his eyes around, spotting a trickle of water leaking down one wall, and walked over to wash both blade and cloak clean.

Jonik went to follow; Mother's Mercy needed a shower as well. Through the walls, he could hear the water moving, rushing like blood through this boundless body of an underworld. Gerrin said it had all seeped down from above, through stone and soil, due to all the rains, and everywhere the walls were dripping and wet, glistening darkly against the glowing moss and fungi.

Sir Owen came over to join them, wetting the hem of his cloak to wipe his sword clean. He cringed at the foul smell of black blood and innards. "So, where now?"

"*Up*," Gerrin said at once. His voice was a weary grunt. "It's past time we go back. We told Harden three days."

Jonik could care less what they told Harden, in truth, much as he liked the old sellsword. They had gone much too deep and much too far to go all the way back now. "We keep going," he said, in a voice that brooked no dissent on the matter. "If Harden wants to go for help, let him. We have a duty to fulfil and going back will only waste time. And we don't know how long we've been down here. It's probably been longer than three days already."

Down in this maze beneath the earth, it was impossible to say when the sun set and moon rose, whether it was dusk or dawn, noon or night. They only had their instincts to guide them, and Jonik's told him that three-day window had elapsed some time ago.

"Harden is not our concern, Gerrin," he went on, misliking the old knight's sullen silence. "If he's got any sense, he'll give us more time. Three days was never going to be enough."

"Then you should have said so," Gerrin came back. "This place is too large. We need more men."

"We don't need more men. We only need me." Jonik was convinced of that now. His written fate, the one seen and recorded by Thala, had ended at the Shadowfort, but that did not mean he had no destiny to fulfil. He had told his cousin Amilia that they could forge their own fate now, and this was his. Finding that blade and bringing it back to the refuge. "The Mistblade is down here, I know it," he said. "I can hear it, Gerrin. We're getting closer."

His old mentor did not much like those words. "That's what worries me. It's already in your head, Jonik. Working its deceptions and tricks. I'm afraid of what will happen if we find it."

Jonik gave him a hard frown. "We have to find it. Why else are we here?" The old man was aggravating him now. "I'm not going to let the blade corrupt me, Gerrin. I've been through that. It won't happen again."

The former Shadowmaster gave him a long look, searching deep into his eyes. "I hope so, Jonik, I do. But if it does…"

"It won't."

"If it does.."

"It won't," Jonik said again, firmer. "But if you're so worried about it, perhaps you should carry it instead? You have the strength, we know that. *You* be the guardian, Gerrin. I'd be more than happy to spare myself the burden."

The man's eyes were uncertain. That was not a responsibility he wanted, Jonik knew, and it wasn't one he wished to foist on him either. This was his task, his duty, and he would see it done.

"We have to go further down," he said, putting the debate to one side. "We can decide on all that once we find it. But we have to find it first."

He turned away from his mentor, looking around the cave. There were two further passages aside from the one they had taken to get here, and the one that led down to the beetle lair. One was tight and narrow, a squeeze to get through. The other was broad and low, and would require that they duck, perhaps even crawl. Either could take them to a dead end…or a plunging drop too perilous to climb…or grow too tight that they must turn back…or open out into another of these larger caverns…or lead to some other peril that had not yet faced. In the end they would not know until they tried, and oft as not selecting one passage from another had become no more than a lottery.

All Jonik knew was that the Mistblade was *lower*. Where, he could not say. Just somewhere lower than here. "This one," he said, looking at the tunnel with the low ceiling. "We'll have to walk in a crouch. I'll lead." He stepped forward.

He knew the others would follow, and duly they did, moving to his heel as he bent his back and ducked inside. The space was cramped, and he could feel the rock ceiling brushing the top of his hair as he went. Within twenty short paces it got worse. "We'll have to crawl," he called back. He went down onto all fours and peered into the darkness. He could see no glow ahead, the way was dark as pitch and unnerving. "Owen. Light a torch and hand it forward."

He waited for the knight to see it done, cutting a spark with flint and steel and setting the top of the torch ablaze. Jonik reached back and took it from his grasp, holding it forward to light the way as he crawled. The tunnel snaked back and forward, almost too uniformly, as though some great serpent had gouged it out, and its walls were smooth. Jonik had heard tales of great worms that wriggled through the depths of the Wings, creating tunnels and passages beneath the fiery mountains that took root upon those islands. Some were colossal, the singers said, and had burrowed all the way to the north during the War of the Gods, forging tunnels a thousand leagues long through which Agarath's armies could march to war. Jonik wondered now if some of them had remained when they got here. Not the giant worms, perhaps, but some lesser offspring. Had *they* made these tunnels? Were they still alive down here, lurking in these depths?

The thought drew a shudder up his spine, and suddenly he was peering forward, worried that some great fleshy worm might come sliding around the corner, its open mouth ringed in razor-sharp teeth, ready to devour him. The thought even made him pause for a moment, long enough for Gerrin to call, "What's the trouble?" from behind him. "Is it too tight up ahead?"

"It's tight enough as it is," Sir Owen said, squirming along. "If we have to turn around…"

"We won't," Jonik declared. He did not know if that was true or not, but he said it anyway, hoping. His good faith was rewarded another fifty metres later, as he came around another bend and sighted an opening a little way ahead. He breathed out in relief. "I can see the exit. We're close." For a moment he'd feared the tunnel might go on and on, narrowing so much that they'd be forced down onto their bellies like those worms he was afraid to meet, but no, the end was near. He shuffled awkwardly, armour scraping on stone, until at last the tunnel widened at the mouth, enough for him to crouch, exiting into a much larger cavern.

There was a short drop to reach the floor, no more than three metres. Jonik communicated that to the others and then clambered out, dropping to the ground with an echoing *thud*. Some bits of grit and loose rock came falling from the ceiling, clattering as they landed. Once Gerrin and Owen had followed him down, Jonik instructed the Oak to leave a leaf so they remembered which tunnel it was.

"We're not likely to forget," Gerrin muttered. "Most tunnels don't come out twelve feet above the ground."

"It's good practice," Jonik replied. Every time they exited a tunnel, or took a turning at some fork, they always left a large maple leaf on the ground, weighed down by a stone to make sure it did not blow away in a draught, so they knew the way back. By now there must be a hundred or more leaves scattered about this maze.

Jonik stepped forward to look around, holding the torch high before him. Its flickering orange light danced on the walls, throwing shadows from tumbles of rock. The cavern was roughly circular in shape, its walls weeping with moisture. Creeping vines fell from a ceiling thirty feet high, and up there he could see a narrow shaft, a hole that led to some upper level. Jonik could not say how deep they were. The main cavern had been over two hundred metres beneath the surface, but by now they might be four or five times deeper than that. The heat suggested so, rising through the vents. On the surface the days had turned bitter cold, but down here the air was muggy and close. Somewhere below them, he could hear the sound of rushing water.

"You might want to put out the torch, Jonik," Gerrin told him. "There's moss enough here to see."

He had the right of that. The glare of the flame only caused the bio-glow of the moss to shy away. It was better to douse the fire and let and their eyes adjust.

He saw a small pool of standing water ahead, its surface rippling as moisture dripped from above to a sound of *tap tap tapping*, a sound heard everywhere here. He stepped forward and plunged the torch into the pool, and the cavern fell abruptly dark. Gradually, the moss came alive, filling the air with its ethereal glow, chasing away the gloom. On the far wall, Jonik saw some strange creature skitter away, half spider and half lizard, moving inhumanly fast. The hair rose on the back of his neck. There was more movement elsewhere, more spider-lizards scuttling away into the shadows.

"*Ghekantulas*," Gerrin said, behind him. "I've read about them before. They're harmless."

"Tell my eyes," Sir Owen Armdall said. "Those things send a shiver up my spine. The way they move…" He gave a shudder.

Gerrin only laughed. "Most people mislike insects and arachnids. We all share that psychological aversion. It's because they're so different from us."

"Alien," Jonik said. *Like this place.* That they were so large only made them all the more disturbing. "So…ghekantulas. Let me guess… a cross between geckos and tarantulas? What genius thought that up?"

"Some old explorer," Gerrin said, shrugging. "Forget his name. He saw them in the old iron mines beneath the Three Peaks, I recall."

Sir Owen had a troubled look on his face. "You don't imagine there are any creatures down here that eat maple leaves, do you? These bugs…what *do* they eat, exactly?"

"Moss and vines and cave shrubs," Gerrin answered. "Perhaps smaller bugs and insects as well, and the droppings of larger crea-tures." He rubbed his stubbly jaw. "Let's hope maple's off the menu."

"We have the stones if not," Jonik said. The stones they used to weigh down the leaves were always big ones, and they always placed them right at the heart of the tunnel entrance, brushing all others aside, to make certain they stood out. "Even if some bug munches on our leaves, they're not like to gorge themselves on chunks of rock. We'll be fine. Stop fretting. And come, it's this way."

He began walking across the heart of the chamber, toward the opposite wall. There was another opening there, a scar no more than a metre wide, that would take them on from here. He could not see any other way, and not for a moment did the notion of squirming back through that tunnel appeal to him. He would have to later, when they came back this way, but not yet. When he reached the opening, he glanced back to make sure the others were following. Dutifully, they did so, though not without a measure of reluctance. He could almost hear Gerrin's rugged old jaw grinding from here.

Let him brood, he thought. *He'll thank me later when we reach our quarry.*

The tunnel was tight. The metre width soon narrowed to half that, and they were forced to crab along sideways to squeeze through. He could feel the tension in the others as the world gave a shiver, and gritty dust cascaded from the low rock roof above him. The earth was growing less stable as they went deeper, shifting and settling, and Jonik did not imagine all those rains were helping. They seeped into the lands, softening them, nibbling away at rock and stone and soil, forcing great subterranean lakes and rivers to form. He could feel one now, a powerful flow thrashing wildly along beneath him. The earth was quivering from its motion, and it only grew stronger the further along they went.

At last Gerrin vented his fears. "This is folly, Jonik. We'll end up like your grandfather if we keep going like this. Is that how you want this to go? All three of us crushed and trapped?"

"We have our blades," Jonik came back. "We can cut through if we have to."

"You don't know what you're talking about. You cut at one rock, and another will collapse in its place. That's how displacement works."

"I know how displacement works." Jonik could not listen to reason, because it was duty that drove him, not logic. *I swore an oath to Ilith*, he told himself. *I swore to him I would bring him the blades, and I will.* He could not stop, despite the dangers. For the sake of the world and all the people in it, he had no choice but to keep on going.

The passage grew tighter. The rock was scraping at him, front and back, but he was not a fool, no matter what Gerrin thought. He would not lead them needlessly to their deaths if the way became too cramped. Many times they had been forced to turn back and find another way, and the same was true here.

"My lord…" Sir Owen said. Jonik could hear the worry in his voice. "The earth does not feel stable here. If the tunnel collapses…"

"It won't." Jonik crabbed doggedly on, stubbornly refusing to listen. Small pebbles rattled down on him, and he could hear them falling ahead and behind as well. For all he knew, there had been cave-ins and collapses at a dozen other tunnels they'd passed, blocking their way back, but he decided not to voice that concern.

The passage remained tight for a long while, before at last it began to widen, broadening until they could walk along shoulder to shoulder if they wanted. Another thirty paces on it yawned open into a capacious chamber, heavy with greenery, bright with bioluminescent. Nets of tangled plant life had taken root on the rock floor, thriving in this strange and hostile world, and above them the ceiling surged up high into the gloom, its glistening rock only partially glimpsed beyond a shroud of coloured mist. Jonik paused a moment to take a breath. The wonders down here never ceased to amaze him.

"Search for ways out," he said to the others. "Find a passage that will take us down."

"Still down?" Gerrin grunted. "How much deeper must we go?"

Not much, Jonik hoped. But deeper it still must be. "We'll know when we get there," he only said. His eyes roamed the space, seeking enemies, unknown creatures lurking in cracks and shadows. His eyes detected no movement, though above him he could hear *flapping*, twittering, see swirls and eddies in the coloured mist. *Bats*, he thought. They had seen those often enough, most of them of common size and species, but that did not mean some other larger and older variety had not made its lair down here.

"Eyes up," he said. "We're not alone." Harmless as most bats were, some were fond of blood rather than fruit and bugs and might see them as prey. *And if one of Brexatron's brood is here…*

He did not imagine so, not down so deep. The spawn of the giant bat did not care for heat, he knew, though their father had been born to it. That was thousands upon thousands of years ago, a time before time began, when Agarath had forged the colossal black-winged nightmare during his early days of life-creation. Brexatron was his first attempt at creating what would become his dragons, men said, and predated even Drulgar, an ancient horror, hated and reviled by all those who looked upon him.

Centuries after the bat's birth, when Drulgar was forged of fire and rock and rage, Agarath marvelled upon the mastery of his art, and scorned Brexatron as an aberration, casting him from his sight in disgust, so the story went. In his shame and anger, the giant bat fled north, to forge a lair in the northernmost peaks of the Hammersongs, far from his father's disdain. There he brooded on his vengeance, hiding in the mists and the cold and the darkness, biding his time to strike. When next war stirred between the gods, he saw his chance. Flying south in a shroud of black rage and storm clouds he descended upon his father as he sat his fiery throne, piercing the night with his echoing call. Such was the force of the blast from the bat's lungs that Agarath was momentarily deafened, and Brexatron descended. Down he flew, raking at the All-Father's face with his ravening claws, biting with elongated needles for teeth, savaging and scarring him as fire and smoke poured from the wounds.

But it was not enough. From Agarath's lips bellowed a roar, and from the shadows Drulgar came. The dragon god had grown monstrous by then, an untamed power of volcanic rage, and he beat the bat back with fire and fang. Brexatron knew his chance was gone.

736

With another shrill call to cover his retreat, he flew in fear of his younger, bigger brother, returning to his northern lair, and from that day on Drulgar swore that he would hunt and kill him in vengeance.

And so he did. Long years later the pair clashed once more, battling in the skies above the mountains, but not before Brexatron had spawned his brood, forging them from shadow and the will of his hate. Many died defending him against the Dread, but not all, and to this day some still lurked in dark places, it was said, bats as big as small dragons haunting high peaks and woods, living on blood.

Jonik looked around as the story passed through his mind. To him that's all it had ever been, a story, a myth, not to be taken literally, and perhaps there remained some exaggeration in there…*but perhaps not.* If Drulgar was back, and as calamitous as the histories said, anything seemed possible now. And there was always that rumour of one of Braxatron's brood living near the Shadowfort too, he remembered. The older knights and masters had spoken of it when he was a boy. The black menace lurking in the heights.

He took a step into the cavern, picking between the patches of lucent flora, trying to keep to the rocks. It was wetter here than in the other caves he'd seen, the ground spongy and…*hollow*, he thought. The floor beneath him felt thin. He paused, suddenly concerned, and looked around. Gerrin was moving right, Owen left, staying closer to the wall. The ground looked sturdier there. He was about to call out to them when he felt a shudder. There was a sound above him, of grit and small bits of stone coming free from the high ceiling, raining to the floor.

"My lord, watch out," he heard Owen Armdall call out sharply.

He looked up. It was not just grit and pebbles. Right above him, several larger rocks had torn free, plummeting right down to where he stood, slicing through the whirling fogs. Colour flashed as they passed. Blue and green and violet and amber. Jonik dashed away unthinkingly, deeper into the heart of the cavern. The rocks crashed down right where he'd been standing, shattering on impact, striking and bursting and ricocheting away. His rear foot landed on something slimy, and he slipped, reaching out to steady his fall with a leather-gloved hand, godsteel gauntlet beneath. The weight of his plate smashed down hard. He felt the ground crack and sink…

There was a *whooshing* sound, of a heavy object moving. He twisted on the rocks and looked up. A spire of rock was plunging down from above him, some great stone stalactite with a fierce sharp tip, ten feet in length, wreathed in whipping vines. He scrambled away. The earth weakened at his movement; he could feel it crumbling.

"Jonik!" he heard Gerrin roar.

The old knight was stepping out toward him. "No. No, stay back! Stay back!" He tried to get to his feet, to scamper away, but the spire of stone was already on him. It pierced the floor two metres away, cutting down through rock and root and moss…

…and then suddenly the whole world was giving way beneath him, disintegrating, and the roar of the rushing river filled the cavern, bellowing up from below.

Jonik's heart lurched inside him as he felt his weight go down…and then he too was falling, arms flailing for purchase, but there was nothing to hold onto. For a moment he was in freefall, his eyes staring up. He saw Gerrin there, shouting, saw Sir Owen Armdall leap and lurch for safety. Ten metres he fell, twenty, thirty…

…and then he felt the *slap* at his back, felt the water rise up about him, swallowing him whole. He had barely enough time to snatch a breath before he was being dragged right down beneath the surface by the weight of his armour, thrashing with his arms to stay afloat.

It was no use. The metal was too heavy. Down he went, into the black surging waters, two metres, three, four, five…

…the bottom rushed up to meet him. The back of his breastplate smacked against stone, solid stone, rugged and rough, the floor of some lower chamber. He fought to his feet, knelt down, and thrust up, breaching the surface, fighting to take a breath. He flailed wildly, blinking, saw the hole in the cavern high above him. It was moving…he was being pulled downstream. He kicked with all his strength, but it only did so much. The river was wild, waves splashing at its surface, eddying around hidden rocks. He was spun about, felt the summit of some outcrop rake against his armour, reached desperately to grab it and missed.

Then he was under again, the armour taking him down. He fought against it in his folly, wasting precious breath, kicking out. The water stung his eyes, blinding him, twisting and turning him this way and that. He crashed into another rock, gasping, gulping water. There was a grinding, a scraping, and he was on the bottom. He reached out, gripping a crack, planted his feet beneath him and bounded up once more.

The roar of the river rang out as he broke the surface. It echoed differently. He'd entered a tunnel. He could see the ceiling above him, just out of reach. Ahead, the tunnel was narrowing, tightening, the river speeding, the pressure building. Even in his heavy armour the strength of the water was tugging him along, and he was powerless to resist. Moss glowed on the walls, luminous lichen in blinding white. He went down again, reached the bottom, and pressed himself up, and down again and up, and down and up, gasping for a breath each time…and each time the tunnel narrowed…each time the ceiling grew lower, closer. *I'll have no air*, he thought. Soon the water would reach the ceiling, and he'd have no air.

Panic soared, a desperate fear surging through his veins. He went down again, found the floor, and thrust up, gulping as big a breath as he could. The ceiling was close enough to touch. He reached up, hoping to dig his fingers into some crevice, but there was nothing. It was too smooth. *Damn the worms, damn them all.* He might have laughed

738

if he wasn't so afraid. *I'm going to drown,* he thought. *I'm going to drown and they'll never find me.*

The water took him back down. It might be for the last time. He *clunked* against the bottom, a jagged rock cutting at his shoulder, tearing through leather and flesh. Blood reddened the water. He tumbled, scrambling to control himself, to slow. The power of the surf had swelled monstrously, racing through the narrowing passage. He could hear a great roaring sound, rumbling through the rock, like some hulking beast trapped in chains. The very water was starting to bubble and froth. Tremors shook through the walls.

His lungs were afire, desperate for air. He twisted, contorting against the current to get his feet beneath him, and launched himself up for the final time. He realised the folly too late. The ceiling was submerged; there was no air. But he thrust up hard all the same…

…and smacked his skull against the ceiling.

His eyes rolled, brain fogging, all strength leeching from his limbs. The flow took him, throwing him around like a ragdoll. He clattered against the walls, the floor, the roof of the tunnel, his flesh cut and torn in a dozen places. Vaguely, he sensed the blood leaking from a gash in his head. His ears pounded, heart smashing at his ribs. He felt like he was floating, spinning through space, glowing lights in white and green and blue racing past in a blur…

Like stars, he thought, dazed. *Nebulas in the night sky.* He spun end over end, bouncing along the tightening walls, and somewhere in the back of his head he knew he'd soon be stuck. The passage would grow too tight and he would lodge in somewhere, entombed forever, grown over by luminous moss and feasted on by beetles and ghekantulas…

There was nothing he could do but let go. The luminous moss formed into faces, flashing before his eyes. He saw Aleron in his armour, throat opened like a red smile, and his father sitting on that chair in his bedchamber, the Sword of Varinar across his lap, stroking. He saw Elyon in the alley, pleading for him to kill him as well, the rain falling down in sheets of tears. He saw his mother, his mother lying on the slab, white as snow and innocent for the first time in her life. He saw Gerrin's shifting mask; from Shadowmaster to spy to saviour, Gerrin who was the only father he'd ever known. He saw Emeric, with his neat beard and hair and keen golden eyes, sitting in the tavern in Greywater where they'd met, and he saw Turner with his flaxen beard and tan coat, standing on the prow of Invincible Iris with a great beaming grin on his face.

Jack. He saw Jack. Jack his friend, his brother by choice, lying on the beach at Lizard's Laze a lifetime ago, his pale skin reddening in the fierce southern sun and denying it all the while. Devin, brown eyes big as saucers as the serving girl Sapphire told him about the Day of Dawning, when all the girls would frolic naked in the sea. Brax with his smile, a nightmare so full of warmth, and Sid so simple and strong.

Even Grim Pete passed his eyes, up there in his nest, pointing and squawking like the raven he resembled.

And the rest, all of them. Borrus and Mooton and Torvyn and the Blackshaws, Sir Lenard and the Silent Suncoat, Big Mo and Kazil and Cabel and Sir Corbray and Harden, loyal Harden, who wanted so much more for him, and would see that desire cruelly dashed. He thought of the boys, the boys he'd let die, and the others that he'd saved, and he wondered where they were. Henrik and Hopper, Nils and Zacarias and Trent, and the rest they'd led to freedom. Were they safe now? Were they dead? Had they found some place to live and be free? Had they fallen to revolt among themselves, and broken up like some shattered plate?

There were other faces too, passing one and then another and then another. The other prisoners they'd saved from the pits, the faces of the dead staff at Emeric's estate. He remembered Brewilla, whom Emeric had loved so fiercely, her dark face peaceful and beautiful in death. He remembered the hook-handed Patriot called Karlesh, the man who had led the men who killed her. He and his friends had not died peacefully. He had butchered them all, as he'd butchered the Whisperer Ghalto and his men that night at Russet Ridge.

Today, I am death, he had thought, as he slew them one and all. How much death had he brought now, how many men had he killed? All bad, he liked to think, but was that true? *Weren't they all just slaves, like me?*

The faces did not stop, would not stop. They passed him by, tormenting him, reminding him of his follies and failures. He thought of the girl Sapphire again, how pretty she was, how she'd looked at him with those eyes, how his own eyes had shied away. He had never had a woman, never felt a loving touch. He might have stayed on the Golden Isles for a night or two and tasted that pleasure. Maybe even that girl Leshie might have shown him. She was pretty too, and had that willing look when she wasn't mocking him and teasing him and calling him Shadowboy.

But she had that right, didn't she? He was a boy, not a man. A chaste boy and a fool and a failure…that most of all. *I have failed him,* he thought, as the faces finished with Ilith. He saw him clear as if he was standing before him now, Ilith in the body of the heir, radiant in his divinity, but fading, already fading in his strength. There was no time, no matter what Gerrin said. *I swore him my oath, I swore I'd find the blades, and I've failed him. My lord, I am sorry. Forgive me, great Ilith. Forgive me…*

Then the faces were gone, and the light snuffed out, and he drifted into the beyond…

He woke to the sound of splashing water, echoing loudly, lying broken on a bank of wet stone.

His heart gave a powerful beat, as though reviving him, and he heaved and sat up, retching water from his stomach and lungs. A soft glow shone from his armour, silvery blue, the light of the moss soaked into his plate. He had not done that by conscious thought. In the deep darkness of the cave, it was the only light. *Ilith's armour,* he thought. *Ilith's gift.*

I'm alive.

He staggered to his feet, trying to get his bearings. High above him, he could see the faint outline of the river, pouring raucously from the tunnel in a chaotic spout. *It must have spat me out,* he thought, dimly. *I must have been spat out into this cavern.* He was too exhausted to smile, too lost, too alone. Weakly, he called out, "Gerrin…Owen…" but even as he said the names he knew they would not hear. They were too far from here, a world away now. He was all alone in the dark of the depths, but alive. *I'm alive,* he thought again, still struggling to believe it. *But where? Where? How far did I go?*

He looked around. He could not see the ceiling, he could not see the walls. He seemed to have reached the very bottom of the world. The glow of his armour would not last, he knew….without more light to restore it and soak into it, it would begin to weaken and fade, and he had no other light to see, no torch, no way to start a fire.

I have to move, he thought. If he rested, and slept, he might wake in total darkness. It was all he wanted in the world, to lie down and close his eyes, but he couldn't. He needed to keep on going. *One step, and then another,* he told himself. *And then another after that.*

He stumbled away from the spray of the water, moving into the darkness. His armour permitted only a faint glow; enough to light the earth before him a few paces but no more. Over his gauntlets he still wore his gloves, and over his sabatons he wore boots. They were stifling the light of the plate, so he removed them, tossing them away, and that won him a little more luminance, but not much. *Quickly,* he thought. *You must move quickly.*

Step by step, he lurched exhaustedly along, the steel of his sabatons scraping against the rock where before the leather boots had muffled his tread. His legs felt weak as wet parchment, and his body ached all over from the battering he'd taken in the river. Blood leaked from a dozen cuts and grazes, and there was a pounding in his head such as he'd never known. He reached up and his fingers came back slick with blood, and the flesh of his left shoulder had been badly torn.

That almost made him smile. *Like my father,* he thought, wryly. Jonik had cut him right down to the bone using the Nightblade, back when he did not know who Amron Daecar truly was. *Not to me, anyway.* He knew who he was to everyone else. A hero, a greatlord, a titan among men.

His death will save the world, Gerrin had told him, words he'd been commanded to say. Still, all this time later, Jonik couldn't figure out how.

He staggered on. The floor rose before him, some hill within the cavern, or maybe just a large rock, he couldn't say. The roar of the water grew thinner the further he went, and in its place he could hear the sounds of chittering and scuttling, the noise a thousand little legs made as they skittered along the ground.

The sound made his spine tingle. He reached to draw out Mother's Mercy, and a mercy it was to find it still at his hip. In the chaos it might have slid from its scabbard, but it had held fast, and he had his dagger too. The feel of the godsteel helped to fortify him against his fears, the bastard sword sliding from its sodden sheath with a scrape of steel on leather. He swung it about, mists swaying and rising. Beyond the pool of light, he could sense the creatures closing in, but what they were he could not say. More of those beetles? An army of geckantulas? Was he to live through the river only to die by the bug?

Where the light bled to dark, he saw something move, skittering past him, thin and long like a snake with legs, a segmented body winding and weaving. He swung about to follow it, but it was gone, vanishing over the lip of a rock. He heard movement behind, and turned, swinging his blade, and another of the creatures scuttled away into the dark. "Damn you…if you want a taste, I'm here." He tried to shout the words, but they came out feebly. He had barely the strength to raise his voice. How was he going to fight?

He sped his pace such as he could, stumbling and staggering up the slope, pain darting through him with every step. His left shoulder throbbed violently, and blood was running freely from the wound. *Is that what they're after? Blood?* Blood or flesh or bones, what did it matter? He had seen the size of the things, he could hear them out there, gathering in their hundreds. When they came for him, what chance did he have? *Run*, he told himself. *They'll chase you, but you have to run…*

But he couldn't. He had barely enough strength in him to walk and hold up his blade. He was spent. Hopelessly spent. The ground was steepening ahead, and it was all he could do to keep going. The light seemed to be keeping the creatures at bay for now, but he could already feel it draining out of him, bleeding from his armour like the blood from his veins.

Light. He needed light. Was that not why Ilith made this armour for him, imbuing it with the Nightblade's power? Did the demigod not know he might face a trial like this? *No*, he told himself. *How could he have known?* But he wanted to believe it anyway. *Fate*, he thought. *I make my own fate, and Ilith…he is part of that.* He had made this armour to help him. And but for it he would already be dead, battered to death in the river…or devoured by these thousand-legged snakes. *There is fate in that*, he thought. He made himself believe it. *I'm not going to die down here.*

The pool of light around him was growing smaller, thinning and receding. He could hear the creatures behind him, hear them to his left and right, clicking and communicating, but he couldn't see them. They sounded excited, sharing the news of the feast to come. More were coming, pouring over the hill in a tide of scuttling feet. Jonik paused to look back, but saw only blackness behind him now. *How deep am I? Have I entered another world?*

Maybe he'd died in the river after all…died and been spat out into some hell. Perhaps these creatures had been sent to punish him for the things he'd done? They would devour him slowly, feasting on skin and flesh, nibbling as he screamed out in terror and agony. And when he finally died, he would only awaken again, spat out from the river, and the creatures would be closing in…

He shuddered, suddenly cold. *No. I am deeper, that is all. There will be a tunnel ahead, atop this hilly or beyond it, and on the other side I'll find moss and glowing vines and a whole sky full of fireflies.*

He kept that thought in his mind, driving him up the slope, reaching now with his spare hand to climb and clamber. Once or twice his feet gave way beneath him, and he slipped, and he could hear the wave of excitement through the swarm of creatures, as though their time had come, but no…he stood and kept on going, moving as quickly as his body would allow. The creatures shrank back, biding their time. The shield of light was fading…fading…

There was a faint line ahead, rugged and uneven, that marked the top of the hill. Faintly, so faintly, he sensed a shimmer back there in the distance beyond the hill. *Moss*, he thought. *Mushrooms, vines.* It made no matter. If it was light his armour could drink it, and he could keep these devils at bay…

He surged on. The army behind followed, all but nipping at his heels. He could sense them, right there behind him, and turned to slash out randomly with his blade, grunting from the effort. Several of them squeaked and fled, but he caught one before it could retreat, slicing right through it. A spray of blood went swishing from the bastard sword's edge, and two long portions of body spun away into the dark. Ten thousand legs rattled and scampered in pursuit, fighting to devour the corpse. Ten thousand more continued after him, shadows a stride behind.

Jonik, said a voice.

He started. Who was that? Had he dreamed it? Had he been dreaming all along? He turned a full circle, his head throbbing. The shadows kept a pace away, but he could see them there, swarming, gathering, climbing all over one another, hundreds of them, thousands…

Here, the whisper said. *Here…here…here…*

Jonik whirled about. The whisper was coming from ahead, over the hill. He sped onward at once, suddenly running, climbing, scrabbling. The creatures erupted into motion behind him. He felt one dart in and bite at his leg, teeth scraping against armour. Another tried, and another. Then suddenly ten were about his feet, squirming and snapping and coiling, and the light was almost gone. The creatures screamed in frenzy. He stamped down, crushing several with his boots, whipping to cut at them with his sword. But they kept coming, clam-

bering up his legs and stabbing with their claws, and suddenly…
suddenly the light was gone, fading like a dying star, like a torch
guttering out in a darkened chamber, and there was only that glow
ahead, marking the top of the hill…that blue glow beyond it calling
him on.

The creatures were all over him. He shook them off, swinging
Mother's Mercy, grabbing at them with his gauntlets, kicking out with
his feet. His chest and back were protected by his breastplate, but his
shoulders and upper arms were exposed. He felt one bite down upon
the bloody gash in his left shoulder, ripping and licking with a darting
tongue. He shuddered and screamed, twisting to shake the thing away.
Another was climbing his neck. He could feel its legs pricking at his
scalp as it crawled for the cut on his head…

Jonik roared out, throwing his limbs about, dislodging a score, but
twoscore replaced them. They were biting, stabbing, licking, drinking,
washing over him like a tide. He could feel their weight pressing him
down, and he stumbled to a knee. *No…not like this.* He could not die
like this.

He laboured back to his feet, dragging himself on. The lip of the
hill was close. The cavern echoed to his grunts and gasps for breath, to
the wild cheeping of the chasing horde.

Ten more paces, he thought. *Just ten.* His legs lunged onward,
counting them down, *nine, eight, seven*…A fresh wave of creatures
bulged up about him, rising like an ocean swell. He kicked, swinging
through them with arm and blade. *Six, five, four*…The light was
blooming ahead, glimpsed through the writhing swarm. A mist rose
from somewhere lower, blue and brilliant. *Three, two*…He reached the
top, pulling himself up with a grasping hand, lugging his legs behind
him. *One…*

The world fell away sharply beneath him, plunging in a steep
descent. The sudden drop made him dizzy. He lurched back, trying to
find a footing among the mass of squirming bodies, but there were too
many of them, too many, and he slipped, stumbled forward, and went
tumbling over the edge, crashing and rolling down the face of the crag.
He felt sharp snags tear at him, heard the smash of armour ring out
on rock. He hit a ledge, the air punched out of his lungs, rolled over
the side and kept on going.

He could not control his motion. Creatures flew from him, from
arms and shoulders and torso and legs, spinning away into the gloom.
Others clung on, claws digging through flesh and leather, chittering
wildly in his ear. His arm struck a thrust of stone, and Mother's Mercy
spun from his grasp, clattering away into the dark. The last strength of
his blood-bond left him. All his energy was stripped away, flayed like
skin from flesh. His eyes darkened at once, and his thoughts fled him,
and down he went…down down down.

He did not feel the rest.

He did not know how far he fell, or how he came to stop.

But when next he opened his eyes, he was lying bathed in a pool of radiant blue light, and dead creatures lay all about him, sizzling and burning. He could hear the rest of them, but only faintly now, staying far away, chittering in the blackness.

Exhausted, Jonik pressed himself up onto an elbow. His eyes flickered to the source of the light, blinding and beautiful in the dark of the underworld, the most beautiful thing he'd ever seen. The smallest, weakest of smiles touched his lips. He reached out, stretching from the floor to touch it. "I found you…" he croaked. "I…I found you…"

His arm fell back down to the floor. He had no strength in him. He fought to stay awake, to drink in the glow, the power, the warmth, but it was no use. Once more the dark was closing in from the sides of his eyes, but this time he knew he was safe. *He will protect me,* Jonik thought, eyes closing. *They cannot get to me here…here in Vandar's light.*

And there, deep in the bowels of the earth, he gave himself up to sleep. Lying alone in that island of godly blue light, surrounded by an ocean of darkness.

57

Saska

The weather was turning again.

From the window seat of Prince Robbert's cabin Saska could see the dark rainclouds on the horizon, gathering menacingly, the unruly whitecaps on the water frothing and hissing. The waves had not yet grown large enough to trouble them, but that could change in an eye blink. *The weather is as capricious as the gods*, she thought. She'd come to hate both of late.

A pebble *pinged* across the room and Del gave a roar of triumph. "Finally!" He soared to his feet and pointed a finger down at the Butcher, who sat cross-legged on the floor, looking like a giant overgrown child from hell. "You lose, Meshface! You have to do what I tell you now."

The Butcher did not look pleased. "You cheated," he said, unfurling his legs to stand. His tattered red cloak fell down his back in strips. "I do not like being cheated. The last man who did that to me lost his manhood." He leaned forward. "Do you want me to snip you, Dellard? I have made a hundred eunuchs in my time."

The boy was aghast. "I never cheated."

"You did. You crossed the line. Your throw was too close. You cheated."

"I never." Del's eyes shot to Leshie and Jaito, who'd both gotten all of their pebbles into the tin cup already. That had left only Del and the Butcher to battle it out in a fierce finale, throw for throw and stone for stone until both only had one pebble left. On the previous throw, the Butcher's pebble had hit the rim of the tin cup and bounced away when it looked sure to fall inside. The reprieve had granted Del one final chance and the boy had made sure to not miss it. "Did I throw too close?" he asked the others. "I didn't, did I? Tell him I didn't."

"You didn't," Leshie confirmed. "That was fair and square, Parapet. Don't be a baby. Just admit that you lost."

"Never." The Butcher folded his large scarred arms. "I never lose."

"You did this time. You lost and now we get to choose a forfeit for you." Leshie's eyes twinkled with malice. The girl liked conjuring her forfeits, damn her. Saska had decided not to play the game herself for fear of losing again. Leshie's stupid forfeit had only gone and made things awkward with Prince Robbert and frankly she could do without that sort of hassle. It was nice, she had told him, and that was the truth. A nice kiss, and he was a handsome prince. *But a friend, that's all.* She never wanted him to think anything else.

"I will do no forfeit," the Butcher declared adamantly. "I do not do forfeits for cheats and their cronies. Ersella is a crony to the boy Dellard. She is in cahoots with him."

"Jaito will say the same," Del insisted. "He saw as well. I never crossed the line."

"Jaito is an honest boy," the Butcher said. "And honourable. A fine archer, yes, and a finer man. He will speak the truth of this."

"Stop trying to butter him up," Leshie hissed at him. "Jaito saw the same as the rest of us. The shot was fair and you've got to do a forfeit. If you don't we'll throw you over the side and let the sharks eat you."

"The sharks will not eat me. They are afraid of the Butcher."

Leshie showed what she thought of that with a derisive hoot of laughter, then proceeded to jabber on again about forfeits and how the Butcher would do his 'or else'. The Butcher took his leave from the cabin, pronouncing them all liars and cheats. Saska heard it all in snippets only as she turned her eyes back to the window, watching the waves grow taller, wilder, whiter. *An eye blink*, she thought. Already the black clouds were getting closer and she could feel the churn of the water beneath them, the thickening swells as *Hammer* rose and fell with the motion of the sea.

Del was still mumbling about how he *didn't* cross the line when the door knocked and the young midshipman called Finn Rivers entered. He was a stout and sparky boy of thirteen, with a face full of freckles and flappy orange hair who seemed comfortable around everyone, whether prince or pauper, Butcher or Wall. That was the Rasal way. The boy was a Seaborn of strong blood and the protege of Blood-hound Burton, Robbert had said. "Sorry for the intrusion," he chirped jauntily, as he drew to a stop just inside the doorway. "Just to say the weather's roughing up and it might get a little wobbly in here. Captain says to batten down the hatches and sit fast. Do any of you get seasick?"

"Leshie does," Saska told him.

"I do *not*." The girl could be affronted by anything if she felt it made her look weak. The truth didn't seem to have a say in the matter. "I *never* get sick. From the sea or anything."

"You were sick on the crossing of Vandar's Mercy."

"Vandar's Mercy? That was a thousand years ago. I was never sick when I sailed south with Rose and Ranulf, and that was a *much* longer voyage. He'd tell you if he was here."

But he isn't here. Ranulf had spent no more than a few hours in their company before he and Talasha and Cevi went flying off to the north again. *To meet a demigod*, Saska thought. Apparently Eldur wasn't the only one of the Five Followers to have arisen…as Drulgar wasn't the only titan. "You didn't face bad weather on that voyage," Saska reminded the Red Blade. She looked at Finn Rivers, taking matters into her own hands. "Leshie gets seasick. No matter what she says. Do you have a bucket for her to vomit into?"

"I'm not going to vomit."

"You will. You're already looking queasy."

"I shall fetch one," the boy said. He bustled off and returned a moment later with a pail in hand, placing it before Leshie.

She glared at him. "Are you stupid or what? I said I'm not going to…to…" *Hammer* rose up sharply upon a swell and Leshie visibly paled, swallowing her next words.

The midshipman gave a chuckle. "You and that bucket are going to become well acquainted, I feel." He turned back to Saska, smiling. "Is there anything else you need?"

"Some fresh air," she said.

"Oh? I'm not sure that's…"

She wouldn't hear of it. If they were going to spend any length of time cooped up down here she would take some air on deck first.

The wind assaulted her as soon as she stepped up the stair, howling like some dying beast as sea spray hissed across the decks, biting at her cheeks and stinging her eyes. On the main deck scores of soldiers were moving toward the ladders to descend down into *Hammer's* bowels so the sailors might work unimpeded. The first mate Bill Humbert and boatswain George Buckley were going about, shouting for anyone who wasn't required to clear off and find some space below. It was horribly crowded down there, Saska knew, and the soldiers did not look happy. Few had the luxury of space like she did. "I hope you have more buckets aboard," she said to Finn Rivers. Half the men on deck looked green and nauseous and some were already retching.

"We're well supplied." The boy smiled all the while. "You've got good sea legs, my lady," he observed. "Much better than the rest of these Tukorans." He gestured to the soldiers, slipping and stumbling about the decks as they headed for the ladders. "Guess that's the Seaborn in you."

She frowned at him. "Where did you hear about that?"

"There's a rumour going around. Though I knew anyway. I always know a Seaborn when I see one." He puffed his chest out proudly.

Saska chose not to comment on all that as she paced swiftly up the stairs to the quarterdeck. No matter what she did, or had others do for her, eventually the truth of her birth would come pouring forth and when it did it would be like the breaking of a dam and soon everyone

748

would know. She sensed that time was upon them now, with so many men about, and the Surgeon could hardly kill them all. *No, let them find out*, she thought. As much as they had to shield the truth of who she was in the south from those who might use it against her, in the north it would be different. *They have to know who I am. They have to know so they'll accept me and help me.*

One of those people was at the helm with the captain; the Crown Prince of Tukor, Robbert Lukar, who might already be king. He had turned cold on her over the last couple of days, avoiding her gaze and being conveniently busy whenever she sought his company. And all over a silly misunderstanding. Saska was not about to let this awkwardness between them endure. She strode right up to him and slipped her arm through his, in the same way she'd seen Talasha do it. "How about this weather, then?" she said, smiling to make light of it.

It was poorly judged, she knew at once. "I lost two dozen ships to storms…and thousands of men," Robbert said, unamused. "I don't think it's anything to joke about."

"No." It was not a good start. "I just meant…I was trying to…" She was not made for this, she realised. With a tug she drew him aside, away from Burton and Sir Lothar and Lord Gullimer, who were also there, and decided to just speak plainly. "Look, Robb, we need to clear the air. Enough of this awkwardness. It's childish."

"What awkwardness?" he asked, stiffly. "I don't feel awkward. Do you?"

"You've been avoiding me."

"I've been busy. If you haven't noticed, I have an army to manage."

A small army, she thought, *and an even smaller fleet.* It would not serve to say that out loud, though. "I know. You've got a lot on your plate. But we've barely spoken for two days. There are things…there are things you need to know."

That piqued his interest well enough, though he tried to show he didn't care. "Oh? And what are those?"

"You know what. The truth. You said you wanted the truth from me, but I never gave it to you." They'd all been distracted by the return of Talasha and Ranulf, and after that Robbert had given her the cold shoulder. The rest of that day had been spent on preparations to leave. Provisions were gathered and water barrels were filled and the sick were brought aboard. Then the following morning Captain Burton put his finger to the wind, declared the day good for sailing, and off they went in their little fleet of four, cruising beneath the stone sculpture of Calacan and up past the Horn of Aramatia under sails in brown and green and black. Now here they were, one day later, facing rough seas and stormy skies as they pushed on into the Three Bays, making for the Vandarian coast. "I want you to know," Saska finished. "Everything. Like you asked."

749

The prince peered at her doubtfully. "Why now, all of a sudden? Are you trying to keep me onside, is that it?"

Yes, she thought. That was definitely it. But she shook her head. "I've wanted to talk to you for two days, but you never have time for me."

"I've been busy, like I said." He was at risk of seeming petty, he seemed to realise, so raised his chin nobly and said, "Well, you've got my ear now. So you can start by telling me where you're going. *North*, you only said. Well, we're on our way now and it'd be nice if Bloodhound had more to go on than that." He turned his eyes into the teeth of the wind and rain; it was coming down from the north, much colder and sharper than the warm rains they'd had in the south. "We might be able to take you to the Rasalanian coast if we can push through this weather. It isn't so far, and I'd be willing to divert if that's what you want. But you have to tell me now, Saska."

She had no intention of going to Rasalan. There was nothing for her there. "I'll step ashore the same place as you, Robbert," she told him.

His brow furrowed. "We're making for the Marshlands. The fighting could still be fierce there."

"I know."

"And yet you still want to come with us?"

She nodded. What Ranulf told them had changed everything and she knew now where her path would take her. For long months they'd known only that they must find a way north and try to gather the Blades of Vandar, never knowing how they would be reforged. Now they did. They knew who and they knew where, and so far as Rolly said it, they must make for Ilith's refuge at once. Once there they would be able to take stock and consider their next course, but they must get there first. Saska knew what would happen next. Rolly would have her remain there in the mountains while he and others went off to fetch the blades for her. He hadn't said it outright yet but she knew what he was thinking. Why risk her, when there was a hidden sanctuary where she'd be safe, protected by ancient and powerful magic and watched over by a demigod?

There was plenty of sense in that, she knew that of course, but Saska did not want to hide in some mountain while others went out and died for her. No. If she was truly Varin's heir she must act like it, and face what perils she may. *It's my task. My duty*, she told herself. *I have to be the one to gather those blades and persuade their bearers to give them up.*

The lurch of the ship intruded on her thoughts as *Hammer* crashed through a rising wave. That put a pause on their conversation as both Saska and Robbert turned their eyes about. The seas were growing rougher. Hills rose up about them in grey and blue, tipped with snow-white peaks, all moving and undulating chaotically. The skies were turning black with rainclouds and there were flashes of lighting out there.

Saska didn't like what she was seeing. "This is bad," she said. Something tickled at the nape of her neck, some shiver she couldn't put her finger on. She could feel some menace in the air.

Robbert nodded. "It started like this last time." He stepped back over to the helm, Saska following. "Bloodhound. I don't like that look on your face. How bad is this going to get?"

The captain did not answer at once. His nostrils were opening, closing, and his eyes were narrowed to slits. "There's a stink in the air I don't like," he growled. "And not from Sir Lank's breeches either." His eyes swayed over the ocean. "Those whales are still trailing us. Same ones as before. There's good and bad in that."

Saska wasn't certain where the good was. She'd seen hundreds of wrecks over the last few weeks and did not doubt that pods of grouchy greatwhales had been responsible for a good many of them. "Aren't they hostile?" she asked. If they were, they'd have attacked by now. She assumed that must be the 'good' part.

"Not to us," was the captain's answer. "They're here for something else."

Something else. *Something worse.* That would be the 'bad' and they all knew what it was.

"Kraken," Sir Lothar said, swallowing. "Is there a kraken out there, Burton?"

The captain nodded, squinting. "Aye. And a big one."

"Where?" Robbert demanded.

The captain did not need to answer. No sooner had Robbert asked the question than a great splash erupted from the waters off to starboard, sending up a frothing white plume two hundred feet high. A flash of black limbs caught the light, slick and slimy and *enormous*, tussling with a huge shadow that thrashed wildly beneath the waves. Everyone turned at once to look, and down the ship someone bellowed, "Kraken! Kraken!" and a dozen others echoed the cry. In an instant men were rushing to the mounted harpoon guns and handing out throwing spears and tridents, taking their positions at the gunwales, shrill shouts spilling thinly into the air beneath the low deep bellow of the storm.

Sir Lothar Tunney looked out, wide-eyed. If he hadn't soiled his breeches before, perhaps now he had, by that look on his face. "A whale. It…it *killed* a greatwhale like it was nothing."

"Aye. A big one, as I say."

The water was turning red. Through the tumbling black rain Saska could see it bubbling and boiling from below. Fins slashed through the surf, coming and going between the waves as the greatwhales went on the attack. Burton grabbed the wheel and spun it, shouting, "Hard to port!" and *Hammer* turned, groaning and shifting as men set their feet and clung on. Bells rang out from the crow's nest and the main deck, relaying orders to the other ships as *Blood Bear*, *Blackthorn* and *Wild*

Raven all swung about as well, their decks a chaos of rushing, shouting men.

Saska turned to look behind them, her fingers grasping at the gunwale to steady her. Her knuckles were turning white. There was a dry lump in her throat that no amount of swallowing seemed able to shift. The waters back there were a rage of fins and tentacles, shadows and blood. One of the whales was floating dead on the surface, buffeted by hissing white-caps and sheets of salt spray. Blood sluiced out from a thousand sucker-cup cuts and gashes all over its great grey body. It did not look small and yet had been crushed and strangled just like that. *A monster,* Saska thought, shivering. This was no normal kraken.

Sir Kester Droyn raced up the rigging to the crow's nest with a godsteel dagger between his teeth. He scrambled inside and peered out with eagle eyes, snatching the dagger into his grasp. Saska could hear him shouting from up there, his voice cutting through the din of the storm. "Another whale down, Captain!" he bellowed. "I see a dozen out there...they're ramming it...charging..."

Bloodhound nodded, jaw tight, eyes narrow. Saska glimpsed more black arms thrashing from the waters, slapping and swatting and grasping at the whales as they drove in from all sides.

"They're not going to hold it" Droyn called down. "It's too big. They can't match it, Captain!"

"Land!" Sir Lothar Tunney shouted in a panic. "We have to make for land, Burton!"

"There is no land." Bloodhound scanned the waters, judging the seas. Some waves were large enough to turn them over if they were caught on the broadside. "Humbert!" he roared. "Humbert, here, now!"

The first mate came dashing from the main deck, panting. "Cap."

"Shallows? Are there any shallows nearby?"

"Not for miles, Ash. There's no running from this thing."

The captain nodded grimly. That seemed to set his mind on the matter. A crash of footsteps heralded the arrival of Sir Ralston as the Wall came thundering up onto the quarterdeck. He went straight for Saska. "To your cabin," he bellowed at her. "Right now."

She shook her head. "I'm not going anywhere."

"Don't be a fool. There's nothing you can do to help here." The giant was armoured in steel from head to heel and his eyes were steel as well. He went to grab her arm and tugged her toward the stairs. The mists about her silver-blue blade were moving wildly, beating like a heart, faster...faster.

Bloodhound saw them, squinting, then turned his eyes on Saska and said, "You get to your cabin like he says, girl. That kraken...he's here for you."

Saska baulked. "Me?"

"Aye. That blade you carry. Always wondered, but now I know." He craned his neck to look back. "That's *Lorin's Bane* out there."

Saska's heart almost stopped in her chest.

Sir Lothar gave a queasy laugh. "It…it *can't* be. That beast died forty years ago. The king killed it."

"No. It was only wounded. And now it's back for a taste of *queen* instead." Burton waved them all away from him. "Go. Now. And stay away from the windows, girl. The Bane is mine, and I'll have my vengeance. For Lorin," he declared, closing a fist. "I'll finish the job he started."

Saska could not quite believe what she was hearing. *Me. It's here for me.* She reached for her dagger, preparing to throw it away into the surf, but the Wall caught her arm. "It won't do any good. It's you it wants, not that steel." He tugged hard, pulling her away…away from the rush of men on deck and the staring eyes of Robbert Lukar and down the corridor to her cabin. Some of the sellswords had gathered outside the door, sensing trouble.

"What's happening up there?" the Surgeon asked. It was perhaps the first time Saska had seen the man look afraid. The Tigress was with him, and the Butcher and the Baker as well. "I thought I heard someone call out 'kraken'."

"You did. Lorin's Bane has resurfaced." Sir Ralston pulled Saska in through the door, and plonked her down into a chair. Leshie and Del and Jaito were still there. The Red Blade was cradling her bucket like a lover and her skin had gone the colour of curdled milk. She gave a groan and retched as *Hammer* lurched over another wave.

"What do you mean, Lorin's Bane?" demanded the Baker.

"You heard me." The Wall surveyed the sellswords. "Butcher. Tigress. Take guard at the window." The pair looked at one another, scowling. Well, the Butcher scowled. The Tigress's face rarely changed from that long-range, cat-like stare she had, a look that made her seem like the most formidable person in all the world sometimes. "Now. Draw your blades and watch the water. Baker, Surgeon, stay here in the cabin. *Protect* her. I'll return when I can." He marched back through the door.

The sellswords moved into position, the Butcher and the Tigress staying as far apart as the window-width would permit. Which wasn't much. The Baker pushed his golden spectacles up his nose and then scratched his chin with a knuckly finger. "I thought Lorin's Bane was dead."

"It isn't Lorin's Bane," the Surgeon dismissed. "It's just another kraken."

"The captain kills them for a living," Del put in. His eyes were bright with fear, but that thought gave him some hope. "He'll kill this one…won't he?"

Saska nodded and smiled wanly, though she had great cause to doubt it. She'd seen the size of those tentacles and she'd seen the dead whale in the water. Joy came over to sit with her, putting her head in her lap. The starcat's eyes were silver and slitted, anxious like she was. Saska stroked her head to calm her and hoped it would calm herself.

Her stomach was in knots. *It's here for me.* Evil was being drawn to her, a dark to snuff out her light. The beast must have been lurking somewhere far below, awakened by her presence as the ship passed its drowned lair. It hadn't been seen for forty years. Why else would it appear now if not for her, Lorin's granddaughter bearing Lorin's blade?

She stroked at Joy's thick soft fur. *I should take a rowboat out. If it's truly here for me, no one else needs to die.* The thought was fleeting. Even if she did that she was not so naive as to think the rest of them would be spared. The ship was rocking wildly now. Through the window she could see *Blackthorn* moving nearby, dark as night against the dread and dreary skies. The Butcher peered through the glass. "There's something in the water."

Others rushed over to look, the Baker and Del and Jaito all gathering around. Saska remained in her chair, stoking Joy's head. She could not see through them all, but knew what was happening by the sounds they made, of fear and horror and awe. The Tigress was looking out too, hissing. Then suddenly there was a deep groaning sound, some primordial bellow coming up from below and Del gave out a sharp gasp. "Gods…gods…" he said, moving back.

Saska rose and went over, peering through them and saw it. The great bulbous body rising up from the water to wrap *Blackthorn* up in a net of tentacles. She saw them slithering out onto the decks, swiping men aside, saw them wrap and crush and throw them to their doom. They were thicker and longer than she could have imagined. Spears as thin as pins flashed silver against the strangled daylight as men hurled from the decks, and the few mounted guns that *Blackthorn* bore fired out in fury from the gunwales. *She is a toy to it*, Saska thought. *Just a toy.* The masts were torn down, sails falling in tangles of rigging. The waves between the ships rose up to block their view, then fell away again, and rose and fell, and each time the damage was worse. She could see bodies in the water, floating among the debris. *There are hundreds of men aboard*, she thought. *Hundreds.* They were all going to die.

All of a sudden *Hammer* swung to starboard, and all they saw was sea and sky. Saska backed away from the window. She could hear the shouting up on deck, hear the fury of the raging storm. Lightning flickered away in the distance and thunder sang its booming song. The ship turned again, moving to face a large incoming wave and they all braced and held on…all but Del who was thrown from his feet to land hard against the wooden floor. Jaito went to help him up. "He is hurt," he called. "Help me get him to a chair."

Saska hurried over. Her brother had hit his head against something as he fell. There was a gash on his scalp, oozing blood into his long

754

black hair. They set him into a chair, bolted to the floor so it did not move. "Jaito, get a cloth for the bleeding."

The young archer rushed off, tripping and falling himself as the ship bucked and lurched. He scrambled back to his feet, snatching a towel and returning. The Surgeon stepped over. "We must check for fractures." He set about running his hands across Del's neck to make sure the cut was his only wound, then nodded. "Sit him up." He let Saska and Jaito do that as he wrapped the towel around Del's head to make a bandage, his fingers working quickly, deftly.

The others were still at the window, calling out what they saw. "We are going to her aid," the Baker said. "This Bloodhound is mad. He is attacking!"

What choice did they have? They were hardly going to outrun the beast and sometimes it was better to stand and fight.

"The other ships are coming too," the Butcher shouted.

They could hear the bells ringing out above them, relaying orders. The Baker called out something about seeing more greatwhales out there, charging their foe. Leshie stood uneasily to her feet and cast her bucket of vomit aside. "They're helping us," she said, weakly. "They'll kill it for us. They will. I know they will."

Saska hoped so. Together they might overwhelm the creature, enough at least to drive it back down to the depths. She went back to the window. The ship was turning and she saw a flash of *Blackthorn* again, listing badly to one side as the monstrous squid dragged it under. From the decks above them she heard the call of 'fire' and dozens of harpoons and throwing tridents went flinging out toward it, to plunge into its enormous black bulk.

"They do nothing. *Nothing*," the Baker proclaimed. He drew his sword. "We must go to deck. Our godsteel will cut it when it comes for us."

"Brother. We protect the heir." The Butcher put a hand on his shoulder.

"We protect her by killing it." The Baker swept his brother's arm aside and staggered toward the door, bellowing for Umberto and the Gravedigger as he passed outside.

No sooner had he left than he was replaced by Prince Robbert, who came surging inside, dripping wet, a dagger in hand to help steady himself. His eyes swept across the room and landed on Saska. "You're Lorin's heir?" he said. "That's who you are? His grand-daughter?"

Saska nodded. "I wanted to tell you."

"You wanted to *use* me. Did you know this would happen? That monster outside…did you know?"

"Of course she didn't," Leshie shouted at him. "We all thought that thing was dead. Don't be stupid."

Robbert snorted loudly. "You should have told me. You should have told me who you are."

"I was going to. Just now. Before…"

"You should have said earlier. You should have trusted me to know the truth." He took a step toward her. Joy growled at his approach. "So you're not just heir of a duchy, but a kingdom, is that it?"

"She's heir to a *demigod*," Leshie yelled at him. "We're going to gather the blades, *that's* where we're going. To reforge them. Only Saska can wield that weapon."

Robbert frowned. "The Blades of Vandar?"

"Yes! The Blades of Vandar! You think that's easy for her to take, carrying that sort of burden? We're all here to help her, and you should too. That's all our duty, king or commoner. We'll all lay down our lives for her if we must."

"My men *are* dying," Robbert came back. "They're dying out there right now."

"And you blame her for that?" Leshie snarled.

"No, I…"

"You lost almost all your fleet already and that had nothing to do with her. That's the Ever-War. It's the Last Renewal. It's Eldur and it's Agarath and Saska's going to end it all…"

The ship bucked violently, throwing everyone to one side. Saska lost her feet, stumbling into the chair in which Del sat unconscious, grabbing on to steady herself as Leshie went flying into a wall. At the window the Butcher careened to the side, but the Tigress was there to catch him. Robbert and the Surgeon both fell as well, stumbling and tripping and standing up groggily.

On the decks the screams told their story. Lorin's Bane had come.

Saska could not stay down here. She headed for the door, reaching for her sword, but Robbert lurched in her way. "No. Stay here."

"I can fight."

"Stay here." He took her by the shoulders. "If all that's true, we have to protect you. Stay here, Saska. You can't be risked." He met her eyes and made sure she agreed before turning and staggering away.

Leshie stumbled up behind her, taking her hand. "He's right." She sounded winded from her fall. "Come here. With me and Joy. Come here, Sask. This one isn't our fight."

It is my fight. It's all of our fight. Saska let herself be drawn away all the same. She could hear the chaos above, glimpsed the tentacles moving past the window. A flash of lightning outside showed *Blackthorn*, sinking down into the depths in a tangle of sails and ropes and shattered wood. A whale was caught up in its rigging, dead. Hundreds of corpses bobbed in the surf like corks.

She squeezed up against the wall, knees tight to her chest, praying for it all to end. Men were dying on deck, screaming as they were crushed and swept away. A figure went flying past the window, shrieking and flailing his arms. She saw a tentacle arm swing out, saw a mast and sails go spinning away into the sea as men clung to the ropes and rigging. From one long arm black blood was raining from a savage cleave and she wondered if that was Rolly's doing. He would be up there now, greatswords to grasp, hacking and cutting, but against that monster what could he do?

What could any of them do?

The ship heaved and moved again, trembling as the kraken brushed against it with its colossal weight, as though testing this new opponent, even savouring the kill. Joy nuzzled up close, trembling, and Saska wrapped an arm about her shoulders. The ship rocked again, shaken, and Saska squeezed her eyes shut. *This is it.* The kraken was going to gut them from below, tear through *Hammer's* reinforced hull, and they would sink. *He'll take us all down to Daarl's Domain.*

Just like he did my grandfather, Saska thought.

A sudden shout rang out from the window and Saska opened her eyes. The Butcher was stumbling away in fright. Beyond him she saw a great eye appearing, large as an oxcart, an orange eye with veins of red and a black slitted pupil peering in through the glass. Joy arched her back and hissed and the Tigress hissed as well, but Leshie only screamed. There was something knowing in that eye, something yearning. It seemed to widen and dilate as he saw her, found her, and the dagger at her hip was pulsing.

Then suddenly the eye was gone, dipping away as *Hammer* moved again. And in its place the tentacle rose up…and she saw the giant suckers, red with blood and scraps of flesh, saw them opening and closing like a thousand little mouths, ringed with razor-sharp teeth, saw the great black arm slither up past the window, saw it lower and take aim, saw the tip point right at her…

"Down!" cried the Surgeon, seeing it too.

Saska had time enough to plant herself prone on the ground as the tip of the tentacle struck out, smashing through the glass and shattering the wooden frame. Splinters went flying everywhere. She saw the long arm reach out, the tip striking where she'd been, smashing right through the wall behind her…felt the suckers drop down to rest on her back, feeling, touching, *tasting*…

"Foul creature!" The Butcher roared and swung down with his sword, cutting deep into the thick black meat, black blood pouring from the wound. The Tigress hissed and leapt forward, hacking and cutting as the tentacle writhed like a snake, striking out fast and fierce. It struck Leshie in the chest, knocking her back, swept the Butcher's legs from under him. The Tigress was knocked aside, smashed against a wall. The Surgeon shouted a wild cry and attacked, but the arm lashed and swatted him back with a sickening crack as well. None wore their godsteel armour. Without it they were defenceless. Saska surged to her feet and drew out her dagger.

"It's me you want. Me! You leave them all alone!" she screamed.

The tentacle stopped writhing and went still. Its tip seemed to *look* at her, studying, cocking a little to one side. Black inky blood gushed from several deep cleaves, but they were nought but scratches to the beast. She held out her dagger, Varin's dagger. "Is this why you're here?" She moved it to one side, and the tip of the tentacle followed. "If you want it, take it. *Take it!*" she roared.

The tentacle coiled, bunching like a snake preparing to strike. She set her feet, ready to throw the dagger and move. The door was close. It was the only way out…

A flash of lightning burst alive outside, so close now, casting the broken wall of the cabin in a blaze of silver.

Thunder bellowed through the world.

The tentacle swung about, as though looking back out. It quivered, concerned, and all of a sudden retreated, sliding back out through the breach.

Saska frowned. *Calacan?* she thought. She had heard the tale from Talasha, how the eagle god had saved her. The golden lightning, the storm, but this lightning…it was *silver*. Through the shattered window a strong wind was blowing, and she glimpsed…up there in the skies she glimpsed a shape, a figure, passing down through the clouds.

Another strike cast away the gloom, bright and brilliant, and thunder roared its song. Through the storm and the rain Saska could hear the strains of men cheering out above her. She cast her eyes around the cabin. Her men were groaning, rising, maybe injured in some cases but alive. Joy loped over to lick her hand, but she shook her head. "Stay here. Stay with them." She turned and ran through the door.

The main deck was chaos. The mizzen mast was gone, the main mast cracked and falling, the sails twisted and torn. Men were stumbling everywhere, moving between the dead and the dying, the decks slick with blood both red and black. The gunwales were smashed, the mounted scorpions broken, only a pair of them still operational to the fore. Out to sea, Saska glimpsed the shadow of *Wild Raven* being tugged away by the winds, but *Blood Bear* was nowhere to be seen.

And in the skies, a god.

She stared up at him in wonder. Beyond the kraken's reach he floated, held in a cushion of curving air. Silver was his armour, blue his cloak, whipping with his hair, coal black like his beard. From his grasp was raised a long silver sword, embraced by a vortex of swirling mist. Above, the lightning gathered. Below, the kraken quailed.

The men were cheering his name. Saska felt the warmth of a tear snaking down her cheek as her eyes met his, lit silver like a star, radiant, brilliant, beautiful. She smiled and thought that he did too, as he jerked the Windblade yet higher, and then swung down with all his might.

The lightning followed from the skies. Down it came, striking Lorin's Bane in his heaving bulk with a *crack* like the breaking of the world. The kraken gave out a trumpeting, otherworldly roar as the sparks zapped and crackled down its long thick arms. Smoke rose, fizzing and steaming. The beast quivered, thrashing out wildly as men ducked and threw themselves away as another strike was cast upon it, another bone-trembling shatter, another deep rageful roar and then suddenly the monster was in full retreat, its impossible bulk sinking into the turbulent waters, fading as it slithered back away to the depths. The long tentacles trailed after, one and then another and then another, until just like that the seas went still…and a deep hush fell over the world.

Saska stared up in silence. About her men were climbing back to their feet, crawling out from under broken sails and bits of debris. Elyon hovered above them, godlike, embraced in the power of the storm. For a short time he watched the waters, as though to be sure the beast was gone. Then slowly, heroically, he descended, drifting from the skies to land right there before her on the deck. The winds settled, and the glow retreated, and there he stood, older than she remembered him, broader, harder, stronger.

"My lady." He went down to a knee before her.

She lost her breath. "Elyon, I…" She reached out to touch him to make sure he was real. "Stand, please, I don't deserve…"

"You deserve everything." He looked up at her, and something in his piercing eyes told her he already knew. "You deserve *this*."

He presented the Windblade in his upraised palms and laid it down at her feet.

A shiver moved up her spine. She took a half step back, stopped. Others were gathering around. She glimpsed the Wall and the prince and others as well, and thanked the gods they still lived. She wanted to take Elyon's hand and step away, go somewhere private away from everyone else, but no, it was time.

Become who you were born to be. Who you need to be, she told herself. She moved in, and knelt down. Close now, their eyes connected. "Will you help me?" she whispered, for only him to hear. "I don't…I don't know what to do, Elyon."

He smiled that smile she missed. "I'll teach you," he promised. "That's my purpose now, and my path."

"Your path." She blinked at him. Another tear was falling. She wiped it quickly away. "How did you know…"

"I had a letter. Well, *two*. They led me back to you." He looked down at the Windblade for a good long while. "Take it, Saska. It's yours now."

She could feel the eyes upon her. The ripe and worried eyes of the Wall. The troubled eyes of Robbert Lukar. Dozens of others were peering from the decks and broken masts, from the crow's nest and the rigging, watching in wonder and confusion. Most knew her only as her grandmother's heir.

I will show them who I am.

She reached forward with her hand and wrapped her fingers around the Windblade's haft. It felt like that first time, when she first touched godsteel. But more acute. More ancient. More powerful. It felt *right*.

A silence had fallen upon them all, upon the men and upon the seas and the skies, upon all the world about them. Others were coming, gathering. Leshie and the Butcher and the Baker and Sir Bernie, Sir Lothar and Sir Kester and Lord Gullimer and Bloodhound Burton.

All watched, all waited, as she stood and drew the Windblade from the deck. Men exhaled and whispered, astonished, as she heaved and lifted, turning the tip of the blade to the skies, and thrust upward with a wash of light. Silver it spilt, and blue were her eyes, glowing radiant in the gloom.

And all about her, figures fell. Princes and lords and knights, sell-swords and soldiers and Seaborn sailors. One and then another and then another they fell.

To their knees before her, they fell.

EPILOGUE

In the hollow of the mountain was a colossal throne of black obsidian, cast and carved in the shape of a crown.

Barbs rose forth from the arms and back, sharp and thin like the spines of a porcupine, the longest soaring fifty feet high. Between the barbed arms was a smooth stone seat, grand in proportion, accessed by a stair. Upon that seat the Father and the Founder sat, dwarfed in its giant embrace, an embrace to fit a god. His skin was pale as ancient stone, his hair the hue of polished bone, and about his frame swirled crimson robes, the shade of new-drawn blood.

Walkways of rock soared high over the abyss, a lattice of them plunging to rivers of molten fire that spread through the mountain below like arteries through flesh. That fire *was* blood, Sotel Dar knew. The blood of Agarath, giving life to the rock, for the Ashmount was a living thing. A thousand plumes of smoke and steam rose up past the bridges like breath, gathering to pour forth from the open mouth and spread out into the skies above them. The scholar could hear the rumbling thunder up there, the eternal red lightning that swirled and roared in the storm. That storm was Agarath the All-Father, laughing.

High above the world, he watched.

The bridge to the throne was wide, a broad paved road lined with black-armoured knights holding tall black spears in their grasp. Each stood before a short parapet wall, still and silent as a statue, their eyes staring forward, swirling red, spear butts planted between their feet before them.

Between the dragonknight guards came the small delegation; the sunlord and his men, a dozen in sum. Two fire priests went before them, and before *them* walked the High Priest of the Temple of Fire, first of Eldur's earthly servants with his robes of flame and hair of the same, coloured orange and scarlet and red. In his right hand he bore a golden sceptre encrusted with rubies and onyx and at his throat swung a great red diamond, glittering in the firelight, pulsing with power.

He stopped before the steep stair that accessed the crown-throne and bowed low in obeisance. "Great Father. I bring at last your honoured guests." He waited for Eldur to gesture for him to rise and stood, opening an arm to introduce the men from Aramatia. "I present to you Sunlord Elio of House Krator, son of Tullio, a famed Moonrider. And his companion, Sunrider Mar of House Malaan." The other men did not merit a mention. Behind they stood, heads low, eyes fearful. *All shudder in the face of the Father,* Sotel knew.

The sunlord's garb was fine scalemail in bronze with a pattern of black diamonds wrought in the shape of a howling sunwolf, his cloak a shimmer of golden feathers that rippled and fluttered as he moved. He was a cold man, Sotel Dar had heard it said, a man of detachment, cruel and calculating. Yet as he looked upon the Father he quailed like all the rest. "My lord," he murmured, in a strangled voice, moving forward a step until he was eight paces from the throne. There he went down to one knee and lowered his head. "I am your humble servant. I pray thank you for this audience, Great Eldur the Eternal."

"I am not eternal," whispered the demigod in his master's throne. His voice swirled and echoed from the rock walls, reaching, stretching, spreading. "Not anymore." He lifted a palm, calling for Krator to stand. "You may rise, Elio son of Tullio. Tell me why you have come."

Elio Krator stood on trembling legs, his shoulders tight and drawn in. He had been made to wait for long days for this summons, kept in a tower at the base of the mountain as the Father worked his sorceries, delving deep into the powers of life-creation granted by his master's soul. The mastery of such art still eluded him, and would always, Sotel Dar knew. Only the gods could create new life, yet what existed could be twisted, corrupted, strengthened. *And raised from their slumber*, the scholar thought. Down in the depths of the body of the Ashmount, ancient forms still lingered, to be raised and revived for the last clash when it came.

The sunlord cleared his throat. "I come bearing information," he said, trying to give strength to his voice. It came out small all the same, the squeak of an infant in the face of the Founder. "There is a person you want, a…a person you have been trying to find, I am told. I have discovered this person's identity, Great Eldur. Grant me your blessing, and I will speak the name." He paused. "I will tell you all I know."

The corners of Eldur's lips twisted into a smile, lines spreading forth like fine cracks in stone. "My blessing. What blessing is this?"

"I seek…I seek only what I am owed. My own people…I have been betrayed, Great Father. By rights I was to sit the Eagle Chair of Aram, to rule the Duchy of Aramatia…"

Laughter cut him off. "The rule of the duchy? What use is such a rule, Elio Krator, when all will be bathed in flame?"

The sunlord went pale as milk. Sweat leaked from his brow and glistened on his neck. "I was told...I understood that..." He looked at the High Priest, who smiled that sly smile of his and stepped forward. A great red prong of beard twisted from his chin like a horn.

"Never fear, Sunlord," his voice slithered. "Great Eldur speaks only of the test that awaits all man. The flame is symbolic. It is a state of peril in which we all will live, yet a man like you...a *warrior* like you... oh, I think you could do very well."

The weak will be the feast and fodder for the strong, thought the old scholar Sotel Dar. He was weak himself, old and frail, no fighter, no warrior, and his own time was near. He held no fear of it. Death had been a cold breath at the nape of his neck for many years now, yet he had lived long enough to see the Father rise. It was more than he could ever have asked for. The great honour and pride of his life.

"The duchy was only a...a first step," Elio Krator said. His eyes flittered nervously to Eldur again. "It is the rule of the empire I truly seek."

The High Priest spoke again. "You must listen more carefully, Krator. You must open your ears. The duchy is of no significance, nor this empire you wish to rule. All kingdoms and nations and empires will fall, to become broken husks, borderless, filled with fallen cities and burning forts. There is too much *life*, the All-Father decrees, too much life and gluttony and greed, too much excess and overindulgence. The beauty of bare rock has been spoiled. It is mined and tilled and built upon, so more women can whelp men of scant worth. Some are worthy, and the worthy will fight on, clashing in the smoking ruin that this world will become. And in the clash, in the chaos, true joy will be found. That joy can be yours, Krator. For what little time you have."

The sunlord did not seem to know what to say to that. He swallowed, the apple in his throat struggling up and down, then turned to face Eldur, tumbling before him in genuflection. "Great Eldur, I wish only to serve you," he declared pitifully. "Grant me but a...a portion of your strength, and I will overthrow Empress Vesper and take the empire in your name. I vow it, my lord. I will muster all Lumara's strength and march it upon the north. Together, my lord, we shall..."

"Together?" the voice whispered. "*Together*, did you say?"

The sunlord shrank back. "No, my lord. *Great Eldur, no.* I only meant..."

Eldur moved his red eyes. At once men came forth, a pair of dragonknights striding from behind to snatch Elio Krator by the arms. He struggled and gave a cry as they tugged him to one side of the bridge, wrenching his arms back behind him, thrusting his upper body over the edge. His men stirred, and one stepped forward, but a dragonknight came in behind him, pressing a spear through the small of his back to burst out through his belly with an explosion of bone and blood. Others shouted out and went to draw their blades but were skewered and stabbed with violent thrusts, some tripping as they were

763

driven over the edge to tumble down into the molten rivers below, devoured in Agarath's blood.

Krator was screaming all the while, his eyes strained and bulging as he stared down into the abyss. The fat Sunrider Mar Malaan had dropped to the floor, curling into a sphere of sweatstained silk as he sobbed into his fleshy knees. Sotel Dar watched it all impassively from his place beside the Fire Father's throne. He even smiled at what he saw. *Fools,* he thought. *They were fools to have come here.*

"Together, did you say?"

The two dragonknights yanked Elio Krator back from the edge and turned him again to face the Founder. They thrust him to his knees and stood either side of him as his men were slain behind. "Please…my lord. Great Eldur, I never meant…"

Eldur raised a hand to silence him, and at once the slaughter stopped. His fingers were long, pale, sharp-nailed, almost like claws. In a crook of the crown-throne the Soul of Agarath throbbed and pulsed atop his black staff, the colours swirling, shifting. Directly above it, thousands of metres high, the great black fume of clouds was flashing red as Agarath the All-Father watched on, approving. Dragons screeched as they moved through the smog, sometimes diving down through the great mouth of the volcano, their voices echoing, exulting as they twisted and flew between the pillars of smoke. One plunged low, causing cloaks to flutter as he swept past, calling out in a voice only Eldur could understand. What it said made the Fire Father nod. "He is waking," he whispered, speaking almost to himself. "I wonder… who will he seek out first?" His eyes looked into his master's soul and he seemed to see the answer. Whatever it was, it made him smile. Then he looked again at Krator and said, "You came here on your sunwolf, I am told."

The sunlord nodded, desperate. "Yes, Great Lord. We all…all of us…" He glanced back. His men were all dead, save Mar Malaan and three others, who had been thrust down to their knees with spearpoints at their necks. "We rode our sunwolves and starcats," he murmured. "We travelled a…a long way to be here."

"His name. Your wolf."

"Braccaro, my lord."

"I would like you to bring him to me," Eldur said.

A pause. Krator shuddered, terror-filled, and raised his eyes. "Please, my lord, he…he is a good wolf. My men…punish my men for my insolence, and me…even *me*…but him…please…"

"You misunderstand. I wish to help you."

"H-help me…?" he repeated, uncertain. He blinked and stared. "I…I don't…"

"You came to serve. You seek to bring the empire to its knees, and rule in my name." Malice twinkled in the Fire Father's pupil-less gaze. "Then you will need a steed suited to this task, child. Sunwolves are small…noble creatures, but *weak*. I will make Braccaro…stronger, for you." He gestured with a pale palm and his clawed fingers flicked. "Rise."

Krator rose, and the two tall dragonknights behind him drew back, red cloaks rippling. The screech of dragons filled the great chamber and somewhere far off, long leagues away, Sotel Dar could hear the distant thunder of a waking roar, the yawning of a dread-god rising. He smiled at the sound, and ignored the voice inside him that was screaming and crying out a warning, a voice locked deep within. *This world will end*, he thought, *as Agarath wills it. It must end and be renewed. I know that now.*

"Now come here, child," the Fire Father hissed, signalling for Elio Krator to approach the stair. "Come here and whisper to me this name. Up, up the stair. Come and speak it in my ear."

Trembling, Krator scaled the steps, one and then another, until he stood right there before him. A pale hand reached out and draped itself over the sunlord's feathered shoulder. He pulled him in, and turned his head to listen. There was a flutter of white hair as the words whispered through Krator's lips. Then a smile, slowly forming, twisting on the Father's face.

He looked out at his subjects. "Find her," he said.

THE END

The Bladeborn Saga will continue in Book 7 - coming soon!

If you'd be so kind as to leave a review or rating for this book, that would be hugely appreciated. I truly value the support and feedback. Many thanks for reading this far!

Made in the USA
Middletown, DE
05 September 2024

60435623R00458